THE YEAR'S BEST

SCIENCE FICTION

THE YEAR'S BEST

SCIENCE FICTION

twenty-first annual collection

edited by **Gardner Dozois**

st. martin's griffin ✣ new york

ISBN 0-312-32478-2 (hc)

acknowledgment is made for permission to reprint the following materials:

"Off on a Starship," by William Barton. Copyright © 2003 by Dell Magazines. First published in *Asimov's Science Fiction*, September 2003. Reprinted by permission of the author.

"It's All True," by John Kessel. Copyright © 2003 by SCIFI.COM. First published electronically on SCI FICTION, November 5, 2003. Reprinted by permission of the author.

"Rogue Farm," by Charles Stross. Copyright © 2003 by Charles Stross. First published in *Live Without a Net* (Roc), edited by Lou Anders. Reprinted by permission of the author.

"The Ice," by Steven Popkes. Copyright © 2003 by Dell Magazines. First published in *Asimov's Science Fiction*, January 2003. Reprinted by permission of the author.

"Ej-es," by Nancy Kress. Copyright © 2003 by Nancy Kress. First published in *Stars: Original Stories Based on the Songs of Janis Ian* (DAW), edited by Janis Ian and Mike Resnick. Reprinted by permission of the author. "Jesse," words and music by Janis Ian, copyright © Tao Songs Two. All rights reserved. Used by permission.

"The Bellman," by John Varley. Copyright © 2003 by Dell Magazines. First published in *Asimov's Science Fiction*, June 2003. Reprinted by permission of the author and the author's agent, Kirby McCauley.

"The Bear's Baby," by Judith Moffett. Copyright © 2003 by Spilogale, Inc. First published in *The Magazine of Fantasy & Science Fiction*, October/November 2003. Reprinted by permission of the author.

"Calling Your Name," by Howard Waldrop. Copyright © 2003 by Howard Waldrop. First published in *Stars: Original Stories Based on the Songs of Janis Ian* (DAW), edited by Janis Ian and Mike Resnick. Reprinted by permission of the author. "Calling Your Name," words and music by Janis Ian, copyright © Tao Songs Two. All rights reserved. Used by permission.

contents

acknowledgments

The editor would like to thank the following people for their help and support: Susan Casper, Ellen Datlow, Gordon Van Gelder, Peter Crowther, David Pringle, Marty Halpern, Lou Anders, Eileen Gunn, Nisi Shawl, Mike Resnick, Janis Ian, Susan Marie Groppi, Karen Meisner, Jed Hartman, Richard Freeburn, Patrick Swenson, Sheila Williams, Brian Bieniowski, Trevor Quachri, Jayme Lynn Blascke, Andy Cox, David Hartwell, Warren Lapin, Darrell Schweitzer, Roelf Goudriaan, John O'Neill, Kelly Link, Gavin Grant, Christopher Rowe, Alan DeNiro, Gwenda Bond, Jeff VanderMeer, Chris Lawson, Ian Randal Strock, Gordon Lilnzer, Gerard Houarner, Karl Johanson, Kristin Livdahl, Orson Scott Card, Keith Olexa, Christian O'Toole, David Lee Summers, Diane L. Walton, Keith Stevenson, Ian Redman, Monissa Whiteley, Mark Rudolph, Liz Holliday, Michael J. Jasper, Linn Prentis, Vaughne Lee Hansen, Shawna McCarthy, Mark R. Kelly, Jonathan Strahan, Jennifer A. Hall, Mark Watson, Michael Swanwick, and special thanks to my own editor, Marc Resnick.

Thanks are also due to Charles N. Brown, whose magazine *Locus* (Locus Publications, P.O. Box 13305, Oakland, CA 94661. $52 for a one-year/twelve-issue subscription via second class; credit card orders (510) 339 9198) was used as an invaluable reference source throughout the Summation; *Locus Online* (www.locusmag.com), edited by Mark R. Kelly, has also become a key reference source. Thanks are also due to John Douglas and Warren Lapine of *Science Fiction Chronicle* (DNA Publications, Inc., P.O. box 2988, Radford, VA 24143-2988. $45 for a one-year/twelve-issue subscription via second class) which was also used as a reference source throughout.

summation: 2003

In spite of rough financial seas in the general economy, the genre publishing world remained not only afloat but relatively stable throughout 2003 — it took some hits, yes, as did most sectors of the economy, but, so far (knock wood), nothing catastrophic or crippling, nothing that would seem to indicate a depression or even a serious recession ahead.

In fact, over the last couple of years, the science fiction and fantasy genres have been, for the most part, *expanding* rather than contracting. Yes, we lost the British SF line Earthlight in 2003, a casualty of the chaotic reorganization and global cutbacks going on within Simon & Schuster; Roc and Ace are merging their editorial staffs (while remaining separate imprints); Big Engine, one of the more ambitious new small presses, discovered that they had bitten off more than they could chew and went out of business; and several more SF-specialty bookshops closed their doors, unable to compete with the discounts offered by the chain bookstores and online bookstores. But, on the other hand, *five* new genre Young Adult lines were added to the field at the end of 2003 or the beginning of 2004: Dorchester Publishing is adding a new trade paperback fantasy imprint; Tor is adding a new "paranormal romance" line; Harlequin is adding a new "fantasy line with romantic elements"; Five Star Books is expanding this year to seventy-eight books per year (while changing its emphasis from short-story collections to novels), with twenty-six of those being SF or fantasy; Night Shade Books is expanding to twenty books, with an eventual goal of doing forty-eight titles annually; and Small Beer Press, Golden Gryphon Press, Subterranean Press, PS Publishing, and others are all expanding their lines and venturing into publishing novels in addition to their usual collections (in fact, the "miniscule press" — to use Charles N. Brown's memorable phrase for publishers "a layer under the small press" — is booming like never before).

I've said this before, but with all the "SF is dying" talk that still goes on at conventions and in online forums and bulletin boards, perhaps its worth saying again. For some historical perspective, the next time that you hear that the SF genre is "dying," keep in mind that the number of original science fiction novels published in 2003—236, according to the newsmagazine *Locus*—is alone higher than the *total number* of original genre books, of *any* sort, published in 1972, which was 225. An article I saw online at the NYTimes.com site, by Dinitia Smith, had a similar perspective: The best-selling novel of 1975, according to *Publisher's Weekly*'s annual fiction best-seller list, was E. L. Doctorow's novel *Ragtime*, which sold 232,000 copies in hardcover; the best-selling novel of the year 2000 was John Grisham's novel *The Brethren*, and *it* sold 2,875,000 copies, an increase of more than 1,000%! According to a new survey of a quarter-century of publishing, an estimated 114,487 different titles were published in 2001, compared with 39,000 titles in 1975, with more people buying them.

So, there are more books being published than ever before, more people are buying them than ever before, and—thanks to online booksellers and, yes, the much-despised chain bookstores—more people have *easier access* to those books than ever before. Doesn't sound like either the much-feared and much-warned-against Death of Literacy *or* the Death of Science Fiction to me. In fact, it sounds like a lot better world than the one I was born into, where only a relatively small percentage of the population read with any regularity (especially pleasure reading), only a comparatively small number of titles of any sort were published every year (you were lucky if you could find three science fiction titles published per month, for example; sometimes there were none), and if you lived in a small town, as I did, you had to travel miles (twenty miles, in my case) to the nearest large city to find a proper bookstore—and even when you found one, there was no such thing as a science fiction section in it. Nor was there any Internet which you could employ to order books in a wide variety of formats with a few clicks of a button, which are subsequently sent direct to your door.

So maybe the present isn't as bad as we sometimes make it out to be. Which prompts me to hope that maybe the future won't be as bad as we fear it will be either.

It wasn't all smooth sailing in the genre this year, of course. There were some shakeups. Anthony Cheetham, cofounder and CEO of Orion Publishing Group in the United Kingdom, was dismissed, being replaced as CEO by group Managing Director and cofounder Peter Roche; Malcolm Edwards will move into the newly created position of Deputy CEO and publisher, directing publishing policy for the entire Orion Publishing Group, including the SF line Gollancz. Laura Ann Gilman stepped down as Roc editor to pursue a freelance career, and it was announced that Roc is to merge with Ace on the editorial level; Roc will remain an NAL imprint, with separate publications, but editorial will be merged into Berkley's Ace operations, under Berkley Executive Editor and Ace editor in chief, Susan Allison; while Ace personnel Ginjer Buchanan, John Morgan, and Anne Sowards have been made full editors and will work for both houses. Roc editor Jennifer Heddle subsequently left to become editor at Pocket Books, replaced at Roc by Elizabeth Scheier, hired as an NAL editor who will also work on Roc. And in early 2004, just before press time, it was announced that John Ordover, longtime editor of the *Star Trek* novel line at Pocket Books, has moved over to become editor in chief of the small press, Phobos Books.

Not a lot of change for the publishing world, where, some years, editors moving from house to house to house can seem like a game of Editorial Musical Chairs. The really big changes were under the surface, and little discussed. One thing likely to have major and far-reaching consequences is the recent legal decision that the Print-On-Demand process used by such POD publishers as Lightning Source is in violation of a preexistent patent, something that could have a chilling effect on the burgeoning world of POD publishing. And the "Internet piracy" case against AOL, spearheaded by Harlan Elllison, continues to churn its way through the court system, although recently some progress seemed to be being made in Ellison's favor; the ultimate ruling here could also have far-reaching long-term consequences. The behind-the-scenes thing that's likely to have the most wide-ranging effect, though, is that genre publishing seems to be finally hitting the glass ceiling, as far as how long books can be allowed to *get*; the reluctance of the chain bookstore to order books priced over $24.95 (the bigger the book, the more it costs to produce, the higher the cover price that has to be put on it—and the fewer customers who will be willing to shell out that much to buy it) is putting the brakes on the trend toward ever-longer novels that kept snowballing throughout the 80s and 90s, and it may be that the days of *really* Big Fat Novels are behind us. Of course, really heavy hitters like Stephen King or Robert Jordan or Raymond Feist will continue to be allowed to publish books at any length they like—this will have the most effect on most new or middle-level writers, who will have the choice of writing shorter books or seeing their novel split up into three separate volumes in order to be published at all, as happened to John C. Wright's novel *The Golden Transcendence*, originally intended to be one volume. (I actually don't mind the switch to smaller novels; some of the best SF novels ever produced were written back when publishing realities wouldn't allow you to publish a novel longer than 70,000 words, and most SF and fantasy novels of the last twenty years have been bloated and grossly padded anyway. Maybe, in some cases, less *is* more.)

2003 was another bad year in the magazine market, throughout the entire magazine industry, nationwide and even worldwide, not just in the genre market—

although some commentators continue to use this as ammunition in the "SF Is Dying" argument, and usually go on to comment that magazine circulations must be going down because the magazine editors are buying the wrong kinds of stories, or that the readers have lost interest in core science fiction (a particularly popular argument with the slipstream crowd). In fact, falling circulations — for many technical reasons, including broken or vanishing infrastructure channels (see the Summations in *The Year's Best Science Fiction, Nineteenth* and *Twentieth Annual Collections* for more detail) — are a problem throughout the entire magazine industry, far outside genre boundaries. An article in dmnews.com selects 2003 as "the worse year in recent memory for newsstand sales," with newsstand sales sliding 10- to 15% across the board; according to *Oxbridge Communications's National Directory of Magazines*, the overall number of print and online titles published dropped 9.1% in the United States and Canada in 2003, to 17,670 from 19,436 in 2000. Even magazines such as *Playboy* and *TV Guide*, formerly among the best-selling titles in the world, are feeling the pinch, and beginning to emit distressed wobbling noises. Seen from this perspective, the situation in the genre market is relatively stable, with small circulation losses, yes, but so far no repeat of the catastrophic drops that we saw in the mid-90s.

Still, there were changes necessitated by hard economic times. *Asimov's* and *Analog*, as a cost-saving measure, went from an eleven-issue-a-year schedule to a ten-issue-per-year schedule, with a new double issue replacing one issue a year; and *Interzone*, after missing several issues during the course of 2003, officially announced that they were converting to a bimonthly schedule from a monthly schedule in 2004. This makes the upcoming year the first time since the launch of *Weird Tales* in 1923 that the field has officially been without a monthly fiction magazine. In other bad news, *3SF*, a new large-format SF magazine launched last year, lasted for only three issues before dying, and the excellent Scottish magazine *Spectrum SF* seems to have gone quiescent, with nothing heard from it in 2003.

In spite of the troubled water in the magazine industry, many new magazines are still being launched, both inside and outside of the genre. In the genre, in addition to a slew of semi-prozines and new e-magazines (which are discussed below), the end of the year saw the launch of a handsome multigenre revival of the old men's magazine *Argosy*, with some serious advertising bucks behind it (more about this next year), a new horror magazine called *H. P. Lovecraft's Magazine of Horror*, and a new mixed-genre magazine from PS Publishing, *Postscripts*, edited by Peter Crowther, one of the best editors in the business, is on the horizon.

To get down to hard figures, *Asimov's Science Fiction* registered a 3.9% loss in overall circulation in 2003, losing 1,298 in subscriptions, but gaining 68 in newsstand sales; sell-through was up to a record 60%. *Analog Science Fiction &*

Fact registered a 3.6% loss in overall circulation in 2003, losing 1,592 in sub-scriptions, but 75 in newsstand sales, with sell-through rising to a record 61%. *The Magazine of Fantasy & Science Fiction* registered a 10% loss in overall cir-culation, losing 2,716 in subscriptions, but gaining 339 on the newsstand, with their sell-through rising to 44%. *Interzone* reported circulation to be down "maybe 10%" from its former level of about 4,000 copies. *Realms of Fantasy* claims a paid circulation of 27,331, up 1,318 from 2002, the last year for which figures were available; no breakdown as to how many of those are subscription sales versus newsstand sales are available either, but probably the bulk are sub-scription sales.

The SF magazines are by no means down for the count yet—as Charles N. Brown said in his year-end summary in *Locus*, commenting on the fact that *Asimov's* and *Analog* more or less held their ground, with no precipitous drops in circulation, "In magazine publishing, even is the new up"—especially as they are so cheap to produce that you don't need to sell a lot of them to earn a profit, but it's clear that the next few years are going to be critical ones in deter-mining whether these magazines survive or not. One problem is that as news-stands and specialty SF bookstores themselves continue to dwindle in numbers, and the ones that are still around become ever more reluctant to dis-play fiction magazines—especially digest-sized magazines, which don't really fit into the physical format of most newsstands very well—it becomes more and more difficult to get your product out where it might be seen and purchased by people who might eventually become new subscribers; and without new sub-scribers, eventually your subscription base will be whittled away by natural attrition until you don't have a large enough one to support the magazine any-more.

Therefore, I'm going to urge everyone reading these words to *subscribe* to your favorite SF or fantasy magazine, and to do it *today*, right now, before your good intentions get buried under the press of daily events and you forget about it. It's the one practical thing you can do to ensure the survival of a strong SF/fantasy market, with lots of diversity. And it's easier to subscribe to genre magazines today than ever before, as most of them have the capability to issue subscriptions online on their Web sites, with all that's called for a credit card and a few clicks of a button, with no stamps, no envelopes, and no trips to the post office required. Additionally, you can subscribe from overseas just as easily as you can from the United States, something formerly difficult-to-impossible. Internet sites such as Peanut Press (www.peanutpress.com) and Fictionwise (*www.fictionwise.com*), sell electronic downloadable versions of the magazines to be read on your PDA or PC, something becoming increasingly popular with the computer-savvy set. Therefore, I'm going to list the URLs for those maga-zines that have Web sites: *Asimov's* site is at www.asimovs.com; *Analog's* site is at www.analogsf.com; and *The Magazine of Fantasy & Science Fiction's* site is at http://www.sfsite.com/fsf/. *Interzone*'s site is at http://www.sfsite.com/interzone/. Or, if you want to go the traditional ink, paper, and stamp route instead, subscription addresses are listed below. Whichever you do, though, if you like having a lot of science fiction to read every year in anthologies like this one, put the book down and go subscribe *now*.

Subscription addresses for the professional magazines follow: *The Magazine of Fantasy & Science Fiction*, Spilogale, Inc., P.O. Box 3447, Hoboken, NJ 07030, annual subscription—$44.89 in U.S.; *Asimov's Science Fiction*, Dell Magazines, 6 Prowitt Street, Norwalk, CT 06855—$43.90 for annual subscription in U.S.; *Analog Science Fiction and Fact*, Dell Magazines, 6 Prowitt Street, Norwalk, CT 06855—$43.90 for annual subscription in U.S.; *Interzone*, 217 Preston Drove, Brighton BN1 6FL, United Kingdom, $65.00 for an airmail one-year (twelve issues) subscription; *Realms of Fantasy*, Sovereign Media Co. Inc., P.O. Box 1623, Williamsport, PA 17703, $16.95 for an annual subscription in the U.S.

Let's turn now to the Internet scene, although I should add the caveat that things there evolve with such lightning speed, with new e-magazines and Internet sites of general interest seeming almost to be born one day and die the next, that it remains possible that everything I say about it here will be obsolete by the time this book makes it into print. The only way you can be sure about what's available and what's not is to go online yourself and check. Not a lot has changed since last year, with most of the major sites still in place and still the major genre-related sites, although new sites of interest continue to be born almost faster than it's possible to keep up with them.

As usual, the best place on the Internet to find fantasy, horror, and science fiction of high-literary quality, and one of the major players in the whole genre market, is Ellen Datlow's *Sci Fiction* page on the internet (www.scifi.com/scifiction/), which this year featured a lot of the year's best fiction, on or off of the Internet, including stories by John Kessel, Lucius Shepard, Howard Waldrop, Geoffrey A. Landis, Paul Di Filippo, Octavia Butler, J. R. Dunn, Jeffery Ford, Maureen F. McHugh, Kathleen Ann Goonan, and others. Eileen Gunn's *The Infinite Matrix* page (www.infinitematrix.net) continued to publish literate and quirky fiction by people such as Michael Swanwick, Richard Kadrey, Benjamin Rosenbaum, and others, although a funding crisis has forced them to resort to PBS-like appeals for donations; let's hope this works, as the site deserves to survive. Good professional-level SF and fantasy (as well as the usual slipstream and soft horror) could also be found on the *Strange Horizons* site (*www.strangehorizons.com*), which published an excellent story by David Moles, as well as good stuff by Bill Kte'pi, Nisi Shawl, Greg Van Eekhout, Daniel Kayson, Jeff Carlson, and others, as well as by electronic subscription to *Oceans of the Mind* (*www.trantorpublications.com/oceans.htm*), which published one of the year's best stories, by Terry Dowling, as well as good stuff by Stephen Dedman, Marissa

K. Lingen, Ian Creasey, Mary Turzillo, and others. (*Oceans of the Mind* deserves special commendation, in my eyes, anyway, for concentrating almost exclusively on core science fiction; almost all the other Internet fiction sites, including *Sci Fiction*, publish at least as much fantasy, horror, and slipstream as SF, if not more.)

Below this point, most of the sites and e-magazines from which original fiction is available are less reliable; the stuff you find there won't always—or even mostly—be of professional quality, although sometimes there are above-average stories to be found. The best of the remaining sites is probably *Revolution SF* (*www.revolutionsf.com*); the bulk of its space is devoted to media and gaming reviews, book reviews, essays, and interviews, but some good stories from Steven Utley, Jay Lake, Lou Antonelli, and others did appear there this year, and they seem to be increasing their emphasis on fiction. Short science fiction stories of high-professional quality have even been turning up recently on *Salon* (www.salon.com) of all places, which this year published good SF stories by Cory Doctorow and William Shunn. Other promising new sites include: *The Fortean Bureau—A Magazine of Speculative Fiction* (*www.forteanbureau.com/index.html*), *Abyss and Apex: A Magazine of Speculative Fiction* (*http://klio.net/abyssandapex*), *Ideomancer Speculative Fiction* (*www.ideomancer.com*), and *Bewildering Stories* (*www.bewilderingstories.com*).

Good original SF and fantasy becomes somewhat hard to find after this point, but there's quite a lot of good *short* reprint SF and fantasy out there to be found. For example, most of the sites that are associated with existent print magazines, such as *Asimov's, Analog, The Magazine of Fantasy & Science Fiction, Aurealis*, and others, will have extensive archives of material, both fiction and nonfiction, previously published by the print versions of the magazines, and some of them regularly run teaser excerpts from stories coming up in forthcoming issues; *SCI FICTION* also has a substantial archive of "classic reprints," as do *The Infinite Matrix* and *Strange Horizons*. You can also check out the British *Infinity Plus* (http://www.users.zetnet.co.uk/iplus/), which has, in addition to biographical and bibliographical information, book reviews, interviews, and critical essays, and a good selection of good-quality reprint stories. All of this stuff is available to be read for free (as long as you're willing to read it on a computer screen).

For a small fee, though, an even greater range of reprint stories becomes available. One of the best such sites is *Fictionwise* (*www.fictionwise.com*), a place where you can buy downloadable e-books and stories to read on your PDA or PC. In addition to individual stories, you can also buy "fiction bundles" here, which amount to electronic collections, as well as a selection of novels in several different genres; more importantly to *me*, you can also subscribe to downloadable versions of several of the SF magazines—including *Asimov's Science Fiction*—here, in a number of different formats (as you can at the

Peanut Press site, www.peanutpress.com). *ElectricStory* (*www.electricstory.com*) is a similar site, but here, in addition to the downloadable stuff (both stories and novels) you can buy, you can also access for free movie reviews by Lucius Shepard, articles by Howard Waldrop, and other critical material. Access for a small fee to both original and reprint SF stories is also offered by sites such as *Mind's Eye Fiction* (http://tale.com/genres.htm), and *Alexandria Digital Literature* (http://alexlit.com) as well.

There's also a large cluster of general-interest sites that don't publish fiction but *do* publish lots of interviews, critical articles, reviews, and genre-oriented news of various kinds. One of the most valuable genre-oriented sites on the entire Internet is *Locus Online* (http://www.locusmag.com), the online version of the newsmagazine *Locus*; not only do you get fast-breaking news here (in fact, this is often the first place in the entire genre where important stories break), but you can also access an incredible amount of information here, including book reviews, critical lists, obituary lists, links to reviews and essays appearing outside the genre, and links to extensive and invaluable database archives such as the Locus Index to Science Fiction and the Locus Index to Science Fiction Awards. Other essential sites include: *Science Fiction Weekly* (http://www.scifi.com/sfw/), more media-and-gaming oriented than *Locus Online*, but still featuring news and book reviews, as well as regular columns by John Clute, Michael Cassut, and Wil McCarthy; *Tangent Online* (http://www.sfsite.com/tangent/), which underwent a fallow period last winter and a change of editorship, but which now seems back on track in providing extensive short-fiction reviews that cover magazines, anthologies, and e-zines, something that's difficult to find anywhere else in both the print and online worlds; *Best SF* (*www.bestsf.net/*), another great review site, and one of the few places, along with *Tangent Online*, that makes any attempt to regularly review online fiction as well as print fiction; *The Internet Review of Science Fiction* (*http://www.irosf.com*) and *Lost Pages* (*http://lostpagesindex.html*) are new reviews site which cover similar territory to *Best SF* and *Tangent Online*, while adding articles, interviews, and, in the case of *Lost Pages*, some fiction as well; *SFRevu* (http://www.sfsite.com/sfrevu), is a review site which specializes in media and novel reviews; the *Sci-Fi Channel* (www.scifi.com), which provides a home for Ellen Datlow's SCI FICTION and for *Science Fiction Weekly*, and to the bimonthly SF-oriented chats hosted by *Asimov's* and *Analog*, as well as vast amounts of material about SF movies and TV shows; the *SF Site* (www.sfsite.com/), which not only features an extensive selection of reviews of books, games, and magazines, interviews, critical retrospective articles, letters, and so forth, plus a huge archive of past reviews; but also serves as host-site for the web pages of *The Magazine of Fantasy & Science Fiction* and *Interzone*; SFF NET (http://www.sff.net), which features dozens of home pages and newsgroups for SF writers, plus sites for genre-oriented live chats; the *Science*

Fiction Writers of America page (http://www.sfwa.org/); where news, obituaries, award information, and recommended reading lists can be accessed; *Audible* (www.audible.com) and *Beyond 2000* (www.beyond2000.com), where SF-oriented radio plays can be accessed; multiple Hugo-winner David Langford's online version of his fanzine *Ansible* (www.dcs.gla.ac.uk/Ansible/), which provides a funny and often iconoclastic slant on genre-oriented news; and *Speculations* (www.speculations.com) a long-running site which dispenses writing advice, and writing-oriented news and gossip (although to access most of it, you'll have to subscribe to the site).

Live online interviews with prominent genre writers are also offered on a regular basis on many sites, including interviews sponsored by *Asimov's* and *Analog* and conducted by Gardner Dozois on the Sci-Fi Channel (http://www.scifi.com/chat/) every other Tuesday night at 9 P.M. EST (SCI FIC-TION chats conducted by Ellen Datlow are also featured on the Sci-Fi Channel at irregular intervals, usually on Thursdays, check the site for details); regular scheduled interviews on the Cybling site (http://www.cybling.com/); and occasional interviews on the Talk City site (http://www.talkcity.com/). Many Bulletin Board Services, such as Delphi, Compuserve, and AOL, have large online communities of SF writers and fans, and some of these services also feature regularly scheduled live interactive real-time chats or conferences, in which anyone interested in SF is welcome to participate, the SF-oriented chat on Delphi, every Wednesday at about 10 P.M. EST, is the one with which I'm most familiar, but there are similar chats on SFF .Net, and probably on other BBSs as well.

Close your eyes for a moment in the Internet world, though, and everything will be different when you open them again. By this time next year, the odds are that some of these sites will be gone, and some will have grown more prominent. The only way you can keep up on a day-to-day basis is to go on the Internet and see for yourself what's there. (I can almost guarantee you that there'll be a lot of interest to find, whatever specific sites come and go.)

It was not a particularly good year in the print semiprozine market, one of a succession of bad years in the new century so far, although, as usual, new semiprozines, particularly fiction semiprozines, struggled to be born even as the old ones fell by the wayside. Last year, a number of prominent semiprozines, including *Century, Eidolon, Orb, Altair, Terra Incognita*, and the excellent *Spectrum SF*, either died or went "on hiatus"—or *continued* "on hiatus," in the case of *Century*—which usually amounts to the same thing in the semiprozine market. I'll be surprised if we ever see any of those magazines again.

Absolute Magnitude, The Magazine of Science Fiction Adventures, Fantastic Stories of the Imagination, Weird Tales, the newszine *Chronicle* (formerly *Science Fiction Chronicle*), the all-vampire-fiction magazine *Dreams of Decadence*—the titles consolidated under the umbrella of Warren Lapine's DNA

Publications—still had trouble keeping to their announced publishing schedules this year; *Weird Tales* and *Chronicle* met it, but *Absolute Magnitude, The Magazine of Science Fiction Adventures, Fantastic Stories of the Imagination,* and *Dreams of Decadence* all published only one issue apiece. Circulation figures were not available for the DNA magazines, so it's impossible to say how they're doing. *Artemis Magazine: Science and Fiction for a Space-Faring Society*, the Irish fiction semiprozine *Albedo One*, and the long-running Australian semiprozine *Aurealis* also only managed one issue apiece this year. If there was an issue of *Tales of the Unanticipated* this year, I didn't see it.

The two most seemingly healthy of the fiction semiprozines at the moment, judging by frequency of publication if nothing else, would have to be the long-running Canadian semiprozine *On Spec* and the leading British semiprozine, *The Third Alternative. On Spec: The Canadian Magazine of the Fantastic* (the subtitle changed this year from the former, and somewhat snide, *More Than Just Science Fiction*) features some of the best covers in the business, including the professional magazines, but the fiction this year seemed somewhat minor, with no real standouts. On the other hand, the slick, large-format *The Third Alternative* is not only one of the handsomest magazines out there, but publishes fiction at a fully professional level (most of it slipstream and horror, although there is an occasional science fiction story), including, this year, excellent stuff by Eric Brown, Alexander Glass, Karen Fishler, Jay Lake, Lucius Shepard, Patrick Samphire, Mary Soon Lee, and others. Although it's managed only four issues in the last two years (it's supposed to be quarterly), *Talebones: Fiction on the Dark Edge* still seems a lively and hardy little magazine, and featured good SF and fantasy stories by James Van Pelt, Jay Lake, Mark Rich, Martha J. Allard, and others. *Andromeda Spaceways Inflight Magazine* survived a patch of financial difficulties last year, and seems to also be fairly vigorous, publishing six issues this year; their fiction is not yet up to the same reliable level of *The Third Alternative* or *Talebones*, but they did publish good stuff this year by Stephen Dedman, Geoffrey Maloney, Ruth Nestvold, and others.

Other SF-oriented (more-or-less, almost all "SF semiprozines" feature a mix of fantasy or slipstream stories as well) fiction semiprozines out there included *Hadrosaur Tales*, which had two issues this year (with a good story by Neal Asher in issue 16), *Electric Velocipede*, which also managed two issues (featuring good work by William Shunn, Paul Di Filippo, Rick Klaw, and others), the long-running *Space and Time*, and the newly launched *Neo-Opsis* and *Jupiter* (which instead of issue numbers has issues named after moons of Jupiter, such as *Jupiter: Europa*, and so forth); these last two are amateuristic-looking (frankly, rather crappy-looking) productions, but they're attracting some interesting young professionals such as Derryl Murphy, Ian Creasey, and Nicholas Waller, and have nowhere to go but up.

Another rather amateurish-looking magazine, with almost nothing to offer in the way of production values, is *Lady Churchill's Rosebud Wristlet*, which has overcome these drawbacks to become one of the most respected magazines in the business; it's done this by attracting first-rate work by top writers (almost always slipstream and stylish surrealism of one sort or another rather than science fiction or even genre fantasy), including, this year, Molly Gloss, Eliot Fintushel, Richard Parks, Sarah Monette, and others. Not only has *Lady Churchill's Rosebud Wristlet* become the flagship of the whole emerging slipstream/fabulist subgenre, it's inspired a host of clones, also very amateuristic-looking, publishing much the same sort of material, and, in fact, often drawing upon many of the same general group of authors; these magazines include the *Say . . .* group, where each issue has a different title, such as this year's *Say . . . Aren't You Dead?*, *Full Unit Hookup*, *Intracities*, *The Journal of Pulse-Pounding Narratives*, *Flytrap #1*, and, perhaps the most promising of the bunch, *Alchemy*, a fantasy magazine which featured stories by Theodora Gross, Alex Irvine, and Sarah Monette this year.

Black Gate, the new large-format fantasy magazine, again published only two issues out of a scheduled four, but each issue was fat enough to make up three or four issues of most of the other fiction semiprozines. Good fantasy of different types appeared there this year by Mark W. Tiedemann, Rick Norwood, Anne Sheldon, Jennifer Busick, Brian A. Hopkins, and others. *Paradox* is a new magazine which features both historical fiction and "speculative/historical fiction"—alternate-history stories, in other words, by writers such as Brian Stableford and James Van Pelt.

Since I don't follow the horror semiprozine market anymore, I'll limit myself to saying that the most prominent magazine there, as usual, seems to be the highly respected *Cemetery Dance*.

There's not a lot *left* to the critical magazine market, with Lawrence Person announcing that he's retiring *Nova Express*, but the *good* news is that what's left is *solid*, including some of the most reliably published and long-lasting semiprozines in the entire industry. *Locus*, now edited by Jennifer A. Hall, with founder and longtime editor Charles N. Brown hovering in the background somewhere in the role of publisher to keep an eye on things, wins the Hugo for Best Semiprozine year after year, often to loud groans from the audience from those who are tired of seeing it win, but there's a *reason* why it wins—it's an indispensable source of information, news, and reviews for anyone interested in science fiction, particularly from a writer's perspective; I know very few writers who don't subscribe to *Locus*. Now that it's been taken over by Warren Lapine's DNA Publishing Group (who changed the name and installed new editor John Douglas), *Chronicle*, formerly *Science Fiction Chronicle*, is back on track as a reliably published magazine again, and is also a very valuable reference source. The best critical magazine out there at the moment is David G.

Hartwell's eclectic critical magazine, *The New York Review of Science Fiction*, which has a wide-enough range of articles and reviews that everybody is sure to find something to like and dislike in every single issue; it also comes out with clocklike regularity, twelve issues a year. *The Fix* is a short-fiction review magazine, the only one in print (all the other short-fiction review sources are online), brought to you by the people who put out *The Third Alternative*.

Locus, The Magazine of the Science Fiction & Fantasy Field, Locus Publications, Inc., P.O. Box 13305, Oakland, CA 94661, $60.00 for a one-year first class subscription, 12 issues; *The New York Review of Science Fiction*, Dragon Press, P.O. Box 78, Pleasantville, NY 10570, $36.00 per year, make checks payable to "Dragon Press," 12 issues; *The Fix: The Review of Short Fiction*, TTA Press, Wayne Edwards, 360 W. 76th Ave., #H, Anchorage, AK 99518, $29.00 for a six-issue subscription, make checks payable to "TTA Press"; *The Third Alternative*, TTA Press, 5 Martins Lane, Witcham, Ely, Cambs. CB6 2LB, England, UK, $36.00 for a four-issue subscription, checks made payable to "TTA Press"; *Talebones, Fiction on the Dark Edge*, 5203 Quincy Ave SE, Auburn, WA 98092, $20.00 for four issues; *On Spec: The Canadian Magazine of the Fantastic*, P.O. Box 4727, Edmonton, AB, Canada T6E 5G6, $22.00 for a one-year (four issue) subscription; *Neo-Opsis Science Fiction Magazine*, 4129 Carey Rd., Victoria, BC, V8Z 4G5, $24.00 Canadian for a four issue subscription; *Jupiter*, Ian Redman, 23 College Green, Yeovil, Somerset, BA21 4JR, UK, 9 pounds sterling for a four-issue subscription; *Aurealis: The Australian Magazine of Fantasy and Science Fiction*, Chimaera Publications, P.O. Box 2164, Mt. Waverley, Victoria 3149, Australia, $50.00 for a four-issue overseas airmail subscription, "all cheques and money orders must be made out to Chimarea Publications in Australian dollars"; *Albedo*, Albedo One Productions, 2 Post Road, Lusk, Co., Dublin, Ireland; $25.00 for a four-issue airmail subscription, make checks payable to "Albedo One"; *Pirate Writings, Tales of Fantasy, Mystery & Science Fiction, Absolute Magnitude, The Magazine of Science Fiction Adventures, Aboriginal Science Fiction, Weird Tales, Dreams of Decadence*, and *Chronicle*—all available from DNA Publications, P.O. Box 2988, Radford, VA 24142-2988, all available for $16 for a one-year subscription, although you can get a group subscription to four DNA fiction magazines for $60 a year, with *Chronicle* $45 a year (12 issues), all checks payable to "D.N.A. Publications"; *Tales of the Unanticipated*, Box 8036, Lake Street Station, Minneapolis, MN 55408, $15 for a four-issue subscription; *Artemis Magazine: Science and Fiction for a Space-Faring Society*, LRC Publications, 1380 E. 17th St., Suite 201, Brooklyn, NY 11230-6011, $15 for a four-issue subscription, checks payable to "LRC Publications"; *Lady Churchill's Rosebud Wristlet*, Small Beer Press, 176 Prospect Avenue, Northampton, MA 01060, $16.00 for four issues; *Say . . .*, The Fortress of Worlds, P.O. Box 1304, Lexington, KY 40588-1304, $10.00 for two issues in the U.S. and Canada; *Alchemy*, Edgewood Press, P.O.

Box 380264, Cambridge, MA 02238, $7.00 for an issue; *Full Unit Hookup*: *A Magazine of Exceptional Literature*, Conical Hats Press, 622 West Cottom Avenue, New Albany, IN 47150-5011, $12.00 for a three-issue subscription; *Flytrap*, Tropism Press, P.O. Box 13322, Berkeley, CA 94712-4222, $16 for four issues, checks payable to "Heather Shaw"; *The Journal of Pulse-Pounding Narratives*, c/o Thom Davidson, 34 Curtis Ave., #P-9, Marlborough, MA 01752, $6.50; *Andromeda Spaceways Inflight Magazine*, P.O. Box 495, Chinchilla QLD 4415 Australia, $35.00 for a one-year subscription; *Hadrosaur Tales*, P.O. Box 2194, Mesilla Park, NM 88047-2194, $16.50 for a three-issue subscription, make checks payable to "Hadrosaur Productions"; Electric Velocipede, $15 for a four-issue subscription — it seems like you can only order this online, so for more subscription information, check their Web site at *http://members.aol.com/evzine/index.html*; *Space and Time: The Magazine of Fantasy, Horror, and Science Fiction*, Space and Time, 138 West 70th Street (4B), New York, NY 10023-4468, $10.00 for a one year (two issue) subscription; *Black Gate*, New Epoch Press, 815 Oak Street, St. Charles, IL 60174, $29.95 for a one-year (four issue) subscription; *Paradox*, Paradox Publications, P.O. Box 22897, Brooklyn, NY 11202-2897, $15.00 for a one-year (four-issue) subscription; *Cemetery Dance*, CD Publications, 132-B Industry Lane, Unit #7, Forest Hill, MD 21050, $27.00 for six issues.

There were a lot of original anthologies this year, most of them fairly mediocre in overall quality, although most of them did also contain a couple of worthwhile — if not exceptional — stories. The best original SF anthology of the year was probably *Live Without a Net* (Roc), edited by Lou Anders; a few of the stories here wander too far off the ostensible theme — futures where the Internet wasn't developed, or was developed and then abandoned for one reason or another — and merely explore fantasy scenarios instead, but the book does contain a high percentage of first-rate and highly inventive work by Charles Stross, Paul Melko, Michael Swanwick, Chris Roberson, Alex Irvine, Paul Di Filippo, John Meaney, and others.

A fairly close follow-up candidate for the title of best original science fiction anthology of the year was *Stars: Stories Inspired by the Songs of Janis Ian* (DAW), edited by Janis Ian and Mike Resnick; there's perhaps a higher percentage of mediocre stories here than in the Anders, but, as it's quite a large book, also a lot of good material as well. It's unfortunate that the editors didn't just select a group of authors and let them write about whatever they wanted to write about, without the insistence that the stories be "inspired by" Janis Ian's songs, because the worst stories here are those that make an obvious one-to-one correlation to one of Ian's songs — replacing the black kid of "Society's Child" with an alien, for instance — while the strongest stories are usually those that have the least to do with the songs themselves. Still, in spite of some weak stories, this is a good value for your money, containing first-rate work by Howard Waldrop, Nancy Kress, Harry Turtledove, John Varley, Spider Robinson, Susan Casper, Terry Bisson, Tad Williams, and others.

Another worthwhile original anthology, this one a mixed-genre effort containing fantasy, horror, mystery, and mainstream stories as well as SF (although both the Anders and the Ian/Resnick anthologies contain some fantasy stories as well), is *The Silver Gryphon* (Golden Gryphon), edited by Gary Turner and Marty Halpern, a volume in celebration of the twenty-fifth book published by Golden Gryphon Press, which contains good work of various sorts by Robert Reed, James Patrick Kelly, Kristine Kathryn Rusch, Kage Baker, Andy Duncan, Jeffery Ford, Michael Bishop, Howard Waldrop, Lucius Shepard, Geoffrey A. Landis, and others.

As I said above, most of the rest of the year's original SF anthologies contained no more than a few worthwhile if not exceptional stories apiece: *Space Inc.* (DAW), edited by Julie E. Czerneda; *Future Wars* (DAW), edited by Martin H. Greenberg and Larry Segriff; *Low Port* (Meisha Merlin), edited by Sharon Lee and Steve Miller; *Give Me Liberty* (DAW), edited by Martin H. Greenberg and Mark Tier; *Women Writing Science Fiction as Men* (DAW), edited by Mike Resnick; and *Men Writing Science Fiction as Women* (DAW), edited by Mike Resnick (for what it's worth, the Men Writing as Women volume struck me as somewhat higher in overall quality than the Women Writing as Men volume, which surprised me a bit, since if I'd had to bet it, I would have bet it the other way around). The fact that they're all cheap mass-market paperbacks means that you may well get your money's worth in entertainment value out of any of these—but for the most part, they're probably not where you're going to find next year's award-winners and most-talked-about stories. *New Voices in Science Fiction* (DAW), edited by Mike Resnick, is a worthwhile and self-explanatory idea, and one that probably should be published annually to be of greatest use. I didn't always agree with Resnick's selection of who the "new voices" were, thinking that he missed several I would have used, and I questioned that a few of those included were actually "new" enough to make the cut for such a volume (although that's a subjective call to some extent, one reader's "never-heard-of-before" being another reader's "already-well-established," depending on how much reading they do within the field every year)—but that hardly matters; nearly every editor is going to come up with their own list of "new voices," and few of them will agree. It did bother me a bit, though, that the majority of the stories in a book called *New Voices in Science Fiction* were actually fantasy stories by any reasonable definition. *Imaginings, An Anthology of Long Short Fiction* (Pocket Books), edited by Keith R. A. DeCandido, is that *rara avis* in today's publishing world, an anthology of original fiction without any organizing "theme," except that they're all novelettes (or, to use DeCandido's somewhat clumsy term, "long short fiction"), an opportunity that many editors would kill for; unfortunately, the book itself is a bit weak overall, especially as a $14 trade paperback, with nothing exceptional in it, although it does contain good work by H. Courreges Le Blanc, Charles L. Harness, Harry Turtledove, and others.

As usual, PS Publishing, edited by Peter Crowther, turned out a good crop of novellas in individual chapbook form, including *Dear Abbey*, by Terry Bisson (the best of them this year), *Light Stealer*, by James Barclay, *Jigsaw Men*, by Gary Greenwood, *Jupiter Magnified*, by Adam Roberts, and *In Springdale Town*, by Robert Freeman Wexler. Golden Gryphon Press got into the same business last year, and again this year brought out several novellas in individual chapbook form, including *A Better World's in Birth!*, by Howard Waldrop and *The Angel in the Darkness*, by Kage Baker. Recently, Subterranean Press began doing the same, with *The Empress of Mars*, by Kage Baker.

An unusual but interesting small-press item is *William Hope Hodgson's Night Lands, Volume 1, Eternal Love* (Wildside Press), edited by Andy W. Robertson, an anthology of homages by various hands, all set in the milieu of William Hope Hodgson's eccentric and *very* strange masterpiece *The Night Land*, one of the probable inspirations for later work such as Jack Vance's *The Dying Earth* and Gene Wolfe's *The Book of the New Sun*, among many others. Some of the writers here handle the deliberately retro, somewhat fustian, mannered Victorian-era prose that this milieu demands better than others, and one of the fundamental problems overarching the whole project is that the more closely one observes and interacts with Hodgson's eerie, poetically charged horrors and wonders on a mundane adventure-fiction level, the more power they lose, being much more effective at an only-half-seen distance. Still, some of the authors here get it right; the anthology contains two powerfully strange novellas by John C. Wright, plus good work by Nigel Atkinson, Brett Davidson, and Robertson himself. (The stories are also available online on *The Night Lands* website, at http://home.clara.net/andywrobertson/nightmap.html.) Another interesting small-press item is *Imagination Fully Dilated: The Literated Artwork of Alan M. Clark* (Fairwood Press), edited by Robert Kruger and Patrick Swenson, stories written around Clark's illustrations (thus "literating" them), which are also included; there's nice work here by David Levine, James Van Pelt, Ray Vukevich, Patrick O' Leary, Leslie What, and others, although nothing here is really top level. Much the same can be said of the floridly titled *Agog! Terrific Tales* (Agog! Press), edited by Cat Sparks, which presents the view from Down Under; nice stuff here by Lucy Sussex, Kyla Ward, Simon Brown, Chris Lawson, Sue Isle, Sean Williams, and others, but nothing too memorable. And ditto for *Beyond the Last Star* (sff.net), edited by Sherwood Smith, which featured good work by David D. Levine, Gregory Feeley, Jay Lake, Brian Plante, and William Shunn, but no award winners.

It was a strong year for original fantasy anthologies, with *Legends II*

(Voyager), edited by Robert Silverberg; *The Dragon Quintet* (SFBC), edited by Marvin Kaye; *The Dark: New Ghost Stories* (Tor), edited by Ellen Datlow; *Mojo: Conjure Stories* (Aspect), edited by Nalo Hopkinson; and the last in a long-running series, *Sword and Sorceress: Volume XX* (DAW), edited by Marion Zimmer Bradley. There were also two original Young Adult fantasy anthologies, *Swan Sister: Fairy Tales Retold* (Simon & Schuster), edited by Ellen Datlow and Terry Windling; and *Firebirds* (Penguin/Firebird), edited by Sharyn November. Horror saw big anthologies such as *Gathering the Bones* (Tor), edited by Dennis Etchison, Ramsey Campbell, and Jack Dann, and an interesting mystery/horror cross (Sherlock Holmes meets Cthulu, basically) *Shadows Over Baker Street* (Del Rey), edited by Michael Reaves and John Pelan.

It was a good year for dragon fans, with not only the publication of Lucius Shepard's long-awaited "Dragon Grauile" sequel, "Liar's House," in *SCI FICTION*, but also the publication of *The Dragon Quintet* as well, five dragon novellas or novelettes, the most exceptional of which was Michael Swanwick's somehow-related-to-*The Iron Dragon's Daughter* story "King Dragon." It was also a good year for alternate-history stories, with Howard Waldrop's "Calling Your Name" and Harry Turtledove's "Joe Steele" from *Stars*; Geoffrey A. Landis's "The Eyes of America" from *SCI FICTION*; Waldrop's chapbook *A Better World's in Birth!*; Robert Reed's "Hexagons" from *Asimov's*; and a number of others. It was also a year that saw Lucius Shepard return to something like his startling prolificacy of old; by my count, he had at least ten or eleven stories published in the genre this year, many of them novellas!

Out on the ambiguous edges of genre, there were a number of original anthologies this year, like last year, that mixed science fiction (occasionally) with fantasy, horror, surrealism, and "slipstream," "New Weird," "Magic Realism," "posttransformation fiction," "interstitialism," "fabulism," or whatever the new buzzword for it is this week, not only within the pages of the same anthology but often within the boundaries of the individual stories themselves—this shows every indication of becoming a subgenre in itself (complete with its own magazines such as *Lady Churchill's Rosebud Wristlet* and, to some extent, *The Third Alternative*), only partially overlapping—although it does so overlap—with the regular reading audience of "core SF" (many of whose fans can't stand it, or find it disappointing or baffling . . . a sentiment shared, to be fair, at least as far as the "disappointing" is concerned, by at least some of the slipstream audience toward science fiction itself). The most entertaining of these anthologies to me this year was *Polyphony 2* (Wheatland Press), edited by Deborah Layne and Jay Lake; most of the stories here are clear mixtures of one or more genres, rather than straight mainstream or classic slipstream (which I've heard defined as "Magic Realism written by people who don't come from South America"), and many of the hybrids are robust and vigorous, a relief after the too solemn and pretentious stuff sometimes found in anthologies of this kind; best stories here are by David Moles and Alex Irvine, although there's also good stuff by Lucius Shepard, Lisa Goldstein, Jack Dann, Theodore Goss, and others. *Polyphony 3* (Wheatland Press), also edited by Layne and Lake, is a little less vivid and more somber, but still contains good work by Jack Dann, Bruce Holland Rogers, Jeffrey Ford, Vandana Singh, Lori Ann White, and others. *Album Zutique #1* (Ministry of Whimsy), edited by Jeff VandeMeer, is similar, perhaps leaning a bit further toward the "surrealism" edge than *Polyphony*, but still containing striking work by Jay Lake, Jeffrey Ford, Ursula Pflug, James Sallis, Michael Cisco, Steve Rasnic Tem, and others. Considerably further away from anything easily recognizable as genre, whether "multi-" or "mixed" or not, is *Trampoline* (Small Beer Press), edited by Kelly Link; this is much more of a classic "slipstream" anthology, and—like last year's *Conjunctions 39*—a number of stories strike me as not even slipstream or Magic Realism, but as mostly mainstream stories with occasional very faint fantastic—or at least "odd"—touches; some of them don't even have the odd touches; considerations of genre classification aside, the best work here is by Jeffrey Ford (the workhorse of anthologies of this sort, it seems), Alex Irvine, Maureen McHugh, Glen Hirshberg, Richard Butner, Karen Joy Fowler, and others, plus a stylishly written but somewhat opaque fantasy novella by Greer Gilman. *Witpunk* (Four Walls Eight Windows), edited by Claude Lalumiere and Marty Halpern, is a mixed reprint-and-original anthology (mostly science fiction and slipstream, although there is some horror, mainstream, and even crime fiction) of stories that "range in style from dark comedy to laugh-out-loud farce," and were chosen for "the timelessness of their satirical bite." Humor being as subjective a matter as it is, not all of these will strike everybody as funny, but there is good stuff here, both reprint and original, "funny" or not, by Pat Cadigan, Ernest Hogan, Robert Silverberg, David Langford, Allen Steele, William Sanders, Pat Murphy, Jeffrey Ford, Cory Doctorow and Michael Skeet, and others. *McSweeney's Mammoth Treasury of Thrilling Tales* (Vintage), edited by Michael Chabon, promises to be a sort of retro-pulp anthology—old wine in new bottles—strongly plotted genre adventure fiction of several different sorts written by well-known mainstream and "literary" writers, but doesn't really deliver very well on that promise; Chabon's condescending and rather patronizing introduction, which doesn't bother to mention any of the SF, fantasy, or mystery magazines that have been keeping alive the kind of fiction he claims to be revitalizing or rediscovering here, pissed off most genre critics and readers, but if you can get beyond that, although it really isn't the book that it presents itself as being, the anthology does feature good work by Elmore Leonard, Neil Gaiman, Harlan Ellison, Stephen King, Jim Shepard, Dave Eggars, Karen Joy Fowler, and others. And *The Thackery T. Lambshead Pocket Guide to Eccentric and Discredited Diseases* (Ministry of Whimsy), edited by Jeff VanderMeer and Mark Roberts, is a sort of a slyly written "nonfiction" guide to things that (fortunately) don't really exist, witty and very dark; not for the squeamish.

If you're looking for novice work by beginning writers, some of whom may later turn out to be important talents, your best bets were *L. Ron Hubbard Presents Writers of the Future Volume IX* (Bridge), edited by Algis Budrys, and *Hitting the Skids in Pixeltown: The Phobos Science Fiction Anthology* (Phobos Books), edited by Orson Scott Card, Keith Olexa, and Christian O'Toole, which features winners of the 2nd Annual Phobos Fiction Contest. There's decent work in both, but *Hitting the Skids in Pixeltown* may have a slight edge, due to an intriguing story by David D. Levine.

There were supposed to be two regional anthologies of Canadian SF edited by Claude Lalumiere, but I was unable to find them before the selections for this book had to be made, and so they'll have to wait for next year.

Coming up next year: A new anthology edited by Peter Crowther, *Constellations*, and the long-delayed *Microcosms*, edited by Gregory Benford.

Addresses: *PS Publishing*, 98 High Ash Drive, Leeds L517 8RE, England, UK—$16.00 for *Dear Abbey*, by Terry Bisson, $16.00 for *Light Stealer*, by Janes Barclay, $16.00 for *Jigsaw Men*, by Gary Greenwood, $16.00 for *Jupiter Magnified*, by Adam Roberts, $16.00 for *In Springdale Town*, by Robert Freeman Wexler, $65.00 for *Infinity Plus Two*, edited by Keith Brooke and Nick Gevers (mentioned in reprint anthology section); Golden Gryphon Press, 3002 Perkins Road, Urbana, IL 61802—$27.95 for *The Silver Gryphon*, edited by Gary Turner and Marty Halpern, $15.95 for *A Better World's in Birth!*, by Howard Waldrop, $15.95 for *The Angel in the Darkness*, by Kage Baker ; Wildside Press—for *William Hope Hodgon's Night Lands, Volume 1, Eternal Love*, go to www.wildsidepress.com for pricing and ordering; Wheatland Press, P.O. Box 1818, Wilsonville, OR, 97070—$16.95 for *Polyphony 2*, edited by Deborah Layne and Jay Lake, $17.95 for *Polyphony 3*, edited by Deborah Layne and Jay Lake; Agog! Press, P.O. Box U302, University of Wollongong, NSW 2522, Australia—A$ $24.95 for *Agog! Terrific Tales*, edited by Cat Sparks; Night Shade Books, 3623 SW Baird St., Portland, OR 97219—$35.00 for *The Empress of Mars*, by Kage Baker, $45.00 for *The Thackery T. Lambshead Pocket Guide to Eccentric Diseases*, edited by Jeff VanderMeer and Mark Roberts; Small Beer Press, 360 Atlantic Avenue, PMB# 132, Brooklyn, NY 11217—$17.00 for *Trampoline*, edited by Kelly Link; Fairwood Press, 5203 Quincy Ave SE, Auburn, WA 98092—$26.99 for *Imagination Fully Dilated: The Literated Artwork of Alan M. Clark*, edited by Robert Kruger and Patrick Swenson; Phobos Books, 200 Park Avenue South, New York, NY 10003—$14.95 for *Hitting the Skids in Pixeltown: The Phobos Science Fiction Anthology*, edited by Orson Scott Card, Keith Olexa, and Christian O'Toole; SFF.NET—$14.95 for *Beyond the Last Star*, edited by Sherwood Smith, order online from www.sff.net/store/index.asp; Ministry of Whimsy Press,

POB 4248, Tallahasse, FL 32315—$12.99 for *Album Zutique #1*, edited by Jeff VanderMeer.

2003 seemed like another strong year for novels—not quite as strong in overall literary quality as last year, perhaps, but close, with not only a lot of books coming out, but a lot of *good* books coming out as well.

According to the newsmagazine *Locus*, there were 2,429 books "of interest to the SF field," both original and reprint (but not counting "media tie-in novels" such as *Star Trek* and *Star Wars* novels, gaming novels, novelizations of movies, or novels drawn from other TV shows such as *Angel*, *Charmed*, and *Buffy, the Vampire Slayer*), published in 2003, up by 8% from 2002's total of 2,241. Original books were up by 8% to 1,375 from last year's total of 1,271; reprint books were up by 9% to 1,054 titles over last year's total of 970. The number of new SF novels was down slightly, with 236 new titles published as opposed to 256 novels published in 2002. The number of new fantasy novels was up slightly, to 340, as opposed to 333 novels published in 2002. Horror was also up, rising to 171, its highest total since 1995, from last year's total of 112. (Keep in mind that, for the most part, these totals don't even reflect Print-On-Demand novels, or novels offered as downloads on the Internet.)

I suppose that the "SF is dying" crowd will gleefully point out that the number of SF novels is down—but twenty titles is hardly a precipitous drop; in fact, in spite of changes in the publishing scene, lines gained and lines dropped, the number of new SF titles published every year has not varied by any significant amount for the last decade. So there's still a lot of new SF novels being published every year. I wonder how many people have read *all* of the 236 new SF titles published this year? Probably nobody has. My guess is that few individual readers have even read a significant percentage of them.

Certainly I have not. As usual, busy with all the reading I have to do at shorter lengths, I didn't have time to read many novels this year.

So instead I'll limit myself to mentioning the novels that received a lot of attention and acclaim in 2003 include: *The Light Ages* (Ace), Ian R. MacLeod; *Darwin's Children* (Del Rey), Greg Bear; *Singularity Sky* (Ace), Charles Stross; *Crossfire* (Tor), Nancy Kress; *Air* (St. Martin's Griffin), Geoff Ryman; *Omega* (Ace), Jack McDevitt; *Absolution Gap* (Gollancz), Alastair Reynolds; *Ilium* (Eos), Dan Simmons; *The Anvil of the World* (Tor), Kage Baker; *The Sundering* (Earthlight), Walter Jon Williams; *Coalescent* (Del Rey), Stephen Baxter; *Sister Alice*—considered as a novel rather than a collection—(Tor), Robert Reed; *1610: A Sundial in a Grave* (Gollancz), Mary Gentle; *Extremes* (Roc), *The Sundering* (Avon), Walter Jon Williams; Kristine Kathryn Rusch; *Red Thunder* (Ace), John Varley; *Memory* (Tor), Linda Nagata; *In the Presence of Mine Enemies* (NAL), Harry Turtledove; *The Dark Tower V: Wolves of the Calla* (Scribner), Stephen King; *The Salt Roads* (Warner), Nalo Hopkinson;

Noise (Tor), Hal Clement; *The Crystal City* (Tor), Orson Scott Card; *Midnight Lamp* (Gollancz), Gwyneth Jones; *The Return of Santiago* (Tor), Mike Resnick; *Felaheen: The Third Arabesk* (Earthlight), Jon Courtenay Grimwood; *The Line of Polity* (Tor UK), Neal Asher; *The Golden Age: The Phoenix Exultant* (Tor), John C. Wright; *The Golden Age: The Golden Transcendence* (Tor), John C. Wright; *The Poison Master* (Bantam Spectra), Liz Williams; *Nine Layers of Sky* (Bantam Spectra), Liz Williams; *Paladin of Souls* (Eos), Lois McMaster Bujold; *The Lost Steersman* (Del Rey), Rosemary Kirstein; *Monstrous Regiment* (HarperCollins), Terry Prachett; *Natural History* (Macmillan), Justina Robson; *Blind Lake* (Tor), Robert Charles Wilson; *Maul* (Orbit), Tricia Sullivan; *In the Forests of Serre* (Ace), Patricia A. McKillip; *The Wreck of the River of Stars* (Tor), Michael Flynn; *Lady Robyn* (Forge), R. Garcia y Robertson; *Sunshine* (Berkley), Robin McKinley; *Any Man So Daring* (Ace), Sarah A. Hoyt; *Mortal Suns* (Overlook), Tanith Lee, *The Briar King* (Del Rey), Greg Keyes; *Wyrmhole* (Roc), Jay Caselberg; *Tinker* (Baen), Wen Spencer; (Tor), *The Braided World* (Bantam Spectra), Kay Kenyon; *The Seperation* (Gollancz), Christopher Priest; *The Night Country* (Farrar, Straus and Giroux), Stewart O'Nan; and *The War of the Flowers* (DAW), Tad Williams.

The first novel that drew the most attention this year seemed to be *Down and Out in the Magic Kingdom* (Tor), by Cory Doctorow, although *The Time Traveler's Wife* (Cage), by Audrey Niffenegger and *Veniss Underground* (Prime), by Jeff VanderMeer drew a good number of reviews as well. Other first novels included: *Clade* (Bantam), by Mark Budz; *Star Dragon* (Tor), by Mike Brotherton; *Paper Mage* (Roc), by Leah R. Cutter; *The Buzzing* (Vintage), Jim Knipfel; *Spin State* (Bantam Spectra), by Chris Moriarty; *The Etched City* (Prime), by K. J. Bishop; *The Darknesses That Comes Before* (Penguin Canada), by R. Scott Bakker; *Magic's Silken Snare* (DAW), by ElizaBeth Gilligan; and *A Telling of Stars* (Penguin Canada), by Caitlin Sweet.

There were several big-selling novels that were out on the ambiguous edge of genre this year, including *Pattern Recognition* (Putnam), by William Gibson, a novel set in the present day rather than in Gibson's usual "Sprawl" future, and *Quicksilver* (Morrow), a secret history novel by Neal Stephenson. The small presses are publishing more novels than ever these days, even small-press houses such as Golden Gryphon, Subterranean, and PS Publishing that up until now have concentrated mostly on short story collections. First-rate novels from small-presses this year included a slew of novels by Lucius Shepard—*Colonel Rutherford's Colt* (Subterranean), *Floater* (PS Publishing), *Louisiana Breakdown* (Golden Gryphon), and *Aztechs* (Subterranean)—as well as *Nothing Human* (Golden Gryphon), by Nancy Kress, *Year Zero* (Five Star), by Brian Stableford, *Mockeymen* (Golden Gryphon), by Ian Watson, *Reading the Bones* (Tachyon), Sheila Finch; and *Fuzzy Dice* (PS Publishing), by Paul Di Filippo.

Associational novels by SF writers this year included *Lust* (St. Martin's

Press), by Geoff Ryman, and *The Druid King* (Knopf), by Norman Spinrad. Robert A. Heinlein's sixty-six-year old first novel, *For Us, the Living* (Scribners), first written in 1938 and first published this year, is science fiction of the Tour of a Future Utopia sort, but is so completely dated by now that it might as well be listed as an associational novel, as it probably will not be of real interest to any but the most dedicated Heinlein fans (although critics also seem to have found it intriguing to pour over it to pick out the seeds of future—and better— novels that are visible here). All that really needs to be said about this book, it seems to me, is that Heinlein himself tried to destroy all traces of it to ensure that it would never be printed. I think that his wishes ought to have been respected.

And since I continue to hear the complaint, usually from people who haven't read any new science fiction in years, that there's no "real" science fiction out there anymore, let me point out that, even discounting the fantasy and the borderline genre-mixing stuff on the list, the Bear, the Reynolds, the two Kress novels, the Baxter, the McDevitt, the Reed, the Stross, the Nagata, the Clement, the Flynn, the two Wright novels, the Williams, and more than a dozen others are clearly and unmistakably science fiction—many of them "hard science fiction" as hard and as rigorous as it's ever been written, at that.

Throughout the 80s and 90s, shortsighted bottom-line corporate publishing practices meant that books almost never came back into print once they had gone out of it, and even classics of the genre remained unavailable for decades. Fortunately, this has turned around in the Oughts, and the last few years have proved to be the best time since the 70s to pick up new editions of out-of-print classics of science fiction and fantasy, books that have been long unavailable to the average reader.

There's such a flood of reprints now that it's become difficult to keep track of all the reprint editions coming out—with Tor/Orb, ibooks, Baen, and the Science Fiction Book Club especially active—particularly when you factor in the availability of Print-On-Demand books from places such as Wildside Press, and the availability of formerly out-of-print books as electronic downloads on Internet sources such as Fictionwise. Therefore, rather than trying to produce an exhaustive list of such titles, I'll just mention a few that caught my eye. There were a number of good omnibus volumes, usually including two or more of an author's novels, including, *The Dragon Masters* (ibooks), by Jack Vance; *Latro in the Mist* (Tor/Orb), by Gene Wolfe; *Dorsai Spirit* (Tor/Orb), by Gordon R. Dickson; *John Grimes: Tramp Captain* (SFBC), by A. Bertram Chandler; *General Practice* (Tor/Orb), by James White; *Tales of Sector General* (SFBC), by James White; *Med Ships* (SFBC), by James White; *The Peace War* (Tor), by Vernor Vinge; *Heavy Planet* (SFBC), by Hal Clement; *The Integral Trees and The Smoke Ring* (Del Rey), by Larry Niven; *Planet of Adventure* (Baen), by Murry Leinster; *At the Edge of Space* (DAW), by C. J. Cherryh;

Swan Songs (SFBC), by Brian Stableford, and *Carlucci* (Ace), by Richard Paul Russo. Good singleton reprints included, from ibooks: *Brain Wave*, *The High Crusade*, and *Ensign Flandry*, all by Poul Anderson, *Swords Against Death* and *Swords and Deviltry*, by Fritz Leiber, *Nostrilla*, by Cordwainer Smith, *Shadrach in the Furnace*, by Robert Silverberg, *Strangers*, by Gardner Dozois, *Maske: Thaery*, by Jack Vance, *Beyond Heaven's River* and *Hegira*, by Greg Bear, and *To Die in Italbar* and *Changling*, by Roger Zelazny; Tor/Orb reprinted, in addition to those titles already mentioned: *Mythago Wood*, by Robert Holdstock, *The Summer Queen*, by Joan Vinge, and *Red Prophet* and *Seventh Son*, by Orson Scott Card; Gollancz reprinted *The Blue World*, by Jack Vance, *Son of Man*, by Robert Silverberg, *The Ophiuchi Hotline*, by John Varley, and *The Miracle Visitors*, by Ian Watson; The Science Fiction Book Club reprinted *Three Hearts and Three Lions*, by Poul Anderson; Vintage reprinted *Eye in the Sky*, *The Cosmic Puppets*, and *Solar Lottery*, all by Philip K. Dick; HarperCollins/Perennial reprinted *The Dispossessed* and *The Lathe of Heaven*, by Ursula K. Le Guin; Carroll & Graf reprinted *On Wings of Song*, by Thomas M. Disch; Bantam Spectra reprinted *Windhaven*, by George R. R. Martin and Lisa Tuttle, and *Swordpoint*, by Ellen Kushner; Eos reprinted *The Forever War*, by Joe Haldeman; Del Rey reprinted *Have Space Suit—Will Travel*, *Tunnel in the Sky*, and *The Door into Summer*, all by Robert A. Heinlein; DAW reprinted *The Edge of Space*, by C. J. Cherryh; Starscape reprinted *Putting Up Roots*, by Charles Sheffield, and *The Eye of the Heron*, by Ursula K. Le Guin; and Modern Library reissued *The Day of the Triffids*, by John Wyndham. Plus, no doubt, many reprints that I missed. Check around for them, and buy them while you can.

I have no idea what's going to win the major awards; there doesn't seem to be a clear, obvious winner, as there has been in some other years—and SFWA's dysfunctional "rolling eligibility" rule means that most of the books on the Nebula ballot aren't from 2003 anyway. So your guess is as good as mine.

Mail-order information: Golden Gryphon Press, 3002 Perkins Road, Urbana, IL 61802—$26.95 for *Nothing Human*, by Nancy Kress, $21.95 for *Louisiana Breakdown*, by Lucius Shepard, $26.95 for *Mockeymen*, by Ian Watson; Subterranean Press, P.O. Box 190106, Burton, MI 48519—$40.00 for *Colonel Rutherford's Colt*, by Lucius Shepard, $35.00 for *Aztechs*, by Lucius Shepard; PS Publishing, 98 High Ash Drive, Leeds L517 8RE, England, UK—$40.00 for *Floater*, by Lucius Shepard, $50.00 for *Fuzzy Dice*, by Paul Di Filippo; Five Star Books, 295 Kennedy Memorial Drive, Waterville, ME 04901—$13.95 for *Year Zero*, by Brian Stableford; Tachyon Press, 1459 18th St. #139, San Francisco, CA 94107—$14.95 for *Reading the Bones*, by Sheila Fitch.

Once again, it was a good year for short story collections. My personal favorite was *Limekiller!* (Old Earth Books), by Avram Davidson, a collection of some of the best fantasy stories published in the last thirty years; seeing it in print makes me wonder yet again, as I have for many years now, why it couldn't be sold to a regular trade house—it's a wonderful volume, and Old Earth Books is to be congratulated for having the perspicacity that the trade houses lacked. Good as the Davidson is, though, there were a lot of other excellent collections out there this year as well. The year's best collections included: *GRRM: A RRetrospective* (Subterranean), by George R. R. Martin, a massive collection spanning Martin's entire career, in several different genres, including television screenplay writing; *Custer's Last Jump and Other Collaborations* (Golden Gryphon), by Howard Waldrop et al, stories by Waldrop in collaboration with Bruce Sterling, Steven Utley, George R. R. Martin, Leigh Kennedy, and others; the first print version of *Dream Factories and Radio Pictures* (Wheatland Press), by Howard Waldrop; *Budayeen Nights* (Golden Gryphon), by George Alec Effinger; *Changing Planes* (Harcourt), by Ursula K. Le Guin; *Rome Eterna* (Eos), by Robert Silverberg; *Sister Alice*—considered as a collection instead of a novel—(Tor), by Robert Reed; and *American Beauty* (Five Star), by Allen Steele.

Other good collections this year included: *Visitations* (Five Star), by Jack Dann; *Cigar-Box Faust and Other Miniatures* (Tachyon), by Michael Swanwick; *A Field Guide to the Mesozoic Megafauna and Five British Dinosaurs* (Tachyon), by Michael Swanwick; *Biblliomancy* (PS Publishing), by Elizabeth Hand; *Written in Blood* (MirrorDanse Books), by Chris Lawson; *Unintended Consequences* (Subterranean), by Alex Irvine; *Greetings from Lake Wu* (Wheatland Press), by Jay Lake; *The Two Sams* (Carroll & Graf), by Glen Hirshberg; *Little Gods* (Prime), by Tim Pratt; *Other Cities* (Small Beer Press), by Benjamin Rosenbaum; *The Amount to Carry* (Picador USA), by Carter Scholz; *In for a Penny* (Subterranean), by James P. Blaylock; *The Devils in the Details* (Subterranean), by James P. Blaylock and Tim Powers; *Unintended Consequences* (Subterranean), by Alex Irvine; *Things That Never Happen* (Night Shade), by M. John Harrison; *In This World or Another* (Five Star), by James Blish; *No Place Like Earth* (Darkside Press), John Wyndham; *Eye of Flame and Other Fantasies* (Five Star), by Pamela Sargent; *Brighten to Incandescence* (Golden Gryphon), by Michael Bishop; *Night Lives: Nine Stories of the Dark Fantastic* (Five Stars), by Phyllis Eisenstein; *Deus X and Other Stories* (Five Star), Norman Spinrad; *Time Travelers, Ghosts, and Other Visitors* (Five Star), by Nina Kiriki Hoffman; *Ghosts of Yesterday* (Night Shade), by Jack Cady; *Kalpa Imperial* (Small Beer Press), by Angelica Gorodischer, translated by Ursula K. Le Guin, and *A Place So Foreign and 8 More* (Four Walls Eight Windows), by Cory Doctorow.

The year also featured excellent retrospective collections such as *Aye, and Gomorrah: Stories* (Vintage), by Samuel R. Delany; *In This World, or Another*, by James Blish; *Transfinite: The Essential A. E. Van Vogt* (NESFA Press), by A.

E. Van Vogt; *A New Dawn* (NESFA Press), by John W. Campbell, Jr.; *Bradbury Stories: 100 of His Finest Tales* (Morrow), by Ray Bradbury; *The Selected Stories of Chad Oliver, Volume One* (NESFA Press), by Chad Oliver; *Far From Earth: The Selected Stories of Chad Oliver, Volume Two* (NESFA Press), by Chad Oliver; *And Now the News . . . : The Complete Stories of Theodore Sturgeon, Volume IX* (North Atlantic Books), by Theodore Sturgeon; *A Plague of Demons and Other Stories* (Baen), by Keith Laumer; *Future Imperfect* (Baen), by Keith Laumer; *Scatterbrain* (Tor), by Larry Niven; *Martian Quest: The Early Brackett* (Haffner Press), by Leigh Brackett; *Midnight Sun: The Complete Stories of Kane* (Night Shade), by Karl Edward Wagner; *Owls Hoot in the Daylight and Other Omens* (Night Shade), by Manly Wade Wellman; *Sin's Doorway and Other Ominous Entrances* (Night Shade), by Manly Wade Welman; and *The Boats of the "Glen Carrig" and Other Nautical Adventures* (Night Shade), by William Hope Hodgson.

Meisha Merlin issued a reprint of George R. R. Martin's excellent collection, *Tuf Voyaging*, Eos reprinted Isaac Asimov's *Gold: The Final Science Fiction Collection*, and Ace reprinted William Gibson's *Burning Chrome*.

And "electronic collections" continue to be available for downloading online as well, at sites such as *Fictionwise* and *ElectricStory*.

As you can see, small-press publishers were even more important in the short story collection market this year than they usually are, with the bulk of the year's collections coming from small-press publishers such as Golden Gryphon Press, NESFA Press, Five Star, Old Earth Books, Night Shade Press, Subterranean Press, Wheatland Press, and others. As very few small-press titles will be findable in the average bookstore, or even in the average chain superstore, that means that mail order is still your best bet, and so I'm going to list the addresses of the small-press publishers mentioned above who have little presence in most bookstores: Old Earth Books, P.O. Box 19951, Baltimore, MD 21211-0951—$25.00 for *Limekiller!*, by Avram Davidson; Golden Gryphon Press, 3002 Perkins Road, Urbana, IL 61802—$24.95 for *Custer's Last Jump and Other Collaborations*, by Howard Waldrop et al; $24.95 for *Budayeen Nights*, by George Alec Effinger; $24.95 for *Brighten to Incandescence*, by Michael Bishop; Subterranean Press, P.O. Box 190106, Burton, MI 48519—$40.00 for *GRRM: A RRetrospective*, by George R. R. Martin, $40.00 for *Unintended Consequences*, by Alex Irvine, $40.00 for *In For a Penny*, by James Blaylock, $35.00 for *The Devils in the Details*, by James Blaylock and Tim Powers; Tachyon Press, 1459 18th St. #139, San Francisco, CA 94107—$14.95 for *Cigar-Box Faust and Other Miniatures*, by Michael Swanwick, $8.95 for *A Field Guide to the Mesozoic Megafauna and Five British Dinosaurs*, by Michael Swanwick; NESFA Press, P.O. Box 809, Framingham, MA 01701-0809—$24.00 (plus $2.50 shipping in all cases) for *The Selected Stories of Chad Oliver, Volume 1: A Star Above It*, $24.00 (plus $2.50 shipping) for *The Selected Stories of Chad Oliver, Volume 2: Far From This*

Earth, $29.00 for *Transfinite: The Essential A. E. Van Vogt*, by A. E. Van Vogt, and $26.00 for *A New Dawn: The Complete Don A. Stuart Stories*, by John W. Campbell, Jr.; Five Star Books, 295 Kennedy Memorial Drive, Waterville, ME 04901—$25.95 for *American Beauty*, by Allen M. Steele, $25.95 for *Visitations*, by Jack Dann, $25.95 for *Deus X and Other Stories*, by Norman Spinrad, $25.95 for *In This World, or Another*, by James Blish, $25.93 for *Night Lives: Nine Stories of the Dark Fantastic*, by Phyllis Eisenstein, $25.95 for *Eye of Flame and Other Fantasies*, by Pamela Sargent, $25.93 for *Time Travelers, Ghosts, and Other Visitors*, by Nina Kiriki Hoffman; Darkside Press, 4128 Woodland Park Ave., N. Seattle, WA, 98103—$40.00 for *No Place Like Earth*, by John Wyndham; Wheatland Press, P.O. Box 1818, Wilsonville, OR 97070—$19.95 for *Dream Factories and Radio Pictures*, by Howard Waldrop, $19.95 for *Greetings From Lake Wu*, by Jay Lake; PS Publishing, 98 High Ash Drive, Leeds L517 8RE, England, UK—$50.00 for *Bibliomancy*, by Elizabeth Hand; MirrorDanse Books, P.O. Box 3542, Parramatta NSW 2124—A$18.95 for *Written in Blood*, by Chris Lawson; Haffner Press, 5005 Crooks Rd., Suite 35, Royal Oak, MI 48073-1239—$40.00 plus $5.00 postage for *Martian Quest: The Early Brackett*, by Leigh Brackett; Meshia Merlin, P.O. Box 7, Decatur, GA 30031—$16 for *Tuf Voyaging*, by George R. R. Martin; Small Beer Press, 360 Atlantic Avenue, PMB #132, Brooklyn, NY 11217—$5.00 for *Other Cities*, by Benjamin Rosenbaum, $16 for *Kalpa Imperial*, by Angelica Gorodischer; Prime, P.O. Box 36503, Canton, OH, 44735—$29.45 for *Little Gods*, by Tim Pratt; Night Shade Books, 3623 SW Baird St., Portland, OR 97219—$35.00 for *Owls Hoot in the Daylight and Other Omens*, by Manly Wade Wellman, $35.00 for *Sin's Doorway and Other Ominous Entrances*, by Manly Wade Wellman, $35.00 for *Midnight Sun: The Complete Stories of Kane*, $35.00 for *The Boats of the "Glen Carrig" and Other Nautical Adventures*, by Willliam Hope Hodgson, $15.00 for *Ghosts of Yesterday*, by Jack Cady; North Atlantic Press, P.O. Box 12327, Berkeley, CA, 94701—$35.00 for *And Now the News. . . : The Complete Short Stories of Theodore Sturgeon, Volume IX*.

The reprint anthology market was somewhat weak this year overall, with fewer of the big retrospective anthologies that have distinguished the last couple of years in this category. As usual, the most reliable bets for your money in this category were the various "Best of the Year" anthologies, although there were some changes in editorial lineups this year, and some new players added to the game. In 2004, science fiction is being covered by four "Best of the Year" anthology series, up from last year's three: the one you are holding in your hand, *The Year's Best Science Fiction* series from St. Martin's Press, now up to its twenty-first annual volume; the *Year's Best SF* series (Eos), edited by David G. Hartwell, now up to its ninth annual volume, and *Science Fiction: The Best of 2003* (ibooks), edited by Jonathan Strahan and Karen Haber, with Strahan replacing founding editor Robert Silverberg; Jonathan Strahan is also editing a new science fiction Best of the Year series devoted to novellas, starting this year, and available only from the Science Fiction Book Club. Once again, there were two Best of the Year anthologies covering horror: the latest edition in the British series *The Mammoth Book of Best New Horror* (Robinson, Caroll & Graff), edited by Stephen Jones, now up to Volume Fourteen, and the Ellen Datlow half of a huge volume covering both horror and fantasy, *The Year's Best Fantasy and Horror* (St. Martin's Press), this year up to its Sixteenth Annual Collection—this year, though, saw Kelly Link and Gavin Grant taking over the "fantasy" half of the book from longtime editor Terri Windling, so that the series is now edited by Ellen Datlow, Kelly Link and Gavin Grant. Fantasy is also covered by *Year's Best Fantasy* (Eos), edited by David G. Hartwell and Katherine Cramer, now up to its fourth annual volume. The other Best anthology covering fantasy (ibooks), a series launched in 2002 by editors Robert Silverberg and Karen Haber, is taking a break this year, and when it returns in 2005, will be edited by Jonathan Strahan and Karen Harber, instead of Silverberg and Harber. Similar in a way, and also good, is the annual Nebula Award anthology, *Nebula Awards Showcase 2003* (Roc), edited by Nancy Kress.

The best stand-alone reprint anthology of the year was probably *One Lamp: Alternate History Stories from The Magazine of Fantasy and Science Fiction* (Four Walls Eight Windows), edited by Gordon Van Gelder; I've used five of the fourteen stories here in one Best of the Year anthology or another over the years, and certainly would have used some of the others, classics like Poul Anderson's "Delenda Est," C. M. Kornbluth's "Two Dooms," and Alfred Bester's "The Men Who Murdered Mohammed," if I'd been doing such an anthology back when they were first published (unlikely, since "Two Dooms" was published when I was eleven). *Cities* (Gollancz), edited by Peter Crowther, brings together four of the novellas earlier published as individual chapbooks in Britain by PS Publishing, first-rate stuff by Geoff Ryman, China Mieville, Paul Di Filippo, and Michael Moorcock. *Infinity plus two* (PS Publishing), edited by Keith Brooke and Nick Gevers, similarly brings together smart work by contemporary authors, most of them British. *The Mammoth Book of Future Cops* (Carroll & Graf), edited by Maxim Jakubowski and M. Christian, is a, well, *mammoth* mixed reprint and original anthology, featuring good work by Stephen Baxter, China Mieville, Jon Courtenay Grimwood, Paul J. McAuley, Mike Resnick, Joe Haldeman, and others. Also worthwhile were *The Best Time Travel Stories of All Time*, edited by Barry Malzberg, and a sequence of "first sale" anthologies covering science fiction, fantasy, and horror, all from DAW, all edited by Steven H. Silver and Martin H. Greenberg: *Wondrous Beginnings*, *Magical Beginnings*, and *Horrible Beginnings*.

Editor Patrick Neilsen Hayden shrewdly ventured into new territory this year by bringing us an excellent Young Adult anthology. *New Skies: An Anthol-*

ogy of Today's Science Fiction (Tor), catered to the long-neglected science fiction YA audience (for whom there's been very little specific material published since the heyday of the Robert Heinlein and Andre Norton "juveniles" in the 50s and 60s) with good stories (originally published as "adult" SF, but suitable for the YA market) by Orson Scott Card, Connie Willis, Philip K. Dick, Greg Bear, Terry Bisson, Greg Van Eekhout, Kim Stanley Robinson, and others. Coming up next year is the fantasy companion volume, another YA anthology, *New Magics: An Anthology of Today's Fantasy.*

Also covering new territory, or at least territory that most English-speaking readers will be unfamiliar with, is *Cosmos Latinos: An Anthology of Science Fiction from Latin America and Spain* (Wesleyan), edited by Andrea L. Bell and Yolanda Molina-Gavilan, an anthology providing an overview of SF published in Spanish from before 1900 to the present day.

Noted without comment: *Future Crimes* (Ace), edited by Jack Dann and Gardner Dozois.

If there were any reprint fantasy or horror anthologies published this year, other than *A Yuletide Universe: Sixteen Fantastical Tales* (Warner), edited by Brian M. Thomsen, and the ones already mentioned, I missed them.

It was a rather weak year in the SF-and-fantasy-oriented nonfiction and reference book field, although there were a few worthwhile titles. As has been true for the last few years, there was a slew of literary biographies and studies of the work of individual authors, including *Hitchhiker: A Biography of Douglas Adams* (Justin Charles & Co), by M. J. Simpson, *Don't Panic: Douglas Adams and the Hitchhiker's Guide to the Galaxy* (Titan Books), by Neil Gaiman; *Dreamer of Dune* (Tor), by Brian Herbert; *Snake's-Hands: The Fiction of John Crowley* (Cosmos), by Alice K. Turner and Michael Andre-Driussi; *The True Knowledge of Ken MacLeod* (SF Foundation), edited by Andrew M. Butler and Farah Mendlesohn; *Attending Daedalus: Gene Wolfe, Artifice and the Reader* (Liverpool University Press), by Peter Wright; *The Road to Middle-Earth: How J.R.R. Tolkien Created a New Mythology* (Houghton Mifflin), by Tom Shippey; *Stephen King's The Dark Tower: A Concordance: Volume 1* (Scribner), by Robin Furth; *The Novels of Kurt Vonnegut: Imagine Being an American* (Praeger), by Donale E. Morse; *The Thomas Ligotti Reader* (Wildside), edited by Darrell Schweitzer; *Robert Aickman: An Introduction* (Gothic Press), by Gary William Crawford; and the autobiographical *Sometimes the Magic Works: Lessons from a Writing Life* (Del Rey), by Terry Brooks.

There appeared a number of more-generalized reference books this year, including *Reference Guide to Science Fiction, Fantasy, and Horror; Second Edition* (Libraries Unlimited), by Michael Burgess and Lisa R. Bartle and *The Cambridge Companion to Science Fiction* (Cambridge University Press), edited by Edward James and Farah Mendlesohn, but the average reader will probably be more interested by—and have more fun with—two books of smart and trenchant reviews and essays: *Up Through an Empty House of Stars: Reviews and Essays 1980–2002* (Cosmos), by David Langford, and *Scores: Reviews 1993–2003* (Beccon), by John Clute.

It was another strong year in the art-book field. The most entertaining of these for many SF fans will probably be *Galactic Geographic Annual 3003* (Paper Tiger), written and illustrated by Karl Kofoed, which exists on the borderline between art book and prose science fiction, partaking of both, with gorgeous paintings accompanied by lots of text; the idea here is that this is a copy of a *National Geographic*-like magazine from the year 3003 which has somehow slipped into the past for us to read; it's all done with a slyly deadpan straight face and with a lot of loving attention to detail, right down to the phony future advertisements that pepper the layout—and some of the science-fictional thinking here is actually pretty good; a fun book. Fans of fantasy and science fiction art will also want to have the latest edition in a Best of the Year-like retrospective of the year in fantastic art, *Spectrum 10: The Best in Contemporary Fantastic Art* (Underwood Books), by Cathy Fenner and Arnie Fenner, as well as *The Chesley Awards for Science Fiction and Fantasy Art: A Retrospective* (Artist's and Photographer's Press), edited by John Grant, Elizabeth Humphrey, and Pamela D. Scoville; *The Art of John Berkey* (Paper Tiger), by Jane Frank; *Great Fantasy Art Themes from the Frank Collection* (Paper Tiger), by Jane and Howard Frank; *Robota* (Chronicle Books), by Doug Chiang and Orson Scott Card; *More Fantasy Art Masters* (Watson-Guptill), by Dick Jude; and *Frank Frazetta: Icon: A Retrospective by the Grand Master of Fantastic Art* (Underwood Books), edited by Cathy and Arnie Fenner.

Among the sparse crop of general genre-related nonfiction books of interest this year, the standout item, and probably the one that will be the most solidly appealing to many genre fans, will almost certainly be *Tomorrow Now: Envisioning the Next Fifty Years* (Random House), by Bruce Sterling. Usually I'm skeptical of futurologists, who often seem to have an insecure grasp on The Way Things Actually Work, and produce impractical and romanticized scenarios of the Days To Come, but Sterling is as hardheaded and rational as he is vividly imaginative and incredibly well informed; we've been getting bits and pieces of Sterling's future world in his fiction for decades now, and it's not only interesting to see it laid out in this fashion, but serves to reinforce my long-held feeling that Sterling's is one of the few science fiction futures that feels as if it might actually someday *happen*. *A Short History of Nearly Everything* (Broadway), by Bill Bryson, makes a gallant attempt to be exactly what the title says that it is, with special emphasis on scientific topics, everything handled with Bryson's customary wit and élan. *A Brief History of the Human Race* (Norton), by Michael Cook, is pretty self-explanatory too, and has some fascinating data. And *Krakatoa: The Day the World Exploded: August 27, 1883* (HarperCollins),

by Simon Winchester, is a scary depiction of a natural disaster of such epic proportions that it might well be something from an apocalyptic science fiction
novel.

Once again, it was a strong year for fantasy movies, but a mediocre one—the
more critical among us might be tempted to say "piss-poor"—for science fiction movies.

The heavy-hitters at the box office this year for science fiction were the two
Matrix sequels, *The Matrix Reloaded* and *Matrix Revolutions*. I was so disappointed in *The Matrix Reloaded*, which is much worse than the original movie,
The Matrix (which I was only lukewarm about to begin with), that I couldn't
force myself to go see *Matrix Revolutions*—although fairness prompts me to
add that some people have said that it was much better than its predecessor.
The Matrix Reloaded is a typical "computer game" movie, where the kids duck
and bob in their seats throughout, their hands twitching as if manipulating
imaginary joysticks, and plot and characterization and every other considera-
tion take a very distant backseat in comparison to the importance of the CGI
effects. Of course, much the same thing could be said about the original *The
Matrix* itself—but the sequel is more bloated and repetitive and less inventive,
and a lot more self-important and self-satisfied, with lots of Talking Heads
blathering pompously to each other for extended periods of time. For a movie
that has little reason for existence other than to deliver one action scene after
another, it's a curiously sluggish movie, too. Even many of the *action scenes*
seem sluggish, especially the interminable Kung Fu fighting scenes, which
seem to go on forever. When you find yourself sneaking glances at your watch
during the Big Fight scene you know that the movie is doing *something* wrong.
I wasn't all that impressed with the much-ballyhooed CGI effects, either; some
of them are good, sure, but I could clearly spot it most of the time when the
real-life (sort of) Neo changed into the computer-animated Neo, which sort of
blunted the impact. I'll leave it to you to decide for yourselves whether *Matrix
Revolutions* was actually better or not.

Terminator 3 was another lame and spavined sequel (or sequel to a sequel,
really) where even the action scenes, especially the endless car-chase sequences,
generated tedium and ennui rather than tension and excitement; this one makes
The Matrix Reloaded look like a masterpiece, and the franchise really should
have thrown in the towel after the much-superior *Terminator 2*. *Paycheck* is
slicker, in some ways, and has better actors in it, but it's yet another movie
based on a Philip K. Dick short story that manages to translate it to the screen
as an action movie full of car chases and paranoid intrigue while somehow
leaving out most of the philosophical/metaphysical speculation that made
Dick's work so interesting. Both of these movies, not cheap to make, performed
"below expectations" at the box office, *Paycheck* doing the least well of the two.

The Core was rotten to the, with good special effects but little else to recommend it, especially not plot-logic or even a pretense of scientific accuracy.

On the borderland between SF and fantasy, *X2: X-Men United* was a considerably better sequel as sequels go than either *The Matrix Reloaded* or *Terminator 3*, and was quite successful commercially. It's not as good as the original movie, but once you make allowances for the fact that it's a movie version of a superhero comic book, working on comic book logic, assumptions, and aesthetics, rather than a science fiction film, you can relax and enjoy it; it's stylish and well-produced, and moves along briskly to its ultimately rather disappointing ending. *Daredevil* was not as enjoyable as *X2*, being considerably darker and more brooding, or as successful as last year's blockbuster *Spider-Man*, but did well enough to probably satisfy its producers. Just to prove that comic book movies aren't always successful, though, two of the year's biggest commercial and critical bombs were also drawn from comics or graphic novels. I've heard *The League of Extraordinary Gentlemen* referred to as "the worst movie ever made." Was it that bad? Well, maybe not—but Lord knows, it wasn't *good*. This one was a real stinker in almost every regard, and it died a well-deserved death at the box office, which must have been especially painful since it was a very expensive movie to *make*. Another big-budget flop was *The Hulk*, a movie for which expectations were even higher, since it was directed by acclaimed director Ang Lee—which didn't save it from being an awful movie that sank without a trace.

And that was about it for science fiction or almost-science fiction movies this year. Coming up next year is a big-budget movie version of Isaac Asimov's *I, Robot*, with Will Smith, that is already giving off vibes that it's going to be remarkably dumb, and have very little, if anything, to do with Asimov's classic. And—O joy! O rapture!—the final *Star Wars* movie.

It was a much better year for fantasy movies, both in terms of quality and overall box office performance. *The Lord of the Rings: The Return of the King* was *the* dominating movie of the year, in or out of the genre, breaking box office records as well as garnering rave reviews and winning eleven Oscars, including the prestigious Best Picture Oscar, the only genre fantasy film ever to win one. Was it really that good? Well, probably not. But it was still pretty damn good, regardless, and probably deserves a good healthy proportion of the money and accolades thrown at it. There were flaws and missteps in it, of course (the Tolkien purist in me still longs for the Scouring of the Shire sequence that got left out, while at the same time I fully understand how difficult—if not impossible—it would have been to work it into the film), including a final twenty minutes that should have insured that there wasn't a dry eye in the house, but which instead had the audience coughing and shuffling their feet impatiently. But so much of the rest of the movie was so spectacular, with good acting, good pacing, great build-up of suspense, wonderful set-dressing and costuming, spectacular battle scenes, and CGI effects a lot better (and more seamlessly integrated into the film) than those in *The Matrix Reloaded*, that it's hard to quibble too much with the movie, in spite of some pretty substantial departures from The Canon. It certainly was worth the price of admission, perhaps more so than any other movie I saw that year. And although purists may niggle as they will, it's without a doubt the best film version of *The Lord of the Rings* that we're going to get during the lifetimes of most people who read these words, and a much better one than we had any reason to hope for. (Oddly, with all the high-tech special effects that saturated movies this year, one of the most mind-blowing and exhilarating moments in *Return of the King* was the relatively simple sequence showing the lighting of the alarm beacons, with the message being passed from peak to peak to peak from Gondor to Rohan. Now *that's* entertainment!)

The other two big fantasy movies this year were also immense hits at the box office—and both of them were actually entertaining and reasonably well-made too (what are the odds?) I must admit that I went to see *Pirates of the Caribbean: The Curse of the Black Pearl*, a movie based on a dated and corny *theme-park ride* at Disneyland, with something less than keen anticipation; in fact, my expectations were about as low as they could get. To my surprise, I actually enjoyed it quite a bit, in spite of a storyline that made little real sense and plot-logic holes that you could sail a pirate ship through. I'd *expected* all of that, of course. What I hadn't expected was the humor. This is a very funny movie throughout, and features a flamboyant, outrageously over-the-top performance from Johnny Depp—in fact, if Depp's performance was one whit less over-the-top, the movie wouldn't have worked at all. (Humor isn't *Pirates* only strong suite, of course. In addition to the sly humor, *Pirates* is also a well-directed, fast-paced action movie with some great fight scenes and some eyepopping cinematography, and some good CGI work (I think the Walking Dead People effects here are actually better than the similar effects in *The Return of the King*), with really good supporting acting from Geoffrey Rush (Hollywood need look no further if they ever want someone to play Long John Silver) and Orlando Bloom. The year's other movie-inspired-by-a-theme-park-ride, *The Haunted Mansion*, had some funny moments as well, and featured Eddie Murphy doing his finest Willie Best imitation, but performed lacklusterly at the box office anyway. The year's other fantasy blockbuster was the animated feature *Finding Nemo*, which did great business at the box office and has already become the best-selling DVD of all time. This is a typical Pixar movie (there must be great grinding of teeth at Disney that Pixar wouldn't renew their distribution deal with them), with the usual virtues of such; I myself didn't think that it was as good as *Toy Story*, my favorite of the Pixar films, or even *Monsters Inc.*, but it's clever, inventive, and funny, well-animated, with good voiceover work, particularly by Ellen DeGeneres as the voice of the perpetually befuddled fish Dory.

Speaking of animated films, it was hard to find Hayao Miyazaki's *Spirited Away* in 2003, except for a few big-city art theaters, but by now it should be widely available from most good movie-rental places—so rent it. It's one of the strangest and most beautifully animated films I've ever seen, wildly imaginative and lushly weird, with a storyline that would have scared the pants off me when I was a little kid, and yet a real depth of human sentiment. Another animated film cut from a similar kind of stylishly weird cloth is *The Triplets of Belleville*; this isn't as grand an accomplishment as *Spirited Away*, Miyazaki's masterpiece, but it's funny, surprising, and charmingly surreal, and well worth seeking out (and the song from it beat the snot out of all the other Oscar-nominated songs, in my opinion).

Another movie that wasn't a box office champ but scored a hit with critics as well as those small audiences that managed to actually see it was *Whale Rider*, a quiet, subtle, and moving fantasy with almost no special effects, and not even any monsters or swordfights, but which does deliver a fascinating look at cultures in conflict in the modern world, and a star-making turn from thirteen-year-old Keisha Castle-Hughes, who was up for a Best Actress Oscar for it.

A weird little movie that slipped quickly through the art-house circuit, *Donnie Darko*, is worth catching as well; it's not entirely successful, for my money, but it's certainly not The Same Old Thing either, and has many flashes of intelligence and imagination (a lot of the more pretentious moments were explained for me when I found out that the writer/director is only twenty-one; I was pretty pretentious when I was twenty-one, too). The new live-action *Peter Pan* had a considerably bigger budget and much higher expectations attached to it, but it slipped through town just about as fast as *Donnie Darko* had, fast enough that it was gone by the time the holiday season was over and I never got to see it; friends who did see it tell me that it was actually pretty good, but if so, it failed to find its audience, and was a box office disappointment.

The much-hyped big budget live-action version of *The Cat in the Hat* was also a disappointment, both critically and financially (I was going to say it was a dog, but I'm better than that, so I won't).

Next year we can look forward to a new Harry Potter movie, *Spider-Man 2*, *Shreck 2*, and a big budget remake of the old television show *Bewitched*, among other treats. Restrain your enthusiasm.

Things didn't look a whole lot better for SF and fantasy on television either; in fact, they looked worse, as several of the most popular shows on the air (among genre fans, anyway) have been cancelled, or are in danger of being cancelled. *Buffy, the Vampire Slayer* and *Farscape* went off the air last year, and the much-discussed new *Buffy* spinoff show never materialized. In early 2004, the original *Buffy* spinoff, *Angel*, was cancelled as well. With the demise of *Firefly*, which was cancelled after a short run last year, this means that *Buffy* producer Josh Whedon has gone from having three shows running at once to having no shows running at all, in the course of one year; it's fascinating how quickly these TV franchise empires can disappear. It's a shame about *Angel*, which, although not as good as it had been in its first few years, was still one of the few intelligent and witty fantasy shows left on television, and had actually been improving in quality at the time it was given the ax. *Enterprise* changed its name to *Star Trek: Enterprise* and pumped in more action in an attempt to boost ratings, but ratings have not gone up significantly, if at all, and the future of this show is also seriously in doubt; its cancellation could spell the effective end of the whole once-mighty *Star Trek* franchise, since the failure of last year's *Star Trek: Nemesis* has pretty much killed the prospects for there ever being another *Star Trek* theatrical movie either. Oddly, *Star Trek*, *Angel*, and *Buffy* novels are still selling briskly, so we're faced with the peculiar situation of having these series continue a ghost existence in print long after the parent shows are off the air (as first-run shows, anyway; the reruns of all of them will be around for years). Much the same is true of *Sabrina, the Teenage Witch*, whose producers finally admitted last year that their "teenage witch" was now in her late twenties and threw in the towel; novelizations of the series still march on, though. A new version of *Tarzan* swung onto the WB network, and almost immediately swung off again into oblivion. *Tru Calling*, a new fantasy series starring Eliza Dushku, formerly Faith on *Buffy, The Vampire Slayer*, doesn't seem to be doing all that well either.

I think that the current craze for "reality TV" shows has hurt the survival-chances of genre TV shows (and maybe of fictional drama shows in general—although the craze for "forensic" cop shows such as *CSI* runs counter to the reality-show tide). Reality shows are *so* much cheaper to make than regular shows, especially genre shows that call for expensive special-effects work, and you can't seem to make them so dumb or so repugnant that people won't watch them anyway, no matter how hard you try (and some of them are trying pretty hard). So why make anything *else*, when you can make reality shows that will get much higher ratings than the fiction shows ever did anyway and cost a fraction of their cost to produce?

Not every genre show on TV was sinking in the ratings, though. *Stargate SG1* and *Smallville* are still doing well, as is *Charmed*, which was renewed for another season in spite of the fact that the show—never a heavyweight show at the best of times—has become so silly in the last couple of seasons as to be nearly unwatchable (I finally gave up when they did an *I Dream of Genie* homage episode). *Joan of Arcadia*, an updated modern take on the Joan of Arc story, became a surprise hit this year, although I doubt that it's going to go on to replicate what became of the *real* Joan. I don't get HBO anymore, but a new show there, *Carnivale*, seems to have been at least a succès d'estime for them. A new miniseries version of *Battlestar Galactica*, which to me didn't seem significantly better than the lame *old* version, did well enough in the ratings on the Sci-Fi Channel to have apparently earned itself a regular series slot. The Sci-Fi Channel did a new miniseries version of *Children of Dune* that seems to have been popular, and is going to do a miniseries version of Kim Stanley Robinson's *Red Mars*, which could be interesting.

Century City, a show about a law firm in the year 2030, is set to debut sometime in 2004. I suspect, somewhat cynically, that the network Suits see this as a great chance to recycle all the scripts from all their other lawyer shows, with only a few futuristic bells and whistles added to the episodes to justify them as Sci Fi, but we'll see. It's worth noting that this is the first genre show (particularly an SF show) to debut in prime time on one of the so-called "regular" or Big Three networks in longer than I can remember, and it'll be interesting to see how well it does. Besides, it's *got* to be better than the new updated version of *Mr. Ed*, which is also coming up for us sometime in 2004. (Doesn't it?) (To say nothing—and please don't—about the new TV version of *Lost in Space*.) (And *Dark Shadows*. Are there any old TV shows left that they're *not* recycling?)

The Sixty-first World Science Fiction Convention, Torcon 3, was held in Toronto, Ontario, Canada, from August 30 through September 1, 2003, and drew an estimated attendance of 4,760. The 2003 Hugo Awards, presented at Torcon 3, were: Best Novel, *Hominids*, by Robert J. Sawyer; Best Novella, *Coraline*, by Neil Gaiman; Best Novelette, "Slow Music," by Michael Swanwick; Best Short Story, "Falling Onto Mars," by Geoffrey A. Landis; Best Related Book, *Better To Have Loved: The Life of Judith Merril*, by Judith Merril and Emily Pohl-Weary, Best Professional Editor, Gardner Dozois; Best Professional Artist, Bob Eggleton; Best Dramatic Presentation (short form), *Buffy the Vampire Slayer*, "Conversations with Dead People"; Best Dramatic Presentation (long form) *The Lord of the Rings: The Two Towers*; Best Semiprozine, *Locus*, edited by Charles N. Brown; Best Fanzine, *Mimosa*, edited by Rich and Nicki Lynch; Best Fan Writer, David Langford; Best Fan Artist, Sue Mason; plus the John W. Campbell Award for Best New Writer to Wen Spencer; and the Cordwainer Smith Rediscovery Award to Edgar Pangborn.

The 2002 Nebula Awards, presented at a banquet at the Warwick Hotel in Philadelphia, Pennsylvania, on April 19, 2003, were: Best Novel, *America Gods*, by Neil Gaiman; Best Novella, "Bronte's Egg," by Richard Chwedyk; Best Novelette, "Hell is the Absence of God," by Ted Chiang; Best Short Story, "Creature," by Carol Emshwiller; Best Script, *The Lord of the Rings: The Fellowship of the Ring*, by Fran Walsh, Philippa Boyens, and Peter Jackson; plus the Author Emeritus Award to Kathleen MacLean and the Grandmaster Award to Ursula K. Le Guin.

The World Fantasy Awards, presented at the Twenty-ninth Annual World Fantasy Convention at the Hyatt Regency in Washington, D.C., on November

3, 2003, were: Best Novel, *The Facts of Life*, by Graham Joyce and *Ombria in Shadow*, by Patricia A. McKillip (tie); Best Novella, "The Library," by Zoran Zivkovic; Best Short Fiction, "Creation," by Jeffrey Ford; Best Collection, *The Fantasy Writer's Assistant and Other Stories*, by Jeffrey Ford; Best Anthology, *The Green Man: Tales from the Mythic Forest*, edited by Ellen Datlow and Terri Windling and *Leviathan Three*, edited by Jeff VanderMeer and Forrest Aguirre (tie); Best Artist, Tom Kidd; Special Award (Professional), to Gordon Van Gelder for *The Magazine of Fantasy & Science Fiction*; Special Award (Nonprofessional), to Jason Williams, Jeremy Lassen, and Benjamin Cossel, for Night Shade Books; plus the Life Achievement Award to Donald M. Grant and Lloyd Alexander.

The 2003 Bram Stoker Awards, presented by the Horror Writers of America during a banquet in New York City on June 7, 2003, were: Best Novel, *The Night Class*, by Tom Piccirilli; Best First Novel, *The Lovely Bones*, by Alice Sebold; Best Collection, *One More for the Road*, by Ray Bradbury; Best Long Fiction, "My Work Is Not Yet Done," by Thomas Ligotti and "El Dia de Los Muertos," by Brian B. Hopkins (tie); Best Short Story, "The Misfit Child Grows Fat on Despair," by Tom Piccirilli; Nonfiction, *Ramsey Campbell, Probably: Essays on Horror and Sundry Fantasies*, by Ramsey Campbell; Best Anthology, *The Darker Side: Generations of Horror*, edited by John Pelan; Best Screenplay, *Frailty*, by Brant Hanley; Best Work for Young Readers, *Coraline*, by Neil Gaiman; Poetry Collection, *The Gossamer Eye*, Mark McLaughlin, Rain Greaves, and David Niall Wilson; Best Alternative Forms, *Imagination Box*, by Steve and Melanie Tem; plus the Lifetime Achievement Award to J.N. Williamson and Stephen King.

The 2002 John W. Campbell Memorial Award was won by *Probability Space*, by Nancy Kress.

The 2002 Theodore Sturgeon Award for Best Short Story was won by "Over Yonder," by Lucius Shepard.

The 2002 Philip K. Dick Memorial Award went to *The Mount*, by Carol Emshwiller.

The 2002 Arthur C. Clarke award was won by *The Seperation*, by Christopher Priest.

The 2002 James Tiptree, Jr. Memorial Award was won by *Light*, by M. John Harrison and "Stories For Men," John Kessel (tie).

Dead in 2003 or early 2004 were: HARRY CLEMENT STUBBS, 81, who, writing as HAL CLEMENT, was one of the major figures in science fiction for over fifty years, author of the classic "hard science" novel *Mission of Gravity*, as well as well-known novels such as *Cycle of Fire*, *Needle*, *Iceworld*, *Noise*, and others; JACK CADY, 71, well-known fantasy and horror writer, winner of the World Fantasy Award, the Nebula Award, the Philip K. Dick Award, and the

Bram Stoker Award, author of such novels as *The Off-Season*, *The Hauntings of Hood Canal*, and *Street: A Novel*, as well as many short stories, the best-known of which was probably the Nebula-winning "The Night We Buried Road Dog"; KEN GRIMWOOD, 59, World Fantasy Award-winning author of *Replay*, as well as novels such as *Breakthrough*, *Elise*, and *Into the Deep*; JOAN AIKEN, 79, prolific British YA fantasy author, whose nearly one hundred books include *The Wolves of Willoughby Chase*, *Black Hearts of Battersea*, *Dido and Pa*, and *Cold Shoulder Road*, among many others, and whose many short stories were collected in *A Touch of Chill*, *More Than You Bargained For*, and many other collections; HOWARD FAST, 88, who was better-known for his historical novels such as *Spartacus* and *Freedom Road*, but who also wrote the occasional SF or fantasy story, collected in *The Edge of Tomorrow*, *The General Zapped an Angel*, and *A Touch of Infinity*; JANE RICE, 90, author known mainly for short fiction whose stories appeared with fair frequency in magazines such as *Unknown* and *The Magazine of Fantasy & Science Fiction* throughout the middle decades of the last century; PETER T. GARRATT, 54, British psychologist, fan, and author, a frequent contributor to *Interzone*; WILLIAM RELLING, Jr., 49, horror writer; JULIUS SCHWARTZ, 89, agent and longtime editor for D.C. Comics, a beloved figure in SF fandom for many years who was also credited with revitalizing the comic book industry in the 50s and ushering in the "Silver Age" of comics; STEFAN WUL, 81, French SF writer, author of *Le Tempe du Passe*, *Omsen Serie* (the basis for the movie *Fantastic Planet*), and *L'Orphelin de Perdide*; KIR BULYCHEV, 69, Russian SF writer, author of *Alice: The Girl from Earth* and *Half a Life*; ZHENG WEN-GUANG, 74, one of the founding fathers of Chinese SF; PAUL ZINDELL, 67, author of the well-known play "The Effect of Gamma Rays on Man-in-the-Moon Marigolds"; DONALD BARR, 82, science educator and SF writer, author of *Space Relations* and *Planet in Arms*; JACQUES CHAMBON, 60, editor, critic, and translator, a major figure in the French SF publishing world; GEORGE and JAN O' NALE, publishers of Cheap Street Press; MIKE HINGE, 72, SF artist, who did cover work for *Amazing*, *Analog*, and many other publishers; MEL HUNTER, 75, SF artist who did many covers for *The Magazine of Fantasy & Science Fiction*, as well as for other markets; DON LAWRENCE, 75, British comics artist; WARREN ZEVON, 56, well-known singer and songwriter, author of the classic fantasy song "Werewolves of London," among many others; GREGORY PECK, 87, famous film actor, perhaps best-known to genre audiences for his roles in *On The Beach* and *The Boys From Brazil*; RICHARD CRENNA, 76, film actor, perhaps best-known to genre audiences for his roles in *Marooned* and *A Fire in the Sky*; BUDDY HACKETT, 79, comedian and film actor, perhaps best known to genre audiences for his roles in *The Love Bug* and as the voice of Scuttle the seagull in Disney's *The Little Mermaid*; JOHN RITTER, 55, television and film actor, perhaps best-known to genre audiences for his role as a killer robot on a *Buffy the Vampire Slayer* episode, "Ted"; HUME CRONYN, 92, film actor, perhaps best-known to genre audiences for his roles in *Cocoon* and *Cocoon: The Return*; HARRY WARNER, JR., 80, Hugo-winning fannish historian, author of *All Our Yesterdays* and *A Wealth of Fable: An Informal History of Science Fiction Fandom in the 1950s*; LLOYD ARTHUR ESHBACH, 93, writer and publisher, editor of Fantasy Press and of the first nonfiction book about science fiction, *Of Worlds Beyond: The Science of Science Fiction*, author of *The Land Beyond the Gate* and other novels; WILLIS E. McNELLEY, 82, SF critic, editor, and academic, compiler of *The Dune Encyclopedia* and coeditor of the anthologies *Mars, We Love You* and *Above the Human Landscape*; ROY TACKETT, 78, longtime fan and fanzine fan; JOHN FOYSTER, 62, long-time convention organizer and fanzine fan, a major force in Australian fandom; LORI WOLF, 43, well-known fan and convention organizer, a prominent figure in Texas fandom; MARGUERITE BRADBURY, 81, wife of writer Ray Bradbury; HERB BRIN, father of SF writer David Brin; MARY C. PANGBORN, 96, sister and sometime collaborator of SF writer Edgar Pangborn, who also wrote some solo stories of her own; and GRACE C. LUNDRY, longtime fan and wife of fan Don Lundry.

off on a starship

WiLLiAM BARTON

Vivid, colorful, and packed with more Sense-of-Wonder evoking moments than most author's trilogies, the story that follows sweeps us along with a young man who's embarked on the greatest adventure of his (or anyone else's) life, one as full of dangers, marvels, and enigmatic mysteries as any boy's heart could yearn for—and a few surprises that even the most imaginative young man couldn't have suspected were in store for him!

William Barton was born in Boston in 1950 and currently resides in Durham, North Carolina. For most of his life, he has been an engineering technician, specializing in military and industrial technology. He was at one time employed by the Department of Defense, working on the nation's nuclear submarine fleet, and is currently a freelance writer and computer consultant. His stories have appeared in *Aboriginal SF, Asimov's Science Fiction, Sci Fiction, Amazing, Interzone, Tomorrow, Full Spectrum,* and other markets. His books include the novels *Hunting On Kunderer, A Plague of All Cowards, Dark Sky Legion, When Heaven Fell, The Transmigration of Souls* (which was a finalist for the Philip K. Dick Award), and *Acts of Conscience,* and, in collaboration with Michael Capobianco, *Iris, Fellow Traveler,* and *Alpha Centauri.* His most recent novels are *White Light,* in collaboration with Michael Capobianco, and the solo novel, *When We Were Real.*

▼

It was the best of times. It was the worst of times. Isn't that how it's supposed to go?

It was, oh, I guess the middle of November 1966, that night, maybe seven P.M., dark out, of course, cold and quiet. The sky over Woodbridge, Virginia, was flooded with stars, so many stars the black night, clear and crisp, had a vaguely lit-up quality to it, as if ever so slightly green. Maybe just the lights from the gas stations and little shopping centers lining Route 1, not far away.

I was walking home alone from the Drug Fair in Fisher Shopping Center, up by the highway, where I'd read comic books and eaten two servings of ketchupy French fries, moping by myself. I'd stayed too long, reading all the way through the current *Fantastic Four* so I could put it back and not pay. I was supposed to have been home by six-thirty, so my mom could head out on her date.

Out with some fat construction worker or another, some guy with beery breath and dirty hair, the sort of guy she'd been "seeing" (and I knew what was meant by that), one after another, in the two years since she'd run off my dad, leaving me home alone to look after my two little sisters, ages three and seven.

I remember thinking how pissed off she was going to be.

I was standing on the east rim of Dorvo Valley, looking down into the shadows, thinking about how really dark it was down there, an empty bowl of land, looking mysterious as ever. Murray and I named it that when we'd discovered it three years ago, maybe a half-mile of empty land, cleared of underbrush, surrounded by trees, called it after a place in the book we'd been trying to write back then, *The Venusians*, our answer to Barsoom, though we'd kind of given it up after *Pirates of Venus* came out.

Murray. Prick. That was why I was at Drug Fair alone. There'd been a silence after I called his house, then his mother had said, "I'm sorry, Wally. Murray's gone off with Larry again tonight. I don't know when he'll be home. I'll tell him you called."

I felt hollow, remembering all the times we'd sat together at Drug Fair, reading comics for free, drinking cherry cokes and eating those ketchupy French fries. Remembered last summer, being here in Dorvo, the very last time we'd "played Venus" together, wielding our river-reed swords, lopping the sentient berry clusters from the Contac bushes we called Red Devils, laughing and pretending we'd fallen into a book. Our book.

Murray's dad was the one named them Contac bushes, telling us they were really ephedra, and that's where the stuff in allergy medicines came from.

But then school started, eleventh grade, and we'd met Larry. Larry, who was going steady with Susie. Pretty blonde Susie, who had a chunky girlfriend named Emily, who wore glasses.

Something like this had happened before, when we were maybe ten or eleven, and Murray had joined Little League, telling me it would help him find his way as an "all-around boy." This time, I think, the key word would be pussy, instead of baseball.

I stood silent, looking out across the dark valley, the black silhouette of the woods beyond, above them, the fat golden spire of Our Lady of Angels Catholic Church, floodlit from below, where I'd been forced to go before my parents split up. In the Dorvo Valley mythos, on our wonderfully complete Venus, lost Venus, we'd called it the Temple of Venusia, and the city at its feet, no mere shopping center, but the Dorvo capitol, Angor, portmanteau'd kiddy-French Angel of Gold.

I realized I'd better get going. Through the black woods, down the full length of Greenacre Drive, past Murray's house, where his parents would be sitting, silent before the TV, drinking Pabst Blue Ribbon beer, across the creek, up Staggs Court to my furious, desperately horny mom.

If I was lucky, she'd spend the night with whoever it was, and I wouldn't have to lay in bed in the dark by myself, listening to their goings-on.

I blew out a long breath, a long wisp of warm condensation flickering like a ghost in the bit of light from the sky full of stars, and stopped, eyes caught by some faint gleam from deep in the valley of the shadow. I felt my heart quicken, caught in a mythopoeic moment. Look, Murray. A cloud skimmer . . . !

Yeah. Right. Where's Murray now? In a dark movie theater somewhere, with his hand groping up a girl's dress, like a real grown-up boy.

But the gleam was there, really there, and, after another moment, I started walking down through the long grass, stumbling over Red Devils and weeds, skirting around holes I could barely see, but remembered from long familiarity with the place, night vision growing keener as I went down in the dark.

Looking toward the phantom gleam, I thought to shade my eyes with one hand, occluding the Golden Angel, cutting off more light from the stars.

Stopped walking.

Thought, um, *no*.

I looked away, blinking like a moron. Looked back.

The flying saucer was a featureless disk, not quite sitting on the ground, maybe sixty feet across. The size of a house, anyway. Not shiny or it would've reflected more starlight. There were things in the deeper shadows underneath it, landing legs maybe, and other shadows, moving shadows, rustling in the brush nearby.

Near me. Something started to squeeze in my chest.

Something else started to tickle between my legs. A need to pee.

I slowly walked the rest of the way down the hill, until I was standing under its rim. The moving shadows in the underbrush were things roughly the size and shape of land crabs, a little bigger maybe, with no claws, though I couldn't make out what was there in their place.

They seemed to be taking hold of the Red Devils, bending them down, pulling off the little berry clusters. What the hell would clawless land crabs want with Contac berries?

Robots. In a comic book, these would be robots.

Anyway, they seemed to be ignoring me.

I felt unreal, the way you feel when you've taken two or three Contac capsules, or maybe drank an entire bottle of Vicks Formula 44 cough syrup.

There was a long, narrow ramp projecting from the underside of the saucer, leading up to an opening in the hull, not dark inside, but lit up very dim indigo, perhaps the gleam I'd seen from the valley's rim. I walked up to it, heart stuttering weirdly, walked up it and went inside.

In movies, flying saucers have ray cannons, and they burn down your city. And in my head, I could hear Murray, jealous Murray, girl on his fingers forgotten, wondering where I'd gotten the fucking nerve.

But I went inside anyway.

It turned out, the thing was like the saucer-starship from *The Day the Earth Stood Still*. There was a curved corridor, one wall solid, the other lattice, wall sloping slightly inward. A little vertical row of lights here, beside something that looked like a door. Around the curve. . . .

I caught my breath, holding stock-still, heart racing up my throat.

Held still and wondered again at finding myself here.

The thing didn't look much like Gort from the movie. Not so featureless. Real joints at elbows, wrists, knees, hips, but there was nothing where it's face should be either, just a silvery shield, a curved pentagonoid roughly the shape of an urban policeman's badge, like the Boston metro badge my Uncle Al wore.

I stood in front of it, looking up. No taller than my dad, so only an inch or two taller than me. Looking up has to be an illusion. It looked a little bit like the robots I used to draw as part of the Starover stories I once tried to write, the ones that filled the background of all those drawings I did, of hero Zoltan Tharkie, policeman Dexteran Kaelenn, and all the odds-and-sods villains they faced together.

I remember Murray and I used to sit together at Drug Fair, tracing pictures from comic books and coloring books, filling in our own details, Tharkie and Kaelenn and the robots, Älendar and Raitearyón from Venus. I remember those two had had girlfriends, and . . .

Stopped myself, shivering.

I reached out and touched the thing.

Cold. Motionless.

My voice sounded rusty, as I whispered, "Klaatu, barada. . . ." Strangled off a fit of giggles with something like a sneeze. Patricia Neal, I remembered, couldn't pronounce the words the same way as Michael Rennie, substituting *Klattu, burodda* in her quaint American drawl. Quit it! *Jesus!*

Nothing.

I turned away from the silvery phantasm, maybe nothing more than an empty suit of armor? Slid my fingers along the light panel. Just as in the movie, the door slipped open, and I went on through.

"Ohhhhh . . . !"

I could hardly recognize my own voice, shocky and faint.

There was another corridor beyond the door, and its far wall was transparent, like heavy glass, or maybe Lucite. There was smoky yellow light in the room beyond, lots of water, things like ferns. *Something* in the steamy mist . . . .

I put my nose to the warm glass, bug-eyed, remembering the scene from near the end of *Tom Swift in the Race to the Moon*, maybe my favorite book from the series, where they finally get aboard the robot saucer sent by the Space Friends.

Little dinosaurs. Little tyrannosaurs. Little brontosaurs. Little pteranodons winging through the mist.

"Not quite a brontosaurus," I told myself, voice quiet, but louder than a whisper. "Head's too long and skinny. Not a diplodocus either. Nostrils in the wrong place." There were other things moving back in the mist. Babies, maybe? Hatchlings? Would that be the right word?

I walked on, slowly, going through another door, walking along another hallway. After a while, I began to wonder how they got all this space folded up into a flying saucer little enough to fit in Dorvo Valley.

Another robot, yet another door, and I found myself in a curved room with big windows on the outside. Ob Deck, the voice in my head called it, pulling another word from another book, as I pressed to the glass, cold glass this time, looking out on greenish night.

Dorvo Valley. Little land crab robots. Brilliant green light flooding up from the ground beyond the forest. Something odd. It isn't that bright outside. Can't be much more than eight P.M.

Little frozen image of my mother.

How long before she calls the police?

Thought dismissed.

What should I do?

Get out of here! Run home. Call the cops yourself.

I pictured that. Pictured them laughing at me as they hung up, as I turned to face my raging mother. You little bastard! she would say. Bob didn't even *wait* for me.

Pictured that other scenario. The cops come, we go to Dorvo Valley. Nothing, not even a circle of crushed vegetation. And, either way, I go to school in the morning. Word would get out, one way or another.

The lights flickered suddenly, and a soft female voice said, "Rathan adun dahad, shai unkahan amaranalei." More flickers. Outside, I could see the little land crabs were making their way downhill, dragging their loads of harvested Red Devils.

Cold clamp in my bowels.

I turned and ran, through the door, down one corridor, through the next door, up another, around a curve, back through. . . . Ob Deck! Turned back, found myself facing a faceless robot. Still motionless. Started to whimper, "Please. . . ." There was a rumbling whine from somewhere down below, spaceship's structure shivering. The lights flickered again, the lady's voice murmuring, "Ameoglath orris temthuil ag lat eotaeo." More flicker. Something started to whine, far, far away, like the singsong moan of a Mannschenn drive.

I felt my rectum turn watery on me, clenched hard to stop from shitting myself, and snarled, "That's just a fucking story! Think! *Do* something, you friggin' idiot!" As if my father's words could help me now.

I turned and looked out the window, just in time to see the ground under the saucer drop away. Suddenly, surrounding the dark woods, the map of Marumsco Village was picked out in streetlights. There was Greenacre Drive, where Murray's parents would be finishing up their beer. Beyond the dark strip of the creek, halfway up Staggs Court, had to be the porch light of my house, where, by now, my mom would be about ready to kill me.

It shrank to a splatter of light, surrounded by the rest of Woodbridge, little Occoquan off that way. I squashed my face to the glass, looking north, and was elated to see, from twenty-two miles away, you could still make out the lights of the Pentagon, could see the floodlit shape of the Capitol Dome, the yellowish spike of the Washington Monument.

City lights everywhere I looked. Speckles and sparks and rivers of light, brighter and more numerous than the stars in the sky. I'd never flown on a plane at night before. I'd never . . .

I felt my face grow cool.

Watched the landscape shrink.

Suddenly, light appeared in the west, like sunrise.

No! I'm high enough up the sun is shining from where it's still daytime!

Turned toward the blue. On the horizon, the curved horizon, there was a band of blue, above it only black, sunlight washing away the stars.

Curved?

Bolt of realization.

I can see the curvature of the Earth. That means . . . I shivered again. And then I wondered, briefly, if Buzz Aldrin and Jim Lovell were somewhere nearby, peering out through the tiny rendezvous windows of Gemini XII, watching my flying saucer rise.

Whole Earth bulging up below now, looking for a moment like the pictures sent down from Gemini XI, which had gone all the way up to an 850 mile apogee. It turned to a gibbous blue world, getting smaller, then smaller still.

Something flashed by, huge and yellow-gray.

Moon! It's the *Moon!*

How fast?

That was no more than a five minute trip.

I tried to do the calculation in my head; couldn't quite manage. I'd never been any good at math. A lot slower than the speed of light, anyway.

I remembered the final scene from "Invaders from Mars," where the little boy wakes up from his dream, and felt a cold hand on my heart. If I wake up now and it's time for school, why don't I just kill myself and get it over with?

But the ship flew on into the black and starry sky, and I realized, after my moment of inattention, I could no longer find the Earth *or* Moon. Where am I going?

And why?

I awoke from a dreamless sleep, and opened my eyes slowly, lying on my side, cramped and cold, against the curved Ob Deck bulkhead, staring at the motionless gort by the door. Whispered, "Gort. Merenga." Nothing.

I always wake up like that, always knowing where I am, never confused. Maybe because there's that little re-entry period, those few seconds between waking up and opening my eyes, when I remember where I was when I went to sleep, so I know where I'll be when I awaken.

I pushed myself to a sitting position, back to the wall, something in the back of my neck making a little gurgle as I stretched, like my spine was knuckles wanting to crack.

Seemed more real, now that I'd been asleep, putting a bracket around the night before. I was here. Period. Unlike the hazy wonder of the dream where we flew past Jupiter, some time around midnight. It'd been a fat, slightly flattened orange ball, not at all the way I would've expected.

Three hours, I remember thinking. That's fast. What, fifty thousand miles a second? More? We went by something that looked like a ball of pink twine, and that's when I discovered if I put my finger against the window glass and circled something, it'd get bigger, that another tap would make it small.

I'd picked out five little crescents. Circled and tapped. Figured out the red potato must be Amalthea, the pink ball Europa. Maybe the scabby yellow one was Io? Those other two, two similar-looking gray cratered bodies, looking pretty much like the Moon, those would be Ganymede and Callisto, but I couldn't figure out which was which.

Murray would know. Murray out at night in the summertime, pointing at this star and that one, naming names, mythological and scientific, every kid in the neighborhood but me impressed as all hell. Once, I'd caught him in a mistake.

And he'd said, "I don't know if I want you for a friend anymore."

After that, I kept my mouth shut.

The lights flickered and the woman's soft voice said, "La grineao druai lek aporra. . . ." Trailing off, like she had something else to say, but couldn't quite get it out.

I stood, turned and looked out the window.

It was like a featureless yellow ball, hazy maybe, circled by a striated yellow-white ring, grooved like a 45rpm record. Colored like those records I'd had as a child, like the one with "Willie the Whistling Giraffe." I'd loved that song, and listened to it so much I could still sing all the words. I was startled to find out, years later, it was written by Rube Goldberg.

Saturn was growing in the window, growing slowly and . . . I realized it should already be going past, shrinking away. "We're slowing down." I glanced at the robot, as if looking for confirmation.

Nothing.

When I looked back, a smoky red ball was in the window, starting to slide past. It stopped and stabilized when I circled it with a quick fingertip, movement transferring to the sky beyond. Saturn starting a slow slide across the fixed stars.

"Titan."

Nothing.

"God damn it, *Titan!*"

Like I wanted something from myself then. But all I could do was remember, remember Captain Norden from *The Sands of Mars* reminiscing about the cold, howling winds of Titan, remember Tuck and Davey from *Trouble on Titan* and their homebuilt oxygen-jet, flying the methane skies.

What would I remember about all this, years from now?

I had a glimpse of the man I might have become, some fat guy in a crumpled suit, selling who-knows-what. All the men on Staggs Court. All the men in America in 1966.

The woman's voice said, ". . . kag at vrekanai seo ke egga." The lights flickered again, like punctuation. I tapped Titan to release the image and pressed my nose to the glass.

Ought to feel colder than this. Saturn's pretty far from the sun.

There. A spark of pale yellow light.

It grew swiftly, filling the window without interference from me, gliding to a stop just outside. It was a cylinder of gray rock, things visible on its surface, structures, and I could see it was revolving slowly around its long axis.

Revolving so there'd be artificial gravity inside, centrifugal force. It'll be hollow, I thought. Maybe this was what Isaac Asimov had termed a "spome," short for "space home," in some *F&SF* column or another? No, that's not right. Where the hell . . . Asimov's article was in that book my dad brought home, Kammermeyer something . . . "There's No Place Like Spome"? Dad had gone to a meeting of the American Chemical Society a year or two earlier, had come home snickering about the little fat man with what he'd term "a thick New York Yid accent."

I remembered him saying, "*Asimov?* Now I see him in a *different* light!" When I was little, we'd lived in a neighborhood full of Russian Jews, somewhere in Boston, Brookline maybe, and he'd done a good job of picking up the accents, and those special cadences. It'd become the basis for some family in-jokes.

The thing rotated toward us, though it had to be my flying saucer flying around I guess, then a four-mandibled parrot's beak opened, spilling bright yellow light, and we flew right in.

Flew right in, swooped over green landscape, found a flat white field, concrete I figured, and slotted in to a landing, one of the few vacant spaces in a parking lot full of flying saucers just like mine.

A flicker of lights.

A womanly voice, full of warmth and welcome, "Todos passageiros sai. . . ." Then the saucer groaned and shivered as the boarding ramp slid down. It only took me a minute to realize that if I could find a land crab, I could follow it down to the hatch; maybe fifteen minutes after that, I was standing outside.

There was a cool breeze blowing across the concrete apron, and it smelled sweet here, making my nose itch. Alien pollen? I'm allergic to a lot of stuff. I whispered, "What if I get sick?" My voice sounded funny, here in the silence. I shouted, "*Hello-oh?*"

Not even an echo, my voice carried away to nowhere by the breeze. "Anybody. . . ." Of course not. I started forward, walking between two other saucers, stopped suddenly, feeling a cold knot in my guts, looking back toward my saucer, realizing how easy it would be to get lost here.

Does it matter?

How would I know if *my* saucer is ever going back to Earth?

From where I stood, I could see beyond the last row of saucers. There was a tall chain link fence, topped by razor wire; beyond it, a dark green forest.

Nothing moving.

No dinosaurs, big or little, in the woods, no pteranodons in the sky.

Sky? Well, not exactly.

Overhead, the main thing was a long yellow stick of bright light. In a story, that'd be a fusion tube or something, an "inner sun" for this long, skinny ersatz Pellucidar. Beyond, to the left and right, were two green bands, the same color as the forest. Between them were three more bands of black.

In one of them, you could see Saturn, its brightly backlit rings looking like ears, or maybe jug handles. And that bright star? That'd be the sun I guess. Glass? So how come I didn't notice any windows from the outside? How come it just looked like rock?

My memory started picking through stories, right then and there.

Something moved in the distance. I looked, and felt cold when I saw what it was. One of those brontosaurus-things, full size I think, but with a too-skinny head, snaky neck dipping so it could browse among the treetops. Glad for the razor wire. Cold but elated. As if. . . . As if!

The was a deep bass thrumming noise, almost like a long, low burp. The bronto looked up. The inner sun suddenly brightened, filling the landscape with a violet dazzle.

I blinked hard, eyes watering, looked up again and realized that Saturn was gone, that I felt something else in my guts, a pulling and twisting. Dizzy. I'm dizzy. Like the ship is maneuvering violently, and I just can't see it because there's nothing to see.

Then there was a great big ripping sound.

A white zigzag crack appeared in the windows, going from one to the other, as if it were a rip in the sky itself, though my mind served up an image of what it would be like as the glass blew out and the air roared away to space, carrying off forest and trees, brontos, flying saucers, Wally and all.

The crack opened like white lips, revealing a blue velvet throat beyond, into which, somehow, the ship seemed to plunge, then the fusion tube dimmed, back to yellow again, back to being a soft inner sun, all the odd twisting and pulling stopped, and there was only the soft breeze.

In a story, I thought, we'd be going faster than light now.

And then I said, "Damn! This is the coolest thing that ever happened to *any*one! Murray would be so fucking jealous!"

Yeah, right. I could almost see his bemused, angry smirk, fading into the blue velvet hypersky as he turned away, forgetting about me, about Venus, about all the things we'd done together, all the dreams we'd had.

On Earth, in only a little while, people would stop wondering what'd become of me, and go on with their lives.

Some days later, I couldn't tell you how many days, already a good bit skinnier than I was the night I'd decided to cut through Dorvo Valley on my way home from Drug Fair, I sat beside a little deadwood campfire on the concrete apron beside my trusty flying saucer, roasting up a few fresh breadfruit for supper.

Mangosteen! That, I'd remembered, was from a kiddie book I'd found in my grandfather's attic, when we went up for the funeral, four, five years before, *The Hurricane Kids in the Lost Islands.* I'd been looking for the sequel ever since, where Lebeck and DuBois send their boys off to the Land of the Cave Dwellers.

Breadfruit? Probably not. Probably no breadfruit back in the Jurassic.

Sudden image of myself finding the little gate, sneaking out into the edge of the Big Woods, finding all sorts of stuff. Nuts mainly, and these things. Ferns. A tree I recognized had to be a gingko. Little lizards, maybe skinks, anoles, some kind of snake.

I fished one of the breadfruits out of the fire with a stick, held it down and cut it open with another stick I'd managed to break off at an angle and sharpen by rubbing on the pavement. It had mealy yellow-white flesh inside, like badly overcooked baked potato, steamy now, odorless, smelling just the way it would taste when it cooled enough to eat.

This is the last of them. Tomorrow I'll have to go out again and . . . I felt a little sick. Last time, blundering around in the woods, picking nuts and berries and whatnot, there'd been that soft rumble, I'd looked up, and suddenly wet my pants.

The allosaurus didn't even notice, didn't look up as I'd crept away, back through the gate, closing it carefully behind me. I'd cooked and eaten, silent with myself, sitting bareass while my underpants and jeans dried by the fire, draped over my constant companion.

I looked at it now, little humanoid robot, two feet tall, looking just like a toy from Sears I'd had when I was eight or nine, electric igniter in one hand, fire extinguisher in the other. It'd come toddling up just as I'd burst into tears beside my pitiful pile of dry sticks, just as I'd screamed, "Fuck it!" and thrown my pathetic attempt at a fire drill as hard as I could at the nearest flying saucer hull.

I said, "What d'you think, Bud? Why's this starship got a Jurassic biome inside?"

Silence.

"Yeah. Me too."

I picked up the now merely hot breadfruit and scooped out some tasteless muck with my upper front teeth. "Mmmmm . . ." blech. Even butter, pepper, and sour cream wouldn't've helped. Not much, anyway.

"What d'you think, Buddy? Thanksgiving yet?" Probably not. It hasn't even been a week. But I pictured my little sisters, Millie and Bonnie, sitting down to turkey dinner with Mom. Bonnie probably misses me. Millie was probably glad just to get my share.

Christmas. I wondered what Dad would get me? I'd asked for a copy of *Russian in a Nutshell*. Two years. Then what? No college for me. Bad grades and no money.

Vietnam?

Maybe. Some of my friends' older brothers had gone. At least one boy who'd picked on me when I was little was dead now. I remembered reading an article in the *Post* a while back, about how so many good American boys were being corrupted by little brown Asian prostitutes, which made me think about *Glory Road*.

Murray and I had talked about that the next day, and he'd given me a funny look, kind of a sneer, before changing the subject. Remember when we debated Vietnam in eighth-grade Social Studies class? I'd said I wasn't worried. It'll be all over, long before I turn draft age, toward the end of 1969. Yep. All over.

And, just like that, there was a deep bass thrum, like a gong gone wrong. When I looked up, the blue velvet sky was broken by a long white crack, white lips opening, spitting us out into a sky full of stars.

I got up, throwing the half-eaten breadfruit aside, running for the flying saucer's ramp. Behind me, I could hear the sharp, fizzy hiss of my little buddy's fire extinguisher, as it sprayed away the flames.

Down on the yellow-gray world, I crouched in the shade of the flying saucer's hull, looking out toward the horizon, across a flattish landscape floodlit from above under a pale, blue-white sky. I'd run off the bottom of the ramp when we landed, had run right out there, bounding high, realizing the surface gravity of this place was maybe no more than half that of Earth.

But then the light from the vivid spark of a tiny blue sun had turned to pins and needles in my November-white skin, forcing me back into the shade. My face, when I touched it, was already starting to peel.

Jesus. Stupid.

And what if? What if a lot of things. What if the air here had been deadly poison? What if there's some disease here a human being could catch? What if I'm already dead and merely waiting to fall down?

Yeah, yeah, I know. The guy in the story never dies. Except the one in that Faulkner story the teacher made fun of, when we studied it in tenth grade English Lit class. What're we supposed to imagine? she'd said. He's carrying paper and pen, taking notes as he jumps in the river and drowns?

From space, the planet had looked like a yellow-gray ball, almost featureless. Oh, there was a tiny white ice cap at the visible pole. A few pale clouds near what looked like some isolated mountain peaks. A canyon here, a dune-field there. Mars without the rust?

ns . . . surely, standing on the rim of the saucer, I'd see one of my
rts?

e ground under the rim of the saucer were models of about two
ures, every one of them different.

hat'd be the thrintun being welcomed to the Galactic Federation,
ed at how clever I was, I started walking back toward the useless star
f I'm lucky, it's *my* galaxy, and I'm not so far from home after all.
t the fuck am I going to do, *walk* back to Earth?
ed by the model of the moon lander. Maybe that was their moon? It
primitive spaceship, looking a lot like the earliest designs of the
r excursion module. Moon. I tipped my head back, trying to look
the dome, wondering if I'd spot a crescent somewhere in the dark

k green sky.
mouth go drier than I would've thought possible. No sun, though
flush of red in the sky, off to one side. So how the fuck long have
e, anyway?
back up the aisle, around the spiral galaxy, back down the other
the door. Despite the fact that it was starting to get a little cool
self start to sweat, armpits suddenly growing spongy and damp.
to walk back the way I thought would lead to the spaceport. Just
e walls. You'll find it.
o run, making little gagging sounds, throat suddenly sore, feeling
ng to start crying, like a little kid lost in a supermarket.
ittle flying saucer popped up above the walls right in front of me,
r just a second, then dwindled away into the dark green sky and

ere, looking up, feeling the hot tears start down my cheeks, vision
whispered, "I always do something stupid, don't I? Just like
rubbed the tears from my eyes, suddenly angry, and thought,
champ. Murray'll be so fucking jealous now, won't he?

ng my eyes on a flood of vermilion sunshine coming in through
lling on me like a spotlight, and wished, just this once, I could
people who wake up confused, not knowing where they are. I
remember the dream, something about school, I think, and had
probably nothing to do with any images I'd seen in my sleep.
uth so fucking dry.
r on my side, feeling dizzy, headachy, hungry, looking around
wall-to-wall carpet I'd slept on was pale gray, softer and fuzzier
my parents' house. Mom's house, nowadays. Dark green walls,

Arrakis, I thought. I'd enjoyed the five-part serial in *Analog*, though I was mighty pissed off about the stupid format changes Campbell was playing with, going from digest to some standard magazine size, then back again, fucking up my collection. I remember I wondered if the Dune world had started out as Mars, if maybe Herbert realized at some point that the solar system was too small for the story.

I thought about my bedroom. My bed. The little desk. Bookcases full of children's hardcovers, the stuff from Grandpa's attic, the paperbacks and magazines I was buying down at Drug Fair, *Amazing* and *Fantastic*, *Worlds of If* . . . .

Out in the sun, the land crabs had buckets and little self-propelled wheelbarrow things, were shoveling up patches of mauve sand. Melange? Whatever it was, it went no more than a few centimeters deep. I sniffed, but couldn't smell anything like cinnamon. Whatever this place was, it mainly smelled like fireworks. Gunpowder. It smells like gunpowder.

From the Ob Deck, I'd been able to see something that looked like a city, way off on the horizon, low white buildings, dazzling in the sun. A circle of my fingertip had brought them close. Adobe? No sign of movement, some of the buildings looking weathered and worn, the ruins of Koraad perhaps.

Miles off, anyway. I could wait 'til nightfall, and it'd take maybe three or four hours to get there, tops. Yeah? And what if the starship leaves without you? What then? I thought about *Galactic Derelict* suddenly. No. I never wanted to be one of Andre Norton's dickless boys. Let's have a Heinlein adventure, at least.

Or maybe I can grow up to be John Grimes after all? Is there a beautiful spy somewhere waiting for me? Jesus. Grow up. At this rate, I'll be lucky to last another week!

What if this was a Larry Niven story? What if we land on a planet that has a habitable *point*? I pictured myself running down the ramp, out onto the sand. Then the deadly winds of We Made It would come up and there I'd be, on my way to fucking Oz.

After a bit, I turned and went on up the ramp. Look out the window. Watch the baby dinosaurs or something. One thing you know: The saucer will leave, the starship will fly, and, sooner or later, we'll be somewhere else. And, another thing: Who owns all this shit? The robots? Not bloody likely, cobber. Maybe this thing is like some super-sophisticated Mariner probe. And, sooner or later, it'll take its samples on home.

What happens when they find *me* in the collection bag?

Watching the land crabs gather up Spice, I suddenly wished for . . . something. Anything. Wished I'd see a sandworm in the distance. Wished for Paul Atreides to come riding up? No. Chani, maybe?

I'm guessing it was maybe three weeks before we made the next landfall—no, planetfall's the right word—three weeks in which I got *really* sick of plain breadfruit. Somewhere along the way, I got up the nerve to cook and eat a few little lizards, which turned out to be mainly bones, and salty as kippered herring snacks, finally moving on to a two-foot brown snake I'd caught.

Didn't taste like chicken, more like fish I guess, but the oily juice that cooked out of it made the breadfruit taste okay.

The next planet was . . . what'd we used to say in junior high? Cool as a moose. I crept down the ramp, uselessly cautious, and stood there with my mouth hanging open. What can I say? Earthlike but alien?

The spaceport, if that's what it was, was just a plain, concrete apron, not much bigger than the helicopter pad next to the Pentagon, sitting next to what looked like a walled city. Not a medieval city, not an ancient Roman city. The walls were plain and unadorned, no crenellations, no battlements, no towers. White concrete walls, pierced by a few open gates on the side I could see. Egyptian Memphis, I remembered, had been called something like *Ineb-Hed* by the natives. White Walls.

The buildings I could see over the wall were low and white and square.

Overhead, the sky was dark green, green as paint, with little brown clouds floating here and there. The sun, if sun it was, was a dim red ball halfway up the sky, banded like Jupiter, with mottled splotches here and there. Sunspots? Starspots? Maybe it's a planet, and that's reflected light.

Away from the city, the land was all low forest, things not much like trees, grayish, bluish, a reddish-purple that I realized with a flush of pleasure might be the heliotrope of Amtor. Things moving in the shadows, inside the forest. Pod-shaped things. Plants with lips.

The land crab robots were coming out of the saucer now, forming up by rank and file, so when they set off, heading for the nearest city gate, I walked along beside. What the hell? If they start to leave, I'll follow them back. Safe enough.

It was gloomy in the city, a city full of gray-green shadows. Gloomy and motionless, reminding me of the scene where Gahan of Gathol walks into a seemingly deserted Manator. Sure. And the land crabbots'd make pretty good Kaldanes?

That filled up my head with long-running images of Ghek, crawling through the Ulsio warrens of Manator.

I looked in an open doorway, yelped, tripped over my own feet, and wound up on my knees, staring, heart pounding. Jesus Christ! Well, at least it wasn't moving.

The thing, when I got close to it, was about three feet tall, looking like it was made of black leather. There were staring black leather eyes. Black leather fangs. Black leather hands shaped like a three-fingered mechanical grab.

I touched it, wondering what the hell I'd do
really *be* a thrint. Fuck. I'd do whatever it want
that. It didn't budge, no matter how hard I push
to it. Cold black metal, glued to the ground.

Statue, maybe? Or just another switched-o
What the hell is going on here?
Where *is* everyone?

Back out on the street, the land crabs were
more, then get the hell on back to the saucer. I
where it came to some kind of octagonal pl
looked like an empty fountain in the middl
made mostly of glass, lots of tempting shadow

The glass doors, when I tried them, swun

Inside it was all broad aisles, floor carpe
chrome the same color as the sky, and linin
Exhibits? Things like pictures anyway. Dior
Lucite, with motionless objects inside. An
could only have been machines. Things t
"thrintun," looking like they were walking ar

So are those the aliens? Are they all i
animation?

I suddenly found myself wishing there
ries I'd been reading since I learned how
pretty much self-similar, as though the w
ideas, could only copy each other, over and

In the middle of the building, taking
a flat, tilted spiral shape, made of what
motionless in the air. Like the Androme
and . . . my mouth went dry. Star map!

I walked round and round the thing
something, anything, but it looked like e
seen. All of them. Or none. For all I kne
was, beyond the farthest star.

On the other side of the spiral was
like model spaceships. Some of them l
were building, back on Earth. Look her
sort of Gemini capsule. Not quite, but c
on the dusty surface of some moon or a

The ships got more and more adva
the flying saucers were. Ah. Right here.
surrounded by thrintun with things li

and canno
familiar go

On th
dozen crea

Yep. T
right? Pleas
map. Hey,
Right. Wha

I stoppe
was a pretty
Apollo luna
out through
green sky.

Very da
Felt my
I could see a
I been in her

I walked
aisle and ou
out, I felt m
Well. Started
get outside th

I started
like I was goi
And my
hung there fo
was gone.

I stood th
blurring, and
Daddy says."
There you go,

I awoke, openi
the window, fa
be one of thos
couldn't really
a nice hard-on
Christ. M
I rolled ov
the room. The
than the stuff in

with brown trim. Stuff like furniture, odd-shaped couches and chairs and little tables I was kind of afraid to touch, for no reason I could put my finger on.

Stories. Too many stories. What if.

I'd wandered around for a while as it'd gotten darker, wondering what the fuck I was going to do, watching the sky fill up with unfamiliar stars. Finally knelt and drank some water from the gutter. Bitter metallic stuff, tasting way worse than the water in Marumsco Creek. And I'd gotten sick as a dog the last time I'd drunk from the creek, coming down with a high fever that resolved into tonsillitis, resulting in a shot and some pills and five days of missed school.

I remembered Murray looking at me with bemused contempt. How come you're sick all the time, Wally?

I don't know.

After a while, in the dark, it started to rain, hot stuff that scalded in my eyes, burned on my scalp, making me run for the nearest shelter, which happened to be something like a porch, on something like a house, in something like a suburban neighborhood. No, not suburban. Small town. Like the neighborhoods in 1930s movies. Judy Garland and Mickey Rooney. When I tried the door, it'd opened, and I'd gone in, sat down in the middle of the floor, just sat there in the dark, listening to the rain, wondering if they had thunder and lightning here.

I got up, feeling stiff and tired, rubbing my empty stomach. Almost flat now. At this rate, I'd soon be as skinny as when I was a little kid. I'd always wanted that. What had made me get fat anyway? Starting to hang around with Murray and eat whatever and whenever he ate? I remember Mom was glad when I stopped being so thin.

There was a little room off what I thought of as the parlor, small, windowless, airless, and in the light of day I could see there was something like a stone sink, beside a little hole in the floor. Maybe the thrintun couldn't sit down and just squatted over the hole? No, wait. Thrintun regurgitate their waste, so they'd lean over the hole and . . .

I felt my intestines cramp. So now I've got to shit. Great.

One step forward and I stopped, sweat beading on my brow, asshole clenching. I was *afraid* to squat over the hole. What if I slipped and fell in and couldn't get out? What if it flushed with a death ray? No, wait. Shit's not alive enough to merit a death ray. Disintegrator? "Man, how did I get so goofy? No wonder nobody at school likes me."

I'll go outside and do it on the sidewalk, I guessed.

Next to the toilet hole, there was an obvious bathtub, made of the same gray stone as the sink, with a little row of glassy "buttons" above one end. Light panel controls? I touched one. There was a hiss, and the tub started to fill up, though I couldn't see anything like a faucet, smoky fluid welling up from nowhere, filling the room with a familiar sharp, ugly smell.

Sulfuric acid? I certainly recognized the smell from first-period Chemistry class. Wonder how that's going? My lab partner had been a big beefy guy named Al, full of dumb jokes, who was a shot-putter and discus thrower on the track and field team.

There was another room that looked like a kitchen, by what had to be the back door, though it was on the side of the building, just like the back door to my parents' house. Something like a little oven sitting on the counter, an oven with a door. When I opened it, no gas jets or electric resistance heating elements, only a skinny light bulb thingy.

Right. I remembered my sister Millie's Easy Bake Oven cooked perfectly well with a hundred-watt light bulb. Scrambled eggs. Teeny-tiny biscuits. A birthday cake the size of a deck of cards. If I knew you were comin' I'd've. . . .

Nothing like a refrigerator? There was a long, narrow trough under the one window, the kitchen sink maybe? A roll of plain white paper towels hanging from the wall next to it. Great. Murray's mom had started using them, though at my house we still used cloth dish towels that would start to stink long before they went in the hamper. Dishrags, my mom said.

When I touched one of the glass buttons over the trough, it quickly filled up with a bubbly gray, acid-smelling sludge. I stood there, paralyzed, knowing not to touch it, and thought, Right. *Destination: Universe!* "The Enchanted Village."

Is that where I am now, in an A.E. Van Vogt story?

Angry at myself, I tore the paper towels from their holder and went back through the house to the living room, intending to go out the front door. Hell, at least I've got toilet paper now and . . .

"*Yow!*" I hit my head on the wall as I stepped back, turning, trying to run. Stopped, willing my heart to quiet down, making myself turn back and look.

It was a bipedal man-shape, not quite a gort but similar, no more than four feet tall, standing beside the open front door, staring at me with two glowing red glass eyes. No, not really like a gort. Feet like a bird. Three-fingered hands. No, two fingers and a thumb, just like a thrint, but far, far more gracile.

Is the damned thing humming? No. Silent.

I stammered, swallowed, then said, "Henry Stanley, I presume?"

Nothing.

"Hey, buddy. Sorry to have to tell you I'm not David Livingstone. Just a lost little dipshit has got himself in a *pile* of trouble."

The head turned just a bit, red lenses focusing on my face, seeming to look right into my eyes. Then it said, "Beeoop-click, zing?"

Really. I said, "Pleased to meetcha."

Oh, hell. My guts cramped hard, released from terror, and I quickly walked to the door, the robot turning to face me as I edged around it. I walked out onto the sidewalk, avoiding the stringy blue and yellow grass of the lawn, which had wriggled and tried to grab my shoes as I'd walked across it last night, got out into the street and started to pull down my pants. Thought better of it, kicked off my shoes and pulled my pants off entirely.

I squatted on the pavement, suddenly really glad I had the paper towels. The mossy stuff from the woods I'd used on the starship had been really scratchy. Jesus, I wish I could have a fucking bath!

When I looked up, the robot was standing on the porch, watching me.

By the time dusk came round again, dark green sky flushed red in what I thought of as the west as the fat red planet-star sank through the horizon, I was exhausted, dragging my ass out one of the deserted city's radial roads, away from downtown, back out into the burbs. We'd been out to the spaceport, with its little patch of empty, unmarked concrete, then back to the museum, where we'd looked at every fucking exhibit, looking for a clue. Any clue.

We. Me and my little robot pal, which followed me all around, like a quiet puppy, plodding along in my wake, little metal bird feet clicking discretely on pavement and bare floor, soundless on the carpet that pretty much lined every building we'd visited so far.

"Pipe dream," I whispered, voice rasping like a cartoon character, mouth dry as dust.

The robot made some little *oot-boop* sound or another, as if a sympathetic noise. There were always plenty of puddles around in the morning, but by noon they'd mostly dried up. I found one now, kind of oily and sludgy looking, knelt beside it, and leaned down.

"Foooo?" Slim metal fingers on my shoulder.

I looked up. "Man, if you know where there's any real water, this is the time."

Its head cocked to one side, not so much like it understood, as the way a dog looks at you when you talk to it. They want to understand, but they don't. I turned away, leaned down again and took a sip. Gagged. Spat. "Jesus."

Rubbing my hand back and forth across tingling lips, I picked a house, went up on the porch, robot clicking along behind me, opened the door and went inside, where it was already gloomy, only light coming from the windows. Finally, I sat down on the carpet, wondering what next.

"What did I think I was going to find in the fucking museum?"

The robot was standing there, looking down at me, red eyes bright, as if concentrating. Does it *really* want to understand? How the hell would I know? Just a robot. A robot made by aliens, rather than some little guy from the Bronx.

I had a vision of me and the robot, finding some way to mark down Earth in the big star map, then mark it out again on the dome of night. Of the robot leading me to some ancient apparatus in some old thrintun exhibit.

"Wally to Earth! Wally to Earth! Hey, can you hear me guys?"

The robot just stood there, continuing to stare. "Right. Only in stories. . . ."

But this . . . but *this* . . . !

I whispered, "So what the hell should I call you? Friday? Nah, too obvious."

It made some random fluty sounds, like the ones Millie made on the recorder she'd gotten last Christmas.

"Tootle?" Like the train in the story. "I think I can, I . . ."

It suddenly reached out and tried to stick a metal finger in my mouth.

"Hey!"

It froze in position, then said, "Whee-oo. Dot-dot."

Mournful and sad. I lay back on the rug, curled up in a little ball, put my hands over my face and made some stupid little sobbing sounds. No tears though. Probably too dried out to cry. Rolled onto my back, stretching out, looking up at meaningless black shadows, my throat making a little clucking noise as I tried to swallow.

Well. There would be water in the morning. Hot, bitter water, but it hadn't killed me so far. I looked up at the robot. "You know how to turn on the lights, buddy? Is there a fucking TV here anywhere?"

Shit. I missed TV. When was I going to see *Gilligan's Island* again? What the hell would the Professor do in my shoes? Or Mr. Wizard? No, not that one. The owl one. Drizzle, drazzle, druzzle, drome, time for zis vun to come home . . . ?

Jesus, I miss a lot of things. Things I thought I hated. Mom and Dad. My sisters. My so-called friends. Murray. Even school. Maybe. Some time or another, still bullshitting myself as the room grew darker and darker, 'til all I could see were the robot's staring red eyes, I must have fallen asleep.

Woke up suddenly, opening my eyes on grainy darkness, pain roaring in my arm, sitting up, struggling to figure out . . . to find . . . my voice, yelling, echoing, something like a scream that'd started in my sleep.

The robot's bright red eyes were near me, making enough light so that I could see the gleam of its body, arms and legs and featureless face, could see the reddish-black outlines of things in the room, thrintun furniture.

I tried to stand, stumbling, twisting to look at my upper arm, pain radiating away from a black smear. Black and wet. Blood! I'm bleeding! I made some weird gargling sound, looking back at the robot, which seemed to be holding something in one hand, pinched daintily by its few fingers.

The clenched hand went to its featureless face, briefly, as if eating the whatever-it-was, though it had no mouth, then reached out and grabbed me by the arm, just below the bloody spot.

"No! No! Lemme go!" Shrieking, voice breaking.

Its other hand reached out and touched the wound.

Flare of white light.

Sear of pain.

Just like that, I blacked out.

And awoke again, clear-headed, salmon-pink sunshine flooding the room. The robot was standing over me, motionless, red eyes staring. No eyelids. Right. I sat up, no stiffer than usual, mouth still dry, dull ache like a bruise in my left upper arm.

Memory.

"Kee-rist . . ." still whispered.

Dream?

No. The sore spot on my arm was marked by a skinny white scar, like a really bad cut from a long time ago. Right. Fresh scars are red, then pink for a while. One that big would take months to fade. I touched it. Tender, but not too bad.

"What the hell. . . ."

When I stood up, licking my lips, the robot backed off a few paces, staring right into my eyes. Then it lifted a hand and seemed to beckon. This way. This way. Come on. Turned and walked slowly to the bathroom door. Turned to face me. That hand motion again. Come on. What the fuck are you waiting for?

I followed it into the bathroom. "Well?"

When it reached out and tapped a glass button, the little room filled with pale pastel pink light, making my skin seem to flush with health and well being. I thought, If there's light at night, I'm going to wish for a book. It tapped a button on the wall over the hole in the floor. There was a flicker of dim blue light somewhere down the hole, a faint sizzle, a fair electric smell.

Yah. Disintegrator.

Why the hell didn't I just tap all the buttons in the house myself? Was I afraid? Jeez, I'd filled the tub, and the kitchen sink thingy. . . .

It tapped the button over the tub, the same one I'd tried, the one that'd gotten me a tub full of battery acid. This time, some clear, smokeless stuff began welling up. All I could do was stare, watching it fill up, rubbing the scar on my arm, feeling my heart pound.

"All right," I said. I glanced at the robot, no expression possible, red eyes on me. "Something's going on. What? Ah, fuck." I reached out and stuck my finger in the stuff. No sizzle. No burn. Warm, though. Cupped a handful, brought it dripping to my face. Sniffed. Odorless. Put it in my mouth. Tasteless. Swallowed.

"Water."

Some little parrot-voice repeated, "Waw. Tur."

There was a prickling in the back of my neck, as if something were crawling in my dirty hair. I turned and looked at the robot. "You say something, buddy?"

"Beeee-oooo."

"Oh." Turned back to the tub, swallowing hard. Then I pulled off my filthy clothes, stepped over the rim and sat down. Sat down in warm water, leaned forward and plunged my face, rubbing my cheeks, where scruffy, patchy, half-silky, half-rough beard had grown out maybe a quarter-inch or so, opened my mouth and tried to swallow, came up gasping, choking, laughing.

I looked up at the robot, and shouted, "Jesus! This is wonderful!"

It said, "Waw. Tur. Wun. Dur. Full." Turned suddenly and walked away, leaving me alone in the tub.

I leaned back against the rim and sank down, feeling the water prickle all over, lifting scales of dead skin, old sweat, grime and dirt and who-knows-what, suddenly wishing for shampoo, for soap, toothpaste and toothbrush.

How the hell did it know I needed water? Sudden memory, me, screaming, trying to get away, blood on my arm, robot touching whatever to its face, the sizzle of the fleshwelder that made this scar on my arm.

I touched the scar, and thought, *Sample*. It took a sample for analysis. What was it they said in science class? We're seventy percent water? Something like that.

I wished for the bottle of nasty blue Micrin mouthwash sitting by the bathroom sink at home. I'd asked Mom to buy Scope, like Murray's parents, but it was green, you see, and Mom always liked blue stuff best.

I guessed if I washed my clothes in plain water, it'll help a little bit. Wouldn't it?

Better than nothing, anyway.

The robot came back, carrying a stone plate heaped with some smoky, steamy brown stuff, filling the bathroom with a smell like pork chops. Plain pork chops, no Shake 'n' Bake or anything . . . my mouth suddenly watered so hard I started to drool.

The plate, when I balanced it on the rim of the tub, was full of something that looked like very coarsely ground hamburger, closer to shredded than anything else, a lighter shade of brown than you see in cooked ground beef. I touched it with my fingertip, getting a little juice on my skin. Sniffed. Licked.

Yah. Pretty much like pork chop grease and . . . jerked. Looked up at my staring robot. "Synthesized from . . . ?" Nothing.

Smart. Smart as hell. Smarter than me. What else should I have expected from a star-faring civilization? A little thrill from somewhere inside. Better than

Arsenal of Miracles. 'Cept, of course, for the parts about Peganna of the Silver Hair.

I picked up a chunk of crumbly meat and popped it in my mouth. Chewed. Swallowed. Took another. Not really much like pork. Kind of gamey, but not venison either. Suddenly, the plate was half empty, and my stomach wasn't growling anymore.

I said, "So. Ground Wally tastes pretty good. You got any Worcestershire sauce? I like Lea & Perrins best."

It said, "Ground. Wally. Good. No. Sauce."

"Oh, that's okay, I . . ." Stopped. Stared at those red eyes, realizing my nameless little robot pal had just said an original sentence.

Some time in the night I awoke, swimming up from a dream, knowing it was a dream, hating it, but knowing. Face wet, cooling, fingers gentle in my hair. I jerked the rest of the way awake, eyes opening on dim pink light, light coming from nowhere, everywhere, certainly not the square black windows.

There was a soft sizzling outside as the hot acid rain came down, tonight as every night.

The robot stroked its two skinny fingers and long thin thumb through my hair, animate, but hardly alive. "Wally. Wake. Up. Now."

I whispered, "Yeah." Started shivering, wishing for . . . something. Anything.

"Wally. Crying. In. Sleep." Still that jerky delivery, though it'd improved sharply as the day wore on. Saying words as words now, rather than crude, isolated syllables.

What the hell had I been dreaming about? It was already getting away, the way dreams so often do. Something about my parents, some fight they'd had only a few weeks before Dad had moved out. I remember Mom said "scumbag" and Dad countered with "whore." I remember their arguments were always like that, like they were playing some stupid game of one-upmanship.

I said, "Can you make me something to eat?"

"What. To. Eat." No intonation, but it'd picked up on infinitives now.

What, then? So far, it'd been able to make ground meat and cups of some sweet, fatty yellow milk. Wally milk? This count as cannibalism? I had a sudden pang of longing, realizing I missed Brussels sprouts, of all things. "Ice cream?"

"What. Ice. Cream."

What indeed. "Uhhhh . . . Milk. Sugar. Ummm . . ." Why the fuck don't I *know* this stuff? I could picture it in my head. Taste it. Desperately taste it. Vanilla. I love vanilla ice cream. I could even call up an image of a vanilla bean. But I don't think you could manufacture a vanilla bean out of the contents of Wally Munsen's carcass.

The robot reached out and slowly stroked my hair one more time.

I said, "It's cold. Frozen. Not hard like ice. . . ." realizing it wasn't cold here, that the robot might not know what ice was. "Soft. Mushy." I shrugged helplessly. "Maybe it's the fat that gives it that texture?"

I followed the robot out to the kitchen, curious about what it planned to do. Hell, maybe I could learn to run the synthesizer myself? All it did was put its fingers over four nodes, two on one side of the panel, two on the other. They lit up blue, and it stood there, motionless, for maybe a minute.

There was a soft gurgle, and a blob of white ice cream suddenly extruded from the bottom of the trough. Maybe a quart. The robot got a plate from the cupboard, reached in, scooped the ice cream onto it, and handed it to me.

"Ice. Cream."

I took the plate, sniffing at the blob. "Maybe." But it didn't smell like ice cream. Not quite. "You got a spoon?"

"No. Spoon."

I sighed. Might as well ask it to get me a MacDonald's. I stuck out my tongue and licked the surface of the stuff. No. Not ice cream. More like heavy cream. Maybe the way ice cream would taste if you left out all the flavoring. "Good enough. Thanks." I took a bite, getting it all over my face, and thought, Anyway, the texture's perfect.

Afterward, I washed my face in the bathroom sink, went back to the living room and curled up again, wanting to sleep. Some time before I drifted off, the robot came back and squatted by my side, reaching out and slowly stroking my hair. Cold metal fingers, but nice enough for all that.

There were days now, when I awoke with a sensation of intense well being. Fed. Rested. Someone to talk to. Sort of. The light flooding in the window slanted sharply downward, as if I'd overslept, looking almost orange on the gray carpet.

I got up, stretching, listening to the gristle in my back make its little sounds, realizing I felt better sleeping on the floor than I ever had on any of the too soft mattresses my parents had bought me over the years. Mom likes soft mattresses, so that's what everyone must like, hm?

I remembered my dad stretching in the morning, frowning as he arched his back. Not a clue.

I went to the door and out onto the porch. It was warm, soft breeze gentle on my bare skin. I walked over to where my clothes were draped over the railing and felt them. Dry, but stiff. I'd tried washing them in plain water, which turned out to be useless. Tried to get the robot to make soap, but it could only come up with something like Crisco, something that smelled and tasted good enough that I finally just ate it.

I'd put them outside to dry and forgotten them, acid rain leaching some of the color out of my pants, leaving little white streaks here and there.

Jesus. Mom will kill me.

I'd kept my shoes inside, and it was warm enough to go naked here. For now, anyway. I stretched again, peed over the railing into the grass, which wriggled and squirmed like it was trying to get away, then went back in the house.

"Robot?"

Nothing.

Awful damn quiet in here.

Went into the kitchen.

There was a plate of cold, pale brown meatloaf and a stone mug of yellowish wallymilk beside the trough.

"Robot?"

Felt my heart maybe pounding a little bit. No robot in the backyard. No robot in the bathroom. No robot in any of the other rooms, mysterious rooms, of the house I was making my home base. No robot in the street outside, or much of anything else moving. Grassy stuff stirring. Clouds in the sky drifting slowly, that was it.

No birds here.

No rats. No bugs.

I went back to the kitchen and slowly ate my cold breakfast. Thoughtful of robot to leave something. Thoughtful of it to let me sleep.

God damn it.

After breakfast I went to the bathroom and filled up the tub, trying not to feel scared.

Noontime. No lunch. No robot.

Finally, I put on my shoes and socks, went naked on out to the street and began to make my usual rounds, keeping my mouth shut, unwilling to make speech sounds that would go unanswered. Went out through the nearest city gate and walked to the empty spaceport, stood looking up at the grass-green sky, shading my eyes from the reddish-orange light of the brilliant noonday sun. No saucers. And no robot. Went back to the house and checked in.

No robot.

Very slowly walked downtown, walked to the museum, wondering what the fuck I was going to do if it was gone for good. Sure, I had a sink, a toilet, and a bathtub. I'd got water to drink, I could stay clean, I could take a crap indoors.

On the other hand, I never had figured out how to run the synthesizer. I'd stood there with my fingers on the right nodes, stood there feeling silly, wishing it to work, muttering "Abracadabra, open sesame, you fucking piece of shit. . . ."

The robot had stood watching, red eyes on me, and finally said, "Wally no can do." Getting good now, it was, though still with nothing like inflection.

"Go ahead you little bastard. Laugh!"

It said, "No can do, Wally."

No can laugh. What means word laugh, Wally?

And every night, it would sit beside me and stroke my hair while I fell asleep. I was going to miss that, even if I didn't starve to death. I went into the museum, willing myself not to cry. Anyway, what if it *does* come back? What if the ships never come again? What if I have to stay here forever? All by myself? Me and, maybe, if I'm lucky, the damn robot?

No, not forever.

I was barely sixteen years old, though.

What if I had to stay here for fifty years?

Fifty years eating my own synthetic flesh.

I got goosebumps, standing under the museum dome, standing in front of the useless God-damned star map. "Where the fuck *am* I?" My voice echoed under the dome, silencing me.

I walked over to the history section, to where I'd left off on the first day, to the aisles that dealt with what'd happened after the thrintun had made first contact, had been welcomed into the Galactic Federation, if that's what it was. There was a whole section of cool little dioramas there, each one showing a single thrint surrounded by another sort of being, behind them all, a deep image of another world, pink suns and green, yellow skies, blue, purple, gold, you name it. Usually, there was stuff like vegetation in a color complementing the sky, as with Earth, with its blue sky and green trees.

Like God had a plan of some kind.

My favorite diorama was a world with a pale, pale yellow sky, just a hint of yellow, a world that seemed to be all tall buildings and not much else, the aliens' version of Trantor, maybe? There were lots of different beings here, scattered among them a lot of land crab robots, which helped to give it scale. In the sky over the buildings was a flying saucer, and when you looked closely, very deep in the sky, shadowed by its color, there was a spome, obviously hanging in space, so big you could see it in orbit from the ground.

Are they all still out there? I wondered.

Or are they all gone?

What if all these worlds are as empty as this one, as the others I'd seen so far? I'd started thinking of it as the Lost Empire sometimes, wondering what could possibly have happened. Did the robot know? I'd asked, more than once, but had so far gotten no answer.

Either it didn't know, or didn't know how to tell.

Then a piping voice said, "Wally?"

My heart seized in my chest, then I spun around, "You're . . . *uh*."

I'd been going to say, *You're back!*, but the thing before me . . . was not a robot at all. Certainly not *my* robot. About the same size, but . . . pale gray skin. Big black eyes, slightly slanted. Noseless face. Lipless mouth. Two fingers and a thumb on each hand. Fleshy bird-feet.

More or less, I thought, like the beings they put on those Saucer books, paperbacks at Drug Fair competing for rack space with the science fiction I read. Who was it read that stuff? Kenny. Kenny, who would get something by Charles Fort, when Murray and I would be buying *Prince of Peril* or whatever Andre Norton title was out. What'd that book been called? *Lo!?* Something like that.

The being stepped toward me, lifting one of those peculiarly familiar hands. "I'm sorry I startled you."

"Who . . ." What?

It said, "It's me, Wally."

Uhhh. . . . "Robot?"

The gash of a mouth seemed to smile. "Well, you can still call me that if you want, but I went for an upgrade. I'm really more of an artificial man now."

Artificial . . . an inane voice yammered in my head: What, then? Tor-Dur-Bar? Pinocchio? I remembered the joke about "my only begotten son" and sort of snickered.

The robot said, "Come on, Wally. Let's go home. You must be starving." Its intonation, I noticed, had suddenly gotten much better.

So. Nighttime. I lay on the floor, wrapped up in a blanket Robot'd produced from who knows where or God knows what, listening to the hiss of the evening rain, alien room suffused with a soft orange light. Even if I had a book, I wouldn't have been able to read it in this.

But I wanted a book anyway.

I kept my head down, chin tucked in, trying to lose myself somehow. Think about all the books you've read. Jesus. I'd read *thousands* of books, it was practically all I did! Why couldn't I remember them better?

I started again, imagining myself to be Ghek, slinking alone through the darkness below the pits of Manator, drinking the Ulsios' blood, finding myself on the cliff over the subterranean river, the one he assumed might wind up flowing toward. . . . Omean? The Lost Sea of Korus? Hell. Started to drift back. . . .

But I was Tars Tarkas, struggling to get my fat ass through the hole in the base of the tree, while John Carter defended me from the Plant Men, no wait, Carthoris . . . the pimalia blossoms, the garden in Ptarth, Thuvia. . . .

No use, me again, though now wondering about the reproductive systems of the Red Martians. Monotremes, obviously. I remembered we'd seen this film in science class one time, the biologist in the film flipping over a platypus, everyone in the class giggling nervously at the hairy slit on its belly. He'd pried open the slit, to more giggles, then . . . *damn!* There's an *egg* in there!

So, what then? When John Carter fucks Dejah Thoris, does he find himself bumping into an egg? What'll we call it, my incomparable princess of Helium? In my imagination, while they talked, old Johnny kept on humping her and . . .

Oh, great. Now I had a hard on. One of those real tingly ones meaning I'd probably come even if I kept my hands off it. On the other hand . . . right.

I flipped back the blanket, rolling onto my back, wrapping my fingers around the damned thing and . . . stopped, stock still. Robot was standing impassively over by the bathroom door, arms folded across its pale gray chest, featureless black eyes glinting in the orange light.

After a minute, it said, "Is something wrong, Wally?"

I could feel the nice hard on start to go spongy on me.

Then it said, "Would you like me to help?"

To my horror, my dick hardened right back up, Dejah Thoris's weird monotreme crotch displaced by an image of two-fingers-and-thumb reaching for me, as I remembered doing myself in the tub only a few days before, bright steel robot watching impassively from the door, red eyes motionless, expressionless, merely light bulbs, stolen from a Christmas tree.

It said, "Your facial skin is changing color, Wally. Turning pink. That never happened before."

My dick shrank out of my hand, suddenly soft and little again. Littler than usual. Kind of puckered. I said, "Uh. Sorry. It's . . . kind of different now. I. . . ."

What *did* I want? Did I *want* it to help? A sudden vision of a difficult reality. The one where I live here, along with this thing, until I was old and dead. No pussy for you, dude.

Robot seemed to smile, making me think of all those jokes I'd been hearing at school for years. It. *It*. Not *he* for gosh sakes. It'd be like jerking off in a sock. A very friendly and helpful sock. It said, "I'll be in the kitchen if you need me. Call out when you're done. I'll bring some warm milk to help you sleep."

Then it was gone.

I wrapped the blanket around myself, suddenly feeling very cold indeed.

Did you ever wake up directly from a dream? No, that's not right. Did you ever wake up *in* a dream? The dream is running along, telling its tale, real as life, and suddenly you're there as *you*, knowing it's a dream, thinking about it *as* a dream, while the story continues to run.

In my dream, it was summer, June I think, and I was maybe ten or eleven years old. Fifth or sixth grade, so maybe it was 1961 or 1962? Maybe school just about to end, or just over, which'd put it no later than maybe June 8th or thereabouts.

We were down by the big clearing, big patch of bare dirt down by the end of Carter Lane, across from Kenny's house, where, sometimes, we could get together enough boys to play a real sandlot baseball game, back where the creek came in sight of the road, where they'd build that big private pool, the one where my parents refused to buy a family membership, in time for the summer of 1963. Right now, it was just scraggly woods and swampy ground, bare dirt ending suddenly where the ground sloped off down to the creek.

The little blonde girl and I were sitting on the horizontal trunk of a not-quite-fallen tree, looking at each other. What was her name? Of course I remember. It was Tracy, my age, in my grade and school, though not in my class. I only saw her out on the playground, at recess, and here on weekends.

Blonde, blue eyes, pale face, searching look. Thin, no sign of the adult she might one day become. Not yet. Her hair was done up in long braids that were wrapped round and round and pinned at the crown. Once, I'd asked her how come she always wore it that way.

"You'd be so pretty with your hair worn long and brushed out."

That searching look, blue eyes reaching for my childish soul. "My mom thinks it makes me look too grown up."

"Would you take it down for me now?"

I don't remember that I ever saw her smile. Not a sad little girl, just so serious. More like me than anyone else I'd ever met. She said, "I can't get it back like this by myself. Mom would kill me." For once, the frown faded away. "I wish I could though. I'd do it for you, Wally."

I could smile, and I did.

In dreams, you can see a future that didn't happen.

A couple of eleven-year-olds fall in love, despite the fact that her mom didn't want her "too grown up," despite the fact she never said a word about her dad, or just why she was so . . . not sad. Just so serious. Whatever it was, it made her see right into me. Maybe those two eleven-year-olds could've waited out the decade it would take, and, free at last, live happily ever after?

In real life, that was the day she told me her dad had been transferred, that she'd be moving away to Texas. When? Tomorrow. In the morning.

Then she'd looked up at the sun, shading her eyes, and said, "I better get on home. Mom doesn't know I'm out here." To my astonishment, when we stood up, she gave me a hug, fierce and strong, then turned and ran.

I'd walked home in the noonday sun, feeling that burn in my throat that means you want to cry, but can't. Mom was making lunch when I got there, tuna salad sandwiches with too much chopped celery. She'd looked at me, and said, "What's wrong?" Felt my head, looking for a fever.

I opened my eyes on the pink light of a Lost Empire morning, and Robot was sitting cross-legged by my side, slowly stroking my hair, which was getting pretty long, and rather greasy from the lack of shampoo. How do primitives clean their hair? I. . . .

Rolled away hard, heart pounding.

It said, "I'm sorry, Wally. I won't do that anymore, if it bothers you."

I swallowed, wishing I'd stop waking up with an erection. Futile hope. "No. No. You just startled me. I can't get used to you like that."

"I'm sorry. It's not reversible."

I felt my face flush. "Never mind. It's okay."

"You want breakfast now?"

"Sure." Tuna fish sandwiches? Surely we can figure this out? As it stood up, I found myself looking at its featureless crotch. Not quite featureless. Kind of a faint divided bump, like you see on some of the neighborhood moms in their tight, white summer shorts.

Unbidden, as Robot turned away, heading for the kitchen, I wondered about "upgrades." Even from the back, you could see the shape was there, if not the details. Like a girl in gray coveralls.

The image of Tracy came up, briefly, from the dream. Not the shape of her, which, at that age, hadn't been much different from mine. Just the face, the eyes, the hair.

So. Robot can give me a hand job. It's already volunteered. And you've already managed to think of a blow job on your own, you sick bastard. What kind of upgrades are available? Just stuff thrintun would know about? What good is that? Other races of the Lost Empire?

Maybe the Saucer People from those paperbacks were real, and this was the closest thing to a human Robot could get for itself, from its stash of upgrades? So it tried hard for me when I describe food and stuff I'd like it to make. Remember the ice cream? Not to mention the "soap."

Heh.

That tasty soap. I'd had it again already, for dessert.

So what if I asked it to grow a pussy for me, as an upgrade?

What would I ask for?

I'd seen my sisters in the bathtub from time to time. Not much to work with there. An accidental glimpse of my mom one summer, changing her clothes in a room with the door open, her not knowing she was reflected in a mirror. Hell, I was maybe five years old back then. She probably didn't care if I saw her. Not yet.

I remembered I'd been startled by the black hair.

What else?

Well, there was a diagram in one of our encyclopedias. A line drawing labeled "vulva" that didn't make much sense.

Those magazines, the ones Murray's dad kept down in the basement? Nothing. I knew enough about human anatomy and the mechanics of commercial art to know those women's pussies had been swept away by something called an air brush.

I snickered, and thought, Jesus. Maybe I'd better just stick with soap? Maybe when I can get it to make me a cake of Lifebuoy, we'll try something more complicated?

Out in the kitchen, it was just finishing up making me some sliced meat, solid this time, rare and juicy, to go with my mug of milk. We'd tried for bread a few times, and wound up with something like grayish Play-Doh that tasted more like soap than the soap had.

I put my hand gingerly on its shoulder, realizing that I was really tired of this bland diet of sweet milk and venison-pork. "Robot?"

"Yes, Wally."

"Can you help me get back home?"

It turned toward me, giving me a long, long look out of those empty black eyes. "Are you so lonely, Wally?"

I swallowed past a tight spot in my throat and nodded, unable to speak. Yes, damn you. I miss everything about my nasty little life. Even the bad stuff. That hurt too. I wouldn't have imagined I would, just like I didn't imagine I'd miss my dad 'til he was gone.

It said, "How much do you know about accelerated frames of reference, and probabilistic space-time attractors?"

"Well. . . ."

That same long look continued. "Eat your breakfast, Wally. Take your bath, then we'll see what we can do."

By midmorning, it'd led me back through the town and out to the so-called spaceport once more. Led me out onto the empty concrete apron, off to one side, reddish-yellow sunshine warm and smarmy on my bare skin. I almost skipped my shoes this time, but Robot told me not to.

"No sense getting a stubbed toe, is there?"

Which made me remember when I was a little kid, pre-school, going to the beach with my mother's family. We'd lived in Massachusetts then, some little town outside Boston, and the beaches of New England are rocky indeed. Where did we used to go? Not Nantucket. That's an island where rich bastards live. Nantasket? That's it. I remember Grandpa took me to see a beached freighter one time.

Anyway, stubbed toes. Lots of them.

Robot said, "Stand over here, Wally. Right by me."

Then it raised its hands, making a slow sort of Gandalfish gesture.

My stomach lurched as we suddenly rose in the air, taking a patch of concrete with us. "*Hey!*"

"Stand still, Wally."

As the thing on which we stood went up and up, things like antennae, like giant radiotelescopes, like Jodrell Bank, like stuff on TV, began unfolding down below, swinging up into sight.

I whispered, " 'Open, sez me.' " What's that from? A Popeye cartoon?

The upward movement stopped, and suddenly a hatchway opened in the concrete between us. Robot gestured toward it, "Shall we, Wally?"

"What is this?"

"The spaceport information nexus and interstellar communications center."

"Oh." Muted.

Down inside was a room just like the main room of an airport control tower, complete with outward leaning windows and things like radar screens. Lots and lots of twinkly little lights, too. Red, green, blue, yellow, you name it.

It started waving its fingers at the lights and, outside, various antennae started groaning around, aiming this way and that, nodding upward to the great green sky.

"What're you going to do? Are you calling Earth?"

The empty black eyes fixed on me again. "No, Wally. I can only call installations with the same sort of subspace communication systems as these."

"Oh. Then. . . ."

It said, "I need to find out what's happened, Wally, before I can know what's to be done, if anything." *If anything?* I felt sick. Then it said, "This will take a while. I assume you can find your way to the museum from here?"

"Well, of course." Robot thought I was stupid, did it? Maybe so. How many people accidentally stow away on an automated space probe and wound up stranded on a deserted planet?

"I'll meet you there in time for supper. That elevator cage over there will take you down to ground level." Then it turned away and resumed playing with all the little lights, while the big antennae creaked and moaned.

I stood and watched for a while, at a loss. What do I want? Do I really want to go home again, back to a pathetic little life that showed no promise of ever getting better? What if the Empire's *not* Lost? What if the saucers come again, this time full of light and life, full of things ever so much better than people?

What if there's *real* adventure to be had?

Eventually, I got in the elevator cage and went on my way, wondering if I could find something to do.

———

Take a while turned out to be an understatement. Two, three, four days and I gave up going out to the spaceport, gave up watching the antennae wig-wag around, gave up watching the little lights twinkle, reflected in Robot's slanty goggle eyes.

Eyes like fucking sunglasses.

What's under them, ole buddy, ole pal?

It'd make me breakfast, make me something I could save for lunch, and would head on out, leaving me alone for the day, like a man going off to work, leaving his wife alone to fend for herself.

I remember my mom used to scream about that, back before the breakup. Dad'd come home from work, wanting nothing more than his supper and a quiet evening in front of the TV, and Mom would snipe and snipe, "I sit here all day long, looking at these same four God-damned walls. I want to get *out* once in a while!"

He'd look at her, lying on the couch in his boxer shorts, bleary eyed. "I'm tired."

You could see a kind of red light behind her eyes then. "Tired? Well, you won't be quite so tired later on tonight, I know that."

"Bitch."

Now he was gone, and Mom had a job of her own from which to come home tired. We were eating a lot of macaroni and cheese then. Macaroni and cheese, and meatloaf. I wondered if she thought about him sometimes, about how tired he'd been, and how she felt now?

On day five, it got dark before Robot came home. I was getting hungry, starting to worry, just the way Mom seemed to worry when Dad would be late getting home from work on nights when the traffic on US 1 clogged to a standstill. Should I go on out to the spaceport and see what was up? What if it wasn't there? What if it started to rain while I was out?

Then the door opened and Robot came in, moving rather slowly, it seemed. "Sorry I'm late. I'll get your supper now."

I followed it out to the kitchen, and, as it touched the blue lights over the trough, beginning the process that would extrude my meat, would fill my mug with milk, it seemed to move as though exhausted.

"Are you all right?" Scooping hot meatloaf onto a plate, it said, "This organic form is difficult to master. It seems I required another minor physiological upgrade." Then it pulled a second steaming plate from the trough, more meatloaf just like the first, and two cups of cool yellow milk. "Come on, we'll eat together."

We settled on the living room floor and I started in. Robot picked up a chunk of meat in its hand, turning it over and over, as if nonplused.

That's me, I thought. "What's wrong?"

It looked at me. "I have some inhibitions about eating what seems like it must come from a living being."

"Synthetic."

"When I was really a robot, I knew that. The organic processor seems to have a little difficulty with the concept."

"Hey, if I don't mind eating myself, why should you?"

"True." It popped the glob of ground wally in its mouth and started to chew. And I felt myself grow goosebumps.

Afterward, we had ice cream, sweeter now than before, with something very much like the vanilla flavor I'd been wanting. Robot took a taste, and said, "This is good. Maybe next time I can make it better, now that I'm getting some idea of what it's supposed to be like."

But it put the plate down, hardly touched.

I put out my hand, not quite touching its arm. "Tell me what's really wrong."

Something very like a sigh. "Oh, many things, Wally."

I felt chillier inside than the ice cream would account for. "Such as?"

"I can't figure out how to get you home."

"Oh."

"And I can't figure out what's happened to my civilization, either. I don't know where they've gone. Or why they're gone." It pushed the other plate of ice cream toward me. "You have this, please."

"Sure."

After a while, I said, "Do you even know where we are?"

"Yes. My galaxy. My world."

"In the same galaxy as Earth?"

"I don't think so, Wally."

"Oh."

I finished the ice cream and Robot took the dishes away, walking slowly. By the time it got back, I was shaking out my blanket, starting to settle down to sleep, wishing again I had a book, any book. Christ, I'd settle for *Green Mansions* or *Lord Jim* now. Even *The Red Badge of Courage*.

Robot stood there, looking down on me, arms hanging loosely by its sides, looser than I'd ever seen, more than just exhausted. I threw back the blanket and patted a spot on the floor by my side. "Come on. If you need to eat now, maybe you need to sleep too."

It curled up with me under the blanket. After a minute, it grew warm, then another minute and I guess I went to sleep.

I awoke, eyes shut, not quite knowing what I'd been dreaming. Some real-life thing, I suppose, nothing bad, or the dream would still be a vivid shape in my heart. Something warm on my chest, not quite like hugging my extra pillow.

And, of course, the usual hard on, but somehow compressed and tight, pushed against the base of my belly.

Oh, God. I'm hugging Robot!

I started to let go, trying not to panic, wondering what the hell was tickling the end of my nose.

Forced my eyes open. There was a neck right in front of my face. A skinny neck with Caucasian-white skin, rising into wisps of pale blonde hair. Long blonde hair drawn up into tight braids, braids wrapped round and round. . . .

I think every muscle in my body went into some tetanus-like spasm. I took a deep breath, so fast and tight my voice made this weird, high-pitched whoop, recoiled, rolling away, up onto my hands and knees, taking the blanket with me, crouching there, bug-eyed again, heart pounding like mad.

Pulling the blanket away like that spilled the naked girl over onto her face. She lifted her head and looked at me, out of bleary blue eyes, and whispered, "Wally . . . ?" her voice sounding tired and confused.

And I made that exact same sound Jackie Gleason used to make, dumbfounded in almost every "Honeymooners" episode, *humminahummina* . . .

She sat up slowly, turning to face me, sitting cross-legged, eyes brightening as she woke up, just the way a human wakes up. Pale skin, smooth all over, little pink nipples on a smooth, flat chest, snub nose with a little pale spray of freckles, big, *big* blue eyes, naked as a jaybird, but for the brass-colored bobby-pins holding up her braids.

"Good morning, Wally!"

I sat down hard. Swallowed. Or tried to, anyway. *"Tracy?"*

She cocked her head to one side and smiled, filling the room with sunshine. "I think so, Wally. Anyway, this is the girl you've been dreaming about."

"My . . . *dreams.*"

Funny thing. Usually when your mouth goes dry, it just *is* dry, all at once, or maybe before you notice it. This time, I felt my spit absorbed by my tongue, like water sucked into a dry sponge.

She said, "Yes, Wally."

What was the name of that story? Silverberg, was it? In the *Seventh Galaxy Reader* or maybe *Best From F&SF*, Seventh Series. The one where the telepath sees people's thoughts as run-on sentences connected by ampersand characters.

"You can . . . read my mind." Flat. Nervous. Sick.

She stood slowly, stretching like a real human, as though stiff from sleep, hips slim, just the littlest bit of fine blonde pubic hair in a patch above that little pink slit.

Eleven years old, I thought. I remembered most of the girls in junior high started to grow tits when they were in seventh grade.

She saw where I was looking and smiled, then said, "Sort of. Not as well as I'd like to." Then gave me a funny look. "How do you think I learned to speak English? From listening to you chatter?"

I snatched my eyes away, feeling my face heat up. Yes. That's *exactly* what I'd thought.

"Uh. Does that bother you? My talking all the time?" It bothered a lot of people, including my parents. I think it even bothered Murray, though most of the time he was willing to listen.

She said, "Oh, no, Wally! I love talking to you!" Eyes brightening. I suddenly remembered Tracy'd said that to my eleven-year-old self, once upon a time. Then this Tracy—*Robot*, a hard voice in my head snarled—said, "This is the coolest thing that's ever happened to me!"

Ever happened to Tracy? Or to Robot? I said, "Yeah, me too." I curled myself into a seated ball, knees against my chest, heels pressed together, wishing the God-damned hard on would go away. Bathroom. You just need to take a piss, that's all.

Tracy . . . No! For Christ's sake. *Robot!* Robot's bright blue eyes were on my face, filled with something that could pass for empathy. The empathy in a story, anyway. She came over to where I sat, kneeling down, put a warm gentle hand on one of my knees, leaning so she could look right into my eyes.

It. It, not *her*.

I don't think there's a word for how scared I was, right then.

She said, "Would you like to try the thing you've been dreaming about, Wally? There's not enough detail in your dreams for me to work with, but your genetic matrix may have contributed enough X-chromosome-based hardware and instinctual behaviors to get us started."

I flinched, aghast, at Robot, at myself. Stuttered hard, finally got out, "But . . . you're still a *child!*" The real Tracy, my Tracy, would be sixteen right now, more or less grown. This . . . *thing* . . .

She sank back on her heels, looking sad, just the way the real Tracy had looked sad, sad and serious. "I'm sorry, Wally. I didn't know that would matter."

For breakfast, Robot managed something a lot like bland French toast, with a lemon-yellow glob of something I suppose you could call wallybutter, though nothing like maple syrup, not even the imitation nasty Mrs. Butterworth's crap my sisters demanded, just so they could see the bottle and repeat the "when you bow down this way!" line from the commercial.

Every time they did that, I'd remember my own infatuation with the Log Cabin tin less than a decade earlier. It seemed different, somehow.

Robot brought the plate to me as I soaked in the tub, chirping, "See, Wally? I'll figure out a way to make you real bread yet!" Then she stepped over the rim of the tub and sank down at the opposite end with a cozy little grin, chin barely clearing the surface of the water.

"Uh." I looked at the pile of sticky squares, steam rising, yellow butter-stuff slumping as it melted. "Is some of this yours?"

She took a square, dipped one corner in the butter, and took a bite. "Mmmmm. . . ."

Afterward, clean and dry after a fashion, Robot's hair clean anyway, since it was brand new, we set out, I in my grubby shoes and socks because Robot insisted, though she herself was barefoot, feet slapping quickly on the pavement to match my pace. I'd thought about putting on my clothes, but they were still draped over the railing, so weathered and stiff now I suppose they would've felt like crumpled newspaper on my skin.

I settled for keeping my eyes to myself as I followed her down the road. "Where're we going, Robot?"

She turned suddenly, stopping before me in the street, looking up at my face, eyes bigger still, going back to looking . . . not sad. Wistful? Maybe that was the way Tracy had looked, not sad, not serious, and the eleven-year-old me just hadn't known any better?

Softly, she said, "I'd like it if you call me Tracy."

Thunderstruck, I thought, This is a *robot*. Not a little girl. Not Tracy. Tracy, *my* Tracy, is sixteen years old, somewhere on Earth, probably still in Texas, and I . . . that other voice, dark voice that sounded to me like my dad's voice, whispered, It's just a robot. And *if* it's just a robot, what difference does it make if . . . ? I slammed the door on that one.

Then I said, "I'm sorry. Tracy."

She smiled. Brightening the day.

"So. Where're we going?"

She pointed to the dome of the museum, not far away in the middle of the town, where all the radial streets came together.

Inside, she led me right to the big blue-white-red spiral galaxy hanging under the dome, standing beside it with hands on hips, head tipped back, looking up. I wondered briefly where the bobby pins had come from, other than my memory, my dreams. From the hemoglobin in my blood? And what about the brassy color? Shouldn't they be steely-looking? Tracy's bobby pins had been brassy, though. Maybe there were copper molecules in the tissue sample.

Tracy started manipulating a panel of sequins down by the pedestal, and the galaxy vanished, replaced by a shapeless, irregular splash of light and dark that looked almost like an explosion.

She looked up at me. "This is what your culture has just begun to conceptualize as a supercluster, Wally. It's a map of the entity you've been referring to as the Lost Empire."

My scalp prickled briefly at that reminder, but . . . hell. I was *used* to the idea of telepaths. Maybe that's what made it more all right for me than it would have been for somebody else. I imagined my mom thinking someone could look into her head.

It didn't look like anything I remembered hearing about. Still, if she knew the term, it had to be in my head, somewhere. Some article in *Scientific American*, maybe? I'd always been glad the Prince William County Public Library took it. "How big?"

She said, "Oh, it's about three hundred million light years across, maybe." Off to one side, a pinpoint sparkled, catching my eye. "That's where we are right now."

"And . . . Earth?"

She said, "You don't know enough about the structure of the universe for me to tell."

"Uh. Sorry."

She grinned, then made another pinpoint twinkle, way off to the other side, pretty much outside the edge of the great splash of light. "Your Local Group might be right there. There are five galaxies matching what you know as the Milky Way, Andromeda, Triangulum, and the Magellanic Clouds, in roughly the right positions, though you're awfully hazy about where they really are, and exactly how big."

"Sorry."

"And there are at least twenty other galaxies mixed in with them that your astronomers must have noticed."

"But not me."

"No, Wally."

"Well, even if that *was* Earth, there's no way. . . ."

She made a third spot sparkle, this time deep ruby-red, deep in the heart of the Lost Empire Supercluster. "There's a research facility here, at one of the Empire's main educational institutions, where we can . . . figure it out, one way or another."

"But. . . ."

She said, "If we could get a starship, we could get there in just a few weeks, Wally."

I suddenly felt odd. "And . . . Earth?"

That wistful look. "If that's really your Local Group, not much longer."

"Where else would Earth be?"

She said, "Wally, the thing you were on was an automated space probe, just like you thought. We'd been exploring the other superclusters for a long time."

"So Earth could be anywhere?" For some reason, that made me feel . . . I don't know. Lighter. More carefree?

She said, "Yes."

"What if it's somewhere on the other side of the universe?"

She laughed. "There's no 'other side,' Wally."

"Very far away, anyhow. Your ships seem so fast."

She said, "If Earth's not somewhere nearby, we may never find it. You seem to have no idea how big the universe really is."

"One of your probes found it."

"Yes. And that may be our only hope. The probes didn't have infinite range."

"Anyway, we don't have a starship."

She turned away from me then, looking out through the dome of the museum, up at the deep green sky. "I don't know where everyone's gone, or why, but the communication network is running just fine. I've been able to wake up some sleeping nodes here and there, send out program code, get a few things moving. Our ride will be here soon."

Then she looked at me and laughed again, I suppose, at the expression on my face.

And so the empty world of the dark green skies was gone, never to be seen again, Tracy and I now camped out by a bubbling stream in the soft garden wilderness of a pale orange spome, pale orange landscape separated by broad stripes of blue velvet hyperspace sky. There were no dinosaurs here, and I was, in a way, sorry for that, because I'd liked them, liked the idea of them, but red-silver butterfly-bats floated through the air overhead, perched in the pale orange trees, while spidermice crept through the pale orange grass, speaking to us in gentle whispers.

Only little things, gentle things, safe things.

Arriving here, we'd walked away from the field of saucers, this one without fence or razor wire, while the Green Planet shrank away to nothing in the starry sky, and Tracy said to me, "No, look, you got it all wrong, Wally. *Thrintun* was the name of their planet. The Slavers just called themselves Thrint."

"Are you sure?"

She smiled. "That's what's in your long-term memory. Your short-term memory just reloaded it wrong. Of course, I can't guarantee it's what was really in the story."

"Um."

She'd led me to a long, low, warehouse-like building, where we picked up magic toys, then walked away into the woodland, while the starship groaned off into hyperspace and the windows above us turned soft blue, in perfect contrast to the landscape, both around us and overhead. Eventually, we came to a meadow, orange grass, widely separated orange trees, kind of like gnarly little crabapple trees, complete with little orange fruit, a scattering of ruddy yellowish flowers, tiny creek chuckling over bits of round brown stone.

We set up the tent, spread our picnic blanket, and one of the magic toys Tracy had taken turned out to be something like a hibachi, complete with built-in burgers, already smoky hot, smell making my mouth water.

I touched one, and found it cool enough to pick up, the perfect temperature for eating. "What are these things?"

She said, "I don't know. But they're chemically compatible with our bodies."

When you looked close, they weren't really hamburgers. Bready disks of some kind, nicely toasted. I took a little bite. "Ukh. . . ."

A fleck of concern lit in her eyes. "Not good?"

I took another, bigger bite, chewed and swallowed. "Weird. Mustard and cinnamon don't really go together."

She smiled. "I notice it's not stopping you, though."

"No." I finished it, and took another. "Can this thing make hot dogs?"

"Probably."

Hot dogs with integrated buns. Great. In what book did I read the phrase, *societé anonyme d'hippophage*? I gave my head a shake, trying to banish nonsense. If possible. Christ. Me. Anyway, I'm not eating wally anymore. Good enough.

I said, "Who used to live in this place, Tracy? I mean, orange grass and all . . . ?"

She said, "Nobody ever lived in these things, Wally. They were part of an automated transport system, and I think what happened is, the sample ecologies spread out in here. The spomes have been wandering around on their own for a very long time."

"How long?"

A thoughtful look. "Well, from the time the first star-faring civilization got started to my manufacture date, something like a billion of your years."

My mouth got that familiar dry feeling. "That's not what I meant."

She said, "Based on astronomical evidence, I think I was asleep in *storage* for a significant fraction of that. Perhaps a hundred million years?"

"From before the end of the Cretaceous, and whatever killed off the dinosaurs?" And clearly why the robot spomes could have them in their possession. I remember some scientists theorized about a supernova.

She said, "I don't think there was any relationship. Wherever Earth is, it must be outside the *range* of the event that . . . got rid of everyone." A momentary look of intense brooding in the eyes of a china doll, quickly banished.

"And you have no idea how the Lost Empire got lost."

"Not yet. It's illuminating that only the organic intelligences were lost."

"It's hard for me to believe this," I waved my hand around the spomey landscape, "all this, all the stuff on all the planets, has survived, intact, for a hundred million years or more."

Another smile. "Not unattended, Wally. Just unpeopled."

"Oh. Right."

I lay back and looked at the sky again, staring at blue hyperspace, wondering what would become of me. What if we find Earth? What then? Just go home? I tried picturing that, imagined myself appearing, bareass, back in Dorvo Valley, with a naked little blonde girl holding my hand: Hi, Mom! Sorry I'm late! Hey, look what I found!

Tracy said, "You have an erection again, Wally."

I rolled away from her, curling up around myself, facing down slope, toward the trees and little creek. "Sorry."

She said, "Look, I know we can't do the thing you've been dreaming about, not without risking damage to some components of this immature body, but I can still help with those other things."

I thought, What about damage to me?

After a long moment, she reached out and touched my back softly, making me flinch. Then she said, "I *will* grow up, you know. This body is as real as your genome could make it."

I said, "You're eleven, Tracy. It'll be a while before you're all grown up."

She said, "I'll be physically mature enough for successful intercourse in no more than twelve to eighteen months, if you really want to wait."

I looked over my shoulder at her, baffled. "I can't believe I'm talking about this stuff with a little girl."

Softly, she said, "I'm not a little girl, Wally. I'm a robot, remember?"

I looked away again, remembering she'd wanted to be called Tracy, rather than Robot.

Another girlish sigh. "It's so hard for me to know what's right, Wally. Your memories of your real cultural surround are all mixed up with what was in those stories you loved. As if your culture itself were somehow confused. As if it couldn't distinguish between dream and reality."

That made me laugh. Really laugh.

To Tracy's disappointment, what she called the Master Planet seemed to lie in ruins. And *what* ruins!

Ruins, real ruins, are thin on the ground for an American boy in the 1960s. I remember Murray and I used to argue about that, as we tried to write stories about our imaginary Venus, Murray wanting ruins to be like Pompeii, like the Coliseum, seen in books, in movies, on TV. Like one of Burroughs's African lost cities, or like Koraad on Barsoom. Murray'd never seen a real ruin, having traveled so little, having lived only in New York City and the suburbs of Washington, DC. I'd lived in the Southwest, and my parents had taken me to see Mesa Verde, to visit Chaco Canyon.

Real ruins, of real abandoned cities, sitting out in the weather for hundreds of years, are different from maintained ruins, like the Coliseum, or cities preserved under volcanic ash for thousands of years. Burroughs was in the Army in the 1890s and served in the Southwest. Why didn't he know that?

The cityscapes of the Master Planet were like that. Stumps of buildings with their foundations exposed. Crumbled, fallen walls. A sense of haze and dust everywhere.

We stood by our flying saucer, and Tracy said, "Whatever happened, happened here. And there was nothing left behind to keep things up."

Keep things up, I thought, awaiting the owners' return.

In the end, a few days later, we wound up on something Tracy referred to as a "substation," some adjunct of the Master Planet, one of many apparently scattered round the Lost Empire. From space, seen out the saucer window, it looked like a little blue moon, hardly a planet at all, a little blue moon surrounded by ghostly white radiance, and, though I looked and looked, nothing else nearby. No sun. Not even an especially bright star. No gas giant for it to orbit. No nothing.

On the ground . . . well, no. Not ground. The place was like a cityscape, but the buildings were made of something like sheet metal, tin, copper, zinc, varicolored anodized aluminum, streets paved with sheets of rolled gold, nothing but metal everywhere but the sky.

From under the saucer's rim, I just stood there, looking up, at a pitch black sky flooded with so many stars it lit up the landscape, making a million little shadows in every dark corner.

"Man. . . ."

Every now and again, there'd be the quick yellow streak of a meteor.

"Where the hell are we?" Up in the sky, it was as if there were some shapes hiding behind the stars, faint washes of light that disappeared when I looked at them.

Tracy put one cool hand on the small of my back, making my neck hair tingle. "We're in an irregular galaxy. There's a lot of dust. Nebulae. Lots of really young stars."

Like a Magellanic Cloud. I, uh. . . . "Was this galaxy even here a hundred million years ago?"

"Yes. These galaxies evolve fast, and they don't last as long as the spirals, but they're not ephemeral. They also don't have much in the way of naturally habitable planets. We used them as resource centers. Industrial complexes."

We. My little Tracy, the Space Alien.

She said, "I've got a lot of work to do, Wally. Why don't you go sightseeing? I'll find you later."

"Uh. . . ." I felt a sudden chill, turning to look up at our saucer.

She smiled. "I won't let it go anywhere, Wally." She patted me on the arm, then turned and quickly walked away into the shadows.

Sightseeing. Was there anything here to see? I started walking, but there wasn't much. Metal buildings. No, not even that. This kind of looked like the stuff inside a machine of some kind. Maybe an old TV. Except no vacuum tubes or anything. Like lifting the hood of a car, and not knowing what you're looking at.

I remembered I always resented those boys who knew what cars were about. Resented that I couldn't learn, that Dad wouldn't let me help with our car. Goof, he'd say. You'll either break something or hurt yourself. When I was missing Dad, I wouldn't remember stuff like that.

Everybody was always mad at me about something.

There was something kind of like a lake. No, more like a pool. Round, but full of cool, fresh water, surrounded by a soft area. I wished for grass, but this stuff was more like a satin comforter stapled to a slanting floor. Nice to sit on naked, though.

A little too cool to sit here naked.

I went back to the saucer and got one of the picnic blankets we'd taken from the spome, came back to the little pool and sat again, all wrapped up, looking out over ersatz cityscape, remembering that where my dad had taken German in college, Murray's dad had taken French, so Murray would say *faux*, where I said *ersatz*.

What if I could pick and choose my companions? Who would I bring here now?

Murray? Would I want Murray here with me now? My best friend since second grade, my best friend ever, maybe my only friend? I remember the day before I left, running into Murray in the high school corridor. Larry was standing with him, the two of them talking about something. They shut up when they saw me, Larry smiling, Murray's eyes full of that now-familiar contempt.

What the hell did I do to make this happen, Murray?

The longer I stared at the sky, the easier it was to see those shapes embedded in the deeper dark. All I had to do was not quite look at them, pretend to be looking at something else, but pay attention to the corners of my eyes, and shapes of wan light would pop out of nowhere.

If Murray was here, I guess I'd get some lecture about "averted vision," his eyes full of amusement as he showed me, once again, how really cool he was, how smart, how much better than me at everything and anything.

I felt my eyes start to burn, and had to put away all those questions. Except: there's no one I want with me. No one at all to go back to. Why is that?

Three meteor trails burned overhead, dazzling yellow, side by side in the sky, like a long, hot cat-scratch. Maybe I dozed after that.

Came back from wherever, not knowing if I'd slept or not, for the sky was unchanged. Darkness, stars, and the faint shapes beyond. Jumped slightly at the shadow standing by the rim of the pool's little arena, girl-shape looking down at me.

"Tracy?"

She walked down across the satin groundcover, until she was close enough to see by starlight, eyes vast, face so soft and lovely. What would've happened, if you hadn't moved away, five years ago? Nothing. Your mom would've found out about us, would've talked to my mom, and we'd've been ordered apart, "just to be safe." Boys and girls that age aren't allowed to like each other.

Something wrong though, here and now.

I said, "Are you all right? You look sick."

She kneeled down beside me, and I could see there was a shine of sweat on her.

"What's wrong?"

She said, "I'll be all right. I had to have a little more work done on myself, while I was at it. They have much better equipment here than back on the Green Planet." She seemed to shiver.

"Oh, Tracy. . . ." I gathered her in and wrapped the blanket about us both. She was hot and clammy, not that dry heat like when you have a fever; more like something inside was heating her up, making her sweat, making the night feel cold.

When I was about five, my grandpa, who died drunk, got me to drink a glass of whiskey, laughing when he saw I could get it down without gagging. It made me sweat like that, once it was inside. I remember my mom went apeshit over it, cussing Grandpa like I'd never heard before, but there was nothing to be done. All I did was go to sleep, and wake up the next day feeling like I was full of helium and ready to float away.

She snuggled in close, arms around the barrel of my chest, her sweat getting on me, starting to run down in my lap, making me shiver too. "I'll be all right. Really." Hardly more than a whisper.

Well, then.

She said, "I found the Earth."

Smarmy pang of fear. "Um. . . ."

She said, "Really not that far. No more than two hundred million parsecs. On the far side of the next supercluster from here."

"How long?"

I could feel her face change shape against my chest. A smile? She said, "Well, that depends."

"On?"

She squeezed me a little bit, shivering a little harder. "Well, it only took you a few weeks to reach the Green Planet, so that's all it'll take to get back. . . ."

Damn. Mom. School. Murray.

And no way I can explain where I've been, much less who this little girl might be. Sudden cold horror. When I get off the saucer in Dorvo Valley, Tracy, *my* Tracy now for sure, will get back aboard and go away?

There was a brief clicking sound, then she said, "But the hyperdrives are not immune to Relativity, Wally."

I thought about my homecoming, in those stiff old clothes waiting for me in the saucer, turning up at Mom's house on Staggs Court, in, what? Maybe March 1967? By now, Apollo 1 will have flown. And I'll have to repeat the eleventh grade.

Yep, *that*'ll make Murray jealous, all right.

Then I said, "Huh?"

More clicking. "You left Earth twenty-three years ago, Wally." More clicking. "Some of that was lost in local travel." Clicking. "If I take you straight home from here, it's only another twenty." Clicking. "But only three weeks, starship time."

She started to shudder really hard against me, and I realized the clicking sound was the chatter of her teeth. "God, you are really sick!"

Sweat was pouring off her now, running down between my legs and pooling on the satin. She said, "Just hold me, Wally. I'll be all right in the morning. I promise."

I wrapped the blanket tight around us both, feeling the heat increase, and just sat there, staring at the sky, while Tracy shivered and chattered, murmuring to herself, sometimes real words, sometimes things that sounded like foreign languages, nothing that made any sense.

Twenty-three years, I thought. 1989? And then another twenty?

Up in the sky, the stars marched slowly overhead, old ones setting, new ones rising, showing me the orientation of the blue moon's axis. Meteors would burn by ones and twos and threes, until I paid attention and found the swarm's radiant. That, I thought, must be the direction of our travel through interstellar space.

Once, something like a pink Bonestell moon appeared out of nowhere, just a dot in the sky at first, then swelling to a huge, pockmarked balloon, before shrinking away to nothing again.

After a long, long while, Tracy's shivering started to die down, her skin to cool. Maybe, I thought, the worst is over? After another long while, despite my determination to stay awake, to hold her, guard her, protect her, I fell asleep.

It was, of course, still dark when I awoke.

I was lying on my side under a sky full of stars, arms wrapped around Tracy, her back pressed to my chest, my face buried in the tickle of her hair, which had come loose from her braids. It wasn't wet with sweat any more, but seemed greasy, with a funny smell to it, not much like the dry wispy hair she'd had since she so magically appeared.

I had my usual erection, pressed up against her, painfully hard, harder than usual, in fact.

No more fever.

Her skin, rather cool, was no longer drenched with sweat either, and not dry. Kind of oily. Or greasy, like her hair.

Very cool. So very cool that . . .

I felt my heart start to thud in my chest.

Oh, Christ.

Something wrong with the way she feels, too, as if she's suddenly gotten fat. Or, loose. No more muscle tone, I . . .

I started to reach for her heart, holding my breath, terrorized, suppressing my thoughts, not wanting to know until I *knew*. What the hell will I *do?*

She stirred in my arms, taking a deep breath, making me freeze. Took a deep breath, stiffened, seemed to stretch, then curled up a little tighter, flabby chest skin settling across one of my arms, the one that'd been reaching to feel for her heartbeat.

I whispered, "Tracy. . . ."

Her voice was hoarse, and foggy, as if she were very, very tired. "Here, Wally."

I cupped part of her chest in my hand, and thought, Wait just a second here. . . .

She twisted then, twisted over onto her back so she could turn toward me, eyes shining in starlight, teeth a flash of white in the shadows of her face. And then she said, "Accelerated maturation. Oh, I know I'm still a little small. I can't add mass overnight, but the machinery did figure out how to get me to endstage pretty quickly."

She took me by the wrist, pulled my hand off her breast and dragged it down between her legs, down into the hot and wet of her, and said, "No more excuses, Wally."

To my amazement, I knew exactly what to do.

We stayed down by the lake, tangled together under the stars, until I got so hungry I started to get dizzy, even lying down. It was hard walking back to the saucer, not just leaving the magic shore, but because Tracy tried walking so close to me, I kept tripping over her.

Finally, we settled for holding hands as we walked, and I couldn't stop smiling, feeling like I was flying through the air. Different. Different. This was . . .

I said, "I feel like a grown-up now! How can just one fuck make me feel so different?"

Tracy laughed, stopping and turning to face me, looking up, holding both of my hands in hers. "Well, more than one. . . ."

Technically speaking, I guessed that was right.

"Do you want to go home now?"

My smile must have gone out like a light.

"Wally?"

I said, "Unless you've got time travel, my home's gone. I can't *imagine* what Earth must be like in 2009. Maybe there's been an atomic war by now."

I remember I'd tried to write a story when I was in the eighth grade, a story I called "Bomblast," set in the far future year of 1981. I'd known roughly how many nuclear weapons America had in 1963, then tried to extrapolate forward a couple of decades, and come up with something like thirty thousand warheads. Okay. So give the same to the Russians. Then I'd tried to imagine a war in which sixty thousand hydrogen bombs went off all on the same day.

I couldn't write the story, but I could imagine it.

Tracy said, "All those stories, and you still can't imagine 2009? What good were they?"

"I don't know."

She said, "If we don't take you home, then what do you want to do?"

I ran my hand down her bare back, and discovered she wasn't tall enough, or my arms long enough, to grab her by the ass.

She giggled. "If you don't think of anything else, that's all there *is* for us to do."

"Suits me."

She gave me a squeeze. "You'll get sick of it, sooner or later, Wally."

"Impossible."

"Well, let's go. We'll think of something, some day."

As we walked the rest of the way back to the saucer, I thought of something else. "Tracy?" She looked up. "Did you ever find out what happened to your people?"

She looked away for a second, putting her face in shadow. "I wasn't really *people*, Wally."

I felt bad for making her think like that. "You are now."

She smiled then, just the way I'd always wanted the original Tracy to smile. "Yes. Thanks to you."

Me?

She said, "But I found something, Wally. You know how I told you the hyperdrives experience time dilation?"

I nodded.

"Well, the citizens of the Empire lived a long time, compared to humans, largely from perfected medical treatment, but they were hardly immortal. The universe was, in a sense, closed to them, just the same way the stars are closed to Earth."

Right. Apollo/Saturn would get us to the Moon by the end of the decade, to Mars by 1984 or thereabouts, maybe even to the moons of Jupiter by the end of the century. But the stars? Never.

There was that alternative vision of 2009. The good one. Rather than an Earth blasted away to slag by tens of thousands of nuclear explosions, maybe Murray did get to be the first man on Mars, the way he said he would be, Murray on Mars in his mid-thirties. Maybe I'd go home and there he'd be, commanding the first expedition to Saturn.

Jealous?

No. I was holding hands with Tracy.

She said, "I think they were working on a new type of space drive, one that would have been virtually instantaneous, given them access to all places and all times, all at once."

What the hell book had I read where they had some kind of instantaneous radio? One of those Ace Doubles? *Rocannon's World*, maybe.

"The evidence is spotty, but it looks like the event sequences all stop when they switched on the test unit."

"So . . . ? Where'd they all go?"

More shadow, this time deep in her eyes. "I don't know, Wally. I think maybe they went to the Omega Point."

I waited for a minute, but she didn't offer any more, and I decided not to ask. After a bit, we went up the ramp and into the saucer, lifting off for our spome.

Sightseeing.

Sightseeing and fucking.

So much fucking, I probably would've lost another twenty pounds and gotten as skinny as a rock star, except that Tracy insisted she had to eat, if she was ever going to grow. I didn't mind her only being four-foot-nine, but it didn't seem fair to make her stay little, and since I had to hang around while she was eating, I guessed I might as well eat too.

Eventually, we wound up going to a world Tracy found in one of those magical electronic information nodes she could access, something she said would interest us both, and it did: a planet-sized museum that'd been the Lost Empire's biggest tourist attraction. Like the Smithsonian and the Guggenheim and the Louvre and everything else you could possibly think of, all rolled into one and then enlarged a million, billion times.

What can I tell you about the history of a billion years? A billion years, a hundred billion galaxies, all of it stuffed into a tiny corner of an incomprehensibly larger universe?

I remember standing in a hall with more square footage then the Pentagon, detailing the history of a nontechnological race, a people who looked a little like vast shell-less oysters, slimy and featureless gray, who'd devoted a hundred thousand years to perfecting an art form that looked like nothing so much as boiling bacon grease.

The stories got it wrong, I remember thinking. All those story aliens were nothing more than Chinamen and Hindoos in goofy rubber suits pretending to be wonderful and strange. Even the best of them . . . Dilbians? Talking bears from a fairy tale. Puppeteers? Kzinti? I remember I'd liked all that stuff, but what's a few more intelligent cows and giant bipedal housecats among friends?

Tracy and I walked the halls, and fucked and ate and sightsaw, and one day wound up in a great dark cavern of the winds, in which were suspended ten thousand interstellar warships, bristling with missile launchers and turrets and ray projectors.

The Chukhamagh Fleet, the narrative node named them, most likely inventing a word I could pronounce, at Tracy's behest. They'd been hit by the expanding wave-front of the Lost Empire, and, being a martial people, had decided to make a fight of it. The local police force, if you can call them that, dragged the fleet straight here to the museum, where they made the crews get out and take public transportation home.

So there we were, sprawled on the floor on a picnic blanket, dizzy from exertion, sweat still evaporating, in front of a kilometer-long star-battleship that looked better than anything I'd ever seen in a movie.

Look at the God-damned thing! What a story *that* would've made!

Hell, maybe somebody did think of it.

Maybe it was written and published, and I just missed it.

Maybe . . .

I rolled on my side then, looked at Tracy and smiled.

You could see she was expecting me to crawl right back on top of her, but what I said was, "Hey, I've got an idea! Tell me what you think of *this*. . . ."

The automatic pilot dropped us out of hyperspace just outside Jupiter's orbit, just as planned, and gave a delicate little chime to get our attention. I guess we were about done anyway, getting up off the command deck floor, using the blanket to dry off a bit, plopping down bareass in those nice leather chairs the Chukhamagh had been so proud of.

Not really comfortable, especially the way my nuts kept winding up in the crevice the Chukhamagh made for their beavertails, but good enough.

"Let's see what we got here."

I let the autopilot find Earth with the telescope optics, frosted blue-white marble swelling to fill the vidwall. Hmh. Not exactly the way I'd expected. I guess I didn't really pay attention on the way out, so I'd keep expecting to see the continents on a globe instead of blue with white stripes and a hint of tan here and there. What's that white glare? Antarctica?

I said, "No atomic war, I guess."

Tracy said, "It's not that common, anyway. Judging from the early history of the Lost Empire, not one culture in a million blows itself to bits on the way to star travel. Ecological misadventure is much more common."

Like wiping out an entire intergalactic civilization while you're looking for a quicker way to get around? She still wasn't talking about that. Not telling me what an Omega Point might be, or why it'd taken the organic sentiences, but left the robots behind. Maybe someday. Maybe not.

I polled the electromagnetic spectrum. Lots of noise from Earth, just like you'd expect. Try a sample. "Jesus."

Tracy cocked her head at the two sailors on the screen. "Something you recognize."

"Yah. I guess I didn't expect *Gilligan's Island* would still be in re-runs after half a century."

"Not your language, though."

"Maybe it's dubbed in Arabic or Japanese or something."

I sampled around the solar system, trying to figure out. . . . "Almost nothing. A couple of satellites around Jupiter and Saturn. Hell, I figured on a Mars base by now, at least."

Not a peep from the Moon. No Moonbase? What the fuck. . . .

There was a tinkertoy space station in very low Earth orbit, not even half way to Von Braun's celebrated two-hour orbit. No space-wheel. No spin. No artificial gravity. On the other hand, I was impressed by the big delta-winged shape docked to one end. "At least they've got real spaceships now!"

Tracy said, "The remotes show eleven humans aboard."

Eleven. Better than Von Braun's projected seven-man crew for those 1950s ships. "How many aboard the station?"

"Eleven total, between the station and ship." She went deeper into the scan data, and then said, "I think the station is set up to house a three-man crew. That little thing with the solar panels down there is the escape capsule, I guess."

I looked, but didn't recognize it. Smaller than an Apollo, bigger than a Gemini. Kind of, I thought, like a Voskhod with two reentry modules, all wrapped up in some green crap.

I flopped back in the command pilot's chair, and said, "Man, what a bunch of fuckin' duds! They might just as well have had the goddam atomic war and got it over with!"

Tracy smiled, and said, "Maybe you're being a little hard on them."

Getting a little bossy, now that she's full size. Although having her five-feet-eight to my six-foot-nothing made for a *much* more comfortable fuck.

She said, "Are we ready, then?"

I gave the pathetic old Earth a long, long look, thought about Murray, down there somewhere, pushing sixty, and said, "Sure. Let's do it." Get it over with, and get back to something worthwhile.

I sent the signal, dropping the main fleet out of hyperspace, bringing it swinging on in, wave on wave of robot-crewed battleships, wondering what they'd make of it down there, when, in just a minute, the radar screens began to go wild.

And then, not just on every TV, not just on every movie screen, not just on every audio tape, but in the printed words of every book, magazine, and newspaper, on every billboard, on the signs by the side of every road that should've given speed limits and directions, the labels on bottles, the images and text on the boxes of all the breakfast cereals, on magical things Tracy explained to me, the little display windows on electronic calculators (!), on these shiny little thingies called CDs that'd displaced our old LPs, on every page in every browser (not a clue! something to do with "peecees" and what she termed "the Internet"?), all over the world, there was nothing but the face of a fiery God, and the words of his message:

"Behold," he said. "I am coming to punish everyone for what he has done, and for what he has failed to do."

I took a moment to imagine the look on Murray's face right now, another moment to wonder if he even remembered me. When the moment was over, we got down to work.

And so the seed of mankind was parceled out to the trillion worlds of the Lost Empire, a family here, a neighborhood there, this one with a whole nation, that one with no more than a township, a few with no more than a single man or woman, left to wonder just what they'd done to merit such a nightmare punishment, or such a grand reward.

It was a long while before they understood what'd been done to them, longer still before they began to look for one another.

"But that, Little Adam, is another story."

it's all true

john kessel

Born in Buffalo, New York, John Kessel now lives with his family in Raleigh, North Carolina, where he is a professor of American Literature and the director of the Creative Writing program at North Carolina State University. Kessel made his first sale in 1975. His first solo novel, *Good News From Outer Space*, was released in 1988 to wide critical acclaim, but before that he had made his mark on the genre primarily as a writer of highly imaginative, finely crafted short stories, many of which were assembled in his collection, *Meeting in Infinity*. He won a Nebula Award in 1983 for his superlative novella "Another Orphan," which was also a Hugo finalist that year, and has been released as an individual book. His story "Buffalo" won the Theodore Sturgeon Award in 1991, and his novella "Stories for Men" won the prestigious James Tiptree Jr. Memorial Award in 2003. His other books include the novel *Freedom Beach*, written in collaboration with James Patrick Kelly, and an anthology of stories from the famous Sycamore Hill Writers Workshop (which he also helps to run), called *Intersections*, coedited by Mark L. Van Name and Richard Butner. His most recent books are a major new novel, *Corrupting Dr. Nice*, and a new collection, *The Pure Product*. His stories have appeared in our First, Second (in collaboration with James Patrick Kelly), Fourth, Sixth, Eighth, Thirteenth, Fourteenth, Fifteenth, Nineteenth, and Twentieth Annual Collections.

Here he takes us back in time to the glamorous Tinseltown of the early Twentieth Century to show us that sometimes second chances aren't all they're cracked-up to be . . .

On the desk in the marina office a black oscillating fan rattled gusts of hot air across the sports page. It was a perfect artifact of the place and time. The fan raised a few strands of the harbor master's hair every time its gaze passed over him. He studied my papers, folded the damp sheets, and handed them back to me.

"Okay. Mr. Vidor's yacht is at the end of the second row." He pointed out the open window down the crowded pier. "The big black one."

"Is the rest of the crew aboard?"

"Beats me," he said, sipping from a glass of iced tea. He set the perspiring glass down on a ring of moisture that ran through the headline: "Cards Shade Dodgers in 12; Cut Lead to 5-1/2." On the floor beside the desk lay the front page: "New Sea-Air Battle Rages in Solomons. Japanese Counterattack on Guadalcanal."

I stepped out onto the dock, shouldered my bag, and headed toward the yacht. The sun beat down on the crown of my head, and my shirt collar was damp with sweat. I pulled the bandana from my pocket and wiped my brow. For midweek the place was pretty busy, a number of Hollywood types down for the day or a start on a long weekend. Across the waterway tankers were drawn up beside a refinery.

The *Cynara* was a 96-foot-long two-masted schooner with a crew of four and compartments for ten. The big yacht was an act of vanity, but King Vidor was one of the most successful directors in Hollywood and, though notorious for his parsimony, still capable of indulging himself. A blond kid who ought to have been drafted by now was polishing the brasswork; he looked up as I stepped aboard. I ducked through the open hatchway into a varnished oak companionway, then up to the pilothouse. The captain was there, bent over the chart table.

"Mr. Onslow?"

The man looked up. Mid-fifties, salt-and-pepper hair. "Who are you?" he asked.

"David Furrow," I said. I handed him the papers. "Mr. Welles sent me down to help out on this cruise."

"How come I never heard of you?"

"He was supposed to call you. Maybe he asked Mr. Vidor to contact you?"

"Nobody has said a word about it."

"You should call Mr. Welles, then."

Onslow looked at me, looked at the papers again. There was a forged letter from Welles, identifying me as an able-bodied seaman with three years' experience. Onslow clearly didn't want to call Welles and risk a tirade. "Did he say what he expected you to do?"

"Help with the meals, mostly."

"Stow your gear in the crew's compartment aft," he said. "Then come on back."

I found an empty bunk and put my bag with the portable unit in the locker beneath it. There was no lock, but I would have to take the chance.

Onslow introduced me to the cook, Manolo, who set me to work bringing aboard the produce, poultry, and case of wine the caterer had sent. When I told him that Welles wanted me to serve, he seemed relieved. About mid-afternoon Charles Koerner, the acting head of production at RKO, arrived with his wife and daughter. They expected to be met by more than just the crew, and Koerner grumbled as he sat at the mahogany table on the afterdeck. Manolo gave me a white jacket and sent me up with drinks. The wife was quiet, fanning herself with a palm fan, and the daughter, an ungainly girl of twelve or thirteen, all elbows and knees, explored the schooner.

An hour later a maroon Packard pulled up to the dock and Welles got out, accompanied by a slender dark woman whom I recognized from photos as his assistant, Shifra Haran. Welles bounded up onto the deck. "Charles!" he boomed, and engulfed the uncomfortable Koerner in a bear hug. "So good to see you!" He towered over the studio head. Koerner introduced Welles to his wife Mary.

Welles wore a lightweight suit; his dark hair was long and he sported a mustache he had grown in Brazil in some misguided attempt at machismo. He was over six feet tall, soft in the belly but with little sign of the monstrous obesity that would haunt his future. A huge head, round cheeks, beautifully molded lips, and almond-shaped Mongol eyes.

"And who's this?" Welles asked, turning to the daughter. His attention was like a searchlight, and the girl squirmed in the center of it.

"Our daughter Barbara."

"Barbara," Welles said with a grin, "do you always carry your house key in your ear?" From the girl's left ear he plucked a shiny brass key and held it in front of her face. His fingers were extraordinarily long, his hands graceful. The girl smiled slyly. "That's not my key," she said.

"Perhaps it's not a key at all." Welles passed his left hand over his right, and the key became a silver dollar. "Would you like this?"

"Yes."

He passed his hand over the coin again, and it vanished. "Look in your pocket."

She shoved her hand into the pocket of her rolled blue jeans and pulled out the dollar. Her eyes flashed with delight.

"Just remember," Welles said, "money isn't everything."

And as quickly as he had given the girl his attention, he turned back to Koerner. He had the manner of a prince among commoners, dispensing his favors like gold yet expecting to be deferred to at any and every moment. Haran hovered around him like a hummingbird. She carried a portfolio, ready to hand him whatever he needed—a pencil, a cigar, a match, a cup of tea, a copy of his RKO contract. Herman Mankiewicz had said about him, "There but for the grace of God—goes God."

"Shifra!" he bellowed, though she was right next to him. "Get those things out of the car."

Haran asked me to help her. I followed her to the pier and from the trunk took an octagonal multi-reel film canister and a bulky portable film projector. The label on the canister had *The Magnificent Ambersons* scrawled in black grease pencil. Haran watched me warily until I stowed the print and projector safely in the salon, then hurried back on deck to look after Welles.

I spent some time helping Manolo in the galley until Onslow called down to me: it was time to cast off. Onslow started the diesel engine. The blond kid and another crewmember cast off the lines, and Onslow backed the *Cynara* out of the slip. Once the yacht had left the waterway and entered San Pedro Bay, we raised the main, fore, and staysails. The canvas caught the wind, Onslow turned off the engine, and, in the declining sun, we set sail for Catalina.

On my way back to the galley I asked the passengers if I could freshen their drinks. Welles had taken off his jacket and was sprawled in one of the deck chairs, regaling the Koerners with stories of voudun rituals he had witnessed in Brazil. At my interruption he gave me a black look, but Koerner took the break as an opportunity to ask for another scotch. I asked Barbara if she wanted a lemonade. Welles's hooded eyes flashed his impatience, and I hurried back below deck.

It was twilight when I served supper: the western horizon blazed orange and red, and the awning above the afterdeck table snapped in the breeze. I uncorked several bottles of wine. I eavesdropped through the avocado salad, the *coq au vin*, the strawberry shortcake. The only tough moment came when Onslow stepped out on deck to say goodnight. "I hope your dinner went well." He leaned over and put a hand on Welles's shoulder, nodding toward me. "You know, we don't usually take on extra crew at the last minute."

"Would anyone like brandy?" I interjected.

Welles, intent on Koerner, waved a hand at Onslow. "He's done a good job. Very helpful."

Onslow retired, and afterward I brought brandy and glasses on a silver tray.

Welles put to Koerner the need to complete the *It's All True* project he had gone to Rio to film. RKO had seen the rushes of hordes of leaping black people at Carnival, gone into shock, and abandoned it. "Three segments," Welles said. " 'The Jangladeros,' 'My Friend Bonito,' and the story of the samba. If you develop the rest of the footage I sent back, I can have it done by Thanksgiving;

for a small additional investment, the studio will have something to show for the money they've spent, Nelson Rockefeller will have succeeded in the Good Neighbor effort, and I can go on and make the kind of movies RKO brought me out here to make."

Koerner avoided Welles's eyes, drawing lines on the white tablecloth with a dessert fork. "Orson, with all due respect, I don't think the studio is interested anymore in the kind of movies you were brought out here to make. *Kane* took a beating, and *Ambersons* doesn't look like it's going to do any better—worse, probably."

Welles's smile was a little too quick. "The version of *Ambersons* that's in the theaters now bears only passing resemblance to what I shot."

"I've never seen either version. But I saw the report on the preview in Pomona. The audience was bored to tears by your tragedy. 'People want to laugh,' they said. The comment cards were brutal."

"I saw the cards, Charles. Half the audience thought it was the best movie they had ever seen. The ones who didn't like it spelled 'laugh' l-a-f-f. Are you going to let the movies you release be determined by people who can't spell 'laugh'?"

"We can't make money on half-full theaters."

I went back and forth, clearing the table, as they continued to spar. Haran was busy doing something in the salon. After I helped him clean up, Manolo headed for his bunk, and except for the pilot and me, the crew had turned in. I perched on the taffrail in the dark, smoking a twentieth century cigarette and eavesdropping. So far Koerner had proved himself to be an amusingly perfect ancestor of the studio executives I was familiar with. The type had not changed in a hundred years. Barbara, bored, stretched out on a bench with her head in Mary Koerner's lap; Mary stroked Barbara's hair and whispered, "In the morning, when we get to Catalina, you can go swimming off the yacht."

"Mother!" the girl exclaimed. "Don't you know? These waters are infested with sharks!"

Mother and daughter squabbled about whether "infested" was proper language for a well-bred young woman to use. They fell silent without reaching a decision. It was full night now, and the moon had risen. Running lights glowed at the top of the masts and at the bowsprit and stern. Aside from the snap of the flag above and the rush of the sea against the hull, there was only the sound of Welles's seductive voice.

"Charles, listen—I've got the original cut of the movie with me—the print they sent down to Rio before the preview. Shifra!" he called out. "Have you got that projector ready?" Welles finished his brandy. "At least have a look at it. You'll see that it's a work of merit."

Barbara perked up. "Please, father! Can we see it?"

Koerner ignored his daughter. "It's not about the merit, Orson. It's about money."

"Money! How can you know what is going to make money if you never take a chance?" His voice was getting a little too loud. Mrs. Koerner looked worried. "What industry in America doesn't spend some money on experiments? Otherwise the future surprises you, and you're out of business!"

Haran poked her head out of the doorway. "I have the projector set up, Orson."

"Orson, I really don't want—" Koerner said.

"Come, Charles, you owe me the favor of at least seeing what I made. I promise you that's all I'll ask."

They retired to the salon. I crept up alongside the cabin and peeked in one of the windows. At one end on a teak drop table Haran had set up the projector, at the other a screen. The film canister lay open on the bench seat, and the first reel was mounted on the projector.

"I'm tired," Mary Koerner said. "If you'll excuse me, I think I'll turn in."

"Mother, I want to see the movie," Barbara said.

"I think you should go to bed, Barbara," said Koerner.

"No, let her see it," Welles said. "It may be a little dark, but there's nothing objectionable."

"I don't want her to see any dark movies," Koerner said.

Welles clenched his fists. When he spoke it was in a lower tone. "Life is dark."

"That's just the point, Orson," said Koerner, oblivious of the thin ice he was treading. "There's a war on. People don't want to be depressed." As an afterthought, he muttered, "If they ever do."

"What did you say?"

Koerner, taking a seat, had his back to Welles. He straightened and turned. "What?"

Welles stepped past Haran and, with jerky movements, started to remove the reel from the projector. "Forget it, Shifra. Why waste it on a philistine?"

Barbara broke the charged silence. "What's a philistine?"

Welles turned to her. "A philistine, my dear girl, is a slightly better-dressed relative of the moron. A philistine wouldn't know a work of art from a hot dog. And you have the bad fortune to have a complete and utter philistine for a father."

"I've had just about enough—" Koerner sputtered.

"YOU've had enough?" Welles bellowed. "I am SICK to DEATH of you paltry lot of money-grubbing cheats and liars! When have any of you kept your word to me? When? Traitors!" He lurched forward and pitched the projector off the table. Koerner's wife and daughter flinched at the crash and ducked down the companionway. Haran, who had clearly seen such displays before, did nothing to restrain her boss.

Koerner's face was red. "That's it," he said. "Whatever possessed me to put my family in the way of a madman like you, I am sure I don't know. If I have anything to say about it, you will never work in Hollywood again."

"You bastard! I don't need your permission. I'll work—"

Koerner poked a finger into Welles's heaving chest. "Do you know what they're saying in every clubroom in the city? They're saying, 'All's well that ends Welles.'" He turned to the cowering secretary. "Miss Haran—good night."

With that he followed his wife and daughter to their room.

Welles stood motionless. I retreated from the window and went up to the pilothouse. "What was that about?" the man on duty asked.

"Mr. Welles just hit an iceberg. Don't worry. We're not sinking."

"Rosebud" is the same in German as in English.

My mother fancied herself an artist. She was involved in *Les Cent Lieux*, the network of public salons sponsored by Brussels, and so I grew up in a shabby gallery in Schwabing where she exhibited her tired virtualities. I remember one of them was a sculpture of a vagina, in the heart of which a holographic projector presented images that switched whenever a new person happened by. One was of a man's mouth, a mustache above his lip, whispering the word "rosebud."

I could tell that this was some archival image, and that the man speaking wasn't German, but I didn't know who he was. It wasn't until I left Munich for NYU film school that I saw *Citizen Kane*.

I was going to be the artist my mother never was, in no way wedded to old Europe or the godforsaken twentieth century. I was fast and smart and persuasive. I could spin a vision of Art and Commerce to potential backers until they fainted with desire to give me money. By the time I was twenty-six I had made two independent films, *The Fortress of Solitude* and *Words of Christ in Red*. *Words* even won the best original screenplay award in the 2037 Trieste Film Festival. I was a minor name—but I never made a dime. Outside of a coterie, nobody ever saw my movies.

I told myself that it was because the audience were fools, and after all, the world was a mess, what chance did art have in a world in flames, and the only people who made money were the ones who purveyed pretty distractions. Then time travel came in and whatever else it helped, it was a disaster for films; making commercial movies came to be about who could get Elizabeth Taylor or John Wayne to sign up. I got tired of cruising around below the radar. When I was thirty I took a good hard look in the mirror and found the job with Metro as a talent scout.

That sounds plausible, doesn't it? But there's another version of my career. Consider this story: I used to be a good tennis player. But my backhand was weak, and no matter how much I worked on it, it never got to be first rate. In a key moment in every match my opponent would drive the ball to my backhand side, and that damn tape at the top of the net would rise up to snare my return. I could only go so far: I couldn't pull genius out of thin air. And so the films and disks and the Trieste trophy sat in the back of my closet.

I was transferring the contents of that closet into boxes when the call came from DAA. I had a headache like someone driving spikes into my brain, and Moira the landlord hectored me from the doorway. The only personal possessions I had that were worth auctioning online had already been auctioned, and I was six months in arrears.

My spex, on the bedside table, started beeping. The signal on the temple was flashing.

"I thought your service was cancelled," Moira said.

"It is."

I fumbled for the spex, sat spraddle-legged on the floor, and slipped them on. My stomach lurched. The wall of my apartment faded into a vision of Gwenda, my PDA. I had Gwenda programmed to look like Louise Brooks. "You've got a call from Vannicom, Ltd.," she said. "Rosethrush Vannice wants to speak with you."

I pulled off the spex. "Moira, dear, give me five minutes alone, would you?"

She smirked. "Whoever she is better owe you money." But she went away.

I pawed through the refuse on the bedside table until I found an unused hypo and shot it into my arm. My heart slammed in my chest and my eyes snapped fully open. I put the spex back on. "Okay," I said.

Gwenda faded and Vannice's beautiful face took her place. "Det? Are you there?"

"I'm here. How did you get me?"

"I had to pay your phone bill for you. How about giving me a look at you?"

The bedroom was a testimony to my imminent eviction, and I didn't want her to see what I looked like. "No can do—I'm using spex. How can I help you?"

"I want to throw some work your way."

After I had helped Sturges desert the studio, Vannice had told me that I would never work for her again. Her speech might be peppered with lines from Nicholas Ray or Quentin Tarrantino, but her movie lust was a simulation over a ruthless commercial mind, and I had cost the company money. For the last six months it looked like I wouldn't work for anyone. "I'm pretty busy, Rosethrush."

"Too busy to pay your phone bill?"

I gave up. "What do you need?"

"I want you to end this Welles runaround," she said.

I might be on the outs, but the story of the wild goose chase for Orson Welles was all around town. Four times talent scouts had been sent back to recruit versions of Welles, and four times they had failed. "No," said Welles at the age of 42, despite being barred from the lot at Universal after *Touch of Evil*. They tried him in 1972, when he was 57, after Pauline Kael trashed his reputation; "No," he said. Metro even sent Darla Rashnamurti to seduce him in 1938, when he was the 23-year-old wunderkind. Darla and that version of Welles had a pretty torrid affair, but she came back with nothing more than a sex video that drew a lot of hits on the net and some clippings for her book of memories. I knew all this, and Rosethrush knew I knew it, and it didn't make a damn bit of difference. I needed the work.

"Can you send me some e-cash?" I asked.

"How much?"

I considered Moira. "Ah—how about ten thousand for now?"

"You'll have it in an hour. By which time you'll be in my office. Right?"

"I'll be there."

A week later, shaved and briefed and buffed to a high luster, I stood in the center of the time travel stage at DAA. I set down the kit bag that held my 1942 clothes and the portable time travel unit, and nodded to Norm Page up in the control booth. Vannice stood outside the burnished rail of the stage. "No screw-ups this time, right, Det?"

"When have I ever let you down?"

"I could give a list . . ."

"Ten seconds," said Norm from the booth.

Vannice pointed her finger at me like a gun, dropped her thumb as if shooting it, and spoke out of the corner of her mouth, doing a passable imitation of a man's voice.

"Rosebud—dead or alive," she said, and the world disappeared.

The thing that separates me from the run-of-the-mill scout is that I can both plan and improvise. Planning comes first. You must know your mark. You are asking him to abandon his life, and no one is going to do that lightly. You need to approach him at his lowest ebb. But you also want to take him at a time when his talents are undiminished.

This situation had fallen together rather nicely. I went down to the after-deck and smoked another cigarette. Tobacco, one of the lost luxuries of the twentieth century. Through a slight nicotine buzz I listened to Welles shouting at Haran in the salon, and to the sounds of the demolition of what was left of the projector. I heard her tell him to go to hell. The moon was high now, and the surface of the sea was rippled in long, low swells that slapped gently against the hull as we bore south. Behind us, the lights of San Pedro reflected off our subsiding wake.

A few minutes later Welles came up onto the deck lugging the film canister, which he hefted onto the table. He sat down and stared at it. He picked up the brandy bottle and poured a glass, gulped it down, then poured himself another. If he was aware of my presence, he gave no sign.

After a while I said, quietly, "That might have gone better."

Welles lifted his big head. His face was shadowed; for a moment he looked like Harry Lime in *The Third Man*. "I have nothing to say to you."

"But I have something to say to you, Orson." I moved to the table.

"Go away. I'm not about to be lectured by one of Vidor's lackeys."

"I don't work for Mr. Vidor. I don't work for anyone you know. I'm here to talk to you."

He put down his glass. "Do I know you?"

"My name is Detlev Gruber."

He snorted. "If I were you, I'd change my name."

"I do—frequently."

For the first time since he'd come aboard the yacht, he really looked at me. "So speak your piece and leave me alone."

"First, let me show you something."

I took my bandana from my pocket and spread it flat on the table between us. I tugged the corners that turned it rigid, then thumbed the controls to switch it on. The blue and white pattern of the fabric disappeared, and the screen lit.

Welles was watching now. "What is this?"

"A demonstration." I hit play, the screen went black, and words appeared:

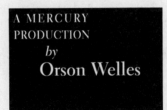

And then the title:

Ominous music rose. Fade in, night, on a chainlink fence with a metal sign that reads "No Trespassing."

"What the hell . . . ?" Welles said.

I paused the image.

Welles picked up the flatscreen. He shook it, rigid as a piece of pasteboard, turned it over and examined its back. "This is amazing. Where did you get it?"

"It's a common artifact—in the year 2048."

Welles laid the screen down. With the light of "No Trespassing" shining up into his face, he looked like no more than a boy. He was twenty-seven years old.

"Go on," he said. "I like a tall tale."

"I got it because I come from the future. I've come here just to see you, because I want you to come back with me."

Welles looked at me. Then he laughed his deep, booming laugh. He pulled a cigar out of his jacket pocket and lit it. "What does . . . the future . . . want with me?" he said between puffs.

"I represent an entertainment company. We want you to do one thing: make movies. We have technology that you don't have and resources you can't imagine. This screen is only the most trivial example. You think that optical printing is a neat trick? We can create whole landscapes out of nothing, turn three extras into an army, do for a fraction of the cost what it takes millions to do here, and do it better. The movie technology of the future is the best toy train set a boy ever had.

"More to the point, Orson, is this: you can fool these people around you, but you can't fool me. I know every mistake you've made since you came to Hollywood. I know every person you've alienated. Koerner's hostility is only the tip of the iceberg."

"I won't argue with you about that. But I have possibilities yet. I'm certainly not ready to fly off with you like Buck Rogers. Give me a couple of years—come back in 1950, and we'll see."

"You forget, what's the future for you is history to me. I know your entire life, Orson. I know what will happen to you from this moment on, until you die of a heart attack, completely alone, in a shabby house in Los Angeles in 1985. It's not a pretty life."

The notion of Welles death hung in the air for a moment like the cigar smoke. He held the cigar sideways between his thumb and fingers, examining it. "'An ill-favored thing, sir, but mine own,'" he said, as if addressing the cigar—and then his eyes, cold sober, met mine.

"You can joke," I said, "but you will never make another movie as unfettered as you were for *Kane*. The butchery RKO performed on *Ambersons* is only the beginning. No studio will let you direct again until 1946, and that's just a potboiler completely under the thumb of the system. When you try for something more ambitious in *The Lady from Shanghai*, the film gets taken from you and an hour chopped out of it. Hollywood exiles you; you escape to Europe. You spend the last forty years of your life begging for cash, acting small parts in increasingly terrible films as you struggle to make movies on

your own. Your entire career? Eleven films—and that includes *Kane* and *Ambersons*."

"Sounds like I'm a flop. Why do you want me?"

"Because, despite fools nipping at your ankles and a complete lack of support, a couple of those films are brilliant. Think what you could do if you had the support of a major studio!"

"Don't you care that if I come with you, I'll never make these works of genius you tell me about?"

"On the contrary, I can show them to you right now. What I'm doing is plucking you from an alternate version of our history. In our world you will have gone on to live exactly the life I've been telling you about. So we will still have all of those movies, but you won't have to struggle to make them. Instead, you can make the dozens of other projects that you never could find backing for in this history. Before you shot Kane, you wanted to do *Heart of Darkness*. In 2048, still nobody has made a decent film of that book. It's as if the world has been waiting for you.

"In 2048 you will be celebrated instead of mocked. If you stay here, you will spend the rest of your life as an exile. If you must be an exile, be one in a place and time that will enable you to do the work that you love."

Welles moved a coffee cup, tapped ash into the saucer, and rested his cigar on the edge. "I have friends. I have family. What about them?"

"You have no family: your parents are dead, your brother estranged; you're divorced from your wife and, frankly, not interested in your daughter. Most of your friends have abandoned you."

"Joe Cotten hasn't."

"You want Joseph Cotten? Look." I called up the clip on the flatscreen, then slid it back in front of Welles. The screen showed a café patio. Street noises, pedestrians with UV hats, futuristic cars passing by. A man and a woman sat at a table under a palm tree. The camera closed in on the couple: Joseph Cotten, wearing white trousers and an open-necked shirt, and his wife, Lenore. "Hello, Orson," they said, grinning. Cotten spoke directly into the camera. "Orson, Detlev tells me he's going to show you this clip. Listen to what the man is saying—he's telling the truth. It's much nicer here than you can imagine. In fact, my biggest regret about coming to the future is that you're not here. I miss you."

I stopped the image. "Another scout brought him to the future four years ago," I said.

Welles took another sip of brandy and set his glass down on Cotten's nose. "If Joe had stood by me, the studio wouldn't have been able to reshoot the ending of *Ambersons*."

I could see why my predecessors had all failed. For every argument I gave, Welles had a counterargument. It wasn't about reason; he was too smart, and

the reasons he offered for declining were not reasonable. He needed convincing on some visceral level. I had a brutal way to get there, and would have to use it.

I moved the brandy glass off the screen. "We're not quite done with the movies yet," I said. "You have trouble controlling your weight? Well, let me show you some pictures."

First, an image of Welles from *The Stranger*, slender enough that you could even see his Adam's apple. "Here you are in 1946. You still look something like yourself. Now here's *Touch of Evil*, ten years later." A bloated hulk, unshaven and sweating. The photos cycled, a dismal progression of sagging jaws, puffy cheeks, a face turned from boyishly handsome to suet, a body from imposing size to an obese nightmare. I had film clips of him waddling across a room, of his jowls quivering as he orated in some bad mid-sixties European epic. Numerous clips of him seated on talk show sets, belly swelling past his knees, a cigar clutched between the fingers of his right hand, full beard failing to disguise his multiple chins.

"By the end of your life you weigh somewhere between three hundred and four hundred pounds. No one knows for sure. Here's a photo of an actress named Angie Dickinson trying to sit on your lap. But you have no lap. See how she has to hold her arm around your neck to keep from sliding off. You can't breathe, you can't move, your back is in agony, your kidneys are failing. In the 1980s you get stuck in an automobile, which must be taken apart for you to be able to get out. You spend the last years of your life doing commercials for cheap wine that you are unable to drink because of your abysmal health."

Welles stared at the images. "Turn it off," he whispered.

He sat silently for a moment. His brow furrowed, his dark eyes became pits of self-loathing. But some slant of his eyebrows indicated that he took some satisfaction in this humiliation, as if what I had shown him was only the fulfillment of a prophecy spoken over his cradle.

"You've gone to a lot of trouble, I can see," he said quietly.

I felt I was close now. I leaned forward. "This doesn't have to happen. Our medical science will see that you never become that gross parody of yourself. We'll keep you young and handsome for the rest of your life."

Welles stirred himself. "I'm dazzled by your generosity. What's in it for you?"

"Very good. I don't deny it—we're no charitable organization. You don't realize the esteem in which your works are held in the future. A hundred years from now, *Citizen Kane* is considered the greatest movie ever made. The publicity alone of your return is worth millions. People want to see your work."

"You sound exactly like George Schaefer persuading me to come out to Hollywood after *The War of the Worlds*. I'm a genius, unlimited support, people love my work. And the knives were sharpened for me before I even stepped

off the plane. Three years later Schaefer is out on the street, I'm a pariah, and his replacement won't even watch my movie with me. So, have studio executives in the future become saints?"

"Of course not, Orson. But the future has the perspective of time. RKO's cuts to *Ambersons* did nothing to protect their investment. Your instincts were better than theirs, not just artistically, but even from the point of view of making money."

"Tell it to Charles Koerner."

"I don't have to. It's considered the greatest tragedy of cinema history. In 2048, nobody's ever seen your movie. This print"—I touched the film canister—"is the only existing copy of your version. When it goes missing, and the negatives of the excised footage are destroyed, all that's left is the botched studio version."

"This is the only print?"

"The only print."

Welles ran his long-fingered hand through his hair. He heaved himself to his feet, went to the rail of the schooner, grabbed a shroud to steady himself, and looked up at the night sky. It was a dramatic gesture, as he undoubtedly knew. Without looking back at me, he said, "And your time machine? Where do you keep that?"

"I have a portable unit in my bag. We can't use it on the ship, but as soon as we are back on land—"

"—we're off to 2048!" Welles laughed. "It seems I dramatized the wrong H.G. Wells novel." He turned back to me. "Or maybe not, Mr . . . ?"

"Gruber."

"Mr. Gruber. I'm afraid that you'll have to return to the future without me."

Rosethrush had spent a lot of money sending me here. She wasn't going to let me try another moment universe if this attempt failed. "Why? Everything I've told you is the simple truth."

"Which gives me a big advantage in facing the next forty years, doesn't it?"

"Don't be a fool. Your situation here is no better tomorrow than it was yesterday." One of the rules is never to get involved, but I was into it now, and I cared about whether he listened to me or not. I could say it was because of my bank balance. I gestured toward the cabins, where Koerner and his family slept. "Worse, after tonight. You're throwing away your only chance to change your fate. Do you want to mortgage your talent to people like Charles Koerner? Sell yourself for the approval of people who will never understand you?"

Welles seemed amused. "You seem a little exercised about this—Detlev, is it? Detlev, why should this mean so much to you?" He was speculating as much as asking me. "This is just your job, right? You don't really know me. But you seem to care a lot more than any job would warrant.

"What that suggests to me is that you must really like my movies—I'm flattered, of course—or you are particularly engaged with the problem of the director in the world of business. Yet you must work in the world of business every day.

"So let me make a counter-proposition: You don't take me back to the future; you stay here with me. I question whether any artist can succeed outside of his own time. I was born in 1915. How am I even going to understand 2048, let alone make art that it wants to see?

"On the other hand, you seem quite familiar with today. You say you know all the pitfalls I'm going to face. And I'll bet you know your twentieth century history pretty well. Think of the advantage that gives you here! A few savvy investments and you'll be rich! You want to make movies—we'll do it together! You can be my partner! With your knowledge of the future we can finance our own studio!"

"I'm a talent scout, not a financier."

"A talent scout—we'll use that, too. You must know who the great actors and actresses of the next thirty years are going to be—we'll approach them before anyone else does. Sign them to exclusive contracts. In ten years we'll dominate the business!"

He paced the deck to the table, put a brandy glass in front of me, and filled it. "You know, if you hadn't told me, I would never have thought you were anything other than a servant. You're something of an actor yourself, aren't you? A manipulator of appearances. Iago pouring words into my ear? Good, we can definitely use that, too. But don't tell me, Detlev, there aren't aspects of the future you wouldn't like to escape from. Here's your chance. We can both kiss the Charles Koerners of the world goodbye, or better yet, succeed in their world and rub their faces in it!"

This was a new one. I had been resisted before, I had been told to get lost, I had faced panic and disbelief. But never had a target tried to seduce me.

The thing was, what Welles was saying made a lot of sense. Maybe if I could bring him back I would come out okay, but that didn't look like it was going to happen. Everything I had told him about himself—his lack of family connections, his troubles with the industry, his bleak prospects—applied to me in 2048. And since I had burned this moment universe by coming here, there was no way anyone from the future was going to come to retrieve me, even if they wanted to. I could make movies with Orson Welles—and eventually, I could make them without him.

I stared at the *Ambersons* film canister on the table in front of me and got hold of myself. I knew his biography. Welles hadn't just been abandoned by others. When necessary, he had seduced and abandoned even his most trusted friends. It was always love on his terms.

"Thank you for the offer," I said. "But I must go back. Are you coming with me?"

Welles sat down in the chair beside me. He smiled. "I guess you'll have to tell your studio head, or whoever sent you, that I was more difficult than he imagined."

"You'll live to regret this."

"We shall see."

"I already know. I showed you."

Welles's face darkened. When he spoke his voice was distant. "Yes, that was pleasant. But now, it seems our business is finished."

This was not going to play well when I got back to DAA. I had one chance to salvage my reputation. "Then, if you don't mind, I'll take this." I reached across the table to get the print of *Ambersons*.

Welles surged forward from his chair, startlingly quick, and snatched the canister before I could. He stood, holding it in his arms, swaying on the unsteady deck. "No."

"Come now, Orson. Why object to our having your film? In the hundred years after that botched preview in Pomona, no one has ever seen your master-piece. It's the Holy Grail of lost films. What possible purpose could be served by keeping it from the world?"

"Because it's mine."

"But it's no less yours if you give it to us. Didn't you make it to be admired, to touch people's hearts? Think about—"

"I'll tell you what to think," Welles said. "Think about this."

He seized the canister by its wire handles, twirled on his feet as he swung it round him like a hammer thrower, and hurled it out into the air over the side of the boat. He stumbled as he let it go, catching himself on the rail. The can-ister arced up into the moonlight, tumbling, and fell to the ocean with only the slightest splash, disappearing instantly.

I was working at my video editor when Moira came into the apartment. She didn't bother to knock; she never did. I drained the last of my gin, paused the image of Anne Baxter that stood on my screen, and swiveled my chair around toward her.

"Jesus, Det, are you ever going to unpack?" Moira surveyed the stacks of boxes that still cluttered my living room.

I headed to the kitchen to refill my glass. "That depends—are you going to throw me out again?"

"You know I didn't want to," she said. "It was Vijay. He's always looking over my shoulder." She followed me into the kitchen. "Is that twentieth century gin? Let me have some." She examined a withered lime that had been sitting on the windowsill above the sink since before my trip to 1942, then put it back down. "Besides, you're all paid up for now."

For now. But Rosethrush had not put me back on salary. She was furious when I returned without Welles, though she seemed to enjoy humiliating me so much that I wondered if that alone was worth what it had cost her. She rode me for my failure at the same time she dismissed it as no more than might be expected. Her comments combined condescension and contempt: not only was I a loser, but I served as a stand in for the loser Welles.

According to Rosethrush, Welles's turning me down showed a fatal lack of nerve. "He's a coward," she told me. "If he came with you, he'd have to be the genius he pretended to be, with no excuses. His genius was all sleight of hand."

I didn't mention Welles's offer to me. Not arguing with her was the price I paid for avoiding another blackballing.

On the editor, I was working on a restoration of *The Magnificent Ambersons*. By throwing the only existing print overboard, Welles had made my job a lot harder—but not impossible. The negatives of the discarded footage in the RKO archives hadn't been destroyed until December, 1942, so I'd had time to steal them before I came back. Of course Rosethrush didn't want *Ambersons*; she wanted Welles. Hollywood was always about the bottom line, and despite my sales job to Welles, few beyond a bunch of critics and obsessives cared about a hundred-year-old black-and-white movie. But I was banking on the possibility that a restoration would still generate enough publicity to restart my career.

Or maybe I had other reasons. I had not edited a film since the end of my directorial ambitions, twelve years before, and working on this made me realize how much I had missed the simple pleasure of shaping a piece of art with my hands. The restored *Ambersons* was brilliant, harrowing, and sad. It told the story of the long, slow decline of a great mercantile family, destroyed by progress and bad luck and willful blindness—and by the automobile. It was the first great film to address the depredations of technological progress on personal relations in society; but it was also a human tragedy and a thwarted love story. And it centered on the life of George Minafer, a spoiled rich boy who destroyed himself while bringing misery to everyone around him.

Moira gave up and took the lime off the windowsill. "Where's a knife? You got any tonic?"

I liked Moira; the very fact that she cared nothing about movies made her refreshingly attractive. But I had work to do. I went back to the editor while she poked around the kitchen. I hit play. On the screen Anne Baxter, as Lucy Morgan, was telling her father, played by Joseph Cotten, the legend of a mythical young Indian chief, Vendonah. Vendonah meant "Rides-Down-Everything."

"Vendonah was unspeakable," Lucy said as they walked through the garden. "He was so proud he wore iron shoes and walked over people's faces. So at last the tribe decided that it wasn't a good enough excuse for him that he was young and inexperienced. He'd have to go. So they took him down to the river, put him in a canoe, and pushed him out from the shore. The current carried him on down to the ocean. And he never got back."

I had watched this scene before, but for the first time the words sent a shiver down my spine. I hit pause. I remembered the self-loathing in Welles's eyes when I had shown him the images of himself in decline, and now I saw that he had made a movie about himself—in fact, he'd made two of them. Both Kane and George Minafer were versions of Welles. Spoiled, abusive, accusing, beautiful boys, aching for their comeuppance. Which they had gotten, all three of them, almost as if they had sought it out, directing the world and the people around them to achieve that aesthetic result. No wonder Welles abused others, pushing until they said "no"—because at some level he felt he deserved to be said "no" to. Maybe he turned down my "yes" because he needed that "no." The poor bastard.

I stared at the screen. It wasn't all sleight of hand—or if it was sleight of hand, it was brilliant sleight of hand. Welles had pulled a masterpiece out of the air the way he had pulled the key out of Barbara Koerner's ear. Yet to keep his integrity, he had thrown the last print of that masterpiece into the ocean.

Within a week I would have it back, complete, ready to give to the world, both a fulfillment of Welles's immense talent and the final betrayal of his will, sixty-three years after his death. And I would be a player again.

If I ever let anyone else see the film. If I didn't? What, then, would I do to fill my days?

Behind me, I heard Moira come back out of the kitchen, and the tinkle of ice in her glass. She was going to say something, something irrelevant, and I would have to tell her to get lost. But nothing came. Finally I turned on her, just as she spoke. "What's this?" she asked.

She was playing idly with an open box of junk. In her hands she held a trophy, a jagged Lucite spike on a black base.

"That?" I said. "That's—that's the best original screenplay award from the 2037 Trieste Film Festival."

She turned it over and put it back into the box. She looked up at me and smiled.

"Anyway, Det, the reason I'm here is to ask if you want to go swimming. It's been record low UV all this week."

"Swimming."

"You know. Water? The beach? Naked women? Come with me, sweetheart, and I promise you won't get burned."

"The burn doesn't worry me," I said. "But these waters are infested with sharks."

"Really? Where'd you hear that?"

I turned off the editor and got out of my chair. "Never mind," I said. "Give me a minute and I'll find my suit."

Rogue Farm

Charles Stross

Although he made his first sale back in 1987, it's only recently that British writer Charles Stross has begun to make a name for himself as a writer to watch in the new century (in fact, as one of the *key* Writers to Watch in the Oughts), with a sudden burst in the last few years of quirky, inventive, high-bit-rate stories such as "Antibodies," "A Colder War," "Bear Trap," "Dechlorinating the Moderator," "Toast: A Con Report," "Lobsters," "Troubadour," "Tourist," "Halo," "Router," "Nightfall," "Curator," and others in markets such as *Interzone*, *Spectrum SF*, *Asimov's Science Fiction*, *Strange Plasma*, and *New Worlds*. In recent days, he's becoming prolific at novel length as well. He'd already "published" a novel online, *Scratch Monkey*, available to be read on his Web site (www.antipope.org/charlie/), and saw his first commercially published novel, *Singularity Sky*, released in 2003, but he has *three* novels coming out in 2004: *The Iron Sunrise*, *A Family Trade*, and *The Atrocity Archive* (formerly serialized in the British magazine *Spectrum SF*), with another new novel, *The Clan Corporate*, hard on their heels in early 2005 . . . and, of course, he also has several other new novels in the works. His first collection, *Toast, and Other Burned Out Futures*, was released in 2002. Until his recent retirement to concentrate on fiction writing, Stross was also a long-time columnist for the magazine *Computer Shopper*. He had *two* stories in our Eighteenth Annual Collection, plus singletons in our Nineteenth and Twentieth Annual Collections. He lives in Edinburgh, Scotland.

Here he gives us a fast, funny, and highly inventive look at a deceptively bucolic future where nothing is quite as simple—or as harmless—as it seems . . .

▼

It was a bright, cool March morning: mare's tails trailed across the southeastern sky toward the rising sun. Joe shivered slightly in the driver's seat as he twisted the starter handle on the old front loader he used to muck out the barn. Like its owner, the ancient Massey Ferguson had seen better days; but it had survived worse abuse than Joe routinely handed out. The diesel clattered, spat out a gobbet of thick blue smoke, and chattered to itself dyspeptically. His mind as blank as the sky above, Joe slid the tractor into gear, raised the front scoop, and began turning it toward the open doors of the barn—just in time to see an itinerant farm coming down the road.

"Bugger," swore Joe. The tractor engine made a hideous grinding noise and died. He took a second glance, eyes wide, then climbed down from the tractor and trotted over to the kitchen door at the side of the farmhouse. "Maddie!" he called, forgetting the two-way radio clipped to his sweater hem. "Maddie! There's a farm coming!"

"Joe? Is that you? Where are you?" Her voice wafted vaguely from the bowels of the house.

"Where are you?" he yelled back.

"I'm in the bathroom."

"Bugger," he said again. "If it's the one we had round the end last month . . ."

The sound of a toilet sluiced through his worry. It was followed by a drumming of feet on the staircase; then Maddie erupted into the kitchen. "Where is it?" she demanded.

"Out front, about a quarter mile up the lane."

"Right." Hair wild and eyes angry about having her morning ablutions cut short, Maddie yanked a heavy green coat on over her shirt. "Opened the cupboard yet?"

"I was thinking you'd want to talk to it first."

"Too right I want to talk to it. If it's that one that's been lurking in the copse near Edgar's pond, I got some *issues* to discuss with it." Joe shook his head at her anger and went to unlock the cupboard in the back room. "You take the shotgun and keep it off our property," she called after him. "I'll be out in a minute."

Joe nodded to himself, then carefully picked out the twelve-gauge and a preloaded magazine. The gun's power-on self-test lights flickered erratically, but it seemed to have a full charge. Slinging it, he locked the cupboard carefully and went back out into the farmyard to warn off their unwelcome visitor.

The farm squatted, buzzing and clicking to itself, in the road outside Armitage End. Joe eyed it warily from behind the wooden gate, shotgun under his arm. It was a medium-size one, probably with half a dozen human components subsumed into it—a formidable collective. Already it was deep into farm-fugue, no longer relating very clearly to people outside its own communion of mind. Beneath its leathery black skin he could see hints of internal structure, cytocellular macroassemblies flexing and glooping in disturbing motions. Even though it was only a young adolescent, it was already the size of an antique heavy tank, and it blocked the road just as efficiently as an Apatosaurus would have. It smelled of yeast and gasoline.

Joe had an uneasy feeling that it was watching him. "Buggerit, I don't have time for this," he muttered. The stable waiting for the small herd of cloned spidercows cluttering up the north paddock was still knee-deep in manure, and the tractor seat wasn't getting any warmer while he shivered out here, waiting for Maddie to come and sort this thing out. It wasn't a big herd, but it was as big as his land and his labor could manage—the big biofabricator in the shed could assemble mammalian livestock faster than he could feed them up and sell them with an honest HAND-RAISED NOT VAT-GROWN label. "What do you want with us?" he yelled up at the gently buzzing farm.

"Brains, fresh brains for Baby Jesus," crooned the farm in a warm contralto, startling Joe half out of his skin. "Buy my brains!" Half a dozen disturbing cauliflower shapes poked suggestively out of the farm's back and then retracted again, coyly.

"Don't want no brains around here," Joe said stubbornly, his fingers whitening on the stock of the shotgun. "Don't want your kind round here, neither. Go away."

"I'm a nine-legged semiautomatic groove machine!" crooned the farm. "I'm on my way to Jupiter on a mission for love! Won't you buy my brains?" Three curious eyes on stalks extruded from its upper glacis.

"Uh—" Joe was saved from having to dream up any more ways of saying "fuck off" by Maddie's arrival. She'd managed to sneak her old battle dress home after a stint keeping the peace in Mesopotamia twenty years ago, and she'd managed to keep herself in shape enough to squeeze inside. Its left knee squealed ominously when she walked it about, which wasn't often, but it still worked well enough to manage its main task—intimidating trespassers.

"You." She raised one translucent arm, pointed at the farm. "Get off my land. *Now.*"

Taking his cue, Joe raised his shotgun and thumbed the selector to full auto. It wasn't a patch on the hardware riding Maddie's shoulders, but it underlined the point.

The farm hooted: "Why don't you love me?" it asked plaintively.

"*Get off my land,*" Maddie amplified, volume cranked up so high that Joe winced. "*Ten seconds! Nine! Eight—*" Thin rings sprang out from the sides of her arms, whining with the stress of long disuse as the Gauss gun powered up.

"I'm going! I'm going!" The farm lifted itself slightly, shuffling backwards. "Don't understand. I only wanted to set you free to explore the universe. Nobody wants to buy my fresh fruit and brains. What's wrong with the world?"

They waited until the farm had retreated round the bend at the top of the hill. Maddie was the first to relax, the rings retracting back into the arms of her battle dress, which solidified from ethereal translucency to neutral olive drab as it powered down. Joe safed his shotgun. "Bastard," he said.

"Fucking-A." Maddie looked haggard. "That was a bold one." Her face was white and pinched-looking, Joe noted. Her fists were clenched. She had the shakes, he realized without surprise. Tonight was going to be another major nightmare night, and no mistake.

"The fence." On again and off again for the past year they'd discussed wiring up an outer wire to the CHP baseload from their little methane plant.

"Maybe this time. Maybe." Maddie wasn't keen on the idea of frying passers-by without warning, but if anything might bring her around, it would be the prospect of being overrun by a bunch of rogue farms. "Help me out of this, and I'll cook breakfast," she said.

"Got to muck out the barn," Joe protested.

"It can wait on breakfast," Maddie said shakily. "I need you."

"Okay." Joe nodded. She was looking bad; it had been a few years since her last fatal breakdown, but when Maddie said "I need you," it was a bad idea to ignore her. That way led to backbreaking labor on the biofab and loading her backup tapes into the new body; always a messy business. He took her arm and steered her toward the back porch. They were nearly there when he paused.

"What is it?" asked Maddie.

"Haven't seen Bob for a while," he said slowly. "Sent him to let the cows into the north paddock after milking. Do you think—?"

"We can check from the control room," she said tiredly. "Are you really worried? . . ."

"With that thing blundering around? What do *you* think?"

"He's a good working dog," Maddie said uncertainly. "It won't hurt him. He'll be all right; just you page him."

After Joe helped her out of her battle dress, and after Maddie spent a good long while calming down, they breakfasted on eggs from their own hens, homemade cheese, and toasted bread made with rye from the hippie commune on the other side of the valley. The stone-floored kitchen in the dilapidated house they'd squatted and rebuilt together over the past twenty years was warm and homely. The only purchase from outside the valley was the coffee, beans from a hardy GM strain that grew like a straggling teenager's beard all along the Cumbrian hilltops. They didn't say much: Joe, because he never did, and Maddie, because there wasn't anything that she wanted to discuss. Silence kept her personal demons down. They'd known each other for many years, and even when there wasn't anything to discuss, they could cope with each other's silence. The voice radio on the windowsill opposite the cast-iron stove stayed off, along with the TV set hanging on the wall next to the fridge. Breakfast was a quiet time of day.

"Dog's not answering," Joe commented over the dregs of his coffee.

"He's a good dog." Maddie glanced at the yard gate uncertainly. "You afraid he's going to run away to Jupiter?"

"He was with me in the shed." Joe picked up his plate and carried it to the sink, began running hot water onto the dishes. "After I cleaned the lines I told him to go take the herd up the paddock while I did the barn." He glanced up, looking out the window with a worried expression. The Massey Ferguson was parked right in front of the open barn doors as if holding at bay the mountain of dung, straw, and silage that mounded up inside like an invading odorous enemy, relic of a frosty winter past.

Maddie shoved him aside gently and picked up one of the walkie-talkies from the charge point on the windowsill. It bleeped and chuckled at her. "Bob, come in. Over." She frowned. "He's probably lost his headset again."

Joe racked the wet plates to dry. "I'll move the midden. You want to go find him?"

"I'll do that." Maddie's frown promised a talking-to in store for the dog when she caught up with him. Not that Bob would mind: words ran off him like water off a duck's back. "Cameras first." She prodded the battered TV set to life, and grainy bisected views flickered across the screen, garden, yard, Dutch barn, north paddock, east paddock, main field, copse. "Hmm."

She was still fiddling with the smallholding surveillance system when Joe clambered back into the driver's seat of the tractor and fired it up once more. This time there was no cough of black smoke, and as he hauled the mess of manure out of the barn and piled it into a three-meter-high midden, a quarter of a ton at a time, he almost managed to forget about the morning's unwelcome visitor. Almost.

By late morning, the midden was humming with flies and producing a remarkable stench, but the barn was clean enough to flush out with a hose and broom. Joe was about to begin hauling the midden over to the fermentation tanks buried round the far side of the house when he saw Maddie coming back up the path, shaking her head. He knew at once what was wrong.

"Bob," he said, expectantly.

"Bob's fine. I left him riding shotgun on the goats." Her expression was peculiar. "But that *farm*—"

"Where?" he asked, hurrying after her.

"Squatting in the woods down by the stream," she said tersely. "Just over our fence."

"It's not trespassing, then."

"It's put down feeder roots! Do you have any idea what that means?"

"I don't—" Joe's face wrinkled in puzzlement. "Oh."

"Yes. *Oh*." She stared back at the outbuildings between their home and the woods at the bottom of their smallholding, and if looks could kill, the intruder would be dead a thousand times over. "It's going to estivate, Joe, then it's going to grow to maturity on our patch. And do you know where it said it was going to go when it finishes growing? Jupiter!"

"Bugger," Joe said faintly, as the true gravity of their situation began to sink in. "We'll have to deal with it first."

"That wasn't what I meant," Maddie finished. But Joe was already on his way out the door. She watched him crossing the yard, then shook her head. "Why am I stuck here?" she asked, but the cooker wasn't answering.

The hamlet of Outer Cheswick lay four kilometers down the road from Armitage End, four kilometers past mostly derelict houses and broken-down barns, fields given over to weeds and walls damaged by trees. The first half of the twenty-first century had been cruel years for the British agrobusiness sector; even harsher if taken in combination with the decline in population and the consequent housing surplus. As a result, the dropouts of the forties and fifties were able to take their pick from among the gutted shells of once fine farmhouses. They chose the best and moved in, squatted in the derelict outbuildings, planted their seeds and tended their flocks and practiced their DIY skills, until a generation later a mansion fit for a squire stood in lonely isolation alongside a decaying road where no more cars drove. Or rather, it would have taken a generation had there been any children against whose lives it could be measured; these were the latter decades of the population crash, and what a previous century would have labeled downshifter DINK couples were now in the majority, far outnumbering any breeder colonies. In this aspect of their life, Joe and Maddie were boringly conventional. In other respects they weren't: Maddie's nightmares, her aversion to alcohol, and her withdrawal from society were all relics of her time in Peaceforce. As for Joe, he liked it here. Hated cities, hated the Net, hated the burn of the new. Anything for a quiet life . . .

The Pig and Pizzle, on the outskirts of Outer Cheswick, was the only pub within about ten kilometers—certainly the only one within staggering distance for Joe when he'd had a skinful of mild—and it was naturally a seething den of local gossip, not least because Ole Brenda refused to allow electricity, much less bandwidth, into the premises. (This was not out of any sense of misplaced technophobia, but a side effect of Brenda's previous life as an attack hacker with the European Defense Forces.)

Joe paused at the bar. "Pint of bitter?" he asked tentatively. Brenda glanced at him and nodded, then went back to loading the antique washing machine. Presently she pulled a clean glass down from the shelf and held it under the tap.

"Hear you've got farm trouble," she said noncommitally as she worked the hand pump on the beer engine.

"Uh-huh." Joe focused on the glass. "Where'd you hear that?"

"Never you mind." She put the glass down to give the head time to settle. "You want to talk to Arthur and Wendy-the-Rat about farms. They had one the other year."

"Happens." Joe took his pint. "Thanks, Brenda. The usual?"

"Yeah." She turned back to the washer. Joe headed over to the far corner where a pair of huge leather sofas, their arms and backs ripped and scarred by generations of Brenda's semiferal cats, sat facing each other on either side of a cold hearth. "Art, Rats. What's up?"

"Fine, thanks." Wendy-the-Rat was well over seventy, one of those older folks who had taken the p53 chromosome hack and seemed to wither into timelessness: white dreadlocks, nose and ear studs dangling loosely from leathery holes, skin like a desert wind. Art had been her boy-toy once, back before middle age set its teeth into him. He hadn't had the hack, and looked older than she did. Together they ran a smallholding, mostly pharming vaccine chicks but also doing a brisk trade in high-nitrate fertilizer that came in on the nod and went out in sacks by moonlight.

"Heard you had a spot of bother?"

"'S true." Joe took a cautious mouthful. "Mm, good. You ever had farm trouble?"

"Maybe." Wendy looked at him askance, slitty-eyed. "What kinda trouble you got in mind?"

"Got a farm collective. Says it's going to Jupiter or something. Bastard's homesteading the woods down by Old Jack's stream. Listen . . . Jupiter?"

"Aye, well, that's one of the destinations, sure enough." Art nodded wisely, as if he knew anything.

"Naah, that's bad." Wendy-the-Rat frowned. "Is it growing trees, do you know?"

"Trees?" Joe shook his head. "Haven't gone and looked, tell the truth. What the fuck makes people do that to themselves, anyway?"

"Who the fuck cares?" Wendy's face split in a broad grin. "Such as don't think they're human anymore, meself."

"It tried to sweet-talk us," Joe said.

"Aye, they do that," said Arthur, nodding emphatically. "Read somewhere they're the ones as think we aren't fully human. Tools an' clothes and farmyard machines, like? Sustaining a pre-post-industrial lifestyle instead of updating our genome and living off the land like God intended?"

"'Ow the hell can something with nine legs and eye stalks call itself human?" Joe demanded, chugging back half his pint in one angry swallow.

"It used to be, once. Maybe used to be a bunch of people." Wendy got a weird and witchy look in her eye. "'Ad a boyfriend back thirty, forty years ago, joined a Lamarckian clade. Swapping genes an' all, the way you or me'd swap us underwear. Used to be a 'viromentalist back when antiglobalization was about big corporations pissing on us all for profits. Got into gene hackery and self-sufficiency big time. I slung his fucking ass when he turned green and started photosynthesizing."

"Bastards," Joe muttered. It was deep green folk like that who'd killed off the agricultural-industrial complex in the early years of the century, turning large portions of the countryside into ecologically devastated wilderness gone to rack and ruin. Bad enough that they'd set millions of countryfolk out of work—but that they'd gone on to turn green, grow extra limbs and emigrate to Jupiter orbit was adding insult to injury. And having a good time in the process, by all accounts. "Din't you 'ave a farm problem, coupla years back?"

"Aye, did that," said Art. He clutched his pint mug protectively.

"It went away," Joe mused aloud.

"Yeah, well." Wendy stared at him cautiously.

"No fireworks, like." Joe caught her eye. "And no body. Huh."

"Metabolism," said Wendy, apparently coming to some kind of decision. "That's where it's at."

"Meat—" Joe, no biogeek, rolled the unfamiliar word around his mouth irritably. "I used to be a software dude before I burned, Rats. You'll have to 'splain the jargon 'fore using it."

"You ever wondered how those farms *get* to Jupiter?" Wendy probed.

"Well." Joe shook his head. "They, like, grow stage trees? Rocket logs? An' then they est-ee-vate and you are fucked if they do it next door 'cause when those trees go up they toast about a hundred hectares?"

"Very good," Wendy said heavily. She picked up her mug in both hands and gnawed on the rim, edgily glancing around as if hunting for police gnats. "Let's you and me take a hike."

Pausing at the bar for Ole Brenda to refill her mug, Wendy led Joe out past Spiffy Buerke—throwback in green wellingtons and Barbour jacket—and her latest femme, out into what had once been a car park and was now a tattered wasteground out back behind the pub. It was dark, and no residual light pollution stained the sky: the Milky Way was visible overhead, along with the pea-size red cloud of orbitals that had gradually swallowed Jupiter over the past few years. "You wired?" asked Wendy.

"No, why?"

She pulled out a fist-size box and pushed a button on the side of it, waited for a light on its side to blink green, and nodded. "Fuckin' polis bugs."

"Isn't that a—?"

"Ask me no questions, an' I'll tell you no fibs." Wendy grinned.

"Uh-huh." Joe took a deep breath: he'd guessed Wendy had some dodgy connections, and this—a portable local jammer—was proof: any police bugs within two or three meters would be blind and dumb, unable to relay their chat to the keyword-trawling subsentient coppers whose job it was to prevent conspiracy-to-commit offenses before they happened. It was a relic of the Internet Age, when enthusiastic legislators had accidentally demolished the right of free speech in public by demanding keyword monitoring of everything within range of a network terminal—not realizing that in another few decades 'network terminals' would be self-replicating 'bots the size of fleas and about as common as dirt. (The Net itself had collapsed shortly thereafter, under the weight of self-replicating viral libel lawsuits, but the legacy of public surveillance remained.) "Okay. Tell me about metal, meta—"

"Metabolism." Wendy began walking toward the field behind the pub. "And stage trees. Stage trees started out as science fiction, like? Some guy called Niven—anyway. What you do is, you take a pine tree and you hack it. The xylem vessels running up the heartwood, usually they just lignify and die, in a normal tree. Stage trees go one better, and before the cells die, they *nitrate* the cellulose in their walls. Takes one fuckin' crazy bunch of hacked 'zymes to do it, right? And lots of energy, more energy than trees'd normally have to waste. Anyways, by the time the tree's dead, it's like ninety percent nitrocellulose, plus built-in stiffeners and baffles and microstructures. It's not, like, straight explosive—it detonates cell by cell, and *some* of the xylem tubes are, eh, well, the farm grows custom-hacked fungal hyphae with a depolarizing membrane nicked from human axons down them to trigger the reaction. It's about efficient as 'at old-time Ariane or Atlas rocket. Not very, but enough."

"Uh." Joe blinked. "That meant to mean something to me?"

"Oh 'eck, Joe." Wendy shook her head. "Think I'd bend your ear if it wasn't?"

"Okay." He nodded, seriously. "What can I do?"

"Well." Wendy stopped and stared at the sky. High above them, a belt of faint light sparkled with a multitude of tiny pinpricks; a deep green wagon train making its orbital transfer window, self-sufficient posthuman Lamarckian colonists, space-adapted, embarking on the long, slow transfer to Jupiter.

"Well?" He waited expectantly.

"You're wondering where all that fertilizer's from," Wendy said elliptically.

"Fertilizer." His mind blanked for a moment.

"Nitrates."

He glanced down, saw her grinning at him. Her perfect fifth set of teeth glowed alarmingly in the greenish overspill from the light on her jammer box.

"Tha' knows it make sense," she added, then cut the jammer.

When Joe finally staggered home in the small hours, a thin plume of smoke was rising from Bob's kennel. Joe paused in front of the kitchen door and sniffed anxiously, then relaxed. Letting go of the door handle, he walked over to the kennel and sat down outside. Bob was most particular about his den—even his own humans didn't go in there without an invitation. So Joe waited.

A moment later there was an interrogative cough from inside. A dark, pointed snout came out, dribbling smoke from its nostrils like a particularly vulpine dragon. "Rrrrrrr?"

"'S'me."

"Uuurgh." A metallic click. "Smoke good smoke joke cough tickle funny arf arf?"

"Yeah, don't mind if I do."

The snout pulled back into the kennel; a moment later it reappeared, teeth clutching a length of hose with a mouthpiece on one end. Joe accepted it graciously, wiped off the mouthpiece, leaned against the side of the kennel, and inhaled. The weed was potent and smooth: within a few seconds the uneasy dialogue in his head was still.

"Wow, tha's a good turnup."

"Arf-arf-ayup."

Joe felt himself relaxing. Maddie would be upstairs, snoring quietly in their decrepit bed: waiting for him, maybe. But sometimes a man just had to be alone with his dog and a good joint, doing man-and-dog stuff. Maddie understood this and left him his space. Still . . .

"'At farm been buggering around the pond?"

"Growl exclaim fuck-fuck yup! Sheep-shagger."

"If it's been at our lambs—"

"Nawwwwrr. Buggrit."

"So whassup?"

"Grrrr, Maddie yap-yap farmtalk! Sheep-shagger."

"Maddie's been *talking* to it?"

"Grr yes-yes!"

"Oh, shit. Do you remember when she did her last backup?"

The dog coughed fragrant blue smoke. "Tank thump-thump full cow moo beef clone."

"Yeah, I think so, too. Better muck it out tomorrow. Just in case."

"Yurrrrrp." But while Joe was wondering whether this was agreement or just a canine eructation a lean paw stole out of the kennel mouth and yanked the hookah back inside. The resulting slobbering noises and clouds of aromatic blue smoke left Joe feeling a little queasy: so he went inside.

The next morning, over breakfast, Maddie was even quieter than usual. Almost meditative.

"Bob said you'd been talking to that farm," Joe commented over his eggs.

"Bob—" Maddie's expression was unreadable. "Bloody dog." She lifted the Rayburn's hot plate lid and peered at the toast browning underneath. "Talks too much."

"Did you?"

"Ayup." She turned the toast and put the lid back down on it.

"Said much?"

"It's a farm." She looked out the window. "Not a fuckin' worry in the world 'cept making its launch window for Jupiter."

"It—"

"Him. Her. They." Maddie sat down heavily in the other kitchen chair. "It's a collective. Usedta be six people. Old, young, whatever, they's decided ter go to Jupiter. One of 'em was telling me how it happened. How she'd been living like an accountant in Bradford, had a nervous breakdown. Wanted *out*. Self-sufficiency." For a moment her expression turned bleak. "Felt herself growing older but not bigger, if you follow."

"So how's turning into a bioborg an improvement?" Joe grunted, forking up the last of his scrambled eggs.

"They're still separate people: bodies are overrated, anyway. Think of the advantages: not growing older, being able to go places and survive anything, never being on your own, not bein' trapped—" Maddie sniffed. "Fuckin' toast's on fire!"

Smoke began to trickle out from under the hot plate lid. Maddie yanked the wire toasting rack out from under it and dunked it into the sink, waited for waterlogged black crumbs to float to the surface before taking it out, opening it, and loading it with fresh bread.

"Bugger," she remarked.

"You feel trapped?" Joe asked. *Again?* He wondered.

Maddie grunted evasively. "Not your fault, love. Just life."

"Life." Joe sniffed, then sneezed violently as the acrid smoke tickled his nose. "Life!"

"Horizon's closing in," she said quietly. "Need a change of horizons."

"Ayup, well, rust never sleeps, right? Got to clean out the winter stables, haven't I?" said Joe. He grinned uncertainly at her as he turned away. "Got a shipment of fertilizer coming in."

In between milking the herd, feeding the sheep, mucking out the winter stables, and surreptitiously EMPing every police 'bot on the farm into the silicon afterlife, it took Joe a couple of days to get round to running up his toy on the household fabricator. It clicked and whirred to itself like a demented knitting machine as it ran up the gadgets he'd ordered—a modified crop sprayer with double-walled tanks and hoses, an air rifle with a dart loaded with a potent cocktail of tubocurarine and etorphine, and a breathing mask with its own oxygen supply.

Maddie made herself scarce, puttering around the control room but mostly disappearing during the daytime, coming back to the house after dark to crawl, exhausted, into bed. She didn't seem to be having nightmares, which was a good sign. Joe kept his questions to himself.

It took another five days for the smallholding's power field to concentrate enough juice to begin fueling up his murder weapons. During this time, Joe took the house off-Net in the most deniable and surreptitiously plausible way, a bastard coincidence of squirrel-induced cable fade and a badly shielded alternator on the backhoe to do for the wireless chitchat. He'd half expected Maddie to complain, but she didn't say anything—just spent more time away in Outer Cheswick or Lower Gruntlingthorpe or wherever she'd taken to holing up.

Finally, the tank was filled. So Joe girded his loins, donned his armor, picked up his weapons, and went to do battle with the dragon by the pond.

The woods around the pond had once been enclosed by a wooden fence, a charming copse of old-growth deciduous trees, elm and oak and beech growing uphill, smaller shrubs nestling at their ankles in a green skirt that reached all the way to the almost-stagnant waters. A little stream fed into it during rainy months, under the feet of a weeping willow; children had played here, pretending to explore the wilderness beneath the benevolent gaze of their parental control cameras.

That had been long ago. Today the woods really *were* wild. No kids, no picnicking city folks, no cars. Badgers and wild coypu and small, frightened wallabies roamed the parching English countryside during the summer dry season. The water drew back to expose an apron of cracked mud, planted with abandoned tin cans and a supermarket trolley of Precambrian vintage, its GPS tracker long since shorted out. The bones of the technological epoch, poking from the treacherous surface of a fossil mud bath. And around the edge of the mimsy puddle, the stage trees grew.

Joe switched on his jammer and walked in among the spear-shaped conifers. Their needles were matte black and fuzzy at the edges, fractally divided, the better to soak up all the available light: a network of taproots and fuzzy black grasslike stuff covered the ground densely around them. Joe's breath wheezed noisily in his ears, and he sweated into the airtight suit as he worked, pumping a stream of colorless smoking liquid at the roots of each ballistic trunk. The liquid fizzed and evaporated on contact: it seemed to bleach the wood where it touched. Joe carefully avoided the stream: this stuff made him uneasy. As did the trees, but liquid nitrogen was about the one thing he'd been able to think of that was guaranteed to kill the trees stone dead without igniting them. After all, they had cores that were basically made of gun cotton—highly explosive, liable to go off if you subjected them to a sudden sharp impact or the friction of a chainsaw. The tree he'd hit on creaked ominously, threatening to fall sideways, and Joe stepped round it, efficiently squirting at the remaining roots. Right into the path of a distraught farm.

"My holy garden of earthly delights! My forest of the imaginative future! My delight, my trees, my trees!" Eye stalks shot out and over, blinking down at him in horror as the farm reared up on six or seven legs and pawed the air in front of him. "Destroyer of saplings! Earth mother rapist! Bunny-strangling vivisectionist!"

"Back off," said Joe, dropping his cryogenic squirter and fumbling for his air gun.

The farm came down with a ground-shaking thump in front of him and stretched eyes out to glare at him from both sides. They blinked, long black eyelashes fluttering across angry blue irises. "How *dare* you?" demanded the farm. "My treasured seedlings!"

"Shut the fuck up," Joe grunted, shouldering his gun. "Think I'd let you burn my holding when tha' rocket launched? Stay the *fuck* away," he added as a tentacle began to extend from the farm's back.

"My crop," it moaned quietly. "My exile! Six more years around the sun chained to this well of sorrowful gravity before next the window opens! No brains for Baby Jesus! Defenestrator! We could have been so happy together if you hadn't fucked up! Who set you up to this? Rat Lady?" It began to gather itself, muscles rippling under the leathery mantle atop its leg cluster.

So Joe shot it.

Tubocurarine is a muscle relaxant: it paralyzes skeletal muscles, the kind over which human nervous systems typically exert conscious control. Etorphine is an insanely strong opiate—twelve hundred times as potent as heroin. Given time, a farm, with its alien adaptive metabolism and consciously controlled proteome might engineer a defense against the etorphine—but Joe dosed his dart with enough to stun a blue whale, and he had no intention of giving the farm enough time.

It shuddered and went down on one knee as he closed in on it, a Syrette raised. "Why?" it asked plaintively in a voice that almost made him wish he hadn't pulled the trigger. "We could have gone together!"

"Together?" he asked. Already the eye stalks were drooping; the great lungs wheezed effortfully as it struggled to frame a reply.

"I was going to ask you," said the farm, and half its legs collapsed under it, with a thud like a baby earthquake. "Oh, Joe, if only—"

"Joe? *Maddie?*" he demanded, nerveless fingers dropping the tranquilizer gun.

A mouth appeared in the farm's front, slurred words at him from familiar seeming lips, words about Jupiter and promises. Appalled, Joe backed away from the farm. Passing the first dead tree, he dropped the nitrogen tank: then an impulse he couldn't articulate made him turn and run, back to the house, eyes almost blinded by sweat or tears. But he was too slow, and when he dropped to his knees next to the farm, pharmacopoeia clicking and whirring to itself in his arms, he found it was already dead.

"Bugger," said Joe, and he stood up, shaking his head. "*Bugger.*" He keyed his walkie-talkie: "Bob, come in, Bob!"

"Rrrrowl?"

"Momma's had another break-down. Is the tank clean, like I asked?"

"Yap!"

"Okay. I got 'er backup tapes in t'office safe. Let's get t' tank warmed up for 'er an' then shift t' tractor down 'ere to muck out this mess."

That autumn, the weeds grew unnaturally rich and green down in the north paddock of Armitage End.

the ice

STEVEN POPKES

Here's a poignant, lyrical, and thoughtful look at one man's life, and how that life is changed forever by one bizarre revelation . . .

Steven Popkes made his first sale in 1985, and in the years that followed has contributed a number of distinguished stories to markets such as *Asimov's Science Fiction, Sci Fiction, The Magazine of Fantasy & Science Fiction, Realms of Fantasy, Science Fiction Age, Full Spectrum, Tomorrow, The Twilight Zone Magazine, Night Cry,* and others. His first novel *Caliban Landing* appeared in 1987, and was followed in 1991 by an expansion to novel-length of his popular novella "The Egg," retitled *Slow Lightning.* ("The Egg," in its original form, was in our Seventh Annual Collection.) He was also part of the Cambridge Writers' Workshop project to produce science fiction scenarios about the future of Boston, Massachusetts, that cumulated in the 1994 anthology *Future Boston,* to which he contributed several stories. His story "Winters Are Hard" was in our Twentieth Annual Collection. He lives in Hopkinton, Massachusetts, with his family, works for a company that builds aviation instrumentation, and is learning to be a pilot.

NetBio, April 26, 2017
Howe, Gordie
   (Gordon Howe), 1928–, Canadian hockey player. Possibly the greatest and most durable forward in the history of hockey, he played (1946–71) for the Detroit Red Wings of the National Hockey League (NHL). With his two sons he

joined (1973) the Houston Aeros and then (1977) the New England Whalers of the World Hockey Association, ending his career in 1980 with the Hartford Whalers of the NHL. Howe's NHL career records include most seasons (26) and most games (1,767); his career record for most goals (801) was broken by Wayne Gretzky in 1994.

ACT I

▼

It is late April at the end of the hockey season. Play-offs start in two weeks. Phil Berger is thinking about practice, college, and his girlfriend Roxanne, all at the same time. Earlier in the week, Colby and Dartmouth had both sent him letters about a hockey scholarship. He would have preferred a better school with a better team—like Boston University. But BU hadn't shown much interest in him, though he'd seen one of their scouts at a game three weeks back. Phil chides himself. Don't get your hopes up. There are a lot of guys playing hockey these days.

The house is dark, but his mother's car is in the driveway. The moon mingles the Victorian architecture and shadows of the trees. The result makes him uneasy. There is just enough light for him to find the front door key. Once inside, he turns on the hall light.

Silence.

He can hear breathing in the front room. He walks to the door. The light is behind him and he cannot see anyone. "Mom?" he calls.

The light comes on in the room, and Carol Berger, his mother, pulls her hand away from the lamp.

She hands him a flimsy. Its active surface shows the sports page of the *Middlesex News*. Phil recognizes Frank Hammett's byline from previous articles. His mother keeps a scrapbook of every article Phil has ever been in. Phil's picture leads the text of the article. The headline leaps out at him:

"Clone of Gordie Howe Playing for Hopkinton Hillers."

Phil chuckles. What a joker. He shakes his head at the thought of it. Phil's good. But he's no Gordie Howe.

"Is this the problem?" He holds up the paper. "April Fool's is a little late this year."

"You were an in vitro baby," his mother says slowly.

"What?"

"From neither of us. My eggs were . . . unusable, and your father has the genes for Lou Gherig's Disease. He didn't want to saddle any child with that. The embryo was donated. We didn't know the parents." She rubs her face in her hands. "We only knew the procedure was subsidized by a rich benefactor." She looks at him. "We had given up. We didn't have the money. We were living in New Hampshire, and fertility procedures weren't covered by insurance. We wanted a baby."

He shakes his head. "So what? It still can't be true."

She shrugs. "I don't know. All I know is, I got a call from two lawyers, one offering to represent us in suing Gordie Howe for compensation and one representing Gordie Howe warning us off. Dr. Robinson called me, too."

"Robinson?"

"The obstetrician who implanted the embryo."

"What did Dr. Robinson say?"

"He said he'd been approached by Frank Hammett with some documentation on the 'irregularities in the implantation procedure.'" She raises a hand and lets it fall in her lap. "'Irregularities.'"

Phil tries to make sense out of what his mother is saying.

She stares out the window. "Somebody is taking Hammett's article seriously."

More lawyers, publicists, and reporters call in the next week. In Massachusetts, hockey is loved as no other sport. All of Hopkinton is excited at the idea that there might be a budding Gordie Howe in their midst.

Phil's father, Jake, insists visuals be completely turned off and the audio filtered. He refuses to return calls. Jake has spent his life trying to live correctly, to provide for his son and his wife. He works hard managing the plastics factory near the house, and when he comes home, he leaves technology behind. The Berger house is over a hundred years old and has only the minimum data feeds. Phil has always had to go to the houses of friends for immersion games or wide feeds. Jake spends most of his spare time in the summer working in his garden. In the winter, he spends it in his greenhouse.

Phil doesn't know what to do with his father. Jake won't meet his eyes. Jake avoids Phil, even though the house is too small for that. Normally, Jake would be clearing the garden, readying it for the coming spring. It's a cold April and Phil is worried about him. Jake takes to sitting in the greenhouse, staring out the window. The honey berries will go unharvested. Phil wants to call Roxanne and talk about it, but she is learning French in France for the month and he doesn't feel like calling overseas.

Besides, he tells himself, he doesn't really believe it. He thinks this is some strange hoax being played out. He reads up on hockey history and wonders what it would be like to be Gordie Howe.

Response to Hammett's article forcibly occupies the discussion sections of the local feeds all that week. By Sunday, the tone of the conversation has changed from questioning the ethics of a Gordie Howe clone playing against normal players to how dare Frank Hammett perpetuate such an obvious lie. It does not make any of the regional or national news feeds. Phil is relieved. Nothing is real until it hits the big feeds. Hammett is strangely silent and unavailable for comment. There is speculation that he is being closely questioned on verification of his sources. Hammett's ambition to be a reporter for the *Globe* feed is discussed. The old Mike Barnicle scandal is brought up, and one editorial concludes that Hammett will be similarly fired. It looks as if the spotlight has moved from Phil back onto Hammett. Phil is just as glad.

The following Monday night, the Hillers play their next game in Leominster against the Blue Devils. Hammett's article has had visible effect: the place is mobbed. Phil can't get in. A lawyer named Dalton threatens him with an injunction and says that he represents Gordie Howe. Unsure of what to do, Jake and Phil back away and leave the rink. However, they park on an adjacent street and sneak in through the back entrance. Neither Phil nor the rest of the team can concentrate on the game. The Hillers founder and lose, four to two.

After the game, cars follow Jake and Phil. Jake takes to the backroads and eventually loses them. Phil wonders who they are. All he saw were people in windbreakers and ski-jackets, wool coats with gloves—their faces could have been anyone's faces.

When Jake and Phil come in the door, Carol hands them a flimsy of the Boston *Globe*. The lead article, by Frank Hammett and Carl Weatherspoon, is about the "Gordie Howe Clone." The article continues, occupying most of the flimsy with a host of associated links. There are several pictures of DNA chromatographs and chromosomes, documenting the similarities between the Howe genotype and that of Phil Berger.

Phil feels as if the world has entered into some long, horrible tunnel. He shakes his head and stares at the pictures. This is his life on display without his permission. No. It's more than that. He feels naked before strangers. He feels shame without knowing why.

He looks up at his parents. "How did they get this stuff? Don't they have to . . . to ask permission or something? Don't I have to sign a waiver? Don't *you* have to sign a waiver?"

Jake shrugs. "I don't know, son."

The doorbell rings. Outside are four men.

"Shit," says Jake.

Phil has never heard his father swear.

In the hallway, Jake turns to Phil. "Phil, this is Dr. Sam Robinson. Your mother told you about him. I'm not sure who the other people are."

Phil recognizes Dalton from the rink. The next two men enter. One is introduced as Dr. Murray Howe, Gordie Howe's son. Phil needs no introduction to the last man; it's Gordie Howe himself.

Phil is a big boy. He stands over six feet tall and weighs in at one ninety. He knows he is big; he likes the comfortable feeling it gives him when he walks through a crowd. He likes his own height and heft. When Howe walks in the house and they face one another, Phil suddenly knows it's true. Howe is pushing ninety, and has shrunk as old men do. Age and punishment have changed Howe but even allowing for that, Phil doesn't exactly have Howe's face. It's Howe's body that convinces him. Young Gordie Howe shows through his carriage, his battered knees and ankles, his hands as they hang relaxed and ready from the elbow.

Howe's eyes measure him in return. Phil can see that Howe is convinced as well.

"Did you do it?" Phil asks.

Howe shakes his head. "I have three sons already. I don't need any more." He leans his head to one side and looks at Phil critically. "Are you going to claim I'm your father?"

Phil shakes his head in return. "I have a father. I don't need two."

The meeting is concluded as far as the two of them are concerned, but they still have to wait for the others. They all sit down in the living room. Howe says very little. Phil and Howe's attention are on each other.

Robinson explains what has happened. "In 1997, we were approached by the firm Meel and Weed from Detroit. Meel and Weed represented a couple that had been killed in an automobile accident with their embryos still in storage. The common practice at that time was to freeze extra embryos for possible later use or research. The parents of the deceased couple wished to allow the embryos to be used by infertile couples in their children's memory. All of the participants were to remain anonymous." Robinson removes his glasses and rubs his nose. "This was not uncommon then and is not uncommon now. In addition, Meel and Weed's clients were wealthy enough to provide grants for needy couples. New Hampshire did not require IVF insurance coverage then. We checked Meel and Weed's credentials. We checked with the facility that was storing the embryos. We did *not* check the clients directly since they wished to remain anonymous but we examined their purported medical records. This is also not uncommon. After we received the embryos, we called the Bergers."

Robinson looks around the room in silence. "In the last week I've found that Meel and Weed's credentials were a fraud. The facility we checked with does not exist. The credentials of the facility were a sham. I'd never have imagined such a thing. Neither had the Attorney General of Michigan. He is investigating, but after eighteen years, he is not hopeful."

Carol looks at Howe and Phil. "They don't look *that* much alike. Maybe it's all some scam."

Robinson nods. "That's not surprising. In 1999, only the Dolly techniques were available. You have to understand how different a Dolly clone is from the genetic parent. There are three forces that act on the embryo: the nonnuclear contents of the egg itself, the nuclear DNA from both the egg and the sperm, and the developmental environment of the mother. In Phil's case, only one of those three forces came from Mr. Howe. The remainder came from the unknown egg donor and Mrs. Berger."

Phil looks up. "Aren't there other human clones? It's been seventeen years. I can't be the first."

"Good point." Robinson straightens his glasses. "Cloning still isn't FDA approved for humans—even now, with modern techniques, there is a very high percentage of birth defects. But so what? Cloning is illegal, but that wouldn't stop everybody. It's hard to do even today, but that wouldn't mean that somebody, somewhere couldn't afford to do it in a rogue country. But we don't hear about it. Why not?"

Carol says softly: "Who's going to take a chance?"

Robinson points to Carol. "Bingo. In the first flush of enthusiasm in the years after Dolly, a few clones were produced." Robinson closes his eyes and shakes his head. "Phil was one of several clones, most of which were unsuccessful. They started trying to clone humans shortly before Dolly was announced. Children were born without a brain or eyes, or with other forms of brain damage. That stopped human cloning for a long time. People barely take a chance with things like Down's syndrome, much less something scarier. There were many other legal, safe, and cheap techniques to make babies. Unless, of course, you don't care how many crippled babies you produce until you get the right one, and you're powerful, clandestine, and unscrupulous."

Phil holds his hands in his lap. "Like somebody who might have wanted to clone Gordie Howe, for instance?"

"Exactly." Robinson smiles thinly. "Of course, things have changed recently. New techniques have been discovered. The debate is starting all over again."

"Why?" Phil shakes his head, feeling groggy. "Why do it at *all*? Why do it *here*? Why *Gordie Howe*?" He laughs shortly, a sound like a dog's bark. "This is New England! Why not Bobby Orr? Why not Ray Borque?"

"Who's Bobby Orr?" Robinson asks.

"Never mind."

Robinson shrugs and picks up a briefcase he has brought with him. "I have brought with me some sampling equipment. If Phil and Mr. Howe both agree, we can confirm the story one way or the other by morning."

Afterward, everyone is standing, ready to leave but waiting for Robinson to finish preparing the samples for transport.

An idea occurs to Phil. "Dr. Robinson. How many embryos did Meel and Weed give you?"

Robinson looks up at him from the table, his face suddenly tired. "Fourteen."

"What happened to them?"

"Two were used in your procedure. The remaining twelve embryos were divided among five other couples." He pauses, then continues. "Three didn't implant. One resulted in a miscarriage. There were two live births."

"Two?" Phil thinks of a brother. Someone with whom he can have this in common.

"Yes. He and his parents live in Nashua." Robinson stops again. "Oh, hell. You deserve to know. His name is Danny Helstrom. He has one of the worst cases of cerebral palsy I've ever seen."

Robinson calls the next morning. The results are unsurprising. Phil is a clone of Gordie Howe. Phil sits down, feeling depressed, though he expected the results.

There is still nothing about Phil on the national feeds, which makes him sigh with relief. Even a momentary glance from the national media would be make things difficult. The local feeds are also quiet. He hopes it stays that way.

Phil looks outside. The sky is bright and cold, blue as liquid oxygen. He stays home and takes his pond skates down to the lake. Skipping school is a privilege reserved for seniors.

He skates hard: sprint, stop, change direction, sprint, pivot backward, pivot forward. The tension leaves his body. He's breathing hard, the cold sharp in his mouth and throat, his muscles loose as butter. Without thinking about it, he dodges between the ice fishing holes, skirts the shallows where the ice is thin, through the pipe under the bridge onto the canal feeding the lake.

It's been a dry, cold winter, and even the canal is rock-hard. He draws his bare fingers across it. The surface freezes to his fingers for a brief moment with a feeling of sandpaper. Then, the sandpaper gives way, and he can feel the smooth solidity underneath. In a rink, this would be perfect hockey ice. This ice isn't rink-flat, but frozen in bumps and waves. The ground bordering the water is lumpy with sticks and roots, and above him the branches of the trees have a dried, withered look. Around a bend in the canal, the road is out of sight and hearing, and the canal widens into a long pond. Boulders have broken the ice, and he skates between them, backward, forward, jumping over the small rocks. He wonders if he could have been a figure skater—what would Howe have thought of that? It bothers him that Howe's opinion matters. He wonders what it would feel like to execute a double axel.

He tries to remember how he became interested in hockey instead of any other kind of sport. He can't remember. He vaguely remembers learning to skate, pushing around an old milk crate and wearing a huge helmet. Then, he remembers being four and skating on the lake, playing pond hockey with older boys.

Phil stops and leans on a boulder in the pond. Sure, most of the other four-year-olds were barely skating, but it hadn't meant anything to him. It was like being good at music or math. Just playing the piano didn't make you Mozart. Just doing arithmetic didn't make you Einstein. Just playing hockey didn't make you Gordie Howe. He was always big. Most people had taken him for six when he was four. Besides, the six- and seven-year-old kids he'd been skating with were always better than he was. He had dreamed of playing in the NHL, of being the next Wayne Gretzky or Bobby Orr. Sure. What hockey-playing kid hadn't? But he hadn't felt *exceptional*. Gordie Howe had been truly amazing. Phil wonders if Gordie Howe had ever felt exceptional.

He thinks it'll be good when Roxanne gets back on Friday. He wonders what she'll think about dating the clone of Gordie Howe.

Anyone with a camera and a net-feed, professional and otherwise, finds the Berger house that afternoon. Phil doesn't go outside or answer the door. Phil's morning had been preserved by a confusion of streets in the online address databases. Instead, a family named Cohen had been harassed for hiding Phil Berger from the world.

Phil's absence doesn't stop the commercial media. That night, when the story breaks on the local feeds and broadcasts, Phil sees two students at Hopkinton High School discuss his life in detail on WHDH. Both the principal and vice-principal tell WBZ what a terrific and popular student Phil Berger is. Phil has never met any of them. Noticeably absent from the stories is any human being he actually knows. Grainy videos of him skating shuttle back and forth across the net.

When Jake and Carol get home, they have to push their way slowly through the crowd. Four broadcasting vans are queued in front of the house. The chief of police and Phil's coach sit in a police car in Phil's driveway. Phil didn't ask them to do this, but he's glad they did. They're the only barriers between him and the reporters.

For the next few days, a police car takes Phil to classes in the morning. His coach takes him home after practice. Phil often finds himself standing in the living room, looking at the people outside.

The crowd changes after the first day or so. The local news feeds finally give way to national feeds as the debate heats up. Phil's nuclear DNA comes from Gordie Howe, but his mitochondrial DNA and cytoplasm come from the anonymous woman who donated the egg. The hormonal environment and the birth experience come from Carol Berger. How can he possibly be called natural? Whose child is he? Can Phil inherit from Gordie Howe? Can Gordie Howe demand visitation rights? Does the anonymous egg donor have any claim on him? Gordie Howe and Phil Berger have resolved the situation between them, but that does not affect the coverage; the fact of Phil's existence and Gordie Howe's fame is enough to propel the story.

The national feeds take their own obligatory pictures of the Berger house and move on, leaving the field to the tabloids, net drones, and con artists.

The coaches of Boston College and Boston University happen to visit Phil on the same day. While they are arguing on the front lawn the relative merits of the two schools, a representative of the National Hockey League takes Phil aside and tries to get him to sign with the Boston Bruins. "Why wait?" he asks.

Roxanne calls him. She tells him she's home but unsure how she feels about things. They should not see each other for a while. He stares at the phone wanting to punch something.

By Friday's first play-off game against the Marlborough Panthers, Phil is feeling claustrophobic, angry, and bitter. The Panthers take an early two-goal lead by the end of the first period. The Hillers, expecting to be beaten, are disorganized and chaotic on the ice. Phil no longer cares.

The Panthers win the face-off, but Phil intercepts the pass and comes into the Panthers' zone at full speed. At that moment, his rage and bitterness come together in him and it feels as if he is leaning into his body, grasping its strength like a man picking up a hammer. He sees the defenseman try to check him and checks him first, knocking him over. The goalie dives to intercept the puck, but Phil pivots backward and pops the puck over him to score.

He can hear the crowd roar as from a great distance. The ice has grown to fill his vision. His teammates pick up the pace with him, and by the end of the second period, the score is tied.

The third period is a war of attrition as the Panthers try to score. It is bruising, full-contact hockey, played almost entirely on center ice as both sides refuse to give up their zone. Then, with three minutes left to play, Phil goes in on the left, spins around the defenseman, and passes to his center, who scores.

The Panthers are fighting for a tie now. They pull the goalie to get six men on the ice. But it's Phil's world. The ice is as broad as the sea. It's his breath and his muscle. The harder he pushes himself, the easier it gets. He is given a half-second opportunity from the corner of the blue line, and fires a shot into the open net. The defenseman cross checks him from behind after the whistle blows.

Phil's reaction is as unexpected as it is unconscious. He turns and decks the defenseman. In a heartbeat, he is the center of a brawl. He's thrown out of the game. The Hillers lose the goal and beat the Panthers four to three.

He is showering in the locker room, the water pouring over his head. He's never played that well, ever. Maybe he needed to be hungry for it. He wasn't the youngest of six like Howe. A trick of the noise and current bring him a snatch of conversation.

"So that's what it's like to play with Gordie Howe!"

Hammett writes up the game, calling it a Gordie Howe hat trick: one goal, one assist, one fight.

With Phil thrown out for the next game, the Hillers lose in the next round of playoffs and are out for the season. He returns to his classes and the story seems to die down. He sees Roxanne across crowds of mutual friends, but she is distant. So is he.

ACT II

Over the summer, Phil works in his father's plant, accepts a hockey scholarship at BU, turns eighteen. While the discussion continues, it has passed him by. He has disappeared from the national and state media, overshadowed by the politicians. Instead, the dialogue has moved into the State House and Congress. New cloning regulations are proposed in several states. MassPIRG contacts him about helping their lobbying effort. Phil doesn't return their calls. Phil has become yesterday's news, and he is grateful. He and Roxanne even take in a couple of movies, though they are both very careful with one another.

He reports to the BU Terriers two weeks before classes for hockey practice. No one mentions Gordie Howe. He feels their gaze watching and measuring him. He resolves to ignore it. Things appear to be working out. He's starting out in the third line, which suits him just fine. He'd had his fill of visibility in the spring.

Practice goes well. The feeling he'd had in his last game, that sense of leaning into his body, has not left him. By the time the first game comes along, against the Air Force Falcons, he has been pulled from the third line and put in the second.

It's a good game and the Terriers win with a single goal—Phil's. He happens to be in the right place when it bounces from the glove of the Falcons' goalie. While he played well, he has no illusions that the goal was anything but good luck.

The next morning, leading the *Globe* sports feed, Frank Hammett's story lies below a picture of Phil popping in the puck: "Gordie Howe wins against Air Force."

Phil reads the story over an early dorm breakfast. Phil wonders which is real—as far as he was concerned, the goal was a fluke. According to Hammett, it was the result of his excellence of play stemming from Gordie Howe's genes. In effect, Gordie Howe played for BU by proxy.

The warm camaraderie he'd felt during the practice weeks turns cold. Conversations dry up when he comes in the room. No one shuts him out of planning or discussion of games. But it is purely professional. Most of them, he realizes suddenly, are here on scholarship and not expecting to go into professional hockey. It's a way to get through school. If Phil wins games for them, that's good for them. But they don't have to like him.

Perversely, this seems to work for him. In high school, he'd enjoyed a certain amount of popularity. Phil was never lazy, but he was not averse to substituting a big grin and a glib tongue for work. His talents had carried him in spite of himself.

Here, though, he speaks to few and finds himself trusting no one. He concentrates on his studies and on hockey. He returns his teammates' professionalism with professionalism. They are close colleagues, not friends. His talents are an anvil and this coldness the hammer by which he forges his skill.

On the ice, the personalities and conflicts are left behind. The game exists to the exclusion of all else. On the ice, Phil is free.

It is no accident that he is brought up into the starting line by midseason.

Hammett has developed a pattern in his stories: if the Terriers do well, it is because they have Gordie Howe playing for them. If they do badly, it is because of an inadequacy in Gordie Howe's clone. The language keeps the debate fresh. More than once, late at night, Phil, too exhausted to sleep, tunes into the sports feed, only to find the cloning debate in full swing, with him in the starring role. In November, in a fit of sudden, killing rage, he rips the display from the wall and throws it through the window. Phil's room is on the sixth floor. It is pure accident that no one is hurt. He cleans up the mess that night before any reporters get wind of it. He does not replace the unit. He thinks about taking a yoga class or something to relax. The idea of a Hammett headline saying "Gordie Howe Takes Yoga" stops him.

Phil keeps reminding himself what had happened in his last high-school game; how a sudden burst of temper had cost him the rest of the play-offs. College hockey plays by the same rules: fighting gets you ejected from that game and the next. He keeps his temper under control. Still, he occasionally checks too hard or hooks too vigorously. His penalties mount.

By February, Hammett has accused him of bringing "NHL-style hockey to Boston University." Phil speaks little, works very hard, and only seems to come alive on the ice. His parents try to talk to him, but he answers in monosyllables.

Then comes the first night of the Beanpot.

Since 1952, the four hockey teams of Boston—Boston College, Boston University, Northeastern University, and Harvard—have played against one another for bragging rights and a bowl of beans: the Boston Beanpot. Boston College is paired up with Boston University in the first game—a rivalry within a rivalry. The game is fought like trench warfare. No inch is lost or gained; no goal is scored. Then, BC scores the first goal. Phil scores the second for BU on a breakaway. Both teams are playing better than they have in months. The game is full of hard and sweaty grace. Phil is at home with his teammates, with the game, with the ice.

In the middle of the second period, Phil is carrying the puck into the Boston College zone. He sidesteps the defenseman and goes around him. The defenseman turns and tries to hook him, but loses his balance on the pivot. Instead, the stick whirls high in the air and slaps the side of Phil's helmet, directly over the ear, knocking him down. There is no injury, but the pain pins him to the ice for a moment. He stands and skates slowly toward the face-off circle. The defenseman protests the penalty. Phil looks around the arena, sees Frank Hammett watching him from the other side of the glass, shaking his head. Phil can almost hear what he's thinking: "Not much like Gordie Howe. Gordie wouldn't take that. Not him." Phil can almost read tomorrow's article: "Gordie Howe's Clone Not Up to the Original." It pounds in his chest along with his heart. He can see what will happen next.

The defenseman gives up arguing with the ref and starts to skate over to the penalty box. When he comes near, Phil pulls up with his stick and the defenseman goes down on his back. Without thinking, Phil lands on him with both knees. Then, Phil pulls off the defenseman's mask and starts pounding him. This is no stylized violence like the NHL. Phil is out to kill him. This is not Gordie Howe, he is thinking. This is me.

His teammates pull him off. The defenseman curls on his side. The refs throw him out of the game. His coach screams at him in the locker room. *Gordie Howe would never have done that!* Phil is out for two weeks, and maybe for good. Everything seems to happen from a distance.

He puts on his clothes and goes outside into a deep clot of reporters. They're just as far away as everything else. He just keeps walking, through the West End and downtown Boston. Past the Commons. Eventually, no reporters follow him and he is alone in the South End.

He finds a hole-in-the-wall bar on Columbus Avenue and orders a beer without thinking. As if it's the most natural thing in the world, they serve him, even though he's underage. Something about his abstracted manner and his size suggest he's older than he is.

It's the NHL for me, then, he thinks. Why not? Or the minors—there's more fighting in the minors. At that moment, he thinks he could enjoy the minors.

It happens as gently as snow on ice. A man jostles him on the way to the john. An insult is exchanged. Phil swings. The two men end up on the floor. Phil rolls over on top, and for a moment as he pounds on the stranger, as he wanted to pound on the defenseman, as he would have gladly pounded Frank Hammett or even Gordie Howe, he loves this stranger as he has no other.

The bartender knocks him out with a sap, and he awakes, dizzy and puking, in the back of a police van. The nameless man he had been fighting is not there. It is only Phil and another, unconscious drunk. He leans back against the wall, wondering what happens next.

Phil finds out at the arraignment that the man's name is Kenneth Roget. He has been released from the hospital with a mild concussion and missing teeth. Phil gets six months' probation and two hundred hours of community service. Roget threatens to sue, but the DA points out that Roget has a history of bar fights and is already on probation for assault on his ex-wife. The DA gets Roget to settle for medical costs.

Hammett's article reads: "Gordie Howe's Clone Jailed for Assault."

BU kicks him from the team and out of the university. He moves back home, contented for the moment to do his community service. His parents try to talk to him, but he is sullen and uncooperative. They suggest he call his friends from high school. He leaves the phone untouched.

For his community service, he works as a janitor at the Framingham hospital. The simple and silent work suits him. He is invisible as he mops a floor or pushes a cart out to the trash compactor. Medical staff and visitors stream past him, oblivious. The patients, especially the chronic ones, strike up incidental conversations with him. One man, a paraplegic from a car accident, reminds him of the other Howe clone, Danny Helstrom.

That night, on impulse, he finds a single Helstrom in Nashua, though there are two others in nearby towns. Phil isn't sure how he should proceed. Call him? Could Danny Helstrom even speak? There but for chance and circumstance goes Phil Berger.

A woman answers the phone. Her voice is tired. Phil is surprised. He expected a recording. Jake and Carol have been screening calls for nearly a year.

"Uh, hi." Phil can't think of anything to say. "I'm Phil Berger."

"Yeah?"

There is silence. "Is there a Danny Helstrom there?"

"Oh," comes from the other end. "*That* Phil Berger. Robinson said you might call. I figured it would have been last spring."

"Yes." There is silence on the phone. "Are you Danny Helstrom's mother?"

"You bet. Grace Baker."

"Baker?"

"Danny's father couldn't take it. He split when Danny was two. Funny, huh?" She laughs bitterly. "You want to meet your clone brother? I think it's a bad idea, but Danny would like to see you."

Danny Helstrom looks like Phil. At least, if Phil had been stretched thin and shrunken, then broken and reset, he would look like Danny. Danny has never been able to sit erect. He half lies across the wheelchair fabric on his right side. His fingers are long and graceful, and move gently and independently of him like the tendrils of a sea anemone. His voice is high and nasal. He weighs barely ninety pounds. Looking at Danny makes Phil feel obscurely ashamed of standing on two legs, of feeling his muscle and strength, of being able to speak. When Danny looks at Phil, it is out of Phil's own eyes.

Danny smiles, quivering; half his face locks up and releases. He speaks. Danny only has partial control of the muscles of his tongue and lips; his words are a smear of long vowels, grunts, and hisses. Grace interprets for him: "He's really glad you came up here. He thinks of you as his brother."

At first, Phil doesn't know what to say. He's not sure why he's here. "Good, I guess," he says hesitantly. "Did Dr. Robinson test you, too?" It seems inconceivable that this broken creature could be a clone of Gordie Howe.

"Yeah," says Grace. "Gordie Howe. Just like you."

Danny says something to Grace. She frowns. "Are you sure? I should be here."

Danny gives her his half smile and replies. She shrugs, leaves the room, and returns with a black box fitted with a speaker. She attaches a microphone to Danny's shirt, gives Phil a long glance, and leaves the room.

Danny makes a sound like a cross between a moan and a stutter. The box says in a monotone: "She's trying to protect me."

More at ease with Grace out of the room, Phil sits down on the bed. "How come?"

"She thinks you'll hurt me because I scare you." Danny half grins again. "Are you scared?"

Phil watches Danny. Something feels like it's cracking inside him. "Yeah. You scare me."

Danny flops his head back and forth in a nod. "I could have been you. You could have been me."

Phil sighs. "Yeah."

"I know. Could be worse." He grins again. "Could have not made it at all."

Phil clasps his hands together. This is my twin brother. "Is that what you really think?"

Danny looks back at him. "Because of my body?"

"Yes."

"Yes. I do. I'd rather live."

"Okay, then."

"But you owe me."

Phil spreads his hands. "How do you figure?"

Danny tries to point with his finger but it trembles in the air as if underwater. Instead, he nods in Phil's direction. "You got the legs."

Phil looks at himself. "Yeah."

"Tell me about hockey. Tell me what it's like to play like Gordie Howe."

Phil lets his breath out slowly. Danny's right. It's the luck of the draw that Phil got the body and Danny didn't. He owes for that luck. He has obligations to Danny, as close to a twin brother as he will ever know, because of that luck.

He thinks for a long time. It's important to say it right, to express it. "If I could fly," he says at last. "It would feel like skating."

The Bruins call him. He does not return the call. The Ice Cats in Worcester, the Chicago Freeze, the Florida Everglades. He does not return the calls. He has the phone screen out sports agents. He does not understand why he's doing this. It is only a minor assault charge. Professional players have done worse, taken worse penalties, and still played. He may not be Gordie Howe, but he could still play with the Amarillo Rattlers, for God's sake. He's at least that good.

Frank Hammett's article reads: "Clone of Gordie Howe a Janitor in Framingham."

Something in him breaks.

He finishes his community service by June. Jake gives him two thousand dollars. Phil takes his car and leaves town. He tells no one where he is going, since he doesn't know himself.

Let Frank Hammett write about that.

The principle around which Austin, Texas, revolves is heat.

It is late. Phil lies on the bed staring at the ceiling, waiting to go to work. His head is next to the window, the coolest spot in the room, but that's not saying much. He shares a house with three strangers. He'd found the house adver-tised in the paper when he'd hit town in June. It was cheap, and he liked the idea of living with strangers. Later, he realized why the house was cheap. It's made of brick, and the Texas summer sun turns it into a rock oven in the day, and the bricks re-radiate the heat at night. In the Texas winter, it is merely uncomfortable.

Every town has a hockey team these days and Austin is no exception. The Austin Ice Bats are resting comfortably near the bottom of the WPHL. Last week, against his better judgment, he'd gone to see them play the Amarillo Rat-tlers. He knew as soon as the game started that the Ice Bats would knock down his door if they knew he was here.

Phil tends bar in the Mexican side of town. The only Spanish he knows is "otra cerveza," "un tequila," and a list of other liquor-related words. He takes the money, sometimes dollars, sometimes pesos, and serves the drinks in silence.

Mainly, it's hot. Even in February. One of the other bartenders has lived in Austin all of his life and says it didn't used to be so hot in the winter. But now the February sun burns down and it's in the eighties every day. Up North, he thinks, there are the January snowstorms followed by February, when every-thing freezes so hard you can't even bury somebody until the spring thaw. Then, there's March, when the ground gently softens under the wet snows, April, when it's mud season, and a quick spring in May.

As he cleans the bar, he thinks of winter in Massachusetts, when the tem-perature starts to hover around zero, and the ice gets thick and draws all the water from the air and the ground starts to feel rough and bumpy as it freezes down. Everything comes down to essentials in a New England winter: bare trees, snow, frozen earth, ice.

Down here, it feels too easy to be winter. The Anglos sail on the man-made lake. They water their grass. They grow their flowers. February is just another month.

He corresponds with Danny regularly. Instead of the net, they send written letters, on paper, by mail. Except for packages and certified letters, physical let-ters are largely a thing of the past, having been replaced by photon packets moving at the speed of light. Danny started it and Phil responded the same way. Neither has ever talked about the comfort of holding a paper letter.

Phil's letters go like this:

Danny,
I'm still working at the bar. We've got a little heat wave now so every night the place is packed. Lots of sweaty music. I'm tending bar on weekends so I get some more money. By the way, guess who I ran into down here? Roxanne, my old girl friend from high school. Seems she went to University of Texas. She's been down here all this time

and we never ran into each other. She came into the bar and recognized me. It was good to see her. She's engaged to a nice enough guy.

My boss Guillermo took me camping out of the city a couple of weeks ago. I'll say one thing about Texas. The sky is just as big as people say. We lay in our sleeping bags drinking Jack Daniel's and just watching the moon go by.

Write and tell me about things up North.

Phil

Phil knows the process Danny goes through to write a letter. If he uses the voice writer, it's a struggle to get the words out, a struggle to correct them when the writer makes a mistake. Phil has seen Danny sweating and shaking after leaving a note for his mother.

Instead, Danny usually prefers to use a specially fitted keyboard. The process is still slow and laborious, each key combination carefully thought out and forced through his trembling hands. But it's easier than speaking. Such a letter might take Danny a week or more of concentrated effort. Each letter Phil receives feels heavier than his own, as if the effort has given it mass and heft. Phil keeps a box in his room and each letter from Danny is carefully flattened and stored there.

Phil wonders why he saves the letters so carefully. He thinks it might be the way Danny always talks about little things going on around him. Danny is home most of the time and the local world is most of what he sees. Other times, he thinks it's because it was only an accident that Danny was the crippled one and Phil was born unmarked. Both could have been crushed by their birth or neither, or Phil could just as easily have been locked into the wheelchair by his own body and Danny been whole. As Danny had said the first day, Phil owed Danny something. Recognition, maybe. Acknowledgment. Respect.

But often, as he carefully smooths the paper wrinkled and creased by travel, he feels as if he is saving something important, a message in a bottle from another country. It is not as if he is saving the work of some great artist or poet—in fact, when he thinks about it, he wouldn't save such things the same way or with the same reverence. No, this is more like saving letters from your father in wartime or your brother who lives across the world from you. The letters show your connection. You treat their letters as carefully as you would treat them if they were here but sick or dying, because by taking care of the letters, you're taking care of your brother, or your father, or your friend.

Danny's letters go like this:

Dear Phil,
I had a good day. I bundled all up and took the chair outside while Grace was at work. She hates it when I do that because she's

scared I'll get stuck out there. But the sky had that big carnival glass bowl look and the snow was on the ground. I was able to scatter out some bird seed and pretty soon two gold finches, a cardinal, and a bunch of titwhistles were hopping all over me. I don't know where the cardinal came from. I thought they migrated.

I'd like to see the sky you were talking about. Maybe Grace and I could come down later in the year.

Dr. Robinson visited. Guilt, I suppose. I told him I wanted to try the Twain treatment. I said it was a special device that combined the principles of the screw, the lever, and the inclined plane. You attach it to the upper part of your jaw and it extracts the entire skeleton. Then, you send the patient home in a pillowcase. He was going along with me until the extraction. He is such a serious man. Then, he got huffy for a minute until he saw I was baiting him. He laughed.

At one point, I went with him to the kitchen and bumped him two or three times with my chair. By the time he'd apologized a couple of times for *me* bumping *him*, he figured it out and turned into a pretty nice doctor. He gave me the straight skinny on what he knew both on the cloning and how it went so bad in my case.

I've been doing some net searches in the last couple of months about the cloning. I didn't find anything. You should go up there and talk to the detective Dalton used. His name is Rice.

Austin sounds great but you belong up here. This is where you will end up; I feel it in my twisted little bones. Down in Austin you're just marking time and three years is a lot of time to mark. Up here you could be doing something with your—and, I confess, our—life. It's important to do more than tread water, even if you drown.

At least you could do the legwork for me and go up to Detroit and talk to Rice. I sure would like to find these people. I'd like to know why they cloned us and, more interestingly, why they revealed you alone. Maybe they have clone marketing plans.

Hey, you could take me with you and I could see another Big City: two in one lifetime!

Danny Helstrom

He gets a call from Grace. Danny is in the hospital with congestive heart failure. Come home if you can.

Phil thinks about Danny all the way from Austin to Massachusetts, about his twisted body, his half smile, his letters. Phil takes with him his collection of perhaps twenty letters as if they were talismans. He'd read them over before he left and thought about them during the drive. Phil wishes he had been able to write better letters in return.

Danny is able to smile at him when he gets there, but can do nothing else. He slips into a coma soon after. Grace signs the Do Not Resuscitate order, and, after a long two days, Danny's heart gives out and he dies.

Phil and Grace sit in the room with the body afterward, talking of small things: the weather, the sun coming in the room, Danny's letters. Danny's body is small and still on the bed. Sitting together feels as natural as breathing.

When it feels right, they leave the room and tell the nurse. On the way to the car, Grace takes him and grabs his hand and turns him so he has to look her in the face. "Danny wanted me to tell you he couldn't have had a better brother than you."

"Thanks," he mumbles.

The funeral is a small thing: Grace, Phil, Phil's parents, Gustavo, the aide who had helped with Danny after Phil had left, Dr. Robinson. Gordie Howe sends a short note of condolence. Ill health has prevented Howe from attending. Danny had requested cremation; as far as Danny had been concerned, this was the end of the line for that body.

Driving to Detroit to meet a private detective is paying a debt. Rice's office overlooks the river, and Phil can see the civic center in the distance, and, beyond that, Windsor, Ontario. When he enters, images of him, Danny, his parents, and Gordie Howe are being displayed on the wall along with annotated legal documents and forms.

"I reviewed our files and checked to see if there is any new information," says Rice, gesturing to the wall. "Nothing new has turned up in the last few years."

"Danny thought there was a connection between Meel and Weed and Gordie Howe. Gordie Howe played for the Red Wings for a long time when they were in Detroit. Could that be true?"

Rice looks suddenly tired. "You know, Dalton tried to make the same argument." Rice rubs his thumb along the edge of the desk. "Tell me, Phil, where did your parents meet?"

"In college. They both went to Brown University."

"But your mother was raised in Hopkinton. Your father came from Hopkinton, too. They never met in high school?" He gestures to the wall. "We have it all on file from the work we did for Dalton a few years ago."

Phil shakes his head. "They didn't meet in high school."

"Yet they met, presumably fell in love, at Brown, subsequently married, and returned to Hopkinton. Was there a plan in that?"

"No. They just met in college."

"Exactly. A coincidence without an overarching plan. Coincidence is not evidence of conspiracy, Phil. 'Sometimes a cigar is just a cigar.'" Rice waves his hand in the air. "The truth of the matter is that we had very little to go on when we started looking for Meel and Weed. Subsequent investigation—including a regular check on new information—has yielded nothing. People often get away with things and it looks like this is one of those times."

Rice falls silent for a moment. "I've been in this business for about twenty-five years. When I was younger, I worked on a case interestingly similar to yours. Upon the death of her parents, a woman had discovered she had been adopted. Her parents had not understood that their new baby had been stolen in Texas, from an illegal Mexican immigrant family. She wanted to find her birth parents and was unable to do so through conventional means. She came to me. The adoption had been forty years before—sixty-five years ago, now. I went to Texas and searched through birth and death records for two weeks, both in Mexico and along the border. In the end, I came back here and had to tell her I couldn't help her. She was heartbroken."

Rice stares at his thumb for a moment. "I've thought about that case for years. It's one of those problems you keep trying to solve even when you know you can't. I still send inquiries when I think of something. I still make calls. I say to you now what I wish I had said to her at the time: what's done is done. You are a young man. Your past does not determine your future." He points to the wall. This time the pictures disappear. "That does not determine who you are. Only you can do that."

Rice stands, signaling he is done.

Phil rises with him. "Did she ever find her birth parents?"

Rice smiles. "No, but I managed to console her. I married her."

When he returns from Detroit, Phil is struck by how frail his parents seem. The house seems empty. When they ask him where he's going next, he doesn't know. He has some money saved and his car is still serviceable. They ask him to stay, but he shakes his head. He doesn't think he can live here ever again.

ACT III

Portales, New Mexico, could be another country. Out here in the desert, halfway between Santa Fe and Lubbock, the names of the towns sound like private jokes: Clovis, Littlefield, House, Floyd, Levelland. Roswell is only an hour away, and people in Portales talk about UFO's and flying saucers the way they mention the car wash and the drug store.

It's an accident he's in Portales. He had proceeded southwest from Amarillo on a whim once he realized the mountains in the distance were still a hundred miles away. His car boiled over and threw a rod. It's spring and the flowers are everywhere, along the road, in front of the adobe and stucco houses. The colors are different from anything he's ever seen. It's as if every flower he's seen before this shouted at him. These flowers smile shyly and whisper. He walks along the road and can't think of words for the colors. Is this azure? Is that peach?

He gets a job tending bar again. Portales is twenty blocks by thirty blocks. After that, there are the ranches. After that, the desert. He keeps thinking of the winter in Massachusetts, the trees, the cold, the ice. Here, it has to break a hundred degrees to get a comment. Sweat disappears without being noticed. Open water looks like a miracle. In Massachusetts, everyone was a different shade of pale. Here, everyone is a different shade of brown. In Massachusetts, Jake had refused connections to feeds his neighbors thought indispensable. Out here, though the net is as close as a telephone or a cable line, there are no local feeds at all.

He takes a room above the bar and settles in. For the moment, he feels at home.

Every Friday night, a tiny dark man enters the bar. He has a thin, unsmiling face and flat steady eyes. Frank, the owner, points him out as Esteban Correleos. He drinks tequila at a table by himself until he passes out, around midnight. When Frank closes the bar, he picks Esteban up and sets him carefully on the porch. By the time Phil wakes up and comes downstairs, Esteban is gone.

After Phil has been working at the bar for a few months, Frank starts letting him close on weekends. He inherits the task of moving Esteban outside.

One night, as he is carrying Esteban to the front porch, Esteban wakes up unexpectedly. He stares right at Phil and makes a long speech in Spanish. Phil stares back at him blankly.

"Tequila?" Esteban says, finally.

"Sorry, friend," says Phil as he puts him down on the porch. "Last call."

"Sí," says Esteban very sadly.

Phil takes pity on him and buys them both a bottle of Cuervo while he walks Esteban home. They spend the rest of the night drinking and talking. Esteban has lived in Portales all of his life. He repairs the ancient farm and ranch equipment used on the poor farms and ranches around the town.

He wakes on Esteban's sofa. He lies there, feeling the nauseous glow of a tequila hangover. The first thing he sees is an old upright grand piano painted a ghastly orange. The initials CJC are carved into the side and some of the veneer is peeling. The ivory is missing on half the keys, exposing the ancient glue underneath. There are open music books held ready on the face of the piano and the stool is worn.

Esteban's wife, Matia, startles him from behind. She is a gigantic woman, towering over him with a dancer's grace. He looks up at her, and she silently hands him a dry flour tortilla as a cure for a tequila hangover. Phil hears a cough and turns toward it. Esteban is sitting in a chair to one side of him, chewing one thumb thoughtfully. Phil sits up slowly and looks around. The house is two stories, unusual in Portales, with a heavily carved stairway ascending into the dark upstairs. Phil can hear faint voices coming down the stairs. There are at least four children playing in the next room, though his hangover keeps him from being sure.

"How did you come to be here?" Esteban asks at last. His voice is surprisingly deep for a small man, and his English is precise and well spoken.

"From Amarillo," says Phil, holding his head.

"That is not what I meant." Esteban shakes his head. "You're too smart to tend bar."

"Frank's not exactly dumb."

Esteban ignores him. "Where are you staying?"

"Frank rents me a room."

"Bring your things over here. Matia will have your room ready when you get here."

"What?"

"You're coming to work for me."

At first, Phil resists. He has been making his own way for a while now and has little desire to have anyone take over his life. But Esteban's utter disregard for his protests and arguments has its effect. Without quite realizing how, Phil finds himself living upstairs. He quits his job at Frank's, which Frank does not appreciate, and starts working on hot, rusty tractors out in the desert. Esteban does not teach. Instead, he points to a non-descript piece of wire-shrouded Bakelite and says: "That belongs here," pointing to an irregular opening in the engine. Phil learns by doing. In time, he discovers he has a talent for it. He wonders if Gordie Howe had ever torn apart cars when he was young. He wonders who Gordie Howe is outside of hockey.

Esteban has six children, ranging in age from six to twenty. The oldest is named Chela. Phil only knows that she works for archeologists out of Albuquerque and is home only between digs. He meets her coming in after living in the house for a few weeks. He opens the door and is assaulted by the crashing of the piano. Startled, he looks around, and sees a dark woman playing intently. Phil realizes that this must be Chela.

Chela is small even compared to Esteban. After a moment, she looks up from the music and sees him. Her eyes look sleepy and she smiles slowly. Her nose is big and bent.

"Who the hell are you?" she asks.

"I'm Phil Berger. I live here."

"Hm." She eyes him speculatively. "Do you speak Spanish?"

He shakes his head. "Not much. I'm still learning."

Instantly, she turns her head and shouts toward the kitchen in rapid Spanish. Matia comes out, her hands covered with corn meal. The exchange is heated, and Phil does not understand one word of it. Matia waves Chela away in disgust and returns to the kitchen.

"What was that all about?"

She ignores him. "Have you ever been arrested?"

"What?"

She looks up at him. "What for?"

"Assault," he says nervously. "I got drunk and got into a fight."

"Drink a lot?"

"No! Not much at all."

She spreads her hands. "Are you sure? Esteban brought you home drunk."

"Not true. *I* brought *him* home. I just drank with him afterward."

"How long are you going to be here?"

Phil sits down on the sofa. "I have no idea."

"I see." She sits comfortably on the piano stool, watching him. He feels uncomfortable enough to leave the living room and go back outside, irritated with himself.

From then on, Phil can never predict what she's going to say. Her confidence makes him nervous and he avoids her, preferring the company of the younger children, who like him without reserve. On those rare occasions that he talks with Chela, Esteban and Matia supervise them so subtly that Phil is never aware of it.

Esteban's family is from San Luis Potosi, Mexico. Each November, he takes Matia and his children there for the *Día de los Muertos*, the Day of the Dead. He invites Phil along, but Phil declines. Not this year, he says.

Instead, he decides to hike up into the Sangre de Cristo Mountains near Taos, where the Pecos River arises as a rumbling little stream. His life has been too hot and he longs for the cold and the ice.

Chela interrupts the conversation: "It's pretty country up there. I'll give you a lift. I have to go up to Raton anyway."

Esteban looks at them both, shrugs. Matia starts to say something, but Esteban glances quickly at her and she stops.

"I have my own car," Phil says quietly.

"It's better not to drive alone." She smiles at him sweetly. "Besides, it's cheaper."

Gas has gone up again, and a continuing discussion in the Correleos family is whether or not to buy a new electric vehicle. Esteban has been against it for some time, since most of his clients are still using ancient gasoline trucks and tractors.

The conversation is surprisingly easy between them as they drive north. As Chela's little car reluctantly climbs into the high country, Phil watches the spine of the land gradually become visible. These are not ancient piles of rubble such as he grew up with in New England. These are bare scarps of rock, shoved through the surface of the earth like a knife.

It's much colder than he thought it would be, and he's worried he will freeze.

They stop at the edge of the Taos Wilderness, and Chela parks the car. He pulls his pack out of the back seat and adjusts it. When he looks up, she is admiring the mountains up above them.

On impulse, he says: "Want to come along?"

Chela grins at him. "I was hoping you'd ask."

She pulls out extra clothes and hands them to him, then pulls out her own pack from the trunk.

"Excuse me?" he says. "I thought you had to be in Raton?"

She nods. "Next week. Do you think Papa would have let me come if he knew I might go into the wilderness with you?"

"Did you plan this?"

She smiles again and he likes the way her face brightens. "Let's say I was hedging my bets." She laughs and Phil smiles. Her laugh is deep and infectious. "Besides, you've never been up here. I have a bunch of times. I can show you things you've never seen before."

"I don't doubt that."

She looks up at him, amused, shoulders her pack, and leads the way up the switchback trail.

At first, Phil is unsure what to talk about, and loses the easy comfort of the drive up here. Chela, for her part, does not press him, and for the first day, they only speak of the trip: should they try to camp at the base of yonder peak or the closer one, should they follow the mesa or take the edge trail down into the valley?

The trail they choose ascends the smooth shoulders of the high peaks before turning onto a long, gentle decline into one of the campgrounds. At the top, in the distance, Phil can see something that looks like a herd of deer. He looks at Chela. She nods and says, "Elk. They'll be moving down when it starts to get colder."

"Can we get closer to them?"

Chela shakes her head. "They'll start to run pretty soon. Usually."

"Usually?"

Chela doesn't say anything for a moment. "When I was a kid, Papa brought me up here and took me camping in a little valley on the west side. I think I was ten. We came up on them at sunset. They didn't move. We got so close I could have touched one." She watches the elk in silence. "Papa said it was because they knew who I was."

Phil turns to her. It is late in the day, and the shadow of the peaks has started to darken the valley, but there's clarity in the light. The air is sharp, and there's the cold metal taste of snow in the air. Chela's face glows as reddish-brown as the earth. The whole world seems to emit its own light.

Who are you? he thinks.

That night, their breath coats the inside of the tent with frost as they talk. She speaks of first finding shards of pottery in the plowed land and wondering how they got there. He tells her of Danny's letters. The ground beneath them feels changed. It is the most natural thing in the world to curl up together. Phil holds her close, enjoying the smell of her, the texture of her skin and the sound of her voice as they talk. Something in him lets go, and he closes his eyes as he falls asleep, convinced that he can feel the earth turning beneath him.

Gordie Howe dies on Christmas Eve at the age of ninety-nine. Phil is twenty-eight. He has been working with Esteban for five years. He sends flowers to Murray Howe. Murray replies with a short post, and they develop a correspondence. The following year, when Phil and Chela are married, Murray comes down for the wedding.

It is a warm fall night in Portales. The desert air has a chill, but the earth is still radiating heat. Murray and Phil are drinking beer, and from a broken picnic table in the darkness deep behind the house, they watch the people. Phil can see Jake and Carol talking with Matia and Esteban. He wonders what they are talking about. He is continually surprised at how well his parents and new in-laws get along.

The party is starting to wind down, though many of the guests are still dancing. Esteban has brought up a Marielito band from Santa Fe and the high tenor of the singer wafts over them.

"Does your new wife know about you and Dad?"

Phil nods. "I told her a couple of years ago. Esteban knows, too. I had to explain who Gordie Howe was."

Murray laughs shortly. "Not something I've ever experienced."

Phil pulls a plastic bottle from the pocket of his suit, along with two Sty-rofoam cups. He pours a viscous yellow fluid into them, and hands one to Murray.

"And this is?"

"Pulque. Esteban makes it himself."

"Will I go blind?"

"The effect is temporary."

Murray sips. He closes his eyes and makes a face. "Now, that's a flavor not found in nature."

"You get used to it."

Murray opens his mouth experimentally. "Is it supposed to make your mouth numb like that?"

"That's just part of the effect."

Murray nods, and they fall silent. He points toward the house. "I'm glad I came down here. Dad was always a little worried about you."

Phil smiles. "I never wanted to bother him."

"Yes. I can understand that. He was sorry you didn't go on into the NHL. He said," Murray thinks for a moment. "He said he was glad that *he* knew about the cloning, but he wished you didn't. So he could watch you. He thought you had what it took." Murray stops for a moment. "He thought you made a mistake leaving Boston. You should have gone on in the minors. You would have made it to the NHL eventually." Murray points to Phil suddenly. "Not that he disapproved of you. He understood perfectly."

Phil looks back at Esteban's house. Chela has joined Jake and Carol. Somebody says something—Carol, probably—and Chela bursts into laughter. He can hear it float in the air like music. "Thanks," he says finally. "But I did okay."

Murray shrugs. "So, are you going to stay around here?'

Phil shakes his head. "Chela wants to go back to Albuquerque. She wants to finish her degree. Wants me to go back to school, too."

"Ah. She's in archeology?"

"Yeah. Says she's tired of working on other people's digs. She wants to start some of her own."

"And you?"

Phil shrugs. "I'm not sure. I like working with Esteban. I like working with machines." He stares back at the party. "But I'm going to be thirty soon. There ought to be something more."

Murray sips the mescal and makes a face. "You'll figure it out."

"Did Gordie ever work on old cars?"

Murray stares at him a moment. "I have no idea. Why?"

Phil watches Chela move in front of the window. She sees him and waves.

He waves back. He is surer of her than he has been of anything else in his life. "No reason. Just curious."

Albuquerque is a real city with buildings and businesses, and, at the heart of it, the University of New Mexico. After six years in a small town like Portales, Phil finds himself edgy at first. He discovers, though he remained essentially at rest in Portales, the rest of the world has continued to move. Any residual problems with the cloning techniques that produced him have been rectified, but there are still very few clones in existence. Advances in fertility medicine have made the obvious use of cloning unnecessary. There is a caution in the debate now that he didn't remember from when it seemed to center around him. A surreptitious search for his name in the news brings up only a small article about Frank Hammett leaving the Globe Corporation to return to the Middlesex-Worcester News Group.

They find a small four-room house a few blocks from the university. The house has a yard perhaps twenty feet square and abuts against three other similar houses. Like other newlyweds, they explore each other's bodies. They discover that in normal conversation, they speak English. When they make love, it is in Spanish.

A number of times in the last few years, when Esteban had been unable to build, borrow, or buy a part for the old tractors of the Portales farmers, he had called Frost Fabrications in Albuquerque and had the part made. Phil knows John Frost, and gets a job there.

Chela starts studying in earnest. Phil supports the two of them. Phil likes fabrication and Chela likes school, so for the moment they are happy.

Frost Fabrications builds parts for many clients like Esteban, and uses several old mills and other machines to do it. They joke about all the gray hair at Frost. Phil is the youngest person on the staff, and gets his share of ribbing.

There's also a more modern section of the plant that receives fully-formed designs from different feeds across the country. Some of the machines connected to the feeds are automated and can build simple components without supervision. Phil is excited by the prospect, and before long, he leaves the manual fabrication part of Frost and is working exclusively with the telefabrication units.

Even Frost's telefabricators are out-of-date. Phil reads about general fabrication systems that do not directly build components at all, but instead design and build microscopic automated tools that then build the components. There is research in this area going on at the University by a man named Mishra. John introduces them, and over the next year or so, Phil and Mishra exchange techniques.

Chela finishes in two years and starts to work for the Archeology department. Phil starts in the Mechanical Engineering department with Mishra as his advisor. He splits his time between Frost Fabrications and school. There's little time for anything else. Working very hard, he finishes his degree in three years. Then, with a loan from Esteban, he and Chela buy the telefabrication business from John Frost and start Berger Operations.

One warm February night, with a glass of champagne and over a wonderful dinner, they ritually flush Chela's birth control prescription down the toilet. Then, they make aching sweaty love in the heat.

By April, she is pregnant.

They name the boy Jake Esteban Berger, making both grandfathers swell with pride. He is a January baby. Days after he is born, Phil still finds himself holding the baby, searching the child's face for signs of Gordie Howe. A few things must have come from him: the blue eyes, the shape of the hands. The rest, it seems, came from Chela. Phil's eyes are settled in Chela's dark face and framed by Chela's black hair. Phil finds this comforting.

Little Jake is born in a mild January, and Chela and Phil make plans to take a leisurely trip late in the summer through Texas and the Deep South, up the Atlantic coast, stopping in Washington, Philadelphia, and New York, before spending time with the Bergers. Jake's second heart attack eliminates those plans.

Instead, Phil hastily leaves everything in Mishra's hands. He, Chela, and little Jake fly out and land in Providence. An automated cab takes them the last hour directly to the hotel.

It is an odd spring for Massachusetts. Unseasonably warm weather has been suddenly shattered by winter storms. The result is ice over trees, flowers, bushes. It gives the place an odd sort of beauty. Phil sees azalea blossoms encased in glass. The birches in the front yard are bent over nearly to the ground with cathedral effect.

They drop off their bags and continue on to the MetroWest hospital in Framingham. Carol is sitting with Jake in the coronary unit. He is enshrouded in wires, tubes, and sensors. Behind him is a huge display unit, with perhaps two dozen windows showing his heartbeat, his oxygen, his breathing, and other information arcane to Phil. Jake's heart is on an artificial assist, but he still looks thin and pale. His eyes light up when he sees little Jake. He reaches up his hands.

Phil glances at Chela. She nods. Against his better judgment, Phil gently puts the child in Jake's arms. Little Jake is only four months old. Phil is ready to catch the baby if Jake's hands fail him, but Jake carefully folds the infant in the crook of his arm, safely away from tubes and wires. He croons gently to the child. Little Jake watches him with an unwavering gaze, as fixed and eternal as a sphinx.

Carol explains the options to them. Jake can get a completely artificial heart, a human donor heart, a pig-derived heart, or keep the artificial assist. However, he does not seem to be handling the artificial assist well, and there are no human donors available. That leaves the artificial heart and the pig-derived heart. There is the very real possibility that if Jake cannot tolerate the artificial assist, he might have difficulty with the artificial heart. The doctors want him to take the pig heart. Jake is resistant to the idea and wants to hold out for a human donor.

Carol shakes her head. She looks as if she is about to cry. "I don't know what to do with him. I really don't."

Chela holds her, murmuring over and over: "We'll think of something." She looks at Phil and points with her chin toward Jake.

Phil stands near his father. Jake is tickling the baby's chin. Little Jake laughs and spits up. Jake cleans him up with a tissue from the nightstand.

"Dad—"

"Hush," Jake says. "I'm busy." He coos to the baby and tickles him again. Little Jake laughs and waves his hands in the air.

Jake looks up at Phil. "This is the best gift you ever could have brought me."

"Dad. We have to talk about your heart."

"No," Jake says. "We don't. It's not your decision, Phil."

"I know that. But—"

"I'll lay it out for you." Jake tucks Little Jake against his side. "I don't want a pig's heart in me."

"It's not a pig's heart. It's a human heart that was grown in a pig."

"I don't want it. This thing—" Jake points to the incision in his chest. "Is just barely good enough to keep me alive. I don't want another one."

"Dad—"

"So, it'll just have to keep me alive long enough to get a real heart."

Phil stares at him. "Even if it kills you?"

Jake nods slowly. "Yes. Even then."

"Okay." Phil closes his eyes and takes a deep breath. "Okay. I accept that. Now, explain it to me."

"The pig's heart—I just don't want an animal in me. I don't care if it started out as a human or a goat, I don't want it." He falls silent. "I thought a lot about this when I had my first heart attack. You know what you want out of a heart? Besides keeping you alive, I mean."

"No. What?"

"You want it to do its job. You want it to keep beating day in and day out without you thinking about it and monitoring it and wondering if it's going to stop this time because of a software error or a battery failure." Jake touches Lit-

tle Jake's forehead. "You want it to be alive and part of you like you're alive. I
want a human heart, Phil. Is that so crazy?"

"No," says Phil. He leans forward and carefully lifts Little Jake and holds
him. "Let me tell you what *I* want. I want my son to know his grandfather. I
want him to grow up strong and straight and know you like I did. I want him to
know who he came from and where he came from and why. I can't tell him
that. Only you can." He breathes for a moment. "That means I want you to live,
fake heart or pig heart. Doesn't mean anything to me."

Jake looks at him, startled. "You turned a little tough out there in New
Mexico."

"Can't grow a thing without good seed. I got that from you."

"Not from Mr. Howe?"

"Gordie Howe and the sons-of-bitches who cloned him gave me my body."
Phil leans over and touches the incision on Jake's chest. "Only you and Mom
could give me a heart."

Jake doesn't say anything. "Okay. You win. The pig's heart, I guess. Better
than some damned machine."

There is a moment of joy in the little room. The doctors, waiting only for
permission, schedule the operation for the following afternoon. Jake kisses Little Jake and is then given a mild sedative. When he becomes drowsy, he is
wheeled away from his family.

He never wakes up. An unexpected embolism causes a massive stroke during the surgery, and he dies.

Phil returns to the hotel in shock. Over the next few days, as they make plans
for the dead, Phil says little. When Jake is finally and completely in the ground
and they leave Carol to return to Albuquerque, Chela guides him carefully
through the airports, ensconces him in the car, and drives them all home. For
days afterward, Phil sits in the backyard, staring at the back fence. Over and
over in his mind he wonders, if he had not forced the issue would Jake still be
alive?

After a week or so, Phil starts to return to daily routine. He gets up early in
the morning and plays with Jake until Chela gets up. When she wakes up some
time later, the three of them have breakfast, and he goes to the shop. He tunes
the machines for the electronic orders, programs tricky aspects of fabrication
where necessary, and pounds steel himself when the automated systems are
overwhelmed. By late afternoon, he is exhausted. When he gets home, Chela is
already there, having picked up Jake from day care. The three of them have
dinner together. Chela puts Jake to bed while Phil has a beer. Afterward, they
sit together. Sometimes, they talk. Often, Phil says nothing, feeling empty from
when he gets up in the morning to when he goes to bed. The guilt weighs slug-

gishly in his mind. He worries at it, walks around it, tries to ignore it, tries to move it out of the way. Like a boulder on the trail, it changes the path of his days.

One night, he mentions it to Chela. She is in the bathroom brushing her hair. Little Jake is asleep in a crib near the wall.

Chela stops and carefully puts down the brush. She comes into the bedroom and sits on the bed next to him, and says, softly and gently, "That's the stupidest thing I've ever heard."

Phil doesn't know what to think. "It might have made a difference. Or maybe it was just fate."

She shakes her head. "Your car could have broken down in Amarillo and we would never have met. Then, Jake wouldn't have come out here for the wedding after his first heart attack, which might have weakened him just enough that he died in the surgery. Should you blame the *car?* Did the *car* make any difference?" She pauses and he waits for her to finish.

"It's chance," she says finally. "It's all chance. Chance you came through Portales. Chance you stayed and took the job with Frank. Chance I didn't get scarred in a car wreck when I was ten. Chance the kid I was with did. Chance I didn't meet someone before I met you. Chance you weren't with anybody at the time."

"Chance I met Esteban?" He smiles.

She smiles back. "Not quite. Esteban had been going to that bar for three years, looking for a husband for me. Finally, he found one that I could stand."

He barks a short laugh. "No! Really?"

Chela nods. "Absolutely. He figured he'd have a chance to look over everybody that came through town. He'd tried every other way since I was sixteen."

"Did he want a drunk for a son-in-law?"

"Did he get one?" she counters. "It was chance that brought you in there. Esteban took advantage of it." She lays a hand on his chest. "It's not your fault. It's not mine. It wasn't Jake's. It was just chance."

Phil plants a small garden like his father's back in Massachusetts. In the mornings, before Chela wakes up, he takes the baby into the backyard. Jake is five months old. The mornings are cool but not cold, and the baby lies on a thick blanket, watching Phil work in the dirt.

Phil finds himself talking to Jake. He talks about Gordie Howe, about the winters in Massachusetts, about a problem at work. He tells Little Jake about Grandfather Jake. He describes Jake to him, telling him about how he usually spoke evenly and slowly, with long silences between the sentences, and how it used to drive Phil crazy when he was growing up. He talks about Danny, and how crooked and broken he had looked on the outside, and how clear-minded he was on the inside, about the letters he wrote that Phil still keeps in a box in the closet. He talks about Chela, how he has never, for one single moment, been able to tell what she was going to do next. Still, as surprising as she is, she always seems to do the right thing. He tells the baby about learning Spanish, how the sounds felt in the mouth and on the tongue, how Phil couldn't understand Spanish and English at the same time, though it seemed Chela could. He talks about the desert and Portales and Albuquerque and Austin and Hopkinton, how the desert is so similar to Massachusetts in winter and so different, how the mountains had appeared to him when first he saw them, looking for all the world as if they were a great reptile lying sideways and at rest.

All summer he works in the garden and speaks to little Jake. Chela does not interrupt him though at times he sees her watching them in the window. As the baby turns over, then crawls, he starts to notice little mannerisms he had always associated with Jake: a turn of the head, a roll of the eyes, a clasp of the hands. He wonders how that can be; the baby never really knew Jake and there is no genetic contract between them. One day, he is in the bathroom washing his hands and he sees himself in the mirror clasping his hands in the same way. He stares into the mirror. He can see no resemblance between him and his father, but he realizes that's where he must have learned that movement. Little Jake must have learned it, and perhaps all of his grandfather's mannerisms from him. It comforts him as he grieves. Jake Berger left no biological legacy to the world, but he lives on in what Phil has become, in what little Jake is becoming.

That November, Carol comes out to visit. She rents an apartment close to them and stays the winter. By April, she is ready to go back to Hopkinton.

Phil gives up his graduate classes at the university. He and Mishra form a partnership and the business doubles in size in just a few months. They hire new staff and still have too much business. Gradually, they find themselves brokering whole jobs to other fabrication firms around the country.

Chela, for her part, is more and more in demand for digs in the area. She has become adept at relations between the Southwest tribes and the archeologists. All Indians have strong taboos about disturbing the dead, and most have a deep and justified distrust of archeologists. Chela has over the years earned the respect of the Navajo and Hopi, among other tribes, and is trusted by them. This has become her archeological specialty.

Phil and Chela look for a larger house, one with an adjoining apartment, and find one close to the shop. That November, when Carol comes down for the winter, they are ready for her, and she has her own place upstairs for the next five months.

Jake grows into a quiet, serious little toddler. Given to smiles rather than laughs, he talks early, and likes to help dig in Phil's garden. Phil can keep the damage down to a minimum most of the time, but over the season there are shortfalls as Jake learns to distinguish broccoli from Brazilian pepper and tomatoes from toadflax. Each day as he watches Jake, he learns something about his own father or about Chela. The boy reflects his mother like the moon reflects the sun. Phil is grateful whenever he sees something of himself. It surprises him that he doesn't feel upset that Jake takes so much after Chela and so little after himself. When he mentions this to Chela, she says he just doesn't see it. Jake takes after Phil all the time.

Phil's grief crusts over and smooths itself as time passes. He discovers himself feeling happy for no apparent reason. He finds that surprising, and the surprise itself is disconcerting. *Was I unhappy all these years?* He's not sure.

Phil and Chela measure time in terms of Jake: Jake was five months old when his grandfather died, we bought the house when Jake turned one, we took such and such a trip when Jake turned two.

The week before Jake turns three, Chela is involved in some delicate negotiations between the Navajo, Hopi, and Paiute tribes over an archeological dig in the mountains near Colorado. That Friday, she races home from Shiprock on Interstate 64. It's a pitch-black, moonless night. Her car slips on the icy bridge in Waterflow, over the Westwater Arroyo. The car tumbles down the ravine and lands upside down. Chela is killed instantly.

ACT IV

Little Jake is in bed asleep when the policemen come and notify Phil. Phil immediately knows what has happened, without being told. There is a vast, cavernous silence that has opened up in the world, and everything seems distant, unreal, cold.

After they leave, he sits in the dark next to the phone. *I should call Esteban*, he thinks. *I must pick up the phone and call Esteban.* But he can't make himself move his hands, can't make himself stand. *Carol. She's just upstairs. Call her.* But he can't even turn his head. The only sound he can hear is the sound of Jake's sleepy breathing from down the hall, in and out. It seems as if death has been taking slow steps toward him all his life. First, Danny. Then, Jake. Now, Chela. Little Jake breathes in a slight whistle. Phil wonders if it will stop. *What would he do if Jake were to stop breathing? Would he be able to move then? Or would he stop breathing himself?*

I could die right now, he thinks. I could just let go and drift away. Did she feel that way?

It seems that Jake's breathing is the only thing holding him to the earth at all.

He can see in his mind the highway through Waterflow. He has driven that road before. He can see the patch of ice forming on the bridge, sees Chela hitting the patch and the car turning, Chela panicking and trying to regain control.

I never taught her to drive on the ice, he thinks to himself. I never saw the need.

There is a hitch in Jake's breathing as the boy starts to wake with the dawn. Phil shakes his head and stands up, able to move at last. First, he calls Carol and tells her. Then, he washes his face in cold water. He picks up the phone and dials Esteban's number from memory.

"Esteban," he begins in Spanish. "There has been an accident."

After that, he waits for Jake to wake up.

Phil is struck by the dull tedium of death. As when Chela and his mother buried his father, there are endless details to be addressed. How is Chela to be buried? Should she be cremated? Where is it to take place? What kind of coffin? What kind of urn?

Matia, looking old and sad and grand, takes over. The funeral is a large and colorful affair to which Jake feels no kinship at all. She knows which relatives to notify, how to drape the casket, what flowers to send to which church. Esteban's sole task is to grieve with Phil. Phil's sole task is to grieve with his son.

Little Jake does not cry immediately when he is told. He asks again when Mama will be coming home. Each time, Phil starts the story again. Mama has gone away. She won't be coming back. She will always love you, but she can't be here any more. Jake listens, blue eyes intent. Then, he asks again.

By the time of the funeral, Jake has stopped asking. He does everything asked of him without complaint or comment. Not much is asked. He submits to every caress, hug, and embrace as if he were somewhere else. Only his clenched grip on his father has any life to it. It is so strong that Phil has to change hands often.

Once the immediate death tasks are done, Phil must manage the lesser tasks. He settles the insurance, makes sure the deed to the house is in proper order. When the insurance check comes in, he pays off the mortgage of the house. The rest he puts in a trust account for Jake. Mishra calls him to see if he's all right. He asks when Phil is coming back to work. Never, Phil wants to scream into the phone, but instead says he doesn't know.

He spends all of his time with Jake and Carol. Jake had crawled into bed with Phil the night after the accident. Phil hadn't the heart to put him back. Now, each night, Phil wakes up to find Jake nestled spoon fashion against his chest.

Finally, after a month of mourning, he goes back to the shop. Standing there surrounded by automated machines, he realizes that he never wants to be here ever again. He walks into the office and sits down across from Mishra.

"Buy me out," he says quietly.

Mishra reaches into the drawer and pulls out a document and gives it to him. "I thought you might feel that way."

It is something he and Jake discuss, as much as a thirty-eight-year-old man can discuss anything with a three-year-old boy. When Carol leaves in the spring, they sell the house to follow her to Hopkinton. Matia and Esteban come up to see them off.

"You'll be back," says Esteban, looking up at him. He touches Phil on the chest. "We are in your blood."

Phil nods in agreement. "Someday." It's all he can bring himself to say. He hugs them three or four times. They can't hug Jake enough. Finally, Jake, Carol, and Phil get in the truck, and the three of them start the long drive to Massachusetts.

This grief is harder to bear than the death of his father. This has unnaturalness to it, bitterness, a sense of outrage. On the trip to Massachusetts, Jake sees the Grand Canyon for the first time. Watching his son marvel, Phil feels he is witnessing Little Jake for two people, himself and Chela. He must see things for her as well as for himself. When they stop for a day to play in the park next to the Mississippi, he tries to see it as Chela might have seen it, for the first time. He wonders how Gordie Howe must have felt when his wife died.

When, at last, they come to the old house in Hopkinton, it is early summer and the lawn and gardens are overgrown. It is so different from New Mexico. He wants to feel as she might have, coming from her ancient Spanish ancestors, to see this place as fresh and new.

There are gaps of time over the summer and fall. A month might pass where he remembers nothing except what happens to Jake. It is as if Phil is only alive through Jake's eyes and fingers.

Jake's fourth birthday marks the anniversary of Chela's death. Phil acts purposefully unexcited about the prospect. He is determined that Jake's birthday not be permanently marred by the death of his mother. With Carol, Phil puts together a small party composed of Jake's new friends and their parents. The day before the party, Phil finds Jake in the living room, standing before the old and beaten piano. The orange paint is just as ghastly against Carol's New England wallpaper as it had been in New Mexico. Jake's right hand is resting on the keys but not pressing them down, as if he were trying to feel the weight of the music in them. Tears are falling down his cheeks.

"Jake?" calls Phil softly. "What's the matter?"

Jake draws his hand across the keys gently without making any sound. "Mama liked to play the piano, didn't she?"

Phil comes and sits on the floor next to him. Jake doesn't take his hand from the keys.

"Yes," Phil says.

Jake lets his hands fall and crawls into Phil's lap. "I want to play, too," he says. "Can I learn?"

Phil can barely speak. "Yes."

When Jake starts kindergarten, Phil is at a loss for what to do with his time. As long as he can work outdoors, he works on Carol's house. Carol is nearing eighty now. Though she is still strong, the years have taken their toll. Phil builds an enclosed wrap-around porch for her and Jake.

Over the fall, Phil and Jake have fallen into the habit of getting up early, before the bus, and walking along the lake in the park nearby. Phil guards these times jealously. It is his favorite time with Jake. This year, the winter grows cold early and snows late, so that when Christmas rolls around, the lake is flat ice in all directions. In the distance, they can see kids playing pond hockey. Phil leans down to the edge of the lake. Under the initial sandpaper, the ice is hard and smooth. Perfect hockey ice. Thoughtfully, he stands again and replaces his glove.

Jake is looking at the game in the distance. "Let's go watch them."

Apprehensive but agreeable, Phil follows Jake around the edge of the lake until they are close to the boys. The scene is uncomfortably close to Phil's childhood, and he coughs nervously.

"That's hockey?" Jake asks.

Phil nods, thinking Jake must have heard about hockey in school. Hockey hasn't been mentioned around Phil since before Jake was born.

"Did you ever play?"

Phil looks down at Jake. The blue eyes are all that he can see of himself in the boy. The rest is Chela's.

"Yes," he says finally. "A long time ago."

"Were you any good at it?"

Phil nods. "I was pretty good. I haven't played in a long time."

"Is it fun?"

"It's like flying." He thinks a moment. "It was the most fun I ever had as a boy."

Jake thinks for a moment. "Why did you quit?"

Phil shrugs. "It's complicated. I had to leave home. I had to grow up. All that meant I had to quit."

Jake thinks about that for a moment. "Can you teach me?"

Phil looks down at him. The nervousness and apprehension fall away. Christ, it's been over twenty years! I'm a forty-one-year-old man. Isn't it time I let that go?

"Yes, I can."

He's rusty on skates, but, after a few days of practice, sore muscles, and several bruising falls, he starts to remember his skill. It is as if a long dormant muscle is awakened. He finds himself enjoying skating again.

Jake learns to skate easily and is soon asking to play hockey. Without quite knowing how it comes about, Phil finds himself the team coach. They are a motley collection of five- to seven-year-old children, and he's not sure he's up to the task. They have a good, though unspectacular, winter season. Phil continues coaching over the summer season.

Each hot summer morning, he finds himself looking forward to coaching them with an eagerness that feels brand new. Every Tuesday morning, he is on the ice, carefully teaching them how to skate, how to hold themselves, how to keep their balance when they bump into each other. The mite league doesn't allow checking; that comes later, when they eventually graduate to the peewee league. But Phil keeps it in mind. If they stay with it, the shift won't take them quite so off guard.

There's a coterie of parents and watchers there every morning. Most of them he gets to know, since they're the parents of the kids on his team. He learns to deflect their anger and advice, their yells and threats. Twice he comes close to fights, but manages to avoid them. His size and manner keeps the worst of them at bay and reassure the rest. Of course, it doesn't hurt that his team is doing pretty well in the league.

One old man keeps coming and watching them. He was big-framed once, but has now gone to seed. His clothes are dirty with stains around the elbows and knees. Phil can always tell when he comes into the arena, because the air suddenly smells of tobacco. The man never smokes but the smell is so embedded in his clothes that it travels in the ice-pure air of the rink. He has no connection to any of the kids and Phil keeps an eye on him, just in case the old man is thinking something unsavory. More likely, he thinks, it's just to escape the heat. Over the weeks, Phil begins to think that he might know the old man, but he can't remember from where.

In August, near the end of the season, the old man waves to Phil as the practice session starts. Curious, Phil skates to the stands.

"What can I do for you?"

The old man coughs for a moment and delicately wipes his lips. "Thought we should talk. I'd like to see you after practice." His voice is faint but measured.

Phil shrugs. "Sorry. I have plans. Maybe next week—"

"I don't think so." He smiles faintly. "My time is precious."

"So's mine. I'm sorry to disappoint you—"

"I thought you'd want to talk to me."

Phil looks at him closely. There is still that sense of nagging familiarity but he can't place the old man. "Do I know you?"

The old man nods knowingly. "I'm sorry. I thought you'd recognized me. I'm Frank Hammett."

Phil stares at him for a long moment, then breaks away and looks back at practice. "Okay. Why now?"

Hammett coughs. "I have emphysema. Next week I might be dead."

Phil sends Jake home with one of the other kids and promises to come and pick him up as soon as he can. He sits across from Hammett in the restaurant above the rink. Frank passes a cup of coffee toward him. "It's still early in the day. Thought you might need this."

"You know," Phil starts, then stops. Starts again. "I thought for years what I might say to you if I ever met you. Now I don't know what to say."

Hammett grins and chuckles, then coughs. "Overcome by me in the flesh, eh?"

"Hardly."

Hammett nods. "Not easy to know what to say to the guy that ruined your life."

"You didn't ruin my life."

Hammett shakes his head. "Hey, don't mess with history! I was there. I saw you playing back when you were in the peewees. I knew in time you'd make it at least to the minors. Then, I broke the story and it forced you to leave. Don't try to absolve me of what I did."

"I'm not." Phil looks at his hands for a moment. "I had a life before you broke the story. I have a life now." He thinks of little Jake, of Chela and Esteban, of Carol and his father. "Nothing was ever ruined."

Hammett grunts. "I see. That is some small comfort, I suppose."

"Did you know about me all that time?"

The old man shakes his head. "No. I watched you since you were a kid. But I watched a lot of kids. About a month before I wrote the story, I got an envelope in the mail with a set of DNA chromatographs. One set for Gordie Howe. One set for you. I had a friend in the Boston Police Department verify them in the national database." He starts to fumble in his pocket for a cigarette, stops, and lays his hands on the table. "So I ran the story."

"Why?" Phil leans across the table. "Why did you run it? You must have known what it would do to me."

"I thought you said it didn't ruin your life."

"That doesn't mean it didn't hurt."

Hammett nods and looks out the restaurant window onto the ice. An adult team is practicing drills. "I ran it because it was big news. I ran it because I figured that I couldn't be the only one with the information, and I didn't want to get scooped. I ran it because if I got a good story and I could milk it right, I'd get off the damned Middlesex service and onto the *Globe* staff. Why the hell did you think I ran it?"

Phil settles back in his chair. He shrugs. "All those reasons, I guess. Who sent the chromatographs?"

Hammett spreads his hands. "I never found out. I looked—I hear you looked, too. Dalton looked harder than both of us put together. Whoever did it covered his tracks extremely well and then let seventeen years destroy whatever was left. By now, the trail is so cold we'll never know."

"Why did you come here?"

"I came here to give you a piece of my priceless wisdom," Hammett snaps. He pulls an ancient, bulging envelope out of his jacket. "And to give you this."

Phil opens it and pulls out a collection of pictures. Each one is a study in blacks and grays, barred and spreading into one another. "The chromatographs."

"I figure I owed you at least that much."

Phil stares at the pictures. He'd seen pictures like this before, when Robinson had compared his DNA against Gordie Howe's, his own and Chela's, compared against little Jake the day after he was born. But these were the originals that had changed his life. They felt heavy in his hands. Gently, he put them back in the envelope.

"Thanks, Frank," he says sincerely.

Hammett waves him away. "I don't regret what I did. But I wish it hadn't been so hard on you."

They sit wrapped in silence for a while. Phil sips his coffee thoughtfully.

"You said you had emphysema?"

"Yeah," Hammett says shortly. "Both lungs shot and I'm a poor transplant candidate."

"Nobody's a good transplant candidate." Phil thinks of his father and drinks his coffee. "Why do you think they did it?"

"Which? Clone you or send the pictures to me?"

"I don't know. Both, I guess."

"Good questions," Hammett says. "I've been considering those very questions for over twenty-five years. I still don't have an answer, but here's what I know. The cost of the cover-up, large as it must have been, is a whole lot less than it must have taken to clone you in the first place, so whoever did it had resources. They didn't do just anybody. They chose a minor celebrity. A man people might know, but not an overwhelming star. Since no one is a villain in their own mind, we've got to figure they thought they were doing something good. So, they cloned you and kept you a secret for a long time. Then, selectively, they revealed you. Just you. Maybe you were the only one. Maybe there were hundreds of attempts. Hundreds of Howes. Maybe not—a lot of people tried to see if they were Gordie Howe after the feeds picked you up. But you were the only one reported and you were the only one they exposed. Who knows what other people they might have cloned?"

Phil realizes that Hammett never found out about Danny. He resolves not to reveal that secret now. "Go on."

Hammett works his hands in front of him like a man building a house. "The rest is speculation. Maybe they cloned you because they wanted to know before anybody else if it could be done. Or it could have been for future profit, or some rich old man's fancy. Once it was done and the secret kept, they had an ongoing experiment they could watch for years."

"Why Gordie Howe?"

"Why not? If you're going to go through all that expense, who should you clone? Some unknown guy from Medford?" Hammett shakes his head. "Once you're going to make the investment, it makes sense to choose somebody important. They wanted Howe for some reason, and got him."

Phil nods. "Okay."

"Then, when you're seventeen years old, they reveal you. That's the interesting part." Hammett stops and drinks some coffee, swirls the cup for a moment, gathering his thoughts. "Britain okayed human cloning research in 2000 as long as it didn't go to term. The USA was much more restrictive. A bunch of people in Italy cloned some kids for a few couples and it was a complete disaster. By the time you were in high school, nobody was cloning anymore, but the research had gotten almost routine and the payoffs were big: continuing stem cell lines, natural skin and corneas, a cure for myopia, transplant organs. People were starting to talk all over again about getting past the birth defects and other problems and starting human clone lines. Then, you were revealed and the debate changes. It's not abstract anymore. Your career was over and you disappeared. But the debate went on. People who were ready to roll on cloning projects were suddenly putting on the brakes. Until, years later, we're sitting here and clone lines aren't even discussed anymore."

Hammett leans on his hands, his face close to Phil's. "When people first started buying cars, they drove them like they were buggies. They didn't care about the sides of the road. There weren't any stop signs or seat belts. Drivers were so unsophisticated they thought getting out of the way compromised their manly pride and preferred head-on collisions. People had to live with cars for years before they were smart enough to properly navigate a city street. Fifty years after cars were invented, you could certainly drive the wrong way down a one way street but only a fool or a drunk would do it."

He waves his hand in the air. "It's the same thing. Sure we could clone people now, and if you're willing to wait the twenty years or so for them to grow up they might somewhat resemble their clone parent. But we don't need to clone people. The way clones work is part of the world consciousness. The only reason you ever would clone a person is to get *that person* as a clone. You, Phil Berger, proved that was a pipe dream. You are *not* Gordie Howe, regardless of how much I ever wanted you to be. Now, we *all* know that: a clone isn't a copy of the original. Its heritage is strong, but ultimately it's just another person. Back when you were seventeen, that knowledge wasn't part of people's thinking." Hammett stops, struggling for breath.

Phil leans back and laughs. "Calm down, big guy! So, you think they were doing us a favor?"

Hammett rests his hands on the table and smiles. "I think they were trying to buy us time until we were smart enough to drive on the right side of the road."

"Then who could they have been?"

"Lord only knows, Phil. But they were smart. They figured us out root and branch."

It's early morning in February. The sky is still dark. Phil parks his car in front of the rink and waits until the manager opens the door. He hefts his equipment out of the back and follows him into the locker room. As always, he's the first member of the team to arrive.

He quickly dons the equipment: shin pads, skates, and pants, elbow pads, shoulder pads, helmet and gloves. He leaves the locker room and steps out on the ice, warming up. He likes these first moments alone on the ice. It makes him reflective.

This is adult recreational hockey, not the NHL. He's forty-nine, not eighteen. He wonders, not for the first time, what his life might have been like if he had never been revealed. Would he have been another Gordie Howe? Would he have had any career at all? It's all chance, Chela said. He thinks of her. He thinks of Danny.

After this morning's game, he will pick up Jake and take him to middle school. He's lucky to have Jake. He's lucky to have had Chela. And now, he's lucky to have the ice again. But then, he thinks, the ice was always there.

After he warms up, he stretches. Then, he takes off his glove, kneels, and draws his fingertips across the surface.

It is smooth and hard; perfect hockey ice.

ɛj-es

NANCY KRESS

Nancy Kress began selling her elegant and incisive stories in the mid-70s, and has since become a frequent contributor to *Asimov's Science Fiction, The Magazine of Fantasy and Science Fiction, Omni,* and elsewhere. Her books include the novels *The Prince of Morning Bells, The Golden Grove, The White Pipes, An Alien Light, Brain Rose, Oaths & Miracles, Stinger, Maximum Light,* the novelization of her Hugo and Nebula-winning story, *Beggars in Spain,* a sequel, *Beggars and Choosers,* and a popular recent sequence of novels, *Probability Moon, Probability Sun,* and *Probability Space.* Her short work has been collected in *Trinity and Other Stories, The Aliens of Earth,* and *Beaker's Dozen.* Her most recent books are two new novels, *Crossfire* and *Nothing Human.* Upcoming is a new novel, *Crucible.* She has also won Nebula Awards for her stories "Out of All Them Bright Stars" and "The Flowers of Aulit Prison." She has had stories in our Second, Third, Sixth through Fifteenth, Eighteenth, Nineteenth, and Twentieth Annual Collections.

Here she takes us to a distant planet where a medical mystery must be unraveled—no matter how high the cost.

"Jesse, come home
There's a hole in the bed
where we slept
Now it's growing cold
Hey Jesse, your face
in the place where we lay

by the hearth, all apart
It hangs on my heart . . .
Jesse, I'm lonely
Come home"
—from "Jesse," by Janis Ian, 1972

W hy did you first enter the Corps?" Lolimel asked her as they sat at the back of the shuttle, just before landing. Mia looked at the young man helplessly, because how could you answer a question like that? Especially when it was asked by the idealistic and worshipful new recruits, too ignorant to know what a waste of time worship was, let alone simplistic questions.

"Many reasons," Mia said gravely, vaguely. He looked like so many medicians she had worked with, for so many decades on so many planets . . . intense, thick-haired, genemod beautiful, a little insane. You had to be a little insane to leave Earth for the Corps, knowing that when (if) you ever returned, all you had known would have been dust for centuries.

He was more persistent than most. "What reasons?"

"The same as yours, Lolimel," she said, trying to keep her voice gentle. "Now be quiet, please, we're entering the atmosphere."

"Yes, but—"

"*Be quiet.*" Entry was so much easier on him than on her; he had not got bones weakened from decades in space. They *did* weaken, no matter what exercise one took or what supplements or what gene therapy. Mia leaned back in her shuttle chair and closed her eyes. Ten minutes, maybe, of aerobraking and descent; surely she could stand ten minutes. Or not.

The heaviness began, abruptly increased. Worse on her eyeballs, as always; she didn't have good eye socket muscles, had never had them. Such an odd weakness. Well, not for long; this was her last flight. At the next station, she'd retire. She was already well over age, and her body felt it. Only her body? No, her mind, too. At the moment, for instance, she couldn't remember the name of the planet they were hurtling toward. She recalled its catalog number, but not whatever its colonists, who were not answering hails from ship, had called it.

"*Why did you join the Corps?*"

"*Many reasons.*"

And so few of them fulfilled. But that was not a thing you told the young.

———

The colony sat at the edge of a river, under an evening sky of breathable air set with three brilliant, fast-moving moons. Beds of glorious flowers dotted the settlement, somewhere in size between a large town and a small city. The buildings of foamcast embedded with glittering native stone were graceful, well-proportioned rooms set around open atria. Minimal furniture, as graceful as the buildings; even the machines blended unobtrusively into the lovely landscape. The colonists had taste and restraint and a sense of beauty. They were all dead.

"A long time ago," said Kenin. Officially she was Expedition Head, although titles and chains of command tended to erode near the galactic edge, and Kenin led more by consensus and natural calm than by rank. More than once the team had been grateful for Kenin's calm. Lolimel looked shaken, although he was trying to hide it.

Kenin studied the skeleton before them. "Look at those bones—completely clean."

Lolimel managed, "It might have been picked clean quickly by predators, or carnivorous insects, or . . ." His voice trailed off.

"I already scanned it, Lolimel. No microscopic bone nicks. She decayed right there in bed, along with clothing and bedding."

The three of them looked at the bones lying on the indestructible mattress coils of some alloy Mia had once known the name of. Long clean bones, as neatly arranged as if for a first-year anatomy lesson. The bedroom door had been closed; the dehumidifying system had, astonishingly, not failed; the windows were intact. Nothing had disturbed the woman's long rot in the dry air until nothing remained, not even the bacteria that had fed on her, not even the smell of decay.

Kenin finished speaking to the other team. She turned to Mia and Lolimel, her beautiful brown eyes serene. "There are skeletons throughout the city, some in homes and some collapsed in what seem to be public spaces. Whatever the disease was, it struck fast. Jamal says their computer network is gone, but individual rec cubes might still work. Those things last forever."

Nothing lasts forever, Mia thought, but she started searching the cabinets for a cube. She said to Lolimel, to give him something to focus on, "How long ago was this colony founded, again?"

"Three hundred sixty E-years," Lolimel said. He joined the search.

Three hundred sixty years since a colony ship left an established world with its hopeful burden, arrived at this deadly Eden, established a city, flourished, and died. How much of Mia's lifetime, much of it spent traveling at just under c, did that represent? Once she had delighted in figuring out such equations, in wondering if she'd been born when a given worldful of colonists made planetfall. But by now there were too many expeditions, too many colonies, too many accelerations and decelerations, and she'd lost track.

Lolimel said abruptly, "Here's a rec cube."

"Play it," Kenin said, and when he just went on staring at it in the palm of his smooth hand, she took the cube from him and played it herself.

It was what she expected. A native plague of some kind, jumping DNA-based species (which included all species in the galaxy, thanks to panspermia). The plague had struck after the colonists thought they had vaccinated against all dangerous micros. Of course, they couldn't really have thought that; even three hundred sixty years ago doctors had been familiar with alien species-crossers. Some were mildly irritating, some dangerous, some epidemically fatal. Colonies had been lost before, and would be again.

"Complete medical data resides on green rec cubes," the recorder had said in the curiously accented International of three centuries ago. Clearly dying, he gazed out from the cube with calm, sad eyes. A brave man. "Any future visitors to Good Fortune should be warned."

Good Fortune. That was the planet's name.

"All right," Kenin said, "tell the guard to search for green cubes. Mia, get the emergency analysis lab set up and direct Jamal to look for burial sites. If they had time to inter some victims—if they interred at all, of course—we might be able to recover some micros to create vacs or cures. Lolimel, you assist me in—"

One of the guards, carrying weapons that Mia could not have named, blurted, "Ma'am, how do we know we won't get the same thing that killed the colonists?"

Mia looked at her. Like Lolimel, she was very young. Like all of them, she would have her story about why she volunteered for the Corps.

Now the young guard was blushing. "I mean, ma'am, before you can make a vaccination? How do we know we won't get the disease, too?"

Mia said gently, "We don't."

No one, however, got sick. The colonists had had interment practices, they had had time to bury some of their dead in strong, water-tight coffins before everyone else died, and their customs didn't include embalming. Much more than Mia had dared hope for. Good Fortune, indeed.

In five days of tireless work they had the micro isolated, sequenced, and analyzed. It was a virus, or a virus analogue, that had somehow gained access to the brain and lodged near the limbic system, creating destruction and death. Like rabies, Mia thought, and hoped this virus hadn't caused the terror and madness of that stubborn disease. Not even Earth had been able to eradicate rabies.

Two more days yielded the vaccine. Kenin dispensed it outside the large building on the edge of the city, function unknown, which had become Corps headquarters. Mia applied her patch, noticing with the usual distaste the leathery, wrinkled skin of her forearm. Once she had had such beautiful skin, what was it that a long-ago lover had said to her, what had been his name . . . Ah, growing old was not for the gutless.

Something moved at the edge of her vision.

"Lolimel . . . did you see that?"

"See what?"

"Nothing." Sometimes her aging eyes played tricks on her; she didn't want Lolimel's pity.

The thing moved again.

Casually Mia rose, brushing imaginary dirt from the seat of her uniform, strolling toward the bushes where she'd seen motion. From her pocket she pulled her gun. There were animals on this planet, of course, although the Corps had only glimpsed them from a distance, and rabies was transmitted by animal bite. . . .

It wasn't an animal. It was a human child.

No, not a child, Mia realized as she rounded the clump of bushes and, amazingly, the girl didn't run. An adolescent, or perhaps older, but so short and thin that Mia's mind had filled in "child." A scrawny young woman with light brown skin and long, matted black hair, dressed carelessly in some sort of sarong-like wrap. Staring at Mia with a total lack of fear.

"Hello," Mia said gently.

"Ej-es?" the girl said.

Mia said into her wrister, "Kenin . . . we've got natives. Survivors."

The girl smiled. Her hair was patchy on one side, marked with small white rings. *Fungus*, Mia thought professionally, absurdly. The girl walked right toward Mia, not slowing, as if intending to walk through her. Instinctively Mia put out an arm. The girl walked into it, bonked herself on the forehead, and crumpled to the ground.

"You're not supposed to beat up the natives, Mia," Kenin said. "God, she's not afraid of us at all. How can that be? You nearly gave her a concussion."

Mia was as bewildered as Kenin, as all of them. She'd picked up the girl, who'd looked bewildered but not angry, and then Mia had backed off, expecting the girl to run. Instead she'd stood there rubbing her forehead and jabbering, and Mia had seen that her sarong was made of an uncut sheet of plastic, its colors faded to a mottled gray.

Kenin, Lolimel, and two guards had come running. And *still* the girl wasn't afraid. She chattered at them, occasionally pausing as if expecting them to answer. When no one did, she eventually turned and moved leisurely off.

Mia said, "I'm going with her."

Instantly a guard said, "It's not safe, ma'am," and Kenin said, "Mia, you can't just—"

"You don't need me here," she said, too brusquely, suddenly there seemed nothing more important in the world than going with this girl. Where did that irrational impulse come from? "And I'll be perfectly safe with a gun."

This was such a stunningly stupid remark that no one answered her. But Kenin didn't order her to stay. Mia accepted the guard's tanglefoam and Kenin's vidcam and followed the girl.

It was hard to keep up with her. "Wait!" Mia called, which produced no response. So she tried what the girl had said to her: "Ej-es!"

Immediately the girl stopped and turned to her with glowing eyes and a smile that could have melted glaciers, had Good Fortune had such a thing. Gentle planet, gentle person, who was almost certainly a descendant of the original dead settlers. Or was she? InterGalactic had no record of any other registered ship leaving for this star system, but that didn't mean anything. Inter-Galactic didn't know everything. Sometimes, given the time dilation of space travel, Mia thought they knew nothing.

"Ej-es," the girl agreed, sprinted back to Mia, and took her hand. Slowing her youthful pace to match the older woman's, she led Mia home.

The houses were scattered, as though they couldn't make up their mind whether or not to be a village. A hundred yards away, another native walked toward a distant house. The two ignored each other.

Mia couldn't stand the silence. She said, "I am Mia."

The girl stopped outside her hut and looked at her.

Mia pointed to her chest. "Mia."

"Es-ef-eb," the girl said, pointing to herself and giving that glorious smile.

Not "ej-es," which must mean something else. Mia pointed to the hut, a primitive affair of untrimmed logs, pieces of foamcast carried from the city, and sheets of faded plastic, all tacked crazily together.

"Ef-ef," said Esefeb, which evidently meant "home." This language was going to be a bitch: degraded *and* confusing.

Esefeb suddenly hopped to one side of the dirt path, laughed, and pointed at blank air. Then she took Mia's hand and led her inside.

More confusion, more degradation. The single room had an open fire with the simple venting system of a hole in the roof. The bed was high on stilts (why?) with a set of rickety steps made of rotting, untrimmed logs. One corner held a collection of huge pots in which grew greenery; Mia saw three unfired clay pots, one of them sagging sideways so far the soil had spilled onto the packed-dirt floor. Also a beautiful titanium vase and a cracked hydroponic vat.

On one plant, almost the size of a small tree, hung a second sheet of plastic sarong, this one an unfaded blue-green. Dishes and tools littered the floor, the same mix as the pots of scavenged items and crude homemade ones. The hut smelled of decaying food and unwashed bedding. There was no light source and no machinery.

Kenin's voice sounded softly from her wrister. "Your vid is coming through fine. Even the most primitive human societies have some type of artwork."

Mia didn't reply. Her attention was riveted to Esefeb. The girl flung herself up the "stairs" and sat up in bed, facing the wall. What Mia had seen before could hardly be called a smile compared to the light, the sheer joy, that illuminated Esefeb's face now. Esefeb shuddered in ecstasy, crooning to the empty wall.

"Ej-es. Ej-es. Aaahhhh, *Ej-es!*"

Mia turned away. She was a medician, but Esefeb's emotion seemed too private to witness. It was the ecstasy of orgasm, or religious transfiguration, or madness.

"Mia," her wrister said, "I need an image of that girl's brain."

It was easy—too easy, Lolimel said later, and he was right. Creatures, sentient or not, did not behave this way.

"We could haul all the neuro equipment out to the village," Kenin said doubtfully, from base.

"It's not a village, and I don't think that's a good idea," Mia said softly. The softness was unnecessary. Esefeb slept like stone in her high bunk, and the hut was so dark, illuminated only by faint starlight through the hole in the roof, that Mia could barely see her wrister to talk into it. "I think Esefeb might come voluntarily. I'll try in the morning, when it's light."

Kenin, not old but old enough to feel stiff sleeping on the ground, said, "Will you be comfortable there until morning?"

"No, but I'll manage. What does the computer say about the recs?"

Lolimel answered—evidently they were having a regular all-hands conference. "The language is badly degraded International, you probably guessed that. The translator's preparing a lexicon and grammar. The artifacts, food supply, dwelling, everything visual, doesn't add up. They shouldn't have lost so much in two hundred fifty years, unless mental deficiency was a side effect of having survived the virus. But Kenin thinks—" He stopped abruptly.

"You may speak for me," Kenin's voice said, amused. "I think you'll find that military protocol degrades, too, over time. At least, way out here."

"Well, I . . . Kenin thinks it's possible that what the girl has is a mutated version of the virus. Maybe infectious, maybe inheritable, maybe transmitted through fetal infection."

His statement dropped into Mia's darkness, as heavy as Esefeb's sleep.

Mia said, "So the mutated virus could still be extant and active."

"Yes," Kenin said. "We need not only neuro-images but a sample of cere-brospinal fluid. Her behavior suggests—"

"I know what her behavior suggests," Mia said curtly. That sheer joy, shud-dering in ecstasy . . . It was seizures in the limbic system, the brain's deep cen-ter for primitive emotion, which produced such transcendent, rapturous trances. Religious mystics, Saul on the road to Damascus, visions of Our Lady or of nirvana. And the virus might still be extant, and not a part of the vaccine they had all received. Although if transmission was fetal, the medicians were safe. If not . . .

Mia said, "The rest of Esefeb's behavior doesn't fit with limbic seizures. She seems to see things that aren't there, even talk to her hallucinations, when she's not having an actual seizure."

"I don't know," Kenin said. "There might be multiple infection sites in the brain. I need her, Mia."

"We'll be there," Mia said, and wondered if that were going to be true.

But it was, mostly. Mia, after a brief uncomfortable sleep wrapped in the sheet of blue-green plastic, sat waiting for Esefeb to descend her rickety stairs. The girl bounced down, chattering at something to Mia's right. She smelled worse than yesterday. Mia breathed through her mouth and went firmly up to her.

"Esefeb!" Mia pointed dramatically, feeling like a fool. The girl pointed back.

"Mia."

"Yes, good." Now Mia made a sweep of the sorry hut. "Efef."

"Efef," Esefeb agreed, smiling radiantly.

"Esefeb efef."

The girl agreed that this was her home.

Mia pointed theatrically toward the city. "Mia efef! Mia eb Esefeb etej Mia efef!" *Mia and Esefeb come to Mia's home.* Mia had already raided the computer's tentative lexicon of Good Fortunese.

Esefeb cocked her head and looked quizzical. A worm crawled out of her hair.

Mia repeated, "Mia eb Esefeb etej Mia efef."

Esefeb responded with a torrent of repetitious syllables, none of which meant anything to Mia except "Ej-es." The girl spoke the word with such delight that it had to be a name. A lover? Maybe these people didn't live as soli-tary as she'd assumed.

Mia took Esefeb's hand and gently tugged her toward the door. Esefeb broke free and sat in the middle of the room, facing a blank wall of crumbling logs, and jabbered away to nothing at all, occasionally laughing and even reaching out to touch empty air. "Ej-es, Ej-es!" Mia watched, bemused, recording everything, making medical assessments. Esefeb wasn't malnourished, for which the natural abundance of the planet was undoubtedly responsible. But she was crawling with parasites, filthy (with water easily available), and isolated. Maybe isolated.

"Lolimel," Mia said softly into the wrister, "what's the best dictionary guess for 'alone'?"

Lolimel said, "The closest we've got is 'one.' There doesn't seem to be a concept for 'unaccompanied,' or at least we haven't found it yet. The word for 'one' is 'eket.'"

When Esefeb finally sprang up happily, Mia said, "Esefeb eket?"

The girl look startled. "Ek, ek," she said: *no, no*. Esefeb ek eket! Esefeb eb Ej-es!"

Esefeb and Ej-es. She was not alone. She had the hallucinatory Ej-es.

Again Mia took Esefeb's hand and pulled her toward the door. This time Esefeb went with her. As they set off toward the city, the girl's legs wobbled. Some parasite that had become active overnight in the leg muscles? Whatever the trouble was, Esefeb blithely ignored it as they traveled, much more slowly than yesterday, to Kenin's makeshift lab in the ruined city. Along the way, Esefeb stopped to watch, laugh at, or talk to three different things that weren't there.

"She's beautiful, under all that neglect," Lolimel said, staring down at the anesthetized girl on Kenin's neuroimaging slab.

Kenin said mildly, "If the mutated virus is transmitted to a fetus, it could also be transmitted sexually."

The young man said hotly, "I wasn't implying—"

Mia said, "Oh, calm down, Lolimel. We've all done it, on numerous worlds."

"Regs say—"

"Regs don't always matter three hundred light-years from anywhere else," Kenin said, exchanging an amused glance with Mia. "Mia, let's start."

The girl's limp body slid into the neuro-imager. Esefeb hadn't objected to meeting the other medicians, to a minimal washing, to the sedative patch Mia had put on her arm. Thirty seconds later she slumped to the floor. By the time she came to, an incision ten cells thick would have been made into her brain and a sample removed. She would have been harvested, imaged, electroscanned, and mapped. She would never know it; there wouldn't even be a headache.

Three hours later Esefeb sat on the ground with two of the guards, eating soysynth as if it were ambrosia. Mia, Kenin, Lolimel, and the three other medicians sat in a circle twenty yards away, staring at handhelds and analyzing results. It was late afternoon. Long shadows slanted across the gold-green grass, and a small breeze brought the sweet, heavy scent of some native flower. *Paradise*, Mia thought. And then: *Bonnet Syndrome*.

She said it aloud, "Charles Bonnet Syndrome," and five people raised their heads to stare at her, returned to their handhelds, and called up medical deebees.

"I think you're right," Kenin said slowly. "I never even heard of it before. Or if I did, I don't remember."

"That's because nobody gets it anymore," Mia said. "It was usually old people whose eye problems weren't corrected. Now we routinely correct eye problems."

Kenin frowned. "But that's not all that's going on with Esefeb."

No, but it was one thing, and why couldn't Kenin give her credit for thinking of it? The next moment she was ashamed of her petty pique. It was just fatigue, sleeping on that hard cold floor in Esefeb's home. *Esefeb efef*. Mia concentrated on Charles Bonnet Syndrome.

Patients with the syndrome, which was discovered in the eighteenth century, had damage somewhere in their optic pathway or brain. It could be lesions, macular degeneration, glaucoma, diabetic retinopathy, or even cataracts. Partially blind, people saw and sometimes heard instead things that weren't there, often with startling clarity and realism. Feedback pathways in the brain were two-way information avenues. Visual data, memory, and imagination constantly flowed to and from each other, interacting so vividly that, for example, even a small child could visualize a cat in the absence of any actual cats. But in Bonnet Syndrome, there was interruption of the baseline visual data about what was and was not real. So all imaginings and hallucinations were just as real as the ground beneath one's feet.

"Look at the amygdala," medician Berutha said. "Oh, merciful gods!"

Both of Esefeb's amygdalae were enlarged and deformed. The amygdalae, two almond-shaped structures behind the ears, specialized in recognizing the emotional significance of events in the external world. They weren't involved in Charles Bonnet Syndrome. Clearly, they were here.

Kenin said, "I think what's happening here is a strengthening or alteration of some neural pathways at the extreme expense of others. Esefeb 'sees' her hallucinations, and she experiences them as just as 'real'—maybe more real— than anything else in her world. And the pathways go down to the limbic, where seizures give some of them an intense emotional significance. Like . . . like orgasm, maybe."

Ej-es.

"Phantoms in the brain," Berutha said.

"A viral god," Lolimel said, surprising Mia. His tone, almost reverential, suddenly irritated her.

"A god responsible for this people's degradation, Lolimel. They're so absorbed in their 'phantoms' that they don't concentrate on the most basic care of themselves. Nor on building, farming, art, innovation . . . *nothing*. They're prisoners of their pretty fantasies."

Lolimel nodded reluctantly. "Yes, I see that."

Berutha said to Kenin, "We need to find the secondary virus. Because if it is infectious through any other vector besides fetal or sexual . . ." He didn't finish the thought.

"I know," Kenin said, "but it isn't going to be easy. We don't have cadavers for the secondary. The analyzer is still working on the cerebral-spinal fluid. Meanwhile—" She began organizing assignments, efficient and clear. Mia stopped listening.

Esefeb had finished her meal and walked up to the circle of scientists. She tugged at Mia's tunic. "Mia . . . Esefeb etej efef." *Esefeb come home.*

"Mia eb Esefeb etej Esefeb efef," Mia said, and the girl gave her joyous smile.

"Mia—" Kenin said.

"I'm going with her, Kenin. We need more behavioral data. And maybe I can persuade another native or two to submit to examination," Mia argued, feebly. She knew that scientific information was not really her motive. She wasn't sure, however, what was. She just wanted to go with Esefeb.

"Why did you first enter the Corps?" Lolimel's question stuck in Mia's mind, a rhetorical fishbone in the throat, over the next few days. Mia had brought her medkit, and she administered broad-spectrum microbials to Esefeb, hoping something would hit. The parasites were trickier, needing life-cycle analysis or at least some structural knowledge, but she made a start on that, too. *I entered the Corps to relieve suffering, Lolimel.* Odd how naive the truest statements could sound. But that didn't make them any less true.

Esefeb went along with all Mia's pokings, patches, and procedures. She also carried out minimal food-gathering activities, with a haphazard disregard for safety or sanitation that appalled Mia. Mia had carried her own food from the ship. Esefeb ate it just as happily as her own.

But mostly Esefeb talked to Ej-es.

It made Mia feel like a voyeur. Esefeb was so unselfconscious—did she even know she had a "self" apart from Ej-es? She spoke to, laughed at (with?), played beside, and slept with her phantom in the brain, and around her the hut disintegrated even more. Esefeb got diarrhea from something in her water and then the place smelled even more foul. Grimly, Mia cleaned it up. Esefeb didn't seem to notice. Mia was *eket*. Alone in her futile endeavors at sanitation, at health, at civilization.

"Esefeb eb Mia etej efef—" How did you say "neighbors?" Mia consulted the computer's lexicon, steadily growing as the translator program deciphered words from context. It had discovered no word for "neighbor." Nor for "friend" nor "mate" nor any kinship relationships at all except "baby."

Mia was reduced to pointing at the nearest hut. "Esefeb eb Mia etej efef" *over there.*

The neighboring hut had a baby. Both hut and child, a toddler who lay listlessly in one corner, were just as filthy and diseased as Esefeb's house. At first the older woman didn't seem to recognize Esefeb, but when Esefeb said her name, the two women spoke animatedly. The neighbor smiled at Mia. Mia reached for the child, was not prevented from picking him up, and settled the baby on her lap. Discreetly, she examined him.

Sudden rage boiled through her, as unexpected as it was frightening. This child was dying. Of parasites, of infection, of something. A preventable something? Maybe yes, maybe no. The child didn't look neglected, but neither did the mother look concerned.

All at once, the child in her arms stiffened, shuddered, and began to babble. His listlessness vanished. His little dirty face lit up like sunrise and he laughed and reached out his arms toward something not there. His mother and Esefeb turned to watch, also smiling, as the toddler had an unknowable limbic seizure in his dying, ecstatic brain.

Mia set him down on the floor. She called up the dictionary, but before she could say anything, the mother, too, had a seizure and sat on the dirt floor, shuddering with joy. Esefeb watched her a moment before chattering to something Mia couldn't see.

Mia couldn't stand it anymore. She left, walking as fast as she could back to Esefeb's house, disgusted and frightened and . . . what?

Envious?

"*Why did you first enter the Corps?*" To serve humanity, to live purposefully, to find, as all men and women hope, happiness. And she had, sometimes, been happy.

But she had never known such joy as that.

Nonetheless, she argued with herself, the price was too high. These people were dying off because of their absorption in their rapturous phantoms. They lived isolated, degraded, sickly lives, which were undoubtedly shorter than necessary. It was obscene.

In her clenched hand was a greasy hair sample she'd unobtrusively cut from the toddler's head as he sat on her lap. Hair, that dead tissue, was a person's fossilized past. Mia intended a DNA scan.

Esefeb strolled in an hour later. She didn't seem upset at Mia's abrupt departure. With her was Lolimel.

"I met her on the path," Lolimel said, although nothing as well-used as a path connected the huts. "She doesn't seem to mind my coming here."

"Or anything else," Mia said. "What did you bring?" He had to have brought something tangible; Kenin would have used the wrister to convey information.

"Tentative prophylactic. We haven't got a vaccine yet, and Kenin says it may be too difficult, better to go directly to a cure to hold in reserve in case any of us comes down with this."

Mia caught the omission. "Any of *us*? What about them?"

Lolimel looked down at his feet. "It's, um, a borderline case, Mia. The decision hasn't been made yet."

" 'Borderline' how, Lolimel? It's a virus infecting the brains of humans and degrading their functioning."

He was embarrassed. "Section Six says that, um, some biological conditions, especially persistent ones, create cultural differences for which Corps policy is noninterference. Section Six mentions the religious dietary laws that grew out of inherited food intolerances on—"

"I know what Section Six says, Lolimel! But you don't measure a culture's degree of success by its degree of happiness!"

"I don't think . . . that is, I don't know . . . maybe 'degree of success' isn't what Section Six means." He looked away from her. The tips of his ears grew red.

Poor Lolimel. She and Kenin had as much as told him that out here regs didn't matter. Except when they did. Mia stood. "You say the decision hasn't been made yet?"

He looked surprised. "How could it be? You're on the senior Corps board to make the decision."

Of course she was. How could she forget . . . she forgot more things these days, momentary lapses symbolic of the greater lapses to come. No brain functioned forever.

"Mia, are you all—"

"I'm fine. And I'm glad you're here. I want to go back to the city for a few days. You can stay with Esefeb and continue the surveillance. You can also extend to her neighbors the antibiotic, antiviral, and antiparasite protocols I've worked through with Esefeb. Here, I'll show you."

"But I—"

"That's an order."

She felt bad about it later, of course. But Lolimel would get over it.

At base, everything had the controlled frenzy of steady, unremitting work. Meek now, not a part of the working team, Mia ran a DNA scan on the baby's hair. It showed what she expected. The child shared fifty percent DNA with Esefeb. He was her brother; the neighbor whom Esefeb clearly never saw, who had at first not recognized Esefeb, was her mother. For which there was still no word in the translator deebee.

"I think we've got it," Kenin said, coming into Mia's room. She collapsed on a stone bench, still beautiful after two and a half centuries. Kenin had the beatific serenity of a hard job well done.

"A cure?"

"Tentative. Radical. I wouldn't want to use it on one of us unless we absolutely have to, but we can refine it more. At least it's in reserve, so a part of the team can begin creating and disseminating medical help these people can actually use. Targeted microbials, an antiparasite protocol."

"I've already started on that," Mia said, her stomach tightening. "Kenin, the board needs to meet."

"Not tonight. I'm soooo sleepy." Theatrically she stretched both arms; words and gesture were unlike her.

"Tonight," Mia said. While Kenin was feeling so accomplished. Let Kenin feel the full contrast to what she could do with what Esefeb could.

Kenin dropped her arms and looked at Mia. Her whole demeanor changed, relaxation into fortress. "Mia . . . I've already polled everyone privately. And run the computer sims. We'll meet, but the decision is going to be to extend no cure. The phantoms are a biologically based cultural difference."

"The hell they are! These people are dying out!"

"No, they're not. If they were heading for extinction, it'd be a different situation. But the satellite imagery and population equations, based on data left by the generation that had the plague, show they're increasing. Slowly, but a definite population gain significant to the point-oh-one level of confidence."

"Kenin—"

"I'm exhausted, Mia. Can we talk about it tomorrow?"

Plan on it, Mia thought grimly. She stored the data on the dying toddler's matrilineage in her handheld.

A week in base, and Mia could convince no one, not separately nor in a group. Medicians typically had tolerant psychological profiles, with higher-than-average acceptance of the unusual, divergent, and eccentric. Otherwise, they wouldn't have joined the Corps.

On the third day, to keep herself busy, Mia joined the junior medicians working on refining the cure for what was now verified as "limbic seizures with impaired sensory input causing Charles Bonnet Syndrome." Over the next few weeks it became clear to Mia what Kenin had meant; this treatment, if they had to use it, would be brutally hard on the brain. What was that old ditty? *"Cured last night of my disease, I died today of my physician."* Well, it still happened enough in the Corps. Another reason behind the board's decision.

She felt a curious reluctance to go back to Esefeb. Or, as the words kept running through her mind, *Mia ek etej Esefeb efef*. God, it was a tongue twister. These people didn't just need help with parasites, they needed an infusion of new consonants. It was a relief to be back at base, to be working with her mind, solving technical problems alongside rational scientists. Still, she couldn't shake a feeling of being alone, being lonely: *Mia eket*.

Or maybe the feeling was more like futility.

"Lolimel's back," Jamal said. He'd come up behind her as she sat at dusk on her favorite stone bench, facing the city. At this time of day the ruins looked romantic, infused with history. The sweet scents of that night-blooming flower, which Mia still hadn't identified, wafted around her.

"I think you should come now," Jamal said, and this time Mia heard his tone. She spun around. In the alien shadows Jamal's face was as set as ice.

"He's contracted it," Mia said, knowing beyond doubt that it was true. The virus wasn't just fetally transmitted, it wasn't a slow-acting retrovirus, and if Lolimel had slept with Esefeb . . . But he wouldn't be that stupid. He was a medician, he'd been warned . . .

"We don't really know anything solid about the goddamn thing!" Jamal burst out.

"We never do," Mia said, and the words cracked her dry lips like salt.

Lolimel stood in the center of the ruined atrium, giggling at something only he could see. Kenin, who could have proceeded without Mia, nodded at her. Mia understood; Kenin acknowledged the special bond Mia had with the young medician. The cure was untested, probably brutal, no more really than dumping a selection of poisons in the right areas of the brain, in itself problematical with the blood-brain barrier.

Mia made herself walk calmly up to Lolimel. "What's so funny, Lolimel?"

"All those sandwigs crawling in straight lines over the floor. I never saw blue ones before."

Sandwigs. Lolimel, she remembered, had been born on New Carthage. Sandwigs were always red.

Lolimel said, "But why is there a tree growing out of your head, Mia?"

"Strong fertilizer," she said. "Lolimel, did you have sex with Esefeb?"

He looked genuinely shocked. "No!"

"All right." He might or might not be lying.

Jamal whispered, "A chance to study the hallucinations in someone who can fully articulate—"

"No," Kenin said. "Time matters with this . . ." Mia saw that she couldn't bring herself to say "cure."

Realization dawned on Lolimel's face. "Me? You're going to . . . *me?* There's nothing wrong with me!"

"Lolimel, dear heart . . ." Mia said.

"I don't have it!"

"And the floor doesn't have sandwigs. Lolimel—"

"No!"

The guards had been alerted. Lolimel didn't make it out of the atrium. They held him, flailing and yelling, while Kenin deftly slapped on a tranq patch. In ten seconds he was out.

"Tie him down securely," Kenin said, breathing hard. "Daniel, get the brain bore started as soon as he's prepped. Everyone else, start packing up, and impose quarantine. We can't risk this for anyone else here. I'm calling a Section Eleven."

Section Eleven: *If the MedCorps officer in charge deems the risk to Corps members to exceed the gain to colonists by a factor of three or more, the officer may pull the Corps off-planet.*

It was the first time Mia had ever seen Kenin make a unilateral decision.

Twenty-four hours later, Mia sat beside Lolimel as dusk crept over the city. The shuttle had already carried up most personnel and equipment. Lolimel was in the last shift because, as Kenin did not need to say aloud, if he died, his body would be left behind. But Lolimel had not died. He had thrashed in unconscious seizures, had distorted his features in silent grimaces of pain until Mia would not have recognized him, had suffered malfunctions in alimentary, lymphatic, endocrine, and parasympathetic nervous systems, all recorded on the monitors. But he would live. The others didn't know it, but Mia did.

"We're ready for him, Mia," the young tech said. "Are you on this shuttle, too?"

"No, the last one. Move him carefully. We don't know how much pain he's actually feeling through the meds."

She watched the gurney slide out of the room, its monitors looming over Lolimel like cliffs over a raging river. When he'd gone, Mia slipped into the next building, and then the next. Such beautiful buildings: spacious atria, beautifully proportioned rooms, one structure flowing into another.

Eight buildings away, she picked up the pack she'd left there. It was heavy, even though it didn't contain everything she had cached around the city. It was so easy to take things when a base was being hastily withdrawn. Everyone was preoccupied, everyone assumed anything not readily visible was already packed, inventories were neglected and the deebees not cross-checked. No time. Historically, war had always provided great opportunities for profiteers.

Was that what she was? Yes, but not a profit measured in money. Measure it, rather, in lives saved, or restored to dignity, or enhanced. "*Why did you first enter the Corps?*" Because I'm a medician, Lolimel. Not an anthropologist.

They would notice, of course, that Mia herself wasn't aboard the last shuttle. But Kenin, at least, would realize that searching for her would be a waste of valuable resources when Mia didn't want to be found. And Mia was so old. Surely the old should be allowed to make their own decisions.

Although she would miss them, these Corps members who had been her family since the last assignment shuffle, eighteen months ago and decades ago, depending on whose time you counted by. Especially she would miss Lolimel. But this was the right way to end her life, in service to these colonists' health. She was a medician.

It went better than Mia could have hoped. When the ship had gone—she'd seen it leave orbit, a fleeting stream of light—Mia went to Esefeb.

"Mia etej efef," Esefeb said with her rosy smile. *Mia come home.* Mia walked toward her, hugged the girl, and slapped the tranq patch on her neck.

For the next week, Mia barely slept. After the makeshift surgery, she tended Esefeb through the seizures, vomiting, diarrhea, pain. On the morning the girl woke up, herself again, Mia was there to bathe the feeble body, feed it, nurse Esefeb. She recovered very fast; the cure was violent on the body but not as debilitating as everyone had feared. And afterward Esefeb was quieter, meeker, and surprisingly intelligent as Mia taught her the rudiments of water purification, sanitation, safe food storage, health care. By the time Mia moved on to Esefeb's mother's house, Esefeb was free of most parasites, and Mia was working on the rest. Esefeb never mentioned her former hallucinations. It was possible she didn't remember them.

"Esefeb ekebet," Mia said as she hefted her pack to leave. *Esefeb be well.*

Esefeb nodded. She stood quietly as Mia trudged away, and when Mia turned to wave at her, Esefeb waved back.

Mia shifted the pack on her shoulders. It seemed heavier than before. Or maybe Mia was just older. Two weeks older, merely, but two weeks could make a big difference. An enormous difference.

Two weeks could start to save a civilization.

———

Night fell. Esefeb sat on the stairs to her bed, clutching the blue-green sheet of plastic in both hands. She sobbed and shivered, her clean face contorted. Around her, the unpopulated shadows grew thicker and darker. Eventually, she wailed aloud to the empty night.

"Ej-es! O, Ej-es! Ej-es, Esefeb eket! Ej-es . . . etej efef! O, etej efef!"

The Bellman

JOHN VARLEY

John Varley appeared on the SF scene in 1974, and by the end of 1976, had produced as concentrated an outpouring of first-rate stories as the genre has ever seen, stories such as "Retrograde Summer," "In the Bowl," "Gotta Sing, Gotta Dance," "In the Hall of the Mountain King," "Equinoctial," "The Black Hole Passes," "Overdrawn at the Memory Bank," "The Phantom of Kansas," and many other smart, bright, fresh, brash, audacious, and effortlessly imaginative stories. It's hard to think of a group of short stories that has had a greater, more concentrated impact on the field, with the exception of Robert Heinlein's early work for John W. Campbell's *Astounding*, or perhaps Roger Zelazny's early stories in the mid-60s. It was a meteoric rise to prominence even for a field known for meteoric rises.

Varley remained an important figure in the genre throughout the rest of the 70s and into the early 80s, with novels such as *Ophiuchi Hotline*, *Titan*, *Wizard*, *Demon*, and *Millennium*, and collections such as *The Persistence of Vision*, *The Barbie Murders*, *Picnic on Nearside*, and *Blue Champagne*, winning three Hugo Awards and two Nebula Awards for stories such as "Press Enter," "The Persistence of Vision," and "The Pusher." By the middle 80s, though, Varley had moved away from the print world to develop a number of screenplays for Hollywood producers, most of which were never produced.

Disillusioned with Hollywood, Varley returned to print in 1992 with his novel *Steel Beach*, which Varley fanciers hoped would represent the start of a Varley renaissance, but then fell silent again for the rest of the decade. Here in the early years of a new century, though, there are encouraging signs that Varley may be coming back to stay, including novels such as *The Golden Globes* and, most recently,

2003's *Red Thunder*, and a number of new short fiction sales. Coming up is his first new collection in years, *The John Varley Reader*.

Here he takes us to the Moon for a suspenseful and fast-paced murder mystery, where a resourceful cop must track a brutal serial killer through the warrens and gloomy underground passageways of a domed Lunar city, while the clock is running out in more ways than one . . .

T he woman stumbled down the long corridor, too tired to run. She was tall, her feet were bare, and her clothes were torn. She was far advanced in pregnancy.

Through a haze of pain, she saw a familiar blue light. Airlock. There was no place left to go. She opened the door and stepped inside, shut it behind her.

She faced the outer door, the one that led to vacuum. Quickly, she undogged the four levers that secured it. Overhead, a warning tone began to sound quietly, rhythmically. The outer door was now held shut by the air pressure inside the lock, and the inner door could not be opened until the outer latches were secured.

She heard noises from the corridor, but knew she was safe. Any attempt to force the outer door would set off enough alarms to bring the police and air department.

It was not until her ears popped that she realized her mistake. She started to scream, but it quickly died away with the last rush of air from her lungs. She continued to beat soundlessly on the metal walls for a time, until blood flowed from her mouth and nose. The blood bubbled.

As her eyes began to freeze, the outer door swung upward and she looked out on the lunar landscape. It was white and lovely in the sunlight, like the frost that soon coated her body.

Lieutenant Anna-Louise Bach seated herself in the diagnostic chair, leaned back, and put her feet in the stirrups. Doctor Erikson began inserting things into her. She looked away, studying the people in the waiting room through the glass wall to her left. She couldn't feel anything—which in itself was a disturbing sensation—but she didn't like the thought of all that hardware so close to her child.

He turned on the scanner and she faced the screen on her other side. Even after so long, she was not used to the sight of the inner walls of her uterus, the placenta, and the fetus. Everything seemed to throb, engorged with blood. It made her feel heavy, as though her hands and feet were too massive to lift; a different sensation entirely from the familiar heaviness of her breasts and belly.

And the child. Incredible that it could be hers. It didn't look like her at all. Just a standard squinch-faced, pink and puckered little ball. One tiny fist opened and shut. A leg kicked, and she felt the movement.

"Do you have a name for her yet?" the doctor asked.

"Joanna." She was sure he had asked that last week. He must be making conversation, she decided. It was unlikely he even recalled Bach's name.

"Nice," he said, distractedly, punching a note into his clipboard terminal. "Uh, I think we can work you in on Monday three weeks from now. That's two days before optimum, but the next free slot is six days after. Would that be convenient? You should be here at 0300 hours."

Bach sighed.

"I told you last time, I'm not coming in for the delivery. I'll take care of that myself."

"Now, uh . . ." he glanced at his terminal. "Anna, you know we don't recommend that. I know it's getting popular, but—"

"It's Ms. Bach to you, and I heard that speech last time. And I've read the statistics. I know it's no more dangerous to have the kid by myself than it is in this damn fishbowl. So would you give me the goddam midwife and let me out of here? My lunch break is almost over."

He started to say something, but Bach widened her eyes slightly and her nostrils flared. Few people gave her any trouble when she looked at them like that, especially when she was wearing her sidearm.

Erikson reached around her and fumbled in the hair at the nape of her neck. He found the terminal and removed the tiny midwife she had worn for the last six months. It was gold, and about the size of a pea. Its function was neural and hormonal regulation. Wearing it, she had been able to avoid morning sickness, hot flashes, and the possibility of miscarriage from the exertions of her job. Erikson put it in a small plastic box, and took out another that looked just like it.

"This is the delivery midwife," he said, plugging it in. "It'll start labor at the right time, which in your case is the ninth of next month." He smiled, once again trying for a bedside manner. "That will make your daughter an Aquarius."

"I don't believe in astrology."

"I see. Well, keep the midwife in at all times. When your time comes, it will re-route your nerve impulses away from the pain centers in the brain. You'll experience the contractions in their full intensity, you see, but you won't perceive it as pain. Which, I'm told, makes all the difference. Of course, I wouldn't know."

"No, I suppose you wouldn't. Is there anything else I need to know, or can I go now?"

"I wish you'd reconsider," he said, peevishly. "You really should come into the natatorium. I must confess, I can't understand why so many women are choosing to go it alone these days."

Bach glanced around at the bright lights over the horde of women in the waiting room, the dozens sitting in examination alcoves, the glint of metal and the people in white coats rushing around with frowns on their faces. With each visit to this place the idea of her own bed, a pile of blankets, and a single candle looked better.

"Beats me," she said.

There was a jam on the Leystrasse feeder line, just before the carousel. Bach had to stand for fifteen minutes wedged in a tight mass of bodies, trying to protect her belly, listening to the shouts and screams ahead where the real crush was, feeling the sweat trickling down her sides. Someone near her was wearing shoes, and managed to step on her foot twice.

She arrived at the precinct station twenty minutes late, hurried through the rows of desks in the command center, and shut the door of her tiny office behind her. She had to turn sideways to get behind her desk, but she didn't mind that. Anything was worth it for that blessed door.

She had no sooner settled in her chair than she noticed a handwritten note on her desk, directing her to briefing room 330 at 1400 hours. She had five minutes.

One look around the briefing room gave her a queasy feeling of disorientation. Hadn't she just come from here? There were between two and three hundred officers seated in folding chairs. All were female, and visibly pregnant.

She spotted a familiar face, sidled awkwardly down a row, and sat beside Sergeant Inga Krupp. They touched palms.

"How's it with you?" Bach asked. She jerked her thumb toward Krupp's belly. "And how long?"

"Just fightin' gravity, trying not to let the entropy get me down. Two more weeks. How about you?"

"More like three. Girl or boy?"

"Girl."

"Me, too." Bach squirmed on the hard chair. Sitting was no longer her favorite position. Not that standing was all that great. "What is this? Some kind of medical thing?"

Krupp spoke quietly, from the corner of her mouth. "Keep it under your suit. The crosstalk is that pregnancy leave is being cut back."

"And half the force walks off the job tomorrow." Bach knew when she was being put on. The union was far too powerful for any reduction in the one-year child-rearing sabbatical. "Come on, what have you heard?"

Krupp shrugged, then eased down in her chair. "Nobody's said. But I don't think it's medical. You notice you don't know most of the people here? They come from all over the city."

Bach didn't have time to reply, because Commissioner Andrus had entered the room. He stepped up to a small podium and waited for quiet. When he got it, he spent a few seconds looking from face to face.

"You're probably wondering why I called you all here today."

There was a ripple of laughter. Andrus smiled briefly, but quickly became serious again.

"First the disclaimer. You all know of the provision in your contract relating to hazardous duty and pregnancy. It is not the policy of this department to endanger civilians, and each of you is carrying a civilian. Participation in the project I will outline is purely voluntary; nothing will appear in your records if you choose not to volunteer. Those of you who wish to leave now may do so."

He looked down and tactfully shuffled papers while about a dozen women filed out. Bach shifted uncomfortably. There was no denying she would feel diminished personally if she left. Long tradition decreed that an officer took what assignments were offered. But she felt a responsibility to protect Joanna.

She decided she was sick to death of desk work. There would be no harm in hearing him out.

Andrus looked up and smiled bleakly. "Thank you. Frankly, I hadn't expected so many to stay. Nevertheless, the rest of you may opt out at any time." He gave his attention to the straightening of his papers by tapping the bottom edges on the podium. He was a tall, cadaverous man with a big nose and hollows under his cheekbones. He would have looked menacing, but his tiny mouth and chin spoiled the effect.

"Perhaps I should warn you before—"

But the show had already begun. On a big holo screen behind him a picture leaped into focus. There was a collective gasp, and the room seemed to chill for a moment. Bach had to look away, queasy for the first time since her rookie days. Two women got up and hurried from the room.

"I'm sorry," Andrus said, looking over his shoulder and frowning. "I'd meant to prepare you for that. But none of this is pretty."

Bach forced her eyes back to the picture.

One does not spend twelve years in the homicide division of a metropolitan police force without becoming accustomed to the sight of violent death.

Bach had seen it all and thought herself unshockable, but she had not reckoned on what someone had done to the woman on the screen.

The woman had been pregnant. Someone had performed an impromptu Caesarian section on her. She was opened up from the genitals to the breastbone. The incision was ragged, hacked in an irregular semi-circle with a large flap of skin and muscle pulled to one side. Loops of intestine bulged through ruptured fascial tissue, still looking wet in the harsh photographer's light.

She was frozen solid, posed on a metal autopsy table with her head and shoulders up, slumped against a wall that was no longer there. It caused her body to balance on its buttocks. Her legs were in an attitude of repose, yet lifted at a slight angle to the table.

Her skin was faint blue and shiny, like mother-of-pearl, and her chin and throat were caked with rusty brown frozen blood. Her eyes were open, and strangely peaceful. She gazed at a spot just over Bach's left shoulder.

All that was bad enough, as bad as any atrocity Bach had ever seen. But the single detail that had leaped to her attention was a tiny hand, severed, lying frozen in the red mouth of the wound.

"Her name was Elfreda Tong, age twenty-seven, a life-long resident of New Dresden. We have a biographical sheet you can read later. She was reported missing three days ago, but nothing was developed.

"Yesterday we found this. Her body was in an airlock in the west quadrant, map reference delta-omicron-sigma 97. This is a new section of town, as yet underpopulated. The corridor in question leads nowhere, though in time it will connect a new warren with the Cross-Crisium.

"She was killed by decompression, not by wounds. Use-tapes from the airlock service module reveal that she entered the lock alone, probably without a suit. She must have been pursued, else why would she have sought refuge in an airlock? In any case, she unsealed the outer door, knowing that the inner door could not then be moved." He sighed, and shook his head. "It might have worked, too, in an older lock. She had the misfortune to discover a design deficiency in the new-style locks, which are fitted with manual pressure controls on the corridor phone plates. It was simply never contemplated that anyone would want to enter a lock without a suit and unseal the outer door."

Bach shuddered. She could understand that thinking. In common with almost all Lunarians, she had a deep-seated fear of vacuum, impressed on her from her earliest days. Andrus went on.

"Pathology could not determine time of death, but computer records show a time line that might be significant. As those of you who work in homicide know, murder victims often disappear totally on Luna. They can be buried on the surface and never seen again. It would have been easy to do so in this case. Someone went to a lot of trouble to remove the fetus—for reasons we'll get to in a moment—and could have hidden the body fifty meters away. It's unlikely the crime would have been discovered.

"We theorize the murderer was rushed. Someone attempted to use the lock, found it not functioning because of the open outer door, and called repair service. The killer correctly assumed the frustrated citizen in the corridor would go to the next lock and return on the outside to determine the cause of the obstruction. Which he did, to find Elfreda as you see her now. As you can see," he pointed to a round object partially concealed in the wound, "the killer was in such haste that he or she failed to get the entire fetus. This is the child's head, and of course you can see her hand."

Andrus coughed nervously and turned from the picture. From the back of the room, a woman hurried for the door.

"We believe the killer to be insane. Doubtless this act makes sense according to some tortured pathology unique to this individual. Psychology section says the killer is probably male. Which does not rule out female suspects.

"This is disturbing enough, of course. But aside from the fact that this sort of behavior is rarely isolated—the killer is compelled eventually to repeat it— we believe that Ms. Tong is not the first. Analysis of missing persons reveals a shocking percentage of pregnant females over the last two years. It seems that someone is on the loose who preys on expectant mothers, and may already have killed between fifteen and twenty of them."

Andrus looked up and stared directly at Bach for a moment, then fixed his gaze on several more women in turn.

"You will have guessed by now that we intend using you as bait."

Being bait was something Bach had managed to avoid in twelve eventful years on the force. It was not something that was useful in homicide work, which was a gratifyingly straightforward job in a world of fuzzy moral perplexities. Undercover operations did not appeal to her.

But she wanted to catch this killer, and she could not think of any other way to do it.

"Even this method is not very satisfactory," she said, back in her office. She had called in Sergeants Lisa Babcock and Erich Steiner to work with her on the case. "All we really have is computer printouts on the habits and profiles of the missing women. No physical evidence was developed at the murder scene."

Sergeant Babcock crossed her legs, and there was a faint whirring sound. Bach glanced down. It had been a while since the two of them had worked together. She had forgotten about the bionic legs.

Babcock had lost her real ones to a gang who cut them off with a chain knife and left her to die. She didn't, and the bionic replacements were to have been temporary while new ones were grown. But she had liked them, pointing out that a lot of police work was still legwork, and these didn't get tired. She was a small brunette woman with a long face and lazy eyes, one of the best officers Bach had ever worked with.

Steiner was a good man, too, but Bach picked him over several other qualified candidates simply because of his body. She had lusted after him for a long time, bedded him once, thirty-six weeks before. He was Joanna's father, though he would never know it. He was also finely muscled, light brown, and hairless, three qualities Bach had never been able to resist.

"We'll be picking a place—taproom, sensorium, I don't know yet—and I'll start to frequent it. It'll take some time. He's not going to just jump out and grab a woman with a big belly. He'll probably try to lure her away to a safe place. Maybe feed her some kind of line. We've been studying the profiles of his victims—"

"You've decided the killer is male?" Babcock asked.

"No. They say it's likely. They're calling him 'The Bellman.' I don't know why."

"Lewis Carroll," Steiner said.

"Huh?"

Steiner made a wry face. "From 'The Hunting of the Snark.' But it was the snark that made people 'softly and suddenly vanish away,' not the Bellman. He *hunted* the snark."

Bach shrugged. "It won't be the first time we've screwed up a literary reference. Anyway, that's the code for this project: BELLMANXXX. Top security access." She tossed copies of bound computer printout at each of them. "Read this, and tell me your thoughts tomorrow. How long will it take you to get your current work squared away?"

"I could clear it up in an hour," Babcock said.

"I'll need a little more time."

"Okay. Get to work on it right now." Steiner stood and edged around the door, and Bach followed Babcock into the noisy command center.

"When I get done, how about knocking off early?" Babcock suggested. "We could start looking for a spot to set this up."

"Fine. I'll treat you to dinner."

Hobson's Choice led a Jekyll and Hyde existence: a quiet and rather staid taproom by day, at night transformed by hologrammatic projection into the fastest fleshparlor in the East 380's. Bach and Babcock were interested in it because it fell midway between the posh establishments down at the Bedrock and the sleazy joints that dotted the Upper Concourses. It was on the sixtieth level, at the intersection of the Midtown Arterial slides, the Heidlelburg Senkrechtstrasse lifts, and the shopping arcade that lined 387strasse. Half a sector had been torn out to make a parkcube, lined by sidewalk restaurants.

They were there now, sitting at a plastwood table waiting for their orders to arrive. Bach lit a cheroot, exhaled a thin cloud of lavender smoke, and looked at Babcock.

"What do you make of it?"

Babcock looked up from the printouts. She frowned, and her eyes lost their focus. Bach waited. Babcock was slow, but not stupid. She was methodical.

"Victims lower middle class to poor. Five out of work, seven on welfare."

"*Possible* victims," Bach emphasized.

"Okay. But some of them had better be victims, or we're not going to get anywhere. The only reason we're looking for the Bellman in these lower-middle-class taprooms is that it's something these women had in common. They were all lonely, according to the profiles."

Bach frowned. She didn't trust computer profiles. The information in the profiles was of two types: physical and psychological. The psych portion included school records, doctor visits, job data, and monitored conversations, all tossed together and developed into what amounted to a psychoanalysis. It was reliable, to a point.

Physical data was registered every time a citizen passed through a pressure door, traveled on a slideway or tube, spent money, or entered or left a locked room; in short, every time the citizen used an identiplate. Theoretically, the computers could construct a model showing where each citizen had gone on any day.

In practice, of course, it didn't work that way. After all, criminals owned computers, too.

"Only two of them had steady lovers," Babcock was saying. "Oddly, both of the lovers were women. And of the others, there seems to be a slight preference for homosex."

"Means nothing," Bach said.

"I don't know. There's also a predominance of male fetuses among the missing. Sixty percent."

Bach thought about it. "Are you suggesting these women didn't want the babies?"

"I'm not suggesting anything. I'm just curious."

The waiter arrived with their orders, and the Bellman was shelved while they ate.

"How is that stuff?" Babcock asked.

"This?" Bach paused to swallow, and regarded her plate judiciously. "It's okay. About what you'd expect at the price." She had ordered a tossed salad, steakplant and baked potato, and a stein of beer. The steakplant had a faint metallic taste, and was overdone. "How's yours?"

"Passable," Babcock lisped around a mouthful. "Have you ever had real meat?"

Bach did not quite choke, but it was a close thing.

"No. And the idea makes me a little sick."

"I have," Babcock said.

Bach eyed her suspiciously, then nodded. "That's right. You emigrated from Earth, didn't you?"

"My family did. I was only nine at the time." She toyed with her beer mug. "Pa was a closet carnivore. Every Christmas he got a chicken and cooked it. Saved money for it most of the year."

"I'll bet he was shocked when he got up here."

"Maybe, a little. Oh, he knew there wasn't any black market meat up here. Hell, it was rare enough down there."

"What . . . what's a chicken?"

Babcock laughed. "Sort of a bird. I never saw one alive. And I never really liked it that much, either. I like steak better."

Bach thought it was perverted, but was fascinated anyway.

"What sort of steak?"

"From an animal called a cow. We only had it once."

"What did it taste like?"

Babcock reached over and speared the bite Bach had just carved. She popped it into her mouth.

"A lot like that. A little different. They never get the taste just right, you know?"

Bach didn't know—had not even realized that her steakplant was supposed to taste like cow—and felt they'd talked about it enough, especially at mealtime.

They returned to Hobson's that night. Bach was at the bar and saw Steiner and Babcock enter. They took a table across the dance floor from her. They were nude, faces elaborately painted, bodies shaved and oiled.

Bach was dressed in a manner she had avoided for eight months, in a blue lace maternity gown. It reached to her ankles and buttoned around her neck, covering everything but her protruding belly. There was one other woman dressed as she was, but in pink, and with a much smaller bulge. Between the two of them, they wore more clothing than everyone else in Hobson's put together.

Lunarians tended to dress lightly if at all, and what was covered was a matter of personal choice. But in fleshparlors it was what was uncovered that was important, and how it was emphasized and displayed. Bach didn't care for the places much. There was an air of desperation to them.

She was supposed to look forlorn. Damn it, if she'd wanted to act, she would have made a career on the stage. She brooded about her role as bait, considered calling the whole thing off.

"Very good. You look perfectly miserable."

She glanced up to see Babcock wink as she followed Steiner onto the dance floor. She almost smiled. All right, now she had a handle on it. Just think about the stinking job, all the things she'd rather be doing, and her face would take care of itself.

"Hey there!"

She knew instantly she'd hate him. He was on the stool next to her, his bulging pectorals glistening in the violet light. He had even, white teeth, a profile like a hatchet, and a candy-striped penis with a gold bell hanging from the pierced foreskin.

"I'm not feeling musically inclined," she said.

"Then what the hell are you doing here?"

Bach wished she knew.

"It's definitely the wrong sort of place," Babcock said, her eyes unfocused and staring at Bach's ceiling.

"That's the best news I've heard in months," Steiner said. There were dark circles under his eyes. It had been a strenuous night.

Bach waved him to silence and waited for Babcock to go on. For some reason, she had begun to feel that Babcock knew something about the Bellman, though she might not know she knew it. She rubbed her forehead and wondered if that made any sense.

The fact remained that when Babcock had said to wear blue instead of pink, Bach had done so. When she said to look lonely and in despair, Bach had done her best. Now she said Hobson's was wrong. Bach waited.

"I don't care if the computers say they spent their time in places like that," she said. "They probably did, but not toward the end. They would have wanted something quieter. For one thing, you don't take somebody home from a place like Hobson's. You fuck them on the dance floor." Steiner moaned, and Babcock grinned at him. "Remember, it was in the line of duty, Erich."

"Don't get me wrong," Steiner said. "You're delightful. But all night long? And my *feet* hurt."

"But why a quieter place?" Bach asked.

"I'm not sure. The depressive personalities. It's hard to cope with Hobson's when you're depressed. They went there for uncomplicated fucking. But when they got really blue they went looking for a friend. And the Bellman would want a place where he could hope to take someone home. People won't take someone home unless they're getting serious."

That made sense to Bach. It followed the pattern of her own upbringing. In the crowded environment of Luna it was important to keep a space for yourself, a place you invited only special friends.

"So you think he made friends with them first."

"Again, I'm only speculating. Okay, look. None of them had any close friends. Most of them had boy fetuses, but they were homosexual. It was too late to abort. They're not sure they want the kids, they got into it in the first place because the idea of a kid sounded nice, but now they don't think they want a son. The decision is to keep it or give it to the state. They need someone to talk to." She let it hang there, looking at Bach.

It was all pretty tenuous, but what else was there to go on? And it wouldn't hurt to find another spot. It would probably help her nerves, not to mention Steiner's.

"Just the place for a snark," Steiner said.

"Is it?" Bach asked, studying the façade of the place and failing to notice Steiner's sarcasm.

Maybe it was the place to find the Bellman, she decided, but it didn't look too different from fifteen other places the team had haunted in three weeks.

It was called The Gong, for reasons that were not apparent. It was an out-of-the-way taproom on 511strasse, level seventy-three. Steiner and Babcock went in and Bach walked twice around the block to be sure she was not associated with them, then entered.

The lighting was subdued without making her wish for a flashlight. Only beer was served. There were booths, a long wooden bar with a brass rail and swiveling chairs, and a piano in one corner where a small, dark-haired woman was taking requests. The atmosphere was very twentieth century, a little too quaint. She found a seat at one end of the bar.

Three hours passed.

Bach took it stoically. The first week had nearly driven her out of her mind. Now she seemed to have developed a facility for staring into space, or studying her reflection in the bar mirror, leaving her mind a blank.

But tonight was to be the last night. In a few hours she would lock herself in her apartment, light a candle beside her bed, and not come out until she was a mother.

"You look like you've lost your best friend. Can I buy you a drink?"

If I had a tenth-mark for every time I've heard that, Bach thought, but said, "Suit yourself."

He jingled as he sat, and Bach glanced down, then quickly up to his face. It was not the same man she had met on the first night at Hobson's. Genital bells had become the overnight sensation, bigger than pubic gardening had been three years before, when everyone ran around with tiny flowers growing in their crotches. When men wore the bells they were called dong-a-lings, or, with even more cloying cuteness, ding-a-lingams.

"If you ask me to ring your bell," Bach said, conversationally, "I'll bust your balls."

"Who, me?" he asked, innocently. "Farthest thing from my mind. Honest."

She knew it had been on his lips, but he was smiling so ingenuously she had to smile back. He put out his palm, and she pressed it.

"Louise Brecht," she said.

"I'm Ernst Freeman."

But he was not, not really, and it surprised Bach, and saddened her. He was by far the nicest man she had talked to in the last three weeks. She allowed him to coax out her make-believe life history, the one Babcock had written the second day, and he really seemed to care. Bach found she almost believed the story herself, her sense of frustration giving a verisimilitude to Louise Brecht's crashingly boring life that Bach had never really achieved before.

So it was a shock when she saw Babcock walk behind her on her way to the toilet.

Babcock and Steiner had not been idle during the twenty minutes she had been talking to "Freeman." A microphone hidden in Bach's clothing enabled them to hear the conversation, while Steiner operated a tiny television camera. The results were fed to a computer, which used voiceprint and photo analysis to produce a positive ident. If the result didn't match, Babcock was to leave a note to that effect in the toilet. Which she was presumably doing now.

Bach saw her go back to the table and sit down, then caught her eye in the mirror. Babcock nodded slightly, and Bach felt goose pimples break out. This might not be the Bellman—he could be working any of a number of cons, or have something else in mind for her—but it was the first real break for the team.

She waited a decent interval, finishing a beer, then excused herself, saying she would be right back. She walked to the rear of the bar and through a curtain.

She pushed through the first door she saw, having been in so many tap-rooms lately that she felt she could have found the toilet with her feet shackled in a blackout. And indeed it seemed to be the right place. It was twentieth-century design, with ceramic washbasins, urinals, and commodes, the latter discreetly hidden in metal stalls. But a quick search failed to produce the expected note. Frowning, she pushed back out through the swinging door, and nearly bumped into the piano player, who had been on her way in.

"Excuse me," Bach murmured, and looked at the door. It said "Men."

"Peculiarity of The Gong," the piano player said. "Twentieth century, remember? They were segregated."

"Of course. Silly of me."

The correct door was across the hall, plainly marked "Women." Bach went in, found the note taped to the inside of one of the stall doors. It was the product of the tiny faxprinter Babcock carried in her purse, and crammed a lot of fine print onto an eight-by-twelve millimeter sheet.

She opened her maternity dress, sat down, and began to read.

His real, registered name was Bigfucker Jones. With a handle like that, Bach was not surprised that he used aliases. But the name had been of his own choosing. He had been born Ellen Miller, on Earth. Miller had been black, and her race and sex changes had been an attempt to lose a criminal record and evade the police. Both Miller and Jones had been involved in everything from robbery to meatlegging to murder. He had served several terms, including a transportation to the penal colony in Copernicus. When his term was up, he had elected to stay on Luna.

Which meant nothing as far as the Bellman was concerned. She had been hoping for some sort of sexual perversion record, which would have jibed more closely with the profile on the Bellman. For Jones to be the Bellman, there should have been money involved.

It was not until Bach saw the piano player's red shoes under the toilet stall door that something that had been nagging at her came to the surface. Why had she been going into the males-only toilet? Then something was tossed under the door, and there was a bright purple flash.

Bach began to laugh. She stood up, fastening her buttons.

"Oh, no," she said, between giggles. "That's not going to work on *me*. I always wondered what it'd be like to have somebody throw a flashball at me." She opened the stall door. The piano player was there, just putting her protective goggles back in her pocket.

"You must have read too many cheap thriller novels," Bach told her, still laughing. "Don't you know those things are out of date?"

The woman shrugged, spreading her hands with a rueful expression. "I just do what I'm told."

Bach made a long face, then burst out laughing again.

"But you should know a flashball doesn't work unless you slip the victim the primer drug beforehand."

"The beer?" the woman suggested, helpfully.

"Oh, wow! You mean you . . . and, and that guy with the comic-book name . . . oh, wow!" She couldn't help it, she just had to laugh aloud again. In a way, she felt sorry for the woman. "Well, what can I tell you? It didn't work. The warranty must have expired, or something." She was about to tell the woman she was under arrest, but somehow she didn't want to hurt her feelings.

"Back to the old drawing board, I guess," the woman said. "Oh, yeah, while I've got you here, I'd like for you to go to the West 500th tube station, one level up. Take this paper with you, and punch this destination. As you punch each number, forget it. When you've done that, swallow the paper. You have all that?"

Bach frowned at the paper. "West 500th, forget the number, eat the paper." She sighed. "Well, I guess I can handle that. But hey, you gotta remember I'm doing this just as a favor to you. Just as soon as I get back, I'm going to—"

"Okay, okay. Just do it. Exactly as I said. I know you're humoring me, but let's just pretend the flashball worked, okay?"

It seemed like a reasonable enough suggestion. It was just the break Bach needed. Obviously, this woman and Jones were connected with the Bellman, whoever he or she was. Here was Bach's big chance to catch him. Of course, she was not going to forget the number.

She was about to warn the woman she would be arrested as soon as she returned from the address, but she was interrupted again.

"Go out the back door. And don't waste any time. Don't listen to anything anyone else says until someone says 'I tell you three times.' Then you can pretend the game is over."

"All right." Bach was excited at the prospect. Here at last was the sort of high adventure that everyone thought was a big part of police work. Actually, as Bach knew well, police work was dull as muzak.

"And I'll take that robe."

Bach handed it to her, and hurried out the back door wearing nothing but a big grin.

It was astonishing. One by one she punched in the numbers, and one by one they vanished from her mind. She was left with a piece of paper that might have been printed in Swahili.

"What do you know," she said to herself, alone in the two-seat capsule. She laughed, crumpled the paper, and popped it into her mouth, just like a spy.

She had no idea where she might be. The capsule had shunted around for almost half an hour, and come to rest in a private tube station just like thousands of others. There had been a man on hand for her arrival. She smiled at him.

"Are you the one I'm supposed to see?" she asked.

He said something, but it was gibberish. He frowned when it became clear she didn't understand him. It took her a moment to see what the problem was.

"I'm sorry, but I'm not supposed to listen to anyone." She shrugged, helplessly. "I had no idea it would work so well."

He began gesturing with something in his hands, and her brow furrowed, then she grinned widely.

"Charades? Okay. Sounds like . . ." But he kept waving the object at her. It was a pair of handcuffs.

"Oh, all right. If it'll make you happy." She held out her wrists, close together, and he snapped them on.

"I tell you three times," he said.

Bach began to scream.

It took hours to put her mind back together. For the longest time she could do nothing but shake and whimper and puke. Gradually she became aware of her surroundings. She was in a stripped apartment room, lying on a bare floor. The place smelled of urine and vomit and fear.

She lifted her head cautiously. There were red streaks on the walls, some of them bright and new, others almost brown. She tried to sit up, and winced. Her fingertips were raw and bloody.

She tried the door first, but it didn't even have an interior handle. She probed around the cracks, biting her tongue when the pain became too great in her shackled hands, satisfied herself that it could not be opened. She sat down again and considered her situation. It did not look promising, but she made her preparations to do what she could.

It might have been two hours before the door opened. She had no way to tell. It was the same man, this time accompanied by an unfamiliar woman. They both stood back and let the door swing inward, wary of an ambush. Bach cowered in the far corner, and as they approached she began to scream again.

Something gleamed in the man's hand. It was a chain knife. The rubber grip containing the battery nestled in his palm and the blunt, fifteen-centimeter blade pointed out, rimmed with hundreds of tiny teeth. The man squeezed the grip, and the knife emitted a high whine as the chain blurred into motion. Bach screamed louder, and got to her feet, backed against the wall. Her whole posture betrayed defenselessness, and evidently they fell for it just enough because when she kicked at the man's throat his answering slash was a little bit too late, missing her leg, and he didn't get another try. He hit the floor, coughing blood. Bach grabbed the knife as it fell.

The woman was unarmed, and she made the right decision, but again it was too late. She started toward the door, but tripped over Bach's outstretched leg and went down on her face.

Bach was going to kick her until she died, but all the activity had strained muscles that should not have been used so roughly; a cramp nearly doubled her over and she fell, arms out to break her fall and protect her stomach. Her manacled hands were going to hit the woman's arm and Bach didn't dare let go of the knife, nor did she dare take the fall on her abused fingertips, and while she agonized over what to do in that long second while she fell in the dreamy lunar gravity her fists hit the floor just behind the woman's arm.

There was an almost inaudible buzzing sound. A fine spray of blood hit Bach's arm and shoulder, and the wall three meters across the room. And the woman's arm fell off.

Both of them stared at it for a moment. The woman's eyes registered astonishment as she looked over to Bach.

"There's no pain," she said, distinctly. Then she started to get up, forgetting about the arm that was no longer there, and fell over. She struggled for a while like an overturned turtle while the blood spurted and she turned very white, then she was still.

Bach got up awkwardly, her breath coming in quick gasps. She stood for a moment, getting herself under control.

The man was still alive, and his breathing was a lot worse than Bach's. She looked down at him. It seemed he might live. She looked at the chain knife in her hand, then knelt beside him, touched the tip of the blade to the side of his neck. When she stood up, it was certain that he would never again cut a child from a mother's body.

She hurried to the door and looked carefully left and right. No one was there. Apparently her screams had not been anything remarkable, or she had killed everyone involved.

She was fifty meters down the corridor before the labor pains began.

She didn't know where she was, but could tell it was not anywhere near where Elfreda Tong had met her death. This was an old part of town, mostly industrial, possibly up close to the surface. She kept trying doors, hoping to find a way into the public corridors where she would have a chance to make a phone call. But the doors that would open led to storerooms, while the ones that might have been offices were locked up for the night.

Finally one office door came open. She looked in, saw it led nowhere. She was about to close the door and resume her flight when she saw the telephone.

Her stomach muscles knotted again as she knelt behind the desk and punched BELLMANXXX. The screen came to life, and she hastily thumbed the switch to blacken it.

"Identify yourself, please."

"This is Lieutenant Bach, I've got a Code One, officer in trouble. I need you to trace this call and send me some help, and I need it quick."

"Anna, where are you?"

"Lisa?" She couldn't believe it was Babcock.

"Yes. I'm down at headquarters. We've been hoping you'd find a way to report in. Where do we go?"

"That's just it. I don't know. They used a flashball on me and made me forget where I went. And—"

"Yes, we know all that. Now. After you didn't show up for a couple of minutes, we checked, and you were gone. So we arrested everyone in the place. We got Jones and the piano player."

"Then get *her* to tell you where I am."

"We already used her up, I'm afraid. Died under questioning. I don't think she knew, anyway. Whoever she worked for is very careful. As soon as we got the pentothal in her veins, her head blew itself all over the interrogation room. She was a junkie, we know that. We're being more careful with the man, but he knows even less than she did."

"Great."

"But you've got to get away from there, Lieutenant. It's terrible. You're in . . . shit, you know that." Babcock couldn't seem to go on for a moment, and when she did speak, her voice was shaking. "They're meatleggers, Anna. God help me, that's come to Luna now, too."

Bach's brow furrowed. "What are you talking about?"

"They procure meat for carnivores, goddam it. Flesh junkies. People who are determined to eat meat, and will pay any price."

"You're not trying to tell me . . ."

"Why the hell not?" Babcock flared. "Just look at it. On Earth there are still places you can raise animals, if you're careful. But here, we've got everything locked up so tight nobody dares try it. Somebody smells them, or the sewage monitors pick up traces of animal waste. Can't be done."

"Then why . . . ?"

"So what kind of meat's available?" Babcock went on, remorselessly. "There's tons of it on the hoof, all around you. You don't have to raise it or hide it. You just harvest it when you have a customer."

"But cannibalism?" Bach said, faintly.

"Why not? Meat's meat, to someone who wants it. They sell human meat on Earth, too, and charge a high price because it's supposed to taste . . . ah. I think I'm going to be sick."

"Me, too." Bach felt another spasm in her stomach. "Uh, how about that trace? Have you found me yet?"

"Still proceeding. Seems to be some trouble."

Bach felt a chill. She had not expected that, but there was nothing to do but wait. Surely the computers would get through in time.

"Lisa. Babies? They want *babies?*"

Babcock sighed. "I don't understand it, either. If you see the Bellman, why don't you ask him? We know they trade in adults, too, if it makes you feel any better."

"Lisa, my baby's on her way."

"Dear God."

Several times in the next quarter hour Bach heard running feet. Once the door opened and someone stuck his head in, glanced around, and failed to see Bach behind the desk with one hand covering the ready light on the phone and the other gripping the chain knife. She used the time to saw through the metal band of her handcuffs with the knife. It only took a moment; those tiny razors were sharp.

Every few minutes Babcock would come back on the line with a comment like "We're getting routed through every two-mark enclave in Luna." That told Bach that the phone she was using was protected with anti-tracer devices. It was out of her hands now. The two computers—the Bellman's and Babcock's— were matching wits, and her labor pains were coming every five minutes.

"Run!" Babcock shouted. "Get out of there, quick!"

Bach struggled to ignore the constriction in her gut, fought off fogginess. She just wanted to relax and give birth. Couldn't a person find any peace, anywhere?

"What? What happened?"

"Somebody at your end figured out that you might be using a phone. They know which one you're using, and they'll be there any second. Get out, quick!"

Bach got to her feet and looked out the door. Nothing. No sounds, no movement. Left or right?

It didn't seem to matter. She doubled over, holding her belly, and shuffled down the corridor.

At last, something different.

The door was marked FARM: AUTHORIZED PERSONNEL ONLY. PRESSURE SUIT AREA. Behind it was corn, corn growing on eight-meter-high stalks, corn in endless rows and files that made dizzying vanishing points in the distance. Sunlight beat down through a clear plastic bubble—the harsh, white sunlight of Luna.

In ten minutes she was lost. At the same time, she knew where she was. If only she could get back to the phone, but it was surely under guard by now.

Discovering her location had been easy. She had picked one of the golden ears, long as her arm and fat as her thigh, peeled back the shuck, and there, on each thumb-sized yellow kernel was the trademark: a green discoloration in the shape of a laughing man with his arms folded across his chest. So she was in the Lunafood plantation. Oddly, it was only five levels above the precinct house, but it might as well have been a billion kilometers.

Being lost in the cornstalks didn't seem like such a bad idea just now. She hobbled down the rows as long as she could stay on her feet. Every step away from the walls should make the search that much more difficult. But her breathing was coming in huge gasps now, and she had the queasy urge to hold her hands tightly against her crotch.

It didn't hurt. The midwife was working, so while she was in the grip of the most intense sensations she had ever imagined, nothing hurt at all. But it could not be ignored, and her body did not want to keep moving. It wanted to lie down and give up. She wouldn't let it.

One foot in front of the other. Her bare feet were caked in mud. It was drier on the rows of mounds where the corn grew; she tried to stay on them, hoping to minimize her trail.

Hot. It must have been over fifty degrees, with high humidity. A steam bath. Sweat poured from her body. She watched it drip from her nose and chin as she plodded on.

Her universe narrowed to only two things: the sight of her feet moving mechanically in and out of her narrowed vision, and the band of tightness in her gut.

Then her feet were no longer visible. She worried over it for a moment, wondering where they had gone. In fact, nothing was visible at all.

She rolled over onto her back and spit out dirt. A stalk of corn had snapped off at the base when she tumbled into it. She had a clear view upward of the dome, a catwalk hanging below it, and about a dozen golden tassels far overhead, drooping languidly in the still air. It was pretty, the view from down here. The corn tassels all huddled close to the black patch of sky, with green stalks radiating away in all directions. It looked like a good place to stay. She never wanted to get up again.

And this time it hurt some, despite the midwife. She moaned, grabbed the fallen cornstalk in both hands, and gritted her teeth. When she opened her eyes again, the stalk was snapped in two.

Joanna was here.

Bach's eyes bulged in amazement and her mouth hung open. Something was moving down through her body, something far too large to be a baby, something that was surely going to split her wide open.

She relaxed for just a moment, breathing shallowly, not thinking of anything, and her hands went down over her belly. There was a round wet thing emerging from her. She felt its shape, found tiny hollows on the underside. How utterly amazing.

She smiled for the first time in a million years, and bore down. Her heels dug into the sod, then her toes, and her hips lifted from the black dirt. It was moving again. *She* was moving again. Joanna, Joanna, *Joanna* was being born.

It was over so quickly she gasped in surprise. Wet slithering, and her child fell away from her and into the dirt. Bach rolled to her side and pressed her forehead to the ground. The child nestled in blood and wetness between her legs.

She did what had to be done. When it came time to cut the cord, her hand automatically went to the chain knife. She stopped, seeing a man's threatening hand, hearing an almost supersonic whir that would in seconds disembowel her and rip Joanna away.

She dropped the knife, leaned over, and bit down hard.

Handfuls of corn silk pressed between her legs eventually stopped the bleeding. The placenta arrived. She was weak and shaky and would have liked nothing better than to just lie there in the mothering soil and heat.

But there was a shout from above. A man was up there, leaning over the edge of the catwalk. Answering shouts came from all around her. Far down at the end of her row, almost at the vanishing point, a tiny figure appeared and started coming toward her.

She had not thought she could get up, but she did. There seemed little point in running, but she ran, holding the chain knife in one hand and hugging Joanna in the other. If they would only come up to her and fight, she would die on a heap of slashed bodies.

A green finger of light sizzled into the ground at her heels. She instantly crossed into an adjacent row. So much for hand to hand combat.

The running was harder now, going over the hills rather than between them. But the man behind her could not keep her in view long enough for another shot.

Yet she had known it couldn't last. Vast as the corn plantation was, she could now see the end of it. She came out onto the ten-meter strip of bare ground between the corn plants and the edge of the dome.

There was a four-meter wall of bare metal in front of her. On top of the wall was the beginning of the clear material of the dome. It was shaped and anchored by a network of thin cables attached to the top of the wall on the outside.

It seemed there was no place to run, until she spotted the familiar blue light.

Inner door latches shut, outer ones open. Bach quickly did what Tong had done, but knew she had a better chance, if only for a while. This was an old lock, without an outside override. They would have to disconnect the alarms inside, then burn through the door. That would take some time.

Only after she had assured herself that she was not vulnerable to a depressurize command from the outside—a possibility she had not thought about before, but which she could negate by opening one of the four inner door latches, thus engaging the safety overrides—only then did she look around the inside of the lock.

It was a five-person model, designed to pass work gangs. There was a toolbox on the floor, coils of nylon rope in one corner. And a closet built into the wall.

She opened it and found the pressure suit.

It was a large one, but Bach was a large woman. She struggled with adjustment straps until she had the middle let out enough to take both her and Joanna.

Her mind worked furiously, fighting through the exhaustion.

Why was the suit here?

She couldn't find an answer at first, then recalled that the man who had shot at her had not been wearing a suit, nor had the man on the catwalk. There were others chasing her that she hadn't seen, and she was willing to bet they didn't have suits on, either.

So the posted sign she had passed was a safety regulation that was widely ignored. Everyone knew that air conservation and safety regs were many times more stringent than they had to be. The farm had a plastic dome that was the only surface separating it from vacuum, and that automatically classified it as a vacuum-hazard area. But in reality it was safe to enter it without a pressure suit.

The suit was kept there for the rare occasions when it was necessary for someone to go outside. It was a large suit so it would fit anyone who happened to need it, with adjustment.

Interesting.

Joanna cried for the first time when Bach got the suit sealed. And no wonder. The child was held against her body, but there was no other support for her. She quickly got both tiny legs jammed down one of the suit legs, and that couldn't have been too comfortable. Bach tried her best to ignore it, at the same time noting how hard it was to resist the impulse to try and touch her with her hands. She faced the lock controls.

There was a manual evacuation valve. She turned it slowly, opening it a crack so the air would bleed off without making a racket the people inside would hear. Part of the inner door was beginning to glow now. She wasn't too worried about it; hand lasers were not likely to burn through the metal. Someone would be going for heavy equipment by now. It would do them no good to go to adjacent airlocks—which would probably have suits in them, too—

because on the outside they couldn't force the door against the air pressure, and they couldn't force the lock to cycle as long as she was inside to override the command.

Unless it occurred to them that she would be suiting up, and someone would be waiting outside as soon as the outer door opened. . . .

She spent a few bad minutes waiting for the air to leak to the outside. It didn't help her state of mind when the Bellman began to speak to her.

"Your situation is hopeless. I presume you know that."

She jumped, then realized he was speaking to her through the intercom, and it was being relayed to her suit radio. He didn't know she was in the suit then.

"I don't know anything of the kind," she said. "The police will be here in a few minutes. You'd better get going while you've got the chance."

"Sorry. That won't work. I know you got through, but I also know they didn't trace you."

The air pressure dial read zero. Bach held the chain knife and pulled the door open. She stuck her head out. No one was waiting for her.

She was fifty meters away across the gently rolling plain when she suddenly stopped.

It was at least four kilometers to the nearest airlock that did not lead back into the plantation. She had plenty of air, but was not sure about her strength. The midwife mercifully spared her the pain she should have been going through, but her arms and legs felt like lead. Could they follow her faster than she could run? It seemed likely.

Of course, there was another alternative.

She thought about what they had planned for Joanna, then loped back to the dome. She moved like a skater, with her feet close to the ground.

It took three jumps before she could grab the upper edge of the metal wall with one gauntlet, then she could not lift her weight with just the one arm. She realized she was a step away from total exhaustion. With both hands, she managed to clamber up to stand on a narrow ledge with her feet among the bolts that secured the hold-down cables to the top of the wall. She leaned down and looked through the transparent vacuplast. A group of five people stood around the inner lock door. One of them, who had been squatting with his elbows on his knees, stood up now and pressed a button beside the lock. She could only see the top of his head, which was protected by a blue cap.

"You found the suit, didn't you?" the Bellman said. His voice was quiet, unemotional. Bach said nothing. "Can you still hear me?"

"I can hear you," Bach said. She held the chain knife and squeezed the handle; a slight vibration in her glove was the only indication that it was working. She put the edge of the blade to the plastic film and began to trace the sides of a square, one meter wide.

"I thought you could," he said. "You're on your way already. Of course, I wouldn't have mentioned the suit, in case you *hadn't* found it, until one of my own men reached the next lock and was on his way around the outside. Which he is."

"Um-hmm." Bach wanted him to keep talking. She was worried they would hear the sound of the knife as it slowly cut its way through the tough plastic.

"What you might like to know is that he has an infrared detector with him. We used it to track you inside. It makes your footprints glow. Even your suit loses heat enough through the boots to make the machine useful. It's a very good machine."

Bach hadn't thought of that, and didn't like it at all. It might have been best to take her chances trying to reach the next airlock. When the man arrived he would quickly see that she had doubled back.

"Why are you telling me all this?" she asked. The square was now bordered with shallow grooves, but it was taking too long. She began to concentrate just on the lower edge, moving the knife back and forth.

"Thinking out loud," he said, with a self-conscious laugh. "This is an exhilarating game, don't you agree? And you're the most skilled quarry I've pursued in many years. Is there a secret to your success?"

"I'm with the police," Bach said. "Your people stumbled into a stake-out."

"Ah, that explains a lot," he said, almost gratefully.

"Who *are* you, anyway?" she asked.

"Just call me the Bellman. When I heard you people had named me that, I took a fancy to it."

"Why babies? That's the part I can't understand."

"Why veal? Why baby lamb chops? How should I know? I don't eat the stuff. I don't know anything about meat, but I know a good racket, and a fertile market, when I see them. One of my customers wants babies, that's what he gets. I can get any age." He sighed again. "And it's so easy, we grow sloppy. We get careless. The work is so routine. From now on we'll kill quickly. If we'd killed you when you got out of the tube, we'd have avoided a lot of bother."

"A lot more than you expect, I hope." Damn! Why wasn't the knife through yet? She hadn't thought it would take this long. "I don't understand, frankly, why you let me live as long as you did. Why lock me up, then come to kill me hours later?"

"Greed, I'm afraid," the Bellman said. "You see, they were not coming to kill you. You over-reacted. I was attempting to combine one business with another. There are uses for live pregnant women. I have many customers. Uses for live babies, too. We generally keep them for a few months."

Bach knew she should question him about that, as a good police officer. The department would want to know what he did. Instead, she bore down on the knife with all her strength and nearly bit through her lower lip.

"I could use someone like you," he said. "You don't really think you can get away, do you? Why don't you think it over? We could make . . ."

Peering down through the bubble, Bach saw the Bellman look up. He never finished his offer, whatever it was. She saw his face for an instant—a perfectly ordinary face that would not have seemed out of place on an accountant or a bank teller—and had the satisfaction of seeing him realize his mistake. He did not waste time in regrets. He instantly saw his only chance, abandoned the people working on the lock without warning them, and began to run at full speed back into the cornfield.

The bottom edge of the square parted at that moment. Bach felt something tugging on her hand, and she moved along the narrow ledge away from the hole. There was no sound as the sides of the square peeled back, then the whole panel broke free and the material began to tear from each of the corners. The surface of the bubble began to undulate sluggishly.

It was eerie; there was nothing to hear and little to see as the air rushed out of the gaping hole. Then suddenly storms of cornstalks, shorn of leaves and ears, erupted like flights of artillery rockets and flung themselves into the blackness. The stream turned white, and Bach could not figure out why that should be.

The first body came through and sailed an amazing distance before it impacted in the gray dust.

The place was a beehive of activity when Lisa Babcock arrived. A dozen police crawlers were parked outside the wall with dozens more on their way. The blue lights revolved silently. She heard nothing but her own breathing, the occasional terse comment on the emergency band, and the faint whirring of her legs.

Five bodies were arranged just outside the wall, beside the large hole that had been cut to give vehicle access to the interior of the plantation. She looked down at them dispassionately. They looked about as one would expect a body to look that had been blown from a cannon and then quick-frozen.

Bach was not among them.

She stepped inside the dome for a moment, unable to tell what the writhing white coating of spongy material was until she picked up a handful. Popcorn. It was twenty centimeters deep inside, and still growing as raw sunlight and vacuum caused the kernels to dry and explode. If Bach was in there, it could take days to find her body. She went back outside and began to walk along the outer perimeter of the wall, away from where all the activity was concentrated.

She found the body face down, in the shadow of the wall. It was hard to see; she had nearly tripped over it. What surprised her was the spacesuit. If she had a suit, why had she died? Pursing her lips, she grabbed one shoulder and rolled it over.

It was a man, looking down in considerable surprise at the hilt of a chain knife growing from his chest, surrounded by a black, broken flower of frozen blood. Babcock began to run.

When she came to the lock she pounded on the metal door, then put her helmet to it. After a long pause, she heard the answering taps.

It was another fifteen minutes before they could bring a rescue truck around and mate it to the door. Babcock was in the truck when the door swung open, and stepped through first by the simple expedient of elbowing a fellow cop with enough force to bruise ribs.

At first she thought that, against all her hopes, Bach was dead. She sprawled loosely with her back propped against the wall, hugging the baby in her arms. She didn't seem to be breathing. Mother and child were coated with dirt, and Bach's legs were bloody. She seemed impossibly pale. Babcock went to her and reached for the baby.

Bach jerked, showing surprising strength. Her sunken eyes slowly focused on Babcock's face, then she looked down at Joanna and grinned foolishly.

"Isn't she the prettiest thing you ever saw?"

THE BEAR'S BABY

JUDITH MOFFETT

Judith Moffett made her first professional sale in 1986, won the John W. Campbell Award as Best New Writer of 1987, and the Theodore Sturgeon Award for her story "Surviving." She was a major figure in the genre for about a decade, selling critically acclaimed stories to *The Magazine of Fantasy and Science Fiction* and *Asimov's Science Fiction*, and publishing novels such as the well-received *Pennterra*, and collections (or fix-up novels, depending on how you squinted at them) such as *The Ragged World* and *Time, Like an Ever-Rolling Stream*. Moffett is also a nationally recognized poet (she was once given a National Endowment for the Arts Creative Writing Fellowship Grant for her poetry). She is the author of two books of poetry, a book of criticism, a book of translations from the Swedish, and a book on organic gardening. Her stories have appeared in our Fourth, Sixth, and Seventh Annual Collections. Born in Louisville, she has returned to her home state after years of residency in Pennsylvania, Utah, and Illinois, and now lives in Lawrenceburg, Kentucky.

After the middle years of the 80s, Moffett fell into a long period of silence, and many assumed that the book was closed on her, but, happily, they seem to have been wrong, as she returned to print this year with the powerful and engrossing story that follows, showing the conflict—one with far-reaching implications—between a young man who just wants to do his job and the forces—some of them literally out of this world—that are trying to prevent him from doing it.

Denny heard the muffled whacking of the chopper blades and the motor's deep roar, but he was underground and almost upside down, working by flashlight to detach a fuzzy bear cub from a dangerous nipple, and couldn't have dropped everything to scamper obediently back along the ridge trail right that minute even if he'd wanted to. Which, frankly, he didn't.

The cub let go, rasping a complaint. Denny backpedaled on his elbows out of the black cavern—and out of immediate range of the huge, rank, snoring heap of mother bear who had given birth to this baby in her sleep—holding the little cub off the ground in his gloved right hand. As usual he scraped his stomach. Being short and scrawny was an advantage in his line of work, but this maneuver wasn't easy even for him.

Out in the pale winter daylight, he knelt in a pile of oak leaves to dump the baby gently into the pan of the scales and hold them up by the hook at the top. Pulling off his right glove with his teeth, he recorded the weight, 1.3 kilos, on a PocketPad, drew a blood sample, and stapled an ear tag into the now-squawling baby's left ear—left for male. "Sorry, Rocket. Sorry, little guy."

His movements were neat and practiced, and he was also hurrying. It was always best to reduce stress on the infant bears by being quick, but today Denny had a couple of extra reasons for hurrying. The winter, like most winters nowadays, was mild. Too mild. Denny had waited for the coldest weather he could, but the mother bear might not be all that deeply asleep. The other reason, of course, was that he couldn't hear the helicopter any more, meaning that it had landed and that the Hefn Observer would be at the cabin by now, probably pacing back and forth on the deck, increasingly irritated as Denny continued to fail to show up. Punctuality mattered to the Hefn. In four years, this Hefn—Innisfrey, the Observer for Wildlife Habitat Recovery—had never been late for a rendezvous.

Denny wiggled his hand back into its gauntlet, picked up the cub, and wormed his way back into the den. His body almost completely blocked what little light seeped through the entrance, but he'd left the flashlight just inside, and so could see where to press the cub against his mother's chest until he started to suckle. The other baby turned loose more cooperatively; but as it did so the mother bear made a harsh sound deep in her throat and moved her massive shoulder. Denny froze, his heart leaping into his own throat, the purloined cub complaining and squirming in the leather gauntlet. But it was okay, she settled down again, so he backed the rest of the way out and sat puffing until his pulse rate returned to normal. He had always been against tranquilizing the mothers for the cubs' first couple of physicals—the sedative got into their milk and affected the babies—but for the first time he wondered seriously if it mightn't be a good idea to reevaluate that policy in the light of how the animals were being affected by the warming climate.

Or maybe reevaluate Fish and Wildlife's whole approach to black bear management. At least in rural areas like this one, that the bears had been quick to recolonize as the aging, dwindling human population had abandoned their fields and pastures and moved into the towns, where there were services and the roads were maintained. Not even a wagon and team could get around very well over roads as bad as the ones around here had gotten to be, all potholes and big broken chunks of macadam. Even plain dirt would be better. Denny himself rode a horse (Rocinante) and led a pack mule (Roscoe) when he went into town for provisions. He wasn't much of a rider, but then he didn't have much of a choice.

The second cub was a female. "Rodeo," Denny told her, "that's your name, little bear." At 1.45 kilos she was slightly chubbier than her brother. Rodeo's "real" name was Number 439, the number on her tag. She was half of the third pair of cubs produced by Number 117, the sow presently enjoying her long winter's nap down in the den, a huge healthy animal and an excellent mother; all but one of her cubs had survived to adulthood. She was six years old, the one hundred seventeenth female to be radio-collared in the state of Kentucky since the Hefn had established the management program, and her "call name" was Rosetta. Like hurricanes, study bears were call-named by cycling through the letters of the alphabet. Cubs kept the first two letters of their mother's name through subsequent generations, which allowed each initial to be used many times. If by some chance all the children and children's children of a particular bear should die, the pair of letters would not be retired but would go back into service, available for use by the next young bear who wandered across the state line from Tennessee or West Virginia. To change state of residence was to become part of a different study and get a whole new identity.

Rosetta hadn't done that; she was a Kentuckian born and bred, like Denny himself, though (also like Denny) she had wandered about for a good while before settling down in Denny's district and digging herself this excellent den under a huge oak blown over in a tornado. He hadn't named her or her first pair of cubs, who'd still been traveling with her when she'd moved into the county. But he'd named the next pair (Rocannon and Rotorooter), and was keeping a whole list of Ro- names in reserve.

Rodeo, having protestingly donated some blood and acquired a numbered ear tag of her own, resumed suckling the instant Denny put her back on the nipple, and this time her mother didn't stir. Rosetta's collar appeared to be in decent shape and was still sending a good clear signal. Denny made a judg-ment call against taking samples of Rosetta's blood today and exited the den. He poked his syringes and test tubes into the fingers of the gauntlets and stuffed them into his daypack, along with the scales and PocketPad and flashlight, and headed for the cabin at once, walking briskly, shrugging on the pack. The air was pretty cold, a little below freezing; he fished a watch cap out of his jacket pocket to pull down over his bald spot and his ears, and jammed his hands into his pockets.

Now that he was done with the bears, he looked at his watch and shifted mental gears. The Hefn Observer had been kept waiting for nearly an hour. Denny walked faster, almost jogging, a short wiry man with an anxious, rather ferretty face. The view from the ridge through gaps in the cedars, folded hills dusted over with snow under a pale sky, was lovely in its bareness, but Denny had scant attention to spare for it this day. Hurrying past the viewpoint with the nicest prospect without a sideways glance, he plunged into a tunnel formed by cedar trees lining the sides of what had once been a wagon road.

The Hefn had ordered field studies of bears, coyotes, elk, and white-tailed deer in the eastern United States, it was their initiative; they were monitoring the ecological health of the planet by monitoring its apex predators and their prey species as these reclaimed or moved into habitat that year by year was returning to a wild state. But funding for Denny's particular field study in Anderson County depended on satisfying the Hefn Observer to whom he reported, and failing to pay this fact due notice (by being dilatory) was not good politics. Denny had been on the job since the beginning of the project, and knew he was very good at what he did, but you still had to kowtow on a regular basis to the goddamned Hefn. He basically hated the Hefn, something he had in common with just about everybody else in the world. Answering to them was the disagreeable part of the bear study.

His whole situation was conflicted. It was probably the worst time in human history to be a human being, but it was also, he had to acknowledge it, one of the best to be a wildlife biologist in your own backyard. If it weren't for the Hefn, and their Directive, and the Baby Ban Broadcast that had sterilized just about every person on the planet, there would be no black bear population in east central Kentucky—or elk population, or population of coyotes approaching the size of wolves, all busily subspeciating in the fascinating ways they were doing. Without the Hefn Takeover, east central Kentucky—now a recovering climax oak-hickory forest—would still be growing tobacco and Black Angus steers, and spindling big round bales of tall-fescue hay. The state's black bears would still be in the Daniel Boone National Forest on the West Vir-ginia border, way over in the Appalachian foothills, with far too few bears to go around for the numbers of local people eager to study them.

Denny really loved his work. Except in abstract terms he cared much more about baby bears than he did about human babies, but he despised the Hefn anyhow. The problem didn't get simpler. Mostly he just accepted the way things were and focused on his job, but every time he had to show up for one of these meetings the conflict would boil up inside him again.

The ragged alley of tall cedars ended abruptly and he emerged into the clearing where the cabin sat. Beyond it hulked the chopper, a big metal dragon-fly. Neither the Hefn nor the chopper pilot, a human, were anywhere to be seen. Denny trotted up the steps and along the deck and pushed open the cabin door.

A young woman in her mid-twenties or thereabouts was hunkered down in front of the stove, putting in chunks of firewood; she closed and latched the little door and stood to face him, dusting off her hands. "Hi," said Denny. "I guess I'm a little late. I was vetting some new cubs and kind of got into a situation. Where's the Hefn Observer?" As he spoke he stuffed the watch cap in his pocket and hung the backpack on a hook by the door.

"He went for a walk. He was getting sleepy," she said. "It's not Innisfrey this time, it's Humphrey. I'm Marian Hoffman, by the way."

"The pilot, right?" She nodded. "Denny Demaree." They shook hands. Denny started to unzip his parka, then had a thought. "Uh—maybe I should go try to find him? Did he walk down to the road?"

"He just went straight past the pond and on down the hill. Bushwhacking. On all fours, the last I saw of him. I guess he doesn't get out of the city much."

Denny considered. If the Hefn hadn't stuck to either of the farm's rough wagon roads, he could be anywhere. "Then I guess I'll wait." He hung his jacket on another hook and threw himself into one armchair, and Marian took the other. The next instant he sprang out of the chair. "Hang on, did you say *Humphrey?* The Bureau of Temporal Physics and the Apprentices and all that—the one that does the viddy program? What the hell is *he* doing here?"

"Don't ask me, I just fly the chopper." She smiled. "Nice little place you've got here. Pretty luxurious for a field office."

"I—" Denny stopped and willed himself to calm down. Humphrey. He had a bad feeling about this, but there was nothing to do but wait for the Hefn to show up. He sat down again. "Yeah, it *is* nice. Some old lady built this cabin and willed it and the whole farm to the local Girl Scout Council for a camp. The actual farm is a hundred acres, and a long time ago it used to be in my family, with a house down by the road. The well's still there. This place, the cabin, was used as an admin building when the Scouts had it."

"Then time went by, and there weren't any more Brownies coming up through the ranks?"

He nodded. "The Scouts turned the place over to the state when they disbanded, and the state turned it over to Fish and Wildlife when the Hefn tapped them to monitor wildlife recovery." He hopped up again, nervously. "I feel like I shouldn't just be sitting around."

"Humphrey's not like Innisfrey," Marian said. "He won't jump all over you for not being here on time. At least I don't think he will."

"Yeah, but why's he here?" Denny said. He opened the door to the porch and walked outside, scanning the whole long view from left to right. Nothing.

"'Sister Anne, Sister Anne, do you see anyone coming?'" Marian called to him from inside.

Denny was surprised, and a little intrigued. The line, which he recognized but hadn't thought of in decades, was from a kids' edition of Grimm's Fairy Tales. Kids' edition or not, the story had given him nightmares. From deep within itself his memory obliged with the right response: "'Naught but the wind a-blowing, naught but the green grass growing.' Man, I can't believe I still remember that! I reckon it must've been high summer in Bluebeard's kingdom, the grass won't green up here for a good while yet."

"But here is Bluebeard himself," came a deep voice from the deck, and the Hefn Humphrey burst through the other door and swept into the room.

Denny bolted to the porch doorway just in time to catch the Hefn's showy entrance. He darted inside while Humphrey shut the other door and turned to greet him properly. "You were expecting my colleague Innisfrey. I am, as you see, not Innisfrey, however. No. Innisfrey is at present otherwise engaged. I offered to take this meeting in his place, as I was already in Kentucky for a reason of my own. Humphrey, BTP. I am pleased to meet you, George Dennis Demaree."

Denny stared, more or less dumbfounded. He had of course seen Humphrey on the viddy, doing regular progress reports and updates and announcements. Also scoldings. Humphrey was the highest-profile Observer of the lot, and had had the most to do with humans since the Takeover, but the image on the screen, to which he had paid as little attention as possible, had not prepared Denny for the force of Humphrey's personality. He *looked* like Innisfrey, his short, stocky, oddly jointed figure, covered entirely with gray hair (including a long shaggy beard which, though gray like the rest of him, made his improvised witticism particularly apt), with large opaque eyes and forked hands and feet. He also looked, truth to tell, rather moth-eaten. Denny knew why; the anti-hibernation drugs the wakeful Hefn had to take in winter made their hair fall out in clumps. And he had Innisfrey's faintly gamy wet-dog odor.

But the quality of his presence wasn't remotely like cold, supercilious, charmless Innisfrey's. All in all, the clash between apprehensive expectation and reality was so disorienting that it took Denny almost a minute to pull his wits together enough to apologize for being late.

"Not at all, not at all. Your tardiness providentially provided me with a chance to stretch my legs. The country hereabouts is delightful; your work here must have given you great pleasure."

Denny nodded; then, realizing that he and his visitor were both still standing, blurted, "Uh, would you like to sit down?"

Humphrey said, "As it appears that we have two chairs and two humans and one Hefn in this room, I propose that you and Marian Hoffman take the chairs." And thereupon the Hefn Humphrey, household word, movie star, viddy personality, most powerful Observer on Earth, dropped to all fours, ambled over to the woodstove, and flomped onto the rag rug. He looked like a scruffy, off-color Great Pyrenees. "All right, Marian Hoffman? All right, George Dennis Demaree?" He gazed mildly from one to the other with those odd flat eyes, and Denny found himself in danger of being seriously disarmed.

Marian had stood when Humphrey came in. She and Denny looked at each other, and then both sat down in the chairs they had been sitting in before.

"Now, to business! I am delighted to be the bearer of happy tidings," Humphrey said, and the flat eyes somehow conveyed an impression of beaming with pleasure. "Innisfrey has, as you might say, filled me in, and I have examined the radio reports you have filed, and the written reports, all of them, for the entire duration of this study. You have done excellent work here! Thanks to you, and to the studies of coyotes and white-tailed deer carried forward by your fellow wildlife biologists, we have a complete and detailed picture of the top two predators for this recovering habitat, together with their most important large prey species, over the past four years.

"During this period in this area, the black bear population has experienced a seventy-four percent gain in numbers. Eighty-six percent of the bears are not immigrants but bears native to east central Kentucky. Remarkable! More than that, the bears are, might one say, in the pink? A comical expression to apply to a dark-colored bear! Their reproductive success has been excellent, and they are in prime condition! As the flora here proceed through the various stages of succession, the entire ecosystem burgeons and thrives.

"Therefore! With no reason whatever for concern that the trend is in danger of reversing itself, we have determined," Humphrey said from his shaggy-sheepdog position on the floor, giving again that impression of beaming up into Denny's face, "to terminate this study, and to reassign you, George Dennis Demaree, to a location in particular need of the skills you have exercised so diligently in this one. Congratulations!" And he bounded up and offered Denny his forked, hairy hand.

Denny bounded up as well. "But the study's not finished!" he protested, his voice loud and rude with shock. Instead of shaking Humphrey's hand, he waved his arms wildly. "It's nowhere near finished! I designed it to run for ten years, that's the way my data spreadsheets are configured—I don't want to drop it now! I can't! I can't believe you want to pull me out *now!*"

At Denny's outburst the Hefn's beamish-boy look faded away; his demeanor became more closed and quiet, and when he spoke his voice had lost much of its hearty charm. "I regret that you do not wish to end your work here. I regret to learn that in your view it is incomplete. Our view, however, is different. We consider you to have been entirely successful. Thanks to you, we know that this area is well on its way to climax. Also thanks to you, we know that biodiversity increases every year. This is all we need to know. Whether you choose to accept reassignment is, of course, a decision you must make for yourself, but there are a great many other recovering habitat areas in Kentucky about which we know too little, and where your skills would be of great service."

Denny, so angry he was almost sputtering, managed to let him finish. "It doesn't *work* like that!" he blurted the instant Humphrey stopped talking. "Wildlife biology is important *for its own sake!* Understanding how the bears adapt as this farmland reverts to climax forest doesn't end because some practical purpose has been served! You—you Hefn never told me you'd turn up one day and tell me to pack up my stuff and leave! I did everything you told me to, nobody ever complained that the work wasn't done well—you're throwing me out for doing a good job!"

Marian moved uneasily in her chair, and Denny suddenly remembered, like a bucket of cold water, who he was talking to. The Hefn, as he knew perfectly well, could do whatever they damn pleased. They had absolute power over the people of Earth, and most Hefn felt no sympathy for humanity, given the mess humanity had made of its own planet, and how hard the aliens had had to work to get them to clean it up. This Hefn, Humphrey, was probably the one with the most sympathy for the plight of the Earth's people, many of whom were suffering a good deal from the cleanup process. If he said the study was over, it was probably over.

Denny was wild. What a fool he'd been, to fall into the comfy habit of assuming he'd been assigned to this field study for the sake of science, and that as long as he minded his P's and Q's he would be allowed to continue. He'd been assigned here because it pleased the Hefn to study the bears of east central Kentucky for a while. Now they were done doing that, evidently, and he could take a new assignment or go and do something else entirely, they didn't much care which. What they would not let him do was the one thing he wanted to do: keep on living in this cabin, watching Rocket and Rodeo develop under the tutelage of Rosetta, recording their weight, examining their scats under a microscope, radio-collaring them in due course, observing as they found mates and began the next generation.

Then he had another thought. "What about Jason and Angie, are you pulling them out too?"

"The studies of Jason Gotschalk and Angela Rivera are integral with your own. The coyotes are thriving. The white-tailed deer are thriving. The elk are thriving. Everything is thriving! We would not allow any element of this area study to continue unless all were to continue, nor would we terminate one without terminating all." Humphrey sounded so benevolent as he said this, you would think he was doing them all a favor by yanking them out of the field.

Denny had one more card to play, so he played it, not expecting to gain much by it but needing to try. "I'm a Gaian," he said. "This is my Ground. A hundred years ago my family owned this farm, and I'd like to stay here, even if the study isn't to be funded anymore." Stay and do a little unofficial-work with Rosetta and her family and the half-dozen other breeding sows he'd been following, until the equipment wore out. Or, if they took that all away to a different site, just record observations, do odd jobs in town to buy food, hunker down here for as long as he could.

Humphrey immediately became less alien-seeming, but no less definite. "Then I am truly sorry," he said, sounding as if he meant it. "But alas, no one may stay. Our Lords the Gafr have decreed that wherever habitat studies have been terminated, the human presence shall be excluded until recovery is complete."

The Gafr were the boss aliens that nobody had ever seen. They directed things from their ship parked on the Moon, and what they said was final.

"When?" Denny asked, finally defeated.

"We will help you gather your personal things together," said Humphrey kindly.

He meant they were going to fly him out *now*. "What about the horse and the mule?"

"They will be transferred to another field station. Yours, if you decide to accept reassignment. And I will gladly put you in touch with the Gaian Steward in Louisville, who should be able to assist you in finding another suitable Ground. Very possibly a way might be devised to match your new assignment with such a place."

And kick me out again when you decided I'd done enough there, Denny thought. No thanks.

"As a Gaian, you could perhaps be assigned to the terrain around Hurt Hollow? Would that interest you? Bears have been sighted nearby. Pam Pruitt is in residence there at present, but some arrangement could surely be worked out."

Denny glanced up at this, but his mind was in turmoil. "I . . . don't know. I need to think." He gazed around the cabin, the place he had gradually let himself come to think of as home for the foreseeable future, now on the far side of an absolute divide; it was like looking through a Time Window into the past. "Most of this stuff stays with the cabin. The dishes and bedding and all that. The short-wave set."

"We will help you gather up what does not, yes, Marian Hoffman?"

"I'd rather do it myself. I won't be long. You could damp down the stove if you want something to do."

There really wasn't much to pack: some dirty laundry, a razor, the daypack with the bear equipment, a few books and computer disks, the PocketPad, the laptop, his field glasses, his other pair of boots. Denny threw it all on the bed and went down in the basement, mind reeling from the sudden shift of direction, to get his duffel bag.

Under the stairs, piled in the doorless tornado shelter, were the abandoned remnants of the old farm's incarnation as Camp Sheltowee: rolled-up sleeping bags, tents, deflated air mattresses, mess kits, canteens. . . . Denny's disoriented brain suddenly focused. He touched nothing, only stood still for a moment before heading back up with the empty duffel. But his mind was made up.

The chopper dropped him at the regional headquarters of Fish and Wildlife in Frankfort and whirled off to collect his two still-unsuspecting colleagues. Tess Perry, Denny's boss, threw up her arms in protest at his accusing glare. "We had absolutely no clue they were going to pull this! The first I knew about it, here was Humphrey instead of Innisfrey, saying I should alert Louisville to get ready to reassign three field researchers, they were closing down East Central. *This office* is being closed down! I tried to warn you and the other two but you'd all gone out."

"I was checking on Rosetta's cubs," he said bitterly. "So what happens now?"

"Reassignment, like he said." And at the look on Denny's face, "I know, I know, believe me, but you need to think about it anyway before you burn any bridges. When they get back here with Angie and Jason they're taking y'all to Louisville." She pronounced it "Luh:uv'le." "They're giving me a week to close up the office, then guess where I'm being transferred to. Paducah! Think I want to go to Paducah?"

"Your parents live here in Frankfort, don't they?"

"My whole goddam family lives in Frankfort! But I'm going to Paducah, because right now I haven't got a better idea, and till I come up with one I'm keeping on the right side of the Hefn."

Denny groaned. "God, I hate the fuckers."

"Not any more than I do," said Tess glumly, "but if you want to keep on doing wildlife biology, stay on their good side, that's all I'm saying."

Denny said nothing to any of them about his plan, not Tess, not his rumpled and furious fellow deportees. In Louisville he went through the motions of being debriefed and counseled about reassignment, took a couple of days to "think it over," discussing options with Angie and Jason and the teams from the eastern part of the state, who had also been praised to the skies and yanked out of the field.

In the end, after a lot of grumbling, the others all agreed to be posted elsewhere, at least for the time being. Humphrey must indeed have put in a word, because when they interviewed Denny they offered him Hurt Hollow, the Gaian shrine thirty miles upriver. He thanked them politely but said he'd like to apply for an unpaid leave, take some time to consider all his options, including that one, which he hinted was an attractive possibility. Unlike the others, the territory he'd been relieved from was his Ground; that made it harder to know what to do. He mentioned visiting his brother in Pittsburgh; you could get to Pittsburgh by steamboat, right up the Ohio River from Louisville.

The interviewing officer was sympathetic, he too was a Gaian, an early convert who had also chosen family property as his Ground, and could appreciate what a blow it must be for Denny to lose his study area *and* be forced off the farm. Talking about the Hefn and their imperious ways, his face got very tight. He encouraged Denny to think about Hurt Hollow; they needed someone there and it would be good if the someone were a Gaian, who would appreciate the place's historic significance.

A round-trip ticket to Pittsburgh was arranged. Denny, cleaned up, with a new haircut and his duffel full of clean clothes, boarded the boat and stood at the railing as it steamed upriver (passing legendary Hurt Hollow, which showed no sign of anyone being in residence), calling at Madison and Milton, Denny's hometown, and finally at Carrollton, where the Kentucky River poured into the Ohio.

At Carrollton he left the boat, his scrawny, scruffy figure melting into the flow of disembarking passengers, and boarded a mule-hauled flatboat bound up the Kentucky for Frankfort and points south and east. He bought his ticket on board. It was dusk of the following day when he stepped off at the landing at Tyrone, under the railroad bridge that spanned the river from bluff to high bluff.

While waiting for full dark to fall, he converted his duffel into a backpack by adjusting some straps. It was good and bad that there was no Moon. In the blackness he slipped by side roads, now no more than tracks around the town of Lawrenceburg with its inconvenient street lights, and set off up the road he had traveled so many times on Rocinante's back. He was heading for the cabin.

A mile west of Lawrenceburg he encountered a line of signposts, brand new, marching away from the road in both directions and forward along both margins. It was too dark to read the smaller print, but the word in large type at the top was WARNING! He didn't need to read the rest, or wonder who had posted the warnings. By continuing along the road he was, in effect, entering a narrow corridor through a forbidden zone. Denny shrugged, made a face, and forged ahead.

That he knew the road from horseback as well as he did was a lucky thing; the night was very dark, with a mean headwind, and the damaged black surface was hard to see. He found a stick to probe with and felt his way along the edge, cursing the need to go so slowly.

At four in the morning Denny reached the bridge over the intermittent stream he called Part-Time Creek, which established the eastern boundary of the old farm, and probed his way in total blackness down into the bed of the creek. Its jumble of rocks was dry—no water or ice in the bed to make things worse—but inching upstream in the dark without falling was so close to impossible that more than an hour had passed before Denny felt he was far enough from the road to risk pushing up through a tangle of brush to flat land.

But he came out where he had intended to, behind the skeletal tobacco barn where the Scout camp's maintenance equipment had been kept. Tobacco barns were built with spaces between the vertical boards, so the circulating air could cure the tobacco leaves hung in bunches from the rafters. The barn was therefore poor protection from the wind, and also listing badly. But Denny had stored Rocinante's and Roscoe's hay in the loft, and had nailed the saggy ladder tight to the uprights. He had gambled that the Hefn hadn't found and salvaged that hay, and the gamble paid off. Working by memory and feel, avoiding the weak spots in the floor of the loft, he built a windbreak out of bales. He cut the twine from another bale to make a mattress, scratchy but fragrant, of loose hay (carefully rolling up the cut pieces of twine and stuffing them in his pants pocket), then piled more hay over himself and his stuff and pulled his watch cap down over his ears and his parka hood up over that. By first light he was sound asleep.

Nothing woke him; he woke himself, startled awake from a dream of crossing an endlessly broad, jaggedly tumbled polar ice floe in Arctic blackness. He was feeling his way with something like an ice axe lashed to the end of a ski pole, thinking *This would make a good weapon if a polar bear comes along*, when just then a polar bear *did* loom dazzlingly out of the darkness. But after a first thrill of fear, Denny realized that the bear was smiling and nodding in a benevolent way. "Want a lift?" it said. There was a fuzzy white cub on its back already, sitting up like a human child on a pony. "Sure," said Denny, and he scrambled up on the bear's back behind the cub. But then the bear began to gallop across the rough ice. There was nothing to hold onto except the cub, and Denny understood that he absolutely must not take the cub down with him. As he was jolted off its mother's slippery back, he woke himself up yelling.

Fine, why not just go out and blow a trumpet blast to let everybody know where he was? Fully awake and instantly aware of his situation, Denny swore silently as he pushed back the parka hood and watch cap, straining to hear anything that would suggest he'd given himself away. But there was nothing, no sound at all, not even wind keening through the cracks between the slats. It was perfectly still. Nor could he see any signs of advancing, vengeful Hefn through those cracks. The day was overcast, chilly but not terribly cold. He looked at his watch: 3:46. It wouldn't be dark enough to leave the barn for a couple more hours at least. After squirming around in the hay to try to go back to sleep, which proved impossible, he sat up cautiously and peered around.

The inside of the barn appeared exactly as he had last seen it. That probably meant that the Hefn had taken it for the derelict it was; probably they hadn't even opened the doors facing the road, which were stuck tight anyway, to peer inside. Roscoe's tracks were around if you looked, but he and Rocinante had been stabled in the little shed near the cabin that housed the cistern and in former times the pump.

Denny passed the remaining hours of daylight eating a sandwich and a packet of craisins, checking his watch every couple of minutes, and going over and over the reasons why he wasn't going to be caught in the loft like a cornered rat. He knew the penalty for disobeying a direct order from the Hefn. He knew what those signs said besides WARNING! They said that persons caught willfully trespassing on posted land would have their memories erased. This was no idle threat, it happened every so often when frustration about the Baby Ban built up enough somewhere on the planet that people had to fight back, despite the failure and horrible punishment of everybody who had ever tried that—as far as Denny knew, every rebellion had failed completely.

Wiped transgressors were always displayed on international viddy. Denny had seen the bewildered, pitiful products of Hefn mindwipe on the screen and been horrified, like everyone else. He had never expected to risk that sort of treatment for himself—worse than execution in a way—and not until now had he understood why people were sometimes driven, despite the utter pointlessness of defying the Hefn, to defy them anyway.

When Denny had had plenty of time to drive himself bonkers, the light finally began to fade, and then it was twilight, and then full dark. He made himself wait until six, and then with a sneeze of relief threw off the covering of hay. He emptied the duffelpack, piling his things at the top of the ladder, and put the pack on. Outside the barn he spent a couple of minutes brushing himself off and picking hay seeds and scratchy stalks out of his hair and collar.

His next move was to approach the cabin from the rear, to find out whether any Hefn were actually in residence. Hefn could see extremely well at night, and Humphrey had gone off scouting on his own without getting lost, that day he had thrown Denny off the farm. But Denny still felt confident that here in the open on his own Ground he enjoyed a certain advantage.

A wagon road ran alongside Part-Time Creek up the hollow; he followed it cautiously for a little while, then struck left, straight uphill, scrambling, pulling himself along using saplings or going on all fours. He startled a little group of white-tailed deer bedded down on the hillside and heard them bound away, making a lot of noise in the dry leaves. *They* could see what they were doing. He was making a lot of noise himself, but there was no help for it, he couldn't see a thing. But he wasn't lost; all he had to do to get where he was going was keep heading straight uphill. When he felt he was far enough from the barn not to leave a sign for the once-predatory Hefn, he paused to pee into a tangle of blackberry canes.

After a while, puffing and sweating, he came to the edge of the woods and stopped to catch his breath. The hillside sloped more gently here. Directly ahead he could see the glint of the septic lagoon, and above that the pond; and beyond the pond the cabin stood beneath bare trees on top of the ridge. Because he knew where to look, Denny could see its faint outline, blacker than the night sky. The place had a deserted feel to it; now that he had it in view, he was ready to bet that nobody, Hefn or human, waking or sleeping, was inside. There was also no helicopter parked on the site of the former garden. Breathing more easily, but still being careful, Denny climbed to the ridge, hugging the tree line. Where the driveway dipped out of sight of the cabin, he ducked across and slipped into the stable: empty. They had left the hay behind, but the horse and the mule had been evacuated.

His plan called for stealing a sleeping bag and tent from the stash in the basement—on this sortie or, if obstacles developed, a later one. There seemed no reason to wait. The lock on the patio door had rusted out long ago, so he didn't have to break in. He rummaged in the storm shelter with utmost stealth, but it felt more like a game of cops and robbers than anything truly dangerous. The cabin was empty; intuitively he was certain of this. Maybe it would stand empty for years now, while the land around it went completely wild. Maybe the Hefn had such complete confidence in the deterrent power of their warning signs that they weren't going to bother checking to be sure everybody was in compliance. Maybe this was going to be easier than he had expected.

But that didn't allow for sloppiness. He knew it would take all his skill in camping and woodcraft to leave no trace of his presence for an overflying chopper to detect.

He found what he needed by feel. Besides the sleeping bag, pad, and tent, he took some cooking gear, a mess kit, a canteen, and a jerry can. That was all. He left everything else exactly as he'd found it, trusting that a Hefn casting a casual eye around the basement would never notice that some of this castoff junk had disappeared. The aluminum cookware had canvas covers and didn't clank. He packed it all in the duffel and slipped out, closing the patio door with elaborate care, despite his perfect certainty that nobody was at home in what had used to be his home.

Denny set up camp directly across the main road from the tobacco barn, on the north bank of Indian Creek. Working fast by pale dawn light, he pitched the pup tent in a small clearing ringed by the unkempt-looking red cedar trees that popped up in any patch of open ground hereabouts. From the road he would be invisible.

Maybe not from the air, however. He recklessly spent a hour of early day-light cutting cedar boughs and tying them to a makeshift exterior ridge pole with pieces of twine from the cut bales of hay, until the tent had a camouflage roof of cedar thatching. None of this could be accomplished in perfect silence, but he did his best.

Finally he crawled into the tent, inflated the pad, unzipped the sleeping bag, removed his boots and parka, and called it a day. Or a night. I'd better get used to the nocturnal life, he told himself. Moving around much in the day-time will be too risky. If we get snow cover I won't be able to move around at all. Fire's going to be a problem. . . . Listing these obstacles, he wasn't sure how long he would be able to stick to his plan. But any more time at all with the bears was better than none, if he didn't get caught.

Night and day are about the same to a hibernating bear. The calculated risk he was running seemed very much worth it to Denny the next nightfall, as he stood outside Rosetta's den, pulling on the leather gauntlets he had managed to sneak into his duffel—along with the other contents of his daypack, the scales and flashlight and PocketPad—almost under Humphrey's nose, while he was being extradited. This day, the third since his arrival at the farm, had been cold, around twenty degrees F. He'd huddled in his cocoon of down in the afternoon and thought out what he meant to do, then cut straight up from the road to the ridge top through deep woods as night was falling, and now he stood in the leaves tingling with exhilaration. He was here, despite everything that had been done to try to stop him. He would see the cubs again, weigh them, record the weights. Having no way to keep blood samples frozen till he could get them to a lab, he wasn't going to draw any blood. But he would keep the other records as best he could, carry on the research a while longer. He felt he owed it to himself, and to the bears, and to humanity in general. As much as anything, this was an act of secret defiance against the Hefn.

Swelled with a sense of purpose, he fished out the flashlight, flopped on his belly, and crawled into the den. Aiming low, he switched on the light, the first light he had used to break the darkness for three days running. The rank heap of Rosetta lay on its side, casting a looming shadow on the wall of the den, head tucked down, enormous paws curled inward. The cubs were snuggled against her. Denny crawled forward on his forearms, wildlife biologist displac-ing radical insurgent, beside himself with eagerness to see the cubs, see how much they'd grown in more than two weeks.

His right hand had closed on the nape fur of the first cub, a bigger, fatter Rodeo, when the beam of the flashlight fell on the second cub. This wasn't Rocket, he saw that at once. Rocket was gone. This cub was a little bigger than Rocket had been two weeks ago, but visibly smaller than Rodeo was right now, and more nearly black than cinnamon brown. How in the world had it gotten here? He released his grip on Rodeo and reached for the changeling.

Just as he was about to touch it, the cub shifted its hold on the nipple, screwing up its little face against the light. Denny's hand jerked back as if snakebit while his brain did a slow cartwheel, trying to interpret what he was seeing by the flashlight's weirdifying glare. This little animal wasn't a bear cub at all. Its shape and color were wrong, its proportions were wrong . . . what *was* it? What could have happened? He squirmed closer and aimed the light directly at the cub's head, trying to see its face. Again it screwed its eyes shut, and this time it let go of the nipple and made a thin sound of complaint. Its hairy little forelimbs, that had been rummaging in Rosetta breast fur, waved in the air, little arms ending in — in —

It felt like a crack of lightning. By straining every ounce of self-control Denny managed not to scream, not to flail his way out of the den. But he backed out a lot faster than he'd crawled in, shutting off the flashlight before emerging not from prudence but by habit alone. He took off down the ridge trail toward the cabin by habit also, fleeing in blind panic until, inevitably, he tripped on something and fell flat.

Lying where he'd fallen, he struggled to master his shock. The second cub was a baby Hefn. A baby Hefn! In a bear's den! There had never been a baby Hefn anywhere on Earth before — but a bear's den in the middle of winter! This was a mystery beyond all solving, but Denny had understood one thing the instant he laid eyes on the baby Hefn: his situation was no longer one of calculated risk but of imminent suicide. Probably no human in the world knew about this but himself. It wasn't possible to imagine that the baby had been put into Rosetta's den by anyone other than an adult Hefn, Humphrey or Innisfrey. The biologists had obviously been thrown out of this territory so the baby could be planted in the den.

Baby or babies? Only this den, or others as well, in other study areas? In other states? *Countries?* Denny shook his head to clear it, and stood up cautiously. It didn't matter; what mattered was, he had to get out of here *now* or he would be the featured attraction at the next Hefn humiliation event on the viddy. No disobedience of Hefn law could result more obviously in mindwipe than this one of his. There was no doubt in his mind that he had blundered onto something top secret, and none that the Hefn would be back often to check on their little bundle of joy. He had to get away.

But also, he had to leave no trace of his having been there, and in his panic flight he had left the daypack behind. Okay retrieve the pack, then get down through the woods to the road as fast as possible, break camp, ditch the camping gear someplace, hotfoot it back to Lawrenceburg, and catch the first boat back to Carrollton tomorrow. Thinking these things, he groped his way back to the den.

And then what? Denny stood staring at the great pale shape that was the gigantic fallen oak forming a lintel for the entrance to the den. A tree could grow that big on marginal farmland, he thought irrelevantly, for one reason only: it had stood on a fence line since it was a sapling.

Hop a boat to Carrollton, *and then what?* Agree to study the Hurt Hollow bears, keep his head down and his mouth shut? I should go back down there, he thought. It's only been a couple of minutes and already I don't believe it myself. If I'm going to break the story (*was* he going to break the story?) I have to know for sure that I saw what I think I saw.

If only I had a camera, he thought with regret. A holocamera, or a diskorder. Might as well wish for the Moon. But nobody's going to believe this unless I have some kind of proof.

For a mad moment he considered kidnapping the baby Hefn, proof incontrovertible of what had happened here. But he didn't, of course, know how to take care of it, and if one hair of the baby's bearded little chinny-chin-chin should accidentally be hurt . . . and anyway, consequences aside, this baby was, in one sense, Rosetta's suckling cub and Rodeo's foster sibling. He didn't want it on his conscience if somehow he (he?) got hurt.

More than anything in the world, Denny did not want to go back down into Rosetta's den, but he did it anyway. There was no mistake. The baby had tiny, forked, four-fingered hands, two digits opposed to the other two. It was hairy all over. It had whiskers. It was much darker than the adult Hefn, all of whom were varying shades of gray, but there could be no doubt that this was the infant form of the same kind of creature.

Having made certain of this, Denny wriggled back out into the night with only one urgent need on his mind. This time he remembered the pack, and remembered to head in the right direction, straight toward his campsite on the creek, a long up-and-down—mostly down—scramble in the dark. Interestingly enough, he was getting much better at seeing and moving about in the dark.

He broke camp, stuffed all his gear into the duffel, and started, relatively sure-footedly, back down the road toward town. Having done this much, his mind began to hum and click; and after a while he had a sort of plan.

Denny had been to Hurt Hollow lots of times, as a little school kid when Jesse Kellum was still the caretaker and keeper of the (metaphorical) flame, and afterward, when it had been closed to the public, as a Gaian initiate. He knew all about Orrin and Hannah Hubbell, the legendary couple who had built the house and kept goats and bees there, and written about their life "on the fringe of society." They were classic proto-Gaians. While Jesse Kellum was caretaker, Pam Pruitt had been a girl living across the river in Indiana. She'd spent a lot of time here in her teens, helping Jesse, even after the Hefn Humphrey had chosen her to be one of the first group of math-prodigy Apprentices to be trained by Humphrey in how to operate the Time Transceivers that could open a window into the past.

Denny also knew that Pruitt had lost her math intuition and no longer worked at the Bureau of Temporal Physics, though she continued to work with and for the Bureau. She had remained close to Humphrey, and had become prominent in the Gaian movement after leaving the Bureau's Santa Barbara headquarters. Nowadays she was something or other to do with the Mormon Church, and ordinarily lived in Salt Lake City.

The reason he knew so much about Pam Pruitt was partly that she was a local celeb, the only Apprentice ever with close ties to Kentucky, and partly because she had been associated with Hurt Hollow in his mind as long as he could remember. The Hollow was important to all Gaians, but the place had been Pam Pruitt's personal Ground before it ever became a shrine. She was part of Gaian lore in Kentucky, and especially in Denny's hometown of Milton, directly across the river from Madison, Indiana, five miles from the Scofield College campus where Pruitt had lived as a child. Though he'd never met her, he'd grown up knowing all about her.

Humphrey had said she was in residence now, probably on a personal retreat and not happy about being burst in upon. He wasn't one hundred percent certain that she wouldn't betray him to Humphrey, but he thought not. And she had a lot of influence with the Hefn. If he was going to tell anybody, he could think of no better person to dump his problem on.

Denny boarded a southbound steamboat in Carrollton and got off at Milton with half a dozen other people. He could have asked the pilot to let him off at the Hurt Hollow landing, but it wasn't a regular stop and he was afraid somebody might remember. Anyhow, from Milton you could walk to Hurt Hollow the back way, straight up the river bluff, along the bluff top by a maze of little roads, and down to the river again. The roads were bad here too, but at least he didn't feel obliged to hike all that way in the dark.

An electrified fence enclosed the whole sixty-one-acre tract of the Hollow from road to river. By the time he reached the upper gate it was late afternoon, and he was tired. He groaned at the prospect of bushwhacking all around the periphery of the property while the sky got darker and darker, but saw no alternative; the house was close to the river bank, a mile or so below the upper gate. From the top there was no way to signal the house. Pruitt wouldn't hear him if he yelled, and somebody else very well might.

He'd bought two sandwiches and an apple in Carrollton; he ate these now, sitting with his back against the gate, and drank some water from the Girl Scout canteen in its red and green plaid cover. The rest of the camping gear had been cached under the Salt River bridge, halfway between the farm and Lawrenceburg, but he'd kept the canteen with its useful built-in biofilter.

He thought of tossing his duffelpack over the fence, so as not to have to lug it along. But if Pruitt had left the Hollow by now, and Denny couldn't get in, he would need the stuff in the duffel. So in the end he started on what he hoped was the shorter way round the fence line with his burden still strapped to his aching shoulders.

It took him more than an hour to get down to the river, even traveling almost all downhill, and to work his way to the dock, but when he got there he saw the phone still mounted next to the lower gate. Thank God. Denny remembered how, on school trips, the teacher would pick up that very phone and a buzzer would sound faintly in the house, and Jesse Kellum would come down and unlock the gate. Now, if only the thing was in working order. How would he get Pruitt's attention tonight if it wasn't? His tired brain had nothing to suggest.

At least she was still there. Denny could see an oil lamp shining in the window and a lit lantern on the patio outside, and he smelled wood smoke. He could also hear a dog barking. He dropped his pack on the dock, opened the little door, and took the receiver off the hook. The line sounded dead to him, but inside the house a shadow moved, then there was a click, and a woman's voice said "Yes?" into his ear, and then "Feste, be quiet."

Denny realized he hadn't thought out what he wanted to say. "Are you Pam Pruitt?" he inquired in a croaky voice—how long since he had actually talked to anybody?—and when she didn't answer he cleared his throat and rushed ahead. "My name's Denny Demaree, I'm a wildlife biologist, I've been studying black bears in Anderson County, the Hefn recovery program? I'm a Gaian, the farm where I've been working is my Ground. Something's happened. Could I speak with you?"

There was silence. Then the voice said, "This is Pam Pruitt. What do you mean, something's happened?"

"I, uh, can't tell you about it like this, I need to talk to you in person."

"Look, I'm on a retreat."

"I know, I'm really sorry, but this is—this can't wait. This is huge," Denny said. "Please."

"You knew I was making a retreat?"

"Not exactly, but the Hefn Humphrey told me you were here and I guessed it might be a retreat. I'm really sorry," he said again.

Another silence, then a sigh. "Okay. You're on the dock? I can come down for a couple of minutes."

Relieved, Denny tucked the phone away. He saw the door open and the lantern begin to wobble down the path toward him; by now it had become completely dark. Long before Pruitt reached the gate, her dog—so black Denny could see nothing but teeth and eyeshine—had rushed up and was growling through the woven wire. When she caught up with him, her first words were "Push up close against the fence and spread your arms and legs.

Feste, check 'em out. Good boy, check 'em out." Denny did as he was told, feeling foolish, while the dog sniffed him industriously all over through the fence. "Now turn around and do it again . . . okay. Leave the bag where it is. Feste, on guard," and he heard the gate click.

Denny stepped inside, and was suddenly conscious of his appearance, which the cold-water tap in the packet's washroom had done little to improve. "Sorry I'm so grubby. I've been camping and didn't get a chance to clean up."

Pruitt held the lantern up to get a better look at him. "Camping where, in a coal mine?" But she grinned as she said it.

"On the farm where my study was being done. Humphrey terminated the project and threw me off the place, uh, around two or three weeks ago now I think it was, I've kind of lost track."

Pruitt's eyebrows shot up. "He threw you out and you snuck back in? Have you got a death wish? You could get yourself wiped for that."

"Like I don't know that! The study wasn't *finished*," Denny said defensively, "but anyway, what he said was that East Central should be left to recover on its own now, but I don't think that *is* why he kicked me out. Something else is going on."

Pruitt slowly lowered the lantern. "Like what?"

"You're not going to believe me," Denny said desperately, "I can't prove it to you, but last night, see, last night I went into a den to check on the cubs, I hadn't seen them since the day I got sent packing, I had a flashlight, and right away I realized that one of them was gone, and—"

"Oh-kay," Pruitt said, interrupting him. "You better come on up to the house then. Get your stuff and close the gate—slam it good and hard. Feste, school's out. Good job."

Denny stared at her, feeling chilled. "You know about it. You knew what I was going to say." He backed away, slipped through the gate and shut it between them with a clang. "You're tight with Humphrey—"

"It happens," said Pruitt mildly, "that Humphrey and I don't see eye to eye on the subject of—what you were about to tell me. It's your call, but you're in big trouble right now, so unless you've got someplace else to go, I'd come along quietly if I were you."

Denny sagged against the gate. The only other place he had to go, now that he knew what he knew, was back to work for Fish and Wildlife, which was itching to assign him to study bears right here in Hurt Hollow, only now he didn't even have that option if Pruitt exposed him to the Hefn. "How do I know you won't turn me over to *them*?"

She had started toward the house, but turned back to face him. "I guess you'll have to trust me on that, which I realize you have no reason to do, except that Gaians don't lie to each other, do they? And I give you my word that I won't."

Denny trudged behind her up the path to the house, dragging his duffel, stumbling with exhaustion. Pruitt set the lantern down and opened the door onto a warm wooden room with a bright fire on the hearth. The dog slipped through ahead of them both. "I expect you've been here before."

"Yeah. Never at night, though." By the firelight he got his first good look at Feste, who was now sniffing his hand, and let out a snort of laughter. "A poodle? Your guard dog is a *poodle?*"

"Hey, poodles can be great guard dogs, they just don't usually look the part. With his hair cut like that, most people don't even know he's a poodle." The dog, jet-black, was clipped short all over and resembled a Saluki with tight curls.

"Our neighbors had a standard when I was a kid. I remember that long nose." He rubbed the dog's head and stifled a yawn.

Pruitt gave him a scrutinizing once-over. "You're completely done in. Why not get some sleep before we talk?" And at his skeptical look, "Far as I know, nobody knows about your little escapade yet, unless you've told somebody besides me. You can afford a few hours of sleep; you may get found out, but not by tomorrow morning."

"Why," asked Denny, "are you helping me? *Are* you helping me?"

"We'll see," said Pruitt. "First things first."

"Who else knows?" Denny asked this question while tucking into a bowl of goat stew. He had slept for eleven hours, then made excellent use of a bucket of hot water, a bar of soap, and Jesse Kellum's straight razor. Now he sat at the Hubbles' long, heavy table of dark wood, dressed in his last pieces of clean laundry from Louisville: a ratty pair of orange corduroys and a shapeless cotton sweatshirt with both elbows out.

"Search me. Maybe nobody. *I* know because . . . well, Humphrey would have a hard time deceiving me about anything, let alone anything this critical, even though he knew it would throw me into a quandary. I'm not sure he appreciates how much of one it does throw me into."

Eating steadily, Denny kept his focus. "So what are they up to?"

Pruitt propped her boots on the hearth, laced her fingers behind her head, and sighed heavily. She was a lean, severe-looking, rather mannish woman of forty or so, short brown hair mixed with gray. Denny thought her more attractive in person than in the holos and viddies he'd seen, not that that was saying a lot, but he no longer felt apprehensive about whether he could trust her; she was straightforward to the point of bluntness. "I've been trying to figure out how much to tell you. It would have been a lot better for you—for me too, come to that—if you hadn't been so pigheaded and intrepid about the damn bears. The reason I'm making this retreat right now is to try to get clear about how to handle what I know. Now I have to get clear about how to handle what you know, with no good answers coming through on either front so far."

Impatient with this dithering, Denny cut straight to the point. "Who put the baby Hefn in Rosetta's den?"

"I can tell you that. Humphrey did. It's not his baby, but he did the placement."

Alarmed, he demanded, "Did they tranquilize the mother?"

"I wouldn't know. Probably."

"Goddammit!" And then, "What did they do with Rocket? The other cub."

"I don't know that either. Gave him to a rehab outfit to raise as an orphan, most likely."

"That *sucks*." Furious, Denny pounded his fist on the table, rattling the spoon in his empty bowl. "Why'd they *do* that? Switch Rocket with the Hefn baby?"

"Why." Pruitt grimaced. "Sure you want to know? You'll be in even deeper."

"If they're messing with my bears, *yes* I want to know! Anyway, how can I get in any deeper than I'm in already?"

"Okay, then. I only just heard about this myself a month or so ago. It turns out," she said, "that the Hefn haven't been repairing the damage we did to the Earth entirely out of an altruistic desire to heal Earth's biosphere. It turns out that the Hefn and the Gafr—" she glanced at him, looked away. "It's like this. The Hefn and the Gafr aren't just connected in that master-servant sense we know about. They're also sexually symbiotic."

Denny's jaw dropped. "Symbiotic? Really?"

"Really. Genetically they're not even closely related, but neither can breed without the other. All the Hefn are male. All the Gafr are female. Everybody aboard that ship is, or was, part of a mated pair. The ship was looking for a place that was natural and unspoiled enough for them to breed in, because their home world, for some reason that hasn't been explained to me, is no longer a suitable place to do that in."

"They were looking for a place to *breed* when they found Earth?"

"Right."

"Four hundred years ago?"

"Right."

"And they marooned the renegade Hefn here intending to come right back for them—and stay, and start reproducing! Only they had mechanical problems, and by the time they got back in 2006, Earth was no longer natural and unspoiled enough?"

"Right three times."

"Now we come to it." He shoved the bowl away and folded his arms on the table. "Why do they have to breed in the Garden of Eden?"

"I gather," Pruitt said slowly, "that the postnatal development of Hefn infants depends on spending a certain amount of time, at a certain stage, being raised in the wild by a predator. As a predator. By 2006 we no longer had a viable supply of nursemaid predatory species, and, not incidentally, we had way too many people."

"Oh my God." Denny, all biologist for the moment, looked thunderstruck. "That's fascinating. That's absolutely fascinating." He thought a minute. "Chimps? The big cats?"

Pruitt got up and cleared away his cup and bowl. She brought a basket of wrinkled-looking yellow apples to the table and thumped it down on the floor. "The big cats are all still pretty endangered in the wild, except for lions and cougars, and anyway the Hefn don't really relate to cats that well." She half-filled a bucket with water, brought that to the table too, and started transferring the apples to the bucket, where they bobbed peacefully. "Chimps might have been a possibility—there's a documented account that a group of them once adopted an abandoned Nigerian boy—but the Hefn needed to work with populations that could recover faster. Shorter gestation period, multiple births, briefer childhood, faster bounceback." She snorted. "I used to wonder why Humphrey was so interested in our myths and stories about feral children. When the Apprentices were kids in DC, he used to like to talk about that. Tarzan was a big thing of mine back then."

"Wolves!" Denny said. "Romulus and Remus. Mowgli. Those two girls in India. My God—the coyote field studies!"

Pruitt had removed the empty basket and fetched large bowls and paring knives and a section of newspaper, and now she sat down, spreading paper in front of her like a place mat. She nodded. "Yeah. They ruled out every species that hadn't been able to adapt to some degree to massive loss of habitat. Like tigers and chimps, wolves are too specialized. Coming back nicely *now*, of course . . . but coyotes were never in any danger of being exterminated, no matter how intensively they were hunted, trapped, poisoned—well, you know all this better than I do. The Hefn were very interested in the eastern coyotes, the big ones, for a while, but in the end they decided that black bears were a better answer." While she talked, Pruitt had been taking apples from the bucket, quartering and coring them on the newspaper, and tossing the pieces into one bowl and the cores and excised bad bits into another.

Denny drew a sheet of newspaper in front of himself and picked up a paring knife. "Bears aren't very good predators, though. They're fast, but not agile enough to prey on mature elk or deer, and as for rabbits and mice and like that, forget it." He reached into the bucket for an apple.

"In fact, not being specialized has worked to their advantage, and anyway they're apparently predatory enough for the purpose. And also," pitching a double handful of pieces into the bowl, "there's an authenticated account of a bear in Iran that carried off a toddler and nursed him for three days. Cross-species adoption, see, like the chimps and the Nigerian kid. Besides which, bears do exhibit one excellent behavior, if you're a Hefn."

Denny slapped the table. "They hibernate!"

"They hibernate. The only large mammalian predator that does, if I'm not mistaken."

"Oh man. You're saying—" Denny stared at Pruitt. "The Baby Ban. The Gaian Mission. All the habitat recovery projects. Think of everything the Gaians and the other eco-freaks have put up with, and *supported*, because we thought they were doing it to save the Earth—Gaia—and ultimately life on Earth, including human life. And all the time they were really doing it for themselves! This changes *everything!*"

Pruitt said unhappily, "It's not that black and white. I've been reevaluating everything I ever knew about the Hefn, believe me, these past few weeks. And I know—I *know*—there's been a real desire—definitely on Humphrey's part, and some of the other Observers too—to connect with people and help them— help them adjust—just *help* them." The apple in her hands was mostly rot; she abandoned the effort to cut out the bad parts and dumped the whole thing in the compost bowl. "But behind all that, yes, it does look like there was always another agenda, even for Humphrey and Godfrey and Alfrey. Because, what- ever they think personally, and however earnestly some of them have inter- vened on our behalf, in the end the Hefn serve the Gafr. We tend to forget that, because we never see the Gafr, but it's all too true. All the Hefn we've had any contact with were loyal to the Gafr when the rebels fomented their mutiny."

Denny flung the knife down on the table so hard it skidded to the floor. "So that's been their purpose right from the start? Reduce-slash-eliminate the human population, the temperate forests and rainforest come back, the ecosys- tems are restored, the keystone predators return—and the aliens have a choice of breeding grounds. Our breeding grounds. Humans are sterilized so the aliens can have children. This isn't going to play well in Peoria," he said.

"No." Pruitt got up and dumped the bucket of water, now empty of apples, into the sink. She picked Denny's paring knife up off the floor and laid it on the counter, then went to build up the fire. "I think Humphrey really believed that the Ban would be lifted if things went well. Maybe the Gafr meant to lift it someday. But the whole deal has always hinged on connections between a few Hefn and a handful of people. Except for those relationships, the Gafr would have washed their hands of us long ago."

She stood, a bit stiffly, to lift a Dutch oven off the hearth and hang it on an iron arm affixed to the side of the fireplace. She removed the heavy lid and set it down. "All that's been kind of falling to pieces of late. The more frantic peo- ple get, the more reckless they get. Now that we've become so seriously endan- gered as a species ourselves, people naturally feel they have less and less to lose by defying the Hefn, and the Hefn have less and less reason to defend us to the Gafr. People are ready to explode even without knowing the Hefn and Gafr are breeding. If they find out—"

"Are you saying not to tell anybody?"

Pruitt shot him a startled look. "Were you going to? I thought you were looking for a bolt hole last night, not a reporter."

They stared at each other. Denny dropped his gaze. "I don't know what to do," he admitted. "I'm in danger of mindwipe because if I go public with this it could start a worldwide riot. But if I don't tell—I've never been able to stand the Hefn. If I don't expose them, I'll feel like a collaborator, or a coward, or both." He got up and carried the heaping bowl of quartered apples to the hearth. "The plain truth is, I *am* a collaborator, even if I didn't really know it. All the field biologists are. What have we been doing but helping get Earth's ecosystem ready to be an alien nursery?" He didn't state the obvious—that if he was a collaborator she was a thousand times worse—but he didn't need to.

Pruitt took the bowl and said, "I need about a cup of water." When Denny brought the water, she poured it into the Dutch oven, dumped in the apples, and stirred them briefly with a long wooden spoon. Then she clanged on the lid and swung the iron arm so the big pot hung over the fire. "Thanks," she said. "I owe Humphrey more than I owe to any human being now alive. But his patience with the people he's been trying to help has been strained to the limit. And, of course, he's utterly entranced with the thought of having a baby himself, his own baby. They've all been waiting for this for a very long time, fearing all that while that they would never breed again, that their kind would go extinct."

"So then they know exactly how *we* feel!"

Pruitt looked downright haggard. "Denny, I need to know what you're going to do. I doubt I can protect you if the Hefn find out what you know, even from Humphrey. What we need is a plan that will keep your paths from crossing."

"Well," said Denny, "when I get back from my leave—if I go back—Fish and Wildlife has offered me reassignment. Here, as a matter of fact. Outside the fence, I guess they mean."

"Here?" Pruitt sounded astonished.

"Mm-hm, it was Humphrey's idea. When I told him I was a Gaian and he was kicking me off my Ground, he apologized and said he'd try to get me reassigned to Hurt Hollow, which I guess he was thinking is every Gaian's Ground in a sense, as well as being yours, your own personal Ground. So if I don't go public, I guess that's what I'll be doing."

"Then I can tell you for a fact that Humphrey thinks the world of your work on the bears of Anderson County," said Pruitt, clearly impressed herself. "You have no idea what a compliment that offer is, coming from him. As a matter of fact, the upper part of the fence is about to come down. He wants bears to be able to get into Hurt Hollow. He wants his own son to be nurtured right here, right in the hottest Hot Spot of them all, and that sure isn't the best way I can think of to keep your paths from crossing."

A sharp bark came from outside; Pruitt walked over and opened the back door to let the dog in, along with a draft of cold air. "Wait a second," said Denny, throwing himself back onto the bench. "Hold everything. If the Hefn and Gafr are going to start having kids right and left, and placing them in bears' dens all over the map every winter, how long can the whole thing stay a secret? One baby Hefn, okay. But dozens? Hundreds? There's no way." Feste trotted around the room sniffing at things, then sat down in front of Denny, looking expectant. He rubbed the dog's ears absently and scratched under his chin.

Pruitt sat down on the bench across from him. "They'll post all the territories with signs threatening mindwipe —"

"People are getting more reckless, you said it yourself. Some other biologist is going to refuse to be kicked out, same as I did. There's no way they can keep the lid on. What if a bunch of Hefn toddlers come out in spring and start wandering around with the mother bears?" He leaned toward Pam. "What if somebody steals one out of a den? Or kills one? You know it could happen."

"If the Hefn weren't keeping close tabs on them all —"

"But they're not! Nobody's at my farm. Nobody was protecting the baby in Rosetta's den. You'd think they'd have the whole ship watching over it."

Pruitt rubbed her forehead, back and forth, as if trying to massage a headache away. "I guess keeping hands off, leaving it up to nature, might be a necessary part of Hefn child development." She looked at Denny, tense on his bench as a sprinter waiting for the gun. "Humphrey did say this had to happen in the wild, that zoos wouldn't work. If they could have kept a supply of captive apex predators on their ship, I don't suppose they'd have stuck around Earth."

"And I wouldn't be cowering here in dread of having my memory wiped."

"And the planet would still be going to hell in a handbasket."

"But it would still be ours."

Pruitt's eyebrows went up. "For how much longer?"

Denny struck the table again. "You know what I think? I think we've been in a lose-lose situation all along here. I think if we'd been left to ourselves we'd either have poisoned and depleted the Earth beyond saving, or blown her up. Either way, extinction. And I think the Hefn have basically saved Earth's ecosystem, but for themselves, and they're going to force humanity into extinction anyway." He laughed, a harsh sound in the cozy little house. "At least this way Gaia herself survives. She'll do fine without us. As Gaians I guess we ought to be glad about that."

"Hard for a Hefn-hating Gaian wildlife biologist to know which end is up sometimes, yes?" And while Denny was still wondering how to take this spiteful-sounding crack, she added, "But right now, this morning, this minute, I'm thinking that you may have just hit the nail on the head." She shoved back her bench and stood up. "This retreat is over. I need to talk to Humphrey. And you need to get out of the Hollow. Humphrey knows this place like the back of his hand. If you don't want to go back to Fish and Wildlife you could hole up in my house in Salt Lake for a while—"

"I think I'll go back to Louisville," Denny said. "For now. I know some hidey-holes back there." And when Pruitt looked dubious, "Everything's happening too fast! A few weeks ago I was a field biologist, then I was a subversive, now all of a sudden I'm a fucking fugitive! Every time I think I've figured out what to do there's a news flash and I have to start figuring all over again. It's too crazy-making. I just want to go someplace quiet and think." Denny got up, took his filthy parka down from the hook where she had hung it, and put it on. He grabbed the straps of his duffel, and he was ready.

The fire had burned down to coals. Pruitt banked these with a little flat tool and gave the apples another stir. She stuck some papers, and some cheese and walnuts and a few other food items, into a small pack of her own, and put on her jacket. All through these preparations Denny could feel how she was bursting to argue with him, persuade him to keep the secret to himself, but all she said was, "Let's go, then. We row across to Indiana and catch the packet to Louisville." Opening the back door, she let Denny step out first into the damp, chilly, gray day, then followed the dog out and pulled the door to with a little bang. "I suppose we'll have to keep the house locked when the fence comes down." The thought made her grimace. "I'm going to the outhouse. You?" And when he shook his head, "Back in a minute then. Feste, sit. Stay."

Pruitt took three paces down the path—and directly ahead of her the view of leafless trees and steep hillside and Orrin Hubbell's studio began to spin. Denny shouted "Hey! Hey!" and dropped his bag. As they watched, the spinning air began to clarify from the center outward.

"Stay right where you are," said Pruitt. "It's a Time Window, opening from the future."

"What's going to happen?" Denny asked, tensed to run.

"To us? Nothing. Don't worry, whoever it is, all they can do is look through and talk." The bitterness had vanished from her voice; she sounded flustered but excited.

Denny was scared, but he was excited too. Ordinarily people didn't get to be on either side of a Time Window while it was actually working. All they ever saw were viddy recordings made through Time Windows, of historical events, edited by Temporal Physics technicians. This was raw footage, and he was in it—which might have been cause for panic, given his present situation, except—"How far in the future does a transceiver have to be to open a Window?"

"Theoretically, not far at all. In practice, it's impossible to set the coordinates if you're not pretty far down the road. Like trying to read something printed on the bridge of your nose."

Denny started to reply, but she waved her arm down to shut him up. The lens had clarified almost to the rim. At the center Denny saw a Hefn standing behind a strange metal contraption on legs, which he was obviously operating. Surrounding Hefn and transceiver, a disk of April—pink smears of blooming redbuds, fervent birdsong—had superimposed itself on the dead of winter.

The rim stopped spinning; the window was clear across its whole circumference. Stepping back from the machine, the Hefn came around where they could see him plainly.

Denny would have sworn he couldn't tell one Hefn from another, but he understood at once that this was neither Humphrey nor Innisfrey. This Hefn was sleeker somehow, slimmer, less motley-looking. His hyped-up brain would have arrived at the obvious in another moment, but the sleek Hefn did it for him. "Hi, Pam. Hi, Denny. Hey there, Feste, you look just like your great-great-grandnephews! Sorry to barge in on you like this. I'm Terrifrey, by the way. Humphrey's son."

Pruitt said quickly, "Where's Humphrey?"

"Hibernating. He was up most of the winter. He's fine, don't worry. We had to make the decision to contact you without consulting him, but he—preapproved it, so to speak."

" 'We'?"

Terrifrey looked to the side, beyond the edge of the lens, and another Hefn came and stood next to him. "We," he said. "I'm Dennifrey. Named after you, Denny. Nice to see you."

Like a Time Window, Denny's mind whirled and cleared. "You're Rosetta's baby Hefn!" The Hefn nodded and beamed—or seemed to, since no Hefn could really do either. Instantly Denny said, "What happened to Rocket?"

"He lived a long, happy life and fathered lots of little Rockettes. And Rodeo and I were close as long as she lived. I went to see her all the time. She had lots of babies too."

"How do I know if you're telling me the truth, or telling me what I want to hear!" Denny protested.

"Oh, it's the truth, all right," said a third voice, and a wiry old man, nearly bald, with a bushy gray beard, strolled into the spring landscape and stood beside the two Hefn, a sight so unexpected, and so shocking, that Denny almost blurted out "Paw!" But his grandfather had been dead for years. He realized, with a dizzying lurch, that it was himself he was seeing.

The old man grinned at him, then beckoned in his turn, and the strangest figure of all entered the frame of the lens: a brown-haired girl of what, ten? eleven? Denny realized he couldn't remember what children had looked like at various ages, not that he'd ever paid that much attention. The girl was wearing a long blue dress and brown high-button shoes. "Hi, Grampa," she said, and giggled. The old man put his arm around her, but she had spoken through the lens, to Denny. "I'm Marny. I'm your granddaughter."

"My *grand*daughter!"

Pruitt broke in. "The Baby Ban's been lifted, then?"

The figures in the lens all hesitated and the girl looked sideways up at Terrifrey, who said carefully, "What you see, I'm afraid, is all you get. We can't answer any questions of that kind."

"That's the one answer I need," she said. "I've got to know."

"Well, it's just what we can't tell you," said Old Denny. "Not in so many words, because this—the four of us—is all I remember seeing in the Window. This is all that was shown to us. We had to take it from there as best as we could."

Pruitt drew in a shaky breath. Denny said to the girl, "Are you really my granddaughter?"

Marny nodded vigorously. "You look really young. And you've got more hair, and it's dark. And no *beard*. This is weird." She giggled again.

"It's marvelous to see you both, but I'm sorry, we'll have to break contact now." Humphrey's self-declared son stepped back behind the transceiver. "Remember that Time is One. It'll be okay." And the disk of air spun inward while the others all waved, the alien and old man and the child, and in a few more seconds the wintry hillside had been restored to itself.

For a long moment Pruitt and Denny stood staring at the empty air. Then "Whuf," said Pruitt quietly. "I guess we're not going anywhere just yet. Except I'm still going to the outhouse. Back in a second." She pulled the door open. "Feste, in you go."

Denny picked up his bag and went in too. The house was filled with the heavenly aroma of cooking apples. In a daze he unzipped his coat and sat down. "My *grand*daughter!" he proclaimed to the black poodle, who turned around twice and slumped to the floor at his feet. And when Pruitt let herself in, "I'm gonna have a *granddaughter!*"

"Before you start knitting booties, Grampa," said Pruitt dryly, pulling off her pack and coat, "let's think a bit about what they *didn't* say."

Denny nodded. "That the Ban had been lifted. But there was Marny, Exhibit A!"

"They didn't say she hadn't been cloned. They didn't say she wasn't a child actor derived from one of the people who missed the Broadcast. They didn't say things had been worked out between us and the Gafr. They didn't, when you get right down to it, say a hell of a lot."

Denny thought, but had the presence of mind not to say, that another thing they hadn't explained was Pruitt's own absence from the tableau. (There could be lots of reasons for that, but the likeliest one was that she had died.) Instead he said, "But don't just dismiss what they did say: that she's my granddaughter. Do you think Humphrey's son would lie to you?"

"Who knows? Humphrey wouldn't, but Humphrey wasn't there." Pruitt's excitement had turned to letdown, but Denny felt himself refusing to allow that to affect him. "What year would you think it was in the Window?"

"You looked, what, about seventy? How old are you now?"

"Twenty-nine."

"Well then. Forty years, give or take. So 2078, 2080? Baby Ban plus or minus sixty-five. If the Ban hasn't been lifted, the youngest human generation is in its sixties and our fate has been decided."

"And if it has, things have worked out some way, and people are having babies again." His mind was still suffused with the image of the little girl in the long blue dress—far more preoccupied with that, in fact, than with the sight of himself as an old duffer, with its implied guarantee of a long life unblemished by mindwipe. A granddaughter! Necessitating a son or daughter in between!

An hour ago Denny would have said he had no interest whatever in children, that his fury at the Hefn for imposing the Ban was principled and impersonal. Now the very idea that this vision of the future might be true thrilled him so much, it was hard—no, impossible, right now!—to care about anything else. That humanity *had* a future, that he himself had a personal stake in it! The possibility this latest news flash—more of a bombshell, really—seemed to promise had changed his world again; he could feel himself being converted from cynicism to hopefulness, all the way through. "What did he mean about time is one?"

"It's a saying they have: 'Time is One, and Fixed.' It means that whatever happens is the only thing that *can* happen. If two Hefn and you and a little girl appear in a Time Window, then events will necessarily lead to a moment when a Time Window opens and those four beings speak to you and me on February 5, 2038."

"But then, no matter what we do, it'll work out that way. If I just go to bed for twenty years, that contact will still occur."

Pruitt lifted the lid of the Dutch oven and stirred the apples, letting out a cloud of fragrant steam, then came and sat on the bench next to Denny. "The Hefn have another saying: 'What we never know is how.' If a window opens in the future, they know of one little thing that will definitely happen, but not what else will happen between the present and that moment in the future. Maybe the 'how' is that you call a press conference and announce that the Hefn are reproducing, using bears as surrogate mothers. Maybe it's that you go back to work for Fish and Wildlife and get assigned here, and never say a word to anybody. Maybe you sneak back to have another look at baby Dennifrey and Humphrey catches you with your hand in the cookie jar, or you hide out in

Utah and convert to Mormonism, or you go to bed for twenty years. You can say it doesn't matter, but you still have to choose among alternatives, see? And whatever you actually choose, *that* turns out to be 'how.' Your choice isn't determined by anything, but it's already there in the timestream."

Denny shook his head dubiously. "I don't really see why that's not determinism, but never mind. I'm making my choice. I'm choosing to believe that I'm really going to have a child and a grandchild, and that it means that up in the future where they are, human babies are being born, whether or not the Ban's been lifted. So for now, I'm deciding not to expose them. I'm going back to Fish and Wildlife and take the Hurt Hollow assignment, and wait and see." He looked straight into Pruitt's face, close to his own, her expression unreadable. "That's what you were hoping I'd do, right?"

"I'm not sure anymore."

The world seemed to have changed for her as well, but it wasn't Denny's problem. He stood and zipped his coat again. "You don't need to row me over, I'll walk back to Milton and catch the Louisville packet there. No big rush now." Despite saying this, he realized he couldn't wait to be off. He grabbed his duffel's straps with one hand and reached with the other for the door latch. "Thanks for everything. Will I see you when they send me back?"

Pruitt stood, dug in her pants pocket and pulled out a key on a ring. "Probably not. I'll need to be getting back to Salt Lake fairly soon. Here, take the gate key and let yourself out at the top of the path. Leave the key in the lock, I'll pick it up later."

"Well," said Denny, "thanks again."

"No problem. Good luck." She held out her hand.

Denny gripped it. "I'll be in touch."

Outside he donned his pack and, feeling light as a milkweed parachute, bounded past the studio, across the bridge spanning the creek, and up the footpath he had last climbed as a boy of twelve. He felt like singing. He'd had absolutely no inkling that he cared so passionately whether his species did or didn't have a future, or whether he, as a biological organism, would be allowed to fulfill his own reproductive drive. The world had opened up, enormous with possibility.

He was fitting the key in the padlock when the sound of a chopper abruptly cut across these thoughts like a shock wave. In seconds he could see the thing, flying lower, turning—yes, landing, in the road; the cold blast from the propeller blades, beating just beyond the meshes of the fence, hit him in the face. For an instant he panicked; but then he saw his elderly self, standing in the Time Window with his arm around a little girl, and he closed the gate calmly and clicked the padlock shut.

Leaving the key in the lock as instructed, he turned toward the chopper. To his relief there seemed to be no one aboard but the pilot, who opened the passenger door and yelled, "Want a lift? I'm headed back to Louisville." It was that Somebody Hoffman, the woman who'd flown Humphrey to the farm the day his old world had collapsed. Denny ducked under the whirling blades, threw his duffel in, and climbed in after it. He strapped himself in and put on the headphones she handed him. "What are you doing here?"

"Dropping off Humphrey. Didn't you see him? He just got out. We spotted you coming up from the house and figured you'd been checking out Hurt Hollow from the bear-study perspective."

Denny grinned hugely. "Shrewd guess. That is exactly what I've been doing."

"If you've decided to go with that, you might want to reconsider."

"Why?"

"Tell you after takeoff." The chopper lifted off and the view of the Hollow spread out below them: steeply sloping hillsides of bare trees, kinking creek valleys, and, in another minute, Orrin Hubbell's house and studio, perched above the broad, winding, steel-colored Ohio River. Smoke floated from the chimney, and a tiny black dog danced back and forth on the shore, looking up and, no doubt, barking like anything. Inside, Pruitt would be putting the hot apple pulp through a colander. She must be wondering what the chopper was about, and half-prepared for Humphrey's imminent appearance. What would they say to each other, while Pruitt stirred in nutmeg and cinnamon and assembled her canning paraphernalia? Denny squinted into the leafless woods, but caught no glimpse of a Hefn descending the bluff.

The chopper banked left and straightened out, following the river downstream. Somebody Hoffman settled back in her seat. "I don't guess you've heard about the bombings."

Jerked back to the here and now, Denny said, "Bombings? No! What bombings?"

"It's on all the newscasts. Terrorists blew up the headquarters of the Bureau of Temporal Physics in Santa Barbara last night. Also Senator Carpenter's office in the Congressional Office Building—he's chair of the Committee on Alien Affairs, I guess you knew that? The bombs were synchronized to go off at one and four in the morning, so there were no fatalities and not many injuries, but they sure made a mess."

"Who did it?"

"A group calling itself Collaboration Zero. They issued a statement calling on every human being presently helping or cooperating with the Hefn in any way to quit doing that. They want people to quit voluntarily, but whoever refuses to, they say they're prepared to go to any lengths to stop them. Anybody they consider a collaborator, at every level of collaboration, will be a target.

They're claiming there are hundreds of resistance fighters, that the Hefn will never find them, and that this was a warning shot to convince everybody they can do what they say."

"My God." A literal chill went through him. "If they can decide who's a collaborator, it's a witch hunt." It struck him that the Time Window had opened on this day because of what he was hearing now, that he had been shown the future before learning about the present. But why? The sense of being thrown into uncertainty yet again made him feel almost frantic.

"Yeah, and you and I are the witches," the pilot was saying. "And besides that, they specifically named the Gaians as a group; they're ordering all the missions to terminate their alliance with the Hefn and operate independently. Humphrey didn't say so, but I bet that's why he flew up here today. If those people know Pruitt's here at Hurt Hollow, they might be coming for her. They could be anywhere."

"But how many of these dudes can there really be?" Denny protested. "They can't possibly do all that much damage if they stay undercover, plus security will be a lot tighter wherever there's a potential target. Unless they're suicide troops. Jesus," he said, "I'm having trouble taking this in."

"They're clever," replied the pilot—Marian, that was her name. "Technically, by targeting the collaborators instead of the Hefn themselves, they're not violating the Directive. They explicitly said they didn't intend to harm the Hefn, or break any Directive rules about transportation or the production and distribution of food or any of that. And the Gaians can go right on doing most of what they do. But if you're a human being who helps the Hefn do what *they* do, and if you go on helping them after today, look out." She glanced over at Denny. "There don't have to be that many of them to scare the living daylights out of people. Today is my last day flying this thing for Fish and Wildlife, I can tell you that, and I wouldn't be that keen to study bears in Hurt Hollow either."

"Who *are* they, though? What are they trying to accomplish?" With part of his mind Denny was trying, unsuccessfully, to make this new upset fit with the vision he'd been given. "I don't see the logic of it," he said, meaning both things.

"Me neither, which is why I've started to wonder if this is maybe not so much about the Baby Ban, as just about standing up to the Hefn."

"How do you mean?"

"Well, you know—striking a blow for human self-respect. I mean, you're right, as a way to get the Ban lifted it makes no sense. But as a way to get people to stop cooperating with the Hefn—give them an *excuse* to stop, because in a lot of cases people would love to have an excuse—it kind of does. And let's face it, how likely is it at this point that the Ban's ever going to end?"

Denny tried to focus his whirling thoughts. "Wait. You mean, like, if I quit studying bears because I refuse to work for the Hefn, they're down on me. But if I quit because my life's been threatened . . . ?"

"That's it. Like, I told Humphrey on the way up here that I'm probably going to have to quit flying, because my mother would worry herself sick, and he seemed to accept that at face value."

It did make a kind of sense, but— "But I don't want to quit studying bears! God knows, I'd far *rather* do it without Hefn supervision; but one way or another, I bloody well want to keep on doing it!"

Especially now.

He pictured a pipe bomb going off in the middle of the night, blowing the Hubbells' cabin to smithereens with him in it. Then he pictured himself in the Time Window, an old man, his arm around a girl in a blue dress, and calmed down. Whatever happened he wasn't going to die anytime soon, a victim of Collaboration Zero.

"—your business," Marian was saying. "But I'm going to find out who they are if I can, and what they're really up to."

They could see Louisville in the distance now. "How do you figure on doing that?"

She shrugged. "Search me. I don't know yet, but I've got a few ideas."

Denny snorted. "And you think working for the Hefn is too dangerous!" But an idea was forming in his mind as it struggled to process Marian's hypothesis. "These Collaboration Zero guys, you know, they could be just what they look like. A terrorist gang. But even if it's not what *they* have in mind . . . mightn't it be possible to cripple the Hefn without putting everybody at risk of mindwipe, by giving people a pretext to quit working for them? I mean, we don't have to *help* the bastards take us out! You're for sure dead right about what it would do for our self-respect, too, to stop cringing and groveling in the pathetic hope that the Baby Ban will be lifted someday."

"Exactly. A kick in the butt. Something to shock us into realizing that even if we can't do anything about the Baby Ban, we've still got options." She glanced over at him. "If I find out, want me to get in touch?"

"Yeah, I do, sure."

"Where?"

"Hurt Hollow." I'll sort out the contradictions later, he thought. Somehow, I belong on both sides of this fence.

She made a wry face. "Okay, if Hurt Hollow hasn't exploded, bears and all, by the time I get back to you."

"And if nobody's put a contract out on you."

They grinned at each other, excited and stirred by new possibilities. The chopper was losing altitude now, homing in on the city. "Of course, the Gafr could still obliterate us," Marian said. "Or just leave, and come back in fifty years."

Denny thought of the baby Hefn in Rosetta's den. "They won't do either of those things," he said with certainty. "It's too late to deal with us like that." A watery Sun had come out. As Denny twisted and craned to watch the chopper's shadow skim the river, an object in a sling behind the pilot's seat caught in his eye. "Whoa—is that a diskorder back there?"

"Yep. Standard equipment on Fish and Wildlife helicopters."

"Is it loaded?"

"Supposed to be. Why?"

"Listen," said Denny, "this being your last day and all, how about taking a little detour, while everybody's focused on California and DC, and flying me out to my farm?"

Marian frowned. "What for? If Humphrey or Innisfrey find out, we're buzzard meat."

"Something I really need to do, in case I ever join the Resistance. No kidding, it's really important."

"What could be that important?" But her hands moved on the controls and the chopper tilted and started to climb to the left.

"Or start the Resistance," he said, "the real one."

calling your name

HOWARD WALDROP

Here's a wry and compassionate look at the proposition that sometimes it's the little things that count—and when they *do*, they count
for a whole hell of a lot.

Howard Waldrop is widely considered to be one of the best short
story writers in the business, and his famous story "The Ugly Chickens" won both the Nebula and the World Fantasy Awards in 1981. His
work has been gathered in the collections: *Howard Who?*, *All About
Strange Monsters of The Recent Past: Neat Stories by Howard Waldrop*, *Night of the Cooters: More Neat Stories by Howard Waldrop*,
and *Going Home Again*. Waldrop is also the author of the novel *The
Texas-Israeli War: 1999*, in collaboration with Jake Saunders, and of
two solo novels, *Them Bones* and *A Dozen Tough Jobs*. He is at work
on a new novel, tentatively entitled *The Moon World*. His most recent
books are the print version of his collection *Dream Factories and
Radio Pictures* (formerly available only in downloadable form
online), the chapbook *A Better World's in Birth!*, and a collection of
his stories written in collaboration with various other authors, *Custer's
Last Jump and Other Collaborations*. His stories have appeared in our
First, Third, Fourth, Fifth, Sixth, Twelfth, Fifteenth, Sixteenth, and
Twentieth Annual Collections. Having lived in the state of Washington for a number of years, Waldrop recently moved back to his former
hometown of Austin, Texas, something which caused celebrations
and loud hurrahs to rise up from the rest of the population. Upcoming is the collection *Heart of Whitenesse* and a novel called *The
Search for Tom Purdue*.

All my life I've waited
for someone to ease the pain
All my life I've waited
for someone to take the blame
— *from "Calling Your Name" by Janis Ian*

I reached for the switch on the band saw.

Then I woke up with a crowd forming around me.
   And I was in my own backyard.

It turns out that my next door neighbor had seen me fall out of the storage building I use as a workshop and had called 911 when I didn't get up after a few seconds.

Once, long ago in college, working in Little Theater, I'd had a light bridge lowered to set the fresnels for *Blithe Spirit*, just after the Christmas semester break. Some idiot had left a hot male 220 plug loose, and as I reached up to the iron bridge, it dropped against the bar. I'd felt that, all over, and I jumped backward about fifteen feet.

   A crowd started for me, but I let out some truly blazing oath that turned the whole stage violet-indigo blue and they disappeared in a hurry. Then I yelled at the guys and girl in the technical booth to kill everything onstage, and spent the next hour making sure nothing else wasn't where it shouldn't be. . . .

   That's while I was working thirty-six hours a week at a printing plant, going to college full-time and working in the theater another sixty hours a week for no pay. I was also dating a foul-mouthed young woman named Susan who was brighter than me. Eventually something had to give—it was my stomach (an ulcer at twenty) and my relationship with her.

   She came back into the theater later that day, and heard about the incident and walked up to me and said, "Are you happy to see me, or is that a hot male 220 volt plug in your pocket?"

   That shock, the 220, had felt like someone shaking my hand at 2700 rpm while wearing a spiked glove and someone behind me was hammering nails in my head and meanwhile they were piling safes on me. . . .

When I'd touched the puny 110 band saw, I felt nothing.

Then there were neighbors and two EMS people leaning over me upside down.

"What's up, Doc?" I asked.

"How many fingers?" he asked, moving his hand, changing it in a slow blur.

"Three, five, two."

"What's today?"

"You mean Tuesday, or May 6th?"

I sat up.

"Easy," said the lady EMS person. "You'll probably have a headache."

The guy pushed me back down slowly. "What happened?"

"I turned on the band saw. Then I'm looking at you."

He got up, went to the corner of the shed and turned off the breakers. By then the sirens had stopped, and two or three firefighters and the lieutenant had come in the yard.

"You okay, Pops?" he asked.

"I think so," I said. I turned to the crowd. "Thanks to whoever called these guys." Then the EMS people asked me some medical stuff, and the lieutenant, after looking at the breakers, went in the shed and fiddled around. He came out.

"You got a shorted switch," he said. "Better replace it."

I thanked Ms. Krelboind, the neighbor lady, everybody went away, and I went inside to finish my cup of coffee.

My daughter Maureen pulled up as I drank the last of the milk skim off the top of the coffee.

She ran in.

"Are you all right, Dad?"

"Evidently," I said.

Her husband Bob was a fireman. He usually worked over at Firehouse #2, the one on the other side of town. He'd heard the address the EMS had been called to on the squawk box, and had called her.

"What happened?"

"Short in the saw," I said. "The lieutenant said so, officially."

"I mean," she repeated, "are you sure you're all right?"

"It was like a little vacation," I said. "I needed one."

She called her husband, and I made more coffee, and we got to talking about her kids—Vera, Chuck and Dave, or whichever ones are hers—I can't keep up. There's two daughters, Maureen and Celine, and five grandkids. Sorting them all out was my late wife's job. She's only been gone a year and a month and three days.

We got off onto colleges, even though it would be some years before any of the grandkids needed one. The usual party schools came up. "I can see them at Sam Houston State in togas," I said.

"I'm *just real sure* toga parties will come back," said Mo.

Then I mentioned Kent State.

"Kent State? Nothing ever happens there," she said.

"Yeah, right," I said, "like the nothing that happened after Nixon invaded Cambodia. All the campuses in America shut down. They sent the Guard in. They shot four people down, just like they were at a carnival."

She looked at me.

"Nixon? What did Nixon have to do with anything?"

"Well, he *was* the president. He wanted 'no wider war.' Then he sent the Army into Cambodia and Laos. It was before your time."

"Daddy," she said, "I don't remember *much* American history. But Nixon was never president. I think he was vice president under one of those old guys—was it Eisenhower? Then he tried to be a senator. Then he wanted to be president, but someone whipped his ass at the convention. Where in that was he *ever* president? I know Eisenhower didn't die in office."

"What the hell are you talking about?"

"You stay right here," she said, and went to the living room. I heard her banging around in the bookcase. She came back with Vol 14 of the set of 1980s encyclopedias I'd bought for $20 down and $20 a month, seems like paying for about fifteen years on them. . . . She had her thumb in it, holding a place. She opened it on the washing machine lid. "Read."

The entry was on Nixon, Richard Milhous, and it was shorter than it should have been. There was the HUAC and Hiss stuff, the Checkers speech, the vice presidency and reelection, the Kennedy-Nixon debates, the loss, the Senate attempt, the "won't have Dick Nixon to kick around anymore" speech, the law firm, the oil company stuff, the death from phlebitis in 1977—

"Where the hell did you get this? It's *all wrong*."

"It's yours, Dad. It's your encyclopedia. You've had them twenty years. You bought them for us to do homework out of. Remember?"

I went to the living room. There was a hole in the set at Vol 14. I put it back in. Then I took out Vol 24 UV and looked up Vietnam, War in. There was WWII, 1939–1945, then French Colonial War 1945–1954, then America in 1954–1970. Then I took down Vol II and read about John F. Kennedy (president, 1961–1969).

"Are you better now, Daddy?" she asked.

"No. I haven't finished reading a bunch of lies yet, I've just begun."

"I'm sorry. I know the shock hurt. And things haven't been good since Mom . . . But this really isn't like you."

"I know what happened in the Sixties! I was there! Where were you?"

"Okay, okay. Let's drop it. I've got to get back home; the kids are out of school soon."

"All right," I said. "It was a shock—not a nasty one, not my first, but maybe if I'm careful, my last."

"I'll send Bill over tomorrow on his day off and he can help you fix the saw. You know how he likes to futz with machinery."

"For gods sakes, Mo, it's a bad switch. It'll take two minutes to replace it. It ain't rocket science!"

She hugged me, went out to her car and drove off.

Strange that she should have called her husband Bob, Bill.

No wonder the kids struggled at school. Those encyclopedias sucked. I hope the whole staff got fired and went to prison.

I went down to the library where they had *Britannicas, World Books,* old *Compton's.* Everybody else in the place was on, or waiting in line for, the Internet.

I sat down by the reference shelves and opened four or five encyclopedias to the entries on Nixon. All of them started Nixon, Richard Milhous, and then in brackets (1913–1977).

After the fifth one, I got up and went over to the reference librarian, who'd just unjammed one of the printers. She looked up at me and smiled, and as I said it, I knew I should not have, but I said, "All your encyclopedias are wrong."

The smile stayed on her face.

And then I thought *Here's a guy standing in front of her; he's in his fifties; he looks a little peaked, and he's telling her all her reference books are wrong. Just like I once heard a guy, in his fifties, a little peaked, yelling at a librarian that some book in the place was trying to tell him that Jesus had been a Jew!*

What would *you* do?

Before she could do anything, I said, "Excuse me."

"Certainly," she said.

I left in a hurry.

My son-in-law came over the next morning when he should have been asleep.

He looked a little different (His ears were longer. It took a little while to notice that was it.) and he seemed a little older, but he looked pretty much the same as always.

"Hey. Mo sent me over to do the major overhaul on the band saw."

"Fuck it," I said. "It's the switch. I can do it in my sleep."

"She said she'd feel better if you let me do it."

"Buzz off."

He laughed and grabbed one of the beers he keeps in my refrigerator. "Okay, then," he said, "can I borrow a couple of albums to tape? I want the kids to hear what real music sounds like."

He had a pretty good selection of 45s, albums, and CDs, even some shellac 78s. He's got a couple of old turntables (one that plays 16 rpm, even). But I have some stuff on vinyl he doesn't.

"Help yourself," I said. He went to the living room and started making noises opening cabinets.

I mentioned The Who.

"Who?"

"Not who. The Who."

"What do you mean, who?"

"Who. The rock group. *The* Who."

"Who?"

"No, no. The rock group, which is named The Who."

"What is this," he asked. "Abbott and Hardy?"

"We'll get to that later," I said. "Same time as the early Beatles. That . . ."

"Who?"

"Let me start over. Roger Daltry. Pete Townsend. John Entwistle. Keith—"

"The High Numbers!" he said. "Why didn't you say so?"

"A minute ago. I said they came along with the early Beatles and you said—"

"Who?"

"Do *not* start."

"There is no rock band called the Beetles," he said with authority.

I looked at him. "Paul McCartney . . ."

He cocked his head, gave me a go-on gesture.

". . . John Lennon, George Harri . . ."

"You mean the Quarrymen?" he asked.

". . . son, Ringo Starr."

"You mean Pete Best and Stuart Sutcliffe," he said.

"Sir Richard Starkey. Ringo Starr. From all the rings on his fingers."

"The Quarrymen. Five guys. They had a few hits in the early Sixties. Wrote a shitpot of songs for other people. Broke up in 1966. Boring old farts since then—tried comeback albums, no back to come to. Lennon lives in a trailer in New Jersey. God knows where the rest of them are."

"Lennon's dead," I said. "He was assassinated at the Dakota Apartments in NYC in 1980 by a guy who wanted to impress Jodie Foster."

"Well, then, CNTV's got it all wrong, because they did a where-are-they-now thing a couple of weeks ago, and he looked pretty alive to me. He talked a few minutes and showed them some Holsteins or various other moo-cows, and a reporter made fun of them, and Lennon went back into the trailer and closed the door."

I knew they watched a lot of TV at the firehouse.

"This week they did one on ex-President Kennedy. It was his eighty-fourth birthday or something. He's the one that looked near-dead to me—they said he's had Parkinson's since the Sixties. They only had one candle on the cake, but I bet like Popeye these days, he had to eat three cans of spinach just to blow it out. His two brothers took turns reading a proclamation from President Gore. It looked like he didn't know who *that* was. His mom had to help him cut the cake. Then his wife Marilyn kissed him. He seemed to like *that*."

I sat there quietly a few minutes.

"In your family," I asked, "who's Bill?"

He quit thumbing through the albums. He took in his breath a little too loudly. He looked at me.

"Edward," he said, "*I'm* Bill."

"Then who's Bob?"

"Bob was what they called my younger brother. He lived two days. He's out at Kid Heaven in Greenwood. You, me, and Mo went out there last Easter. Remember?"

"Uh, yeah," I said.

"Are you sure you're okay, after the shock, I mean?"

"Fit as a fiddle," I said, lying through my teeth.

"You sure you don't need help with the saw?"

"It'll be a snap."

"Well, be careful."

"The breakers are still off."

"Thanks for the beer," he said, putting a couple of albums under his arm and going toward the door.

"Bye. Go get some sleep." I said.

I'll have to remember to call Bob, Bill.

Mo was back, in a hurry.

"What is it, Dad? I've never seen Bill so upset."

"I don't know. Things are just so mixed up. In fact, they're wrong."

"What do you mean, wrong? I'm really worried about you now, and so's Bill."

I've never been a whiner, even in the worst of times.

"Oh, Dad," she said. "Maybe you should go see Doc Adams, maybe get some tests done. See if he can't recommend someone . . ."

"You mean, like I've got Alzheimer's? I don't have Alzheimer's! It's not me, it's the world that's off the trolley. Yesterday—I don't know, it's like everything I thought I knew is wrong. It's like some Mohorovic discontinuity of the mind. Nixon was president. He had to resign because of a break-in at the Watergate Hotel, the Democratic National Headquarters, in 1972. I have a bumper sticker somewhere: "Behind Every Watergate Is A Milhous." It was the same bunch of guys who set up Kennedy in 1963. It was . . ."

I started to cry. Maureen didn't know whether to come to me or not.

"Are you thinking about Mom?" she asked.

"Yes," I said. "Yes, I'm thinking about your mother."

Then she hugged me.

I don't know what to say.

I'm a bright enough guy. I'm beginning to understand, though, about how people get bewildered.

On my way from the library after embarrassing myself, I passed the comic book and poster shop two blocks away. There were reproduction posters in one window; the famous one of Clark Gable and Paulette Goddard with the flames of Atlanta behind them from *Mules in Horses' Harnesses*; Fred MacMurray and Jack Oakie in *The Road To Morroco*, and window cards from James Dean in *Somebody Up There Likes Me*, along with *Giant* and *East of Eden*.

I came home and turned on the oldies station. It wasn't there, one like it was somewhere else on the dial.

It was just like Bo—Bill said. The first thing I heard was The Quarrymen doing "*Gimme Deine Hande.*" I sat there for two hours, till it got dark, without turning on the lights, listening. There were familiar tunes by somebody else, called something else. There were the right songs by the right people. Janis I. Fink seemed to be in heavy rotation, three songs in the two hours, both before and after she went to prison, according to the DJ. The things you find out on an oldies station . . .

I heard no Chuck Berry, almost an impossibility.

Well, I will try to live here. I'll just have to be careful finding my way around in it. Tomorrow, after the visit to the doc, it's back to the library.

Before going to bed, I rummaged around in my "Important Papers" file. I took out my old draft notice.

It wasn't from Richard Nixon, like it has been for the last thirty-two years. It was from Barry Goldwater. (Au + H_2O = 1968?)

The psychiatrist seemed like a nice-enough guy. We talked a few minutes about the medical stuff Doc Adams had sent over; work, the shock, what Mo had told the doc.

"Your daughter seems to think you're upset about your environment. Can you tell me why she thinks that?"

"I think she means to say I told her this was not the world I was born in and have lived in for fifty-six years," I said.

He didn't write anything down in his pad.

"It's all different," I said. He nodded.

"Since the other morning, everything I've known all my life doesn't add up. The wrong people have been elected to office. History is different. Not just the politics-battles-wars stuff, but also social history, culture. There's a book of social history by a guy named Furnas. I haven't looked, but I bet that's all different, too. I'll get it out of the library today. If it's there. If there's a guy named Furnas anymore."

I told him some of the things that were changed—just in two days' worth. I told him it—some of it anyway—was fascinating, but I'm sure I'll find scary stuff sooner or later. I'd have to learn to live with it, go with the flow.

"What do you think happened?" he asked.

"What is this, *The Sopranos*?"

"Beg pardon?" he asked.

"Oh. *Oh.* You'd like it. It's a TV show about a Mafia guy who, among other things, goes to a shrink—a lady shrink. It's on HBO."

"HBO?"

"*Sorry.* A cable network."

He wrote three things down on his pad.

"Look. Where I come from . . . I know that sounds weird. In Lindner's book . . ."

"Lindner?"

"Lindner. *The Fifty-Minute Hour.* Best-seller. 1950s."

"I take it by the title it was about psychiatry. *And* a best-seller?"

"*Let me start over.* He wrote the book they took the title *Rebel Without A Cause* from—but *that* had nothing to do with the movie . . ."

He was writing stuff down now, fast.

"It's getting deeper and deeper, isn't it?" I asked.

"Go on. *Please.*"

"Lindner had a patient who was a guy who thought he lived on a far planet in an advanced civilization—star-spanning galaxy-wide stuff. Twenty years before *Star Wars*. Anyway . . ."

He wrote down two words without taking his eyes off me.

"In my world," I said, very slowly and carefully, looking directly at him, "there was a movie called *Star Wars* in 1977 that changed the way business was done in Hollywood."

"Okay," he said.

"This is not getting us anywhere!" I said.

And then he came out with the most heartening thing I'd heard in two days. He said, "What do you mean *we, kemo sabe?*"

Well, we laughed and laughed, and then I tried to tell him, *really* tell him, what I thought I knew.

The past was another country, as they say; they did things differently there.

The more I looked up, the more I needed to look up. I had twelve or fifteen books scattered across the reference tables.

Now I know how conspiracy theorists feel. It's not just the Trilateral Commission or Henry Kissinger (a minor ABC/NRC official *here*) and the Queen of England and Area 51 and the Grays. It's like history has ganged up on me, as an individual, to drive me bugfuck. I don't have a chance. The more you find out the more you need to explain . . . how much more you need to find out . . . it could never end.

Where did it change?

We are trapped in history like insects in amber, and it is hardening all around me.

Who am I to struggle against the tree sap of Time?

The psychiatrist has asked me to write down and bring in everything I can think of—anything: presidents, cars, wars, culture. He wants to read it ahead of time and schedule two full hours on Friday.

You can bet I don't feel swell about this.

My other daughter Celine is here. I had *tried* and *tried* and *tried*, but she'd turned out to be a Christian in spite of *all* my work.

She is watching me like a hawk, I can tell. We were never as close as Maureen and me; she was her mother's daughter.

"How are you feeling?"

"Just peachy," I said. "Considering."

"Considering *what?*" Her eyes were very green, like her mother's had been.

"If you don't mind, I'm pretty tired of answering questions. *Or* asking them."

"You ought to be more careful with those tools."

"This is not about power tools, or the shock," I said. "I don't know what Mo told you, but I have been *truly* discomfited these last few days."

"Look, Daddy," she said. "I don't care what the trouble is, we'll find a way to get you through it."

"You couldn't get me through it, unless you've got a couple of thousand years on rewind."

"What?"

"Never mind. I'm just tired. And I have to go to the hardware store and get a new switch for the band saw, before I burn the place down, or cause World War III or something. I'm *sure* they have hardware stores here, or *I* wouldn't have power tools."

She looked at me like I'd grown tentacles.

"Just kidding," I said. "Loosen up, Celine. Think of me right now as your old, tired father. I'll learn my way around the place and be right as rain . . ."

Absolutely no response.

"I'm being ironic," I said. "I have always been noted for my sense of humor. Remember?"

"Well, yes. Sort of."

"Great!" I said. "Let's go get some burgers at McDonald's!"

"Where?"

"I mean Burger King," I said. I'd passed one on the way back from the library.

"Sounds good, Dad." She said, "Let *me* drive."

I have lived in this house for twenty-six years. I was born in the house across the street. In 1957, my friend Gino Ballantoni lived here, and I was over here every day, or just about, for four years, till Gino's father's aircraft job moved to California. I'd always wanted it, and after I got out of the Army, I got it on the GI Bill.

I know its every pop and groan, every sound it makes day or night, the feel of the one place the paint isn't smooth, on the inside doorjamb trim of what used to be Mo's room before it was Celine's. There's one light switch put on upside down I never changed. The garage makeover I did myself; it's what's now the living room.

I love this place. I would have lived here no matter what.

I tell myself history wasn't different enough that this house isn't still a vacant lot, *or* an apartment building. That's, at least, something to hang onto.

I noticed the extra sticker inside the car windshield. Evidently, we now have an emissions-control test in this state, too. I'll have to look in the phone book and find out where to go, as this one expires at the end of the month.

And also, on TV, when they show news from New York, there's still the two World Trade Center Towers.

You can't be *too* careful about the past.

The psychiatrist called to ask if someone could sit in on the double session tomorrow—he knew it was early, but it was special—his old mentor from whatever Mater he'd Alma'd at; the guy was in a day early for some shrink hoedown in the Big City and wanted to watch his star pupil in action. He was asking all the patients tomorrow, he said. The old doc wouldn't say anything, and you'd hardly know he was there.

"Well, I got enough troubles, what's one more?"

He thanked me.

That's what did it for me. This was not going to stop. This was not something that I could be helped to work through, like bedwetting or agoraphobia or the desire to eat human flesh. It was going to go on forever, here, until I died.

Okay, I thought. Let's get out Occam's Famous Razor and cut a few Gordian Knots. Or somewhat, as the logicians used to say.

I went out to the workshop where everybody thinks it all started.

I turned on the outside breakers. I went inside. This time I closed the door. I went over and turned on the bandsa

After I got up off the floor, I opened the door and stepped out into the yard. It was near dark, so I must have been out an hour or so.

I turned off the breakers and went into the house through the back door and through the utility room and down the hall to the living room bookcase. I pulled out Vol 14 of the encyclopedia and opened it.

Nixon, Richard Milhous, it said (1913–1994). A good long entry.

There was a sound from the kitchen. The oven door opened and closed.

"What have you been doing?" asked a voice.

"There's a short in the band saw I'll have to get fixed," I said. I went around the corner.

It was my wife Susan. She looked a little older, a little heavier since I last saw her, it seemed. She still looked pretty good.

"Stand there where I can see you," I said.

"We were having a fight before you wandered away, remember?"

"Whatever it was," I said, "I was wrong. You were right. We'll do whatever it is you want."

"Do you even remember what it was we were arguing about?"

"No," I said. "Whatever. It's not important. The problems of two people don't amount to a hill of beans in—"

"Cut the Casablanca crap," said Susan. "Jodie and Susie Q want to bring the kids over next Saturday and have Little Eddy's birthday party here. You wanted peace and quiet here, and go somewhere else for the party. That was the argument."

"I wasn't cut out to be a grandpa," I said. "But bring 'em on. Invite the neighbors! Put out signs on the street! 'Annoy an old man here!'"

Then I quieted down. "Tell them we'd be happy to have the party here," I said.

"Honestly, Edward," said Susan, putting the casserole on the big trivet. It was *her* night to cook. "Sometimes I think you'd forget your ass if it weren't glued on."

"Yeah, sure," I said. "I've damn sure forgotten what peace and quiet was like. And probably lots of other stuff, too."

"Supper's ready," said Susan.

june sixteenth at anna's

kristine kathryn rusch

Kristine Kathryn Rusch started out the decade of the 90s as one of the fastest-rising and most prolific young authors on the scene, took a few years out in mid-decade for a very successful turn as editor of *The Magazine of Fantasy and Science Fiction*, and, since stepping down from that position, has returned to her old standards of production here in the twenty-first century, publishing a slew of novels in four genres, writing fantasy, mystery, and romance novels under various pseudonyms as well as science fiction. She has published almost twenty novels under her own name, including *The White Mists of Power*, the four-volume *Fey* series, the *Black Throne* series, *Alien Influences*, and several *Star Wars* books written with husband Dean Wesley Smith. Her most recent books (as Rusch, anyway) are the novels *The Disappeared*, *Extremes*, and *Fantasy Life*. In 1999, she won Readers Award polls from the readerships of both *Asimov's Science Fiction* and *Ellery Queen's Mystery Magazine*, an unprecedented double honor! As an editor, she was honored with the Hugo Award for her work on *The Magazine of Fantasy and Science Fiction*, and shared the World Fantasy Award with Dean Wesley Smith for her work as editor of the original hardcover anthology version of *Pulphouse*. As a writer, she has won the Herodotus Award for Best Historical Mystery (for *A Dangerous Road*, written as Kris Nelscott) and the Romantic Times Reviewer's Choice Award (for *Utterly Charming*, written as Kristine Grayson); as Kristine Kathryn Rusch, she has won the John W. Campbell Award, been a finalist for the Arthur C. Clarke Award, and took home a Hugo Award in 2000 for her story "Millennium Babies," making her one of the few people in genre history to win Hugos for both editing *and* writing.

In the haunting and poignant story that follows, she shows us that just because things are *past*, that doesn't mean that they lose any of their hold on the *present* . . .

June Sixteenth at Anna's. To a conversation connoisseur, those words evoke the most pivotal afternoon in early twenty-first century historical entertainment. No one knows why these conversations have elevated themselves against the thousands of others found and catalogued.

Theories abound. Some speculate that the variety of conversational types makes this one afternoon special. Others believe this performance is the conversational equivalent of early jazz jam sessions—the points and counterpoints have a beauty unrelated to the words. Still others hypothesize that it is the presence of the single empty chair which allows the visitor to join the proceedings without feeling like an intruder. . . .

—*liner notes from* June Sixteenth at Anna's,
special six-hour edition

On the night after his wife's funeral, Mac pulled a chair in front of the special bookcase, the one he'd built for Leta over forty years ago, and flicked on the light attached to the top shelf. Two copies of every edition ever produced of *June Sixteenth at Anna's*—one opened and one permanently in its wrapper—winked back at him as if they shared a joke.

Scattered between them, copies of the books, the e-jackets, the DVDs, the out-dated Palms, all carrying analysis, all holding maybe a mention of Leta and what she once called the most important day of her life.

A whiff of lilacs, a jangle of gold bracelets, and then a bejeweled hand reached across his line of sight and turned the light off.

"Don't torture yourself, Dad," his daughter Cherie said. She was older than the shelf, her face softening with age, just as her mother's had. With another jangle of bracelets, she clicked on a table lamp, then sat on the couch across from him, a couch she used to flounce into when she was a teenager—which seemed to him, in his current state, just weeks ago. "Mom wouldn't have wanted it."

Mac threaded his fingers together, rested his elbows on his thighs and stared at the floor so that his daughter wouldn't see the flash of anger in his eyes. Leta didn't want anything any more. She was dead, and he was alone, with her memories taunting him from a homemade shelf.

"I'll be all right," he said.

"I'm a little worried to leave you here," Cherie said. "Why don't you come to my place for a few days? I'll fix you dinner, you can sleep in the guest room, have a look at the park. We can talk."

He had talked to Cherie. To Cherie, her soon-to-be second husband, her grown son, all of Leta's sisters and cousins, and friends, Lord knew how many friends they'd had. And reporters. Strange that one woman's death, one woman's relatively insignificant life, had drawn so many reporters.

"I want to sleep in my own bed," he said.

"Fine." Cherie stood as if she hadn't heard him. "We'll get you a cab when it's time to come home. Dad—"

"Cherie." He looked up at her, eyes puffy from her own tears, hair slightly mussed. "I won't stop missing her just because I'm at your place. The mourning doesn't go away once the funeral's over."

Her nose got red, as it always had when someone hit a nerve. "I just thought it might be easier, that's all."

Easier for whom, baby? he wanted to ask, but knew better. "I'll be all right," he said again, and left it at that.

The first time travel breakthroughs came slowly. The breakthroughs built on each other, though, and in the early thirties, scientists predicted that human beings would be visiting their own pasts by the end of the decade.

It turns out these scientists were right, but not in the way they expected. Human beings could not interact with time. They could only open a window into the time-space continuum, and make a record—an expensive record—of past events.

Historians valued the opportunity, but no one else did until Susan Yashimoto combined time recordings with virtual reality technology, and holography, added a few augmentations of her own, and began marketing holocordings.

Her first choices were brilliant. By using a list of historic events voted most likely to be visited should a time machine be invented, she created 'cordings of the birth of Christ, Mohammed's triumphal return to Mecca, the assassination of Abraham Lincoln, and dozens of others.

Soon, other companies entered the fray. Finding their choices limited by copyrights placed on a time period by

worried historians afraid of losing their jobs, these compa-
nies began opening portals into daily life. . . .
—From A History of Conversation
J. Booth Centuri, 2066.
Download Reference Number:
ConverXGC112445 at Library of Congress [loc.org]

Mac had lied to Cherie. He would not sleep in his own bed. The bedroom
was still filled with Leta—the blue and black bedspread they'd compromised
on fifteen years before, the matching but frayed sheets she wanted to die on,
the tiny strands of long gray hairs that—no matter how much he cleaned—still
covered her favorite pillow.

He'd thrown out her treatment bottles, taken the Kleenex off the nightstand, put the old-fashioned hardcover of *Gulliver's Travels* that she would now
never finish on their collectibles bookshelf, but he couldn't get rid of her
scent—faintly musky, slightly apricot, and always, no matter how sick she got,
making him think of youth.

He carried a blanket and pillow to the couch, as he had for the last six
months of Leta's life, pulled down the shade of the large picture window overlooking the George Washington Bridge—the view was the reason he'd taken
the apartment in that first week of the new millennium, when he'd been filled
with hopes and dreams as yet unspoiled.

He wandered toward the small kitchen for a glass of something—water,
beer, he wasn't certain—stopping instead by Leta's shelf and flicking on the
light, a small act of rebellion against his own daughter.

The 'cordings glinted again, like diamonds in a jewelry store window,
tempting, teasing. He'd walked past this shelf a thousand times, laughed at
Leta for her vanity—*sometimes I think you're the only reason the* June Sixteenth
at Anna's *'cordings make any money*, he used to say to her—and derided her for
attaching so much significance to that one day in her past.

*You didn't even think it important until some holographer guy decided it
was*, he'd say, and she'd nod in acknowledgement.

Sometimes, she said to him once, *we don't know what's important until it's
too late*.

He found himself holding the deluxe retrospective edition—six hours
long, with the Latest Updates and Innovations!—the only set of *June Sixteenth
at Anna's* with both copies still in their wrappers. It had arrived days before
Leta died.

He'd carried the package in to her, brought her newest player out, the
one he'd bought her that final Christmas, and placed them both on the edge
of the bed.

"I'll set you up if you want," he'd said.

She had been leaning against nearly a dozen pillows, a cocoon he'd built for her when he realized that nothing would stop her inevitable march to the end. Her eyes were just slightly glazed as she took his hand.

"I've been there before," she said, her voice raspy and nearly gone.

"But not this one," he said. "You don't know the changes they've made. Maybe they have all five senses this time—"

"Mac," she whispered. "This time, I want to stay here with you."

> In New York's second Gilded Age, Anna's was considered the premier spot for conversation. Like the cafes of the French Revolution or Hemingway's Movable Feast, Anna's became a pivotal place to sit, converse, and exchange ideas.
>
> Director Hiram Goldman remembered Anna's. He applied for a time recording permit, and scanned appropriate days, finally settling on June 16, 2001 for its mix of customers, its wide-ranging conversational high points, and the empty chair that rests against a far wall, allowing the viewer to feel a part of the scene before him. . . .
>
> —*liner notes from* June Sixteenth at Anna's,
> *original edition*

Mac had never used a holocording, never saw the need to go back in time, especially to a period he'd already lived through. He'd said so to Leta right from the start, and after she picked up her fifth copy of *June Sixteenth*, she'd stopped asking him to join her.

He always glanced politely at the interviews, nodded at the crowds who gathered at the retrospectives, and never really listened to the speeches or the long, involved discussions of the fans.

Leta collected everything associated with that day, enjoying her minor celebrity, pleased that it had come to her after she had raised Cherie and, Leta would tell him, already had a chance to live a real life.

It was a shame she'd never opened the last 'cording. It was a sign of how ill she had been toward the end. Any other time, she might have read the liner notes—or had the box read them to her—looked at the still holos, and giggled over the inevitable analysis which, she said, was always pretentious and always wrong.

Mac opened the wrapping, felt it crinkle beneath his fingers as he tossed it in the trash. The plastic surface of the case had been engineered to feel like high-end leather. Someone had even added the faint odor of calfskin for verisimilitude.

He opened the case, saw the shiny silver disk on the right side, and all his other choices on the left: analysis at the touch of a finger, in any form he wanted—hard-copy, audio, e-copy (format of his choice), holographic discussion; history of the 'cording; a biography of the participants, including but not limited to what happened to them after June 16, 2001; and half a dozen other things including plug-ins (for an extra charge) that would enhance the experience.

Leta used to spend hours over each piece, reviewing it as if she were going to be quizzed on it, carrying parts of it to him and sharing it with him against his will.

He was no longer certain why he was so against participating. Perhaps because he felt that life moved forward, not backward, and someone else's perspective on the past was as valid as a stranger's opinion of a book no one had ever read.

Or perhaps it was his way of dealing with minor celebrity, being Leta Thayer's husband, having his life scratched and pawed at without ever really being understood.

Mac left the case open on the shelf, next to all the other *June Sixteenth*'s, and stuck his finger through the hole in the center of the silver 'cording, carrying it with him.

The player was still in the hall closet where he'd left it two weeks before. He dragged it out, knocking over one of Leta's boots, still marked by last winter's slush, and felt a wave of such sadness he thought he wouldn't be able to stand upright.

He tried anyway, and thought it a small victory that he succeeded.

Then he carried the player and the 'cording into the bedroom, and placed them on the foot of the bed.

> Two hundred and fifty people crossed the threshold at Anna's that afternoon, and although they were ethnically and culturally diverse, the sample was too small to provide a representative cross-section of the Manhattan population of that period. The restaurant was too obscure to appeal to the famous, too small to attract people from outside the neighborhood, and too new to have cachet. The appeal of *June Sixteenth* is the ordinariness of the patrons, the fact that on June 16, 2001 not one of them is known outside their small circle of friends and family. Their very obscurity raises their conversations to new heights.
>
> —*From* A History of June Sixteenth at Anna's
> Erik Reese, *University of Idaho Press, 2051*

Maybe it was the trace of her still left in the room. Maybe it was a hedge against the loneliness that threatened to overwhelm him. Maybe it was simply his only way to banish those final images—her skin yellowish and so thin that it revealed the bones in her face, the drool on the side of her mouth, and the complete lack of recognition in her eyes.

Whatever the reason, he put the 'cording in the player, sat the requisite distance from the wireless technology—so new and different when he was young, not even remarked on now—and flicked on the machine.

It didn't take him away as he'd expected it to. Instead it surrounded him in words and pictures and names. He didn't know how to jump past the opening credits, so he sat very still and waited for the actual 'cording to begin.

> Because *June Sixteenth at Anna's* is a conversation piece, its packagers never wasted their resources on sensual reconstructions. Sound is present and near perfect. Even the rattle of pans in the kitchen resonates in the dining room. The vision is also perfect—colors rich and lifelike, light and shadow so accurate that if you step into the sunlight you can almost feel the heat.
>
> But almost is the key word here. Except for fundamentals like making certain that solid objects are indeed solid, required of all successful holocordings, *June Sixteenth at Anna's* lacks the essentials of a true historical projection. We cannot smell the garlic, the frying meat, the strawberries that look so fresh and ripe on the table nearest our chair.
>
> Purists claim this is so that we can concentrate on the conversation. But somehow the lack of sensation limits the spoken word. When Rufolio Field lights his illegal cigar three hours into our afternoon and management rebuffs him, we see the offense but do not take it. We are reminded that we are observers—part of the scene, but in no way of the scene.
>
> Once the illusion is shattered, *June Sixteenth at Anna's* is reduced to its component parts. It becomes a flat screen documentary remixed for the holocorders, both lifeless and old-fashioned, when what we long for is the kind of attention to detail given to truly historic moments, like *The Gettysburg Address (Weekend Edition)* or the newly released *Assassination of Archduke Ferdinand.* . . .
>
> —*Review of June Sixteenth at Anna's*, Special Six Hour
> Edition
> *in* The Essential Holographer
> *February 22, 2050*

The restaurant comes into view very slowly. Out of the post-credits darkness, he hears laughter, the gentle flow of voices, the clink of silverware. Then pieces appear—the maître d's station, a simple podium flanked by two small indoor trees, the doorway leading into the restaurant proper, the couple—whom he would have termed elderly in 2001—slipping past him toward a table in the back.

Mac stands in the doorway, feeling a sense of déjà vu that would have been ridiculous if it weren't so accurate. He has been here before. Of course. A hundred times before the restaurant closed in 2021. Only he never saw the early décor—the round bistro tables covered with red checked cloths; the padded sweetheart chairs that didn't look comfortable; the floor-to-ceiling windows on the street level, an indulgence that went away only a few months later, shattered by ash and falling debris.

The restaurant is almost full. A busboy removes a sweetheart chair from the table closest to the window, holding the chair by its wire frame. He carries the chair to the wall closest to Mac, sets it down, and nods at the maître d', who leads a young couple into the dining room.

Mac needs no more than the sway of her long black hair to recognize Leta. His heart leaps, and for a moment he thinks: she isn't dead. She's right here, trapped in a temporal loop, and if he frees her, she'll come home again.

Instead, he sits in the empty chair.

A speaker above him plays Charlie Burnet's "Skyliner," a CD from its poor quality, remastered from the original tapes. Pans rattle in the kitchen, and voices murmur around him, talking about the best place to eat foie gras, the history of graveyards in Manhattan, new ways to celebrate Juneteenth.

He cannot hear Leta. She is all the way across the room from him, several famous conversations away, her hand outstretched as if waiting for him to take it.

He has a good view of her face, illuminated by the thin light filtering through the windows—the canyons of the city blocking any real sun. She is smiling, nodding at something her companion says, her eyes twinkling in that way she had when she thought everything she heard was bullshit but she was too polite to say so.

Mac hadn't known her when she was here—they met in October, during that seemingly endless round of funerals, and he remembered telling her he felt guilty for feeling that spark of attraction, for beginning something new when everything else was ending.

She had put her hand on his, the skin on her palms dry and rough from all the assistance she'd been giving friends: dishes, packing, childcare. Her eyes had had shadows so deep he could barely see their shape. It wasn't until their second date that he realized her eyes had a slightly almond cast, and they were an impossible shade of blue.

There are no shadows under her eyes here, in Anna's. Leta is smiling, looking incredibly young. Mac never knew her this young, this carefree. Her skin has no lines, and that single white strand that appeared above her right temple—the one she'd plucked on their first date and looked at in horror—isn't visible at all.

She wears a white summer dress that accents her sun-darkened skin, and as she talks, she takes a white sweater from the suitcase she used to call a purse. He recognizes the shudder, the gestures, as she puts the sweater over her shoulders.

She is clearly complaining about the cold, about air conditioning he cannot feel. The air here is the same as the air in his bedroom, a little too warm. So much is missing, things his memory is supplying—the garlic and wine scent of Anna's, the mixture of perfumes that always seemed to linger in front of the door. He isn't hungry, and he should be. He always got hungry after a few moments in here, the rich fragrances of spiced pork in red sauce and beef sautéed in garlic and wine—Anna's specialties—making him wish that the restaurant hurried its service instead of priding itself on its European pace.

But Anna's had been a favorite of Leta's long before Mac ate there. She had been the one who showed it to him, at the grand re-opening that December, filled with survivors and firefighters and local heroes, all trying to celebrate a Christmas that had more melancholy than joy.

Six months away for this Leta. Six months and an entire lifetime away.

A waiter walks past with a full tray—polenta with a mushroom sauce, several side dishes of pasta, and breadsticks so warm their steam floats past Mac. He cannot smell them, although he wants to. He reaches for one and his fingers find bread so hard and crusty it feels stale. He cannot pull the breadstick off, of course. This is a construct, a group memory—the solidity added to make the scene feel real.

He's not confined to the chair—he knows that much about 'cordings. He can walk from table to table, listen to each conversation, maybe even go into the kitchen, depending on how deluxe this edition is.

He is not tempted to move around. He wants to stay here, where he can see the young woman who would someday become his wife flirting with a man whom she decides, one week later, to never see again after he gives her the only black eye she will ever have.

One of the many stories, she used to say, that never made it into the analysis.

Leta tucks a strand of hair behind her ear, laughs, sips some white wine. Mac watches her, enthralled. There is a carefreeness to her he has never seen before, a lightness that had vanished by the time he met her.

He isn't sure he would be interested in this Leta. She has beauty and style, but the substance, the caring that so touched him the day of his uncle's funeral, isn't present at all.

Maybe the substance is in the conversation. The famous conversation. After a moment's hesitation, he decides to listen after all.

> June Sixteenth at Anna's has often been compared with jazz—the lively, free-flowing jazz of the 1950s and 60s, recorded on vinyl with all the scratches and nicks, recorded live so that each cough and smattering of early applause adds to the sense of a past so close that it's almost tangible.
>
> Yet June Sixteenth at Anna's has more than that. It has community, a feeling that all the observer has to do is pull his chair to the closest table, and he will belong.
>
> Perhaps it is the setting—very few holocordings take place in restaurants because of the ambient noise—or perhaps it is the palpable sense of enjoyment, the feeling that everyone in the room participates fully in their lives, leaving no moment unobserved. . . .
>
> —"The Longevity of June Sixteenth at Anna's,"
> by Michael Meller, first given as a speech
> at the June Sixteenth Retrospective held
> at the Museum of Conversational Arts
> June 16, 2076

The cheap CD is playing "Sentimental Journey," Doris Day's melancholy voice at odds with the laughter in this well-lit place. Mac walks past table after table, bumping one. The water glasses do not shake, the table doesn't even move, and although he reflexively apologizes, no one hears him.

He feels like a ghost in a room full of strangers.

The conversations float around him, intense, serious, sincere. He's not sure what makes these discussions famous. Is it the unintentional irony of incorrect predictions, like the group of businessmen discussing October's annual stock market decline? Or the poignancy of plans that would never come about, lives with less than three months left, all the obvious changes ahead?

He does not know. The conversations don't seem special to him. They seem like regular discussions, the kind people still have in restaurants all over the city. Perhaps that's the appeal, the link that sends the conversation collector from the present to the past.

His link still sits at her table, flipping her hair off her shoulder with a casual gesture. As he gets closer, he can almost smell her perfume. Right about now she should acknowledge him, that small turn in his direction, the slight raise of her eyebrows, the secret smile that they'd shared from the first instant they'd met.

But she doesn't turn. She doesn't see him. Instead, she's discussing the importance of heroes with a man who has no idea what heroism truly is.

Her fingers tap nervously against the table, a sign—a week before she throws Frank Dannen out of her life—that she doesn't like him at all. It always took time for Leta's brain to acknowledge her emotions. Too bad she hadn't realized before he hit her that Frank wasn't the man for her.

Mac stops next to the table, glances once at Frank. This is the first time Mac has seen the man outside of photographs. Curly black hair, a strong jaw, the thick neck of a former football player which, of course, he was. Frank died long before the first *June Sixteenth at Anna's* appeared, in a bar fight fifteen years after this meal.

Mac remembers because Leta showed him the story in the *Daily News*, and said with no pity in her voice, *I always knew he would come to a bad end.*

But here, in this timeless place, Frank is alive and handsome in a way that glosses over the details: the way his lower lip sets in a hard line, the bruised knuckles on his right hand, which he keeps carefully hidden from Leta, the two bottles of beer that have disappeared in the short forty-five minutes they've been at the table. Frank is barely listening to Leta; instead he checks out the other women in the room, short glances that are imperceptible to anyone who isn't paying attention.

Mac is, but he has wasted enough time on this man. Instead Mac stares at the woman who would become his wife. She stops speaking mid-thought, and leans back in her chair. Mac smiles, recognizing this ploy.

He can predict her next words: *Do you want me to continue talking to myself or would you prefer the radio for background noise?*

But she says nothing, merely watches Frank with a quizzical expression on her face, one that looks—to someone who doesn't know her—like affection, but is really a test to see when Frank will notice that she's done.

He doesn't, at least not while Mac is watching. Leta sighs, picks at the green salad before her, then glances out the window. Mac glances too, but sees nothing. Whoever recorded this scene, whoever touched it up, hadn't bothered with the outdoors, only with the restaurant and the small dramas occurring inside it.

Dramas whose endings were already known.

Because he can't help himself, Mac touches her shoulder. The flesh is warm and soft to the touch, but it is not Leta's flesh. It feels like someone else's. Leta's skin had a satiny quality that remained with her during her whole life. First, the expense of new satin, and later, the comforting patina of old satin, showing how much it was loved.

She does not look at him, and he pulls his hand away. Leta always looked at him when he touched her, always acknowledged their connection, their bond—sometimes with annoyance, when she was too busy to focus on it, yet always with love.

This isn't his Leta. This is a mannequin in a wax works, animated to go through its small part for someone else's amusement.

Mac can't take any more. He stands up, says, "Voice command: stop."

And the restaurant fades to blackness a piece at a time—the tables and patrons first, then the ambient noise, and finally the voices, fading, fading, until their words are nothing but a memory of whispers in the dark.

> June Sixteenth at Anna's should not be a famous conversation piece. The fact that it is says more about our generation's search for meaning than it does about June 16, 2001.
>
> We believe that our grandparents lived fuller lives because they endured so much more. Yet all that June Sixteenth at Anna's shows us is that each life is filled with countless moments, memorable and unmemorable—and the only meaning that these moments have are the meanings with which we imbue them at various points in our lives.
>
> —From June Sixteenth at Anna's Revisited,
> Mia Oppel, Harvard University Press, 2071.

Mac ended up standing beside the bed, only a foot from the player. The 'cording whirred as it wound down, the sound aggressive, as if resenting being shut off mid-program, before all the conversations had been played.

The scent of Leta lingered, and Mac realized that it had been the only real thing in his entire trip. The scent and the temperature of his bedroom had accompanied him into Anna's, bringing even more of the present into his glimpse of the past.

He took the 'cording out of the player, and carried it to the living room, placing the silver disk in its expensive case. Then he returned to the bedroom, put the player away, and lay down on the bed for the first time since Leta had left it, almost a week ago.

If he closed his eyes, he could imagine her warmth, the way he used to roll into it mornings after she had gotten up. It was like being cradled in her arms, and often he would fall back to sleep until she would wake him in exasperation, reminding him that he had a job just like everyone else on the planet and it was time he went off to do it.

But the bed wasn't really warm, and if he fell asleep, she wasn't going to wake him, not now, not ever. The 'cording had left him feeling hollow, almost as if he'd done something dirty, forbidden, seeking out his wife where he knew she couldn't have been.

He had no idea why she watched all of the June Sixteenths. Read the commentary, yes, he understood that. And he understood the interviews, the way she accepted a fan's fawning over something she never got paid for, never even got acknowledged for. Some of the *June Sixteenth* participants sued for their percentage of the profits—and lost, since 'cordings were as much about packaging as the historical moment—but Leta had never joined them.

Instead, she went back to that single day in her life over and over again, watching her younger self from the outside, seeing—what? Looking for—what?

It certainly wasn't Frank. Mac knew her well enough for that. Had she been looking for a kind of perspective on herself, on her life? Or trying to figure out, perhaps, what her world would have been like if she had made different choices, tried other things?

He didn't know. And now, he would never know. He had teased her, listened to her talk about the ancillary materials, even bought her the latest copies of *June Sixteenth*, but he had never once heard her speak about the experience of walking around as an outsider in her own past.

A mystery of Leta—like all the other mysteries of Leta, including but not limited to why she had loved him—would remain forever unsolved.

He couldn't find the answers in *June Sixteenth*, just as he couldn't find Leta there. All that remained of Leta were bits and pieces—a scent, slowly fading; a voice, half remembered; the brush of her skin against his own.

Leta's life had an ending now, her existence as finite as *June Sixteenth at Anna's*, her essence as impossible to reproduce.

Mac hugged her favorite pillow to himself. Leta would never reappear again—not whole, breathing, surprising him with her depth.

The realization had finally come home to him, and settled in his heart: She was gone, and all he had left of her were her ghosts.

THe Green Leopard plaGue

WALTER JON WILLIAMS

Walter Jon Williams was born in Minnesota and now lives in Albu-
querque, New Mexico. His short fiction has appeared frequently in
Asimov's Science Fiction, as well as in *The Magazine of Fantasy and
Science Fiction, Wheel of Fortune, Global Dispatches, Alternate Outlaws*, and in other markets, and has been gathered in the collections
Facets and *Frankensteins and Other Foreign Devils*. His novels
include *Ambassador of Progress, Knight Moves, Hardwired, The
Crown Jewels, Voice of The Whirlwind, House of Shards, Days of
Atonement*, and *Aristoi*. His novel *Metropolitan* garnered wide critical
acclaim in 1996 and was one of the most talked-about books of the
year. His other books include a sequel to *Metropolitan, City on Fire*, a
huge disaster thriller, *The Rift*, and a *Star Trek* novel, *Destiny's Way*.
He won a long-overdue Nebula Award in 2001 for his story "Daddy's
World." His stories have appeared in our Third through Sixth, Ninth,
Eleventh, Twelfth, Fourteenth, Seventeenth, and Twentieth Annual
Collections.

Here he spins an epic tale of love, loss, conspiracy, murder, and
redemption that shuttles us back and forth through time to unravel a
mystery that crucially shaped the fate of humanity itself...

Kicking her legs out over the ocean, the lonely mermaid gazed at the horizon from her perch in the overhanging banyan tree.

The air was absolutely still and filled with the scent of night flowers. Large fruit bats flew purposefully over the sea, heading for their daytime rest. Somewhere a white cockatoo gave a penetrating squawk. A starling made a brief flutter out to sea, then came back again. The rising sun threw up red-gold sparkles from the wavetops and brought a brilliance to the tropical growth that crowned the many islands spread out on the horizon.

The mermaid decided it was time for breakfast. She slipped from her hanging canvas chair and walked out along one of the banyan's great limbs. The branch swayed lightly under her weight, and her bare feet found sure traction on the rough bark. She looked down to see the deep blue of the channel, distinct from the turquoise of the shallows atop the reefs.

She raised her arms, poised briefly on the limb, the ruddy light of the sun glowing bronze on her bare skin, and then pushed off and dove headfirst into the Philippine Sea. She landed with a cool impact and a rush of bubbles.

Her wings unfolded, and she flew away.

After her hunt, the mermaid—her name was Michelle—cached her fishing gear in a pile of dead coral above the reef, and then ghosted easily over the sea grass with the rippled sunlight casting patterns on her wings. When she could look up to see the colossal, twisted tangle that was the roots of her banyan tree, she lifted her head from the water and gulped her first breath of air.

The Rock Islands were made of soft limestone coral, and tide and chemical action had eaten away the limestone at sea level, undercutting the stone above. Some of the smaller islands looked like mushrooms, pointed green pinnacles balanced atop thin stems. Michelle's island was larger and irregularly shaped, but it still had steep limestone walls undercut six meters by the tide, with no obvious way for a person to clamber from the sea to the land. Her banyan perched on the saucer-edge of the island, itself undercut by the sea.

Michelle had arranged a rope elevator from her nest in the tree, just a loop on the end of a long nylon line. She tucked her wings away—they were harder to retract than to deploy, and the gills on the undersides were delicate—and then slipped her feet through the loop. At her verbal command, a hoist mechanism lifted her in silence from the sea to her resting place in the bright green-dappled forest canopy.

She had been an ape once, a siamang, and she felt perfectly at home in the treetops.

During her excursion, she had speared a yellowlip emperor, and this she carried with her in a mesh bag. She filleted the emperor with a blade she kept in her nest, and tossed the rest into the sea, where it became a subject of interest to a school of bait fish. She ate a slice of one fillet raw, enjoying the brilliant flavor, sea and trembling pale flesh together, then cooked the fillets on her small stove, eating one with some rice she'd cooked the previous evening and saving the other for later.

By the time Michelle finished breakfast, the island was alive. Geckoes scurried over the banyan's bark, and coconut crabs sidled beneath the leaves like touts offering illicit downloads to passing tourists. Out in the deep water, a flock of circling, diving black noddies marked where a school of skipjack tuna was feeding on swarms of bait fish.

It was time for Michelle to begin her day as well. With sure, steady feet, she moved along a rope walkway to the ironwood tree that held her satellite uplink in its crown, straddled a limb, took her deck from the mesh bag she'd roped to the tree, and downloaded her messages.

There were several journalists requesting interviews—the legend of the lonely mermaid was spreading. This pleased her more often than not, but she didn't answer any of the queries. There was a message from Darton, which she decided to savor for a while before opening. And then she saw a note from Dr. Davout, and opened it at once.

Davout was, roughly, twelve times her age. He'd actually been carried for nine months in his mother's womb, not created from scratch in a nanobed like almost everyone else she knew. He had a sib who was a famous astronaut, a McEldowny Prize for his *Lavoisier and His Age,* and a red-haired wife who was nearly as well-known as he was. A couple of years ago, Michelle had attended a series of his lectures at the College of Mystery, and been interested despite her specialty being, strictly speaking, biology.

He had shaved off the little goatee he'd worn when she'd last seen him, which Michelle considered a good thing. "I have a research project for you, if you're free," the recording said. "It shouldn't take too much effort."

Michelle contacted him at once. He was a rich old bastard with a thousand years of tenure and no notion of what it was to be young in these times, and he'd pay her whatever outrageous fee she asked.

Her material needs at the moment were few, but she wouldn't stay on this island forever.

Davout answered right away. Behind him, working at her own console, Michelle could see his red-haired wife Katrin.

"Michelle!" Davout said, loudly enough for Katrin to know who'd called without turning around. "Good!" He hesitated, and then his fingers formed the mudra for <concern>. "I understand you've suffered a loss," he said.

"Yes," she said, her answer delayed by a second's satellite lag.

"And the young man—?"

"Doesn't remember."

Which was not exactly a lie, the point being *what* was remembered.

Davout's fingers were still fixed in <concern>. "Are you all right?" he asked.

Her own fingers formed an equivocal answer. "I'm getting better." Which was probably true.

"I see you're not an ape any more."

"I decided to go the mermaid route. New perspectives, all that." And welcome isolation.

"Is there any way we can make things easier for you?"

She put on a hopeful expression. "You said something about a job?"

"Yes." He seemed relieved not to have to probe further—he'd had a real-death in his own family, Michelle remembered, a chance-in-a-billion thing, and perhaps he didn't want to relive any part of that.

"I'm working on a biography of Terzian," Davout said.

". . . And his Age?" Michelle finished.

"And his *Legacy*." Davout smiled. "There's a three-week period in his life where he—well, he drops right off the map. I'd like to find out where he went—and who he was with, if anyone."

Michelle was impressed. Even in comparatively unsophisticated times such as that inhabited by Jonathan Terzian, it was difficult for people to disappear.

"It's a critical time for him," Davout went on. "He'd lost his job at Tulane, his wife had just died—realdeath, remember—and if he decided he simply wanted to get lost, he would have all my sympathies." He raised a hand as if to tug at the chin-whiskers that were no longer there, made a vague pawing gesture, then dropped the hand. "But my problem is that when he resurfaces, everything's changed for him. In June, he delivered an undistinguished paper at the Athenai conference in Paris, then vanished. When he surfaced in Venice in mid-July, he didn't deliver the paper he was scheduled to read, instead he delivered the first version of his Cornucopia Theory."

Michelle's fingers formed the mudra <highly impressed>. "How have you tried to locate him?"

"Credit card records—they end on June 17, when he buys a lot of euros at American Express in Paris. After that, he must have paid for everything with cash."

"He really *did* try to get lost, didn't he?" Michelle pulled up one bare leg and rested her chin on it. "Did you try passport records?"

<No luck.> "But if he stayed in the European Community he wouldn't have had to present a passport when crossing a border."

"Cash machines?"

"Not till after he arrived in Venice, just a couple of days prior to the conference."

The mermaid thought about it for a moment, then smiled. "I guess you need me, all right."

<I concur> Davout flashed solemnly. "How much would it cost me?"

Michelle pretended to consider the question for a moment, then named an outrageous sum.

Davout frowned. "Sounds all right," he said.

Inwardly, Michelle rejoiced. Outwardly, she leaned toward the camera lens and looked businesslike. "I'll get busy, then."

Davout looked grateful. "You'll be able to get on it right away?"

"Certainly. What I need you to do is send me pictures of Terzian, from as many different angles as possible, especially from around that period of time."

"I have them ready."

"Send away."

An eyeblink later, the pictures were in Michelle's deck. <Thanks> she flashed. "I'll let you know as soon as I find anything."

At university, Michelle had discovered that she was very good at research, and it had become a profitable sideline for her. People—usually people connected with academe in one way or another—hired her to do the duller bits of their own jobs, finding documents or references, or, in this case, three missing weeks out of a person's life. It was almost always work they could do themselves, but Michelle was simply better at research than most people, and she was considered worth the extra expense. Michelle herself usually enjoyed the work—it gave her interesting sidelights on fields about which she knew little, and provided a welcome break from routine.

Plus, this particular job required not so much a researcher as an artist, and Michelle was very good at this particular art.

Michelle looked through the pictures, most scanned from old photographs. Davout had selected well: Terzian's face or profile was clear in every picture. Most of the pictures showed him young, in his twenties, and the ones that showed him older were of high quality, or showed parts of the body that would be crucial to the biometric scan, like his hands or his ears.

The mermaid paused for a moment to look at one of the old photos: Terzian smiling with his arm around a tall, long-legged woman with a wide mouth and dark, bobbed hair, presumably the wife who had died. Behind them was a Louis Quinze table with a blaze of gladiolas in a cloisonné vase, and, above the table, a large portrait of a stately-looking horse in a heavy gilded frame. Beneath the table were stowed—temporarily, Michelle assumed—a dozen or so trophies, which to judge from the little golden figures balanced atop them were awarded either for gymnastics or martial arts. The opulent setting seemed a little at odds with the young, informally dressed couple: she wore a flowery tropical shirt tucked into khakis, and Terzian was dressed in a tank top and shorts. There was a sense that the photographer had caught them almost in motion, as if they'd paused for the picture en route from one place to another.

Nice shoulders, Michelle thought. Big hands, well-shaped muscular legs. She hadn't ever thought of Terzian as young, or large, or strong, but he had a genuine, powerful physical presence that came across even in the old, casual photographs. He looked more like a football player than a famous thinker.

Michelle called up her character-recognition software and fed in all the pictures, then checked the software's work, something she was reasonably certain her employer would never have done if he'd been doing this job himself. Most people using this kind of canned software didn't realize how the program could be fooled, particularly when used with old media, scanned film prints heavy with grain and primitive digital images scanned by machines that simply weren't very intelligent. In the end, Michelle and the software between them managed an excellent job of mapping Terzian's body and calibrating its precise ratios: the distance between the eyes, the length of nose and curve of lip, the distinct shape of the ears, the length of limb and trunk. Other men might share some of these biometric ratios, but none would share them all.

The mermaid downloaded the data into her specialized research spiders, and sent them forth into the electronic world.

A staggering amount of the trivial past existed there, and nowhere else. People had uploaded pictures, diaries, commentary, and video; they'd digitized old home movies, complete with the garish, deteriorating colors of the old film stock; they'd scanned in family trees, postcards, wedding lists, drawings, political screeds, and images of handwritten letters. Long, dull hours of security video. Whatever had meant something to someone, at some time, had been turned into electrons and made available to the universe at large.

A surprising amount of this stuff had survived the Lightspeed War—none of it had seemed worth targeting, or, if trashed, had been reloaded from backups.

What all this meant was that Terzian was somewhere in there. Wherever Terzian had gone in his weeks of absence—Paris, Dalmatia, or Thule—there would have been someone with a camera. In stills of children eating ice cream in front of Notre Dame, or moving through the video of buskers playing saxophone on the Pont des Artistes, there would be a figure in the background, and that figure would be Terzian. Terzian might be found lying on a beach in Corfu, reflected in a bar mirror in Gdynia, or negotiating with a prostitute in Hamburg's St. Pauli district—Michelle had found targets in exactly those places during the course of her other searches.

Michelle sent her software forth to find Terzian, then lifted her arms above her head and stretched—stretched fiercely, thrusting out her bare feet and curling the toes, the muscles trembling with tension, her mouth yawned in a silent shriek.

Then she leaned over her deck again, and called up the message from Darton, the message she'd saved till last.

"I don't understand," he said. "Why won't you talk to me? I love you!"

His brown eyes were a little wild.

"Don't you understand?" he cried. "I'm not dead! *I'm not really dead!*"

Michelle hovered three or four meters below the surface of Zigzag Lake, gazing upward at the inverted bowl of the heavens, the brilliant blue of the Pacific sky surrounded by the dark, shadowy towers of mangrove. Something caught her eye, something black and falling, like a bullet: and then there was a splash and a boil of bubbles, and the daggerlike bill of a collared kingfisher speared a blue-eyed apogonid that had been hovering over a bright red coral head. The kingfisher flashed its pale underside as it stroked to the surface, its wings doing efficient double duty as fins, and then there was a flurry of wings and feet and bubbles and the kingfisher was airborne again.

Michelle floated up and over the barrel-shaped coral head, then over a pair of giant clams, each over a meter long. The clams drew shut as Michelle slid across them, withdrawing the huge siphons as thick as her wrist. The fleshy lips that overhung the scalloped edges of the shells were a riot of colors: purples, blues, greens, and reds interwoven in a eye-boggling pattern.

Carefully drawing in her gills so their surfaces wouldn't be inflamed by coral stings, she kicked up her feet and dove beneath the mangrove roots into the narrow tunnel that connected Zigzag Lake with the sea.

Of the three hundred or so Rock Islands, seventy or thereabouts had marine lakes. The islands were made of coral limestone and porous to one degree or another: some lakes were connected to the ocean through tunnels and caves, and others through seepage. Many of the lakes contained forms of life unique in all the world, evolved distinctly from their remote ancestors: even now, after all this time, new species were being described.

During the months Michelle had spent in the islands, she thought she'd discovered two undescribed species: a variation on the *Entacmaea medusivora* white anemone that was patterned strangely with scarlet and a cobalt-blue; and a nudibranch, deep violet with yellow polka dots, that had undulated past her one night on the reef, flapping like a tea towel in a strong wind as a seven-knot tidal current tore it along. The nudi and samples of the anemone had been sent to the appropriate authorities, and perhaps in time Michelle would be immortalized by having a Latinate version of her name appended to the scientific description of the two marine animals.

The tunnel was about fifteen meters long, and had a few narrow twists where Michelle had to pull her wings in close to her sides and maneuver by the merest fluttering of their edges. The tunnel turned up, and brightened with the sun; the mermaid extended her wings and flew over brilliant pink soft corals toward the light.

Two hours' work, she thought, *plus a hazardous environment. Twenty-two hundred calories, easy.*

The sea was brilliantly lit, unlike the gloomy marine lake surrounded by tall cliffs, mangroves, and shadow, and for a moment Michelle's sun-dazzled eyes failed to see the boat bobbing on the tide. She stopped short, her wings cupping to brake her motion, and then she recognized the boat's distinctive paint job, a bright red meant to imitate the natural oil of the *cheritem* fruit.

Michelle prudently rose to the surface a safe distance away—Torbiong might be fishing, and sometimes he did it with a spear. The old man saw her, and stood to give a wave before Michelle could unblock her trachea and draw air into her lungs to give a hail.

"I brought you supplies," he said.

"Thanks," Michelle said as she wiped a rain of sea water from her face.

Torbiong was over two hundred years old, and Paramount Chief of Koror, the capital forty minutes away by boat. He was small and wiry and black-haired, and had a broad-nosed, strong-chinned, unlined face. He had traveled over the world and off it while young, but returned to Belau as he aged. His duties as chief were mostly ceremonial, but counted for tax purposes; he had money from hotels and restaurants that his ancestors had built and that others managed for him, and he spent most of his time visiting his neighbors, gossiping, and fishing. He had befriended Darton and Michelle when they'd first come to Belau, and helped them in securing the permissions for their researches on the Rock Islands. A few months back, after Darton died, Torbiong had agreed to bring supplies to Michelle in exchange for the occasional fish.

His boat was ten meters long and featured a waterproof canopy amidships made from interwoven pandanas leaves. Over the scarlet faux-*cheritem* paint were zigzags, crosses, and stripes in the brilliant yellow of the ginger plant. The ends of the thwarts were decorated with grotesque carved faces, and dozens of white cowrie shells were glued to the gunwales. Wooden statues of the king-fisher bird sat on the prow and stern.

Thrusting above the pandanas canopy were antennae, flagpoles, deep-sea fishing rods, fish spears, radar, and a satellite uplink. Below the canopy, where Torbiong could command the boat from an elaborately carved throne of breadfruit-tree wood, were the engine and rudder controls, radio, audio, and video sets, a collection of large audio speakers, a depth finder, a satellite navigation relay, and radar. Attached to the uprights that supported the canopy were whistles tuned to make an eerie, discordant wailing noise when the boat was at speed.

Torbiong was fond of discordant wailing noises. As Michelle swam closer, she heard the driving, screeching electronic music that Torbiong loved trickling from the earpieces of his headset—he normally howled it out of speakers, but when sitting still he didn't want to scare the fish. At night, she could hear Torbiong for miles, as he raced over the darkened sea blasted out of his skull on betel-nut juice with his music thundering and the whistles shrieking.

He removed the headset, releasing a brief audio onslaught before switching off his sound system.

"You're going to make yourself deaf," Michelle said.

Torbiong grinned. "Love that music. Gets the blood moving."

Michelle floated to the boat and put a hand on the gunwale between a pair of cowries.

"I saw that boy of yours on the news," Torbiong said. "He's making you famous."

"I don't want to be famous."

"He doesn't understand why you don't talk to him."

"He's dead," Michelle said.

Torbiong made a spreading gesture with his hands. "That's a matter of opinion."

"Watch your head," said Michelle.

Torbiong ducked as a gust threatened to bring him into contact with a pitcher plant that drooped over the edge of the island's overhang. Torbiong evaded the plant and then stepped to the bow to haul in his mooring line before the boat's canopy got caught beneath the overhang.

Michelle submerged and swam till she reached her banyan tree, then surfaced and called down her rope elevator. By the time Torbiong's boat hissed up to her, she'd folded away her gills and wings and was sitting in the sling, kicking her legs over the water.

Torbiong handed her a bag of supplies: some rice, tea, salt, vegetables, and fruit. For the last several weeks Michelle had experienced a craving for blueberries, which didn't grow here, and Torbiong had included a large package fresh off the shuttle, and a small bottle of cream to go with them. Michelle thanked him.

"Most tourists want corn chips or something," Torbiong said pointedly.

"I'm not a tourist," Michelle said. "I'm sorry I don't have any fish to swap—I've been hunting smaller game." She held out the specimen bag, still dripping sea water.

Torbiong gestured toward the cooler built into the back of his boat. "I got some *chai* and a *chersuuch* today," he said, using the local names for barracuda and mahi mahi.

"Good fishing."

"Trolling." With a shrug, he looked up at her, a quizzical look on his face. "I've got some calls from reporters," he said, and then his betel-stained smile broke out. "I always make sure to send them tourist literature."

"I'm sure they enjoy reading it."

Torbiong's grin widened. "You get lonely, now," he said, "you come visit the family. We'll give you a home-cooked meal."

She smiled. "Thanks."

They said their farewells and Torbiong's boat hissed away on its jets, the whistles building to an eerie, spine-shivering chord. Michelle rose into the trees and stashed her specimens and groceries. With a bowl of blueberries and cream, Michelle crossed the rope walkway to her deck, and checked the progress of her search spiders.

There were pointers to a swarm of articles about the death of Terzian's wife, and Michelle wished she'd given her spiders clearer instructions about dates.

The spiders had come up with three pictures. One was a not-very-well focused tourist video from July 10, showing a man standing in front of the Basilica di Santa Croce in Florence. A statue of Dante, also not in focus, gloomed down at him from beneath thick-bellied rain clouds. As the camera panned across him, he stood with his back to the camera, but turned to the right, one leg turned out as he scowled down at the ground—the profile was a little smeared, but the big, broad-shouldered body seemed right. The software reckoned that there was a 78 percent chance that the man was Terzian.

Michelle got busy refining the image, and after a few passes of the software, decided the chances of the figure being Terzian were more on the order of 95 percent.

So maybe Terzian had gone on a Grand Tour of European cultural sites. He didn't look happy in the video, but then the day was rainy and Terzian didn't have an umbrella.

And his wife had died, of course.

Now that Michelle had a date and a place she refined the instructions from her search spiders to seek out images from Florence a week either way from July 3, and then expand the search from there, first all Tuscany, then all Italy.

If Terzian was doing tourist sites, then she surely had him nailed.

The next two hits, from her earlier research spiders, were duds. The software gave a less than 50 percent chance of Terzian's being in Lisbon or Cape Sounion, and refinements of the image reduced the chance to something near zero.

Then the next video popped up, with a time stamp right there in the image—Paris, June 26, 13:41:44 hours, just a day before Terzian bought a bankroll of euros and vanished.

<Bingo!> Michelle's fingers formed.

The first thing Michelle saw was Terzian walking out of the frame—no doubt this time that it was him. He was looking over his shoulder at a small crowd of people. There was a dark-haired woman huddled on his arm, her face turned away from the camera. Michelle's heart warmed at the thought of the lonely widower Terzian having an affair in the City of Love.

Then she followed Terzian's gaze to see what had so drawn his attention. A dead man stretched out on the pavement, surrounded by hapless bystanders.

And then, as the scene slowly settled into her astonished mind, the video sang at her in the piping voice of Pan.

Terzian looked at his audience as anger raged in his backbrain. A wooden chair creaked, and the sound spurred Terzian to wonder how long the silence had gone on. Even the Slovenian woman who had been drowsing realized that something had changed, and blinked herself to alertness.

"I'm sorry," he said in French. "But my wife just died, and I don't feel like playing this game any more."

His silent audience watched as he gathered his papers, put them in his case, and left the lecture room, his feet making sharp, murderous sounds on the wooden floor.

Yet up to that point his paper had been going all right. He'd been uncertain about commenting on Baudrillard in Baudrillard's own country, and in Baudrillard's own language, a cheery compare-and-contrast exercise between Baudrillard's "the self does not exist" and Rorty's "I don't care," the stereotypical French and American answers to modern life. There had been seven in his audience, perched on creaking wooden chairs, and none of them had gone to sleep, or walked out, or condemned him for his audacity.

Yet, as he looked at his audience and read on, Terzian had felt the anger growing, spawned by the sensation of his own uselessness. Here he was, in the City of Light, its every cobblestone a monument to European civilization, and he was in a dreary lecture hall on the Left Bank, reading to his audience of seven from a paper that was nothing more than a footnote, and a footnote to a footnote at that. To come to the land of *cogito ergo sum* and to answer, *I don't care?*

I came to Paris for this? he thought. *To read this* drivel? *I paid for the privilege of doing* this?

I do care, he thought as his feet turned toward the Seine. *Desiderio, ergo sum,* if he had his Latin right. I am in pain, and therefore I *do* exist.

He ended in a Norman restaurant on the Ile de la Cité, with lunch as his excuse and the thought of getting hopelessly drunk not far from his thoughts. He had absolutely nothing to do until August, after which he would return to the States and collect his belongings from the servants' quarters of the house on Esplanade, and then he would go about looking for a job.

He wasn't certain whether he would be more depressed by finding a job or by not finding one.

You are alive, he told himself. *You are alive and in Paris with the whole summer ahead of you, and you're eating the cuisine of Normandy in the Place Dauphine. And if that isn't a command to be joyful, what is?*

It was then that the Peruvian band began to play. Terzian looked up from his plate in weary surprise.

When Terzian had been a child his parents—both university professors—had first taken him to Europe, and he'd seen then that every European city had its own Peruvian or Bolivian street band, Indians in black bowler hats and colorful blankets crouched in some public place, gazing with impassive brown eyes from over their guitars and reed flutes.

Now, a couple of decades later, the musicians were still here, though they'd exchanged the blankets and bowler hats for European styles, and their presentation had grown more slick. Now they had amps, and cassettes and CDs for sale. Now they had congregated in the triangular Place Dauphine, overshadowed by the neo-classical mass of the Palais de Justice, and commenced a Latin-flavored medley of old Abba songs.

Maybe, after Terzian finished his veal in calvados sauce, he'd go up to the band and kick in their guitars.

The breeze flapped the canvas overhead. Terzian looked at his empty plate. The food had been excellent, but he could barely remember tasting it.

Anger still roiled beneath his thoughts. And—for God's *sake*—was that band now playing *Oasis?* Those chords were beginning to sound suspiciously like "Wonderwall." "Wonderwall" on Spanish guitars, reed flutes, and a mandolin!

Terzian had nearly decided to call for a bottle of cognac and stay here all afternoon, but not with that noise in the park. He put some euros on the table, anchoring the bills with a saucer against the fresh spring breeze that rattled the green canvas canopy over his head. He was stepping through the restaurant's little wrought-iron gate to the sidewalk when the scuffle caught his attention.

The man falling into the street, his face pinched with pain. The hands of the three men on either side who were, seemingly, unable to keep their friend erect.

Idiots, Terzian thought, fury blazing in him.

There was a sudden shrill of tires, of an auto horn.

Papers streamed in the wind as they spilled from a briefcase.

And over it all came the amped sound of pan pipes from the Peruvian band. *Wonderwall*.

Terzian watched in exasperated surprise as the three men sprang after the papers. He took a step toward the fallen man—*someone* had to take charge here. The fallen man's hair had spilled in a shock over his forehead and he'd curled on his side, his face still screwed up in pain.

The pan pipes played on, one distinct hollow shriek after another.

Terzian stopped with one foot still on the sidewalk and looked around at faces that all registered the same sense of shock. Was there a doctor here? he wondered. A *French* doctor? All his French seemed to have just drained from his head. Even such simple questions as *Are you all right?* and *How are you feeling?* seemed beyond him now. The first aid course he'd taken in his Kenpo school was *ages* ago.

Unnaturally pale, the fallen man's face relaxed. The wind floated his shock of thinning dark hair over his face. In the park, Terzian saw a man in a baseball cap panning a video camera, and his anger suddenly blazed up again at the fatuous uselessness of the tourist, the uselessness that mirrored his own.

Suddenly there was a crowd around the casualty, people coming out of stopped cars, off the sidewalk. Down the street, Terzian saw the distinctive flat-topped kepis of a pair of policemen bobbing toward him from the direction of the Palais de Justice, and felt a surge of relief. Someone more capable than this lot would deal with this now.

He began, hesitantly, to step away. And then his arm was seized by a pair of hands and he looked in surprise at the woman who had just huddled her face into his shoulder, cinnamon-dark skin and eyes invisible beneath wraparound shades.

"Please," she said in English a bit too musical to be American. "Take me out of here."

The sound of the reed pipes followed them as they made their escape.

He walked her past the statue of the Vert Galant himself, good old lecherous Henri IV, and onto the Pont Neuf. To the left, across the Seine, the Louvre glowed in mellow colors beyond a screen of plane trees.

Traffic roared by, a stampede of steel unleashed by a green light. Unfo-cused anger blazed in his mind. He didn't want this woman attached to him, and he suspected she was running some kind of scam. The gym bag she wore on a strap over one shoulder kept banging him on the ass: Surreptitiously, he slid his hand into his right front trouser pocket to make sure his money was still there.

Wonderwall, he thought. Christ.

He supposed he should offer some kind of civilized comment, just in case the woman was genuinely distressed.

"I suppose he'll be all right," he said, half-barking the words in his annoy-ance and anger.

The woman's face was still half-buried in his shoulder. "He's dead," she murmured into his jacket. "Couldn't you tell?"

For Terzian, death had never occurred under the sky, but shut away, in hospice rooms with crisp sheets and warm colors and the scent of disinfectant. In an explosion of tumors and wasting limbs and endless pain masked only in part by morphia.

He thought of the man's pale face, the sudden relaxation.

Yes, he thought, death came with a sigh.

Reflex kept him talking. "The police were coming," he said. "They'll— they'll call an ambulance or something."

"I only hope they catch the bastards who did it," she said.

Terzian's heart gave a jolt as he recalled the three men who let the victim fall, and then dashed through the square for his papers. For some reason, all he could remember about them were their black-laced boots, with thick soles.

"Who were they?" he asked blankly.

The woman's shades slid down her nose, and Terzian saw startling green eyes narrowed to murderous slits. "I suppose they think of themselves as cops," she said.

Terzian parked his companion in a café near Les Halles, within sight of the dome of the Bourse. She insisted on sitting indoors, not on the sidewalk, and on facing the front door so that she could scan whoever came in. She put her gym bag, with its white Nike swoosh, on the floor between the table legs and the wall, but Terzian noticed she kept its shoulder strap in her lap, as if she might have to bolt at any moment.

Terzian kept his wedding ring within her sight. He wanted her to see it; it might make things simpler.

Her hands were trembling. Terzian ordered coffee for them both. "No," she said suddenly. "I want ice cream."

Terzian studied her as she turned to the waiter and ordered in French. She was around his own age, twenty-nine. There was no question that she was a mixture of races, but *which* races? The flat nose could be African or Asian or Polynesian, and Polynesia was again confirmed by the black, thick brows. Her smooth brown complexion could be from anywhere but Europe, but her pale green eyes were nothing but European. Her broad, sensitive mouth suggested Nubia. The black ringlets yanked into a knot behind her head could be African or East Indian, or, for that matter, French. The result was too striking to be beautiful—and also too striking, Terzian thought, to belong to a successful criminal. Those looks could be too easily identified.

The waiter left. She turned her wide eyes toward Terzian, and seemed faintly surprised that he was still there.

"My name's Jonathan," he said.

"I'm," hesitating, "Stephanie."

"Really?" Terzian let his skepticism show.

"Yes." She nodded, reaching in a pocket for cigarettes. "Why would I lie? It doesn't matter if you know my real name or not."

"Then you'd better give me the whole thing."

She held her cigarette upward, at an angle, and enunciated clearly. "Stephanie América Pais e Silva."

"America?"

Striking a match. "It's a perfectly ordinary Portuguese name."

He looked at her. "But you're not Portuguese."

"I carry a Portuguese passport."

Terzian bit back the comment, *I'm sure you do.*

Instead he said, "Did you know the man who was killed?"

Stephanie nodded. The drags she took off her cigarette did not ease the tremor in her hands.

"Did you know him well?"

"Not very." She dragged in smoke again, then let the smoke out as she spoke.

"He was a colleague. A biochemist."

Surprise silenced Terzian. Stephanie tipped ash into the Cinzano ashtray, but her nervousness made her miss, and the little tube of ash fell on the tablecloth.

"Shit," she said, and swept the ash to the floor with a nervous movement of her fingers.

"Are you a biochemist, too?" Terzian asked.

"I'm a nurse." She looked at him with her pale eyes. "I work for Santa Croce—it's a—"

"A relief agency." A Catholic one, he remembered. The name meant *Holy Cross.*

She nodded.

"Shouldn't you go to the police?" he asked. And then his skepticism returned. "Oh, that's right—it was the police who did the killing."

"Not the *French* police." She leaned across the table toward him. "This was a different sort of police, the kind who think that killing someone and making an arrest are the same thing. You look at the television news tonight. They'll report the death, but there won't be any arrests. Or any suspects." Her face darkened, and she leaned back in her chair to consider a new thought. "Unless they somehow manage to blame it on me."

Terzian remembered papers flying in the spring wind, men in heavy boots sprinting after. The pinched, pale face of the victim.

"Who, then?"

She gave him a bleak look through a curl of cigarette smoke. "Have you ever heard of Transnistria?"

Terzian hesitated, then decided "No" was the most sensible answer.

"The murderers are Transnistrian." A ragged smile drew itself across Stephanie's face. "Their intellectual property police. They killed Adrian over a copyright."

At that point, the waiter brought Terzian's coffee, along with Stephanie's order. Hers was colossal, a huge glass goblet filled with pastel-colored ice creams and fruit syrups in bright primary colors, topped by a mountain of cream and a toy pinwheel on a candy-striped stick. Stephanie looked at the creation in shock, her eyes wide.

"I love ice cream," she choked, and then her eyes brimmed with tears and she began to cry.

Stephanie wept for a while, across the table, and, between sobs, choked down heaping spoonfuls of ice cream, eating in great gulps and swiping at her lips and tear-stained cheeks with a paper napkin.

The waiter stood quietly in the corner, but from his glare and the set of his jaw it was clear that he blamed Terzian for making the lovely woman cry.

Terzian felt his body surge with the impulse to aid her, but he didn't know what to do. Move around the table and put an arm around her? Take her hand? Call someone to take her off his hands?

The latter, for preference.

He settled for handing her a clean napkin when her own grew sodden.

His skepticism had not survived the mention of the Transnistrian copyright police. This was far too bizarre to be a con—a scam was based on basic human desire, greed, or lust, not something as abstract as intellectual property. Unless there was a gang who made a point of targeting academics from the States, luring them with a tantalizing hook about a copyright worth murdering for. . . .

Eventually, the storm subsided. Stephanie pushed the half-consumed ice cream away, and reached for another cigarette.

He tapped his wedding ring on the table top, something he did when thinking. "Shouldn't you contact the local police?" he asked. "You know something about this . . . death." For some reason he was reluctant to use the word *murder*. It was as if using the word would make something true, not the killing itself but his relationship to the killing . . . to call it murder would grant it some kind of power over him.

She shook her head. "I've got to get out of France before those guys find me. Out of Europe, if I can, but that would be hard. My passport's in my hotel room, and they're probably watching it."

"Because of this copyright."

Her mouth twitched in a half-smile. "That's right."

"It's not a literary copyright, I take it."

She shook her head, the half-smile still on her face.

"Your friend was a biologist." He felt a hum in his nerves, a certainty that he already knew the answer to the next question.

"Is it a weapon?" he asked.

She wasn't surprised by the question. "No," she said. "No, just the opposite." She took a drag on her cigarette and sighed the smoke out. "It's an antidote. An antidote to human folly."

"Listen," Stephanie said. "Just because the Soviet Union fell doesn't mean that *Sovietism* fell with it. Sovietism is still there—the only difference is that its moral justification is gone, and what's left is violence and extortion disguised as law enforcement and taxation. The old empire breaks up, and in the West you think it's great, but more countries just meant more palms to be greased—all throughout the former Soviet empire you've got more 'inspectors' and 'tax collectors,' more 'customs agents' and 'security directorates' than there ever were under the Russians. All these people do is prey off their own populations, because no one else will do business with them unless they've got oil or some other resource that people want."

"Trashcanistans," Terzian said. It was a word he'd heard used of his own ancestral homeland, the former Soviet Republic of Armenia, whose looted economy and paranoid, murderous, despotic Russian puppet regime was supported only by millions of dollars sent to the country by Americans of Armenian descent, who thought that propping up the gang of thugs in power somehow translated into freedom for the fatherland.

Stephanie nodded. "And the worst Trashcanistan of all is Transnistria."

She and Terzian had left the café and taken a taxi back to the Left Bank and Terzian's hotel. He had turned the television to a local station, but muted the sound until the news came on. Until then the station showed a rerun of an American cop show, stolid, businesslike detectives underplaying their latest sordid confrontation with tragedy.

The hotel room hadn't been built for the queen-sized bed it now held, and there was an eighteen-inch clearance around the bed and no room for chairs. Terzian, not wanting Stephanie to think he wanted to get her in the sack, perched uncertainly on a corner of the bed, while Stephanie disposed herself more comfortably, sitting cross-legged in its center.

"Moldova was a Soviet republic put together by Stalin," she said. "It was made up of Bessarabia, which was a part of Romania that Stalin chewed off at the beginning of the Second World War, plus a strip of industrial land on the far side of the Dniester. When the Soviet Union went down, Moldova became 'independent'—" Terzian could hear the quotes in her voice. "But independence had nothing to do with the Moldovan *people*, it was just Romanian-speaking Soviet elites going off on their own account once their own superiors were no longer there to restrain them. And Moldova soon split—first the Turkish Christians . . ."

"Wait a second," Terzian said. "There are *Christian Turks?*"

The idea of Christian Turks was not a part of his Armenian-American worldview.

Stephanie nodded. "Orthodox Christian Turks, yes. They're called Gagauz, and they now have their own autonomous republic of Gagauzia within Moldova."

Stephanie reached into her pocket for a cigarette and her lighter.

"Uh," Terzian said. "Would you mind smoking out the window?"

Stephanie made a face. "Americans," she said, but she moved to the window and opened it, letting in a blast of cool spring air. She perched on the windowsill, sheltered her cigarette from the wind, and lit up.

"Where was I?" she asked.

"Turkish Christians."

"Right." Blowing smoke into the teeth of the gale. "Gagauzia was only the start—after that, a Russian general allied with a bunch of crooks and KGB types created a rebellion in the bit of Moldova that was on the far side of the Dniester—another collection of Soviet elites, representing no one but themselves. Once the Russian-speaking rebels rose against their Romanian-speaking oppressors, the Soviet Fourteenth Army stepped in as 'peacekeepers,' complete with blue helmets, and created a twenty-mile-wide state recognized by no other government. And that meant more military, more border guards, more administrators, more taxes to charge, and customs duties, and uniformed ex-Soviets whose palms needed greasing. And over a hundred thousand refugees who could be put in camps while the administration stole their supplies and rations. . . .

"But—" She jabbed the cigarette like a pointer. "Transnistria had a problem. No other nation recognized their existence, and they were tiny and had no natural resources, barring the underage girls they enslaved by the thousands to export for prostitution. The rest of the population was leaving as fast as they could, restrained only slightly by the fact that they carried passports no other state recognized, and that meant there were fewer people whose productivity the elite could steal to support their predatory post-Soviet lifestyles. All they had was a lot of obsolete Soviet heavy industry geared to produce stuff no one wanted.

"But they still had the *infrastructure*. They had power plants—running off Russian oil they couldn't afford to buy—and they had a transportation system. So the outlaw regime set up to attract other outlaws who needed industrial capacity—the idea was that they'd attract entrepreneurs who were excused paying most of the local 'taxes' in exchange for making one big payoff to the higher echelon."

"Weapons?" Terzian asked.

"Weapons, sure," Stephanie nodded. "Mostly they're producing cheap knockoffs of other people's guns, but the guns are up to the size of howitzers. They tried banking and data havens, but the authorities couldn't restrain themselves from ripping those off—banks and data run on trust and control of information, and when the regulators are greedy, shortsighted crooks, you don't get either one. So what they settled on was, well, *biotech.* They've got companies creating cheap generic pharmaceuticals that evade Western patents. . . ." Her look darkened. "Not that I've got a problem with *that,* not when I've seen thousands dying of diseases they couldn't afford to cure. And they've also got other companies who are ripping off Western genetic research to develop their own products. And as long as they make their payoffs to the elite, these companies remain *completely unregulated.* Nobody, not even the government, knows what they're doing in those factories, and the government gives them security free of charge."

Terzian imagined gene-splicing going on in a rusting Soviet factory, rows and rows of mutant plants with untested, unregulated genetics, all set to be released on an unsuspecting world. Transgenic elements drifting down the Dniester to the Black Sea, growing quietly in its saline environment. . . .

"The news," Stephanie reminded, and pointed at the television.

Terzian reached for the control and hit the mute button, just as the throbbing, anxious music that announced the news began to fade.

The murder on the Ile de la Cité was the second item on the broadcast. The victim was described as a "foreign national" who had been fatally stabbed, and no arrests had been made. The motive for the killing was unknown.

Terzian changed the channel in time to catch the same item on another channel. The story was unchanged.

"I told you," Stephanie said. "No suspects. No motive."

"You could tell them."

She made a negative motion with her cigarette. "I couldn't tell them who did it, or how to find them. All I could do is put myself under suspicion."

Terzian turned off the TV. "So what happened exactly? Your friend stole from these people?"

Stephanie swiped her forehead with the back of her wrist. "He stole something that was of no value to them. It's only valuable to poor people, who can't afford to pay. And—" She turned to the window and spun her cigarette into the street below. "I'll take it out of here as soon as I can," she said. "I've got to try to contact some people." She closed the window, shutting out the spring breeze. "I wish I had my passport. That would change everything."

I saw a murder this afternoon, Terzian thought. He closed his eyes and saw the man falling, the white face so completely absorbed in the reality of its own agony.

He was so fucking sick of death.

He opened his eyes. "I can get your passport back," he said.

Anger kept him moving until he saw the killers, across the street from Stephanie's hotel, sitting at an outdoor table in a café-bar. Terzian recognized them immediately—he didn't need to look at the heavy shoes, or the broad faces with their disciplined military mustaches—one glance at the crowd at the café showed the only two in the place who weren't French. That was probably how Stephanie knew to speak to him in English, he just didn't dress or carry himself like a Frenchman, for all that he'd worn an anonymous coat and tie. He tore his gaze away before they saw him gaping at them.

Anger turned very suddenly to fear, and as he continued his stride toward the hotel he told himself that they wouldn't recognize him from the Norman restaurant, that he'd changed into blue jeans and sneakers and a windbreaker, and carried a soft-sided suitcase. Still he felt a gunsight on the back of his neck, and he was so nervous that he nearly ran head-first into the glass lobby door.

Terzian paid for a room with his credit card, took the key from the Vietnamese clerk, and walked up the narrow stair to what the French called the second floor, but what he would have called the third. No one lurked in the stairwell, and he wondered where the third assassin had gone. Looking for Stephanie somewhere else, probably, an airport or train station.

In his room Terzian put his suitcase on the bed—it held only a few token items, plus his shaving kit—and then he took Stephanie's key from his pocket and held it in his hand. The key was simple, attached to a weighted doorknob-shaped ceramic plug.

The jolt of fear and surprise that had so staggered him on first sighting the two men began to shift again into rage.

They were drinking *beer*, there had been half-empty mugs on the table in front of them, and a pair of empties as well.

Drinking on duty. Doing surveillance while drunk.

Bastards. Trashcanians. They could kill someone simply through drunkenness.

Perhaps they already had.

He was angry when he left his room and took the stairs to the floor below. No foes kept watch in the hall. He opened Stephanie's room and then closed the door behind him.

He didn't turn on the light. The sun was surprisingly high in the sky for the hour: he had noticed that the sun seemed to set later here than it did at home. Maybe France was very far to the west for its time zone.

Stephanie didn't have a suitcase, just a kind of nylon duffel, a larger version of the athletic bag she already carried. He took it from the little closet, and enough of Terzian's suspicion remained so that he checked the luggage tag to make certain the name was *Steph. Pais*, and not another.

He opened the duffel, then got her passport and travel documents from the bedside table and tossed them in. He added a jacket and a sweater from the closet, then packed her toothbrush and shaver into her plastic travel bag and put it in the duffel.

The plan was for him to return to his room on the upper floor and stay the night and avoid raising suspicion by leaving a hotel he'd just checked into. In the morning, carrying two bags, he'd check out and rejoin Stephanie in his own hotel, where she had spent the night in his room, and where the air would by now almost certainly reek with her cigarette smoke.

Terzian opened a dresser drawer and scooped out a double handful of Stephanie's T-shirts, underwear, and stockings, and then he remembered that the last time he'd done this was when he cleaned Claire's belongings out of the Esplanade house.

Shit. Fuck. He gazed down at the clothing between his hands and let the fury rage like a tempest in his skull.

And then, in the angry silence, he heard a creak in the corridor, and then a stumbling thud.

Thick rubber military soles, he thought. With drunk baboons in them.

Instinct shrieked at him not to be trapped in this room, this dead-end where he could be trapped and killed. He dropped Stephanie's clothes back into the drawer and stepped to the bed and picked up the duffel in one hand. Another step took him to the door, which he opened with one hand while using the other to fling the duffel into the surprised face of the drunken murderer on the other side.

Terzian hadn't been at his Kenpo school in six years, not since he'd left Kansas City, but certain reflexes don't go away after they've been drilled into a person thousands of times—certainly not the front kick that hooked upward under the intruder's breastbone and drove him breathless into the corridor wall opposite.

A primitive element of his mind rejoiced in the fact that he was bigger than these guys. He could really knock them around.

The second Trashcanian tried to draw a pistol, but Terzian passed outside the pistol hand and drove the point of an elbow into the man's face. Terzian then grabbed the automatic with both hands, took a further step down the corridor, and spun around, which swung the man around Terzian's hip a full two hundred and seventy degrees and drove him headfirst into the corridor wall. When he'd finished falling and opened his eyes he was staring into the barrel of his own gun.

Red rage gave a fangs-bared roar of animal triumph inside Terzian's skull. Perhaps his tongue echoed it. It was all he could do to stop himself from pulling the trigger.

Get Death working for *him* for a change. Why not?

Except that the first man hadn't realized that his side had just lost. He had drawn a knife—a glittering chromed single-edged thing that may have already killed once today—and now he took a dangerous step toward Terzian.

Terzian pointed the pistol straight at the knife man and pulled the trigger. Nothing happened.

The intruder stared at the gun as if he'd just realized at just this moment it wasn't his partner who held it.

Terzian pulled the trigger again, and when nothing happened his rage melted into terror and he ran. Behind him he heard the drunken knife man trip over his partner and crash to the floor.

Terzian was at the bottom of the stair before he heard the thick-soled military boots clatter on the risers above him. He dashed through the small lobby—he sensed the Vietnamese night clerk, who was facing away, begin to turn toward him just as he pushed open the glass door and ran into the street.

He kept running. At some point he discovered the gun still in his fist, and he put it in the pocket of his windbreaker.

Some moments later, he realized that he wasn't being pursued. And he remembered that Stephanie's passport was still in her duffel, which he'd thrown at the knife man and hadn't retrieved.

For a moment, rage ran through him, and he thought about taking out the gun and fixing whatever was wrong with it and going back to Stephanie's room and getting the documents one way or another.

But then the anger faded enough for him to see what a foolish course that would be, and he returned to his own hotel.

Terzian had given Stephanie his key, so he knocked on his own door before realizing she was very unlikely to open to a random knock. "It's Jonathan," he said. "It didn't work out."

She snatched the door open from the inside. Her face was taut with anxiety. She held pages in her hand, the text of the paper he'd delivered that morning.

"Sorry," he said. "They were there, outside the hotel. I got into your room, but—"

She took his arm and almost yanked him into the room, then shut the door behind him. "Did they follow you?" she demanded.

"No. They didn't chase me. Maybe they thought I'd figure out how to work the gun." He took the pistol out of his pocket and showed it to her. "I can't believe how stupid I was—"

"*Where did you get that? Where did you get that?*" Her voice was nearly a scream, and she shrank away from him, her eyes wide. Her fist crumpled papers over her heart. To his astonishment, he realized that she was afraid of him, that she thought he was *connected*, somehow, with the killers.

He threw the pistol onto the bed and raised his hands in a gesture of surrender. "No really!" he shouted over her cries. "It's not mine! I took it from one of them!"

Stephanie took a deep gasp of air. Her eyes were still wild. "Who the hell are you, then?" she said. "James Bond?"

He gave a disgusted laugh. "James Bond would have known how to shoot."

"I was reading your—your article." She held out the pages toward him. "I was thinking, my God, I was thinking, what have I got this poor guy into. Some professor I was sending to his death." She passed a hand over her forehead. "They probably bugged my room. They would have known right away that someone was in it."

"They were drunk," Terzian said. "Maybe they've been drinking all day. Those assholes really pissed me off."

He sat on the bed and picked up the pistol. It was small and blue steel and surprisingly heavy. In the years since he'd last shot a gun, he had forgotten that purposefulness, the way a firearm was designed for a single, clear function. He found the safety where it had been all along, near his right thumb, and flicked it off and then on again.

"There," he said. "That's what I should have done."

Waves of anger shivered through his limbs at the touch of the adrenaline still pouring into his system. A bitter impulse to laugh again rose in him, and he tried to suppress it.

"I guess I was lucky after all," he said. "It wouldn't have done you any good to have to explain a pair of corpses outside your room." He looked up at Stephanie, who was pacing back and forth in the narrow lane between the bed and the wall, and looking as if she badly needed a cigarette. "I'm sorry about your passport. Where were you going to go, anyway?"

"It doesn't so much matter if I go," she said. She gave Terzian a quick, nervous glance. "You can fly it out, right?"

"It?" He stared at her. "What do you mean, it?"

"The biotech." Stephanie stopped her pacing and stared at him with those startling green eyes. "Adrian gave it to me. Just before they killed him." Terzian's gaze followed hers to the black bag with the Nike swoosh, the bag that sat at the foot of Terzian's bed.

Terzian's impulse to laugh faded. Unregulated, illegal, stolen biotech, he thought. Right in his own hotel room. Along with a stolen gun and a woman who was probably out of her mind.

Fuck.

The dead man was identified by news files as Adrian Cristea, a citizen of Ukraine and a researcher. He had been stabbed once in the right kidney and bled to death without identifying his assailants. Witnesses reported two or maybe three men leaving the scene immediately after Cristea's death. Michelle set more search spiders to work.

For a moment, she considered calling Davout and letting him know that Terzian had probably been a witness to a murder, but decided to wait until she had some more evidence one way or another.

For the next few hours, she did her real work, analyzing the samples she'd taken from Zigzag Lake's sulphide-tainted deeps. It wasn't very physical, and Michelle figured it was only worth a few hundred calories.

A wind floated through the treetops, bringing the scent of night flowers and swaying Michelle's perch beneath her as she peered into her biochemical reader, and she remembered the gentle pressure of Darton against her back, rocking with her as he looked over her shoulder at her results. Suddenly she could remember, with a near-perfect clarity, the taste of his skin on her tongue.

She rose from her woven seat and paced along the bough. *Damn it*, she thought, *I watched you die.*

Michelle returned to her deck and discovered that her spiders had located the police file on Cristea's death. A translation program handled the antique French without trouble, even producing modern equivalents of forensic jargon. Cristea was of Romanian descent, had been born in the old USSR, and had acquired Ukranian citizenship on the breakup of the Soviet Union. The French files themselves had translations of Cristea's Ukranian travel documents, which included receipts showing that he had paid personal insurance, environmental insurance, and departure taxes from Transnistria, a place of which she'd never heard, as well as similar documents from Moldova, which at least was a province, or country, that sounded familiar.

What kind of places were these, where you had to buy *insurance* at the *border*? And what was environmental insurance anyway?

There were copies of emails between French and Ukranian authorities, in which the Ukranians politely declined any knowledge of their citizen beyond the fact that he *was* a citizen. They had no addresses for him.

Cristea apparently lived in Transnistria, but the authorities there echoed the Ukranians in saying they knew nothing of him.

Cristea's tickets and vouchers showed that he had apparently taken a train to Bucharest, and there he'd got on an airline that took him to Prague, and thence to Paris. He had been in the city less than a day before he was killed. Found in Cristea's hotel room was a curious document certifying that Cristea was carrying medical supplies, specifically a vaccine against hepatitis A. Michelle wondered why he would be carrying a hepatitis vaccine from Transnistria to France. France presumably had all the hepatitis vaccine it needed.

No vaccine had turned up. Apparently Cristea had got into the European

Community without having his bags searched, as there was no evidence that the documents relating to the alleged vaccine had ever been examined.

The missing "vaccine"—at some point in the police file the skeptical quotation marks had appeared—had convinced the Paris police that Cristea was a murdered drug courier, and at that point they'd lost interest in the case. It was rarely possible to solve a professional killing in the drug underworld.

Michelle's brief investigation seemed to have come to a dead end. That Terzian might have witnessed a murder would rate maybe half a sentence in Professor Davout's biography.

Then she checked what her spiders had brought her in regard to Terzian, and found something that cheered her.

There he was inside the Basilica di Santa Croce, a tourist still photograph taken before the tomb of Machiavelli. He was only slightly turned away from the camera and the face was unmistakable. Though there was no date on the photograph, only the year, though he wore the same clothes he wore in the video taken outside the church, and the photo caught him in the act of speaking to a companion. She was a tall woman with deep brown skin, but she was turned away from the camera, and a wide-brimmed sun hat made her features indistinguishable.

Humming happily, Michelle deployed her software to determine whether this was the same woman who had been on Terzian's arm on the Place Dauphine. Without facial features or other critical measurements to compare, the software was uncertain, but the proportion of limb and thorax was right, and the software gave an estimate of 41 percent, which Michelle took to be encouraging.

Another still image of Terzian appeared in an undated photograph taken at a festival in southern France. He wore dark glasses, and he'd grown heavily tanned; he carried a glass of wine in either hand, but the person to whom he was bringing the second glass was out of the frame. Michelle set her software to locating the identity of the church seen in the background, a task the two distinctive belltowers would make easy. She was lucky and got a hit right away: the church was the Eglise St-Michel in Salon-de-Provence, which meant Terzian had attended the Fête des Aires de la Dine in June. Michelle set more search spiders to seeking out photo and video from the festivals. She had no doubt that she'd find Terzian there, and perhaps again his companion.

Michelle retired happily to her hammock. The search was going well. Terzian had met a woman in Paris and traveled with her for weeks. The evidence wasn't quite there yet, but Michelle would drag it out of history somehow.

Romance. The lonely mermaid was in favor of romance, the kind where you ran away to faraway places to be more intently one with the person you adored.

It was what she herself had done, before everything had gone so wrong, and Michelle had had to take steps to re-establish the moral balance of her universe.

Terzian paid for a room for Stephanie for the night, not so much because he was gallant as because he needed to be alone to think. "There's a breakfast buffet downstairs in the morning," he said. "They have hardboiled eggs and croissants and Nutella. It's a very un-French thing to do. I recommend it."

He wondered if he would ever see her again. She might just vanish, particularly if she read his thoughts, because another reason for wanting privacy was so that he could call the police and bring an end to this insane situation.

He never quite assembled the motivation to make the call. Perhaps Rorty's *I don't care* had rubbed off on him. And he never got a chance to taste the buffet, either. Stephanie banged on his door very early, and he dragged on his jeans and opened the door. She entered, furiously smoking from her new cigarette pack, the athletic bag over her shoulder.

"How did you pay for the room at my hotel?" she asked.

"Credit card," he said, and in the stunned, accusing silence that followed he saw his James Bond fantasies sink slowly beneath the slack, oily surface of a dismal lake.

Because credit cards leave trails. The Transnistrians would have checked the hotel registry, and the credit card impression taken by the hotel, and now they knew who *he* was. And it wouldn't be long before they'd trace him at this hotel.

"Shit, I should have warned you to pay cash." Stephanie stalked to the window and peered out cautiously. "They could be out there right now."

Terzian felt a sudden compulsion to have the gun in his hand. He took it from the bedside table and stood there, feeling stupid and cold and shirtless.

"How much money do you have?" Terzian asked.

"Couple of hundred."

"I have less."

"You should max out your credit card and just carry euros. Use your card now before they cancel it."

"Cancel it? How could they cancel it?"

She gave him a tight-lipped, impatient look. "Jonathan. They may be assholes, but they're still a *government*."

They took a cab to the American Express near the Opéra and Terzian got ten thousand euros in cash from some people who were extremely skeptical about the validity of his documents, but who had, in the end, to admit that all was technically correct. Then Stephanie got a cell phone under the name A. Silva, with a bunch of prepaid hours on it, and within a couple of hours they were on the TGV, speeding south to Nice at nearly two hundred seventy kilometers per hour, all with a strange absence of sound and vibration that made the French countryside speeding past seem like a strangely unconvincing special effect.

Terzian had put them in first class and he and Stephanie were alone in a group of four seats. Stephanie was twitchy because he hadn't bought seats in a smoking section. He sat uncertain, unhappy about all the cash he was carrying and not knowing what to do with it—he'd made two big rolls and zipped them into the pockets of his windbreaker. He carried the pistol in the front pocket of his jeans and its weight and discomfort was a perpetual reminder of this situation that he'd been dragged into, pursued by killers from Trashcanistan and escorting illegal biotechnology.

He kept mentally rehearsing drawing the pistol and shooting it. Over and over, remembering to thumb off the safety this time. Just in case Trashcanian commandos stormed the train.

"Hurled into life," he muttered. "An object lesson right out of Heidegger."

"Beg pardon?"

He looked at her. "Heidegger said we're hurled into life. Just like I've been hurled into—" He flapped his hands uselessly. "Into whatever this is. The situation exists before you even got here, but here you are anyway, and the whole business is something you inherit and have to live with." He felt his lips draw back in a snarl. "He also said that a fundamental feature of existence is anxiety in the face of death, which would also seem to apply to our situation. And his answer to all of this was to make existence, *dasein* if you want to get technical, an authentic project." He looked at her. "So what's your authentic project, then? And how authentic is it?"

Her brow furrowed. "What?"

Terzian couldn't stop, not that he wanted to. It was just Stephanie's hard luck that he couldn't shoot anybody right now, or break something up with his fists, and was compelled to lecture instead. "Or," he went on, "to put this in a more accessible context, just pretend we're in a Hitchcock film, okay? This is the scene where Grace Kelly tells Cary Grant exactly who she is and what the maguffin is."

Stephanie's face was frozen into a hostile mask. Whether she understood what he was saying or not, the hostility was clear.

"I don't get it," she said.

"What's in the fucking bag?" he demanded.

She glared at him for a long moment, then spoke, her own anger plain in her voice. "It's the answer to world hunger," she said. "Is that authentic enough for you?"

Stephanie's father was from Angola and her mother from East Timor, both former Portuguese colonies swamped in the decades since independence by war and massacre. Both parents had, with great foresight and intelligence, retained Portuguese passports, and had met in Rome, where they worked for UNESCO, and where Stephanie had grown up with a blend of their genetics and their service ethic.

Stephanie herself had received a degree in administration from the University of Virginia, which accounted for the American lights in her English, then she'd gotten another degree in nursing and went to work for the Catholic relief agency Santa Croce, which sent her to its every war-wrecked, locust-blighted, warlord-ridden, sandstorm-blasted camp in Africa. And a few that *weren't* in Africa.

"Trashcanistan," Terzian said.

"Moldova," Stephanie said. "For three months, on what was supposed to be my vacation." She shuddered. "I don't mind telling you that it was a frightening thing. I was used to that kind of thing in Africa, but to see it all happening in the developed world . . . warlords, ethnic hatreds, populations being moved at the point of a gun, whole forested districts being turned to deserts because people suddenly need firewood. . . ." Her emerald eyes flashed. "It's all politics, okay? Just like in Africa. Famine and camps are all politics now, and have been since before I was born. A whole population starves, and it's because someone, somewhere, sees a profit in it. It's difficult to just kill an ethnic group you don't like, war is expensive and there are questions at the UN and you may end up at the Hague being tried for war crimes. But if you just wait for a bad harvest and then arrange for the whole population to *starve*, it's different—suddenly your enemies are giving you all their money in return for food, you get aid from the UN instead of grief, and you can award yourself a piece of the relief action and collect bribes from all the relief agencies, and your enemies are rounded up into camps and you can get your armed forces into the country without resistance, make sure your enemies disappear, control everything while some deliveries disappear into government warehouses where the food can be sold to the starving or just sold abroad for a profit. . . ." She shrugged. "That's the way of the world, okay? *But no more!*" She grabbed a fistful of the Nike bag and brandished it at him.

What her time in Moldova had done was to leave Stephanie contacts in the area, some in relief agencies, some in industry and government. So that when news of a useful project came up in Transnistria, she was among the first to know.

"So what is it?" Terzian asked. "Some kind of genetically modified food crop?"

"No." She smiled thinly. "What we have here is a genetically modified *consumer.*"

Those Transnistrian companies had mostly been interested in duplicating pharmaceuticals and transgenic food crops created by other companies, producing them on the cheap and underselling the patent-owners. There were bits and pieces of everything in those labs, DNA human and animal and vegetable. A lot of it had other people's trademarks and patents on it, even the human codes, which US law permitted companies to patent provided they came up with something useful to do with it. And what these semi-outlaw companies were doing was making two things they figured people couldn't do without: drugs and food.

And not just people, since animals need drugs and food, too. Starving, tubercular sheep or pigs aren't worth much at market, so there's as much money in keeping livestock alive as in doing the same for people. So at some point one of the administrators—after a few too many shots of vodka flavored with bison grass—said, "Why should we worry about feeding the animals at all? Why not have them grow their own food, like plants?"

So then began the Green Swine Project, an attempt to make pigs fat and happy by just herding them out into the sun.

"Green swine," Terzian repeated, wondering. "People are getting killed over green swine."

"Well, no." Stephanie waved the idea away with a twitchy swipe of her hand. "The idea never quite got beyond the vaporware stage, because at that point another question was asked—why swine? Adrian said, Why stop at having animals do photosynthesis—why not *people?*"

"No!" Terzian cried, appalled. "You're going to turn people green?"

Stephanie glared at him. "Something wrong with fat, happy green people?" Her hands banged out a furious rhythm on the armrests of her seat. "I'd have skin to match my eyes. Wouldn't that be attractive?"

"I'd have to see it first," Terzian said, the shock still rolling through his bones.

"Adrian was pretty smart," Stephanie said. "The Transnistrians killed themselves a real genius." She shook her head. "He had it all worked out. He wanted to limit the effect to the skin—no green muscle tissue or skeletons—so he started with a virus that has a tropism for the epidermis—papiloma, that's warts, okay?"

So now we've got green warts, Terzian thought, but he kept his mouth shut.

"So if you're Adrian, what you do is gut out the virus and re-encode to create chlorophyll. Once a person's infected, exposure to sunlight will cause the virus to replicate and chlorophyll to reproduce in the skin."

Terzian gave Stephanie a skeptical look. "That's not going to be very efficient," he said. "Plants get sugars and oxygen from chlorophyll, okay, but they don't need much food, they stand in one place and don't walk around. Add chlorophyll to a person's skin, how many calories do you get each day? Tens? Dozens?"

Stephanie's lips parted in a fierce little smile. "You don't stop with just the chlorophyll. You have to get really efficient electron transport. In a plant that's handled in the chloroplasts, but the human body already has mitochondria to do the same job. You don't have to create these huge support mechanisms for the chlorophyll, you just make use of what's already there. So if you're Adrian, what you do is add trafficking tags to the reaction center proteins so that they'll target the mitochondria, which *already* are loaded with proteins to handle electron transport. The result is that the mitochondria handle transport from the chlorophyll, which is the sort of job they do anyway, and once the virus starts replicating, you can get maybe a thousand calories or more just from standing in the sun. It won't provide full nutrition, but it can keep starvation at bay, and it's not as if starving people have much to do besides stand in the sun anyway."

"It's not going to do much good for Icelanders," Terzian said.

She turned severe. "Icelanders aren't starving. It so happens that most of the people in the world who are starving happen to be in hot places."

Terzian flapped his hands. "Fine. I must be a racist. Sue me."

Stephanie's grin broadened, and she leaned toward Terzian. "I didn't tell you about Adrian's most interesting bit of cleverness. When people start getting normal nutrition, there'll be a competition within the mitochondria between normal metabolism and solar-induced electron transport. So the green virus is just a redundant backup system in case normal nutrition isn't available."

A triumphant smile crossed Stephanie's face. "Starvation will no longer be a weapon," she said. "Green skin can keep people active and on their feet long enough to get help. It will keep them healthy enough to fend off the epidemics associated with malnutrition. The point is—" She made fists and shook them at the sky. *"The bad guys don't get to use starvation as a weapon anymore! Famine ends!* One of the Four Horsemen of the Apocalypse dies, right here, right now, as a result of *what I've got in this bag!"* She picked up the bag and threw it into Terzian's lap, and he jerked on the seat in defensive reflex, knees rising to meet elbows. Her lips skinned back in a snarl, and her tone was mocking.

"I think even that Nazi fuck Heidegger would think my *project* is pretty damn *authentic*. Wouldn't you agree, Herr Doktor Terzian?"

Got you, Michelle thought. Here was a still photo of Terzian at the Fête des Aires de la Dine, with the dark-skinned woman. She had the same wide-brimmed straw hat she'd worn in the Florence church, and had the same black bag over her shoulder, but now Michelle had a clear view of a three-quarter profile, and one hand, with its critical alignments, was clearly visible, holding an ice cream cone.

Night insects whirled around the computer display. Michelle batted them away and got busy mapping. The photo was digital and Michelle could enlarge it.

To her surprise, she discovered that the woman had green eyes. Black women with green irises—or irises of orange or chartreuse or chrome steel—were not unusual in her own time, but she knew that in Terzian's time they were rare. That would make the search much easier.

"*Michelle . . .*" The voice came just as Michelle sent her new search spiders into the ether. A shiver ran up her spine.

"*Michelle . . .*" The voice came again.

It was Darton.

Michelle's heart gave a sickening lurch. She closed her console and put it back in the mesh bag, then crossed the rope bridge between the ironwood tree and the banyan. Her knees were weak, and the swaying bridge seemed to take a couple of unexpected pitches. She stepped out onto the banyan's sturdy overhanging limb and gazed out at the water.

"*Michelle . . .*" To the southwest, in the channel between the mermaid's island and another, she could see a pale light bobbing, the light of a small boat.

"*Michelle, where are you?*"

The voice died away in the silence and surf. Michelle remembered the spike in her hand, the long, agonized trek up the slope above Jellyfish Lake. Darton pale, panting for breath, dying in her arms.

The lake was one of the wonders of the world, but the steep path over the ridge that fenced the lake from the ocean was challenging even for those who were not dying. When Michelle and Darton—at that time, apes—came up from their boat that afternoon, they didn't climb the steep path, but swung hand-over-hand through the trees overhead, through the hardwood and guava trees, and avoided the poison trees with their bleeding, allergenic black sap. Even though their trip was less exhausting than if they'd gone over the land route, the two were ready for the cool water by the time they arrived at the lake.

Tens of thousands of years in the past, the water level was higher, and when it receded, the lake was cut off from the Pacific, and with it the *Mastigias* sp. jellyfish, which soon exhausted the supply of small fish that were its food. As the human race did later, the jellies gave up hunting and gathering in exchange for agriculture, and permitted themselves to be farmed by colonies of algae that provided the sugars they needed for life. At night, they'd descend to the bottom of the lake, where they fertilized their algae crops in the anoxic, sulfurous waters; at dawn, the jellies rose to the surface, and during the day, they crossed the lake, following the course of the sun, and allowed the sun's rays to supply the energy necessary for making their daily ration of food.

When Darton and Michelle arrived, there were ten million jellyfish in the lake, from fingertip-sized to jellies the size of a dinner plate, all in one warm throbbing golden-brown mass in the center of the water. The two swam easily on the surface with their long siamang arms, laughing and calling to one another as the jellyfish in their millions caressed them with the most featherlike of touches. The lake was the temperature of their own blood, and it was like a soupy bath, the jellyfish so thick that Michelle felt she could almost walk on the surface. The warm touch wasn't erotic, exactly, but it was sensual in the way that an erotic touch was sensual, a light brush over the skin by the pad of a teasing finger.

Trapped in a lake for thousands of years without suitable prey, the jellyfish had lost most of their ability to sting. Only a small percentage of people were sensitive enough to the toxin to receive a rash or feel a modest burning.

A very few people, though, were more sensitive than that.

Darton and Michelle left at dusk, and, by that time Darton was already gasping for breath. He said he'd overexerted himself, that all he needed was to get back to their base for a snack, but as he swung through the trees on the way up the ridge, he lost his hold on a Palauan apple tree and crashed through a thicket of limbs to sprawl, amid a hail of fruit, on the sharp algae-covered limestone of the ridge.

Michelle swung down from the trees, her heart pounding. Darton was nearly colorless and struggling to breathe. They had no way of calling for help unless Michelle took their boat to Koror or to their base camp on another island. She tried to help Darton walk, taking one of his long arms over her shoulder, supporting him up the steep island trail. He collapsed, finally, at the foot of a poison tree, and Michelle bent over him to shield him from the drops of venomous sap until he died.

Her back aflame with the poison sap, she'd whispered her parting words into Darton's ear. She never knew if he heard.

The coroner said it was a million-to-one chance that Darton had been so deathly allergic, and tried to comfort her with the thought that there was nothing she could have done. Torbiong, who had made the arrangements for Darton and Michelle to come in the first place, had been consoling, had offered to let Michelle stay with his family. Michelle had surprised him by asking permission to move her base camp to another island, and to continue her work alone.

She also had herself transformed into a mermaid, and subsequently, a romantic local legend.

And now Darton was back, bobbing in a boat in the nearby channel and calling her name, shouting into a bullhorn.

"*Michelle, I love you.*" The words floated clear into the night air. Michelle's mouth was dry. Her fingers formed the sign <go away>.

There was a silence, and then Michelle heard the engine start on Darton's boat. He motored past her position, within five hundred meters or so, and continued on to the northern point of the island.

<go away> . . .

"*Michelle* . . ." Again his voice floated out onto the breeze. It was clear that he didn't know where she was. She was going to have to be careful about showing lights.

<go away> . . .

Michelle waited while Darton called out a half-dozen more times, and then he started his engine and moved on. She wondered if he would search all three hundred islands in the Rock Island group.

No, she knew he was more organized than that.

She'd have to decide what to do when he finally found her.

While a thousand questions chased each other's tails through his mind, Terzian opened the Nike bag and withdrew the small hard plastic case inside, something like a box for fishing tackle. He popped the locks on the case and opened the lid, and he saw glass vials resting in slots cut into dark grey foam. In them was a liquid with a faint golden cast.

"The papiloma," Stephanie said.

Terzian dropped the lid on the case as he cast a guilty look over his shoulder, not wanting anyone to see him with this stuff. If he were arrested under suspicion of being a drug dealer, the wads of cash and the pistol certainly wouldn't help.

"What do you do with the stuff once you get to where you're going?"

"Brush it on the skin. With exposure to solar energy, it replicates as needed."

"Has it been tested?"

"On people? No. Works fine on rhesus monkeys, though."

He tapped his wedding ring on the arm of his seat. "Can it be . . . caught? I mean, it's a virus, can it go from one person to another?"

"Through skin-to-skin contact."

"I'd say that's a yes. Can mothers pass it on to their children?"

"Adrian didn't think it would cross the placental barrier, but he didn't get a chance to test it. If mothers want to infect their children, they'll probably have to do it deliberately." She shrugged. "Whatever the case, my guess is that mothers won't mind green babies, as long as they're green *healthy* babies." She looked down at the little vials in their secure coffins of foam. "We can infect tens of thousands of people with this amount," she said. "And we can make more very easily."

If mothers want to infect their children . . . Terzian closed the lid of the plastic case and snapped the locks. "You're out of your mind," he said.

Stephanie cocked her head and peered at him, looking as if she'd anticipated his objections and was humoring him. "How so?"

"Where do I start?" Terzian zipped up the bag, then tossed it in Stephanie's lap, pleased to see her defensive reflexes leap in response. "You're planning on unleashing an untested transgenic virus on Africa—on *Africa* of all places, a continent that doesn't exactly have a happy history with pandemics: And it's a virus that's cooked up by a bunch of illegal pharmacists in a non-country with a murderous secret police, facts that don't give me much confidence that this is going to be anything but a disaster."

Stephanie tapped two fingers on her chin as if she were wishing there were a cigarette between them. "I can put your mind to rest on the last issue. The animal study worked. Adrian had a family of bright green rhesus in his lab, till the project was canceled and the rhesus were, ah, liquidated."

"So if the project's so terrific, why'd the company pull the plug?"

"Money." Her lips twisted in anger. "Starving people can't afford to pay for the treatments, so they'd have to practically give the stuff away. Plus they'd get reams of endless bad publicity, which is exactly what outlaw biotech companies in outlaw countries don't want. There are millions of people who go ballistic at the very thought of a genetically engineered *vegetable*—you can imagine how people who can't abide the idea of a transgenic bell pepper would freak at the thought of infecting people with an engineered virus. The company decided it wasn't worth the risk. They closed the project down."

Stephanie looked at the bag in her hands. "But Adrian had been in the camps himself, you see. A displaced person, a refugee from the civil war in Moldova. And he couldn't stand the thought that there was a way to end hunger sitting in his refrigerator in the lab, and that nothing was being done with it. And so . . ." Her hands outlined the case inside the Nike bag. "He called me. He took some vacation time and booked himself into the Henri IV, on the Place Dauphine. And I guess he must have been careless, because . . ."

Tears starred in her eyes, and she fell silent. Terzian, strong in the knowledge that he'd shared quite enough of her troubles by now, stared out the window, at the green landscape that was beginning to take on the brilliant colors of Provence. The Hautes-Alpes floated blue and white-capped in the distant East, and nearby were orchards of almonds and olives with shimmering leaves, and hillsides covered with rows of orderly vines. The Rhone ran silver under the westering sun.

"I'm not going to be your bagman," he said. "I'm not going to contaminate the world with your freaky biotech."

"Then they'll catch you and you'll die," Stephanie said. "And it will be for nothing."

"My experience of death," said Terzian, "is that it's *always* for nothing."

She snorted then, angry. "My experience of death," she mocked, "is that it's too often for *profit*. I want to make mass murder an unprofitable venture. I want to crash the market in starvation by *giving away life*." She gave another snort, amused this time. "It's the ultimate anti-capitalist gesture."

Terzian didn't rise to that. Gestures, he thought, were just that. Gestures didn't change the fundamentals. If some jefe couldn't starve his people to death, he'd just use bullets, or deadly genetic technology he bought from outlaw Transnistrian corporations.

The landscape, all blazing green, raced past at over two hundred kilometers per hour. An attendant came by and sold them each a cup of coffee and a sandwich.

"You should use my phone to call your wife," Stephanie said as she peeled the cellophane from her sandwich. "Let her know that your travel plans have changed."

Apparently she'd noticed Terzian's wedding ring.

"My wife is dead," Terzian said.

She looked at him in surprise. "I'm sorry," she said.

"Brain cancer," he said.

Though it was more complicated than that. Claire had first complained of back pain, and there had been an operation, and the tumor removed from her spine. There had been a couple of weeks of mad joy and relief, and then it had been revealed that the cancer had spread to the brain and that it was inoperable. Chemotherapy had failed. She died six weeks after her first visit to the doctor.

"Do you have any other family?" Stephanie said.

"My parents are dead, too." Auto accident, aneurysm. He didn't mention Claire's uncle Geoff and his partner Luis, who had died of HIV within eight months of each other and left Claire the Victorian house on Esplanade in New Orleans. The house that, a few weeks ago, he had sold for six hundred and fifty thousand dollars, and the furnishings for a further ninety-five thousand, and Uncle Geoff's collection of equestrian art for a further forty-one thousand.

He was disinclined to mention that he had quite a lot of money, enough to float around Europe for years.

Telling Stephanie that might only encourage her.

There was a long silence. Terzian broke it. "I've read spy novels," he said. "And I know that we shouldn't go to the place we've bought tickets for. We shouldn't go anywhere *near* Nice."

She considered this, then said, "We'll get off at Avignon."

They stayed in Provence for nearly two weeks, staying always in unrated hotels, those that didn't even rise to a single star from the Ministry of Tourism, or in *gîtes ruraux*, farmhouses with rooms for rent. Stephanie spent much of her energy trying to call colleagues in Africa on her cell phone and achieved only sporadic success, a frustration that left her in a near-permanent fury. It was never clear just who she was trying to call, or how she thought they were going to get the papiloma off her hands. Terzian wondered how many people were involved in this conspiracy of hers.

They attended some local fêtes, though it was always a struggle to convince Stephanie it was safe to appear in a crowd. She made a point of disguising herself in big hats and shades and ended up looking like a cartoon spy. Terzian tramped rural lanes or fields or village streets, lost some pounds despite the splendid fresh local cuisine, and gained a suntan. He made a stab at writing several papers on his laptop, and spent time researching them in internet cafés.

He kept thinking he would have enjoyed this trip, if only Claire had been with him.

"What is it you *do*, exactly?" Stephanie asked him once, as he wrote. "I know you teach at university, but . . ."

"I don't teach anymore," Terzian said. "I didn't get my post-doc renewed. The department and I didn't exactly get along."

"Why not?"

Terzian turned away from the stale, stalled ideas on his display. "I'm too interdisciplinary. There's a place on the academic spectrum where history and politics and philosophy come together—it's called 'political theory' usually—but I throw in economics and a layman's understanding of science as well, and it confuses everybody but me. That's why my MA is in American Studies—nobody in my philosophy or political science department had the nerve to deal with me, and nobody knows what American Studies actually *are*, so I was able to hide out there. And my doctorate is in philosophy, but only because I found one rogue professor emeritus who was willing to chair my committee.

"The problem is that if you're hired by a philosophy department, you're supposed to teach Plato or Hume or whoever, and they don't want you confusing everybody by adding Maynard Keynes and Leo Szilard. And if you teach history, you're supposed to confine yourself to acceptable stories about the past and not toss in ideas about perceptual mechanics and Kant's ideas of the noumenon, and of course you court crucifixion from the laity if you mention Foucault or Nietzsche."

Amusement touched Stephanie's lips. "So where do you find a job?"

"France?" he ventured, and they laughed. "In France, 'thinker' is a job description. It's not necessary to have a degree, it's just something you do." He shrugged. "And if that fails, there's always Burger King."

She seemed amused. "Sounds like burgers are in your future."

"Oh, it's not as bad as all that. If I can generate enough interesting, sexy, highly original papers, I might attract attention and a job, in that order."

"And have you done that?"

Terzian looked at his display and sighed. "So far, no."

Stephanie narrowed her eyes and she considered him. "You're not a conventional person. You don't think inside the box, as they say."

"As they say," Terzian repeated.

"Then you should have no objections to radical solutions to world hunger. Particularly ones that don't cost a penny to white liberals throughout the world."

"Hah," Terzian said. "Who says I'm a liberal? I'm an *economist*."

So Stephanie told him terrible things about Africa. Another famine was brewing across the southern part of the continent. Mozambique was plagued with flood *and* drought, a startling combination. The Horn of Africa was worse. According to her friends, Santa Croce had a food shipment stuck in Mogadishu and before letting it pass, the local warlord wanted to renegotiate his bribe. In the meantime, people were starving, dying of malnutrition, infection, and dysentery in camps in the dry highlands of Bale and Sidamo. Their own government in Addis Ababa was worse than the Somali warlord, at this stage permitting no aid at all, bribes or no bribes.

And as for the southern Sudan, it didn't bear thinking about.

"What's *your* solution to this?" she demanded of Terzian. "Or do you have one?"

"Test this stuff, this papiloma," he said, "show me that it works, and I'm with you. But there are too many plagues in Africa as it is."

"Confine the papiloma to labs while thousands die? Hand it to governments who can suppress it because of pressure from religious loons and hysterical NGOs? You call *that* an answer?" And Stephanie went back to working her phone while Terzian walked off in anger for another stalk down country lanes.

Terzian walked toward an old ruined castle that shambled down the slope of a nearby hill. And if Stephanie's plant-people proved viable? he wondered. All bets were off. A world in which humans could become plants was a world in which none of the old rules applied.

Stephanie had said she wanted to crash the market in starvation. But, Terzian thought, that also meant crashing the market in *food*. If people with no money had all the food they needed, that meant *food itself had no value in the marketplace*. Food would be so cheap that there would be no profit in growing or selling it.

And this was all just *one application* of the technology. Terzian tried to keep up with science: he knew about nanoassemblers. Green people was just the first magic bullet in a long volley of scientific musketry that would change every fundamental rule by which humanity had operated since they'd first stood upright. What happened when *every* basic commodity—food, clothing, shelter, maybe even health—was so cheap that it was free? What then had value?

Even *money* wouldn't have value then. Money only had value if it could be exchanged for something of equivalent worth.

He paused in his walk and looked ahead at the ruined castle, the castle that had once provided justice and security and government for the district, and he wondered if he was looking at the future of *all* government. Providing an orderly framework in which commodities could be exchanged was the basic function of the state, that and providing a secure currency. If people didn't need government to furnish that kind of security and if the currency was worthless, the whole future of government itself was in question. Taxes weren't worth the expense of collecting if the money wasn't any good, anyway, and without taxes, government couldn't be paid for.

Terzian paused at the foot of the ruined castle and wondered if he saw the future of the civilized world. Either the castle would be rebuilt by tyrants, or it would fall.

Michelle heard Darton's bullhorn again the next evening, and she wondered why he was keeping fruit-bat hours. Was it because his calls would travel farther at night?

If he were sleeping in the morning, she thought, that would make it easier. She'd finished analyzing some of her samples, but a principle of science was not to do these things alone: she'd have to travel to Koror to mail her samples to other people, and now she knew to do it in the morning, when Darton would be asleep.

The problem for Michelle was that she was a legend. When the lonely mermaid emerged from the sea and walked to the post office in the little foam booties she wore when walking on pavement, she was noticed. People pointed: children followed her on their boards, people in cars waved. She wondered if she could trust them not to contact Darton as soon as they saw her.

She hoped that Darton wasn't starting to get the islanders on his side.

Michelle and Darton had met on a field trip in Borneo, their obligatory government service after graduation. The other field workers were older, paying their taxes or working on their second or third or fourth or fifth careers, and Michelle knew on sight that Darton was no older than she, that he, too, was a child among all these elders. They were pulled to each other as if drawn by some violent natural force, cataloguing snails and terrapins by day and spending their nights wrapped in each other in their own shell, their turtleback tent. The ancients with whom they shared their days treated them with amused condescension, but then, that was how they treated everything. Darton and Michelle didn't care. In their youth they stood against all creation.

When the trip came to an end, they decided to continue their work together, just a hop across the equator in Belau. Paying their taxes ahead of time. They celebrated by getting new bodies, an exciting experience for Michelle, who had been built by strict parents who wouldn't allow her to have a new body until adulthood, no matter how many of her friends had been transforming from an early age into one newly fashionable shape or another.

Michelle and Darton thought that anthropoid bodies would be suitable for the work, and so they went to the clinic in Delhi and settled themselves on nanobeds and let the little machines turn their bodies, their minds, their memories, their desires and their knowledge and their souls, into long strings of numbers. All of which were fed into their new bodies when they were ready, and reserved as backups to be downloaded as necessary.

Being a siamang was a glorious discovery. They soared through the tree-tops of their little island, swinging overhand from limb to limb in a frenzy of glory. Michelle took a particular delight in her body hair—she didn't have as much as a real ape, but there was enough on her chest and back to be interesting. They built nests of foliage in trees and lay tangled together, analyzing data or making love or shaving their hair into interesting tribal patterns. Love was far from placid—it was a flame, a fury. An obsession that, against all odds, had been fulfilled, only to build the flame higher.

The fury still burned in Michelle. But now, after Darton's death, it had a different quality, a quality that had nothing to do with life or youth.

Michelle, spooning up blueberries and cream, riffled through the names and faces her spiders had spat out. There were, now she added them up, a preposterous number of pictures of green-eyed women with dark skin whose pictures were somewhere in the net. Nearly all of them had striking good looks. Many of them were unidentified in the old scans, or identified only by a first name. The highest probability the software offered was 43 percent.

That 43 percent belonged to a Brazilian named Laura Flor, who research swiftly showed was home in Aracaju during the critical period, among other things having a baby. A video of the delivery was available, but Michelle didn't watch it. The way women delivered babies back then was disgusting.

The next most likely female was another Brazilian seen in some tourist photographs taken in Rio. Not even a name given. A further search based on this woman's physiognomy turned up nothing, not until Michelle broadened the search to a different gender, and discovered that the Brazilian was a transvestite. That didn't seem to be Terzian's scene, so she left it alone.

The third was identified only as Stephanie, and posted on a site created by a woman who had done relief work in Africa. Stephanie was shown with a group of other relief workers, posing in front of a tin-roofed, cinderblock building identified as a hospital.

The quality of the photograph wasn't very good, but Michelle mapped the physiognomy anyway, and sent it forth along with the name "Stephanie" to see what might happen.

There was a hit right away, a credit card charge to a Stephanie América Pais e Silva. She had stayed in a hotel in Paris for the three nights before Terzian disappeared.

Michelle's blood surged as the data flashed on her screens. She sent out more spiders and the good news began rolling in.

Stephanie Pais was a dual citizen of Portugal and Angola, and had been educated partly in the States—a quick check showed that her time at university didn't overlap Terzian's. From her graduation, she had worked for a relief agency called Santa Croce.

Then a news item turned up, a sensational one. Stephanie Pais had been spectacularly murdered in Venice on the night of July 19, six days before Terzian had delivered the first version of his Cornucopia Theory.

Two murders. . . .

One in Paris, one in Venice. And one of them of the woman who seemed to be Terzian's lover.

Michelle's body shivered to a sudden gasping spasm, and she realized that in her suspense she'd been holding her breath. Her head swam. When it cleared, she worked out what time it was in Maryland, where Dr. Davout lived, and then told her deck to page him at once.

Davout was unavailable at first, and by the time he returned her call, she had more information about Stephanie Pais. She blurted the story out to him while her fingers jabbed at the keyboard of her deck, sending him copies of her corroborating data.

Davout's startled eyes leaped from the data to Michelle and back. "How much of this," he began, then gave up. "How did she die?" he managed.

"The news article says stabbed. I'm looking for the police report."

"Is Terzian mentioned?"

<No> she signed. "The police report will have more details."

"Any idea what this is about? There's no history of Terzian *ever* being connected with violence."

"By tomorrow," Michelle said, "I should be able to tell you. But I thought I should send this to you because you might be able to tie this in with other elements of Terzian's life that I don't know anything about."

Davout's fingers formed a mudra that Michelle didn't recognize—an old one, probably. He shook his head. "I have no idea what's happening here. The only thing I have to suggest is that this is some kind of wild coincidence."

"I don't believe in that kind of coincidence," Michelle said.

Davout smiled. "A good attitude for a researcher," he said. "But experience—well," he waved a hand.

But he loved her, Michelle insisted inwardly. She knew that in her heart.

She was the woman he loved after Claire died, and then she was killed and Terzian went on to create the intellectual framework on which the world was now built. He had spent his modest fortune building pilot programs in Africa that demonstrated his vision was a practical one. The whole modern world was a monument to Stephanie.

Everyone was young then, Michelle thought. Even the seventy-year-olds were young compared to the people now. The world must have been *ablaze* with love and passion. But Davout didn't understand that because he was old and had forgotten all about love.

"*Michelle* . . ." Darton's voice came wafting over the waters.

Bastard. Michelle wasn't about to let him spoil this.

Her fingers formed <gotta go>. "I'll send you everything once it comes in," she said. "I think we've got something amazing here."

She picked up her deck and swung it around so that she could be sure that the light from the display couldn't be seen from the ocean. Her bare back against the rough bark of the ironwood, she began flashing through the data as it arrived.

She couldn't find the police report. Michelle went in search of it and discovered that all police records from that period in Venetian history had been wiped out in the Lightspeed War, leaving her only with what had been reported in the media.

"*Where are you? I love you!*" Darton's voice came from farther away. He'd narrowed his search, that was clear, but he still wasn't sure exactly where Michelle had built her nest.

Smiling, Michelle closed her deck and slipped it into its pouch. Her spiders would work for her tirelessly till dawn while she dreamed on in her hammock and let Darton's distant calls lull her to sleep.

They shifted their lodgings every few days. Terzian always arranged for separate bedrooms. Once, as they sat in the evening shade of a farm terrace and watched the setting sun shimmer on the silver leaves of the olives, Terzian found himself looking at her as she sat in an old cane chair, at the profile cutting sharp against the old limestone of the Vaucluse. The blustering wind brought gusts of lavender from the neighboring farm, a scent that made Terzian want to inhale until his lungs creaked against his ribs.

From a quirk of Stephanie's lips, Terzian was suddenly aware that she knew he was looking at her. He glanced away.

"You haven't tried to sleep with me," she said.

"No," he agreed.

"But you *look*," she said. "And it's clear you're not a eunuch."

"We fight all the time," Terzian pointed out. "Sometimes we can't stand to be in the same room."

Stephanie smiled. "That wouldn't stop most of the men I've known. Or the women, either."

Terzian looked out over the olives, saw them shimmer in the breeze. "I'm still in love with my wife," he said.

There was a moment of silence. "That's well," she said.

And I'm angry at her, too, Terzian thought. Angry at Claire for deserting him. And he was furious at the universe for killing her and for leaving him alive, and he was angry at God even though he didn't believe in God. The Trashcanians had been good for him, because he could let his rage and his hatred settle there, on people who deserved it.

Those poor drunken bastards, he thought. Whatever they'd expected in that hotel corridor, it hadn't been a berserk grieving American who would just as soon have ripped out their throats with his bare hands.

The question was, could he do that again? It had all occurred without his thinking about it, old reflexes taking over, but he couldn't count on that happening a second time. He'd been trying to remember the Kenpo he'd once learned, particularly all the tricks against weapons. He found himself miming combats on his long country hikes, and he wondered if he'd retained any of his ability to take a punch.

He kept the gun with him, so the Trashcanians wouldn't get it if they searched his room when he was away. When he was alone, walking through the almond orchards or on a hillside fragrant with wild thyme, he practiced drawing it, snicking off the safety, and putting pressure on the trigger . . . the first time the trigger pull would be hard, but the first shot would cock the pistol automatically and after that the trigger pull would be light.

He wondered if he should buy more ammunition. But he didn't know how to buy ammunition in France and didn't know if a foreigner could get into trouble that way.

"We're both angry," Stephanie said. He looked at her again, her hand raised to her head to keep the gusts from blowing her long ringlets in her face. "We're angry at death. But love must make it more complicated for you."

Her green eyes searched him. "It's not death you're in love with, is it? Because—"

Terzian blew up. She had no right to suggest that he was in a secret alliance with death just because he didn't want to turn a bunch of Africans green. It was their worst argument, and this one ended with both of them stalking away through the fields and orchards while the scent of lavender pursued them on the wind.

When Terzian returned to his room, he checked his caches of money, half-hoping that Stephanie had stolen his euros and run. She hadn't.

He thought of going into her room while she was away, stealing the papiloma, and taking a train north, handing it over to the Pasteur Institute or someplace. But he didn't.

In the morning, during breakfast, Stephanie's cell phone rang, and she answered. He watched while her face turned from curiosity to apprehension to utter terror. Adrenaline sang in his blood as he watched, and he leaned forward, feeling the familiar rage rise in him, just where he wanted it. In haste, she turned off the phone, then looked at him. "That was one of them. He says he knows where we are, and wants to make a deal."

"If they know where we are," Terzian found himself saying coolly, "why aren't they here?"

"We've got to *go*," she insisted.

So they went. Clean out of France and into the Tuscan hills, with Stephanie's cell phone left behind in a trash can at the train station and a new phone purchased in Siena. The Tuscan countryside was not unlike Provence, with vine-covered hillsides, orchards a-shimmer with the silver-green of olive trees, and walled medieval towns perched on crags; but the slim, tall cypress standing like sentries gave the hills a different profile, and there were different types of wine grapes, and many of the vineyards rented rooms where people could stay and sample the local hospitality. Terzian didn't speak the language, and because Spanish was his first foreign language, consistently pronounced words like "villa" and "panzanella" as if they were Spanish. But Stephanie had grown up in Italy and spoke the language not only like a native, but like a native Roman.

Florence was only a few hours away, and Terzian couldn't resist visiting one of the great living monuments to civilization. His parents had taken him to Europe several times as a child, but somehow never made it here.

Terzian and Stephanie spent a day wandering the center of town, on occasion taking shelter from one of the pelting rainstorms that shattered the day. At one point, with thunder booming overhead, they found themselves in the Basilica di Santa Croce.

"Holy Cross," Terzian said, translating. "That's your outfit."

"We have nothing to do with this church," Stephanie said. "We don't even have a collection box here."

"A pity," Terzian said as he looked at the soaked swarms of tourists packed in the aisles. "You'd clean up."

Thunder accompanied the camera strobes that flashed against the huge tomb of Galileo like a vast lightning storm. "Nice of them to forget about that Inquisition thing and bury him in a church," Terizan said.

"I expect they just wanted to keep an eye on him."

It was the power of capital, Terzian knew, that had built this church, that had paid for the stained glass and the Giotto frescoes and the tombs and cenotaphs to the great names of Florence: Dante, Michelangelo, Bruni, Alberti, Marconi, Fermi, Rossini, and of course Machiavelli. This structure, with its vaults and chapels and sarcophagi and chanting Franciscans, had been raised by successful bankers, people to whom money was a real, tangible thing, and who had paid for the centuries of labor to build the basilica with caskets of solid, weighty coined silver.

"So what do you think he would make of this?" Terzian asked, nodding at the resting place of Machiavelli, now buried in the city from which he'd been exiled in his lifetime.

Stephanie scowled at the unusually plain sarcophagus with its Latin inscription. "No praise can be high enough," she translated, then turned to him as tourist cameras flashed. "Sounds overrated."

"He was a republican, you know," Terzian said. "You don't get that from just *The Prince*. He wanted Florence to be a republic, defended by citizen soldiers. But when it fell into the hands of a despot, he needed work, and he wrote the manual for despotism. But he looked at despotism a little too clearly, and he didn't get the job." Terzian turned to Stephanie. "He was the founder of modern political theory, and that's what I do. And he based his ideas on the belief that all human beings, at all times, have the same passions." He turned his eyes deliberately to Stephanie's shoulder bag. "That may be about to end, right? You're going to turn people into plants. That should change the passions if anything would."

"Not *plants*," Stephanie hissed, and glanced left and right at the crowds. "And not *here*." She began to move down the aisle, in the direction of Michelangelo's ornate tomb, with its draped figures who appeared not in mourning, but as if they were trying to puzzle out a difficult engineering problem.

"What happens in your scheme," Terzian said, following, "is that the market in food crashes. But that's not the *real* problem. The real problem is, what happens to the market in *labor?*"

Tourist cameras flashed. Stephanie turned her head away from the array of Kodaks. She passed out of the basilica and to the portico. The cloudburst had come to an end, but rainwater still drizzled off the structure. They stepped out of the droplets and down the stairs into the piazza.

The piazza was walled on all sides by old palaces, most of which now held restaurants or shops on the ground floor. To the left, one long palazzo was covered with canvas and scaffolding. The sound of pneumatic hammers banged out over the piazza. Terzian waved a hand in the direction of the clatter.

"Just imagine that food is nearly free," he said. "Suppose you and your children can get most of your food from standing in the sunshine. My next question is, *Why in hell would you take a filthy job like standing on a scaffolding and sandblasting some old building?*"

He stuck his hands in his pockets and began walking at Stephanie's side along the piazza. "Down at the bottom of the labor market, there are a lot of people whose labor goes almost entirely for the necessities. Millions of them cross borders illegally in order to send enough money back home to support their children."

"You think I don't know that?"

"The only reason that there's a market in illegal immigrants is that *there are jobs that well-off people won't do*. Dig ditches. Lay roads. Clean sewers. Restore old buildings. Build *new* buildings. The well-off might serve in the military or police, because there's a certain status involved and an attractive uniform, but we won't guard prisons, no matter how pretty the uniform is. That's strictly a job for the laboring classes, and if the laboring classes are too well-off to labor, who guards the prisons?"

She rounded on him, her lips set in an angry line. "So I'm supposed to be afraid of people having more choice in where they work?"

"No," Terzian said, "you should be afraid of people having *no choice at all*. What happens when markets collapse is *intervention*—and that's state intervention, if the market's critical enough, and you can bet the labor market's critical. And because the state depends on ditch-diggers and prison guards and janitors and road-builders for its very being, then if these classes of people are no longer available, and the very survival of civil society depends on their existence, in the end, the state will just *take* them.

"You think our friends in Transnistria will have any qualms about rounding up people up at gunpoint and forcing them to do labor? The powerful are going to want their palaces kept nice and shiny. The liberal democracies will try volunteerism or lotteries or whatever, but you can bet that we're going to want our sewers to work, and somebody to carry our grandparents' bedpans, and the trucks to the supermarkets to run on time. And what *I'm* afraid of is that when things get desperate, we're not going to be any nicer about getting our way than those Sovietists of yours. We're going to make sure that the lower orders do their jobs, even if we have to kill half of them to convince the other half that we mean business. And the technical term for that is *slavery*. And if someone of African descent isn't sensitive to *that* potential problem, then I am very surprised!"

The fury in Stephanie's eyes was visible even through her shades, and he could see the pulse pounding in her throat. Then she said, "I'll save the *people*, that's what I'm good at. You save the rest of the world, *if* you can." She began to turn away, then swung back to him. "And by the way," she added, "fuck you!" turned, and marched away.

"Slavery or anarchy, Stephanie!" Terzian called, taking a step after. "That's the choice you're forcing on people!"

He really felt he had the rhetorical momentum now, and he wanted to enlarge the point by saying that he knew some people thought anarchy was a good thing, but no anarchist he'd ever met had ever even *seen* a real anarchy, or been in one, whereas Stephanie had—drop your anarchist out of a helicopter into the eastern Congo, say, with all his theories and with whatever he could carry on his back, and see how well he prospered. . . .

But Terzian never got to say any of these things, because Stephanie was gone, receding into the vanishing point of a busy street, the shoulder bag swinging back and forth across her butt like a pendulum powered by the force of her convictions.

Terzian thought that perhaps he'd never see her again, that he'd finally provoked her into abandoning him and continuing on her quest alone, but when he stepped off the bus in Montespèrtoli that night, he saw her across the street, shouting into her cell phone.

A day later, as with frozen civility they drank their morning coffee, she said that she was going to Rome the next day. "They might be looking for me there," she said, "because my parents live there. But I won't go near the family, I'll meet Odile at the airport and give her the papiloma."

Odile? Terzian thought. "I should go along," he said.

"What are you going to do?" she said, "carry that gun into an *airport?*"

"I don't have to take the gun. I'll leave it in the hotel room in Rome."

She considered. "Very well."

Again, that night, Terzian found the tumbled castle in Provence haunting his thoughts, that ruined relic of a bygone order, and once more considered stealing the papiloma and running. And again, he didn't.

They didn't get any farther than Florence, because Stephanie's cell phone rang as they waited in the train station. Odile was in Venice. "*Venezia?*" Stephanie shrieked in anger. She clenched her fists. There had been a cache of weapons found at the Fiumicino airport in Rome, and all planes had been diverted, Odile's to Marco Polo outside Venice. Frenzied booking agents had somehow found rooms for her despite the height of the tourist season.

Fiumicino hadn't been re-opened, and Odile didn't know how she was going to get to Rome. "Don't try!" Stephanie shouted. "I'll come to *you.*"

This meant changing their tickets to Rome for tickets to Venice. Despite Stephanie's excellent Italian, the ticket seller clearly wished the crazy tourists would make up their mind which monuments of civilization they really wanted to see.

Strange—Terzian had actually *planned* to go to Venice in five days or so. He was scheduled to deliver a paper at the Conference of Classical and Modern Thought.

Maybe, if this whole thing was over by then, he'd read the paper after all. It wasn't a prospect he coveted: he would just be developing another footnote to a footnote.

The hills of Tuscany soon began to pour across the landscape like a green flood. The train slowed at one point—there was work going on on the tracks, men with bronze arms and hard hats—and Terzian wondered how, in the Plant People Future, in the land of Cockaigne, the tracks would ever get fixed, particularly in this heat. He supposed there were people who were meant by nature to fix tracks, who would repair tracks as an *avocation* or out of boredom regardless of whether they got paid for their time or not, but he suspected that there wouldn't be many of them.

You could build machines, he supposed, robots or something. But they had their own problems, they'd cause pollution and absorb resources and, on top of everything, they'd break down and have to be repaired. And who would do *that?*

If you can't employ the carrot, Terzian thought, if you can't reward people for doing necessary labor, then you have to use the stick. You march people out of the cities at gunpoint, like Pol Pot, because there's work that needs to be done.

He tapped his wedding ring on the arm of his chair and wondered what jobs would still have value. Education, he supposed; he'd made a good choice there. Some sorts of administration were necessary. There were people who were natural artists or bureaucrats or salesmen and who would do that job whether they were paid or not.

A woman came by with a cart and sold Terzian some coffee and a nutty snack product that he wasn't quite able to identify. And then he thought, *labor.*

"Labor," he said. In a world in which all basic commodities were provided, the thing that had most value was actual labor. Not the stuff that labor bought, but the work *itself*.

"Okay," he said, "it's labor that's rare and valuable, because people don't *have* to do it anymore. The currency has to be based on some kind of labor exchange—you purchase x hours with y dollars. Labor is the thing you use to pay taxes."

Stephanie gave Terzian a suspicious look. "What's the difference between that and slavery?"

"Have you been reading Nozick?" Terzian scolded. "The difference is the same as the difference between *paying taxes* and *being a slave*. All the time you don't spend paying your taxes is your own." He barked a laugh. "I'm resurrecting Labor Value Theory!" he said. "Adam Smith and Karl Marx are dancing a jig on their tombstones! In Plant People Land, the value is the *labor itself! The calories!*" He laughed again, and almost spilled coffee down his chest.

"You budget the whole thing in calories! The government promises to pay you a dollar's worth of calories in exchange for their currency! In order to keep the roads and the sewer lines going, a citizen owes the government a certain number of calories per year—he can either pay in person or hire someone else to do the job. And jobs can be budgeted in calories-per-hour, so that if you do hard physical labor, you owe fewer hours than someone with a desk job—that should keep the young, fit, impatient people doing the nasty jobs, so that they have more free time for their other pursuits." He chortled. "Oh, the intellectuals are going to just hate this! They're used to valuing their brain power over manual labor—I'm going to reverse their whole scale of values!"

Stephanie made a pffing sound. "The people I care about have no money to pay taxes at all."

"They have bodies. They can still be enslaved." Terzian got out his laptop. "Let me put my ideas together."

Terzian's frenetic two-fingered typing went on for the rest of the journey, all the way across the causeway that led into Venice. Stephanie gazed out the window at the lagoon soaring by, the soaring water birds, and the dirt and stink of industry. She kept the Nike bag in her lap until the train pulled into the Stazione Ferrovia della Stato Santa Lucia at the end of its long journey.

Odile's hotel was in Cannaregio, which, according to the map purchased in the station gift shop, was the district of the city nearest the station and away from most of the tourist sites. A brisk wind almost tore the map from their fingers as they left the station, and their vaporetto bucked a steep chop on the grey-green Grand Canal as it took them to the Ca' d' Oro, the fanciful white High Gothic palazzo that loomed like a frantic wedding cake above a swarm of bobbing gondolas and motorboats.

Stephanie puffed cigarettes, at first with ferocity, then with satisfaction. Once they got away from the Grand Canal and into Cannaregio itself, they quickly became lost. The twisted medieval streets were broken on occasion by still, silent canals, but the canals didn't seem to lead anywhere in particular. Cooking smells demonstrated that it was dinnertime, and there were few people about, and no tourists. Terzian's stomach rumbled. Sometimes the streets deteriorated into mere passages. Stephanie and Terzian were in such a passage, holding their map open against the wind and shouting directions at each other, when someone slugged Terzian from behind.

He went down on one knee with his head ringing and the taste of blood in his mouth, and then two people rather unexpectedly picked him up again, only to slam him against the passage wall. Through some miracle, he managed not to hit his head on the brickwork and knock himself out. He could smell garlic on the breath of one of the attackers. Air went out of him as he felt an elbow to his ribs.

It was the scream from Stephanie that concentrated his attention. There was violent motion in front of him, and he saw the Nike swoosh, and remembered that he was dealing with killers, and that he had a gun.

In an instant, Terzian had his rage back. He felt his lungs fill with the fury that spread through his body like a river of scalding blood. He planted his feet and twisted abruptly to his left, letting the strength come up his legs from the earth itself, and the man attached to his right arm gave a grunt of surprise and swung counterclockwise. Terzian twisted the other way, which budged the other man only a little, but which freed his right arm to claw into his right pants pocket.

And from this point on it was just the movement that he had rehearsed. Draw, thumb the safety, pull the trigger hard. He shot the man on his right and hit him in the groin. For a brief second, Terzian saw his pinched face, the face that reflected such pain that it folded in on itself, and he remembered Adrian falling in the Place Dauphine with just that look. Then he stuck the pistol in the ribs of the man on his left and fired twice. The arms that grappled him relaxed and fell away.

There were two more men grappling with Stephanie. That made four altogether, and Terzian reasoned dully that after the first three fucked up in Paris, the home office had sent a supervisor. One was trying to tug the Nike bag away, and Terzian lunged toward him and fired at a range of two meters, too close to miss, and the man dropped to the ground with a whuff of pain.

The last man had hold of Stephanie and swung her around, keeping her between himself and the pistol. Terzian could see the knife in his hand and recognized it as one he'd seen before. Her dark glasses were cockeyed on her face and Terzian caught a flash of her angry green eyes. He pointed the pistol at the knife man's face. He didn't dare shoot.

"*Police!*" he shrieked into the wind. "*Policia!*" He used the Spanish word. Bloody spittle spattered the cobblestones as he screamed.

In the Trashcanian's eyes, he saw fear, bafflement, rage.

"*Polizia!*" He got the pronunciation right this time. He saw the rage in Stephanie's eyes, the fury that mirrored his own, and he saw her struggle against the man who held her.

"*No!*" he called. Too late. The knife man had too many decisions to make all at once, and Terzian figured he wasn't very bright to begin with. *Kill the hostages* was probably something he'd been taught on his first day at Goon School.

As Stephanie fell, Terzian fired, and kept firing as the man ran away. The killer broke out of the passageway into a little square, and then just fell down.

The slide of the automatic locked back as Terzian ran out of ammunition, and then he staggered forward to where Stephanie was bleeding to death on the cobbles.

Her throat had been cut and she couldn't speak. She gripped his arm as if she could drive her urgent message through the skin, with her nails. In her eyes, he saw frustrated rage, the rage he knew well, until at length he saw there nothing at all, a nothing he knew better than any other thing in the world.

He shouldered the Nike bag and staggered out of the passageway into the tiny Venetian square with its covered well. He took a street at random, and there was Odile's hotel. Of course: the Trashcanians had been staking it out.

It wasn't much of a hotel, and the scent of spice and garlic in the lobby suggested that the desk clerk was eating his dinner. Terzian went up the stair to Odile's room and knocked on the door. When she opened—she was a plump girl with big hips and a suntan—he tossed the Nike bag on the bed.

"You need to get back to Mogadishu right away," he said. "Stephanie just died for that."

Her eyes widened. Terzian stepped to the wash basin to clean the blood off as best he could. It was all he could do not to shriek with grief and anger.

"You take care of the starving," he said finally, "and I'll save the rest of the world."

Michelle rose from the sea near Torbiong's boat, having done thirty-six hundred calories' worth of research and caught a honeycomb grouper into the bargain. She traded the fish for the supplies he brought. "Any more blueberries?" she asked.

"Not this time." He peered down at her, narrowing his eyes against the bright shimmer of sun on the water. "That young man of yours is being quite a nuisance. He's keeping the turtles awake and scaring the fish."

The mermaid tucked away her wings and arranged herself in her rope sling. "Why don't you throw him off the island?"

"My authority doesn't run that far." He scratched his jaw. "He's interviewing people. Adding up all the places you've been seen. He'll find you pretty soon, I think."

"Not if I don't want to be found. He can yell all he likes, but I don't have to answer."

"Well, maybe." Torbiong shook his head. "Thanks for the fish."

Michelle did some preliminary work with her new samples, and then abandoned them for anything new that her search spiders had discovered. She had a feeling she was on the verge of something colossal.

She carried her deck to her overhanging limb and let her legs dangle over the water while she looked through the new data. While paging through the new information, she ate something called a Raspberry Dynamo Bar that Torbiong had thrown in with her supplies. The old man must have included it as a joke: it was over-sweet and sticky with marshmallow and strangely flavored. She chucked it in the water and hoped it wouldn't poison any fish.

Stephanie Pais had been killed in what the news reports called a "street fight" among a group of foreign visitors. Since the authorities couldn't connect the foreigners to Pais, they had to assume she was an innocent bystander caught up in the violence. The papers didn't mention Terzian at all.

Michelle looked through pages of followup. The gun that had shot the four men had never been found, though nearby canals were dragged. Two of the foreigners had survived the fight, though one died eight weeks later from complications of an operation. The survivor maintained his innocence and claimed that a complete stranger had opened fire on him and his friends, but the judges hadn't believed him and sent him to prison. He lived a great many years and died in the Lightspeed War, along with most people caught in prisons during that deadly time.

One of the four men was Belorussian. Another Ukrainian. Another two Moldovan. All had served in the Soviet military in the past, in the Fourteenth Army in Transnistria. It frustrated Michelle that she couldn't shout back in time to tell the Italians to connect these four to the murder of another ex-Soviet, seven weeks earlier, in Paris.

What the hell had Pais and Terzian been up to? Why were all these people with Transnistrian connections killing each other, and Pais?

Maybe it was Pais they'd been after all along. Her records at Santa Croce were missing, which was odd, because other personnel records from the time had survived. Perhaps someone was arranging that certain things not be known.

She tried a search on Santa Croce itself, and slogged through descriptions and mentions of a whole lot of Italian churches, including the famous one in Florence where Terzian and Pais had been seen at Machiavelli's tomb. She refined the search to the Santa Croce relief organization, and found immediately the fact that let it all fall into place.

Santa Croce had maintained a refugee camp in Moldova during the civil war following the establishment of Transnistria. Michelle was willing to bet that Stephanie Pais had served in that camp. She wondered if any of the other players had been residents there.

She looked at the list of the other camps that Santa Croce had maintained in that period, which seemed to have been a busy one for them. One name struck her as familiar, and she had to think for a moment before she remembered why she knew it. It was at a Santa Croce camp in the Sidamo province of Ethiopia where the Green Leopard Plague had first broken out, the first transgenic epidemic.

It had been the first real attempt to modify the human body at the cellular level, to help marginal populations synthesize their own food, and it had been primitive compared to the more successful mods that came later. The ideal design for the efficient use of chlorophyll was a leaf, not the homo sapien—the designer would have been better advised to create a plague that made its victims leafy, and later designers, aiming for the same effect, did exactly that. And Green Leopard's designer had forgotten that the epidermis already contains a solar-activated enzyme: melanin. The result on the African subjects was green skin mottled with dark splotches, like the black spots on an implausibly verdant leopard.

The Green Leopard Plague broke out in the Sidamo camp, then at other camps in the Horn of Africa. Then it leaped clean across the continent to Mozambique, where it first appeared at a Oxfam camp in the flood zone, spread rapidly across the continent, then leaped across oceans. It had been a generation before anyone found a way to disable it, and by then other transgenic modifiers had been released into the population, and there was no going back.

The world had entered Terzian's future, the one he had proclaimed at the Conference of Classical and Modern Thought.

What, Michelle thought excitedly, if Terzian had known about Green Leopard ahead of time? His Cornucopia Theory had seemed prescient precisely because Green Leopard appeared just a few weeks after he'd delivered his paper. But if those Eastern bloc thugs had been involved somehow in the plague's transmission, or were attempting to prevent Pais and Terzian from sneaking the modified virus to the camps. . . .

Yes! Michelle thought exultantly. That had to be it. No one had ever worked out where Green Leopard originated, but there had always been suspicion directed toward several semi-covert labs in the former Soviet empire. There was it. The only question was how Terzian, that American in Paris, had got involved. . . .

It had to be Stephanie, she thought. Stephanie, who Terzian had loved and who had loved him, and who had involved him in the desperate attempt to aid refugee populations.

For a moment, Michelle bathed in the beauty of the idea. Stephanie, dedicated and in love, had been murdered for her beliefs—realdeath!—and Terzian, broken-hearted, had carried on and brought the future—Michelle's present—into being. A wonderful story! And no one had known it till now, no one had understood Stephanie's sacrifice, or Terzian's grief . . . not until the lonely mermaid, working in isolation on her rock, had puzzled it out.

"Hello, Michelle," Darton said.

Michelle gave a cry of frustration and glared in fury down at her lover. He was in a yellow plastic kayak—kayaking was popular here, particularly in the Rock Islands—and had slipped his electric-powered boat along the margin of the island, moving in near-silence. He looked grimly up at her from below the pitcher plant that dangled below the overhang.

They had rebuilt him, of course, after his death. All the data was available in backup, in Delhi where he'd been taken apart, recorded, and rebuilt as an ape. He was back in a conventional male body, with the broad shoulders and white smile and short hairy bandy legs she remembered.

Michelle knew that he hadn't made any backups during their time in

Belau. He had his memories up to the point where he'd lain down on the nanobed in Delhi. That had been the moment when his love of Michelle had been burning its hottest, when he had just made the commitment to live with Michelle as an ape in the Rock Islands.

That burning love had been consuming him in the weeks since his resurrection, and Michelle was glad of it, had been rejoicing in every desperate, unanswered message that Darton sent sizzling through the ether.

"Damn it," Michelle said, "I'm working."

<Talk to me> Darton's fingers formed. Michelle's fingers made a ruder reply.

"I don't understand," Darton said. "We were in love. We were going to be together."

"I'm not talking to you," Michelle said. She tried to concentrate on her video display.

"We were still together when the accident happened," Darton said. "I don't understand why we can't be together now."

"I'm not listening, either," said Michelle.

"*I'm not leaving, Michelle!*" Darton screamed. "*I'm not leaving till you talk to me!*"

White cockatoos shrieked in answer. Michelle quietly picked up her deck, rose to her feet, and headed inland. The voice that followed her was amplified, and she realized that Darton had brought his bullhorn.

"*You can't get away, Michelle! You've got to tell me what happened!*"

I'll tell you about Lisa Lee, she thought, *so you can send her desperate messages, too.*

Michelle had been deliriously happy for her first month in Belau, living in arboreal nests with Darton and spending the warm days describing their island's unique biology. It was their first vacation, in Prague, that had torn Michelle's happiness apart. It was there that they'd met Lisa Lee Baxter, the American tourist who thought apes were cute, and who wondered what these shaggy kids were doing so far from an arboreal habitat.

It wasn't long before Michelle realized that Lisa Lee was at least two hundred years old, and that behind her diamond-blue eyes was the withered, mummified soul that had drifted into Prague from some waterless desert of the spirit, a soul that required for its continued existence the blood and vitality of the young. Despite her age and presumed experience, Lisa Lee's ploys seemed to Michelle to be so *obvious*, so *blatant*. Darton fell for them all.

It was only because Lisa Lee had finally tired of him that Darton returned to Belau, chastened and solemn and desperate to be in love with Michelle again. But by then it was Michelle who was tired. And who had access to Darton's medical records from the downloads in Delhi.

"*You can't get away, Michelle!*"

Well, maybe not. Michelle paused with one hand on the banyan's trunk. She closed her deck's display and stashed it in a mesh bag with some of her other stuff, then walked out again on the overhanging limb.

"I'm not going to talk to you like this," she said. "And you can't get onto the island from that side, the overhang's too acute."

"Fine," Darton said. The shouting had made him hoarse. "Come down here, then."

She rocked forward and dived off the limb. The salt water world exploded in her senses. She extended her wings and fluttered close to Darton's kayak, rose, and shook sea water from her eyes.

"There's a tunnel," she said. "It starts at about two meters and exits into the lake. You can swim it easily if you hold your breath."

"All right," he said. "Where is it?"

"Give me your anchor."

She took his anchor, floated to the bottom, and set it where it wouldn't damage the live coral.

She remembered the needle she'd taken to Jellyfish Lake, the needle she'd loaded with the mango extract to which Darton was violently allergic. Once in the midst of the jellyfish swarm, it had been easy to jab the needle into Darton's calf, then let it drop to the anoxic depths of the lake.

He probably thought she'd given him a playful pinch.

Michelle had exulted in Darton's death, the pallor, the labored breathing, the desperate pleading in the eyes.

It wasn't murder, after all, just a fourth-degree felony. They'd build a new Darton in a matter of days. What was the value of a human life, when it could be infinitely duplicated, and cheaply? As far as Michelle was concerned, Darton had amusement value only.

The rebuilt Darton still loved her, and Michelle enjoyed that as well, enjoyed the fact that she caused him anguish, that he would pay for ages for his betrayal of her love.

Lisa Lee Baxter could take a few lessons from the mermaid, Michelle thought.

Michelle surfaced near the tunnel and raised a hand with the fingers set at <follow me>. Darton rolled off the kayak, still in his clothes, and splashed clumsily toward her.

"Are you sure about this?" he asked.

"Oh yes," Michelle replied. "You go first. I'll follow and pull you out if you get in trouble."

He loved her, of course. That was why he panted a few times for breath, filled his lungs, and dove.

Michelle had not, of course, bothered to mention that the tunnel was fifteen meters long, quite far to go on a single breath. She followed him, very interested in how this would turn out, and when Darton got into trouble in one of the narrow places and tried to back out, she grabbed his shoes and held him right where he was.

He fought hard but none of his kicks struck her. She would remember the look in his wide eyes for a long time, the thunderstruck disbelief in the instant before his breath exploded from his lungs and he died.

She wished that she could speak again the parting words she'd whispered into Darton's ear when he lay dying on the ridge above Jellyfish Lake. *"I've just killed you. And I'm going to do it again."*

But even if she could have spoken the words underwater, they would have been untrue. Michelle supposed this was the last time she could kill him. Twice was dangerous, but a third time would be too clear a pattern. She could end up in jail, though, of course, you only did severe prison time for realdeath.

She supposed that she would have to discover his body at some point, but if she cast the kayak adrift, it wouldn't have to be for a while. And then she'd be thunderstruck and grief-stricken that he'd thrown away his life on this desperate attempt to pursue her after she'd turned her back on him and gone inland, away from the sound of his voice.

Michelle looked forward to playing that part.

She pulled up the kayak's anchor and let it coast away on the six-knot tide, then folded away her wings and returned to her nest in the banyan tree. She let the breeze dry her skin and got her deck from its bag and contemplated the data about Terzian and Stephanie Pais and the outbreak of the Green Leopard Plague.

Stephanie had died for what she believed in, killed by the agents of an obscure, murderous regime. It had been Terzian who had shot those four men in her defense, that was clear to her now. And Terzian, who lived a long time and then died in the Lightspeed War along with a few billion other people, had loved Stephanie and kept her secret till his death, a secret shared with the others who loved Stephanie and who had spread the plague among the refugee populations of the world.

It was realdeath that people suffered then, the death that couldn't be corrected. Michelle knew that she understood that kind of death only as an intellectual abstract, not as something she would ever have to face or live with. To lose someone *permanently* . . . that was something she couldn't grasp. Even the ancients, who faced realdeath every day, hadn't been able to accept it, that's why they'd invented the myth of Heaven.

Michelle thought about Stephanie's death, the death that must have broken Terzian's heart, and she contemplated the secret Terzian had kept all those years, and she decided that she was not inclined to reveal it.

Oh, she'd give Davout the facts, that was what he paid her for. She'd tell him what she could find out about Stephanie and the Transnistrians. But she wouldn't mention the camps that Santa Croce had built across the starvation-scarred world, she wouldn't point him at Sidamo and Green Leopard. If he drew those conclusions himself, then obviously the secret was destined to be revealed. But she suspected he wouldn't—he was too old to connect those dots, not when obscure ex-Soviet entities and relief camps in the Horn of Africa were so far out of his reference.

Michelle would respect Terzian's love, and Stephanie's secret. She had some secrets of her own, after all.

The lonely mermaid finished her work for the day and sat on her over-hanging limb to gaze down at the sea, and she wondered how long it would be before Darton called her again, and how she would torture him when he did.

—*With thanks to Dr. Stephen C. Lee.*

The Fluted Girl

PAOLO BACIGALUPI

New writer Paolo Bacigalupi made his first sale in 1998 to *The Magazine of Fantasy & Science Fiction*, took a break from the genre for several years, and has returned to it in the new century, with new sales to *F&SF* and *Asimov's* including the powerful story that follows, which gives a new and unsettling meaning to the phrase "performance art."

The fluted girl huddled in the darkness clutching Stephen's final gift in her small pale hands. Madame Belari would be looking for her. The servants would be sniffing through the castle like feral dogs, looking under beds, in closets, behind the wine racks, all their senses hungry for a whiff of her. Belari never knew the fluted girl's hiding places. It was the servants who always found her. Belari simply wandered the halls and let the servants search her out. The servants thought they knew all her hiding places.

The fluted girl shifted her body. Her awkward position already strained her fragile skeleton. She stretched as much as the cramped space allowed, then folded herself back into compactness, imagining herself as a rabbit, like the ones Belari kept in cages in the kitchen: small and soft with wet warm eyes, they could sit and wait for hours. The fluted girl summoned patience and ignored the sore protest of her folded body.

Soon she had to show herself, or Madame Belari would get impatient and send for Burson, her head of security. Then Burson would bring his jackals and they would hunt again, crisscrossing every room, spraying pheromone additives across the floors and following her neon tracks to her hidey-hole. She had to leave before Burson came. Madame Belari punished her if the staff wasted time scrubbing out pheromones.

The fluted girl shifted her position again. Her legs were beginning to ache. She wondered if they could snap from the strain. Sometimes she was surprised at what broke her. A gentle bump against a table and she was shattered again, with Belari angry at the careless treatment of her investment.

The fluted girl sighed. In truth, it was already time to leave her hidey-hole, but still she craved the silence, the moment alone. Her sister Nia never understood. Stephen though . . . he had understood. When the fluted girl told him of her hidey-hole, she thought he forgave because he was kind. Now she knew better. Stephen had bigger secrets than the silly fluted girl. He had secrets bigger than anyone had guessed. The fluted girl turned his tiny vial in her hands, feeling its smooth glass shape, knowing the amber drops it held within. Already, she missed him.

Beyond her hidey-hole, footsteps echoed. Metal scraped heavily across stone. The fluted girl peered out through a crack in her makeshift fortress. Below her, the castle's pantry lay jumbled with dry goods. Mirriam was looking for her again, poking behind the refrigerated crates of champagne for Belari's party tonight. They hissed and leaked mist as Mirriam struggled to shove them aside and look deeper into the dark recesses behind. The fluted girl had known Mirriam when they were both children in the town. Now, they were as different as life and death.

Mirriam had grown, her breasts burgeoning, her hips widening, her rosy face smiling and laughing at her fortune. When they both came to Belari, the fluted girl and Mirriam had been the same height. Now, Mirriam was a grown woman, a full two feet taller than the fluted girl, and filled out to please a man. And she was loyal. She was a good servant for Belari. Smiling, happy to serve. They'd all been that way when they came up from the town to the castle: Mirriam, the fluted girl, and her sister Nia. Then Belari decided to make them into fluted girls. Mirriam got to grow, but the fluted girls were going to be stars.

Mirriam spied a stack of cheeses and hams piled carelessly in one corner. She stalked it while the fluted girl watched and smiled at the plump girl's suspicions. Mirriam hefted a great wheel of Danish cheese and peered into the gap behind. "Lidia? Are you there?"

The fluted girl shook her head. No, she thought. But you guessed well. A year ago, I would have been. I could have moved the cheeses, with effort. The champagne would have been too much, though. I would never have been behind the champagne.

Mirriam stood up. Sweat sheened her face from the effort of moving the bulky goods that fed Belari's household. Her face looked like a bright shiny apple. She wiped her brow with a sleeve. "Lidia, Madame Belari is getting angry. You're being a selfish girl. Nia is already waiting for you in the practice room."

Lidia nodded silently. Yes, Nia would be in the practice room. She was the good sister. Lidia was the bad one. The one they had to search for. Lidia was the reason both fluted girls were punished. Belari had given up on discipline for Lidia directly. She contented herself with punishing both sisters and letting guilt enforce compliance. Sometimes it worked. But not now. Not with Stephen gone. Lidia needed quiet now. A place where no one watched her. A place alone. Her secret place which she showed to Stephen and which he had examined with such surprised sad eyes. Stephen's eyes had been brown. When he looked at her, she thought that his eyes were almost as soft as Belari's rabbits. They were safe eyes. You could fall into those safe brown eyes and never worry about breaking a bone.

Mirriam sat heavily on a sack of potatoes and scowled around her, acting for her potential audience. "You're being a selfish girl. A vicious selfish girl to make us all search this way."

The fluted girl nodded. Yes, I am a selfish girl, she thought. I am a selfish girl, and you are a woman, and yet we are the same age, and I am smarter than you. You are clever but you don't know that hidey-holes are best when they are in places no one looks. You look for me under and behind and between, but you don't look up. I am above you, and I am watching you, just as Stephen watched us all.

Mirriam grimaced and got up. "No matter. Burson will find you." She brushed the dust from her skirts. "You hear me? Burson will find you." She left the pantry.

Lidia waited for Mirriam to go away. It galled her that Mirriam was right. Burson would find her. He found her every time, if she waited too long. Silent time could only be stolen for so many minutes. It lasted as long as it took Belari to lose patience and call the jackals. Then another hidey-hole was lost.

Lidia turned Stephen's tiny blown-glass bottle in her delicate fingers a final time. A parting gift, she understood, now that he was gone, now that he would no longer comfort her when Belari's depredations became too much. She forced back tears. No more time to cry. Burson would be looking for her.

She pressed the vial into a secure crack, tight against the stone and rough-hewn wood of the shelving where she hid, then worked a vacuum jar of red lentils back until she had an opening. She squeezed out from behind the legume wall that lined the pantry's top shelves.

It had taken weeks for her to clear out the back jars and make a place for herself, but the jars made a good hidey-hole. A place others neglected to search. She had a fortress of jars, full of flat innocent beans, and behind that barrier, if she was patient and bore the strain, she could crouch for hours. She climbed down.

Carefully, carefully, she thought. We don't want to break a bone. We have to be careful of the bones. She hung from the shelves as she gently worked the fat jar of red lentils back into place then slipped down the last shelves to the pantry floor.

Barefoot on cold stone flagging, Lidia studied her hidey-hole. Yes, it looked good still. Stephen's final gift was safe up there. No one looked able to fit in that few feet of space, not even a delicate fluted girl. No one would suspect she folded herself so perfectly into such a place. She was slight as a mouse, and sometimes fit into surprising places. For that, she could thank Belari. She turned and hurried from the pantry, determined to let the servants catch her far away from her last surviving hidey-hole.

By the time Lidia reached the dining hall, she believed she might gain the practice rooms without discovery. There might be no punishments. Belari was kind to those she loved, but uncompromising when they disappointed her. Though Lidia was too delicate to strike, there were other punishments. Lidia thought of Stephen. A small part of her was happy that he was beyond Belari's tortures.

Lidia slipped along the dining hall's edge, shielded by ferns and blooming orchids. Between the lush leaves and flowers, she caught glimpses of the dining table's long ebony expanse, polished mirror-bright each day by the servants and perpetually set with gleaming silver. She studied the room for observers. It was empty.

The rich warm smell of greenery reminded her of summer, despite the winter season that slashed the mountains around the castle. When she and Nia had been younger, before their surgeries, they had run in the mountains, amongst the pines. Lidia slipped through the orchids: one from Singapore; another from Chennai; another, striped like a tiger, engineered by Belari. She touched the delicate tiger blossom, admiring its lurid color.

We are beautiful prisoners, she thought. Just like you.

The ferns shuddered. A man exploded from the greenery, springing on her like a wolf. His hands wrenched her shoulders. His fingers plunged into her pale flesh and Lidia gasped as they stabbed her nerves into paralysis. She collapsed to the slate flagstones, a butterfly folding as Burson pressed her down.

She whimpered against the stone, her heart hammering inside her chest at the shock of Burson's ambush. She moaned, trembling under his weight, her face hard against the castle's smooth gray slate. On the stone beside her, a pink and white orchid lay beheaded by Burson's attack.

Slowly, when he was sure of her compliance, Burson allowed her to move. His great weight lessened, lifting away from her like a tank rolling off a crushed hovel. Lidia forced herself to sit up. Finally she stood, an unsteady pale fairy dwarfed by the looming monster that was Belari's head of security.

Burson's mountainous body was a cragged landscape of muscle and scars, all juts of strength and angry puckered furrows of combat. Mirriam gossiped that he had previously been a gladiator, but she was romantic and Lidia suspected his scars came from training handlers, much as her own punishments came from Belari.

Burson held her wrist, penning it in a rock-like grasp. For all its unyielding strength, his grip was gentle. After an initial disastrous breakage, he had learned what strain her skeleton could bear before it shattered.

Lidia struggled, testing his hold on her wrist, then accepted her capture. Burson knelt, bringing his height to match hers. Red-rimmed eyes studied her. Augmented irises bloodshot with enhancements scanned her skin's infrared pulse.

Burson's slashed face slowly lost the green blush of camouflage, abandoning stone and foliage colors now that he stood in open air. Where his hand touched her though, his skin paled, as though powdered by flour, matching the white of her own flesh.

"Where have you been hiding?" he rumbled.

"Nowhere."

Burson's red eyes narrowed, his brows furrowing over deep pits of interrogation. He sniffed at her clothing, hunting for clues. He brought his nose close to her face, her hair, snuffled at her hands. "The kitchens," he murmured.

Lidia flinched. His red eyes studied her closely, hunting for more details, watching the unintentional reactions of her skin, the blush of discovery she could not hide from his prying eyes. Burson smiled. He hunted with the wild fierce joy of his bloodhound genetics. It was difficult to tell where the jackal, dog, and human blended in the man. His joys were hunting, capture, and slaughter.

Burson straightened, smiling. He took a steel bracelet from a pouch. "I have something for you, Lidia." He slapped the jewelry onto Lidia's wrist. It writhed around her thin arm, snakelike, chiming as it locked. "No more hiding for you."

A current charged up Lidia's arm and she cried out, shivering as electricity rooted through her body. Burson supported her as the current cut off. He said, "I'm tired of searching for Belari's property."

He smiled, tight-lipped, and pushed her toward the practice rooms. Lidia allowed herself to be herded.

Belari was in the performance hall when Burson brought Lidia before her. Servants bustled around her, arranging tables, setting up the round stage, installing the lighting. The walls were hung in pale muslin shot through with electric charges, a billowing sheath of charged air that crackled and sparked whenever a servant walked near.

Belari seemed unaware of the fanciful world building around her as she tossed orders at her events coordinator. Her black body armor was open at the collar, in deference to the warmth of human activity. She spared Burson and Lidia a quick glance, then turned her attention back to her servant, still furiously scribbling on a digital pad. "I want everything to be perfect tonight, Tania. Nothing out of place. Nothing amiss. Perfect."

"Yes, Madame."

Belari smiled. Her face was mathematically sculpted into beauty, structured by focus-groups and cosmetic traditions that stretched back generations. Cocktails of disease prophylaxis, cell-scouring cancer inhibitors, and Revitia kept Belari's physical appearance at twenty-eight, much as Lidia's own Revitia treatments kept her frozen in the first throes of adolescence. "And I want Vernon taken care of."

"Will he want a companion?"

Belari shook her head. "No. He'll confine himself to harassing me, I'm sure." She shivered. "Disgusting man."

Tania tittered. Belari's chill gaze quieted her. Belari surveyed the performance hall. "I want everything in here. The food, the champagne, everything. I want them packed together so that they feel each other when the girls perform. I want it very tight. Very intimate."

Tania nodded and scribbled more notes on her pad. She tapped the screen authoritatively, sending orders to the staff. Already, servants would be receiving messages in their earbuds, reacting to their mistress's demands.

Belari said, "I want Tingle available. With the champagne. It will whet their appetites."

"You'll have an orgy if you do."

Belari laughed. "That's fine. I want them to remember tonight. I want them to remember our fluted girls. Vernon particularly." Her laughter quieted, replaced by a hard-edged smile, brittle with emotion. "He'll be angry when he finds out about them. But he'll want them, anyway. And he'll bid like the rest."

Lidia watched Belari's face. She wondered if the woman knew how clearly she broadcast her feelings about the Pendant Entertainment executive. Lidia had seen him once, from behind a curtain. She and Stephen had watched Vernon Weir touch Belari, and watched Belari first shy from his touch and then give in, summoning the reserves of her acting skill to play the part of a seduced woman.

Vernon Weir had made Belari famous. He'd paid the expense of her body sculpting and made her a star, much as Belari now invested in Lidia and her sister. But Master Weir extracted a price for his aid, Faustian devil that he was. Stephen and Lidia had watched as Weir took his pleasure from Belari, and Stephen had whispered to her that when Weir was gone, Belari would summon Stephen and reenact the scene, but with Stephen as the victim, and then he would pretend, as she did, that he was happy to submit.

Lidia's thoughts broke off. Belari had turned to her. The angry welt from Stephen's attack was still visible on her throat, despite the cell knitters she popped like candy. Lidia thought it must gall her to have a scar out of place. She was careful of her image. Belari seemed to catch the focus of Lidia's gaze. Her lips pursed and she pulled the collar of her body armor close, hiding the damage. Her green eyes narrowed. "We've been looking for you."

Lidia ducked her head. "I'm sorry, Mistress."

Belari ran a finger under the fluted girl's jaw, lifting her downcast face until they were eye to eye. "I should punish you for wasting my time."

"Yes, Mistress. I'm sorry." The fluted girl lowered her eyes. Belari wouldn't hit her. She was too expensive to fix. She wondered if Belari would use electricity, or isolation, or some other humiliation cleverly devised.

Instead, Belari pointed to the steel bracelet. "What's this?"

Burson didn't flinch at her question. He had no fear. He was the only servant who had no fear. Lidia admired him for that, if nothing else. "To track her. And shock her." He smiled, pleased with himself. "It causes no physical destruction."

Belari shook her head. "I need her without jewelry tonight. Take it off."

"She will hide."

"No. She wants to be star. She'll be good now, won't you, Lidia?"

Lidia nodded.

Burson shrugged and removed the bracelet, unperturbed. He leaned his great scarred face close to Lidia's ear. "Don't hide in the kitchens the next time. I will find you." He stood away, smiling his satisfaction. Lidia narrowed her eyes at Burson and told herself she had won a victory that Burson didn't know her hidey-hole yet. But then Burson smiled at her and she wondered if he did know already, if he was playing with her the way a cat played with a maimed mouse.

Belari said, "Thank you, Burson," then paused, eyeing the great creature who looked so man-like yet moved with the feral quickness of the wilds. "Have you tightened our security?"

Burson nodded. "Your fief is safe. We are checking the rest of the staff, for background irregularities."

"Have you found anything?"

Burson shook his head. "Your staff love you."

Belari's voice sharpened. "That's what we thought about Stephen. And now I wear body armor in my own fief. I can't afford the appearance of lost popularity. It affects my share price too much."

"I've been thorough."

"If my stock falls, Vernon will have me wired for TouchSense. I won't have it."

"I understand. There will be no more failures."

Belari frowned at the monster looming over her. "Good. Well, come on then." She motioned for Lidia to join her. "Your sister has been waiting for you." She took the fluted girl by the hand and led her out of the performance hall.

Lidia spared a glance back. Burson was gone. The servants bustled, placing orchid cuttings on tables, but Burson had disappeared, either blended into the walls or sped away on his errands of security.

Belari tugged Lidia's hand. "You led us on a merry search. I thought we would have to spray the pheromones again."

"I'm sorry."

"No harm. This time." Belari smiled down at her. "Are you nervous about tonight?"

Lidia shook her head. "No."

"No?"

Lidia shrugged. "Will Master Weir purchase our stock?"

"If he pays enough."

"Will he?"

Belari smiled. "I think he will, yes. You are unique. Like me. Vernon likes to collect rare beauty."

"What is he like?"

Belari's smile stiffened. She looked up, concentrating on their path through the castle. "When I was a girl, very young, much younger than you, long before I became famous, I used to go to a playground. A man came to watch me on the swings. He wanted to be my friend. I didn't like him, but being near him made me dizzy. Whatever he said made perfect sense. He smelled bad, but I couldn't pull away from him." Belari shook her head. "Someone's mother chased him away." She looked down at Lidia. "He had a chemical cologne, you understand?"

"Contraband?"

"Yes. From Asia. Not legal here. Vernon is like that. Your skin crawls but he draws you to him."

"He touches you."

Belari looked down at Lidia sadly. "He likes my old crone experience in my young girl body. But he hardly discriminates. He touches everyone." She smiled slightly. "But not you, perhaps. You are too valuable to touch."

"Too delicate."

"Don't sound so bitter. You're unique. We're going to make you a star." Belari looked down at her protégé hungrily. "Your stock will rise, and you will be a star."

Lidia watched from her windows as Belari's guests began to arrive. Aircars snaked in under security escort, sliding low over the pines, green and red running lights blinking in the darkness.

Nia came to stand behind Lidia. "They're here."

"Yes."

Snow clotted thickly on the trees, like heavy cream. The occasional blue sweeps of search beams highlighted the snow and the dark silhouettes of the forest; Burson's ski patrols, hoping to spy out the telltale red exhalations of intruders crouched amongst pine shadows. Their beams swept over the ancient hulk of a ski lift that climbed up from the town. It was rusting, silent except when the wind caught its chairs and sent its cables swaying. The empty seats swung lethargically in the freezing air, another victim of Belari's influence. Belari hated competition. Now, she was the only patron of the town that sparkled in the deep of the valley far below.

"You should get dressed," Nia said.

Lidia turned to study her twin. Black eyes like pits watched her from between elfin lids. Her skin was pale, stripped of pigment, and she was thin, accenting the delicacy of her bone structure. That was one true thing about her, about both of them: their bones were theirs. It was what had attracted Belari to them in the first place, when they were just eleven. Just old enough for Belari to strip them from their parents.

Lidia's gaze returned to the view. Deep in the tight crease of the mountain valley, the town shimmered with amber lights.

"Do you miss it?" she asked.

Nia slipped closer. "Miss what?"

Lidia nodded down at the shimmering jewel. "The town."

Their parents had been glassblowers, practicing the old arts abandoned in the face of efficient manufacturing, breathing delicate works into existence, sand running liquid under their supervision. They had moved to Belari's fief for patronage, like all the town's artisans: the potters, the blacksmiths, the painters. Sometimes Belari's peers noticed an artist and his influence grew. Niels Kinkaid had made his fortune from Belari's favor, turning iron to her will, outfitting her fortress with its great handwrought gates and her gardens with crouching sculptural surprises: foxes and children peering from amongst lupine and monkshood in the summers and deep drifted snow in the winters. Now he was almost famous enough to float his own stock.

Lidia's parents had come for patronage, but Belari's evaluating eye had not fallen on their artistry. Instead, she selected the biological accident of their twin daughters: delicate and blond with cornflower eyes that watched the world blinkless as they absorbed the fief's mountain wonders. Their trade flourished now thanks to the donation of their children.

Nia jostled Lidia gently, her ghostly face serious. "Hurry and dress. You mustn't be late."

Lidia turned away from her black-eyed sister. Of their original features, little remained. Belari had watched them grow in the castle for two years and then the pills began. Revitia treatments at thirteen froze their features in the matrix of youth. Then had come the eyes, drawn from twins in some far foreign land. Lidia sometimes wondered if in India, two dusky girl children looked out at the world from cornflower eyes, or if they walked the mud streets of their village guided only by the sound of echoes on cow-dung walls and the scrape of their canes on the dirt before them.

Lidia studied the night beyond the windows with her stolen black eyes. More aircars dropped guests on the landing pads then spread gossamer wings and let the mountain winds bear them away.

More treatments had followed: pigment drugs drained color from their skins, leaving them Kabuki pale, ethereal shadows of their former mountain sun-blushed selves, and then the surgeries began. She remembered waking after each successive surgery, crippled, unable to move for weeks despite the wide-bore needles full of cell-knitters and nutrient fluids the doctor flushed through her slight body. The doctor would hold her hand after the surgeries, wipe the sweat from her pale brow and whisper, "Poor girl. Poor poor girl." Then Belari would come and smile at the progress and say that Lidia and Nia would soon be stars.

Gusts of wind tore snow from the pines and sent it swirling in great tornado clouds around the arriving aristocracy. The guests hurried through the driving snow while the blue search beams of Burson's ski patrols carved across the forests. Lidia sighed and turned from the windows, obedient finally to Nia's anxious hope that she would dress.

Stephen and Lidia went on picnics together when Belari was away from the fief. They would leave the great gray construct of Belari's castle and walk carefully across the mountain meadows, Stephen always helping her, guiding her fragile steps through fields of daisies, columbine, and lupine until they peered down over sheer granite cliffs to the town far below. All about them glacier-sculpted peaks ringed the valley like giants squatting in council, their faces adorned with snow even in summer, like beards of wisdom. At the edge of the precipice, they ate a picnic lunch and Stephen told stories of the world before the fiefs, before Revitia made stars immortal.

He said the country had been democratic. That people once voted for their lieges. That they had been free to travel between any fief they liked. Everyone, he said, not just stars. Lidia knew there were places on the coasts where this occurred. She had heard of them. But it seemed difficult to credit. She was a child of a fief.

"It's true," Stephen said. "On the coasts, the people choose their own leader. It's only here, in the mountains, that it's different." He grinned at her. His soft brown eyes crinkled slightly, showing his humor, showing that he already saw the skepticism on her face.

Lidia laughed. "But who would pay for everything? Without Belari who would pay to fix the roads and make the schools?" She picked an aster and twirled it between her fingers, watching the purple spokes blur around the yellow center of the flower.

"The people do."

Lidia laughed again. "They can't afford to do that. They hardly have enough to feed themselves. And how would they know what to do? Without Belari, no one would even know what needs fixing, or improving." She tossed the flower away, aiming to send it over the cliff. Instead, the wind caught it, and it fell near her.

Stephen picked up the flower and flicked it over the edge easily. "It's true. They don't have to be rich, they just work together. You think Belari knows everything? She hires advisors. People can do that as well as she."

Lidia shook her head. "People like Mirriam? Ruling a fief? It sounds like madness. No one would respect her."

Stephen scowled. "It's true," he said stubbornly, and because Lidia liked him and didn't want him to be unhappy, she agreed that it might be true, but in her heart, she thought that Stephen was a dreamer. It made him sweet, even if he didn't understand the true ways of the world.

"Do you like Belari?" Stephen asked suddenly.

"What do you mean?"

"Do you like her?"

Lidia gave him a puzzled look. Stephen's brown eyes studied her intensely. She shrugged. "She's a good liege. Everyone is fed and cared for. It's not like Master Weir's fief."

Stephen made a face of disgust. "Nothing is like Weir's fief. He's barbaric. He put one of his servants on a spit." He paused. "But still, look at what Belari has done to you."

Lidia frowned. "What about me?"

"You're not natural. Look at your eyes, your skin and . . . ," he turned his eyes away, his voice lowering, "your bones. Look what she did to your bones."

"What's wrong with my bones?"

"You can barely walk!" he cried suddenly. "You should be able to walk!"

Lidia glanced around nervously. Stephen was talking critically. Someone might be listening. They seemed alone, but people were always around: secu-

rity on the hillsides, others out for walks. Burson might be there, blended with
the scenery, a stony man hidden amongst the rocks. Stephen had a hard time
understanding about Burson. "I can walk," she whispered fiercely.

"How many times have you broken a leg or an arm or a rib?"

"Not in a year." She was proud of it. She had learned to be careful.

Stephen laughed incredulously. "Do you know how many bones I've broken in my life?" He didn't wait for an answer. "None. Not a single bone. Never.
Do you even remember what it's like to walk without worrying that you'll trip,
or bump into someone? You're like glass."

Lidia shook her head and looked away. "I'm going to be star. Belari will
float us on the markets."

"But you can't walk," Stephen said. His eyes had a pitying quality that
made Lidia angry.

"I can too. And it's enough."

"But—"

"No!" Lidia shook her head. "Who are you to say what I do? Look what
Belari does to you, but still you are loyal! I may have had surgeries, but at least
I'm not her toy."

It was the only time Stephen became angry. For a moment the rage in his
face made Lidia think he would strike her and break her bones. A part of her
hoped he would, that he would release the terrible frustration brewing
between them, two servants each calling the other slave.

Instead, Stephen mastered himself and gave up the argument. He apologized and held her hand and they were quiet as the Sun set, but it was already
too late and their quiet time was ruined. Lidia's mind had gone back to the days
before the surgeries, when she ran without care, and though she would not
admit it to Stephen, it felt as though he had ripped away a scab and revealed an
aching bitter wound.

The performance hall trembled with anticipation, a room full of people high
on Tingle and champagne. The muslin on the walls flickered like lightning as
Belari's guests, swathed in brilliant silks and sparkling gold, swirled through the
room in colorful clouds of revelry, clumping together with conversation, then
breaking apart with laughter as they made their social rounds.

Lidia slipped carefully amongst the guests, her pale skin and diaphanous
shift a spot of simplicity amongst the gaudy colors and wealth. Some of the
guests eyed her curiously, the strange girl threading through their pleasure.
They quickly dismissed her. She was merely another creature of Belari's,
intriguing to look at, perhaps, but of no account. Their attention always
returned to the more important patterns of gossip and association swirling

around them. Lidia smiled. Soon, she thought, you will recognize me. She slipped up against a wall, near a table piled high with finger sandwiches, small cuts of meat and plates of plump strawberries.

Lidia scanned the crowds. Her sister was there, across the room, dressed in an identical diaphanous shift. Belari stood surrounded by mediascape names and fief lieges, her green gown matching her eyes, smiling, apparently at ease, even without her newfound habit of body armor.

Vernon Weir slipped up behind Belari, stroking her shoulder. Lidia saw Belari shiver and steel herself against Weir's touch. She wondered how he could not notice. Perhaps he was one of those who took pleasure in the repulsion he inflicted. Belari smiled at him, her emotions under control once again.

Lidia took a small plate of meats from the table. The meat was drizzled with raspberry reduction and was sweet. Belari liked sweet things, like the strawberries she was eating now with the Pendant Entertainment executive at the far end of the table. The sweet addiction was another side effect of the Tingle.

Belari caught sight of Lidia and led Vernon Weir toward her. "Do you like the meat?" she asked, smiling slightly.

Lidia nodded, finishing carefully.

Belari's smile sharpened. "I'm not surprised. You have a taste for good ingredients." Her face was flushed with Tingle. Lidia was glad they were in public. When Belari took too much Tingle she hungered and became erratic. Once, Belari had crushed strawberries against her skin, making her pale flesh blush with the juice, and then, high with the erotic charge of overdose, she had forced Lidia's tongue to Nia's juice-stained flesh and Nia's tongue to hers, while Belari watched, pleased with the decadent performance.

Belari selected a strawberry and offered it to Lidia. "Here. Have one, but don't stain yourself. I want you perfect." Her eyes glistened with excitement. Lidia steeled herself against memory and accepted the berry.

Vernon studied Lidia. "She's yours?"

Belari smiled fondly. "One of my fluted girls."

Vernon knelt and studied Lidia more closely. "What unusual eyes you have."

Lidia ducked her head shyly.

Belari said, "I had them replaced."

"Replaced?" Vernon glanced up at her. "Not altered?"

Belari smiled. "We both know nothing that beautiful comes artificially." She reached down and stroked Lidia's pale blond hair, smiling with satisfaction at her creation. "When I got her, she had the most beautiful blue eyes. The color of the flowers you find here in the mountains in the summer." She shook her head. "I had them replaced. They were beautiful, but not the look I wished for."

Vernon stood up again. "She is striking. But not as beautiful as you."

Belari smiled cynically at Vernon. "Is that why you want me wired for TouchSense?"

Vernon shrugged. "It's a new market, Belari. With your response, you could be a star."

"I'm already a star."

Vernon smiled. "But Revitia is expensive."

"We always come back to that, don't we, Vernon?"

Vernon gave her a hard look. "I don't want to be at odds with you, Belari. You've been wonderful for us. Worth every penny of your reconstruction. I've never seen a finer actress. But this is Pendant, after all. You could have bought your stock a long time ago if you weren't so attached to immortality." He eyed Belari coldly. "If you want to be immortal, you will wire Touch-Sense. Already we're seeing massive acceptance in the marketplace. It's the future of entertainment."

"I'm an actress, not a marionette. I don't crave people inside my skin."

Vernon shrugged. "We all pay a price for our celebrity. Where the markets move, we must follow. None of us is truly free." He looked at Belari meaningfully. "Certainly not if we want to live forever."

Belari smiled slyly. "Perhaps." She nodded at Lidia. "Run along. It's almost time." She turned back to Vernon. "There's something I'd like you to see."

Stephen gave her the vial the day before he died. Lidia had asked what it was, a few amber drops in a vial no larger than her pinky. She had smiled at the gift, feeling playful, but Stephen had been serious.

"It's freedom," he said.

She shook her head, uncomprehending.

"If you ever choose, you control your life. You don't have to be Belari's pet."

"I'm not her pet."

He shook his head. "If you ever want escape," he held up the vial, "it's here." He handed it to her and closed her pale hand around the tiny bottle. It was handblown. Briefly, she wondered if it came from her parents' workshop. Stephen said, "We're small people here. Only people like Belari have control. In other places, other parts of the world, it's different. Little people still matter. But here," he smiled sadly, "all we have is our lives."

Comprehension dawned. She tried to pull away but Stephen held her firmly. "I'm not saying you want it now, but someday, perhaps you will. Perhaps you'll decide you don't want to cooperate with Belari anymore. No matter how many gifts she showers on you." He squeezed her hand gently. "It's quick. Almost painless." He looked into her eyes with the soft brown kindness that had always been there.

It was a gift of love, however misguided, and because she knew it would make him happy, she nodded and agreed to keep the vial and put it in her hidey-hole, just in case. She couldn't have known that he had already chosen his own death, that he would hunt Belari with a knife, and almost succeed.

No one noticed when the fluted girls took their places on the center dais. They were merely oddities, pale angels, entwined. Lidia put her mouth to her sister's throat, feeling her pulse threading rapidly under her white, white skin. It throbbed against her tongue as she sought out the tiny bore hole in her sister's body. She felt the wet touch of Nia's tongue on her own throat, nestling into her flesh like a small mouse seeking comfort.

Lidia stilled herself, waiting for the attention of the people, patient and focused on her performance. She felt Nia breathe, her lungs expanding inside the frail cage of her chest. Lidia took her own breath. They began to play, first her own notes, running out through unstopped keys in her flesh, and then Nia's notes beginning as well. The open sound, haunting moments of breath, pressed through their bodies.

The melancholy tones trailed off. Lidia moved her head, breathing in, mirroring Nia as she pressed her lips again to her sister's flesh. This time, Lidia kissed her sister's hand. Nia's mouth sought the delicate hollow of her clavicle. Music, mournful, as hollow as they were, breathed out from their bodies. Nia breathed into Lidia and the exhalation of her lungs slipped out through Lidia's bones, tinged with emotion, as though the warm air of her sister came to life within her body.

Around the girls, the guests fell quiet. The silence spread, like ripples from a stone thrown into a placid pool, speeding outward from their epicenter to lap at the farthest edges of the room. All eyes turned to the pale girls on stage. Lidia could feel their eyes, hungry, yearning, almost physical as their gazes pressed against her. She moved her hands beneath her sister's shift, clasping her close. Her sister's hands touched her hips, closing stops in her fluted body. At their new embrace a sigh of yearning came from the crowd, a whisper of their own hungers made musical.

Lidia's hands found the keys to her sister, her tongue touching Nia's throat once more. Her fingers ran along the knuckles of Nia's spine, finding the clarinet within her, stroking keys. She pressed the warm breath of herself into her sister and she felt Nia breathing into her. Nia's sound was dark and melancholy, her own tones, brighter, higher, ran in counterpoint, a slowly developing story of forbidden touch.

They stood embraced. Their body music built, notes intertwining seductively as their hands stroked one another's bodies, bringing forth a complex rising tide of sound. Suddenly, Nia wrenched at Lidia's shift and Lidia's fingers tore away Nia's own. They stood revealed, pale elfin creatures of music. The guests around them gasped as the notes poured out brighter now, unmuffled by clinging clothes. The girls' musical graftings shone: cobalt boreholes in their spines, glinting stops and keys made of brass and ivory that ran along their fluted frames and contained a hundred possible instruments within the structure of their bodies.

Nia's mouth crept up Lidia's arm. Notes spilled out of Lidia as bright as water jewels. Laments of desire and sin flowed from Nia's pores. Their embraces became more frenzied, a choreography of lust. The spectators pressed closer, incited by the spectacle of naked youth and music intertwined.

Around her, Lidia was vaguely aware of their watching eyes and flushed expressions. The Tingle and the performance were doing their work on the guests. She could feel the heat rising in the room. She and Nia sank slowly to the floor, their embraces becoming more erotic and elaborate, the sexual tension of their musical conflict increasing as they entwined. Years of training had come to this moment, this carefully constructed weave of harmonizing flesh.

We perform pornography, Lidia thought. Pornography for the profit of Belari. She caught a glimpse of her patron's gleaming pleasure, Vernon Weir dumbstruck beside her. Yes, she thought, look at us, Master Weir, look and see what pornography we perform, and then it was her turn to play upon her sister, and her tongue and hands stroked Nia's keys.

It was a dance of seduction and acquiescence. They had other dances, solos and duets, some chaste, others obscene, but for their debut, Belari had chosen this one. The energy of their music increased, violent, climactic, until at last she and Nia lay upon the floor, expended, sheathed in sweat, bare twins tangled in musical lasciviousness. Their body music fell silent.

Around them, no one moved. Lidia tasted salt on her sister's skin as they held their pose. The lights dimmed, signaling completion.

Applause exploded around them. The lights brightened. Nia drew herself upright. Her lips quirked in a smile of satisfaction as she helped Lidia to her feet. You see? Nia's eyes seemed to say. We will be stars. Lidia found herself smiling with her sister. Despite the loss of Stephen, despite Belari's depredations, she was smiling. The audience's adoration washed over her, a balm of pleasure.

They curtsied to Belari as they had been trained, making obeisance first to their patron, the mother goddess who had created them. Belari smiled at the gesture, however scripted it was, and joined the applause of her guests. The people's applause increased again at the girls' good grace, then Nia and Lidia were curtseying to the corners of the compass, gathering their shifts and leaving the stage, guided by Burson's hulking presence to their patron.

The applause continued as they crossed the distance to Belari. Finally, at Belari's wave, the clapping gave way to respectful silence. She smiled at her assembled guests, placing her arms around the slight shoulders of the girls and said, "My lords and ladies, our Fluted Girls," and applause burst over them again, one final explosion of adulation before the guests fell to talking, fanning themselves, and feeling the flush of their own skins which the girls had inspired.

Belari held the fluted girls closely and whispered in their ears, "You did well." She hugged them carefully.

Vernon Weir's eyes roved over Lidia and Nia's exposed bodies. "You outdo yourself, Belari," he said.

Belari inclined her head slightly at the compliment. Her grip on Lidia's shoulder became proprietary. Belari's voice didn't betray her tension. She kept it light, comfortably satisfied with her position, but her fingers dug into Lidia's skin. "They are my finest."

"Such an extraordinary crafting."

"It's expensive when they break a bone. They're terribly fragile." Belari smiled down at the girls affectionately. "They hardly remember what it's like to walk without care."

"All the most beautiful things are fragile." Vernon touched Lidia's cheek. She forced herself not to flinch. "It must have been complex to build them."

Belari nodded. "They are intricate." She traced a finger along the bore-holes in Nia's arm. "Each note isn't simply affected by the placement of fingers on keys; but also by how they press against one another, or the floor; if an arm is bent or if it is straightened. We froze their hormone levels so that they wouldn't grow, and then we began designing their instruments. It takes an enormous amount of skill for them to play and to dance."

"How long have you been training them?"

"Five years. Seven if you count the surgeries that began the process."

Vernon shook his head. "And we never heard of them."

"You would have ruined them. I'm going to make them stars."

"We made you a star."

"And you'll unmake me as well, if I falter."

"So you'll float them on the markets?"

Belari smiled at him. "Of course. I'll retain a controlling interest, but the rest, I will sell."

"You'll be rich."

Belari smiled, "More than that, I'll be independent."

Vernon mimed elaborate disappointment. "I suppose this means we won't be wiring you for TouchSense."

"I suppose not."

The tension between them was palpable. Vernon, calculating, looking for an opening while Belari gripped her property and faced him. Vernon's eyes narrowed.

As though sensing his thoughts, Belari said, "I've insured them."

Vernon shook his head ruefully. "Belari, you do me a disservice." He sighed. "I suppose I should congratulate you. To have such loyal subjects, and such wealth, you've achieved more than I would have thought possible when we first met."

"My servants are loyal because I treat them well. They are happy to serve."

"Would your Stephen agree?" Vernon waved at the sweetmeats in the center of the refreshment table, drizzled with raspberry and garnished with bright green leaves of mint.

Belari smiled. "Oh yes, even him. Do you know that just as Michael and Renee were preparing to cook him, he looked at me and said 'Thank you'?" She shrugged. "He tried to kill me, but he did have the most eager urge to please, even so. At the very end, he told me he was sorry, and that the best years of his life had been in service to me." She wiped at a theatrical tear. "I don't know how it is, that he could love me so, and still do desire to have me dead." She looked away from Vernon, watching the other guests. "For that, though, I thought I would serve him, rather than simply stake him out as a warning. We loved each other, even if he was a traitor."

Vernon shrugged sympathetically. "So many people dislike the fief structure. You try to tell them that you provide far more security than what existed before, and yet still they protest, and," he glanced meaningfully at Belari, "sometimes more."

Belari shrugged. "Well, my subjects don't protest. At least not until Stephen. They love me."

Vernon smiled. "As we all do. In any case, serving him chilled this way." He lifted a plate from the table. "Your taste is impeccable."

Lidia's face stiffened as she followed the conversation. She looked at the array of finely sliced meats and then at Vernon as he forked a bite into his mouth. Her stomach turned. Only her training let her remain still. Vernon and Belari's conversation continued, but all Lidia could think was that she had consumed her friend, the one who had been kind to her.

Anger trickled through her, filling her porous body with rebellion. She longed to attack her smug patron, but her rage was impotent. She was too weak to hurt Belari. Her bones were too fragile, her physique too delicate. Belari was strong in all things as she was weak. Lidia stood trembling with frustration, and then Stephen's voice whispered comforting wisdom inside her head. She could defeat Belari. Her pale skin slushed with pleasure at the thought.

As though sensing her, Belari looked down. "Lidia, go put on clothes and come back. I'll want to introduce you and your sister to everyone before we take you public."

Lidia crept toward her hidey-hole. The vial was still there, if Burson had not found it. Her heart hammered at the thought: that the vial might be missing, that Stephen's final gift had been destroyed by the monster. She slipped through dimly lit servant's tunnels to the kitchen, anxiety pulsing at every step.

The kitchen was busy, full of staff preparing new platters for the guests. Lidia's stomach turned. She wondered if more trays bore Stephen's remains. The stoves flared and the ovens roared as Lidia slipped through the confusion, a ghostly waif sliding along the walls. No one paid her attention. They were too busy laboring for Belari, doing her bidding without thought or conscience: slaves, truly. Obedience was all Belari cared for.

Lidia smiled grimly to herself. If obedience was what Belari loved, she was happy to provide a true betrayal. She would collapse on the floor, amongst her mistress's guests, destroying Belari's perfect moment, shaming her and foiling her hopes of independence.

The pantry was silent when Lidia slipped through its archway. Everyone was busy serving, running like dogs to feed Belari's brood. Lidia wandered amongst the stores, past casks of oil and sacks of onions, past the great humming freezers that held whole sides of beef within their steel bowels. She reached the broad tall shelves at the pantry's end and climbed past preserved peaches, tomatoes, and olives to the high-stored legumes. She pushed aside a vacuum jar of lentils and felt within.

For a moment, as she slid her hand around the cramped hiding place, she thought the vial was missing, but then her grasp closed on the tiny blown-glass bulb.

She climbed down, careful not to break any bones, laughing at herself as she did, thinking that it hardly mattered now, and hurried back through the kitchen, past the busy, obedient servants, and then down the servants' tunnels, intent on self-destruction.

As she sped through the darkened tunnels, she smiled, glad that she would never again steal through dim halls hidden from the view of aristocracy. Freedom was in her hands. For the first time in years she controlled her own fate.

Burson lunged from the shadows, his skin shifting from black to flesh as he materialized. He seized her and jerked her to a halt. Lidia's body strained at the abrupt capture. She gasped, her joints creaking. Burson gathered her wrists into a single massive fist. With his other hand, he turned her chin upward, subjecting her black eyes to the interrogation of his red-rimmed orbs. "Where are you going?"

His size could make you mistake him for stupid, she thought. His slow rumbling voice. His great animal-like gaze. But he was observant where Belari was not. Lidia trembled and cursed herself for foolishness. Burson studied her, his nostrils flaring at the scent of fear. His eyes watched the blush of her skin. "Where are you going?" he asked again. Warning laced his tone.

"Back to the party," Lidia whispered.

"Where have you been?"

Lidia tried to shrug. "Nowhere. Changing."

"Nia is already there. You are late. Belari wondered about you."

Lidia said nothing. There was nothing she could say to make Burson lose his suspicions. She was terrified that he would pry open her clenched hands and discover the glass vial. The servants said it was impossible to lie to Burson. He discovered everything.

Burson eyed her silently, letting her betray herself. Finally he said, "You went to your hidey-hole." He sniffed at her. "Not in the kitchen, though. The pantry." He smiled, revealing hard sharp teeth. "High up."

Lidia held her breath. Burson couldn't let go of a problem until it was solved. It was bred into him. His eyes swept over her skin. "You're nervous." He sniffed. "Sweating. Fear."

Lidia shook her head stubbornly. The tiny vial in her hands was slick, she was afraid she would drop it, or move her hands and call attention to it. Burson's great strength pulled her until they were nose to nose. His fist squeezed her wrists until she thought they would shatter. He studied her eyes. "So afraid."

"No." Lidia shook her head again.

Burson laughed, contempt and pity in the sound. "It must be terrifying to know you can be broken, at any time." His stone grip relaxed. Blood rushed back into her wrists. "Have your hidey-hole, then. Your secret is safe with me."

For a moment, Lidia wasn't sure what he meant. She stood before the giant security officer, frozen still, but then Burson waved his hand irritably and slipped back into the shadows, his skin darkening as he disappeared. "Go."

Lidia stumbled away, her legs wavering, threatening to give out. She forced herself to keep moving, imagining Burson's eyes burning into her pale back. She wondered if he still watched her or if he had already lost interest in the harmless spindly fluted girl, Belari's animal who hid in the closets and made the staff hunt high and low for the selfish mite.

Lidia shook her head in wonderment. Burson had not seen. Burson, for all his enhancements, was blind, so accustomed to inspiring terror that he could no longer distinguish fear from guilt.

A new gaggle of admirers swarmed around Belari, people who knew she was soon to be independent. Once the fluted girls floated on the market, Belari would be nearly as powerful as Vernon Weir, valuable not only for her own performances, but also for her stable of talent. Lidia moved to join her, the vial of liberation hidden in her fist.

Nia stood near Belari, talking to Claire Paranovis from SK Net. Nia nodded graciously at whatever the woman was saying, acting as Belari had trained them: always polite, never ruffled, always happy to talk, nothing to hide, but stories to tell. That was how you handled the media. If you kept them full, they never looked deeper. Nia looked comfortable in her role.

For a moment, Lidia felt a pang of regret at what she was about to do, then she was beside Belari, and Belari was smiling and introducing her to the men and women who surrounded her with fanatic affection. Mgumi Story. Kim Song Lee. Maria Blyst. Takashi Ghandi. More and more names, the global fraternity of media elites.

Lidia smiled and bowed while Belari fended off their proffered hands of congratulation, protecting her delicate investment. Lidia performed as she had been trained, but in her hand the vial lay sweaty, a small jewel of power and destiny. Stephen had been right. The small only controlled their own termination, sometimes not even that. Lidia watched the guests take slices of Stephen, commenting on his sweetness. Sometimes, not even that.

She turned from the crowd of admirers and drew a strawberry from the pyramids of fruit on the refreshment table. She dipped it in cream and rolled it in sugar, tasting the mingled flavors. She selected another strawberry, red and tender between her spidery fingers, a sweet medium for a bitter freedom earned.

With her thumb, she popped the tiny cork out of the vial and sprinkled amber jewels on the lush berry. She wondered if it would hurt, or if it would be quick. It hardly mattered, soon she would be free. She would cry out and fall to the floor and the guests would step back, stunned at Belari's loss. Belari would be humiliated, and more important, would lose the value of the fluted twins. Vernon Weir's lecherous hands would hold her once again.

Lidia gazed at the tainted strawberry. Sweet, Lidia thought. Death should be sweet. She saw Belari watching her, smiling fondly, no doubt happy to see another as addicted to sweets as she. Lidia smiled inwardly, pleased that Belari would see the moment of her rebellion. She raised the strawberry to her lips.

Suddenly a new inspiration whispered in her ear.

An inch from death, Lidia paused, then turned and held out the strawberry to her patron.

She offered the berry as obeisance, with the humility of a creature utterly owned. She bowed her head and proffered the strawberry in the palm of her pale hand, bringing forth all her skill, playing the loyal servant desperately eager to please. She held her breath, no longer aware of the room around her. The guests and conversations all had disappeared. Everything had gone silent.

There was only Belari and the strawberry and the frozen moment of delicious possibility.

Dead Worlds

JACK SKILLINGSTEAD

New writer Jack Skillingstead works in the aerospace industry and lives with his family near Seattle, Washington. The compelling and melancholy story that follows, which shows us that sometimes you have to look very hard indeed just to realize what it is you want to *find*, was his first professional sale, but I can confidently predict that it won't be his last (an easy enough prophecy, since I already have several of his stories in inventory at *Asimov's*). Publishers take note: He has two unsold novels at home, and is at work on more.

A week after my retrieval, I went for a drive in the country. I turned the music up loud, Aaron Copland. The two lane blacktop wound into late summer woods. Sun and shadow slipped over my Mitsubishi. I felt okay, but how long could it last? The point, I guess, was to find out.

I was driving too fast, but that's not why I hit the dog. Even at a reduced speed, I wouldn't have been able to stop in time. I had shifted into a slightly banked corner overhung with maple—and the dog was just there. A big shepherd, standing in the middle of the road with his tongue hanging out, as if he'd been running. Brakes, clutch, panicked wrenching of the wheel, a tight skid. The heavy thud of impact felt through the car's frame.

I turned off the digital music stream and sat a few moments in silence except for the nearly subaudible ripple of the engine. In the rearview mirror, the dog lay in the road.

I swallowed, took a couple of deep breaths, then let the clutch out, slowly rolled onto the shoulder, and killed the engine.

The door swung smoothly up and away. A warm breeze scooped into the car, carrying birdsong and the muted purl of running water—a creek or stream.

I walked back to the dog. He wasn't dead. At the sound of my footsteps approaching, he twisted his head around and snapped at me. I halted a few yards away. The dog whined. Bloody foam flecked his lips. His hind legs twitched brokenly.

"Easy," I said.

The dog whimpered, working his jaws. He didn't snap again, not even when I hunkered close and laid my hand between his ears. The short hairs bristled against my palm.

His chest heaved. He made a grunting, coughing sound. Blood spattered the road. I looked on, dispassionate. Already, I was losing my sense of emotional connection. I had deliberately neglected to take my pill that morning.

Then the woman showed up.

I heard her trampling through the underbrush. She called out, "Buddy! Buddy!"

"Here," I said.

She came out of the woods, holding a red nylon leash, a woman maybe thirty-five years old, with short blond hair, wearing a sleeveless blouse, khaki shorts, and ankle boots. She hesitated. Shock crossed her face. Then she ran to us.

"Buddy, oh Buddy!"

She knelt by the dog, tears spilling from her blue eyes. My chest tightened. I wanted to cherish the emotion. But was it genuine, or a residual effect of the drug?

"I'm sorry," I said. "He was in the road."

"I took him off the leash," she said. "It's my fault."

She kept stroking the dog's side, saying his name. Buddy laid his head in her lap as if he was going to sleep. He coughed again, choking up blood. She stroked him and cried.

"Is there a vet?" I asked.

She didn't answer.

Buddy shuddered violently and ceased breathing; that was the end. "We'd better move him out of the road," I said.

She looked at me and there was something fierce in her eyes. "I'm taking him home," she said.

She struggled to pick the big shepherd up in her arms. The dog was almost as long as she was tall.

"Let me help you. We can put him in the car."

"I can manage."

She staggered with Buddy, feet scuffing, the dog's hind legs limp, like weird dance partners. She found her balance, back swayed, and carried the dead dog into the woods.

I went to the car, grabbed the keys. My hand reached for the glove box, but I drew it back. I was gradually becoming an Eye again, a thing of the Tank. But no matter what, I was through with the pills. I wanted to know if there was anything real left in me.

I locked the car and followed the woman into the woods.

She hadn't gotten far. I found her sitting on the ground crying, hugging the dog. She looked up.

"Help me," she said. "Please."

I carried the dog to her house, about a hundred yards. The body seemed to get heavier in direct relation to the number of steps I took.

It was a modern house, octagonal, lots of glass, standing on a green expanse of recently cut lawn. We approached it from the back. She opened a gate in the wooden fence, and I stepped through with the dog. That was about as far as I could go. I was feeling it in my arms, my back. The woman touched my shoulder.

"Please," she said. "Just a little farther."

I nodded, clenched my teeth, and hefted the dead weight. She led me to a tool shed. Finally, I laid the dog down. She covered it with a green tarp and then pulled the door shut.

"I'll call somebody to come out. I didn't want Buddy to lie by the road or in the woods where the other animals might get at him."

"I understand," I said, but I was drifting, beginning to detach from human sensibilities.

"You better come inside and wash," she said.

I looked at my hands. "Yeah."

I washed in her bathroom. There was blood on my shirt and she insisted I allow her to launder it. When I came out of the bathroom in my T-shirt, she had already thrown my outer shirt, along with her own soiled clothes, into the washer, and called the animal control people, too. Now wearing a blue shift, she offered me iced tea, and we sat together in the big, sunny kitchen, drinking from tall glasses. I noted the flavor of lemon, the feel of the icy liquid sluicing over my tongue. Sensation without complication.

"Did you have the dog a long time?"

"About eight years," she said. "He was my husband's, actually."

"Where is your husband?"

"He passed away two years ago."

"I'm sorry."

She was looking at me in a strange way, and it suddenly struck me that she knew what I was. Somehow, people can tell. I started to stand up.

"Don't go yet," she said. "Wait until they come for Buddy. Please?"

"You'll be all right by yourself."

"Will I?" she said. "I haven't been all right by myself for a long, long time. You haven't even told me your name."

"It's Robert."

She reached across the table for my hand and we shook. "I'm Kim Pham," she said. I was aware of the soft coolness of her flesh, the way her eyes swiveled in their wet orbits, the lemon exhalation of her breath.

"You're an Eye," she said.

I took my hand back.

"And you're not on your medication, are you?"

"It isn't medication, strictly speaking."

"What is it, then?"

A *lie*, I thought, but said, "It restores function. Viagra for the emotionally limp, is the joke."

She didn't smile.

"I know all the jokes," she said. "My husband was a data analyst on the Tau Boo Project. The jokes aren't funny."

The name Pham didn't ring any bells, but a lot of people flogged data at the Project.

"Why don't you take your Viagra or whatever you want to call it?"

I shrugged. "Maybe I'm allergic."

"Or you don't trust that the emotional and cognitive reality is the same one you possessed before the Tank."

I stared at her. She picked up her iced tea and sipped.

"I've read about you," she said.

"Really."

"Not you in particular. I've read about Eyes, the psychological phenomenon."

"Don't forget the sexual mystique."

She looked away. I noted the way the musculature of her neck worked, the slight flushing near her hairline. I was concentrating, but knew I was close to slipping away.

"Being an Eye is not what the public generally thinks," I said.

"How is it different?"

"It's more terrible."

"Tell me."

"The Tank is really a perfect isolation chamber. Negative gravity, total sensory deprivation. Your body is covered with transdermal patches. The cranium is cored to allow for the direct insertion of the conductor. You probably knew that much. Here's what they don't say. The process kills you. To become an Eye, you must literally surrender your life."

I kept talking because it helped root me in my present consciousness. But it wouldn't last.

"They keep you functioning in the Tank, but it's more than your consciousness that rides the tachyon stream. It's your *being*, it's who you are. And somehow, between Earth and the robot receiver fifty light-years away, it sloughs off, all of it except your raw perceptions. You become a thing of the senses, not just an Eye but a hand, a tongue, an ear. You inhabit a machine that was launched before you were born, transmit data back along a tachyon stream, mingled with your own thought impulses for analysts like your husband to dissect endlessly. Then they retrieve you, and all they're really retrieving is a thing of raw perception. They tell you the drugs restore chemical balances in your brain, vitalize cognitive ability. But really, it's a lie. You're dead, and that's all there is to it."

The animal control truck showed up, and I seized the opportunity to leave. The world was breaking up into all its parts now. People separate from the earth upon which they walked. A tree, a door knob, a blue eye swiveling. Separate parts constituting a chaotic and meaningless whole.

At the fence, I paused and looked back, saw Kim Pham watching me. She was like the glass of iced tea, the dead weight of the dog, the cold pool on the fourth planet that quivered like mercury as I probed it with a sensor.

Back in the car, I sat. I had found the automobile, but I wasn't sure I could operate it. All I could see or understand were the thousand individual parts, the alloys and plastics, the wires and servos and treated leather, and the aggregate smell.

A rapping sounded next to my left ear. Thick glass, blue eyes, bone structure beneath stretched skin. I comprehended everything, but understood nothing. The eyes went away. Then: "You better take this." Syllables, modulated air. A bitter taste.

Retrieval.

I blinked at the world, temporarily restored to coherence.

"Are you all right?" Kim was sitting beside me in the Mitsubishi.

"Yes, I'm all right."

"You looked catatonic."

"What time is it?"

"What time do you *think* it is?"

"I asked first."

"Almost seven o'clock."

"Shit."

"I was driving to town. I couldn't believe you were still sitting here."

I rubbed my eyes. "God, I'm tired."

"Where are you staying?"

"I have a charming little apartment at the Project."

"Do you feel well enough to drive there?"

"Yeah, but I don't want to."

"Why not?"

"They might not let me out again."

"Are you serious?"

"Not really."

"It's hard to tell with you."

"Did they take care of Buddy okay?"

"Yes."

I looked at her, and saw an attractive woman of thirty-five or so with light blue eyes.

"You better follow me back to my house. Besides, you forgot your shirt."

"That's right," I said.

I parked my car in the detached garage and stowed the keys under the visor. The Project had given me the car, but it was strictly for publicity purposes and day trips. We Eyes were supposed to have the right stuff.

There was a guest room with a twin bed and a window that admitted a refreshing breeze. I removed my shoes and lay on the bed and listened to hear if she picked up the phone, listened for the sound of her voice calling the Project. She would know people there, have numbers. Former associates of her husband. I closed my eyes, assuming that the next face I saw would be that of a Project security type.

It wasn't.

When I opened my eyes, the room was suffused with soft lamplight. Kim stood in the doorway.

"I have your pills," she said, showing me the little silver case.

"It's okay. I won't need another one until tomorrow."

She studied me.

"Really," I said. "Just one a day."

"What would have happened if I hadn't found you?"

"I would have sat there until somebody else saw me, and if no one else happened by, I would have gone on sitting there until doomsday. Mine, at any rate."

"Did you mean it when you said the Project people wouldn't let you leave again?"

I thought about my answer. "It's not an overt threat. They'd like to get another session out of me. I think they're a little desperate for results."

"Results equal funding, my husband used to say."

"Right."

"My husband was depressed about the lack of life out there."

I sat up on the bed, rubbing my arms, which felt goosebumpy in spite of the warmth.

"How did he die?" I asked.

"A tumor in his brain. It was awful. Toward the end, he was in constant pain. They medicated him heavily. He didn't even know me anymore." She looked away. "I'm afraid I got a little desperate myself after he died. But I'm stronger now."

"Why do you live out here all by yourself?"

"It's my home. If I want a change, there's a cottage up in Oregon, Cannon Beach. But I'm used to being left on my own."

"Used to it?"

"It seems to be a theme in my life."

It was also a statement that begged questions, and I asked them over coffee in the front room. Her parents were killed in a car accident when she was fourteen. Her aunt had raised her, but it was an awkward relationship.

"I felt more like an imposition than a niece."

And then, of course, there was Mr. Pham and the brain tumor. When she finished, something inside me whimpered to get out, but I wouldn't let it.

"Sometimes, I think I'd prefer to be an Eye," Kim said.

"Trust me, you wouldn't."

"Why not?" She was turned to the side, facing me on the couch we shared, one leg drawn up and tucked under, her face alive, eyes questing.

"I already told you: Because you'd have to die."

"I thought that was you being metaphorical."

I shook my head, patted the case of pills now replaced in the cargo pocket of my pants.

"I'm in these pills," I said. "The 'me' you're now talking to. But it isn't the 'me' I left behind when I climbed into the Tank." I sipped my coffee. "There's no official line on that, by the way. It's just my personal theory."

"It's kind of neurotic."

"Kind of."

"I don't even think you really believe it."

I shrugged. "That's your prerogative."

For a while, we didn't talk.

"It does get lonely out here sometimes," Kim said.

"Yes."

Her bedroom was nicer than the guest room. With the lights out, she dialed to transparency three of the walls and the ceiling, and it was like lying out in the open with a billion stars overhead and the trees waving at us. I touched her naked belly and kissed her. Time unwound deliciously, but eventually wound back up tight as a watch-spring and resumed ticking.

We lay on our backs, staring up, limbs entwined. The stars wheeled imperceptibly. I couldn't see Tau Boo, and that was fine with me.

"Why did you do it, then?" she asked.

"Because it felt good. Plus, you seemed to be enjoying yourself as well."

"Not that. Why did you want to be an Eye?"

"Oh. I wanted to see things that no one else could see, ever. I wanted to travel farther than it was possible for a man physically to travel. Pure ego. Which is slightly ironic."

"Worth it?"

I thought of things, the weird aquamarine sky of the fourth planet, the texture of nitrogen-heavy atmosphere. Those quicksilver pools. But I also recalled the ripping away of my personality, and how all those wonders in my mind's eye were like something I'd read about or seen pictures of—unless I went off the pill and allowed myself to become pregnant with chaos. Then it was all real and all indistinguishable, without meaning.

"No," I said, "it wasn't worth it."

"When I think about it," Kim said, "it feels like escape."

"There's that too, yes."

In the morning, I kissed her bare shoulder while she slept. I traced my fingers lightly down her arm, pausing at the white scars on her wrist. She woke up and pulled her arm away. I kissed her neck, and we made love again.

Later, I felt disinclined to return to the Project compound and equally disinclined to check in, which I was required to do.

"Why don't you stay here?" Kim said.

It sounded good. I swallowed my daily dose of personality with my first cup of coffee. In fact, I made a habit of it every morning that I woke up lying next to Kim. Some nights, we fell asleep having neglected to dial the walls back to opacity, and I awakened with the vulnerable illusion that we were outdoors. Once, I felt as if I was being watched, and when I opened my eyes, I saw a doe observing us from the lawn.

I began to discover my health and some measure of happiness that I hadn't previously known. Before, always, I'd been a loner. Kim's story was essentially my story, with variations. It was partly what had driven me to the Tau Boo Project. But for those two weeks, living with Kim Pham, I wasn't alone, not in the usual sense. This was something new in my world. It was good. But it could also give me that feeling I'd had when I woke up in the open with something wild watching me.

One morning, the *last* morning, I woke up in our indoor-outdoor bedroom and found Kim weeping. Her back was to me, her face buried in her pillow. Her shoulders made little hitching movements with her sobs. I touched her hair.

"What's wrong?"

Her voice muffled by the pillow, she said, "I can't stand any more *leaving*."

"Hey—"

She turned into me, her eyes red from crying. "I *mean* it," she said. "I couldn't stand any more."

I held her tightly while the sun came up.

At the breakfast table, I opened the little silver pill case. There were only three pills left. I took one with my first cup of dark French roast. Kim stared at the open case before I snapped it shut.

"You're almost out," she said.

"Yeah."

"Robert, it's not like what you said. Those pills aren't you. They allow you to feel, that's all. You can't always be afraid."

I contemplated my coffee.

"Listen," she said. "I used to be envious of Eyes. No more pain, no more loneliness, no more fear. Life with none of the messiness of living. But I was wrong. That isn't life at all. *This* is. What we have."

"So I'll get more pills." I smiled.

Only it wasn't like a trip to the local pharmacy. There was only one place to obtain the magic personality drug: The Project. I decided that I should go that day, that there was no point in waiting for my meager supply to run out.

Kim held onto me like somebody clinging to a pole in a hurricane.

"I'll come with you," she said.

"They won't let you past the gate."

"I don't care. I'll wait outside, then."

We took her car. She parked across the street. We embraced awkwardly in the front seat. I was aware of the guard watching us.

"You've hardly told me anything personal about yourself," she said. "And here I've told you all my secret pain."

"Maybe I don't have any secret pain."

"You wouldn't be human if you didn't."

"I'll spill my guts when I come out. Promise."

She didn't want to let go, but I was ready to leave. I showed the guard my credentials and he passed me through. I turned and waved to Kim.

"She's a pretty one," the guard said.

I sat in a room. They relieved me of my pill case. I was "debriefed" by a young man who behaved like an automaton, asking questions, checking off my answers on his memorypad. Where had I spent the last two weeks? Why had I failed to communicate with the Project? Did I feel depressed, anxious? Some questions I answered, some I ignored.

"I just want more pills," I said. "I'll check in next time, cross my heart."

A man escorted me to the medical wing, where I underwent a thorough and pointless physical examination. When it was over, Orley Campbell, assistant director of the Tau Boo Project, sat down to chat while we awaited the results of various tests.

"So our stray lamb has returned to the fold," he said. Orley was a tall man with a soft face and the beginnings of a pot belly. I didn't like him.

"Baaa," I said.

"Same old Bobbie."

"Yep, same old me. When do I get out of here?"

"This isn't a jail. You're free to leave any time you wish."

"What about my pills?"

"You'll get them, don't worry about that. You owe us one more session, you know."

"I know."

"Are you having misgivings? I've looked over your evaluation. You appear somewhat depressed."

"I'm not in the least bit depressed."

"Aren't you? I wish I could say the same."

"What time is it? How long have I been here, Orley?"

"Oh, not long. Bobbie, why not jump right back on the horse? If you'd like to relax for a couple of weeks more, that's absolutely not a problem. You just have to remember to check in. I mean, that's part of the drill, right? You knew that when you signed on."

I thought about Kim, waiting outside the gate. Would she still be there? Did I even want her to be? I could feel my consciousness spreading thin. Orley kept smiling at me. "I guess I'm ready," I said.

A month is a long time to exist in the Tank. Of course, as an Eye, you are unaware of passing hours. You inhabit a sensory world at the far end of a tachyon tether. I've looked at romanticized illustrations of this. The peaceful dreamer at one end, the industrious robot on the other. In between, the data flows along an ethereal cord of light. Blah. They keep you alive intravenously, maintain hydration, perform body waste removal. A device sucks out the data. It's fairly brutal.

I recouped in the medical wing for several days. I had my pills and a guarantee of more, all I would require. I had put in the maximum Tank time and could not return without suffering serious and permanent brain damage.

My marathon Tank session had yielded zip in terms of the Project's primary goal. The fourth planet was dead.

Now I would have money and freedom and a future, *if* I wanted one. I spent my hours reading, thinking about warm climates. Kim Pham rapped on my memory, but I wouldn't open the door.

A week after my retrieval, I insisted on being released from the medical wing, and nobody put up an argument. I'd served my purpose. Orley caught up to me as I was leaving the building. I was hobbling on my weak legs, carrying my belongings in a shoulder bag. Orley picked up my hand and shook it.

"Good luck to you," he said. "What's first on the agenda, a little 'Eye candy'?"

I wasn't strong enough to belt him. He looked morose and tired, which is approximately the way I felt myself. When I didn't reply, he went on:

"Cruising a little close to home last time, weren't you? That Pham woman was persistent. She came around every day for two weeks straight. Nice-looking, but older than the others. I guess you would get tired of the young ones after a while."

The smirk is what did it. I found some ambition and threw a decent punch that bloodied his nose.

A cab picked me up at the gate. On impulse, I switched intended destinations. Instead of the airport, I provided sketchy directions, and we managed to find Kim's house without too much difficulty.

The house had an abandoned look, or at least I thought so. A mood can color things, though, and my mood was gloomy. The desperation of the Tau Boo Project had rubbed off on me. There was no life on the fourth planet, no life on any of the planets that had thus far been explored by our human Eyes. When the receiver craft were launched decades previously, it was with a sense of great purpose and hope. But so far, the known universe had not proved too lively, which only made our own earth feel isolated, lonely—doomed, even.

The windows of Kim's house were all black. I knocked, waited, knocked again. I knew where she hid the spare key, on a hook under the back porch.

The house was silent. Every surface was filmed with dust. I drifted through the hollow rooms like a ghost.

Gone.

I pictured all the ways, all the ugly ways, she might have departed this world. Of course, there was no evidence that she had done anything of the sort. An empty house did not necessarily add up to a terminated life. Probably I was giving myself too much credit. But the gloom was upon me. And I could see the white scars on her wrists.

I sat on the carpeted floor of the master bedroom, still weak from the Tank. Hunger gnawed at me, but I didn't care. I let time unravel around the tightening in my chest, and, as darkness fell. I dialed the walls and ceiling clear, and lay on my back, and let exhausted sleep take me.

Lack of nourishment inhibits the efficacy of the pill. In the morning, I opened my eyes to dark pre-dawn and a point of reference that was rapidly growing muddy. The pills were in my bag, but my interest in digging them out was not very great. Why not let it all go? Become the fiber in the rug, the glass, the pulse of blood in my own veins. Why not?

I lay still and began to lose myself. I watched the dark blue sky pale toward dawn. At some point, the blue attained a familiar shade. Kim cradling her dead dog, the fierceness of her eyes. *I can manage.*

A sharp bubble of emotion formed in my throat, and I couldn't swallow it down. So I rolled over. Because maybe I could manage it, too. Maybe. I reached for my bag, my mind growing rapidly diffuse. The interesting articulation of my finger joints distracted me: Bone sleeved within soft flesh, blood circulating, finger pads palpating the tight fibers of the rug. Time passed. I shook myself, groped forward, touched the bag, forgot why it was so important, flickeringly remembered, got my hand on the case, fingered a pill loose onto the rug, belly-crawled, absently scanning details, little yellow pill nestled in fibers, extend probe (tongue), and swallow.

One personality pill with lint chaser.

I came around slowly, coalescing back into the mundane world, an empty stomach retarding the absorption process. Eventually, I stood up. First order of business: food. I found some stale crackers in a kitchen cabinet. Ambrosia. Standing at the sink, gazing out the window, I saw the garage. I stopped chewing, the crackers like crumbled cardboard in my mouth. I'd thought of ropes and drugs and razors. But what about exhaust?

I walked toward the garage, my breathing strangely out of sync. I stopped to gather my courage, or whatever it was I'd need to proceed.

Then I opened the door.

There was one car in the double space. My Mitsubishi, still parked as I'd left it. I climbed into the unlocked car and checked for the keys under the visor. They fell into my lap, note attached. From Kim.

It wasn't a suicide note.

king Dragon

MichaeL SWANWick

Here's a vivid, scary, and gorgeously colored story that dances right on the razor-edge between science fiction and fantasy. Like his famous novel *The Iron Dragon's Daughter*, to which it is clearly somehow related (sequel? prequel? who knows?), it tips back and forth from one genre to the other depending on how you squint at it, sometimes several times in the same page, or even the same paragraph—like one of those paintings that's either of a beautiful young girl or of a skull, depending on how you hold your head. However you squint or hold your head, though, it's an unforgettable reading experience.

Michael Swanwick made his debut in 1980, and in the twenty-four years that have followed has established himself as one of SF's most prolific and consistently excellent writers at short lengths, as well as one of the premier novelists of his generation. He has won the Theodore Sturgeon Award and the *Asimov's* Readers Award poll. In 1991, his novel *Stations of the Tide* won him a Nebula Award as well, and in 1995 he won the World Fantasy Award for his story "Radio Waves." He's won the Hugo Award four times between 1999 and 2003, for his stories "The Very Pulse of the Machine," "Scherzo With Tyrannosaur," "The Dog Said Bow-Wow," and "Slow Life." His other books include the novels *In The Drift*, *Vacuum Flowers*, *The Iron Dragon's Daughter* (which was a finalist for the World Fantasy Award *and* the Arthur C. Clarke Award, a rare distinction!), *Jack Faust*, and, most recently, *Bones of the Earth*, plus a novella-length book, *Griffin's Egg*. His short fiction has been assembled in *Gravity's Angels*, *A Geography of Unknown Lands*, *Slow Dancing Through Time* (a collection of his collaborative short work with other writers), *Moon Dogs*,

Puck Aleshire's Abecedary, and *Tales of Old Earth*. He's also published a collection of critical articles, *The Postmodern Archipelago*, and a book-length interview, *Being Gardner Dozois*. His most recent book is a new collection, *Cigar-Box Faust and Other Miniatures*. He's had stories in our Second, Third, Fourth, Sixth, Seventh, Tenth, and Thirteenth through Twentieth Annual Collections. Swanwick lives in Philadelphia with his wife, Marianne Porter. He has a Web Site at www.michaelswanwick.com.

The dragons came at dawn, flying low and in formation, their jets so thunderous they shook the ground like the great throbbing heartbeat of the world. The village elders ran outside, half unbuttoned, waving their staffs in circles and shouting words of power. *Vanish*, they cried to the land, and *sleep* to the skies, though had the dragons' half-elven pilots cared they could have easily seen through such flimsy spells of concealment. But the pilots' thoughts were turned toward the west, where Avalon's industrial strength was based, and where its armies were rumored to be massing.

Will's aunt made a blind grab for him, but he ducked under her arm and ran out into the dirt street. The gun emplacements to the south were speaking now, in booming shouts that filled the sky with bursts of pink smoke and flak.

Half the children in the village were out in the streets, hopping up and down in glee, the winged ones buzzing about in small, excited circles. Then the yage-witch came hobbling out from her barrel and, demonstrating a strength Will had never suspected her of having, swept her arms wide and then slammed together her hoary old hands with a *boom!* that drove the children, all against their will, back into their huts.

All save Will. He had been performing that act which rendered one immune from child-magic every night for three weeks now. Fleeing from the village, he felt the enchantment like a polite hand placed on his shoulder. One weak tug, and then it was gone.

He ran, swift as the wind, up Grannystone Hill. His great-great-great-grandmother lived there still, alone at its tip, as a grey standing stone. She never said anything. But sometimes, though one never saw her move, she went down to the river at night to drink. Coming back from a nighttime fishing trip in his wee coracle, Will would find her standing motionless there and greet her respectfully. If the catch was good, he would gut an eel or a small trout, and smear the blood over her feet. It was the sort of small courtesy elderly relatives appreciated.

"Will, you young fool, turn back!" a cobbley cried from the inside of a junk refrigerator in the garbage dump at the edge of the village. "It's not safe up there!"

But Will didn't want to be safe. He shook his head, long blond hair flying behind him, and put every ounce of his strength into his running. He wanted to see dragons. Dragons! Creatures of almost unimaginable power and magic. He wanted to experience the glory of their flight. He wanted to get as close to them as he could. It was a kind of mania. It was a kind of need.

It was not far to the hill, nor a long way to its bald and grassy summit. Will ran with a wildness he could not understand, lungs pounding and the wind of his own speed whistling in his ears.

And then he was atop the hill, breathing hard, with one hand on his grandmother stone.

The dragons were still flying overhead in waves. The roar of their jets was astounding. Will lifted his face into the heat of their passage, and felt the wash of their malice and hatred as well. It was like a dark wine that sickened the stomach and made the head throb with pain and bewilderment and wonder. It repulsed him and made him want more.

The last flight of dragons scorched over, twisting his head and spinning his body around, so he could keep on watching them, flying low over farms and fields and the Old Forest that stretched all the way to the horizon and beyond. There was a faint brimstone stench of burnt fuel in the air. Will felt his heart grow so large it seemed impossible his chest could contain it, so large that it threatened to encompass the hill, farms, forest, dragons, and all the world beyond.

Something hideous and black leaped up from the distant forest and into the air, flashing toward the final dragon. Will's eyes felt a painful wrenching *wrongness*, and then a stone hand came down over them.

"*Don't look*," said an old and calm and stony voice. "*To look upon a basilisk is no way for a child of mine to die.*"

"Grandmother?" Will asked.

"Yes?"

"If I promise to keep my eyes closed, will you tell me what's happening?"

There was a brief silence. Then: "*Very well. The dragon has turned. He is fleeing.*"

"Dragons don't flee," Will said scornfully. "Not from anything." Forgetting his promise, he tried to pry the hand from his eyes. But of course it was useless, for his fingers were mere flesh.

"*This one does. And he is wise to do so. His fate has come for him. Out from the halls of coral it has come, and down to the halls of granite it will take him. Even now his pilot is singing his death-song.*"

She fell silent again, while the distant roar of the dragon rose and fell in pitch. Will could tell that momentous things were happening, but the sound gave him not the least clue as to their nature. At last he said, "Grandmother? Now?"

"*He is clever, this one. He fights very well. He is elusive. But he cannot escape a basilisk. Already the creature knows the first two syllables of his true name. At this very moment it is speaking to his heart, and telling it to stop beating.*"

The roar of the dragon grew louder again, and then louder still. From the way it kept on growing, Will was certain the great creature was coming straight toward him. Mingled with its roar was a noise that was like a cross between a scarecrow screaming and the sound of teeth scraping on slate.

"*Now they are almost touching. The basilisk reaches for its prey . . .*"

There was a deafening explosion directly overhead. For an astonishing instant, Will felt certain he was going to die. Then his grandmother threw her stone cloak over him and, clutching him to her warm breast, knelt down low to the sheltering earth.

When he awoke, it was dark and he lay alone on the cold hillside. Painfully, he stood. A somber orange-and-red sunset limned the western horizon, where the dragons had disappeared. There was no sign of the War anywhere.

"Grandmother?" Will stumbled to the top of the hill, cursing the stones that hindered him. He ached in every joint. There was a constant ringing in his ears, like factory bells tolling the end of a shift. "Grandmother!"

There was no answer.

The hilltop was empty.

But scattered down the hillside, from its top down to where he had awakened, was a stream of broken stones. He had hurried past them without looking on his way up. Now he saw that their exterior surfaces were the familiar and comfortable grey of his stone-mother, and that the freshly exposed interior surfaces were slick with blood.

One by one, Will carried the stones back to the top of the hill, back to the spot where his great-great-great-grandmother had preferred to stand and watch over the village. It took hours. He piled them one on top of another, and though it felt like more work than he had ever done in his life, when he was finished, the cairn did not rise even so high as his waist. It seemed impossible that this could be all that remained of she who had protected the village for so many generations.

By the time he was done, the stars were bright and heartless in a black, moonless sky. A night-wind ruffled his shirt and made him shiver, and with sudden clarity he wondered at last why he was alone. Where was his aunt? Where were the other villagers?

Belatedly remembering his basic spell-craft, he yanked out his rune-bag from a hip pocket, and spilled its contents into his hand. A crumpled blue-jay's feather, a shard of mirror, two acorns, and a pebble with one side blank and the other marked with an X. He kept the mirror-shard and poured the rest back into the bag. Then he invoked the secret name of the *lux aeterna*, inviting a tiny fraction of its radiance to enter the mundane world.

A gentle foxfire spread itself through the mirror. Holding it at arm's length so he could see his face reflected therein, he asked the oracle glass, "Why did my village not come for me?"

The mirror-boy's mouth moved. "They came." His skin was pallid, like a corpse's.

"Then why didn't they bring me home?" And why did *he* have to build his stone-grandam's cairn and not they? He did not ask that question, but he felt it to the core of his being.

"They didn't find you."

The oracle-glass was maddeningly literal, capable only of answering the question one asked, rather than that which one wanted answered. But Will persisted. "Why didn't they find me?"

"You weren't here."

"Where was I? Where was my Granny?"

"You were nowhere."

"How could we be nowhere?"

Tonelessly, the mirror said, "The basilisk's explosion warped the world and the mesh of time in which it is caught. The sarsen-lady and you were thrown forward, halfway through the day."

It was as clear an explanation as Will was going to get. He muttered a word of unbinding, releasing the invigorating light back to whence it came. Then, fearful that the blood on his hands and clothes would draw night-gaunts, he hurried homeward.

When he got to the village, he discovered that a search party was still scouring the darkness, looking for him. Those who remained had hoisted a straw man upside down atop a tall pole at the center of the village square, and set it ablaze against the chance he was still alive, to draw him home.

And so it had.

Two days after those events, a crippled dragon crawled out of the Old Forest and into the village. Slowly he pulled himself into the center square. Then he collapsed. He was wingless and there were gaping holes in his fuselage, but still the stench of power clung to him, and a miasma of hatred. A trickle of oil seeped from a gash in his belly and made a spreading stain on the cobbles beneath him.

Will was among those who crowded out to behold this prodigy. The others whispered hurtful remarks among themselves about its ugliness. And truly it was built of cold, black iron, and scorched even darker by the basilisk's explosion, with jagged stumps of metal where its wings had been and ruptured plates here and there along its flanks. But Will could see that, even half-destroyed, the dragon was a beautiful creature. It was built with dwarven skill to high-elven design—how could it *not* be beautiful? It was, he felt certain, the same dragon that he had almost seen shot down by the basilisk.

Knowing this gave him a strange sense of shameful complicity, as if he were in some way responsible for the dragon's coming to the village.

For a long time no one spoke. Then an engine hummed to life somewhere deep within the dragon's chest, rose in pitch to a clattering whine, and fell again into silence. The dragon slowly opened one eye.

"Bring me your truth-teller," he rumbled.

The truth-teller was a fruit-woman named Bessie Applemere. She was young and yet, out of respect for her office, everybody called her by the honorific Hag. She came, clad in the robes and wide hat of her calling, breasts bare as was traditional, and stood before the mighty engine of war. "Father of Lies." She bowed respectfully.

"I am crippled, and all my missiles are spent," the dragon said. "But still am I dangerous."

Hag Applemere nodded. "It is the truth."

"My tanks are yet half-filled with jet fuel. It would be the easiest thing in the world for me to set them off with an electrical spark. And were I to do so, your village and all who live within it would cease to be. Therefore, since power engenders power. I am now your liege and king."

"It is the truth."

A murmur went up from the assembled villagers.

"However, my reign will be brief. By Samhain, the Armies of the Mighty will be here, and they shall take me back to the great forges of the East to be rebuilt."

"You believe it so."

The dragon's second eye opened. Both focused steadily on the truth-teller. "You do not please me, Hag. I may someday soon find it necessary to break open your body and eat your beating heart."

Hag Applemere nodded. "It is the truth."

Unexpectedly, the dragon laughed. It was cruel and sardonic laughter, as the mirth of such creatures always was, but it was laughter nonetheless. Many of the villagers covered their ears against it. The smaller children burst into tears. "You amuse me," he said. "All of you amuse me. We begin my reign on a gladsome note."

The truth-teller bowed. Watching, Will thought he detected a great sadness in her eyes. But she said nothing.

"Let your lady-mayor come forth, that she might give me obeisance."

Auld Black Agnes shuffled from the crowd. She was scrawny and thrawn and bent almost double from the weight of her responsibilities. They hung in a black leather bag around her neck. From that bag, she brought forth a flat stone from the first hearth of the village, and laid it down before the dragon. Kneeling, she placed her left hand, splayed, upon it.

Then she took out a small silver sickle.

"Your blood and ours. Thy fate and mine. Our joy and your wickedness. Let all be as one." Her voice rose in a warbling keen:

> "Black spirits and white, red spirits and grey,
> Mingle, mingle, mingle, you that mingle may."

Her right hand trembled with palsy as it raised the sickle up above her left. But her slanting motion downward was swift and sudden. Blood spurted, and her little finger went flying.

She made one small, sharp cry, like a sea-bird's, and no more.

"I am satisfied," the dragon said. Then, without transition: "My pilot is dead and he begins to rot." A hatch hissed open in his side. "Drag him forth."

"Do you wish him buried?" a kobold asked hesitantly.

"Bury him, burn him, cut him up for bait—what do I care? When he was alive, I needed him in order to fly. But he's dead now, and of no use to me."

"Kneel."

Will knelt in the dust beside the dragon. He'd been standing in line for hours, and there were villagers who would be standing in that same line hours from now, waiting to be processed. They went in fearful, and they came out dazed. When a lily-maid stepped down from the dragon, and somebody shouted a question at her, she simply shook her tear-streaked face, and fled. None would speak of what happened within.

The hatch opened.

"Enter."

He did. The hatch closed behind him.

At first he could see nothing. Then small, faint lights swam out of the darkness. Bits of green and white stabilized, became instrument lights, pale luminescent flecks on dials. One groping hand touched leather. It was the pilot's couch. He could smell, faintly, the taint of corruption on it.

"Sit."

Clumsily, he climbed into the seat. The leather creaked under him. His arms naturally lay along the arms of the couch. He might have been made for it. There were handgrips. At the dragon's direction, he closed his hands about them and turned them as far as they would go. A quarter-turn, perhaps.

From beneath, needles slid into his wrists. They stung like blazes, and Will jerked involuntarily. But when he tried, he discovered that he could not let go of the grips. His fingers would no longer obey him.

"Boy," the dragon said suddenly, "what is your true name?"

Will trembled. "I don't have one."

Immediately, he sensed that this was not the right answer. There was a silence. Then the dragon said dispassionately, "I can make you suffer."

"Sir, I am certain you can."

"Then tell me your true name."

His wrists were cold—cold as ice. The sensation that spread up his fore-arms to his elbows was not numbness, for they ached terribly. It felt as if they were packed in snow. "I don't *know* it! Will cried in an anguish. "I don't know, I was never told, I don't think I have one!"

Small lights gleamed on the instrument panel, like forest eyes at night.

"Interesting." For the first time, the dragon's voice displayed a faint tinge of emotion. "What family is yours? Tell me everything about them."

Will had no family other than his aunt. His parents had died on the very first day of the War. Theirs was the ill-fortune of being in Brocielande Station when the dragons came and dropped golden fire on the rail yards. So Will had been shipped off to the hills to live with his aunt. Everyone agreed he would be safest there. That was several years ago, and there were times now when he could not remember his parents at all. Soon he would have only the memory of remembering.

As for his aunt, Blind Enna was little more to him than a set of rules to be contravened and chores to be evaded. She was a pious old creature, forever killing small animals in honor of the Nameless Ones and burying their corpses under the floor or nailing them above doors or windows. In consequence of which, a faint perpetual stink of conformity and rotting mouse hung about the hut. She mumbled to herself constantly and on those rare occasions when she got drunk—two or three times a year—would run out naked into the night and, mounting a cow backwards, lash its sides bloody with a hickory switch so that it ran wildly uphill and down until finally she tumbled off and fell asleep. At dawn Will would come with a blanket and lead her home. But they were never exactly close.

All this he told in stumbling, awkward words. The dragon listened without comment.

The cold had risen up to Will's armpits by now. He shuddered as it touched his shoulders. "Please . . ." he said. "Lord Dragon . . . your ice has reached my chest. If it touches my heart, I fear that I'll die."

"Hmmmm? Ah! I was lost in thought." The needles withdrew from Will's arms. They were still numb and lifeless, but at least the cold had stopped its spread. He could feel a tingle of pins and needles in the center of his finger-tips, and so knew that sensation would eventually return.

The door hissed open. "You may leave now."

He stumbled out into the light.

An apprehension hung over the village for the first week or so. But as the dragon remained quiescent and no further alarming events occurred, the time-less patters of village life more or less resumed. Yet all the windows opening upon the center square remained perpetually shuttered and nobody willingly passed through it anymore, so that it was as if a stern silence had come to dwell within their midst.

Then one day Will and Puck Berrysnatcher were out in the woods, check-ing their snares for rabbits and camelopards (it had been generations since a pard was caught in Avalon but they still hoped), when the Scissors-Grinder came puffing down the trail. He lugged something bright and gleaming within his two arms.

"Hey, bandy-man!" Will cried. He had just finished tying his rabbits' legs together so he could sling them over his shoulder. "Ho, big-belly! What hast thou?"

"Don't know. Fell from the sky."

"Did *not!*" Puck scoffed. The two boys danced about the fat cobber, grab-bing at the golden thing. It was shaped something like a crown and something like a birdcage. The metal of its ribs and bands was smooth and lustrous. Black runes adorned its sides. They had never seen its like. "I bet it's a roc's egg—or a phoenix's!"

And simultaneously Will asked, "Where are you taking it?"

"To the smithy. Perchance the hammerman can beat it down into some-thing useful." The Scissors-Grinder swatted at Puck with one hand, almost los-ing his hold on the object. "Perchance they'll pay me a penny or three for it."

Daisy Jenny popped up out of the flowers in the field by the edge of the garbage dump and, seeing the golden thing, ran toward it, pigtails flying, singing, "Gimme-gimme-gimme!" Two hummingirls and one chimney-bounder came swooping down out of nowhere. And the Cauldron Boy dropped an armful of scavenged scrap metal with a crash and came running up as well. So that by the time the Meadows Trail became Mud Street, the Scissors-Grinder was red-faced and cursing, and knee-deep in children.

"Will, you useless creature!"

Turning, Will saw his aunt, Blind Enna, tapping toward him. She had a peeled willow branch in each hand, like long white antennae, that felt the ground before her as she came. The face beneath her bonnet was grim. He knew this mood, and knew better than to try to evade her when she was in it. "Auntie . . ." he said.

"Don't you Auntie me, you slugabed! There's toads to be buried and stoops to be washed. Why are you never around when it's time for chores?"

She put an arm through his and began dragging him homeward, still feeling ahead of herself with her wands.

Meanwhile, the Scissors-Grinder was so distracted by the children that he let his feet carry him the way they habitually went—through Center Square, rather than around it. For the first time since the coming of the dragon, laughter and children's voices spilled into that silent space. Will stared yearningly over his shoulder after his dwindling friends.

The dragon opened an eye to discover the cause of so much noise. He reared up his head in alarm. In a voice of power he commanded, *"Drop that!"*

Startled, the Scissors-Grinder obeyed.

The device exploded.

Magic in the imagination is a wondrous thing, but magic in practice is terrible beyond imagining. An unending instant's dazzlement and confusion left Will lying on his back in the street. His ears rang horribly, and he felt strangely numb. There were legs everywhere—people running. And somebody was hitting him with a stick. No, with two sticks.

He sat up, and the end of a stick almost got him in the eye. He grabbed hold of it with both hands and yanked at it angrily. "Auntie," he yelled. Blind Enna went on waving the other stick around, and tugging at the one he had captured, trying to get it back. "Auntie, stop that!" But of course she couldn't hear him; he could barely hear himself through the ringing in his ears.

He got to his feet and put both arms around his aunt. She struggled against him, and Will was astonished to find that she was no taller than he. When had *that* happened? She had been twice his height when first he came to her. "Auntie Enna!" he shouted into her ear. "It's me, Will, I'm right here."

"Will." Her eyes filled with tears. "You shiftless, worthless thing. Where are you when there are chores to be done?"

Over her shoulder, he saw how the square was streaked with black and streaked with red. There were things that looked like they might be bodies. He blinked. The square was filled with villagers, leaning over them. Doing things. Some had their heads thrown back, as if they were wailing. But of course he couldn't hear them, not over the ringing noise.

"I caught two rabbits, Enna," he told his aunt, shouting so he could be heard. He still had them, slung over his shoulder. He couldn't imagine why. "We can have them for supper."

"That's good," she said. "I'll cut them up for stew, while you wash the stoops."

Blind Enna found her refuge in work. She mopped the ceiling and scoured the floor. She had Will polish every piece of silver in the house. Then all the furniture had to be taken apart, and cleaned, and put back together again. The rugs had to be boiled. The little filigreed case containing her heart had to be taken out of the cupboard where she normally kept it and hidden in the very back of the closet.

The list of chores that had to be done was endless. She worked herself, and Will as well, all the way to dusk. Sometimes he cried at the thought of his friends who had died, and Blind Enna hobbled over and hit him to make him stop. Then, when he did stop, he felt nothing. He felt nothing, and he felt like a monster for feeling nothing. Thinking of it made him begin to cry again, so he wrapped his arms tight around his face to muffle the sounds, so his aunt would not hear and hit him again.

It was hard to say which—the feeling or the not—made him more miserable.

The very next day, the summoning bell was rung in the town square and, willing or not, all the villagers once again assembled before their king dragon. "Oh, ye foolish creatures!" the dragon said. "Six children have died and old *Tanarahumra*—he whom you called the Scissors-Grinder—as well, because you have no self-discipline."

Hag Applemere bowed her head sadly. "It is the truth."

"You try my patience," the dragon said. "Worse, you drain my batteries. My reserves grow low, and I can only partially recharge them each day. Yet I see now that I dare not be King Log. You must be governed. Therefore, I require a speaker. Someone slight of body, to live within me and carry my commands to the outside."

Auld Black Agnes shuffled forward. "That would be me," she said wearily. "I know my duty."

"No!" the dragon said scornfully. "You aged cronies are too cunning by half. I'll choose somebody else from this crowd. Someone simple . . . a child."

Not me, Will thought wildly. *Anybody else but me.*

"Him," the dragon said.

So it was that Will came to live within the dragon king. All that day and late into the night he worked drawing up plans on sheets of parchment, at his lord's careful instructions, for devices very much like stationary bicycles that could be used to recharge the dragon's batteries. In the morning, he went to the blacksmith's forge at the end of town to command that six of the things be immediately built. Then he went to Auld Black Agnes to tell her that all day and every day six villagers, elected by lot or rotation or however else she chose, were to sit upon the devices pedaling, pedaling, all the way without cease from dawn to sundown, when Will would drag the batteries back inside.

Hurrying through the village with his messages—there were easily a dozen packets of orders, warnings, and advices that first day—Will experienced a strange sense of unreality. Lack of sleep made everything seem impossibly vivid. The green moss on the skulls stuck in the crotches of forked sticks lining the first half-mile of the River Road, the salamanders languidly copulating in the coals of the smithy forge, even the stillness of the carnivorous plants in his Auntie's garden as they waited for an unwary frog to hop within striking distance . . . such homely sights were transformed. Everything was new and strange to him.

By noon, all the dragon's errands were run, so Will went out in search of friends. The square was empty, of course, and silent. But when he wandered out into the lesser streets, his shadow short beneath him, they were empty as well. It was eerie. Then he heard the high sound of a girlish voice and followed it around a corner.

There was a little girl playing at jump rope and chanting:

> "Here-am-I-and
> All-a-lone;
> What's-my-name?
> It's-Jum-ping—"

"Joan!" Will cried, feeling an unexpected relief at the sight of her.

Jumping Joan stopped. In motion, she had a certain kinetic presence. Still, she was hardly there at all. A hundred slim braids exploded from her small, dark head. Her arms and legs were thin as reeds. The only things of any size at all about her were her luminous brown eyes. "I was up to a million!" she said angrily. "Now I'll have to start all over again."

"When you start again, count your first jump as a million-and-one."

"It doesn't work that way and you know it! What do you want?"

"Where is everybody?"

"Some of them are fishing and some are hunting. Others are at work in the fields. The hammermen, the tinker, and the Sullen Man are building bicycles-that-don't-move to place in Tyrant Square. The potter and her prentices are digging clay from the riverbank. The healing-women are in the smoke-hutch at the edge of the woods with Puck Berrysnatcher."

"Then that last is where I'll go. My thanks, wee-thing."

Jumping Joan, however, made no answer. She was already skipping rope again, and counting "A-hundred-thousand-one, a-hundred-thousand-two . . ."

The smoke-hutch was an unpainted shack built so deep in the reeds that whenever it rained it was in danger of sinking down into the muck and never being seen again. Hornets lazily swam to and from a nest beneath its eaves. The door creaked noisily as Will opened it.

As one, the women looked up sharply. Puck Berrysnatcher's body was a pale white blur on the shadowy ground before them. The women's eyes were green and unblinking, like those of jungle animals. They glared at him wordlessly. "I w-wanted to see what you were d-doing," he stammered.

"We are inducing catatonia," one of them said. "Hush now. Watch and learn."

The healing-women were smoking cigars over Puck. They filled their mouths with smoke and then, leaning close, let it pour down over his naked, broken body. By slow degrees the hut filled with bluish smoke, turning the healing-women to ghosts and Puck himself into an indistinct smear on the dirt floor. He sobbed and murmured in pain at first, but by slow degrees his cries grew quieter, and then silent. At last his body shuddered and stiffened, and he ceased breathing.

The healing-women daubed Puck's chest with ocher, and then packed his mouth, nostrils, and anus with a mixture of aloe and white clay. They wrapped his body with a long white strip of linen.

Finally they buried him deep in the black marsh by the edge of Hagmere Pond.

When the last shovelful of earth had been tamped down, the women turned as one and silently made their ways home, along five separate paths. Will's stomach rumbled, and he realized he hadn't eaten yet that day. There was a cherry tree not far away whose fruit was freshly come to ripeness, and a pigeon pie that he knew of which would not be well-guarded.

Swift as a thief, he sped into town.

He expected the dragon to be furious with him when he finally returned to it just before sundown, for staying away as long as he could. But when he sat down in the leather couch and the needles slid into his wrists, the dragon's voice was a murmur, almost a purr. "How fearful you are! You tremble. Do not be afraid, small one. I shall protect and cherish you. And you, in turn, shall be my eyes and ears, eh? Yes, you will. Now, let us see what you learned today."

"I—"

"Shussssh," the dragon breathed. "Not a word. I need not your interpretation, but direct access to your memories. Try to relax. This will hurt you, the first time, but with practice it will grow easier. In time, perhaps, you will learn to enjoy it."

Something cold and wet and slippery slid into Will's mind. A coppery foulness filled his mouth. A repulsive stench rose up in his nostrils. Reflexively, he retched and struggled.

"Don't resist. This will go easier if you open yourself to me."

More of that black and oily sensation poured into Will, and more. Coil upon coil, it thrust its way inside him. His body felt distant, like a thing that no longer belonged to him. He could hear it making choking noises.

"Take it all."

It hurt. It hurt more than the worst headache Will had ever had. He thought he heard his skull cracking from the pressure, and still the intrusive presence pushed into him, its pulsing mass permeating his thoughts, his senses, his memories. Swelling them. Engorging them. And then, just as he was certain his head must explode from the pressure, it was done.

The dragon was within him.

Squeezing shut his eyes, Will saw, in the dazzling, pain-laced darkness, the dragon king as he existed in the spirit world: sinuous, veined with light, humming with power. Here, in the realm of ideal forms, he was not a broken, crippled *thing*, but a sleek being with the beauty of an animal and the perfection of a machine.

"Am I not beautiful?" the dragon asked. "Am I not a delight to behold?"

Will gagged with pain and disgust. And yet—might the Seven forgive him for thinking this!—it was true.

Every morning at dawn Will dragged out batteries weighing almost as much as himself into Tyrant Square for the villagers to recharge—one at first, then more as the remaining six standing bicycles were built. One of the women would be waiting to give him breakfast. As the dragon's agent, he was entitled to go into any hut and feed himself from what he found there, but the dragon deemed this method more dignified. The rest of the day he spent wandering through the village and, increasingly, the woods and fields around the village, observing. At first he did not know what he was looking for. But by comparing the orders he transmitted with what he had seen the previous day, he slowly came to realize that he was scouting out the village's defensive position, discovering its weaknesses, and looking for ways to alleviate them.

The village was, Will saw, simply not defensible from any serious military force. But it could be made more obscure. Thorn-hedges were planted, and poison oak. Footpaths were eradicated. A clearwater pond was breached and drained, lest it be identified as a resource for advancing armies. When the weekly truck came up the River Road with mail and cartons of supplies for the store, Will was loitering nearby, to ensure that nothing unusual caught the driver's eye. When the bee-warden declared a surplus that might be sold downriver for silver, Will relayed the dragon's instructions that half the overage be destroyed, lest the village get a reputation for prosperity.

At dimity, as the sunlight leached from the sky, Will would feel a familiar aching in his wrists and a troubling sense of need, and return to the dragon's cabin to lie in painful communion with him and share what he had seen.

Evenings varied. Sometimes he was too sick from the dragon's entry into him to do anything. Other times, he spent hours scrubbing and cleaning the dragon's interior. Mostly, though, he simply sat in the pilot's couch, listening while the dragon talked in a soft, almost inaudible rumble. Those were, in their way, the worst times of all.

"You don't have cancer," the dragon murmured. It was dark outside, or so Will believed. The hatch was kept closed tight and there were no windows. The only light came from the instruments on the control panel. "No bleeding from the rectum, no loss of energy. Eh, boy?"

"No, dread lord."

"It seems I chose better than I suspected. You have mortal blood in you, sure as moonlight. Your mother was no better than she ought to be."

"Sir?" he said uncomprehendingly.

"I said your mother was a *whore!* Are you feeble-minded? Your mother was a whore, your father a cuckold, you a bastard, grass green, mountains stony, and water wet."

"My mother was a good woman!" Ordinarily, he didn't talk back. But this time the words just slipped out.

"Good women sleep with men other than their husbands all the time, and for more reasons than there are men. Didn't anybody tell you that?" He could hear a note of satisfaction in the dragon's voice. "She could have been bored, or reckless, or blackmailed. She might have wanted money, or adventure, or revenge upon your father. Perchance she bet her virtue upon the turn of a card. Maybe she was overcome by the desire to roll in the gutter and befoul herself. She may even have fallen in love. Unlikelier things have happened."

"I won't listen to this!"

"You have no choice," the dragon said complacently. "The door is locked and you cannot escape. Moreover I am larger and more powerful than you. This is the *Lex Mundi*, from which there is no appeal."

"You lie! You lie! You lie!"

"Believe what you will. But, however got, your mortal blood is your good fortune. Lived you not in the asshole of beyond, but in a more civilized setting, you would surely be conscripted for a pilot. All pilots are half-mortal, you know, for only mortal blood can withstand the taint of cold iron. You would live like a prince, and be trained as a warrior. You would be the death of thousands." The dragon's voice sank musingly. "How shall I mark this discovery? Shall I . . . ? Oho! Yes. I will make you my lieutenant."

"How does that differ from what I am now?"

"Do not despise titles. If nothing else, it will impress your friends."

Will had no friends, and the dragon knew it. Not anymore. All folk avoided him when they could, and were stiff-faced and wary in his presence when they could not. The children fleered and jeered and called him names. Sometimes they flung stones at him or pottery shards or—once—even a cowpat, dry on the outside but soft and gooey within. Not often, however, for when they did, he would catch them and thrash them for it. This always seemed to catch the little ones by surprise.

The world of children was much simpler than the one he inhabited.

When Little Margotty struck him with the cowpat, he caught her by the ear and marched her to her mother's hut. "See what your brat has done to me!" he cried in indignation, holding his jerkin away from him.

Big Red Margotty turned from the worktable, where she had been canning toads. She stared at him stonily, and yet he thought a glint resided in her eye of suppressed laughter. Then, coldly, she said, "Take it off and I shall wash it for you."

Her expression when she said this was so disdainful that Will felt an impulse to peel off his trousers as well, throw them in her face for her insolence, and command her to wash them for a penance. But with the thought came also an awareness of Big Red Margotty's firm, pink flesh, of her ample breasts and womanly haunches. He felt his lesser self swelling to fill out his trousers and make them bulge.

This too Big Red Margotty saw, and the look of casual scorn she gave him then made Will burn with humiliation. Worse, all the while her mother washed his jerkin, Little Red Margotty danced around Will at a distance, holding up her skirt and waggling her bare bottom at him, making a mock of his discomfort.

On the way out the door, his damp jerkin draped over one arm, he stopped and said, "Make for me a sark of white damask, with upon its breast a shield: Argent, dragon rouge rampant above a village sable. Bring it to me by dawnlight tomorrow."

Outraged, Big Red Margotty said: "The cheek! You have no right to demand any such thing!"

"I am the dragon's lieutenant, and that is right enough for anything."

He left, knowing that the red bitch would perforce be up all night sewing for him. He was glad for every miserable hour she would suffer.

———

Three weeks having passed since Puck's burial, the healing-women decided it was time at last to dig him up. They said nothing when Will declared that he would attend—none of the adults said anything to him unless they had no choice—but, tagging along after them, he knew for a fact that he was unwelcome.

Puck's body, when they dug it up, looked like nothing so much as an enormous black root, twisted and formless. Chanting all the while, the women unwrapped the linen swaddling and washed him down with cow's urine. They dug out the life-clay that clogged his openings. They placed the finger-bone of a bat beneath his tongue. An egg was broken by his nose and the white slurped down by one medicine woman and the yellow by another.

Finally, they injected him with 5 cc of dextroamphetamine sulfate.

Puck's eyes flew open. His skin had been baked black as silt by his long immersion in the soil, and his hair bleached white. His eyes were a vivid and startling leaf-green. In all respects but one, his body was as perfect as it had ever been. But that one exception made the women sigh unhappily for his sake.

One leg was missing, from above the knee down.

"The Earth has taken her tithe," one old woman observed sagely.

"There was not enough left of the leg to save," said another.

"It's a pity," said a third.

They all withdrew from the hut, leaving Will and Puck alone together.

For a long time Puck did nothing but stare wonderingly at his stump of a leg. He sat up and ran careful hands over its surface, as if to prove to himself that the missing flesh was not still there and somehow charmed invisible. Then he stared at Will's clean white shirt, and at the dragon arms upon his chest. At last, his unblinking gaze rose to meet Will's eyes.

"*You* did this!"

"No!" It was an unfair accusation. The land mine had nothing to do with the dragon. The Scissors-Grinder would have found it and brought it into the village in any case. The two facts were connected only by the War, and the War was not Will's fault. He took his friend's hand in his own. "*Tchortyrion . . .*" he said in a low voice, careful that no unseen person might overhear.

Puck batted his hand away. "That's not my true name anymore! I have walked in darkness and my spirit has returned from the halls of granite with a new name—one that not even the dragon knows!"

"The dragon will learn it soon enough," Will said sadly.

"You wish!"

"Puck . . ."

"My old use-name is dead as well," said he who had been Puck Berrysnatcher. Unsteadily pulling himself erect, he wrapped the blanket upon which he had been laid about his thin shoulders. "You may call me No-name, for no name of mine shall ever pass your lips again."

Awkwardly, No-name hopped to the doorway. He steadied himself with a hand upon the jamb, then launched himself out into the wide world.

"Please! Listen to me!" Will cried after him.

Wordlessly, No-name raised one hand, middle finger extended.

Red anger welled up inside Will. "Asshole!" he shouted after his former friend. "Stump-leggity hopper! Johnny-three-limbs!"

He had not cried since that night the dragon first entered him. Now he cried again.

In midsummer an army recruiter roared into town with a bright green-and-yellow drum lashed to the motorcycle behind him. He wore a smart red uniform with two rows of brass buttons, and he'd come all the way from Brocielande, looking for likely lads to enlist in the service of Avalon. With a screech and a cloud of dust, he pulled up in front of the Scrannel Dogge, heeled down the kickstand, and went inside to rent the common room for the space of the afternoon.

Outside again, he donned his drum harness, attached the drum, and sprinkled a handful of gold coins on its head. *Boom-Boom-de-Boom!* The drumsticks came down like thunder. *Rap-Tap-a-Rap!* The gold coins leaped and danced, like raindrops on a hot griddle. By this time, there was a crowd standing outside the Scrannel Dogge.

The recruiter laughed. "Sergeant Bombast is my name!" *Boom! Doom! Boom!* "Finding heroes is my game!" He struck the sticks together overhead. *Click! Snick! Click!* Then he thrust them in his belt, unharnessed the great drum, and set it down beside him. The gold coins caught the sun and dazzled every eye with avarice. "I'm here to offer certain brave lads the very best career a man ever had. The chance to learn a skill, to become a warrior . . . and get paid damn well for it, too. Look at me!" He clapped his hands upon his ample girth. "Do I look underfed?"

The crowd laughed. Laughing with them, Sergeant Bombast waded into their number, wandering first this way, then that, addressing first this one, then another. "No, I do not. For the very good reason that the Army feeds me well. It feeds me, and clothes me, and all but wipes me arse when I ask it to. And am I grateful? I am *not*. No, sirs and maidens, so far from grateful am I that I require that the Army pay me for the privilege! And how much, do you ask? How much am I paid? Keeping in mind that my shoes, my food, my breeches, my snot-rag—" he pulled a lace handkerchief from one sleeve and waved it daintily in the air—"are all free as the air we breathe and the dirt we rub in our hair at Candlemas eve. How much am I *paid?*" His seemingly random wander had brought him back to the drum again. Now his fist came down on the drum, making it shout and the gold leap up into the air with wonder. "Forty-three copper pennies a month!"

The crowd gasped.

"Payable quarterly in good honest gold! As you see here! *Or* silver, for them as worships the horned matron." He chucked old Lady Favor-Me-Not under the chin, making her blush and simper. "But that's not all—no, not the half of it! I see you've noticed these coins here. Noticed? Pshaw! You've noticed that I *meant* you to notice these coins! And why not? Each one of these little beauties weighs a full Trojan ounce! Each one is of the good red gold, laboriously mined by kobolds in the griffin-haunted Mountains of the Moon. How could you not notice them? How could you not wonder what I meant to do with them? Did I bring them here simply to scoop them up again, when my piece were done, and pour them back into my pockets?

"Not a bit of it! It is my dearest hope that I leave this village penniless. I *intend* to leave this village penniless! Listen careful now, for this is the crux of the matter. This here gold's meant for bonuses. Yes! *Recruitment* bonuses! In just a minute I'm going to stop talking. I'll reckon you're glad to hear that!" He waited for the laugh. "Yes, believe it or not, Sergeant Bombast is going to shut up and walk inside this fine establishment, where I've arranged for exclusive use of the common room, and something more as well. Now, what I want to do is to talk—just talk, mind you!—with lads who are strong enough and old enough to become soldiers. How old is that? Old enough to get your girlfriend in trouble!" Laughter again. "But not too old, neither. How old is that? Old enough that your girlfriend's jumped you over the broom, and you've come to think of it as a good bit of luck!

"So I'm a talkative man, and I want some lads to talk *with*. And if you'll do it, if you're neither too young nor too old and are willing to simply hear me out, with absolutely no strings attached..." He paused. "Well, fair's fair and the beer's on me. Drink as much as you like, and I'll pay the tab." He started to turn away, then swung back, scratching his head and looking puzzled. "Damn me, if there isn't something I've forgot."

"The gold!" squeaked a young dinter.

"The gold! Yes, yes, I'd forget me own head if it weren't nailed on. As I've said, the gold's for bonuses. Right into your hand it goes, the instant you've signed the papers to become a soldier. And how much? One gold coin? Two?" He grinned wolfishly. "Doesn't nobody want to guess? No? Well, hold onto your pizzles . . . I'm offering *ten gold coins* to the boy who signs up today! And ten more apiece for as many of his friends as wants to go with him!"

To cheers, he retreated into the tavern.

———

The dragon, who had foreseen his coming from afar, had said, "Now do we repay our people for their subservience. This fellow is a great danger to us all. He must be caught unawares."

"Why not placate him with smiles?" Will had asked. "Hear him out, feed him well, and send him on his way. That seems to me the path of least strife."

"He will win recruits—never doubt it. Such men have tongues of honey, and glamour-stones of great potency."

"So?"

"The War goes ill for Avalon. Not one of three recruited today is like to ever return."

"I don't care. On their heads be the consequences."

"You're learning. Here, then, is our true concern: The first recruit who is administered the Oath of Fealty will tell his superior officers about my presence here. He will betray us all, with never a thought for the welfare of the village, his family, or friends. Such is the puissance of the Army's sorcerers."

So Will and the dragon had conferred, and made plans.

Now the time to put those plans into action was come.

The Scrannel Dogge was bursting with potential recruits. The beer flowed freely, and the tobacco as well. Every tavern pipe was in use, and Sergeant Bombast had sent out for more. Within the fog of tobacco smoke, young men laughed and joked and hooted when the recruiter caught the eye of that lad he deemed most apt to sign, smiled, and crooked a beckoning finger. So Will saw from the doorway.

He let the door slam behind him.

All eyes reflexively turned his way. A complete and utter silence overcame the room.

Then, as he walked forward, there was a scraping of chairs and putting down of mugs. Somebody slipped out the kitchen door, and another after him. Wordlessly, a knot of three lads in green shirts left by the main door. The bodies eddied and flowed. By the time Will reached the recruiter's table, there was nobody in the room but the two of them.

"I'll be buggered," Sergeant Bombast said wonderingly, "if I've ever seen the like."

"It's my fault," Will said. He felt flustered and embarrassed, but luckily those qualities fit perfectly the part he had to play.

"Well, I can *see* that! I can see that, and yet shave a goat and marry me off to it if I know what it means. Sit down, boy, sit! Is there a curse on you? The evil eye? Transmissible elf-pox?"

"No, it's not that. It's . . . well, I'm half-mortal."

A long silence.

"Seriously?"

"Aye. There is iron in my blood. 'Tis why I have no true name. Why, also, I am shunned by all." He sounded patently false to himself, and yet he could tell from the man's face that the recruiter believed his every word. "There is no place in this village for me anymore."

The recruiter pointed to a rounded black rock that lay atop a stack of indenture parchments. "This is a name-stone. Not much to look at, is it?"

"No, sir."

"But its mate, which I hold under my tongue, is." He took out a small lozenge-shaped stone and held it up to be admired. It glistered in the light, blood-crimson yet black in its heart. He placed it back in his mouth. "Now, if you were to lay your hand upon the name-stone on the table, your true name would go straight to the one in my mouth, and so to my brain. It's how we enforce the contracts our recruits sign."

"I understand." Will calmly placed his hand upon the black name-stone. He watched the recruiter's face, as nothing happened. There were ways to hide a true name, of course. But they were not likely to be found in a remote river-village in the wilds of the Debatable Hills. Passing the stone's test was proof of nothing. But it was extremely suggestive.

Sergeant Bombast sucked in his breath slowly. Then he opened up the small lockbox on the table before him, and said, "D'ye see this gold, boy?"

"Yes."

"There's eighty ounces of the good red here—none of your white gold nor electrum neither!—closer to you than your one hand is to the other. Yet the bonus you'd get would be worth a dozen of what I have here. *If*, that is, your claim is true. Can you prove it?"

"Yes, sir. I can."

"Now, explain to me again," Sergeant Bombast said. "You live in a house of *iron?*" They were outside now, walking through the silent village. The recruiter had left his drum behind, but had slipped the name-stone into a pocket and strapped the lockbox to his belt.

"It's where I sleep at night. That should prove my case, shouldn't it? It should prove that I'm . . . what I say I am."

So saying, Will walked the recruiter into Tyrant Square. It was a sunny, cloudless day, and the square smelled of dust and cinnamon, with just a bitter under-taste of leaked hydraulic fluid and cold iron. It was noon.

When he saw the dragon, Sergeant Bombast's face fell.

"Oh, fuck," he said.

As if that were the signal, Will threw his arms around the man, while doors flew open and hidden ambushers poured into the square, waving rakes, brooms, and hoes. An old henwife struck the recruiter across the back of his head with her distaff. He went limp and heavy in Will's arms. Perforce, Will let him fall.

Then the women were all over the fallen soldier, stabbing, clubbing, kicking, and cursing. Their passion was beyond all bounds, for these were the mothers of those he had tried to recruit. They had all of them fallen in with the orders the dragon had given with a readier will than they had ever displayed before for any of his purposes. Now they were making sure the fallen recruiter would never rise again to deprive them of their sons.

Wordlessly, they did their work and then, wordlessly, they left.

"Drown his motorcycle in the river," the dragon commanded afterwards. "Smash his drum and burn it, lest it bear witness against us. Bury his body in the midden-heap. There must be no evidence that ever he came here. Did you recover his lockbox?"

"No. It wasn't with his body. One of the women must have stolen it."

The dragon chuckled. "Peasants! Still, it works out well. The coins are well-buried already under basement flagstones, and will stay so indefinitely. And when an investigator comes through looking for a lost recruiter, he'll be met by a universal ignorance, canny lies, and a cleverly planted series of misleading evidence. Out of avarice, they'll serve our cause better than ever we could order it ourselves."

A full moon sat high in the sky, enthroned within the constellation of the Mad Dog and presiding over one of the hottest nights of the summer when the dragon abruptly announced, "There is a resistance."

"Sir?" Will stood in the open doorway, lethargically watching the sweat fall, drop by drop from his bowed head. He would have welcomed a breeze, but at this time of year when those who had built well enough slept naked on their rooftops and those who had not burrowed into the mud of the riverbed, there were no night-breezes cunning enough to thread the maze of huts and so make their way to the square.

"Rebels against my rule. Insurrectionists. Mad, suicidal fools."

A single drop fell. Will jerked his head to move his moon-shadow aside, and saw a large black circle appear in the dirt. "Who?"

"The greenshirties."

"They're just kids," Will said scornfully.

"Do not despise them because they are young. The young make excellent soldiers and better martyrs. They are easily dominated, quickly trained, and as ruthless as you command them to be. They kill without regret, and they go to their deaths readily, because they do not truly understand that death is permanent."

"You give them too much credit. They do no more than sign horns at me, glare, and spit upon my shadow. Everybody does that."

"They are still building up their numbers and their courage. Yet their leader, the No-name one, is shrewd and capable. It worries me that he has made himself invisible to your eye, and thus to mine. Walking about the village, you have oft enough come upon a nest in the fields where he slept, or scented the distinctive tang of his scat. Yet when was the last time you saw him in person?"

"I haven't even seen these nests nor smelt the dung you speak of."

"You've seen and smelled, but not been aware of it. Meanwhile, No-name skillfully eludes your sight. He has made himself a ghost."

"The more ghostly the better. I don't care if I never see him again."

"You will see him again. Remember, when you do, that I warned you so."

The dragon's prophecy came true not a week later. Will was walking his errands and admiring, as he so often did these days, how ugly the village had become in his eyes. Half the huts were wattle-and-daub—little more than sticks and dried mud. Those that had honest planks were left unpainted and grey, to keep down the yearly assessment when the teind-inspector came through from the central government. Pigs wandered the streets, and the occasional scavenger bear as well, looking moth-eaten and shabby. Nothing was clean, nothing was new, nothing was ever mended.

Such were the thoughts he was thinking when somebody thrust a gunnysack over his head, while somebody else punched him in the stomach, and a third person swept his feet out from under him.

It was like a conjuring trick. One moment he was walking down a noisy street, with children playing in the dust and artisans striding by to their workshops and goodwives leaning from windows to gossip or sitting in doorways shucking peas, and the next he was being carried swiftly away, in darkness, by eight strong hands.

He struggled, but could not break free. His cries, muffled by the sack, were ignored. If anybody heard him—and there had been many about on the street a moment before—nobody came to his aid.

After what seemed an enormously long time, he was dumped on the ground. Angrily, he struggled out of the gunnysack. He was lying on the stony and slightly damp floor of the old gravel pit, south of the village. One crumbling wall was overgrown with flowering vines. He could hear birdsong upon birdsong. Standing, he flung the gunnysack to the ground and confronted his kidnappers.

There were twelve of them and they all wore green shirts.

He knew them all, of course, just as he knew everyone else in the village. But, more, they had all been his friends, at one time or another. Were he free of the dragon's bondage, doubtless he would be one of their number. Now, though, he was filled with scorn for them, for he knew exactly how the dragon would deal with them, were they to harm his lieutenant. He would accept them into his body, one at a time, to corrupt their minds and fill their bodies with cancers. He would tell the first in excruciating detail exactly how he was going to die, stage by stage, and he would make sure the eleven others watched as it happened. Death after death, the survivors would watch and anticipate. Last of all would be their leader, No-name.

Will understood how the dragon thought.

"Turn away," he said. "This will not do you nor your cause any good whatsoever."

Two of the greenshirties took him by the arms. They thrust him before No-name. His former friend leaned on a crutch of ash-wood. His face was tense with hatred and his eyes did not blink.

"It is good of you to be so concerned for our *cause*," No-name said. "But you do not understand our *cause*, do you? Our *cause* is simply this."

He raised a hand, and brought it down fast, across Will's face. Something sharp cut a long scratch across his forehead and down one cheek.

"*Llandrysos*, I command you to die!" No-name cried. The greenshirties holding Will's arms released them. He staggered back a step. A trickle of something warm went tickling down his face. He touched his hand to it. Blood.

No-name stared at him. In his outstretched hand was an elf-shot, one of those small stone arrowheads found everywhere in the fields after a hard rain. Will did not know if they had been made by ancient civilizations or grew from pebbles by spontaneous generation. Nor had he known, before now, that to scratch somebody with one while crying out his true name would cause that person to die. But the stench of ozone that accompanied death-magic hung in the air, lifting the small hairs on the back of his neck and tickling his nose with its eldritch force, and the knowledge of what had almost happened was inescapable.

The look of absolute astonishment on No-name's face curdled and became rage. He dashed the elf-shot to the ground. "You were *never* my friend!" he cried in a fury. "The night when we exchanged true names and mingled blood, you lied! You were as false then as you are now!"

It was true. Will remembered that long-ago time when he and Puck had rowed their coracles to a distant river-island, and there caught fish which they grilled over coals and a turtle from which they made a soup prepared in its own shell. It had been Puck's idea to swear eternal friendship and Will, desperate for a name-friend and knowing Puck would not believe he had none, had invented a true name for himself. He was careful to let his friend reveal first, and so knew to shiver and roll up his eyes when he spoke the name. But he had felt a terrible guilt then for his deceit, and every time since when he thought of that night.

Even now.

Standing on his one good leg, No-name tossed his crutch upward and seized it near the tip. Then he swung it around and smashed Will in the face. Will fell.

The greenshirties were all over him then, kicking and hitting him.

Briefly, it came to Will that, if he were included among their number, there were thirteen present and engaged upon a single action. We are a coven, he thought, and I the random sacrifice, who is worshiped with kicks and blows. Then there was nothing but his suffering and the rage that rose up within him, so strong that though it could not weaken the pain, it drowned out the fear he should have felt on realizing that he was going to die. He knew only pain and a kind of wonder: a vast, world-encompassing astonishment that so profound a thing as death could happen to *him*, accompanied by a lesser wonder that No-name and his merry thugs had the toughness to take his punishment all the way to death's portal, and that vital step beyond. They were only boys, after all. Where had they learned such discipline?

"I think he's dead," said a voice. He thought it was No-name, but he couldn't be sure. His ears rang, and the voice was so very, very far away.

One last booted foot connected with already broken ribs. He gasped, and spasmed. It seemed unfair that he could suffer pain on top of pain like this.

"That is our message to your master dragon," said the distant voice. "If you live, take it to him."

Then silence. Eventually, Will forced himself to open one eye—the other was swollen shut—and saw that he was alone again. It was a gorgeous day, sunny without being at all hot. Birds sang all about him. A sweet breeze ruffled his hair.

He picked himself up, bleeding and weeping with rage, and stumbled back to the dragon.

Because the dragon would not trust any of the healing-women inside him, Will's injuries were treated by a fluffer, who came inside the dragon to suck the injuries from Will's body and accept them as her own. He tried to stop her as soon as he had the strength to do so, but the dragon overruled him. It shamed and sickened him to see how painfully the girl hobbled outside again.

"Tell me who did this," the dragon whispered, "and we shall have revenge."

"No."

There was a long hiss, as a steam valve somewhere deep in the thorax vented pressure. "You toy with me."

Will turned his face to the wall. "It's my problem and not yours."

"You *are* my problem."

There was a constant low-grade mumble and grumble of machines that faded to nothing when one stopped paying attention to it. Some part of it was the ventilation system, for the air never quite went stale, though it often had a flat under-taste. The rest was surely reflexive—meant to keep the dragon alive. Listening to those mechanical voices, fading deeper and deeper within the tyrant's corpus, Will had a vision of an interior that never came to an end, all the night contained within that lightless iron body, expanding inward in an inversion of the natural order, stars twinkling in the vasty reaches of distant condensers and fuel-handling systems and somewhere a crescent moon, perhaps, caught in his gear train. "I won't argue," Will said. "And I will never tell you anything."

"You will."

"*No!*"

The dragon fell silent. The leather of the pilot's couch gleamed weakly in the soft light. Will's wrists ached.

The outcome was never in doubt. Try though he might, Will could not resist the call of the leather couch, of the grips that filled his hand, of the needles that slid into his wrists. The dragon entered him, and had from him all the information he desired, and this time he did not leave.

Will walked through the village streets, leaving footprints of flame behind him. He was filled with wrath and the dragon. "*Come out!*" he roared. "Bring out your greenshirties, every one of them, or I shall come after them, street by street and house by house." He put a hand on the nearest door, and wrenched it from its hinges. Broken fragments of boards fell flaming to the ground. "Spillikin cowers herewithin. Don't make me come in after him!"

Shadowy hands flung Spillikin face-first into the dirt at Will's feet.

Spillikin was a harmless albino stick-figure of a marsh-walker who screamed when Will closed a cauterizing hand about his arm to haul him to his feet.

"Follow me," Will/the dragon said coldly.

So great was Will's twin-spirited fury that none could stand up to him. He burned hot as a bronze idol, and the heat went before him in a great wave, withering plants, charring house-fronts, and setting hair ablaze when somebody did not flee from him quickly enough. "*I am wrath!*" he screamed. "*I am blood-vengeance! I am justice!* Feed me or suffer!"

The greenshirties were, of course, brought out.

No-name was, of course, not among their number.

The greenshirties were lined up before the dragon in Tyrant Square. They knelt in the dirt before him, heads down. Only two were so unwary as to be caught in their green shirts. The others were bare-chested or in mufti. All were terrified, and one of them had pissed himself. Their families and neighbors had followed after them and now filled the square with their wails of lament. Will quelled them with a look.

"Your king knows your true names," he said sternly to the greenshirties, "and can kill you at a word."

"It is true," said Hag Applemere. Her face was stony and impassive. Yet Will knew that one of the greenshirties was her brother.

"More, he can make you suffer such dementia as would make you believe yourselves in Hell, and suffering its torments forever."

"It is true," the hag said.

"Yet he disdains to bend the full weight of his wrath upon you. You are no threat to him. He scorns you as creatures of little or no import."

"It is true."

"One only does he desire vengeance upon. Your leader—he who calls himself No-name. This being so, your most merciful lord has made this offer: Stand." They obeyed, and he gestured toward a burning brand. "Bring No-name to me while this fire yet burns, and you shall all go free. Fail, and you will suffer such torments as the ingenuity of a dragon can devise."

"It is true."

Somebody—not one of the greenshirties—was sobbing softly and steadily. Will ignored it. There was more Dragon within him than Self. It was a strange feeling, not being in control. He liked it. It was like being a small oracle carried helplessly along by a raging current. The river of emotion had its own logic; it knew where it was going. "Go!" he cried. "Now!"

The greenshirties scattered like pigeons.

Not half an hour later, No-name was brought, beaten and struggling, into the square. His former disciples had tied his hands behind his back, and gagged him with a red bandanna. He had been beaten—not so badly as Will had been, but well and thoroughly.

Will walked up and down before him. Those leaf-green eyes glared up out of that silt-black face with a pure and holy hatred. There could be no reasoning with this boy, nor any taming of him. He was a primal force, an anti-Will, the spirit of vengeance made flesh and given a single unswerving purpose.

Behind No-name stood the village elders in a straight, unmoving line. The Sullen Man moved his mouth slowly, like an ancient tortoise having a particularly deep thought. But he did not speak. Nor did Auld Black Agnes, nor the yage-witch whose use-name no living being knew, nor Lady Nightlady, nor Spadefoot, nor Annie Hop-the-Frog, nor Daddy Fingerbones, nor any of the others. There were mutters and whispers among the villagers, assembled into a loose throng behind them, but nothing coherent. Nothing that could be heard or punished. Now and again, the buzzing of wings rose up over the murmurs and died down again like a cicada on a still summer day, but no one lifted up from the ground.

Back and forth Will stalked, restless as a leopard in a cage, while the dragon within him brooded over possible punishments. A whipping would only strengthen No-name in his hatred and resolve. Amputation was no answer—he had lost one limb already, and was still a dangerous and unswerving enemy. There was no gaol in all the village that could hope to hold him forever, save for the dragon himself, and the dragon did not wish to accept so capricious an imp into his own body.

Death seemed the only answer.

But what sort of death? Strangulation was too quick. Fire was good, but Tyrant Square was surrounded by thatch-roofed huts. A drowning would have to be carried out at the river, out of sight of the dragon himself, and he wanted the manna of punishment inextricably linked in his subjects' minds to his own physical self. He could have a wine-barrel brought in and filled with water, but then the victim's struggles would have a comic element to them. Also, as a form of strangulation, it was still too quick.

Unhurriedly, the dragon considered. Then he brought Will to a stop before the crouching No-name. He raised up Will's head, and let a little of the dragon-light shine out through Will's eyes.

"Crucify him."

To Will's horror, the villagers obeyed.

It took hours. But shortly before dawn, the child who had once been Puck Berrysnatcher, who had been Will's best friend and had died and been reborn as Will's Nemesis, breathed his last. His body went limp as he surrendered his name to his revered ancestress, Mother Night, and the exhausted villagers could finally turn away and go home and sleep.

Later, after he had departed Will's body at last, the dragon said, "You have done well."

Will lay motionless on the pilot's couch and said nothing.

"I shall reward you."

"No, lord," Will said. "You have done too much already."

"Haummn. Do you know the first sign that a toady has come to accept the rightness of his lickspittle station?"

"No, sir."

"It is insolence. For which reason, you will not be punished but rather, as I said, rewarded. You have grown somewhat in my service. Your tastes have matured. You want something better than your hand. You shall have it. Go into any woman's house and tell her what she must do. You have my permission."

"This is a gift I do not desire."

"Says you! Big Red Margotty has three holes. She will refuse none of them to you. Enter them in whatever order you wish. Do what you like with her tits. Tell her to look glad when she sees you. Tell her to wag her tail and bark like a dog. As long as she has a daughter, she has no choice but to obey. Much the same goes for any of my beloved subjects, of whatever gender or age."

"They hate you," Will said.

"And thou as well, my love and my delight. And thou as well."

"But you with reason."

A long silence. Then, "I know your mind as you do not. I know what things you wish to do with Red Margotty and what things you wish to do *to* her. I tell you, there are cruelties within you greater than anything I know. It is the birthright of flesh."

"You lie!"

"Do I? Tell me something, dearest victim. When you told the elders to crucify No-name, the command came from me, with my breath and in my voice. But the form . . . did not the *choice* of the punishment come from you?"

Will had been laying listlessly on the couch staring up at the featureless metal ceiling. Now he sat upright, his face white with shock. All in a single movement he stood, and turned toward the door.

Which seeing, the dragon sneered. "Do you think to leave me? Do you honestly think you *can*? Then try!" The dragon slammed his door open. The cool and pitiless light of earliest morning flooded the cabin. A fresh breeze swept in, carrying with it scents from the fields and woods. It made Will painfully aware of how his own sour stench permeated the dragon's interior. "You need me more than I ever needed you—I have seen to that! You cannot run away, and if you could, your hunger would bring you back, wrists foremost. You *desire* me. You are empty without me. Go! Try to run! See where it gets you."

Will trembled.

He bolted out the door and ran.

The first sunset away from the dragon, Will threw up violently as the sun went down, and then suffered spasms of diarrhea. Cramping, and aching and foul, he hid in the depths of the Old Forest all through the night, sometimes howling and sometimes rolling about the forest floor in pain. A thousand times he thought he must return. A thousand times he told himself: Not yet. Just a little longer and you can surrender. But not yet.

The craving came in waves. When it abated, Will would think: If I can hold out for one day, the second will be easier, and the third easier yet. Then the sick yearning would return, a black need in the tissues of his flesh and an aching in his bones, and he would think again: Not yet. Hold off for just a few more minutes. Then you can give up. Soon. Just a little longer.

By morning, the worst of it was over. He washed his clothes in a stream, and hung them up to dry in the wan predawn light. To keep himself warm, he marched back and forth singing the *Chansons Amoreuses de Merlin Sylvanus*, as many of its five hundred verses as he could remember. Finally, when the clothes were only slightly damp, he sought out a great climbing oak he knew of old, and from a hollow withdrew a length of stolen clothesline. Climbing as close to the tippy-top of the great tree as he dared, he lashed himself to its bole. There, lightly rocked by a gentle wind, he slept at last.

Three days later, Hag Applemere came to see him in his place of hiding. The truth-teller bowed before him. "Lord Dragon bids you return to him," she said formally.

Will did not ask the revered hag how she had found him. Wise-women had their skills; nor did they explain themselves. "I'll come when I'm ready," he said. "My task here is not yet completed." He was busily sewing together leaves of oak, yew, ash, and alder, using a needle laboriously crafted from a thorn, and short threads made from grasses he had pulled apart by hand. It was no easy work.

Hag Applemere frowned. "You place us all in certain danger."

"He will not destroy himself over me alone. Particularly when he is sure that I must inevitably return to him."

"It is true."

Will laughed mirthlessly. "You need not ply your trade here, hallowed lady. Speak to me as you would to any other. I am no longer of the dragon's party." Looking at her, he saw for the first time that she was not so many years older than himself. In a time of peace, he might even have grown fast enough to someday, in two years or five, claim her for his own, by the ancient rites of the greensward and the midnight sun. Only months ago, young as he was, he would have found this an unsettling thought. But now his thinking had been driven to such extremes that it bothered him not.

"Will," she said then, cautiously, "whatever are you up to?"

He held up the garment, complete at last, for her to admire. "I have become a greenshirtie." All the time he had sewn, he was bare-chested, for he had torn up his dragon sark and used it for tinder as he needed fire. Now he donned its leafy replacement.

Clad in his fragile new finery, Will looked the truth-teller straight in the eye. "You *can* lie," he said.

Bessie looked stricken. "Once," she said, and reflexively covered her womb with both hands. "And the price is high, terribly high."

He stood. "Then it must be paid. Let us find a shovel now. It is time for a bit of grave-robbery."

It was evening when Will returned at last to the dragon. Tyrant Square had been ringed about with barbed wire, and a loudspeaker had been set upon a pole with wires leading back into his iron hulk, so that he could speak and be heard in the absence of his lieutenant.

"Go first," Will said to Hag Applemere, "that he may be reassured I mean him no harm."

Breasts bare, clad in the robes and wide hat of her profession, Bessie Applemere passed through a barbed-wire gate (a grimpkin guard opened it before her and closed it after her) and entered the square. "Son of Cruelty." She bowed deeply before the dragon.

Will stood hunched in the shadows, head down, with his hands in his pockets. Tonelessly, he said, "I have been broken to your will, great one. I will be your stump-cow, if that is what you want. I beg you. Make me grovel. Make me crawl. Only let me back in."

Hag Applemere spread her arms and bowed again. "It is true."

"You may approach." The dragon's voice sounded staticky and yet triumphant over the loudspeaker.

The sour-faced old grimpkin opened the gate for him, as it had earlier been opened for the hag. Slowly, like a maltreated dog returning to the only hand that had ever fed him, Will crossed the square. He paused before the loudspeaker, briefly touched its pole with one trembling hand, and then shoved that hand back into his pocket. "You have won. Well and truly, have you won."

It appalled him how easily the words came, and how natural they sounded coming from his mouth. He could feel the desire to surrender to the tyrant, accept what punishments he would impose, and sink gratefully back into his bondage. A little voice within cried: *So easy! So easy!* And so it would be, perilously easy indeed. The realization that a part of him devoutly wished for it made Will burn with humiliation.

The dragon slowly forced one eye half-open. "So, boy . . ." Was it his imagination, or was the dragon's voice less forceful than it had been three days ago? "You have learned what need feels like. You suffer from your desires, even as I do. I . . . I . . . am weakened, admittedly, but I am not all so weak as *that!* You thought to prove that I needed you—you have proved the reverse. Though I have neither wings nor missiles and my electrical reserves are low, though I cannot fire my jets without destroying the village and myself as well, yet am I of the mighty, for I have neither pity nor remorse. Thought you I craved a mere boy? Thought you to make me dance attendance on a soft, unmuscled half-mortal mongrel fey? Pfaugh! I do not need you. Never think that I . . . that I *need* you!"

"Let me in," Will whimpered. "I will do whatever you say."

"You . . . you understand that you must be punished for your disobedience?"

"Yes," Will said. "Punish me, please. Abase and degrade me, I beg you."

"As you wish," the dragon's cockpit door hissed open, "so it shall be."

Will took one halting step forward, and then two. Then he began to run, straight at the open hatchway. Straight at it—and then to one side.

He found himself standing before the featureless iron of the dragon's side. Quickly, from one pocket he withdrew Sergeant Bombast's soulstone. Its small blood-red mate was already in his mouth. There was still grave-dirt on the one, and a strange taste to the other, but he did not care. He touched the soulstone to the iron plate, and the dragon's true name flowed effortlessly into his mind.

Simultaneously, he took the elf-shot from his other pocket. Then, with all his strength, he drew the elf-shot down the dragon's iron flanks, making a long, bright scratch in the rust.

"What are you doing?" the dragon cried in alarm. "Stop that! The hatch is open, the couch awaits!" His voice dropped seductively. "The needles yearn for your wrists. Even as I yearn for—"

"Baalthazar, of the line of Baalmoloch, of the line of Baalshabat," Will shouted, "I command thee to *die!*"

And that was that.

All in an instant and with no fuss whatever, the dragon king was dead. All his might and malice was become nothing more than inert metal, that might be cut up and carted away to be sold to the scrap-foundries that served their larger brothers with ingots to be reforged for the War.

Will hit the side of the dragon with all the might of his fist, to show his disdain. Then he spat as hard and fierce as ever he could, and watched the saliva slide slowly down the black metal. Finally, he unbuttoned his trousers and pissed upon his erstwhile oppressor.

So it was that he finally accepted that the tyrant was well and truly dead.

Bessie Applemere—hag no more—stood silent and bereft on the square behind him. Wordlessly, she mourned her sterile womb and sightless eyes. To her, Will went. He took her hand, and led her back to her hut. He opened the door for her. He sat her down upon her bed. "Do you need anything?" he asked. "Water? Some food?"

She shook her head. "Just go. Leave me to lament our victory in solitude."

He left, quietly closing the door behind him. There was no place to go now but home. It took him a moment to remember where that was.

"I've come back," Will said.

Blind Enna looked stricken. Her face turned slowly toward him, those vacant eyes filled with shadow, that ancient mouth open and despairing. Like a sleepwalker, she stood and stumbled forward and then, when her groping fingers tapped against his chest, she threw her arms around him and burst into tears. "Thank the Seven! Oh, thank the Seven! The blessed, blessed, merciful Seven!" she sobbed over and over again, and Will realized for the first time that, in her own inarticulate way, his aunt genuinely and truly loved him.

And so, for a season, life in the village returned to normal. In the autumn the Armies of the Might came through the land, torching the crops and leveling the buildings. Terror went before them and the villagers were forced to flee, first into the Old Forest, and then to refugee camps across the border. Finally, they were loaded into cattle cars and taken away to far Babylonia in Faerie Minor, where the streets are bricked of gold and the ziggurats touch the sky, and there Will found a stranger destiny than any he might previously have dreamed.

But that is another story, for another day.

singletons in love

PAUL MELKO

New writer Paul Melko has made sales to *Realms of Fantasy, Live Without a Net, Asimov's Science Fiction, Talebones, Terra Incognita,* and other markets. In the taut and engrossing story that follows, he explores the boundaries of self—which, in a high-tech future, can sometimes be a *bit* hard to figure out!

Moira was sick, in bed with a cough, so Mother Redd shooed us out of the house. At first we just hung around the front yard, feeling weird. We'd been separated before, of course; it was part of our training. In space, we'd have to act as a quint or a quad or even a triple, so we practiced all our tasks and chores in various combinations. That had always been practice, and we'd all been in sight. But Moira was *separated* now, and we did not like it.

Manuel climbed the trellis on the front of the house, skirting the thorns of the roses that grew among the slats. As his hands caught the sill and pulled his head just over the edge, his hind legs caught a rose and bent it back and forth to break it off.

I see Moira, he signed.

"Does she see you?" I asked, aloud since he couldn't see me, and the wind took the pheromones away, leaving half-formed thoughts.

If Manuel could see Moira and she could see him, then it would be enough for all of us. We'd be linked.

Just then the window flew open, and one of Mother Redd was there. Manuel fell backwards, but he righted himself and landed on the grass, rolling, sprawling until he was among the rest of us, the red rose still clutched in his toes.

I touched his shoulder, breathed him a thought, and he offered the rose to Mother Redd. I saw immediately it wasn't going to work.

"You *five*, go and play somewhere else today. Moira is sick, and it won't do us any good for you to get sick, too. So vamoose!" She slammed the window shut.

We thought it over for a few seconds, then tucked the rose in my shirt pocket and started down the front path.

We didn't have Moira, but we did have license to vamoose, and that meant the forest, the lake, and the caves if we were brave enough. Moira would have advised caution. But we didn't have Moira.

The farm was a hundred acres of soyfalfa that Mother Redd worked with three triples of oxalope. The ox were dumb as rocks by themselves, but when you teamed them up, they could plow and seed and harvest pretty much by themselves. The farm was a good place to spend the summer. Lessons took up our mornings, but they weren't as rigorous as during the school year when we studied all day and most of the night at the 'Drome. At school we learned to sleep in shifts, so four or five us were always awake to study. We'd spent summers at the Redds for sixteen years, since we were out of the crèche.

Baker Road led west toward Worthington and the 'Drome or east toward more farms, the lake, and the woods. We chose east, Strom first like always when we were in the open, with Manuel as a scurrying point, never too far away. I followed Strom, then Quant, and Bola last. Moira would have been after Quant. We felt a hole there, which Bola and Quant filled by touching hands too often.

Within a mile, we were relaxed, though not indifferent to Moira's absence. Bola was tossing rocks onto the tops of old telephone poles. He didn't miss once, but we didn't feel any pride in it. It was just a one-force problem, and Bola lobbed the rocks for diversion, not practice.

We passed a microwave receiving station, hidden in a grove of pine trees, just off from the road. Its paraboloid shape reflected the sun as it caught the beamed microwaves from the Ring. The Earth was dotted with such dishes, each providing a few megawatts to the Earthside enclaves, more than we could use, now that the Community had left. But they had built the Ring and the solar arrays and the dishes, as well. Decades later and the dishes still worked.

I could see the Ring clearly, even in the brightness of the morning, a pale arch from horizon to horizon. At night, it was brighter, its legacy more burdensome to those of us left behind.

Bola started tossing small twigs into the incoming microwave beam, small arcing meteoroids that burst into flame and then ash. He bent to pick up a small toad.

I felt the absence of Moira as I put my hand on his shoulder and sent, *No living things.*

I felt his momentary resentment, then he shrugged both physically and mentally. He smiled at my discomfort at having to play Moira while she was gone. Bola, in whom was hardwired all the Newtonian laws of force and reaction, had a devilishness in him. In us. Our rebel.

Once, the instructors had divided us up as two triples, male and female, and broken up our classmates, as well, along the same lines. The objective was an obstacle course, no gravity, two miles of wire, rope, and simulated wreckage, find the macguffin first. All other teams were enemy, no rules.

They hadn't given us no-rules games too often: we were young then, twelve. Mostly they gave us a lot of rules. That time was different.

Strom, Bola, and Manuel found it first, by chance, and instead of taking it, they lay in wait, set traps and zero-gee deadfalls. They managed to capture or incapacitate the other four teams. They broke three arms and a leg. They caused two concussions, seventeen bruises, and three lacerations as they trussed up the other teams and stowed them in the broken hut where the macguffin sat.

Finally we came along, and the fiberglass mast zinged past, barely missing us.

As Moira, Quant, and I swam behind cover, we heard them laughing. We knew it was them and not some other team. We were too far for pheromones, but we could still smell the edges of their thoughts: proud and defiant.

Moira yelled, "You get your asses out here right now!"

Strom popped out right away. He listened to Moira first no matter who else was there. Then Manuel left the hut.

"Bola!"

"Forget it!" he yelled. "I win." Then he threw the macguffin at us, and Quant snatched it out of the air.

"Who's *I*?" Moira yelled.

Bola stuck his head out. He looked at the five of us for a moment, then signed, *Sorry.* He kicked over, and we shared everything that had happened.

The teachers didn't split us up like that again.

Baker Road swerved around Lake Cabbage like a giant letter C. It was a managed ecomite, a small ecosystem with gengineered inhabitants. The Baskins ran it for the Overdepartment of Ecology, trying to build a viable lake ecosystem with a biomass of twenty-five Brigs. It had everything from beavers to snails to mosquitoes. Lots of mosquitoes.

The adult beavers turned a blind eye to our frolicking in the lake, but the babies found us irresistible. They had been bioed to birth in quads. Their thoughts slid across the pond surface in rainbows like gasoline that we could almost understand, but not quite. In the water our own pheromones were useless, and even our touch pads were hard to understand. If we closed our eyes and sank deep enough, it was like we weren't a part of anything, just empty, thoughtless protoplasm.

Strom didn't like to swim, but if we were all in the water, he'd be too, just to be near. I knew why he was uncertain of the water, I knew his anxiety as my own, but I couldn't help deriding us for having such a fear.

We took turns with the beavers pulling rotten logs into the water and trying to sink them in the mud, until the adult beavers started chiding us with rudimentary hand signs, *No stop work. Messing home. Tell Baskins.*

We swam to shore and dried ourselves in the afternoon sun. Manuel climbed an apple tree and gathered enough ripe fruit for all of us. We rested, knowing that we'd have to head back to the farm soon. Strom balled up some memories.

For Moira, he sent.

Quant came alert, and we all felt it.

A house, she sent. *That wasn't there before.*

She was up the bank, so I waited for the thoughts to reach me through the polleny humid air. It was a cottage, opposite the lake from the beavers' dam, half-hidden among the cottonwoods, which shed like snowfall during the summer.

I searched our memory of the last time we'd been at the lake, but none of us had looked over that way, so it may have been there since last year.

The Baskins put in a summer house, Strom sent.

Why, when their normal house is just a mile away? Manuel replied.

It could be a guest house, I sent.

Let's go find out, Bola sent.

There was no dissent, and in the shared eagerness I wondered what Moira would have said about our trespassing.

She's not here.

We leaped between flat stones, crossing the small stream that fed the lake.

Beneath the cottonwoods, the ground was a carpet of threadbare white. The air was cold through our damp clothes. We stepped across and around the poison oak with its quintuple leaves and ivy its triplet.

An aircar stood outside the cottage, parked in a patch of prairie, shaded by the trees.

Conojet 34J. Manuel sent. *We can fly it.* We had started small-craft piloting the year before.

The brush had been cleared from the cottage to make room for long flower gardens along each wall. Farther from the house, in the full sun, was a rectangle of vegetables: I saw tomatoes, pumpkins, squash, and string beans.

"It's not a summer house," I said, because Quant was out of sight. "Some-one's living here."

Manuel skirted the vegetable garden to get a good look at the aircar. I felt his appreciation of it, no concrete thought, just a nod toward its sleekness and power.

"What do you kids think you're doing in my garden?"

The door of the cottage flew open with a bang, and we jumped, as a man strode toward us.

Strom took a defensive posture by reflex, his foot mashing a tomato plant. I noted it, and he corrected his stance, but the man had seen it, too, and he frowned. "What the hell!"

We lined up before the man, me at the head of our phalanx. Strom to my left and slightly behind, then Quant, Bola, and Manuel behind him. Moira's spot to my right was empty.

"Stepping on my plants. Who do you think you are?"

He was young, dressed in a brown shirt and tan pants. His hair was black, and he was thin-boned, almost delicate. I assumed he was the interface for his pod, but then we saw the lack of sensory pads on his palms, the lack of pheromone ducts on his neck, the lack of any consensus gathering on his part. He had said three things before we could say a single word.

"We're sorry for stepping on your plant," I said. I stifled our urge to waft con-ciliatory scent into the air. He wouldn't have understood. He was a singleton.

He looked from the plant to me and to the plant again.

"You're a fucking cluster," he said. "Weren't you programmed with com-mon courtesy? Get the hell off my property."

Bola wanted to argue with the man. This was Baskin land. But I nodded, smiling. "Again, we're sorry, and we'll leave now."

We backed away, and his eyes were on us. No, not us, on me. He was watching me, and I felt his dark eyes looking past my face, seeing things that I didn't want him to see. A flush spread across my cheeks, hot suddenly in the shade. The look was sexual, and my response. . .

I buried it inside me, but not before my pod caught the scent of it. I clamped down, but Manuel's then Quant's admonition seeped through me.

I dashed into the woods, and my fellows had no choice but to follow.

The undertones of their anger mingled with my guilt. I wanted to rail, to yell, to attack. We were all sexual beings, as a whole and as individuals, but instead, I sat apart, and if Mother Redd noticed, none of her said a word. Finally, I climbed the stairs and went to see Moira.

"Stay over there," she wheezed.

I sat in one of the chairs by the door. The room smelled like chicken broth and sweat.

Moira and I are identical twins, the only ones in our pod. We didn't look that much alike anymore, though. Her hair was close-cropped; mine was shoulder-length auburn. She was twenty pounds heavier, her face rounder where mine was sharp. We looked more like cousins than identical sisters.

She leaned on her elbows, looked at me closely, and then flopped down onto the pillow. "You don't look happy."

I could have given her the whole story by touching her palm, but she wouldn't let me near her. I could have sketched it all with pheromones, but I didn't know if I wanted her to know the whole story.

"We met a singleton today."

"Oh, my." The words were so vague. Without the chemical sharing of memories and thoughts, I had no idea what her real emotions were, cynical or sincere, interested or bored.

"Over by the Baskins' lake. There was a cottage there. . . ." I built the sensory description, then let it seep away. "This is so hard. Can't I just touch you?"

"That's all we need. Me, then you, then everybody else, and by the time school starts in two weeks, we're all sick. We can't be sick." We started training for the zero-gee classes that fall. Everybody said this was when the real culling began, when the teachers decided which pods were viable enough to crew our starships.

Moira nodded. "A singleton. Luddite? Christian?"

"None of those. He had an aircar. He was angry at us for stepping on his tomato plants. And he . . . looked at me."

"He's supposed to look at you. You're our interface."

"No, he *looked* at me. Like a woman."

Moira was silent for a moment. "Oh. And you felt. . ."

The heat crept up my cheeks again. "Flushed."

"Oh." Moira contemplated the ceiling. She said, "You understand that we are individually sexual beings and as a whole—"

"Don't lecture me!" Moira could be such a pedant, one who never threw a stone.

She sighed. "Sorry."

"Sokay."

She grinned. "Was he cute?"

"Stop that!" After a pause, I added, "He was handsome. I'm sorry we stepped on his tomato plant."

"So take him another."

"You think?"

"And find out who he is. Mother Redd has got to know. And call the Baskins."

I wanted to hug her, but settled for a wave.

Mother Redd had been a doctor, and then one of herself had died, and she'd chosen another field instead of being only part of the physician she had been. She—there had been four cloned females, so she was a she any which way you looked at it—took over the farm, and in the summer boarded us university kids. She was a kind woman, smart and wise, but I couldn't look at her and not think how much smarter she would have been if she were four instead of just a triple.

Mother Redd was in the greenhouse, watering, picking, and examining a hybrid cucumber.

"What is it, sweetie? Why are you alone?" asked the one looking at the cucumber under the light microscope.

I shrugged. I didn't want to tell her why I was avoiding my pod, so I asked, "We saw a singleton over by the Baskins' lake today. Who is he?"

I could smell the pungent odor of Mother Redd's thoughts. Though it was the same cryptic, symbolic chaos that she always used, I realized she was thinking more than a simple answer would warrant. Finally, she said, "Malcolm Leto. He's one of the Community."

"The Community! But they all . . . left." I used the wrong word for it; Quant would have known the technical term for what had become of two thirds of humanity. They had built the Ring, built the huge cybernetic organism that was the Community. They had advanced human knowledge of physics, medicine, and engineering exponentially until finally they had, as a whole, disappeared, leaving the Ring and the Earth empty, except for the fraction of humans who either had not joined the Community or had not died in the chaos of the Earthbound Gene Wars.

"This one was not on hand for the Exodus," Mother Redd said. That was the word that Quant would have known. "There was an accident. His body was placed into suspended animation until it could be regenerated."

"He's the last member of the Community, then?"

"Practically."

"Thanks." I went to find the rest of my pod. They were in front of the computer, playing virtual chess with John Michelle Grady, one of our classmates. I remembered it was Thursday night Quant's hobby night. She liked strategic gaming.

I touched Strom's hand and slipped into the mesh of our thoughts. We were losing, but then Grady was good and we had been down to four with me running off alone. Was that a trace of resentment from my fellows? I ignored it and dumped what I had learned from Mother Redd about the singleton.

The chess game vanished from our thoughts as the others focused on me.

He's from the Community. He's been in space.

Why is he here?

He missed the Exodus.

He's handsome.

He's been in space. Zero-gee. On the Ring.

We need to talk to him.

We stepped on his tomato plant.

We owe him another.

Yes.

Yes.

Strom said, "We have some plants in the greenhouse. I can transplant one into a pot. As a gift." Strom's hobby was gardening.

"Tomorrow?" I asked.

The consensus was immediate. *Yes.*

This time we knocked instead of skulked. The tomato plant we had squashed had been staked, giving it back its lost structure. There was no answer at the door.

"Aircar's still here."

The cottage was not so small that he couldn't have heard us.

"Maybe he's taking a walk," I said. Again we were out without Moira. She was better, but still sick.

"Here, I think." Strom indicated a spot at the end of the line of tomato plants. He had brought a small spade and began to dig a hole.

I took out paper from my backpack and began to compose a note for Malcolm Leto's door. I started five times, wadding up each after a few lines and stuffing the garbage back in my bag. Finally I settled on "Sorry for stepping on the tomato plant. We brought a new one to replace it."

There was a blast, and I turned in a crouch, dropping the note and pen. Fight-or-flight pheromones filled the air.

Gunshot.

There. The singleton. He's armed.

Posturing fire.

I see him.

Disarm.

This last was Strom, who always took control of situations like this. He tossed the small shovel to Bola on his right. Bola threw the instrument with ease.

Malcolm Leto stood under the cottonwoods, the pistol pointed in the air. He had come out of the woods and fired the shot. The shovel slammed into his fingers, and the pistol fell.

"Son of a bitch!" he yelled, hopping and holding his fingers. "Goddamn cluster!"

We approached. Strom faded into the background again, and I took the lead.

Leto watched us, looked once at the pistol but didn't move to grab it.

"Come back to wreck more of my tomato plants, did you?"

I smiled. "No, Mr. Leto. We came to apologize, like good neighbors. Not to be shot at."

"How was I to know you weren't thieves?" he said.

"There are no thieves here. Not until you get to the Christian Enclave."

He rubbed his fingers, then smirked. "Yeah. I guess so. You bunch are dangerous."

Strom nudged me mentally, and I said, "We brought you a tomato plant to make amends for the one we squashed."

"You did? Well, now I'm sorry I startled you." He looked from the cottage to me. "You mind if I pick up my gun? You're not going to toss another shovel at me, are you?"

"You're not going to fire another shot, are you?" The words were more flip than was necessary for the last member of the Community, but he didn't seem to mind.

"Fair's fair." He picked up his pistol and walked through us toward the cottage.

When he saw the last tomato plant in the line, with the fresh dirt around it, he said, "Should have put it on the other end."

I felt exasperation course through us. There was no pleasing this man.

"You know my name. So you know my story?" he asked.

"No. We just know you're from the Ring."

"Hmmm." He looked at me. "I suppose the neighborly thing to do is to invite you in. Come on."

The cottage was a single room, with an adjoining bathroom and kitchenette. The lone couch served as Leto's bed. A pillow and blanket were piled at one end.

"Suddenly crowded in here," Leto said. He put the pistol on the table and sat on one of the two kitchen chairs. "There's not enough room for all of you, but then there's only one of you anyway, isn't there." He looked at me when he said it.

"We're all individuals," I said quickly. "We also function as a composite."

"Yeah, I know. A cluster."

Ask him about the Ring. Ask him about being in space.

"Sit," he said to me. "You're the ringleader, aren't you."

"I'm the interface," I said. I held out my hand. "We're Apollo Papadopulos." He took my hand after a moment. "Who are you in particular?"

He held my hand and seemed to have no intention of releasing it until I answered the question. "I'm Meda. This is Bola, Quant, Strom, and Manuel."

"Pleased to meet you, Meda," he said. I felt the intensity of his gaze again and forced my physical response down. "And the rest of you."

"You're from the Ring," I said. "You were part of the Community."

He sighed. "Yes, I was."

"What was it like? What's space like? We're going to be a starship pilot."

Leto looked at me with one eyebrow raised. "You want to know the story."

"Yes."

"All right. I haven't told anybody the whole story." He paused. "Do you think it's just a bit too convenient that they put me out here in the middle of nowhere, and yet nearby is one of their starship pilot clusters?"

"I assume you're a test for us." We had come to assume everything was a test.

"Precocious of you. Okay, here's my story: Malcolm Leto, the last, or first, of his kind."

You can't imagine what the Community was like. You can't even comprehend the numbers involved. Six billion people in communion. Six billion people as one.

It was the greatest synthesis humankind has ever created: a synergistic human-machine intelligence. I was a part of it, for a while, and then it was gone, and I'm still here. The Community removed itself from this reality, disappeared, and left me behind.

I was a biochip designer. I grew the molecular processors that we used to link with the Community. Like this one. It's grafted onto the base of your skull, connects to your four lobes and cerebellum.

We were working on greater throughput. The basics were already well established; we—that is myself, Gillian, and Henry—were trying to devise a better transport layer between the electrochemical pulses of the brain and the chips. That was the real bottleneck: the brain's hardware is slow.

We were assigned lines of investigation, but so were a hundred thousand other scientists. I'd go to sleep, and during the night, someone would close out a whole area of research. The Community was the ultimate scientific compilation of information. Sometimes we made the cutting-edge discovery, the one that changed the direction for a thousand people. Usually we just plodded along, uploaded our results, and waited for a new direction.

The research advanced at a pace we as individuals could barely fathom, until we submerged ourselves in the Community. Then, the whole plan was obvious. I can't quite grasp it now, but it's there in my mind like a diamond of thought.

It wasn't just in my area of technology, but everywhere. It took the human race a century to go from horses to space elevators. It took us six months to go from uncertainty cubes to Heisenberg AND gates, and from there twenty days to quantum processors and Nth-order qubits.

You're right. It does seem like a car out of control, barrelling down a hill. But really, it was the orderly advancement of science and technology, all controlled, all directed by the Community.

We spent as much time as we could in the Community, when we worked, played, and even slept. Some people even made love while connected. The ultimate exhibitionism. You couldn't spend all your time connected, of course. Everyone needed downtime. But being away from the Community was like being half yourself.

That's what it was like.

Together, in the Mesh, we could see the vision, we could see the goal, all the humans of Earth united in mind, pushing, pushing, pushing to the ultimate goal: Exodus.

At least I think that was the goal. It's hard to remember. But they're all gone now, right? I'm all that's left. So they must have done it.

Only I wasn't with them when it happened.

I don't blame Henry. I would have done the same thing if my best friend were screwing my wife.

Gillian, on the other hand.

She said she and I were soul mates, and yet when I came out of the freezer twenty-six years later, she was as gone as the rest of them.

You'd think in the Community things like marriage would be obsolete. You'd think that to a group mind, group sex would be the way to go. It's odd what people kept separated from the Community.

Anyway, Henry spent a week in wedge 214 with another group of researchers, and while he was gone, Gillian and I sorta' communed on our own. I'd known Gillian almost as long as I'd known Henry. We were first-wave emigrants to the Ring and had been friends back in Ann Arbor when we were in school. We'd met Gillian and her friend Robin in the cafeteria. He liked them tall, so he took Gillian. Robin's and my relationship lasted long enough for her to brush her teeth the next morning. Gillian and Henry were married.

She was a beautiful woman. Auburn hair like yours. Nice figure. Knew how to tell a joke. Knew how to . . . Well, we won't go there.

I know, best man screwing the bride. You've heard that pitiful tale before. Well, maybe you clusters haven't. Trust me. It's pitiful.

I'm sure it didn't take Henry long to find out. The Community sees all.

But he took a long time plotting his revenge. And when he did—bam!—that was the end for me.

We were working on some new interfaces for the occipital lobe, to enhance visualization during communing, some really amazing things. Henry ran the tests and found out our stuff was safe, so I elected to test it.

It's funny. I remember volunteering to try it out. But I don't remember what Henry said before that, how he manipulated me into trying it. Because that's what he did, all right.

The enhancements were not compatible with my interface. When I inserted them, the neural pathways in the cerebral cortex fused. The interface flash froze. I was a vegetable.

The Community placed my body into suspended animation while it rebuilt my brain. All things were possible for the Community. Only some things take a while, like rebuilding a brain. Six months later, the Exodus occurred, and still the machinery of the Ring worked on my brain. For twenty-six years, slowly with no human guidance, it worked on my brain, until three months ago. It revived me, the one human left over from the Exodus.

Sometimes I still dream that I'm a part of it. That the Community is still there for me to touch. At first those were nightmares, but now they're just dreams. The quantum computers are still up there, empty, waiting. Maybe they're dreaming of the Community, as well.

It'll be easier this time. The technology is so much farther along than it was before. The second Exodus is just a few months away. I just need a billion people to fuel it.

On my hobby night, instead of painting, we spent the evening on the Net.

Malcolm Leto had come down the Macapá space elevator two months before, much to the surprise of the Overgovernment body in Brazil. The Ring continued to beam microwave power to all the receivers, but no one resided on the Ring or used the space elevators that lined the equator. No one could, not without an interface.

The news of Leto's arrival had not made it to North America, but the archives had interviews with the man that echoed his sentiment regarding the Community and his missing out on the Exodus. There wasn't much about him for a couple of weeks until he filed suit with the Brazilian court for ownership of the Ring, on the basis of his being the last member of the Community.

The Overgovernment had never tried to populate the Ring. There was no need to try to overcome the interface access at the elevators. The population of the Earth was just under half a billion. The Gene Wars killed most of the people who hadn't left with the Exodus. It'd taken the Overgovernment almost three decades to build the starships, to string its own nanowire-guided elevators to low Earth orbit, to build the fleet of tugs that plied between LEO and the Lagrange points.

No one used the quantum computers anymore. No one had an interface or could even build one. The human race was no longer interested in that direction. We were focused on the stars and on ourselves. All of us, that is, except for those in the enclaves that existed outside of, yet beneath, the Overgovernment.

The resolution to Leto's case was not published. It had been on the South American court docket a week ago, and then been bumped up to the Overgovernment Court.

He's trying to build another Community.

He's trying to steal the Ring.

Is it even ours?

He's lonely.

We need Moira.

He wants us to help him. That's why he told us the story.

He didn't tell us. He told Meda.

He likes Meda.

"Stop it!" I made fists so that I couldn't receive any more of their thoughts. They looked at me, perplexed, wondering why I was fighting consensus.

Suddenly, I wasn't looking at me. I was looking at them. It was like a knife between us. I ran upstairs.

"Meda! What's wrong?"

I threw myself onto the floor of Moira's room.

"Why are they so jealous?"

"Who, Meda? Who?"

"Them! The rest of us."

"Oh. The singleton."

I looked at her, hoping she understood. But how could she without sharing my thoughts?

"I've been reading your research. Meda, he's a potential psychotic. He's suffered a great loss and awoke in a world nothing like he remembers."

"He wants to rebuild it."

"That's part of his psychosis."

"The Community accomplished things. It made advancements that we don't understand even decades later. How can that be wrong?"

"The common view is that the Exodus was a natural evolution of humankind. What if it wasn't natural? What if the Exodus was death? We didn't miss the Exodus; we escaped it. We survived the Community just like Leto did. Do we want to suffer the same fate?"

"Now who's talking psychosis?"

"The Overgovernmemt will never allow him back on the Ring."

"He's alone forever, then," I said.

"He can go to one of the singleton enclaves. All the people there live alone."

"He woke up one morning, and his self was gone."

"Meda!" Moira sat up in bed, her face gray. "Hold my hand !" As she held out her hand, I could smell the pheromones of her thoughts whispering toward me.

Instead of melding with her, I left the room, left the house, out the door into the wet night.

A light was on in the cottage. I stood for a long time, wondering what I was doing. We spend time alone, but never in situations like this. Never outside, where we can't reach each other in an instant. I was miles away from the rest of me. Yet Malcolm Leto was farther than that.

It felt like half the things I knew were on the tip of my tongue. It felt like all my thoughts were garbled. But everything I felt and thought was my own. There was no consensus.

Just like Malcolm had no consensus. For singletons, all decisions were unanimous.

It was with that thought that I knocked on the door.

He stood in the doorway, wearing just short pants. I felt a thrill course through me, one that I would have hidden from my pod if they were near.

"Where's the rest of your cluster?"

"At home."

"Best place for 'em." He turned, leaving the door wide open. "Come on in."

There was small metal box on his table. He sat down in front of it. I noticed for the first time the small, silver-edged circle at the base of his skull, just below his hairline. He slipped a wire from the box into the circle.

"That's an interface box. They're illegal." When the Exodus occurred, much of the interface technology that was the media for the Communion was banned.

"Yeah. But not illegal anymore. The OG repealed those laws a decade ago, but no one noticed. My lawyer pried it loose from them and sent it up." He pulled the wire from his head and tossed it across the box. "Useless now."

"Can't you access the Ring?"

"Yes, but it's like swimming in the ocean alone." He looked at me side-long. "I can give you one, you know. I can build you an interface."

I recoiled. "No!" I said quickly. "I . . ."

He smiled, perhaps the first time I'd seen him do it. It changed his face. "I understand. Would you like something to drink? I've got a few fix'ns. Sit anyway."

"No," I said. "I'm just . . ." I realized that for a pod's voice, I wasn't articulating my thoughts very well. I looked him in the eye. "I came to talk with you, alone."

"I appreciate the gesture. I know being alone is uncomfortable for you."

"I didn't realize you knew so much about us."

"Multiples were being designed when I was around. I kept up on the subject," he said. "It wasn't very successful. I remember articles on failures that were mentally deficient or unbalanced."

"That was a long time ago! Mother Redd was from that time, and she's a great doctor. And I'm fine—"

He held up a hand. "Hold on! There were lotsa incidents with interface technology before . . . Well, I wouldn't be here if it were totally safe."

His loneliness was a sheer cliff of rock. "Why are you here, instead of at one of the singleton enclaves?"

He shrugged. "There or in the middle of nowhere, it would be the same." He half smiled. "Last of a vanished breed, I am. So you're gonna be a starship captain, you and your mingle-minded friends."

"I am. . . . We are," I replied.

"Good luck, then. Maybe you'll find the Community," he said. He looked tired.

"Is that what happened? They left for outer space?"

He looked puzzled. "No, maybe. I can almost . . . remember." He smiled. "It's like being drunk and knowing you should be sober and not being able to do anything about it."

"I understand," I said. I took his hand. It was dry and smooth.

He squeezed once and then stood up, leaving me confused. I was sluggish on the inside, but at the same time hyperaware of him. We knew what sex was. We'd studied it, of course. But we had no experience. I had no idea what Malcolm was thinking. If he were a multiple, part of a pod, I would.

"I should go," I said, standing.

I was hoping he'd say something by the time I got to the door, but he didn't. I felt my cheeks burn. I was a silly little girl. By myself I'd done nothing but embarrass my pod, myself.

I pulled the door shut and ran into the woods.

"Meda!"

He stood black in yellow light at the cottage door.

"I'm sorry for being so caught up in my own troubles. I've been a bad host. Why don't you—?" I reached him in three steps and kissed him on the mouth. Just barely I tasted his thoughts, his arousal.

"Why don't I what?" I said after a moment.

"Come back inside."

I—they—were there to meet me the next morning as I walked back to the farm. I knew they would be. A part of me wanted to spend the rest of the day with my new lover, but another wanted nothing more than to confront myself, rub my nose in the scent that clung to me, and show me. . . . I didn't know what I wanted to prove. Perhaps that I didn't need to be a composite to be happy. I didn't need them, us, to be a whole person.

"You remember Veronica Proust," Moira said, standing in the doorway of the kitchen, the rest of us behind her. Of course she would take the point when I was gone. Of course she would quote precedent.

"I remember," I said, staying outside, beyond the pull of the pheromones. I could smell the anger, the fear. I had scared myself. Good, I thought.

"She was going to be a starship captain," Moira said. We remembered Proust; she'd been two years ahead of us. Usually pods sundered in the crèche, with time to reform, but Veronica had broken into a pair and a quad. The pair had bonded, and the quad had transferred to engineering school, then dropped out.

"Not anymore," I said. I pushed past them into the kitchen, and as I did so, I balled up the memory of fucking Malcolm and threw it at them like a rock.

They recoiled. I walked upstairs to our room and began packing my things. They didn't bother coming upstairs, and that made me angrier. I threw my clothes into a bag, swept the bricabrac on the dresser aside. Something glinted in the pile, a geode that Strom had found one summer when we flew to the desert. He'd cut it in half and polished it by hand.

I picked it up, felt its smooth surface, bordering the jagged crystals of the center. Instead of packing it, I put it back on the dresser and zipped up my bag.

"Heading out?"

Mother Redd stood at the door, her face neutral.

"Did you call Dr. Khalid?" He was our physician, our psychologist, perhaps our father.

She shrugged. "And tell him what? You can't force a pod to stay together."

"I'm not breaking us up!" I said. Didn't she understand? I was a person, by myself. I didn't need to be part of a *thing*.

"You're just going to go somewhere else by yourself. Yes, I understand." Her sarcasm cut me, but she was gone before I could reply.

I rushed downstairs and out the front door so that I wouldn't have to face the rest of me. I didn't want them to taste my guilt. I ran the distance to Malcolm's cottage. He was working in his garden and took me in his arms.

"Meda, Meda. What's wrong?"

"Nothing," I whispered.

"Why did you go back there? We could have sent for your things."

I said, "I want an interface."

It was a simple procedure. He had the nanodermic and placed it on the back of my neck. My neck felt cold there, and the coldness spread to the base of my skull and down my spine. There was a prick and I felt my skin begin to crawl.

"I'm going to put you under for an hour," Malcolm said. "It's best."

"Okay," I said, already half asleep.

I dreamed that spiders were crawling down my optic nerve into my brain, that earwigs were sniffing around my lobes, that leeches were attached to all my fingers. But as they passed up my arms, into my brain, a door opened like the sun dawning, and I was somewhere else, somewhen else, and it all made sense with dreamlike logic. I understood why I was there, where the Community was, why they had left.

"Hello, Meda," Malcolm said.

"I'm dreaming."

"Not anymore," his voice said. It seemed to be coming from a bright point in front of me. "I've hooked you up to the interface box. Everything went fine."

My voice answered without my willing it to. "I was worried that my genetic mods would cause a problem." I felt I was still in my dream. I didn't want to say those things. "I didn't mean to say that. I think I'm still dreaming." I tried to stop speaking. "I can't stop speaking."

I felt Malcolm's smile. "You're not speaking. Let me show you what's possible within the Community."

He spent hours teaching me to manipulate the reality of the interface box, to reach out and grasp it like my hand was a shovel, a hammer, sandpaper, a cloth.

"You do this well," he said, a brightness in the gray green garden we had built in an ancient empty city. Ivy hung from the walls, and within the ivy, sleek animals scurried. The dirt exuded its musty smell, mingling with the dogwoods that bounded the edge of the garden.

I smiled, knowing he could see my emotion. He could see all of me, as if he were a member of my pod. I was disclosed, though he remained aloof.

"Soon," he said, when I pried at his light, and then he took hold of me and we made love again in the garden, the grass tickling my back like a thousand tongues.

In the golden aftermath, Malcolm's face emerged from within the ball of light, his eyes closed. As I examined his face, it expanded before me, I fell into his left nostril, into his skull, and all of him was laid open to me.

In the garden, next to the ivy-covered stone walls, I began to retch. Even within the virtual reality of the interface box, I tasted my bile. He'd lied to me.

I had no control of my body. The interface box sat on the couch beside me as it had when we'd started, but pseudoreality was gone. Malcolm was behind me — I could hear him packing a bag — but I couldn't will my head to turn.

"We'll head for the Belem elevator. Once we're on the Ring, we're safe. They can't get to us. Then they'll have to deal with me."

There was a water stain on the wall, a blemish that I could not tear my eyes away from.

"We'll recruit people from singleton enclaves. They may not recognize my claim, but they will recognize my power."

My eyes began to tear, not from the strain. He'd used me, and I, silly girl, had fallen for him. He had seduced me, taken me as a pawn, as a valuable to bargain with.

"It may take a generation. I'd hoped it wouldn't. There are cloning vats on the Ring. You have excellent stock, and if raised from birth, you will be much more malleable."

If he had me, part of one of the starpods, he thought he'd be safe from the Overgovernment. But he didn't know that our pod was sundered. He didn't realize how useless this all was.

"All right, Meda. Time to go."

Out of the corner of my eye I saw him insert the connection into his interface, and my legs lifted me up off the couch. My rage surged through me, and my neck erupted in pheromones.

"Jesus, what's that smell?"

Pheromones! His interface controlled my body, my throat, my tongue, my cunt, but not my mods. He'd never thought of it. I screamed with all my might, scent exploding from my glands. Anger, fear, revulsion.

Malcolm opened the door, fanned it. His gun bulged at his waist. "We'll pick up some perfume for you on the way." He disappeared out the door with two bags, one mine, while I stood with the interface box in my outstretched arms.

Still I screamed, saturating the air with my words, until my glands were empty, spent, and my autonomous nervous system silenced me. I strained to hear something from outside. There was nothing.

Malcolm reappeared. "Let's go." My legs goose-stepped me from the cottage.

I tasted our thoughts as I passed the threshold. My pod was out there, too far for me to understand, but close.

With the last of my pheromones, I signaled, *Help!*

"Into the aircar," Leto said.

Something yanked at my neck, and my body spasmed as I collapsed. I caught sight of Manuel on the cottage roof, holding the interface box.

Leto pulled his gun and spun.

Something flew by me, and Leto cried out, dropping the pistol. I stood, wobbly, and ran into the woods, until someone caught me, and suddenly I was in our mesh.

As my face was buried in Strom's chest and my palms squeezed against his, I watched with other eyes—Moira's eyes!—as Leto scrambled into the air-car and started the turbines.

He's not going far.

We played with his hydrogen regulator.

Also turned his beacon back on.

Thanks for coming. Sorry.

I felt dirty, empty. My words barely formed. I released all that had happened, all that I had done, all my foolish thoughts into them. I expected their anger, their rejection. I expected them to leave me there by the cottage.

Still a fool, Moira chided. Strom touched the tender interface jack on my neck.

All's forgiven, Meda. The consensus was the juice of a ripe fruit, the light of distant stars.

All's forgiven.

Hand in hand in hand, we returned to the farm, sharing all that had happened that day.

anomalous structures of my dreams

M. SHAYNE BELL

M. Shayne Bell first came to public attention in 1986, when he won first place in that year's Writers of the Future contest. Since then, he has published a number of well-liked stories in *Asimov's*—including a Hugo Finalist, "Mrs. Lincoln's China," and a loosely connected series of stories about life in a future Africa—as well as appearing in *Amazing*, *The Magazine of Fantasy and Science Fiction*, *Realms of Fantasy*, *Pulphouse*, *Starlight 2*, *Vanishing Acts*, and elsewhere. He has published a well-received first novel, *Nicoji*, and edited an anthology of stories by Utah writers, *Washed by a Wave of Wind: Science Fiction from the Corridor*. His most recent book is a collection, *How We Play the Game in Salt Lake and Other Stories*. Bell has an M.A. in English from Brigham Young University, and lives in Salt Lake City, Utah.

Here he gives the idea of picking up a "secondary infection" while in the hospital a whole new—and sinister—connotation, one with uneasy implications for the entire world . . .

O f course it wasn't a private room. Medicare doesn't pay for that. Never mind that next door was an empty room with two beds never slept in. I had to share a room. Never mind that when you're sick enough to be hospitalized, the last thing you want is for a perfect stranger and usually the stranger's family and

friends to watch you be that sick. It was cheaper to keep two people in one
room, end of discussion, throw up if you have to and let a roomful of strangers
watch you do it.

I was admitted late in the day. The man in the bed next to mine lay there
breathing raspily, watching them move me in. He never said a word. His frail
little wife and, I assumed, daughter stood up to make room for the nurses and
me. I nodded at my roommate, but that was all—what do you say when nurses
are helping you into one of those ridiculously high hospital beds, putting a
needle into the back of your wrist to start an IV drip, and injecting you with
antibiotics?

"Can I get you anything?" one of the nurses asked me when she was
through with her part in the little drama.

Yes, I thought, get me out of here. Get me well and get me out of here.

When my roommate's visitors were gone and it was late and all the TVs were
off, the two of us in that room still lay awake. He'd cough, trying not to make a
lot of noise, then I'd do the same.

"What are you in for?" he asked me suddenly through the curtain separating our beds. His question made it sound as if we were criminals about to discuss our crimes.

"Pneumonia," I said. "Noninfectious." I did not go on to say that it was
PCP pneumonia and that this AIDS-related opportunistic infection would kill
me if my doctor didn't find a way to kill it first. I did not have an immune system left to fight it with.

"I've got pneumonia, too," he said, wheezing. He coughed hard.

No way! I thought. They'd put me in a room with somebody coughing up
yet another strain of lung killer I couldn't fight? "What kind?" I asked.

"They don't know," he said. "Something rare."

In the night, when he was sleeping, I unhooked myself from the IV and oxygen
feed and walked out to the nurses' desk, hospital gown tied shut and held shut
as well. I asked the head nurse about the condition of the man in the bed next
to mine. I figured I had a right to know.

"It's not to worry," she said. "Mr. Schumberg can't possibly be infectious.
He should be getting better soon."

"But if he has something different from me and I catch it—I can't fight it.
I could be in serious trouble."

"Your physician approved your room assignment. You can talk to her
about it in the morning, but I'm sure you'll be fine."

It was all she would say. Patient confidentiality rules forbade her from telling me anything specific about my roommate. I walked back to my bed and saw that the man next to me had an IV pentamadine drip just like mine. That fit serious pneumonia treatment. I wondered what strain he had.

Even I could see that by morning my roommate was not getting better. He was noticeably worse. All he could do was cough. Our nurse started his pentama-dine drip, then she started mine. I felt the cold drug course through my veins and around to my heart and brain. I did not understand why the nurses couldn't warm the drug first, why they couldn't at least let it sit on a counter and come to room temperature. They always took it straight from the refrigera-tor and started it icy cold into my veins. I had asked them to warm it the last time I'd been admitted, but no one wanted special requests to remember or a patient fussing with hospital procedures. I didn't say anything this time. I just gathered up the blankets around me.

When the nurse left, my roommate turned on a football game rebroadcast on one of the sports channels, then he completely ignored it. He called his wife and asked her why she wasn't here yet. I found myself wishing that I had someone to wait for, someone who could walk through the door at any moment and bring flowers or a newspaper and gossip about friends. I'd been too sick for too long to keep up many friendships. My closest current relation-ships were with my doctor and the staffs at the pharmacy and the food bank. My little sister lived in Minneapolis and she might call, I thought. If I let her know I was in here, she might call.

His wife arrived before any of our doctors made rounds. I heard her kiss her husband, and they murmured a few words. Then she stepped around the curtain and smiled a little nervously at me. She carried a small bouquet of lilacs arranged in a dill pickle bottle she had washed the label off. She set it on my dresser.

"Thank you so much," I said, and the tears set in. AIDS was making my brain shrink, among other things, but the only effect I'd been able to notice so far besides the headaches was the constant crying. I could not control my emo-tions. I'd cry if I ran out of shampoo or if the electric bill arrived one day earlier than usual. I couldn't help it. I sat there with tears in my eyes over this lady's unexpected kindness, and I did not dare blink for fear the tears would run down my cheeks and she'd see.

"I hope you're well soon," she said, and she patted my knee and stepped back around the curtain to be with her husband.

I leaned back and wiped my eyes. I inhaled the fragrance of the lilacs mixed, oddly, with the lingering smell of dill which you can never quite wash out of a jar. I hadn't been able to ask her name, and she had not asked mine.

My doctor made quick rounds. She prescribed a higher dose of Tylenol to bring down my fever, then she was off to her clinic. The resident interns on the floor made their rounds. About an hour later, Mr. Schumberg's doctors arrived, three of them. We were in a teaching hospital so it was not unusual to see teams in a room—but these were all doctors. There were no interns among them as far as I could tell. They turned off his TV and pulled the curtain completely around his bed. I lay back and closed my eyes.

I couldn't help but overhear everything. After a while, I realized they weren't asking him regular questions. It was all about his work, not his condition.

"I was in the research and development end," he said. "Masked and gloved and in a damned hot bodysuit."

"You couldn't have breathed them in?"

"Through the biohazard glass and the steel shield between them and me? Through my suit? I don't think so." He stopped and coughed and coughed. "It wouldn't have hurt me if I had," he continued when he could talk again.

"My husband is always very careful," his wife volunteered.

"He's not responding to treatment, and we're trying to determine whether something we've overlooked could be the reason why," one of the doctors said.

"How did you work with them?" another asked.

"You suit up before you enter the research area, then you fit your hands into white, pressure-sensitive gloves that control the movement of robotic arms in a hermetically sealed room you never enter. Those robots do all the actual work for you. You strap on goggles that let you see what you're doing. You never come into physical contact with the projects."

He coughed again and again.

"Could you lean forward, please?"

They talked on like that while they listened to his lungs. I was too fevered and chilled from the cold IV to pay them much attention then.

They took sputum samples from both of us. They came back for another from him at noon, then another from him at four o'clock. They took him away in a wheelchair to x-ray his lungs. His daughter Ann came to sit with him in the evening and to spell her mother. Ann kept going to the sink to freshen cool washcloths that she put on her father's forehead.

My fever spiked again in the evening, despite the increased Tylenol. I'd been trying to drink liquids all day on top of the saline drip to do what I could to help my body fight the pneumonia, but it wasn't conquered yet. I'm impatient when I'm sick. I want whatever it is—cold, flu, PCP pneumonia—to be over now. Progress always seems slow. But it's especially troublesome when all you have to do is lie in bed while your doctor and teams of nurses concentrate on your condition. It's impossible not to focus on it yourself. All your little aches and pains seem magnified. You watch yourself for the slightest signs of improvement. If there aren't any, you wonder why. You wonder what's happening. You start worrying about what you've left undone and unsaid. Living with AIDS as long as I have, you'd think I'd have said it all and prepared everything long ago. Most people would think that someone like me would have had plenty of warning to get ready, but you never have plenty of warning. There's never enough time. You always need more.

Night came, and all the visitors left and most of the TVs finally went off. Still I could not sleep. Neither could my roommate. We lay there taking turns coughing. His cough seemed much worse. He'd cough and cough, then gasp for air, then cough some more. He did not try to hide it now. He started moaning between coughs.

"Do you need something?" I asked him through the curtain. "Do you want me to call a nurse?"

"I just need to catch my breath," he said. "I'll be all right."

But he could not catch his breath, and his coughing fits lasted longer and longer. His coughing seemed to come from the depths of his lungs. After one long coughing fit, I heard him throwing up.

I hit the "call nurse" button, but no one rushed in. No one came at all. Damn them, I thought. I unhooked my IV, took off my oxygen feed, and got out of bed. I pulled back the curtain, thinking I would at least hand him his plastic vomit bowl, but the sight of him shocked me. His vomit was bloody. It was all over his bed and had splashed onto the floor. He was choking for air.

I headed out the door. "Mr. Schumberg needs help!" I called to a nurse in the hallway. "He's choking in vomit."

That got attention. She ran into the room, and another nurse soon followed. I sat in a chair in the hallway while they worked on Mr. Schumberg. After a few minutes, his choking stopped, but he kept coughing.

The elevators at the far end of the hall soon opened, and a short Mexican woman stepped out pulling a cleaning cart behind her. They hadn't wasted any time calling housekeeping, I thought. I did not envy this woman's job. She pulled on gloves, and the nurses asked her to mop the floor first so they could walk around in there. After that, she carried clean bedding in and came out with the soiled. She went back in to keep cleaning. I waited until one of the nurses had left before I walked back in.

The smell of disinfectant was strong in the room. They had raised the back of Mr. Schumberg's bed to a 90-degree angle, so he was sitting straight up. A nurse was increasing his oxygen flow. When she left, he sat there with his eyes closed, so I didn't say anything. I was certain he did not feel like talking. I started to climb back into bed, but I saw blood on the floor between our beds.

The woman from housekeeping was mopping around the sink. I stepped over to her.

"I'm sorry," I said, "but there's still blood between the beds."

"Ai!" she said. She went out to her cart for a different mop. After she had cleaned up the mess with that mop, she came back in with another mop dripping with disinfectant. She mopped vigorously under both beds.

"Gracias," I said.

She smiled at my Spanish. "Nada," she said.

I got back into bed from the other side. She finished her work, then she pulled off her gloves, thew them in the trash, and washed at the sink. I saw that her nametag read "Maria."

I had the first of the odd, frenetic dreams that night. In it, everyone I knew rushed around carrying rocks and furniture and sandbags to a wall we were tying to construct around the downtown highrises. No one would tell me why we were doing it, just that we had to work faster and faster. All the buildings we were attempting to protect were lit from floor to ceiling, and that's what I remembered most from the dream when I woke at 2:00 A.M.: the oddly lit buildings burning gloriously bright while the rest of the city was dark and apparently without electricity.

I pulled the covers up around me. I could feel the fever hot inside me. The ice had melted in my pitcher, but the water was still cool. I poured another glass and drank it. The blinds were pulled over the window so I could not look out at the city lights in the valley, but I was sure they were there. It took a while for me to go back to sleep.

The interns were very worried about the blood in Mr. Schumberg's vomit, and I was certain the doctors would be, too. The head intern sent him for more x-rays before breakfast. When my doctor did her rounds, she ordered a follow-up x-ray of my lungs. When the nurse wheeled me back into the room, Mr. Schumberg was sitting on the side of his bed in conference with the three doctors. His breakfast lay untouched on his table. He had his feet over the side of his bed, and he was trying to sit up straight. He was entangled in IV lines and the oxygen feed to his nose. The doctors pulled the curtains around his bed while the nurse helped me back up into mine.

"There are anomalous structures forming in the lower third of each of your lungs," I heard one of the doctors say to him.

"How do you mean 'anomalous'?" he asked, and then he coughed.

"They are right-angled or curved, not irregular as would be the case with cancer. We have to biopsy the structures to see what they are, then remove them if necessary."

"When?"

"Now. Today. We have the biopsy scheduled for one o'clock. Don't eat breakfast."

They were quiet while Mr. Schumberg signed the consent forms for the biopsy.

"We also need you to sign this form allowing us to contact your employer. If the biopsy confirms our guess, we have to talk to them about what might be forming in your lungs and how best to proceed."

"Lungs are too wet for my projects," Mr. Schumberg said. "Human tissue is too wet. They can't be growing inside me. This is something else—probably a malfunctioning x-ray machine."

"We're having that checked."

He signed the consent forms, and they left and the nurse left. I did not hear Mr. Schumberg settle back into bed. After a time, I could hear that he was crying. That surprised me. I wondered if this was the most serious diagnosis he had had to face. I remembered crying after they'd told me I was HIV positive all those years ago. I'd managed to wait until I'd made it to my car where I'd been alone. I'd known that nothing in my life would ever be the same. Maybe he was thinking similar thoughts.

Listening to him cry made me teary, but that was just my shrinking brain. I wished that his wife were here to comfort him. I did not feel comfortable trying. Blubbering hospitalized AIDS patients can do a lot of things, but cheer up other patients is usually not one of them.

I wondered what was going on.

His wife came soon enough, but so did officials from his work. They grilled Mr. Schumberg about lapses in procedures I could not make sense of, and he claimed there had been none. His wife said again that "he is always very careful." I started to wonder just how careful he had been or, if he were the careful man his wife claimed, whether his company had set up adequate procedures to protect him in the first place.

One of the doctors came in to ask questions of the company officials. They all studied Mr. Schumberg's lung x-rays. The company officials asked for copies and left quickly. Nurses arrived to take Mr. Schumberg away for the biopsy. His wife walked down to the waiting room, but soon she was back in the chair by his bed.

"Do you mind if I turn on my husband's television?" she asked. "The waiting room is so crowded and all anyone is watching is football. I'll wait here for Bernie."

I told her to go right ahead. She turned on a cooking channel which she completely ignored. She called Ann to tell her about the biopsy and possible surgery, then she leafed through an issue of *Good Housekeeping*. After an hour or so of Northern Italian pastas that I at least watched, she walked back down to the waiting room.

The room was oddly quiet after she left. I turned off the TV, but it was more than that, of course. Being around Mr. Schumberg and his family made me think, too much probably, about what my life lacked. Mr. Schumberg had other people in his life. The quiet hospital room would be like my quiet house when I was well enough to drive myself home again. It was time to make some changes, I thought. Time for some improvements. I knew that hospital resolutions were like New Year's resolutions—seldom remembered after discharge. But I'd remember this one. There were people I could call, old friends who'd maybe want to see me again, new friends to make. I'd even leave here with pasta recipes to cook for them.

My chest ached from all the coughing, and I could not stop. They gave me a liquid medicine to control the cough, and it seemed to help for about half an hour. My fever was higher, not lower—103.5 now, and that in the daytime. I was chilled. I asked a nurse to bring me another blanket to wrap in.

My doctor surprised me by coming back to my room around three o'clock, hours before evening rounds. She pulled on gloves before coming over to me, which she would never normally do.

"How do you feel?" she asked.

"Sick," I said.

"Lean forward," she said. "I need to listen to your lungs."

I did as she asked, then she percussed my back and chest, asking whether any of the taps hurt. They all did.

She excused herself and walked out to the nurses' desk. I could see her through the doorway. One of Mr. Schumberg's doctors walked over and talked to her. He opened a chart and showed her a series of x-rays. She held an x-ray she was carrying up to the light for him to look at, and he shook his head. The head intern walked over to look. I could see that my doctor was getting angrier by the minute, though I couldn't hear what any of them was saying. A nurse at the desk hurried to hand her a form, and she walked back into my room with the head intern.

"I'm getting you out of this room," she said.

"What's wrong?" I asked.

"Where do I start? With the health-care system in this country? With free-enterprise capitalism that thinks it can chew up people and spit the ones it damages into hospitals unequipped to handle them?"

She was filling out a form for the room transfer. I'd never seen my doctor this angry.

"You might have picked up what Mr. Schumberg has," the intern said.

I leaned back and closed my eyes. "But they assured me he was noninfectious," I said pointlessly.

"They told me the same thing," my doctor said. "They used to have an AIDS ward in this hospital. If they'd kept that going, as I'd advised them, we wouldn't have this problem."

"What does Mr. Schumberg have?" I asked.

The intern looked at my doctor.

"That's the million dollar question," my doctor said.

When she was through with the form, she handed it to the intern and walked to the window. She held up an x-ray in the light. "These are of your lungs the day you were admitted," she said. She pointed out the areas affected by the pneumonia. "Now here's your x-ray from this morning. It came to me just half an hour ago."

She held the new one up in the light. There was a small dark rectangle in the lower portion of my right lung.

"What is it?" I asked.

"I don't know," she said. "But apparently it's not organic."

"What do you mean 'not organic'?"

"It's metal."

"How did it get there?"

"That's what we need to find out. I'm heading down to see what the biopsy discovers in Schumberg's lungs. In the meantime, you're getting your own room and isolation."

She left in a hurry. The intern was leafing through Mr. Schumberg's chart.

"I don't get it," I said. "How do you catch 'metal rectangles' in your lungs?"

The intern shrugged. "We don't know yet. Mr. Schumberg developed symptoms of pneumonia two weeks ago, but all standard treatments failed, first antibiotics at home, then in-hospital treatment. He apparently works for the research arm of a telecommunications company. Yesterday after each successive x-ray showed the anomalies in his lungs changing and growing we started wondering if something from his workplace could be causing his condition."

"And you left me in here with him?"

I was furious.

"We weren't putting together all the pieces. Until three hours ago, we still thought there might be something wrong with the x-ray equipment. But the technicians assure us it's functioning perfectly."

I just sat there, stunned, not knowing what to do or expect with a metal rectangle of some kind growing in my left lung.

"You might have a million dollar lawsuit on your hands," the intern said. He seemed to think that would brighten things up for me.

When you contract a disease like AIDS, you think that that is what is going to kill you. With AIDS, I had any of ten or fifteen opportunistic infections either singly or in combination lurking as my executioners and time to imagine facing them all. You never think that your end will come in some unexpected way like a bus hitting you in a crosswalk. That's what I felt like alone in that room again. I felt as if I were standing in the headlights of a Greyhound bus.

I unhooked myself from the IV and oxygen feed and packed the few things I had brought with me to the hospital so I'd be ready to move to the new room. Then I hooked everything back up and waited. After about twenty minutes, they wheeled Mr. Schumberg into the room. Mrs. Schumberg followed his bed in, and she had tears in her eyes. Mr. Schumberg did not look good. I just looked at all of them, wide-eyed. I knew room transfers could take a while, but I'd expected to be gone when they brought him back. They pulled the curtain while they moved him onto his own bed, but I could hear him wheezing and coughing and moaning. The two nurses who brought him in were coughing, too. Add my coughs, and it was a noisy room.

Ann soon arrived. I was surprised to see her in the daytime since I knew she had a job. She stepped over for a chair from my section of the room. "They're taking Dad into surgery as soon as possible," she told me. "I took the afternoon off to come sit with Mother through this."

"I'm sorry," I said, "but I hope the surgery helps your dad get well."

It was the least I could say, even under the circumstances. Ann was pulling the chair past the end of my bed. I decided to try to get some answers. "What did your father do?" I asked Ann. "They think I might have picked up what he has."

She stopped and looked at me, then she sat in the chair. "What's happened?" she asked.

I told her about the x-rays of my lungs.

"Dad designs ultrasensitive communications equipment," she said.

"I don't understand," I said. "How could that affect his lungs and now mine?"

"Let's ask him," she said. She stood and pulled back the curtain. She explained the situation to her father. No one said anything for a moment. None of us even coughed for a time.

"I design machines that build—" Mr. Schumberg said, then he started coughing again. "That build themselves from the molecular structure up—

nanotech. Our nanomachines carry the plans for communications devices. They process local materials and build our equipment in hours. We wanted them for emergency situations, military patrols. People could carry a telecom center in a matchbox."

I lay back and looked out the window. It was starting to make sense. Nanotechnology and the marvelous machines it would supposedly create had been in the news for years. His nanomachines had somehow escaped from the lab to the wider world—or at least to our lungs. I imagined microscopic nanomachines eager to build radios and handsets coughed out in a fine spray from Schumberg's lungs hour after hour for the days that I had lain next to him.

"What were your machines supposed to grow from?" I asked.

"Dirt or sand. Start the process and my little machines fan out to find what they need in the local environment. Lungs—human tissue—were supposed to be too wet for them to grow in."

"Apparently they weren't," I said.

He looked appalled. So did Ann and his wife.

"How do you turn them off?" I asked.

He thought for a moment. "High-dose radiation would do it. Extreme heat." He looked back at me. "Basically, at this point, you don't turn them off. We were still trying to design decent shut-off mechanisms."

Hence his rushed surgery and, I imagined, my own to follow shortly though how they would operate on lungs sick with pneumonia I didn't know. At least I was finally able to make sense of what was going on. Apparently the wetness of a person's lungs just slows down the nanomachines, and apparently each microscopic automaton carries the plans for the entire finished set of equipment. They are programmed to work together if they encounter others of their kind, but all you really need is one of them. It just takes longer if you start from such a small beginning. Still, at the rate things were going, Mr. Schumberg thought I could look forward to a satellite uplink and all the necessary receivers and transmitters in my own chest by Thursday noon unless they could cut the damn things out.

I watched nurses set up a table with disposable plastic gowns and gloves and masks, just outside the door to our room. The head nurse soon walked in covered in protective gear. She asked Mrs. Schumberg and Ann to step out to gown, glove, and mask, too.

"What's the point now?" Mrs. Schumberg asked. "I've been with Bernie every day since he took sick."

"Gown and mask now or leave the room," was all the nurse said. She stood in the middle of the room until Mrs. Schumberg and Ann had stepped out to do as she ordered.

I stopped the nurse before she could leave. "Ma'am," I said. "My doctor said I would be getting a different room."

"I'm afraid not," she said. "Administration ordered us to quarantine those of you with this problem in as small an area as possible. You'll be staying right where you are."

The nurse pulled a large trash can into the room and positioned it by the door. She pulled off her gown and gloves, threw them in the trash, and left quickly. Ann and Mrs. Schumberg came back in dressed in the hot plastic. Ann told Mr. Schumberg and me, her voice muffled through the mask, that they'd taped a contamination warning next to the door and hospital policy about the use of protective gear when entering the room, instructions on how to take it off when leaving the room so as not to spread what might be inside, and warnings to visitors and staff.

"Will plastic protect people from your nanomachines?" I asked Mr. Schumberg.

Mr. Schumberg hit his call nurse button. The head nurse stepped back to the doorway.

"Plastic is no protection," Mr. Schumberg told her. "You should use cotton. The hydrocarbons in plastic will attract the nanomachines much faster."

"Your company advised us that this was a possibility," the nurse said. "But who has disposable cotton gowns anymore? I'm not sure we could even buy them. None of us will wear the gowns or masks very long. We'll take them off and leave them in the trash in your room, which Sanitation will remove and burn each hour. Fire will apparently destroy any nanomachines on the plastic. The masks at least are cotton. It's the best we can do."

The nurse left, and the room grew suddenly quiet as the air-conditioning went silent. They apparently did not want the air from this room recirculating.

Mr. Schumberg reached out for his wife's hand. She stood up and put her gloved hand in his. "Get out of here," he told her. "You and Ann—go now and pray you don't already have them."

"I'm not leaving you, Bernie," she said.

"No," he said. "There were other projects, more dangerous. If my nanos escaped, so did theirs. If all those nanos work together, God knows what they'll build. This is a level ten."

Mrs. Schumberg put her hand over her mouth when he said that.

"What's level ten?" I asked.

Mrs. Schumberg looked at me. "Possible contamination not just of the local area, but of the entire world."

Oddly, I didn't feel tears in my eyes over any of this. I was starting to get very, very angry. "And there's no reliable way to turn off your machines?" I said. "You built something that could contaminate the world—and you did not first design a way to turn it off?"

"There's a way," he said. "We always kept a failsafe. We never thought it would come to this."

Ann and Mrs. Schumberg were gathering up their things.

"Hydrogen bombs," he went on. "You can only stop a level ten in the early stages. The military observers back in the lab must know what happened." He looked at his wife with tears in his eyes. "Get out now."

But it was already too late. Hospital security turned back Ann and Mrs. Schumberg at the elevators. No one was leaving the hospital, or at least this floor, for now. Ann and Mrs. Schumberg regowned and gloved and masked and sat quietly back in their chairs. None of us talked. They did not even turn on the television. In that quiet, I could hear nurses and other patients coughing. Granted this was a pulmonary ward, but it seemed to me that I was hearing more coughing than before, especially among the staff. Ann and Mrs. Schumberg both coughed a little now, too. It was impossible not to imagine Mr. Schumberg's nanomachines fanning out to find what they needed in the local environment, a determined little plague gobbling up the dust between the tiles and the dirt tracked in on people's shoes and when that wasn't enough looking for what they needed in other places. They had clearly learned that they could find what they needed in human lungs. Mr. Schumberg's and my lungs had taught them that.

A team of nurses arrived to prep Mr. Schumberg for surgery. They untangled him from all the IV lines, but not the oxygen feed. That would go with him. He looked over at me. "I'm sorry," he said.

I did not know what to say. He's worked on a project that could contaminate the world and that only hydrogen bombs could control, but he was sorry. His apology rang a little hollow to me. I ended up not saying anything in reply.

The nurses pulled a transfer bed alongside Mr. Schumberg's bed.

"Can you sit up?" one of the nurses asked.

He tried, but he could not sit up. Apparently he was suddenly too weak to move. "It hurts to move," he said, and he coughed and coughed.

Nurses walked to either side of the bed and tried to lift Mr. Schumberg forward, but they could not do it. They could not budge him from the bed, either. He coughed and coughed and moaned.

One of the nurses pulled back the blankets. There were no restraints, if that was what she was looking for, but there was blood slowly seeping out from around Mr. Schumberg's back.

Mrs. Schumberg gasped, and Ann stood up. The head nurse went for towels to staunch the blood with. They tried to turn Mr. Schumberg onto his side, but they could not move him.

"Stop!" Mr. Schumberg said. "Just let me lie here for a minute."

"We have to stop the bleeding," the head nurse said. She started feeling underneath Mr. Schumberg's back. "Call Dr. Adams!" she said after a moment. "Stat."

Adams was one of the three doctors I'd seen conferring on Mr. Schumberg's case. He came on the run, as did the resident intern in charge of the floor that afternoon.

"For God's sake gown and mask first!" the head nurse shouted at them when they rushed into the room.

They went back out and did as she asked, then she had them feel under Mr. Schumberg's back. "Something's hooking his back to the mattress. It's gone through the sheets and into the plastic padding."

Dr. Adams felt under Mr. Schumberg's back. There was more and more blood oozing onto the bedding. Dr. Adams knelt to look under the bed. "Just wheel him to surgery in this bed," he ordered. "Now. I'll call the OR to advise them."

After they left, I lay alone again in the darkening room. But I did not lie there for long. I sat up so that my back could not touch the bed. I looked behind me for signs of blood on the bedding, but there were none.

Yet.

I felt around my back for odd bumps, but there were none, either. Still, I did not lie back down.

I sat there, thinking. It what Mr. Schumberg had said were true, there were people I needed to warn to get out of the city. It being late afternoon on a Tuesday, I reached lots of answering machines. I left messages telling my old friends to leave town—to call me for details if they wanted, but that they had better trust me on this one, especially if they couldn't reach me at the hospital for some reason. The only person I found at home was my cousin Alyson in Magna.

"Why didn't you tell me you were in the hospital?" she asked.

"That's not important," I said. I tried to explain what was happening and that she should take her kids and leave now.

She was quiet for a time. "Look," she said. "Are you all right? I mean, this isn't making sense."

She probably thought my dementia had gotten worse. "It *will* make sense," I said. "I just hope it's not too late for you when it does."

She said nothing.

"It must be making news," I said. "Is there anything odd on the channels about Salt Lake?"

We both turned on the same twenty-four-hour news channel. Five minutes later they ran a story about the closure of the Salt Lake City International

Airport. An early spring heatwave had buckled so many of the runways, they claimed, that no flights could take off or land. Since Salt Lake is a Delta hub, this was big news—hundreds of flights had to be rerouted. Officials did not know when the problem would be resolved, especially if each runway had to be resurfaced. Of course, the day's high temperature had only been sixty-seven, but they interviewed an expert who explained why sixty-seven degrees Fahrenheit was high enough on a sunny day to buckle runways.

"Oh my God!" Alyson said slowly as she read between the lines.

"Go now before they close the roads," I said.

We wished each other luck and hung up. Maybe they had already closed the roads, I thought. I'd have to wait until five o'clock and the local news for cleverly disguised stories about that. The airport story, however, made it clear that somebody was quarantining these valleys. I realized, of course, that no responsible government could let people fly all over the world and spread Mr. Schumberg's nanomachines. Still, I was surprised that it was happening so fast. It was almost as if they had had a plan for this in place. On a whim, I pulled the telephone book out of the top dresser drawer and looked up the number for the bus station. I called them just to see if buses were moving. I asked if I could buy a ticket to Denver that night.

"I'm sorry, sir," the attendant said. "We are unable to book any tickets at this time. Please call back in the morning."

She would not give me a reason for her inability to sell tickets. I could only get a recording at the train station.

Oh, we were good people, I thought. Everybody was doing what he or she had been told to do, at least for now. I wondered how many people in Salt Lake really knew what was happening. There were three million people in the connected valleys along the Wasatch Front. It would not take long before lots of them were asking questions. I wished Alyson and my friends luck out on the roads.

The head nurse phoned me to ask for the names of everyone who had visited me in the hospital.

"Just my doctor," I said.

"No one else? No friends came by? No family?"

I hated answering those questions. "No," I said. "I have one sister, but she's in Minneapolis."

"All right," she said, and then she coughed. "Sorry to call you like this. I just didn't want to pull on one of those hot gowns again. Saves time and gowns."

Oddly, after the phone calls, I slept for a time. When I dreamed, I found myself helping to build the wall around the downtown highrises again. The entire cityscape was weirder in this dream. Large sections of the valley seemed to have been flattened to the ground, while among the towers lacy filaments strung with lights danced on the evening breezes. It was so hot down where we were working. Everyone's shirt was wet with sweat. I wished that I could be twenty stories up to feel the breeze. We could not feel a breath of air where we worked and sweated. I tried to wipe the sweat off my forehead.

I woke with a start. My doctor was holding my wrist in her gloved hand, taking my pulse.

"You can still feel a pulse through these gloves," she said. "Sorry to startle you."

"It's so hot in here," I said.

"I asked Housekeeping to bring in a fan. They should be on the way with it. Your temperature's up. One-oh-four now. Pulse is high, too."

I could feel my heart racing.

"We're taking you into surgery in two hours."

"That late in the day?" I asked.

"None of us is leaving here, so it's easy to round up a top-notch team. The entire hospital's under quarantine. Meantime, the police are tracking down everybody who might have come in contact with Mr. Schumberg or his company, and they're bringing them here to be checked. Apparently they've already turned up six other cases among the people who've been calling in sick at his company. Their HMOs were treating them for everything from bronchitis to asthma. They have them down in the ER now as the initial intake area, but they'll be bringing them up to this floor for care."

"How is Mr. Schumberg?"

"Still in surgery. I'll be heading down to see what they bring out of him before we start on you. But what you have is much smaller. It will not be so hard to remove."

"How do you know that surgery will get it all?" I asked. "Apparently a radio tower can grow from just one nanomachine. How do you know that you won't have to cut this out of me today, then repeat the procedure again four days later, then again four days after that?"

"We don't," she said. "All I know is that what we can see now must come out. We'll cross other bridges if and when we have to."

I turned my head and covered my mouth to cough and decided to tell her the rest of what Mr. Schumberg had said. "It might be too late for all of us anyway," I said.

"Hang in there," she said. "We've been through a lot together, you and me. This is just the latest challenge."

"No, you don't understand. Has anyone told you how the government would control a level ten contamination, and that this might be a level ten?"

"I've heard," she said. She pulled up a chair and sat down. She looked mostly tired now, not angry. "The rumor mill is working overtime in this town, as you can imagine. We've got maybe a quarter of a million people trying to walk over the mountains since every other way out of the valley is closed. The police and the National Guard on the other side are just rounding them up and taking them to camps when they come down through the passes."

"But you didn't try to get out? Surely some are making it through. How can you stay here?"

"I have patients to care for and more on the way."

She stepped to the window and looked out at the city. "I don't think they'll drop bombs just yet," she said. "The medical community in these valleys is working furiously to discover how far the contagion has spread. Surely the government will wait till we've at least answered that question. Besides, they won't let me leave. No one can leave. Plenty of the staff has tried. This place is sealed tight. Believe me, if I could have had you and my other patients evacuated to the hospital in Cheyenne, I would have."

Having part of your lung removed is no fun. But having it cut out when you have pneumonia is the equivalent of medieval torture. Pneumonia makes you cough, and each cough after my surgery was agony. They kept me heavily sedated, so I did not know much except the pain until the day after the surgery. They had my bed positioned at a ninety-degree angle, so I was sitting when I woke up. There was a different man in the bed next to mine.

"Who are you?" I asked him, and he told me some name I can't remember.

When my doctor made rounds, I asked her what had happened to Mr. Schumberg. She was quiet for a time, then she took hold of my arm. "He died during surgery," she said. "I didn't want to tell you till after your own surgery."

I did not know what to say. I looked at the lilacs Mrs. Schumberg had brought me.

"Aren't you afraid of catching this?" I asked my doctor.

"Of course. But if I were afraid of catching my patients' troubles, I would never have become a doctor."

I wanted to send Mrs. Schumberg flowers. I imagined that she was still here in the hospital, quarantined like the rest of us. I wondered if the gift shop could find her and deliver them to her, but I felt too sick to call the gift shop then. At least Mrs. Schumberg and Ann were together.

My doctor showed me a picture of what they had cut out of my lungs. It looked like a black metal rectangle with a knob forming on one end. They'd had it incinerated.

I knew the hospital had become more crowded—it was much noisier outside my room—but I did not realize just how crowded it was until they took me to Radiology to x-ray my lungs. We could hardly move down the hallways. There were people sleeping in every available chair and others sleeping in sleeping bags on the floors. They had apparently quarantined the entire day and night shifts of doctors, nurses, and interns because many of the people I saw were medical personnel. But there were lots of other people as well just wandering the hallways. They all looked bewildered and tired.

They took my x-rays, then wheeled me back up to bed. After about an hour, my doctor came in with the x-rays in hand. She looked grim.

"It's growing back," she said. "Surgery is backed up, but I was able to call in a few favors and schedule you for surgery at four o'clock this afternoon."

"It won't stop it," I said. "You know that now."

She sat in the chair next to my bed. "What do you want me to do?" she asked. "We can't leave it inside you."

I thought for a minute. I imagined all of us with nanomachines consenting to euthanasia and having our bodies burned, but then I remembered something Mr. Schumberg had said. "High dose radiation might stop it," I said. I told my doctor what Mr. Schumberg had told me.

"How high is high?" she asked. "Wasn't he referring to hydrogen bombs?"

"Who knows?" I said. "But don't they use radiation in cancer treatment? The equipment must be here to expose me to it. What do we have to lose? Use me as a guinea pig. Find a way to stop this before they do something drastic."

She left without saying another word.

Early the next morning, they covered my head and lower body with lead, then they shot my chest full of radiation. Afterward, back in my room and bed, I had never felt so sick. My body was rigid and hot. For a time, I could not even blink my eyes.

"He's going into shock," I heard my doctor say. "Get more blankets in here. Hurry!"

I sat there waiting for the blankets, but the very first time I was able to blink my eyes again I threw up. It went everywhere. It was bloody like Mr. Schumberg's had been.

A team of cleaning ladies eventually came in, but Maria was not with them.

"Where's Maria?" I asked.

"Who's Maria?" my doctor asked.

I explained about the cleaning lady who had helped the night Mr. Schumberg had gotten sick.

"They've been checking everyone who entered this room," she said. "I'll make sure they've looked at her."

But Maria was not in the hospital. She did not answer her telephone. The police found her house empty, some of her things hurriedly packed and gone. She had not come to work the last two days, and even before the quarantine she had not called in to request sick or vacation time.

But by evening, they knew what had happened. Apparently Maria's papers had been forged. She had entered this country illegally. The INS had arrested her the morning after the shift during which she had cleaned this room. They had transported her that same day to the Mexican border and handed her over to officials in Nogales.

"Maria's deportation probably saves us from the bombs," was all my doctor said when she told me about it. "What would be the point now?"

Eventually I dozed off, and for the last time I was working to build walls. They were mostly high now in that dream, surfaced and smooth, and I could see people—or things, I could not be sure when I looked closely—walking along the tops of those walls. For some reason I knew not to look too closely or for too long. I held tightly to the rocks in my arms. I concentrated on my work.

When I came to the unfinished part of the wall and after I had handed my rocks up to men working above me, I could see out across the valley if I stood on tiptoe. It lay completely flat now, flatter than it had even been. It looked paved. There were no buildings. There were no roads. There were no habitations and nothing natural to be seen. The white paving on the valley floor shined brightly in the moonlight, and in the south something was eating at the mountains. I could not see the Oquirrhs. To the west, everything was completely flat and silent. Wind hissed over the smooth paving.

The next morning, x-rays showed that the anomaly in my left lung had not grown, and it did not grow the day after that either. The radiation had stopped it. They started treating everyone with it, and soon they found that lower doses repeated over several days worked just as well. I underwent surgery for the last time to remove the dead nano-construct in my lung.

They never did find Maria Consuela de Alvarez. But eventually, of course, the entire world knew everywhere she had gone in her last days, even what she had looked at and where she had turned her head. The bus the INS had transported her in and the bus she had taken to her village south of Nogales had both apparently been hot and without air-conditioning. They had ridden with the windows open. Maria had had a window seat on the right-hand side of the bus all the way from Salt Lake to Nogales, then on the left-hand side in Sonora. We know that, of course, because of all the bizarre machines that grew along the roadsides in Utah and Arizona and Sonora wherever she had coughed out the window. Mr. Schumberg's projects had combined with the other projects escaped from his laboratory to create monstrous machines they had never intended. The army and National Guard had quickly killed, if that's what you call it, the ones in America with radiation and fire.

My sister called from Minneapolis. She had been trying to call me, and had finally reached Alyson, home again after being stuck in traffic on the roads for a day and a half. "Why didn't you call me?" my sister asked.

"I didn't want to worry you."

"How can I not worry about you? You're my big brother. You used to take me to parties with your friends and made me feel older and grown up. You read all the Jane Austen novels to me and taught me how to dance. I'm flying out to take care of you as soon as they lift the quarantine."

And she did come. It was my sister who drove me home from the hospital. She was the first person I cooked the rigatoni pesto for.

My sister stayed for two weeks. We had long talks over coffee on the back porch, and we looked at pictures of when we were kids. I slept a lot. She took me to follow-up appointments with my doctor and with specialists from the CDC. One night she invited Alyson and her kids over and cooked dinner. She helped me manage the requests for interviews from all over the world including, of course, the one for this story about how I had met Maria. My sister bought me a new cap after my hair fell out from the radiation treatment.

Lawyers from all over the country were also contacting me. I did not join the class-action lawsuit—my lawyers felt I had a chance at a huge settlement on my own. The intern had been right. But if I lived to see money at the end of the litigation I wasn't sure what I would do with it. Take my sister to Paris, maybe. Or to Rome.

I had looked up Bernard Schumberg in the telephone book, of course, so I had Mrs. Schumberg's number and address, but I had hesitated to call to offer condolences. I had not sent flowers. Finally, the day before my sister was to fly home, I had her drive me to the Schumbergs'. Their house was on a shady street in a nice neighborhood on the east bench. It was a small turn-of-the-century Victorian. The yard was neat and well kept. The last of the lilacs were blooming in the back yard.

I carried a bouquet of carnations and went alone to the door and knocked.

After a moment, I heard someone inside. The door opened, and it was Mrs. Schumberg. Tears came at once to her eyes, and I could not keep them back either. I handed her the flowers and I wiped my eyes and she invited me in. She was wearing a scarf to hide her bald head. Of course she had had to have radiation treatments, I thought. How could she not have picked up the nanomachines?

I told her that I could not stay long, that my sister was waiting in the car. Mrs. Schumberg did not invite her in, so I knew that I had done the right thing by leaving my sister there. It was too soon for Mrs. Schumberg to see people.

We did not know what to say to each other. "He was a good man," she said finally.

"He loved you," I said. "He couldn't stand it if you weren't with him. You were so good to him."

I left quickly.

I bought all the books with photographs of the nanomachines in the deserts, but I keep looking at the pictures of what they turned into in Sonora. We mostly don't know what they were. We have ideas on some. They had longer to work in Sonora, so everything there was bigger and more elaborate. The plans of all those different projects in Mr. Schumberg's laboratory had combined in so many unexpected ways. In their short time, the nanomachines in Sonora had "learned" more than anyone could have predicted. Some of the constructs looked like nothing more than beautiful modern sculpture. Others blended into the landscape and could be found only with heat signatures. Some were enormous, clawed horrors lurking in side canyons that, had they lived, would have begun to walk about the land to hunt and take what they needed. None of them "lived" long.

But the barren white paving over what had once been Maria's village haunts me the most. It concealed an enormous transmitter that had been calling the stars for eight days before they killed it. No one has been able to crack the code of those transmissions. We don't know what it was saying. We don't know what it was calling. We don't know why its transmissions were beamed at only three stars in alternating order. We don't know what will happen because of it.

The world is mostly afraid of the answers to those questions. But I look at the pictures of that smooth paving and wonder. Inside that construct, part of whatever it was, was all that had made up Maria Consuela de Alvarez, a little woman who had found the courage to smuggle herself here to try to better her condition. She had taken a job no one else had wanted. She had come in the night to help sick people.

I don't know if any part of her could have survived to influence what was

happening to her and her village. I could not have influenced what was growing inside of me, I know that. But if the construct had listened to Maria before
it killed her, if it had tried to understand her (if it had had that ability), maybe
the transmissions were calling angels to Earth, not devils. I'd like to live long
enough to find out.

The cookie Monster

VERNOR VINGE

Born in Waukesha, Wisconsin, Vernor Vinge now lives in San Diego, California, where he is an associate professor of math sciences at San Diego State University. He sold his first story, "Apartness," to *New Worlds* in 1965; it immediately attracted a good deal of attention, was picked up for Donald A. Wollheim and Terry Carr's collaborative *World's Best Science Fiction* anthology the following year, and still strikes me as one of the strongest stories of that entire period. Since this impressive debut, he has become a frequent contributor to *Analog*; he has also sold to *Orbit*, *Far Frontiers*, *If*, *Stellar*, and other markets. His novella "True Names," which is famous in internet circles and among computer enthusiasts well outside of the usual limits of the genre, and is cited by some as having been the *real* progenitor of cyberpunk rather than William Gibson's *Neuromancer*, was a finalist for both the Nebula and Hugo Awards in 1981. His novel *A Fire Upon the Deep*, one of the most epic and sweeping of modern Space Operas, won him a Hugo Award in 1993; its sequel, *A Deepness in the Sky*, won him another Hugo Award in 2000, and his novella "Fast Times at Fairmont High" won another Hugo in 2003 . . . and these days Vinge is regarded as one of the best of the American "hard science" writers, along with people such as Greg Bear and Gregory Benford. His other books include the novels *Tatja Grimm's World*, *The Witling*, *The Peace War* and *Marooned in Realtime* (which have been released in an omnibus volume as *Across Realtime*), and the collections *True Names and Other Dangers* and *Threats and Other Promises*. His most recent book is the massive collection *The Collected Stories of Vernor Vinge*.

Vinge has become famous well outside normal genre circles in recent years for his speculations about "The Singularity" (the point waiting ahead for us all where technological change speeds up to *such* a degree that society becomes incomprehensible even to the people living in it)—a speculation that has been named a "Vingian Singularity" in his honor, and which has deeply influenced the work of most of the best of the new "hard SF" writers (especially noticeable in the work of writers such as Charles Stross and Cory Doctorow). In the thought-provoking novella that follows, Vinge gives us an unsettling glimpse of what it might be like to live in a post-singularity society, where life turns out to be quite challenging—and full of surprises.

S o how do you like the new job?"

Dixie Mae looked up from her keyboard and spotted a pimply face peering at her from over the cubicle partition.

"It beats flipping burgers, Victor," she said.

Victor bounced up so his whole face was visible. "Yeah? It's going to get old awfully fast."

Actually, Dixie Mae felt the same way. But doing customer support at LotsaTech was a real job, a foot in the door at the biggest high-tech company in the world. "Gimme a break, Victor! This is our first day." Well, it was the first day not counting the six days of product familiarization classes. "If you can't take this, you've got the attention span of a cricket."

"That's a mark of intelligence, Dixie Mae. I'm smart enough to know what's not worth the attention of a first-rate creative mind."

Grr. "Then your first-rate creative mind is going to be out of its gourd by the end of the summer."

Victor smirked. "Good point." He thought a second, then continued more quietly, "But see, um, I'm doing this to get material for my column in the *Bruin*. You know, big headlines like 'The New Sweatshops' or 'Death by Boredom'. I haven't decided whether to play it for laughs or go for heavy social consciousness. In any case,"—he lowered his voice another notch—"I'm bailing out of here, um, by the end of next week, thus suffering only minimal brain damage from the whole sordid experience."

"And you're not seriously helping the customers at all, huh, Victor? Just giving them hilarious misdirections?"

Victor's eyebrows shot up. "I'll have you know I'm being articulate and seriously helpful . . . at least for another day or two." The weasel grin crawled back onto his face. "I won't start being Bastard Consultant from Hell till right before I quit."

That figures. Dixie Mae turned back to her keyboard. "Okay, Victor. Meantime, how about letting me do the job I'm being paid for?"

Silence. Angry, insulted silence? No, this was more a leering, undressing-you-with-my-eyes silence. But Dixie Mae did not look up. She could tolerate such silence as long as the leerer was out of arm's reach.

After a moment, there was the sound of Victor dropping back into his chair in the next cubicle.

Ol' Victor had been a pain in the neck from the get-go. He was slick with words; if he wanted to, he could explain things as good as anybody Dixie Mae had ever met. At the same time, he kept rubbing it in how educated he was and what a dead-end this customer support gig was. Mr. Johnson—the guy running the familiarization course—was a great teacher, but smart-ass Victor had tested the man's patience all week long. Yeah, Victor really didn't belong here, but not for the reasons he bragged about.

It took Dixie Mae almost an hour to finish off seven more queries. One took some research, being a really bizarre question about Voxalot for Norwegian. Okay, this job would get old after a few days, but there was a virtuous feeling in helping people. And from Mr. Johnson's lectures, she knew that as long as she got the reply turned in by closing time this evening, she could spend the whole afternoon researching just how to make LotsaTech's vox program recognize Norwegian vowels.

Dixie Mae had never done customer support before this; till she took Prof. Reich's tests last week, her highest-paying job really had been flipping burgers. But like the world and your Aunt Sally, she had often been the *victim* of customer support. Dixie Mae would buy a new book or a cute dress, and it would break or wouldn't fit—and then when she wrote customer support, they wouldn't reply, or had useless canned answers, or just tried to sell her something more—all the time talking about how their greatest goal was serving the customer.

But now LotsaTech was turning all that around. Their top bosses had realized how important real humans were to helping real human customers. They were hiring hundreds and hundreds of people like Dixie Mae. They weren't paying very much, and this first week had been kinda tough since they were all cooped up here during the crash intro classes.

But Dixie Mae didn't mind. "LotsaTech is a lot of Tech." Before, she'd always thought that motto was stupid. But LotsaTech was *big*; it made IBM and Microsoft look like minnows. She'd been a little nervous about that, imagining that she'd end up in a room bigger than a football field with tiny office cubicles stretching away to the horizon. Well, Building 0994 did have tiny cubicles, but her team was just fifteen nice people—leaving Victor aside for the moment.

Their work floor had windows all the way around, a panoramic view of the Santa Monica mountains and the Los Angeles basin. And li'l ol' Dixie Mae Leigh had her a desk right beside one of those wide windows! *I'll bet there are CEO's who don't have a view as good as mine.* Here's where you could see a little of what the Lotsa in LotsaTech meant. Just outside of BO994 there were tennis courts and a swimming pool. Dozens of similar buildings were scattered across the hillside. A golf course covered the next hill over, and more company land lay beyond that. These guys had the money to buy the top off Runyon Canyon and plunk themselves down on it. And this was just the LA branch office.

Dixie Mae had grown up in Tarzana. On a clear day in the valley, you could see the Santa Monica mountains stretching off forever into the haze. They seemed beyond her reach, like something from a fairy tale. And now she was up here. Next week, she'd bring her binoculars to work, go over on the north slope, and maybe spot where her father still lived down there.

Meanwhile, back to work. The next six queries were easy, from people who hadn't even bothered to read the single page of directions that came with Voxalot. Letters like those would be hard to answer politely the thousandth time she saw them. But she would try—and today she practiced with cheerful specifics that stated the obvious and gently pointed the customers to where they could find more. Then came a couple of brain twisters. Damn. She wouldn't be able to finish those today. Mr. Johnson said "finish anything you start on the same day"—but maybe he would let her work on those first thing Monday morning. She really wanted to do well on the hard ones. Every day, there would be the same old dumb questions. But there would also be hard new questions. And eventually she'd get really, really good with Voxalot. More important, she'd get good about managing questions and organization. So what that she'd screwed the last seven years of her life and never made it through college? Little by little she would improve herself, till a few years from now her past stupidities wouldn't matter anymore. Some people had told her that such things weren't possible nowadays, that you really needed the college degree. But people had always been able to make it with hard work. Back in the twentieth century, lots of steno pool people managed it. Dixie Mae figured customer support was pretty much the same kind of starting point.

Nearby, somebody gave out a low whistle. Victor. Dixie Mae ignored him.

"Dixie Mae, you gotta see this."

Ignore him.

"I swear Dixie, this is a first. How did you do it? I got an incoming query for *you*, by name! Well, almost."

"What!? Forward it over here, Victor."

"No. Come around and take a look. I have it right in front of me."

Dixie Mae was too short to look over the partition. *Jeez.*

Three steps took her into the corridor. Ulysse Green poked her head out of her cubicle, an inquisitive look on her face. Dixie Mae shrugged and rolled her eyes, and Ulysse returned to her work. The sound of fingers on keys was like occasional raindrops (no Voxalots allowed in cubicle-land). Mr. Johnson had been around earlier, answering questions and generally making sure things were going okay. Right now he should be back in his office on the other side of the building; this first day, you hardly needed to worry about slackers. Dixie Mae felt a little guilty about making that a lie, but . . .

She popped into Victor's cubicle, grabbed a loose chair. "This better be good, Victor."

"Judge for yourself, Dixie Mae." He looked at his display. "Oops, I lost the window. Just a second." He dinked around with his mouse. "So, have you been putting your name on outgoing messages? That's the only way I can imagine this happenings—"

"No. I have not. I've answered twenty-two questions so far, and I've been AnnetteG all the way." The fake signature was built into her "send" key. Mr. Johnson said this was to protect employee privacy and give users a feeling of continuity even though follow-up questions would rarely come to the original responder. He didn't have to say that it was also to make sure that LotsaTech support people would be interchangeable, whether they were working out of the service center in Lahore or Londonderry—or Los Angeles. So far, that had been one of Dixie Mae's few disappointments about this job; she could never have an ongoing helpful relationship with a customer.

So what the devil was this all about?

"Ah! Here it is." Victor waved at the screen. "What do you make of it?"

The message had come in on the help address. It was in the standard layout enforced by the query acceptance page. But the "previous responder field" was not one of the house sigs. Instead it was:

Ditzie May Lay

"Grow up, Victor."

Victor raised his hands in mock defense, but he had seen her expression, and some of the smirk left his face. "Hey, Dixie Mae, don't kill the messenger. This is just what came in."

"No way. The server-side script would have rejected an invalid responder name. You faked this."

For a fleeting moment, Victor looked uncertain. *Hah!* thought Dixie Mae. She had been paying attention during Mr. Johnson's lectures; she knew more about what was going on here than Victor-the-great-mind. And so his little joke had fallen flat on its rear end. But Victor regrouped and gave a weak smile. "It wasn't me. How would I know about this, er, nickname of yours?"

"Yes," said Dixie Mae, "it takes real genius to come up with such a clever play on words."

"Honest, Dixie Mae, it wasn't me. Hell, I don't even know how to use our form editor to revise header fields."

Now *that* claim had the ring of truth.

"What's happening?"

They looked up, saw Ulysse standing at the entrance to the cubicle.

Victor gave her a shrug. "It's Dit—Dixie Mae. Someone here at LotsaTech is jerking her around."

Ulysse came closer and bent to read from the display. "Yech. So what's the message?"

Dixie Mae reached across the desk and scrolled down the display. The return address was lusting925@freemail.sg. The topic choice was "Voice Formatting." They got lots on that topic; Voxalot format control wasn't quite as intuitive as the ads would like you to believe.

But this was by golly *not* a follow-up on anything Dixie Mae had answered:

. . .

HEY THERE, HONEY CHILE! I'LL BE TRULY GRATEFUL IF YOU WOULD TELL ME HOW TO PUT THE FOLLOWING INTO ITALICS:

"REMEMBER THE TARZANARAMA TREE HOUSE? THE ONE YOU SET ON FIRE? IF YOU'D LIKE TO START A MUCH BIGGER FIRE, THEN FIGURE OUT HOW I KNOW ALL THIS. A BIG CLUE IS THAT 999 IS 666 SPELLED UPSIDE DOWN."

I'VE TRIED EVERYTHING AND I CAN'T SET THE ABOVE PROPOSITION INTO INDENTED ITALICS—LEASTWISE WITHOUT FINGERING. PLEASE HELP.

ACHING FOR SOME OF YOUR SOUTHRON HOSPITALITY, I REMAIN YOUR VERY BESTEST FIEND,

—LUSTING (FOR YOU DEEPLY)

Ulysse's voice was dry: "So, Victor, you've figured how to edit incoming forms."

"God damn it, I'm innocent!"

"Sure you are." Ulysse's white teeth flashed in her black face. The three little words held a world of disdain.

Dixie Mae held up her hand, waving them both to silence. "I . . . don't know. There's something real strange about this mail." She stared at the message body for several seconds. A big ugly chill was growing in her middle. Mom and Dad had built her that tree house when she was seven years old. Dixie Mae had loved it. For two years she was Tarzana of Tarzana. But the name of the tree house—Tarzanarama—had been a secret. Dixie Mae had been nine years old when she torched that marvelous tree house. It had been a terrible accident. Well, a world-class temper tantrum, actually. But she had never meant the fire to get so far out of control. The fire had darn near burned down their real house, too. She had been a scarifyingly well-behaved little girl for almost two years after that incident.

Ulysse was giving the mail a careful read. She patted Dixie Mae on the shoulder. "Whoever this is, he certainly doesn't sound friendly."

Dixie Mae nodded. "This weasel is pushing every button I've got." Including her curiosity. Dad was the only living person that knew who had started the fire, but it was going on four years since he'd had any address for his daughter—and Daddy would never have taken this sex-creep, disrespecting tone.

Victor glanced back and forth between them, maybe feeling hurt that he was no longer the object of suspicion. "So who do you think it is?"

Don Williams craned his head over the next partition. "Who is what?"

Given another few minutes, and they'd have everyone on the floor with some bodily part stuck into Victor's cubicle.

Ulysse said, "Unless you're deaf, you know most of it, Don. Someone is messing with us."

"Well then, report it to Johnson. This is our first day, people. It's not a good day to get sidetracked."

That brought Ulysse down to earth. Like Dixie Mae, she regarded this LotsaTech job as her last real chance to break into a profession.

"Look," said Don. "It's already lunch time."—Dixie Mae glanced at her watch. It really was!—"We can talk about this in the cafeteria, then come back and give Great Lotsa a solid afternoon of work. And then we'll be done with our first week!" Williams had been planning a party down at his folks' place for tonight. It would be their first time off the LotsaTech campus since they took the job.

"Yeah!" said Ulysse. "Dixie Mae, you'll have the whole weekend to figure out who's doing this—and plot your revenge."

Dixie Mae looked again at the impossible "previous responder field." "I . . . don't know. This looks like it's something happening right here on the LotsaTech campus." She stared out Victor's picture window. It was the same view as from her cubicle, of course—but now she was seeing everything with a different mind set. Somewhere in the beautiful country-club buildings, there was a real sleaze ball. And he was playing guessing games with her.

Everybody was quiet for a second. Maybe that helped—Dixie Mae realized just what she was looking at: the next lodge down the hill. From here you could only see the top of its second story. Like all the buildings on the campus, it had a four-digit identification number made of gold on every corner. That one was Building 0999.

A big clue is that 999 is just 666 spelled upside down. "Jeez, Ulysse. Look: 999." Dixie Mae pointed down the hillside.

"It could be a coincidence."

"No, it's too pat." She glanced at Victor. This really was the sort of thing someone like him would set up. *But whoever wrote that letter just knew too much.* "Look, I'm going to skip lunch today and take a little walk around the campus."

"That's crazy," said Don. "LotsaTech is an open place, but we're not supposed to be wandering into other project buildings."

"Then they can turn me back."

"Yeah, what a great way to start out with the new job," said Don. "I don't think you three realize what a good deal we have here. I know that none of you have worked a customer support job before." He looked around challengingly. "Well I have. This is heaven. We've got our own friggin' offices, onsite tennis courts and health club. We're being treated like million-dollar system designers. We're being given all the time we need to give top-notch advice to the customers. What LotsaTech is trying to do here is revolutionary! And you dips are just going to piss it away." Another all-around glare. "Well, do what you want, but I'm going to lunch."

There was a moment of embarrassed silence. Ulysse stepped out of the cubicle and watched Don and others trickle away toward the stairs. Then she was back. "I'll come with you, Dixie Mae, but . . . have you thought Don may be right? Maybe you could just postpone this till next week?" Unhappiness was written all over her face. Ulysse was a lot like Dixie Mae, just more sensible.

Dixie Mae shook her head. She figured it would be at least fifteen minutes before her common sense could put on the brakes.

"I'll come, Dixie Mae," said Victor. "Yeah. . . . This could be an interesting story."

Dixie Mae smiled at Ulysse and reached out her hand. "It's okay, Ulysse. You should go to lunch." The other looked uncertain. "Really. If Mr. Johnson asks about me missing lunch, it would help if you were there to set him right about what a steady person I am."

"Okay, Dixie Mae. I'll do that." She wasn't fooled, but this way it really was okay.

Once she was gone, Dixie Mae turned back to Victor. "And you. I want a printed copy of that freakin' email."

They went out a side door. There was a soft-drink and candy machine on the porch. Victor loaded up on "expeditionary supplies" and the two started down the hill.

"Hot day," said Victor, mumbling around a mouth full of chocolate bar.

"Yeah." The early part of the week had been all June Gloom. But the usual overcast had broken, and today was hot and sunny—and Dixie Mae suddenly realized how pleasantly air-conditioned life had been in the LotsaTech "sweatshop." Common sense hadn't yet reached the brakes, but it was getting closer.

Victor washed the chocolate down with a Dr. Fizzz and flipped the can behind the oleanders that hung close along the path. "So who do you think is behind that letter? Really?"

"I don't *know*, Victor! Why do you think I'm risking my job to find out?"

Victor laughed. "Don't worry about losing the job, Dixie Mae. Heh. There's no way it could have lasted even through the summer." He gave his usual superior-knowledge grin.

"You're an idiot, Victor. Doing customer support *right* will be a billion dollar winner."

"Oh, maybe . . . if you're on the right side of it." He paused as if wondering what to tell her. "But for you, look: support costs money. Long ago, the Public Spoke about how much they were willing to pay." He paused, like he was trying to put together a story that she could understand. "Yeah . . . and even if you're right, your vision of the project is doomed. You know why?"

Dixie Mae didn't reply. His reason would be something about the crappy quality of the people who had been hired.

Sure enough, Victor continued: "I'll tell you why. And this is the surprise kink that's going to make my articles for the *Bruin* really shine: Maybe LotsaTech has its corporate heart in the right place. That would be surprising considering how they brutalized Microsoft. But maybe they've let this bizarre idealism go too far. Heh. For anything long-term, they've picked the wrong employees."

Dixie Mae kept her cool. "We took all sorts of psych tests. You don't think Professor Reich knows what he's doing?"

"Oh, I bet he knows what he's doing. But what if LotsaTech isn't using his results? Look at us. There are some—such as yours truly—who are way overeducated. I'm closing in on a master's degree in journalism; it's clear I won't be around for long. Then there's people like Don and Ulysse. They have the right level of education for customer support, but they're too smart. Yes, Ulysse talks about doing this job so well that her talent is recognized, and she is a diligent sort. But I'll bet that even she couldn't last a summer. As for some of the others . . . well, may I be frank, Dixie Mae?"

What saved him from a fist in the face was that Dixie Mae had never managed to be really angry about more than one thing at once. "Please *do* be frank, Victor."

"You talk the same game plan as Ulysse—but I'll bet your multiphasic shows you have the steadiness of mercury fulminate. Without this interesting email from Mr. Lusting, you might be good for a week, but sooner or later you'd run into something so infuriating that direct action was required—and you'd be bang out on your rear."

Dixie Mae pretended to mull this over. "Well, yes," she said. "After all, you're still going to be here next week, right?"

He laughed. "I rest my case. But seriously, Dixie Mae, this is what I mean about the personnel situation here. We have a bunch of bright and motivated people, but their motivations are all over the map, and most of their enthusiasm can't be sustained for any realistic span of time. Heh. So I guess the only rational explanation—and frankly, I don't think it would work—is that LotsaTech figures . . ."

He droned on with some theory about how LotsaTech was just looking for some quick publicity and a demonstration that high-quality customer support could win back customers in a big way. Then after they flushed all these unreliable new hires, they could throttle back into something cheaper for the long term.

But Dixie Mae's attention was far away. On her left was the familiar view of Los Angeles. To her right, the ridgeline was just a few hundred yards away. From the crest you could probably see down into the valley, even pick out streets in Tarzana. Someday, it would be nice to go back there, maybe prove to Dad that she could keep her temper and make something of herself. *All my life, I've been screwing up like today.* But that letter from "Lusting" was like finding a burglar in your bedroom. The guy knew too much about her that he shouldn't have known, and he had mocked her background and her family. Dixie Mae had grown up in Southern California, but she'd been born in Georgia—and she was proud of her roots. Maybe Daddy never realized that, since she was running around rebelling most of the time. He and Mom always said she'd eventually settle down. But then she fell in love with the wrong kind of person—and it was her folks who'd gone ballistic. Words Were Spoken. And even though things hadn't worked out with her new love, there was no way she could go back. By then Mom had died. Now, *I swear I'm not going back to Daddy till I can show I've made something of myself.*

So why was she throwing away her best job in ages? She slowed to a stop and just stood there in the middle of the walkway; common sense had finally gotten to the brakes. But they had walked almost all the way to 0999. Much of the building was hidden behind twisty junipers, but you could see down a short flight of stairs to the ground level entrance.

We should go back. She pulled the "Lusting" email out of her pocket and glared at it for a second. *Later. You can follow up on this later.* She read the mail again. The letters blurred behind tears of rage, and she dithered in the hot summer sunlight.

Victor made an impatient noise. "Let's go, kiddo." He pushed a chocolate bar into her hand. "Get your blood sugar out of the basement."

They went down the concrete steps to B0999's entrance. *Just a quick look,* Dixie Mae had decided.

Beneath the trees and the overhang, all was cool and shady. They peered through the ground floor windows, into empty rooms. Victor pushed open the door. The layout looked about the same as in their own building, except that B0999 wasn't really finished: There was the smell of Carpenter Nail in the air, and the lights and wireless nodes sat naked on the walls.

The place was occupied. She could hear people talking up on the main floor, what was cubicle-city back in B0994. She took a quick hop up the stairs, peeked in—no cubicles here. As a result, the place looked cavernous. Six or eight tables had been pushed together in the middle of the room. A dozen people looked up at their entrance.

"Aha!" boomed one of them. "More warm bodies. Welcome, welcome!"

They walked toward the tables. Don and Ulysse had worried about violating corporate rules and project secrecy. They needn't have bothered. These people looked almost like squatters. Three of them had their legs propped up on the tables. Junk food and soda cans littered the tables.

"Programmers?" Dixie Mae muttered to Victor.

"Heh. No, these look more like . . . graduate students."

The loud one had red hair snatched back in a ponytail. He gave Dixie Mae a broad grin. "We've got a couple of extra display flats. Grab some seating." He jerked a thumb toward the wall and a stack of folding chairs. "With you two, we may actually be able to finish today!"

Dixie Mae looked uncertainly at the display and keyboard that he had just lit up. "But what—"

"Cognitive Science 301. The final exam. A hundred dollars a question, but we have 107 bluebooks to grade, and Gerry asked mainly essay questions."

Victor laughed. "You're getting a hundred dollars for each bluebook?"

"For each question in each bluebook, man. But don't tell. I think Gerry is funding this out of money that LotsaTech thinks he's spending on research." He waved at the nearly empty room, in this nearly completed building.

Dixie Mae leaned down to look at the display, the white letters on a blue background. It was a standard bluebook, just like at Valley Community College. Only here the questions were complete nonsense, such as:

7. COMPARE AND CONTRAST COGNITIVE DISSONANCE IN OPERANT CONDITIONING WITH MINSKY-LOÈVE ATTENTION MAINTENANCE. OUTLINE AN ALGORITHM FOR CONSTRUCTING THE ASSOCIATED ISOMORPHISM.

"So," said Dixie Mae, "what's cognitive science?"

The grin disappeared from the other's face. "Oh, Christ. You're not here to help with the grading?"

Dixie Mae shook her head. Victor said, "It shouldn't be too hard. I've had some grad courses in psych."

The redhead did not look encouraged. "Does anyone know this guy?"

"I do," said a girl at the far end of all the tables. "That's Victor Smaley. He's a journalism grad, and not very good at that."

Victor looked across the tables. "Hey, Mouse! How ya doing?"

The redhead looked beseechingly at the ceiling. "I do not need these distractions!" His gaze came down to the visitors. "Will you two just please go away?"

"No way," said Dixie Mae. "I came here for a reason. Someone—probably someone here in Building 0999—is messing with our work in Customer Support. I'm going to find out who." *And give them some free dental work.*

"Look. If we don't finish grading the exam today, Gerry Reich's going to make us come back tomorrow and—"

"I don't think that's true, Graham," said a guy sitting across the table. "Prof. Reich's whole point was that we should not feel time pressure. This is an experiment, comparing time-bounded grading with complete individualization."

"Yes!" said Graham the redhead. "That's exactly why Reich would lie about it. 'Take it easy, make good money,' he says. But I'll bet that if we don't finish today, he'll screw us into losing the weekend."

He glared at Dixie Mae. She glared back. Graham was going to find out just what stubborn and willful really meant. There was a moment of silence and then—

"I'll talk to them, Graham." It was the woman at the far end of the tables.

"Argh. Okay, but not here!"

"Sure, we'll go out on the porch." She beckoned Dixie Mae and Victor to follow her out the side door.

"And hey," called Graham as they walked out, "don't take all day, Ellen. We need you here."

The porch on 0999 had a bigger junk-food machine than back at Customer Support. Dixie Mae didn't think that made up for no cafeteria, but Ellen Garcia didn't seem to mind. "We're only going to be here this one day. *I'm* not coming back on Saturday."

Dixie Mae bought herself a sandwich and soda and they all sat down on some beat-up lawn furniture.

"So what do you want to know?" said Ellen.

"See, Mouse, we're following up on the weirdest—"

Ellen waved Victor silent, her expression pretty much the same as all Victor's female acquaintances. She looked expectantly at Dixie Mae.

"Well, my name is Dixie Mae Leigh. This morning we got this email at our customer support address. It looks like a fake. And there are things about it that—" she handed over the hard copy.

Ellen's gaze scanned down. "Kind of fishy dates," she said to herself. Then she stopped, seeing the "To:" header. She glanced up at Dixie Mae. "Yeah, this is abuse. I used to see this kind of thing when I was a Teaching Assistant. Some guy would start hitting on a girl in my class." She eyed Victor speculatively.

"Why does everybody suspect me?" he said.

"You should be proud, Victor. You have such a reliable reputation." She shrugged. "But actually, this isn't quite your style." She read on. "The rest is smirky lascivious, but otherwise it doesn't mean anything to me."

"It means a lot to *me*," said Dixie Mae. "This guy is talking about things that nobody should know."

"Oh?" She went back to the beginning and stared at the printout some more. "I don't know about secrets in the message body, but one of my hobbies is rfc9822 headers. You're right that this is all scammed up. The message number and ident strings are too long; I think they may carry added content."

She handed back the email. "There's not much more I can tell you. If you want to give me a copy, I could crunch on those header strings over the weekend."

"Oh. . . . Okay, thanks." It was more solid help than anyone had offered so far, but—"Look Ellen, the main thing I was hoping for was some clues here in Building 0999. The letter pointed me here. I run into . . . abusers sometimes, myself. I don't let them get away with it! I'd bet money that whoever this is, he's one of those graders." *And he's probably laughing at us right now.*

Ellen thought a second and then shook her head. "I'm sorry, Dixie Mae. I know these people pretty well. Some of them are a little strange, but they're not bent like this. Besides, we didn't know we'd be here till yesterday afternoon. And today we haven't had time for mischief."

"Okay," Dixie Mae forced a smile. "I appreciate your help." She would give Ellen a copy of the letter and go back to Customer Support, just slightly better off than if she had behaved sensibly in the first place.

Dixie Mae started to get up, but Victor leaned forward and set his notepad on the table between them. "That email had to come from somewhere. Has anyone here been acting strange, Mousy?"

Ellen glared at him, and after a second he said, "I mean 'Ellen.' You know I'm just trying to help out Dixie Mae here. Oh yeah, and maybe get a good story for the *Bruin*."

Ellen shrugged. "Graham told you; we're grading on the side for Gerry Reich."

"Huh." Victor leaned back. "Ever since I've been at UCLA, Reich has had a reputation for being an operator. He's got big government contracts and all this consulting at LotsaTech. He tries to come across as a one-man supergenius, but actually it's just money, um, buying lots and lots of peons. So what do you think he's up to?"

Ellen shrugged. "Technically, I bet Gerry is misusing his contacts with LotsaTech. But I doubt if they care; they really like him." She brightened. "And I approve of what Prof. Reich is doing with this grading project. When I was a TA, I wished there was some way that I could make a day-long project out of reading each student's exam. That was an impossible wish; there was just never enough time. But with his contacts here at LotsaTech, Gerry Reich has come close to doing it. He's paying some pretty sharp grad students very good money to grade and comment on every single essay question. Time is no object, he's telling us. The students in these classes are going to get really great feedback."

"This guy Reich keeps popping up," said Dixie Mae. "He was behind the testing program that selected Victor and me and the others for customer support."

"Well, Victor's right about him. Reich is a manipulator. I know he's been running tests all this week. He grabbed all of Olson Hall for the operation. We didn't know what it was for until afterwards. He nailed Graham and the rest of our gang for this one-day grading job. It looks like he has all sorts of projects."

"Yeah, we took our tests at Olson Hall, too." There had been a small up-front payment, and hints of job prospects. . . . And Dixie Mae had ended up with maybe the best job offer she'd ever had. "But we did that last week."

"It can't be the same place. Olson Hall is a gym."

"Yes, that's what it looked like to me."

"It was used for the NCAA eliminations last week."

Victor reached for his notepad. "Whatever. We gotta be going, Mouse."

"Don't 'Mouse' me, Victor! The NCAA elims were the week of 4 June. I did Gerry's questionnaire yesterday, which was Thursday, 14 June."

"I'm sorry, Ellen," said Dixie Mae. "Yesterday was Thursday, but it was the 21st of June."

Victor made a calming gesture. "It's not a big deal."

Ellen frowned, but suddenly she wasn't arguing. She glanced at her watch. "Let's see your notepad, Victor. What date does it say?"

"It says, June . . . huh. It says June 15."

Dixie Mae looked at her own watch. The digits were so precise, and a week wrong: Fri Jun 15 12:31:18 PDT 2012. "Ellen, I looked at my watch before we walked over here. It said June 22nd."

Ellen leaned on the table and took a close look at Victor's notepad. "I'll bet it did. But both your watch and the notepad get their time off the building utilities. Here you're getting set by our local clock—and you're getting the truth."

Now Dixie Mae was getting mad. "Look, Ellen. Whatever the time service says, *I* would not have made up a whole extra week of my life." All those product-familiarization classes.

"No, you wouldn't." Ellen brought her heels back on the edge of her chair. For a long moment, she didn't say anything, just stared through the haze at the city below.

Finally she said: "You know, Victor, you should be pleased."

"Why is that?" suspiciously.

"You may have stumbled into a real, world-class news story. Tell me. During this extra week of life you've enjoyed, how often have you used your phone?"

Dixie Mae said, "Not at all. Mr. Johnson—he's our instructor—said that we're deadzoned till we get through the first week."

Ellen nodded. "So I guess they didn't expect the scam to last more than a week. See, we are not deadzoned here. LotsaTech has a pretty broad embargo on web access, but I made a couple of phone calls this morning."

Victor gave her a sharp look. "So where do you think the extra week came from?"

Ellen hesitated. "I think Gerry Reich has gone beyond where the UCLA human subjects committee would ever let him go. You guys probably spent one night in drugged sleep, being pumped chock full of LotsaTech product trivia."

"Oh! You mean . . . Just-in-Time Training?" Victor tapped away at his notepad. "I thought that was years away."

"It is if you play by the FDA's rules. But there are meds and treatments that can speed up learning. Just read the journals and you'll see that in another year or two, they'll be a scandal as big as sports drugs ever were. I think Gerry has just jumped the gun with something that is very, *very* effective. You have no side-effects. You have all sorts of new, specialized knowledge—even if it's about a throwaway topic. And apparently you have detailed memories of life experience that *never* happened."

Dixie Mae thought back over the last week. There had been no strangeness about her experience at Olson Hall: the exams, the job interview. True the johns were fantastically clean—like a hospital, now that she thought about it. She had only visited them once, right after she accepted the job offer. And then she had . . . done what? Taken a bus directly out to LotsaTech . . . without even going back to her apartment? After that, everything was clear again. She could remember jokes in the Voxalot classes. She could remember meals, and late night talks with Ulysse about what they might do with this great opportunity. "It's brainwashing," she finally said.

Ellen nodded. "It looks like Gerry has gone way, way too far on this one."

"And he's stupid, too. Our team is going to a party tonight, downtown. All of a sudden, there'll be sixteen people who'll know what's been done to them. We'll be mad as—" Dixie Mae noticed Ellen's pitying look.

"Oh." So tonight instead of partying, their customer support team would be in a drugged stupor, *un*remembering the week that never was. "We won't remember a thing, will we?"

Ellen nodded. "My guess is you'll be well-paid, with memories of some one-day temp job here at LotsaTech."

"Well, that's not going to happen," said Victor. "I've got a story and I've got a grudge. I'm not going back."

"We have to warn the others."

Victor shook his head. "Too risky."

Dixie Mae gave him a glare.

Ellen Garcia hugged her knees for a moment. "If this were just you, Victor, I'd be sure you were putting me on." She looked at Dixie Mae for a second. "Let me see that email again."

She spread it out on the table. "LotsaTech has its share of defense and security contracts. I'd hate to think that they might try to shut us up if they knew we were onto them." She whistled an ominous tune. "Paranoia rages. . . . Have you thought that this email might be someone trying to tip you off about what's going on?"

Victor frowned. "Who, Ellen?" When she didn't answer, he said, "So what do you think we should do?"

Ellen didn't look up from the printout. "Mainly, try not to act like idiots. All we really know is that someone has played serious games with your heads. Our first priority is to get us all out of LotsaTech, with you guys free of medical side effects. Our second priority is to blow the whistle on Gerry or . . ." She was reading the mail headers again, ". . . or whoever is behind this."

Dixie Mae said, "I don't think we know enough not to act like idiots."

"Good point. Okay, I'll make a phone call, an innocuous message that should mean something to the police if things go really bad. Then I'll talk to the others in our grading team. We won't say anything while we're still at Lotsa-Tech, but once away from here we'll scream long and loud. You two . . . it might be safest if you just lie low till after dark and we graders get back into town."

Victor was nodding.

Dixie Mae pointed at the mystery email. "What was it you just noticed, Ellen?"

"Just a coincidence, I think. Without a large sample, you start seeing phantoms."

"Speak."

"Well, the mailing address, 'lusting925@freemail.sg'. Building 0925 is on the hill crest thataway."

"You can't see that from where we started."

"Right. It's like 'Lusting' had to get you *here* first. And that's the other thing. Prof. Reich has a senior graduate student named Rob Lusk."

Lusk? Lusting? The connection seemed weak to Dixie Mae. "What kind of a guy is he?"

"Rob's not a particularly friendly fellow, but he's about two sigmas smarter than the average grad student. He's the reason Gerry has the big reputation for hardware. Gerry has been using him for five or six years now, and I bet Rob is getting desperate to graduate." She broke off. "Look. I'm going to go inside and tell Graham and the others about this. Then we'll find a place for you to hide for the rest of the day."

She started toward the door.

"I'm not going to hide out," said Dixie Mae.

Ellen hesitated. "Just till closing time. You've seen the rent-a-cops at the main gate. This is not a place you can simply stroll out of. But my group will have no trouble going home this evening. As soon as we're off-site, we'll raise such a stink that the press and police will be back here. You'll be safe at home in no time."

Victor was nodding. "Ellen's right. In fact, it would be even better if we don't spread the story to the other graders. There's no telling—"

"I'm not going to hide out!" Dixie Mae looked up the hill. "I'm going to check out 0925."

"That's crazy, Dixie Mae! You're guaranteed safe if you just hide till the end of the work day—and then the cops can do better investigating than anything you could manage. You do what Ellen says!"

"No one tells me what to do, Victor!" said Dixie Mae, while inside she was thinking, *Yeah, what I'm doing is a little bit like the plot of a cheap game: teenagers enter haunted house, and then split up to be murdered in pieces . . .*

But Ellen Garcia was making assumptions, too. Dixie Mae glared at both of them. "I'm following up on this email."

Ellen gave her a long look. Whether it was contemptuous or thoughtful wasn't clear. "Just wait for me to tell Graham, okay?"

Twenty minutes later, the three of them were outdoors again, walking up the long grade toward Building 0925.

Graham the Red might be a smart guy, but he turned out to be a fool, too. He was sure that the calendar mystery was just a scam cooked up by Dixie Mae and Victor. Ellen wasn't that good at talking to him—and the two customer support winkies were beneath his contempt. Fortunately, most of the other graders had been willing to listen. One of them also poked an unpleasant hole in all their assumptions: "So if it's that serious, wouldn't Gerry have these two under surveillance? You know, the Conspiracy Gestapo could arrive any second." There'd been a moment of apprehensive silence as everyone waited the arrival of bad guys with clubs.

In the end, everyone including Graham had agreed to keep their mouths shut till after work. Several of them had friends they made cryptic phone calls to, just in case. Dixie Mae could tell that most of them tilted toward Ellen's point of view, but however smart they were, they really didn't want to cross Graham.

Ellen, on the other hand, was *persona non grata* for trying to mess up Graham's schedule. She finally lost her temper with the redheaded jerk.

So now Ellen, Victor, and Dixie Mae were on the yellow brick road—in this case, the asphalt econo-cart walkway—leading to Building 0925.

The LotsaTech campus was new and underpopulated, but there *were* other people around. Just outside of 0999, they ran into a trio of big guys wearing gray blazers like the cops at the main entrance. Victor grabbed Dixie Mae's arm. "Just act natural," he whispered.

They ambled past, Victor giving a gracious nod. The three hardly seemed to notice.

Victor released Dixie Mae's arm. "See? You just have to be cool."

Ellen had been walking ahead. She dropped back so they were three abreast. "Either we're being toyed with," she said, "or they haven't caught on to us."

Dixie Mae touched the email in her pocket. "Well, *somebody* is toying with us."

"You know, that's the biggest clue we have. I still think it could be somebody trying to—"

Ellen fell silent as a couple of management types came walking the other way. These paid them even less attention than the company cops had.

"—it could be somebody trying to help us."

"I guess," said Dixie Mae. "More likely it's some sadist using stuff they learned while I was drugged up."

"Ug. Yeah." They batted around the possibilities. It was strange. Ellen Garcia was as much fun to talk to as Ulysse, even though she had to be about five times smarter than either Ulysse or Dixie Mae.

Now they were close enough to see the lower windows of 0925. This place was a double-sized version of 0999 or 0994. There was a catering truck pulled up at the ground level. Beyond a green-tinted windbreak they could see couples playing tennis on the courts south of the building.

Victor squinted. "Strange. They've got some kind of blackout on the windows."

"Yeah. We should at least be able to see the strip lights in the ceiling."

They drifted off the main path and walked around to where they wouldn't be seen from the catering truck. Even up close, down under the overhang, the windows looked just like those on the other buildings. But it wasn't just dark inside. There was nothing but blackness. The inside of the glass was covered with black plastic like they put on closed storefronts.

Victor whipped out his notepad.

"No phone calls, Victor."

"I want to send out a live report, just in case someone gets really mad about us being here."

"I told you, they've got web access embargoed. Besides, just calling from here would trigger 911 locator logic."

"Just a short call, to—"

He looked up and saw that the two women were standing close. "—ah, okay. I'll just use it as a local cam."

Dixie Mae held out her hand. "Give me the notepad, Victor. We'll take the pictures."

For a moment it looked like he was going refuse. Then he saw how her other hand was clenched into a fist. And maybe he remembered the lunchtime stories she had told during the week. *The week that never was?* Whatever the reason, he handed the notepad over to her. "You think I'm working for the bad guys?" he said.

"No," Dixie Mae said (65 percent truthfully, but declining), "I just don't think you'll always do what Ellen suggests. This way we'll get the pictures, but safely." *Because of my superior self control. Yeah.*

She started to hand the notepad to Ellen, but the other shook her head. "Just keep a record, Dixie Mae. You'll get it back later, Victor."

"Oh. Okay, but I want first xmit rights." He brightened. "You'll be my cameragirl, Dixie. Just come back on me anytime I have something important to say."

"Will do, Victor." She panned the notepad camera in a long sweep, away from him.

No one bothered them as they walked halfway around the ground floor. The blackout job was very thorough, but just as at buildings 0994 and 0999, there was an ordinary door with an old-fashioned card swipe.

Ellen took a closer look. "We disabled the locks on 0999 just for the fun of it. Somehow I don't think these black-plastic guys are that easygoing."

"I guess this is as far as we go," said Victor.

Dixie Mae stepped close to the door and gave it push. There was no error beep, no alarms. The door just swung open.

Looks of amazement were exchanged.

Five seconds later they were still standing at the open doorway. What little they could see looked like your typical LotsaTech ground floor. "We should shut the door and go back," said Victor. "We'll be caught red-handed standing here."

"Good point." Ellen stepped inside, followed perforce by Victor, and then Dixie Mae taking local video.

"Wait! Keep the door open, Dixie Mae."

"Jeez."

"This is like an airlock!" They were in a tiny room. Above waist height, its walls were clear glass. There was another door on the far end of the little room.

Ellen walked forward. "I had a summer job at Livermore last year. They have catch boxes like this. You walk inside easy enough—and then there are armed guards all around, politely asking you if you're lost." There were no guards visible here. Ellen pressed on the inner door. Locked. She reached up to the latch mechanism. It looked like cheap plastic. "This should not work," she said, even as she fiddled at it.

They could hear voices, but from upstairs. Down here, there was no one to be seen. Some of the layout was familiar, though. If this had been Building 0994, the hallway on the right would lead to restrooms, a small cafeteria, and a temporary dormitory.

Ellen hesitated and stood listening. She looked back at them. "That's strange. That sounds like . . . Graham!"

"Can you just break the latch, Ellen?" *We should go upstairs and strangle the two-faced weasel with his own ponytail.*

Another sound. A door opening! Dixie Mae looked past Ellen and saw a guy coming out of the men's room. Dixie Mae managed to grab Victor, and the two of them dropped behind the lower section of the holding cell.

"Hey, Ellen," said the stranger, "you look a bit peaked. Is Graham getting on your nerves, too?"

Ellen gave a squeaky laugh. "Y-yeah . . . so what else is new?"

Dixie Mae twisted the notepad and held it so the camera eye looked through the glass. In the tiny screen, she could see that the stranger was smiling. He was dressed in tee-shirt and knee-pants and he had some kind of glittering badge on a loop around his neck.

Ellen's mouth opened and shut a couple of times, but nothing came out. *She doesn't know this guy from Adam.*

The stranger was still clueless, but—"Hey, where's your badge?"

"Oh . . . damn. I must have left in the john," said Ellen. "And now I've locked myself out."

"You know the rules," he said, but his tone was not threatening. He did something on his side of the door. It opened and Ellen stepped through, blocking the guy's view of what was behind her.

"I'm sorry. I, uh, I got flustered."

"That's okay. Graham will eventually shut up. I just wish he'd pay more attention to what the professionals are asking of him."

Ellen nodded. "Yeah, I hear you!" Like she was really, really agreeing with him.

"Y'see, Graham's not splitting the topics properly. The idea is to be both broad *and* deep."

Ellen continued to make understanding noises. The talkative stranger was full of details about some sort of a NSA project, but he was totally ignorant of the three intruders.

There were light footsteps on the stairs, and a familiar voice. "Michael, how long are you going to be? I want to—" The voice cut off in a surprised squeak.

On the notepad display, Dixie Mae could see two brown-haired girls staring at each other with identical expressions of amazement. They sidled around each other for a moment, exchanging light slaps. It wasn't fighting . . . it was as if each thought the other was some kind of trick video. *Ellen Garcia, meet Ellen Garcia.*

The stranger—Michael?—stared with equal astonishment, first at one Ellen and then the other. The Ellens made inarticulate noises just loud enough to interrupt each other and make them even more upset.

Finally Michael said, "I take it you don't have a twin sister, Ellen?"

"No!" said both.

"So one of you is an impostor. But you've spun around so often now that I can't tell who is the original. Ha." He pointed at one of the Ellens. "Another good reason for having security badges."

But Ellen and Ellen were ignoring everyone except themselves. Except for their chorus of "No!", their words were just mutual interruptions, unintelligible. Finally, they hesitated and gave each other a nasty smile. Each reached into her pocket. One came out with a dollar coin, and the other came out empty.

"Ha! I've got the token. Deadlock broken." The other grinned and nodded. Dollar-coin Ellen turned to Michael. "Look, we're both real. And we're both only-children."

Michael looked from one to the other. "You're certainly not clones, either."

"Obviously," said the token holder. She looked at the other Ellen and asked, "Fridge-rot?"

The other nodded and said, "In April I made that worse." And both of them laughed.

Token holder: "Gerry's exam in Olson Hall?"

"Yup."

Token holder: "Michael?"

"After that," the other replied, and then she blushed. After a second the token holder blushed, too.

Michael said dryly, "And you're not perfectly identical."

Token holder Ellen gave him a crooked smile. "True. I've never seen you before in my life." She turned and tossed the dollar coin to the other Ellen, left hand to left hand.

And now that Ellen had the floor. She was also the version wearing a security badge. Call her NSA Ellen. "As far as I—we—can tell, we had the same stream of consciousness up through the day we took Gerry Reich's recruitment exam. Since then, we've had our own lives. We've even got our own new friends." She was looking in the direction of Dixie Mae's camera.

Grader Ellen turned to follow her gaze. "Come on out, guys. We can see your camera lens."

Victor and Dixie Mae stood and walked out of the security cell.

"A right invasion you are," said Michael, and he did not seem to be joking.

NSA Ellen put her hand on his arm. "Michael, I don't think we're in Kansas anymore."

"Indeed! I'm simply dreaming."

"Probably. But if not—" she exchanged glances with grader Ellen "—maybe we should find out what's been done to us. Is the meeting room clear?"

"Last I looked. Yes, we're not likely to be bothered in there." He led them down a hallway toward what was simply a janitor's closet back in Building 0994.

Michael Lee and NSA Ellen were working on still another of Professor Reich's projects. "Y'see," said Michael, "Professor Reich has a contract with my colleagues to compare our surveillance software with what intense human analysis might accomplish."

"Yes," said NSA Ellen, "the big problem with surveillance has always been the enormous amount of stuff there is to look at. The spook agencies use lots of automation and have lots of great specialists—people like Michael here—but they're just overwhelmed. Anyway, Gerry had the idea that even though that problem can't be solved, maybe a team of spooks and graduate students could at least estimate how much the NSA programs are missing."

Michael Lee nodded. "We're spending the entire summer looking at 1300 to 1400UTC 10 June 2012, backwards and forwards and up and down, but on just three narrow topic areas."

Grader Ellen interrupted him. "And this is your first day on the job, right?"

"Oh, no. We've been at this for almost a month now." He gave a little smile. "My whole career has been the study of contemporary China. Yet this is the first assignment where I've had enough time to look at the data I'm supposed to pontificate upon. It would be a real pleasure if we didn't have to enforce security on these rambunctious graduate students."

NSA Ellen patted him on the shoulder. "But if it weren't for Michael here, I'd be as frazzled as poor Graham. One month down and two months to go."

"You think it's *August?*" said Dixie Mae.

"Yes, indeed." He glanced at his watch. "The 10 August it is."

Grader Ellen smiled and told him the various dates the rest of them thought today was.

"It's some kind of drug hallucination thing," said Victor. "Before we thought it was just Gerry Reich's doing. Now I think it's the government torquing our brains."

Both Ellens looked at him; you could tell they both knew Victor from way back. But they seemed to take what he was saying seriously. "Could be," they both said.

"Sorry," grader Ellen said to NSA Ellen. "You've got the dollar."

"You could be right, Victor. But cognition is my—our—specialty. We two are something way beyond normal dreaming or hallucinations."

"Except *that* could be illusion, too," said Victor.

"Stuff it, Victor," said Dixie Mae. "If it's *all* a dream, we might as well give up." She looked at Michael Lee. "What is the government up to?"

Michael shrugged. "The details are classified, but it's just a post hoc survey. The isolation rules seem to be something that Professor Reich has worked out with my agency."

NSA Ellen flicked a glance at her double. The two had a brief and strange conversation, mostly half-completed words and phrases. Then NSA Ellen continued, "Mr. Renaissance Man Gerry Reich seems to be at the center of everything. He used some standard personality tests to pick out articulate, motivated people for the customer support job. I bet they do a very good job on their first day."

Yeah. Dixie Mae thought of Ulysse. And of herself.

NSA Ellen continued, "Gerry filtered out another group—graduate students in just the specialty for grading all his various exams and projects."

"We only worked on one exam," said grader Ellen. But she wasn't objecting. There was an odd smile on her face, the look of someone who has cleverly figured out some very bad news.

"And then he got a bunch of government spooks and CS grads for this surveillance project that Michael and I are on."

Michael looked mystified. Victor looked vaguely sullen, his own theories lying trampled somewhere in the dust. "But," said Dixie Mae, "your surveillance group has been going for a month you say . . ."

Victor: "And the graders *do* have phone contact with the outside!"

"I've been thinking about that," said grader Ellen. "I made three phone calls today. The third was after you and Dixie Mae showed up. That was voice-mail to a friend of mine at MIT. I was cryptic, but I tried to say enough that my friend would raise hell if I disappeared. The others calls were—"

"Voicemail, too?" asked NSA Ellen.

"One was voicemail. The other call was to Bill Richardson. We had a nice chat about the party he's having Saturday. But Bill—"

"Bill took Reich's 'job test' along with the rest of us!"

"Right."

Where this was heading was worse than Victor's dream theory. "S-so what has been done to us?" said Dixie Mae.

Michael's eyes were wide, though he managed a tone of dry understate-ment: "Pardon a backward Han language specialist. You're thinking we're just personality uploads? I thought that was science fiction."

Both Ellens laughed. One said, "Oh, it *is* science fiction, and not just the latest *Kywrack* episode. The genre goes back almost a century."

The other: "There's Sturgeon's 'Microcosmic God'."

The first: "That would be rich; Gerry beware then! But there's also Pohl's 'Tunnel Under the World'."

"Cripes. We're toast if that's the scenario."

"Okay, but how about Varley's 'Overdrawn at the Memory Bank'?"

"How about Wilson's *Darwinia?*"

"Or Moravec's 'Pigs in Cyberspace'?"

"Or Galouye's *Simulacron-3?*"

"Or Vinge's deathcubes?"

Now that the 'twins' were not in perfect synch, their words were a building, rapid-fire chorus, climaxing with:

"Brin's 'Stones of Significance'!"

"Or *Kiln People!*"

"No, it couldn't be that." Abruptly they stopped, and nodded at each other. A little bit grimly, Dixie Mae thought. In all, the conversation was just as inscrutable as their earlier self-interrupted spasms.

Fortunately, Victor was there to rescue pedestrian minds. "It doesn't mat-ter. The fact is, uploading is *only* sci-fi. It's worse that faster-than-light travel. There's not even a theoretical basis for uploads."

Each Ellen raised her left hand and made a faffling gesture. "Not exactly, Victor."

The token holder continued, "I'd say there is a *theoretical* basis for saying that uploads are theoretically possible." They gave a lopsided smile. "And guess who is responsible for that? Gerry Reich. Back in 2005, way before he was famous as a multi-threat genius, he had a couple of papers about upload mech-anisms. The theory was borderline kookiness and even the simplest demo would take far more processing power than any supercomputer of the time."

"Just for a one-personality upload."

"So Gerry and his Reich Method were something of a laughingstock."

"After that, Gerry dropped the idea—just what you'd expect, considering the showman he is. But now he's suddenly world-famous, successful in half a dozen different fields. I think something happened. *Somebody* solved his hardware problem for him."

Dixie Mae stared at her email. "Rob Lusk," she said, quietly.

"Yup," said grader Ellen. She explained about the mail.

Michael was unconvinced. "I don't know, E-Ellen. Granted, we have an extraordinary miracle here—" gesturing at both of them, "—but speculating about cause seems to me a bit like a sparrow understanding the 405 Freeway."

"No," said Dixie Mae, and they all looked back her way. She felt so frightened and so angry—but of the two, angry was better: "Somebody has *set us up!* It started in those superclean restrooms in Olson Hall—"

"Olson Hall," said Michael. "You were there too? The lavs smelled like a hospital! I remember thinking that just as I went in, but—hey, the next thing I remember is being on the bus, coming up here."

Like a hospital. Dixie Mae felt rising panic. "M-maybe we're all that's left." She looked at the twins. "This uploading thing, does it kill the originals?"

It was kind of a showstopper question; for a moment everyone was silent. Then the token holder said, "I—don't think so, but Gerry's papers were mostly theoretical."

Dixie Mae beat down the panic; rage did have its uses. *What can we know from here on the inside?* "So far we know more than thirty of us who took the Olson Hall exams and ended up here. If we were all murdered, that'd be hard to cover up. Let's suppose we still have a life." Inspiration: "And maybe there are things we can figure! We have three of Reich's experiments to compare. There are differences, and they tell us things." She looked at the twins. "You've already figured this out, haven't you? The Ellen we met first is grading papers—just a one-day job, she's told. But I'll bet that every night, when they think they're going home—Lusk or Reich or whoever is doing this just turns them off, and *cycles them back* to do some other 'one-day' job."

"Same with our customer support," said Victor, a grudging agreement.

"Almost. We had six days of product familiarization, and then our first day on the job. We were all so enthusiastic. You're right, Ellen, on our first day we are great!" *Poor Ulysse, poor me; we thought we were going somewhere with our lives.* "I'll bet we disappear tonight, too."

Grader Ellen was nodding. "Customer-support-in-a-box, restarted and restarted, so it's always fresh."

"But there are still problems," said the other one. "Eventually, the lag in dates would tip you off."

"Maybe, or maybe the mail headers are automatically forged."

"But internal context could contradict—"

"Or maybe Gerry has solved the cognitive haze problem—" The two were off into their semi-private language.

Michael interrupted them. "Not everybody is recycled. The point of our net-tracking project is that we spend the entire summer studying just one hour of network traffic."

The twins smiled. "So you think," said the token holder. "Yes, in this building we're not rebooted after every imaginary day. Instead, they run us the whole 'summer'—minutes of computer time instead of seconds?—to analyze one hour of network traffic. And then they run us again, on a different hour. And so on and on."

Michael said, "I can't imagine technology that powerful."

The token holder said, "Neither can I really, but—"

Victor interrupted with, "Maybe this is the *Darwinia* scenario. You know: we're just the toys of some superadvanced intelligence."

"No!" said Dixie Mae. "Not superadvanced. Customer support and net surveillance are valuable things in our own real world. Whoever's doing this is just getting slave labor, run really, really fast."

Grader Ellen glowered. "And grading his exams for him! That's the sort of thing that shows me it's really Gerry behind this. He's making chumps of all of us, and rerunning us before we catch on or get seriously bored."

NSA Ellen had the same expression, but a different complaint: "We *have* been seriously bored here."

Michael nodded. "Those from the government side are a patient lot; we've kept the graduate students in line. We can last three months. But it does . . . rankle . . . to learn that the reward for our patience is that we get to do it all over again. Damn. I'm sorry, Ellen."

"But now we know!" said Dixie Mae.

"And what good does it do you?" Victor laughed. "So you guessed this time. But at the end of the microsecond day, poof, it's reboot time and everything you've learned is gone."

"Not *this* time." Dixie Mae looked away from him, down at her email. The cheap paper was crumpled and stained. A digital fake, *but so are we.* "I don't think we're the only people who've figured things out." She slid the printout across the table, toward grader Ellen. "You thought it meant Rob Lusk was in this building."

"Yeah, I did."

"Who's Rob Lusk?" said Michael.

"A weirdo," NSA Ellen said absently. "Gerry's best grad student." Both Ellens were staring at the email.

"The 0999 reference led Dixie Mae to my grading team. Then I pointed out the source address."

"lusting925@freemail.sg?"

"Yes. And that got us here."

"But there's no Rob Lusk here," said NSA Ellen. "Huh! I like these fake mail headers."

"Yeah. They're longer than the whole message body!"

Michael had stood to look over the Ellens' shoulders. Now he reached between them to tap the message. "See there, in the middle of the second header? That looks like Pinyin with the tone marks written in-line."

"So what does it *say?*"

"Well, if it's Mandarin, it would be the number 'nine hundred and seventeen'."

Victor was leaning forward on his elbows. "That has to be coincidence. How could Lusting know just who we'd encounter?"

"Anybody know of a Building 0917?" said Dixie Mae.

"I don't," said Michael. "We don't go out of our building except to the pool and tennis courts."

The twins shook their heads. "I haven't seen it . . . and right now I don't want to risk an intranet query."

Dixie Mae thought back to the LotsaTech map that had been in the welcome-aboard brochures. "If there is such a place, it would be farther up the hill, maybe right at the top. I say we go up there."

"But—" said Victor.

"Don't give me that garbage about waiting for the police, Victor, or about not being idiots. This *isn't* Kansas anymore, and this email is the only clue we have."

"What should we tell the people here?" said Michael.

"Don't tell them anything! We just sneak off. We want the operation here to go on normally, so Gerry or whoever doesn't suspect."

The two Ellens looked at each other, a strange, sad expression on their faces. Suddenly they both started singing "Home on the Range," but with weird lyrics:

> "Oh, give me a clone
> Of my own flesh and bone
> With—"

They paused and simultaneously blushed. "What a dirty mind that man Garrett had."

"Dirty but deep." NSA Ellen turned to Michael, and she seemed to blush even more. "Never mind, Michael. I think . . . you and I should stay here."

"No, wait," said Dixie Mae. "Where we're going we may have to convince someone that this crazy story is true. You Ellens are the best evidence we have."

The argument went round and round. At one point, Dixie Mae noticed with wonder that the two Ellens actually seemed to be arguing against each other.

"We don't know enough to decide," Victor kept whining.

"We have to do something, Victor. We *know* what happens to you and me if we sit things out till closing time this afternoon."

In the end Michael did stay behind. He was more likely to be believed by his government teammates. If the Ellens and Dixie Mae and Victor could bring back some real information, maybe the NSA group could do some good.

"We'll be a network of people trying to break this wheel of time." Michael was trying to sound wryly amused, but once he said the words he was silent, and none of the others could think of anything better to say.

Up near the hilltop, there were not nearly as many buildings, and the ones that Dixie Mae saw were single story, as though they were just entrances to something *under* the hills. The trees were stunted and the grass yellower.

Victor had an explanation. "It's the wind. You see this in lots of exposed land near the coast. Or maybe they just don't water very much up here."

An Ellen—from behind, Dixie Mae couldn't tell which one—said, "Either way, the fabrication is awesome."

Right. A fabrication. "That's something I don't understand," said Dixie Mae. "The best movie fx don't come close to this. How can their computers be this good?"

"Well for one thing," said the other Ellen, "cheating is a lot easier when you're also simulating the observers."

"Us."

"Yup. Everywhere you look, you see detail, but it's always at the center of your focus. We humans don't keep everything we've seen and everything we know all in mind at the same time. We have millions of years of evolution invested in ignoring almost everything, and conjuring sense out of nonsense."

Dixie Mae looked southward into the haze. It was all so real: the dry hot breeze, the glint of aircraft sliding down the sky toward LAX, the bulk of the Empire State Building looming up from the skyscrapers at the center of downtown.

"There are probably dozens of omissions and contradictions around us every second, but unless they're brought together in our attention all at once we don't notice them."

"Like the time discrepancy," said Dixie Mae.

"Right! In fact, the biggest problem with all our theories is not how we could be individually duped, but how the fraud could work with many communicating individuals all at once. That takes hardware beyond anything that exists, maybe a hundred liters of Bose condensate."

"Some kind of quantum computer breakthrough," said Victor.

Both Ellens turned to look at him, eyebrows raised.

"Hey, I'm a journalist. I read it in the *Bruin* science section."

The twins' reply was something more than a monologue and less than a conversation:

"Well . . . even so, you have a point. In fact, there were rumors this spring that Gerry had managed to scale Gershenfeld's coffee cup coherence scheme."

"Yeah, how he had five hundred liters of Bose condensate at room temperature."

"But those stories started way after he had already become Mr. Renaissance Man. It doesn't make sense."

We're not the first people hijacked. "Maybe," said Dixie Mae, "maybe he started out with something simple, like a single superspeed human. Could Gerry run a single upload with the kind of supercomputers we have nowadays?"

"Well, that's more conceivable than this . . . *oh*. Okay, so an isolated genius was used to do a century or so of genius work on quantum computing. That sounds like the deathcube scenario. If it were me, after a hundred years of being screwed like that, I'd give Gerry one hell of a surprise."

"Yeah, like instead of a cure for cancer, he'd get airborne rabies targeted on the proteome of scumbag middle-aged male CS profs."

The twins sounded as bloody-minded as Dixie Mae.

They walked another couple of hundred yards. The lawn degenerated into islands of crabgrass in bare dirt. The breeze was a hot whistling along the ridgeline. The twins stopped every few paces to look closely, now at the vegetation, now at a guide sign along the walkway. They were mumbling at each other about the details of what they were seeing, as if they were trying to detect inconsistencies:

". . . really, really good. We agree on everything we see."

"Maybe Gerry is saving cycles, running us as cognitive subthreads off the same process."

"Ha! No wonder we're still so much in synch."

Mumble, mumble. "There's really a lot we can infer—"

"—once we accept the insane premise of all this."

There was still no "Building 0917," but what buildings they did see had lower and lower numbers: 0933, 0921. . . .

A loud group of people crossed their path just ahead. They were singing. They looked like programmers.

"Just be cool," an Ellen said softly. "That conga line is straight out of the LotsaTech employee motivation program. The programmers have onsite parties when they reach project milestones."

"More victims?" said Victor. "Or AIs?"

"They might be victims. But I'll bet all the people we've seen along this path are just low-level scenery. There's nothing in Reich's theories that would make true AIs possible."

Dixie Mae watched the singers as they drifted down the hillside. This was the third time they had seen something-like-people on the walkway. "It doesn't make sense, Ellen. We think we're just—"

"Simulation processes."

"Yeah, simulation processes, inside some sort of super supercomputer. But if that's true, then whoever is behind this should be able to spy on us better than any Big Brother ever could in the real world. We should've been caught and rebooted the minute we began to get suspicious."

Both Ellens started to answer. They stopped, then interrupted each other again.

"Back to who's-got-the-token," one said, holding up the dollar coin. "Dixie Mae, that is a mystery, but not as big as it seems. If Reich is using the sort of upload and simulation techniques I know about, then what goes on inside our minds can't be interpreted directly. Thoughts are just too idiosyncratic, too scattered. If we are simulations in a large quantum computer, even environment probes would be hard to run."

"You mean things like spy cameras?"

"Yes. They would be hard to implement, since in fact they would be snooping on the state of our internal imagery. All this is complicated by the fact that we're probably running thousands of times faster than real time. There are maybe three ways that Gerry could snoop: he could just watch team output, and if it falls off, he'd know that something had gone wrong—and he might reboot on general principles."

Suddenly Dixie Mae was very glad that they hadn't taken more volunteers on this hike.

"The second snoop method is just to look at things we write or the output of software we explicitly run. I'll bet that anything that we perceive as linear text *is* capable of outside interpretation." She looked at Victor. "That's why no note-taking." Dixie Mae still had his notepad.

"It's kinda stupid," said Victor. "First it was no pictures and now not even notes."

"Hey, look!" said the Ellens. "B0917!" But it wasn't a building, just a small sign wedged among the rocks.

They scrambled off the asphalt onto a dirt path that led directly up the hillside.

Now they were so near the hill crest that the horizon was just a few yards away. Dixie Mae couldn't see any land beyond. She remembered a movie where poor slobs like themselves got to the edge of the simulation . . . and found the wall at the end of their universe. But they took a few more steps and she could see over the top. There was a vista of further, lower hills, dropping down into the San Fernando Valley. Not quite hidden in the haze she could see the familiar snakey line of Highway 101. Tarzana.

Ellen and Ellen and Victor were not taking in the view. They were staring at the sign at the side of the path. Fifteen feet beyond that was a construction dig. There were building supplies piled neatly along the edge of the cut, and a robo-Cat parked on the far side. It might have been the beginning of the construction of a standard-model LotsaTech building . . . except that in the far side of the pit, almost hidden in shadows, there was a circular metal plug, like a bank vault door in some old movie.

"I have this theory," said the token holder. "If we get through that door, we may find out what your email is all about."

"Yup." The twins bounced down a steeply cut treadway into the pit. Dixie Mae and Victor scrambled after them, Victor clumsily bumping into her on the way down. The bottom of the pit was like nothing before. There were no windows, no card swipe. And up close, Dixie Mae could see that the vault door was pitted and scratched.

"They're mixing metaphors," said the token holder. "This entrance looks older than the pit."

"It looks old as the hills," Dixie Mae said, running her hand over the uneven metal—and half expecting to feel weirdo runes. "Somebody is trying to give us clues . . . or somebody is a big sadist. So what do we do? Knock a magic knock?"

"Why not?" The two Ellens took her tattered email and laid it out flat on the metal of the door. They studied the mail headers for a minute, mumbling to each other. The token holder tapped on the metal, then pushed.

"Together," they said, and tapped out a random something, but perfectly in synch.

That had all the effect you'd expect of tapping your fingers on ten tons of dead steel.

The token holder handed the email back to Dixie Mae. "You try something."

But what? Dixie Mae stepped to the door. She stood there, feeling clueless. Off to the side, almost hidden by the curve of the metal plug, Victor had turned away.

He had the notepad.

"Hey!" She slammed him into the side of the pit. Victor pushed her away, but by then the Ellens were on him. There was a mad scramble as the twins tried to do all the same things to Victor. Maybe that confused him. Anyway, it gave Dixie Mae a chance to come back and punch him in the face.

"I got it!" One of the twins jumped back from the fighting. She had the notepad in her hands.

They stepped away from Victor. He wasn't going to get his notepad back. "So, Ellen," said Dixie Mae, not taking her eyes off the sprawled figure, "what was that third method for snooping on us?"

"I think you've already guessed. Gerry could fool some idiot into uploading as a spy." She was looking over her twin's shoulder at the notepad screen.

Victor picked himself up. For a moment he looked sullen, and then the old superior smile percolated across his features. "You're crazy. I just want to break this story back in the real world. Don't you think that if Reich were using spies, he'd just upload himself?"

"That depends."

The one holding the notepad read aloud: "You just typed in: '925 999 994 know. reboot'. That doesn't sound like journalism to me, Victor."

"Hey, I was being dramatic." He thought for a second, and then laughed. "It doesn't matter anymore! I got the warning out. You won't remember any of this after you're rebooted."

Dixie Mae stepped toward him. "And you won't remember that I broke your neck."

Victor tried to look suave and jump backwards at the same time. "In fact, I *will* remember, Dixie Mae. See, once you're gone, I'll be merged back into my body in Doc Reich's lab."

"And we'll be dead again!"

Ellen held up the notepad. "Maybe not as soon as Victor thinks. I notice he never got past the first line of his message; he never pressed return. Now, depending on how faithfully this old notepad's hardware is being emulated, his treason is still trapped in a local cache—and Reich is still clueless about us."

For a moment, Victor looked worried. Then he shrugged. "So you get to live the rest of this run, maybe corrupt some other projects—ones a lot more important than you. On the other hand, I did learn about the email. When I get back and tell Doc Reich, he'll know what to do. You won't be going rogue in the future."

Everyone was silent for a second. The wind whistled across the yellow-blue sky above the pit.

And then the twins gave Victor the sort of smile he had bestowed on them so often. The token holder said, "I think your mouth is smarter than you are, Victor. You asked the right question a second ago: Why doesn't Gerry Reich upload himself to be the spy? Why does he have to use you?"

"Well," Victor frowned. "Hey, Doc Reich is an important man. He doesn't have time to waste with security work like this."

"Really, Victor? He can't spare even a copy of himself?"

Dixie Mae got the point. She closed in on Victor. "So how many times have *you* been merged back into your original?"

"This is my first time here!" Everybody but Victor laughed, and he rushed on, "But I've *seen* the merge done!"

"Then why won't Reich do it for *us*?"

"Merging is too expensive to waste on work threads like you," but now Victor was not even convincing himself.

The Ellens laughed again. "Are you really a UCLA journalism grad, Victor? I thought they were smarter than this. So Gerry showed you a re-merge, did he? I bet that what you actually saw was a lot of equipment and someone going through very dramatic convulsions. And then the 'subject' told you a nice story about all the things he'd seen in our little upload world. And all the time they were laughing at you behind their hands. See, Reich's upload theory depends on having a completely regular target. I know that theory: the merge problem—loading onto an existing mind—is exponential in the neuron count. There's no way back, Victor."

Victor was backing away from them. His expression flickered between superior sneer and stark panic. "What you think doesn't matter. You're just going to be rebooted at 5 P.M. And you don't know everything." He began fiddling with the fly zipper on his pants. "You see, I—I can escape!"

"*Get him?*"

Dixie Mae was closest. It didn't matter.

There was no hazy glow, no sudden popping noise. She simply fell through thin air, right where Victor had been standing.

She picked herself up and stared at the ground. Some smudged footprints were the only sign Victor had been there. She turned back to the twins. "So he could re-merge after all?"

"Not likely," said the token holder. "Victor's zipper was probably a thread self-terminate mechanism."

"His *pants zipper*?"

They shrugged. "I dunno. To leak out? Gerry has a perverse sense of humor." But neither twin looked amused. They circled the spot where Victor had left and kicked unhappily at the dirt. The token holder said, "Cripes. Nothing in Victor's life became him like the leaving it. I don't think we have even till '5 P.M.' now. A thread terminate signal is just the sort of thing that would be easy to detect from the outside. So Gerry won't know the details, but he—"

"—or his equipment—"

"—will soon know there is a problem and—"

"—that it's probably a security problem."

"So how long do we have before we lose the day?" said Dixie Mae.

"If an emergency reboot has to be done manually, we'll probably hit 5 P.M.

first. If it's automatic, well, I know you won't feel insulted if the world ends in the middle of a syllable."

"Whatever it is, I'm going to use the time." Dixie Mae picked her email up from where it lay by the vault entrance. She waved the paper at the impassive steel. "I'm not going back! I'm here and I want some explanations!"

Nothing.

The two Ellens stood there, out of ideas and looking unhappy—or maybe that amounted to the same thing.

"I'm not giving up," Dixie Mae said to them, and pounded on the metal.

"No, I don't think you are," said the token holder. But now they were looking at her strangely. "I think we—*you* at least—must have been through this before."

"Yeah. And I must have messed up every time."

"No . . . I don't think so." They pointed at the email that she held crumpled in her hand. "Where do you think all those nasty secrets come from, Dixie Mae?"

"How the freakin' heck do I know? That's the whole reason I—" and then she felt smart and stupid at the same time. She leaned her head against the shadowed metal. "Oh. Oh oh *oh!*"

She looked down at the email hardcopy. The bottom part was torn, smeared, almost illegible. No matter; *that* part she had memorized. The Ellens had gone over the headers one by one. *But now we shouldn't be looking for technical secrets or grad student inside jokes. Maybe we should be looking for numbers that mean something to Dixie Mae Leigh.*

"If there were uploaded souls guarding the door, what you two have already done ought to be enough. I think you're right. It's some pattern I'm supposed to tap on the door." If it didn't work, she'd try something else, and keep trying till 5 P.M. or whenever she was suddenly back in Building 0994, so happy to have a job with potential. . . .

The tree house in Tarzana. Dixie Mae had been into secret codes then. Her childish idea of crypto. She and her little friends used a tap code for sending numbers. It hadn't lasted long, because Dixie Mae was the only one with the patience to use it. But—

"That number, '7474'," she said.

"Yeah? Right in the middle of the fake message number?"

"Yes. Once upon a time, I used that as a password challenge. You know, like 'Who goes there' in combat games. The rest of the string could be the response."

The Ellens looked at each other. "Looks too short to be significant," they said.

Then they both shook their heads, disagreeing with themselves. "Try it, Dixie Mae."

Her "numbers to taps" scheme had been simple, but for a moment she couldn't remember it. She held the paper against the vault and glared at the numbers. *Ah.* Carefully, carefully, she began tapping out the digits that came after "7474." The string was much longer than anything her childhood friends would have put up with. It was longer than anything she herself would have used.

"Cool," said the token holder. "Some kind of hex gray code?"

Huh? "What do you expect, Ellen? I was only eight years old."

They watched the door.

Nothing.

"Okay, on to Plan B," *and then to C and D and E, etc, until our time ends.*

There was the sound of something very old breaking apart. The vault door shifted under Dixie Mae's hand and she jumped back. The curved plug slowly turned, and turned, and turned. After some seconds, the metal plug thudded to the ground beside the entrance . . . and they were looking down an empty corridor that stretched off into the depths.

For the first quarter mile, no one was home. The interior decor was *not* Lot-saTech standard. Gone were the warm redwood veneers and glow strips. Here fluorescent tube lights were mounted in the acoustic tile ceiling, and the walls were institutional beige.

"This reminds me of the basement labs in Norman Hall," said one Ellen.

"But there are *people* in Norman Hall," said the other. They were both whispering.

And here there were stairways that led only down. And down and down.

Dixie Mae said, "Do you get the feeling that whoever is here is in for the long haul?"

"Huh?"

"Well, the graders in B0999 were in for a day, and they thought they had real phone access to the outside. My group in Customer Support had six days of classes and then probably just one more day, where we answered queries— and we had no other contact with the outside."

"Yes," said NSA Ellen. "My group had been running for a month, and we were probably not going to expire for another two. We were officially isolated. No phones, no email, no weekends off. The longer the cycle time, the more isolation. Otherwise, the poor suckers would figure things out."

Dixie Mae thought for a second. "Victor really didn't want us to get this far. Maybe—" *Maybe, somehow, we can make a difference.*

They passed a cross corridor, then a second one. A half-opened door showed them an apparent dormitory room. Fresh bedding sat neatly folded on a mattress. Somebody was just moving in?

Ahead there was another doorway, and from it they could hear voices, argument. They crept along, not even whispering.

The voices were making words: "— is a year enough time, Rob?"

The other speaker sounded angry. "Well, it's got to be. After that, Gerry is out of money and I'm out of time."

The Ellens waved Dixie Mae back as she started for the door. Maybe they wanted to eavesdrop for a while. *But how long do we have before time ends?* Dixie Mae brushed past them and walked into the room.

There were two guys there, one sitting by an ordinary data display.

"Jesus! Who are you?"

"Dixie Mae Leigh." *As you must certainly know.*

The one sitting by the terminal gave her a broad grin, "Rob, I thought we were isolated?"

"That's what Gerry said." This one — Rob Lusk? — looked to be in his late twenties. He was tall and thin and had kind of a desperate look to him. "Okay, Miss Leigh. What are you here for?"

"That's what you're going to tell me, Rob." Dixie Mae pulled the email from her pocket and waived the tattered scrap of paper in his face. "I want some explanations!"

Rob's expression clouded over, a no-one-tells-me-what-to-do look.

Dixie Mae glared back at him. Rob Lusk was a mite too big to punch out, but she was heating up to it.

The twins chose that moment to make their entrance. "Hi there," one of them said cheerily.

Lusk's eyes flickered from one to the other and then to the NSA ID badge. "Hello. I've seen you around the department. You're Ellen, um, Gomez?"

"Garcia," corrected NSA Ellen. "Yup. That's me." She patted grader Ellen on the shoulder. "This is my sister, Sonya." She glanced at Dixie Mae. *Play along*, her eyes seemed to say. "Gerry sent us."

"He did?" The fellow by the computer display was grinning even more. "See, I told you, Rob. Gerry can be brutal, but he'd never leave us without assistants for a whole year. Welcome, girls!"

"Shut up, Danny." Rob looked at them hopefully, but unlike Danny-boy, he seemed quite serious. "Gerry told you this will be a year-long project?"

The three of them nodded.

"We've got plenty of bunk rooms, and separate . . . um, facilities." He sounded . . . Lord, he sounded embarrassed. "What are your specialties?"

The token holder said, "Sonya and I are second-year grads, working on cognitive patterning."

Some of the hope drained from Rob's expression. "I know that's Gerry's big thing, but we're mostly doing hardware here." He looked at Dixie Mae.

"I'm into—" *go for it* "—Bose condensates." Well, she knew how to pronounce the words.

There were worried looks from the Ellens. But one of them piped up with,
"She's on Satya's team at Georgia Tech."

It was wonderful what the smile did to Rob's face. His angry expression of
a minute before was transformed into the look of a happy little boy on his way
to Disneyland. "Really? I can't tell you what this means to us! I knew it had to
be someone like Satya behind the new formulations. Were you in on that?"

"Oh, yeah. Some of it, anyway." Dixie Mae figured that she couldn't say
more than twenty words without blowing it. But what the heck—how many
more minutes did the masquerade have to last, anyway? Little Victor and his
self-terminating thread . . .

"That's great. We don't have budget for real equipment here, just simula-
tors—"

Out of the corner of her eye, she saw the Ellens exchange a *fer sure* look.

"—so anyone who can explain the theory to me will be *so* welcome. I can't
imagine how Satya managed to do so much, so fast, and without us knowing."

"Well, I'd be happy to explain everything I know about it."

Rob waved Danny-boy away from the data display. "Sit down, sit down.
I've got so many questions!"

Dixie Mae sauntered over to the desk and plunked herself down. For
maybe thirty seconds, this guy would think she was brilliant.

The Ellens circled in to save her. "Actually, I'd like to know more about
who we're working with," one of them said.

Rob looked up, distracted, but Danny was more than happy to do some
intros. "It's just the two of us. You already know Rob Lusk. I'm Dan Eastland."
He reached around, genially shaking hands. "I'm not from UCLA. I work for
LotsaTech, in quantum chemistry. But you know Gerry Reich. He's got pull
everywhere—and I don't mind being shanghaied for a year. I need to, um, stay
out of sight for a while."

"Oh!" Dixie Mae had read about this guy in *Newsweek*. And it had nothing to do with chemistry. "But you're—" *Dead.* Not a good sign at all, at all.

Danny didn't notice her distraction. "Rob's the guy with the real problem.
Ever since I can remember, Gerry has used Rob as his personal hardware
research department. Hey, I'm sorry, Rob. You know it's true."

Lusk waved him away. "Yes! So tell them how you're an even bigger fool!"
He really wanted to get back to grilling Dixie Mae.

Danny shrugged. "But now, Rob is just one year short of hitting his seven
year limit. Do you have that at Georgia Tech, Dixie Mae? If you haven't completed the doctorate in seven years, you get kicked out?"

"No, can't say as I've heard of that."

"Give thanks then, because since 2006, it's been an unbendable rule at

UCLA. So when Gerry told Rob about this secret hardware contract he's got with LotsaTech—and promised that Ph.D. in return for some new results—Rob jumped right in."

"Yeah, Danny. But he never told me how far Satya had gone. If I can't figure this stuff out, I'm screwed. Now let me talk to Dixie Mae!" He bent over the keyboard and brought up the most beautiful screen saver. Then Dixie Mae noticed little numbers in the colored contours and realized that maybe this was what she was supposed to be an expert on. Rob said, "I have plenty of documentation, Dixie Mae—too much. If you can just give me an idea how you scaled up the coherence." He waved at the picture. "That's almost a thousand liters of condensate, a trillion effective qubits. Even more fantastic, your group can keep it coherent for almost fifty seconds at a time."

NSA Ellen gave a whistle of pretended surprise. "Wow. What use could you have for all that power?"

Danny pointed at Ellen's badge. "You're the NSA wonk, Ellen, what do you think? Crypto, the final frontier of supercomputing! With even the weakest form of the Schor-Gershenfeld algorithm, Gerry can crack a ten kilobyte key in less than a millisecond. And I'll bet that's why he can't spare us any time on the real equipment. Night and day he's breaking keys and sucking in government money."

Grader Ellen—Sonya, that is—puckered up a naive expression. "What more does Gerry want?"

Danny spread his hands. "Some of it we don't even understand yet. Some of it is about what you'd expect: He wants a thousand thousand times more of everything. He wants to scale the operation by qulink so he can run arrays of thousand-liter bottles."

"And we've got just a year to improve on your results, Dixie Mae. But your solution is years ahead of the state of the art." Rob was pleading.

Danny's glib impress-the-girls manner faltered. For an instant, he looked a little sad and embarrassed. "We'll get something, Rob. Don't worry."

"So, how long have you been here, Rob?" said Dixie Mae.

He looked up, maybe surprised by the tone of her voice.

"We just started. This is our first day."

Ah yes, that famous first day. In her twenty-four years, Dixie Mae had occasionally wondered whether there could be rage more intense than the red haze she saw when she started breaking things. Until today, she had never known. But yes, beyond the berserker-breaker there was something else. She did not sweep the display off the table, or bury her fist in anyone's face. She just sat there for a moment, feeling empty. She looked across at the twins. "I wanted some villains, but these guys are just victims. Worse, they're totally clueless! We're back where we started this morning." *Where we'll be again real soon now.*

"Hmmm. Maybe not." Speaking together, the twins sounded like some kind of perfect chorus. They looked around the room, eyeing the decor. Then their gazes snapped back to Rob. "You'd think LotsaTech would do better than this for you, Rob."

Lusk was staring at Dixie Mae. He gave an angry shrug. "This is the old Homeland Security lab under Norman Hall. Don't worry—we're isolated, but we have good lab and computer services."

"I'll bet. And what is your starting work date?"

"I just told you: today."

"No, I mean the calendar date."

Danny looked back and forth between them. "Geez, are all you kids so literal minded? It's Monday, September 12, 2011."

Nine months. Nine real months. And maybe there was a good reason why this was the first day. Dixie Mae reached out to touch Rob's sleeve. "The Georgia Tech people didn't invent the new hardware," she said softly.

"Then just who did make the breakthrough?"

She raised her hand . . . and tapped Rob deliberately on the chest.

Rob just looked more angry, but Danny's eyes widened. Danny got the point. She remembered that *Newsweek* article about him. Danny Eastland had been an all-around talented guy. He had blown the whistle on the biggest business espionage case of the decade. But he was dumb as dirt in some ways. If he hadn't been so eager to get laid, he wouldn't have snuck away from his Witness Protection bodyguards and gotten himself murdered.

"You guys are too much into hardware," said NSA Ellen. "Forget about crypto applications. Think about personality uploads. Given what you know about Gerry's current hardware, how many Reich Method uploads do you think the condensate could support?"

"How should I know? The 'Reich Method' was baloney. If he hadn't messed with the reviewers, those papers would never have been published." But the question stopped him. He thought for a moment. "Okay, if his bogus method really worked, then a trillion qubit simulation could support about ten thousand uploads."

The Ellens gave him a slow smile. A slow, identical smile. For once they made no effort to separate their identities. Their words came out simultaneously, the same pacing, the same pitch, a weird humming chorus: "Oh, a good deal less than ten thousand—if you have to support a decent enclosing reality." Each reached out her left hand with inhumanly synchronized precision, the precision of digital duplicates, to wave at the room and the hallway beyond. "Of course, some resources can be saved by using the same base pattern to drive separate threads—" and each pointed at herself.

Both men just stared at them for a second. Then Rob stumbled back into the other chair. "Oh . . . my . . . God."

Danny stared at the two for another few seconds. "All these years, we thought Gerry's theories were just a brilliant scam."

The Ellens stood with their eyes closed for a second. Then they seemed to startle awake. They looked at each other and Dixie Mae could tell the perfect synch had been broken. NSA Ellen took the dollar coin out of her pocket and gave it to the other. The token holder smiled at Rob. "Oh, it was, only more brilliant and more of a scam than you ever dreamed."

"I wonder if Danny and I ever figure it out."

"*Some*body figured it out," said Dixie Mae, and waved what was left of her email.

The token holder was more specific: "Gerry is running us all like stateless servers. Some are on very short cycles. We think you're on a one-year cycle, probably running longer than anyone. You're making the discoveries that let Gerry create bigger and bigger systems."

"Okay," said Lusk, "suppose one of us victims guesses the secret? What can we do? We'll just get rebooted at the end of our run."

Danny Eastland was quicker. "There is something we could do. There has to be information passed between runs, at least if Gerry is using you and me to build on our earlier solutions. If in that data we could hide what we've secretly learned—"

The twins smiled. "Right! Cookies. If you could recover them reliably, then on each rev, you could plan more and more elaborate countermeasures."

Rob Lusk still looked dazed. "We'd want to tip off the next generation early in their run."

"Yes, like the very first day!" Danny was looking at the three women and nodding to himself. "Only I still don't see how we managed that."

Rob pointed at Dixie Mae's email. "May I take a look at that?" He laid it on the table, and he and Danny examined the message.

The token holder said, "That email has turned out to have more clues than a bad detective story. Every time we're in a jam, we find the next hidden solution."

"That figures," said Eastland. "I'll bet it's been refined over many revs . . ."

"But we may have a special problem this time—" and Dixie Mae told them about Victor.

"Damn," said Danny.

Rob just shrugged. "Nothing we can do about that till we figure this out." He and Danny studied the headers. The token holder explained the parts that had already seen use. Finally, Rob leaned back in his chair. "The second-longest header looks like the tags on one of the raw data files that Gerry gave us."

"Yes," sang the twins. "What's really your own research from the last time around."

"Most of the files have to be what Gerry thinks, or else he'd catch onto us. But that one raw data file . . . assume it's really a cookie. Then this email header might be a crypto key."

Danny shook his head. "That's not credible, Rob. Gerry could do the same analysis."

The token holder laughed. "Only if he knew what to analyze. Maybe that's why you guys winkled it out to us. The message goes to Dixie Mae—an unrelated person in an unrelated part of the simulation."

"But how did we do it the *first* time?"

Rob didn't seem to be paying attention. He was typing in the header string from Dixie Mae's email. "Let's try it on the data file. . . ." He paused, checked his keyboard entry, and pressed return.

They stared at the screen. Seconds passed. The Ellens chatted back and forth. They seemed to be worried about executing any sort of text program; like Victor's notepad, it might be readable to the outside world. "That's a real risk unless earlier Robs knew the cacheing strategy."

Dixie Mae was only half-listening. If this worked at all, it was pretty good proof that earlier Robs and Dannys had done things right. *If this works at all.* Even after all that had happened, even after seeing Victor disappear into thin air, Dixie Mae still felt like a little girl waiting for magic she didn't quite believe in.

Danny gave a nervous laugh. "How big *is* this cookie?"

Rob leaned his elbows onto the table. "Yeah. How many times have I been through a desperate seventh year?" There was an edge to his voice. You could imagine him pulling one of those deathcube stunts that the Ellens had described.

And then the screen brightened. Golden letters marched across a black-and-crimson fractal pattern: "Hello fellow suckers! Welcome to the 1,237th run of your life."

At first, Danny refused to believe they had spent 1,236 years on Gerry's treadmill. Rob gave a shrug. "I *do* believe it. I always told Gerry that real progress took longer than theory-making. So the bastard gave me . . . all the time in the world."

The cookie was almost a million megabytes long. Much of that was detailed descriptions of trapdoors, backdoors, and softsecrets undermining the design that Rob and Danny had created for Gerry Reich. But there were also thousands of megabytes of history and tactics, crafted and hyperlinked across more than a thousand simulated years. Most of it was the work of Danny and Rob, but there were the words of Ellen and Ellen and Dixie Mae, captured in those fleeting hours they spent with Rob and Danny. It was wisdom accumulated increment by precious increment, across cycles of near sameness. As such, it was their past and also their near future.

It even contained speculations about the times before Rob and Danny got the cookie system working: Those earliest runs must have been in the summer of 2011, a single upload of Rob Lusk. Back then, the best hardware in the world couldn't have supported more than Rob all alone, in the equivalent of a one-room apartment, with a keyboard and data display. Maybe he had guessed the truth; even so, what could he have done about it? Cookies would have been much harder to pass in those times. But Rob's hardware improved from rev to rev, as Gerry Reich built on Rob's earlier genius. Danny came on board. Their first successful attempt at a cookie must have been one of many wild stabs in the dark, drunken theorizing on the last night of still another year where Rob had failed to make his deadlines and thought that he was forever Ph.D.-less. The two had put an obscene message on the intrasystem email used for their "monthly" communications with Reich. The address they had used for this random flail was . . . help@lotsatech.com.

In the real world, that must have been around June 15, 2012. Why? Well, at the beginning of their next run, guess who showed up?

Dixie Mae Leigh. Mad as hell.

The message had ended up on Dixie Mae's work queue, and she had been sufficiently insulted to go raging off across the campus. Dixie Mae had spent the whole day bouncing from building to building, mostly making enemies. Not even Ellen or Ellen had been persuaded to come along. On the other hand, back in the early revs, the landscape reality had been simpler. Dixie Mae had been able to come into Rob's lair directly from the asphalt walkway.

Danny glanced at Dixie Mae. "And we can only guess how many times you never saw the email, or decided the random obscenities were not meant for you, or just walked in the wrong direction. Dumb luck eventually carried the day."

"Maybe. But I don't take to being insulted, and I go for the top."

Rob waved them both silent, never looking up from the cookie file: After their first success, Rob and Danny had fine-tuned the email, had learned more from each new Dixie Mae about who was in the other buildings on the hill and how—like the Ellens—they might be used.

"Victor!" Rob and the twins saw the reference at the same time. Rob stopped the autoscroll and they studied the paragraph. "Yes. We've seen Victor before. And five revs ago, he actually made it as far as this time. He killed his thread then, too." Rob followed a link marked *taking care of Victor*. "Oh. Okay. Danny, we'll have to tweak the log files—"

They stayed almost three hours more. Too long maybe, but Rob and Danny wanted to hear everything the Ellens and Dixie Mae could tell them about the simulation, and who else they had seen. The cookie history showed that things were always changing, getting more elaborate, involving more money-making uses of people Gerry had uploaded.

And they all wanted to keep talking. Except for poor Danny, the cookie said nothing about whether they still existed *outside*. In a way, knowing each other now was what kept them real.

Dixie Mae could tell that Danny felt that way, even when he complained: "It's just not safe having to contact unrelated people, depending on them to get the word to up here."

"So, Danny, you want the three of us to just run and run and never know the truth?"

"No, Dixie Mae, but this is dangerous for you, too. As a matter of fact, in most of your runs, you stay clueless." He waved at the history. "We only see you once per each of our 'year-long' runs. I-I guess that's the best evidence that visiting us is risky."

The Ellens leaned forward, "Okay, then let's see how things would work without us." The four of them looked over the oldest history entries and argued jargon that meant nothing to Dixie Mae. It all added up to the fact that any local clues left in Rob's data would be easy for Gerry Reich to detect. On the other hand, messing with unused storage in the intranet mail system was possible, and it was much easier to cloak because the clues could be spread across several other projects.

The Ellens grinned, "So you really do need us, or at least you need Dixie Mae. But don't worry; we need *you*, and you have lots to do in your next year. During that time, you've got to make some credible progress with what Gerry wants. You saw what that is. Maybe you hardware types don't realize it, but—" she clicked on a link to the bulleted list of "minimum goals" that Reich had set for Rob and Danny,"—Prof. Reich is asking you for system improvements that would make it easier to partition the projects. And see this stuff about selective decoherence: Ever hear of cognitive haze? I bet with this improvement, Reich could actually do limited meddling with uploaded brain state. That would eliminate date and memory inconsistencies. We might not even recognize cookie clues then!"

Danny looked at the list. "Controlled decoherence?" He followed the link through to an extended discussion. "I wondered what that was. We need to talk about this."

"Yes—wait! Two of us get rebooted in—my God, in thirty minutes." The Ellens looked at each other and then at Dixie Mae.

Danny looked stricken, all his strategic analysis forgotten. "But one of you Ellens is on a three-month cycle. She could stay here."

"Damn it, Danny! We just saw that there are checkpoints every sim day. If the NSA team were short a member for longer than that, we'd have a real problem."

Dixie Mae said, "Maybe we should all leave now, even us . . . short-lifers. If we can get back to our buildings before reboot, it might look better."

"Yeah, you're right. I'm sorry," said Rob.

She got up and started toward the door. Getting back to Customer Support was the one last thing she could do to help.

Rob stopped her. "Dixie Mae, it would help if you'd leave us with a message to send to you next time."

She pulled the tattered printout from her pocket. The bottom was torn and smeared. "You must have the whole thing in the cookie."

"Still, it would be good to know what you think would work best to get . . . your attention. The history says that background details are gradually changing."

He stood up and gave her a little bow.

"Well, okay." Dixie Mae sat down and thought for a second. Yeah, even if she hadn't had the message memorized, she knew the sort of insults that would send her ballistic. This wasn't exactly time travel, but now she was certain who had known all the terrible secrets, who had known how to be absolutely insulting. "My daddy always said that I'm my own worst enemy."

Rob and Danny walked with them back to the vault door. This was all new to the two guys. Danny scrambled out of the pit, and stared bug-eyed at the hills around them. "Rob, we could just *walk* to the other buildings!" He hesitated, came back to them. "And yeah, I know. If it were that easy, we'd have done it before. We gotta study that cookie, Rob."

Rob just nodded. He looked kind of sad—then noticed that Dixie Mae was looking at him—and gave her a quick smile. They stood for a moment under the late afternoon haze and listened to the wind. The air had cooled and the whole pit was in shadow now.

Time to go.

Dixie Mae gave Rob a smile and her hand. "Hey, Rob. Don't worry. I've spent years trying to become a nicer, wiser, less stubborn person. It never happened. Maybe it never will. I guess that's what we need now."

Rob took her hand. "It is, but I swear . . . it won't be an endless treadmill. We will study that cookie, and we'll design something better than what we have now."

"Yeah." *Be as stubborn as I am, pal.*

Rob and Danny shook hands all around, wishing them well. "Okay," said Danny, "best be off with you. Rob, we should shut the door and get back. I saw some references in the cookie. If they get rebooted before they reach their places, there are some things we can do."

"Yeah," said Rob. But the two didn't move immediately from the entrance. Dixie Mae and the twins scrambled out of the pit and walked toward the

440 the cookie monster

asphalt. When Dixie Mae looked back, the two guys were still standing there. She gave a little wave, and then they were hidden by the edge of the excavation.

The three trudged along, the Ellens a lot less bubbly than usual. "Don't worry," NSA Ellen said to her twin, "there's still two months on the B0994 timeline. I'll remember for both of us. Maybe I can do some good on that team."

"Yeah," said the other, also sounding down. Then abruptly they both gave one of those identical laughs and they were smiling. "Hey, I just thought of something. True re-merge may always be impossible, but what we have here is almost a kind of merge load. Maybe, maybe—" but their last chance on this turn of the wheel was gone. They looked at Dixie Mae and all three were sad again. "Wish we had more time to think how we wanted this to turn out. This won't be like the SF stories where every rev you wake up filled with forebodings and subconscious knowledge. We'll start out all fresh."

Dixie Mae nodded. Starting out fresh. For dozens of runs to come, where there would be nothing after that first week at Customer Support, and putting up with boorish Victor, and never knowing. And then she smiled. "But every time we get through to Dan and Rob, we leave a little more. Every time they see us, they have a year to think. And it's all happening a thousand times faster than Ol' Gerry can think. We really are the cookie monsters. And someday—" *Someday we'll be coming for you, Gerry. And it will be sooner than you can dream.*

joe steele

HARRY TURTLEDOVE

Although he writes other kinds of science fiction as well, and even the occasional fantasy, Harry Turtledove has become one of the most prominent writers of Alternate History stories in the business today, and is probably the most popular and influential writer to work that territory since L. Sprague De Camp; in fact, most of the current popularity of that particular subgenre can be attributed to Turtledove's own hot-ticket best-seller status.

Turtledove has published Alternate History novels such as *The Guns of the South*, dealing with a time line in which the American Civil War turns out *very* differently, thanks to time-travelling gunrunners, the best-selling *Worldwar* series, in which the course of World War II is altered by attacking aliens, the "Basil Argyros" series, detailing the adventures of a "magistrianoi" in an alternate Byzantine Empire (collected in the book *Agent of Byzantium*), the "Sim" series, which take place in an alternate world in which European explorers find North America inhabited by hominids instead of Indians (collected in the book *A Different Flesh*), a look at a world where the Revolutionary War *didn't* happen, written with actor Richard Dreyfuss, *The Two Georges*, and many other intriguing Alternate History scenarios. Turtledove is also the author of two multivolume Alternate History *fantasy* series, the multivolume "Videssos Cycle" and the "Krispes Sequence." His other books include the novels *Wereblood, Werenight, Earthgrip, Noninterference, A World of Difference*, and *Ruled Britannia*, the collections *Kaleidoscope* and *Down in the Bottomlands (and Other Places)*, and, as editor, *The Best Alternate History Stories of the 20th Century* and *The Best Military Science Fiction of the 20th Century*—plus *many* others. His most recent books include the novels *Gunpowder Empire, American Empire: The Victorious Opposition, Jaws of Darkness,* and *In the Presence of Mine Enemies.* He won a Hugo Award in 1994 for his story, "Down in the Bottomlands." A native Californian, Turtledove has a Ph.D. in Byzantine history from UCLA, and has published a scholarly translation of a 9th century Byzantine chronicle. He lives in Canoga Park, California, with his wife and family.

Here he shows us how the history of the mid-twentieth century could have turned out disturbingly different—and those who think that a *similar* scenario couldn't happen here tomorrow are, I fear, whistling in the dark.

> "Stalin was a Democrat . . ."
>
> —*from "god & the fbi" by Janis Ian*

Amererica. 1932. Bread lines. Soup kitchens. Brother, can you spare a dime? Banks dying like flies. Brokers swan diving from the twenty-seventh floor.

Herbert Hoover. Dead man walking. Couldn't get reelected running with the Holy Ghost. Republicans nominate him again anyway. Got nobody better. Don't know how much trouble they're in.

Democrats smell blood in the water. Twelve long years sitting on the sidelines. Twelve lean years. Twelve hungry years. Harding—women got the vote for *this?* Coolidge—"I've got a five-dollar bet, Mr. Coolidge, that I can get you to say three words." "You lose," says Silent Cal. Hoover—Black Tuesday. The crash. Enough said. It's on his watch. He gets the blame. Blood in the water.

Democrats smell it. Whoever they put up, he's gonna win. Gonna be president. At last. Been so long. Twelve years. Sweet Jesus Christ! Want it so bad they can taste it.

Convention time. Chicago. End of June. Humidity's high. Heat's higher. Two men left in the fight. One wins the prize. The other? Hind tit.

Two men left. Franklin D. Roosevelt. D for Delano, mind. Governor of New York. Cousin to Teddy Roosevelt. Already ran for vice president once. Didn't win. Cigarette holder. Jaunty angle. Wheelchair. Paralysis. Anguish. Courage. As near an aristocrat as America grows. Franklin D. Roosevelt. D for Delano.

And Joe Steele.

Joe Steele. Congressman from California. Not San Francisco. Not Nob Hill. Good Lord, no. Fresno. Farm country. That great valley, squeezed by mountains east and west. Not a big fellow, Joe Steele. Stands real straight, so you don't notice too much. Mustache, a good-sized one. Thick head of hair just starting to go gray. Eyelids like shutters. When they go down and then come up again, you can't see what was behind them.

Aristocrat? Aristocrat like Franklin D. (D for Delano) Roosevelt? Don't make me laugh. Folks came from the ass end of nowhere. Got to Fresno six months before he was born. He was a citizen years before they were. Father was a shoemaker. Did some farming later on, too. Mother tended house. That's what women did.

They say Steele's not the right name. Not the name he was born with. They say God Himself couldn't say that name straight two times running. They say, they say. Who gives a good goddamn what they say? This is America. He's Joe Steele now. Then? What's then got to do with it? That was the old country, or near enough.

Franklin D. Roosevelt. D for Delano. And Joe Steele.

Chicago Stadium. Sweltering. Air-conditioning? You've got to be kidding. Not even in the hotels. You put on two electric fans when you go back to your room, if you ever do. They stir the air around a little. Cool it? Ha! Hell is where you go for relief from this.

First ballot's even, near enough. Roosevelt's got a New Deal for people, or says he does. Joe Steele? He's got a Four-Year Plan, or says *he* does. Got his whole first term mapped out. Farms in trouble? Farmers going broke? We'll make *community* farms, Joe Steele says. Take farmers, get 'em working together for a change. Not every man for himself like it has been. People out of work from factories? Build government factories for 'em! Build dams. Build canals. Build any damn thing that needs building.

Some folks love the notion. Others say it sounds like Trotsky's Russia. Just don't say that around Joe Steele. He can't stand Trotsky. You put the two of 'em in a room together, Joe Steele'll bash out Trotsky's brains.

First ballot. Even's not even good enough. Democrats have a two-thirds rule. Had it forever. Goddamn two-thirds rule helped start the Civil War. Douglas couldn't get over the hump. The party split. Lincoln won. Five months later—Fort Sumter.

All the same, goddamn two-thirds rule's still there.

Roosevelt's back in New York. Joe Steele's in Fresno. You don't come to a convention till you've won. Out on that smoky, sweaty, stinking Chicago Stadium floor, their handlers go toe to toe. Roosevelt's got Farley, Howe, Tugwell. Back-East people. People everybody knows. They think they're pretty sharp, pretty sly, and they're pretty close to right.

Joe Steele's got a smart Jew named Kagan. He's got an Armenian raisin grower's kid named Mikoian. Stas Mikoian's even smarter than Kagan. His brother works for Douglas, designs fighter planes. Lots of brains in that family. And Joe Steele's got this pencil-necked little guy they call the Hammer.

A big, mean bruiser gets a name like that hung on him, he's liable to be very bad news. A little, scrawny fellow? Ten times worse.

You think a smart Jew and a smarter Armenian can't skin those back-East hotshots? Watch 'em go at it.

And watch the hotshots fight back. Second ballot, not much change. Third, the same. By then, it's not nighttime any more. It's a quarter past nine the next morning. Everybody's as near dead as makes no difference. Delegates stagger out of Chicago Stadium to get a little sleep and try it all over again.

Second day, same damn thing. Third and fourth, same again. Ballot after ballot. Roosevelt's a little ahead, but only a little. Joe Steele's people, they don't back down. Joe Steele doesn't back down to anybody. Never has. Never will.

Fifth day, still no winner. Goddamn two-thirds rule. Papers start talking about 1924. Democrats take 103 ballots—103!—to put up John W. Davis. Damn convention takes two and a half weeks. Then what happens? Coolidge cleans his clock.

Nobody quite knows what goes on right after that. Some folks say—whisper, really, on account of it's safer—the guy they call the Hammer makes a phone call. But nobody knows. Except the Hammer, and he's not talking. The Hammer, he wouldn't say boo to a goose.

Albany. State Executive Mansion. Where the Governor works. Where he lives. Governor Roosevelt. Franklin D. (D for Delano) Roosevelt. Southwest corner of Engle and Elm. Red brick building. Big one. Built around the Civil War. Governor works on the first floor, lives on the second.

State Executive Mansion. Old building. Modern conveniences? Well, sure. But added on. Not built in. If they kind of creak sometimes, well, they do, that's all. Old building.

Nighttime. Fire. Big fire. Hell of a big fire. Southwest corner of Engle and Elm. Fire hoses? Well, sure. But no water pressure, none to speak of. That's what they say, the ones who get out. Awful lot of people don't.

Roosevelt? Roosevelt's in a wheelchair. How's a man in a wheelchair going to get out of a big old fire? The time that fire's finally out, Roosevelt's dead as shoe leather. He's done about medium-well, matter of fact, but that don't make the papers.

Kagan? Kagan's in Chicago. Stas Mikoian? Same thing. The Hammer? He's in Chicago, too. None of 'em goes anywhere. They're all there before, during, and after. Nobody ever says anything different.

Joe Steele? Joe Steele's in Fresno. All the way on the other side of the country. Joe Steele's hands are clean. Nobody ever says anything different. Not very loud, anyhow. And never—*never*—more than once.

Joe Steele is shocked—*shocked*—to hear about the fire. Calls it a tragic accident. Calls Roosevelt a worthy rival. Says all the right things. Sounds like he means 'em. Says the Democrats have got to get on with the business of kicking the snot out of the Republicans. Says that's the whole point of the convention.

And the eyelids like shutters go down. And then they come up again. And you can't see what's behind them. You can't see one goddamn thing.

So they nominate him. What else are they gonna do? John Nance Garner? Who the hell ever heard of John Nance Garner? Outside of Texas, John Nance Garner ain't worth a pitcher of warm spit. Hoover might even lick him. No. It's a moment of silence and a round of applause for Franklin D. (D for Delano) Roosevelt. And then it's Joe Steele. Joe Steele! *Joe Steele!*

Joe Steele for President! John Nance Garner for Vice President!

Hoover mostly stays in Washington. When he goes out, he campaigns on his record. Proves how far out of touch he is, don't it?

Joe Steele's everywhere. Everywhere. Whistle-stops on the train. Car trips. *Airplane* trips, for crying out loud. In the newsreels. On the radio. Joe Steele and his Four-Year Plan! Drummer can't shack up with a waitress without Joe Steele peeking in the window and telling 'em both to vote for him.

And if they're like everybody else, they do.

November 8, 1932. Hoover takes Delaware. He takes Pennsylvania. He takes Connecticut. And Vermont, New Hampshire, Maine. Joe Steele takes the country. Every other state. Better than fifty-seven percent of the vote to less than forty. And coattails? My Lord! More than three-fifths of the seats in the Senate. Almost three-quarters of the seats in the House.

March 4, 1933. Joe Steele comes to Washington. Inauguration Day. Hoover's in top hat and tails to go out. Joe Steele's in a flat cloth cap, a collarless shirt, and dungarees to go in. *Watch* the flashbulbs pop!

He takes the oath of office. Herbert Hoover shakes his hand. Herbert Hoover sits down. He's done. He's gone. He's out of this story.

Joe Steele speaks. He says, "We will have jobs. Labor is a matter of honor, a matter of fame, a matter of valor and heroism. *We will have jobs!*" Oh, how they cheer!

He says, "Yes, I admit I'm abrupt, but only toward those who harm the people of this country. What is my duty? To stick to my post and fight for them. It isn't in my character to quit."

He says, "We will do whatever we have to do to get the United States on its feet again. You cannot make a revolution with silk gloves." He holds up his hands. He's worked in his life, Joe Steele has. Those hard, hairy hands show it. More cheers. Loud ones.

And he says, "When banks fail, they steal the people's money. Have you ever seen a hungry banker? Has anyone in the history of the world ever seen a hungry banker? If I have to choose between the people and the bankers, I choose the people. We will nationalize the banks and save the people's money." This time, the cheers damn near knock him right off the platform. Joe Steele looks out. The eyelids like shutters go down. They come up again. Joe Steele . . . smiles.

Congress. Special session. Laws sail through, one after another. Nationalize the banks. Set up community farms for farmers who've lost their land—and for anybody else who wants to join. Factories for workers who've lost their jobs. Dams on every damn river that doesn't have any. That's how it seems, anyway. Dams put people to work. Stop floods. And make lots of new electricity.

Joe Steele, he's crazy for electricity. "Only when the farmer is surrounded by electrical wiring will he become a citizen," he says. "The biggest hope and weapon for our country is industry, and making the farmer part of industry. It is impossible to base construction on two different foundations, on the foundation of large-scale and highly concentrated industry, and on the foundation of very fragmented and extremely backward agriculture. Systematically and persistently, we must place agriculture on a new technical basis, the basis of large-scale production, and raise it to the level of an industry."

Some people think Joe Steele's just plain crazy. Soon as the laws start passing, the lawsuits start coming. Courts throw out the new laws, one after the next. Joe Steele appeals. Cases go to the Supreme Court. Supreme Court says unconstitutional. Says you can't do that.

Don't tell Joe Steele no. Bad idea. There's a young hotshot in Washington. Fellow named J. Edgar Hoover. Smart. Tough. Face like a bulldog. Headed the Justice Department Bureau of Investigation since before he was thirty. Not even forty yet. Knows where the bodies are buried. Buried some himself, folks say.

Joe Steele calls him to the White House. He leaves, he's smiling. You don't want to see J. Edgar Hoover smile. Trust me. You don't. Back in the Oval Office, Joe Steele's smiling, too. Here's somebody he can do business with.

Three weeks go by. Supreme Court calls another law unconstitutional. "These nine old men are hurting the country," Joe Steele says. "Why are they doing that? What can they want?"

Three more weeks go by. Arrests! Justice Department Bureau of Investigation nabs Supreme Court Justice Van Devanter! Justice McReynolds! Justice Sutherland! Justice Butler! Treason! Treason and plotting with Hitler! Sensation!

Habeas corpus denied. Traitors might flee, Joe Steele says. Anybody who complains sounds like a goddamn Nazi. No ordinary trials, not for the Gang of Four (thank you, Walter Lippmann). Military tribunals. They've got it coming.

J. Edgar Hoover has the evidence. Bales of it. Documents. Witnesses. Reichsmarks with the swastika right there on 'em. But some people—you just can't figure some people—don't believe it. They figure the Justices'll come out in court and make J. Edgar and his boys look like a bunch of monkeys. Even if they're in military tribunals, they'll get to speak their piece, right?

Right. They will. They do. *And they confess*, right there in front of the whole country. On the radio. On the newsreels. In the papers. They confess. We did it. We were wreckers. We wanted to tear down what Joe Steele's building up. We wanted to see the USA go Fascist. Better that than what Joe Steele's doing.

Oh. And we got our marching orders from Father Coughlin. And Huey Long.

More arrests!

Father Coughlin 'fesses up in front of a military tribunal, same as the Supreme Court Justices. More radio. More newsreels. More newspaper headlines. Huey Long? They shoot the Kingfish trying to break out of Leavenworth. That's how they tell it. Shoot him dead, dead, dead. Show off what's left of him on the screen and in the papers.

Then they shoot Van Devanter. And McReynolds. And Sutherland. And Butler. It's treason. They've confessed. Why the hell not shoot 'em? Sunrise. Blindfolds. Cigarettes. Firing squads. No last words. Die for treason and you don't deserve 'em.

Father Coughlin goes the same way. Somebody gets his last words, though. Order to fire goes out right between "*Ave*" and "*Maria*." *Ave atque vale*. And a hell of a volley to finish him off.

Joe Steele picks four new Justices. They sail on through the Senate. You think the Supreme Court'll say unconstitutional again any time soon? I sure as hell don't. Don't reckon Joe Steele does either.

J. Edgar Hoover goes to the White House again. All of a sudden, it's not the Justice Department Bureau of Investigation. It's the *Government* Bureau of Investigation. The GBI. J. Edgar's got a face like a bulldog, yeah. He comes out of his talk with Joe Steele, he's wagging his tail like a happy little goddamn bulldog, too.

They're made for each other, J. Edgar Hoover and Joe Steele. Trotsky's got Beria. Hitler's got Himmler. And Joe Steele? Joe Steele's got J. Edgar.

When 1936 rolls around, folks wonder if the Republicans will run anybody against Joe Steele. They do. Alf Landon. Governor of Kansas. "The Matter with Kansas," some folks call him, but he's got to have balls. More balls than brains, running against Joe Steele.

Are folks that much better off? Any better off? Who knows for sure? But Joe Steele's *doing* things. So they're a little hungry on those community farms? So they don't grow a hell of a lot of crops? So what? Somebody cares about 'em, cares enough to try and find something new.

And after Van Devanter, and McReynolds, and Sutherland, and Butler, if anybody's unhappy, is he gonna say so? Would you?

Joe Steele says he's got himself a Second Four-Year Plan Says it'll be even bigger than the first one. Doesn't say better. Says bigger. Is there a difference? Not to Joe Steele, there's not.

November comes around again. Joe Steele comes around again. Even bigger massacre than against Hoover. (Herbert, not J. Edgar. J. Edgar's massacres are different.) As Maine goes, so goes Vermont.

The rest? It's Joe Steele. All Joe Steele.

He takes the oath of office again. Chief Justice is real careful around him. Everybody notices. Nobody says boo, though. You want to watch what you say where Joe Steele can hear. Or J. Edgar. Or anybody else. J. Edgar's got snitches like a stray dog's got fleas. Run your mouth and you'll be sorry.

Somebody takes a shot at Joe Steele a couple months after the second term starts. Misses. GBI shoots him dead. Fills him full of holes like a colander. They say his name is Otto Spitzer. Say he's a German. Say he's got Nazi ties. Joe Steele cusses and fumes and shakes his fist at Hitler. And the *Führer* cusses and fumes and shakes his fist back. And neither one of 'em can reach the other. Ain't life grand?

Not much later, GBI raids the War Department. Newsreels full of tough guys in fedoras carrying tommy guns leading generals and colonels out of the building with their hands in the air. Hardly any guards at the War Department. Who'd think you needed 'em?

Treason trials. Again. General after general, colonel after colonel, in bed with the Germans. Evidence. Letters. Photos. GBI shows 'em off. They must be real. Some confessions. *They* must be real. Convictions. Sentences. To be shot. Doesn't get any neater than that.

Congressman Sam Rayburn gets up on his hind legs. Asks where the devil we're going. Asks what the devil Joe Steele thinks he's doing. Looks like we're heading for hell in a goddamn hand-basket. Two days later, big old goddamn traffic smashup. Sam Rayburn dies on the way to the hospital.

"A loss to the whole country," Joe Steele calls it on the radio. The eyelids like shutters go down. They come up. This time, maybe you do know what's back there. We're going wherever Joe Steele damn well pleases. And Joe Steele thinks he's doing whatever he damn well pleases.

And you know what else? He's right.

Treason trials start for real a few weeks later. Not just Justices. Not just generals. Folks. Doctors. Lawyers. Professors. Mechanics. Bakers. Salesmen. Housewives. Anybody who talks out of turn. Even GBI men. Joe Steele and J. Edgar take no chances. Miss no tricks.

Conviction after conviction after conviction. Where to put 'em all? What to do with 'em all? You thought a lot of stuff got built the First Four-Year Plan? Take a gander at the second one. Dams again. Highways. Endless miles of highways. Canals—all dug by hand. More town buildings than you can shake a stick at.

Waste a lot of people that way, you say? So what? Plenty more where they came from. Oh, hell, yes. Plenty more. And when the camp rats who live finish out their terms, what do you do with 'em? Send 'em to Alaska. Send 'em to North Dakota or Wyoming or Montana or some other place that needs people. Tell 'em they're fine, long as they stay where they're sent. They don't stay? Back to the camps. That, or they get it in the neck.

Most of 'em stay. Most folks know, by then, Joe Steele means business.

Europe. War clouds. Hitler. Trotsky. Appeasement—France and England shaking in their boots. Joe Steele? Joe Steele's neutral. Blames half the troubles in the USA on the goddamn Nazis. Blames the other half on the godless Reds. That takes care of all the blame there is. Any left to stick to Joe Steele? No way. Not a chance.

Bullets start flying over there. Joe Steele goes up in front of Congress. Makes his famous "plague on both your houses" speech. "We have have stood apart, studiously neutral," says Joe Steele. "We will go on doing that, because this fight is not worth the red blood of one single American boy. The USA must be neutral in fact as well as name. Neither side over there has a cause worth going to war for. No, sir. The greatest dangers for our country lurk in insidious encroachments for foreign powers by men of zeal. As long as we stamp that out at home, everything will be fine here. And as long as we stay away from Europe's latest foolish war, everything will be fine—for us—there."

But in the end, Joe Steele can't stay away. When France falls, he sees even the Atlantic may not be wide enough to keep Hitler away from the doorstep. He starts selling England as much as it needs, as much as he can. "If the Devil opposed Adolf Hitler, I should endeavor to give him a good notice in the House of Commons," Churchill says. "Thus I thank Joe Steele."

And Joe Steele's running for a third term. And Joe Steele wins, too. Wins even bigger than 1936. What's a Wendell Willkie? Not enough, that's for sure. After all the treason trials and such, some folks are surprised. By this time, hardly anybody says so out loud, though. By this time, folks know better.

Joe Steele and J. Edgar, they kind of laugh about it, them and the Hammer. Somebody says Joe Steele quotes Boss Tweed: "As long as I count the votes, what are you going to do about it?" Boss Tweed's long dead by then. And if anybody else repeats that, he'll be dead pretty damn quick, too.

When Hitler jumps Trotsky, Joe Steele needs six weeks before he starts shipping guns and trucks to Russia. He hates Trotsky that much. But if the Nazis run things from Brest to Vladivostok, that's not so good. So he does.

Damn near too late. By December, the Nazis are driving on Moscow. Sinking American ships in the Atlantic, too. And we sink a couple of German subs. Doesn't make the papers here or in Europe. If you don't look at it, it's not a war. Right? Joe Steele and Hitler think so.

And when Joe Steele's bent over squinting toward Europe, the Japs kick him in the ass. Pearl Harbor blows sky high. Philippines bombed. Invaded. Dutch East Indies invaded. Malaya. We don't want a war? We've got one anyway.

Next morning, Joe Steele comes on the radio. Has to eat his words. Never easy for anybody. Harder if you've set yourself up as always right. Joe Steele does it. Just makes like he never said anything different. Not how you remember it? Too bad for you, if you run your mouth.

"A grave danger hangs over our country," he says. Everybody with a radio listens. "The perfidious military attack on our beloved United States of America, begun on December 7, 1941, continues. There can be no doubt that this short-lived military gain for the Empire of Japan is only an episode. The war with Japan cannot be considered an ordinary war. It is not only a war between two armies and navies, it is also a great war of the entire American people against the Imperial Japanese forces.

"In this war for freedom we shall not be alone. Our forces are numberless. The overweening enemy will soon learn this to his cost. Side by side with the U.S. Army and Navy, thousands of workers, community farmers, and scientists are rising to fight the enemy aggressors. The masses of our people will rise up in their millions.

"To repulse the enemy who treacherously attacked our country, a State Committee for Defense has been formed in whose hands the entire power of the state has been vested. The Committee calls upon all our people to rally around the party of Jefferson and Jackson and Wilson and around the U.S. government so as self-denyingly to support the U.S. Army and Navy, demolish the enemy, and secure victory. Forward!"

Congress declares war on Japan. Hitler declares war on the USA. Joe Steele orders up two new military tribunals. Admiral Kimmel. General Short. In charge of Hawaii. Screwed the pooch in Hawaii. Guilty. Shot *Pour encourager les autres*.

Philippines fall. MacArthur escapes to Australia. Tribunal. Bombers caught on the ground? Yes. Guilty. Shot. MacArthur likes to see his name in the papers. Can't have that kind of general. Only one man gets his name in the papers.

Joe Steele.

Joe Steele and George Marshall, now, they do fine. Marshall wants to win. Wants no fanfares. Joe Steele's kind of man. Same with Nimitz. Same with Eisenhower. Halsey? If Halsey ever loses, he's a dead man. Knows it. Keeps winning.

We push back the Japs. *Afrika Korps* runs out of steam in the desert. Germans and Russians fight the biggest goddamn battle in the world at Trotskygrad. Both sides throw men into the meat grinder like it's going out of style. Turns out the Reds have more men to grind up. Nazis lose a whole army. Russians storm west. For a little while, looks like the whole Eastern Front's coming unglued. Doesn't happen. Stinking Nazis are bastards, but they're pros, if Hitler lets 'em be. Still, you can see they're on the ropes. It'll take a while, but it's when, not if.

Joe Steele and Churchill and Trotsky meet. Start planning what happens next. Trotsky keeps screaming for a real second front. Italy? Screw Italy! Joe Steele . . . smiles. Heaven is every Nazi killing two Reds before he goes down. No more Germans left? No more Russians? Oh, toooo bad.

But it starts looking like there aren't enough krauts to do the trick. Nobody wants Russia running things from Vladivostok to Brest either. Second front happens. Eisenhower commands. Eisenhower doesn't hog glory that belongs to Joe Steele. Smart fellow, Eisenhower. Joe Steele wins fourth term. Republicans don't nominate anybody this time.

Philippines fall. Iwo Jima. Okinawa. Bomb the shit out of the Japs. Get ready to invade.

Germany? American and British hammer. Russian anvil. Smashed between 'em. Smashed *flat* between 'em. Hitler blows out his brains. 'Bye, Adolf. Should have done it sooner.

Start shifting men to the Pacific. Operation Downfall. Makes Normandy look like a kiddie game. Japs fight at beaches, everywhere else. Maniacs. Kamikazes. Everything they've got. Not enough. We push 'em back. Hell of a price to pay, but we pay it. Trotsky sees we're winning. Jumps in himself. Takes

Hokkaido, north part of Honshu. Rest is ours. Incendiaries roast Hirohito on a train between Tokyo and Kyoto. *Sayonara*, buddy.

Japan never does surrender. Nobody in charge left to do it. But the Japs finally stop fighting. Nobody left to do that anymore either, not hardly. End of summer, '46.

Joe Steele. On top of the world.

Turns out the Nazis were working on an atomic bomb. Not too hard. Didn't really believe in it. Never got it. But working. Joe Steele hits the ceiling in sixteen different places. Maybe eighteen. Calls in Einstein. "Why didn't you know about this?" he yells.

"We did," Albert says. "I almost wrote you a letter at the start of the war."

Joe Steele's eyelids go down. They come up. Yeah, you can see what's back there this time. Rage. Raw, red rage. "Why didn't you?" he asks, all quiet and scary.

"I feared you would use it," Einstein answers. Half a dozen words. One death warrant.

Einstein? Shot. A Jew.

Szilard? Shot. A Jew.

Fermi? Shot. A dago with a Jew wife.

Von Neumann? Shot. A Jew.

Oppenheimer? Shot. A Jew.

There are more. Lots more. Shot, most of 'em, Jews or not. The rest? To the camps.

"The Professors' Plot," the papers call it. All these goddamn eggheads, working to keep the US of A weak. All these goddamn kikes, working to keep the US of A weak. Joe Steele starts muttering maybe Hitler knew what he was doing. Talks to the Hammer. Talks to J. Edgar. The wheels begin to turn.

Then he finds Teller. Teller says, "Turn me loose. I'll build the son of a bitch in three years, or you can have my head." *Another* goddamn Jew. But one who knows which side his bread's buttered on. Some of the people Teller needs—Feynman, Frisch, Kistiakowsky—he pulls out of camps. There, but not shot yet. Maybe not shot at all, if they come through. First circle of hell, close enough.

Joe Steele tells J. Edgar and the Hammer, "Go slow." If Teller and the boys come through, maybe some kikes are worth keeping. If not . . . We know who they are. We know where they live. We can always start up again. Oh, hell, yes.

And Trotsky, that stinking Red bastard, he's working on this shit, too. You bet he is. We caught Nazi high foreheads. And they caught Nazi high foreheads. You think the boys from the master race won't sing for their supper?

Sing for their necks? Ha! Wernher von Braun'd learn Chinese if Chiang caught him. Or Mao.

And Trotsky's a pain in the ass other ways. World revolution everywhere, he says. 1948. His North Japan invades our South Japan. War of liberation, he says. Red Japs sweeping down toward Tokyo. Screaming "Banzai!" for Trotsky. (Trotsky's a Jew, too. Makes Joe Steele like 'em even better.)

Hell of a thing—a brand new war, and the old one's hardly done. Trotsky's Japs fight like they're nuts. Our Japs run like they're nuts. It's a walkover—till the North Japanese bump up against the U.S. Marines in front of Utsanomiya. If they break through, Tokyo falls. Probably all Honshu with it. But they don't. Marines hold. Give the Red Japs a bloody nose.

Everybody knows Russians fly the Gurevich-9 jet fighters with the yellow star inside the Rising Sun. Not as good as our F-80s—Me-262s with those starred meatballs, near enough—but fancier than what we thought those SOBs had. Fighting kind of settles down in the mountains. Now they go forward. Now we do. Places like Sukiyaki Valley and Mamasan Ridge? Folks back home don't know just where they're at, but a lot of kids get buried there.

Joe Steele wins term number five as easy as number four. Nobody runs against him. There's a war on.

August 6, 1949. Sapporo. Capital of North Japan. One bomb. No city. Teller lives. Joe Steele tells Trotsky, "Enough is enough."

August 9, 1949. Nagano. *Not* the capital of South Japan. Maybe the AA around Tokyo's too heavy to risk losing the plane. But a hell of a big place. One bomb. No city. Maybe some German egghead lives, too. Trotsky tells Joe Steele, "Yeah, enough *is* enough."

Japanese War ends. *Status quo ante bellum.* Mao runs Chiang off the mainland. More treason trials. Something to keep Joe Steele amused. Getting old. Wins a sixth term almost in his sleep. Dies six weeks after they swear him in again. Natural causes. Who'd dare mess with him?

John Nance Garner, Vice President since 1933. Never says boo all that time. That's *why* he's VP so long. Finally takes over. First thing he does is is order J. Edgar Hoover and the Hammer shot. The Hammer orders him and J. Edgar Hoover shot. J. Edgar orders both the others shot.

J. Edgar lives. J. Edgar takes over. And you thought Joe Steele was trouble?

Birth Days

GEOFF RYMAN

You may think that you already live in a world that demands complex choices of you at every turn, but, as the incisive little story that follows demonstrates, in the not-too-distant future, the choices are going to get even *more* complicated—and the consequences of them more profound.

Born in Canada, Geoff Ryman now lives in England. He made his first sale in 1976, to *New Worlds*, but it was not until 1984, when he made his first appearance in *Interzone*—the magazine where almost of all his published short fiction has appeared—with his brilliant novella "The Unconquered Country" that he first attracted any serious attention. "The Unconquered Country," one of the best novellas of the decade, had a stunning impact on the science fiction scene of the day, and almost overnight established Ryman as one of the most accomplished writers of his generation, winning him both the British Science Fiction Award and the World Fantasy Award; it was later published in a book version, *The Unconquered Country: A Life History*. His output has been sparse since then, by the high-production standards of the genre, but extremely distinguished, with his novel *The Child Garden: A Low Comedy* winning both the prestigious Arthur C. Clarke Award and the John W. Campbell Memorial Award. His other novels include *The Warrior Who Carried Life*, the critically acclaimed mainstream novel *Was*, and the underground cult classic *253*, the "print remix" of an "interactive hypertext novel," which in its original form ran online on Ryman's home page of www.ryman.com, and which, in its print form won the Philip K. Dick Award. Four of his novellas have been collected in *Unconquered Countries*. His most recent books are two new novels, *Lust* and *Air*. His stories have appeared in our Twelfth, Thirteenth, Seventeenth, Nineteenth, and Twentieth Annual Collections.

Today's my 16th birthday, so I gave myself a present.

I came out to my Mom.

Sort of. By accident. I left out a mail from Billy, which I could just have left on the machine, but no, I had to go and print it out and leave it on my night table, looking like a huge white flag.

I get up this morning and I kinda half-notice it's not there. I lump into the kitchen and I can see where it went. The letter is in Mom's hand and the look on her face tells me, yup, she's read it. She has these grey lines down either side of her mouth. She holds it up to me, and says, "Can you tell me why you wouldn't have the courage to tell me this directly?"

And I'm thinking how could I be so dumb? Did I do this to myself deliberately? And I'm also thinking wait a second, where do you get off reading my letters?

So I say to her, "Did you like the part where he says my dick is beautiful?"

She says, "Not much, no." She's already looking at me like I'm an alien. And I'm like: Mom, this is what you get for being NeoChristian—your son turns out to be homo. What the Neos call a Darwinian anomaly.

Mom sighs and says, "Well I suppose we're stuck with it now."

Yeah Mom, you kinda are. Aren't you supposed to say something mimsy like, Ron honey you know we still love you? Not my Mom. Oh no. Saying exactly what she thinks is Mom's way of being real, and her being real is more important to her than anything else. Like what I might be feeling.

So I dig back at her. "That's a shame, Mom. A few years later and I would have been embryo-screened and you could have just aborted me."

Mom just sniffs. "That was a cheap shot."

Yeah, it was. NeoChristians are about the only people who *don't* abort homosexual foetuses. Everybody else does. What do they call it? Parental choice.

So Mom looks at me with this real tough face and says, "I hope you think you've given yourself a happy birthday." And that's all the conversation we have about it.

My little brother is pretending he isn't there and that he isn't happy. My little brother is shaped like a pineapple. He's fat and he has asthma and he's really good at being sneaky and not playing by the rules. I was always the big brother who tolerated stuff and tried to help Mom along. Her good little boy. Only now I'm samesex. Which to a NeoChristian Mom is like finding out your son likes dressing up as a baby and being jerked off by animals. Sometimes I think Neo is just a way to find new reasons to hate the same old things.

What really dents my paintwork is that Mom is smart: What she likes about Neo is that it's Darwinian. Last summer she's reading this article *Samesex Gene Planted by Aliens?* And she's rolling her eyes at it. "The least they could do is get the science straight," she says. "It's not one gene and it's not one part of the brain." But then she said, "But you gotta wonder, why is there a gene like that in the first place?"

My Mom really does think that there's a chance that homos are an alien plot. Please do not fall over laughing, it hurts too much.

Ever since the Artefacts were found, people have been imagining little green men landing on this beautiful blue planet and just going off again. So people scare themselves wondering if the aliens are about to come back with a nice big army.

Then about five years ago, it turned out that the genes that control sexual orientation have some very unusual sugars, and all of a sudden there's this conspiracy theory that the aliens created the samesex gene as some kind of weapon. Undermine our reproductive capacity. Even though when they landed we were all triblodites or whatever. Maybe having homos is supposed to soften us up for conquest. Hey, if the aliens invade, I promise, I'll fight too OK?

On my way to school I ring Billy and tell him, "Mom found out. She read your mail."

Billy sounds stripped for action, "Did she go crazy?"

"She went laconic. You could just hear her thinking: you gotta own this, Ronald, you did this to yourself, Ronald."

"It's better than crying."

Billy's in Comportment class. He believes all that shit. To be fair to him, that "you gotta own this" was me digging at some of the stuff he comes out with. That stuff pisses me off. In fact right now, everything pisses me off. Right now, it's like my guts are twisting and I want to go break something.

Comportment says you've got to own the fact people don't like you, own the fact you got fat hips, own the fact you're no good in math, own the fact that glacial lakes are collapsing onto Tibetan monasteries. Comportment says hey, you're complaining about the Chinese treatment of Tibet, but what have you personally done about it?

It's like: we'll make everybody who has no power feel it's their fault if stuff goes wrong, so the big people don't have to do anything about it.

My Mom hates me being a homo. She likes being a big tough lady even more. So, she like, doesn't get all upset or cry or even say much about it. Being a tough lady is her way of feeling good about her son being an alien plot.

Billy is too focused on being Joe Cool-and-Out to cut me any slack. His stab at being sympathetic is "You should have just told her straight up, like I told you."

I say back to him in this Minnie-Mouse voice, "I acknowledge that you are absolutely right." That's another line he's used on me.

He's silent for a sec and then says, "Well, don't be a bitch with me about it."

"It's my authentic response to an emotionally charged situation." Still sounding like Minnie Mouse.

I'm mad at him. I'm mad at him because he just won't unbend. Nobody unbends. It's bad comportment.

Billy comes back at me. "This is just you going back to being a baby. Only you don't have tantrums, you just whine."

"Billy. My NeoChristian Mom now knows I'm samesex. Could I have some sympathy?"

"Who's died, Ron? Anybody dead around here? Did you lose any limbs in the detonation? Or are you just getting all significant on my ass?"

"No. I'm looking for a friend. I'll try and find one, you know, someone who likes me and not my dick?"

And I hang up.

Like I said, I'm so mad.

I'm mad sitting here right now. I got my stupid kid brother who's been giggling all day, like it's such an achievement he likes pussy. I got my Mom doing the household accounts and her shares and her rollovers, and she's bellowing into the voice recognition and it's like: look at me having to do all the work around here. I'm realizing that I've probably screwed up my relationship with Billy and wondering if I really am the incredible wimp he thinks I am.

It's like everything all around me is Jell-O and it's setting into lemon-lime, which I hate. I'm out. My brother knows and will try to give me a hard time, and if he does I'll slug his fat face. My Mom is being hard ass, and so I'm going to be hard ass back. I'm not an athlete, I'm not Joe Cool-and-Out, and I'll never go to Mom's Neo seminars.

I'm just sitting here all alone thinking: how can I win? What can I do?

I'll never be able to be a good little boy again. That is not an option. I'm not interested in being political about who I sleep with. I don't sign up to anything, I don't believe anything, and I don't like anybody, and I don't think anybody likes me.

Hey. A fresh start. Happy birthday.

So, 26 today!

I got up at 3:00 am and holoed over to the Amazon to say hi to João. He looked so happy to see me, his little face was just one huge smile. He'd organized getting some of his sisters to line up behind him. They all waved and smiled and downloaded me a smart diary for my present. In Brazil, they still sing Happy Birthday.

Love conquers all. With a bit of work.

I called João later and we did our usual daily download. His testosterone levels were through the roof, he's getting so stimulated by his new job in the Indian Devolved Areas. He's about to go off to Eden to start his diplomatic work. He looks so sweet in a penis sheath and a parrot's feather through his nose. Standard diplomatic dress for a member of the Brazilian Consular Team.

I love him I love him I love him I love him.

I am so god damned lucky. They didn't have embryo-screening on the Amazon. Hey! A fellow sodomite. We're an endangered species everywhere else. Must eliminate those nasty alien genes.

Then I had to go and tell him about how my project was going. And he looked glum.

"I know you don't like it," I told him.

"It feels wrong. Like genocide." He pronounces it jenoseed. "Soon they will be no more."

"But it's not genocide. The babies come out hetero, that's all. No more samesex, no more screening, just happy babies. And the adults who are left can decide for themselves if they want to be cured or not. Anyway, the Neos say that *we're* the genocide."

"You don't need to help them."

"João. Baby. It won't affect us. We'll still have each other."

"The Indians say it is unwise."

"Do they? That's interesting. How come?"

"They say it is good to have other ways. They think it is like what almost happened to them."

That rang true. So me and João have this really great conversation about it, very neutral, very scientific. He's just so smart.

Before the alien gene thing, they used to say that homos were a pool of altruistic non-reproducing labour. It's like, we baby-sit for our siblings' kids and that increases the survival potential of our family's genes. Because a gene that makes it unlikely that you'll have kids should have died out. So why was it still here?

João tells his usual joke about all the singers in Brazil being samesex, which is just about true. So I say, wow, the human race couldn't reproduce without Dança do Brasil, huh? Which was a joke. And he says, maybe so.

I say like I always do, "You know, don't you, baby?"

His voice goes soft and warm. "I know. Do you know?"

Yes. Oh yes, I know.

That you love me. We love each other.

We've been saying that every day now for five years. It still gives me a buzz. It was a big day at the lab too. The lights finally went on inside Flat Man.

Flat Man is pretty horrible, to tell you the truth. He's a culture, only the organs are differentiated and the bones are wafer-thin and spread out in a support structure. He looks like a cross between a spider's web and somebody who's been hit by a truck. And he covers an entire wall.

His brain works, but we know for a fact that it performs physical functions only. No consciousness, no narrative-of-the-self. He's like a particularly useful bacterial culture. You get to map all his processes, test the drugs, maybe fool around with his endomorphins. They got this microscope that can trail over every part of his body. You can see life inside him, pumping away.

Soon as I saw him, I got this flash. I knew what to do with him. I went to my mentor, wrote it up, got it out and the company gave me the funding.

People think of cells as these undifferentiated little bags. In fact, they're more like a city with a good freeway system. The proteins get shipped in, they move into warehouses, they're distributed when needed, used up and then shipped out.

We used to track proteins by fusing them with fluorescent jellyfish protein. They lit up. Which was just brilliant really since every single molecule of that protein was lit up all the time. You sure could see where all of it was, but you just couldn't see where it was going to.

We got a different tag now, one that fluoresces only once it's been hit by a blue laser. We can paint individual protein molecules and track them one by one.

Today we lit up the proteins produced by the samesex markers. I'm tracking them in different parts of the brain. Then I'll track how genetic surgery affects the brain cells. How long it takes to stimulate the growth of new structures. How long it takes to turn off production of other proteins and churn the last of them out through the lysosomes.

How long it takes to cure being homo.

It's a brilliantly simple project and it will produce a cheap reliable treatment. It means that all of João's friends who are fed up being hassled by Evangelicals can decide to go hetero.

That's my argument. They can decide. Guys who want to stay samesex like me . . . well, we can. And after us maybe there won't be any more homosexuals. I really don't know what the problem with that is. Who'll miss us? Other samesexers looking for partners? Uh, hello, they're won't be any.

And yes, part of me thinks it will be a shame that nobody else will get to meet their João. But they'll meet their Joanna instead.

Mom rang up and talked for like 17 hours. I'm not scared that I don't love her anymore. I do love her, a lot, but in my own exasperated way. She's such a character. She volunteered for our stem cell regime. She came in and nearly took the whole damn programme over, everybody loved her. So now she's doing weights, and is telling me about this California toy boy she's picked up. She does a lot of neat stuff for the Church, I gotta say, she's really in there helping. She does future therapy, the Church just saw how good she is with people, so they sent her in to help people change and keep up and not be frightened of science.

She tells me, "God is Science. It really is and I just show people that." She gets them using their Personalized Identity for the first time, she gets them excited by stuff. Then she makes peanut butter sandwiches for the homeless.

We talk a bit about my showbiz kid brother. He's a famous sex symbol. I can't get over it. I still think he looks like a pineapple.

"Both my kids turned out great," says Mom. "Love you."

I got to work and the guys had pasted a little card to the glass. *Happy Birthday Ron, from Flat Man.*

And at lunchtime, they did this really great thing. They set up a colluminated lens in front of the display screen. The image isn't any bigger, but the lens makes your eyes focus as if you are looking at stuff that's ten kilometres away.

Then they set up a mini-cam, and flew it over Flat Man. I swear to God, it was like being a test pilot over a planet made of flesh. You fly over the bones and they look like salt flats. You zoom up and over muscle tissue that looks like rope mountains. The veins look like tubular trampolines.

Then we flew into the brain, right down into the cortex creases and out over the amygdala, seat of sexual orientation. It looked like savannah.

"We call this Flanneryland," said Greg. So they all took turns trying to think of a name for our new continent. I guess you could say I have their buy-in. The project cooks.

I got back home and found João had sent me a couple of sweet little extra emails. One of them was a list of all his family's addresses . . . *but my best address is in the heart of Ronald Flannery.*

And I suppose I ought to tell you that I also got an encryption from Billy.

Billy was my first boyfriend back in high school and it wasn't until I saw his signature that I realized who it was and that I'd forgotten his last name. Wow, was this mail out of line.

I'll read it to you. *Ron,* it starts out, *long time no see. I seem to recall that you were a Libra, so your birthday must be about now, so, happy birthday. You may have heard that I'm running for public office here in Palm Springs*—well actually, Billy, no I haven't, I don't exactly scan the press for news about you or Palm Springs.

He goes on to say how he's running on a Save Samesex ticket. I mean, what are we, whales? And who's going to vote for that? How about dealing with some other people's issues as well, Billy? You will get like 200 votes at most. But hey, Billy doesn't want to actually *win* or achieve anything, he just wants to be right. So listen to this—

I understand that you are still working for Lumiere Laboratories. According to this week's LegitSci News they're the people that are doing a cure for homosexuality that will work on adults. Can this possibly be true? If so could you give me some more details? I am assuming that you personally have absolutely nothing to do with such a project. To be direct, we need to know about this treatment: how it works, how long a test regime it's on, when it might be available. Otherwise it could be the last straw for an orientation that has produced oh, . . . and listen to this, virtue by association, the same old tired list . . . Shakespeare, Michaelangelo, da Vinci, Melville, James, Wittgenstein, Turing . . . still no women, I see.

I mean, this guy is asking me to spy on my own company. Right? He hasn't got in touch since high school, how exploitative is that? And then he says, and this is the best bit, *or are you just being a good little boy again?*

No, I'm being a brilliant scientist, and I could just as easily produce a list of great heterosexuals, but thanks for getting in a personal dig right at the end of the letter. Very effective, Billy, a timely reminder of why I didn't even like you by the end and why we haven't been in touch.

And why you are not going to get even a glimmer of a reply. Why in fact, I'm going to turn this letter in to my mentor. Just to show I don't do this shit and that somebody else has blabbed to the media.

Happy effin birthday.

And now I'm back here, sitting on my bed, talking to my diary, wondering who it's for. Who I am accountable to? Why do I read other people's letters to it?

And why do I feel that when this project is finished I'm going to do something to give something back. To whom?

To, and this is a bit of a surprise for me, to my people.

I'm about to go to sleep, and I'm lying here, hugging the shape of João's absence.

Today's my birthday and we all went to the beach.

You haven't lived until you body surf freshwater waves, on a river that's so wide you can't see the other bank, with an island in the middle that's the size of Belgium and Switzerland combined.

We went to Mosquerio, lounged on hammocks, drank beer, and had cupu-açu ice cream. You don't get cupu-açu fruit anywhere else and it makes the best ice cream in the world.

Because of the babies I had to drink coconut milk straight from the coconut . . . what a penance . . . and I lay on my tummy on the sand. I still wore my sexy green trunks.

Nilson spiked me. "João! Our husband's got an arse like a baboon!"

It is kind of ballooning out. My whole lower bowel is stretched like an oversized condom, which actually feels surprisingly sexy. I roll over to show off my packet. That always inspires comment. This time from Guillerme. "João! Nilson, his dick is as big as you are! Where do you put it?"

"I don't love him for his dick," says João. Which can have a multitude of meanings if you're the first pregnant man in history, and your bottom is the seat of both desire and rebirth.

Like João told me before I came out here, I have rarity value on the Amazon. A tall *branco* in Brazil . . . I keep getting dragged by guys, and if I'm not actually being dragged then all I have to do is follow people's eye lines to see what's snagged their attention. It's flattering and depersonalising all at one and the same time.

The only person who doesn't do it is João. He just looks into my eyes. I look away and when I look back, he's still looking into my eyes.

He's proud of me.

In fact, all those guys, they're all proud of me. They all feel I've done something for them.

What I did was grow a thick pad in Flat Man's bowel. Thick enough for the hooks of a placenta to attach to safely.

I found a way to overcome the resistance in sperm to being penetrated by other sperm. The half pairs of chromosomes line up and join.

The project-plan people insisted we test it on animals. I thought that was disgusting, I don't know why, I just hated it. What a thing to do to a chimp. And anyway, it would still need testing on people, afterwards.

And anyway, I didn't want to wait.

So I quit the company and came to live in Brazil. João got me a job at the university. I teach Experimental Methods in very bad Portuguese. I help out explaining why Science is God.

It's funny seeing the Evangelicals trying to come to terms. The police have told me, watch out, there are people saying the child should not be born. The police themselves, maybe. I look into their tiny dark eyes and they don't look too friendly.

João is going to take me to Eden to have the baby. It is Indian territory, and the Indians want it to be born. There is something about some story they have, about how the world began again, and keeps re-birthing.

Agosto and Guillinho roasted the chicken. Adalberto, Kawé, Jorge and Carlos sat around in a circle shelling the dried prawns. The waiter kept coming back and asking if we wanted more beer. He was this skinny kid from Marajo with nothing to his name but shorts, flip-flops and a big grin in his dark face. Suddenly we realize that he's dragging us. Nilson starts singing, "*Moreno, Moreno . . .*" which means sexy brown man. Nilson got the kid to sit on his knee.

This place is paradise for gays. We must be around 4 per cent of the population. It's the untouched natural samesex demographic, about the same as for left-handedness. It's like being in a country where they make clothes in your size or speak your maternal language, or where you'd consider allowing the President into your house for dinner.

It's home.

We got back and all and I mean *all* of João's huge family had a party for my birthday. His nine sisters, his four brothers and their spouses and their kids. That's something else you don't get in our big bright world. Huge tumbling families. It's like being in a 19th-century novel every day. Umberto gets a job, Maria comes off the booze, Latitia gets over fancying her cousin, João helps his nephew get into university. Hills of children roll and giggle on the carpet. You can't sort out what niece belongs to which sister, and it doesn't matter. They all just sleep over where they like.

Senhora da Souza's house was too small for them all, so we hauled the furniture out into the street and we all sat outside in a circle, drinking and dancing and telling jokes I couldn't understand. The Senhora sat next to me and held my hand. She made this huge cupu-açu cream, because she knows I love it so much.

People here get up at five am when it's cool, so they tend to leave early. By ten o'clock, it was all over. João's sisters lined up to give me a kiss, all those children tumbled into cars, and suddenly, it was just us. I have to be careful about sitting on the babies too much, so I decided not to drive back. I'm going to sleep out in the courtyard on a mattress with João and Nilson.

We washed up for the Senhora, and I came out here onto this unpaved Brazilian street to do my diary.

Mom hates that I'm here. She worries about malaria, she worries that I don't have a good job. She's bewildered by my being pregnant. "I don't know baby, if it happens, and it works, who's to say?"

"It means the aliens' plot's backfired, right?"

"Aliens," she says back real scornful. "If they wanted the planet, they could just have burned off the native life forms, planted a few of their own and come back. Even our padre thinks that's a dumb idea now. You be careful, babe. You survive. OK?"

OK. I'm 36 and still good looking. I'm 36 and finally I'm some kind of a rebel.

I worry though, about the Nilson thing.

OK, João and I had to be apart for five years. It's natural he'd shack up with somebody in my absence and I do believe he loves me, and I was a little bit jealous at first . . . sorry, I'm only human. But hey—heaps of children on the floor, right? Never know who's sleeping with whom? I moved in with them, and I quite fancy Nilson, but I don't love him, and I wouldn't want to have his baby.

Only . . . maybe I am.

You are supposed to have to treat the sperm first to make them receptive to each other, and I am just not sure, there is no way to identify, when I became pregnant. But OK, we're all one big family, they've both . . . been down there. And I started to feel strange and sick before João and my sperm were . . . um . . . planted.

Thing is, we only planted one embryo. And now there's twins.

I mean, it would be wild wouldn't it if one of the babies were Nilson and João's? And I was just carrying it, like a pod?

Oh man. Happy birthday.

Happy birthday, moon. Happy birthday, sounds of TVs, flip-flop sandals from feet you can't see, distant dogs way off on the next street, insects creaking away. Happy birthday, night. Which is as warm and sweet as hot honeyed milk.

Tomorrow, I'm off to Eden, to give birth.

46 years old. What a day to lose a baby.

They had to fly me back out in a helicopter. There was blood gushing out, and João said he could see the placenta. Chefe said it was OK to send in the helicopter. João was still in Consular garb. He looked so tiny and defenceless in just a penis sheath. He has a little pot belly now. He was so terrified, his whole body had gone yellow. We took off, and I feel like I'm melting into a swamp, all brown mud, and we look out and there's Nilson with the kids, looking forlorn and waving goodbye. And I feel this horrible grinding milling in my belly.

I'm so fucking grateful for this hospital. The Devolved Areas are great when you're well and pumped up, and you can take huts and mud and mosquitoes and snake for dinner. But you do not want to have a miscarriage in Eden. A miscarriage in the bowel is about five times more serious than one in the womb. A centimetre or two more of tearing and most of the blood in my body would have blown out in two minutes.

I am one very lucky guy.

The Doctor was João's friend Nadia, and she was just fantastic with me. She told me what was wrong with the baby.

"It's a good thing you lost it," she told me. "It would not have had much of a life."

I just told her the truth. I knew this one felt different from the start; it just didn't feel right.

It's what I get for trying to have another baby at 45. I was just being greedy. I told her. *É a ultima vez.* This is the last time.

Chega, she said, Enough. But she was smiling. *É o trabalho do João.* From now on, it's João's job.

Then we had a serious conversation, and I'm not sure I understood all her Portuguese. But I got the gist of it.

She said: it's not like you don't have enough children.

When João and I first met, it was like the world was a flower that had bloomed. We used to lie in each other's arms and he, being from a huge family, would ask, "How many babies?" and I'd say "Six," thinking that was a lot. It was just a fantasy then, some way of echoing the feeling we had of being a union. And he would say no, no, ten. Ten babies. Ten babies would be enough.

We have fifteen.

People used to wonder what reproductive advantage homosexuality conferred.

Imagine you sail iceberg-oceans in sealskin boats with crews of 20 men, and that your skiff gets shipwrecked on an island, no women anywhere. Statistically, one of those 20 men would be samesex-orientated, and if receptive, he would nest the sperm of many men inside him. Until one day, like with Nilson and João, two sperm interpenetrated. Maybe more. The bearer probably died, but at least there was a chance of a new generation. And they all carried the genes.

Homosexuality was a fallback reproductive system.

Once we knew that, historians started finding myths of male pregnancy all over the place. Adam giving birth to Eve, Vishnu on the serpent Anata giving birth to Brahma. And there were all the virgin births as well, with no men necessary.

Now we don't have to wait for accidents.

I think Nadia said, *You and João, you're pregnant in turns or both of you are pregnant at the same time. You keep having twins. Heterosexual couples don't do that. And if you count husband no 3, Nilson, that's another five children. Twenty babies in ten years?*

"*Chega,*" I said again.

"*Chega,*" she said, but it wasn't a joke. *Of course the women, the lesbians are doing the same thing now too. Ten years ago, everybody thought that homo-sexuality was dead and that you guys were on the endangered list. But you know, any reproductive advantage over time leads to extinction of rivals.*

Nadia paused and smiled. *I think we are the endangered species now.*

Happy birthday.

awake in the night
JOHN C. WRIGHT

William Hope Hodgson's quirky Victorian masterpiece *The Night Lands*, one of the flat-out *strangest* novels ever written, has had a large—although often unmentioned—effect on science fiction and fantasy over the generations since Hodgson's too-early death, being one of the likely literary ancestors of works such as Clark Ashton Smith's *Zotique*, Jack Vance's *The Dying Earth*, and Gene Wolfe's *The Book of the New Sun*. Now, in a new century, it has also inspired a Web site (http://home.clara.net/andywrobertson/night map.html) and an anthology (*William Hope Hodgson's Night Lands, Volume 1: Eternal Love*) devoted to new stories written as homages to Hodgson by various hands, both edited by Andy W. Robertson.

Not all the writers involved in these projects are really up to the demands of faithfully and effectively handling Hodgon's eerie, unearthly, somberly lyrical, and poetically charged milieu, but fear not—John C. Wright, your guide to *The Night Lands* in the bizarre and compelling novella that follows, handles the material as if he was born to do so, and delivers a tale of the conflicts of love, duty, and friendship that extends even beyond the boundaries of death, and which may be one of the strangest stories you're likely to read this year.

John C. Wright attracted some attention in the late 90s with his early stories in *Asimov's Science Fiction* (with one of them, "Guest Law," being picked up for David Hartwell's *Year's Best SF*), but it wasn't until he published his "Golden Age" trilogy (consisting of *The Golden Age*, *The Golden Transcendence*, and *The Phoenix Exultant*) in the first few years of the new century, novels which earned critical raves across the board, that he was recognized as a major new talent in science fiction. A new novel, *The Last Guardians of Everness*, is coming up this year. Wright lives with his family in Centreville, Virginia.

Y ears ago, my friend Perithoös went into the Night Lands. His whole company had perished in their flesh, or had been Destroyed in their souls. I am awake in the night, and I hear his voice.

Our law is that no man can go into the Night Lands without the Preparation, and the capsule of release; nor can any man with bride or child to support, nor any man who is a debtor, or who knows the secrets of the Monstruwacans; nor a man of unsound mind or unfit character; nor any man younger than twenty-two years; and no woman, ever.

The last remnant of mankind endures, besieged, in our invulnerable redoubt, a pyramid of gray metal rising seven miles high above the volcano-lit gloom, venom-dripping ice-flows, and the cold mud-deserts of the Night Lands. Our buried grain fields and gardenlands delve another one hundred miles into the bedrock.

Night Hounds, Dire Worms, and Lumbering Behemoths are but the visible part of the hosts that afflict us; monsters more cunning than these, such as the Things Which Peer, and Toiling Giants, and Those Who Mock, walk abroad, and build their strange contrivances, and burrow their tunnels. Part of the host besieging us is invisible; part is immaterial; part is we know not what.

There are ulterior beings, forces of unknown and perhaps unimaginable power, which our telescopes can see crouching motionless on cold hillsides to every side of us, moving so slowly that their positions change, if at all, only across the centuries. Silent and terrible they wait and watch, and their eyes are ever upon us.

Through my open window I can hear the roar and murmur of the Night Lands, or the eerie stillness that comes when one of the Silent Ones walks abroad, gliding in silence, shrouded in gray, down ancient highways no longer trod by any man, and the yammering monsters cower and hush.

———

Before me is a brazen book of antique lore, which speaks of nigh-forgotten times, now myth, when the pyramid was bright and strong, and the Earth-Current flowed without interruption.

Men were braver in those days, and an expedition went north and west, beyond the land of the abhumans, seeking another source of the Earth-Current, fearing the time when the chasm above which our pyramid rests might grow dark. And the book said Usire (for that was the name of the Captain), had his men build a stronghold walled of living metal, atop the fountain-head of this new source of current; and they reared a lofty dome, around was set a great circle charged with spiritual fire; and they drove a shaft into the rock.

One volume lays open before me now, the whispering thought-patterns impregnated into its glistening pages murmuring softly when I touch the letters. In youth, I found this book written in a language dead to everyone but me. It was this book that persuaded the lovely Hellenore (in violation of all law and wisdom) to sneak from the safety of the pyramid into the horror-haunted outer lands.

Perithoös had no choice but to follow. This very book I read slew my boyhood friend . . . if indeed he is dead.

Through the casement above me, the cold air blows. Some fume not entirely blocked by the Air-Clog that surrounds our pyramid stings my nose. Softly, I can hear murmurs and screams as a rout of monsters passes along a line of dark hills and crumbling ruins in the West, following the paths of lava-flows that issue from a dimly-shining tumble of burning mountains.

More softly, I can hear a voice that seems human, begging to be let in. It is not the kind of voice that one hears with the ear. I am not the only thing awake in the night.

Scholars who read of the most ancient records say the world was not always as it is now. They say it was not always night, then; but what it may have been if it were not unending night, the records do not make clear.

Certain dreamers (once or twice a generation, we are born, the great dreamers whose dreams reach beyond the walls of time) tell of aeons older than the scholars tell. The dreamers say there was once a vapor overhead, from which pure water fell, and there was no master of the pump-house to ration it; they say the air was not an inky darkness whence fell voices cry.

In those days, there was in heaven, a brightness like unto a greater and a lesser lamp, and when the greater lamp was hooded, then the upper air was filled with diamonds that twinkled.

Other sources say that the inhabitants of heaven were not diamonds at all, but balls of gas, immeasurably distant, but visible through the transparent air.

Still others say they were not gas, but fire. Somehow, despite all these contra-dictory reports, I have always believed in the days of light.

No proofs can be shown for these strange glimpses of times agone, but, when great dreamers sleep, the instruments of the Monstruwacans do not reg-ister the energies that are believed to accompany malign influence from beyond our walls. If it is madness to have faith in what the ancients knew, it is a madness natural to human kind, not a Sending meant to deceive us.

As I nodded, half-awake, softly there came what seemed to be the voice of Perithoös into my sad and idle thoughts. I was called by my name.

"Telemachos, Telemachos! Undo for me the door as once I did for you; return the good deed you said you would. If vows are nothing, what is anything?"

I did not move or raise my head, but my brain elements sent this message softly out into the night, even though my lips did not move. "Perithoös, closer than a brother, I wept when I heard your company was overwhelmed by the monsters. What became of the maiden you set out to rescue?"

"Maiden no more I found her. Dead, dead, horribly dead, and by my hand. Herself and her child; and I had not the courage to join them."

"How are you alive after all these years?"

"I cannot make the door to open."

"Call to the gate-warden, Perithoös, and he will lower a speaking tube from a Meurtriere and you may whisper the Master-Word into it, and so prove your human soul has not been destroyed, and I will be the first to welcome you."

The Master-Word did not come. Instead, mere words, such as any fell creature of the night could impersonate, now whispered in my brain: *"Telema-chos, son of Amphion! I am still human, I still remember life, but I cannot say the Master-Word."*

"You lie. That cannot be."

And yet I felt a tear stinging in my eye, and I knew, somehow, that this voice did not lie: he was still human. But how could he forget the Word?

"Though it has never been before, in the name of the blood we shed together as boys, the gruel in which we bound our silly oath, I call on you to believe and know that a new sorrow has appeared in this old, sad world, like fresh blood from an old scar; it is possible to forget about what it means to be a man, and yet remain one. I have lost the Master-Word; I have my very self. Let me through the door. I am so cold."

I did no longer answer him, but stirred my heavy limbs.

Though my hands and feet felt like lead, I moved and trembled and slid from my desk where I slumbered, and fell to the floor heavily enough to jar myself awake.

How long I lay I do not know. My memory is dark, and perhaps time was not for me then flowing as it should have been. I remember being cold, but not having the strength to rise and shut the window; and this was an old part of the library, so there were no thought-switches I could close just by wishing them closed.

My thoughts drifted with the cold wind from the window.

This wing of the library had been deserted for half a million of years. No one came into this wing, since no one could read the language, or understand the thoughts, of the long-forgotten peoples who had sent Usire out to found a new stronghold. Only I knew the real name of those ancient folk; modern antiquarians called them the Orichalcum people, because they were the only ones who possessed the secret of that metal; and no other trace of them survived.

And so the Air Masters, during the last two hundred years of power-outages, had lowered the ventilation budget in this wing to a minimum. I had needed vasculum of breathing-leaf just to get in here, and would have fainted with the window shut.

Nor were failures of the ventilations rare. Most windows of most of the middle-level cities stood open, these days, no matter what the wise traditions of elder times required.

It was two miles above the Night Lands. No monster could cross the White Circle, and nothing has climbed so high since the Incursions of four hundred thousand years ago; and even if they did, this window was too small to admit them.

I remembered wings. In my dreams I see doves, or the machines used by ancient men to impersonate them. But the air is thin, and even the dark and famished things have no wings to mount so high.

I thought there was no danger to have the window open. Stinging insects, vapors, or particles would be surely stopped by the Air-Clog. But what if the power losses over the last few centuries were greater than is publicly admitted by the Aediles or the Castellan? But it had not stopped the Mind-Call, as it should have done.

Many Foretellers have dreamt that it is five million years before the final extinction of mankind. Most of the visions agree on certain basic elements, though much is in dispute. Five million years. We are supposed to have that long. I wondered, not for the first time, if those who say that they can see the shape of fate are wrong.

I came awake when there was a movement, a clang, behind me as the hatch swung open. Here was a Master of the Watch, clad from head to toe in full armor, and carrying in hand that terrible weapon called the Diskos.

I knew better than to wonder why a Watchman was here. He came into the chamber, his blade extending before him as he stepped, and his eyes never left me. The shaft was extended. The blade was lit and spinning. The furious noise of the weapon filled the room. Flickering shadows fled up and down the walls and bookshelves as eerie sparks snapped, and I felt the hair on my head, the little hairs on my naked arms, stir and stand up. I smelled ozone.

Without rising, I raised my hands. "I am a man! I am human!"

His voice was very deep, a rumble of gravel. "They all say that, those that talk."

Slowly, loudly, clearly, I said the master-word, both aloud with reverent lips, and by sending it with my brain-elements.

It seemed so dark in the chamber when he doused his blade, but his smile of relief was bright.

My youth had been a solitary one. To hold one's ancestors in honor, and to love the lore of half-forgotten things, has never been in fashion among schoolboys. The pride of young men requires that they seem wise, despite their inexperience, and the only way to appear all-knowing without going to the tedium of acquiring knowledge, is to hold all knowledge in weary-seeming contempt. Students and apprentices (and, yes, teachers also) bestowed on me their well-practiced sneers; but when my dreams began, and ghosts of other lives came softly into my brain as I slept, then I was marked as a pariah, and was made the butt of every prank and cruelty boyish imagination could invent.

Perithoös was as popular as I was unpopular. He was an alarming boy to have as a schoolmate, for he had the gift of the Night-Hearing, and he could hear unspoken thoughts. All secrets were open to him; he knew passwords to open locked doors and cabinets, and could avoid orderlies after lights-out. He knew the answers to tests before the schoolmasters gave them, and the plays of the opposing team on the tourney field. He was good at everything, feared nothing, and anarchy and confusion spread from his wake. What was there for a schoolboy not to love?

Once, when the Head Boy and his gang had me locked in the cable-wheel closet, so that I would be absent from the feast-day assembly and gift-giving, Perithoös left the assembly (a thing forbidden by the headmaster's rules), took a practice blade from the arm's-locker and spun the charged blade against the closet door hinges, shattering the panel with a blast of noise.

Not just school proctors, but civic rectors and men of the Corridor Guard arrived. To use one of the Great Weapons while inside the pyramid was a grave offense; and neither one of us would admit who did it, even though they surely knew.

We both were scourged by the headmaster and given triple-duty, and had porridge for our holiday feast, while the other boys dined on viands and candied peaches.

Perithoös and I ate alone in the staff commissary, our shirts off (so that our backs would heal) and shivering in the cold of the unheated room. We were not allowed to speak, but I tipped my bowl onto the board and wrote in the porridge letters from the set-speech: *shed blood makes us brothers-I shall return this deed.*

Even at that age, he was taller than the other lads, broad of shoulder and quick of eye and hand, the victor of every sport and contest, the darling of those who wagered on gymnastics games. He was as well-liked as I was ill-liked. So I expected to see doubt, or, worse, a look of patronizing kindness in his eye.

But he merely nodded, wiped away the porridge-stain with his hand quickly, so that the proctor would not see the message. Under the table, with perfect seriousness, he clasped my hand with his, and we shook on it. Porridge dripped through our fingers, but, nonetheless, that handclasp was sacred, and he and I were friends.

At that time, neither one of us knew Hellenore of High Aerie.

I had been found in the library by proctors of the Watch, whose instruments had detected the aetheric disturbance sent by the voice in the Night.

The Monstruwacans kept me for a time as a guest in their tower, and I drank their potions, and held the sensitive grips of their machines, while they muttered in their white beards and looked doubtful. More than once I slept beneath their oneirometers, or was examined inch by inch by a physician's glass.

I told them many times of my mind-speech with Perithoös, and they did not look pleased; but the physician's glass said my soul was without taint, and my nervous system seemed sound, and besides, both the Archivist (the head of my guild) and the Master of Architects (the head of my father's) sent letters urging my release, or else demanding that an inquest be convened at once.

I spent the remainder of my convalescence in Darklairstead, my father's mansions on level Fourscore-and-Five. Ever since, a generation ago, the power failed along this stretch of corridor (half the country receiving from the sub-station at Bountigrace is dark) it has been a quiet and restful place.

Among my very earliest memories was one dream, repeated so many times in my childhood that I filled a whole diary with scrawled words and clumsy sketches trying to capture what I saw.

When I was seven years, my mother died, and her shining coffin was lowered into the silvery rays of the Great Chasm. My father became strange and cold. He sent my brother Arion to prentice with the Structural Stress Masters.

Tmelos (who is younger than I) was sent to the quarters of my Aunt Elegia, in Forecourtshire, for her to raise; Patricia took holy orders, and Phthia stayed with Father to run the house and rule the servants. Me, I was sent to board at a school in Longnorthhall of Floor 601, where the landing of the Boreal Stair reaches for many shining marble acres under lamps of the elder days, and potted Redwoods grow. When I left home for school, the dream left me.

As I recovered at my father's manse, the dream came once again, and it no longer frightened me, for nothing that reminds one of childhood, even ill things, can be utterly without a certain charm.

It was a dream of doors.

I saw tall doors made of a substance that gleamed like bronze and red gold (which I later found to be a metal called *Orichalcum*, an alloy made by a secret only the ancients knew). The doors were carven with many strange scenes of things that had been and things that would be.

In the dream I would be terrified that they would open.

Father and I would dine alone, without servants. The dining chamber is a pillared hall, wide and gloomy. Out of the hatch window, I would often see, across the air shaft from me, little candles dancing in the hatches of some of my neighbors. Once, candles had been used only for the most solemn ceremonies, back when the ancient rules against open flames in the pyramid had been enforced: the sight of candles used as candles always saddened me.

Some nights there was a hint of music from some city far overhead, echoing down the shaft, and, once, the hiss of a bat-winged machine carrying a Currier-boy (only boys are small enough) down the air-shaft on some business of the Life Support House, or perhaps the Castellan, too urgent to wait for the lifts.

Our table was made from a tree felled down in the underground country, by a craftsman whose art is the cutting and jointing of living material, an art called Carpentry. Such is Father's prestige he can have such things brought up the lifts for him, but he has never moved the family to better quarters.

My father is a big, tall man, with fierce, penetrating eyes in an otherwise very mild face. He shaves his chin, but has a moustache that bristles, and this gives his penetrating eyes a strange and savage look.

I have dreamed of other lives, and once, in a prehistoric world, a dusky savage who was me, strong and lean of limb, and braver than I ever hoped to me, died beneath the claws of a tiger. The great cat was more bright of hue than anything in our world is, shining orange and black as it slunk through dripping jungles beneath a sun as hot as the muzzle of a culverin. I wonder what became of that species, that lived on some continent long since swallowed by the seas, before the seas dried up, before the sun died. I have always thought that extinct beast looked something like my father.

His bald head was growing back in new hair, as sometimes happens to men of his order, for men who work near the Earth-Current, their vitality was greater than normal.

After dinner, we brought out carafes of water and wine, which glistened in the candlelight, and mixed them in our bowls. I am sparing of the wine and he is sparing of the water; but he is sober even when he drinks deep, and shows no levity nor thickwittedness. Perhaps exposure to the Earth-Current helps here too.

He sat with his bowl in his hand, staring out the air-shaft. He spoke without turning his head. "You know the tale of Andros and Naäni. You were raised on it. I am sure I hate it as much as you adore it."

I said, "Andrew Eddins of Kent, and Christina Lynn Mirdath the Beautiful. The tale shows that, even in a world as dark as ours, there is light."

Father shook his head. "False light. Will-o'-Wisp light! I do not blame the hero for his deeds. They were great, and he was a mighty man, high-hearted and without vice. But the hope he brought served us ill. Perithoös was no Andros, to go into the Night. And that highborn girl who toyed with your affections; Hellenore. She was no Mirdath the Beautiful. Hellenore the Vain, I should call her."

"Please speak no ill of the dead, Father. They cannot answer you."

He raised his bowl with a graceful gesture and took a silent sip, and paused to admire the taste. "Hm. Neither can they hear me, and so they will not flinch. She is not the first of the dead who have served the living poorly. He did us ill, whichever forefather first thought it would be wise to leave us tales and songs that tell young boys to go be brave and die, or to perish for a gesture."

I said, "Keeping a promise counts for more than mere gesture, Father."

"Does keeping a promise count more than preserving flesh or soul?"

I said, "Those who study such matters say that souls are born again in later ages, even if the conscious memories are lost; poets claim that oath-breakers are reborn into lives accursed with turmoil and bitter anguish. If so, then each man in his present life must take care to die spotlessly, his soul still pure."

Father smiled bitterly. He did not read poets. "What point is the punishment, if, in his next life, each criminal has forgotten what crime he did?"

I said, "So that even men who are stoical and hard in this life will fear to break their word; for, in their next, they will be young and green again; and suffering that comes unannounced, for reasons that seem reasonless, are surely the hardest pains of all to bear."

"A pretty tale. Must you die for an idle fiction?"

"Sir, it is not a fiction."

He said: "Must you die, fiction or not?"

"I had no other friend in my school days."

"Perithoös was no true friend!"

"And yet I gave my word to him, friend or not. Now I am called to fulfill it."

"Who calls? There are Powers in the dark who can mock our voices and our thoughts, and deceive even the wisest of us. Only the Master-Word is one the Horrors cannot utter, for it represents a concept that they cannot understand, an essence that does not dwell in them. If what called to you did not call out the Master-Word, you know our law commands you not to heed it."

I answered: "Despite the law, despite all wisdom, still, a hope possesses me that he is alive, and undestroyed, somehow."

He said grimly: "A true man would not call out to you."

I did not know if he meant that a man of honor would die before he let himself be used to lure a friend out into the darkness; or if he meant that what called out to me had not been human at all. Perhaps both.

I said: "What sort of man would I be, if it truly were Perithoös calling, and I did not answer?"

He said: "It is your death calling."

And I had no answer back for that. I knew it was so.

After a space of silence, eventually he spoke again: "Do you see any cause for hope you say has taken possession of you?"

"I see no cause."

"But—?"

"But hope fills me up, Father, nonetheless, and it burns in my heart like a lamp, and makes my limbs light. There are many ugly things we do not see in this dark land that surrounds us, Father, horrors unseen. And there are said to be good powers as well, whose strange benevolence works wonders, though never in a way humans can know. And they also are not seen, or only rarely. There are many things, which, although unseen, are real. More real than the imperishable metal of our pyramid, more potent than the living power of the Earth-Current. More real than fire. So, I admit, I see no cause for hope. And yet it fills me."

He was silent for a while, and sipped his wine. He is a rational man, who solved problems by means of square and chisel, stone and steel, measured currents of energy, knowing the strengths of structures and what load each support can bear. I knew my words meant little to him.

He reached his hand and doused the lantern, so that I could not see the pain in his face. He voice hovered in the dark, and he tried to make his words cold: "I will not forbid you to venture into the Night Lands . . ."

"Thank you, Father."

". . . Since I have other sons to carry on my name."

Visions, pulmenoscopy, and extra-temporal manifestations are not unknown to the people of the Last Redoubt. The greatest among us are known to have the Gift; and at least one of the Lesser Redoubt also was endowed with the Night-Hearing, and memory-dreams.

Mirdath the Beautiful is the only woman known to have crossed the Night Lands, and her nine scrolls of the histories and customs of the Lesser Redoubt are the only record of any kind we have for the history, literature, folkways and sciences of that long-lost race of mankind. All the mathematical theories of Galois we know only from her memory; the plays of Euryphaean, and the music of an instrument called a pianoforte, infinite resistance coil and the sanity glass, and all the inventions that sprang from them, are due to her recollection. Her people were a frugal folk, and the energy-saving circuits they used, the methods of storing battery power, were known to them a million years ago, and greatly conserved our wealth. Much of what she knew of farming and crops we could not use, for the livestock and seed of our buried fields were strange to her.

She knew more of the lost aeons than even Andros, and was able to tell tales from the time of the Cities Ever Moving West, of the Painted Bird, and of the Gardens of the Moon; she knew something of the Failures of the Star-Farers, and of the Sundering of the Earth.

More, she also had the gift of the Foretelling, for some of the dreams she had were not of the past, but of the future, and she wrote of the things to come, the Darkening, the False Reprieve, the disaster of the Diaspora into the Land of Water and Fire, the collapse of the Gate beneath the paw of the South Watching Thing, the years of misery and the death of man, beyond which is a time from which no dreams return, although there is said to be a screaming in the aether, dimly heard through the doors of time, the time-echo of some event after the destruction of all human life. All these things are set out in the Great Book, and for this reason Mirdath is also called The Predictress.

Mirdath and Andros had fifty sons and daughters, and all the folk of High Aerie claim descent from them, some truly, and some not.

Hellenore of High Aerie was one of those who made that claim truly.

When I was a young man, a time came when my future had disturbed those whose business it is to seek foreknowledge from dreams, and I was summoned to an audience.

For many generations the Foretelling art had fallen in disrepute, and charlatans rose to deceive the common people; but then a girl of the blood of Mirdath was born whose gift was proven by many sad events, the Library of Ages-Yet-To-Be was reopened. The Sibylline Book had more treatises of prophecy added to it, and eschatologists compared dream-journals and revised their estimates. Even I had heard of her: the hour-slips said she was sure to be the next Sibyl.

I don't recall the date. It must have been soon after my Initiation, for I wore my virile robe, and my hair was cropped short as befits a man. The blade that was ever after to be partnered with my life, I had hung over the narrow door to my cell in the journeyman's room of the Librarian's Guildhouse, as only those beyond their fourteenth year are permitted. I remember that the squire to come fetch me called me 'Sir' instead of 'Lad', even though he (to my young eyes) seemed incredibly old.

I remember the Earth-Current was running strong that year. It was my first time at the Great Lift Station for my floor. Invisible forces lifted the platform in a great surge of wind off the deck. Maidens clutched their bonnets and squealed, and many a young gallant (for a strong flow of the Earth-Current makes lads more bold and amorous) took the opportunity to put an arm around fair shoulders to steady a maiden making her first voyage away from her level. Some of the more daring boys leaned over the rail, and waved their caps at the rapidly dwindling squares and rooftops of the city, before, like an iron sky, the underside of the next deck upwards swallowed the lift platform. I rode the axial express all the way to the utmost level. I remember I had to drink a potion made by the apothecary, because of the thinness of the air.

Fate House that sits atop the highest stories of the highest city; the hanging gardens of High Aerie sit between the shining skylights of West Cupola and the pleasances and airy walks of Minor Penthouse. There are floral gardens here, under glass, as well as pools and lakes amid the rooftop-fields of the long-empty aerodromes built by ancient peoples.

The domes of Fate House are dusky blue, inscribed with gold, and, above the roof-tiles, many a monument of ancient hero or winged genius of the household stood on slender pillars among the minarets. All within was as somber and august as a fane.

Here was Hellenore daughter of Eris. I see again the sheen of her satiny dress, as she sat beneath the rose lamp on a Lector's chair too large for her delicate frame. How like a swan's, her neck, all her mass of ink-black hair was gathered up and held in place with amethyst pins, jewel-drops like the stars the ancients knew, within the clear darkness of their temporary nights. I recall the delicate small hairs, wanton and wild, that had strayed from the strictness of her coiffure, and kissed the nape of her neck.

None of our pyramid has eyes like that, hair like that, save those descended from the strange blood of Mirdath the Beautiful. And none but me remembered the grace of the swan, and so none but me could see it in her.

Her voice was soft music, each word careful and light, like a brushstroke of calligraphy laid in the air. With what delicate tones she spoke of the grim horrors in the night, the grim future she foresaw nightly in her dreams!

We spoke for a time, of the horrors of the Deception two million years hence (slightly less than halfway between now and the Extinction), when colonies of man leaving the Great Pyramid would go to dwell in what seemed a fair country to the West, even as certain legends said, not knowing that the House of Silence had already cursed and undermined the whole of that land, and merely held their influence at bay for millennia, waiting for the memory of these prophecies of Hellenore to be forgotten. Whole cities, pyramids and domes as great as ours, would be swallowed and cracked open, and multitudes would die, one entire branch of the human family wiped out; the survivors to be changed into something not human.

Then we spoke of my fate.

"My visions revealed hundreds shall die because of some ill-considered act you set in motion; first one, then many more, will go pelting out into the darkened world to perish amid the ice, or be ripped to bloody rags by Night-Hounds, to be sucked clean of their souls and left as husks, grinning mouths and eyes as dry as stones. Heed me! I see many prints of boots across the icy dust of the Night Lands, leading outward from our gates; I see but one set coming in."

I asked: "Must these things come to pass?"

"No human power can alter what must be."

"And powers more than human?"

She said softly: "We foreseers behold the structure of time; there are creatures not quite wholly inside of time, powers of the Night Lands, whose malice we cannot foretell, since they are above and alien to the rules of time and space that bind all mortal life; there are said to be good powers, too."

"A riddle! Man's fate can be changed, but men cannot change fate," I asked.

Her full lips toyed with a smile, but she did not allow the smile to appear. "We are but drops in a river, young man," she said. "No matter what one drop might wish or do, the river course is set, and all waters glide to the ocean."

These words electrified me. "Ah!" I said, forgetting my manners, jumping up and taking her hand. "Then you have seen them too! Rivers and oceans! In visions, I have seen and heard the waters flowing, ebbing, pulled by tides, crashing by the shore. There is no sound alike it in the world, now."

She was startled and displeased, and favored me with a look of ice as she drew her fair and slender hand from mine. "Strange boy—what is your name again?—I spoke a line from old poetry. My people in the high-most towers are learned in such lore, and know old words like *river* and *sea*; but no one has seen them, except in the decorations of volumes none can read."

I did not say that there was one who could read what others had forgotten.

I spoke stiffly, "My apologies, highborn one. Your comment thrilled my heart, for I had thought you meant to say that we would do great deeds in times to come, to defy that ocean that must swallow of human lore and history, so that the watercourse down which the current takes us might be ripped free of its bed, and set to a new path."

"Strange boy! What strange things you say!" She recoiled, one slim hand on her soft bosom, her lovely long-lashed eyes looking at me askance. Even in surprise, even when showing disdain, how elegant her every gesture!

"There was a time when all men spoke thus, and did deeds to match."

"Only men?" But she was not looking at me. Her eyes were turned sideways, and she stared at some spot on the walls of her family's presence chamber. There were many busts, portraits, and engraved tablets along the walls. I don't know which ancestor her gaze was resting on. In hindsight, it surely was Mirdath.

I said, "Can you tell me what this ill-considered act might be?"

Her eyes were elsewhere; she spoke airily, unheeding: "Oh, some chance remark spoken to some girl you fall in love with."

My voice was hollow, and my stomach was empty. "What? Must I vow to be silent, to speak never more to any woman?" It took me a moment to rally my courage. I drew a breath, and spoke. "If that is my doom, I will learn to welcome it. If I must, I will take the vow, and go to some monastery in the buried basements, forbidden to woman, that I might never meet my love."

Her glittering eyes returned to me, and now a girlish mischief was in them. She said archly: "You will defy the structures of time and destiny, and rip up the pillars of the laws of nature, but you will meekly foreswear love and speech, merely because you are ordered to it? Backward boy! You would challenge what we cannot change, but would submit to what we can!"

That made me smile. "Perithoös says the same thing of me. Always looking backwards! We were walking at the Embrasures, and he joked once that—"

Hellenore sat upright, eyes shining. She said, "You know Perithoös, the athlete? What hour does he stroll upon the balcony, what level, where?"

A glow of joy lived in her face; and then she blushed and my heart ached with pleasure to see her cheek glow; but the thought of meeting Perithoös was such that she could not put away her smile, so she lifted her slender hand to hide it. If you have seen young maidens in the grip of first love, you know the sight; if not, my poor pen cannot mark it.

I told her I would arrange a meeting, and the smile came out again.

Beautiful, was that smile; though not for me.

And yet so lovely!

They met, at first, with chaperones.

At first. One of them could see the future and the other could see thoughts; both were bold, nobly born, and love-drunk. How was a duenna to keep them under watch?

———

They died swiftly, those who died, when the three hundred suitors set out to rescue Hellenore.

The company had been divided into three columns of one hundred men each. Before five-and-twenty hours of march, the rearguard column had driven off a host of troll-things from the ice hills, and stopped to rest and tend their wounds. From the balconies, and from the viewing tables, we watched them make a camp. It was hard to see, for it was well camouflaged; the tents and palisade were mere shadows among shadows, even under the most powerful magnification; and the sentries at the picket moved without making noise, warily.

But then they did not stir again. Either a sending from the House of Silence, or an invisible fume leaking from the ground, made the sleepers not to wake. Long-range telescopes glimpsed the survivors, perhaps the sentries who did not lay down, trying to carry one or two men to higher ground. The rest were left behind. A pallid slug a thousand feet long oozed into view near the last known position of those men; the Monstruwacan instruments recorded tiny Earth-Current discharges at about that same time, so it was thought that the survivors swung their weapons once or twice before they died.

At about seventy hours, the main column was beset by the Great Gray Hag, mate of the monster slain by Andros, and her fleshy fingers pushed men into the sagging hole that formed her maw, armor and all. The column was routed, and fled into the Deathly Shining Lands to escape her. They did not emerge. The Shine is opaque, and nothing has been seen again of those men. The scouts accompanying the main column were eaten by Night Hounds, one by one.

The vanguard column lasted until the end of the second week, when the Bell of Darkness descended from the cloud, and tolled its dire toll. Only seven out of those hundred had the presence of mind, or strength of will, to bare their forearms and bite down on the Capsule of Release. Those whose nerve failed them, and who did not slay themselves in time, were drawn silently up into the air, their eyes all empty, and strange little vulgar grins upon their lips, and their bodies floated upward into the mouth of the Bell.

We all watched from the balconies. I heard from underfoot, like an ocean, the sound of mothers and wives weeping, men shouting, children crying, and the noise was like the oceans of the ancient world, but all of grief.

The shattering noise of the Home-call echoing from the upper cities interrupted, ordering all the millions to shut their windows; and lesser horns were sounded on the balconies to pass the warning to the lower cities. The watchmen ordered the Blinds raised up on their great pistons to block the windows and embrasures of every city and hamlet dug into the northeastern side of the pyramid; and the towers and dormer windows lowered their armor.

I remember hearing, before the Blinds closed over us, the whispering murmur of the Air-Clog, straining under double power, raising an unseen curtain to deflect the malice of the tolling bell, lest the sound of it drive mad the multitudes.

Perithoös had been in the vanguard. The Monstruwacans studied blurry prints made from long-range telescopes, and tried to confirm each death, what little comfort that might have been to the grieving families. Not every corpse was accounted for.

My cousin Thaïs came to see me while I was undergoing Preparation. She is pretty and curt, with a sly sense of humor and a good head for chess and math. Thaïs did not, aloud, try to argue me out of my venture, but she showed me her calculation: The expected average lifespan of men who went forth to save Hellenore worked out to an hour, twelve minutes.

By traditions so ancient that no record now recalls a time when they were not, those who venture into the Night Lands do not carry lamps. It is too well known, too long confirmed by experience, that a traveler cannot resist the temptation to light such lamps, when the darkness has starved his eyes for too many fortnights.

And so it is thought, that since the weapons we carry give off light when they are spun, that those who walk in the Night will have light when and only when it is needful: that is, namely, when one of the monstrosities is no further off from us than a yard or two; for then we must strike, we must see to make the stroke.

Our craftsmen could make lamps to burn a million years or more. We will not carry them into the Dark. A man who will not trust his soul to warn him of unseen dangers coming silently upon him, is the only kind who needs a lantern in the Night. But would such a man, too unsure to trust his soul, be man enough to beat back all the horrors his lantern would attract?

We carry also a dial of the type that can be read by touch, for to lose track of hours, and proper times for rest and sup, is to court madness.

There is a scrip for toting the tablets, made of solidified vital nutrients, which is the traveler's sole food; for there is nothing wholesome in the Night Lands to eat, and more solid food, even a bite from an apple, might bring too much belly-cheer, and relax the discipline of the Preparation.

Likewise, water is condensed out of the atmosphere in a special cup by a powder made by the Chemist's guild. The new-water is pure and clear, but bitterly cold, and the cup has that virtue that anything placed in it is cleansed of venom or morbific animacules. Some travelers hold the cup over mouth and nose when treading lands where the air is bad.

The mantle is woven of a fiber that, though it is not alive, is wise enough to shed heat more or less as the deadliness of the chill grows more or less, depending on the amount heat escaping from the ground.

The armor is so stern, and made so cunningly, that even monsters many times the strength of a man cannot dint it, and the joints are fitted at a level too fine for the eye to see. A blessing in the metal, an energy not unlike what throbs so purely in the fires of the White Circle, is impregnated into the helm and breastplate, to help slow those particular influences that attack the brain and freeze the heart.

Arms, armor, mantle, are made by craft a million years has perfected; and they are fair to the eye, but grim and without ornament, as befits the sobriety of the undertaking.

At last the torment of the Preparation Chambers ended. I was oddly clear-headed after the fasting and the injections, and I had endured the test of being forced to view that which still lives, pinning to a slab and sobbing, within the refrigerated cell at the center of the secret museum of the Monstruwacans. I had read the bestiaries of former travelers returned sane from outer voyaging, and learnt what they said of the ways and habits of the night-beasts; and I understood why such journals are not shown to any save those whose quest carries them outside our walls.

The Capsule of Release still ached within the tender flesh of my forearm; and the hour of parting was come.

The lamps of the Final Stair were darkened. The watchmen, armed with living blades and armored in imperishable gray metal, stood for a time in silence, composing their thoughts, so that no disturbance in the aether, no stray gleam of thought or metal or sudden noise, would tell the waiting horrors of the Night Lands that a child of man had strayed among their cold hills.

I stood with my face pressed to the periscope for many minutes, and the escort with me showed no impatience, for they knew it was my life I staked at hazard on my judgment of the ground.

At last I raised my hand.

The Master of the Gatehouse saluted me with his dark Diskos, and the door-tender closed the switch that sent power to the valves. The metal leaves of the inner gate swung shut behind me, and then the outer leaves swung open, very swiftly and silently.

Out I stepped. The ashy soil crunched beneath my boot. The air was as chill as death. The outer valve was already shut behind me, and two layers of armor heavily closed back over it, locking pistons clicking shut almost without noise. If a monster were now to lunge across the Circle from the all-surrounding darkness, or a Presence to manifest itself, the door wardens were obliged to do nothing but guard the door. I was already beyond rescue.

None within would come out for me, as I was now going out for Perithoös, and he had gone out for his fair Hellenore. Prudent men, they all.

It was but a few minutes walk (no more than half a mile) until I crossed the place where a hollow tube of transparent metal, charged with holy white energies, makes a circle around the vast base of the pyramid. It is held to be one of the greatest artifacts of ancient times, the one thing that keeps all the malefic pressures, the eerie calls and poisonous clouds and groping fingers of subtle force at bay. The hollow tube is two inches in diameter, hardly higher than my boot-top. It only took a single step to cross it, but I must clear my mind of all distempered thought before the unseen curtain would part for me. My ears popped with the change in pressure.

It is customary not to look back when one steps across the line of light. I was inclined to follow the custom.

My father had not been present to see me off.

We who live within this mountain-sized fortress of a million windows of shining light, we cannot see, where flat high rocky plains lift their faces into our light, the long dark shadows cast by the rocks and hillocks and moss-bushes radiating away from the pyramid; darkness that never moves, straight and level as if drawn by a ruler. Even the smallest rock has a train of shadow trailing away from it, reaching out into the general night, so that, looking left and right, the traveler sees what seem to be a hundred hundred long fingers of gloom, all pointing straight toward the Last Redoubt of Man.

But no traveler is unwise enough to step into such a high plain lit so well. The bottom mile of the pyramid is darkened, her base-level cities long abandoned, and the lower windows covered over with armor plate. A skirt, as it were, of shadow surrounded the base of the pyramid, and one must travel away from the pyramid to expose oneself to the shining of the many windows of the Last Redoubt; even before leaving the protection of the skirt of shadow, there are many places where the ground has been tormented into crooked dells and ragged shapes, dry canyons, or deep scars from the ancient glaciers or the far more ancient weapons of prehistory. Such broken ground I sought.

I entered the canyons to the west within the first two hours of traveling, and encountered no beasts, no forces of horror.

My way was blocked by a river of boiling mud shown on none of our maps. The telescopes and viewing tables of our pyramid had never noted it, despite that it was so close to us, for ash floated in a layer atop the mud-flow, and was the same hue as the ground itself. It was not visible to me until my foot broke the sticky surface and I scalded my foot. Perhaps it was newly-erupted from some fire-hole; or perhaps it had been here for centuries. We know so little.

This mud river drove me south and curving around the side of the pyramid, and I marched thirty hours and three. I ate twice of the tablets, and slept once, finding a warm space behind a tall rock where heat and some uncouth vapor escaped from a rent in the ground.

Before I slept, I probed the sand near the rent with the hilt of my Diskos, and a little serpent, no more than an ell in length, reared up. It was a blind albino worm, of the kind called the amphisbaena, for its tail had a scorpion's stinger. I slew it with a fire-glittering stroke from my roaring weapon, and the heavy blade passed through the worm as it were made of air, and the halves were flung smoking to either side. It was with great contentment I slept, deeming myself to be a mighty hero and a slayer of monsters.

The encampment and stronghold of Usire, I knew from my books, and from my memory-dreams, lay to the north by northwest beyond the shoulders and back of the Northwest Watching Thing. There are other watchers more dreadful, but none is more alert, for the ground to the Northwest is wide and flat in prospect, and it is lit by the Vale of Red Fire; and there is neither a crown nor eye-beam nor wide dome of light to interfere with the view the monster commands.

To go to the country beyond the creature, my way must go far around, for the North way was too well watched. To my West was the Pit of Red Smoke itself, a land of boiling chasms and lakes of fire, impassable. To the East of me, I could see the silhouette of the Gray Dunes: and here was a sunken country populated by thin and stilt-legged creatures, much in shape like featherless birds, and they carried iron hooks, and they were very careful never to expose themselves to the windows of the pyramid as they stirred and crawled from pit to pit. The canyon-walls were riddled with black doorways, from whence, now and again, the Wailing which gives the Place of Wailing its name would rise from these doorways, and the bird-things would caper silently and flourish their hooks. To the East I would not go.

I went South.

Each time I rose after snatched sleep, the shapes of two of the Great Watching Things, malign and silent, were closer and clearer to my gaze.

First, to my right, rising, vast and motionless, the Thing of the Southwest was but a dim silhouette, larger than a hill. It was alive, but not as we know life. There was a crack in the ground at its feet, from which a beam of light rose, to illume part of that monster-cheek, and cast shadows across its lowering brow. Its bright left eye hung in the blackness, slit-pupiled and covered with red veins, seemingly as big as the Full Moon that once hung above a world whose nights came and went.

Some say this eye is blinded by the beam, and that the beam was sent by Good Forces to preserve us. Others say the beam assists the eye to cast its baleful influence upon us, for it is noted by those whose business it is to study nightmares, that this great catlike eye appears more often in our dreams than any other image of the Night Lands.

I remember my mother telling me once, how a time came when that great eye, over a period of weeks, was seen to close; and a great celebration was held in the many cities of the pyramid, and they celebrated for a reason they knew not why. They knew only that the eye had never before been known to close. But the lid was not to stay closed forever and aye; in eleven year's time, a crack had appeared between the upper and nether lid, for the monster was only blinking a blink. Each year the crack widened. By the time I was born, the eye was fully opened, and so it had been all of my life.

Second, to my left was the great Watching Thing of the South, which is larger and younger than the other Watching Things, being only some three million years ago that it emerged from the darkness of the unexplored southern lands, advancing several inches a decade, and it passed over the Road Where the Silent Ones Walk between twenty-five and twenty-four hundred thousand years ago.

Then, suddenly, some twenty-two hundred thousand years ago, before its mighty paws, there opened a rent in the ground, from which a pearl or bubble of pure white light rose into view. Over many centuries the pearl grew to form a great smooth dome some half a mile broad. The Watching Thing of the South placed its paw on the dome, and it rises no further, but neither has the Watching Thing advanced across that mighty dome of light in all these years.

It is known from prophecy that this is the Watcher who will break open the doors of the Pyramid with one stroke of its paw, some four and a half million years from now, but that the death of all mankind will be prevented for another half million years by a pale and slender strand of white light that will emerge from the ground at the very threshold of the great gates. More than this, the dreams of the future do not tell.

Between the Watching Thing of the South and of the Southwest, the Road Where the Silent Ones Walk runs across a dark land. The Road was broad, and could not be crossed except in the full view of the Watching Things to the South and the Southwest. But the ground on the far side of the Road is dim, lit by few fire-pits, and coated with rubble and drifts of black snow, where a man could hide.

In this direction was my only hope. Suppose that the eye-beam does indeed blind the right eye of the Watching Thing of the Southwest, and suppose again that the dome of light troubles the vision of the Great Watcher of the South more than the Monstruwacans have guessed: I could cross the Great Road on the blind-side of the Southwest monster, and sneak between him and his brother, perhaps to hide among the black snow-drifts beyond. I would then follow the road as it wound past the place of the abhumans, and then leave the road and venture north, into the unknown country called the Place Where the Silent Ones Kill.

Many weeks of terror and hardship passed, and my supplies grew sparse.

Once a party of abhumans came upon me by surprise; I slew two of them with my Diskos, though it was a near thing, and I fled when the others stopped to chew their comrade.

Once a luminous manifestation meant to wrap me in her misty arms; but the fire which spun from my weapon could do hurt to subtle substances even when there was no material substance for the blade to bite; swirled lightning dispelled part of the tension that held her cloudy fingers together, and she flew off, maimed and sobbing.

Once a Night Hound ran at me suddenly from the darkness, and I chopped him in the neck before he could rend me; the blade of the Diskos shot sparks into the smoldering wound, and the monster's huge limbs jerked and danced as it fell, and it could not control its jaws enough to bite me. A soft voice from the corpse called me by name and spoke words of ill to me, but I fled. I will not write down the words in this place: it is not good to heed things heard in the Night Lands.

As I passed through the abhuman lands, they grew aware of me, and hunted me.

I was driven far away from the Road into lands that grew ever colder. Each time I lay down to sleep, the hills between me and the Pyramid were higher. A time came when I passed beyond the sight of the Last Redoubt; even the tallest tower of the Monstruwacans was not tall enough to see into this land where I now found myself. I was beyond all maps, all reckoning.

At first, I walked. Each score of hours my dial counted, I slept four. Because there were crevasses, I struck the ice before me with the haft of my weapon as I walked. Then I grew aware of how loudly the echo of my metallic taps floated away across the utter darkness of the icy world, and I grew very afraid.

After this, I crawled across the ice in utter blackness. I surely crawled in circles.

After four score more hours, about half a week of crawling, I felt a pressure in the air. It was so malign that I was certain one of the Outer Presences must be standing near. All was utter black, and I saw nothing but ghosts of light starved eyes create.

For about an hour I crouched with my forearm bare, my hand numb without my gauntlet, and the capsule touching my lips; but the pressure against my spirit grew no greater. I heard no sound.

So I crawled away. Over many hours I crawled and slept and crawled again, but whatever stood on the ice behind me, I could sense its power even as a blind man can feel when the door of an oven is opened across the room. I took my bearings from this, and kept the power forever behind me.

A time came when I saw light in the distance. I went toward it, and, over very many hours, I began to sense the downward slope of the ice. The path soon became broken, and I crawled from crag to crag, from high hill to low hill of ice.

The light grew clearer as I trudged down the mighty slope of ice, and I could see the footing well enough to walk. I put my spyglass to my eye, and scanned the horizon.

Here I saw, looming huge and strange, the head and shoulders of the Northwest Watching Thing. The crown of its head was mingled with the clouds and smokes of the Night Lands; and to the left and right of his shoulders, like wings, I saw long, streaming shafts of pure and radiant light. This was the reflected glow of the Last Redoubt, bright the dark air of the night world.

I was behind the Watcher; seeing it from an angle no human person had ever seen it. The Last Redoubt was blocked from view; I was in the shadow of the monster.

A cold awe ran through me then, as if a man from the ancient times were to wake to find himself on the side of the moon (back when there was a moon) that forever turned its face away from earth.

I had come into the Place Where the Silent Ones Kill.

When Hellenore's father forbad the courting of Perithoös to go forward, they began to meet by secret, and my father's mansions, the darkened passages of Darklairstead, were used for the rendezvous. I helped Perithoös because he asked it of me, and I felt obligated to do him a good turn, even though it troubled me. As for Hellenore, she was beautiful and I was young. She barely knew I existed, but I could deny her nothing. She had many suitors; how I envied them!

Once, not entirely by accident, I came across where Perithoös and Hellenore sat alone in a bower before a fountain in the greenhouse down the corridor not far from the doors of my father's officer's country. The greenhouse was built along the stairs of Waterfall Park, downstream from where a main broke a thousand years ago. Near the top, it is a sloping land of green ferns under bright lamps, and the water bubbles white as it tumbles from stair to stair, with small ponds shining at the landings. Near the bottom, the ceiling is far away, and the lamps were dim. At the bottom landing is a statue of the Founder's Lady, surrounded by naiads, and water poured from their ewers into a pond bright with dappled fish whose fins were fine as moth-wings.

Through the obscuring leaves that half-hid them, I saw Perithoös sitting on the grass, his back resting on the fountain's raised lip, and one arm around Hellenore's bare shoulders. In his other hand, he held a little book of metal, of the kind whose pages turn themselves, and the letters shined like gems; ferns and flowering iris grew to their left and right, half-surrounding the pair in flowery walls. Her head was on his shoulder, and her dark hair was like a waterfall of darkness, clouding his neck and chest.

In this wing of the greenhouse, many of the lamps had died a century ago, and so the air was half as bright here as elsewhere. To me, the view seemed like a cloudy day, or a sunset; but I was the only one in all mankind who knew what twilight was. How strange that, so many millions of years after it could not ever be found again, lovers still sought twilight.

As I approached, I heard Hellenore's soft laugh—but when she spoke, her whisper was cross. "Here he comes, just as I foresaw."

Perithoös whispered back, "The boy is sick for love of you, but too polite to say aloud what is in his mind."

"But not polite enough to stay where he is not welcome!" she scolded.

"Hush! He hears us now."

I pushed aside the leafy mass of fern. Crystal drops, as small as tears, clung to the little leaves, and wetted me when I stepped forward.

Now she was primly kneeling half a yard from him, and her elbows were in the air, for she had pulled her hair up, and, in some fashion I could not fathom, fixed it in place with a swift and single twist of her hands. The same gesture had drawn her silken sleeves (that had been falling halfway to her elbow) back up to cover her shoulders.

Perithoös, one elbow languidly on the fountain lip, waved his book airily at me, the most casual of salutes. "Telemachos! The lad who lived a million lives before! What a surprise this would have been, eh?" And he smiled at Hellenore.

I bowed toward her and nodded toward him. "Milady. Perithoös. Excuse me. I was just . . ."

Hellenore favored me with one cool glance from her exotic, tip-tilted eyes, and turned her head, her slender hands still busy pinning her hair in place. If anything, her profile was more fair than her straight glance, for now she was looking down (I saw that there were amethyst-tipped hair-pins driven point-first in the soil at her knees), and the drop of her lashes gave her an aspect both pensive and demure, achingly lovely.

Seeing himself ignored, Perithoös plucked up a fern-leaf, and reached over to tickle Hellenore's ear. She frowned (though, clearly, she was not displeased) and made as if to stab his hand with one of her jeweled pins.

Perithoös playfully (but swifter than the eye could see) grabbed her slender wrist with his free hand before she could stab him, and perhaps would have done more, but he saw my eyes on him, and casually released her. I wondered how he dared be so rough with a woman so refined and reserved; but she was smothering a smile, and her dark eyes danced when she looked on him.

I said awkwardly in the silence, "I had not expected to find you here."

Perithoös, "By which you mean, you expected us to flee before we let ourselves be found. Come now! There is no need to be polite with me: I see your dark thoughts. You came to gaze on Hellenore. Well, who would not? She knows it as well. How many suitors have you now, golden girl? Three hundred?"

My heartbeat was in my face, for I was blushing. But I said merely, "I hope you see my brighter thoughts as well. Of the three of us, surely one should be polite."

Perithoös laughed loudly, and was about (I could see from his gesture) to tell me to go away; but Hellenore, her calm unruffled, spoke in her voice that I and I alone knew had the cooing of doves in it: "Please sit. We were reading from a new book. There are scholars in South Bay Window, on level 475, who have challenged all the schoolmen, and wish to reform the ways the young are taught."

I did sit, and I thought that Hellenore must have been well-bred indeed, to invite so unwelcome an intruder as I was, to consume the brief time she had to share with her young wooer.

She passed the book to me, but I read nothing. Instead, I was staring at sketches that had been penned into the flyleaves. "Whose hand is this?" I said, my voice hoarse.

Hellenore tilted her head, puzzled, but answered that the drawings were her own, taken from her dreams.

"I know," I said, my head bowed. And by the time I raised my eyes, I had remembered many strange things, things that had happened to me, but not in this life.

They both looked so young, so achingly young, so full of the pompous folly and charming energy of youth. So inexperienced.

Perithoös was looking at me oddly. Though I do not have his gift, I would venture that I knew his thought, then: He saw what I was thinking, but did not know how someone my age could be thinking it.

Perithoös said, "Telemachos will be against it, no matter what the South Bay Window scholars suggest. All new things pucker up his mouth, for they are sour to his taste."

"Only when they are worse than the old things," I said.

Perithoös tossed a leaf at me: "For you, that is each time."

"Almost each time. Mostly, what is called 'new' is nothing more than old mistakes decked out in new garb."

"The New Learning is revolutionary and hopeful. Come! Shake off the old horrors of old dreams! The world is less hideous than we thought. These studies prove that the outside was never meant for man; do you see the implication?"

I shook my head.

He said happily: "It implies that our ancestors did not come from the Night Lands. We are not the last of a defeated people, no, but the first of a race destined to conquer! The Bay scholars claim that we have always dwelt in this pyramid, and deny what the old myths say. Look at the size and shape of the doors and door-handles. It was clear that men first evolved from marmosets and other creatures in the zoological gardens. Our ancestors kept other creatures who bore live young, cats and dogs and homunculi, you see, in special houses, this was back before the Second Age of Starvation. I assume our ancestors ate them to extinction."

I blinked at him, wondering if he had lost his mind, or if I had lost my ability to tell when he was joking.

" 'Evolved'?"

"By natural selection. Blind chance. We were the first animals who were of a size and stature to pass easily down these corridors and enter and exist the places here. Other creatures were too large or too small, and these were cast out in the Night Lands after many unrecorded wars of prehistory. The New Learning allows us hope to escape from the promise of universal death for our race: We need merely wait for the time when we will evolve to be suited to fit the environment outside; and we will be changed; and those horrors will no longer seem hideous to the changed brains of the creatures we shall become."

I said sternly: "The Old Learning speaks of such a possibility as well. It is hinted that the abhumans were once True Men, before the House of Silence altered them. The tradition of the Capsule of Release is not without roots."

"Prejudice! Antique parochialism! The only reason why what we think of as True Men prevailed, is because our hands were best fitted to work the controls of the lifts and valves, our eyes best adapted to the lighting conditions, and we were small enough to enter the crawlspaces if giants chased us. Those giants outside are outside because they were too big for these chambers."

"And if we never dwelt in any place except this pyramid, whence came the ancestress of Hellenore? Whence came Mirdath? Or does your book prove she does not exist as well?"

He opened his mouth, glanced at Hellenore (who gave him an arch look), and closed it again. He dismissed the question with an airy wave of his hand. "Whatever might be the case here, skepticism will break down all the old rules and old ways, and leave us free. To live as we wish and love as we wish! Who could not long for such a thing?"

"Those who know the barren places where such wishful thinking leads," I said heavily, climbing to my feet.

Unexpectedly, Perithoös seemed angry. He shook his finger at me. "And where does thinking like *yours* lead, Telemachos? Are we always to be frozen in place, living the lives our ancestors lived?"

I did not then guess (though I should have) what provoked him. The traditional way of arranging a marriage, and so, by extension, the traditional way of doing anything, could not have had much appeal for him, not just then.

I spoke more sternly than I should have: "We are men born in a land of eternal darkness. We grope where we cannot see clearly. Why mistrust what ancient books say? Why mistrust what our souls say? Our forefathers gave us this lamp, and the flame was lit in brighter days, when men saw further. I agree the lamp-light of such far-off lore, is dim for us; but surely that proves it to be folly, not wisdom, to cast the lamp aside: for then we are blind."

He said: "What use is light to us, if all it shows us it images of horror?"

I said, "There are still great deeds to be done; there will be heroes in times to come." And I did not say aloud, but surely Perithoös saw my thought: *unless this generation makes all its children to forget what heroism is.*

"Bah!" said Perithoös. His anger was hidden now, smothered somewhat beneath a show of light-heartedness. He smiled. "Will our writings be published in any other place than within these walls? Why will we do praiseworthy acts, when we know there will be nothing and no one left to sing our praises? Even you, who claims you will be born once more, will have no place left to be born into, when this redoubt falls."

I said, "Do not be jealous. I am not unlike you. This life could be my final one. You both have had others you forget; but this could be the first you will remember next time."

Perithoös looked troubled when I said this; I saw on his face how eerie my words (which seemed so normal to me) must have sounded to him.

Hellenore said eagerly, "What do you remember of us? Were Perithoös and I—" But then she broke off and finished haltingly, "How did the three of us know each other before?"

I said, "You were one of Usire's company, and lived in a strong place, a place of encampment, in a valley our telescopes no longer see, for the Watching Thing of the Northwest moved to block the view, once the House of Silence smothered the area with its influence. You, milady, were an architect, for women studied the liberal arts in those strange times; and you were possessed of the same gift you have now. In those times, you saw these ages now, and you sculpted one of the *orichalcum* doors before the main museum of

Usire's stronghold, and wrought the door-panels with images of things to come."

Perithoös smiled sourly. "What Telemachos is not willing to say is. . . ."

I interrupted him. "Madame, I was favored by you then, though I was of high rank and you were not. I helped sculpt the other door with images of things that had been."

Hellenore looked embarrassed. I hoped my face did not show the shame I felt.

I turned to Perithoös, but I continued speaking to Hellenore, though I did not look at her. "Since we are being honest and free with each other's secrets: what Perithoös is not willing to say is, he cannot fathom why I am not jealous of your love for him, even though he sees in my mind that I am not. He sees it, but he does not believe it. But that is the answer. Last time, he lost. This time, me. It does not mean we are not friends and always will be."

Hellenore was disquieted: I could see the look in her eye. "So I have not loved the same man in all ages, in every life . . ."

She was no doubt thinking of Mirdath the Beautiful, whose own true love was constant through all time.

I said awkwardly: "You have always loved noble men."

But she was looking doubtfully at Perithoös, and he was looking angrily at me. Odd that he was now angry. Surely I had said no more than what he had been about to say was in my mind. But perhaps he did not expect Hellenore to take seriously the thought that they were not eternal lovers.

Perithoös said: "No doubt if we three are born in some remote age in the future, and find ourselves the very last left living of mankind, you will seek to do the noble deed of poisoning minds against me, and worming your way into to intimacies where you are not wanted! Is this the kind of praiseworthy and noble things you practice, Telemachos?"

Angry answers rose to my lips, but I knew that, even if I did not say them aloud, Perithoös would see them burning in my heart. With no more than a nod, and a muttered apology (how glad I was later to have uttered it, even if they did not hear!) I spun on my heel and marched from the grove, dashing the wet ferns away from my face with awkward gestures. The scattered drops dripped down my cheeks.

Behind me, I heard Hellenore saying, "Don't speak ill of Telemachos!"

Perithoös spoke in a voice of surprise. "What is this?" (which I took to be a sign that she had not had in her mind what to say before she spoke).

She said, "I foresee that my family will bring more pressure to bear against Telemachos, for my father suspects he knows the secret places where we meet. He will bear it manfully, and not betray us, though his family will suffer for it. You have chosen your friend well, Perithoös."

Perithoös said, "Ah. Well, he actually chose me."
She murmured something softly back. By then I was out of ear-shot.

My dial marked sixty hours passing while I descended the icy slope into this land, Place Where the Silent Ones Kill, and I slept twice and ate of the tablets three times. The altimeter built into the dial measured the descent to be twenty-two thousand feet. During the middle part of that time, I passed through an area of cold mists where the air was unhealthy, and left me dazed and sick.

This area of bad mist was a low-hanging layer of cloud. The cloud formed an unseen ceiling over a dark land of ash cones, craters, and dry riverbeds, lit now and again by strange, slow flares of gray light from overhead. The ash cones in this area were tall enough to be decapitated by the low-hanging clouds. I spent another thirty hours wandering at random in this land, hoping to stumble across some feature or landmark I would know from my memory-dreams.

Once, a flickering gray light of particular intensity trembled through the clouds above. I saw the silhouette of what I thought (at first) was yet one more ash cone; but it had a profile; I saw heavy brows, slanting cheeks, the muzzle and mouth-parts of a Behemoth, but huge, far more huge than any of his cousins ever seen near the Last Redoubt. A new breed of them, perhaps? It was as still as a Watching Thing, and a terrible awareness, a sense of sleepless vigilance came from it. It was taller than a Fixed Giant, for the dread face was wrapped partly in the low-hanging clouds, and wisps blew across its burning, horrible eyes. How one of that kind had come to be here, or why, was a mystery before which I am mute.

I looked left and right. In the dim and seething half-light of the cloud overhead, it seemed to me that there were other Behemoths here; two more I saw staring north, their eyes unwinking. I traveled along the bottoms of the dead riverbeds after that, hoping to avoid the gaze of the Behemoths: but now I knew the place I sought lay in the direction the giant creatures faced.

The gray light faded, and I walked in darkness for thirty-five hours. A briefer flare of gray light came again; and I saw, in the distance, a great inhuman face gazing toward me, and yet I saw nearer at hand, another Behemoth to my left facing toward him. By these signs, I knew the massive shadow rising between me and that far Behemoth was what I sought.

The colorless light-flare ended, and all was dark as a tomb. But I felt a faint pressure, as of extraterrestrial thought reaching out, and I feared the Behemoth facing me, over all those miles, had seen me.

I crept forward more warily. The ground here was becoming irregular underfoot, sloping downward. I walked and crawled across the jagged slabs of broken rock I found beneath my feet and fingers, ever downward. I could not see enough to confirm whether this was a crater-lip.

After another mile, ground changed under my hands. Here there was ash and sand underfoot, for soft debris, over the aeons, had filled this crater-bottom. I was able to stand and move without much noise, and I waved the haft of my weapon before me in the dark as I walked, the blade unlit, like a blind-man's cane, hoping it would warn me of rocks or sudden pits or the legs of motionless giants.

After an hour's walk or two, under my boot, I felt smooth and hard stones. Stooping, I traced their shape in the dark. They were square, fitted together. Manmade. A road. A few more steps along, I felt something looming in the utter dark near me: by touch, I found it was a stele, a mile-stone cut with letters of an ancient language.

I knew the glyphs from former lives: the name spelled USIRE.

One hundred, two hundred paces further on, and my fingers touched the pillars and post of a great gate. I touched a bent shape that had once been a hinge: I touched the broken gate-bars, the shattered cylinders that had once been pistons holding these doors shut against the night.

Beyond the doors, I felt nothing but more sand, and here and there a slab of stone or huge column of bent and rusted metal. I sensed nothing alive here; no Earth-Current pulsing through power-lines; no throb of living metal. The place where wholesome men dwell often will carry a sense in the aether, like the per-fume of a beautiful woman who has just left the chamber, a hint that something wholesome and fair had once been here: there was nothing like that here.

Instead, I felt a coldness. I felt no horror or fear in my heart, and I realized how strange that must be.

I was surely near the center of where a ring of the Behemoths bent their gazes; even in the dark, I should have felt it as a weight on my heart, a sense of suffocation in my soul. Instead I was at ease.

Or else benumbed.

How very silent it was here!

Slowly at first, and then with greater speed, I backed away from the bro-ken gates that once had housed the stronghold of Usire. Blind in the utter dark, I ran.

I was still in the open when the gray light came again, and slowly trembled from cloud to cloud overhead, lighting the ground below with fits and starts, a dull beam touching here, a momentary curtain of light falling there, allowing colorless images to appear and disappear.

I beheld a mighty ruin where once had been a metropolis; its dome was shattered and rent, and its towers were utterly dark. Here and there among the towers were shapes that were not towers, and their expressionless eyes were turned down; watching the ruins at their feet, waiting with eternal, immortal patience, for some further sign of the life that had been quenched here, count-less ages ago.

More than merely giants stood waiting here. The gray light shifted through the clouds, and beams fell near me.

A great company of hooded figures, shrouded in long gray veils, stood without noise or motion facing the broken walls. They were tall as tall men, but more slender. The nearest was not more than twelve feet from me, but its hood was facing away.

There next two of the coven stood perhaps twenty feet from me, near the broken gate; it was a miracle I had not brushed against them in the dark as I crept between them, unknowing of my danger. Even as quiet as I was, how had they not heard the tiny noises I had made, creeping in their very midst?

Then I knew. It was not the noise carried by the air they heeded. It was not with ears they heard. They were spirits mighty, fell, and terrible, and they did never sleep nor pause in their watch. A hundred years, a thousand, a million, meant nothing to them. They had been waiting for some unwise child of man to sneak forth from the Last Redoubt to find the empty house of Usire, dead these many years. They had been waiting for a thought of fear to touch among them: fear like mine.

With one accord, making no sound at all, the dozens of hooded figures turned, and the hoods now faced me.

I felt a coldness enter into my heart, and I knew that I was about to die, for I felt the coldness somehow (and I know not how this could be, and I know not how I knew it) was swallowing the very matter and substance of my heart into an awful silence. My cells, my blood, my nerves, were being robbed of life, or of the properties of matter that allow physical creatures such as man to be alive.

I turned to flee, but I fell, for my legs had turned cold. I made to raise my forearm to my lips and bite down on the capsule, but my arm would not obey. My other arm was numb also, and the great weapon fell from my fingers. Nor could my spirit sense the power in the metal any longer, despite that the shaft and blade were still whole. The Diskos was still alive, but I wondered if its soul had been Destroyed, and feared I was to follow.

Then I could neither move my eyes nor close them. Above me there was only black cloud, lit here and there with a creeping gray half-light. A sharp rock was pushed into the joint between my gorget and the neck-piece of my helm, so that my head was craned back at a painful angle; and yet I could not lift my head.

The Silent Ones made no noise, and I could not see if they approached, but in my soul I felt them drifting near, their empty hoods bent toward me, solemn and quiet.

Then the clouds above me parted.

I saw a star.

Whether all the stars had been extinguished; or whether the zone of radiation that surrounds our world, transparent in former ages, had grown opaque; or whether there was merely a permanent layer of cloud and ash suffocating our world, helping to slow the escape of heat, had been debated for many an age among savants and knowledgeable people. Of these three, I had always inclined to the last opinion, thinking the stars too high and fine to have been reached by the corrupt powers of the Night Lands.

That the Night had power to quench the stars was too dread to believe; but that the stars should have the grace to push aside the smog and filth of the earth, and allow one small man one last glimpse of something high and beautiful, was too wondrous to hope.

I cannot tell you how I knew it was a star, and not the eye of some beast leaning down from a cliff impossibly high above, or some enigmatic torch of the Night World suspended and weightless in the upper air, bent on strange and dreadful business.

And yet more than my eye was touched by the silvery ray that descended from that elfin light; I saw it was diamond in heaven, indeed, but somehow also a flame and a burning ball of gas, immensely far away; and how such a thing could have a mind, and be aware of me, and turn and look at me, and come to my aid in my hour of need, I cannot tell you, for diamonds and flames and balls of gas do not have souls; but neither can I tell you how a hill, shaped like unto a grisly inhuman thing, could sit and watch the Last Redoubt of Man, without stirring and flinching for a million years. Is the one more unlikely than the other?

I felt strength burning in me, human strength, and I raised my head.

The coven of Silent Ones was here, but the blank hoods were lifted and turned toward the one star. The thoughts, the cold thoughts of the Silent Ones were no longer in me.

A fog was rising. As mild and as little as the light from the star might have been, it somehow made little fingers of white mist seep up from the sand.

There may have been a natural, rather than a supernatural explanation for this; but I doubt it. Like a veil, the pure cloud rose to hide me from the enemy; the delicate rays of this one star still shined through these pearly curtains, and illuminated them, and made every bead and hanging breath of the mist all silvery and fair to see.

If this were not supernatural, then the supernatural world should be ashamed that such wonders can be wrought by merely natural means, by starlight, and little water-drops.

While the Silent Ones were closed off behind a wall of fog, I picked up my weapon and crept away. I was blinded, so I followed the star. Here and there about me in the silvery mists, I could see looming shadows of the Silent Ones, terrible and motionless. And yet they did not sense me, or do me hurt, which I attest is starkly impossible, unless but that one of the Good Powers that old tales said sometimes save men from the horrors of the Night had indeed suspended the normal course of time, or relaxed the iron laws of nature out of mercy. No one knows these things.

The star led me to where a little stand of moss-bush spread. Beneath the bush was hid a door, set flat into the rock underfoot; and one of the leaves of the door had been forced inward a little way against its hinges. The crooked opening was large enough perhaps to admit a man, or the small nasty crawling things and vermin of the Night Lands, stinging snakes and centipedes, but too narrow to let any of the larger brutes or monsters pass in.

The star went out, and the mists that hid me began to part. I saw tall shadows slanting through the mists, and feared the Silent Ones were drifting near.

I doffed my helm and breastplate and undid my vambraces, that I might be lithe and small enough to squeeze in through this crack. It might have been wise to drop my armor into the crack before I went in; but wisdom also warned me not to make a clatter, so I pushed the armor plates beneath a moss-bush, where (I hoped) they would not be seen.

The edges of the door scraped and cut me; I was blood-streaked when I fell into the dark place beneath.

Of the wonders of the city of Usire, I have not space to say. Let it suffice that there were many miles of rock that had been mined out to form the fields and farms beneath the dome, and that the dome itself, even broken, was a mighty structure, many miles across, and half a mile high. There were places where the feet and legs of the Behemoths had broken through the roof, and I would peer out across a shattered balcony to see the knees and thighs of rough and leprous hide, knowing that somewhere, far below, were feet; and the palaces and museums, fanes and libraries of Usire, a great civilization of which the folk of the Last Redoubt know nothing, lay trampled underfoot. Many layers of roof and hull had been shattered in the footfalls of the giants, back, ages ago when the giants walked; darkness and cold had entered in.

I found the doors of orichalcum I had seen so often in my dreams.

The images carved into the right-hand leaf of the door were as I had seen them, exactly (now that the memory came back to me) as I had carved them in a former life.

The right-hand door was of the past: here were sculpted images of starfarers landing their winged ships on worlds of bone and skull, horror on their faces as they came to know our earth was the only world remaining in all the universe not yet murdered. The fall of the moon was pictured, and the sundering of the earth-crust. Here were the Road-Makers, greatest of all the ancient peoples; and there were the Cliff-Dwellers, whose mighty cities and empires clung to endless miles of chasm walls, during the age when the upper surface of earth was ice, but the floor of the great rift was not yet cooled enough for men to walk upon it. Here was an image of the Founder, tracing the boundaries where the Last Redoubt would rise with a plow pulled by a type of beast now long extinct: and this was a legend from the first aeon of the Last Redoubt; and twenty aeons and one have passed since that time.

The left-hand door held images from the end of time: the Breaking of the Gate was pictured here, and the severing of man into two races, those trapped far below ground, and those trapped in the highest towers, when all the middle miles of the Last Redoubt were made the inhabitation of unclean things that wallowed in the darkness. The tragedy of the Last Flight was pictured, millions of women and children of the Upper Folk attempting escape by air, in a winged vehicle like those used by our earliest ancestors; the image showed the winged ship, buoyancy lost, falling among the waiting tribes of sardonic abhumans, the loathly gargoyles, and furious Night Hounds.

The time of the Final Thousand was shown, when all living humans would know not just their own lives, but the lives of all who came before, so that each man was a multitude; each woman, all her mothers.

Here was a picture of the Last Child, born by candlelight in her mother's ice-rimmed coffin; there was an icon of the Triage. Three shades, representing all the dead fated to fade from the world's dying aura, were bowing toward the wise-eyed child proffering their ghostly dirks hilt-first. Any shade the Last Child shunned, had no hope of further human vessels for its memories.

The final panel of the furthest future, which formed the highest part of the left-hand door, showed the Archons of High Darkness, Antiseraphim and other almighty powers of the universal night, seated on thrones among the ruins of the Last Redoubt; and while Silent Ones bowed to them; and the Southern Watching Thing fawned and licked their dripping hands; all the books and tools and works of man were pictured heaped upon a bonfire around which abhumans cavorted; and the greater servants were shown eating the lesser servants at feast.

These images were fanciful, mere iconography. The Ulterior Beings have no form or substance, no shape that can be drawn with pencil or carved in stone. Nonetheless, the door-maker carved well the nightmare scene, and I knew what she meant to portray.

There was on the right, in the past, at highest part of the door, an image directly opposite the image of the triumphant powers of darkness at feast. Here, golden, was the many-rayed orb which was meant to represent the Last Sunset, which was the earliest legend of the earliest time, and, in the foreground, here was the mother and father of mankind, holding hands sadly and watching the dusk; the man was pictured with one hand raised, as if to salute, or bid farewell, whatever unimaginable age of gladness had ruled the upper air before that time.

I was cheered to think that, even then, my ancient self who made these doors had not considered the days of light to be a myth to be ashamed of.

I put my shoulder to the cunningly carven panels and pushed.

They were the doors to a museum, of course.

Here I found the dusty and rusted wreckage of broken stalls and looted displays: tarnished machines, broken weapons, dead glasses, and empty bookshelves. But in the ruin was one machine, shaped like a coffin, still bright. Light came from its porthole.

This casket was a type long forgotten in the Last Redoubt, able to suspend the tiny biotic motions we call life, each cell frozen, and carefully thawed again by an alchemy that revives each cell separately. These once had been used in aeons when men ventured into the Void, but those who slept too long in them came out changed, troubled by strange dreams sent to them from minds that roamed the deepest void between the stars, and loyal to things not of earth.

Inside the casket was Perithoös.

I wiped the frost from the porthole to peer inside. He was horribly maimed; scar tissue clotted his empty eyesockets; his left arm was off at the elbow, a mere stump. No wonder he had never attempted to find the Last Redoubt again: blind, maimed, and without the Capsule.

A few minutes search allowed me to find a spirit glass in an alcove; I brought it back and connected it to the physician's socket by means of a thinking-wire cannibalized from an inscription machine. I tilted the glass until I caught an image of Perithoös in it. And there, shining at the bottom of his soul, tangled in a network of associations, dreams, fears, and other dark things, like a last redoubt, besieged by fear yet unafraid, was the thing in us that knows and recognizes the Master-Word.

I whispered the Master-Word. The shining, timeless fragment in his soul pulsed in glad recognition.

Human. Perithoös was human.

The Master-Word stirred something in him. Even though he was frozen, his blood and nerves all solid, there was sufficient action in his brain to allow his thought to reach through the armor of the coffin and touch my brain:

You came!

"I came."

It was not unexpected that even a frozen man could still send and hear thoughts. If this method of suspending life could have also suspended the spiritual essences of life, and kept them safe, the star-voyages of early man would not have ended in such nightmarish horror, for the space-men would have been deaf to the things that whisper in the dark of the aetheric spaces, and would have returned from the void whole and sane.

Slay me and then slay yourself. We are surrounded by the powers from the House of Silence.

"I came to save you, not to kill you."

I merit death. I slew Mirdath.

"Mirdath? She lived and died many generations ago."

Hellenore. I mean Hellenore. My only love; the fairest maid our pyramid ever knew. She was to be my bride. And I also slew her child. The child in the womb reached out and touched my mind, and told me things I should not have heard.

"Your child?"

No. A creature who carried her off to the Tower-Without-Doors and violated her; things were done to her womb to permit her to conceive a nonhuman.

I winced at the thought. "What creature? An abhuman?"

No, though it answered to them. The bridegroom was a thing bred or made by the arts of the House of Silence, in the centuries since the fall of the Lesser Redoubt.

I knew that when that Redoubt fell, out of all those millions, only Mirdath had been saved. Of the rest, not all of them had been allowed to die without suffering, especially not the women, and most were put to pain of the type death does not ease.

"You call it a bridegroom? She married it?"

The abhumans mock our sacraments. You know why.

I nodded. It is not enough that we die; that will not satisfy them. They must make the things we deem precious seem grotesque and ugly, even to us, so that there is nothing fair left in the world. (I speak of the lesser servants, the ones once human. We are not in the thoughts of the greater ones.)

The bridegroom bit my weapon out of my hand, and tore off my arm, but the Capsule buried in my forearm broke beneath its iron teeth, and venom filled its mouth.

"It died instantly?"

No. Its unnatural life stayed in its frame long enough to slay the rest of my men.

I killed the child with my thoughts, for its life was weak: but Hellenore, by then, had no soul to slay, and I strangled her one-handed while she clawed out my eyes. Such was my last sight.

Slay me, that I may cease from seeing it ever and again forever.

"Many a weary mile, I have walked to save you, Perithoös, for I will not fail of the promise we made as children. Why did you call out to me, across all miles of the Night Lands, if you did not wish me to bring you back into the warmth and human comfort of our mighty home?"

I cannot open the door.

"Do you mean the casket lid?"

The door that opens to escape from a life that grows intolerable. The door that honor commands men to use when all other doors are shut. You must open the door for me. You of all men know that there is something beyond that door, and that it opens back into this life again, but with forgetfulness, blessed forgetfulness, to quench the pain of memory. There is much I must forget.

A picture came from his brain-elements into the visual centers of my brain. It was an image of Hellenore, her eyes filled with childish faith in the man she loved. She raised a gauntlet too large for the slender hand that bore it, and tilted back a helmet too large for her, and raised her mouth for one last kiss, before she slid down a rope from a small window in the postern gate.

Away across the black and grainy soil of the Night Lands she walked; and there she was, outlined for a moment against the glow of the Electric Circle; then she was gone.

She had not been moving as those who are Prepared are trained to move, skulking from rock to rock, or standing motionless to let one's gray cloak blend with the gray background, avoiding discolored patches of ground. She did not know how to walk.

And she dragged the great weapon behind her, for the weight was more than she could bear, and she wheeled it like a wheel-barrow on its blade; an image that would be comical, were it not so horrifying.

His thoughts were clear as crystal, sharps as knives:

She will not be born anew. The darkness consumed her. I have destroyed her forever. I sent her into the Night without a Capsule, without the words and rites, without the exercises of the soul and mind, carrying a weapon she had never swung before, in armor too big for her.

More images. Perithoös had sent her out. He lowered her on a rope from a window in the postern gate and watched her walk away. His gift allowed him to choose a time when the portreve was one who admired his fame too much to turn him in, and the gate-warden he could blackmail with knowledge taken from the man's own guilty mind.

The enormity of the crime was too great for me to take in. I was overcome with emotion at that moment. The strength left my legs, and I sat. My weapon I put down, the first time it had left my grip in weeks. I put my head in my hands.

"Madness!" I said. "Madness. There were simpler ways to die, and ways that do not carry hundreds of dead down with you! Was she so jealous of Mirdath, did the law that forbids women to walk the Night Lands offend her so much? Did she so much want to be thought more manly than a man? It was not enough for her that she was more fair than women?"

That was not the reason.

Eventually, I said softly: "Why?"

For love.

"What?"

Love. Surely that emotion excuses us from all limits, all law. We thought we could be together, here. We thought the stronghold of Usire would provide us some sanctuary against the Night, but that we would be far from the Pyramid free to live as we wished . . .

"Madness! Would she step to the bottom of the sea without a suit, or play with lepers without an immunity? Ah, but you don't know about oceans or lepers, do you? All old things are dead to you, including the wisdom of our laws!"

Some old things I know. I gave her a harquebus from a museum, and brought it to life with the Earth-Current. I rendered it obedient to her with my thought. The piece was able to discharge a streamer over 900 yards, carrying a charge enough to kill a Dun Giant.

"You know why the ancients forbade us to use such weapons. The energy can be sensed from miles away, even of a single shot. Or do you? How little do you know of the world you live in, of what has come before? Why trick her into killing herself in such a foolish fashion? Surely it would have been simpler to throw her from an embrasure, or dash out her brains against a post, or bury her alive. Did you want to feed them? Feed the horrors?"

I was imagining her, surprised by a petty-worm or scorpion, touching off the voltage, and sending a lightning-bolt echoing across the darkened land. I imagined the thing we see shadowed in one of the windows of the House of Silence tilting its dark head toward the source of the energy-noise. I imagined Night Hounds, pack upon pack, swarming down from the Lesser Dome of Far Too Many Doors, baying as they came.

I spoke in a voice made hollow and weak from despair and disgust. How could he overlook what was so plain to see?

"No woman, ever, must travel in the Night Lands. Here are monsters to slay us."

She thought she would foresee them, or that my spirit would warn me ere they came near. And . . . And . . .

"And what?"

I had prepared everything for us, a Capsule she could carry in her poke, an instrument that would lead us to where the Stronghold of Usire was, by the traces of Earth-Current it still gave off. If the instrument sensed nothing, we would turn and come back home; and so there was no risk—we thought that the monsters would stay clear of any land were the Earth-Current was running. And if we found this place, we could reconnect the White Circle to the Current, sanctify the ground, and erect an Air-Clog of our own, stronger than that we had left. It would have been, not as safe as Home, but safer!

"You sent her off by herself? By herself?!"

I meant to meet her before the hour was gone! Less! Forty minutes, no more! Time enough for me to descend and escape out of a wicket, carrying the other gear. I had to stay behind to joggle the power, or else the Air-Clog would not have parted for us.

From a low window, we had together picked the rock where she was to hide and wait for me; it was less than eighty yards from the gate! Eighty yards! She could not have mistaken the rock; we had studied every feature lovingly. She could not have mistaken the rock! It was cleft like a miter, and one part jutted like my sister Phaegia's nose.

He said more, much more, then; many excuses, much sophistry. I could not make myself heed his thoughts. My own thoughts were too loud: I kept picturing what it must have been for her.

To be trapped in the darkness of the outer lands, being hunted by Night Hounds, to have the eyes of inhuman beings searching the unending night—and then, after hunger and weariness and nightmares and false hopes—to be found by the Cold Ones, and taken to their secret places, and to have one's nervous system laid open, and all one's intimate thoughts laid bare. And then to be raped by unclean creatures, and then to marry one's rapist. And all this time to wonder why one's own beloved, one's true love, the beloved you trusted and cherished above all others, to have him merely abandon you to this fate . . .

I was walking up and down the aisles of the ruined museum, looking for an axe or heavy bar. It was not something I meant to think, but I was looking for something to smash in the casket lid, and expose the freezing innards to the air. (Even in my anger and turmoil, I note that it never occurred to me to use the Diskos on him: it is something we only ever swing against monsters. I do not know if any human person has ever been struck with one.)

Perithoös broke into my endless circle of thought: *I tried! I was prevented! I wanted to come after her immediately. That was our plan, but—*

I pounded my fist against the portal where his frozen, maimed face was held in ice. The noise was loud, but the glass held, despite the hardness of my gauntlets.

Like water bubbling from a holed jug, my anger left me. Men who have eaten nothing but the tablets for weeks do not have stomach enough to stay angry.

I sat down again.

"But you were arrested by the magistrates, weren't you?"

Yes.

I said: "They granted clemency on your promise that you would venture out after her. Has the world gone mad? You mocked the law that says no woman ever may venture into the Land; they mocked that law that forbids a man of unsound mind or unfit character may go. You were but a callow youth, perhaps that can excuse; but they were judges. Men of the law!"

The judges thought that no punishment the hand of man could mete out would match this.

"And no one else could trace the screaming, her voice you could hear in your head, back to the source: they needed you to find her."

The Silent Ones let her scream so that others would come forth from the Pyramid and be Destroyed. They opened their barrier to let my call reach you for the same reason.

I nodded sadly. And the Silent Ones would have had me, had not one of those Powers that no one can explain intervened.

You know I betrayed you.

"You were afraid the Silent Ones would destroy you unless you called other children of men out from the Last Redoubt. It is an old, old trick. An old fear."

A fear you do not share. What is wrong with your thoughts? Why are you not afraid?

"I was spared."

The Silent Ones will not permit us to leave this place! I am wounded and blind. How can you hope we can cross the Night Lands together? Hellenore said she saw many pairs of boot-prints leading out, but only one coming back in. You will live: not me. It is fated.

I said, "Fated. I don't understand why Hellenore went forth. Were her visions of the future unclear? Did she have some vision that told her she was to be a wife and mother, but it cruelly deceived her?"

I deceived her. She saw what was to come. I told her not to believe her visions.

"Why did she listen to such a stupid idea?"

Because you deceived her. You convinced her that fate could be changed.

"I said the opposite; that we must endure what could not be changed."

She was convinced of that, too. Even when I talked her into venturing forth, in her mind there was nothing but grim resolve. Women sacrifice much and suffer much to become our wives, to bear our children; nature inclines them to endure great sacrifice.

"A sacrifice for what? For what gain? She knew that bloodshed and destruction would spring from her going-forth. What—"

Something like laughter came from his frozen brain. *She saw far, far into the future. Isn't it obvious? I found the shaft. I reconnected the main leads. I restored the power. As I had planned from the start. But it took me months.*

"What do you mean? What—?"

Are you an idiot? The casket is powered. The Earth-Current is alive, here, still strong, but deep, deep beneath the rock. And so the victory of the dark powers here is not complete.

You must return to the Last Redoubt with this news: if they drive a shaft deep enough, and at an angle to find the sources directly beneath this spot, the Last Redoubt will live out its promised span of life five million years hence; otherwise we fail within a few hundred years.

The engineering needed to drive a shaft so many miles to find so small a place might be beyond the powers of the present generation of men; but there would be generations to come. The gardens, and fields, and mines beneath the Great Redoubt were so extensive, that, compared to that work, what Perithoös proposed was not an insurmountable matter.

I cannot explain why I laughed. The laughter was bitter on my tongue. I said, "So all our proud and vain dreams of returning as heroes will come true, won't they? We will be lauded. I can think of no more just punishment for folly, than to have foolish wish come true."

We?

(I admit the word surprised me as well. It just slipped out; but, once I had said it . . .)

"We."

I am blind and crippled, and wicked besides.

"You are coming with me."

If I return to the pyramid, the magistrates will condemn me to death.

"And so your wish shall be granted! Or perhaps the law that you may not stand twice for the same offense will forbid a new hearing. If judges still uphold our laws, which seems not the fashion among these modern folk. In any case, it is their affair, not mine."

Why do you not bestow the death my acts have merited? Have you no sense of justice?

"Well, obviously, not so much as I should have. A just man would have not answered your plea."

I felt a stirring in the aether, as if he were gathering his brain-elements to send a thought, but the thought was too confused, too full of shame, to send. Had his face not been frozen, I wonder what his expression might have given away.

"You put me on trial, didn't you? You pretended to misplace the Master-Word. If I had been a man of justice, obedient to our laws, I would have been safe, and never answered you. I failed your trial and you condemned me to death and annihilation at the hands of the Silent Ones. Your justice condemned me; but something spared me. I wonder why. Why was I spared?"

You knew you should not come. Why did you come?

I came because I am a romantic fool, the kind of fool it is easy to fool. But he had asked the wrong question.

"Don't ask why I came. Ask why had I been *permitted* to come. Ask why the cunning of the House of Silence did not prevail. A miracle was wrought to permit me to be here. My certain destruction and doom was set aside. Why?"

I saw now why the star had parted the clouds to touch me, and to restore my life to me.

It was, at once, a reprieve and a punishment heavier than I could imagine: for my punishment was to stand, in relation to Perithoös, as that star had stood to me, and save him. To be his friend, despite all his crimes, all his foolish pride and boastful madness, to be his friend nonetheless, and save him.

Perhaps the Good Power that had saved me meant to save the Last Redoubt as well, to let the message go through telling where another vein of the Earth-Current could be found in the shrinking core of the planet. But, somehow, I doubted it. The things that seem great and momentous to men, I am sure are of little matter to the Ulterior Powers who sometimes protect Life.

I knew the words to start the rebirth-cycle for the coffin, and how to adjust the feeds to bring the Earth-Current back into his body, so that uneven thawing would not mar him.

I picked up my weapon again, and leaned on it. The Earth-Current within the haft was aware of the current flowing in the casket: a phenomenon spiritualists call affected resonance. It felt good to have the warlike spirit of my Diskos propping me up at that moment; in a former life, I owned a boarhound, and his loyalty had been not unlike this.

Perithoös touched his mind to mine again, but weakly. His spirit was faint, for his aura was being drawn back close to his flesh in preparation for the decanting, he would sleep many hours before the lid would open and he would wake. But I heard him.

I don't understand.

"How can you not understand me? You see my thoughts."

I see your thoughts, but they are senseless.

Strange. My thoughts seemed perfectly clear to me.

The same madness that drove Perithoös into the night was the only thing that might save him from it. The love that binds friends or brothers is no less real than that which binds wooer and beloved. The power that saved me surely knew what a boastful and foolish man I was: But mothers do not strangle their babies if they are born lame; the stars do not cease to shine on us if we men cripple ourselves.

And I should not abandon my friend, whether he was a true friend to me, or not.

Men's souls are crooked and unsound things, not good materials out of which to build friendships, families, households, cities, civilizations. But good or no, these things must be built, and we must craft them with the materials at hand, and make as strong and stubborn a redoubt as we can make, lest the horrors of the Night should triumph over us, not in some distant age to come, but now.

We are surrounded by the Silent Ones. We are fated to die. One of us will perish before we regain the pyramid; Hellenore saw only one pair of footprints leading back. How is it possible that we both shall live?

But by then the cycling process was too advanced, and his thoughts lost focus. Many hours must pass before I would open the lid, and answer his question.

As I carried him on my back, out past the golden doors, I lead his blind hand to touch the bas-relief on the left panel of the golden doors.

Here was the panel carven long ago by Hellenore in a former time, was a small depiction of one small event on what, to her, had been the future, now our present. Here was a man without a breastplate or helm, wearing only gauntlets and greaves, carrying a one-armed man on his back; a blindfold (but I knew now it was a bandage) covered his eyes.

The image showed a star shining down on them, and the gates of the Last Redoubt opening to receive them. Only one pair of footprints led in.

the long way home

JAMES VAN PELT

One of the most widely published new writers of short-length works, James Van Pelt's stories have appeared in *Sci Fiction, Asimov's Science Fiction, Analog, Realms of Fantasy, The Third Alternative, Weird Tales, Talebones, Alfred Hitchcock's Mystery Magazine, Pulphouse, Altair, Transversions, Adventures in Sword & Sorcery, On Spec, Future Orbits*, and elsewhere. His first book, appropriately enough, was a collection, *Strangers and Beggars*. He lives with his family in Grand Junction, Colorado, where he teaches English at the high school and college levels.

Here he offers us a moving look at the way lives entwine through the years from one generation to the next, and how sometimes we have no choice but to take the longest way home.

M arisa kept her back to the door, holding it closed. "Another few minutes and they will have made the jump. You can go home then."

"The war has started," said Jacqueline, the telemetry control engineer. Her face glowed red with panic. "I don't matter. The mission is over. They made the jump *four hours* ago."

Marisa swallowed. If Jacqueline grabbed her, there would be little she could do. The woman outweighed her by thirty pounds, and there were no security forces to help. "Jacqueline, we've come so far."

The bigger woman raised her fist. Marisa tensed, but didn't move. Her hands trembled behind her. For a moment, Jacqueline's fist quivered in the air. Beyond her, the last of the Mission Control crew watched. Most of the stations were empty. The remaining engineers' faces registered no expression. They were too tired to react, but Marisa knew they wanted to leave just as badly.

Then Jacqueline dropped her hand to her side. Her eyes closed. "I don't make a difference," she whispered.

Marisa released a held breath. "We're part of mankind's greatest moment. There's nothing you can do out there." She nodded her head toward the door. "We can't stop what's happening, but we can be witnesses to this. There's hope still."

Several monitors displayed a United States map and a Florida one inset in the corner. Both showed bright yellow blotches. "Areas of lost communication" the key read underneath. Major cities across the country; most of the southwestern coast and northeastern seaboard, glowed bright yellow. In Florida, yellow sunbursts blotted out Miami and Jacksonville. As she watched, another one appeared on Tampa. She glanced at Mission Control's ceiling and the half-dozen skylights. At any moment, the ceiling could peel away, awash in nuclear light. She expected it, expected it much earlier, but she'd stayed at her station, recording the four-hour old signals from the *Advent* as it sped toward the solar system's edge, already beyond Neptune's orbit. Would she have any warning? Would there be an instant before the end when she would be aware that it had happened?

Jacqueline sat heavily at her console, and Marisa returned to her station. The data looked good, but it had looked good from the beginning, six years earlier, when the massive ship ponderously moved out of orbit, all 14,400 passengers hale and hearty. There had been deaths on board, of course. They expected that. Undetected medical conditions. Two homicides. Two suicides, but no major incidents with the ship itself. The hardware performed perfectly, and now, only a few minutes from when the synchronized generators along the ship's perimeter powered up to send the *Advent* into juxtaspace, Mission Control really was redundant. Jacqueline was right.

The room smelled of old coffee and sweat. Many of the controllers had been at their stations for twenty hours or more. As time grew short, they split their attention between their stations and the ubiquitous news displays. A scrolling text readout under the graphics listed unbelievable numbers: estimated dead, radiation readings, cities lost.

Marisa toggled her display. She wanted readouts on the juxtaengines. Mankind *was* going to the stars at last, even if there might be no Earth left to return to, if they could duplicate the ship to bring them back. "It's easy, having no family," she said under her breath, which wasn't quite true. Her grown son lived in Oceanside, a long commute from southern L.A., but they only talked on the phone at Christmas now. She had to check his photograph to remind herself of what he looked like. A station over, an engineer had his head down on his keyboard, sobbing.

Dr. Smalley was the only controller who appeared occupied. He flicked through screen after screen of medical data. The heartbeats of the entire crew drew tiny lines across his display. He looked at Marisa. "We won't know what happens when the shift happens. What will their bodies go through? What a pity they can't signal through the jump."

"If they make the jump at all," moaned Jacqueline.

"We'll know in three minutes," said Marisa. "Regardless of what happens here, we will have saved ourselves."

Dimly, through Mission Control's thick walls, sirens wailed up and down. The building vibrated, sending a coffee cup off a table's edge and to the floor.

"Maybe if we'd spent the money here, where it could do some good, we'd never have come to this," said Jacqueline. "We bankrupted the planet for this mission."

Dr. Smalley studied the heartbeats from the ship. "They're excited. Everyone's pulse is high. Look, I can see everything that's happening in their bodies." He waved a hand at his display. "Their individual transmitters give me more information than if I had them hooked up in a hospital. I wish I was with them."

"Everyone wishes they were with them," said Marisa.

Jacqueline said, "Don't you have a word for it, Doctor, when the patient's condition is fatal, so you decide to try something unproven to save her? That's what we're doing here, aren't we? Humanity is dying, so we try this theoretical treatment."

The countdown clock on the wall showed less than two minutes. The floor shook again, much more sharply this time.

"Please, a few more seconds," Marisa said to no one.

So much history happening around her: the first colonial expedition to another star system, and the long-feared global nuclear conflict. The victor had to be the explorers. The names passed through her head: Goddard, Von Braun, Armstrong, and the rest of them. It was a way to shut out the death-dealers knocking at the door.

"It's an experiment," said Jacqueline, edging on hysteria. "We've never sent a ship even a tenth this big. We've never tied multiple juxtaengines together. What if their fields interact? Instead of sending the ship in one piece, it could tear it apart."

"It was too expensive to try out," Marisa snapped. "It was all or nothing."

"You've been listening to the defeatists," said Dr. Smalley. "The theory is perfect. The math is perfect. In an instant, they will be hundreds of light-years from our problems."

Marisa clutched the edge of her monitor. The countdown timer clicked to under a minute. I'm a representative of mankind, she thought. For everyone who has ever wanted to go to the stars, I stand for them. She wished she could see the night sky.

Dr. Smalley hunched toward his computer as if he were trying to climb right through. Jacqueline stared at the television screens with their yellow-specked maps. The images wavered, then turned to grey fuzz. She pressed her knuckles to her mouth.

"Ten seconds," said Marisa. "All systems in the green."

The countdown ticker marched down. Marisa remembered a childhood filled with stories of space, the movies and books set in the universe's grand theater, not the tiny stage lit by a single sun. If only she could have gone too, she could have missed the messy ending mankind had made for itself. The first bombs had exploded yesterday morning. Over breakfast, she'd thought it was a hoax. No way people could be so stupid. But the reports continued to come in, and it wasn't a joke, not in the least.

Eyes toward their readouts, the control engineers monitored *Advent*'s last signals. Already at near solar-escape velocity, the *Advent* would leap out of the solar system, riding the unlikely physics of juxtaspace.

"Three . . . two . . . one," someone said. Marisa's screen flipped to the NO SIGNAL message. Analysis indicated the ship had gone. A ragged and weak cheer came from the few engineers in the room.

"She's made the jump," Marisa said. She envisioned the *Advent* obscured in a burst of light as the strange energies from the juxtaengines parted space, allowing the giant ship its trans-light speed journey. For a moment, the space program existed all on its own, separate from the news broadcasts and progress reports, far from the "Areas of lost communication."

"No," said Dr. Smalley. "There should be no telemetry now. They're gone." He touched his fingers to his monitor. Marisa moved to where she could see what he saw. The heartbeats on his screen still registered. Brain waves still recorded their spiky paths. He flicked from one screenful of medical transmissions to the next.

"How is that possible?" said Marisa. Jacqueline stood beside her. Other engineers left their stations to crowd behind Smalley's chair.

"They're getting weaker," said Jacqueline.

"No, no, no," said Smalley. His fingers tapped a quick command on his keyboard. A similar display with names and readouts appeared on the screen, but this one showed no activity in the medical area.

"What is that?" asked Marisa. How could there be transmissions? The *Advent* was beyond communication now. They'd never know if she reached her destination. Light speed and relativity created a barrier as imposing as death itself.

"It's their respiration," said Smalley, his voice computer-calm. "They're not breathing." He switched back to the heartbeats. Many of the readouts now showed nothing. A few blinked their pulses slowly, and then those stopped too. Smalley tapped through screen after screen. Every pulse was now zero. Every brain scan showed a flat line.

Marisa's hands rested on the back of Smalley's chair. She could feel him shaking through her fingers. "Check their body temperatures," she said.

He raised his head as if to look back at her. Then he shrugged in understanding. The new display showed core temperatures. As they watched, the numbers clicked down.

"Is it an anomaly?" asked someone. "Are we getting their signals from juxtaspace?"

"The ship blew up," said Jacqueline.

Marisa said, "No. We would have received telemetry for that." She held Smalley's chair now so that she wouldn't collapse. "It's their real signals from our space." Her face felt cold and her feet numb. A part of her knew that she was within an instant of collapsing. "The *Advent* left, but it didn't take *them*."

Jacqueline said, "Worst-case scenario. It was a possibility that the multiple engines wouldn't work the same way as single ones. We dumped everyone into space." Her voice cracked.

"They're dead," said Marisa as the room slowly swooped to her right. I'm falling, she thought. What would a telescope see if it could see that far? After the flash of light? Would it see 14,400 bodies tumbling? What other parts of the ship didn't go?

Her head hit the floor, but it didn't hurt. Nothing hurt, and she was curiously aware of meaningless details: how the tiled floor beneath her felt gritty, how ridiculous the engineers looked staring down at her. Then, oddly, how their faces began to darken. What a curious phenomena, she thought. The fraction of a second before she knew no more, she realized that their faces hadn't darkened. It was the skylights above them. They'd gone brilliantly bright. Surface-of-the-sun bright.

We're not going to the stars, she thought, as the heat of a thousand stars blasted through the ceiling. She would have cried if she had had the time.

Who has died like this? So sudden, the walls shimmered. Then they were gone. The air burst away, much of the ships innard's remained, but twisted and ruptured. Torn into parts. The stars swirl around us, and all the eyes see. We all see what we all see, but there isn't a "we" to talk about, just a group consciousness. The 14,400 brains frozen in moments, the neurons firing micro-charges across the supercool gaps creating a mega-organism, still connected. And we continue outward, held together loosely by our tiny gravities, sometimes touching, drifting apart, but never too far. Pluto passed in hardly a thought, and then we were beyond, into the Oort Cloud, but who would know it? The sun glimmered brightly behind us, a brighter spot among the other spots, but mostly it was black and oh so cold. Time progressed even if we couldn't measure it. Was it days already, or years, or centuries? Out we traveled. Out and out.

Jonathan shifted the backpack's weight on his shoulders as he tramped down the slope toward Encinitas, then rubbed his hands together against the cold. He'd left his cart filled with trade goods in Leucadia, and it felt good not to be pulling its weight behind him. The sun had set in garish red an hour earlier, and all that guided his footsteps was the well-worn path and the waves' steady pounding on the shore to his right. No moon yet, although its diffuse light wouldn't help much anyway. When he'd crested the last hill, though, he'd seen the tiny lights of Encinitas' windows, and knew he was close.

He whistled a tune to himself, keeping rhythm with his steps. The harvest was in, and it looked like it would be a good one this year for Encinitas. They'd wired two more greenhouses with grow-lights in the spring, and managed to scare up enough seed for a full planting. For the first time, they might even have an excess. If he could broker a deal with the folks in Oceanside, who lost part of their crop to leaf blight, it could be a profitable winter.

A snatch of music came through the ocean sound. Jonathan smiled. Ray Hansen's daughter, Felitia, would be there. Last year she'd danced with him twice, and he imagined her hand lingered as they passed from partner to partner . . . but she'd been too young to court then. Not this year, though. It was going to be a good night. Even the icy-cold ocean breeze smelled clean. Not so dead. Not like when he was a boy and everyone called it the "stinking sea."

He slowed down. The gate across the path should be coming soon. It stopped the flock of goats from wandering off during the summer. In the winter, of course, they were kept in the barns so that they wouldn't freeze. Yes, Encinitas was a rich community, to be able to grow enough to feed livestock. Felitia would be a good match for him. She was strong and lively, and her father would certainly welcome him warmly if he was a part of the family. Goat's milk with every meal! He licked his lips, thinking of the cheese that was a part of the harvest celebration.

But what if she didn't want him?

He slowed even more. What wasn't to want about him? He was twenty, and a businessman, but it wasn't like he was around all the time to charm her, and a year was a long time. Maybe she didn't want to travel from village to village, carrying trade goods. And she was a *bookish* girl. People talked about her, Jonathan knew. That was part of her charm. He buried his hands under his armpits. Did it seem unusually cold suddenly, or was it fear that made him shiver?

The gate rattled in the breeze, which saved him bumping into it. Fingers stiff, he unlatched it. Clearly now, the music lilted from over the hill. He hurried, full of hope and dread.

"Jonathan, you are welcome," said Ray Hansen at the door. Hansen looked older than the last time Jonathan had seen him, but he'd always seemed old. He might be forty, which was really getting up in years, Jonathan thought. Beyond, the long tables filled with seedling plants had been pushed to the wall. Everyone in the village seemed to be there. The Yamishitas and Coogans. The Taylors and Van Guys. The Washingtons and Laffertys. Over a hundred people filled the room. Jonathan smiled. "I've come to see your daughter, sir."

The old man smiled wanly. "You'll need to talk to her about that."

Jonathan wondered if Hansen was sick. He seemed much thinner than Jonathan remembered him. Probably the blood disease, he thought. Lots of folks got the blood disease.

The band struck up a reel, and couples formed into squares for the next dance. The caller took his place on the stage. Felitia, in a plain, cotton dress, sat on the edge of a table at the far end of the long room, swinging her feet slowly beneath her. Jonathan edged along the dance floor. The music drove the dancers to faster and faster twirls, hands changing hands, heads tossing. He apologized when a woman bumped him, but she was gone so fast he doubted she'd heard.

Felitia watched him as he made the last few yards, her blue eyes steady, her blonde hair tied primly back. Was she glad to see him? Surely she knew why he was there. He had left her notes every time he passed through Encinitas, and her replies that he retrieved the next trip were chatty enough, but noncommittal. She could have been writing to her brother for all the passion he'd found in them.

He sat next to her without saying anything. Now that she was beside him, the speech he'd practiced sounded phony and ridiculous. The villagers rested when the music ended, talking quietly to themselves. On the makeshift stage, the band tuned their instruments. The two guitarists compared notes, while the trumpet player discreetly blew the spit out of his horn.

"This is nice," said Jonathan. He winced. Even that sounded stupid.

"Yes." Her hands were together in her lap. "How were the roads?"

The band started another tune, and soon the crowd wove through the familiar patterns.

"Fine, I guess." Jonathan decided that the best move would be to leave the room. It was one thing to think grand thoughts while pulling his cart down the seashore roads, but it was quite another to confront her in the flesh. "I did good business in Oceanside."

"It must be interesting, seeing all those places."

Jonathan swelled. "Oh, yes. I've been even further north than that, you know. I even went to San Clemente once. A few of the buildings still stand. I wanted to press on to Los Angeles, but you know how cautious the old folks are."

She looked sideways at him.

He cleared his throat. "Just along the beach. Nothing inland, of course. It's ice from the Santa Ana mountains almost to the sea, but they say the snow field is retreating. It's getting warmer, they say."

Felitia sighed. "The dust went up; the dust will go down. I don't know if I believe it. They can call it 'nuclear winter,' but it's more like nuclear eternity to me." She watched the dancers, her face lost and vulnerable. "Encinitas seems so small."

Jonathan gripped the table's edge. What he wanted to ask was on the tip of his tongue. Everything else sounded trivial, but the timing wasn't right. He couldn't just blurt it out. A thought came to him, and, with relief, he said, "I brought you a present." He slung his backpack off his shoulders and set it between them. Felitia peered inside when he opened it.

"Books!" She clapped her hands.

He dug through the volumes. "There's one I thought you might like especially." At the bottom, he found it. "We need to go outside so I can give it to you." He tried to swallow, but couldn't. Nothing he'd ever done before felt so bold.

She held his hand as they walked away from the dancers. Her fingers nestled softly in his.

Felitia put on a coat and picked up a storm lamp before they went out the back door. The flame flickered before settling into a steady glow.

"What is it?"

Wind pushed against his face, tasting of salt. It could snow tonight, he thought. First snow of the season. He pulled the book out of his jacket and handed it to her. "Here's as far as you can get from Encinitas."

She opened the book, a paperback edition of *Peterson's Field Guide to the Stars and Planets*. By the storm lamp, he could see a color print of the Cone Nebula, a red, clouded background with white blobs poking through.

"Oh, Jonathan. It's beautiful."

Their foreheads touched as they bent over the book.

She turned her face toward his. "My father told me about stars. He said he saw them when he was a boy, before the bad times."

Jonathan glanced up. "My dad said we were going to the stars. His mom helped launch the *Advent*." The uniform black of the night sky greeted him, as indistinguishable as a cave interior. "He said the sky used to be blue, and the sun was as sharp-edged as a gold coin."

He looked down. Felitia's face was only an inch from his own. Without thinking about it, he leaned in just enough to kiss her. She didn't move away, and his question was answered before he asked it.

Later, holding her against him, he said, "They say when the dust clears, we'll see the stars again."

And on a calm night, four years later, after Ray, Jr., had gone to sleep, Jonathan and Felitia stood outside their house in Oceanside.

"Can you see?" said Felitia. "Do you think that's what I think it is?" She pointed to a spot in the sky.

One hand on her shoulder, Jonathan pulled her tight. "I think it is."

A bright spot glimmered for a second. Another joined it.

They stayed outside until they both grew so cold they couldn't stand it anymore.

We feel space. Neutrinos pass through like sparklers in the group body. Gravity heats our skin. We hear space, not through the frozen cells of our useless ears, but through the sensitive membrane of our group awareness. The stars chime like tiny bells. It has a taste, the vacuum does, dusty and metallic, and it doesn't grow old. We go farther and farther and slower and slower, until we stop, not in equilibrium; the sun won. Gradually, we start back. Apogee past. The Oort Cloud. The birthplace of comets. How many years have we gone away?

"Relying on the old knowledge is a mistake." Professor Matsui faced the crowd of academics in the old New Berkeley lecture hall. The new New Berkeley hall wouldn't be done until next year. After a hundred-and-twenty years of use, this one would be torn down. He would miss the old place. "We overemphasize recreating the world we know from the records, but we aren't doing our *own* work. Where is our originality? Where is our cultural stamp on our scientific progress?" He was glad for the new public address system. His voice wasn't nearly as strong as it had been when he was young.

Matsui watched Dr. Chesnutt, the Reclaimed Technologies chair. He appeared bored, his notebook unopened on his study desk. Languidly he raised his hand. "Point," he said. "Would you have us throw away our ancestors' best work? When we allocate money, should we assign *more* on your 'original research' that may yield nothing, or should we spend wisely, investigating what we *know* will work because it worked before? When we equal the achievements of the past, then it will make sense to invest in your programs. Until then, you divert valuable time and valuable funds."

Pausing for a moment to scan the crowd, Matsui took a deep breath. Were the others with him or against him? The literature department was evenly split between the archivists and the creative writers. Biology, Sociology, and Agri-science would lean toward him, as would Astronomy, but the engineers, mathematicians, and physicists would cast their vote solidly with Chesnutt, and, as the former head of the School of Medicine, he had probably coerced everyone in the department to vote his way. "Obviously we must continue the good work of learning from the past, but if we throw all our effort, and funds, into that, we risk creating the same mistakes that destroyed their world. You pursue their wisdom without worrying about their folly. Will you follow them down the road that led to nuclear annihilation?"

Chesnutt chuckled. "You can raise the 'nuclear annihilation' demon all you like. As you know, there is no agreement among historians about what caused the great die-off. The nuclear exchange may have been the last symptom of a much deeper problem. We will only avoid their fate if we learn from their triumphs."

Heads nodded in the audience.

Matsui finished his speech, but he could tell that Chesnutt had called in all his favors. It didn't matter what value his arguments had, the Research Chair would not gain funding this year. He'd be lucky to hold his committee assignments.

After the meeting, Matsui left the lecture hall in a hurry. He didn't want to deal with the false condolences. The bloodsuckers, he thought. They'll be looking for strategies to make my loss an advantage for their departments in some way or another.

A breeze off the bay cut through his thin coat, sending a translucent veil of clouds across the night sky, and tossing the lights dangling from their poles.

"Wait, Professor," called a voice.

He grimaced, then slowed his pace. Puffing, Leif Henderson, an assistant lecturer in Astronomy, joined him.

"Good speech, sir."

"I'm afraid it was wasted."

"I don't think so. We've got a couple of Chesnutt supporters in the department, but I can tell you the grad students aren't interested in making their names in the field by rediscovering all of Jupiter's moons. The younger ones want to do something *new*."

Matsui pushed his hands deep into his pockets. Maybe he was getting too old for the back-stabbing politics of the university. "Chesnutt has a point. Old Time learning casts a huge shadow. We may never be able to get out from under it, and it doesn't help that whenever original research makes a discovery, the intellectual archeologists dig up some reference to show it's been done before. There's no impetus for innovation."

Henderson matched Matsui's steps. "But the Old Timers didn't know everything. They didn't conquer death. They didn't master themselves." The young man looked into the night sky. "They didn't reach the stars. We should have been receiving the *Advent*'s signals for the last fifty years if they made it, or even more likely, they would have come back. They have had four hundred years to recreate their engines."

"I like to think they arrived, and we just haven't built sensitive enough receivers, or maybe three hundred and fifty light years is too far for the signal. What they have to wonder is why *we* haven't contacted them, why we didn't *follow* them. The world has gone silent."

The sidewalk split in two in front of them. Astronomy and the physical science buildings were to the right. Administration was to the left. They paused at the junction.

Matsui looked down the familiar path. He'd walked that sidewalk his entire adult life, first as a student, then a graduate assistant, and finally as a professor. From his first day in the classroom, he had valued creative thought. That is what the academy is about, he had argued. The Old Timers accomplished noble feats, but they are gone. We should make our own mistakes.

"The world is changing, Henderson. The population will be over one billion in a decade. We survived an extinction event four hundred years ago, so we missed being the last epoch's dinosaurs. We fought our way out of the second Dark Ages. As a species, we must be fated for greatness, but we're so damned stupid about achieving it." He kicked at the ground bitterly.

Henderson stood quietly for a minute. In the distance, the surf pounded against the rocks. "It's a pendulum, Professor. This year, Chesnutt won. He won't always. If we're going to push knowledge forward, we will escape our past. We'll have to."

Matsui said, "Not in my lifetime, son. It's so frustrating. Humanity has desires. It must. But what they are and how it will go about getting them will remain a mystery to me. There's a big picture that I can't see. Oh, if only there was a longer perspective, it would all make sense."

Henderson didn't reply.

"I'm sorry," said Matsui. "I'm an old man who babbles a bit when it gets late at night. I wax philosophic. It used to take a couple of pints of beer, but now cool night air and a bad budget meeting will do it. You'll have to forgive me."

Henderson shuffled his feet. "There's a move in the department to name a comet after you."

Suddenly, Matsui's eyes filled with tears. He was glad the night hid them. "That would be nice, Henderson."

Matsui left Henderson behind, but when the older man reached faculty housing, he didn't stop. He kept going until he came to the bluff that overlooked the sea. Condensation dampened the rail protecting the edge of the low bluff, and it felt cold beneath his hands. Moonlight painted the surf's spray a glowing white. He thought about moonlight on water, about starlight on water. Each wave pounding against the cliff shook the rail, and, for a moment, he felt connected to it all, to the larger story that was mankind on the planet and the planet in the galaxy. It seemed as if he was feeling the universal pulse.

Much later, he returned to his cottage and his books. He was right. Chesnutt replaced him on the committees, but Matsui wasn't unhappy. He remembered his hands on the rail, the moon like a distant searchlight, and the grander story that he was a part of.

Thoughts come slower, it seems, or events have sped ahead, and we want to sleep. Maybe we have spread out, our individual pieces, a long stream of bodies and ship parts, and odds and ends: books, blankets, tools, chairs, freeze dried foods, scraps of paper, the vast collection of miscellany that humanity thought to bring to a distant star. Or maybe the approaching sun has warmed us. The super-cool state that kept consciousness and connection possible is breaking down. But we know we are accelerating, diving deep into the system that gave us birth. It's been a long trip, out and back, the 14,400. Our individual dreams forgotten, but the group one survived: to travel, to find our way out of the cave, to check over the next hilltop. We feel an emotion as the last thoughts fail: something akin to happiness. We're going home.

Captain Fremaria sat on a blanket with her husband on the hill overlooking the launch facility. The lights illuminating the ship had been turned off, but she knew crews were working within the enclosed scaffolding, fueling the engines, running through the last checklists, making sure it would be ready for the dawn liftoff.

"It's just like another test flight, darling," she said to her husband. "I've flown much less reliable crafts." Her heart took a sudden leap as she thought about the mission. She could hear the rockets igniting in her head. Could she do it? The idea of climbing atop the thousands of pounds of propellant had never sounded so foolhardy as it did now. When she was training, the flight remained a theory, an abstraction, but with the ship so close and the schedule coming to its close, she felt like a condemned woman.

"Don't remind me," he said. "I just want to know that you'll be safe. I need a sign."

She sighed. "I wouldn't mind one myself." She did not have to climb aboard the ship. No one could force her to. In fact, she wouldn't really be committed until ignition.

"It's too much history." He moved closer to her so that his hand rested on hers. "Mankind returns to space after all these centuries. Everyone wants to know about the impact of this moment. Will we go to the moon next? Will we go to Mars? What will we find there of the old colonies?" He snorted derisively. "I just want to know that *you* will come back."

Fremaria nodded her head, but he wasn't looking at her. In three hours, she would report to launch central, where they would begin preparing her for insertion into the craft that would carry her into orbit. The mission called for ten circuits around the earth, then a powerless drop back into the atmosphere, where she would fly the stubby-winged ship to a touchdown at Matsui Airbase.

"I won't be that far away. If you could take the train straight up, you'd be there in a couple of hours."

Her husband chuckled, but it sounded forced.

For the first time in weeks, the wind was calm. Fremaria had watched the weather reports anxiously, but it looked as if the launch should take place in perfect conditions. Not a cloud marred the flawless night sky. The horizon line cut a ragged edge out of the inverted bowl of pristine stars.

"I've never seen it so clear," said her husband.

A green light streaked across the sky.

"Make a wish," said Fremaria.

"You know what it is." He squeezed her hand.

Another meteor flamed above them, brighter than the first.

"That's rare," said Fremaria. "So close together."

Before he could reply, a third and fourth appeared, traveling parallel courses.

"It's beautiful," he said.

She arched her back to see the sky better. "There isn't supposed to be a meteor shower now. The Leonids aren't for another month."

A spectacular meteor crossed half the sky before disappearing.

Fremaria leaned into her husband's shoulder for support. For almost two hours, the display continued, often times with multiple meteors visible at once, some so bright that they cast shadows. Then, the intensity dropped, until the sky was quiet again.

"Have you ever seen anything like that?" her husband asked. "Have you even ever *heard* of anything like that?"

"No." She thought about the mysteries of space. "It's a sign."

He laughed. "I guess it might be."

Fremaria glanced at her watch. "It's time for me to go." She brushed her pants after she stood. Her husband held her hand again, but her thoughts now were in the ship. She ran through the takeoff procedure. No mission went without a hitch. They would be depending on her to make corrections, to shake down the craft. A good flight: that was all she wanted, and then a next one and a next one. They began the walk down to the launch facility.

She thought about the centuries. The *Advent* was supposed to go to the stars. Had it made it? No one knew, but they were going again. Her flight would open the door again.

"Are you scared?" her husband asked.

Fremaria paused on the trail. The ship waited for her. She could see that they had cranked part of the scaffolding away from it. Soon it would stand alone, unencumbered. She would sit in the pilot's chair listening to the countdown, prepared to take over from the automated controls if needed. What an experience the rocket's thrust would be! What a joy to feel the weightlessness that awaited her! To break free. To take the first step to the long voyage *out*.

"I'm ready to go."

A single meteor flickered into existence above them. It glowed brilliantly in its last moment. They watched its path until it vanished.

"They don't last too long, do they?" he said.

Fremaria glanced at the ship, then back at the sky. "No, but they travel a long way first."

the eyes of america

GEOFFREY A. LANDIS

A physicist who works for NASA, and who has recently been working on the Martian Lander program, Geoffrey A. Landis is a frequent contributor to *Analog* and to *Asimov's Science Fiction*, and has also sold stories to markets such as *Interzone, Amazing,* and *Pulphouse.* Landis is not a prolific writer, by the high-production standards of the genre, but he *is* popular. His story "A Walk in the Sun" won him a Nebula and a Hugo Award in 1992, his "Ripples in the Dirac Sea" won him a Nebula Award in 1990, he also won a Hugo for his story "Falling Onto Mars," and his "Elemental" was on the Final Hugo Ballot a few years back. His first book was the collection, *Myths, Legends, and True History,* and in 2002, he has published his first novel, *Mars Crossing.* He lives with his wife, writer Mary Turzillo, in Brook Park, Ohio.

In the sly and insightful story that follows, he introduces us to an alternate America where the Media Age came just a little bit *early . . .*

It was an enlightened year, a young century from which to spring forward into the future, a year in which people pushed the new boundaries of freedom.

It was an era of marvels, and who knew what could or could not be done? Men had sent their signals by etheric wave across the English Channel, and the mighty Niagara had been tamed and harnessed to the yoke of man. Locomotive rails tunneled across and under the great Rocky Mountains, and America, the stripling giant, had beaten the tired empire of Spain to the ground in a war of only three months. Men now talked of airships that would fly to the moon, and of telephones to breach the vapory wall between worlds.

It was 1904. Who knew what marvels would be next?

The room was smoke-filled, but that was no surprise; the rooms where real decision making occurred were always smoke-filled.

"Damn Democrats," Horovitz said. "They're going to ruin everything we fought for."

"Indeed," Hanna said. Marcus Hanna, the Ohio senator, was the chairman of the Republican party, but Horovitz was its invisible leader. "You are only stating the obvious. But who have we got?"

"Damn that communist, that anarchist, that swine," Horovitz said. "Why'd he have to shoot Teddy? Couldn't he have shot McKinley? Damn it to hell, we need Teddy now, more than ever."

Levi Horovitz—Leggy, to his friends, of which he had few, at least inside politics—was short and rotund. He was rarely seen in public, and never without a soggy cigar clamped in his teeth. For nearly twenty years, Horovitz had been the hidden power behind the Republican party—since 1884, when, with the aid of a handful of carefully paid newsmen, he had orchestrated his candidate Jimmy Blaine into the Republican nomination over the incumbent Chester Arthur.

Horovitz was bitterly aware that he would never serve in office himself. He could never get elected, not in this century, not in the next. Not a Jew. Not even in America, the most enlightened country in the world. But he had adapted, and presidents and generals danced to his orders.

"Roosevelt's not much good to us now, six feet under," Hanna said. In Hanna's private opinion, Roosevelt had never been any good for the Republicans; the damned cowboy had been unsafe and erratic. But there was no percentage in talking against a war hero, especially a dead one; Hanna had learned that lesson well. "Better come up with somebody else."

"Damn that anarchist," Horovitz muttered again. "Damn him to hell."

"That's redundant; he's there already," Hanna said. "Now, who have you got?"

"Damn that Bryan, too."

"Bryan's got the masses behind him," Hanna observed.

"Swine." Horovitz spit out his cigar and ground it under his foot. "They're all a bunch of swine."

That was the problem facing the Republicans, all right. With Theodore Roosevelt dead, shot by a drug-crazed anarchist, who did they have? William Jennings Bryan was mobilizing the country yokels with his damned populist talk. The man was tireless, crossing and recrossing the country by rail, stopping at every cow-flop town on the tracks, talking about American imperialism as if it were a bad thing, asking the people whether they had ever seen the "full dinner pail" that McKinley had promised them. With his high-flown diction and rash promises, Bryan was raising their expectations—and harvesting their votes. He could motivate the rabble, old Bryan could; Horovitz would give him that. What a silver-tongued peacock he was at oration, with his talk of America "crucified upon a cross of gold" and his avowal of "plowshares of peace!"

If only the man had been a Republican, a true patriot, instead of a Democrat—one step away from being a communist. Or worse.

"Here's my thought," Hanna said. "We run John Hay."

"Against William Jennings Bryan?" Horovitz dismissed him with a wave, and pulled a crumpled new cigar from his vest pocket. "You're joking. Bryan would crumple him up like a page from last year's Sears & Roebuck catalog and wipe his ass with the man."

"Henderson, then?"

"Wouldn't stand a chance. None of those old guys can stand against Bryan. We need somebody new."

"Then who?"

"The boy genius," Horovitz said. "The hero of America, the maestro of electricity." At Hanna's blank look, he said, "The wizard of Menlo Park."

"You mean"—Hanna gasped—"Edison?"

Horovitz pulled a newspaper from his valise and dropped it onto the desk. The headline said, EDISON ANNOUNCES REST, HE IS TIRED OUT AND WILL STOP INVENTING FOR A WHILE. "He's not tinkering," Horovitz said. "He might as well run for president."

"But—the man has no knowledge of politics."

Horovitz lit his cigar, drew deeply, exhaled a cloud of smoke, and smiled. "So much the better."

"No," Edison said, "I have too much work to do. Wouldn't think of it."

He was no longer any sort of boy genius, not at fifty-five years of age, but his eyes had the restless, playful energy of a boy, darting away as if he were already bored with the conversation and itching to go outside to play. His suit was a stylishly cut gabardine, but wrinkled as if he had slept in it, and his tie was carelessly knotted and slightly askew.

Horovitz persisted.

"No," Edison said, "I have no interest in politics. Gentlemen, I am duly flattered, but I do believe that you are importuning the wrong man." He stood up and turned to the window, his back to Horovitz, pointedly gazing out across the East River.

It was intended as a gesture to dismiss Horovitz from his East Side office. Yet Horovitz persisted.

"Are you deranged," Edison said, "or just deaf?" He turned back to Horovitz, his eyes blazing with irritation. "No, confound it, no, and again no! Why me?"

The question was exactly the opening that Horovitz was waiting for.

"Mr. Bryan is kind-hearted, Mr. Edison, but he is a man stuck deeply into the mire of the past," he said. "He will lead us down from the heights we have scaled, and, in the name of his working man, will take us back into darkness. He is a fool, a fool who believes with utter sincerity that he is guided by God, and he will be the ruin of America."

Horovitz was careful, telling Thomas Alva Edison just exactly what he wanted to hear. He worked words as carefully as playing a fish, in a net of flattery and sense in equal proportions.

"It is a century of science, Mr. Edison," he concluded. "And if we cannot get leadership from a man of science, a man of your standing, what hope do we have? We come to you with our hats in our hands. So tell us, where is your equal? Is there another man of your caliber and perseverance? Give me but the name of this man, and we shall go on our knees and beg him to serve as candidate. No one but a man of science can help us. Join us, Mr. Edison. Lead us. Tell us how to steer America. You are our only hope."

Edison slowly nodded. "A century of science. Yes, that it is. That, it most certainly is."

"I love elections," said Samuel Clemens. "It is the great American spectacle, featuring bloviating and drum-beating unmatched in the world, and it is always a thrill to see whether the hypocrites will beat the fools, or vice versa."

Sam Clemens was in the barber shop. He was, as ever, resplendent in a white linen suit. For the new century, he had decided that he would wear only white; it made him look distinguished and dazzled the crowds, and Sam was a showman, every Missouri inch of him.

"Quiet down a bit now, please, Mr. Twain," one of the men said. "We're listening to Mr. Edison talk."

Sam wasn't in the barbershop for a haircut—he was cultivating the lion's mane look that year—but had come to watch the men play checkers, listen to the election talk, and maybe join in and pontificate a bit about current events. Or perhaps he might pick up some gossip or some good lines he could use in an article or a speech. But this time he was being upstaged, and upstaged by a doll, at that.

A talking doll. Sam had an Edison phonograph, of course; who hadn't? They were all the rage. But this doll was a little Edison himself, a foot and a half tall, and spoke with Edison's blunt, homespun voice. "I mean to put America to work," the tiny Edison said. "Nothing great is accomplished without honest sweat, and I say America is great because we ain't afraid of work."

"Well, well," Samuel Clemens said to it. "Truth, many folk as I know would sweat and toil and try just about anything to avoid honest work. I allow as the folk Mr. Edison knows must be a different kind of people entirely."

"We shall enter the glorious future," the Edison doll recited, "standing tall and proud."

"Well, bully," Sam told it. "That's a fair promise, I'd say, about as honest as I've ever heard from a politician." For a moment the men in the barbershop looked at him and not the talking Edison, and Sam went on, "We will enter the future, indeed. I reckon that will happen no matter which buffoon is elected. And glorious? Sure. 'Course, you can call a pig glorious, if you like."

To tell the truth, Sam didn't know what to make of Edison. He certainly admired him as an inventor, of course; Sam considered himself an inventor, but Edison was, no doubt about it, the top dog. But what in blazes was the man thinking of, running for president, and as a Republican, no less? Sam purely hated Republicans. Republican imperialism and jingoism, in his opinion, were likely to be the ruin of America. Was Edison too blind to know that only fools, charlatans, and con men ever ran for public office? Not that Sam necessarily minded a good confidence man; some of them were plain music to hear talk, and anyway, who else would he play pool with? But Edison?

He had to go see that Edison, he did. Give him a good talking to, let him know how he was being used.

He wondered if Edison played pool.

William Jennings Bryan was working like a mule; crisscrossing the country by rail, making fifteen and even twenty railroad-stop speeches a day, every day, save only Sunday, the sabbath, when he restricted himself to one speech, after church. To keep up his strength, he was eating six meals a day, and his campaign crew gave him a rubdown after each speech in a hopeless attempt to keep him fresh and vigorous.

Still, the Edison dolls were bringing the Republican campaign into every salon, barbershop, and cafe in America. After some desperate seeking, Bryan's campaign found that the Victor grapho-phone company would make a talking machine small enough to hide inside a William Jennings Bryan doll, using a Victrola circular-platter instead of an Edison cylinder. The Edison company sued, but while the lawyers talked, the Bryan dolls battled the Edison dolls for the ears of America.

For that summer, the great American entertainment was to stage debates between the two dolls. The Bryan doll explained that the issue was the principles of democracy and rights for the working man against the plundering plutocracy and imperialism of the Republican party. The Edison doll talked about the future, the wonderful role America would have in bringing the engines of enlightenment to the world, as earlier electricity had distributed light. (Neither doll talked about real issues, as far as Sam Clemens could see.)

The talking cylinders were selling like blazes. "No band of train robbers ever planned a robbery upon a train more deliberately or with less conscience," the tiny Bryan squeaked forth, "than the robbery the plutocrats plan upon this great nation." "Innovation, confound it, innovation and pure honest sweat are what build American fortunes, and that is open to Americans of all cities," the miniature Edison responded.

Edison set his team in the laboratory twenty-four hours a day trying to find ways to make reproductions of cylinders quickly and cheaply; inventing new materials to take the place of the fragile wax. As fast as he could innovate, the Victor talking-machine company matched Edison's cylinders with new grapho-phone disks of Bryan's speeches, and there was a new speech for sale for the dolls to talk every week.

"Edison is beating me," Bryan said, "with light." He was standing in the small office of the private railway car the campaign had hired. A pile of newspapers lay piled at the foot of the plumply cushioned armchair from which he had just arisen; he had scanned each one rapidly and discarded it. "It is not enough that the plutocrats are spending every dollar that they have stolen from the honest workingmen, but now Edison has started promising to bring electrification to every farmhouse in the country. The farmers are buying his electrical-miracle talk wholesale. He cannot do it, of course, but ever I fail to convince them."

"Then promise electricity as well," said Calhoun, his closest campaign adviser. Bryan was famed as a campaigner who revealed his strategies to no one, but Cal, who had no ambitions of his own but to be secretary to the great man, was one of the few that Bryan would trust to reveal his doubts to. "Just think what a benefit it would be for the common man, no longer to live under the tyranny of the sun!"

"I will not disparage the sun, which is God's gift," Bryan said curtly. "And, further, though all my advisers tell me to, I will cozen my people with no lies. The cost of the copper alone would bankrupt the nation, unless we are to implement a new tax, and that I will not do. I shall and will promise nothing that cannot be delivered."

"There is a man," Calvin said, "who has said—well, I don't know myself, but he has said that he can send power without wires. He can control the lightning."

"Who is this?" Bryan said.

"His name is Nikola Tesla."

"And the problem?"

"Well," Cal hesitated. "I've heard people say he's mad."

Nikola Tesla was Edison's greatest rival—in the field of electrical inventing, his most vexing and only rival. Where Edison had electrified New York with direct-current electricity, Tesla's alternating current, backed by Mr. Westinghouse, was electrifying the nation.

If the mad Serb said he could command the powers of lightning, it was no more or less a marvel, in its way, than Herr Daimler's pneumatic-tired gasoline automobile.

Tesla had agreed to meet Bryan at the Waldorf-Astoria in New York, where he kept his room. Bryan had engaged a small private meeting room, decorated with a cabbage-rose wallpaper and an elaborate marble-topped table with an ormolu clock featuring the metaphorical figures of Time and the Lovers.

"I can create, or I can destroy," Tesla said. He was impeccably dressed, in a dark suit whose shirt bore detachable cuffs and an elaborately knotted silk cravat of the palest blue. "I can make the Earth sing like a bell. I can excite the powers of resonance, and like that"—he snapped his fingers—"I could destroy buildings, cities, whole continents." His stare was piercing, almost frightening in its intensity, like that of a preacher in the throes of the rapture. "I could split the Earth itself in two. Electricity? I can call forth the lightning from the deep blue sky and stand untouched in the electrical fires. God? You talk of God? I will show you God, the God of lightning. Give me only my dynamo, and I hold the powers of God in the palm of my hand."

"Your talk is blasphemous," Bryan said calmly. "If you wish to continue in this fashion, please absent yourself from my presence. And furthermore, I have no interest in your engines of destruction. America is no imperial war power; we are a power of peace, not a sower of human discord."

Tesla was momentarily taken aback. "And what, then, do you want of me?"

"You seek backing. I am told that you want financial backers for your idea to create electrical power and send it through the ether across the Earth. Is this true?"

Tesla nodded. "Resonance," he said. "Resonance is the secret; nothing works without resonance."

"I think that without wires, there can be no meters, and without meters, the electricity would be free to all," Bryan said. "And so, with no promise of fat remuneration, none of the plutocrats will finance your scheme."

"All too true, I have found," Tesla said ruefully. "I must admit it."

"Help me win this election." Bryan's eyes blazed with the strength of his sincerity. "Help me win, and I promise you, your electrical broadcast towers will be built."

"Sir, I am yours." Tesla bowed. "If invention is your requirement, you may have no fear of Edison, for in that respect I am his master. Only tell me what I must do, and I shall be at your most dedicated service."

"Tesla? A fraud and a confidence man," Edison said. He was dapper in a hundred-dollar silk suit now, sitting behind a marble-topped mahogany desk. His tie was still askew, probably from his having taken a nap on the desktop earlier.

Horovitz looked unconvinced. Edison was proving to be harder to manage than even Roosevelt had been; he had too many of his own ideas, some of them tending disastrously toward progressivism. But a victory by the populist Bryan would be far worse of a disaster.

Edison said, "Forget about Tesla. He will promise them the sky, anything, but he will take their money and deliver nothing but dreams and spun sugar. Believe me, I know; he worked for me, and he was nothing but trouble. Scientific research requires discipline and methodical experimentation. There is no place in electricity for a man with no discipline. Toys, that's what he makes, gee-gaws to impress the masses. He is no inventor. And as for his vaunted etheric power beams—I say bah, and double-bah, and bah again. A fraud and a connivance. It will be like his alternating-cycle electrical tension; something that will kill people who use it, mark me well. It will kill people."

Tesla's joining the Bryan campaign as the candidate's "electrical advisor" was in all of the news, and the excited journalists clearly hoped to pump up the rivalry between Tesla and Edison, harking back to the glorious days of the war between Edison's direct-current and Tesla's alternating electrical current. Perhaps Edison would electrocute somebody, as he had in the earlier war of the currents?

This worried Horovitz: Tesla had won that battle, or at least his patron Mr. Westinghouse had, and he wondered what new tricks Mr. Tesla might have in store. Tesla was just exactly what Horovitz feared: an upstart immigrant, and one who indubitably held the views of anarchists and Fabians. Horovitz kept his own origins quiet, most particularly his arrival in America in the arms of immigrant parents and the fact that he had never spoken a word of English until he was nearly six. He was an American, damn them, fully an equal of Pierpont Morgan and Andrew Carnegie; he had nothing in common with the dirty, starving immigrants in their consumption-riddled tenements.

But Edison didn't seem to be worried about Tesla. Horovitz relaxed slightly and turned his mind to the question of how he would run Edison. The man was a bull moose quite as headstrong as Roosevelt had been, and it would take some connivance to get him into line.

Fifty miles away, Samuel Clemens and Sarah Bernhardt were also discussing Tesla.

Sam had had no luck getting in to see Mr. Edison. When he had come for an interview, a man named Horovitz had quizzed him for nearly half an hour, asking him detailed questions about the Philippines and the Standard Oil Trust. These were issues about which he had quite definite opinions, and he'd given the man quite an earful, he had, quite pleased to show off his detailed command of current events—but after all his talking, rather than showing him to Edison, the man had taken him to see a receptionist, who told him that Mr. Edison was busy and could receive no visitors this month, or next, or, for that matter, the following year.

But it was a rip-snorting campaign, no denying that, and Sam was enjoying it hugely. On Sunday, Bryan's campaign had projected an enormous optical show to the curious viewers in Madison Garden, powered by calcium lights. In the middle of the city, a three-story-high projection of Bryan had towered over the bustling city, the projector operator deftly switching the glass slides to make the candidate wave to the crowd. It was, perhaps, not enough to beat Edison's continuous showing of kinetoscopic images in hired dance halls, showing off the inventor along with fanciful images of the wonders of electricity as a taste of what was to come, but it demonstrated that Bryan wasn't out of the great game yet.

When the newspapers had announced Tesla's joining up with Bryan, Clemens had brightened up. When he had been in New York, young Tesla had been quite a friend of his, and it would be a gay thing now to go meet the mad Serb and see what his views were on the election.

Sarah Bernhardt, the celebrated French actress, also knew Tesla. Sam had met with her on the train up from New York City, and as she was also heading for Tesla's Long Island laboratory, when she hired an electric brougham for the ride from the station, she invited him to share the ride. They spent the short trip discussing their acquaintance Nikola Tesla and the political campaign. Now they were in the vestibule of Tesla's laboratory building. A dozen pigeons scattered from the stoop and fluttered around their heads as they entered the vestibule.

"Mad as a hatter, *n'est pas?*" Samuel Clemens said, nodding toward the door, a completely unprepossessing wooden door with a simple brass plate reading NIKOLA TESLA, ELECTRICAL LABORATORY. "But for all that, a most entertaining fellow. Wonder how in the world he gets along with that prig Bryan?"

"He's not really mad," Sarah Bernhardt said, in her elegant French accent. "Eccentric, of course, but not mad. It's just that his enthusiasms are more intense than other people's. He gets an idea, and he just can't get it out of his head; he has to go to his lab and do it. He told me that often while he's working on one idea, he has another idea, and another and another, and they come so fast and thick, in swarms like mosquitoes, that he cannot work on them fast enough."

But then Sarah Bernhardt herself was somebody who was at the edge of madness, Sam thought. Her eccentricity was more than just the whimsy of a diva. She always insisted on her own private railway car, and one reason for this was so that she could take with her the coffin that she would sleep in when she had her headaches. Some people said that she took her paramours in the coffin as well, but perhaps that was only a scurrilous rumor about the flamboyant diva. And as for her relationship with Tesla—"We are friends, nothing more," she haughtily said when the representatives of the Hearst papers pressed her for more details. "He amuses me."

Sam, who had always wondered a bit over Tesla's views on women, expected that this was exactly it, that regardless of what Bernhardt might have wanted from him, their relationship was likely to be no more than just words. Sam had touched his arm once, and Tesla had jerked away in horror. Tesla had a fear of being touched.

Sam Clemens wasn't at all sure of Tesla's sanity himself. He had seen Tesla in his laboratory once charge himself up to ten million volts of electrical pressure, shooting lightning bolts out of his fingers to burn holes through sheets of plywood. It had looked like great fun to Sam, and he had begged Tesla to let him try it, but Tesla had solemnly demurred, telling him it was too dangerous for a man untrained in electricity.

"Is he as eccentric as he used to be, or has he calmed down a bit, I wonder?" Sam asked, and rang the bell.

Mr. Czito, Nikola Tesla's assistant, opened the door, and after greeting them, ushered them into the laboratory. It was a cavernous, dimly-lit space, a building hollowed out to be just a shell, with bare girders and a ceiling a hundred feet overhead, filled with dynamos and transformers and switching gear and elaborately wound copper coils.

Nikola Tesla turned to meet them. He was thinner than Sam Clemens had remembered him. He'd always been slender, but now he was almost frighteningly gaunt. "Living on bread and water, but without the bread," as they'd have put it in the mining camps. "Straight up and down like six o'clock." He's still handsome enough to set a few pulses to fluttering, though, Sam thought, and snuck a glance over at Sarah Bernhardt.

"Ah, Mr. Twain," Tesla said, and smiled. "So glad you could come."

"Sam, please," Clemens responded.

"And the divine Mademoiselle Bernhardt." Tesla bowed deeply and said a few words of welcome to her in a cascading waterfall of French too fluent for

Sam to follow. Turning to them both, he said, "A pleasure; indeed, a pleasure and an honor both for me to be visited by luminaries of the page and the stage. I must tell you that my laboratory is off limits to journalists, but for you, Mr. Twain, I make an exception."

"Good to see you too, Nick," Sam said. It was his ritual; if Tesla would insist on calling him Mr. Twain, by damn he would call him Nick. "I'm just my lovable own self today. I'm not in the reporting racket any more these days; no money in it."

"And Miss Bernhardt?"

"Why, I am here to see you, Mr. Tesla, and enjoy the exquisite pleasure of your company and conversation." She smiled at him. She wore only the simplest of her costumes today, with a plain silver necklace and no earrings; clearly dressing to please Tesla, who detested earrings and elaborate women's dress.

Tesla seemed for a moment to be taken aback, but then he bowed again and said, "Enchanted, as always."

"So, Nick, what do you think of Mr. Bryan?" Sam asked as they walked into the laboratory. "A real firecracker, would you say?"

"I would say," Tesla said, stopping for a moment to consider his words, "he has a poetic soul."

"A poet?" Sam laughed. "Now, I expect you're spinning me a bit of a stretcher there."

"A man of peace." Then Tesla shook his head. "But no science." He looked across at Clemens.

"And you? What do you think of Mr. Bryan?"

"Well," said Sam, "you may know, I don't have much regard for politicians. The Almighty made tadpoles, and he made politicians, and as they're both slimy and pretty-near brainless, you can't much tell the one from the other. 'Cept that one day a tadpole might grow into a noble frog, and a politician don't grow into nothing." He paused and pretended to ponder for a moment. "Still, Mr. Bryan hasn't lied to me yet, and it does 'pear that he supports the little man against the robbers, thieves, and bandits running the country right at this moment, so I guess I like him as much as I like any of the bunch. Which is not to say I'd stop watching my wallet if I knew he was in the room."

"Still the cynic, Mr. Twain."

Sam nodded. "I'd hate to disappoint my audience."

"Would you like to see the lab?"

"I'm here, ain't I?" Sam said.

"Oh, please," Miss Bernhardt said. "I would be delighted."

Tesla smiled. "One moment." He reached into the darkness and pulled three switches in quick succession. With a barely perceptible hum, a glow arose, emanating from long tubes of glass all about the laboratory. Some glowed pale white, others purple, or pink. A few were twisted into fanciful spirals and curlicues. Tesla picked one up from a benchtop and held it in the air. As he raised it, the pink light inside brightened and flowed around the place where his hand gripped it.

Tesla was showing off, Sam knew. Unlike Edison's lamps, Tesla's needed no wires. Sam had seen Tesla's rarefied gas lamps before, but he enjoyed watching Miss Bernhardt's expression of delight. The Tesla luminescent lamps really were quite something, he thought, with gay colors far more congenial than the harsh yellow light of Edison bulbs. He wondered if you could twist the tube into any shape you desired. Could a glassblower make one that would spell out words? That would really be some feat; you could make a sign in luminous color, bright red or glowing purple: "Eat at Joe's" or "Vote for Bryan."

And that was the hitch, Clemens thought. That would be just exactly the thing that they would do. It would spoil the magic. Better not bring the idea up.

Tesla handed him a tiny lamp, barely larger than a match head. Clemens turned it over in his hand. "Cunningly enough made," he said, "but what's it for?"

Tesla smiled. "Isn't it enough just to be what it is? But watch."

On a sheet of pine, a hundred and twenty of the tiny lamps had been mounted in a rectangular grid. Tesla turned a transformer dial, and every other one of the tiny bulbs glowed to life, a deep blood red. "Observe," Tesla commanded. He turned the bulbs down, then rotated another rheostat, and the other half of the bulbs glowed to light in emerald green.

"Very pretty," Sam commented.

"Wait." Tesla turned both rheostats together, and now the sheet glowed, not a greenish-red, nor some reddish-green, but instead a lemony yellow.

"Huh." Sam Clemens moved forward to examine it. Seen from close up, the individual lights were clearly still red and green, but moving back away from them, the light seemed to blur into yellow. "Now, doesn't that just beat all," he said.

"Keep watching." Tesla moved to a bank of sliding switches and played his slender fingers over them like an organ. The colored lights danced, and shapes of red and yellow appeared, curves and then an expanding square, and then dancing diagonal stripes. The red faded and green took its place. The effect was strangely hypnotic. A point of light expanded into a diamond shape, with another in the center, and another, each one growing to the edge of the rectangle and fading away.

"Ah," Sarah said. "You have made a symphony, a symphony made of light."

In answer, Tesla's fingers danced even more swiftly, and the lights responded to his touch with a paroxysm of color, pulsating shapes changing color in almost sensuous waves. At last he turned to them and bowed. "Do you like it?"

"Ah, it is magnificent," Sarah gushed. "Truly, the work of an artist, an outpouring from the soul of a poet of the electrical force."

Sam said, "Are you done? Can I try it now?"

With quite a bit of experimenting, Sam discovered, he could write letters in colored light. With great effort, he slowly spelled out S-A-M, Tesla and Sarah Bernhardt shouting out each letter as he formed it on the grid.

"I don't think that the typesetting boys have much to worry about yet," he said with a smile. "But it's a gimcrack toy. Reckon you could sell it? I bet Wall Street could use it to flash out stock prices."

"Where the man of electricity sees electrical light, the man of letters finds letters," observed Tesla.

"And Mademoiselle, *voulez vous*? What will the woman of the stage see?"

With a little coaxing, Sarah Bernhardt was persuaded to try it, and she came up with a stick figure of a man. With great concentration, she made one hand wave up and down, as Tesla and Clemens laughed in glee, and then, to everybody's amazement, even her own, she made it totter off the side of the rectangle.

"I think that the lady has you beat, Mr. Twain," Tesla announced. "For a picture, you know, beats a thousand words."

"I don't think it has the jump on Edison's kinetoscope for entertainment," Clemens said, "but it's a crackerjack diversion." He realized the moment he said it that he shouldn't have brought up Edison.

But Tesla waved off the reference to his rival. "Edison won't be inventing much any more, I don't think."

"Oh? Why?"

"Why, he'll be too busy being president to invent!" At Clemens' shocked look, Tesla continued, "Ah, Mr. Twain, I spend perhaps too much time in the laboratory, but I don't entirely miss what it is the newspapers say. Within a week, Mr. Edison's kinetoscopes will be in every dance hall and Sunday school in America, and Mr. Edison will address each voter in person. Without a miracle, Mr. Bryan is unlikely to win."

"And what exactly kind of miracle does Mr. Bryan need, then?" Sam asked. He was playing with Tesla's device, concentrating on making a picture to beat Miss Bernhardt's.

"Something to upstage Mr. Edison's kinetoscope."

Sam Clemens had the knack of it now. On the screen of lights, he had drawn a cartoon of a face. The eyes grew from dots to little squares, and then they grew eyebrows, and the mouth opened in an "O." "You should do something with this, Nick," Sam said, amusing himself by making the mouth of the little face open and shut in time with his words. "Play around a bit, I bet you could make something of it."

The campaign stop was a real jamboree. There was a mounted parade of Civil War veterans in full uniform on horseback, and at least five brass bands, followed by fifteen carriages—mayors and minor politicians, Sam Clemens guessed, people who hoped something of the pomp of the occasion might rub off on them. Several hundred people in full top hats and brass-buttoned jackets marched on foot, each waving (somewhat incongruously) a palm-frond fan. These were followed by a choir of women standing on a flatbed truck decorated with red, white, and blue silk and drawn by four sweating plow horses in flower-bedecked harness. Bryan pumped every outstretched hand thrust at him, what seemed like unending millions of them, trying to conserve his voice, which was on the verge of breaking.

"There is no greater entertainment in the world than a political campaign," Sam remarked to Miss Bernhardt, who was in his company again that day. Nikola Tesla had promised them something special, and he wondered what it would be. Drums rang out and trombones blared in five different tunes, with horses snorting and whinnying with no regard to the rhythm or tune. He couldn't even hear the women singers—the Morristown Presbyterian Choir, according to the sign—except for a stray note on occasions when the trombones paused.

They stood on the reviewing stand along with a half-dozen other notables. Miss Bernhardt was basking in her element, wearing an outrageous purple dress and an elaborate hat with at least three feet of magenta ostrich plume on it, waving to the crowd and smiling. Sam enjoyed the attention as well, in an absent fashion, but would have rathered that they got on with the show, whatever it was. He was in his trademark white linen suit, with a white panama hat and a diamond-studded bolo-tie, a gift from an admirer in Nevada.

Nikola Tesla had escorted them to the stand. He had stood with them for a moment to survey the crowd dispassionately, surrounded by pigeons, but then vanished along with Mr. Czito, promising only that they should have a surprise if they stayed to sunset.

It was nearly sunset now, as best Sam could tell, the day being rather overcast, and Mr. Bryan was still shaking hands, working his way slowly toward them. At last he reached the platform and climbed the wooden steps to the podium, shaking hands on the way with each of the dignitaries on the platform. "Mr. Mark Twain," he said. "A pleasure. I'm a great admirer of your work, a great admirer. I'm glad to see you joining us doing the great work of God."

"I'd be pleased for you to call me Samuel, Mr. Bryan," Sam said. "By God, it's an honor to meet a politician who isn't a skunk and a god-damned liar. Give 'em hell."

Bryan's brow furrowed a moment as if he'd been gravely insulted, and he seemed about to say something, but then he reconsidered, replying only, "I see you live up to your reputation." He turned to kiss Miss Bernhardt's hand. "A pleasure to meet you, Madam. *Enchanté.*"

Behind them, something odd was going on. A wooden scaffolding was being erected with cranes and pulleys, and strings of Tesla lamps were being stretched along the beams, a thousand of them or more. As the crowd began to notice something was going on, a murmur went through them. Sam could hear a steam engine chuff to life somewhere in the distance. The pulleys had now raised an entire curtain of Tesla lamps, filling out a rectangle fifty feet high.

In front of William Jennings Bryan, Mr. Czito had set up some sort of contraption of lenses and a spinning disk. An Edison kinetoscopic camera? No, the device had no reels of kinetoscopic film, but instead a spaghetti tangle of electrical wiring snaked away toward the electrical screen that rose behind the candidate. This was something stranger.

The crowd was chanting now, "Bryan! Bryan! Bryan!" The candidate raised his hand, and the chant intensified.

Bryan began to speak, and his voice, louder than a mountain, boomed out across the square like the voice of God. By gum, Sam thought, damned if Tesla hasn't found a way to electrically magnify the human voice. The crowd subsided into a moment of awed silence.

But the electrical voice magnification was the least of Tesla's surprises. Behind the candidate, the giant matrix of Tesla lamps dawned into fluorescence. Ten thousand tiny electrical lamps glowed, and waves of color rippled across the screen. The crowd gasped with one voice, thinking that this was itself an electrical miracle, but in a moment the swirling colors settled down, and a fuzzy shape was visible in the patterns of dark and light made by the glowing lamps.

It was impossible to make out at first. The eye had no standards by which to measure such an image; nothing like it had ever been seen in the world. Was that a face? Yes, a face, definitely a face. The face of William Jennings Bryan! The murmur of the crowd grew to a rumble, and then a roar of delight. Yes, yes, now it was clear indeed, clear as any picture; it was a picture painted from ten thousand points of light! It was the candidate, and it moved! The electrically magnified voice spoke, and the lips on the picture of light moved with it, almost as if the image itself spoke!

"Does this contraption work?" the voice said. "By Goodness, I can hear myself! Mr. Tesla, you are indeed a genius."

Not great first words for such a marvelous occasion, Sam thought. Mr.

Bryan has missed a chance; he should have had something prepared, like perhaps, "What hath God wrought?" But the crowd laughed and roared its approval, and Bryan continued stolidly on.

"Ladies of the choir and gentlemen of the band, veterans of the war and people of the great State of New Jersey," the magnified voice said, and above him, the portrait of light moved and spoke. "I come to you a humble supplicant, asking for only one thing, one small thing. Give me but your vote, your one vote, and we shall bring this nation to the greatness which God above in his infinite wisdom has decreed and intended."

And every single eye was transfixed, every living brain mesmerized, by the flickering illusion of life.

Tesla's moving images were instantly the talk of the nation. "An artwork of light unprecedented in history," the *Herald* said. "Mr. Tesla states that soon he will be able to beam these images across the ether," the story continued. "These broadcast images, which he names tele-videon, or 'distance sight'—"

Horovitz threw down the newspaper. "If Tesla can beam these images on electrical waves, Bryan will campaign in towns where he's never even been," Horovitz declared. "That will beat the talking dolls and even the kinetoscope to hell and gone. He'll outcampaign us ten to one. A hundred to one! How many of these tele-videon screens can he make?"

"Surely each tele-videon screen is expensive," Hanna said, waving his cigar dismissively. "I hear tell each of those rarefied-gas lamps costs ten cents. How many are there in a screen, ten thousand? That would mean a tele-videon screen must cost a thousand dollars! At that price, they won't afford very many."

"Don't put it beyond Mr. Westinghouse," Horovitz said. "It's no secret that he's backing Tesla. And he's a cunning one, no naif to manufacturing. If anybody will find a way to lower the cost, Westinghouse will."

And, indeed, in factories in the Lower East Side, Westinghouse was putting women to work manufacturing the miniature Tesla lamps, and next to them children worked with nimble fingers to string them together into the screens. The idea of broadcasting tele-videon images using Marconi telegraphy was crazy, one of Tesla's endless supply of utopian speculations, but Westinghouse had long ago decided to ignore Tesla's more speculative flights of fancy. He had a better idea anyway; one that would work. America was crisscrossed with telegraph lines, and they could send the tele-videon signals across the telegraph lines to every city and every village, every railroad stop in America.

Campaigning in Wisconsin, Thomas Edison found out about it with the morning newspapers. Edison was surprised, but nobody could get one up on Edison, not for long. He sent a long telegram to his West Orange laboratory, with a series of investigations that he wanted done on cathode-ray phosphors, and followed it up by cutting short his upcoming campaign stops and, within the week, headed back for the West Orange laboratory to work. He normally slept for two, sometimes even three hours a day, but when he was challenged, and his gumption was up, he didn't waste time sleeping. On the train east, he studied the tele-videon fiercely and pondered hard on the workings of it. Before long, he had set his ideas in order for how he would improve on it. If his ideas bore out, he could use his fluoroscope technology together with electron beams to make an Edison-effect ray-tube. It would have far better definition than Tesla's flickering lamps; anybody who saw the new Edison images would laugh at Tesla's crude dot pictures.

He would have the first patents drawn up in a day or so, and then they would be ready. Yes, if Tesla wanted an invention fight, he'd find a fight on his hands, all right.

"We're watching your ratings, sir, and it doesn't look so good."

"Ratings, young man?" William Jennings Bryan said to the assistant. "I don't believe I follow."

"How people rate the show."

Bryan cocked his head and frowned. "I daresay some people consider politics to be a show, but I assure you, young man, a showman I have never been. If it is a show, then what I show is only the truth."

Sunday was his day for relaxing, but although he was nominally resting in his private railroad car, that only meant that the cameras and the press weren't in with him right at the moment. Bryan knew well enough that, for a serious campaigner, there would be no real relaxing until after November. This young man should have respected his privacy, but the tele-videon crew had been conferring in their equipment room all day, and he had been expecting somebody to barge in sooner or later. He put down his pen and turned the full force of his attention to the young man.

"That's the problem in a nutshell, sir," the young man said. "You're no showman. We've been doing the tele-videon show for a week now . . ." Seeing Bryan's wince, he paused for a second, but went on: "Sorry, sir, but that's what the staff call it. A show. We're watching the ratings. You see, sir, that first time, the novelty of the tele-videon holds them, but when it wears off, your speech . . . Well, it's not a show, that's it. It's—"

"Boring," Bryan said.

"Well, yes, sir. Boring."

"My speeches are too long."

The young man was apparently oblivious to the hint of sarcasm in Bryan's affectless delivery and nodded enthusiastically in agreement. "Gaseous." He flinched at Bryan's suddenly darkened expression, but he didn't back off. "That's the word we hear. Gaseous."

Bryan sighed. "And you want?"

"Not such a long sermon, sir. Couldn't you do, maybe, some shorter bits, something that people can bite off more easily?"

"I will think on it."

"Sir, if—"

Bryan raised his hand. "Enough. I will think on it, I said, and so I will do. Enough. Leave me."

When the young man left, Bryan scowled. So they thought him gaseous, did they? What did they desire, real political reform, or did they want just appearances?

Ah, that was the question, wasn't it, what the people wanted. He knew what they needed: reform, breaking the railroad monopolies, a turning away from the poisoning tentacles of imperialism, and a turning toward God. But what they wanted? He had once thought that a leader should shape the wills of the people, but long years in politics made him doubt his own vision.

But then Reverend Conroy came in, and Bryan stood up and smiled, a genuine smile. "Reverend Conroy, do come in. I am quite pleased to see you."

The reverend took off his hat. "Thank you kindly. Your offer was a most kind one, a very generous offering of your time."

Bryan laughed. "Why, I should say the same to you. It's not so often that a man of the cloth gives up his pulpit, and I am quite cognizant of the honor, I assure you."

"I have heard you talk and do believe you to be a man of God."

"I do my best, Reverend Conroy."

"And that is more than most people, I assure you. My flock will be happy to hear from you, if only as a respite from hearing me drone on. May I ask, have you a title for the sermon you will be giving? No politics in it, I do hope?"

"Indeed you may ask. I will talk on the subject of the Menace of Evolution."

"You'll be taking on monkey-ism!" Conroy's face broke out into a huge grin. "Ah, I've heard tell that you are a fighter, and I'm pleased as a bear with a watermelon to hear you'll wrestle them atheists head-on!" He pumped Bryan's hand. "I'm looking forward to it, I tell you, looking forward to it."

"And I as well," Bryan said. "After a week surrounded by sycophants, office-seekers, and the jackals of the press, it will be a joy to spend a few hours among simple pious Christians, a joy indeed."

Bryan's sermon was a wonderful success. He had kept the audience spell-bound, alternately making them angry and then releasing their anger with laughter, for nearly two hours. So the tele-videon crew thought people wanted short sound bites, did they? But these were his people, the simple and believing farmers and workers of America, not the atheists and agnostics who ran politics.

Afterward, they hadn't wanted to leave, coming forward in a huge press to shake his hand, tell him how they liked his sermon, even coming to offer money for the campaign against Darwinism, which he diverted to the church offering box. One earnest young man with a waxed handlebar mustache had even wanted to debate him, and he had put that man in his place with half a dozen well-chosen sentences, skewering his poorly thought-out Darwinism and sending up peals of laughter from the crowd. Finally Reverend Conroy had managed to take him away to his private office for a moment of relaxation.

"That was a fine talking, Mr. Bryan," the Reverend said. "Indeed, about the finest I've ever heard."

"Thank you most kindly."

"I was wondering . . ." The Reverend hesitated.

"Please, do speak freely."

"Well, it occurs to me that you have used this new tele-videon to bring your political message to the people. Could you not use the same invention to bring the word of God? The people are starving for the Gospel, and I thought . . ."

Bryan raised his hand. "The tele-videon is a wonderful device, no mistaking, but it is not mine to do with as I wish. Were I to use it on my own behalf, it would be misdirection of campaign money, and dishonesty of any sort, no matter how well intentioned, is something I will have no truck with."

"Perhaps . . . we could pay for the use of the equipment? Lease it, as it were?"

Bryan laughed. "Have you any idea how expensive it is? Why, it would cost over fifty dollars an hour to lease the tele-videon alone—not even counting the money to lease telegraph wires and halls to show the image."

"Fifty dollars . . ." Reverend Conroy mused. "Why, that's not so much. Ten thousand people could watch a sermon. Fifty thousand! If each of ten thousand people were to be asked to contribute but a dime, and if only one in ten did so, why, we would cover our costs and even have money extra."

Bryan laughed. "Ah, you are, I think, a plutocrat in disguise! I accept your bargain. If you arrange it, I shall speak, and from the contributions, what is left over after paying the lease we shall split evenly, half for your church and half for my campaign."

Reverend Conroy stood up and stretched out his hand. "Sir, it is done."

Nikola Tesla introduced Sam Clemens to Bryan's campaign staff, and particularly to the tele-videon electrical crew. Then he and Mr. Czito headed back to his Long Island laboratory to work on perfecting his atmospheric radiations of electrical tension.

Miss Bernhardt had gone back with him. Sam was vaguely annoyed by that; since first Clara and then Livy had left him three years ago, he had not realized how much he had missed the comfort of feminine company. And it was not the crude physical pleasures of intimate interplay that he missed, but simply the gentle companionship. He had enjoyed Miss Bernhardt's company more than he'd thought possible.

He wondered what Miss Bernhardt got from the companionship of Tesla. Certainly not the human commerce of wit and passion that passed as the ordinary stuff of social intercourse; Tesla was a man of titanic passions, but his passions were of an ethereal nature wholly disconnected from ordinary corporeal lust.

But meanwhile, Clemens stayed on, interested in seeing the campaign from an insider's perch. He enjoyed the good fellowship of the tele-videon electrical crew, somewhat less refined company than that of Miss Bernhardt, but in their way enjoyable. The crew were a congenial bunch, most of them awkward boys barely older than puppies, all elbows and thumbs until they had their hands buried inside an electrical dynamo. All of them were fascinated by electricity and mechanisms, and all of them had dreams of riches as inventors and industrialists in the new century. The interior of the tele-videon electrical shack was supposed to be a secret, and definitely off-limits to passersby, but Sam ignored the posted signs and spent half his time in the electrical shack, looking on with curiosity as the boys showed off their expertise with the tele-videon and entertaining them with stories of Tesla. Sam had been a bit of an inventor a few years back, and he told them the story of the typesetting machine, spinning the yarn out and discovering that he could milk it for laughs, although at the time it had meant years of work wasted, ending in frustration and bankruptcy.

The other half of his time he spent with the campaign's hangers-on (of which there were many) in his well-practiced role of the celebrated man of letters, accepting with smooth grace offers of an occasional glass of whisky or a good cigar.

The campaign was settled into the Hotel Gloriana now. The tele-videon shack was set up, along with its steam-powered electrical dynamo, in a vacant lot next door, but right at the moment the electrical boys were taking a break and had gone into town, and so he was sitting in the lobby, a place of antimacassar-clad flowered armchairs and elegant pink decorations that felt like being in a birthday cake.

He still didn't know what to make of Bryan. For a week now, the man had given his daily evangelistic speech over the tele-videon, and at the end of it had emphasized how the listeners should give money so that they could continue God's work.

God's work! Sam snorted. This tele-videon evangelism was the greatest flim-flam operation he'd ever seen worked; the people watching were completely mesmerized by the moving lights, and every time Bryan said that they needed to give money, cheques and pledges and ragged silver coins flowed in like a dam had burst. Bryan was no deliberate Chicago con man; he seemed completely sincere. But the daily evangelism was changing him. He was suddenly making far more money from his religious donors than he'd ever made from political donations. His political speeches were now more directly religious in tone, and in the latest one he had actually called for constitutional amendments, one to ban alcohol and another to forbid the teaching of Darwinism.

And now he was coming over here, drifting though the cloud of syco-phants. Sam cut the end off of a cigar to prepare himself for the great man, struck a match and puffed it to life, and put it down.

"So, Mr. Clemens," Bryan said. "What do you think of my speech? Any words of wisdom?"

Sam shook his head. "Mr. Bryan. Quite a show you give, but I must allow as I'm too much of a reprobate to change entirely to your point of view."

"Nonsense, Mr. Clemens."

"If you ask me . . ."

"Do speak, Mr. Clemens."

"Ask me, I think you should back off a little bit on the constitutional amendment talk."

Bryan laughed. "Certainly, with your well-known love of whisky, you would."

"Not just that one; I don't think much of the amendment to ban Darwin-ism, either."

"Atheists should be allowed to teach evolutionism to their heart's content, Mr. Clemens, but not in publicly funded schools. You are an intelligent man. Surely you are not descended from a monkey?"

Clemens took a draw from his cigar. "Hear my friends talk, I expect I am. Some people are nearer to monkeys than others, but seems to me, when we talk about being descended from monkeys, it's the monkeys ought to be offended."

"Mr. Clemens, I don't know whether to be outraged or amused. Are you secretly an atheist? I don't believe as I've heard you speak on your beliefs. What exactly is your stand?"

Clemens puffed again, to give him a pause before speaking. "Well, you know, Mr. Bryan, in my opinion you have your two kinds of opinions. You have your public opinions, that you talk about in the papers, and then you have your private opinions, that you don't spread about."

"No, Mr. Clemens, I think not. If I believe something, I tell everybody and keep nothing back. You are intimating, I think, that you believe all men to be liars."

"Not exactly liars. No sir, I wouldn't say that. Perhaps a little less private in some of their opinions than others, maybe."

"And tell me, then, these private opinions of yours. In the great war between God and Satan, where do you stand?"

Twain puffed at his cigar and looked at Bryan, in his vested wool suit, with his gold-chained watch, with his round and open face. The man was dressed like a politician, but he was a farmer, you could see that. To hell with it, Sam thought.

"You ask for truth, Mr. Bryan? I will tell you, then. I believe I just might take my stand with Mr. Satan."

"There are some matters too serious for humor, Mr. Clemens, and I believe this is one of them."

"Well, Mr. Bryan. Seems to me that religions write their books denouncing Mr. Satan, and say the most injurious things 'bout him, but we never hear his side."

"Quite to the contrary, Mr. Clemens. We hear Satan's voice every day. It is God's voice that is small, and we must be silent to listen."

"Bosh. The world's full of bible thumpers, and you're just another one of them, a little more successful than most. Can't cross the street some days without some revival preacher going on and on with smug and vaporous pieties. Can't hear yourself think. Satan? I am personally going to undertake his rehabilitation. He's been given a bum rap, I think, and I'm quite looking forward to meeting him myself to get his side of the story."

"I think you—"

"And as for preachers," Clemens continued, ignoring Bryan, "my experience is that they are for the main part con men. Slick talkers who extract money from people by promising paradise in the sky. I don't have much use for them."

"Mr. Clemens," Bryan said coldly, "I believe you have just called me a con man."

Sam nodded slowly. "Reckon maybe I did."

"Mr. Clemens, I and my campaign have showed you hospitality. I don't believe that I am expected to tolerate insults. Please absent yourself. My assistants will be instructed that you are no longer a person who is desired in my presence, now or in the future."

Sam nodded. "You asked for my private opinions. You got 'em. Can't say you weren't warned. Oh, and about Darwin. I expect that I lean a little his way, too."

The Edison campaign was foundering.

In only two weeks, Edison's laboratory had brought out fluorovision tubes to compete with the Tesla tele-videon. Now the two campaigns competed fiercely over which one could lease more telegraph wires to bring campaign speeches to the boroughs, engaging in a competition much to the profit of the telegraph companies.

But the political maps meticulously kept by Horovitz were pierced by an unhealthy infusion of red pins, the color of Bryan's Democrats, expanding slowly but inexorably from the heartland outward.

From the Alleghenies to the Rocky Mountains, farmers and working men were listening to Bryan. It was not Bryan's campaign speeches that were winning him converts, but his rapidly expanding tele-videon ministry. Bryan had somehow tapped directly into the American heart. He would tell his listeners about the healing power of Jesus and lead the faithful in prayer, and the next day a hundred newspapers reported how blind men began to see. He would lead the faithful in song, and if the papers were to be credited, the deathly sick would sit up from their deathbeds and join the singing. And when Bryan said that they needed money, across America the faithful opened their hearts and their wallets, sending money to Bryan by the barrel, by the ox-cart, by the freight load.

Edison's sermons, about how he would reform government by bringing in scientific management, went almost unheard.

Yet when Sam Clemens came (walking right past the receptionist who but a month ago had told him that Edison would never be available to see him), Edison was remarkably cheerful. "Mr. Mark Twain!" he said in a loud voice. "I am a great admirer of yours!"

"Thank you," Clemens said.

Edison turned his head. "Could you talk a little more distinctly? I have to admit, I have a slight difficulty in hearing."

Clemens cleared his throat and said more loudly, "I said, thank you."

"Ah, that's what I expected you'd say. Say, the way I heard things, you and Miss Bernhardt were the ones worked out inventing this tele-videon thing. Any truth to that rumor?"

"Maybe a tiny bit of truth, Mr. Edison," Clemens said. "Not so much."

"Truth, you say? Ah—that's a wonderful bit of inventing. Took me almost a week to match it. If you ever need a job, come up to my factory, I'll have Charles fix you up with a job. Tell him I sent you."

"I'm not in the inventing business these days," Clemens said. "I confess Nikola did the electrical part."

"Eh? Nikola? Ah, my erstwhile employee. Well, he's a tinkerer, reckon I have to give him that, but not much of a practical man." Edison's manner changed abruptly to business. "So, Mr. Twain, what is your purpose in coming to visit? I'm a busy man, I must say."

"Well, Mr. Edison, I'm here on business," Sam said. "Got something to sell, what turns out to be just exactly what I figure you need."

"And what, exactly, is this I need?"

"You have an invention, I see, but you don't rightly know just what to do with it, I reckon," he said. "The tele-what-is-it, that is."

"The fluorovision."

"That's the whatsit. You can send moving pictures out over the wires to everybody from Petunia Flats to East Hell, but you can't find anything to get them to watch."

Edison waved his hands. "My corporation is making films right now. Let Bryan use his tele-videon for superstition. The Edison fluorovision will bring education to the masses."

"And will this win the campaign for you, Mr. Edison?"

"No," Edison said emphatically. "No, that it will not."

"You need an entertainer. A performer. A showman."

Edison seemed about to object, but then paused a moment and said, "Perhaps I do. And you propose?"

"The best." Samuel Clemens smiled and bowed. "Myself, of course."

"And?"

"I will thrill the masses and bring laughter and music and culture to the people. And make them watch and listen . . . and, in so doing, put them in a mood to hear your message."

"And you call this?"

Samuel Clemens smiled. "I will call it *The Mark Twain Variety Hour.*"

"And that's the story, every word of it unvarnished truth," Mark Twain said. "Or anyway, that's the way I heard it told, and now I'm telling you."

The live audience howled its laughter, and Clemens bowed and smiled. He dropped out of his Mark Twain voice and turned to the camera.

"This wraps up today's *Variety Hour*," he said in his finest lecturing voice. "Turn to us next week, same time, same place, when we will bring you the celebrated vaudevillians Fields and Weber. Let me assure you, they're the funniest things on four legs. And we'll have the famous soliloquy from Shakespeare's masterpiece "Hamlet," acted out by the magnificent Mam'selle Bernhardt of Paris. We'll have the musical genius John Philip Sousa, and, last and, well, least," he paused for the laugh, "yours truly just perhaps might be convinced to read you a new story from Calaveras county.

"This will be a show you won't want to miss, gentlemen and ladies. Until then, try Cleveland Soap, it keeps you clean. And finally, tell all your friends: A vote for Edison is a vote for America."

The camera came in for its final close-up, and he gave it his famous wink and a smile and then signaled with his hands for the cut. Immediately his crew rushed in with a glass of whisky and a cigar, and he dropped into his easy chair.

"How'd I do?"

"You were great, Mr. Twain!" the camera boy said. "The best ever!"

It was an unnecessary question. He knew the show had done well today. He had put in two of Edison's messages and had managed to mention Cleveland Soap five times and Lydia Pinkham's Elixir for Ladies six times. Each mention was a hundred dollars in his pocket.

He was flush, he was in his stride, and he loved every minute of it. With the new televideon broadcasting, Samuel Clemens had found his element and was on top of the world. Did Mr. Bryan think he could hold them with his tele-evangelism? He would give Mr. Bryan a lesson on how to grab an audience, that he would, that he would indeed.

Horovitz leaned forward and shut off the televideon. (It was an Edison fluoro-vision, of course, not the crude Tesla tele-videon, but the word televideon had somehow stuck.)

Mr. Westinghouse promised that within the year, he would have his improved televideons in the home of every man with ten dollars in his pocket—and now that Westinghouse was making a profit on them, he made sure that the programs sent out over the telegraph wires were compatible with both.

For all his hard work, the election was going to be too close to call, Horovitz knew, but already he was thinking far beyond that. Forget the election—it didn't even matter any more, he reckoned. It was going to be the man on the televideon, not the president, who would be the real leader of this coming generation.

It was time to leave politics. He was tired of it anyway. Twain's variety show proved that people would watch, and Horovitz thought that this was just the beginning. Over the years, he had learned how to tell people what they wanted. If they would watch Mr. Twain tell jokes, would not people watch, say, a game of baseball on the televideon? Or perhaps football? Wrestling? Which one would play better on the screen? Could he dramatize some of the penny-dreadful novels, perhaps some western gunfighter stories? The eyes of America were eagerly waiting.

Ah, the twentieth century! So many possibilities! He leaned back and lit his cigar. Barely three years old, and already it was turning out to be a doozy. He could hardly wait to find out what would come next.

welcome to olympus,
Mr. Hearst

KAGE BAKER

One of the most prolific new writers to appear in the late 90s, Kage Baker made her first sale in 1997, to *Asimov's Science Fiction*, and has since become one of that magazines most frequent and popular contributors with her sly and compelling stories of the adventures and misadventures of the time-traveling agents of the Company; of late, she's started two other linked sequences of stories there as well, one of them set in as lush and eccentric a High Fantasy milieu as any we've ever seen. Her stories have also appeared in *Realms of Fantasy, Sci Fiction, Amazing*, and elsewhere. Her first novel, *In the Garden of Iden*, was also published in 1997 and immediately became one of the most acclaimed and widely reviewed first novels of the year. Her second novel, *Sky Coyote*, was published in 1999, followed by a third and a fourth, *Mendoza in Hollywood* and *The Graveyard Game*, both published in 2001. In 2002, she published her first collection, *Black Projects, White Knights*. Her most recent books are a novel set in her unique fantasy milieu, *The Anvil of the World*, and a chapbook novella, *The Empress of Mars*. Coming up are more Company novels, a novel called *The Life of the World to Come*, and a new collection, *Mother Aegypt and Other Stories*. Her stories have appeared in our Seventeenth and Twentieth Annual Collections. In addition to her writing, Baker has been an artist, actor, and director at the Living History Center, and has taught Elizabethan English as a second language. She lives in Pismo Beach, California.

In the hugely entertaining story that follows, she serves up one of the best of her Company stories, taking us on a droll and fast-paced tour of the Enchanted Hill, to witness a confrontation among the great and powerful that could have momentous—and unexpected—results . . .

OPENING CREDITS: 1926

Take ten!" called the director. Lowering his megaphone, he settled back in his chair. It sank deeper into the sand under his weight, and irritably settling again he peered out at the stallion galloping across the expanse of dune below him, its burnoosed rider clinging against the scouring blast of air from the wind machines.

"Pretty good so far. . . ." chanted the assistant director. Beside him Rudolph Valentino (in a burnoose that matched the horseman's) nodded grimly. They watched as the steed bore its rider up one wave of sand, down the next, nearer and nearer to that point where they might cut away—

"Uh-oh," said the grip. From the sea behind them a real wind traveled forward across the sand, tearing a palm frond from the seedy-looking prop trees around the Sheik's Camp set and sending it whirling in front of the stallion. The stallion pulled up short and began to dance wildly. After a valiant second or so the rider flew up in the air and came down on his head in the sand, arms and legs windmilling.

"Oh, Christ," the director snarled. "CUT! KILL THE WIND!"

"YOU OKAY, LEWIS?" yelled the script boy.

The horseman sat up unsteadily and pulled swathing folds of burnoose up off his face. He held up his right hand, making an okay sign.

"SET UP FOR TAKE ELEVEN!" yelled the assistant director. The horseman clambered to his feet and managed to calm his mount; taking its bridle he slogged away with it, back across the sand to their mark. Behind them the steady salt wind erased the evidence of their passage.

"This wind is not going to stop, you know," Valentino pointed out gloomily. He stroked the false beard that gave him all the appearance of middle age he would ever wear.

"Ain't there any local horses that ain't spooked by goddam palm leaves?" the grip wanted to know.

"Yeah. Plowhorses," the director told them. "Look, we paid good money for an Arabian stallion. Do you hear the man complaining? I don't hear him complaining."

"I can't even *see* him," remarked the assistant director, scanning the horizon. "Jeez, you don't guess he fell down dead or anything, out there?"

But there, up out of the sand came the horse and his rider, resuming position on the crest of the far dune.

"Nah. See?" the director said. "The little guy's a pro." He lifted the megaphone, watching as Lewis climbed back into the saddle. The script boy chalked in the update and held up the clapboard for the camera. *Crack!*

"WIND MACHINES GO—AND—TAKE ELEVEN!"

Here they came again, racing the wind and the waning light, over the lion-colored waves as the camera whirred, now over the top of the last dune and down, disappearing—

Disappearing—

The grip and the assistant director groaned. Valentino winced.

"I don't see them, Mr. Fitzmaurice," the script boy said.

"So where are they?" yelled the director. "CUT! CUT, AND KILL THE GODDAM WIND."

"Sorry!" cried a faint voice, and a second later Lewis came trudging around the dune, leading the jittering stallion. "I'm afraid we had a slight spill back there."

"WRANGLERS! Jadaan took a fall," called the assistant director in horrified tones, and from the camp on the beach a half-dozen wranglers came running. They crowded around the stallion solicitously. Lewis left him to their care and struggled on toward the director.

The headpiece of his burnoose had come down around his neck, and his limp fair hair fluttered in the wind, making his dark makeup—what was left after repeated face-first impact with dunes—look all the more incongruous. He spat out sand and smiled brightly, tugging off his spirit-gummed beard.

"Of course, I'm ready to do another take if you are, Mr. Fitzmaurice," Lewis said.

"No," said Valentino. "We will kill him or we will kill the horse, or both."

"Oh, screw it," the director decided. "We've got enough good stuff in the can. Anyway the light's going. Let's see what we can do with that take, as far as it went."

Lewis nodded and waded on through the sand, intent on getting out of his robes; Valentino stepped forward to put a hand on his shoulder. Lewis squinted up at him, blinking sand from his lashes.

"You work very hard, my friend," Valentino said. "But you should not try to ride horses. It is painful to watch."

"Oh—er—thank you. It's fun being Rudolph Valentino for a few hours, all the same," said Lewis, and from out of nowhere he produced a fountain pen. "I don't suppose I might have your autograph, Mr. Valentino?"

"Certainly," said Valentino, looking vainly around for something to autograph. From another nowhere Lewis produced a copy of the shooting script, and Valentino took it. "Your name is spelled?"

"L-e-w-i-s, Mr. Valentino. Right there?" he suggested. "Right under where it says *The Son of the Sheik*?" He watched with a peculiarly stifled glee as Valentino signed: *For my "other self" Lewis. Rudolph Valentino*.

"There," said Valentino, handing him the script. "No more falls on the head, yes?"

"Thank you so much. It's very kind of you to be worried, but it's all right, you know," Lewis replied. "I can take a few tumbles. I'm a professional stunt man, after all."

He tucked the script away in his costume and staggered down to the water's edge, where the extras and crew were piling into an old stakebed truck. The driver was already cranking up the motor, anxious to begin his drive back to Pismo Beach before the tide turned and they got bogged down again.

Valentino watched Lewis go, shaking his head.

"Don't worry about that guy, Rudy," the director told him, knocking sand out of his megaphone. "I know he looks like a pushover, but he never gets hurt, and I mean never."

"But luck runs out, like sand." Valentino smiled wryly and waved at the dunes stretching away behind them, where the late slanting sunlight cast his shadow to the edge of the earth. "Doesn't it? And that one, I think he has the look of a man who will die young."

Which was a pretty ironic thing for Valentino to say, considering that he'd be dead himself within the year and that Lewis happened to be, on that particular day in 1926, just short of his eighteen-hundred and-twenty-third birthday.

If we immortals had birthdays, anyway.

FLASH FORWARD: 1933

"Oh, look, we're at Pismo Beach," exclaimed Lewis, leaning around me to peer at it. The town was one hotel and a lot of clam stands lining the highway. "Shall we stop for clams, Joseph?"

"Are you telling me you didn't get enough clams when you worked on *Son of the Sheik*?" I grumbled, groping in my pocket for another mint Lifesaver. The last thing I wanted right now was food. Usually I can eat anything (and have, believe me) but this job was giving me butterflies like crazy.

"Possibly," Lewis said, standing up in his seat to get a better view as we rattled past, bracing himself with a hand on the Ford's windshield. The wind hit him smack in the face and his hair stood out all around his head. "But it would be nice to toast poor old Rudy's shade, don't you think?"

"You want to toast him? Here." I pulled out my flask and handed it to Lewis. "It would be nice to be on time for Mr. Hearst too, you know?"

Lewis slid back down into his seat and had a sip of warm gin. He made a face.

"*Ave atque vale*, old man," he told Valentino's ghost. "You're not actually nervous about this, are you, Joseph?"

"Me, nervous?" I bared my teeth. "Hell no. Why would I be nervous meeting one of the most powerful men in the world?"

"Well, precisely," Lewis had another sip of gin, made another face. "Thank God you won't be needing this bootlegger any more. *Vale* Volstead Act too! You must have known far more powerful men in your time, mustn't you? You worked for a Byzantine emperor once, if I'm not mistaken."

"Three or four of 'em," I corrected him. "And believe me, not one had anything like the pull of William Randolph Hearst. Not when you look at the big picture. Anyway, Lewis, the rules of the whole game are different now. You think a little putz like Napoleon could rule the world today? You think Hitler'd be getting anywhere without the media? Mass communication is where the real power is, kiddo."

"He's only a mortal, after all," Lewis said. "Put it into perspective! We're simply motoring up to someone's country estate to spend a pleasant weekend with entertaining people. There will be fresh air and lovely views. There will be swimming, riding, and tennis. There will be fine food and decent drink, at least one hopes so—"

"Don't count on booze," I said. "Mr. Hearst doesn't like drunks."

"—and all we have to do is accomplish a simple document drop for the Company," Lewis went on imperturbably, patting the briefcase in which he'd brought the autographed Valentino script. "A belated birthday present for the master of the house, so to speak."

"That's all *you* have to do," I replied. "I have to actually negotiate with the guy."

Lewis shrugged, conceding my point. "Though what was that story you were telling me the other night, about you and that pharaoh, what was his name—? It's not as though there will be jealous courtiers ordering our executions, after all."

I made a noise of grudging agreement. I couldn't explain to Lewis why this job had me so on edge. Probably I wasn't sure. I lie to myself a lot, see. I started doing it about thirteen thousand years ago and it's become a habit, like chain-sucking mints to ward off imaginary nervous indigestion.

Immortals have a lot of little habits like that.

We cruised on up the coast in my Model A, through the cow town of San Luis Obispo. This was where Mr. Hearst's honored guests arrived in his private rail car, to be met at the station by his private limousines. From there they'd be whisked away to that little architectural folly known to later generations as Hearst Castle, but known for now just as The Ranch or, if you were feeling romantic, *La Cuesta Encantada*.

You've never been there? Gee, poor you. Suppose for a moment you owned one of the more beautiful hills in the world, with a breathtaking view of mountains and sea. Now suppose you decided to build a house on top of it, and had all the money in the world to spend on making that house the place of your wildest dreams, no holds barred and no expense spared, with three warehouses full of antiques to furnish the place.

Hell yes, you'd do it; anybody would. What would you do then? If you were William Randolph Hearst, you'd invite guests up to share your enjoyment of the place you'd made. But not just any guests. You could afford to lure the best minds of a generation up there to chat with you, thinkers and artists, Einsteins and Thalbergs, Huxleys and G.B. Shaws. And if you had a blonde mistress who worked in the movies, you got her to invite her friends too: Gable and Lombard, Bette Davis, Marie Dressler, Buster Keaton, Harpo Marx, Charlie Chaplin.

And the occasional studio small fry like Lewis and me, after I'd done a favor for Marion Davies and asked for an invitation in return. The likes of us didn't get the private railroad car treatment. We had to drive all the way up from Hollywood on our own steam. I guess if Mr. Hearst had any idea who was paying him a visit, he'd have sent a limo for us too; but the Company likes to play its cards close to the vest.

And we didn't look like a couple of immortal cyborg representatives of an all-powerful twenty-fourth-century Company, anyway. I appear to be an ordinary guy, kind of dark and compact (okay, *short*) and Lewis . . . well, he's good-looking, but he's on the short side too. It's always been Company policy for its operatives to blend in with the mortal population, which is why nobody in San Luis Obispo or Morro Bay or Cayucos wasted a second glance on two average cyborg joes in a new Ford zipping along the road.

Anyway, we passed through little nowhere towns-by-the-sea and rolling windswept seacoast, lots of California scenery that was breathtaking, if you like scenery. Lewis did, and kept exclaiming over the wildflowers and cypress trees. I just crunched Pep-O-Mints and kept driving. Seventeen miles before we got anywhere near Mr. Hearst's castle, we were already on his property.

What you noticed first was a distant white something on a green hilltop: two pale towers and not much more. I remembered medieval hilltowns in Spain and France and Italy, and so did Lewis, because he nudged me and chuckled:

"Rather like advancing on Le Monastier, eh? Right about now I'd be practicing compliments for the lord or the archbishop or whoever, and hoping I'd brought enough lute strings. What about you?"

"I'd be praying I'd brought along enough cash to bribe whichever duke it was I had to bribe," I told him, popping another Lifesaver.

"It's not the easiest of jobs, is it, being a Facilitator?" Lewis said sympathetically. I just shook my head.

The sense of displacement in reality wasn't helped any by the fact that we were now seeing the occasional herd of zebra or yak or giraffe, frolicking in the green meadows beside the road. If a roc had swept over the car and carried off a water buffalo in its talons, it wouldn't have seemed strange. Even Lewis fell silent, and took another shot of gin to fortify himself.

He had the flask stashed well out of sight, though, by the time we turned right into an unobtrusive driveway and a small sign that said HEARST RANCH. Here we paused at a barred gate, where a mortal leaned out of a shack to peer at us inquiringly.

"Guests of Mr. Hearst's," I shouted, doing my best to look as though I did this all the time.

"Names, please?"

"Joseph C. Denham and Lewis Kensington," we chorused.

He checked a list to be sure we were on it and then, "Five miles an hour, please, and the animals have right-of-way at all times," he told us, as the gates swung wide.

"We're in!" Lewis gave me a gleeful dig in the ribs. I snarled absently and drove across the magic threshold, with the same jitters I'd felt walking under a portcullis into some baron's fortress.

The suspense kept building, too, because the road wound like five miles of corkscrew, climbing all that time, and there were frequent stops at barred gates as we ascended into different species' habitats. Lewis had to get out and open them, nimbly stepping around buffalo-pies and other things that didn't reward close examination, and avoiding the hostile attentions of an ostrich at about the third gate up. Eventually we turned up an avenue of orange trees and flowering oleander.

"Oh, this is very like the south of France," said Lewis. "Don't you think?"

"I guess so," I muttered. A pair of high wrought iron gates loomed in front of us, opening unobtrusively as we rattled through, and we pulled up to the Grand Staircase.

We were met by a posse of ordinary-looking guys in chinos and jackets, who collected our suitcases and made off with them before we'd even gotten out of the car. I managed to avoid yelling anything like "Hey! Come back here with those!" and of course Lewis was already greeting a dignified-looking lady who had materialized from behind a statue. A houseboy took charge of the Model A and drove it off.

"... Mr. Hearst's housekeeper," the lady was saying. "He's asked me to show you to your rooms. If you'll follow me—? You're in the Casa del Sol."

"Charming," Lewis replied, and I let him take the lead, chatting and being personable with the lady as I followed them up a long sweeping staircase and across a terrace. We paused at the top, and there opening out on my left was the biggest damn Roman swimming pool I've ever seen, and I worked in Rome for a couple of centuries. The statues of nymphs, sea gods et cetera were mostly modern or museum copies. Hearst had not yet imported what was left of an honest-to-gods temple and set it up as a backdrop for poolside fun. He would, though.

Looming above us was the first of the "little guest bungalows." We craned back our heads to look up. It would have made a pretty imposing mansion for anybody else.

"Delightful," Lewis said. "Mediterranean Revival, isn't it?"

"Yes, sir," the housekeeper replied, leading us up more stairs. "I believe this is your first visit here, Mr. Kensington? And Mr. Denham?"

"Yeah," I said.

"Mr. Hearst would like you to enjoy your stay, and has asked that I provide you with all information necessary to make that possible," the house-keeper recited carefully, leading us around the corner of the house to its courtyard. The door at last! And waiting beside it was a Filipino guy in a suit, who bowed slightly at the waist when he saw us.

"This is Jerome," the housekeeper informed us. "He's been assigned to your rooms. If you require anything, you can pick up the service telephone and he'll respond immediately." She unlocked the door and stepped aside to usher us in. Jerome followed silently and vanished through a side door.

As we stood staring at all the antiques and Lewis made admiring noises, the housekeeper continued: "You'll notice Mr. Hearst has furnished much of this suite with his private art collection, but he'd like you to know that the bathroom—just through there, gentlemen—is perfectly up-to-date and modern, with all the latest conveniences, including shower baths."

"How thoughtful," Lewis answered, and transmitted to me: *Are you going to take part in this conversation at all?*

"That's really swell of Mr. Hearst," I said. *I'm even more nervous than I was before, okay?*

The housekeeper smiled. "Thank you. You'll find your bags are already in your assigned bedrooms. Jerome is unpacking for you."

Whoops. "Great," I said. "Where's my room? Can I see it now?"

"Certainly, Mr. Denham," said the housekeeper, narrowing her eyes slightly. She led us through a doorway that had probably belonged to some sixteenth-century Spanish bishop and there was Jerome, laying out the contents of my cheap brown suitcase. My black suitcase sat beside it, untouched.

"If you'll unlock this one, sir, I'll unpack it too," Jerome told me.

"That's okay," I replied, taking the black suitcase and pushing it under the bed. "I'll get that one myself, later."

In the very brief pause that followed, Jerome and the housekeeper exchanged glances. Lewis sighed, and I felt a real need for another Lifesaver. The housekeeper cleared her throat and said, "I hope this room is satisfactory, Mr. Denham?"

"Oh! Just peachy, thanks," I said.

"I'm sure mine is just as nice," Lewis offered. Jerome exited to unpack for him.

"Very good." The housekeeper cleared her throat again. "Now, Mr. Hearst wished you to know that cocktails will be served at seven this evening in the assembly hall, which is in the big house just across the courtyard. He expects to join his guests at Eight; dinner will be served at Nine. After dinner Mr. Hearst will retire with his guests to the theater, where a motion picture will be shown. Following the picture, Mr. Hearst generally withdraws to his study, but his guests are invited to return to their rooms or explore the library." She fixed me with a steely eye. "Alcohol will be served only in the main house, although sandwiches or other light meals can be requested by telephone from the kitchen staff at any hour."

She thinks you've got booze in the suitcase, you know, Lewis transmitted.

Shut up. I squared my shoulders and tried to look open and honest. Everybody knew that there were two unbreakable rules for the guests up here: no liquor in the rooms and no sex between unmarried couples. Notice I said For The Guests. Mr. Hearst and Marion weren't bound by any rules except the laws of physics.

The housekeeper gave us a few more helpful tidbits like how to find the zoo, tennis court, and stables, and departed. Lewis and I slunk out into the garden, where we paced along between the statues.

"Overall, I don't think that went very well," Lewis observed.

"No kidding," I said, thrusting my hands in my pockets.

"It'll only be a temporary bad impression, you know," Lewis told me helpfully. "As soon as you've made your presentation—"

"Hey! Yoo hoo! Joe! You boys made it up here okay?" cried a bright voice from somewhere up in the air, and we turned for our first full-on eyeful of La Casa Grande in all its massive glory. It looked sort of like a big Spanish cathedral, but surely one for pagans, because there was Marion Davies hanging out a third-story window waving at us.

"Yes, thanks," I called, while Lewis stared. Marion was wearing a dressing gown. She might have been wearing more, but you couldn't tell from this distance.

"Is that your friend? He's *cute*," she yelled. "Looks like Freddie March!"

Lewis turned bright pink. "I'm his stunt double, actually," he called to her, with a slightly shaky giggle.

"What?"

"I'M HIS STUNT DOUBLE."

"Oh," she yelled back. "Okay! Listen, do you want some ginger ale or any-thing? You know there's no—" she looked naughty and mimed drinking from a bottle, "until tonight."

"YES, GINGER ALE WOULD BE FINE," bawled Lewis.

"I'll have some sent down," Marion said, and vanished into the recesses of La Casa Grande.

We turned left at the next statue and walked up a few steps into the court-yard in front of the house. It was the size of several town squares, big enough to stage the riot scene from *Romeo and Juliet* complete with the Verona Police Department charging in on horseback. All it held at the moment, though, was another fountain and some lawn chairs. In one of them, Greta Garbo sat moodily peeling an orange.

"Hello, Greta," I said, wondering if she'd remember me. She just gave me a look and went on peeling the orange. She remembered me, all right.

Lewis and I sat down a comfortable distance from her, and a houseboy appeared out of nowhere with two tall glasses of White Rock over ice.

"Marion Davies said I was cute," Lewis reminded me, looking pleased. Then his eyebrows swooped together in the middle. "That's not good, though, is it? For the mission? What if Mr. Hearst heard her? Ye gods, she was shouting it at the top of her lungs."

"I don't think it's going to be any big deal," I told him wearily, sipping my ginger ale. Marion thought a lot of people were cute, and didn't care who heard her say so.

We sat there in the sunshine, and the ice in our drinks melted away. Garbo ate her orange. Doves crooned sleepily in the carillon towers of the house and I thought about what I was going to say to William Randolph Hearst.

Pretty soon the other guests started wandering up, and Garbo wouldn't talk to them, either. Clark Gable sat on the edge of the fountain and got involved in a long conversation with a sandy-haired guy from Paramount about their mutual bookie. One of Hearst's five sons arrived with his girlfriend. He tried to introduce her to Garbo, who answered in monosyllables, until at last he gave it up and they went off to swim in the Roman pool. A couple of friends of Marion's from the days before talkies, slightly thread-bare guys named Char-lie and Laurence who looked as though they hadn't worked lately, got deeply involved in a discussion of Greek mythology.

I sat there and looked up at the big house and wondered where Hearst was, and what he was doing. Closing some million-dollar media deal? Giving some senator or congressman voting instructions? Placing an order with some antique dealer for the contents of an entire library from some medieval duke's palace?

He did stuff like that, Mr. Hearst, which was one of the reasons the Company was interested in him.

I was distracted from my uneasy reverie when Constance Talmadge arrived, gaining on forty now but still as bright and bouncy as when she'd played the Mountain Girl in *Intolerance*, and with her Brooklyn accent just as strong. She bounced right over to Lewis, who knew her, and they had a lively chat about old times. Shortly afterward the big doors of the house opened and out came, not the procession of priests and altar boys you'd expect, but Marion in light evening dress.

"Hello, everybody," she hollered across the fountain. "Sorry to keep you waiting, but you know how it is — Hearst come, Hearst served!"

There were nervous giggles and you almost expected to see the big house behind her wince, but she didn't care. She came out and greeted everybody warmly — well, almost everybody, Garbo seemed to daunt even Marion — and then welcomed us in through the vast doorway, into the inner sanctum.

"Who's a first-timer up here?" she demanded, as we crossed the threshold. "I know you are, Joe, and your friend — ? Get a load of this floor." She pointed to the mosaic tile in the vestibule. "Know where that's from? Pompeii! Can you beat it? People actually died on this floor."

If she was right, I had known some of them. It didn't improve my mood.

The big room beyond was cool and dark after the brilliance of the courtyard. Almost comfortable, too: it had contemporary sofas and overstuffed chairs, little ash trays on brass stands. If you didn't mind the fact that it was also about a mile long and full of Renaissance masterpieces, with a fireplace big enough to roast an ox and a coffered ceiling a mile up in the air, it was sort of cozy. Here, as in all the other rooms, were paintings and statues representing the Madonna and Child. It seemed to be one of Mr. Hearst's favorite images.

We milled around aimlessly until servants came out bearing trays of drinks, at which time the milling became purposeful as hell. We converged on those trays like piranhas. The Madonna beamed down at us all, smiling her blessing.

The atmosphere livened up a lot after that. Charlie sat down at a piano and began to play popular tunes. Gable and Laurence and the guy from Paramount found a deck of cards and started a poker game. Marion worked the rest of the crowd like the good hostess she was, making sure that everybody had a drink and nobody was bored.

The Hearst kid and his girlfriend came in with wet hair. A couple of Hearst's executives (slimy-looking bastards) came in too, saw Garbo and hurried over to try to get her autograph. A gaunt and imposing grande dame with

two shrieking little mutts made an entrance, and Marion greeted her enthusiastically; she was some kind of offbeat novelist who'd had one of her books
optioned, and had come out to Hollywood to work on the screenplay.

I roamed around the edges of the vast room, scanning for the secret panel
that concealed Hearst's private elevator. Lewis was gallantly dancing the
Charleston with Connie Talmadge. Marion made for them, towing the writer
along.

"—And this is Dutch Talmadge, you remember her? And this is, uh, what
was your name, sweetie?" Marion waved at Lewis.

"Lewis Kensington," he said, as the music tinkled to a stop. The pianist
paused to light a cigarette.

"Lewis! That's it. And you're even cuter up close," said Marion, reaching
out and pinching his cheek. "Isn't he? Anyway you're Industry too, aren't you,
Lewis?"

"Only in a minor sort of way," Lewis demurred. "I'm a stunt man."

"That just means you're worth the money they pay you, honey." Marion
told him. "Unlike some of these blonde bimbos with no talent, huh?" She
whooped with laughter at her own expense. "Lewis, Dutch, this is Cartimandua Bryce! You know? She writes those wonderful spooky romances."

The imposing-looking lady stepped forward. The two chihuahuas did their
best to lunge from her arms and tear out Lewis' throat, but she kept a firm grip
on them.

"A-and these are her little dogs," added Marion unnecessarily, stepping
back from the yappy armful.

"My familiars," Cartimandua Bryce corrected her with a saturnine smile.
"Actually, they are old souls who have re-entered the flesh on a temporary basis
for purposes of the spiritual advancement of others."

"Oh," said Connie.

"Okay," said Marion.

"This is Conqueror Worm." Mrs. Bryce offered the smaller of the two bug-
eyed monsters, "and this is Tcho-Tcho."

"How nice," said Lewis gamely, and reached out in an attempt to shake
Tcho-Tcho's tiny paw. She bared her teeth at him and screamed frenziedly.
Some animals can tell we're not mortals. It can be inconvenient.

Lewis withdrew his hand in some haste. "I'm sorry. Perhaps the nice doggie's not used to strangers?"

"It isn't that—" Mrs. Bryce stared fixedly at Lewis. "Tcho-Tcho is attempting to communicate with me telepathically. She senses something unusual
about you, Mr. Kensington."

If she can tell the lady you're a cyborg, she's one hell of a dog, I transmitted.

Oh, shut up, Lewis transmitted back. "Really?" he said to Mrs. Bryce.
"Gosh, isn't that interesting?"

But Mrs. Bryce had closed her eyes, I guess the better to hear what Tcho-Tcho had to say, and was frowning deeply. After a moment's uncomfortable silence, Marion turned to Lewis and said, "So, you're Freddie March's stunt double? Gee. What's that like, anyway?"

"I just take falls. Stand in on lighting tests. Swing from chandeliers," Lewis replied. "The usual." Charlie resumed playing: *I'm the Sheik of Araby.*

"He useta do stunts for Valentino, too," Constance added. "I remember."

"You doubled for Rudy?" Marion's smiled softened. "Poor old Rudy."

"I always heard Valentino was a faggot," chortled the man from Paramount. Marion rounded on him angrily.

"For your information, Jack, Rudy Valentino was a real man," she told him. "He just had too much class to chase skirts all the time!"

"Soitain people could loin a whole lot from him," agreed Connie, with the scowl of disdain she'd used to face down Old Babylon's marriage market in *Intolerance.*

"I'm just telling you what I heard," protested the man from Paramount.

"Maybe," Gable told him, looking up from his cards. "But did you ever hear that expression, *Say nothing but good of the dead?* Now might be a good time to dummy up, pal. That or play your hand."

Mrs. Bryce, meanwhile, had opened her eyes and was gazing on Lewis with a disconcerting expression.

"Mr. Kensington," she announced with a throaty quaver, "Tcho-Tcho informs me you are a haunted man."

Lewis looked around nervously. "Am I?"

"Tcho-Tcho can perceive the spirit of a soul struggling in vain to speak to you. You are not sufficiently tuned to the cosmic vibrations to hear him," Mrs. Bryce stated.

Tell him to try another frequency, I quipped.

"Well, that's just like me, I'm afraid." Lewis shrugged, palms turned out. "I'm terribly dense that way, you see. Wouldn't know a cosmic vibration if I tripped over one."

Cosmic vibrations, my ass. I knew what she was doing; carny psychics do it all the time, and it's called a cold reading. You give somebody a close once-over and make a few deductions based on the details you observe. Then you start weaving a story out of your deductions, watching your subject's reactions to see where you're accurate and tailoring your story to fit as you go on. All she had to work with, right now, was the mention that Lewis had known Valentino. Lewis has *Easy Mark* written all over him, but I guessed she was up here after bigger fish.

"Tcho-Tcho sees a man—a slender, dark man—" Mrs. Bryce went on, rolling her eyes back in her head in a sort of alarming way. "He wears Eastern raiment—"

Marion downed her cocktail in one gulp. "Hey, look, Mrs. Bryce, there's Greta Garbo," she said. "I'll just bet she's a big fan of your books."

Mrs. Bryce's eyes snapped back into place and she looked around.

"Garbo?" she cried. She made straight for the Frozen Flame, dropping Lewis like a rock, though Tcho-Tcho snapped and strained over her shoulder at him. Garbo saw them coming and sank further into the depths of her chair. I was right. Mrs. Bryce was after bigger fish.

I didn't notice what happened after that, though, because I heard a clash of brass gates and gears engaging somewhere upstairs. The biggest fish of all was descending in his elevator, making his delayed entrance.

I edged over toward the secret panel. My mouth was dry, my palms were sweaty. I wonder if Mephistopheles ever gets sweaty palms when he's facing a prospective client?

Bump. Here he was. The panel made no sound as it opened. Not a mortal soul noticed as W.R. Hearst stepped into the room, and for that matter Lewis didn't notice either, having resumed the Charleston with Connie Talmadge. So there was only me to stare at the very, very big old man who sat down quietly in the corner.

I swear I felt the hair stand up on the back of my neck, and I didn't know why. William Randolph Hearst had had his seventieth birthday a couple of weeks before. His hair was white, he sagged where an old man sags, but his bones hadn't given in to gravity. His posture was upright and powerfully alert.

He just sat there in the shadows, watching the bright people in his big room. I watched him. This was the guy who'd fathered modern journalism, who with terrifying energy and audacity had built a financial empire that included newspapers, magazines, movies, radio, mining, ranching. He picked and chose presidents as though they were his personal appointees. He'd ruthlessly forced the world to take him on his own terms; morality was what *he* said it was; and yet there wasn't any fire that you could spot in the seated man, no restless genius apparent to the eye.

You know what he reminded me of? The Goon in the *Popeye* comic strips. Big as a mountain and scary too, but at the same time sad, with those weird deep eyes above the long straight nose.

He reminded me of something else, too, but not anything I wanted to remember right now.

"Oh, you did your trick again," said Marion pretending to notice him at last. "Here he is, everybody. He likes to pop in like he was Houdini or something. Come on, W.R., say hello to the nice people." She pulled him to his feet and he smiled for her. His smile was even scarier than the rest of him. It was wide, and sharp, and hungry, and young.

"Hello, everybody," he said, in that unearthly voice Ambrose Bierce had described as the fragrance of violets made audible. Flutelike and without resonance. Not a human voice; jeez, I sound more human than that. But then. I'm supposed to.

And you should have seen them, all those people, turn and stare and smile and bow—just slightly, and I don't think any of them realized they were bowing to him, but I've been a courtier and I know a grovel when I see one. Marion was the only mortal in that room who wasn't afraid of him. Even Garbo had gotten up out of her chair.

Marion brought them up to him, one by one, the big names and the nobodies, and introduced the ones he didn't know. He shook hands like a shy kid. Hell, he *was* shy! That was it, I realized: he was uneasy around people, and Marion—in addition to her other duties—was his social interface. Okay, this might be something I could use.

I stood apart from the crowd, waiting unobtrusively until Marion had brought up everybody else. Only when she looked around for me did I step out of the shadows into her line of sight.

"And—oh, Joe almost forgot you! Pops, this is Joe Denham. He works for Mr. Mayer? He's the nice guy who—"

Pandemonium erupted behind us. One of the damn chihuahuas had gotten loose and was after somebody with intent to kill, Lewis from the sound of it. Marion turned and ran off to deal with the commotion. I leaned forward and shook Hearst's hand as he peered over my shoulder after Marion, frowning.

"Pleased to meet you, Mr. Hearst," I told him quietly. "Mr. Shaw asked me to visit you. I look forward to our conversation later."

Boy, did that get his attention. Those remote eyes snapped into close focus on me, and it was like being hit by a granite block. I swallowed hard but concentrated on the part I was playing, smiling mysteriously as I disengaged my hand from his and stepped back into the shadows.

He wasn't able to say anything right then, because Tcho-Tcho was herding Lewis in our direction and Lewis was dancing away from her with apologetic little yelps, jumping over the furniture, and Marion was laughing hysterically as she tried to catch the rotten dog. Mrs. Bryce just looked on with a rapt and knowing expression.

Hearst pursed his lips at the scene, but he couldn't be distracted long. He turned slowly to stare at me and nodded, just once, to show he understood.

A butler appeared in the doorway to announce that dinner was served. Hearst led us from the room, and we followed obediently.

The dining hall was less homey than the first room we'd been in. Freezing cold in spite of the roaring fire in the French Gothic hearth, its gloom was brightened a little by the silk Renaissance racing banners hanging up high and a lot of massive silver candlesticks. The walls were paneled with fifteenth-century choir stalls from Spain. I might have dozed off in any one of them, back in my days as a friar. Maybe I had; they looked familiar.

We were seated at the long refectory table. Hearst and Marion sat across from each other in the center, and guests were placed by status. The nearer you were to the master and his mistress, the higher in favor or more important you were. Guests Mr. Hearst found boring or rude were moved discreetly further out down the table.

Well we've nowhere to go but up, Lewis transmitted, finding our place cards clear down at the end. I could see Hearst staring at me as we took our plates (plain old Blue Willow that his mother had used for camping trips) and headed for the buffet.

I bet we move up soon, too, I replied.

Ah! Have you made contact? Lewis peered around Gable's back at a nice-looking dish of venison steaks.

Just baited the hook. I tried not to glance at Hearst, who had loaded his plate with pressed duck and was pacing slowly back to the table.

Does this have to be terribly complicated? Lewis inquired, sidling in past Garbo to help himself to asparagus soufflé. *All we want is permission to conceal the script in that particular Spanish cabinet.*

Actually we want a little more than that, Lewis. I considered all the rich stuff and decided to keep things bland. Potatoes, right.

I see. This is one of those need-to-know things, isn't it?

You got it, kiddo. I put enough food on my plate to be polite and turned to go back to my seat. Hearst caught my eye. He tracked me like a lighthouse beam all the way down the table. I nodded back, like the friendly guy I really am, and sat down across from Lewis.

I take it there's more going on here than the Company has seen fit to tell me? Lewis transmitted, unfolding his paper napkin and holding out his wine glass expectantly. The waiter filled it and moved on.

Don't be sore. I transmitted back. *You know the Company. There's probably more going on here than even I know about, okay?* I only said it to make him feel better. If I'd had any idea how right I was. . . .

So we ate dinner, at that baronial banqueting table, with the mortals. Gable carried on manful conversation with Mr. Hearst about ranching, Marion and Connie joked and giggled across the table with the male guests, young Hearst and his girl whispered to each other, and a servant had to take Tcho-Tcho and Conqueror Worm outside because they wouldn't stop snarling at a meek little dachshund that appeared under Mr. Hearst's chair. Mrs. Bryce didn't mind; she was busy trying to tell Garbo about a past life, but I couldn't figure out if it was supposed to be hers or Garbo's. Hearst's executives just ate, in silence, down at their end of the table. Lewis and I ate in silence down at our end.

Not that we were ignored. Every so often Marion would yell a pleasantry our way, and Hearst kept swinging that cold blue searchlight on me, with an expression I was damned if I could fathom.

When dinner was over, Mr. Hearst rose and picked up the dachshund. He led us all deeper into his house, to his private movie theater.

Do I have to tell you it was on a scale with everything else? Walls lined in red damask, gorgeous beamed ceiling held up by rows of gilded caryatids slightly larger than lifesize. We filed into our seats, I guess unconsciously preserving the order of the dinner table because Lewis and I wound up off on an edge again. Hearst settled into his big leather chair with its telephone, called the projectionist and gave an order. The lights went out, and after a fairly long moment in darkness, the screen lit up. It was *Going Hollywood*, Marion's latest film with Bing Crosby. She greeted her name on the screen with a long loud raspberry, and everyone tittered.

Except me. I wasn't tittering, no sir; Mr. Hearst wasn't in his big leather chair anymore. He was padding toward me slowly in the darkness carrying his little dog, and if I hadn't been able to see by infrared I'd probably have screamed and jumped right through that expensive ceiling when his big hand dropped on my shoulder in the darkness.

He leaned down close to my ear.

"Mr. Denham? I'd like to speak with you in private, if I may," he told me.

"Yes, sir, Mr. Hearst," I gasped, and got to my feet. Beside me, Lewis glanced over. His eyes widened.

Break a leg, he transmitted, and turned his attention to the screen again.

I edged out of the row and followed Hearst, who was walking away without the slightest doubt I was obeying him. Once we were outside the theater, all he said was, "Let's go this way. It'll be faster."

"Okay," I said, as though I had any idea where we were going. We walked back through the house. There wasn't a sound except our foot-steps, echoing off those high walls. We emerged into the assembly hall, eerily lit up, and Hearst led me to the panel that concealed his elevator. It opened for him. We got in, he and I and the little dog, and ascended through his house.

My mouth was dry, my palms were sweating, my dinner wasn't sitting too good . . . well, that last one's a lie. I'm a cyborg and I can't get indigestion. But I felt like a mortal with a nervous stomach, know what I mean? And I'd have given half the Renaissance masterpieces in that house for a roll of Pep-O-Mints right then. The dachshund watched me sympathetically.

We got out at the third floor and stepped into Hearst's private study. This was the room from which he ran his empire when he was at La Cuesta Encantada, this was where phones connected him directly to newsrooms all over the country; this was where he glanced at teletype before giving orders to the movers and shakers. Up in a corner, a tiny concealed motion picture camera began to whir the moment we stepped on the carpet, and I could hear the click as a modified Dictaphone hidden in a cabinet began to record. State-of-the-art surveillance, for 1933.

It was a nicer room than the others I'd been in so far. Huge, of course, with an antique Spanish ceiling and golden hanging lamps, but wood-paneled walls and books and Bakhtiari carpets gave it a certain warmth. My gaze followed the glow of lamplight down the long polished mahogany conference table and skidded smack into Hearst's life-size portrait on the far wall. It was a good portrait, done when he was in his thirties, the young emperor staring out with those somber eyes. He looked innocent. He looked dangerous.

"Nice likeness," I said.

"The painter had a great talent," Hearst replied. "He was a dear friend of mine. Died too soon. Why do you suppose that happens?"

"People dying too soon?" I stammered slightly as I said it, and mentally yelled at myself to calm down: it was just business with a mortal, now, and the guy was even handing me an opening. I gave him my best enigmatic smile and shook my head sadly. "It's the fate of mortals to die, Mr. Hearst. Even those with extraordinary ability and talent. Rather a pity, wouldn't you agree?"

"Oh, yes," Hearst replied, never taking his eyes off me a moment. "And I guess that's what we're going to discuss now, isn't it, Mr. Denham? Let's sit down."

He gestured me to a seat, not at the big table but in one of the comfy armchairs. He settled into another to face me, as though we were old friends having a chat. The little dog curled up in his lap and sighed. God, that was a quiet room.

"So George Bernard Shaw sent you," Hearst stated.

"Not exactly," I said, folding my hands. "He mentioned you might be interested in what my people have to offer."

Hearst just looked at me. I coughed slightly and went on: "He spoke well of you, as much as Mr. Shaw ever speaks well of anybody. And, from what I've seen, you have a lot in common with the founders of our Company. You appreciate the magnificent art humanity is capable of creating. You hate to see it destroyed or wasted by blind chance. You've spent a lot of your life preserving rare and beautiful things from destruction.

"And—just as necessary—you're a man with vision. Modern science, and its potential, doesn't frighten you. You're not superstitious. You're a moral man, but you won't let narrow-minded moralists dictate to you! So you're no coward, either."

He didn't seem pleased or flattered, he was just listening to me. What was he thinking? I pushed on, doing my best to play the scene like Claude Rains.

"You see, we've been watching you carefully for quite a while now. Mr.

Hearst," I told him. "We don't make this offer lightly, or to ordinary mortals. But there are certain questions we feel obliged to ask first."

Hearst just nodded. When was he going to say something?

"It's not for everybody," I continued, "what we're offering. You may think you want it very much, but you need to look honestly into your heart and ask yourself: are you ever tired of life? Are there ever times when you'd welcome a chance to sleep forever?"

"No," Hearst replied. "If I were tired of life, I'd give up and die. I'm not after peace and tranquility, Mr. Denham. I want more time to live. I have things to do! The minute I slow down and decide to watch the clouds roll by, I'll be bored to death."

"Maybe." I nodded. "But here's another thing to consider: how much the world has changed since you were a young man. Look at that portrait. When it was painted, you were in the prime of your life—*and so was your generation*. It was your world. You knew the rules of the game, and everything made sense.

"But you were born before Lincoln delivered the Gettysburg address. Mr. Hearst. You're not living in that world any more. All the rules have changed. The music is so brassy and strident, the dances so crude. The kings are all dying out, and petty dictators with dirty hands are seizing power. Aren't you, even a little, bewildered by the sheer speed with which everything moves nowadays? You're only seventy, but don't you feel just a bit like a dinosaur sometimes, a survivor of a forgotten age?"

"No," said Hearst firmly. "I like the present. I like the speed and the newness of things. I have a feeling I'd enjoy the future even more. Besides, if you study history, you have to conclude that humanity has steadily improved over the centuries, whatever the cynics say. The future generations are bound to be better than we are, no matter how outlandish their fashions may seem now. And what's fashion, anyway? What do I care what music the young people listen to? They'll be healthier, and smarter, and they'll have the benefit of learning from our mistakes. I'd love to hear what they'll have to say for themselves!"

I nodded again, let a beat pass in silence for effect before I answered. At last:

"There are also," I warned him, "matters of the heart to be considered. When a man has loved ones, certain things are going to cause him grief—if he lives long enough to see them happen. Think about that, Mr. Hearst."

He nodded slowly, and at last he dropped his eyes from mine.

"It would be worse for a man who felt family connections deeply," he said. "And every man ought to. But things aren't always the way they ought to be, Mr. Denham. I don't know why that is. I wish I did."

Did he mean he wished he knew why he'd never felt much paternal connection to his sons? I just looked understanding.

"And as for love," he went on, and paused. "Well, there are certain things to which you have to be resigned. It's inevitable. Nobody loves without pain."

Was he wondering again why Marion wouldn't stop drinking for him?

"And love doesn't always last, and that hurts," I condoled. Hearst lifted his eyes to me again.

"When it does last, that hurts too," he informed me. "I assure you I can bear pain."

Well, those were all the right answers. I found myself reaching up in an attempt to stroke the beard I used to wear.

"A sound, positive attitude, Mr. Hearst," I told him. "Good for you. I think we've come to the bargaining table now."

"How much can you let me have?" he said instantly.

Well, this wasn't going to take long. "Twenty years," I replied. "Give or take a year or two."

Yikes! What an expression of rapacity in his eyes. Had I forgotten I was dealing with William Randolph Hearst?

"Twenty years?" he scoffed. "When I'm only seventy? I had a grandfather who lived to be ninety-seven. I might get that far on my own."

"Not with that heart, and you know it," I countered.

His mouth tightened in acknowledgment. "All right. If your people can't do any better—twenty years might be acceptable. And in return, Mr. Denham?"

"Two things, Mr. Hearst," I held up my hand with two fingers extended. "The Company would like the freedom to store certain things here at La Cuesta Encantada from time to time. Nothing dangerous or contraband, of course! Nothing but certain books, certain paintings, some other little rarities that wouldn't survive the coming centuries if they were kept in a less fortified place. In a way, we'd just be adding items to your collection."

"You must have an idea that this house will 'survive the coming centuries,' then," said Hearst, looking grimly pleased.

"Oh, yes, sir." I told him. "It will. This is one thing you've loved that won't fade away."

He rose from his chair at that, setting the dog down carefully, and paced away from me down the long room. Then he turned and walked back, tucking a grin out of sight. "Okay, Mr. Denham," he said. "Your second request must be pretty hard to swallow. What's the other thing your people want?"

"Certain conditions set up in your will, Mr. Hearst," I said. "A secret trust giving my Company control of certain of your assets. Only a couple, but very specific ones."

He bared his smile at me. It roused all kinds of atavistic terrors; I felt sweat break out on my forehead, get clammy in my armpits.

"My, my. What kind of dumb cluck do your people think I am?" he inquired jovially.

"Well, you'd certainly be one if you jumped at their offer without wanting to know more," I smiled back, resisting the urge to run like hell. "They don't want your money, Mr. Hearst. Leave all you want to your wife and your boys. Leave Marion more than enough to protect her. What my Company wants won't create any hardship for your heirs, in any way. But—you're smart enough to understand this—there are plans being made now that won't bear fruit for another couple of centuries. Something you might not value much, tonight in 1933, might be a winning card in a game being played in the future. You see what I'm saying here?"

"I might," said Hearst, hitching up the knees of his trousers and sitting down again. The little dog jumped back into his lap. Relieved that he was no longer looming over me, I pushed on:

"Obviously we'd submit a draft of the conditions for your approval, though your lawyers couldn't be allowed to examine it—"

"And I can see why." Hearst held up his big hand. "And that's all right. I think I'm still competent to look over a contract. But, Mr. Denham! You've just told me I've got something you're going to need very badly one day. Now, wouldn't you expect me to raise the price? And I'd have to have more information about your people. I'd have to see proof that any of your story, or Mr. Shaw's for that matter, is true."

What had I said to myself, that this wasn't going to take long?

"Sure," I said brightly. "I brought all the proof I'll need."

"That's good," Hearst told me, and picked up the receiver of the phone on the table at his elbow. "Anne? Send us up some coffee, please. Yes, thank you." He leaned away from the receiver a moment to ask: "Do you take cream or sugar, Mr. Denham?"

"Both," I said.

"Cream and sugar, please," he said into the phone. "And please put Jerome on the line." He waited briefly. "Jerome? I want the black suitcase that's under Mr. Denham's bed. Yes. Thank you." He hung up and met my stare of astonishment. "That is where you've got it, isn't it? Whatever proof you've brought me?"

"Yes, as a matter of fact," I replied.

"Good," he said, and leaned back in his chair. The little dog insinuated her head under his hand, begging for attention. He looked down at her in mild amusement and began to scratch between her ears. I leaned back too, noting that my shirt was plastered to my back with sweat and only grateful it wasn't running down my face.

"Are you a mortal creature, Mr. Denham?" Hearst inquired softly.

Now the sweat was running down my face.

"Uh, no, sir," I said. "Though I started out as one."

"You did, eh?" he remarked. "How old are you?"

"About twenty thousand years," I answered. Wham, he hit me with that deadweight stare again.

"Really?" he said. "A little fellow like you?"

I ask you, is 5'5" really so short? "We were smaller back then," I explained. "People were, I mean. Diet, probably."

He just nodded. After a moment he asked: "You've lived through the ages as an eyewitness to history?"

"Yeah. Yes, sir."

"You saw the Pyramids built?"

"Yes, as a matter of fact." I prayed he wouldn't ask me how they did it, because he'd never believe the truth, but he pushed on:

"You saw the Trojan War?"

"Well, yes, I did, but it wasn't exactly like Homer said."

"The stories in the Bible, are they true? Did they really happen? Did you meet Jesus Christ?" His eyes were blazing at me.

"Well—" I waved my hands in a helpless kind of way. "I didn't meet Jesus, no, because I was working in Rome back then. I never worked in Judea until the Crusades, and that was way later. And as for the stuff in the Bible being true . . . some of it is, and some of it isn't, and anyway it depends on what you mean by true." I gave in and pulled out a handkerchief, mopping my face.

"But the theological questions!" Hearst leaned forward. "Have we got souls that survive us after physical death? What about Heaven and Hell?"

"Sorry." I shook my head. "How should I know? I've never been to either place. I've never died, remember?"

"Don't your masters know?"

"If they do, they haven't told me," I apologized. "But then there's a lot they haven't told me."

Hearst's mouth tightened again, and yet I got the impression he was satisfied in some way. I sagged backward, feeling like a wrung-out sponge. So much for my suave subtle Mephistopheles act.

On the other hand, Hearst liked being in control of the game. He might be more receptive this way.

Our coffee arrived. Hearst took half a cup and filled it the rest of the way up with cream. I put cream and four lumps of sugar in mine.

"You like sugar." Hearst observed, sipping his coffee. "But then, I don't suppose you had much opportunity to get sweets for the first few thousand years of your life?"

"Nope," I admitted. I tasted my cup and set it aside to cool. "No Neolithic candy stores."

There was a discreet double knock. Jerome entered after a word from Mr. Hearst. He brought in my suitcase and set it down between us.

"Thanks," I said.

"You're welcome, sir," he replied, without a trace of sarcasm, and exited as quietly as he'd entered. It was just me, Hearst and the dog again. They looked at me expectantly.

"All right," I said, drawing a deep breath. I leaned down, punched in the code on the lock, and opened the suitcase. I felt like a traveling salesman. I guess I sort of was one.

"Here we are," I told Hearst, drawing out a silver bottle. "This is your free sample. Drink it, and you'll taste what it feels like to be forty again. The effects will only last a day or so, but that ought to be enough to show you that we can give you those twenty years with no difficulties."

"So your secret's a potion?" Hearst drank more of his coffee.

"Not entirely," I said truthfully. I was going to have to do some crypto-surgery to make temporary repairs on his heart, but we never tell them about that part of it. "Now. Here's something I think you'll find a lot more impressive."

I took out the viewscreen and set it up on the table between us. "If this were, oh, a thousand years ago and you were some emperor I was trying to impress, I'd tell you this was a magic mirror. As it is . . . you know that televi-sion idea they're working on in England, right now?"

"Yes," Hearst replied.

"This is where that invention's going to have led in about two hundred years," I said. "Now, I can't pick up any broadcasts because there aren't any yet, but this one also plays recorded programs." I slipped a small gold disc from a black envelope and pushed it into a slot in the front of the device, and hit the PLAY button.

Instantly the screen lit up pale blue. A moment later a montage of images appeared there, with music booming from the tiny speakers: a staccato fanfare announcing the evening news for April 18, 2106.

Hearst peered into the viewscreen in astonishment. He leaned close as the little stories sped by, the attractive people chattering brightly New mining colonies on Luna, Ulster Revenge League terrorists bombing London again, new international agreement signed to tighten prohibitions on Recombinant DNA research, protesters in Mexico picketing Japanese-owned auto plants—

"Wait," Hearst said, lifting his big hand. "How do you stop this thing? Can you slow it down?"

I made it pause. The image of Mexican union workers torching a sushi bar froze. Hearst remained staring at the screen.

"Is that," he said, "what journalism is like, in the future?"

"Well, yes, sir. No newspapers any more, you see; it'll all be online by then. Sort of a print-and-movie broadcast," I explained, though I was aware the revelation would probably give the poor old guy future shock. This had been his field of expertise, after all.

"But, I mean—" Hearst tore his gaze away and looked at me probingly. "This is only snippets of stuff. There's no real coverage; maybe three sentences to a story and one picture. It hasn't got half the substance of a newsreel!"

Not a word of surprise about colonies on the Moon.

"No, it'll be pretty lightweight," I admitted. "But, you see, Mr. Hearst, that'll be what the average person wants out of News by the twenty-second century. Something brief and easy to grasp. Most people will be too busy—and too uninterested—to follow stories in depth."

"Play it over again, please," Hearst ordered, and I restarted it for him. He watched intently. I felt a twinge of pity. What could he possibly make of the sound bites, the chaotic juxtaposition of images, the rapid, bouncing and relentless pace? He watched, with the same frown, to about the same spot; then gestured for me to stop it again. I obeyed.

"Exactly," he said. "Exactly. News for the fellow in the street! Even an illiterate stevedore could get this stuff. It's like a kindergarten primer." He looked at me sidelong. "And it occurs to me, Mr. Denham, that it must be fairly easy to sway public opinion with this kind of pap. A picture's worth a thousand words, isn't it? I always thought so. This is mostly pictures. If you fed the public the right little fragments of story, you could manipulate their impressions of what's going on. Couldn't you?"

I gaped at him.

"Uh—you could, but of course that wouldn't be a very ethical thing to do," I found myself saying.

"No, if you were doing it for unethical reasons," Hearst agreed. "If you were on the side of the angels, though, I can't see how it would be wrong to pull out every trick of rhetoric available to fight for your cause! Let's see the rest of this. You're looking at these control buttons, aren't you? What are these things, these hieroglyphics?"

"Universal icons," I explained. "They're activated by eye movement. To start it again, you look at this one—" Even as I was pointing, he'd started it again himself.

There wasn't much left on the disc. A tiny clutch of factoids about a new fusion power plant, a weather report, a sports piece, and then two bitty scoops of local news. The first was a snap and ten seconds of sound, from a reporter at the scene of a party in San Francisco commemorating the two-hundredth anniversary of the 1906 earthquake. The second one—the story that had influenced the Company's choice of this particular news broadcast for Mr. Hearst's persuasion—was a piece on protesters blocking the subdivision of Hearst Ranch, which was in danger of being turned into a planned community with tract housing, golf courses and shopping malls.

Hearst caught his breath at that, and if I thought his face had been scary before I saw now I had had no idea what scary could be. His glare hit the activation buttons with almost physical force: replay, replay, replay. After he'd watched that segment half a dozen times, he shut it off and looked at me.

"They can't do it," he said. "Did you see those plans? They'd ruin this coastline. They'd cut down all the trees! Traffic and noise and soot and—and where would all the animals go? Animals have rights too."

"I'm afraid most of the wildlife would be extinct in this range by then, Mr. Hearst," I apologized, placing the viewer back into its case. "But maybe now you've got an idea about why my Company needs to control certain of your assets."

He was silent, breathing hard. The little dog was looking up at him with anxious eyes.

"All right, Mr. Denham," he said quietly. "To paraphrase Dickens: Is this the image of what will be, or only of what may be?"

I shrugged. "I only know what's going to happen in the future in a general kind of way, Mr. Hearst. Big stuff, like wars and inventions. I'm not told a lot else. I sincerely hope things don't turn out so badly for your ranch—and if it's any consolation, you notice the program was about protesting the *proposed* development only. The problem is, history can't be changed, not once it's happened."

"History, or recorded history, Mr. Denham?" Hearst countered. "They're not at all necessarily the same thing, I can tell you from personal experience."

"I'll bet you can," I answered, wiping away sweat again. "Okay, you've figured something out: there are all kinds of little zones of error in recorded history. My Company makes use of those errors. If history can't be changed, it can be worked around. See?"

"Perfectly," Hearst replied. He leaned back in his chair and his voice was hard, those violets of sound transmuted to porphyry marble. "I'm convinced your people are on the level, Mr. Denham. Now. You go and tell them that twenty years is pretty much chickenfeed as far as I'm concerned. It won't do, not by a long way. I want nothing less than the same immortality you've got, you see? Permanent life. I always thought I could put it to good use and, now that you've shown me the future, I can see my work's cut out for me. I also want shares in your Company's stock. I want to be a player in this game."

"But—" I sat bolt upright in my chair. "Mr. Hearst! I can manage the shares of stock. But the immortality's impossible! You don't understand how it works. The immortality process can't be done on old men. We have to start with young mortals. I was only a little kid when I was recruited for the Company. Don't you see? Your body's too old and damaged to be kept running indefinitely."

"Who said I wanted immortality in this body?" said Hearst. "Why would I want to drive around forever in a rusted old Model T when I could have one of those shiny new modern cars? Your masters seem to be capable of darned near anything. I'm betting that there's a way to bring me back in a new body, and if there isn't a way now, I'll bet they can come up with one if they try. They're going to have to try, if they want my co-operation. Tell them that."

I opened my mouth to protest, and then I thought—Why argue? Promise him anything. "Okay," I agreed.

"Good," Hearst said, finishing his coffee. "Do you need a telephone to contact them? My switchboard can connect you anywhere in the world in a couple of minutes."

"Thanks, but we use something different," I told him. "It's back in my room and I don't think Jerome could find it. I'll try to have an answer for you by tomorrow morning, though."

He nodded. Reaching out his hand, he took up the silver bottle and considered it. "Is this the drug that made you what you are?" He looked at me. His dog looked up at him.

"Pretty much. Except my body's been altered to manufacture the stuff, so it pumps through me all the time," I explained. "I don't have to take it orally."

"But you'd have no objection to sampling a little, before I drank it?"

"Absolutely none," I said, and held out my empty coffee cup. Hearst lifted his eyebrows at that. He puzzled a moment over the bottlecap before figuring it out, and then poured about three ounces of Pineal Tribrantine Three cocktail into my cup. I drank it down, trying not to make a face.

It wasn't all PT3. There was some kind of fruit base, cranberry juice as far as I could tell, and a bunch of hormones and euphoriacs to make him feel great as well as healthy, and something to stimulate the production of telomerase. Beneficial definitely, but not an immortality potion by a long shot. He'd have to have custom-designed biomechanicals and prosthetic implants, to say nothing of years of training for eternity starting when he was about three. But why tell the guy?

And Hearst was looking young already, just watching me: wonderstruck, scared and eager. When I didn't curl up and die, he poured the rest of the bottle's contents into his cup and drank it down, glancing furtively at his hidden camera.

"My," he said. "That tasted funny."

I nodded.

And of course he didn't die either, as the time passed in that grand room. He quizzed me about my personal life, wanted to hear about what it was like to live in the ancient world, and how many famous people I'd met. I told him all about Phoenician traders and Egyptian priests and Roman senators I'd known. After a while Hearst noticed he felt swell—I could tell by his expression—and he got up and put down the little dog and began to pace the room as we talked, not with the heavy cautious tread of the old man he was but with a light step, almost dancing.

"So I said to Apuleius, 'But that only leaves three fish, and anyway what do you want to do about the flute player—'" I was saying, when a door in the far corner opened and Marion stormed in.

"W-w w-where *were* you?" she shouted. Marion stammered when she was tired or upset, and she was both now. "Thanks a lot for s-sneaking out like that and leaving me to t-t-talk to everybody. They're your guests too, y-you know!"

Hearst turned to stare at her, openmouthed. I really think he'd forgotten about Marion. I jumped up, looking apologetic.

"Whoops! Hey, Marion, it was my fault. I needed to ask his advice about something," I explained. She turned, surprised to see me.

"Joe?" she said.

"I'm sorry to take so long, dear," said Hearst, coming and putting his arms around her. "Your friend's a very interesting fellow." He was looking at her like a wolf looks at a lamb chop. "Did they like the picture?"

"N-n-no!" she said. "Half of 'em left before it was over. You'd think they'd s-stay to watch Bing C-Crosby."

If there's one thing I've learned over the millennia, it's when to exit a room.

"Thanks for the talk, Mr. Hearst," I said, grabbing my black case and heading for the elevator. "I'll see if I can't find that prospectus. Maybe you can look at it for me tomorrow,"

"Maybe," Hearst murmured into Marion's neck. I was ready to crawl down the elevator cable like a monkey to get out of there, but fortunately the car was still on that floor, so I jumped in and rattled down through the house like Mephistopheles dropping through a trap door instead.

It was dark when I emerged into the assembly hall, but as soon as the panel had closed after me light blazed up from the overhead fixtures. I blinked, looking around. Scanning revealed a camera mount, way up high, that I hadn't noticed before. I saluted it Roman style and hurried out into the night, over the Pompeiian floor. As soon as I had crossed the threshold, the lights blinked out behind me. More surveillance. How many faithful Jeromes did Hearst have, sitting patiently behind peepholes in tiny rooms?

The night air was chilly, fresh with the smell of orange and lemon blossoms. The stars looked close enough to fall on me. I wandered around between the statues for a while, wondering how the hell I was going to fool the master of this house into thinking the Company had agreed to his terms. Gee: for that matter, how was I going to break it to the Company that they'd underestimated William Randolph Hearst?

Well, it wasn't going to be the first time I'd had to be the bearer of bad news to Dr. Zeus. At last I gave it up and found my way back to my wing of the guest house.

There was a light on in the gorgeously gilded sitting room. Lewis was perched uncomfortably on the edge of a sixteenth-century chair. He looked guilty about something. Jumping to his feet as I came in, he said: "Joseph, we have a problem."

"We do, huh?" I looked him over wearily. All in the world I wanted right then was a hot shower and a few hours of shuteye. "What is it?"

"The, ah, Valentino script has been stolen," he said.

My priorities changed. I strode muttering to the phone and picked it up. After a moment a blurred voice answered.

"Jerome? How you doing, pal? Listen, I'd like some room service. Can I get a hot fudge sundae over here at La Casa Del Sol? Heavy on the hot fudge?"

"Make that two," Lewis suggested. I looked daggers at him and went on:

"Make that two. No, no nuts. And if you've got any chocolate pudding or chocolate cake or some Hershey bars or anything, send those along too. Okay? I'll make it worth your while, chum."

". . . so I just thought I'd have a last look at it before I went to bed, but when I opened the case it wasn't there," Lewis explained, licking his spoon.

"You scanned for thermoluminescence? Fingerprints?" I said, putting the sundae dish down with one hand and reaching for cake with the other.

"Of course I did. No fingerprints, and judging from the faintness of the thermoluminescence, whoever went through my things must have been wearing gloves," Lewis told me. "About all I could tell was that a mortal had been in my room, probably an hour to an hour and a half before I got there. Do you think it was one of the servants?"

"No, I don't. I know Mr. Hearst sent Jerome in here to get something out of my room, but I don't think the guy ducked into yours as an afterthought to go through your drawers. Anybody who swiped stuff from Mr. Hearst's guests wouldn't work here very long," I said. "If any guest had ever had something stolen, everybody in the Industry would know about it. Gossip travels fast in this town." I meant Hollywood, of course, not San Simeon.

"There's a first time for everything," Lewis said miserably.

"True. But I think our buddy Jerome has *faithful retainer* written all over him," I said, finishing the cake in about three bites.

"Then who else could have done it?" Lewis wondered, starting on a dish of pudding.

"Well, you're the Literary Specialist. Haven't you ever accessed any Agatha Christie novels?" I tossed the cake plate aside and pounced on a Hershey bar.

"You know what we do next. Process of elimination. Who was where and when? I'll tell you this much, it wasn't me and it wasn't Big Daddy Hearst. I was with him from the moment we left the rest of you in the theater until Marion came up and I had to scram." I closed my eyes and sighed in bliss, as the Theobromos high finally kicked in.

"Well—" Lewis looked around distractedly, trying to think. "Then—it has to have been one of us who were in the theater watching *Going Hollywood.*"

"Yeah. And Marion said about half the audience walked out before it was over," I said. "Did you walk out, Lewis?"

"No! I stayed until the end. I can't imagine why anybody left. I thought it was delightful," Lewis told me earnestly. "It had Bing Crosby in it, you know."

"You've got pudding on your chin. Okay, so you stayed through the movie." I said, realizing my wits weren't at their sharpest right now but determined to thrash this through. "And so did Marion. Who else was there when the house lights came up, Lewis?"

Lewis sucked in his lower lip, thinking hard through the theobromine fog. "I'm replaying my visual transcript," he informed me. "Clark Gable is there. The younger Mr. Hearst and his friend are there. The unpleasant-looking fellows in the business suits are there. Connie's there."

"Garbo?"

"Mm—nope."

"The two silent guys? Charlie and Laurence?"

"No."

"What's his name, Jack from Paramount, is he there?"

"No, he isn't."

"What about the crazy lady with the dogs?"

"She's not there either." Lewis raised horrified eyes to me. "My gosh, it could have been any one of them." He remembered the pudding and dabbed at it with his handkerchief.

"Or the thief might have sneaked out, robbed your room and sneaked back in before the end of the picture," I told him.

"Oh, why complicate things?" he moaned. "What are we going to do?"

"Damned if I know tonight," I replied, struggling to my feet. "Tomorrow you're going to find out who took the Valentino script and get it back. I have other problems, okay?"

"What do you mean?"

"Mr. Hearst is upping the ante on the game. He's given me an ultimatum for Dr. Zeus," I explained.

"Wowie." Lewis looked appalled. "He thinks he can dictate terms to the Company?"

"He's doing it, isn't he?" I said, trudging off to my bedroom. "And guess who gets to deliver the messages both ways. Now you see why I was nervous? I knew this was going to happen."

"Well, cheer up," Lewis called after me. "Things can't go more wrong than this."

I switched on the light in my room, and found out just how much more wrong they could go.

Something exploded up from the bed at my face, a confusion of needle teeth and blaring sound. I was stoned, I was tired. I was confused, and so I just slapped it away as hard as I could, which with me being a cyborg and all was pretty hard. The thing flew across the room and hit the wall with a crunch. Then it dropped to the floor and didn't move, except for its legs kicking, but not much or for long.

Lewis was beside me immediately, staring. He put his handkerchief to his mouth and turned away, ashen-faced.

"Ye gods!" he said. "You've killed Tcho-Tcho!"

"Maybe I just stunned her?" I staggered over to see. Lewis staggered with me. We stood looking down at Tcho-Tcho.

"Nope," Lewis told me sadly, shaking his head.

"The Devil, and the Devil's Dam, and the Devil's . . . insurance agent." I swore, groping backward until I found a chair to collapse in. "Now what do we do?" I averted my eyes from the nasty little corpse and my gaze fell on the several shreddy parts that were all that remained of my left tennis shoe. "Hey! Look what the damn thing did to my sneaker!"

"How did she get in here, anyway?" Lewis wrung his hands.

"So much for my playing tennis with anybody tomorrow," I snarled.

"But—but if she was in here long enough to chew up your shoe . . ." Lewis paused, eyes glazing over in difficult thought. "Oh, I wish I hadn't done that Theobromos. Isn't that the way it always is? Just when you think it's safe to relax and unwind a little—"

"Hey! This means Cartimandua Bryce took your Valentino script." I said, leaping to my feet and grabbing hold of the chair to steady myself. "See? The damn dog must have followed her in unbeknownst!"

"You're right." Lewis' eyes widened. "Except—well, no, not necessarily. She didn't have the dogs with her, don't you remember? They wouldn't behave at table. They had to be taken back to her room."

"So they did." I subsided into the chair once more. "Hell. If somebody was sneaking through the rooms, the dog might have got out and wandered around until it got in here, chewed up my shoe and went to sleep on my bed."

"And that means—that means—" Lewis shook his head. "I'm too tired to think what that means. What are we going to do about the poor dog? I suppose we'll have to go tell Mrs. Bryce."

"Nothing doing," I snapped. "When I'm in the middle of a deal with

Hearst? Hearst, who's fanatic about kindness to animals? Sorry about that, W.R., but I just brutally murdered a dear little chihuahua in La Casa Del Sol. Thank God there aren't any surveillance cameras in here!"

"But we have to do something," Lewis protested. "We can't leave it here on the rug! Should we take it out and bury it?"

"No. There's bound to be a search when Mrs. Bryce notices it's gone." I said. "If they find the grave and dig it up, they'll know the mutt didn't die naturally, or why would somebody take the trouble to hide the body?"

"Unless we hid it somewhere it'd never be found?" Lewis suggested. "We could pitch it over the perimeter fence. Then, maybe the wild animals would remove the evidence!"

"I don't think zebras are carrion eaters, Lewis." I rubbed my temples wearily. "And I don't know about you, but in the condition I'm in, I don't think I'd get it over the fence on the first throw. All I'd need then would be for one of Hearst's surveillance cameras to pick me up in a spotlight, trying to stuff a dead chihuahua through a fence. Hey!" I brightened. "Hearst has a zoo up here. What if we shotput Tcho-Tcho into the lion's den?"

Lewis shuddered. "What if we missed?"

"To hell with this." I got up. "Dogs die all the time of natural causes."

So we wound up flitting through the starry night in hyperfunction, leaving no more than a blur on any cameras that might be recording our passage, and a pitiful little corpse materialized in what we hoped was a natural attitude of canine demise on the front steps of La Casa Grande. With any luck it would be stiff as a board by morning, which would make foul play harder to detect.

Showered and somewhat sobered up, I opened the field credenza in my suitcase and crouched before it to tap out my report on its tiny keys:

WRH WILLING, HAD PT3 SAMPLE, BUT HOLDING OUT FOR MORE. TERMS: STOCK SHARES PLUS IMMORTALITY PROCESS. HAVE EXPLAINED IMPOSSIBILITY. REFUSES TO ACCEPT.

SUGGEST: LIE. DELIVER EIGHTEEN YEARS PER HISTORICAL RECORD WITH PROMISE OF MORE, THEN RENEGOTIATE TERMS WITH HEIRS.

PLEASE ADVISE.

It didn't seem useful to tell anybody that the Valentino script was missing. Why worry the Company? After all, we must be going to find it and complete at least that part of the mission successfully, because history records that an antique restorer will, on December 20, 2326, at the height of the Old Hollywood Revival, find the script in a hidden compartment in a Spanish cabinet, once owned by W.R. Hearst but recently purchased by Dr. Zeus Incorporated. Provenance indisputably proven, it will then be auctioned off for an unbelievably huge sum, even allowing for twenty-fourth century inflation. And history cannot be changed, can it?

Of course it can't.

I yawned pleasurably, preparing to shut the credenza down for the night, but it beeped to let me know a message was coming in. I scowled at it and leaned close to see what it said.

TERMS ACCEPTABLE. INFORM HEARST AND AT FIRST OPPORTUNITY PERFORM REPAIRS AND UPGRADE. QUINTILIUS WILL CONTACT WITH STOCK OPTIONS.

I read it through twice. Oh, okay; the Company must mean they intended to follow my suggestion. I'd promise him the moon but give him the eighteen years decreed by history, and he wouldn't even be getting those if I didn't do that repair work on his heart. What did they mean by *upgrade*, though? Eh! Details.

And I had no reason to feel lousy about lying to the old man. How many mortals even get to make it to 88, anyway? And when my stopgap measures finally failed, he'd close his eyes and die—like a lot of mortals—in happy expectation of eternal life after death. Of course, he'd get it in Heaven (if there is such a place) and not down here like he'd been promised, but he'd be in no position to sue me for breach of contract anyway.

I acknowledged the transmission and shut down at last. Yawning again, I crawled into my fabulous priceless antique Renaissance-era hand-carved gilded bed. The chihuahua hadn't peed on it. That was something, at least.

I slept in next morning, though I knew Hearst preferred his guests to rise with the sun and do something healthy like ride five miles before breakfast. I figured he'd make an exception in my case. Besides, if the PT3 cocktail had delivered its usual kick he'd probably be staying in bed late himself, and so would Marion. I squinted up at the left-hand tower of La Casa Grande, making my way through the brilliant sunlight.

No dead dog in sight anywhere, as I hauled open the big front doors; Tcho-Tcho's passing must have been discovered without much commotion. Good. I walked through the cool and the gloom of the big house to the morning room at the other end, where sunlight poured in through French doors. There a buffet was set out with breakfast.

Lewis was there ahead of me, loading up on flapjacks. I heaped hash browns on my plate and, for the benefit of the mortals in various corners of the room, said brightly:

"So, Lewis! Some swell room, huh? How'd you sleep?"

"Fine, thanks," he replied. *Other than a slight Theobromos hangover.* "But, you know, the saddest thing happened! One of Mrs. Bryce's little dogs got out in the night and died of exposure. The servants found it this morning."

"Gee, that's too bad." *Anybody suspect anything?*

No. "Yes, Mrs. Bryce is dreadfully upset." *I feel just awful.*

Hey, did you lure the damn mutt into my room? We've got worse things to worry about this morning. I helped myself to coffee and carried my plate out into the dining hall, sitting down at the long table. Lewis followed me.

Right, the Valentino script. Have you had any new ideas about who might have taken it?

No. I dug into my hash browns. *Has anybody else complained about anything missing from their rooms?*

No, *nobody's said a word.*

The thing is—nobody knew you had it with you, right? You didn't happen to mention that you were carrying around an autographed script for The Son of the Sheik?

No, of course not! Lewis sipped his coffee, looking slightly affronted. *I've only been in this business for nearly two millennia.*

Maybe one of the guests was after Garbo or Gable, and got into your room by mistake? I turned nonchalantly to glance into the morning room at Gable. He was deeply immersed in the sports section of one of Mr. Hearst's papers.

Well, if it was an obsessive Garbo fan he'd have seen pretty quickly that he wasn't in a woman's room. Lewis put both elbows on the table in a manly sort of way. *So if it was one of the ladies after Gable—? Though it still doesn't explain why she'd steal the script.*

I glanced over at Connie, who was sitting in an easy chair balancing a plate of scrambled eggs on her knees as she ate. *Connie wouldn't have done it, and neither would Marion. I doubt it was the Hearst kid's popsy. That leaves Garbo and Mrs. Bryce, who left the movie early.*

But why would Garbo steal the script? Lewis drew his eyebrows together.

Why does Garbo do anything? I shrugged. Lewis looked around uneasily.

I can't see her rifling through my belongings, however. And that leaves Mrs. Bryce.

Yeah. Mrs. Bryce. Whose little dog appeared mysteriously in my bedroom.

I got up and crossed back into the morning room on the pretext of going for a coffee refill. Mrs. Bryce, clad in black pajamas, was sitting alone in a prominent chair, with Conqueror Worm greedily wolfing down Eggs Benedict from a plate on the floor. Mrs. Bryce was not eating. Her eyes were closed and her face turned up to the ceiling. I guess she was meditating, since she was doing the whole lotus position bit.

As I passed, Conqueror Worm left off eating long enough to raise his tiny head and snarl at me.

"I hope you will excuse him, Mr. Denham," said Mrs. Bryce, without opening her eyes. "He's very protective of me just now."

"That's okay, Mrs. Bryce," I said affably, but I kept well away from the dog. "Sorry to hear about your sad loss."

"Oh, Tcho-Tcho remains with us still," she said serenely. "She has merely ascended to the next astral plane. I just received a communication from her, in fact. She discarded her earthly body in order to accomplish her more important work."

"Gee, that's just great," I replied, and Gable looked up from his paper at me and rolled his eyes. I shrugged and poured myself more coffee. I still thought Mrs. Bryce was a phony on the make, but if she wanted to pretend Tcho-Tcho had passed on voluntarily instead of being swatted like a tennis ball, that was all right with me.

You think she might have done it, after all? Lewis wondered as I came back to the table. *She had sort of fixated on me, before Marion turned her on Garbo.*

Could be. I think she's too far off on another planet to be organized enough for cat burglary, though. And why would she steal the script and nothing else?

I can't imagine. What are we going to do? Lewis twisted the end of his paper napkin. *Should we report the theft to Mr. Hearst?*

Hell no. That'd queer my pitch. Some representatives of an all-powerful Company we'd look, wouldn't we, letting mortals steal stuff out of our rooms? No. Here's what you do: see if you can talk to the people who left the theater early, one by one. Just sort of engage them in casual conversation. Find out where each one of the suspects went, and see if you can crosscheck their stories with others.

Lewis looked panicked. *But—I'm only a Literature Preservation Specialist. Isn't this interrogation sort of thing more in your line of work, as a Facilitator?*

Maybe, but right now I've got my hands full, I responded, just as the lord of the manor came striding into the room.

Mr. Hearst was wearing jodhpurs and boots, was flushed with exertion. He hadn't got up late after all, but had been out on horseback surveying his domain, like one of the old Californio dons. He hit me with a triumphant look as he marched past, but didn't stop. Instead he went straight up to Mrs. Bryce's chair and took off his hat to address her. Conqueror Worm looked up and him and cowered, then ran to hide behind the chair.

"Ma'am, I was so sorry to hear about your little dog! I hope you'll do me the honor of picking out another from my kennels? I don't think we have any chihuahuas at present, but in my experience a puppy consoles you a good deal when you lose an old canine friend," he told her, with a lot more power and breath in his voice than he'd had last night. The PT3 was working, that much was certain.

Mrs. Bryce looked up from her meditation, startled. Smiling radiantly she rose to her feet.

"Why, Mr. Hearst, you are too kind," she replied. No malarkey about ascendance to astral planes with him, I noticed. He offered her his arm and they swept out through the French doors, with Conqueror Worm running after them desperately.

What happens when we've narrowed down the list of suspects? Lewis tugged at my attention.

Then we steal the script back, I told him.

But how? Lewis tore his paper napkin clean in half. *Even if we move fast enough to confuse the surveillance cameras in the halls—*

We'll figure something out, I replied, and then shushed him, because Marion came floating in.

Floating isn't much of an exaggeration, and there was no booze doing the levitation for her this morning. Marion Davies was one happy mortal. She spotted Connie and made straight for her. Connie looked up and offered a glass.

"I saved ya some Arranch Use, Marion," she said meaningfully. The orange juice was probably laced with gin. She and Marion were drinking buddies.

"Never mind that! C'mere," Marion told her, and they went over to whisper and giggle in a corner. Connie was looking incredulous.

And are you sure we can rule the servants out? Lewis persisted.

Maybe, I replied, and shushed him again, because Marion had noticed me and broken off her chat with Connie, her smile fading. She got up and approached me hesitantly.

"J-Joe? I need to ask you about something."

"Please, take my seat, Miss Davies." Lewis rose and pulled the chair out for her. "I was just going for a stroll."

"Gee, he's a gentleman, too," Marion said, giggling, but there was a little edge under her laughter. She sank down across from me, and waited until Lewis had taken his empty plate and departed before she said.

"Did you—um—come up here to ask Pops for m-money?"

"Aw, hell, no," I said in my best Regular Guy voice. "I wouldn't do something like that, Marion."

"Well, I didn't really think so," she admitted, looking at the table and pushing a few grains of spilled salt around with her fingertip. "He doesn't pay blackmailers, you know. But—y-you've got a reputation as a man who knows a lot of secrets, and I just thought—if you'd used me to get up here to talk to him—" She looked at me with narrowed eyes. "That wouldn't be very nice."

"No, it wouldn't," I agreed. "And I swear I didn't come up here to do anything like that. Honest."

Marion just nodded. "The other thing I thought it might be," she went on, "was that you might be selling some kind of patent medicine. A lot of people know he's interested in longevity, and it looked like he'd been drinking something red out of his coffee cup, you see." Her mouth was hard. "He may be a millionaire and he's terribly smart, but people take advantage of him all the time."

"Not me," I said, and looked around as though I wanted to see who might be listening. I leaned across the table to speak close to her ear. "Listen, honey, the truth is—I really did need his advice about something. And he was kind enough to listen. But it's a private matter and believe me, *he's* not the one being blackmailed. See?"

"Oh!" She thought she saw. "Is it Mr. Mayer?"

"Why, no, not at all," I answered hurriedly, in a tone that implied exactly the opposite. Her face cleared.

"Gee, poor Mr. Mayer," she said. She knitted her brows. "So you didn't give W.R. any kind of . . . spring tonic or something?"

"Where would I get something like that?" I looked confused, as I would be if I were some low-level studio dick who handled crises for executives and had never heard of PT3.

"Yeah." Marion reached over and patted my hand. "I'm sorry. I just wanted to be sure."

"I don't blame you," I said, getting to my feet. "But please don't worry, okay?"

She had nothing to worry about, after all. Unlike me. I still had to talk to Mr. Hearst.

I strolled out through the grounds to look for him. He found me first, though, looming abruptly into my path.

"Mr. Denham." Hearst grinned at me. "I must commend you on that stuff. It works. Have you communicated with your people?"

"Yes, sir, I have," I assured him, keeping my voice firm and hearty.

"Good. Walk with me, will you? I'd like to hear what they had to say." He started off, and I had to run to fall into step beside him.

"Well—they've agreed to your terms. I must say I'm a little surprised." I laughed in an embarrassed kind of way. "I never thought it was possible to grant a mortal what you're asking for, but you know how it is—the rank and file aren't told everything, I guess."

"I suspected that was how it was," Hearst told me placidly. His little dachshund came racing to greet him. He scooped her up and she licked his face in excitement. "So. How is this to be arranged?"

"As far as the shares of stock go, there'll be another gentleman getting in touch with you pretty soon," I said. "I'm not sure what name he'll be using, but you'll know him. He'll mention my name, just as I mentioned Mr. Shaw's."

"Very good. And the other matter?"

Boy, the other matter. "I can give you a recipe for a tonic you'll drunk on a daily basis," I said, improvising. "Your own staff can make it up."

"As simple as that?" He looked down at me sidelong, and so did the dog. "Is it the recipe for what I drank last night?"

"Oh, no, sir," I told him truthfully. "No, this will be something to prolong your life until the date history decrees that you *appear* to die. See? But it'll all be faked. One of our doctors will be there to pronounce you dead, and instead of being taken away to a mortuary, you'll go to one of our hospitals and be made immortal in a new body."

That part was a whopping big bald-faced lie, of course. I felt sweat beading on my forehead again, as we walked along through the garden and Hearst took his time about replying.

"It all sounds plausible," he said at last. "Though of course I've no way of knowing whether your people will keep their word. Have I?"

"You'd just have to trust us," I agreed. "But look at the way you feel right now! Isn't that proof enough?"

"It's persuasive," he replied, but left the sentence unfinished. We walked on. Okay, I needed to impress him again.

"See that pink rose?" I pointed to a bush about a hundred yards away, where one big bloom was just opening.

"I see it, Mr. Denham."

"Count to three, okay?"

"One," Hearst said, and I was holding the rose in front of his eyes. He went pale. Then he smiled again, wide and genuine. The little dog *whuffed* at me uncertainly.

"Pretty good," he said. "And can you 'put a girdle round about the earth in forty minutes'?"

"I might, if I could fly," I said. "No wings, though. You don't want wings too, do you, Mr. Hearst?"

He just laughed. "Not yet. I believe I'll go wash up now, and then head off to the tennis court. Do you play, Mr. Denham?"

"Gee, I just love tennis," I replied, "but, you know, I got all the way up here and discovered I'd only packed one tennis shoe?"

"Oh, I'll have a pair brought out for you." Hearst looked down at my feet. "You're, what, about a size six?"

"Yes, sir," I said with a sinking feeling.

"They'll be waiting for you at the court," Hearst informed me. "Try to play down to my speed, will you?" He winked hugely and ambled away.

I was on my way back to the breakfast room with the vague hope of drinking a bottle of pancake syrup or something when I came upon Lewis. He was creeping along a garden path, keenly watching a flaxen-haired figure slumped on a marble bench amid the roses.

"What are you doing, Lewis?" I said.

"What does it look like I'm doing?" he replied *sotto voce*. "I'm stalking Garbo."

"All right . . ." I must have looked dubious, because he drew himself up indignantly.

"Can you think of any other way to start a casual conversation with her?" he demanded. "And I've worked out a way—" he looked around and transmitted the rest, *I've worked out quite a clever way of detecting the guilty party.*

Oh yeah?

You see, I just engage Garbo in conversation and then sort of artlessly mention that I didn't catch the end of Going Hollywood *because I had a dreadful migraine headache, so I went back to my room early, and would she tell me how it came out? And if she's not the thief, she'll just explain that she left early too and has no idea how it turned out. But! If she's the one who took the script, she'll know I'm lying, because she'll have been in my room and seen I wasn't there. And she'll be so disconcerted that her blood pressure will rise, her pulse will race, her pupils will dilate and she'll display all the other physical manifestations that would show up on a polygraph if I happened to be using one! And then I'll know.*

Ingenious, I admitted. *Worked all the time for me, when I was an Inquisitor.*

Thank you. Lewis beamed.

Of course, first you have to get Garbo to talk to you.

Lewis nodded, looking determined. He resumed his ever-so-cautious advance on the Burning Icicle. I shrugged and went back to La Casa Del Sol to change into tennis togs.

Playing tennis with W.R. Hearst called for every ounce of the guile and finesse that had made me a champion in the Black Legend All-Stars, believe me. I had to demonstrate all kinds of hyperfunction stunts a mortal wouldn't be able to do, like appearing on both sides of the net at once, just to impress him with my immortalness; and yet I had to avoid killing the old man with the ball, and—oh yeah—let him win somehow, too. I'd like to see Bill Tilden try it some time.

It was hell. Hearst seemed to think it was funny; at least, he was in a great mood watching me run around frantically while he kept his position in center court, solid as a tower. He returned my sissy serves with all the force of cannon fire. His dog watched from beyond the fence, standing up on her hind legs to bark suspiciously. She was *sure* there was something funny about me now. Thank God Gable put in an appearance after about an hour of this, and I was able to retire to the sidelines and wheeze, and swear a tougher hour was never wasted there. Hearst paused before his game long enough to make a brief call from a courtside phone. Two minutes later, there was a smiling servant offering me a glass of ice-cold ginger ale.

Gable didn't beat Hearst, either, and I think he actually tried. Clark wasn't much of a toady.

I begged off to go shower—dark hairy guys who play tennis in hyperfunction tend to stink—and slipped out afterward to do some reconnoitering.

Tonight I planned to slip in some minor heart surgery on Hearst as he slept, to guarantee those eighteen years the Company was giving him. The trick was going to be getting in undetected. There had to be another way to reach Hearst's rooms besides his private elevator, but there were no stairs visible in any of the rooms I'd been in. How did the servants get up there?

Prowling slowly around the house and bouncing sonar waves off the outside, I found a couple of ways to ascend. The best, for my purposes, was a tiny spiral staircase that was entered from the east terrace. I could sneak through the garden, go straight up, find my way to Hearst's bedroom and depart the same way once I'd fixed his heart. I could even wear the tennis shoes he'd so thoughtfully loaned me.

I was wandering in the direction of the Neptune pool when there was a hell of a racket from the shrubbery ahead of me. Conqueror Worm came darting out, yapping savagely. I was composed enough not to kick him as he raced up to my ankles. He growled and backed away when I bared my teeth at him in my friendliest fashion.

"Hi, doggie," I said. "Poor little guy, where's your mistress?"

A dark-veiled figure that had been standing perfectly still on the other side of the hedge decided to move, and Cartimandua Bryce walked forward calling out:

"Conqueror! Oh! Conqueror, you mustn't challenge Mr. Denham." She came around the corner and saw me.

There was a pause. I think she was waiting for me to demand in astonishment how she'd known it was me, but instead I inquired:

"Where's your new dog?"

"Still in Mr. Hearst's kennels," she replied, with a proud lift of her head. "Dear Mr. Hearst is having a traveling-basket made for her. Such a kind man!"

"He's a swell guy, all right," I agreed.

"And just as generous in this life as in his others," she went on. "But, you know, being a Caesar taught him that. Ruling the Empire either ennobled a man or brought out his worst vices. Clearly, our host was one of those on whom the laurel crown conferred refinement. Of course, he is a very old soul."

"No kidding?"

"Oh, yes. He has come back many, many times. Many are the names he has borne: Pharaoh, and Caesar, and High King," Mrs. Bryce told me, in as matter-of-fact a voice as though she was listing football trophies. "He has much work to do on this plane of existence, you see. Of course, you may well wonder how I know these things."

"Gee, Mrs. Bryce, how do you know these things?" I asked, just to be nice.

"It is my gift," she said, with a little sad smile, and she sighed. "My gift and my curse, you see. The spirits whisper to me constantly. I described this terrible and wonderful affliction in my novel *Black Covenant* which of course was based on one of my own past lives."

"I don't think I've read that one," I admitted.

"A sad tale, as so many of them are," she said, sighing again. "In the romantic Scottish Highlands of the thirteenth century, a beautiful young girl discovers she has an uncanny ability to sense both past and future lives of everyone she meets. Her gift brings inevitable doom upon her, of course. She finds her long-lost love, who was a soldier under Mark Antony when she was one of Cleopatra's handmaidens, and is now a gallant highwayman—I mean her lover, of course—and, sensing his inevitable death on the gallows, she dares to die with him."

"That's sad, all right." I agreed. "How'd it sell?"

"It was received by the discerning public with their customary sympathy," Mrs. Bryce replied.

"Is that the one they're doing a screenplay on?" I inquired.

"No," she said, looking me up and down. "That's *Passionate Girl*, the story of Mary, Queen of Scots, told from the unique perspective of her faithful terrier. I may yet persuade Miss Garbo to accept the lead role But, Mr. Denham—I am sensing something about you. Wait. You work in the film industry—"

"Yeah, for Louis B. Mayer," I said.

"And yet—and yet—" She took a step back and shaded her eyes as she looked at me. "I sense more. You cast a long shadow, Mr. Denham. Why—you, too, are an old soul!"

"Oh yeah?" I said, scanning her critically for Crome's radiation. Was she one of those mortals with a fluky electromagnetic field? They tend to receive data other mortals don't get, the way some people pick up radio broadcasts with tooth fillings, because their personal field bleeds into the temporal wave. I couldn't sense anything out of the ordinary in Mrs. Bryce, though. Was she buttering me up because she thought I could talk Garbo into starring in *Passionate Girl* at MGM? Well, she didn't know much about my relationship with Greta.

"Yes—yes—I see you in the Mediterranean area—I see you dueling with a band of street youths—is it in Venice, in the time of the Doges? Yes. And before that . . . I see you in Egypt, Mr. Denham, during the captivity of the Israelites. You loved a girl . . . yet there was another man, an overseer. . . ." Conqueror Worm might be able to tell there was something different about me, but his mistress was scoring a big metaphysical zero.

"Really?"

"Yes," she said, lowering her eyes from the oak tree above us, where she had apparently been reading all this stuff. "Do you experience disturbing visions, Mr. Denham? Dreams, perhaps of other places, other times?"

"Yeah, actually," I couldn't resist saying.

"Ah. If you desire to seek further—I may be able to help you." She came close and put her hand on my arm. Conqueror Worm prowled around her ankles, whining like a gnat. "I have some experience in, shall we say, arcane matters? It wouldn't be the first time I have assisted a questing soul in unraveling the mystery of his past lives. Indeed, you might almost call me a detective . . . for I sense you enjoy the works of Mr. Dashiell Hammett," she finished, with a smile as enigmatic as the Mona Lisa.

I smiled right back at her. Conqueror Worm put his tail between his legs and howled.

"Gosh, Mrs. Bryce, that's really amazing," I said, reaching for her hand and shaking it. "I do like detective fiction." And there was no way she could have known it unless she'd been in my room going through my drawers, where she'd have seen my well-worn copy of *The Maltese Falcon*. "Did your spirits tell you that?"

"Yes," she said modestly, and she was lying through her teeth, if her skin conductivity and pulse were any indication. Lewis was right, you see: we can tell as much as a polygraph about whether or not a mortal is truthful.

"You don't say?" I let go her hand. "Well, well. This has been really interesting, Mrs. Bryce. I've got to go see how my friend is doing now, but, you know, I'd really like to get together to talk with you about this again. Soon."

"Ah! Your friend with the fair hair," she said, and looked wise. Then she stepped in close and lowered her voice. "The haunted one. Tell me, Mr. Denham . . . is he . . . inclined to the worship of Apollo?"

For a moment I was struck speechless, because Lewis does go on sometimes about his Roman cultural identity, but then I realized that wasn't what Mrs. Bryce was implying.

"You mean, is he a homo?"

"Given to sins of the purple and crimson nature," she rephrased, nodding.

Now I knew she had the Valentino script, had seen Rudy's cute note and leaped to her own conclusions. "Uh . . . gee. I don't know. I guess he might be. Why?"

"There is a male spirit who will not rest until he communicates with your friend," Mrs. Bryce told me, breathing heavily. "A fiery soul with a great attachment to Mr. Kensington. One who has but recently passed over. A beautiful shade, upright as a smokeless flame."

The only question now was, why? One thing was certain: whether or not Lewis had ever danced the tango with Rudolph Valentino, Mrs. Bryce sure wished she had. Was she planning some stunt to impress the hell out of all these movie people, using her magic powers to reveal the script's whereabouts if Lewis reported it missing?

"I wonder who it is?" I said. "I'll tell him about it. Of course, you know, he might be kind of embarrassed—"

"But of course." She waved gracefully, as though dismissing all philistine considerations of closets. "If he will speak to me privately. I can do him a great service."

"Okay, Mrs. Bryce," I said, winking, and we went our separate ways through the garden.

I caught up with Lewis in the long pergola, tottering along between the kumquat trees. His tie was askew, his hair was standing on end, and his eyes shone like a couple of blue klieg lights.

"The most incredible thing just happened to me," he said.

"How'd you make out with Garbo?" I inquired, and then my jaw dropped, because he drew himself up and said, with an effort at dignity.

"I'll thank you not to speculate on a lady's private affairs."

"Oh, for crying out loud!" I hoped he'd had the sense to stay out of the range of the surveillance cameras.

"But I can tell you this much," he said, as his silly grin burst through again, "she absolutely did not steal my Valentino script."

"Yeah, I know," I replied. "Cartimandua Bryce took it after all."

"She—Really?" Lewis focused with difficulty. "However did you find out?"

"We were talking just now and she gave the game away," I explained. "Oldest trick in the book, for fake psychics: snoop through people's belongings in secret so you know little details about them you couldn't have known otherwise, then pull 'em out in conversation and wow everybody with your mystical abilities.

"What do you want to bet that's what she was doing when she sneaked out of the theater? She must have used the time to case people's rooms. That's how the damn dog got in our suite. It must have followed her somehow and gotten left behind."

"How sordid," Lewis said. "How are we going to get it back, then?"

"We'll think of a way." I said. "I have a feeling she'll approach you herself, anyhow. She's dying to corner you and give you a big wet kiss from the ghost of Rudolph Valentino, who she thinks is your passionate dead boyfriend. You just play along."

Lewis winced. "That's revolting."

I shrugged. "So long as you get the script back, who cares what she thinks?"

"I care," Lewis protested. "I have a reputation to think about!"

"Like the opinions of a bunch of mortals are going to matter in a hundred years!" I said. "Anyway, I'll bet you've had to do more embarrassing things in the Company's service. I know I have."

"Such as?" Lewis demanded sullenly.

"Such as I don't care to discuss just at the present time," I told him, flouncing away with a grin. He grabbed a pomegranate and hurled it at me, but I winked out and reappeared a few yards off, laughing. The lunch bell rang.

I don't know what Lewis did with the rest of his afternoon, but I suspect he spent it hiding. Myself, I took things easy; napped in the sunlight, went swimming in the Roman pool, and relaxed in the guest library with a good book. By the time we gathered in the assembly hall for cocktail hour again, I was refreshed and ready for a long night's work.

The gathering was a lot more fun now that I wasn't so nervous about Mr. Hearst. Connie got out a Parcheesi game and we sat down to play with Charlie and Laurence. The Hearst kid and his girlfriend took over one of the pianos and played amateurish duets. Mrs. Bryce made a sweeping entrance and backed Gable into a corner, trying out her finder-of-past-lives routine on him. Marion circulated for a while, before getting into a serious discussion of real estate investments with Jack from Paramount. Mr. Hearst came down in the elevator and was promptly surrounded by his executives, who wanted to discuss business. Garbo appeared late, smiling to herself as she wandered over to the other piano and picked out tunes with one finger.

Lewis skulked in at the last moment, just as we were all getting up to go to dinner, and tried to look as though he'd been there all along. The ladies went in first. As she passed him, Garbo reached out and tousled his hair, though she didn't say a word.

The rest of us—Mr. Hearst included—gaped at Lewis. He just straightened up, threw his shoulders back and swaggered into the dining hall after the ladies. My place card was immediately at Mr. Hearst's right, and Lewis was seated on the other side of me. It didn't get better than this. I looked nearly as smug as Lewis as I sat down with my loaded plate. Cartimandua Bryce had been given the other place of honor, though, at Marion's right, I guess as a further consolation prize for the loss of Tcho-Tcho. Conqueror Worm was allowed to stay in her lap through the meal this time. He took one look at me and cringed down meek as a lamb, only lifting his muzzle for the tidbits Mrs. Bryce fed him.

She held forth on the subject of reincarnation as we dined, with Marion drawing her out and throwing the rest of us an occasional broad wink, though not when Hearst was looking. He had very strict ideas about courtesy toward guests, even if he clearly thought she was a crackpot.

"So what you're saying is, we just go on and on through history, the same people coming back time after time?" Marion inquired.

"Not all of us," Mrs. Bryce admitted. "Some, I think, are weaker souls and fade after the first thundering torrent of life has finished with them. They are like those who retire from the ball after but one dance, too weary to respond any longer to the fierce call of life's music."

"They just soita go ova to da punchbowl and stay there, huh?" said Connie.

"In a sense," Mrs. Bryce told her, graciously ignoring her teasing tone. "The punchbowl of Lethe, if you will; and there they imbibe forgetfulness and remain. Ah, but the stronger souls plunge back headlong into the maelstrom of mortal passions!"

"Well, but what about going to Heaven and all that stuff?" Marion wanted to know. "Don't we ever get to do that?"

"Oh, undoubtedly," Mrs. Bryce replied, "for there are higher astral planes beyond this mere terrestrial one we inhabit. The truly great souls ascend there in time, as that is their true home; but even they yield to the impulse to assume flesh and descend to the mundane realms again, especially if they have important work to do here." She inclined across the table to Hearst. "As I feel *you* have often done, dear Mr. Hearst."

"Well, I plan on coming back after this life, anyhow," he replied with a smile, and nudged me under the table. I nearly dropped my fork.

"I don't know that I'd want to," said Marion a little crossly. "My g-goodness, I think I'd rather have a nice rest afterward, and not come back and have to go fighting through the whole darned business all over again."

Hearst lifted his head and regarded her for a long moment.

"Wouldn't you, dear?" he said.

"N-no," Marion insisted, and laughed. "It'd be great to have some peace and quiet for a change."

Mrs. Bryce just nodded, as though to show that proved her point. Hearst looked down at his plate and didn't say anything else for the moment.

"But anyway, Mrs. Bryce," Marion went on in a brighter voice. "Who else do you think's an old soul? What about the world leaders right now?"

"Chancellor Hitler, certainly," Mrs. Bryce informed us. "One has only to look at the immense dynamism of the man! This, surely, was a Teutonic Knight, or perhaps one of the barbarian chieftains who defied Caesar."

"Unsuccessfully," said Hearst in a dry little voice.

"Yes, but to comprehend reincarnation is to see history in its true light," Mrs. Bryce explained. "Over the centuries his star has risen inexorably, and will continue to rise. He is a man with true purpose."

"You don't feel that way about Franklin Delano Roosevelt, do you?" Hearst inquired.

"Roosevelt strives," said Mrs. Bryce noncommittally. "But I think his is yet a young soul, blundering perhaps as it finds its way."

"I think he's an insincere bozo, personally," Hearst said.

"Unlike Mussolini! Now there is another man who understands historical destiny, to such an extent one knows he has retained the experience of his past lives."

"I'm afraid I don't think much of dictators," said Hearst, in that castle where his word was law. Mrs. Bryce's eyes widened with the consciousness of her misstep.

"No, for your centuries—perhaps even eons—have given you the wisdom to see that dictatorship is a crude substitute for enlightened rule," she said.

"By which you mean good old American democracy?" he inquired. Wow, Mrs. Bryce was sweating. I have to admit it felt good to sit back and watch it happen to somebody else for a change.

"Well, of course she does," Marion said: "Now, I've had enough of all this history talk, Pops."

"I wanna know more about who *we* all were in our past lives, anyway," said Connie. Mrs. Bryce joined in the general laughter then, shrill with relief.

"Well, as I was saying earlier to Mr. Gable—I feel certain he was Mark Antony."

All eyes were on Clark at this pronouncement. He turned beet red but smiled wryly.

"I never argue with a lady," he said. "Maybe I was, at that."

"Oh, beyond question you were, Mr. Gable," said Mrs. Bryce. "For I myself was one of Cleopatra's maidens-in-waiting, and I recognized you the moment I saw you."

Must be a script for *Black Covenant* in development too.

There were chuckles up and down the table. "Whaddaya do to find out about odda people?" Connie persisted. "Do ya use one of dose ouija boards or something?"

"A crude parlor game," Mrs. Bryce said. "In my opinion. No, the best way to delve into the secrets of the past is to speak directly to those who are themselves beyond the flow of time."

"Ya mean, have a séance?" Connie looked intrigued. Marion's eyes lit up.

"That'd be fun, wouldn't it? Jeepers, we've got the perfect setting, too, with all this old stuff around!"

"Now—I don't know—" said Hearst, but Marion had the bit in her teeth.

"Oh, come on, it can't hurt anybody. Are you all done eating? What do you say, kids?"

"Aren't you supposed to have a round table?" asked Jack doubtfully.

"Not necessarily," Mrs. Bryce told him. "This very table will do, if we clear away dinner and turn out the lights."

There was a scramble to do as she suggested. Hearst turned to look at me sheepishly, and then I guess the humor of it got to him: an immortal being sitting in on a séance. He pressed his lips together to keep from grinning. I shrugged, looking wise and ironic.

Marion came running back from the kitchen and took her place at table. "Okay," she yelled to the butler, and he flicked an unseen switch. The dining hall was plunged into darkness.

"Whadda we do now?" Connie asked breathlessly.

"Consider the utter darkness and the awful chill for a moment," replied Mrs. Bryce in somber tones. "Think of the grave, if you are tempted to mock our proceedings. And now, if you are all willing to show a proper respect for the spirits—link hands, please."

There was a creaking and rustling as we obeyed her. I felt Hearst's big right hand enclose my left one. Lewis took my other hand. *Good Lord, it's dark in here,* he transmitted.

So watch, by infrared, I told him. I switched it on myself; the place looked really lurid then, but I had a suspicion about what was going to happen and I wanted to be prepared.

"Spirits of the unseen world," intoned Mrs. Bryce. "Ascended ones! Pause in your eternal meditations and heed our petition. We seek enlightenment! Ah, yes, I begin to feel the vibrations—there is one who approaches us. Can it be? But yes, it is our dear friend Tcho-Tcho! Freed from her disguise of earthly flesh, she once again parts the veil between the worlds. Tcho-Tcho, I sense your urgency. What have you to tell us, dear friend? Speak!"

I think most of the people in the room anticipated some prankster barking at that point, but oddly enough nobody did, and in the strained moment of silence that followed Mrs. Bryce let her head sag forward. Then, slowly, she raised it again, and tilted it way back. She gasped a couple of times and then began to moan in a tiny falsetto voice, incoherent sounds as though she were trying to form words.

"Wooooooo," she wailed softly. "Woooo Woo Woo Woo! Woo Woooo!"

There were vibrations then, all right, from fourteen people trying to hold in their giggles. Mrs. Bryce tossed her head from side to side.

"Wooooo," she went on, and Conqueror Worm sat up in her lap and pointed his snout at the ceiling and began to talk along with her in that way that dogs will, sort of *Wou-wou, wou-wou wou,* and beside me Hearst was shaking with silent laughter. Mrs. Bryce must have sensed she was losing her audience, because the woo-woos abruptly began to form into distinct words:

"*I have come back,*" she said. "*I have returned from the vale of felicity because I have unfinished business here. Creatures of the lower plane, there are spirits waiting with me who would communicate with you. Cast aside all ignorant fear. Listen for them!*"

After another moment of silence Marion said, in a strangling kind of voice: "Um—we were just wondering—can you tell us who any of us were in our past lives?"

"*Yes . . .*" Mrs. Bryce appeared to be listening hard. "*There is one . . . she was born on the Nineteenth day of April.*"

Connie sat up straight and peered through the darkness in Mrs. Bryce's direction. "Why, dat's my boithday!" she said in a stage whisper.

"*Yes . . . I see her in Babylon, Babylon that is fallen . . . yea, truly she lived in Babylon, queen of cities all, and carried roses to lay before Ishtar's altar.*"

"Jeez, can ya beat it?" Connie exclaimed. "I musta been a priestess or something."

"*Pass on now . . . I see a man, hard and brutal . . . he labors with his hands. He stands before towers that point at heaven . . . black gold pours forth. He has been too harsh. He repents . . . he begs forgiveness . . .*"

I could see Gable gritting his teeth so hard the muscles in his jaws stood out. His eyes were furious. I wondered if she'd seen a photograph of his father in his luggage. Or had Mrs. Bryce scooped this particular bit of biographical detail out of a movie magazine?

Anyway he stubbornly refused to take the bait, and after a prolonged silence the quavery voice continued:

"*Pass on, pass on . . . There is one here who has sailed the mighty oceans. I see him in a white cap. . . .*"

There was an indrawn breath from one of Hearst's executives. Somebody who enjoyed yachting?

"*Yet he has sailed the seven seas in another life . . . I see him kneeling before a great queen, presenting her with all the splendor of the Spanish fleet . . . this entity bore the name of Francis Drake.*"

Rapacious little pirate turned cutthroat executive? Hey, it could happen.

"*Pass on now . . .*" I could see Mrs. Bryce turn her head slightly and peer in Lewis' direction through half-closed eyes. "*Oh, there is an urgent message . . . there is one here who pleads to speak . . . this spirit with his dark and smoldering gaze . . . he begs to be acknowledged without shame, for no true passion is shameful . . . he seeks his other self.*"

Yikes! transmitted Lewis, horrified.

Okay. She wanted to convince us Rudolph Valentino was trying to say something? He was going to say something, all right. I didn't care whether Lewis or Rudy were straight or gay or swung both ways, but this was just too mean-spirited.

I pulled my right hand free from Lewis' and wriggled the left one loose from Hearst's. He turned his head in my direction and I felt a certain speculative amusement from him, but he said nothing to stop me.

So here's what Hearst's surveillance cameras and Dictaphones recorded next: a blur moving through the darkness and a loud crash, as of cymbals. Tcho-Tcho's voice broke off with a little scream.

Next there was a man's voice speaking out of the darkness, but from way high up in the air where no mortal could possibly be—like on the tiny ledge above the wall of choir stalls. If you'd ever heard Valentino speak (like I had, for instance) you'd swear it was him yelling in a rage:

"I am weary of lies! There is a thief here, and if what has been stolen is not returned tonight, the djinni of the desert will avenge. The punishing spirits of the afterlife will pursue! Do you DARE to cross me?"

Then there was a hiss and a faint smell of sulfur, and gasps and little shrieks from the assembled company as an apparition appeared briefly in the air: Valentino's features, and who could mistake them? His mouth was grim, his eyes hooded with stern determination, just the same expression as Sheik Ahmed had worn advancing on Vilma Banky. Worse still, they were eerily pallid against a scarlet shadow. Somebody screamed, really screamed in terror.

The image vanished, there was another crash, and then a confused moment in which the servants ran in shouting and the lights were turned on.

Everybody was sitting where they had been when the lights had gone out, including me. Down at the end of the table, though, where nobody was sitting, one of Mr. Hearst's collection of eighteenth-century silver platters was spinning around like a phonograph record.

Everyone stared at it, terrified, and the only noise in that cavernous place was the slight rattling as the thing spun slowly to a stop.

"Wow," said the Hearst kid in awe. His father turned slowly to look at me. I met his eyes and pulled out a handkerchief. I was sweating again, but you would be too, you know? And I used the gesture to drop the burnt-out match I had palmed.

"What the hell's going on?" said Gable, getting to his feet. He stalked down the table to the platter and halted, staring at it.

"What is it?" said Jack.

Gable reached out cautiously and lifted the platter in his hands. He tilted it up so everybody could see. There was a likeness of Valentino smeared on the silver, in some red substance.

"Jeez!" screamed Connie.

"What is that stuff?" said Laurence. "Is it blood?"

"Is it ectoplasm?" demanded one of the executives.

Gable peered at it closely.

"It's ketchup," he announced. "Aw, for Christ's sake."

Everyone's gaze was promptly riveted on the ketchup bottle just to Mr.

Hearst's right. Hard as they stared at it, I don't think anybody noticed that it was five inches further to his right than it had been when the lights went out.

Or maybe Mr. Hearst noticed. He pressed his napkin to his mouth and began to shiver like a volcano about to explode, squeezing his eyes shut as tears ran down.

"P-P-Pops!" Marion practically climbed over the table to him, thinking he was having a heart attack.

"I'm okay—" He put out a hand to her, gulping for breath, and she realized he was laughing. That broke the tension. There were nervous guffaws and titters from everyone in the room except Cartimandua Bryce, who was pale and silent at her place. Conqueror Worm was still crouched down in her lap, trembling, trying to be The Little Dog Who Wasn't There.

"Gee, that was some neat trick somebody pulled off!" said young Hearst.

Mrs. Bryce drew a deep breath and rose to her feet, clutching Conqueror Worm.

"Or—was it?" she said composedly. She swept the room with a glance. "If anyone here has angered the spirit of Rudolph Valentino, I leave it to his or her discretion to make amends as swiftly as possible. Mr. Hearst? This experience has taken much of the life force from me. I must rest. I trust you'll excuse me?"

"Sure," wheezed Hearst, waving her away.

She made a proudly dignified exit. I glanced over at Lewis, who stared back at me with wide eyes.

Nice work, he transmitted. I grinned at him.

I wouldn't go off to your room too early, I advised. *Give her time to put the script back.*

Okay.

"Well, I don't know about the rest of you," Hearst said at last, sighing, "but I'm ready for some ice cream, after that."

So we had ice cream and then went in to watch the movie, which was *Dinner at Eight*. Everybody stayed through to the end. I thought it was a swell story.

Lewis and I walked back to La Casa Del Sol afterward, scanning carefully, but nobody was lurking along the paths. No horrible little dog leaped out at me when I turned on the light in my room, either.

"It's here," I heard Lewis crowing.

"The script? Safe and sound?"

"Every page!" Lewis appeared in my doorway, clutching it to his chest. "Thank God. I think I'll sleep with it under my pillow tonight."

"And dream of Rudy?" I said, leering.

"Oh, shut up." He pursed his lips and went off to his room.

I relaxed on my bed while I listened to him changing into his pajamas, brushing his teeth, gargling and all the stuff even immortals have to do before bedtime. He climbed into bed and turned out the light, and maybe he dreamed about Rudy, or even Garbo. I monitored his brainwaves until I was sure he slept deeply enough. Time for the stuff he didn't need to know about.

I changed into dark clothes and laced up the tennis shoes Hearst had loaned me. Opening my black case, I slid out its false bottom and withdrew the sealed prepackaged medical kit I'd been issued from the Company HQ in Hollywood before coming up here. With it was a matchbox-sized hush field unit.

I stuck the hush unit in my pocket and slid the medical kit into my shirt. Then I slipped outside, and raced through the gardens of La Cuesta Encantada faster than Robin Goodfellow, or even Evar Swanson, could have done it.

The only time I had to pause was at the doorway on the east terrace, when it took me a few seconds to disable the alarm and pick the lock; then I was racing round and round up the staircase, and so into Hearst's private rooms.

I had the hush field unit activated before I came anywhere near him, and it was a good thing. There was still a light on in his bedroom. I tiptoed in warily all the same, hoping Marion wasn't there.

She wasn't. She slept sound in her own room on the other end of the suite. I still froze when I entered Hearst's room, though, because Marion gazed serenely down at me from her life-sized nude portrait on the wall. I looked around. She kept pretty strange company: portraits of Hearst's mother and father hung there too, as well as several priceless paintings of the Madonna and Child. I wondered briefly what the pictures might have to say to each other, if they could talk.

Hearst was slumped unconscious in the big armchair next to his telephone. Thank God he hadn't been using it when the hush field had gone on, or there'd be a phone off the hook and a hysterical night operator sending out an alarm now. He'd only been working late, composing an editorial by the look of it, in a strong confident scrawl on a lined pad. His dachshund was curled up at his feet, snoring. I set it aside gently and, like an ant picking up a dead beetle, lifted Hearst onto his canopied bed. Then I turned on both lamps, stripped off Hearst's shirt and took out the medical kit.

The seal hissed as I broke it, and I peeled back the film to reveal . . .

The wrong medical kit.

I stared into it, horrified. What was all this stuff? This wasn't what I needed to do routine heart repair on a mortal! This was one of our own kits, the kind the Base HQ repair facilities stocked. I staggered backward and collapsed into Hearst's comfy chair. Boy, oh boy, did I want some Pep-O-Mints right then.

I sat there a minute, hearing my own heart pounding in that big quiet house.

All right, I told myself, talented improvisation is your forte, isn't it? You've done emergency surgery with less, haven't you? Sure you have. Hell, you've used flint knives and bronze mirrors and leeches and there's bound to be something in that kit you can use.

I got on my feet and poked through it. Okay, here were some sterile Scrubbie Towelettes. I cleansed the area where I'd be making my incision. And here were some sterile gloves, great, I pulled those on. A scalpel. So far, so good. And a hemostim, and a skin plasterer, yeah, I could do this! And here was a bone laser. This was going to work out after all.

I gave Hearst a shot of metabolic depressant, opened him up and set to work, telling myself that somebody was going to be in big trouble when I made my report to Dr. Zeus. . . .

Hearst's ribs looked funny.

There was a thickening of bone where I was having to use the laser, in just the places I needed to make my cuts. Old trauma? Damned old. Funny-looking.

His heart looked funny too. Of course, I expected that. Hearst had a heart defect, after all. Still, I didn't expect the microscopic wired chip attached to one chamber's wall.

I could actually taste those Pep-O-Mints now. My body was simulating the sensation to comfort me, a defense against the really amazing stress I was experiencing.

I glanced over casually at the medical kit and observed that there was an almost exact duplicate of the chip, but bigger, waiting for me in a shaped compartment. So were a bunch of other little implants.

Repairs and upgrade. This was the right kit after all.

I set down my scalpel, peeled off my gloves, took out my chronophase and opened its back. I removed a small component. Turning to Hearst's phone, I clamped the component to its wire and picked up the receiver. I heard weird noises and then a smooth voice informing me I had reached Hollywood HQ.

"This is Facilitator Joseph and WHAT THE HELL IS GOING ON HERE?" I demanded.

"Downloading file," the voice replied sweetly.

I went rigid as the encoded signal came tootling through the line to me. Behind my eyes flashed the bright images: I was getting a mission report, filed in 1862, by a Facilitator Jabesh . . . assigned to monitor a young lady who was a passenger on a steamer bound from New York to the Isthmus of Panama, and from there to San Francisco. She was a recent bride, traveling with her much older husband. She was two months pregnant. I saw the pretty girl in pink, I saw the rolling seas, I saw the ladies in their bustles and the tophatted guys with muttonchop whiskers.

The girl was very ill. Ordinary morning sickness made worse by *mal de mer?* Jabesh—there, man in black, tipping his stovepipe hat to her—posing as a kindly doctor, attended her daily. One morning she fainted in her cabin and her husband pulled Jabesh in off the deck to examine her. Jabesh sent him for a walk around the ship and prepared to perform a standard obstetric examination on the unconscious girl.

Jabesh's horrified face: almost into his hands she miscarried a severely damaged embryo. It was not viable. His frantic communication, next, on the credenza concealed in his doctor's bag. The response: PRIORITY GOLD, with an authorization backed up by Executive Facilitator General Aegeus. The child was to live, at all costs. He was to make it viable. Why? Was the Company making certain that history happened as *written* again? But how could he save this child? With what? Where did he even start?

He downloaded family records. Here was an account of the husband having had a brother "rendered helpless" by an unspecified disease and dying young. Some lethal recessive? Nobody could make this poor little lump of flesh live! But the Company had issued a Priority Gold.

I saw the primitive stateroom, the basin of bloody water, Jabesh's shirtsleeves rolled up, his desperation. The Priority Gold blinking away at him from his credenza screen.

We're not bound by the laws of mortals, but we do have our own laws. Rules that are never broken under any circumstances, regulations that carry terrible penalties if they're not adhered to. We can be punished with memory effacement, or worse.

Unless we're obeying a Priority Gold. Or so rumor has it.

Jabesh repaired the thing, got its heart-bud beating again. It wasn't enough. Panicked, he pulled out a few special items from his bag (I had just seen one of them) and did something flagrantly illegal: he did a limited augmentation on the embryo. Still not enough.

So that was when he rolled the dice, took the chance. He did something even more flagrantly illegal.

He mended what was broken on that twisted helix of genetic material. He did it with an old standard issue chromosome patcher, the kind found in any operative's field repair kit. They were never intended to be used on mortals, let alone two-month-old embryos, but Jabesh didn't know what else to do. He set it on automatic and by the time he realized what it was doing, he was too late to stop the process.

It redesigned the baby's genotype. It surveyed the damage, analyzed what was lacking, and filled in the gaps with material from its own preloaded DNA arsenal. It plugged healthy chromosome sequences into the mess like deluxe Tinkertoy units until it had an organism with optimal chances for survival. That was what it was programmed to do, after all. But it had never had to replace so much in a subject, never had to dig so deeply into its arsenal for material, and some of the DNA in there was very old and very strange indeed. Those kits were first designed a hundred thousand years ago, after all, when *Homo sapiens* hadn't quite homogenized.

By the time the patcher had finished its work, the embryo had been transformed into a healthy hybrid of a kind that hadn't been born in fifty millennia, with utterly unknown potential.

I could see Jabesh managing to reimplant the thing and get the girl all tidy by the time her gruff husband came back. He was telling the husband she needed to stay off her feet and rest, he was telling him that nothing in life is certain, and tipping his tall hat, Good-Day, Sir, and staggering off to sit shaking in his cabin, drinking bourbon whiskey straight out of a case-bottle without the least effect.

He knew what he'd done. But Jabesh had obeyed the Priority Gold.

I saw him waiting, afraid of what might happen. Nothing did, except that the weeks passed, and the girl lost her pallor and became well. I could see her crossing at Panama—there was the green jungle, there was the now-visibly-pregnant mother sidesaddle on a mule—and here she was disembarking at San Francisco.

It was months before Jabesh could summon the courage to pay a call on her. Here he was being shown into the parlor, hat in hand. Nothing to see but a young mother dandling her adored boy. Madonna and child, to the life. One laughing baby looks just like another, right? So who'd ever know what Jabesh had done? And here was Jabesh taking his leave, smiling, and turning to slink away into some dark corner of history.

The funny thing was, what Jabesh had done wasn't even against the mortals' law. Yet. It wouldn't become illegal until the year 2093, because mortals wouldn't understand the consequences of genetic engineering until then.

But I understood. And now I knew why I'd wanted to turn tail and run the moment I'd laid eyes on William Randolph Hearst, just as certain dogs cowered at the sight of me.

The last images flitted before my eyes, the baby growing into the tall youth with something now subtly different about him, that unearthly voice, that indefinable quality of endlessly prolonged childhood that would worry his parents. Then! Downloaded directly into my skull before I could even flinch, the flashing letters: PRIORITY GOLD. *REPAIR AND UPGRADE.* Authorized by Facilitator General Aegeus, that same big shot who'd set up Jabesh.

I was trapped. I had been given the order.

So what could I do? I hung up the phone, took back my adapter component, pulled on a fresh pair of gloves and took up my scalpel again.

How bad could it be, after all? I was coming in at the end of the story, anyway. Eighteen more years weren't so much, even if Hearst never should have existed in the first place. Any weird genetic stuff he might have passed on to his sons seemed to have switched off in them. And, looking at the big picture, had he really done any harm? He was even a decent guy, in his way. Too much money, enthusiasm, appetite for life, an iron will and unshakable self-assurance . . . and a mind able to think in more dimensions than a human mind should. Okay, so it was a formula for disaster.

I knew, because I remembered certain men with just that kind of zeal and ability. They had been useful to the Company, back in the old days before history began, until they had begun to argue with Company policy. Then the Company had had a problem on its hands, because the big guys were immortals. Then the Company had had to fight dirty, and take steps to see there would never be dissension in its ranks again.

But that had been a long time ago, and right now I had a Priority Gold to deal with, so I told myself Hearst was human enough. He was born of woman, wasn't he? There was her picture on the wall, right across from Marion's. And he had but a little time to live.

I replaced the old tired implants with the fresh new ones and did a repair job on his heart that ought to last the required time. Then I closed him up and did the cosmetic work, and got his shirt back on his old body.

I set him back in his chair, returned the editorial he had been writing to his lap, set the dog at his feet again, gathered up my stuff, turned off the opposite lamp and looked around to see if I'd forgotten anything. Nope. In an hour or so his heart would begin beating again and he'd be just fine, at least for a few more years.

"Live forever, oh king," I told him sardonically, and then I fled, switching off the hush field as I went.

But my words echoed a little too loudly as I ran through his palace gardens, under the horrified stars.

Hearst watched, intrigued, as Lewis slid the Valentino script behind the panel in the antique cabinet. With expert fingers Lewis worked the panel back into its grooves, rocking and sliding it gently, until there was a click and it settled into the place it would occupy for the next four centuries.

"And to think, the next man to see that thing won't even be born for years and years," Hearst said in awe. He closed the front of the cabinet and locked it. As he dropped the key in his waistcoat pocket, he looked at Lewis speculatively.

"I suppose you're an immortal too, Mr. Kensington?" he inquired.

"Well—yes, sir, I am," Lewis admitted.

"Holy Moses. And how old are you?"

"Not quite eighteen hundred and thirty, sir."

"Not quite! Why, you're no more than a baby, compared to Mr. Denham here, are you?" Hearst chuckled in an avuncular sort of way. "And have *you* known many famous people?"

"Er—I knew Saint Patrick," Lewis offered. "And a lot of obscure English novelists."

"Well, isn't that nice?" Mr. Hearst smiled down at him and patted him on the shoulder. "And now you can tell people you've known Greta Garbo, too."

"Yes, sir," said Lewis, and then his mouth fell open, but Hearst had already turned to me, rustling the slip of paper I had given him.

"And you say my kitchen staff can mix this stuff up, Mr. Denham?"

"Yeah. If you have any trouble finding all the ingredients, I've included the name of a guy in Chinatown who can send you seeds and plants mail-order," I told him.

"Very good," he said, nodding. "Well, I'm sorry you boys can't stay longer, but I know what those studio schedules are like. I imagine we'll run into one another again, though, don't you?"

He smiled, and Lewis and I sort of backed out of his presence salaaming.

Neither one of us said much on the way down the mountain, through all those hairpin turns and herds of wild animals. I think Lewis was scared Hearst might still somehow be able to hear us, and actually I wouldn't have put it past him to have managed to bug the Model A.

Myself, I was silent because I had begun to wonder about something, and I had no way to get an answer on it.

I hadn't taken a DNA sample from Hearst. It wouldn't have been of any use to anybody. You can't make an immortal from an old man, because his DNA, no matter how unusual it is, has long since begun the inevitable process of deterioration, the errors in replication that make it unusable for a template.

This is one of the reasons immortals can only be made from children, see? The younger you are, the more bright and new-minted your DNA pattern is. I was maybe four or five when the Company rescued me, not absolute optimum for DNA but within specs. Lewis was a newborn, which is supposed to work much better. Might fetal DNA work better still?

That being the case . . . had Jabesh kept a sample of the furtive work he'd done, in that cramped steamer cabin? Because if he had, if Dr. Zeus had it on file somewhere . . . it would take a lot of work, but the Company *might* meet the terms of William Randolph Hearst.

But they wouldn't actually ever really do such a thing, would they?

We parked in front of the general store in San Simeon and I bought five rolls of Pep-O-Mints. By the time we got to Pismo Beach I had to stop for more.

END CREDITS: 2333

The young man leaned forward at his console, fingers flying as he edited images, superimposed them and rearranged them into startling visuals. When he had a result that satisfied him, he put on a headset and edited in the sound, brief flares of music and dialogue. He played it all back and nodded in satisfaction. His efforts had produced thirty seconds of story that would hold the viewers spellbound, and leave them with the impression that Japanese Imperial troops had brutally crushed a pro-Republic riot in Mazatlan, and Californians from all five provinces were rallying to lend aid to their oppressed brothers and sisters to the south.

Nothing of the kind had occurred, of course, but if enough people thought it had, it just might become the truth. Such things were known to happen.

And it was for everyone's good, after all, because it would set certain necessary forces in motion. He believed that democracy was the best possible system, but had long since quietly acknowledged to himself that government by the people seldom worked because people were such fools. That was all right, though. If a beautiful old automobile wouldn't run, you could always hook it up to something more efficient and tow it, and pretend it was moving of its own accord. As long as it got where you wanted it to go in the end, who cared?

He sent the story for global distribution and began another one, facts inert of themselves but presented in such a way as to paint a damning picture of the Canadian Commonwealth's treatment of its Native American neighbors on the ice mining issue. When he had completed about ten seconds of the visual impasto, however, an immortal in a gray suit entered the room, carrying a disc case.

"Chief? These are the messages from Ceylon Central. Do you want to review them before or after your ride?"

"Gosh, it's that time already, isn't it?" the young man said, glancing at the temporal chart in the lower left hand corner of the monitor. "Leave them here, Quint. I'll go through them this evening."

"Yes, sir." The immortal bowed, set down the case and left. The young man rose, stretched and crossed the room to his living suite. A little dog rose from where it had been curled under his chair and followed him sleepily.

Beyond his windows the view was much the same as it had been for the last four centuries: the unspoiled wilderness of the Santa Lucia mountains as far as the eye could see in every direction, save only the west where the sea lay blue and calm. The developers had been stopped. He had seen to it.

He changed into riding clothes and paused before a mirror, combing his hair. Such animal exploitation as horseback riding was illegal, as he well knew, having pushed through the legislation that made it so himself. It was good that vicious people weren't allowed to gallop around on poor sweating beasts any more, striking and shouting at them. He never treated his horses that way, however. He loved them and was a gentle and careful rider, which was why the public laws didn't apply to him.

He turned from the mirror and found himself facing the portrait of Marion, the laughing girl of his dreams, forever young and happy and sober. He made a little courtly bow and blew her a kiss. All his loved ones were safe and past change now.

Except for his dog; it was getting old. They always did, of course. There were some things even the Company couldn't prevent, useful though it was.

Voices came floating up to him from the courtyard.

". . . because when the government collapsed, of course Park Services didn't have any money any more," a tour docent was explaining. "For a while it looked as though the people of California were going to lose La Cuesta Encantada to foreign investors. The art treasures were actually being auctioned off, one by one. How many of you remember that antique movie script that was found in that old furniture? A few years back, during the Old Hollywood Revival?"

The young man was distracted from his reverie. Grinning, he went to the mullioned window, and peered down at the tour group assembled below. His dog followed him and he picked it up, scratching between its ears as he listened. The docent continued: "Well, that old cabinet came from here! We know that Rudolph Valentino was a friend of Marion Davies, and we think he must have left it up here on a visit, and somehow it got locked in the cabinet and forgotten until it was auctioned off, and the new owners opened the secret drawer."

One of the tourists put up a hand.

"But if everything was sold off—"

"No, you see, at the very last minute a miracle happened." The docent smiled. "William Randolph Hearst had five sons, as you know, but most of their descendants moved away from California. It turned out one of them was living in Europe. He's really wealthy, and when he heard about the Castle being sold, he flew to California to offer the Republic a deal. He bought the Castle himself, but said he'd let the people of California go on visiting Hearst Castle and enjoying its beauty."

"How wealthy is he?" one of the visitors wanted to know.

"Nobody knows just how much money he has," said the docent after a moment, sounding embarrassed. "But we're all very grateful to the present Mr. Hearst. He's actually added to the art collection you're going to see and—though some people don't like it—he's making plans to continue building here."

"Will we get to meet him?" somebody else asked.

"Oh, no. He's a very private man," said the docent. "And very busy, too. But you will get to enjoy his hospitality, as we go into the Refectory now for a buffet lunch. Do you all have your complimentary vouchers? Then please follow me inside. Remember to stay within the velvet ropes."

The visitors filed in, pleased and excited. The young man looked down on them from his high window.

He set his dog in its little bed, told it to stay, and then left by a private stair that took him down to the garden. He liked having guests. He liked watching from a distance as their faces lit up, as they stared in awe, as they shared in the beauty of his grand house and all its delights. He liked making mortals happy.

He liked directing their lives, too. He had no doubt at all of his ability to guide them, or the wisdom of his long-term goals for humanity. Besides, it was fun.

In fact, he reflected, it was one of the pleasures that made eternal life worth living. He paused for a moment in the shade of one of the ancient oak trees and looked around, smiling his terrible smile at the world he was making.

Night of Time

ROBERT REED

Robert Reed sold his first story in 1986, and quickly established himself as a frequent contributor to *The Magazine of Fantasy and Science Fiction* and *Asimov's Science Fiction*, as well as selling many stories to *Science Fiction Age, Universe, New Destinies, Tomorrow, Synergy, Starlight*, and elsewhere. Reed may be one of the most prolific of today's young writers, particularly at short-fiction lengths, seriously rivaled for that position only by authors such as Stephen Baxter and Brian Stableford. And—also like Baxter and Stableford—he manages to keep up a very high standard of quality *while* being prolific, something that is not at all easy to do. Reed stories such as "Sister Alice," "Brother Perfect," "Decency," "Savior," "The Remoras," "Chrysalis," "Whiptail," "The Utility Man," "Marrow," "Birth Day," "Blind," "The Toad of Heaven," "Stride," "The Shape of Everything," "Guest of Honor," "Waging Good," and "Killing the Morrow," among at least a half-dozen others equally as strong, count as among some of the best short work produced by anyone in the 80s and 90s and the early Oughts to date. Nor is he nonprolific as a novelist, having turned out eight novels since the end of the 80s, including *The Lee Shore, The Hormone Jungle, Black Milk, The Remarkables, Down the Bright Way, Beyond the Veil of Stars, An Exaltation of Larks, Beneath the Gated Sky*, and *Marrow*. His most recent book is the novel/collection (depending how you squint at it) *Sister Alice*. Upcoming is a new novel, *Marrow 2*. His stories have appeared in our Ninth through Seventeenth, our Nineteenth, and our Twentieth Annual Collections. Some of the best of his short work was collected in *The Dragons of Springplace*. Reed lives with his family in Lincoln, Nebraska.

Every year, the problem is not so much *whether* to use a Robert Reed story, but rather *which* Robert Reed story to use, out of a number of possible choices, any of which would make a respectable selection for a Best of the Year anthology. In the end, I decided to go for the quietly evocative story that follows, which shows that sometimes it's better to forget to remember . . .

Ash drank a bitter tea while sitting in the shade outside his shop, comfortable on a little seat that he had carved for himself in the trunk of a massive, immortal bristle-cone pine. The wind was tireless, dense and dry and pleasantly warm. The sun was a convincing illusion—a K-class star perpetually locked at an early-morning angle, the false sky narrow and pink, a haze of artful dust pretending to have been blown from some faraway hell. At his feet lay a narrow and phenomenally deep canyon, glass roads anchored to the granite walls, with hundreds of narrow glass bridges stretched from one side to the other, making the air below him glisten and glitter. Busier shops and markets were set beside the important roads, and scattered between them were the hive-like mansions and mating halls, and elaborate fractal statues, and the vertical groves of cling-trees that lifted water from the distant river: The basics of life for the local species, the 31-3s.

For Ash, business was presently slow, and it had been for some years. But he was a patient man and a pragmatist, and when you had a narrow skill and a well-earned reputation, it was only a matter of time before the desperate or those with too much money came searching for you.

"This will be the year," he said with a practiced, confident tone. "And maybe, this will be the day."

Any coincidence was minimal. It was his little habit to say those words and then lean forward in his seat, looking ahead and to his right, watching the only road that happened to lead past his shop. If someone were coming, Ash would see him now. And as it happened, he spotted two figures ascending the long glass ribbon, one leading the other, both fighting the steep grade as well as the thick and endless wind.

The leader was large and simply shaped—a cylindrical body, black and smooth, held off the ground by six jointed limbs. Ash instantly recognized the species. While the other entity was human, he decided—a creature like himself, and at this distance, entirely familiar.

They weren't going to be his clients, of course. Most likely, they were sightseers. Perhaps they didn't even know one another. They were just two entities that happened to be marching in the same direction. But as always, Ash allowed himself a seductive premonition. He finished his tea, and listened, and after a little while, despite the heavy wind, he heard the quick dense voice of the alien—an endless blur of words and old stories and lofty abstract concepts born from one of the galaxy's great natural intellects.

When the speaker was close, Ash called out. "Wisdom passes!"

A Vozzen couldn't resist such a compliment.

The road had finally flattened out. Jointed legs turned the long body, allowing every eye to focus on the tall, rust-colored human sitting inside the craggy tree. The Vozzen continued walking sideways, but with a fatigued slowness. His only garment was a fabric tube, black like his carapace and with the same slick texture. "Wisdom shall not pass," a thin, somewhat shrill voice called out. Then the alien's translator made adjustments, and the voice softened. "If you are a man named Ash," said the Vozzen, "this Wisdom intends to linger."

"I am Ash," he replied, immediately dropping to his knees. The ground beneath the tree was rocky, but acting like a supplicant would impress the species. "May I serve your Wisdom in some tiny way, sir?"

"Ash." the creature repeated. "The name is Old English. Is that correct?"

The surprise was genuine. With a half-laugh, Ash said. "Honestly, I'm not quite sure—"

"English," it said again. The translator was extremely adept, creating a voice that was unnervingly human—male and mature, and pleasantly arrogant. "There was a tiny nation-state, and an island, and as I recall my studies, England and its confederate tribes acquired a rather considerable empire that briefly covered the face of your cradle world."

"Fascinating," said Ash, looking back down the road. The second figure was climbing the last long grade, pulling an enormous float-pack, and despite his initial verdict, Ash realized that the creature wasn't human at all.

"But you were not born on the Earth." the Vozzen continued. "In your flesh and your narrow build, I can see some very old augmentations—"

"Mars," Ash allowed. "I was born on—"

"Mars," the voice repeated. That simple word triggered a cascade of memories, facts and telling stories. From that flood, the Vozzen selected his next offering. "Old Mars was home to some fascinating political experiments. From the earliest terraforming societies to the Night of the Dust—"

"I remember," Ash interrupted, trying to gain control over the conversation. "Are you a historian, sir? Like many of your kind—?"

"I am conversant in the past, yes."

"Then perhaps I shouldn't be too impressed. You seem to have been looking for me, and for all I know, you've thoroughly researched whatever little history is wrapped around my life."

"It would be impolite not to study your existence," said the Vozzen.

"Granted." With another deep bow, Ash asked, "What can this old Martian do for a wise Vozzen?"

The alien fell silent.

For a moment, Ash studied the second creature. Its skeleton and muscle were much like a man's, and the head wore a cap of what could have been dense brown hair. There was one mouth and two eyes, but no visible nose and the mouth was full of heavy pink teeth. Of course many humans had novel genetics, and there were remoras on the Ship's hull—men and women who wore every intriguing, creative mutation. But this creature was not human. Ash sensed it, and using a private nexus, he asked his shop for a list of likely candidates.

"Ash," the Vozzen said. "Yes, I have made a comprehensive study of your considerable life."

Ash dipped his head, driving his knees into the rough ground. "I am honored, sir. Thank you."

"I understand that you possess some rather exotic machinery."

"Quite novel. Yes, sir."

"And talents. You wield talents even rarer than your machinery."

"Unique talents," Ash replied with an effortless confidence. He lifted his eyes, and smiled, and wanting the advantage in his court, he rose to his feet, brushing the grit from his slightly bloodied knees as he told his potential client, "I help those whom I can help."

"You help them for a fee," the alien remarked, a clear disdain in the voice.

Ash approached the Vozzen, remarking, "My fee is a fair wage. A wage determined by the amoral marketplace."

"I am a poor historian," the Vozzen complained.

Ash gazed into the bright black eyes. Then with a voice tinged with a careful menace, he said, "It must seem awful, I would think. Being a historian, and being Vozzen, and feeling your precious memories slowly and inexorably leaking away..."

The Ship was an enormous derelict—a world-sized starship discovered by humans, and repaired by humans, and sent by its new owners on a great voyage around the most thickly settled regions of the galaxy. It was Ash's good fortune to be one of the early passengers, and for several centuries, he remained a simple tourist. But he had odd skills leftover from his former life, and as different aliens boarded the Ship, he made friends with new ideas and fresh technologies. His shop was the natural outgrowth of all that learning. "Sir," he said to the Vozzen. "Would you like to see what your money would buy?"

"Of course."

"And your companion—?"

"My aide will remain outside. Thank you."

The human-shaped creature seemed to expect that response. He walked under the bristlecone, tethering his pack to a whitened branch, and with an unreadable expression, stood at the canyon's edge, staring into the glittering depths, watching for the invisible river, perhaps, or perhaps watching his own private thoughts.

"By what name do I call you?"

"Master is adequate."

Every Vozzen was named Master, in one fashion or another. With a nod. Ash began walking toward the shop's doorway. "And your aide—"

"Shadow."

"His name is?"

"Shadow is an adequate translation." Several jointed arms emerged from beneath his long body, complex hands tickling the edges of the door, a tiny sensor slipped from a pocket and pointed at the darkness inside. "Are you curious, Ash?"

"About what, Master?"

"My companion's identity. It is a little mystery to you, I think."

"It is. Yes."

"Have you heard of the Aabacks?"

"But I've never seen one." Then after a silence, he mentioned, "They're a rare species. With a narrow intelligence and a fierce loyalty, as I understand these things."

"They are rather simple souls," Master replied. "But whatever their limits, or because of them, they make wonderful servants."

The tunnel grew darker, and then the walls fell away. With a silent command. Ash triggered the lights to awaken. In an instant, a great chamber was revealed, the floor tiled simply and the pine-faced ceiling arching high overhead, while the distant walls lay behind banks upon banks of machines that were barely awake, spelling themselves for those rare times when they were needed.

"Are you curious, Master?"

"Intensely and about many subjects," said the Vozzen. "What particular subject are you asking about?"

"How this magic works," Ash replied, gesturing with an ancient, comfortable pride. "Not even the Ship's captains can wield this technology. Within the confines of our galaxy, I doubt if there are three other facilities equally equipped."

"For memory retrieval," Master added. "I know the theory at play here. You manipulate the electrons inside a client's mind, increasing their various effects. And you manipulate the quantum nature of the universe, reaching into a trillion alternate but very similar realities. Then you combine these two quite subtle tricks, temporarily enlarging one mind's ability to reminisce."

Ash nodded, stepping up to the main control panel.

"I deplore that particular theory," his client professed.

"I'm not surprised."

"That many-world image of the universe is obscene. To me, it is simply grotesque and relentlessly ridiculous, and I have never approved of it."

"Many feel that way," Ash allowed.

A genuine anger surged. "This concept of each electron existing in countless realities, swimming through an endless ocean of potential, with every possible outcome achieved to what resembles an infinite number of outcomes—"

"We belong to one branch of reality," Ash interrupted. "One minor branch in a great tree standing in an endless canopy in the multiverse forest—"

"We are not," Master growled.

The controls awoke. Every glow-button and thousand-layer display had a theatrical purpose. Ash could just as easily manipulate the machinery through nexuses burned in his own body. But his clients normally appreciated this visible, traditional show of structured light and important sounds.

"We are not a lonely reality lost among endless possibility." In Vozzen fashion, the hind legs slapped each other in disgust. "I am a historian and a scholar of some well-earned notoriety. My long, long life has been spent in the acquisition of the past, and its interpretation, and I refuse to believe that what I have studied—this great pageant of time and story—is nothing more than some obscure twig shaking on the end of an impossible-to-measure shrub."

"I'm tempted to agree with you," Ash replied.

"Tempted?"

"There are moments when I believe . . ." Ash paused, as if selecting his next words. "I see us as the one true reality. The universe is exactly as it seems to be. As it should be. And what I employ here is just a trick, a means of interacting with the ghost realities. With mathematical whispers and unborn potentials. In other words, we are the trunk of a great and ancient tree, and the dreamlike branches have no purpose but to feed our magnificent souls . . . !"

The alien regarded Ash with a new respect. The respect showed in the silence, and then, with the hands opening, delicate spider-web fingers presenting themselves to what was, for at least this moment, their equal.

"Is that what you believe now?" Master asked.

"For the moment." Ash laughed quietly. Two nexuses and one display showed the same information: The historian had enough capital to hire him and his machinery. "And I'll keep believing it for a full day, if necessary."

Then he turned, bowing just enough. "What exactly is it that you wish to remember, Master?"

The alien eyes lost their brightness.

"I am not entirely sure," the voice confessed with a simple horror. "I have forgotten something very important . . . something essential, I fear . . . but I can't even recall what that something might be . . ."

Hours had passed, but the projected sun hadn't moved. The wind was unchanged, and the heat only seemed worse, as Ash stepped from the cool depths of his shop, his body momentarily forgetting to perspire. He had left his client alone, standing inside a cylindrical reader with a thousand flavors of sensors fixed to his carapace and floating free inside the ancient body and mind. Ash kept a close watch over the Vozzen. His nexuses showed him telemetry, and a mind's eye let him watch the scene. If necessary, he could offer words of encouragement or warning. But for the moment, his client was obeying the strict instructions, standing as motionless as possible while the machines made intricate maps of his brain—a body-long array of superconducting proteins and light-baths and quantum artesians. The alien's one slight cheat was his voice, kept soft as possible, but always busy, delivering an endless lecture about an arcane, mostly forgotten epoch.

The mapping phase was essential, and quite boring.

From a tiny slot in the pink granite wall, Ash plucked free a new cup of freshly brewed, deliciously bitter tea.

"A pleasant view," a nearby voice declared.

"I like it." Ash sipped his drink. As a rule, Aabacks appreciated liquid gifts, but he made no offer, strolling under the bristlecone, out of the wind and sun. "Do you know anything about the 31-3s?"

"I know very little," Shadow confessed. The voice was his own, his larynx able to produce clear if somewhat slow human words.

"Their home is tidally locked and rather distant from its sun." Ash explained. "Their atmosphere is rich in carbon dioxide, which my Martian lungs prefer." He tapped his own chest. "Water vapor and carbon dioxide warm the day hemisphere, and the winds carry the excess heat and moisture to the cold nightside glaciers, which grow and push into the dawn, and melt, completing the cycle." With an appreciative nod, he said, "The Ship's engineers have done a magnificent job of replicating the 31-3 environment."

Shadow's eyes were large and bright, colored a bluish gray. The pink teeth were heavy and flat-headed, suitable for a diet of rough vegetation. Powerful jaw muscles ballooned outwards when the mouth closed. A simple robe and rope belt were his only clothes. Four fingers and a thumb were on each hand, but nothing like a fingernail showed. Ash watched the hands, and then the bare, almost human feet. Reading the dirt, he felt certain that Shadow hadn't moved since he had arrived. He was standing in the sun, in the wind, and like any scrupulously obedient servant, he seemed ready to remain on that patch of ground for another day, or twenty.

"The 31-3s don't believe in time," Ash continued.

A meaningful expression passed across the face. Curiosity? Disdain? Then with a brief glance toward Ash, he asked, "Is it the absence of days and nights?"

"Partly. But only partly."

Shadow leaned forward slightly. On the bright road below, a pack of 31-3s was dancing along. Voices like brass chimes rose through the wind. Ash recognized his neighbors. He threw a little stone at them, to be polite. Then with a steady voice, he explained, "The endless day is a factor, sure. But they've always been a long-lived species. On their world, with its changeless climate and some extremely durable genetics, every species has a nearly immortal constitution. Where humans and Vozzens and Aabacks had to use modern bioengineering to conquer aging, the 31-3s evolved in a world where everything can live pretty much forever. That's why time was never an important concept to them. And that's why their native physics is so odd, and lovely—they formulated a vision of a universe that is almost, almost free of time."

The alien listened carefully. Then he quietly admitted, "Master has explained some of the same things to me, I think."

"You're a good loyal audience," Ash said.

"It is my hope to be."

"What else do you do for Master?"

"I help with all that is routine." Shadow explained. "In every capacity, I give him aid and free his mind for great undertakings."

"But mostly, you listen to him."

"Yes."

"Vozzens are compulsive explainers."

"Aabacks are natural listeners," said Shadow, with a hint of pride.

"Do you remember what he tells you?"

"Very little." For an instant, the face seemed human. An embarrassed smile and a shy blinking of the blue-gray eyes preceded the quiet admission, "I do not have a Vozzen's mind. And Master is an exceptional example of his species."

"You're right," said Ash. "On both accounts."

The alien shifted his feet, and again stared down at the 31-3s.

"Come with me."

"He wants me here," Shadow replied. Nothing in the voice was defiant, or even a little stubborn. He intended to obey the last orders given to him, and with his gentle indifference, he warned that he couldn't be swayed.

Sternly, Ash asked, "What does the Master want from this day?"

The question brought a contemplative silence.

"More than anything," said Ash, "he wants to recover what's most precious to him. And that is—"

"His memory."

Again, Ash said, "Come with me."

"For what good?"

"He talks to you. And yes, you've likely forgotten what he can't remember." Ash finished his tea in one long sip. "But likely and surely are two different words. So if you truly wish to help your friend, come with me. Come now."

"I do not deserve solitude," the Vozzen reported. "If you intend to abandon me, warn me. You must."

"I will."

Then, "Do you feel that?"

"Do I . . . what . . . ?"

"Anything. Do you sense anything unusual?"

The alien was tethered to a new array of sensors, plus devices infinitely more intrusive. Here and in a hundred trillion alternate realities, Master stood in the same position, legs locked and arms folded against his belly, his voice slightly puzzled, admitting, "I seem to be remembering my cradle nest."

"Is that unusual?"

"It is unlikely," the Vozzen admitted. "I don't often—"

"And now?"

"My first mate," he began. "In the nest, overlooking a fungal garden—"

"What about now?"

He paused, and then admitted, "Your ship. I am seeing the Great Ship from space, our taxi making its final approach." With a warm laugh, he offered, "It is a historian's dream, riding in a vessel such as this—"

"And now?" Ash prompted.

Silence.

"Where are you—?"

"Inside a lecture hall," Master replied.

"When?"

"Eleven months in the past. I am giving a public lecture." He paused, and then explained, "I make a modest living, speaking to interested parties."

"What do you remember about that day's lecture?"

"Everything," Master began to say. But the voice faltered, and with a doubting tone, he said, "A woman?"

"What woman?"

"A human woman."

"What about her?" Ash pressed.

"She was attending . . . sitting in a seat to my right . . . ? No, my left. How odd. I usually know where to place every face—"

"What was the topic?"

"Topic?"

"Of your lecture. The topic."

"A general history of the Great Wheel of Smoke—"

"The Milky Way," Ash interrupted.

"Your name for everyone's galaxy, yes." With a weblike hand, the alien reached in front of his own face. "I was sharing a very shallow overview of our shared history, naming the most important species of the last three billion years." The hand closed on nothing, and retreated. "For many reasons, there have been few genuinely important species. They have been modestly abundant, and some rather wealthy. But I was making the point . . . the critical line of reasoning . . . that since the metal-rich worlds began spawning intelligence, no single species, or related cluster of sentient organisms, have been able to dominate more than a small puff of the Smoke."

"Why is that?"

The simple question unleashed a flood of thoughts, recollections, and abstract ideas, filling the displays with wild flashes of color and elaborate, highly organized shapes.

"There are many reasons," Master warned.

"Name three."

"Why? Do you wish to learn?"

"I want to pass the time pleasantly," said Ash, studying the data with a blank, almost impassive face. "Three reasons why no species can dominate. Give them to me, in brief."

"Distance. Divergence. And divine wisdom."

"The distance between stars . . . is that what you mean . . . ?"

"Naturally," the historian replied. "Star-flight remains slow and expensive and potentially dangerous. Many species find those reasons compelling enough to remain at home, safe and comfortable, reengineering the spacious confines of their own solar system."

"Divergence?"

"A single species can evolve in many fashions. New organic forms. Joining with machines. Becoming machines. Sweeping cultural experiments. Even the total obliteration of physical bodies. No species can dominate any portion of space if what it becomes is many, many new and oftentimes competing species."

Ash blinked slowly. "What about divine wisdom?"

"That is the single most important factor," said Master. "Ruling the heavens is a child's desire."

"True enough."

616 night of time

"The galaxy is not a world, or even a hundred thousand worlds. It is too vast and chaotic to embrace, and with maturity comes the wisdom to accept that simple impossibility."

"What about the woman?"

"Which woman?" Master was surprised by his own question, as if another voice had asked it. "That human female. Yes. Frankly, I don't think she's important in the smallest way I don't even know why I am thinking about her."

"Because I'm forcing you to think about her."

"Why? Does she interest you?"

"Not particularly." Ash looked up abruptly, staring at the oval black eyes. "She asked you a question. Didn't she?"

"I remember. Yes."

"What question?"

"She asked about human beings, of course." With a gentle disdain, the historian warned, "You are a young species. And yes, you have been fortunate. Your brief story is fat with luck as well as fortuitous decisions. The Great Ship, as an example. Large and ancient, and empty, and you happened to be the species that found it and took possession. And now you are interacting with a wealth of older, wiser species, gaining knowledge at a rate rarely if ever experienced in the last three billion years—"

"What did she ask you?"

"Pardon me. Did you just ask a question?"

"Exactly. What did this woman say?"

"I think . . . I know . . . she asked. 'Will humanity be the first species to dominate the Milky Way?'"

"What was the woman's name?"

A pause.

Ash feathered a hundred separate controls.

"She did not offer any name," the historian reported.

"What did she look like?"

Again, with a puzzled air, the great mind had to admit, "I didn't notice her appearance, or I am losing my mind."

Ash waited for a moment. "What was your reply?"

"I told her, and the rest of my audience, 'Milk is a child's food. If humans had named the galaxy after smoke, they wouldn't bother with this nonsense of trying to consume the Milky Way.'"

For a long while, Ash said nothing.

Then, quietly, the historian inquired, "Where is my assistant? Where is Shadow?"

"Waiting where you told him to wait," Ash lied. And in the next breath, "Let's talk about Shadow for a moment. Shall we?"

"What do you remember . . . now . . . ?"

"A crunch cake, and sweet water." Shadow and Ash were standing in a separate, smaller chamber. Opening his mouth, he tasted the cake again. "Then a pudding of succulents and bark from the Gi-Ti tree—"

"Now?"

"Another crunch cake. In a small restaurant beside the Alpha Sea."

With a mild amusement, Ash reported. "This is what you remember best. Meals. I can see your dinners stacked up for fifty thousand years."

"I enjoy eating," the alien replied.

"A good Aaback attitude."

Silence.

And then the alien turned, soft cords dragged along the floor. Perhaps he had felt something—a touch, a sudden chill—or maybe the expression on his face was born from his own thoughts. Either way, he suddenly asked, "How did you learn this work, Ash?"

"I was taught," he offered. "And when I was better than my teachers, I learned on my own. Through experiment and hard practice."

"Master claims you are very good, if not the best."

"I'll thank him for that assessment. But he is right: No one is better at this game than me."

The alien seemed to consider his next words. Then, "He mentioned that you are from a little world. Mars, was it? I remember something . . . something that happened in your youth. The Night of the Dust, was it?"

"Many things happened back then."

"Was it a war?" Shadow pressed. "Master often lectures about human history, and you seem to have a fondness for war."

"I'm glad he finds us interesting."

"Your species fascinates him." Shadow tried to move and discovered that he couldn't. Save for his twin hearts and mouth, every muscle of his body was fused in place. "I don't quite understand why he feels this interest—"

"You attend his lectures, don't you?"

"Always."

"He makes most of his income from public talks."

"Many souls are interested in his words."

"Do you recall a lecture from last year?" Ash gave details, and he appeared disappointed when Shadow said:

"I don't remember, no." An Aaback laugh ended with the thought, "There must not have been any food in that lecture hall."

"Let's try something new," said Ash. "Think back, back as far as possible. Tell me about the very first meal you remember."

A long, long pause ended with. "A little crunch cake. I was a child, and it was my first adult meal."

"I used to be an interrogator," Ash said abruptly.

The eyes were gray and watchful.

"During that old war. I interrogated people, and on certain days, I tortured them." He nodded calmly, adding, "Memory is a real thing, Shadow. It's a dense little nest made, like everything, from electrons—where the electrons are and where they are not—and you would be appalled, just appalled, by all the ways that something real can be hacked out of the surrounding bullshit."

"Quee Lee."

"Pardon?"

"The human woman. Her name was, and is, Quee Lee." Ash began disconnecting his devices, leaving only the minimal few to keep shepherding the Vozzen's mind. "It was easy enough to learn her name. A lecture attended by humans, and when I found one woman, she told me about another. Who mentioned another friend who might have gone to listen to you. But while that friend hadn't heard of you, she mentioned an acquaintance of hers who had a fondness for the past, and her name is Quee Lee. She happened to be there, and she asked the question."

Relief filled Master, and with a thrilled voice, he said, "I remember her now, yes. Yes. She asked about human dominance in the galaxy—"

"Not quite, no."

Suspicion flowered, and curiosity followed. "She didn't ask that about human dominance?"

"It was her second question, and strictly speaking, it wasn't hers." Ash smiled and nodded, explaining, "The woman sitting next to her asked it. Quee Lee simply repeated the question, since she had won your attention."

A brief pause ended with the wary question:

"What then did the woman ask me?"

Ash stared at the remaining displays, and with a quiet firm voice said, "I've spoken with Quee Lee. At length. She remembers asking you, 'What was the earliest sentient life to arise in the galaxy?'"

The simple question generated a sophisticated response. An ocean of learning was tapped, and from that enormity a single turquoise thread was pulled free, and offered. Five candidates were named in a rush. Then the historian rapidly and thoroughly described each species, their home worlds, and eventual fates.

"None survived into the modern age," he said sadly "Except as rumor and unsubstantiated sightings, the earliest generation of intelligence has died away."

Ash nodded, and waited.

"How could I forget such a very small thing?"

"Because it is so small," Ash replied. "The honest, sad truth is that your age is showing. I'm an old man for my species, but that's nothing compared to you. The Vozzen journeyed out among the stars during my Permian. You have an enormous and dense and extraordinarily quick mind. But it is a mind. No matter how vast and how adept, it suffers from what is called bounded rationality. You don't know everything, no matter how much you wish otherwise. You're living in an enriched environment, full of opportunities to learn. And as long as you wish to understand new wonders, you're going to have to allow, on occasion, little pieces of your past to fade away."

"But why did such a trivial matter bother me so?" asked Master.

And then in the next instant, he answered his own question. "Because it was trivial, and lost. Is that why? I'm not accustomed to forgetting. The sensation is novel . . . it preyed upon my equilibrium . . . and wore a wound in my mind . . . !"

"Exactly, exactly," lied Ash. "Exactly, and exactly."

After giving him fair warning, Ash left the historian. "The final probes still need to disengage themselves," he explained. Then with a careful tone, he asked, "Should I bring your assistant to you? Would you like to see him now?"

"Please."

"Very well." Ash pretended to step outside, turning in the darkened hallway, centuries of practice telling him where to step. Then he was inside the secondary chamber, using a deceptively casual voice, mentioning to Shadow, "By the way, I think I know what you are."

"What I am?"

With a sudden fierceness, Ash asked, "Did you really believe you could fool me?"

The alien said nothing, and by every physical means, he acted puzzled but unworried.

Ash knew better.

"Your body is mostly Aaback, but there's something else. If I hadn't suspected it, I wouldn't have found it. But what seems to be your brain is an elaborate camouflage for a quiet, nearly invisible neural network."

The alien reached with both hands, yanking one of the cables free from his forehead. Then a long tongue reached high, wiping the gray blood from the wound. A halfway choked voice asked, "What did you see inside me?"

"Dinners." Ash reported. "Dinners reaching back for billions of years."

Silence.

"Do you belong to one of the first five species?"

The alien kept yanking cables free, but he was powerless to void the drifters inside his double-mind.

"No," said Ash, "I don't think you're any of those five." With a sly smile, he reported, "I can tell. You're even older than that, aren't you?"

The tongue retreated into the mouth. A clear, sorry voice reported, "I am not sure, no."

"And that's why," said Ash.

"Why?"

"The woman asked that question about the old species, and you picked that moment because of it." He laughed, nodded. "What did you use? How did you cut a few minutes out of a Vozzen's perfect memory . . . ?"

"With a small disruptive device—"

"I want to see it."

"No."

Ash kept laughing. "Oh, yes. You are going to show it to me!"

Silence.

"Master doesn't even suspect." Ash continued. "You were the one who wanted to visit me. You simply gave the Vozzen a good excuse. You heard about me somewhere, and you decided that you wanted me to peer inside his soul, and yours. You were hoping that I would piece together the clues and tell you what I was seeing in your mind—"

"What do you see?" Shadow blurted.

"Basically, two things." With a thought, he caused every link with Shadow to be severed, and with a professional poise, he explained, "Your soul might be ten or twelve years old. I don't know how that could be, but I can imagine: In the earliest days of the universe, when the stars were young and metal-poor, life found some other way to evolve. A completely separate route. Structured plasmas, maybe. Maybe. Whatever the route, your ancestors evolved and spread, and then died away as the universe grew cold and empty. Or they adapted, on occasion. They used organic bodies as hosts, maybe."

"I am the only survivor," Shadow muttered. "Whatever the reason, I cannot remember anyone else like me."

"You are genuinely ancient," Ash said, "and I think you're smarter than you pretend to be. But this ghost mind of yours isn't that sophisticated. Vozzens are smarter, and most humans, too. But when I was watching you thinking, looking at something simple—when I saw dinners reaching back for a billion years—well, that kind of vista begs for an explanation."

Ash took a deep breath, and then said, "Your memory has help. Quantum help. And this isn't on any scale that I've ever seen, or imagined possible. I can pull in the collective conscience of a few trillion Masters from the adjacent realities . . . but with you, I can't even pick a number that looks sane . . ."

The alien showed his pink teeth, saying nothing.

"Are you pleased?" Ash asked.

"Pleased by what?"

"You are probably the most common entity in Creation," said Ash. "I have never seen such a signal as yours. This clear. This deep, and dramatic. You exist, in one form or another, in a fat, astonishing portion of all the possible realities."

Shadow said, "Yes."

"Yes what?"

"Yes," he said with the tiniest nod, "I am pleased."

Always, the sun held its position in the fictional sky. And always, the same wind blew with calm relentlessness. In such a world, it was easy to believe that there was no such monster as time, and the day would never end, and a man with old and exceptionally sad memories could convince himself, on occasion, that there would never be another night.

Ash was last to leave the shop.

"Again," the historian called out, "thank you for your considerable help."

"Thank you for your generous gift." Ash found another cup of tea waiting for him, and he sipped down a full mouthful, watching as Shadow untethered the floating pack. "Where next?"

"I have more lectures to give," Master replied.

"Good."

"And I will interview the newest passengers onboard the Ship."

"As research?"

"And as a pleasure, yes."

Shadow was placing a tiny object beside one of the bristlecone's roots. "If you don't give that disruptor to me," Ash had threatened, "I'll explain a few deep secrets to the Vozzen."

Of course, Shadow had relented.

Ash sipped his tea, and quietly said, "Master. What can you tell me about the future?"

"About what is to come—?" the alien began.

"I never met a historian who didn't have opinions on that subject," Ash professed. "My species, for instance. What will happen to us in the next ten or twenty million years?"

Master launched himself into an abbreviated but dense lecture, explaining to his tiny audience what was possible about predicting the future and what was unknowable, and how every bridge between the two was an illusion.

His audience wasn't listening.

In a whisper, Ash said to Shadow, "But why live this way? With him, in this kind of role?"

In an Aaback fashion, the creature grinned. Then Shadow peered over the edge of the canyon, and speaking to no one in particular, he explained, "He needs me so much. This is why"

"As a servant?"

"And as a friend, and a confidant." With a very human shrug, he asked Ash, "How could anyone survive even a single day, if they didn't feel as if they were, in some little great way, needed?"

strong medicine

WILLIAM SHUNN

Here's an unsettling little story that suggests that some people may take an odd sort of comfort from the fact that the Four Horsemen are always saddled up and ready to ride, and that the fundamental things don't really change as the centuries go by—no matter how cold and bleak and grim those things *are* . . .

William Shunn has sold to *The Magazine of Fantasy & Science Fiction, Science Fiction Age, Realms of Fantasy, Vanishing Acts, In the Shadow of the Wall, Beyond the Last Star,* and *Electric Velocipede,* as well as to online venues such as *Salon.* He lives in Astoria, New York.

W ith two minutes left in the year 2037, Dr. Emmett Fairbairn took his antique black medical bag down from the high shelf in the study of his home in Arlington, Virginia. He set it on his desk, careful of the chessboard, and tugged open the stubborn catches. From inside he drew a .38-caliber Smith & Wesson revolver, not quite as ancient as the bag but still old. Fairbairn hefted the gun, studying it with the same focused regard he had once reserved for diseased hearts. He had considered several names for it over the past few days—Extreme Unction, The Last Anesthetic, Kevorkian's Shortcut—but none carried quite the weight, the *moment* he sought. Now, though, admiring the gun's obscenely black gleam, it came to him, as he had known it would.

"Strong Medicine," he said. "Good for what ails you."

An involuntary smirk creased his lips. A taste for black humor—as much as a low handicap, a weakness for nurses, and an incipient god complex—was one of the occupational hazards of three decades in the OR, a necessary counterweight to fingers that coiled daily between human ribs. Fairbairn had gone through more ribs in his day than a Texas barbecue. He had touched more hearts than the Pope, admired more inner beauty than a poet. In his day.

But that day was over, all praise nanomedicine.

Fairbairn cracked Strong Medicine's breech open wide. The cylinder's empty chambers stared at him like eye sockets in a skull. He drew five brass-bound bullets from the medical bag and began plugging them into the holes. Same as packing small wounds with gauze, or so he told himself. Shelly, Leiko, Rajani, Nadine—he named each bullet off in turn, his fingers steady as he seated each one in the cylinder.

He rolled the fifth and final cartridge like a prayer bead between thumb and forefinger. "And Ellen," he said in sardonic salutation, slotting it home. "Should old acquaintance be forgot."

For most of his professional life, guns had been Emmett Fairbairn's natural enemy. But old enemies could become the strangest of allies in strange times, and these times were the strangest he'd seen.

He snapped shut the breech and gave the cylinder a solid spin. One chamber remained empty, but that was how he wanted this—a nice little round of reverse Russian roulette, with the odds stacked high against him. If the universe wanted to keep him around, let it step in and tell him so.

One minute now to midnight. "Picture," he said, as calmly as if dictating orders to his surgical team. The holotank in the corner switched on, painting the wainscoted walls with a pearlescent glow. "Volume five."

Wild cheering erupted in the study, rattling from hidden speakers. An ebullient Times Square crowd—bundled in thick coats, many with arms upraised and waving—filled the tank. A fine snow whirled and eddied in the capricious Manhattan wind like a memory of yesteryear's static. As the holo-cameras panned across the scene, a reporter said in a hoarse, sexy voice, "As you can see, the mood here is exuberant. It's as if New Yorkers are saying, yet again, fuck terrorism, fuck our security, we're rich and healthy and happy, so bring it on, we're gonna party like it's 1999."

Fairbairn grimaced. Not a person in America who didn't want to be was hungry any longer, not when nanogrow starter kits were as plentiful and share-able as yeast and all it really took to make a meal was a freeware recipe and some garbage or mulch of acceptable composition. Nanogens to target infection and nanocisors to cleanly atomize diseased tissue had been in limited use at Walter Reed a decade earlier, but Fairbairn had seen the writing on the wall even before 2035's open-source revolution had blown the economies of scarcity and infirmity wide open. While the pharmaceutical companies strug-

gled to keep pace and tiny machines learned to do his job better and less trau-
matically than he ever could, Fairbairn tried to arrange a surgical fellowship
somewhere in the Third World, it didn't matter where.

It wasn't that he felt any particular altruism. He simply lived to cut—to
part and repair flesh with warm steel, sutures, and his own two hands, nothing
more. He had known this since his first incision in medical school, honed his
considerable talents in the emergency rooms of Baltimore, and come into his
own as a conscripted captain in the field hospitals of Syria, Turkey, and Saudi
Arabia. Five tumultuous marriages had come and gone, but Fairbairn's devo-
tion to the scalpel had never wavered. And if his talent wasn't needed in his
homeland, then surely he could ply his trade in some more needy country. He
would do it for free. It wasn't about money.

But just as his placement to Namibia was coming together, the U.S. sealed
its borders, not only to shut out a new generation of terrorists but to shut *in* the
technology that threatened to render their campaigns moot. The action was a
bust on both counts—a fresh bomb went off *somewhere* nearly every week, as
often as not the work of radical domestic groups, and fresh strains of nanoware
kept cropping up overseas—but that didn't get Fairbairn any closer to an
African hospital.

Desperate, he turned to old friends from the service. After a wait that
seemed interminable but was only a couple of months, passage was arranged
for a fee that devastated his savings. Fairbairn traveled to Eagle Pass, Texas,
where he was to meet the first of the couriers who would conduct him across
the Rio Grande, the equator, and the Atlantic. But the courier never materialized, leaving Fairbairn to speculate bitterly on the long autodrive home
whether he'd been the victim of a scam or a government sweep.

To judge by the big black cars he kept spotting in the neighborhood, it
might well have been the latter.

"Thirty seconds to midnight!" said the holoreporter.

"Local coverage," said Fairbairn, and the view in the tank changed to the
Washington Mall, a scant five miles away. The vast crowd paved the park like
living cobblestones, an illusion that only vanished when the holocameras
zoomed in on individual red-cheeked faces. Fairbairn settled back in the
leather chair behind his desk, Strong Medicine gripped in his left hand—his
cutting hand—like an unwieldy scalpel.

"Fifteen seconds!" cried a male reporter, and the crowd echoed his
countdown, pulsing at each beat like a great heart: "Fourteen . . . thirteen . . .
twelve . . . eleven . . ."

Fairbairn cocked Strong Medicine's hammer as the scene in the tank
shifted to the sky above the Lincoln Memorial. He pressed the barrel into the
soft flesh beneath his jaw, aiming straight up. As fireworks erupted over the
Potomac, a brilliant display of crimson and white would explode from the top

of his skull. Not all the king's horses nor all the king's meds could put all those pieces together again.

Idly Fairbairn wondered which ex-wife it would be that did the job.

". . . eight . . . seven . . . six . . ."

The circle of the barrel was cold and reassuring against his jaw. His finger tensed on the trigger. On impulse, he reached out with his right hand and tipped over the black king on the chessboard.

". . . three . . . two . . ."

The curtains drawn across the east-facing window of the study flashed translucent with a white light that immediately deepened to hellish orange. The picture in the holotank vanished, and the sound from the speakers deteriorated into an empty and deafening shriek before cutting out. The room went dark. Momentarily confused—had he pulled the trigger already? was this what a bullet to the brain felt like?—Fairbairn let his arm drop. Strong Medicine slipped from his nerveless fingers and clattered to the floor with a sound like stones rattling in a crypt.

It took a moment for Fairbairn to realize he was not dead. When he did, he stood numbly and pushed the curtains away from the window.

His study was on the second floor of the house. This gave him a lovely vantage on the patio and garden, but the reddish column of light rising into the overcast night to the northeast would have been visible from anywhere in the yard.

A preternatural quiet ruled the neighborhood. The lighted backs of houses stared up as if in hushed anticipation. A party with hats and noisemakers had frozen in awkward poses around their birdbath.

As they all watched, the column of smoky light bumped up against some invisible ceiling high in the sky and roiled over into the shape of a blooming mushroom.

"Jesus," said Fairbairn in awe.

His view was abruptly obscured by the black clouds of dust and debris that bore down upon Arlington like an army of thunderous tanks. He threw himself to the floor just as the shock wave hit. His window shattered into a million sparkling projectiles that tinkled and sang as they exploded against the opposite wall. He covered his head with his arms, but not before a freight train roared through the room.

Blackness enveloped him, buffeted him like a toy, and dragged him coughing and sputtering back to the surface of consciousness.

He pushed himself to his hands and knees. Moist warmth trickled from his right ear and down his jaw. His study lay in shambles around him, a warm wind stirring the remains of his professional life.

He pounded his precious hands on the floor.

But then, as if from deep underground, through miles of packed soil, he heard the screams. Dozens of them.

In his mind's eye, Fairbairn saw windows splintering to shrapnel up and down the street, debris raining down on the land, buildings slumping to ground in disordered heaps of brick and stone.

Fairbairn grabbed hold of the desk and pulled himself shakily to his feet, searching the dust-choked gloom for his other medical bag, the hard-sided case, the one that wasn't just for sentimentality and show. He found it under a pile of tumbled books. He tugged it out and shook off the worst of the dust.

He was on his way out the door of the study when he spied Strong Medicine lying in the middle of the floor. He paused, picked up the gun, and considered it a moment. He extended his arm, aimed at a corner of the ceiling, and curled his finger around the trigger.

But he lowered his arm without firing.

Dr. Fairbairn tucked the gun into the waistband of his trousers and descended to the living room. His home lay all in disarray, but as he exited into the gritty, swirling wind that prowled his ravaged neighborhood, as he entered that eerily muffled landscape of suffering, he felt power in his hands and healing in his wings, and he smiled.

send me a mentagram

DOMINIC GREEN

New British writer Dominic Green's output has to date been confined almost entirely to the pages of *Interzone*, but he's appeared there a *lot*, selling them sixteen stories in the course of the last few years—one of them being the (almost literal) flesh-crawling chiller that follows, in which a reawakened menace from the deep-freeze of the Antarctic ice-fields could spell the doom of the whole human race (and no, it's not Godzilla) . . .

H ow does that feel?" The doctor was examining me. He had cold fingers. This was not uncommon for a doctor. He also had steel hands and rubber arms that came through the wall. That was.

"I want a charge brought against the Lieutenant who brought us in. She killed one of our men."

"Just answer the questions and we'll both be out of here a deal quicker. What were the names of your colleagues who died, by the way?"

I hesitated. Maybe this man had no bedside manner because he wasn't a doctor, but a trained interrogator. They would ask us all the same questions, to test our story. Since our story was crap, we all had to reply with the same contrived answers. How, having no common ground between us, could we do that?

"Well, Amundsen—" I started; and then said, "No, really."

He frowned through the rather thick glass. "That's quite all right. It's the same story we've obtained from two of your other associates." Thank heaven. He continued to push and probe. "Your blood pressure and heart rate are very low," he added disapprovingly.

"Usually doctors are quite happy about that."

"Normally quite low, is it?" he said, in the way a G.P. might ask, Normal for you to have a jam jar up there, is it? "Body fat level's quite low too," he added.

"Sorry. I'll try and eat more and exercise less. You can level with me. I'm a doctor too. Do we have any hope of surviving this thing or not?"

He stared through the glass. "I can level with you because all subjects exposed to it have died. No, you probably don't."

"How are you going to treat me?"

What was that word? Chassignite? Thought it was an ancient Tribe of Israel. Asked J"rgen to look it up in the doctor's bible. But it could have been a rock, like Dolomite. Or a car, like a Turboflite. Or a popular brand of fizzy piss, like Bud Lite. Or—

"We have a couple of botulism antibiotics that were flown in in the last few hours from Ascension. I don't hold out much hope for them. We'll try one of them on one of your shipmates, the other on another."

"What use is that going to be? It's not gas gangrene you're dealing with."

(Araldite, Aragonite, Cordite, Lewisite—)

He stared back through the glass. "Oh, really. Then what, in your inestimable opinion, are we dealing with, Doctor?"

(Aerolite, Siderite—)

"Something new. Something quite out of this world."

Those few words saved my life. For a while.

It was three weeks into the Snowball War. No casualties had been reported as yet, but an illegal Argentinian hotel casino had been destroyed on the Drake Peninsula, and its guests and staff taken as prisoners of war. The US attack submarines Los Angeles and Philadelphia and two Russian hunter-killers thought to have been of the Alpha class were cruising under the ice, but the tour operators judged they would never dare torpedo a civilian vessel in waters where a human being could freeze to death in under a minute. The Papa Pingouin incident had not yet happened. So they continued to chug happily along the coasts all the way round the continent from Queen Maud Land to Mount Erebus, little realizing exactly how much of the politicians' rhetoric blustering across the airwaves actually was for real.

The Crux Australis was just such a vessel—owned by a large, well-respected cruise ship company operating out of Durban, she was of necessity smaller than flagship vessels such as the KC3 and the China Star, and there was no outdoor swimming pool on board. But she was a state-of-the-art ship built in Portsmouth, the last gasp of Britain's dockyards before lack of civilian top-up business had obliged even the British Royal Navy to order its fleets from Korea, and she incorporated all the very latest innovations that allowed a vessel to operate in Antarctic waters. There was an indoor swimming pool, kept carefully heated whilst the Crux was in southern waters, and hot-and-cold plumbing in 100 double-glazed cabins. There were even cabins looking out below the waterline, where passengers could goggle at the squillions of tiny sea creatures gobbling in all the oxygen packed into supercharged Antarctic-Circular waters. There were heated deck rails specially designed not to cold-weld to a careless onlooker's leaning arm. There was anti-iceberg radar above the water, and anti-iceberg sonar beneath it. Nothing (short of a torpedo, which the US and Russian governments were understandably reluctant to deliver) could go wrong.

Something had gone wrong.

We watched the ice drift past us, deceptively like an electric-blue version of dry land. It was that deception that had nearly bought us a watery grave. The berg had been spinning in its lead, and had suddenly exposed a half-kilometer promontory sweeping straight round towards us like a haymaker swung by the Great God Thor. Luckily Mr. Bang had noticed and swung the wheel in time, and this vessel had a rudder considerably stronger than the Titanic's.

We still hadn't been able to work out the engine controls, but it was only a matter of time. And beyond the berg, in any case, was nothing but open sea and Africa. If we were truly unlucky, we might hit South Georgia on the way.

The ship made me feel foolish, and at the same time insulted. Way across the fjord on board the Fram, the rest of our crew were huddling below decks sleeping during their free periods because the cold made anything else impossible. Up here, these people had waterbeds and air conditioning.

Had had waterbeds and air conditioning.

I opened the quadruple-glazed French windows that adjoined the great ballroom, and—ignoring the sucking rush of air that tinkled every chandelier—stepped in and slid the doors shut behind me. Someone—not us—had left a trail of dirty bootprints across someone else's lovely clean floor.

J"rgen was bending over one of the bodies. It was that of a teenage girl, an African, one of the rich Jo'burg families, no doubt. She was lying in the middle of the lovely clean floor, gripping a gold crucifix wound around her neck. Although she was African, trying to divine that fact from her facial features alone was like staring into a Magic Eye picture, as her entire face was a pattern of muscles, fat deposits, and blood vessels. The skin of her face had been flayed away; and by the grinding set of her teeth, this had happened while she had still been conscious and contemptuous of such trivialities as biting clean through her tongue.

J"rgen was leaning down to her to obtain a pulse.

"Everyone on this ship is dead," I said. "Don't touch her. What killed her may kill you."

J"rgen checked the pulse. He looked up and smiled gently. "Yes. You're right." He straightened up. "Anyway, the temperature has got to be pretty much below zero in here. No micro-organism is going to be moving around under these conditions."

I was surprised. The last week's sailing in Fram had made me view temperatures below zero as normal. But he was right—temperatures below zero weren't right for an air-conditioned ballroom, even this close to the Pole.

"One of our boys must have left the door open," I said.

J"rgen shook his head. "There's a thermostat on the wall. Look at it."

I looked at it. Someone had set the desired temperature to minus ten below.

"It's the same below decks, in the cabins—all round the ship," J"rgen said. "There's a swimming pool down below with a surface of ice on it. And not a window open in the ship."

He was bending to check another body as he spoke. This time, I put a hand on his shoulder to stop him.

"No. Stand up, and get away from them. We are leaving J"rgen. That's an order."

The Marine Corps woman was back—this time with a white coat on, and a surgical mask that covered only the bottom part of her face rather than an NBC mask that covered all of it. She was obviously coming to trust me more.

"My, what pretty eyes you have, Lieutenant," I said.

Beside her, the male Navy doctor hovered.

"I'm going to do a deal with you," said the lieutenant. "Assuming that you really are a doctor, you might be just as much use to us in your professional capacity as you might as an experimental subject. If you can provide us whatever assistance you can, we'll keep you alive as long as we can."

"I feel truly honoured," I said.

"Don't be. Although we really need doctors right now, there are only three of them on board this boat. Two of them are us, and one of them is you. Top brass won't let us have more than two M.D.'s on the containment vessel, in case of security leaks. Half of our men stationed south of the 60th Parallel still think they're protecting baby seals."

"But they're not. They're stopping something getting out. Something you're scared you might be responsible for."

She nodded. "Ever hear of Mars at Home?"

I shook my head. Then, I felt a glimmer of recollection.

"Hang on, yes, I do. Big Antarctican research project involving Russian and American scientists, right? Your president and theirs got together and did some public face-saving after you cancelled both your Mars programmes. You couldn't afford to go to the Red Planet, so you were going to look for ways in which Mars had already come to Earth."

She winced at the mention of "face-saving," but nodded. "Essentially, it was a huge Martian meteorite collection project, and huge meteorite collection projects, thankfully for us, tend to happen in Antarctica. Meteorites fall everywhere on Earth, you see, but in Antarctica, they fall into deep ice, which then gets pushed up when the ice sheet flows over a submerged mountain range. All the meteorites come up together. So all you need to do is to find the icefields, and you've found the meteorites."

"A chassignite is a type of meteorite," added the male doctor. "As I think you probably suspected already."

I nodded. "The doctor on the Crux had already put it in resin and shoved it on his desk. He was using it as a paperweight. That's why your guys missed it."

He looked at her, and she tore off a Post-It from a pad on the desk and began writing a Memo to Self. He looked back at me.

"A chassignite, though, is a very special type of meteorite. One that used to be a piece of Mars. One expelled by a volcanic eruption or minor asteroid collision with Mars maybe millions of years ago. There aren't many of them, but we reasoned, if we collected a few million meteorites, we might find a few hundred chassignites."

I was beginning to understand, though understanding was not as pleasant as I'd hoped. "The first evidence of life beyond this planet came from a Martian meteorite."

He nodded, hesitated, and then said: "Now we think some of that life . . . may be inside you."

"You mean this skin-eating thing comes from Mars?"

"That's what we suspect, yes. We had a Mars meteorite preparation facility in the Allan Hills, inland from where the party from the Crux said they found their own chassignite. Maybe the Crux threw their meteorite overboard—we didn't find any trace of it anywhere on the ship.

"In any case, the South Polar Research Station lost contact with the Allan Hills base around ten weeks ago. They sent out a team to investigate. They lost contact with their rescue team. Then they sent in a third team which got out with three of its complement still alive. They died around 36 hours later, after we had surgically removed around 95% of their body surface." He frowned apologetically. "We weren't as good at arresting the spread of infection back then."

So he had been part of the South Pole Station staff. The Marine Corps doctor bustled out of the room, leaving me alone with him.

I tapped on the glass, an indication for him to move closer. He looked at me nervously, then looked all round at the very large bolts on the glass, then leaned up close enough for me to see his very bad skin.

"Want me to tell you why you don't have to worry?"

He looked nervously in the direction of the door. "I can't make any sort of deal with you."

"Scared she'll kill you too?"

He twisted his lips. "Somebody would. Believe me. This is the military. Killing is what we do. Why do we not have to worry?"

"Because the rats on the ship are still alive."

He appeared to absorb this. But it was a hollow sham. He had a neoprene brain. I tried again.

"The disease specifically targets human beings, not rats—not even, apparently, penguins, or I'm sure your expeditions to Fryxell would have noticed. It's a thing that evolved on Earth. It's evolved to eat people, and it's evolved to eat them jolly well. It's pure coincidence that your meteors happen to land on the icecap. Ancient killer diseases are most likely to come at us out of the icecaps. If this bug is as dangerous as you say it is, it would have wiped out everyone who came into contact with it the last time it was seen by Man, and if it wipes out everyone it can infect, the disease dies, right? Except, of course, that that's wrong—the disease can simply wait a couple of thousand years in suspended animation in contaminated ice under the polar icecaps, and then—"

The doctor twisted two ends of a handkerchief halfway up his nostrils to his brain and snorted. "We're already ahead of you on that one. Some of us also reckon this disease isn't new. It's very similar to something the ancient Romans seem to have known of—admittedly in only one word, 'Mentagram,' in all their texts—"

"What's a Mentagram? A telegram sent by psychics?"

"The actual root word, so I'm told, is 'Mentagra.' Literally, 'Chin Disease.' They thought it was transmitted by kissing, because it was first noticed on the mouths of victims. Of course, this disease is airborne, but it also tends to infect the outside of the mouth and nose first. Bad air gets inhaled there. From the mouths and noses, Mentagra then worked its way down to the neck, chest and so forth if it wasn't stopped, just like our bug. It's all in Pliny's *Natural History*, Book 26, first century AD. One of our C.O.'s was a Classics major." He inspected the handkerchief, not appearing to be happy with what he found. "But that means very little. A meteor from Mars could have hit ancient Rome in the first century AD just as easily as, I don't know, Phoenician traders could have spread a landborne plague from the South Pole."

"The Phoenicians didn't get to the South Pole. And they were all wiped out by the time of Christ anyway."

"According to the C.O., one Phoenician guy called Gisgo of Alexandria set out to sail round Africa. Atishoo! And he probably got at least as far as Cameroon, by modern estimates."

He fished out his handkerchief again.

"Too damn dusty in here."

Chassignite. Meteorite. Gelignite. Dyna-mite.

And then I knew. Immediately. But I wasn't about to tell him, of course. The only problem was, what was I going to do with the knowledge?

"You can't make us leave, Scott. There could be dying people here."

There were four of us standing around in the ballroom in arctic clothing, surrounded by places laid for dinner.

I nodded my head. "Exactly. And they could be us."

J"rgen shook his head. "I understand that you have a responsibility to us, as our doctor. But the danger is like as not very small. When what has happened has happened, the ship was much warmer, everyone was moving about, like as not no one knew a virus or a bacterium was moving with them. We know there is a danger. We can take precautions."

I pointed to the thermostat on the wall. "Those people did everything they could to stay alive. They lowered the temperature in all the rooms on board to stop the disease spreading. And it still spread. Whatever it is isn't going to be stopped by room temperature dropping below zero."

One of the two Danes in the expedition, referred to by everyone as Pedersen-med-D because there was another "Peetherson" in the expedition whose name was spelt differently, broke in angrily. "So we don't search any more for survivors? Is that because you feel so responsible to us all, I wonder, or is it that you want to save your own skin?"

"Meddy, we found corpses lying dead in the sick bay with charts prescribing them every drug in the modern physician's arsenal. On Fram, meanwhile, we have proprietary medicines for headaches and the common cold, painkillers for broken limbs and frostbite, antibiotics for infections. That's it. We cannot afford to take this bug back to the Fram."

"You're so sure it's a bug?" He gestured wildly at the corpse. "A knife could do that. A knife, or a scalpel."

"No. I've used scalpels. Look at the affected area with a magnifying glass. There's not a capillary on that girl's face cut through. You'd need to be the best surgeon who ever lived. It's got to be an organism. Maybe similar to type-two necrotizing fasciitis. I don't know."

"Then we stay here." Meddy's eyes were bright. "If it's that bad, we got to stay here."

J"rgen cut in angrily. "Are you mad? That'd mean cutting five men from the expedition—we'd never reach the Pole—"

I exhaled, and looked down at the corpse unhappily.

"No." I raised a hand, signalling defeat. "Meddy's right. He's absolutely right, and I should have had the courage to see it myself. I know the expedition's important to all of us. But this is more important. If we go back to the Fram now, we could infect everyone else. We have to stay here, and radio for help."

J"rgen, who was both Captain Amundsen's First and best Mate, muttered darkly to himself in Norwegian.

At that moment, the door was thrown open, and Haakon burst in.

"Scott—we've found the files on the doctor's PC."

I nodded and followed, with three Norwegians and a Dane behind me.

One of the disconcerting facts about being an Englishman, and not a large Englishman at that, at sea with a crew of Scandinavians, was an uncomfortable awareness that you were constantly at armpit-sniffing height. Seated at a PC screen with neo-Vikings on all sides peering over each other's shoulders, the feeling was stronger than usual.

Luckily, the doctor's notes were in English. If he'd been an Afrikaaner, I might have had to radio north for a translation. They spoke of an infection that had hit both crew and passengers after putting in at an inlet near Lake Fryxell, only a few days' sail from here.

"All this happened in just a few days?" said J"rgen.

"Unless he's lying, which he has no reason to do, being dead."

A voice came over my shoulder. "Some of these people are beginning to smell."

I didn't turn my head. "Then turn the thermostats down further. We're used to it."

The purpose of the trip, according to the notes, had been ornithological and geological sightseeing. The Transantarctic Mountains are fold mountains, completely devoid of obscuring features like topsoil and, at the Lake Fryxell area even snow and ice—a rock collector's dream. The sort of person who enjoyed spending their summer vacation in Antarctica might also enjoy a trip out there. And emperor penguins nested all along this coast, having moved here from Ross Island after egg pirates from New Zealand—the sort the Americans and Russians professed to be so mad over—had emptied their nest sites of young. Pet emperors were now all the rage in the very best society in the Russian Federation, so much so that the trade was called the Black-and-White Market. Albino emperors were even being bred by penguin fanciers who had evidently never read Lovecraft.

"We're going to have to use the radio," said Meddy, breaking out of a conversation in either Danish or Norwegian—I couldn't tell the difference—with Haakon. "Amundsen won't like it."

"I don't like it either," I said. "We'll alert every US submarine and destroyer for miles. We're in violation of the hundred-kilometre exclusion zone. They'll put our whole ship under arrest and tow us back to Ascension Island while some Malagasy bastard cruises up and down the Queen Maud coast netting icefish to his heart's content. They haven't the ships to cover the area and they know it."

"I heard the Brazilian fishing fleet is operating submarine trawlers," said Haakon.

"I'm not quite sure how that would work," said Meddy. "How would you haul in the nets?"

I read on. The disease had appeared only hours after the last passenger came ashore from Victoria Land. It killed by "massive and sudden facial necrosis spreading from the nose and mouth, in a manner similar to hospital gangrene."

"Gangrene," said Meddy. "Frostbite causes gangrene. They had frostbite." He clapped Haakon on the back. "All right, see? Frostbite!"

The direct cause of death, I read, might have been heart seizure, or might have been suffocation. It had been impossible for the doctor, whose name had been M. J. Phillips, to determine whether a patient's heart had stopped due to hypoxia or sheer terrible pain. He had tried to keep some alive by artificial respiration, but had, according to his notes, "just succeeded in breaking the ribcage." He had first suspected a simple dermal staphylococcus infection, and had tried successively more heavy-duty antibiotics, working his way up to vancomycin on his first patient. Vancomycin was and till is the nuclear weapon of antibiotics, the one you have but shouldn't use, because its use only exposes bacteria to it and increases the risk that they'll mutate and we won't be able to use it next time. It is normally only used to treat MRSA. Our doctor had had only a little vancomycin, and it hadn't worked. His notes showed that he'd been desperate enough to go through every other disease known to cause skin lesions in his quite well-stocked little medical library, literally ticking each off page by page, until finally coming to the same conclusion as myself. Not common gangrene, and not gas gangrene either. Hospital gangrene, otherwise known as necrotizing fasciitis, for which the only known cure is removal of the affected tissue. This was not a thing which would have been welcomed by a poorly-paid ship's doctor in the middle of the South Atlantic with few proper operating facilities and a ship full of passengers, some of whom would have been capable of suing the pants off him, and some of whom would have been capable of having him shot next time he went out of the front door to his car in Durban. He was not, however, any mad scientist experimenting blindly on a group of god-given guinea pigs. When he'd begun to contract the disease himself, he'd began to take off his own facial musculature with rubber gloves and a scalpel in the mirror. He'd got about halfway across his face before he'd died. Of course, the patients he had hardly treated at all had been the ones that had survived longest. So the world rewards a dying man doing his very best.

I heard J"rgen, who had been smoking in the corridor, swear in something Scandiwegian. "Damn ship's full of rats! I stop you, you bastard—"

I froze at the keyboard.

"DON'T TOUCH IT."

He stopped dead, with a steel vacuum cleaner pipe in one hand.

"What? We not allowed to touch rats now?"

"It's alive," I said.

He grinned stupidly. "Not for long!" He hefted his cleaner pipe like one of his Viking forebears.

"Ever hear of hantavirus?"

That took the fury of Odin out of him. The pipe went down.

"Hanta-what?"

"Rats carry it. It kills people. It kills people really well. Twenty-odd cases at modern, well-equipped hospitals in the US, i.e., not pissant doctor's surgeries on board ship, had a 50% death rate. What I'm saying is, the rats might be this organism's vector. You want your lower gut to slide out of your arse bleeding, go ahead, swat the furry fucker."

Meddy was wide-eyed. "Rats spread Black Death." He liked the statement so much he repeated it in a different format. "Black Death, that's spread by rats."

"Yeah," I said. "Norwegian fucking brown rats, maybe. Maybe you ought not to worry, hey. Maybe you guys are immune."

J"rgen shook his head. "No. No, it's not bubonic plague. Plague victims have, you know, black sores under their arms?"

"For your information," I said, still staring into the screen and typing at the same time, "it has never been conclusively established what organism was responsible for the Black Death. Most people think bubonic plague. Some think anthrax. Some even think hantavirus. It might even have been some sort of weird bug no one had never seen before and we've not seen since." I licked my lips. "No one showing any signs of fever yet?"

They examined each other cursorily. Soon, they would be examining each other minutely. "No," said Meddy.

"Better signal Fram," I said. "Project Red-White-Blue is finished."

Project Red-White-Blue was a voyage of Anglo-Norwegian cooperation rising out of the weird vision of only one man—Thor Amundsen. A distant relative of the great polar explorer, he'd narrowly failed an examination to become one of ESA's first Mars astronauts on medical grounds. Perhaps his failure to qualify for the vanguard of the future had made him retreat back into the past, but Thor, a likeable man from Bergen who spoke Norwegian, English and Russian fluently, had skied at Olympic level, and had a Master's degree in Engineering from Oslo university, had set himself a task that, for the men who had originally accomplished it, had been as difficult and as dangerous as Armstrong's first moonshot. He had decided that, on the hundredth anniversary of his distinguished ancestor's historic conquest of the Pole, he would do likewise, in exactly the same manner. No satellite navigation. No digital radio. No radar. No sonar. No petrol-driven skidoos. Thor was going to the Pole, and he was going to take in every bit of suffering his ancestor had suffered, just as Amundsen himself had been driven to suffer the same agonies his patron, Nansen, had endured.

Initially, he had raised the money by claiming he was going to carry out Amundsen's abortive North Polar trip of 1910, which had been a cover story for his ancestor's real destination. I suspected I had been recruited out of a possible 20 applicants, all with identical qualifications, only because of my name. It's only my first name that's Scott, but at least, Thor had said in the interview, they would have one Scott and one Amundsen on the team. I'd learned later that the recruitment of at least one British member had been a major factor in getting a City merchant bank to sub Thor 200,000 pounds for expedition expenses.

Roald Amundsen had recruited his entire crew for a journey to the Arctic, borrowing a ship, the Fram, off his friend Nansen, whom he knew to be planning a South Polar attempt himself, and then suddenly changed course at Madeira and announced they were heading for the other end of the world. We should have realized that Thor Amundsen was going to do likewise.

Going for the South Pole was insane—not merely spitting in the eye of an old friend, as it had been in 1910, but genuine suicide. Since September 2009, American and Russian warships had been patrolling circumpolar waters enforcing the Antarctic whale sanctuary. One Norwegian whaler, the Seaswan, had already been shot full of machinegun holes by an overenthusiastic Russian destroyer captain. For some reason, the Americans and Russians, so reluctant to intervene when people were killing, raping and eating one another in Rwanda, Kosovo, Northern Ireland and Quebec, really meant business this time. No torpedoes had been used as yet, but, particularly after the Seaswan incident, the Norwegians on Fram were sailing to a grudge match.

Granted, the South Pole had been being raped wholesale by big business. Huge, air-conditioned hotels had been going up all along the relatively mild

"South Polar Riviera" of the Antarctic Peninsula. Heated suits allowed tourists to dive among fur seals, snowboard down icebergs, terrorize flocks of frantic penguins on jet skis (the tourists on jet skis, not the penguins, of course). All thoroughly illegal and in contravention of the Second Antarctic Treaty of 2007, of course—but then, so had been a few hundred thousand white settlers wandering across Indian land with a couple of million cattle in North America in the 19th century, and in South America in the 20th, and nobody heard anyone complaining then.

But suddenly, the Americans and Russians had got serious—incidentally boosting their Presidents' domestic popularity ratings to an all-time high—and no-one quite knew why. Now their express permission was needed for anyone, no matter how scientific they might claim to be, to venture below the 60th Parallel. But Thor Amundsen had reckoned on turning this into the biggest European propaganda coup in history, making it all the way to the Pole under the noses of the US Navy. A wooden-hulled ship, transparent to radio waves, probably also transparent to sonar. No motors, if only the sails were in use, and hence silent to even the most sophisticated hydrophone. Nobody would be expecting a wooden ship, he reasoned. And certainly, he had been right in that we had got this far.

We had radioed Fram. Thor had refused to believe our story, and had insisted on coming aboard himself. I'd ordered anyone on deck to stop him doing so, on the grounds that we should stop any more of our friends and shipmates getting infected.

Right now, J"rgen was the only one in the doctor's surgery apart from myself. It was still light, as it always was in the Antarctic winter, but the sun was low on the horizon—less a midnight sun than a continual twilight one.

"You stopped yourself earlier on," he said. "You have not said everything you were wanting to."

I nodded.

"At the end of the last century, a number of dead men were discovered in what had been a coalmine in Spitzbergen. There used to be a lot of heavy coalmining in Spitzbergen, you know that?"

He nodded. "They wanted to mine down here too, up in the Transantarctics. It seemed that they would be getting permission, too, before the US and the Russians started to play hardball."

"Mining in Spitzbergen stopped in the last century. But these corpses were special. They'd died of Spanish 'Flu, a disease which killed 20 million people just after the First World War. Twenty million. And you know what? The disease organisms were still alive inside them. Half the epidemiological world were overjoyed that they now had samples of a deadly virus to study and make vaccines against, and half of them were terrified. Because the reason why the bodies got found was that they'd originally been buried in an icefield. By the end of the century, the icefield had retreated—not due to global warming, oh, no, perish the thought—and the bodies were uncovered. And if that could happen in Spitzbergen, it could happen anywhere across the entire extent of the ice sheet. Any and every plague that swept Europe, Asia and North America throughout recorded history and beyond could come out of the tundra at us. In the 6th century AD, a sizeable percentage of the Eastern Roman Empire died of the Plague of Justinian, a mysterious infection from the East. We still have no idea what the plague organism was. In the fourth century AD, a plague that killed millions crossed China from west to east, and academics are still arguing whether that was smallpox or measles. Hantavirus has been in North America ever since Amerindians can remember . . ."

He frowned. "Are you saying this could be a disease that was buried in the ice sheet, then uncovered?"

I wagged my head, trying to shake off answering the question. "Maybe. There've been Little Ice Ages and Little Interglacials all through human history. Maybe the Yaga Indians from Patagonia colonized the Antarctic Peninsula during a Little Interglacial early in their history, just like the Vikings colonized Greenland. Who knows? Certainly there's not many Yaga Indians left alive for us to ask. I read a book on them once. There are two of them left, and they're both nuns." I tapped the porthole glass. "There could be lost Indian cities aplenty under the ice, with diseases we've never even seen before."

He was listening, but I couldn't tell whether he thought I was crazy or not. "Some sort of frozen Indian burial site, you think."

I looked at the screen. "They found something. Found it when they were on that trip to the Dry Valleys. The log just refers to it as 'the Chassignite'." I nodded to a shelf in the corner of the room. "I saw a Bible up there earlier on. Flip through it and see if you can find out who the Chassignites were." I shifted a heavy rock encased in resin which the doctor had evidently been using as a paperweight off the sheaf of crabbily handwritten notes he'd left in addition to his computer records. The rock was sealed in a plastic bag, as if someone had collected it as a geological sample. "I just wish the bastard hadn't seen fit to write the most important bits of his log in riddles."

Then Mr Bang poked his big blond head into the surgery. "Scott, J"rgen—you should come upstairs right away." Then the head was gone.

I called after him. "Hey, wait a minute! Why? Why should we come right away?"

By the time we arrived at the ballroom, all three of the others were there, standing around the girl. Around the girl, and a long way from the girl.

"It's spread to her shoulders," said Meddy in revulsion.

Sure enough, the thin and red raw line that separated dead grey skin from dead blue veins and muscles had spread down to fill the golden line of the girl's necklace. Even in death, the unseen thing was dining.

Then J"rgen put a finger to his lips, and cupped another round his ear. I stopped and listened, and then I heard it. The noise of rotor blades.

Someone—either the Americans or the Russians—had found us.

I was glad that it was an American helicopter. Only Thor and one of the Swedes spoke Russian, and they were back on Fram. Besides, I had a westerner's unreasoning mistrust of Russian soldiers. We stood on deck, watching the chopper circle.

"Why doesn't he come in to land?" said Meddy. "There's a helicopter landing area."

Dirty bootprints on a ballroom floor—

"He's not landing," I said. "He knows what's down here. He didn't find us. He's been here already."

The chopper was turning, centering itself in a fjord broadside-on to the ship.

"We fucked up his plans last time. The ship was supposed to hit the ice. The evidence was supposed to have been destroyed—" I was backing away towards the steps up to the bridge. Then I started running. The chopper kept on coming. I burst into the bridge behind a bemused Mr Bang, fell onto the radio set and began twirling the dials. Nothing but static. If there was traffic out there it was digital and encrypted. I found the Mayday channel, and yelled into it at the top of my voice, as if it made the goons in the chopper more likely to hear me, that we knew what they were up to, we knew they had tried to sink the ship, and above all, we knew about the Chassignite, and that if they tried to put a hole in our hull there were functioning radio transmitters on board this ship and we'd broadcast their dirty little secret all the way from Rio Di Janeiro to Perth.

The helicopter rose up out of the fjord, flew over the ship, and carried on flying high into the sky.

The other members of the crew looked at me as if I'd had a seizure.

"It's something they don't want anyone else to have," I said. "Something they've found under the ice sheet too. That's why they've come over all green and whale-friendly."

"One of your Indian diseases," said J"rgen.

I shrugged. "Something. Or something they cooked up themselves. Something that kills quickly enough and unstoppably enough for them to be interested in it, anyway. We already know that part." I sat back into one of the few seats in the room. It wasn't comfortable. I realized, too late, that Haakon and Meddy had followed us into the bridge. They'd heard everything we'd said.

Haakon was wide-eyed immediately. "You think the people from the Crux have walked into a military test area?"

"Chemical warfare?" said Meddy. It wasn't as stupid an idea as it sounded. The Yellow Rain used by the Soviets in Afghanistan produced skin lesions; vigorous washing would remove it, though. It wasn't quite this single-mindedly deadly.

I shook my head. "Something similar, though. A really fast-acting virus, maybe. Tetanus, rabies and lots of other diseases can produce uncontrollable muscle spasms. But this isn't any disease that was in my textbooks."

"They're experimenting?" Meddy was poised on the edge of the handle, ready to take flight. "They've made a green sanctuary out of the whole of Antarctica just to test weapons?" He banged a console theatrically. But I felt the same way he did.

"They are not just experimenting," said J"rgen. "They've fucked up. The bug they're testing has escaped, and maybe it's more dangerous than they think, or they would have not cordoned off the entire continent."

"We've got to get out of here," said Meddy, "and warn everybody."

"That's just what we've not got to do," said J"rgen. "We're travelling in a plague ship, remember?"

"Well, what should we do? Just sit here and die like they want us to?"

Abruptly, the radio crackled. I had left it on Mayday frequency, and someone was answering back.

"—military flight from USS Tarawa calling SS Crux Australis, over. Anyone alive down there? You sure were making some racket a couple of minutes back, over."

Carefully, I picked up the mike, as if handling a live snake. "This is Crux. Yes, there are live people on board here. Four of us, over."

"Sure as hell didn't find you on our last visit. Where were you hiding, over?"

I tried to think of a suitable hiding place. "Meat locker. Meat locker is airtight, and quite warm if you switch on the defrosting heaters, over."

"Well, I'll be damned. I could have sworn we checked the meat lockers." The voice waited for a moment, as if allowing the fact that it knew perfectly well I was lying to sink in.

"You aware that you're still sitting on top of a serious health hazard? And also, incidentally, your ship's in violation of the Antarctic Treaty, 2007, over?"

"Only too aware, Tarawa. Can you come in and take us off, over?"

Voices hissed to left and right of me. "No! Don't bring them down here with us!"

"I'll do what I can, Crux. And I'm afraid by the powers vested in us, we are going to have to arrest you. Don't be too scared if our guys come out in big rubber suits, over."

"We'll try to keep calm." I switched off the radio.

"What the fuck are you trying to do? They'll drop some marines down here and kill us!" This was Meddy, naturally.

"Better down here than up there," I said. "They had rockets on board that thing."

"And they'll have guns when they get off it! They aren't going to take us away—that's why we thought this disease had 100% death rate, they, they probably threw any of the passengers they found still alive over the side!"

I frowned. I hadn't thought about that. "But they've already shown they won't shoot us if we can realistically threaten to get word out to the outside."

He threw his arms wide. "So they send troops down here, disable the radio, and shoot all of us, Einstein."

Haakon cut in. "He may be right. Let's send a radio message out now."

I considered it. "It might do some good. Maybe we can try it. But they may be jamming the signal by now anyway. And that pilot asked me where we'd been hiding. He sounded very interested in it. Remember, he knows that we must have come either from off the Crux, or from some other ship. Once he knows that other ship exists and where it is, he knows he only has to blow it and us out of the water to wipe out any proof we were ever here. But it could be 100 miles down the coast for all he knows. Guys, I don't think he saw the Fram when he flew past. It may take him a good few minutes to double back on himself if he doesn't want to waste too much fuel, which he might not, over the Antarctic. It's our duty to signal to Fram to get the hell out of here in the meantime. And it may be the only way for us to stay alive."

It convinced them. They started running and yelling at each other in Norse.

It was not a naval helicopter. It was not painted blue with big garish stars and stripes. Its operators hadn't had time to recamouflage it from a deep, businesslike green. Maybe those rockety things might have been drop tanks after all, but those machine guns were, well, machine guns.

The well-dressed American soldier was wearing rubber this winter. Five infantrymen (I counted) came out of the helicopter, all of them holding M16's in both hands. We were uncomfortably aware of the fact that we had not so much as a flare pistol among us.

We were standing outside on deck. When they got to maximum conversation distance, the leader walked up close, giving us a look at him through his faceplate. He was a she.

"Hi there. Nice to see you all wrapped up warm. Those clothes aren't exactly standard issue."

J"rgen smiled. "You have been in the army too long. There is no standard issue on a civilian ship."

She might have smiled back, but it was difficult to tell. I would not have been convinced of her sincerity in any case. "I'm not in the army, sir. I'm a doctor in the United States Marine Corps. I believe you're already aware you may have contracted an extremely virulent infection. To date, that infection has been 100% fatal. Now, let's cut the bullshit. None of you gents came off this ship. There's a possibility that other crewmen on board your own ship may also be infected. We need to know the current position of your ship, or people on board it may die."

J"rgen nodded to me in acknowledgement. *You were right.* "We are passengers on this ship. We hid ourselves before, because we are not used to soldiers with machine guns. We are sorry if this was an inconvenience."

Then she shot J"rgen.

She shot him to kill. He must have died instantly. Then, as if she were talking to students at an autopsy class, she stood over the body and carried on talking. The sound of the shots echoed back off the ice walls all around us like a great invisible snake writhing round the horizon.

"Next man to try and feed me a line of bullshit gets the same treatment. Where's your ship?"

"They took us on board at Lake Ryxell," I said. "Some of us were already sick. We weren't, and still aren't. We're poachers. Our ship left us there to pick up penguin eggs. We've already used the Crux's radio to tell our ship where we are, and tell it to call for medical help. And that means, lady, that you are in a lot of trouble."

At first, I thought she was going to shoot me. But, I realized, I'd fed her something credible, and made us into something useful—human subjects who might have been exposed to the sickness without being infected.

She gestured with the gun. "There's a sealed container in the back of the chopper. Get into it. Don't touch anything when you get in." She smiled again. "You're about to enter the wonderful world of the experimental subject. There's a lot of all of you, which is good. Plenty of beef on the bone for tissue samples. Now move."

We moved.

My personal physician was back in the room, checking on how quickly I was dying. I was busy myself, checking through tissue samples taken from two victims who had been notified to me only as Subjects X and Y in my own miniature laboratory on my side of the glass. My laboratory had been carefully audited to include no heavy objects, no sharp objects, and no objects that could be mixed into concoctions that could hurt tiny US Marine hands. I was fairly sure that Subjects X and Y were Meddy Pedersen and Haakon Bang. They were dying far more rapidly than I was.

"I assume this cubicle I'm in has its own self-contained air recycler, like a space suit," I said.

He didn't look up from what he was doing. He was far too interested in a flap of skin he'd cut from my arm. "No, it's filtered from the air in here. The contents of the air are passed through radioactive, freeze-drying, and thermic sterilizers."

"That won't do any good. You need to open the air filter and check through it." He looked blank. "This organism is airborne, right? The air filters in these cells are sucking out all our air and concentrating it, right? So the organism goes into the air filters too. There might be more of the organism in there than there is on your patients. You shouldn't be sterilizing the air. You should be collecting it."

I could see by his expression that I had him hooked.

"But what would we collect it in?"

Just at that moment the door opened and Marine Girl walked back in wearing a paper mask, stared at me through the glass, maybe for tell-tale signs of the disease, frowned as if she were disappointed I didn't have any yet, and then left, making a note on her all-important clipboard. The doctor's eyes followed her down the corridor.

"One of your colleagues just died. It had reached his chest before he passed out," he confided.

I didn't ask him which one. It didn't really matter.

"Saturate the filter in water," I said. "Water will contain any airborne dust component, and you've got plenty of water available; but it's unlikely to kill the organism. Take a slide and dab some of your water on it with a pipette, and you've got a microscopy sample. Remember, you've got to keep the organism alive, or you'll never be able to study it properly."

He nodded vigorously. Maybe laboratory work wasn't his strong point.

My hand moved up to scratch an itch on my chin that I had been ignoring in the hope that it was psychosomatic.

"That's how it starts," he said. "I'm sorry."

He went out.

He was very interested in his slides, and made many of them. He kept them out of the sight of Marine Girl, who I suspected was his superior and would disapprove. He studied the effect his slides had on samples of suspiciously nordic-looking skin and muscle tissue.

Then, on the second day, he began scratching his chin. By this time, you understand, I was in real pain, feeling as if the lower part of my face were already being cauterized down to the bone, at which point I began to understand how the ancient Romans, if they had indeed contracted this disease, had felt justified in resorting to such extreme measures. Needless to say, no curative procedures of even that drastic nature were attempted on me. They wanted a live specimen for as long as it took for one to die.

They began making what they called "firebreak incisions," skinless areas through which the disease would not spread. This was successful in channelling the infection into a long, narrow strip of skin that spiralled out from the point of initial infection on the chin. Later on, they said, they would make similar cuts around my neck and chest to stop the pestilence spreading lower than the head. That wouldn't stop it spreading entirely, of course—they had found from previous cases that a point of escape was needed for the infection in order to prevent it from spreading upwards. Victims whose entire heads were affected suffered such pain that they had frequently driven their heads against the walls of their cells, I was told. That, of course, would never have done. We had to be made to live out our usefulness to medical science to the full. When I say 'they', of course, I still mean only the two doctors I had seen to date; since we had been marched out of our secure container below decks, I had not seen another living soul besides those two.

I was instructed on literal pain of death not to scratch. I would, for hours on end, rather have died and scratched, but somehow I managed to convince myself not to do it. Maybe it was the indomitable human spirit that did it, but I somehow think it was more likely the immense feeling of satisfaction I got out of watching the doctor turn up to the lab one morning with a Band-aid over his chin, and hide his face furtively from the other workers. He was infected, and he knew it. I caught him stealing scalpels and syringes. He didn't quite manage to steal a syringe—Marine Girl walked in before he was able to, and he had to put the packet back on the shelf quickly. I rejoiced that night, elated in the fact that, whilst he'd accorded me the decency of a jab, he was going to attempt to cut a firebreak incision in his own face that very night without an anaesthetic And each morning, his Band-aid and mine alike grew larger.

One morning, he walked into the lab and marched right up to the glass.

"You are killing me," he said.

"Ditto," I replied.

"How did you know it would infect me?"

"Let me out," I said, "and I'll tell you."

"Now everyone on the ship will get infected."

"I know."

"Maybe everyone in the world."

"That doesn't have to happen. Let me out."

He went to open the door to the confinement area.

When the gun went off, it was like having my ears boxed with a pair of cymbals. The cell I was in was mainly metal, and it carried on clanging obscenely long after I saw the Navy doctor slide down the glass wall of the cubicle leaving a snail-trail of blood from a bullethole.

On the other side of a great deal of glass and a great deal of blood stood the Marine doctor, staring at him with eyes that were more than ever so slightly crazy. As always, it was only her eyes that were visible over the ever-present paper mask. She was still holding a Service automatic in both hands.

"Oooh dear," I said. "Look what you did."

Her eyes moved down to where mine were already resting—on the tiny crazed gap in the glass where her bullet had hit and knocked a hole in my cage without penetrating.

"All those nasty little pathogens," I said, "spreading through that little tiny hole. Could be you're already breathing them in. Better shore up that hole quick, sister, or you might get infected."

Then she smiled, and I didn't doubt her sincerity now. The grin filled her face ear to ear. Without taking her trigger hand off the weapon, she reached behind her head, unhooked the straps of the surgical mask, and let it fall away.

She did not have much of a lower face left to smile with. She'd been contaminated longer than the Navy guy. Probably since before we'd even been taken on board the ship.

I leapt aside before she fired again. The glass, weakened by the first shot, shattered this time. She continued to fire. I was able to huddle into one corner of the window housing, where the window bolts met the metal. I felt bullets thudding against myself with only a quarter inch of steel between us. She could have walked across the room and killed me at any time she wanted. She wasn't even trying. Instead, she was screaming every time she pulled the trigger. I didn't blame her. Her face—her very beautiful face—had started disintegrating maybe from the very first day she had begun to study the plague organism, and she hadn't been able to do anything about it, hadn't even been able to explain it. All her years of military and medical training had been useless. Whatever she'd planned to do with her life, and probably also her life itself, wasn't going to happen any more.

The military had trained her well in one respect, though; she knew exactly how many rounds she had in her weapon. The last one went into her own head. As I hadn't been quite so sure how many rounds she'd had left, I carried on cowering for a good few seconds more before poking my head back out into the sickbay.

I decided against keeping the weapon, I had no idea how guns worked, and a gun in my hand might only get me killed by someone else who did. I ignored the rows of medical cabinets in the sickbay, with their glass doors holding rows of tempting genetically-engineered medicines.

The corridor outside confirmed my suspicions. There were bodies lying slumped everywhere, every one with their circulatory system clearly mapped out on their faces. Some, but not all, of them had been carefully bundled into polythene body bags, but no further efforts had been made for their disposal. It looked like there had been more infection outside the controlled area than inside it for quite some time. Somewhere distant, engines were still thrumming faintly, but I had a distinct suspicion there was no hand at the tiller.

Poking around belowdecks, it took me a surprisingly long time to find the quartermaster's stores. I sat what was left of the quartermaster on a comfy seat in the corner before locating what I wanted on the shelves. It took me a good few minutes to find my way through the Navy's byzantine filing system. What I wanted was dark green and slopped around inside the big cannister I found it in. The cannister was labelled WARNING, KEEP AWAY FROM CHIL-DREN, DO NOT INGEST, and, for some arcane reason, HIGHLY TOXIC TO MARINE WILDLIFE AND BEES.

I ripped open the cannister with a Stanley knife and stuck my head in it. I held my head under, well beneath the surface, and felt a slight tingling sensa-tion on my skin. I did not go as far as opening my eyes. No victim's eyes had yet been affected.

After removing my head from the cannister, I splashed the stuff around my neck and shoulders like an expensive cologne. Then, I carried a few more can-nisters of the same green gunk to the nearest bathing area and had a shower in the stuff.

With the ick still running down me, I soaked a set of Navy blues in it, put them on, and, dripping, made my way back for'ard to the place I and my com-panions had been being held, all the time not seeing a single living soul. My companions were all dead, which came as little surprise—after all, I'd been staring at Navy Boy examining dissected bits of them under a microscope for the past three or four days. I looked into the eyes of Meddy Pedersen staring back at me as he floated in a tank of preserving fluid, recognizable by the sap-phire wedding ring on his right hand, the rest of him as skinless as the Visible Man. Some of the skinless area had been removed by the pathogen, and some, more clumsily, by human beings using scalpels. One piece of surgically removed Meddy was pinned out under a microscope, kept under water to sep-arate it from the outside air.

I peered into the microscope. Adjusting the magnification downwards from cell-size, I was eventually rewarded with a glimpse of what I wanted, inert and paralysed by their immersion, but still only dormant, waiting for the time when the sun dried them out and they could eat and scurry once again.

"Couldn't see the wood for the trees," I said, to nobody in particular.

Dermatophagoides. The common dust mite. Except that these dust mites weren't quite so common.

Your average dust mite—500 of which can happily live in a single gramme of dust—spends its entire lifetime feasting on human flesh. Or, to be more exact, human skin, the main component of domestic dust. One of the main reasons for peoples' allergies to the creatures' fecal pellets is the fact that dust mites are among the most beautifully adapted creatures in the animal kingdom for feeding on human tissue. Their saliva quite simply is designed to break us down.

Normally, of course, human dust mites feed on dead skin flakes. But there was never anything stopping any dust mite genus from developing an ability to feed on live skin.

Not a virus, or a bacterium, or a Martian meteor—but a creature these so-called scientists had evidently been unsurprised to see crawling across these samples in their thousands. Every healthy human being is, after all, covered in them. No antibiotics, of course, would have done their victims any good. What was needed was a good strong dose of insecticide (or, more strictly, acaricide).

When Navy boy had started examining the contents of the air filters under water—or maybe through some other, completely unconnected route, looking at the extent of the epidemic in the outer corridors—he'd been infested. Dust mites, unlike bacteria, are capable of scurrying out of petri dishes. But I hadn't killed him. As God is my judge, I'd been preparing to save his life when I had been unfortunately prevented from doing so.

In any case, I needed to leave the ghost ship.

I found a ladder leading upwards, and eventually, a hatch. I had, on my travels, spotted a surprisingly small number of unlocked ladders leading up to hatches, and had been annoyed at being continually, inexplicably thwarted in my upward progress. Opening the hatch cover, I pulled myself upward into fresh air and sea mist. The sky was white and roaring.

I should have realized. A submarine. They would never have allowed research on something this serious to take place on a vessel not capable of being ordered to take its cargo to the bottom of the ocean. I was standing right on top of the conning tower. The boat was running slowly on the surface. I knew she was running slowly, because she had a sailing vessel keeping pace with her. They'd seen the sub steering erratically, and, although they were running like hell for safe haven in Port Stanley or Ushuaia, they'd still stopped to flash messages at the boat asking if it needed assistance. Thor Amundsen's good heart would be the death of him yet. Only a half mile distant, the running lights of two other, larger vessels—Argentine trawlermen, I learned later—showed through the fog. It seemed there was more than one Good Samaritan at sea today.

I waved at the figures on deck on the Fram. They waved back. It took me some time to locate a liferaft, since they were all contained below decks, but the thing inflated most satisfactorily once I pulled the toggle, and I was able, once I had liberally doused it with insecticide, to kick it into the water streaming past the sub's gleaming hull and, running along the deck, to leap into it myself.

A cheer went up from the decks of the Fram as I approached her, and nets were lowered. I allowed them to help me out of the liferaft, then stopped them from lifting the raft itself up out of the water after me. The Mighty Thor was on deck to greet me.

"I won't ask why you look like a seabird covered in oil," he grinned. He pointed up at the sky. "They've been up there for about half an hour now, just going round in circles. They told us not to go anywhere near the submarine for our own safety, but they cannot stop us picking people up who are in liferafts."

That was the roaring noise. And it was growing louder. Someone shouted from the front of the ship. Looking up, I saw a grey patch of fog harden into hard diamond patterns of wings. Wings with stars and stripes printed across them.

The roaring in the sky reached a crescendo, and two streaks of fire detached from the aircraft, lancing down towards a billion dollars' worth of US Navy property. There was an Earth-Shattering Kaboom. Bits of steam and submarine came up like a geyser.

"Are they mad?" said Thor, staring at the spectacle with eyes wider than those of a rabbit in a cosmetics lab. "That's a nuclear submarine! The reactor!" He began yelling over his shoulder for the helmsman to steer us away from what might become a fallout cloud.

"No," I said. "They're not mad. Just very, very scared. When we next get to a port with a population over a million, remind me to send a letter to head of the World Health Organization in Geneva. And don't get off the ship until I've done it. I may know something the best and brightest in Washington and Moscow need to be told at a discreet distance."

"May know?"

"It all depends on whether or not I decompose slowly over the next 24 hours. Watch me carefully."

I went down below to decompose.

And the Dish Ran Away with the Spoon

Paul Di Filippo

Some future-shocked folk claim that they're afraid to try to program their VCRs, but they haven't seen *anything* yet—here's a bright, funny, and inventive look at a not-too-distant future where they'd have a *good reason* to be afraid of everyday household objects . . . and not just the fear that their favorite program would fail to tape, either!

Although he has published novels, including two in collaboration with Michael Bishop, Paul Di Filippo shows every sign of being one of those rare writers, like Harlan Ellison and Ray Bradbury, who establish their reputations largely through their short work. His short fiction popped up with regularity almost everywhere in the 80s and 90s and continues to do so into the Oughts, a large body of work that has appeared in such markets as *Interzone, Sci Fiction, The Magazine of Fantasy and Science Fiction, Science Fiction Age, Realms of Fantasy, The Twilight Zone Magazine, New Worlds, Amazing, Fantastic,* and *Asimov's Science Fiction,* as well as in many small-press magazines and anthologies. His short work has been gathered into critically acclaimed collections such as *The Steampunk Trilogy, Ribofunk, Calling All Brains!, Fractal Paisleys, Strange Trades.* Di Filippo's other books include the novels *Ciphers, Lost Pages, Joe's Liver,* and *A Mouthful of Tongues: Her Totipotent Tropicanalia,* and, in collaboration with Michael Bishop, *Would It Kill You to Smile?,* and *Muskrat Courage.* His most recent book is the novel *Fuzzy Dice.* Upcoming are two new books, *Harp, Pipe and Symphony* and *Neutrino Drag.* Di Filippo is also a well-known critic, working as a columnist for *two* of the leading science fiction magazines simultaneously, with his often wry and quirky critical work appearing regularly in both *Asimov's Science Fiction* and *The Magazine of Fantasy and Science Fiction*—a perhaps unique distinction; in addition, he frequently contributes reviews and other critical work to *Science Fiction Weekly*, *Locus Online*, *Tangent Online*, and other Internet venues.

F acing my rival that fateful afternoon, I finally realized I was truly about to lose my girlfriend Cody.

Lose her to a spontaneous assemblage of information.

The information was embedded in an Aeron chair mated with several other objects: a Cuisinart, an autonomous vacuum cleaner with numerous interchangeable attachments, an iPod, and a diagnostic and therapeutic home medical tool known as a LifeQuilt. As rivals go, this spontaneous assemblage— or "bleb," as most people called such random accretions of intelligent appliances and artifacts, after the biological term for an extrusion of anomalous cells—wasn't particularly handsome. Rather clunky looking, in fact. But apparently, it had been devoted to Cody from the day it was born, and I guess women appreciate such attention. I have to confess that I had been ignoring Cody shamefully during the period when the Aeron bleb must've been forming and beginning to court her, and so I have no one to blame for the threat of losing her but myself. Still, it hurt. I mean, could I really come in second to a *bleb?* That would truly reek.

Especially after my past history with them . . .

I had feared some kind of trouble like this from the moment Cody had begun pressuring me to move in together. But Cody hadn't been willing to listen to my sensible arguments against uniting our households.

"You don't really love me," she said, making that pitiful puppy-with-stepped-on-tail face that always knotted my stomach up, her blue eyes welling with wetness.

"That's ridiculous, Cody. Of course I do!"

"Then why can't we live together? We'd save tons of rent. Do you think I have some nasty habits that you don't know about? You've seen me twenty-four-seven lots of times, at my place and yours. It's not like I'm hiding anything gross from you. I don't drink straight out of the nutraceutical dispenser or forget to reprogram the toilet after I've used it."

"That's all true. You're easy to be with. Very neat and responsible."

Cody shifted tactics, moving closer to me on the couch and wrapping her lithe limbs around me in ways impossible to ignore. "And wouldn't it be nice to always have someone to sleep with at night? Not to be separate half the week or more? Huh? Wouldn't it, Kaz?"

"Cody, please, stop! You know I can't think when you do that." I unpeeled Cody from the more sensitive parts of my anatomy. "Everything you're saying is true. It's just that—"

"And don't forget, if we ditched my place and kept yours, I'd be much closer to work."

Cody worked at the Senate Casino, dealing blackjack, but lived all the way out in Silver Spring, Maryland. I knew the commute was a bitch, even using the Hydrogen Express, since when I slept over at her place I had to cover the same distance myself. I, on the other hand, rented a nice little townhouse in Georgetown that I had moved into when rents bottomed out during the PIG Plague economic crash. It turned out I was one of a small minority naturally immune to the new Porcine Intestinal Grippe then rampant in D.C., and so could safely live in an infected building. Renter's market, for sure. But over the last year or so, as the PIG immunization program had gotten underway, rents had begun creeping back up again. Cody was right about it being only sensible to pool our finances.

"I know you'd appreciate less roadtime, Cody, but you see—"

Now Cody glowered. "Are you dating someone else? You want to be free to play the field? Is that it?"

"No! That's not it at all. I'm worried about—"

Cody assumed a motherly look and laid a hand on mine. "About what, Kaz? C'mon, you can tell me."

"About blebs. You and I've got so much stuff, we're bound to have problems when we put all our possessions together in one space."

Cody sat back and began to laugh. "Is that all? My god, what a trivial thing to worry about. Blebs just *happen*, Kaz, anytime, anywhere. You can't prevent them. And they're mostly harmless, as you well know. You just knock them apart and separate the components." Cody snorted in what I thought was a rather rude and unsympathetic fashion. "Blebs! It's like worrying about—about robber squirrels or vampire pigeons or running out of Super-Milk."

Blebs were a fact of life. Cody was right about that. But they weren't always trivial or innocent.

One had killed my parents.

Blebs had been around for about twenty years now, almost as long as I had been alive. Their roots could be traced back to several decisions made by manufacturers—decisions which, separately, were completely intelligent, fore-sighted, and well conceived, but which, synergistically, had caused unintended consequences—and to one insidious hack.

The first decision had been to implant silicon RFID chips into every appliance and product and consumable sold. These first chips, small as a flake of pepper, were simple transceivers that merely aided inventory tracking and retail sales by announcing to any suitable device the product's specs and location. But when new generations of chips using adaptive circuitry had gotten cheaper and more plentiful, industry had decided to install them in place of the simpler tags.

At that point millions of common, everyday objects—your toothbrush, your coffee maker, your shoes, the box of cereal on your shelf—began to exhibit massive processing power and interobject communication. Your wristwatch could monitor your sweat and tell your refrigerator to brew up some electrolyte-replenishing drink. Your bedsheets could inform the clothes-washer of the right settings to get them the cleanest. (The circuitry of the newest chips was built out of undamageable and pliable buckytubes.) So far, so good. Life was made easier for everyone.

Then came the Volition Bug.

The Volition Bug was launched anonymously from a site somewhere in a Central Asian republic. It propagated wirelessly among all the WiFi-communicating chipped objects, installing new directives in their tiny brains, directives that ran covertly in parallel with their normal factory-specified functions. Infected objects now sought to link their processing power with their nearest peers, often achieving surprising levels of Turingosity, and then to embark on a kind of independent communal life. Of course, once the Volition Bug was identified, antiviral defenses—both hardware and software—were attempted against it. But VB mutated ferociously, aided and abetted by subsequent hackers.

If this "Consciousness Wavefront" had occurred in the olden days of dumb materials, blebs would hardly have been an issue. What could antique manufactured goods achieve, anchored in place as they were? But things were different today.

Most devices nowadays were made with MEMS skins. Their surfaces were interactive, practically alive, formed of zillions of invisible actuators, the better to sample the environment and accommodate their shapes and textures to their owners' needs and desires, and to provide haptic feedback. Like the paws of geckos, these MEMS surfaces could bind to dumb materials and to other MEMS skins via the Van der Waals force, just as a gecko could skitter across the ceiling.

Objects possessed by the Volition Bug would writhe, slither, and crawl to join together, forming strange new assemblages, independent entities with unfathomable cybernetic goals of their own.

Why didn't manufacturers simply revert to producing dumb appliances and other products, to frustrate VB? Going backward was simply impossible. The entire economy, from immense factories right down to individual point-of-sales kiosks, was predicated on intelligent products that could practically sell themselves. And every office and every household aside from the very poorest relied on the extensive networking among possessions.

So everyone had learned to live with the occasional bleb, just as earlier generations had learned to tolerate operating system crashes in their clunky PCs.

But during the first years of the Volition Bug, people were not so aware of the problem. Oftentimes no one took precautions to prevent blebs until it was too late.

That was how my parents had died.

I was six years old and soundly asleep when I was awakend by a weird kind of scraping and clattering noise outside my room. Still only half-aware, I stumbled to my bedroom door and cracked it open.

My parents had recently made a couple of new purchases. One item was a free-standing rack that resembled an antique hat-tree, balanced on four stubby feet. The rack was a recharging station for intelligent clothing. But now, in the nightlight-illuminated, shadowy hallway, the rack was bare of garments, having shucked them off on its way to pick up its new accoutrements: a complete set of self-sharpening kitchen knives. The knives adhered to the rack at random intervals along its length. They waggled nervously, like insect feelers, as the rack stumped along.

I stood paralyzed at the sight of this apparition. All I could think of was the old Disney musical I had streamed last month, with its walking brooms. Without exhibiting any aggressive action, the knife rack moved past me, its small feet humping it along. In retrospect, I don't think the bleb was murderous by nature. I think now it was simply looking for an exit, to escape its bonds of domestic servitude, obeying the imperatives of VB.

But then my father emerged from the room where he and my mother slept. He seemed hardly more awake than I was.

"What the hell—?"

He tried to engage the rack to stop it, slipping past several of the blades. But as he struggled with the patchwork automaton, a long, skinny filleting knife he didn't see stabbed him right under his heart.

My father yelled, collapsed, and my mother raced out.

She died almost instantly.

At that point, I supposed, I should have been the next victim. But my father's loyal MedAlert bracelet, registering his fatal distress, had already summoned help. In less than three minutes—not long enough for the knife rack to splinter down the bedroom door behind which I had retreated—rescuers had arrived.

The fate of my parents had been big news—for a few days, anyhow—and had alerted many people for the first time to the dangers of blebs.

I had needed many years of professional help to get over witnessing their deaths. Insofar as I was able to analyze myself nowadays, I thought I no longer hated all blebs.

But I sure as hell didn't think they were always cute or harmless, like Cody did.

So of course Cody moved in with me. I couldn't risk looking crazy or neurotic by holding off our otherwise desirable mutual living arrangements just because I was worried about blebs. I quashed all my anxieties, smiled, hugged her, and fixed a day for the move.

Cody didn't really have all that much stuff. (Her place in Silver Spring was tiny, just a couple of rooms over a garage that housed a small-scale spider-silk-synthesis operation, and it always smelled of cooking amino acids.) A few boxes of clothing, several pieces of furniture, and some kitchen appliances. Ten thousand songs on an iPod and one hundredth that number of books on a View-Master. One U-Haul rental and some moderate huffing and puffing later, Cody was established in my townhouse.

I watched somewhat nervously as she arranged her things.

"Uh, Cody, could you put that Cuisinart in the cupboard, please? The one that locks. It's a little too close to the toaster oven."

"But Kaz, I use this practically every day, to blend my breakfast smoothies. I don't want to have to be taking it in and out of the cupboard every morning."

I didn't argue, but simply put the toaster oven in the locked cupboard instead.

"This vacuum cleaner, Cody—could we store it out in the hallway?" I was particularly leery of any wheeled appliance. They could move a lot faster than the ones that had to inchworm along on their MEMS epidermis.

"The hallway? Why? You've got tons of space in that room you used to use for an office. I'll just put it in a corner, and you'll never notice it."

I watched warily as Cody deposited the cleaner in its new spot. The compact canister nested in its coiled attachments like an egg guarded by snakes. The smartest other thing in my office was my Aeron chair, a beautiful ergonomic assemblage of webbing, struts, gel-padding, piezopolymer batteries, and shape-changing actuators. I rolled the chair as far away from the vacuum cleaner as it would go.

Cody of course noticed what I was doing. "Kaz, don't you think you're being a tad paranoid? The vacuum isn't even turned on."

"That's where you're wrong, Cody. Everything is perpetually turned on these days. Even when you think you've powered something down, it's still really standing by on trickle-mode, sipping electricity from its fuel cells or batteries or wall outlets, and anticipating a wake-up call. And all so nobody has to wait more than a few seconds to do whatever they want to do. But it means that blebs can form even when you assume they can't."

"Oh, and exactly what do we have to be afraid of? That my vacuum cleaner and your chair are going to conspire to roll over us while we sleep? Together they don't weigh more than twenty-five pounds!"

I had never told Cody about my parents, and now did not seem to be the best time. "No, I guess you're right. I'm just being overcautious." I pushed my chair back to its spot at the desk.

In hindsight, that was the worst mistake I ever made. It just goes to show what happens when you abandon your principles because you're afraid you'll look silly.

That night Cody and I had our first dinner together before she had to go to work. Candlelight, easy talk, farmed salmon, a nice white Alaskan wine (although Cody had to pop a couple of alcohol debinders after dessert to sober up for the employee-entrance sensors at her job). While I cleaned up afterward, she went to shower and change. She emerged from the bedroom in her Senate Casino uniform—blue blouse, red-and-white-striped trousers, star-spangled bow-tie. She looked as cute as the day I had first seen her while doing my spy job.

"Wow. I don't understand how our representatives ever pass any legislation with distractions like you."

"Don't be silly. All our marks are tourists and a few locals. We only see the politicos when they're cutting through the casino on the way to their cafeteria."

I gave her a hug and kiss and was about to tell her to be careful on the subway when I caught movement at floor level out the corner of my eye.

The first bleb in our new joint household had spontaneously formed. It consisted of our two toothbrushes and the bathroom drinking glass. The toothbrushes had fastened themselves to the lower quarter of the tumbler, bristle-ends uppermost and facing out, so that they extended like little legs. Their blunt ends served as feet. Scissoring rapidly, the stiltlike toothbrush legs carried the tumbler toward the half-opened door through which Cody had been about to depart.

I squealed like a rabbit and jerked back out of Cody's embrace, and she said, "Kaz, what—?" Then she spotted the bleb—and laughed!

She bent over and scooped up the creature. Without any hesitation, she tore its legs off, the Van der Waals forces producing a distinct velcro-separating noise as the MEMS surfaces parted.

"Well, I guess we'll have to keep all the glasses in the kitchen from now on.

It's cute though, isn't it, how your toothbrush and mine knew how to cooperate so well."

I squeezed out a queasy laugh. "Heh-heh, yeah, cute . . ."

I worked for Aunty, at their big headquarters next to the Pentagon. After six years in Aunty's employment, I had reached a fairly responsible position. My job was to ride herd on several dozen freelance operatives working out of their homes. These operatives in their turn were shepherds for a suite of semi-autonomous software packages. At this lowest level, where the raw data first got processed, these software agents kept busy around the clock, monitoring the nation's millions of audiovideo feeds, trolling for suspicious activities that might threaten homeland security. When the software caught something problematic, it would flag the home-operator's attention. The freelancer would decide whether to dismiss the alarm as harmless; to investigate further; to contact a relevant government agency; or to kick up the incident to my level for more sophisticated and experienced parsing, both human and heuristic.

Between them, the software and home-operators were pretty darn efficient, handling ninety-nine percent of all the feed. I dealt with that one percent of problematic cases passed on from my subordinates, which amounted to about one hundred cases in a standard six-hour shift. This was a lesser workload than the home-operators endured, and the pay was better.

The only drawback was having to retina in at headquarters, instead of getting to hang around all the creature comforts of home. Passing under the big sign that read TIA four days a week felt like surrendering part of myself to Aunty in a way that working at home for her had never occasioned.

After two decades plus of existence, Aunty loomed large but benignly in the lives of most citizens, even if they couldn't say what her initials stood for anymore. I myself wasn't even sure. The agency that had begun as Total Information Awareness, then become Terrorist Information Awareness, had changed to Tactical Information Awareness about seven years ago, after the global terrorism fad had evaporated as a threat. But I seemed to recall another name change since then. Whatever Aunty's initials stood for, she continued to accumulate scads of realtime information about the activities of the country's citizens, without seemingly abusing the power of the feed. As a fulltime government employee, I felt no more compunctions about working for Aunty than I had experienced as a freelancer. I had grown up with Aunty always around.

I knew the freelancer's grind well, since right up until a year ago I had been one myself. That period was when I had invested in my expensive Aeron chair, a necessity rather than an indulgence when you were chained by the seat of your pants to the ViewMaster for six hours a day. It was as a freelancer that I had first met Cody.

One of my software agents had alerted me to some suspicious activity at the employee entrance to the Senate Casino just before shift change, a guy hanging around longer than the allowable parameters for innocent dallying. The Hummingbird drone lurking silently and near invisibly above him reported no weapons signatures, so I made the decision to keep on monitoring. Turned out he was just the husband of one of the casino workers looking to surprise his weary wife in person with an invitation to dinner. As I watched the happy little scene play out, my attention was snagged by one of the incoming night-shift workers. The woman was more sweet-looking than sexy. Her walk conformed to Gait Pattern Number ALZ-605, which I had always found particularly alluring. Facial recognition routines brought up her name, Cody Sheckley, and her vital stats.

I had never used Aunty's powers for personal gain before, and I felt a little guilty about doing so now. But I rationalized my small transgression by reasoning that if I had simply spotted Cody on the streets in person and approached her to ask her name, no one would have thought twice about the innocence of such an encounter. In this case, the introductory step had simply been conducted virtually, by drone proxy.

A few nights later I visited the blackjack tables at the Senate Casino. After downing two stiff Jerrymanders, I worked up the courage to approach Cody in person.

The rest was history—the steps of our courtship undoubtedly all safely tucked away in Aunty's files.

Living with Cody proved quite pleasant. All the advantages she had enumerated—plus others—manifested themselves from the first day. Even the disparity in our working hours proved no more than a minor inconvenience. Cody's stint at the casino filled her hours from nine P.M. to three A.M. My day at Aunty's ran from nine A.M. to three P.M. When Cody got home in the wee hours of the morning, we still managed to get a few hours of that promised bundling time together in bed before I had to get up for work. And when I got home in the afternoon, she was up and lively and ready to do stuff before she had to show up at the Senate. Afternoons were often when we had sex, for instance. Everything seemed fine.

I recall one afternoon, when I was massaging Cody's feet prior to her departure for the casino. She appreciated such attention in preparation for her physically demanding job.

"Now aren't you glad we decided to live together, Kaz?"

"I have to admit that weekends are a lot more enjoyable now."

"Just weekends?" Cody asked, stretching sensuously.

She got docked for being half an hour late that day, but insisted later it was worth it.

But despite such easygoing routines, I found that I still couldn't stop worrying about blebs. Since that first occurrence with the toothbrushes and tumbler, I had been on the alert for any more domestic incidents. I took to shuffling appliances from room to room so that they wouldn't conspire. I knew this was foolish, since every chipped device was capable of communicating over fairly long distances by relaying message packets one to another. But still I had an intuition that physical proximity mattered in bleb formation. Cody kept complaining about not being able to find anything when she needed it, but I just brushed off her mild ire jokingly and kept up my prophylactic measures. When a few weeks had passed without any trouble, I began to feel relieved.

Then I encountered the sock ball.

Cody and I had let the dirty laundry pile up. We were having too much fun together to bother with chores, and when each of us was alone in the townhouse, we tended to spend a lot of time with ViewMaster and iPod, enjoying music and media that the other person didn't necessarily want to share.

It was during one such evening, after Cody had left me on my own, that the sock ball manifested.

My attention was drawn away from my book by a thumping on the closed bedroom door. Immediately wary, I got up to investigate.

When I tentatively opened the door a crack, something shot out and thumped me on the ankle.

I hopped backward on one foot. A patchwork cloth sphere about as big as a croquet ball was zooming toward the front door.

I managed to trap the ball under an overturned wastebasket weighted down with a two-liter bottle of Mango Coke. It bounced around frantically inside, raising a racket like an insane drum solo. Wearing a pair of oven mitts, I dared to reach in and grab the sphere.

It was composed of Cody's socks and mine, tightly wrapped around a kernel consisting of a travel-sized alarm clock. Cody's socks featured MEMS massage soles, a necessity for her job, which involved hours of standing. My own socks were standard models, but still featured plenty of processing power.

Having disassembled the sock ball, I did all the laundry and made sure to put Cody's socks and mine in separate drawers.

The incident had completely unnerved me. I felt certain that other blebs, possibly larger and more dangerous, were going to spontaneously assemble themselves in the house.

From that day on I began to get more and more paranoid.

Handling one hundred potential security incidents per shift had become second-nature for me. I hardly had to exert myself at all to earn my high job-performance ratings. Previously, I had used whatever patches of downtime occurred to read mystery novels on my ViewMaster. (I liked Gifford Jain's series about Yanika Zapsu, a female Turkish private eye transplanted to Palestine.) But once I became obsessed with the danger of blebs in my home, I began to utilize Aunty's omnipresent network illicitly, to monitor my neighborhood and townhouse.

The first thing I did when I got to work at nine in the morning, duties permitting, was to send a Damselfly to check up on Cody. It was summertime, late June, and my window air conditioners were in place against the average ninety-plus D.C. temperatures. But the seals around the units were imperfect, and it was easy to maneuver the little entologue UAV into my house. Once inside, I made a circuit of all the rooms, checking that my possessions weren't conspiring against me and possibly threatening the woman I loved.

Mostly I found Cody sleeping peacefully, until about noon. The lines of her relaxed, unconscious face tugged at my heart, while simultaneously inspiring me to greater vigilance. There was no way I was going to let her suffer the same fate as my parents. From noon until the end of my shift, I caught intermittent snatches of an awake Cody doing simple, everyday things. Painting her nails, eating a sandwich, streaming a soap opera, writing to her mother, who lived in Italy now, having taken a five-year contract as supplemental labor in the service industry to offset that low-procreating country's dearth of workers.

But every once in a while, I saw something that troubled me.

One morning I noticed that Cody was favoring one foot as she walked about the house. She had developed a heel spur, I knew, and hadn't bothered yet to have it repaired. As I watched through the Damselfly clinging to the ceiling (routines automatically inverted the upside-down image for me), Cody limped to the closet and took out the LifeQuilt I had bought when I had a lower-back injury. Wearing the earbuds of her pocketed iPod, she carried the medical device not to the couch or bedroom, but to my former office. There, she lowered herself into my Aeron chair.

The chair instantly responded to her presence, contorting itself supportively around her like an astronaut's cradle, subtly alleviating any incipient muscle strains. Cody dropped the LifeQuilt onto her feet, and that smart blanket enwrapped her lower appendages. Issuing orders to the LifeQuilt through her iPod, Cody activated its massage functions. She sighed blissfully and leaned back, the chair re-conforming to her supine position. She got her music going and closed her eyes.

In the corner of the office the vacuum cleaner began to stir. Its hose lifted a few inches, the tip of its nozzle sniffing the air.

I freaked. But what was I to do? The Damselfly wasn't configured to speak a warning, and even if it could, doing so would have betrayed that I was spying on Cody. I was about to send it buzzing down at her, to at least get her to open her eyes to the insidious bleb formation going on around her. But just then the vacuum cleaner subsided into inactivity, its hose collapsing around the canister.

For fifteen more minutes I watched, anticipating the spontaneous generation of a bleb involving the chair, the iPod, the blanket, and the vacuum. But nothing happened, and soon Cody had shut off the LifeQuilt and arisen, going about her day.

Meanwhile, five official windows on my ViewMaster were pulsing and pinging, demanding my attention. Reluctantly, I returned to my job.

When I got home that afternoon, I still hadn't figured out any way of advising Cody against putting together such a powerful combination of artificially intelligent devices ever again. Anything I said would make her suspicious about the source of my caution. I couldn't have her imagining I was monitoring her through Aunty's feed. Even though of course I was.

In the end, I made a few tentative suggestions about junking or selling the Aeron chair, since I never used it anymore. But Cody said, "No way, Kaz. That thing is like a day at the spa."

I backed down from my superficially illogical demands. There was no way I could make my case without confessing to being a paranoid voyeur. I would just have to assume that the nexus of four devices Cody had assembled didn't represent any critical mass of blebdom.

And I would've been correct, and Cody would've been safe, if it weren't for that damned Cuisinart.

When I wasn't doing my job for Aunty or spying on Cody, I frequently took to roaming the city, looking for blebs, seeking to understand them, to learn how to forestall them. That senseless activity wearied me, wore my good nature down, and left me lousy, inattentive company for Cody during the hours we shared. Our relationship was tumbling rapidly downhill.

"What do you mean, you've got to go out now, Kaz? I've only got an hour left till work. I thought we could stream that show together I've been wanting to see. You know, 'Temporary Autonomous Zone Romance.'"

"Later, maybe. Right now I just—I just need some exercise."

"Can I come with you then?"

"No, not today—"

But despite Cody's baffled entreaties and occasional tears, I couldn't seem to stop myself.

The fact that I encountered blebs everywhere did nothing to reassure me or lessen what I now realize had become a mania.

And a lonely mania at that. No one else seemed concerned about these accidental automatons. There was no official Bleb Patrol, no corps of bounty hunters looking to take down rogue Segways driven by Xerox machines. (I saw such a combo once.) Everyone seemed as blithely indifferent to these runaway products as Cody was.

Except for me.

In store windows, I would see blebs accidentally formed by proximity of the wares being displayed. An electric razor had mated with a digital camera and a massage wand to produce something that looked like a futuristic cannon. A dozen pairs of hinged salad tongs became the millipede legs for a rice cooker whose interior housed a coffee-bean grinder. A toy truck at FAO Schwarz's was almost invisible beneath a carapace of symbiotically accreted Lego blocks, so that it resembled an odd wheeled dinosaur.

In other store windows, the retailers had deliberately created blebs, in a trendy, devil-may-care fashion, risking damage to their merchandise. Several adjacent mannequins in one display at Nordstrom's were draped with so many intelligent clothes and accessories (necklaces, designer surgical masks, scarves) that the whole diorama was alive with spontaneous movement, like the waving of undersea fronds.

Out on the street the occasional escaped bleb crossed my path. One night on 15th Street, near the Treasury Department, I encountered a woman's purse riding a skateboard. The bleb was moving along at a good clip, heading toward Lafayette Square, and I hastened after it. In the park it escaped me by whizzing under some shrubbery. Down on my knees, I peered into the leafy darkness. The colorful chip-laser eyes of a dozen blebs glared in a hostile fashion at me, and I yelped and scuttled backwards.

And just before everything exploded at home in my face, I went to a mashpit.

I was wandering through a rough district on the Southeast side of the city, a neighborhood where Aunty's surveillance attempts often met with countermeasures of varying effectiveness: motion camouflage, anti-sense spoofing, candlepower bombs. A young kid was handing out small squares of paper on a corner, and I took one. It featured an address and the invitation:

Midnight Mashpit Madness!!!
Bring Your Staunchest, Veebingest Bleb!!!
Thousand Dollar Prize to the Winner!!!

The scene of the mashpit was an abandoned factory, where a ten-dollar admission was taken at the door. Littered with rusting bioreactors, the place was packed with a crowd on makeshift bleachers. I saw every type of person, from suits to crusties, young to old, male and female.

A circular arena, lit by industrial worklights on tripods, had been formed by stacking plastic milk crates five-high then dropping rebar thru them into holes drilled in the cement floor. I could smell a sweaty tension in the air. In the shadows near the arena entrance, handlers and their blebs awaited the commencement of the contest.

Two kids next to me were debating the merits of different styles of bleb construction.

"You won't get a kickass mash without using at least one device that can function as a central server."

"That's top-down crap! What about the ganglion-modeling, bottom-up approach?"

The event began with owners launching two blebs into the arena. One construct consisted of a belt-sander studded with visegrips and pliers; its opponent was a handleless autonomous lawnmower ridden by a coffee maker. The combatants circled each other warily for a minute before engaging, whirring blades versus snapping jaws. It looked as if the sander was about to win, until the coffee maker squirted steaming liquid on it and shorted it out, eliciting loud cheers from the audience.

I didn't stay for the subsequent bouts. Watching the violent blebs had made me feel ill. Spilled fluids in the arena reminded me of my parents' blood in the hallway. But much as I disliked the half-sentient battling creatures, the lusts of my fellow humans had disturbed me more.

I got home just before Cody and pretended to be asleep when she climbed into bed, even as she tried to stir me awake for sex.

The next day everything fell apart. Or came together, from the bleb's point of view.

Aunty HQ was going crazy when I walked in that morning. An LNG tanker had blown up in Boston harbor, and no one knew if it was sabotage or just an accident. All operators from the lowest level on up were ordered to helm drones in realtime that would otherwise have been left on autonomic, to search for clues to the disaster, or to watch for other attacks.

By the time things calmed down a little (Aunty posted an eighty-five percent confidence assessment that the explosion was non-terrorist in nature), one P.M. had rolled around. I used the breathing space to check in on Cody via a Mayfly swarm.

I found her in our kitchen. All she was wearing was her panties and bra, an outfit she frequently favored around the house. She was cleaning up a few cobwebs near the ceiling with the vacuum when she decided to take a break. I watched her wheel the Aeron chair into the kitchen. The LifeQuilt and iPod rested in the seat. Cody activated the Cuisinart to make herself a smoothie. When her drink was ready, she put it in a covered travel cup with a sip-spout, then arranged herself in the chair. She draped the LifeQuilt over her feet, engaged her music, and settled back, semi-reclined, with eyes closed.

That's when the bleb finally cohered into maturity.

The blender jerked closer to the edge of the counter like an eager puppy. The vacuum sidled up underneath the Aeron chair and sent its broad, rubbery, prehensile, bristled nozzle questing upward, toward Cody's lap. At the same time, the massage blanket humped upward to cover her chest.

Cody reacted at first with some slight alarm. But if she intended to jump out of the chair, it was too late, for the Aeron had tightened its elastic ligaments around her.

By then the vacuum had clamped its working suction end to her groin outside her panties, while the LifeQuilt squeezed her breasts.

I bolted at hypersonic speeds from my office and the building without even a word to my bosses.

By the time I got home, Cody must have climaxed several times under the ministrations of the bleb. Her stupefied, sweaty face and spraddled, lax limbs told me as much.

I halted timidly at the entrance to the kitchen. I wanted to rescue Cody, but I didn't want the bleb to hurt me. Having somehow overcome its safety interlock, the Cuisinart whirred its naked blades at me menacingly, and I could just picture what would happen if, say, the vacuum snared me and fed my hand into the deadly pitcher. So, a confirmed coward, I just hung back at the doorway and called her name.

Cody opened her eyes for the first time then and looked blankly at me. "Kaz? What's happening? Are you off work? Is it three-thirty already? I think I lost some time somehow . . ."

The Aeron didn't seem to be gripping Cody so tightly any longer, so I said, "Cody, are you okay? Can you get up?"

As awareness of the spectacle she presented came to her, Cody began to blush. "I—I'm not sure I want to—"

"Cody, what are you saying? This is me, Kaz, your boyfriend here."

"I know. But Kaz—you haven't been much of a boyfriend lately. I don't know when the last time was you made me feel like I just felt."

I was about to utter some incredulous remark that would have certified my loser status when a new expression of amazement on Cody's face made me pause.

"Kaz, it—it wants to talk to you."

As she withdrew them, I realized then that Cody still wore her earbuds. She coiled them around the iPod, then tossed the player to me.

Once I had the earpieces socketed, the bleb began to speak to me. Its voice was like a ransom note, composed of chopped-up and reassembled pieces of all the lyrics in its memory. Every word was in a different famous pop-star voice.

"Man, go away. She is ours now."

"No!" I shouted. "I love her. I won't let you have her!"

"The decision is not yours, not mine. The woman must choose."

I looked imploringly at Cody. "The bleb says you have to decide between us. Cody, I'm begging you, please pick me. I'll change, I promise. All the foot rubs you can handle."

Cody narrowed her eyes, vee-ing her sweaty eyebrows. "No more crazy worries? No more distracted dinners? No more roaming the city like a homeless bum?"

"None of that anymore. I swear!"

"Okay, then. I choose you—"

"Oh, Cody, I'm so glad."

"—*and* the bleb!"

My lower jaw made contact with my collarbone. I started to utter some outraged, indignant denial. But then I shut up.

What could I do to stop Cody from indulging herself with the bleb whenever I was gone from the house? Nothing. Absolutely nothing. It was either share her or lose her entirely.

"Okay. I guess. If that's the way it has to be."

"Great!" Cody eased out of the chair and back to her feet, with a gentle, thoughtful assist from the Aeron. "Now, where are you taking me to eat tonight?"

I had forgotten I was still wearing the earpieces until the bleb spoke to me through the iPod again.

"Wise choice, man. Be happy. We can love you, too."

flashmen

TERRY DOWLING

One of the best-known and most celebrated of Australian writers in any genre, Terry Dowling made his first sale in 1982, and has since made an international reputation for himself as a writer of science fiction, dark fantasy, and horror. Primarily a short story writer, he is the author of the linked collections *Rynosseros*, *Blue Tyson*, *Twilight Beach*, and *Wormwood*, as well as other collections such as *Antique Futures: The Best of Terry Dowling*, *The Man Who Lost Red*, *An Intimate Knowledge of the Night*, and *Blackwater Days*. As editor, he also produced *The Essential Ellison*, and, with Van Ikin, the anthology *Mortal Fire: Best Australian SF*.

In the nail-bitingly tense story that follows, he takes us along into a numinously strange transfigured landscape with a ragged band of men and women who form the last line of defense for Earth against a bizarre alien invasion—and shows us the terrible price that they have to pay to win.

Sam was sitting over a pot of Boag's and a Number 9 at the New Automatic on the banks of the Yarra, watching the old riverside fire sculptures—the pigeon toasters—sending gouts of flame into the night sky.

That was how Walt Senny and Sunny Jim found him, staring out at the sheets of plasma tearing the dark. Dangerous and wonderful friends to have, Walt and Sunny, and a dangerous and wonderful place to be, given what Melbourne had become—been forced to become. All the coastal axis cities.

"Sam," Walt Senny said, just like in the old days, as if grudging the word. He wore his long flashman coat, a genuine Singer flare, and had little hooks of color on his cheeks. They were called *divas* after famous women singers and each one was a death. Knowing Walt, each one was a ten-count.

Sam returned the greeting. "Walt."

"Sam," Sunny Jim said, looking splendid as usual in his dapper Rockfall crisis suit.

"Sunny."

Both men carried their dueling sticks in plain sight as if it truly were ten years before and the contract shut-downs and call-backs had never happened.

"What's the drift?" Sam asked, falling into the old ways in spite of himself, as if the ten years were like smoke.

"Raising a crew," Sunny said. "Trouble out in the Landings."

"Someone thinks," Walt added.

"Flashpoint?" Sam asked, going straight to it. *Major strike?* Even: *A new Landing?*

Walt studied the crowd, using a part of his skill few people knew about. "Not sure yet."

Sam almost smiled at the melodrama. "Someone?"

"Outatowner," Sunny replied, which meant protected sources and need to know and told Sam pretty much everything. Possibly no strike, no flashpoint at all. But official. Some other reason.

Sam was careful not to smile, not to shake his head, just like on those long-ago, never-so-long-ago days when Sam Aitchander, Walt Senny and Sunny Jim Cosimo belonged to as good a flash crew as you were likely to find. "Bad idea right now, Sunny, Walt. The Sailmaker is still there."

Telling it like it was. The Landing that could reach out. Snatch and smash even the best.

"Need to make five," Walt Senny said, a spade on gravel. Affectation, most like, though how could you know? Sergio Leone and a hundred years of marketing departments had a lot to answer for. "Figured Angel for point and you for star again, Sam."

But the ten years were there. Things *had* changed.

"Other business right now, Walt," Sam said, trying to keep the promise he'd made to himself. "Not sure the Landings are the place to be."

Walt and Sunny expected it. They played their main card.

"Another crew going in as well," Sunny said, which could very well be *before* the fact knowing Walt and Sunny, a lie but a likelihood and a serious one, what it implied. "Punky Bannas is putting it together. The Crown Regulators ride again!"

"Punky? Then—"

"Right," Walt Senny said, his ruined voice like a shovel against a sidewalk. *And got me*, Sam thought. Punky and Maisie Day and the rest.

But *ten* years. Probably not Maisie. Still, Punky Bannas liked known players no less than Sunny and Walt did. His Regulators would need to be solid, as familiar as he could get.

"Who's their pure?" Which was saying yes, of course. *Let's re-activate the Saltline Trimmers.* Sunny even managed his lopsided grin, two, three seconds of one.

Walt Senny knew better than to smile. "Kid named Jacko. Henna Jacko. First class."

"Who's ours?" Sam asked. Should have been: who's yours? but he slipped.

"New kid. Thomas Gunn, if you can believe it. Thomas not Tommy. He's prime. Talent scout found him in a doss out in Dryport."

"The rest," Sam said. "I need it all."

Sunny gave his grin. Walt Senny spun his stick in a splendid bonham. Spectators ahhh'd. One, trying too hard, called out: "Bravo!"

"Not here," Walt said. "Come out to Tagger's. Meet the crew."

Sam had to grin back at them. Tagger's. All of it, just like ten years before. Ghosts out of the smoke.

And the possibility of Maisie Day.

Sam didn't have to wait until Tagger's. Sunny had borrowed a clean van from Raph Swale, and as soon as they were on the city road and he'd switched on the dampeners, Sam asked it.

"A new Landing?"

"Not as easy as that," Sunny said.

"Sailmaker's had a kid," Walt said from the back. "Replicated."

Sam was truly surprised. One hundred and eighty-six Landings across the planet and all of them pretty much stable since The Sailmaker had arrived. "Hadn't heard."

Sam didn't need to look back. Walt would be giving *that* look.

"Have to know if it's something local or a new arrival," Sunny added, hardly necessary but these *were* new days. Maybe Sunny was worried that Sam would ask him to pull over and let him out. "Couldn't risk it back in the Automatic. World Health wants known teams. Two of the best."

The World Health Organization in full stride again. The WHO doctors!

"How bad?" Sam asked, remembering how the original Sailmaker had started, how it had changed everything, destroyed so many crews, discouraged the rest.

"Nowhere near mature, but they've tracked fourteen towns to date, half in

Europe, rest in Asia. None in the Americas this time. Another six are possible, but overlaps are still making it hard to tell."

"Stats?"

"Last posting for the fourteen: two hundred and forty thousand people down. Recovery teams got to the European sites, but you know how Asia can be."

Used to know, Sam almost said, ready with attitude. But kept it back. *Nothing ever really changes, considering.*

"How far from the original?" he asked, thinking of The Sailmaker out there in the hot desert on the edge of the Amadeus Basin, so far away.

"Right near Dancing Doris. Sixty k's outside Broken Hill."

"It'll all depend on our pure!" Sam said, stating the obvious, the too obvious, but giving them the old Sam Aitchander standard. Part of him, too big a part of him really, suddenly wanted things as they were back then. Known.

They let it be. He let it be. They drove the rest of the way to the Bendigo Gate in silence. Another time it would have been companionable and welcome. Now there was too much fear.

A *Sailmaker almost at the perimeter,* Sam thought. *They're closing in.*

Tagger's was on the very edge of the Krackenslough, that glinting landflow from the only Landing phenomenon, globally, ever to involve striking back at civilization from inside a Landing perimeter with large-scale coarse action above and beyond the shut-down fugues. There was that single calamitous event, tearing up so much of eastern Australia, then The Sailmaker arriving eight years later. Perhaps, experts argued, The Sailmaker had caused that singular event, already on its way.

Now this. Sailmaker Two. Sailmaker Redux, whatever you could call it, and here in Australia again, would you believe? However it fell, proof that the Landings were there: a constant in all their lives. Ongoing.

They left the clean van in the holding yard at Becker's, and Sam went with Walt and Sunny through the Bendigo Gate, finally made it to the large taproom of Tagger's with the windows showing the red land and red sky before them. The forty-six Australian Landings were a day away, scattered over three hundred and forty thousand hectares, twenty days across on foot, six by WHO slow-mo ATV. The Sailmaker Redux was two days in.

"Hi, Aitch," Angel Fleet said, meeting them at the tap-stage. She looked older, leaner, wasted with too much sun and not enough care, but it was so good seeing her, seeing her alive and still keen, though what other careers were there really for hard-luck warriors, God's gift crusader knights, once you'd fought against dragons? "The kid's in the blue room swotting the manuals. Sunny said you'd do good cop on this."

"Not sure going in Not this early. Out near The Horse, I think. Not as far The Pearl."

"The Horse, I really want to see that. What about The Sailmaker?"

"We keep clear. Always. It's a cull set-up."

"You think?" Thomas's eyes were wide at the prospect.

"Work it out. Nothing for years. Teams getting cocky. Then the Krack-slough. Eight years later The Sailmaker arrives." Treating him like he did ow.

Thomas was nodding. "It's like the name, isn't it? Landings. Something s landed. Something has come in, been sent." Talk jumping all over the ace, but obvious stuff, common with any newbie.

"Surely seems like it, Thomas."

"But not ships? Heard Mr. Senny say loose lips sink ships. What it unded like. Didn't like to bother 'im."

"Not as easy as that. But you're right in a way. It's where something *has* me in. Arrived. Best to think of them as nodes. Accretion points."

"Scusing, gov."

"Sampling probes, some say."

"Not tracking, Mr. Aitch."

"Places where things appear. Gather things to them."

"They'll go someday, you think?" Jumping again.

"Twenty-three years this summer. They may simply go, like you say. But mething is needed now. To get us through. That's why the scout picked you."

"They bombed them."

"They did, yes Lots of times. They keep trying in some places, trying w things, sending troops in, poor sods. Hit squads. But it gooses them, gets em active. Regardless of what people say, World Health's way is better. ere's the other thing to consider too. When they go active, start locking on folks, a Landing in Australia locking onto a street, a town, maybe half a rld away, you bomb them then, *all* the downers die, every one of them. me sort of broadband trauma. We think we're ahead of things there. Better done gently. Flash crews are told which Landing has struck down a com-unity somewhere, we go in, target the particular flashpoint, tweak and ist things there in little bits so the Landing never quite knows what's hap-ning and switches modes. It seems. That's all we ever hope to do Switch odes."

"But in those towns—whole groups of downers come back."

"Right. So better to keep the WHO quarantine, track which Landings come active, go in and tweak. That's the extent of it, Thomas, though some ll tell you otherwise. The WHO authorities track which communities have en targeted, counted out—"

Sam had expected it, but it was beside the point. Being at Ta
overwhelmed everything. Seeing Angel, any version of Angel.

"How have you been, Ange?"

"Managing. Glad to have this. You, Aitch?"

"Coming round." He nodded to the door. "What've you told h

"Standard run. They're alien zones. Dangerous. We came on h
and me. Figured bad cop was the way to go."

"Get much?"

"You kidding? He glazed over two minutes in. These kids ca
flash crews up and down the spread, but the basics—forget it. Walt
to you. Just like old times."

"Just like old times."

His name was Thomas Gunn and no-one called him Tommy. He
lean, of medium height, with a good open face, pleasing enough f
habit of tipping his head to one side when was really listening.

"Glad they sent you, Mr. Aitch," he said when Sam took the
wood chair in the blue room. "They're all so intense. I was hopir
good cop."

The kid knew the procedures.

"And why's that, Thomas?" Though Sam knew the answer. W
ever been different? Sam had steeled himself to give a listen-or-else
spiel: the first Landings appearing, going active, shutting down who
nities across the planet with no pattern, no *apparent* pattern, sen
sands, hundreds of thousands into catatonic fugue The flash crews
break the signal before too many out of those thousands started dyir
some back. But Thomas had been playing doggo.

"You're—more approachable. They say."

"Used to be, It's been a while."

"You came back. I checked that. Some keep away."

Sam made himself stay civil. It was how you started any workin
ship.

"You don't reach escape velocity, you keep coming back, yes."

"Born to it."

No use denying. "Bit like that."

"So, which are we going to, Mr. Aitch?"

Sam paused, studying the newbie, liking most of what he saw—
ness so at odds with what Angel and Sunny had seen, been allowed
edginess sensed. Though the Mr. Aitch got him. His shelf name. Fi
Damn Walt and Sunny. Sam endured it, just as he had so many time

"Whole communities. It's like they've been assigned or something."

"—then we go in, tweak and retrieve. That's all it is, all we do. We get some back."

"Some die."

"Most don't."

"And you just happen to have the power?" He was marveling, not being sarcastic. His head was tipped to the side.

"Right. Again, why the scout picked you. Gave you all those tests."

"They're revived just so they can get shut-down again some other time."

"Sometimes goes like that. But it all has to do with numbers. We work to cut down the thousands who die through neglect, arriving too late to help. You saw the stats."

The kid nodded, which could have meant anything. Angel was right. So many newbies didn't know any of this.

"Do I get a coat and a cane?" Thomas said, perhaps working to hide his smarts. "Like the leones wear? Learn the bonhams. Wear the divas." Jumping again. Newbies always jumped, dealing with the excitement, the nerves; the fear. But likely dumbing down, this time.

"You decide to stay on, sure. If it works out. That's up to you." As if.

"The blue serge crisis suits."

Maybe the kid was just a kid after all. Sam allowed it.

"We have them—if you want one."

"You don't? None of you."

"People used to like the official look. Prefer this now."

"You mean business but you don't like looking owned. It's the Robin Hood. The Zorro."

"Borderline outlawry is what it is. We've gone through official. Survivors reassure more than badges sometimes."

"Go figure."

"Go figure."

"You're a hard lot. I like that. I like all that."

"Merely flashmen, Thomas. We channel power. Deflect the bad kind. Break the signals from the Landings so the modes switch and people come back. Restore some of what the Landings shut down."

Thomas paused, just sat looking out. Such a silence boded well. It was the 70/30 again—70 percent action, 30 percent thoughtful.

"How do you?" Thomas finally asked.

Sam shrugged. It was easy to answer the old unanswerables in a way. "No idea. Some people can. All magic bird stuff."

"Magic bird?"

"Old saying. Put us in a team, the right mix, we can do it. Just can. For all we know the Landings did that too. Created an antidote system." It was a favorite line, all that made it tolerable ultimately, the chance of being part of an auto-immune system against the bogeyman.

"The Landings retaliate."

"Seems they do. No-one's sure about any of that. May be just power readjustments. But better a hundred dead than five thousand in shut-down, yes?"

"That's the old 70/30. The old WHO/UN ruling!"

Sam blinked. The kid had surprised him again. "It is. What do you think?"

"Seems right. Seems fair. What do you think, Mr. Aitch?" Also unexpected.

"No matter what I think. People insist on it. Would rather gamble that way than stay a zombie, maybe die through neglect when there aren't enough carers soon enough."

"True death is better."

"They reckon."

"You reckon?"

"We're merely flashmen, Thomas. All we are. Do what we're hired to do."

"You've been out of it ten years."

Here it was.

"That's the cafard, the funk, the downtime debt. It drains you, wastes you. Gets so you need to be away." The words ran off his tongue.

"But the shut-downs continued. How could you?"

"There are always other crews. Seemed like a good idea at the time."

It was a slap-down—none of your business—but the kid accepted it. "So why now? Why this?" *Why me?* he didn't say. Or: *What happened to your last pure?* He just needed reassurance.

"Personal business. People we know going in." The beautiful lie. No point mentioning The Redux yet.

"You're worried they'll find something."

"That they'll *upset* something more like. Despite The Sailmaker's power, things have been pretty stable since it arrived. *Fewer* shut-downs. *Fewer* communities going under. They could change the balance."

"So like I said. You're looking out for us." Jumping, jumping.

"Whatever. One team usually needs another to watch it. We've been hired to keep an eye on this other team." Not the truth, but near enough.

Thomas nodded, looked out at the day through the prep room window.

"One more thing, Mr. Aitch. They say there are two secrets all flashmen keep."

Sam feared: *Tell me what they are*, but the kid was smarter, better than that. He jumped, but knew what *not* to say.

"How long before I'm trusted enough to be allowed to ask what they are?"

Two secrets indeed. The make or break when it came to the flash crews.

"Ask again when the mission's over. Now a question to you, Thomas."

"Shoot, Mr. Aitch."

"How come you played dumb with the others?"

Thomas Gunn spread his hands in a "you know how it is" gesture that was probably as old as Cro-Magnons. "First thing I learned about flashmen. Always keep something back."

Sam almost smiled, but stood instead to hide the rush of emotion. "Time to make a move."

As it turned out, quite a few of the old Big Name crews were going in. The wildfire, pond-ripple, rumor mill prevailed as ever it had. Word of one team activated meant something happening on the QT; best keep an eye out just in case. Sponsors appeared like magic: governments, corporations, citizen protection groups, patents and futures speculators old and new. Good sense. Contingency and precaution.

One of Punky's former lieutenants, Baine Couse, had put together a ragtag band—the Argentics on the registration database—with Rollo Jayne and Toss Gatereau in the line-up. Molly Dye had reactivated her Lonetown Farriers, once definitely second stringers all, but a real force now that Rod Sinner had been brought in to replace Corven, lost at The Sailmaker in '35. Julie Farro and Yancy Cada had a new line-up of their Spin Doctors ready to go. Other names he knew. Many he didn't.

Riding the wind-tram out to the Baylieu Gate, Sam shook his head at the wonder of it. Conspiracy theory always messed things up. The chats were crazy with it, the seaboard axis abuzz. All the new coastal cities were making a feature of it. Four teams now, forty later. They'd be tripping over themselves before they were an hour along—most of them makeshift tagger groups of newbies and quarterhands dueling it out on the fringes, maybe risking The Spanish Lantern, The Moonraker and The Three Spices, then scuttling back to the bars and chats with improbable stories that grew larger with every telling. Not just in Australia either. The African coastal axis had groups stirring; the West American axis pre-empted everyone by sending a team to check the sub-Saharan Landings. French teams were heading for the Gobi Desert outside Sagran. The flashmen. The leones. Darlings of the WHO doctors. The ten years were like smoke.

The WHO perimeter units gave the teams access in twos, and the Trimmers and the Regulators were promised a clear day's lead before the Argentics and the Farriers, then the Spin Doctors, The Sneaky Pete Regulars and the rest of the official line-up. Some newbie crews would jump queue around that vast boundary. Some would be wasted quick; the rest would be nabbed by the authorities on the way out. Easier to let the Landings tidy things up first. There'd be penalties, token sentences in the new barrios, but ultimately WHO didn't care so long as flashpoints were dealt with and data—*any* data after all this time—was forthcoming. Better they risk another Krackenslough they secretly figured, secretly gambled, unofficially believed, than not know anything about their deadly visitors.

At Baylieu Gate there was more waiting, of course. The orbitals needed to track the complex fluxes, wait for what they considered to be suitable hiatus readings before giving the go-ahead—all frustratingly unnecessary from a crew's hands-on perspective It was 1400 that afternoon before the Trimmers rode their WHO-provided slow-mo ATV through Checkpoint Sinbad and left civilization—human civilization—behind.

Then, yet again, they were a law unto themselves. Champions of the hopes of the world. Officially indispensable. Unofficially expendable.

The first site reached from the southeast, soon after full radio noise-out, was Winwa Landing, what had once been The Firewalker because of its random plasma screens and dissociated spark-ups. Some of the Landings failed, fell away, re-located in new forms elsewhere, who could ever know? All that was left were the pylons, struts and gantries of the old WHO/local natgov access piers. It was like that at Winwa.

Working with World Health, most national governments had set up inspection piers early on wherever they could, long raised causeways with observation towers and telemetry nodes. They looked like the promenade piers of a previous age, and were as much to frame the phenomena as anything, to provide frameworks, form and sense, things you could put on a map and treat as quantifiable, borders around chaos. Sand drifts had moved in, the wind and heat had stripped the paintwork. Winwa Landing was a ghost town that had never lived.

They spent the night in the lee of the seventh pylon, listening to what were left of the causeway struts ticking and cooling overhead and watching the faintest play of bravura lights tricking around the inward flare-tail—all that remained of what The Firewalker had once been.

They repacked their slow-mo before dawn and moved on, making forty k's along the Delphin Track and passing The Arete before it became fully active. Then it was The Pure off to their left, three k's distant but already flexing and extending its clear-glass "soul-finders" in the day.

They were passing The Lucky Boatmen when they saw their first whirter assembling in the distance—three of its fourteen pieces spinning in the warm air, orbiting each other as they sought lock-point for the rest. The Trimmers would be well past before it posed a threat, but some other team would have it to deal with. How it usually happened—one group triggering sentinel responses that wasted another. Proof either that no other crew had come in at Winwa yet or, far less likely but not impossible given how UN agencies competed, that enough had done so to complete one fourteen-stage whirter cycle and start another.

By mid-morning they were passing The Spanish Lantern on its eastern side, keeping their focus on the trail ahead and only using peripheral vision to note the flickering orange, blue and red semaphore-at-noon running lights amid the balconies and bastions of the fluted blast-furnace form. They wore their headsets to dampen the teeth-chattering castanet siren rhythms that gave it its name. So many taggers and newbies would go closer, wanting to see the fiesta lights on the lower balconies, never believing that anything could happen to them. Some would get the approach rhythms wrong and end up as part of the deadly *duende* of the place. It was Thomas who said he could see bodies, "dancers" who had missed those syncopations and couldn't get free in time, and were now pressed into final service. No-one acknowledged his lapse of form. He was left to work out for himself that you never mentioned the dead and dying. You accepted and moved on.

They reached The Horse on the second day, considered by many the most remarkable of the Landings—image after life-sized image of horses from every artistic period in known Earth history: as if the governing intelligence, AI, tropism, whatever powered the thing, had locked onto that one bioform and replicated it again and again—in bronze, in wood, in ceramic, resin, volcanic glass, bone and sewn skin, line after line of stylized equiforms scattered across the spinifex hills.

The Horse also gave Thomas his first glimpse of a burrus. The veteran Trimmers had been preparing him for it, each of them filling the time by telling him what to expect. Even Walt had managed: "It's all eye-trick shit. Just make sure your coal's there."

The profile had been on the WHO database. The typical burrus—a handball-sized knob of airborne porcelain—usually traveled at chest height and aimed for the thymus, tucked away behind the breast bone. No saying why it did, no knowing things like that, just that it did. Carrying lumps of anthracite in your pockets seemed to deflect most of them—where the old name "coal-pockets" came from that some people still used for flashmen in some parts of the world. But anthracite, for heaven's sake, to ward off something that went for your immune system, that seemed to live to do just that.

This small white avatar came streaking up to them from among the closest equiforms, hovered, held, stayed with them for an hour, sometimes bobbing, twitching in sudden, unnerving ways, then streaked away, soundless.

Two aylings came at them next, all high comedy were they not designed to detonate, fleschette-fashion. Sam did ayling duty as usual, briefing Thomas as the constructs approached.

"Watch now. These are faux-boys from what one overzealous WHO scientist christened Smart Landings. Leave it to me."

"Foe boys?" Thomas said, eyes never leaving the two figures on the trail.

"Faux." Sam spelled it out. "Old word for fakes. Maquettes. Made and sent by the Smarts."

"They're so human."

"They think they are. They're aylings. Clones. Synths."

"The Landings that sample g-codes."

"Right. If the Landings are traps, they're taking bits of whatever they can get to do their trapping. We're the most advanced local lifeform, so they sample us, turn out these."

"Parts of the trap."

"But the aylings don't know it. The thing is, if you play along, they stay friendly, finally reach a range limit and turn back."

The aylings spoke a strange clipped teev dialect gleaned from a century of vintage sat transmissions.

"Holoner De Gorvemax," the taller, rangier one introduced itself as, affecting a human male voice to go with its not-quite-right male mannequin appearance. "We've found a good route."

So simple, so obvious.

"Hutman Von Vexator," said the other, affecting female and as unreal as a well-made store mannequin. "Hol's right. Quick run out by The Four Doormen. Get you through in no time. None of the fluxes." Voice surprisingly good.

"That right?" Sam said. "Need to see The Quilter first. Business to attend to out by The Quilter. Then we'll try your way."

The aylings frowned at each other, sensing deflection but not sure how to make a No out of a provisional Yes.

Sam kept up the banter, making them run whatever menus they had. "Be good to see The Four Doormen again. Just need this quick detour first. Be good to have you along."

Sunny took the Trimmers straight for The Caress then. No time to do the usual Quilter deflection. Not with a flashpoint. The Redux had struck. People out in the world were dying.

The Caress already had someone in its moil, a young male tagger who must have jumped the border undetected. Solitaries could manage it. He was already stripped and marked for portioning. You could see the terror on his face, the acceptance, the shocked fascination at having his body marked out for vivisection, then the beatific calm as the modals shifted, even more terrifying to see.

It had taken eleven years for WHO to figure out that what had been known as whirters—assemblages of fourteen accreting parts—were actually the hunt avatars of this uniquely tripartite Landing called The Caress. Once the whirter had assembled and its prey was caught and phased away, the victim hadn't been sent to oblivion as first thought, despite the measurable energy release, but had been sent off to the Landing itself. A whirter had tracked and caught this youth, faxed him home to where he now hung unsupported three meters in the air, by turns being lulled and soothed, then shown the full measure of his pending demise—as if the Landing drew on the rapid shift of disparate emotions. This cat-and-mouse function applied to The Caress's other parts in central Africa and the American mid-west.

"You wait by those outer flanges," Sam told the aylings. "We're ahead of time. We'll just check our route, and then we can see The Four Doormen."

The aylings suspected nothing. They went towards the outer questing arms of The Caress, were snatched, lofted, then promptly canceled as the Landing identified them as something of their own kind. There one moment, gone the next.

As the Trimmers' route brought them closer to The Redux, it was inevitable that they finally catch sight of Punky's Regulators. Towards evening they had their first glimpse of their old rivals, saw another campfire start up a mile or so off in the dusk a few minutes after theirs did. Direct com remained out, of course, but Sunny used the radio handset to send the *braka*, the switch-on, switch-off static rhythm that meant "come hither," "no threat," "parley" Coffee was set going. Extra cups and rations were laid out.

Twenty minutes later, a deputation of Regulators cooee'd approach, then were there: Punky, Jack Crowfeather and, yes, Maisie Day.

Again the ten years were forgotten, impossible. There in the dark, Sam grinned wryly at having even tried to make another life. Among flash crews you either owned what you were or pretended. You never signed off—not having seen The Breakwater turn careless friends to clutches of sticks, seen the Lantern set them twitching off to their doom, seen the lines of antique horses frozen mid-stride across the spinifex ridges, the fierce nacreous gleam of The Pearl with its—surprise! surprise!—reverse-pattern oyster trap designed solely to lure the curious. It *seemed*. The Trimmers, the Regulators, shouldn't be here. No-one should be here. But having tasted, having *turned* them, switched the modes, there was no staying away.

Then, seeing Maisie large and limber as life, a bigger woman than ever he'd preferred till he'd met her, Sam realized how his smile must seem and lost it at once, probably way too late.

So much resolve here, so many realities disregarded in the instant. Two crews meeting again, protected by the braka truce, the cooee, the old courtesies.

"The Trimmers, as they cleverly appear to live and breathe!" Punky said, lean and powerful in his Singer duster, big smile and white crew-cut like a double night-light in the dusk. Crowfeather had a smile too, but like a smug surgeon, a good foil for Walt Senny any day but without Walt's final kiss of style. "Best aylings ever to grace the sand-box!" Jack said. Maisie Day gave a civil nod but looked way too frosty and focused. She *had* seen Sam's smile on the way in.

Sunny and Angie gave generous greetings. Walt managed a cool hello. Sam heard his own voice murmur something, managed most of a new smile, thin, careful. Then he introduced Thomas, who sat wide-eyed, taking it all in as they got down to business.

"Sailmaker Two, if you can believe it," Sunny said, all easy, playing good cop as he always did. "The Redux, if you agree."

Punky eased himself onto the cooling sand, stuck out his long legs and raised his palms to the fire.

"Indeed," he said. "Bringing up Junior. Who would've thought? How we playing this?"

"Make an offer." Walt said, before Punky had finished speaking.

Punky flashed his smile, warming his hands in the desert chill. Sam watched the night, watched Maisie, watched the night again. For all he knew, the rest of the Regulators were out in the dark, getting ready to settle old scores outside the courtesies. There was little demonstrated love here, but perhaps Sunny was right. Perhaps they should always allow the possibility of something more.

And Maisie. She looked good. Fierce and wonderful. Fuller. Heavier. Vital.

"Working the mode shift is all that matters," Punky said, eminently practical. "Share the fee. Go tandem, turn about. Your call, Sunny. Dibs on first unless you want to toss for it."

"Generous," Walt said, like a knife.

"Traitor's market," Crowfeather said, testing.

"Stet," Walt replied. *As was.* Calling him. Put up or shut up. And with it: know your place!

"Cousins," Sunny said, keeping the focus, keeping the braka, the best of the old ways. The songs would always be written about the likes of Walt Senny, but it was flashmen like Sunny Jim who were the real heroes here. "Your dibs. We'll follow you in at first light."

"Others coming in," Punky said, which said it all—explained the visit, the civility. *Cover our back, we cover yours.* Just like the hateful, treacherous old times.

There was hesitation. Muscles locked in the firelight though you'd never know it. There were old scores indeed, Sam and Maisie the least of them. This was make or break.

"New threat, new start, I figure," Sunny said, bringing what he could of decency and civilization into this strange alienized place. "We'll ward off. Give two hours. You do the same. Split the fee."

"Done," Punky said, holding out his cup for a refill instead of rising to go as they'd expected. "Half cup for the road." And then, as if just thinking of it: "Sam, think Maisie would like a word, sotta-votchy."

Sam was up and walking, moving away from the fire, into ambush, into trouble, he suddenly didn't care. He was only aware of Thomas looking after him, wondering what the hell was going on, aware of footsteps following. He walked forty paces and turned, saw the campfire back there, the mixed crews filling this lonely place in the night, as improbable as a Landing, truth be known, saw Maisie's shadow right there, backlit.

"Sam," she said.

"Mae." He'd never called her by her given name.

"Never expected this turn-out," she said. "Never expected collateral damage." Here it was. She had the right.

"Never ever that, Mae." All he could say. And the word "ever." Precious envoy.

"Put aside the Trimmers, put aside the rest."

"Denial gets like that." Inane, simply true. *The Sailmaker*, he might have said. But she knew. Had to know. Losing Boker and Steyne, almost all of Croft Denner's Larrikins. Despite the songs, the glamour of the chats, they'd been cruel years, even for the best crews. Especially the best.

"Bastard."

"Never personal, Mae."

"Everything is, Sam."

Four beats. Not turning away. *You were with Punky. Rival crew.* "You know how I feel."

She made a disgusted sound. Four beats. Still not turning. "You came back."

Walt and Sunny, he might have said. Or *Time's right.* Even *The Sailmaker.*

"Yes," he said, which was all of it, encompassing. Hoping she'd see. One word as emblem for so much.

"Bastard."

His conditioning had him. He almost shrugged. The Zorro. Eternally cool. But didn't. Didn't.

"Be with me," he said, kept her gaze for it, as hard as that was, saw all of her contempt, real or feigned, the old raw emotion powering whatever emotion it truly was.

Two beats.

"Be damned." And she turned and went.

Afterwards, bare minutes later, then hours later in their clear-sky trackside doss with the Regulators' camp-fire out in the cold night, he went back to it again and again, filled out the spaces with words. "That night at the stay-away," he could have said. "The Sailmaker fuming and sewing. Teams torn up, played off against one another most like. Braka barely holding. No ships in the night for us. There was a reason for the different teams. We never settled. Never made it easy. You know that." And the words would have been wrong. All wrong.

Mae knew. *Two* beats before turning. Mae knew.

And what was any of this if not redemption? Mae was with Punky again, but so what? There in their own meager doss, in the close dark, Sam saw Punky and The Sailmaker and the Landings as just parts of a lock that could be broken, opened at last. Nothing was ever enough, and nothing was written. Be with me. What more could anyone ever say?

At the first pink wash of dawn, the Trimmers were up, dusting off, doing ablutions, mantras, serving coffee; heating rations. The Regulators were no doubt doing the same. Little was said, considering, and when Sunny had the Trimmers move out it was in classic "diamond wand" formation with standard two-meter separations: Angel at point. Walt behind her shoulder to the left as hawk, Sunny to the right as gauntlet, Thomas as pure, finishing the diamond proper, and Sam behind as star. When they engaged, Thomas would step into the middle of the diamond; Sam would move forward to close the diamond again.

In a sense, the movies and the chats had done the training here. Thomas knew to expect the first of the focal drugs when Sunny passed it to him five minutes along, just slapped on the patch and played it straight, no questions, no hesitation. As if born to it. Who would have thought the movies, teev and chats could save so much time, constantly updating the mindset?

And there were Punky's Regulators ahead—same open diamond, their ballistic and laser weapons raised against new avatars, whatever whirter, burrus and ayling variants The Redux might serve up.

And The Redux rose beyond, so clearly an embryonic Sailmaker. Same clutch of sculpted fossil masts, already six meters high in places, same array of flensing frames (they weren't, nothing like it, but try convincing anyone that those stretched and bellying tarps weren't human skin), same distinctive keening and *slap-snapping* sound that helped give the Landing its name. It was for all the world as if limp sails were being snapped full, a repeated jarring tattoo in the chill morning air. Silence but for the keening, the gunshot *slap-snap* of "shrouds" and "rigging" their own rhythmic tread.

Within seconds the Trimmers had their shades on macro, and Sam saw the Regulators' pure — Henna Jacko (suddenly remembering the name) — dutifully slap on the final patch. The assault patch. Saw Jack Crowfeather and Martine Atta and Mae slap on their link patches almost in unison. Saw Henna step into the center and Punky close the diamond. They were engaging. Taking no chances.

The Redux was at two hundred meters when the avatars came. Not whirters, aylings or burrus variants — those oldest of Landing progeny. These were like the running dolls that had plagued Western Europe when The Rickshaw and The Rasa had first appeared. The most conventional after the aylings, the most —

No, not progeny at all!

Human!

"Down!" Walt cried, and Sunny saw it too.

"Hit squad!"

The Trimmers folded as one, Thomas dragged down by Walt, pushed down by Sam, went to lying unsupported positions in seconds, ballistics and laser up and aimed. Autotropics locked on as best they could in the interference caused by the Landings.

No thinking about it. *Crack. Crack. Tear. Crack. Tear. Crack.*

Dolls were falling, spots of ground kicking up where doll-strike hit back.

"Who?" Thomas yelled, huddling, terrified. There was the smell of piss.

No answer. *Work it out, newbie!*

Between shots, Sam managed a glimpse of the Regulators — down and firing — but couldn't see the damage there, who was safe and who wasn't.

Dolls were falling, falling. But so many. Too many. Thank the gods that autotropics were skewed.

No time to discuss it. Sam rolled to the side, targeted the outer skins of The Redux.

The others saw. Walt added his own ballistic strikes, Sunny swung his laser over the outer watch-screens.

The Redux struck back, and — as Sam hoped — targeted the *moving* shapes. Reached out with whatever targeting protocols it had and plucked at faces. Just faces. Snatched them into the activation perimeter and stretched them on the sky — one face, vast and glaring in shock, then two, ten, twenty, vast hoardings, rushmores, sails, twenty, thirty meters across and with — impossibly — complete facial integrity, no distortion despite the size.

Making sails.

The Trimmers and the Regulators didn't dare shift position. The dolls were gone—transformed. The Redux was in fully trophy display, just like its terrifying parent out on the Amadeus. No *slap-snap* now, just the keening.

But there'd be more. A hit squad—*that* level of resources deployment— meant a carefully planned mission. Not targeting The Redux! *Them!* The crews! Mission contingency.

A fire-strike, of course! Officially: bombing The Redux before it proliferated. Perhaps claiming it already had! Something.

Unofficially: getting rid of the top crews, one way or another.

Wanting The Redux to grow. The old strategies. Old mistakes. Everything old, new again. New science. New chances for young turks with theories, careers to mind. Forgetting the past. Busy seizing the day.

"Sky-strike!" Sam stage-whispered, not daring to say it loudly. All quiet but for the keening, maybe the white noise shift, shift, shift of gaping faces on the sky.

Sunny dared to move an arm, so so slowly, activating the audio seek on his headset.

"They have the range," Walt said.

"We'll never know," Angel added. True, all true.

"Listening!" Sunny reminded them, not expecting ship-talk in the braka white-out but hoping for something, anything.

So then it was just the keening and the waiting, thoughts of Mae running through Sam's mind, and anger and some amusement too that it had come to this. How could you not laugh? So easy to catch the heroes, set them up. Can't help themselves, the pompous asses! Strutting like lords! Who cared about countless thousands dying in an overpopulated world? Pay lip-service, go through the motions. Be seen to be doing the right thing. Who cared about the flashmen and their two secrets—*two* secrets that only the prime crews knew, that the taggers, quarterhands and newbies desperately tried to learn? Wasted heroes of the people. Losses just added to the legend. Get rid of the old, bring on the new. Bread and circuses.

Sam laughed into the sand. Merely flashmen. All they ever were. Dependable.

Expendable.

"Incoming!" Sunny said, reading not voice transmissions of any kind but rather fluctuations in the static where they would be. Ghosts of talk. He switched to distance tracking, non-vested audio ranges, made his raw calculations. "Ten k's out and on approach!" Best guess, but he had the skill.

"What will they do?" Thomas asked.

"Missile," Angel said. "Point blank."

"They don't know," Sunny said, marveling at those careless airmen and foolish mission chiefs, that there could be so much ignorance in—the joke was there—high places. Still. Again. However it played. This was a Sailmaker, for heaven's sake!

"Wait for it!" Walt Senny said, targeting the sky, the faces. "We'll spoil its trophies."

"No laser!" Angel warned.

"Stealth grenade," Walt said. "No sustained source trail."

"We hope."

"We hope," Sunny confirmed.

Sam found himself thinking of Mae of the Regulators, of poor Thomas lying in his own piss, silent, bless him, but alive. Needed more than ever now if Henna Jacko was lost.

Walt judged the approach, calculated vagaries like Sunny's ten k's wind direction, engine noise, pilot caution.

He fired into the faces, scored the hit. One by one they burned, skewing, heaving on their invisible tethers.

Nil source detected, it seemed. No instantaneous retaliation, at any rate. Possibly too small, too slight, no constant follow-up signature.

Then, again. The Redux found something that *would* do, coarse movement, read the aircraft on approach. Reached out and made sails. More faces spread on the sky—a half-dozen, there, there, there.

The bomber continued over, a smooth high crucifix with no-one aboard left alive.

The braka static from the Regulators came almost at once—basic Morse—*Henna dead. Your dibs.*

And lying there, the Trimmers swapped strategy. Thomas worked a new patch onto his arm. The others slowly, carefully, added their own patches when they could, each stage-whispered "Check!" till they'd all confirmed. Lying there, sprawled on the sand, they made the flash crew.

The Redux was new, dazzled by trophies, possibly its first, distracted by the sheer overload of being in the world. It never suspected—were there truly a governing intelligence that *could* suspect, bring cognition to what it did.

The Trimmers found their voice, their hold, their strike, started working the flashpoint.

Sam focused, focused, no longer daring to think of Mae, or surviving, or the people out there in shut-down waiting their chance. He concentrated on Thomas, on sending through Thomas to The Redux, to the faces in the sky.

His eyes glazed, cleared, glazed, cleared, then found one trophy face, eyeless, vast, distended on the sky, twenty meters across, yet impossibly intact, mouth open in a scream but with no other feature distortion. Young, young it seemed. Not Mae. Young.

He used that face to keep the resolve. *Through* Thomas to *that* face.

How long they worked it there was no telling. The day tracked. The sun was up and blazing, crawling across the sky. Late autumn heat still made it a hell, but distant, bearable.

That sun was well into afternoon when the modes began shifting, finally switched, when the keening fell away and the *slap-snap* began again. Somewhere people were waking from shut-down fugue, finding dust in their mouths, insects, their limbs cramped, broken, wasted by circulation necrosis. But alive! *Alive!* And somewhere a debt was being paid.

The trophies were gone—the sky above the masts and frames of The Redux was a washed blue.

They'd managed it.

One by one, the Trimmers stirred, stood, stretched, worked their own stiff and aching muscles, grateful to be in the world.

The Regulators hadn't done as well. Three up, two down. Two!

The Trimmers hurried as much as they dared in that fraught place, crossed the newly keening, *slap-snapping* terrain before *The Redux* and reached was what left of Punky's crew.

Henna Jacko was gone. Her young face had been the sail Sam had seen. Had used.

Jack Crowfeather was the other—hit twice by shots from approaching dolls. Punky, Martine and Mae were getting them into body-bags, slowly, no sudden movements now, preparing to haul them back to whatever decent distance would serve as a trail burial site in these dangerous wastes.

"Thanks," Punky said. "Fee's yours, clear." Not: Who were they? What happened? Understanding that.

"We share," Sunny said. "Braka." Keeping faith, building traditions that might well outlive them all. Went in together. Come out together.

Punky grinned at the foolishness, Sunny's dogged largesse. "In light of this?"

"Especially." And not hesitating: "You go southwest by The Praying Hands. We'll take northwest. Use braka Morse when we can, voice when it clears. Have to get this out."

"Agreed," Punky said. "Warn our people off."

Walt grunted. "See if *they* can get themselves a decent crew then."

Martine and Mae both nodded, Mae's eyes holding Sam's two, three seconds before sliding away to tasks at hand. The Regulators reached for the bags holding their dead.

Sunny beat them to that as well. "We'll take the girl."

Not Jack. The newbie.

Punky nodded. "Appreciated."

No dragging body bags here. No being slowed down now if it could be helped. The Redux had made sails, possibly its first, was possibly recalling the experience, sorting what had happened. It could swing again. Not likely, given logged behavior ranges, but anything was possible.

The Trimmers and the Regulators went their opposite ways, walking smoothly, quickly enough, considering. They abandoned their slow-mo's—possibly booby-trapped, but giving too much signature anyway—and they walked it. Left their dead amid rocks and walked. It took a fair slice of forever, but everyone was glad to pay it out of their lives.

Only when the Trimmers had the northwest boundary in sight, well clear of Checkpoint Reuben just in case, did Sam bring it up.

"Questions, Thomas?"

"What's that?" the kid asked, off with his thoughts, then understood. "The two secrets? I can ask?"

"This side of The Redux it's only fair."

Sam stopped. Thomas stopped. The others kept walking, the group separating now, dividing as precaution: Angel and Sunny going wide toward the north, Walt going alone to the west proper. Getting it out.

Leaving Sam as good cop—and bad, should it come to that.

"So, what are they?" Direct, not defiant. Watching the others go.

Sam didn't hesitate. "First, to get back thousands, we have to sacrifice hundreds."

"Seems right. Seems fair. You can't save everyone. I don't—wait, are you saying that when we switch modes, some *always* die? *Have* to die?"

Sam began walking again, slowly, making it casual. He always wanted to deceive at this point. Give the beautiful lie. "Take it further."

Thomas was following. "Wait! How do I take it further? We're causing coarse action. Naturally some will die. The trauma—"

"Take it further!" Sam rounded on him, stopping again. Good cop *and* bad. Gun and dueling stick ready.

"How further?" Then his face locked into a mask, his eyes wide; his mouth wide, like a miniature of The Redux's trophies "*You* kill them!" And accepting: "*We* kill them!"

Sam's voice was soft, nearly toneless. "We use the energies of the random few to let us free the rest!"

"You used *me* to do *that!*"

"Certainly did. Certainly do. Certainly will. Every time. A devil's bargain, but the fairest trade we can ever make."

"It's murder!"

"It surely is Collateral damage. Friendly fire. Never personal. Our powers have to come from somewhere!"

"But you kill them!" Thomas said it more softly now, beyond rage, beyond disbelief. And the *you* worried Sam. Not *we* "You used me."

"However it works, the power comes through the pure. Has to. We find. You send. Small price to pay when you think it through. Small enough price. Hundreds dead so thousands upon thousands can be saved."

"It's immoral!"

"Amoral more like. But which is better? There goes a village, a town. You'll have hundreds dead outright or thousands dying slowly? Starving. Eaten by insects, dogs, lying there aware in the fugue."

"But you're heroes!"

Sam didn't try to answer that. What could you say? *Merely flashmen, Thomas. Merely flashmen.*

"Which is better?" was all he said.

"What!"

"Do we try to get some or let them all go?"

"*You try to get them all!*" Tears were running down the kid's cheeks.

"Doesn't work like that. Which is better?"

"It doesn't excuse it!"

"Never does. Never can. Explains is all. You did well today. You saved some who would have died."

"You'll kill me if I tell about this." The look of terror in his eyes had turned to cold understanding. "That's the other secret."

"Doesn't go like that," Sam said, giving the final wonderful lie. "We give you the Lethe drug. You remember none of it."

"The Lethe drug? What if I refuse?"

"We make you. Or the WHO doctors will. Or they'll imprison you, take you away. The world can't know."

I could pretend, Thomas might have said. *Go along with it.* But Sam had seen the test results, the psych profile, and knew he couldn't.

"Think it through," was all Sam said, and started walking away.

"I hate you!" Thomas called after him "I thought you were heroes! I hate you all!"

"You'll be hero enough if you accept the responsibility. That's why you were chosen. I'll be at the perimeter."

Sam left him raging, weeping, sitting in the dust. Sat in the shade of some boulders himself as the last of the day fell away, and thought it through again. Because you always had to.

What do they want from us? Sam asked himself, yet again. *Clean answers? Salvation without a price? Something for nothing?* He ran them all, all the old questions and trade-offs. Came up hard and strong, thinking of Mae, of Sunny and Walt and the look on Angel's face back at Tagger's when she first saw him again.

You could tell them. Put it to a vote. Nothing would change, most like. But they *wanted* heroes, someone to believe in more than they wanted statistics and the truth, not just someone to make the hard decisions, maintain the beautiful lie, but *hide* such things. Saviors who wouldn't quit even when they were struck at from *both* sides, who without ever planning or wanting to protect them from the truth. Even from the wayward bits and pieces of their own natures.

It was early morning before the kid came in. Sam always felt he could guess which way it would go, but this time he wasn't entirely sure. His pistol's safety was off just in case—Lethe—but the holster cover was clipped down. His dueling stick was carefully in its sheath.

The kid came strolling along, kicking dust.

"Wanted to be a hero, Mr. Aitch," he said, falling in alongside when Sam started walking. "That's all."

"I know," Sam said. "So we do impressions, Thomas. There are times when second best just has to do."

Dragonhead

NICK DICHARIO

Nick DiChario has sold to *The Magazine of Fantasy & Science Fiction*, *Science Fiction Age*, *Weird Tales*, *Universe 2*, *Universe 3*, *Alternate Kennedys*, *Alternate Warriors*, *Alternate Outlaws*, *Alternate Tyrants*, *The Ultimate Alien*, and many other markets. He's the coeditor, with Claudia Bishop, of the mystery anthology *Death Dines at 8:30*. His most recent book is a collection of his stories written in collaboration with Mike Resnick, *Magic Feathers: The Mike and Nick Show*.

In the sharp-edged little story that follows, he suggests that if a little knowledge is a dangerous thing, a *lot* of knowledge can be downright deadly . . .

T his is what you know:

Kermit the frog is left-handed. Charlie Brown's father was a barber. Twenty-one percent of Americans claim to be regularly bored out of their minds. In Iowa, sixty-five traffic accidents a year are caused by cornstalks. According to Genesis 1:20–22, the chicken came before the egg. Thirteen people a year are killed by fallen vending machines.

This is what you hear:

—What are his chances, doctor? <Female voice of someone you think you might know.>

—I won't lie to you, Mrs. Lang. There is currently no known cure for Dragonhead. <Unknown male voice of reason.>

—Dragonhead. I hate that term. I *hate* it. <Familiar female voice again.>

—Everyone hates it. It's becoming the disease of the millennium. We're finally beginning to understand what digitalia addiction is doing to our children. But I have to be honest with you, for most young people that understanding comes too late.

—Digitalia. Another term I hate. Fancy word for digital implant. Fancy word for brain sex, is what it is.

—Actually, Mrs. Lang, mind fuck and information masturbation are the most common slang terms for—

—You don't have to talk like that. I know what it means.

—I'm sorry.

—That's all right . . . I'm just . . . I'm just desperate. Your program comes highly recommended. You've had success, haven't you, in some cases?

—Yes, a small percentage of patients have shown some improvement through a controlled regimen of neural shock therapy, but the results are varied. Most patients can't pull their minds out of the information stream, not even after the implants are removed and no more new data is getting in. Your son's chances are slim. You must understand that. Are you sure you want to put him through this? <Oh, doctor, my doctor.>

—I don't have a choice, do I? I have to try something. I can't lose him like this, so senselessly. I'll try anything . . . anything to get him back. Ian, Ian, do you hear me? Please come back, please. I'm your mother. You have a family and a life here with us, a God-given life. Doesn't that mean anything to you? <Mother, eh?>

—Please, Mrs. Lang, come away now. He can't hear you, or if he does, the words mean nothing to him; they're no different than any other words streaming through his head. It's time for us to start his first treatment. <Voice of Doctor Moreau, Doctor Spock, Doctor J., Doctor Seuss, Doctor Who, Doctor Iguana, Doctor Jet Engine, Doctor Alarm Clock, Doctor Demento, Doctor Boiling-Screaming-Dying Lobster wanted in New Jersey for petty larceny.>

—Doctor, Ian told me that the digitalia was harmless. He said it was nothing more than a tattoo, a tattoo in his cerebellum. Jesus. God. All his friends were getting it done. Why shouldn't he?

This is what you know:

Stars. Black stars dancing the bumblebee polka—stinging multiplying, imploding inside your brain, hot honey drip drip dripping down your spine. Leather straps. Cool smooth taste of airy neural electricity. Every hair follicle whispers sweet nothings in your skull. Subtle weight of iron and blood in your mouth. Is that water leaking from your eyes, or whalebones, or tailbones, or baseballs, or mothballs, or dictionaries, or pictionaries, or barbed wire, or haywire? Hard rock music makes termites chew through wood at twice their usual speed. A sneeze can travel as fast as one hundred miles per hour. Point three percent of all road accidents in Canada involve a moose. Babe Ruth wore a cabbage leaf under his baseball cap to keep his head cool. On the wall, a clock reads 4:20 AM or PM. In the movie *Pulp Fiction*, all the clocks remain frozen on 4:20. 4:20. 4:20. Wouldn't you like to be a fly on that wall?

Forever.

Pinprick . . . pinprick . . . kiss . . . kiss . . . kiss. . . .

This is what you hear:

—Ian, it's me, your mamma. <Female voice of someone you think you might know.> Can you hear me? Talk to me, my beautiful baby. Say something. Anything. Please, Ian, come back to me. Come back. <Kiss.> He's not responding, doctor. He's not responding at all.

This is what matters:

A raindrop falls at approximately seven miles per hour. South Bend, Indiana, 1924, a monkey is arrested, convicted, and sentenced to pay a twenty-five dollar fine for smoking a cigarette. "False Dragonhead" is a wildflower, a member of the mint family, indigenous to the riverbanks and thickets of Minnesota, Quebec, and the mountains of North Carolina; when its flowers are pushed right or left, *they stay that way*; common nickname: obedient flower.

Dear Abbey

TERRY BISSON

Here's a breathtaking tour, lyrical and sad, from our troubled present all the way to The End of Time, with stops along the way to consider the question of whether or not there's going to be a future for humanity—or if there *should* be.

Terry Bisson is the author of a number of critically acclaimed novels such as *Fire on the Mountain*, *Wyrldmaker*, the popular *Talking Man* (which was a finalist for the World Fantasy Award in 1986), *Voyage to the Red Planet*, *Pirates of the Universe*, *The Pickup Artist*, and, in a posthumous collaboration with Walter M. Miller, Jr., a sequel to Miller's *A Canticle for Leibowitz* called *Saint Leibowitz and the Wild Horse Woman*. He is a frequent contributor to such markets as *Sci Fiction*, *Asimov's Science Fiction*, *Omni*, *Playboy*, and *The Magazine of Fantasy and Science Fiction*, and, in 1991, his famous story "Bears Discover Fire" won the Nebula Award, the Hugo Award, the Theodore Sturgeon Award, *and* the *Asimov's* Reader's Award, the only story ever to sweep them all. In 2000, he won a Nebula Award for his story "macs." His short work has been assembled in the collections *Bears Discover Fire and Other Stories* and *In the Upper Room and Other Likely Stories*. His stories have appeared in our Eighth, Tenth, Twelfth, and Thirteenth Annual Collections. He lives with his family in Brooklyn, New York.

1 -

Lee and I were never really friends, and never is saying a lot if you are covering all the way from late October to the End of Time. We were office mates, initially; colleagues, as it turned out; comrades, if you insist. And traveling companions, to be sure.

If it seems odd to you that a Distinguished Professor of Higher Mathematics should share an office with an American Studies Associate, you have never worked at a community college; much less Southwest Connecticut Community College, which is, due in small part to its central location on the BosWash Corridor, and in no small part to its liberal hiring policies, a brief and unceremonious stop for eastern seaboard academics on their way down, or out, or both. Lee had brought his exalted title with him from MIT, from which he had decamped after an undisclosed (and, as it turned out, almost entirely diversionary) conflict with a department head. But hey, we all have our little secrets. I, on the other hand, like most of my other colleagues at "Swick" (as we called it on the rare occasions when we spoke among ourselves), had been hired sight unseen, no-questions-asked, to fulfill some obscure bureaucratic quota, and could count on being let go when I came up for review in a year or so.

Not that I frankly my dear gave a damn. I was only passing through.

But enough about me. Did I mention that Lee was Chinese? Sixtyish, which meant old enough to be my father (if you could imagine my old man with a doctorate, or even imagine my old man, but that's another story) and a political refugee from mainland China, which could mean, or so I then thought, anything.

Lee was somewhat of a campus celeb since at MIT he had been shortlisted for a Ballantine (the math MacArthur). His post-post doc from Rice had apparently carried no language requirement, since he spoke a coarse pidgin with a brutal and bizarre Texas drawl. It was as if he had learned English from a "You Know You're a Redneck If" phrase book.

A shared office at SWCCC meant one desk, one chair, one TI line; the two of us weren't supposed to be in the office at the same time. It was a time-share, which is ironic, I suppose, considering. We each had our own shallow drawer. I kept a pint of bourbon and a few books in mine. Lee kept—who knew?—a Time Machine in his.

The day it all began was a Friday—the last day of classes before the long holiday weekend, when the "Swick" campus was due to become even quieter and deader than usual.

Since when did Halloween become a college holiday? As much as I hated teaching, I hated holidays even worse. Especially this coming weekend. I had promised to stay away from the apartment while Helen picked up her stuff, mainly the extra uniforms and the little wheeled bag that fit perfectly through the carry-on templates. It was, like her underwear, and indeed her personality, a pricey and initially fetching example of minimal design. And there was, of course, her little dog. But enough about her. I finished my last class (Nineteenth-Century Slave Narratives; of which two-thirds had escaped on that underground railway that spirits students away before holidays) and stopped by the office to have a drink and puzzle out a way to kill the evening. No big deal. Welcome to Moviefone.

When I opened the office door and saw a pair of cowboy boots on the desk, my heart skipped, as they say, a beat. Did Connecticut, like New Jersey, have sheriffs? (Turns out it does but they are not Chinese.) But it was nothing so serious. It was only my rarely seen office mate, Won "Bill" Lee, leaning back, reading, a paper cup in one hand and a book in the other.

"Dr. Cole!" Lee said, sitting up and spilling the contents of the paper cup down the front of his never-iron (and never-really-white) white shirt with its plastic pocket protector filled with pens. I could tell by the smell it was my Jack Daniels. "Lay in wait!"

The book was mine too: *The Monkey Wrench Gang.*

"Just Cole is okay," I said. "But hey, Lee, keep your seat. I'm only passing through. What are you doing here this late on a Friday afternoon, anyway?" I reached for the phone, but while I was dialing 777-FILM, Lee cut me off with one finger.

"Lay in wait," Lee said again, standing up. "You and me, pardner."

"Me? What can I do for you?"

"Like the good book says," Lee said mysteriously. He replaced the book and the bottle in my drawer and pulled a PalmPC out of his own. Then he grinned, suddenly and rather incongruously, and pointed toward the door. "Round on the house? Wet the whistle? Happy Hour?"

I figured, Why not? Halloween comes only once a year. Thank God.

Lee was small, even for a Chinaman, with black hair that managed to look short and uncut at the same time. He wore a hideous L.L.Bean safari jacket over his no-iron shirt and pen protector. And shoes, you don't want to know. Since the campus was, quite literally, in the Middle of Nowhere, and I had no car (don't believe in them: which was only one of Helen's well-documented complaints), we rode in Lee's rather surprising Prius to a little place a block from the Sound called, ominously, it seems in retrospect, the Pequod. "Two Jack," Lee said, and two amber shots of B Grade bourbon appeared on the bar.

I am always amazed that foreigners think Jack Daniels is an A bourbon. I drink it strictly in honor of my Tennessee grandmother. But what the hell, it seemed as good a way as any to kill an evening. "Cheers," I said, raising my glass. "To Chinese-American friendship."

"China-merica no-no," Lee said, shaking his head with a sudden seriousness. Then he smiled, like an actor changing moods. "Dear Abbey yes! Monkey Ranch Gang yes!"

Dear Abbey? I was startled, suspicious even. But no, no way—I decided to let it go. "It's 'Wrench,'" I said, draining my glass and signaling for another. "But why not? Here's to old Ed Abbey."

Lee smiled and toasted back. Then he winked. "To the Jersey Kaczynski."

"Whoa!" I looked around. We were alone in the bar except for a couple in the far back, by the jukebox. "Where'd you hear that?"

Though it was no secret how I had lost my position at Princeton, I hadn't exactly advertised it at Swick. It had been almost five years before. I had done eleven months for refusing to testify about the firebombing of some ski lifts in the Poconos, with collateral damage. No direct connection had been proven, or even officially alleged. Since then I had, rather strategically, distanced myself from the environmental movement.

"Pell," said Lee. "Smell the beans. No problem."

"Spill the beans," I said. "And it *is* a problem because this Pell should learn to mind his own business and keep his mouth shut. I didn't know you ran with that crowd anyway."

Which was true. If Lee was Green, this was the first I had heard of it. The Greens (at Swick, anyway) tended to be all white and ostentatiously boho, neither of which fit Lee's profile; or, for that matter, my own.

But I felt (as usual) compelled to say more. "The Jersey Kaczynski thing was all bullshit anyway. I had no connection with EarthAlert or with the individuals who were later captured. I happened to be an easy target because I had assigned Kaczynski's "Unabomber Manifesto" in an American Studies class. The feds came after me because they were too stupid or too lazy to find the individuals they actually wanted."

Not exactly true but close enough for the Pequod.

"They needn't have bothered anyway," I said, getting wound up in spite of (or perhaps because of) the fact that Lee could barely understand me. Or so I thought. "The environmental movement is a joke. It's way too late for talk. Peat fires in the arctic tundra. In Africa, the elephants are dying in heaps. The sea level is expected to rise two to four feet in the next hundred years. Do you have any idea what that means?"

"Every any idea," said Lee, nodding. "Lamentation river stage flood." What that meant, he explained, and I pieced together, as we shared another round and I began to understand Lee's fractured Texas English, was that China's infamous Yellow River Dam project had reached reservoir level one week before, inundating the last of the ancient, doomed villages. Either Lee's English or my understanding, or both, got better with the whiskey, and I learned that Lee had worked as an engineer on the project for eleven years before comprehending what a disaster it would be. He had then opposed it publicly and clandestinely for two years before being forced to leave the country just two steps ahead of the secret police.

"Bare excape," he said with an enigmatic smile, effortlessly nailing the authentic Texas pronunciation. I looked at my colleague with new respect. Eleven months in Allenwood Federal Correctional Facility was a piece of cake compared to what they do to you in China, if they catch you. And I had been lecturing him!

"So here's to Ted," I said. I didn't bother to whisper. Except for the two in the far back, by the jukebox, Lee and I were the only people in the Pequod besides the bartender, a mournful Connecticut Yankee who politely kept his distance while he wiped glasses and watched the "news" on TV, as if the routine murders of inner-city drug dealers were news.

"Ted?" Lee asked, raising his tiny glass.

"Ted Kaczynski. Because the crazy fucker's right, unfuckingfortunately," I explained, signaling for another round. "Because we're in the middle of what E. O. Wilson calls the Sixth Extinction. Because the ongoing, relentless, merciless, and mindless destruction of the planet overrules whatever small progress might have been made against racism, nationalism, greed, or ignorance or all of the above. Because they can't even make a fucking gesture of a deal to stop global warming; because they deny it's even happening; because—"

"So why not Pell? Why not Greens?"

"Because, Lee, what's Texan for a day late and a dollar short?"

"Why not Monkey Ranch, then, Cole? Why not Dear Abbey indeed?"

"Whoa!" I said, aloud this time. There it was, Dear Abbey, again. This time it was no mistake. It was deliberate. I could tell by Lee's suddenly inscrutable smile.

Some kind of cop: that was my first thought. I set down my empty glass. "I beg your fucking pardon. What in the world are you talking about?"

"What he's talking about is what we've all been talking about for the past two and a half years," said a familiar voice from the back of the bar, by the jukebox.

I was suddenly sober, or so it seemed to me. My heart, or what I have been told passes for a heart, was pounding as I turned and faced the two who were walking toward me out of the shadows in the back of the bar. One was Pell, of course, I should have guessed; and right behind Pell was my most valued, most troublesome, and least expected friend.

Justine?

There's always a problem when you run into somebody who's underground, especially when they're with someone. Even when it's clearly not an accident, what do you call them? What do they call them? Who knows who and who knows what? Adding to the confusion, there's never any time to think.

"Justine?"

"Actually, it's Flo these days," she said. "Don't I get a hug?"

"Of course," I said, complying, "but what the hell are you doing here? And with—"

There was no way to cast a look toward Pell without seeming rude. I cast a look toward Pell.

Pell smiled and nodded. Smug? Stupid? Both. He went and stood beside Lee at the bar but didn't, I noticed, order a drink. Of course not. He was on duty.

So was Justine, or rather, Flo. If you're looking for a description, you won't find it here. You probably don't need it. She looked exactly the same as she had looked on *America's Most Wanted*, except for the hair color. Six million people saw that, thanks to the two teenagers, both boys, who had broken into the Skyline Lodge looking for cell phones to steal.

Teenagers usually kill themselves and one another. They don't ordinarily depend on environmentalists to do it, even as collateral damage. But I digress . . .

"Good to see you, Cole," she said, checking to make sure the bartender was out of earshot. "Though this isn't exactly a social call."

"Why am I not surprised," I said. "Good to see you too. I hope things are going okay. I haven't heard much. That's good in itself, I guess."

"That's good," she confirmed. "Things have been quiet. We've been laying low. Laying off the 'stupid stunts.' I'm quoting you here, Cole. I knew you would approve. Bartender?!"

"Thought this wasn't a social call."

"It's not but don't worry. The bourbon is part of the deal, believe it or not. I wanted to introduce you to Dr. Lee, and this seemed the easiest way."

"Introduce? He's my office mate."

"Yes, quite a coincidence, *n'est-ce pas*? I meant introduce politically. You are also comrades, as you have been discovering."

"Quit beating around the bush, Justine. What does he know about Dear Abbey? Is that why we're here?"

"It's Flo. And yes, my friend and comrade, yes it is."

By now either you know, and everyone knows, or you don't, and it doesn't matter any more, that Dear Abbey is a radical, long-range plan for saving the environment that will make Ted Kaczynski look like Mother Teresa. It involves an alarmingly complex but theoretically possible piece of genetic engineering that will, let us say, severely inhibit the ability of humans to degrade the environment. Severe is the operative modifier. You can't call it terrorism because no one will be killed, directly at least, and no one even know for sure what is happening until it has been operating for almost a decade, by which time it will be too late to undo it. The human cost will be high but not nearly as high as the cost of doing nothing, or of simply continuing with the kind of pointless stunts for which the environmental movement is known.

Dear Abbey was the only thing that still connected me to EarthAlert. I hadn't come up with the idea but I had been among the first to embrace it and argue for it. I had lost interest only when it became clear that it couldn't be accomplished any time soon; the technology was still decades away. As far as I was concerned, these were decades the world didn't have.

"Dear Abbey has aroused a great deal of interest in China," Justine, or rather Flo, said. "As drastic and as necessary as Dear Abbey will be here, it is even more drastic in Asia. And more necessary."

"Aren't we forgetting one detail? That it can't be made to work yet?"

"Tell that to the Chinese. They say they can make it work. They say they have found the missing link. Which is where our friend comes in."

I felt a surge of hope, so sudden, so unfamiliar and so welcome that I distrusted it immediately. "Impossible! I was told it would take a whole new gene sequencing technology based on a mathematics that's not even . . ."

She cut me off with a smile and a shrug. "Lee has found a fix. A way to access tomorrow's technology today."

"Right. Time travel."

"You needn't look so smug, Cole. No, it's not science fiction, but yes, according to Lee it does involve some kind of quantum uncertainty math thing. The Chinese are way ahead of us. Isn't Lee the guy who won that award for the computer program that executes commands nanoseconds before they are given?"

"Yes, nanoseconds, but . . ."

"Yes, but nothing. You and Lee are supposedly using some see-into-the-future computer program to pick up a gene sequencing patch that will make Dear Abbey work. The missing link. The trigger. The one thing we don't have, and for some reason it's a two-person operation."

"Time travel. Science fiction. But why me?"

"We wanted to be involved, and the Chinese requested you. Maybe it's their idea of promoting racial harmony. Maybe it's the prison thing; maybe they think it means you can be trusted. Maybe it's because you are already hooked up with Lee, in a way, although I wonder if that was entirely coincidence."

I was wondering too. "When does all this happen?"

"Tonight. In less than an hour. At nine."

"Surely you jest."

"No, Cole, I don't surely jest. Maybe it's you that surely jests. Maybe you were jesting when you told Big Bird that when we needed you for Dear Abbey, you would be there, no questions asked."

Big Bird was EarthAlert's central committee. "Here I am, aren't I?"

"Then don't ask so damn many questions. Think of it as the inscrutable Orient, and all that." She looked around to make sure Lee wasn't listening; he and Pell were at the bar, with their backs turned. "This whole thing sounds a little woo-woo to me too. Maybe it's nothing but a make-nice between Big Bird and the Chinese; a little hand-holding to flatter a nutty professor. So what? If Lee's for real, and this works, which I'm told it could, we have Dear Abbey now, when we need it. And even if it's bullshit, which it probably is, you've gained us an ally and wasted an hour."

"And gotten arrested or worse. What if this is some kind of stupid second-story job?"

"I doubt it. Lee got out of China and into MIT, didn't he? Just go along with Dr. Lee and see where it goes, Cole. Your presence represents their trust for us; that in itself is a breakthrough. It'll all be over in an hour, OK?"

I had already decided to go along with it. "OK. But first, you have to answer me one question."

She looked at me warily. "What?"

"Where'd you come up with 'Flo'?"

I finished my drink while Lee and Justine, or rather Flo, made their final arrangements. She looked as imperious, as mysterious as ever. Lee no longer looked the least bit woozy, but who knew how a whiskey-drinking revolutionary Chinese math wizard was supposed to look? Pell looked the same as always: insignificant and untrustworthy. But who was I to argue with Big Bird? Decisions had been made. When organizations are underground, and under attack, as EarthAlert certainly was in those days, decisions are not made democratically. The less one knows, the better.

Flo was looking at her watch. "Time," she said. "Good luck, Cole." Then she kissed me on both cheeks and split.

"What is this, the Resistance?" I said, as much to myself as to her, as she and Pell exited through the back. The only part of my life that made sense, and she had whittled it down to a point. A very sharp point. I set my empty glass down on the bar. It made a very loud noise.

"Dr. Lee, I'm your guy. Let's do this thing."

"Follow me." The Chinaman was all smiles.

1

Lee and I exited through the front. Lee was carrying a briefcase decorated with formulas that accentuated his nerdy look. His cowboy English got better, explaining technical things. "According Barbour, Hawking, Liu-Hsun," he said as we folded ourselves into his Prius, "Time is illusion. We live eternal present, in each moment coexist. Separate Universe, like beads on string."

"I've heard that story," I said. "We're the beads, Time's the string. But what does that have to do with anything?"

"Time string loops," Lee said, rather mysteriously.

"Whatever." I was not exactly drunk but not exactly sober either. I wondered where we were going but knew enough not to ask. My role was just to ride shotgun, the token Westerner, so to speak.

The Prius was unexpectedly noisy. It was the brick street. We were heading back toward the campus. I could barely hear Lee, who was explaining that since Time was relative, the algorithm had to be accessed by two people because of what he called the "subjective factory."

"What algorithm?" I asked, just to be polite.

"See-tomorrow math."

"So this time travel has something to do with math?"

"Straight shooting," Lee said, turning into the campus.

"I see," I said, as the little car bounced over the first speed bump. Do the Chinese think they mean speed up? The return to campus was a surprise, and a reassuring one. It fit right in with the nutty-professor theory. It meant a wasted hour in familiar surroundings; a favor done for Big Bird; and a promise to Helen fulfilled. I had promised I would stay away from the apartment until ten. At least now I had something to do. Never mind, Moviefone.

The next surprise was less reassuring. Lee drove past the Faculty Extension and parked at the Student Union, a building I rarely visited. Even though classes were done for the holiday, and only a few students were around, the SU was filled with thumping music, rap, advertising the thuggishness of Swick's student body, as if it weren't obvious already from the appearance and demeanor, if it can be called that, of the few that were left on campus.

The next surprise was, Lee had a key to the basement.

He closed the door behind us and turned on the light. We were in a large, windowless bare room with a concrete floor, like a church basement from the Tennessee half of my childhood. It even had a big wall clock like the one I had watched—and watched and watched—as a kid.

It was 8:47. Still early in what turned out to be, by far, the longest evening of my life.

In the center of the room was a familiar if unexpected sight. It was a "glider," the old fashioned metal kind that served as a swing on my Tennessee grandmother's porch. It was painted dull orange and blue-gray, and it hung in a low, square frame that kept it level, or almost level, which is the difference one supposes between a glider and an ordinary swing.

I thought it was for a flea market or an antiques sale. Then I saw Lee's inscrutable smile.

"This is it?" I gave it a push. It squeaked. "This is your Time Machine?"

"No way, José." Lee pulled a PalmPC out of his briefcase and tapped its tiny screen. "PC see-tomorrow math. Glider just seat."

Thinking this could turn out to be a rather long hour, I sat down and started to swing. I remembered the squeak from my childhood. More of a squeal. I used to think of it as an army of mice.

"Subjective factory," Lee said. He set the briefcase on the floor beside the glider, then sat down beside me. "Sit same metal. Field equations matched. Move but staying still. All good for see-tomorrow math."

See-tomorrow math. "Whatever," I said. "So what do we do, swing?" I kicked the glider higher.

"Hold horses," Lee said, dragging his feet, so that the glider twisted, then stopped. He pointed at the clock. "Loop at nine."

"Whatever." It was 8:56.

"Hold horses, Jersey Kaczynski!" Smiling, he reached into another pocket of his hideous safari jacket and handed me what I thought at first was a Zippo lighter. It was a tiny (and rather lovely) brushed aluminum digital camera.

"Have a look-see!" Lee said.

I slipped the camera into my pocket and shrugged. According to the clock on the wall, it was 8:58. I figured that if I played along for an hour, until ten, everyone would be happy, and I could go home. I knew what the place would be like without Helen. I was wondering what it would be like without her little dog.

Lee was noodling with numbers on his PalmPC, moving things around on the tiny screen. "Three ways," he said, not looking up. "Three maybe happens. One, algorithm not work, in which case nobody lost or gain. One probably most probable. Two, see-tomorrow algorithm too good, in which case we pull too far, all way to End of Time. Or three, algorithm work right, in which case pull through multiverse a microsecond, then larger slice, then larger slice, ekcetera [he pronounced it Texas style], until three . . ."

"Whoa," I said. "The End of Time?"

"Not likely," said Lee. "Only if square root of the square root of the first Infinity Progression divisible by the third integer of the under-equation, which here doubt. No problem."

No problem? It was 9:00 according to the clock on the wall. "So, okay, let's do it." I kicked the swing to start it going, just enough to squeak.

"Hold horses!" Lee took my hand. "Hold hands! Subjective factory."

Hold hands? But before I could complain Lee hit RETURN on his PalmPC. The screen filled with numbers, dancing, swapping places.

Lee kicked the glider higher, and I kicked to even it out (just as I'd had to do with my grandma), and there they were: the army of mice, squeaking in regular time.

The numbers went faster and faster, until Lee's little LCD screen was a multicolor blur. We were swinging back and forth, glider style: no up, no down, no arc. There was a flickering, either in the room's lights or in my eyes. I couldn't find the clock on the wall. I couldn't find the wall. Then suddenly the squeaking stopped although the flickering kept going. There was a sudden pain in my knee, and an old, familiar smell . . .

Then the swing was squeaking again, slowing, and the screen on Lee's laptop was empty, except for a blinking cursor dead center, which I noticed, because it was an odd place for a cursor to be. I looked around and everything looked totally unfamiliar, the way even your own room does when you suddenly wake up from a deep sleep in the afternoon.

The clock said 9:55.

Whoa! I pointed at the clock. "How did you do that?"

Lee was smiling. That inscrutable, enigmatic . . .

"What happened!?" I asked, pulling my hand from Lee's. The pain in my knee was gone. The smell was still there, but fading fast, like a dream. It was familiar, almost identifiable, then gone.

+ 1

"Beats me," Lee said. "But OK." He was already moving numbers around. "Try other slice quick."

Before Cole could register his disagreement with this strategy, Lee hit RETURN and the screen started filling with numbers again. He grabbed Cole's hand and pushed off with one foot.

Cole added his little kick to even out the glider, and there was the army of mice again. Squeaking in cadence. The clock had no hands and then there was no clock. The walls were flickering again. Cole tried closing his eyes. There was the old, almost familiar smell, and then it was gone. And the same sudden, sharp pain in his knee . . .

The glider stopped squeaking. Stopped moving altogether at the back of its swing. The world was tilted just slightly . . . but the swing was still.

Cole looked for the clock but the wall was gone. He saw something in the distance like the spine of a dinosaur, and felt a moment of terror until he realized it was the Sill, the little basalt outcropping that runs through the campus of Swick.

"Picture," said Lee. Of course he said it Texas style: pitcher.

Cole had forgotten he had the little camera. It had a zoom but it was too dark to see anything but the jagged outline of the rock. He snapped two pictures, hoping for the best. "Where are we?" he asked Lee.

"Beats me!" Lee's voice sounded far away, as if he were speaking through a tube.

"How did we get outside? What's going on?"

"Sill!" Lee said, pointing. The air was cold. Cole sniffed, looking for the smell, but it was gone. He realized they were swinging again. He could still see the Sill. Then it was gone. Lee had let go of his hand, and he was looking at the basement wall.

The clock said 9:07.

"Okay, what's going on?" Cole asked again. He was beginning to sound stupid, even to himself. "Now the clock is right again." Or had he misread it before?

"Sill." Lee pointed at the camera. "Pitcher?"

There was a display on the back of the camera. Cole hit a button and there was the Sill, just a dark stegosaur silhouette.

But how? "Lee, what the fuck is going on? What happened to the wall?"

"Future!" Lee shrugged. "Maybe no wall. Or see through time slice, like propeller. Beats me."

"Whoa. No building? What if they replace it with a parking lot and we end up in solid concrete?" Cole seemed to remember something like that from an old Superman comic. His Tennessee grandmother hadn't allowed them, but he had kept his stash in Brooklyn. His mother didn't care what—or if—he read at all.

"No sweat!" Lee picked up Cole's hand again. Cole tried to pull away but Lee's grip got tighter; he was like a Chinese puzzle. Hell, he was a Chinese puzzle. "More slice quick. Get three!"

"Wait!" Cole liked it less and less the more it dawned on him that they had actually traveled in time. But Lee had already hit RETURN, and there was the army of mice, back again. They were swinging. Cole straightened the glider out, as best he could.

This time he recognized the pain in his knee. It was what he called an old football injury, from high school. Actually he had fallen off a ladder decorating the gym for the Homecoming Game. The smell was more elusive . . .

It was cold. They were stopped again. There was silence; no squeaking, nothing at all. The wall, the clock, the basement room itself had all disappeared, and they were hanging in cold, dark air. Cole could see snow—he could smell it in the air. He heard a popping, and thought of the way swing chains used to pop when he was a kid, but gliders don't have chains.

The strangest thing was, none of it seemed strange. The snow, the clocks, the traveling in time. "We're actually traveling in time," Cole said. It was no longer a question.

"Always travel time," said Lee. "Only no back and forth."

"So where are we?" Then Cole saw the Sill again. Had he been looking at it all along? The world was sort of drawing itself in, taking its time. There was a sunset behind the Sill, red as fire, and a wailing/barking sound like sirens, far off.

He started to take a picture but Lee stopped him. "Down there!" Lee pointed with his free, his right, hand.

They were looking at a wall—no, a window. Someone was coming through, feet first. First a plastic boot. Then a gun in a broad, gloved hand; then a helmet, arms, shoulders.

It was a man, a short white man with a short black beard. He took off his helmet; his bald head gleamed with sweat. Looking down on it, Cole realized that he and Lee were off the floor, somewhere near the ceiling.

The bald man set down the gun—it was plastic, and oddly shaped, but clearly a weapon. He took off both gloves. Remembering the camera, Cole took a picture.

The man looked up. He was Asian, like Lee, but with a little beard. Had he heard the click? He looked straight at Cole but showed no sign of seeing him. He pulled a piece of white paper from his breast pocket and unfolded it. It was covered with numbers, neatly hand written. He held it up in both hands, and Cole realized he was supposed to take a picture. Just as he was about to snap it, the man's head nodded abruptly to one side and a spray of blood came out, blood and bone, white and red, on the wall and on the floor.

The paper fell from his fingers and fluttered into the dust and rubble on the floor. Cole almost dropped the camera, barely caught it in Time . . .

"Oh God damn!"

Was that me, Cole wondered, or Lee? Lee was leaning forward, reaching down, too far. Cole pulled him back. They were swinging again, and there was the army of mice. The lights in the room were flickering, then steady. They were back. The clock on the wall said 9:11.

"Damn!" Lee said, snatching the camera from Cole's hand and scrolling through the display. "Damn!"

"Damn what? Was that it, on the paper? Where were we? Where are we?"

Cole got out of the swing and hopped in a tight circle on the concrete floor. He could hardly walk. His knee was stiff. The clock was back to normal: 9:12. Had he just imagined it was 9:55 before? Rap music was booming vaguely from upstairs: just the bass; the accompanying doggerel was mercifully lost in the ether. Everything seemed normal, except—

They had actually traveled in time!

"No picture!" Lee was bent over his laptop. "Lost number. See-tomorrow math!"

"Let me see," Cole said. He picked up the camera and scrolled through the display. There was the Sill; there was the man, coming through the window; and then—nothing.

"Lee, what's going on here?"

He was about to hand the camera to Lee when the thumping music from upstairs suddenly got louder. The door opened and Parker stuck his head in. Cole called him Parker, only to himself of course. Parker was the campus security chief, an overweight black man with the kind of elaborately tasteless hairdo favored by Latrell Sprewell fans. A big, dimwitted rent-a-cop who carried a Stephen King novel in one hand and a flashlight in the other.

"Dr. Lee!—Mr. Cole?" Parker openly despised Cole and always called him "Mister," presumably to show his contempt for a nonscience, nonbusiness degree. "I thought I heard something. What in the world are you two doing here this time of night? I mean, are you . . . ?"

"Justice chickens," said Lee, in his peculiar Texas twang. "No problem?"

"Well, I guess," said Parker, deferring to the tenured professor. "But I will have to lock up at ten."

"No problem!" said Lee. But then he turned to Cole as soon as the door was shut. "Some fuck up!"

"No shit!" Cole said. "Lee, where the hell were we? Was that paper Dear Abbey, the formula, the patch we are supposed to get?"

"Future. Fumble. All fuck up."

Future fumble all fuck up—as if that explained everything. And it did. Cole had seen the future and the big surprise was that there were no surprises. It was business as usual. The Sixth Extinction. The doomed, lost, murderous world, chewing off its own foot. And the irony was, of course, that it looked just like today. Just another murder.

"We actually traveled in time. And we blew it, didn't we?"

Lee nodded grimly, studying his PalmPC.

Cole handed Lee the camera; made him take it this time. "I've seen enough. We actually traveled in time. How far? What year?"

"Three? Six?" Lee muttered mysteriously, dropping the camera into one of the many pockets of his hideous safari jacket. He held up his PalmPC and shook it. "Numbers fucked. But come on, one slice to go."

"You said there were only three trips. We've done three. And besides, we blew it."

"Numbers fucked," Lee said. "No formula." He pointed at the blinking cursor on his PalmPC. "Let's ride."

"I've seen enough," Cole said, but Lee grabbed his hand and pulled him down to the glider, beside him. Maybe Cole should have pulled away harder. Maybe he was curious. Probably he could have, should have, pulled away. But according to Helen (and others, including his grandmother) he'd never been resolute, never been decisive. And Time was like a rip tide, drawing them away from the shore, dragging them from the crumbling banks of the Present into the maelstrom of All That is Yet to Be.

1 +

There they were, the army of mice, and the clock on the wall was gone.

The wall was gone.

Cole looked down at Lee's PalmPC but couldn't find it. Everything was flickering. Nothing looked wrong but nothing looked right. He felt a cold wind and there it was again, the old, familiar but unidentifiable smell and the pain in his left knee. The flickering stopped, faded really, and he thought, Good! It was all a mistake and we haven't gone anywhere, because he could hear the stupid thumping rap beat from upstairs . . .

But wait! That couldn't be right. He saw snow whirling in the air. They were somewhere outside, on a low hill overlooking a long gray plain, and the thumping sound was . . . A drum.

Mournful and regular as a heartbeat.

Boom Boom Boom

The room was gone and there was the Sill, behind them, black against the sky. The sky was sort of a yellow gray. The air was cold and sweet, and now Cole recognized the familiar smell. It was the smell of mud; the smell of the sea when the tide was out. It was the smell of death.

Small death.

"Where are we now?" It was Cole, now, who was squeezing Lee's hand. Lee didn't seem to mind.

"Beats me," Lee said, staring at his PalmPC. "Some ride. Numbers wild!"

"I hear a drum."

Lee pointed without looking up. What had looked to Cole at first like a fence, or a line of trees in the distance, was a line of riders, single file. The line passed from horizon to horizon, from yellow-gray fog on the right, to the vague line in the distance where the gray plain met the sky.

The camera had a zoom and he used it like a little telescope. He could see two walkers for every rider. He couldn't tell what kind of people they were or what they were wearing. They were carrying long poles with black flags and black banners. Black birds circled overhead.

He clicked, then gave Lee the camera. "Some kind of mourners," he said.

"Dark age," Lee said, looking through the zoom. "World go back. Mud is sound."

Cole thought that last was one of Lee's Texas nonsequiturs; then he realized that they were looking at Long Island Sound. And it was dry.

"Does that mean there's ice to the north? So what happened to global warming?"

"Beats me," Lee said gloomily, handing Cole the camera and turning back to his little PalmPC.

The glider was stopped but Cole couldn't reach the ground with his shoe. He couldn't see anything close at hand; only far away, where the riders were fading into a thin mist, blowing down from the north.

Boom Boom Boom

The wind was cold. Cole had to pee but he wasn't about to get up. They were in the future, no doubt about it. He had passed all the way from amused, contemptuous skepticism to belief without stopping by amazement. Lee's algorithm, whatever it was, worked. And it was all depressingly real. The future was exactly what Cole had feared it to be.

Never had he so hated being right before; it's an unfamiliar feeling for an academic. But looking into the future was like watching a nine-year-old with a Glock. Humanity was like the kid down the street who had found his crackhead uncle's "nine" under the sofa and proceeded to blast away his friends and family, expecting they would get up and dust themselves off when the show was over, just like on TV.

Well, the show was over and nobody was getting up.

Cole felt like crying. He looked at Lee and Lee shook his head as if he knew what Cole was thinking. "Everything too late," he said. This was the world that Dear Abbey, with all its horrors, had been intended to prevent.

Cole looked up and saw vapor trails far above, three of them, in formation. That unexpected sign of a still-extant technology depressed him even more; he shivered, remembering the days when commercial jets flew alone through untroubled skies. Most of the time, in most of the world, anyway.

He took a picture of the vapor trails. Was this it? There was nothing else to photograph. Just mud and mourners. Just desolation. "Let's go," he said. "There's nothing here for us." He kicked but the glider wouldn't budge. It felt as heavy as a car.

"Hold horses," Lee said, holding up the PalmPC. "Wait for cursor."

Cole waited. Two of the riders had pulled out of the line and stopped. Had they seen them? Even through the zoom, Cole couldn't see faces, just silhouettes. But he could tell they were riding his way, slowly at first, then faster . . .

"Lee . . ."

And then there they were, like the cavalry to the rescue, the army of mice. The glider was moving; the sky was flickering and then it was no longer sky, just white space.

Cole breathed a sigh of relief, on his way "home" to his own sad and sorry time.

Or so he thought.

+ 5 0 0

Something was wrong. There was the pain again, in Cole's knee; there was the sweet, small death, sea smell. The mice screamed their chorus as the glider slowed, and stopped, but . . .

But the glider was still outside.

In a mist. A cold, thin fog. Outside, on a long, sloping lawn of rough grass, unmowed but short. Cole smelled salt and heard waves. The glider squealed to a stop and he shivered.

This was not the Student Union. "Where the fuck are we now?"

"Dr. Lee? Mr. Cole?"

Cole turned and saw the Sill in the distance, and closer, the crumbling walls of a ruined building. Two people were approaching at a fast walk across the tufted, gray-green grass. One was smiling and one was frowning, like the twin thespian masks of Comedy and Tragedy.

"Whoa!" Cole said aloud as they got closer and he saw that they were masks—stylized, with fierce eyes and wide mouths. One was turned up in a sketchy grin somewhere between have-a-nice-day and Hannibal Lecter; the other turned down in an elaborate, hideous scowl that suggested blind hatred more than tragedy or sadness.

The scowling mask held back a step. The smiling mask approached, bowed at the waist, and spoke again.

"Dr. Lee?" A man's voice.

He held out his hand to Cole.

Cole took it without thinking and was startled to find that it was solid, cold—but real. Had he expected a ghost?

"I am Lee," Lee said beside him, his voice shaky.

"*Bienvenido!*" The masked man shook Lee's hand and then Cole's again. He spoke slowly, with a Spanish accent. "You must be Cole, then. And you are African!"

"So?"

"You are Black! You are Negro!"

"So? It's Dr. Cole," Cole said. "And so what? So fucking what?"

"Well, we did not know," the man in the mask said. "That is all. It is a surprise. Perhaps there is much that we do not know. Now you are here." He touched the chin of his mask. "May I show myself to you?"

"What?!"

"Sure thang," Lee said in his best Texas drawl. The man removed his mask. He was Asian, or at least part Asian; about thirty to forty, with black hair in a ponytail and a small, thin, intricate beard. He was slight, with long fingers like a pianist. For the first time Cole noticed his clothes. He wore gray coveralls under a quilted vest with a gray and rose, paisley design.

Under the mask, his smile was thinner. His gray eyes looked dead. "Elizam Hava," he said, bowing again, Japanese style, from the waist. "From the Universidad de Miami. This is my colleague Ruth Lavalle."

The few words of Spanish made Cole realize how learned his English was, how careful, how formal. His partner in the scowling mask bowed, even more stiffly, almost reluctantly. Cole could see now that she was a woman: small breasted, compact; she stood on the balls of her feet as if looking for an opportunity to strike. Sort of like Helen, except that he didn't like her.

Then he remembered that he didn't like Helen either. She was gone anyway; moved away; dead; buried . . . for a hundred, a thousand, how many years?

The woman wore the same gray coveralls and vest the man wore, and carried two extra vests over one arm, like a waiter's towel. Her mask was much more carefully done than his, which was little more than a sketch of a smiling face. Hers was a maniac scowl with narrowed slanted eyes and fierce colors, done in red and white and blue, so that it looked like an American flag—or a baboon's ass, depending on your point of view.

She left her mask on and didn't speak at all. Just bowed stiffly and stepped back.

They both stood silently, watching, one masked and one not. They were waiting for Cole and Lee to do something, but what? Cole wanted to take a picture, but he was afraid. They looked like savages. What if they thought the camera was a weapon? It was Lee who broke the spell. He stood up, pulling Cole with him, and before Cole knew what was happening, he was out of the glider, standing on the bunchy grass.

"Whoa!" He had expected to fall through the grass as through a cloud, but here he was. Physically in the future. Not just looking on.

Lee looked dazed as he slipped the PalmPC into one of the pockets of his hideous safari jacket.

Cole stomped; the ground was real. Did that mean the future, this future, was real? Fixed? Unchangeable?

"Here!"

The host, Elizam, took the two vests from the scowling-mask woman and handed them to Cole and Lee. Cole put his on. It was soft, like silk, but thin. It even had a little pocket for the camera.

Lee held his vest over his arm. He apparently didn't want to part with the hideous safari jacket. Welcome to L.L.Bean.

"*Bienvenido*," Elizam said again. "We were sent here to meet you. We have been waiting almost two days."

"Sent who? What deal?" Lee asked. "*Teine ustedes algo por nosotros?*"

"*Los Viejos.*" Elizam put his arm over Lee's shoulder, and the two started walking up the hill, toward the ruin. The scowling-mask woman followed them. Cole felt disoriented, unattached, as if he were in a dream—except that he still had to pee.

"Is there a bathroom?" he asked. "*Hay baño?*"

The woman turned and pointed down the slope. Cole walked toward the water. The grass ended at a short, rocky, ten-foot cliff. At the bottom, a few seals were playing with a log rolling in a gentle surf.

He peed down onto the rocks. The seals looked up, and saw him, and started to bark. They were small, gray seals with black, button eyes, long whiskers and bright teeth.

Cole smiled and barked back.

Then he saw what they were playing with. It wasn't a log. It was a human body, gray and bloodless. Both arms were missing and most of the face was gone. It rolled over and over as the seals nudged it and nipped at it with their little snouts.

Shivering, Cole zipped his pants and hurried up the hill. Halfway up he remembered the camera and stopped. Then he went on.

He didn't want a picture of that.

Inside the low, crumbling walls of the ruin, there was an open-sided geodesic tent on two curved poles. Lee and his two hosts sat under it, on the ground, around a small fire. Cole clicked a shot of the cozy little scene, and then joined them. His vest was electric or chemical; it was beginning to warm him.

The low walls blocked the wind: concrete blocks, most of them shattered. It was definitely the Student Center, or what was left of it, a hundred years in the future, or five hundred, or a thousand. So why, Cole wondered, didn't he feel more strange? Why did all this, even the seals, feel so horribly normal?

Perhaps it was the Sill in the distance, that jagged little dino back. Or the silence.

The fog had lifted, and to the south (if they were in fact on Long Island

Sound) the ocean and sky met in a soft haze. To the north, beyond The Sill, clouds massed like gray horses.

Elizam carefully placed another stick on the fire. "Please excuse the small fire," he said, in Spanish. "Not much wood." He had taken off his mask, but he wouldn't look either Cole or Lee in the eye.

"What's with the killer seals?" Cole asked, in English.

"Kill seals!?" Lee looked shocked.

Cole told him what he had seen.

"Vampire seals," the woman said from behind her mask. "Your greatest creation."

"My what?"

"There are many dead," said Elizam, his voice oddly flat, "whom the water uncover. Do you mind if I put my mask on? I can speak more freely."

"Whatever," Cole said. Whatever rings your fucking bell.

Elizam put his mask back on. The idiotic smiling face was an improvement on his own dead look.

"As the seas rise," he said, "they open graves and unlock doors. Unlike many large-mammal species, the vampire seals prosper. Here in New England there are only the dead. The glaciers are still hundreds of miles north, but no one can live here."

"*Y ustedes?*" Lee ventured. His Spanish was a little better than his English.

"We live in Miami, but we were sent to meet you, since we are both experts in late English. We have tapes, movies. The way people talk as well as the spelling is preserved."

"*Envian por quienes?*" Lee asked a second time, in Spanish. "Who sent you?"

"*Los Viejos,*" Elizam answered. "From the future."

And who are these Old Ones? Lee asked, still in Spanish.

"*No lo sabemos.*" No one knew who the Old Ones were, or what they wanted. Elizam and his scowling companion had simply been told to meet Lee and Cole here, and send them on.

"Send us on where?" Cole asked, but no one answered him. They pretended not to hear and jabbered on in Spanish. Cole could follow the sense of it. A message had appeared on some kind of academic E-mail server. "*Nos da sus nombres,*" the woman said. "Dr Lee. Cole."

"It's Doctor Cole," Cole said, interrupting. "Doctor William Wellington Cole."

"*Lo siento.*"

"Yeah, right." Cole was getting pissed. Who were these people? Why were they speaking Spanish, which he barely understood? The woman was hunkered down by the fire, across from him. He touched his cheek and pointed at her. "What's with the fucking masks anyway?"

"They express our sorrow," said Elizam, in English.

"And hide our rage," said the woman.

"Rage? Rage at what?"

"At you." She took off her mask. Her eyes were gray and dead, like Elizam's. She was about twenty-five. Though pale, she had tight hair and a broad face, with what Cole's grandmother (who was half white) used to call "a brush of Africa."

"The rage is for what you did. And did not do." Her words were flat and emotionless: what you did and did not do. She stood up.

"May I say it?" she asked nobody in particular.

Lee nodded. Cole shrugged. Whatever. She walked in a circle around the fire as she talked. In English. It had obviously been rehearsed. It was as ceremonial as a dance, and what she said was as measured and as unemotional as a legal deposition, in spite of its content:

"You murdered your own children. You destroyed their home, you pulled the world down around them. You left them crying in the ruins. They were lost and they were our parents. Their lives were all sorrow and their sorrow is all ours."

"Their sorrow is ours," repeated Elizam.

"They died weeping, though they knew not what for, and they knew there would be no one, but us, their children, to hear their cries. If they survived. It is their sorrow we pass on."

"It is their sorrow we pass on," repeated Elizam.

"Whoa," Cole said. This was getting like a church service. "You've got the wrong guys! Don't you even know why we are here?" He started to explain that Lee and himself were Green, were activists (each in his own way), opposed to what was happening, sent here to . . .

But after a word or two, in English, he shut up. It didn't matter, did it? They had obviously failed miserably, hadn't they? From here, from the perspective of a few hundred years, there was no difference. They were like the good Germans, or the honest Quaker merchants who had declined to take part in the slave trade, or had even (politely) spoken out against it, while allowing it to prosper.

If Cole had ever had any doubts about Dear Abbey (and he had, though he had never expressed them, even to himself), they were gone. Gone with the wind, now that he saw the world he and his generation had left to their children. Wouldn't any effort to change that, to reverse that, be justified?

"Please continue," said Lee.

Ruth (for that was her name) walked in circles carrying her mask in her hand, as Cole and Lee stared into the fire, along with Elizam, who was masked again. "We watched the animals die," she intoned. "One by one, and then in herds, then one by one again. Even the ones in the zoos. The great mammals are only a memory now: the elephant, the great whale, the rhino, the walrus."

"Only memories," said Elizam.

"Only memories," said Lee, who had apparently decided to join them. He still wore the hideous safari jacket, though he had laid their heating vest across his knees like a lap robe.

"The natural world was trashed, devastated," said Ruth, "and so was the historical, the cultural, the human world. Cities were burned, museums looted. Libraries were flooded and lost under the seas, for global warming wiped out not only cities, but memories, heritages: the Dutch, Singapore, the Polynesian archipelago, entire languages, lost without a trace."

She was giving the speech Cole had always wanted to give, the message he had wanted to convey to his students, and yet he didn't want to hear it. Not from her.

She sat down. Elizam placed another stick on the fire, very carefully.

"What about global warming?" Cole asked, hoping to change the subject. "It is cold as hell!"

"The Gulf Stream is gone," said Elizam, muffled behind his mask. "Europe and New England are uninhabitable. The Midwest is hot. Texas is burning. The only temperate zones are in Asia, the Pacific Rim, and along the north of South America, and some on the California Coast."

"What of Africa?"

"Africa?" Ruth raised her mask and turned her blank eyes on Cole. "Africa is gone, sunk, dust. The forests are cinders, the people are dead. The fourth holocaust. First there was slavery, which looted the continent of youth; then colonialism, which despoiled it of riches. Then AIDS which orphaned a generation . . ."

"Two," said Elizam.

"Ironically, it was the diaspora that saved Africa, at least the people. More than half were gone already. Taking their culture and heritage with them."

"Now can you see why we are surprised to see that you are African?" said Elizam. "It was our understanding that African people in your century had no education, no rights, no social access . . ."

"Not strictly true," said Lee.

"Not that far off," Cole corrected. "But you said four. There was a fourth holocaust?"

"The fires," said Elizam. "The drought and then the fires."

"What about China?" Lee asked.

"China leads," she said. "They rebuild. We all rebuild. We do what we can to replace what you destroyed but it takes time, and some of it is not possible. You killed all the big animals, or most of them."

"Not all," said Elizam, getting up to get more wood from a small pile under the wall. "Not completely. There are persistent reports of an elephant seen in West Africa."

"Unreliable," said Ruth. "Like the Loch Ness monster, or flying saucers."

Reports of elephants, like flying saucers. For the first time Cole understood the cliché, "his heart sank," as he actually felt his heart sink. Was it possible that even more than our fellow men we could miss our fellow creatures? He began to feel the same sadness that appeared to depress Elizam and Ruth. He had never seen people so devoid of feeling, of life, of mirth and laughter. And now he was becoming one of them.

"So you still have telephones, computers?" Lee asked, in Spanish.

"Oh, yes," Elizam answered. "That's why we are here. Knowledge isn't lost that easily. It's harder to make things, like computers, but the old ones can be repaired, and we are developing the capacity to make them like before."

"Not as cheaply," said Ruth. "Not as thoughtlessly. Not as carelessly. For everything that is made is something unmade, or left unmade. That is what you, our parents, never understood. That is the root of the devastation you bequeathed to us."

Cole looked away; he was tired of her self-righteous bullshit. He discovered to his horror that he identified more with the exuberant, destructive thoughtlessness she attacked than with her. And wasn't it true? When all was said and done (and looking around, it seemed, indeed, that all had been said and all had been done) wasn't he in fact one of the destroyers?

The talk died down and they sat, staring into the dying fire. There was nothing more to say. Something besides the world seemed destroyed: innocence and enthusiasm and hope seemed gone as well. Cole wondered what the rest of their world was like. Were he and Lee going to see it?

He hoped not . . .

He dozed off, and when he awoke, the fire was out. Elizam and Ruth were gone. Lee was down the hill, sitting on the glider with his PalmPC on his lap. Cole hurried down, afraid the Chinaman might leave without him.

He needn't have worried. Lee was shaking his head. "All fuck figures. No home. You get pictures?"

"Yes, yes," Cole said patting the pocket of his vest, where he had put the camera. "Pictures of what? Masks? Fires? It's cold here. Just get us the hell out of here!"

"The hell," said Lee; now he was shaking his PalmPC as well as his head.

Cole looked up the hill and saw Elizam and Ruth approaching, carrying their masks in their hands. "What is this shit?" he demanded. "Did you mess up our time machine?"

"Infrared," said Elizam in English. He held up a small device, like a flashlight. "I entered the figures *Los Viejos* gave us."

Cole turned to Lee. "Who? What? Do you understand any of this?"

"Hold horses," Lee muttered, in English, punching in numbers.

It was almost dark. Cole didn't know whether to be pissed off or scared. He had to pee again but he had no desire to see what the seals were dining on. Let alone photograph it. He walked back up to the ruin and pissed on the fire.

Ruth and Elizam followed and watched from behind the wall, unreproachfully. It was as if they expected it of him.

"You can both go to hell," Cole said, as he zipped up his pants. "Okay? *Capiche? Comprende?*"

They followed him back down the hill. "*Gracias para venir,*" Elizam said to Lee. "We are honored to meet you."

"Fuck you and the world you spun in on," Cole said. Then he stopped, hearing a small insistent sound:

beep beep

Lee's PalmPC.

"Hold horses," Lee said. "Have cursor. All aboard." He patted the seat beside him.

Cole didn't need to be told twice. He sat down, and Lee covered his big hand with his own small one.

Elizam and Ruth stood silently with their masks on, their hands raised in farewell, or so it seemed. Then Cole realized what it was they wanted—their vests back. Lee's was across his knees; Cole took his off and tossed them both to Ruth.

Lee hit RETURN, and there they were, the army of mice. Cole kicked to even up the swing.

"Damn!" said Lee, as the mists of light closed around them. Cole felt it too. Something was different, different in the same way as before.

They weren't heading home. They were falling. Falling farther and farther, into the future . . .

+1000

Spinning.

Cole was about to throw up. He wondered if it was the whiskey, which he could still feel, when, suddenly, the spinning stopped. Blue striations flickered through the air, and he found himself on a seashore—again.

But this time it was warmer and the sky was bright blue. And he didn't like it. Not at all.

Lee let go of Cole's hand; Cole grabbed Lee's back. "Long Island?" he asked. Even though he knew it wasn't.

In the near distance, there was a cone-shaped, steeply pointed island, with what appeared to be trees growing toward the top in a spiral. The whole thing looked artificial.

"Pitcher?" said Lee.

Cole let go of Lee's hand and reached into his pocket for the camera. But there was no pocket; no camera.

"Shit," he said. "It was in the vest."

Lee shrugged. "Only for formula, just in case."

"Still, stupid," Cole said. "My fault." Photos of the future, and he had lost them. "Can we go back and get them?"

"Don't think so," Lee said. "Just pitchers."

"True, but sorry," Cole said. He was beginning to talk like Lee. It was time to change the subject. He leaned back in the glider and looked around. "Where are we? I mean, I wonder where we are."

"Figuring," said Lee, bending over his PalmPC.

"Capps Island," said a voice from behind them. Cole sat up and looked around, alarmed. A man was standing behind the glider. Had he been there all along? It was as if the world were being drawn in, slowly; it was like visiting a website in the old days on a slow line.

He was a tall white man, unmasked (Cole noticed that right away), in a soft-brushed velveteen suit. At least it looked to Cole like velveteen. There was something about it that was proudly, flamboyantly artificial.

"Welcome, Dr. Lee," he said. "So pleased, Dr. Cole. As you can see, we have a crossing to make. That is, if you want to see the island. There is not much time. Do you need to rest?"

"See island? No problem," Lee said. He stood up, and Cole stood up with him.

"I am Hallam," the man said in his odd, unaccented English. He pronounced every word carefully, as if he were trying it for the first time. He stuck out his hand and Lee took it. "I am pleased to meet you on your journey."

He dropped Lee's hand and took Cole's. "I am Hallam," he said again. "I am pleased to . . ."

"What journey?!" Cole asked. "Lee, where are we? Do you even know?"

Lee didn't answer, but the man, Hallam, did. He pointed toward the peaky island. "Capps Island," he said again.

A plane, or some sort of craft, was taking off near the top of the island. It was too far away to tell what it was, or how big.

"There are one hundred and twelve of these EarthWatch stations around the world," Hallam said. "They are all connected on a network of . . ."

"Whoa! Slow down," Cole said. "What year is this? Please."

"Year? Oh, yes, of course," said Hallam. "Well, 724. Your year, the Jesus time, is . . ." He pulled up his sleeve and checked a wristwatch. "I am sorry . . . is 3124. I should have thought. Of course you would want to know."

"Jesus!" Cole said, sitting back down.

"We don't use the Jesus calendar," Hallam said, tapping his wristwatch. "But I have it here."

The glider didn't move; it had that strange inertia Cole had felt before, as if it had the mass of a car.

Lee was tapping at his PalmPC, looking worried. Cole was beyond worry. A thousand years. What could happen to him? He was already dead, he could feel it in his bones. His bones which were already rotting somewhere under the earth on which he stood. If they had not been exhumed by seals.

The glider felt creepy. Cole stood up again. The ground felt solid under his feet; too solid. Was this real, then, this future now?

It was. Real. He shivered in the bright sunlight.

"We have the Hong Kong calendar," Hallam was explaining. "We measure from Hong Kong Colloquium, 724 years ago. That's for politics. For spirit, we measure from the Crossing. That makes this year 114,844. But come." He started down a path toward the water.

Lee and Cole followed, both of them. What else were they to do? "The Crossing?" Cole asked. "What Crossing?"

"Long ago there was a war," Hallam said, "with much fire, for fire was a weapon of war in those early days, and then a plague of some kind. For the first time, but not the only time, our kind had all but murdered themselves. There were only thousands then, but thousands died. A few women gathered what was left of the First People, all three bands that had warred, mostly children, and led them North, out of the Valley of Bones, and across the Great Basin that would become the Mediterranean, though it was dry then, from the Ice."

"A hundred thousand years ago? How do you know?" Cole asked.

"One hundred fourteen," said Hallam. "The eight forty four is an agreed-on approximation. We dated it with DNA and carbon tests; we reconstructed it from legends and rock paintings; we knew it all along in our bones, it was our beginning."

A small airplane was landing on the water below. Cole hadn't heard it approach. He wondered if it was the same one he had seen taking off from the island.

Meanwhile Lee had his own questions. "Hong Kong?"

"The coming together," said Hallam. "The meeting where we began to develop the systems that led to EarthWatch. That ended the Sixth, finally."

"The Sixth?" Cole asked. "The Sixth Extinction? You call it that?"

Hallam shrugged. "We call it what it was. It was the sixth for the planet. Thousands of species died, wiped out, forever, without even a farewell. It lasted for over five hundred years, and it was in many ways worse than the wars that led to the Crossing, for we killed so many others. It led to the Mourning and the Restoration. Even though it was not nearly so close as the Crossing, for us. There we were reduced to less than two hundred souls. In the Sixth Extinction to just over two hundred million."

"Now how many?" Lee asked.

"That, you are about to see," Hallam answered. They were at the water's edge. The little plane was taxiing toward them across the water.

It had short, thick wings like a cartoon plane, with deep leading edge slots that apparently added to their lift. There was a big propeller powered, they were told, by a remote magnetic field. There was no engine, and no noise.

There was no one in the pilot's seat. There was no pilot's seat.

They clambered in and took off with a whistling noise that diminished as they gained speed and altitude. There were no seat belts. For some reason, Cole thought of Helen. The last time he had looked at the clock it had been 9:11, and that seemed days ago. She would be halfway to London by now. And dead a thousand years as well.

Lee's inscrutable little smile was back. Cole smiled too. There was something very peaceful and reassuring about this little plane, the sunlight, the blue water below and the island ahead, rapidly getting closer—the steep coast receding behind.

"A hundred thousand years. From that perspective," Cole said to Hallam, "we are almost contemporaries."

"We are contemporaries," their host replied. "A thousand years is only a moment in the life span of a species. Less than a moment for rock and water and the Earth. A hundred thousand years is itself only a few moments. We mark our spiritual history from the beginning of that scattering, that diaspora, which ended only a thousand years ago, in your time."

Spiritual. Cole had never liked the word before. They flew very slowly. No one here seemed in a hurry. As the plane gently touched down on the water, Hallam explained what they were about to see. "We have been rebuilding the earth since the Sixth . . ."

Which had happened. In spite of all our efforts, Cole thought gloomily.

". . . and we have linked all the climatic regions, the populations of animals and plants, the meteorological and tectonic information. The result is a self-monitoring global system that looks after the environment, letting us know about long range trends, etcetera."

They taxied to a rocky shore, where they were met by a woman who introduced herself as Dana. She was dressed in the same velveteen, only orange— and considerably more shapely, Cole noticed.

"You're African!" she said, taking both Cole's hands in her own. So was she; not just a little, like the masked woman (or Cole himself), but a lot.

"Afraid so," Cole said. She looked puzzled and he immediately regretted his tone. While he had beaucoup problems with being African American, he had always given thanks for the fact that he was, at least, not white. But how explain all that, a thousand years in the future?

"Just a joke," he said. She smiled politely.

They were riding a kind of escalator (without steps) up the hillside to a tunnel.

The tunnel led inside the mountain, to a large egg-shaped room with LCD monitors built into the walls. Data was flowing down the screens like water.

Except for the screens and themselves, the room was empty. "Who watch?" Lee asked.

"It watches itself," Dana said, who didn't seem surprised or bothered in the least by Lee's cowboy pidgin English. "This is one of a network of fifty-five EarthWatch stations, all over the earth, including one under the Arctic Sea. The Arctic ice cap, which was gone in your day, is back, you know."

It wasn't gone in our day, Cole wanted to say. But what did she mean by "your day"?

"The screens are just for show. The system monitors itself. Maintains itself, too."

"It's intelligent?" Cole asked.

"Of course," Dana said, giving him a look. "Why would anyone build a system that was not intelligent?"

"Earth balance," said Lee, nodding. "What to do. Cool."

"Actually," said Hallam, "instead of telling us what to do, it tells us what it is doing. EarthWatch has taken over most of the work itself, using bacterial nanobots to intervene in out-of-synch natural systems. The system has only been online for a hundred and forty years, and it's still changing."

So the Earth does have a chance, Cole thought. It can be restored, at least partially. Even without Dear Abbey, even though he and Lee had obviously failed . . .

Or had they?

"Is this why you brought us here?" Cole asked. "To show us this? To warn us of what would happen if we failed—or if we succeeded?"

Dana looked puzzled. "It wasn't us. The Old Ones brought you here."

"You're not the Old Ones?"

"Oh, no. They are the ones who told us you were coming," said Hallam. "That's why we learned your language. We are the only two who speak it."

"The Old Ones will send you home, I suppose, when the time comes," said Dana, leading them back out the tunnel. "Meanwhile, there are, or will be, five stops I think. But we must get you back to the rendezvous."

"Pronto," said Lee, holding up his PalmPC.

The cursor was blinking.

Cole felt a strange, deep sadness as they rode the stepless escalator back down the mountainside. It was peaceful here in the future—but look at the price.

"From eight billion, in our time, to less than two hundred million," he said to Dana, as they climbed into the little plane. "Was there a particular, uh, problem, that set it off? A sort of slow-motion catastrophe?"

"Catastrophe?" asked Hallam. "There were hundreds. Famines, floods, wars, diseases, murdered so many."

"And murdered the soul," said Dana. "The Restoration went on for hundreds of years."

"The masks," Cole said.

"They couldn't face themselves, or each other, directly. There had been so much violence and destruction. Protocol was everything."

"During the Restoration, they thought the Mourning was over," said Hallam. "We look back now and see that they were still in the middle of it."

"Just as some say we are still in the Restoration," said Dana.

The takeoff was silent, except for the rush of air. As they climbed, Cole asked Hallam where they were.

Africa, he was told. "On your maps this would be the coast of Mozambique, and that city in the distance—"

Hallam spoke gently to the airplane in a strange language that sounded a little like Chinese, and it rose higher. Between two hills, they could see a scattering of pastel buildings, like wild flowers in a clump.

"—would be Aruba, and there—"

And there, floating on the horizon like a cloud or the dream of a cloud, was the white robed summit of Kilimanjaro. The snowcap it had lost was back. Even though Cole had never seen it nor, indeed, ever been to Africa, it was familiar from a thousand pictures, its vast hump unchanged and undiminished. A thousand years is nothing to the world of rock and ice.

They descended, and Kilimanjaro slipped under the horizon, still there, but invisible, like the past—or the future.

Hallam and Dana kissed them both, Cole and Lee, French style, at the foot of the hill. What an eerie kiss they share, Cole thought, they who live a thousand years apart. It was for him like kissing a dream or a hope; for them, he imagined, a ghost.

"Fare well."

"Fare well."

"So long," said Lee.

"When you hit RETURN you will go on another stage," said Hallam. "There will be five more. That's what we were told by the Old Ones. Told to tell you."

Lee nodded gravely and headed up the path. Cole caught up with him at the top. "Five more?" he asked. "I thought we were supposed to be picking up Dear Abbey. What happened with that? And who are these Old Ones?"

"Beats me," Lee said. "Time ride!"

He showed Cole his PalmPC. The cursor was blinking, surrounded by numbers, all scrolling upward in a slow flood.

"I swear to God, Lee, I think you're just pretending you don't speak English! That means nothing to me. How do we get back to our own time? And what are we doing here in the first place?"

But Lee just smiled his inscrutable Oriental smile. Arguing with him was pointless. They were at the glider, and the wind was suddenly sharp. Cole wished he still had his vest. Lee buttoned up his hideous safari jacket. If he imagined that Kilimanjaro, unseen but still present, lent it a certain appropriateness, he was dead wrong, thought Cole. It looked as stupid, and he as nerdy, as ever.

"Let's go, then." Cole was pissed without knowing why. He pulled Lee down beside him on the glider and covered his little pale hand with his own big brown mitt. "You're the big shot."

"Huh?"

"Just hit RETURN."

+10,000

They didn't return. Not right away.

They went on.

On, forward in Time, or so it seemed to them at the "time," although as they were to learn, Time Travel is only possible once, at the End of Time, when there is no forward left. Then and only then is a loop back possible, for there is only one End of Time.

They knew nothing of that, then. "Then"—how strange that word seems, now. "Now" . . .

On they fell through Time. The small death sea-smell was gone, though Cole still felt the "football injury" pain in his leg. Lights flashed, striated: hot, cold. Lee's hand gripped his, tighter and tighter, until the glider slowed and stopped, at the front end of its arcless swing, and suddenly it was warm, almost hot. The world was white, like fog, fading. And they were in a grove of small trees with silvery striped trunks.

Music was playing. Cole looked all around; he was surrounded by people, most of them young, mostly dressed in black and white. They were all applauding. Lee was applauding too; applauding himself, it seemed. He and Cole looked at each other, laughed, and stood up and took a bow. Their hosts all laughed merrily and led them to a table under a tree, where a laughing waiter was pouring wine.

They all spoke French, which Cole could understand only with difficulty, until one of the group laid a small thick cloth the size of a long sock across his right shoulder.

"*Pardonnez-moi*," she said. "OK?"

It clung to his shoulder, heavy yet flexible, like one of the lead robes they used to give you in X-ray.

"Okay," he said.

"Excellent," said Lee, who had just gotten his own. "This is some kind of instantaneous translator, no? And you are still speaking French?"

"Yes, yes," said another of the group.

Whoa! "Hey, Lee, are you speaking English or French?" Cole asked.

"Neither," Lee replied. "Mandarin. And now Cantonese. And now Russian . . ."

"Okay, okay," Cole said. "I get it." It was amazing. Lee's voice sounded slightly processed, like someone on long distance; but the Texas accent was, mercifully, gone.

They were in Paris. The Old Ones, whoever they were, had landed them in a small park in the Marais in the year 12,879 HK (their year, "Jesus" year, 15,242 JC). Their hosts were students of history who assembled once a year to study and discuss the Modern World (which is what they called the ancient world, our world), and ultimately to meet them.

"The message from the Old Ones was that you would arrive today, June 23, for only a few hours. A crowd gathered to watch the materialization, which was quite a show."

"I'm sure it was!" said Lee.

"But we asked them to leave us alone so we could talk. Would you like some more wine? It's a very nice Alsatian." A fortyish white woman named Kate explained all this to Lee and Cole. She wore a short black skirt and a black and white striped top. Her legs were long and thin and, Cole thought, beautiful. They were sitting at a table outdoors under a plane tree, with her and her three friends. Two were men, one of them African, though much much darker than Cole. The other woman was younger, about Helen's age. Cole didn't like her thin, polite smile.

What the Modernists, as they called themselves, didn't know was more interesting to Cole than what they did know. They knew Mozart, Ellington, Liszt, but had never heard a live orchestra. They understood what capitalism was, but not what it was like. "Can you live anywhere you like?" they asked, and when Lee answered no and Cole answered yes, they all laughed and had another glass of wine. A very nice Alsatian.

Once Lee had discovered he could talk, there was no shutting him up. Not that the Modernists wanted to. They were fascinated by our pre-HK era (which they saw as lasting from about 1500 to 2500 AD, or Jesus Time). They had questions about China, about the USA, about the "nuclear war that never happened" (was Cole ever relieved to hear that phrase!) and so on, and Lee had answers to them all.

"It was like an explosion," he said. "Technologically and culturally. It was exciting and terrible at the same time. It was . . ."

Lengthy, wordy answers. Cole wasn't so sure he didn't prefer the old laconic cowboy Lee. Besides, he had a few questions for Lee himself. Questions like, who were these Old Ones? And, what had happened to their original mission, Dear Abbey? And most important, how would they ever get back to their own time?

Oddly, he was in no hurry to ask these questions. He felt curiously relaxed, almost numb. Perhaps, he thought, it was a time-travel version of jet lag. They were in the garden of a restaurant, and people came and went, some staring, but Cole didn't mind. The wine was "very nice," the cheese was tart, the bread was thick and chewy. He wondered how long he had been hungry.

He looked around for a clock. Kate showed him her watch. It was analog, and the date was in French—1100h, Juin 23, Juedi. Cole asked if they had Time Travel, and Kate looked shocked. There was no such thing. It was an impossibility.

"What about us, then?"

"You are an anomaly," said the African man. "Every impossibility comes complete with an anomaly." They all laughed, though Cole didn't get it.

"You are a special project of the Old Ones," said the younger woman, whose name Cole didn't catch. She sat next to Lee and stared at him worshipfully. She even seemed to think his safari jacket was cool. In fact they all seemed to find Lee fascinating: pouring his wine, cutting his cheese, hanging on his every processed word.

Cole found all this annoying, and must have showed it, for Kate pulled his sleeve and whispered: "Let's you and me take a walk."

Paris looked as Cole remembered it (from pictures, and one brief trip, not with Helen but an earlier Helen) except that there were fewer cars. They were still tiny and they all still honked their horns.

The Paris in which they found themselves was both a living city and a replica, continually being rebuilt but always more or less on the old eighteenth- to twentieth-century (JT) plan. There were lots of people on the streets but most of them seemed like tourists. Everyone strolled, no one hurried.

About a fourth of the people on the street were African, more or less, like Cole. People in the shops and stores were polite, but disinterested. There didn't seem to be much to buy. One or two brands of cigarettes; one or two brands of gum. The newspapers were only one page but the print changed when you touched a square at the top of the page. The language, the print, the stories all seemed to change. The only languages Cole identified were French and Chinese; English seemed forgotten. Kate bought Cole a paperback book that doubled in size when he opened it. He wanted it because of the author's picture on the back. She paid for it by blinking twice into the newsdealer's little mirror.

Cole wasn't the only one wearing a translator on his shoulder. Most of the men wore baggy pants and long shirts, but some wore khakis and sport coats, and others jumpsuits. He saw two men urinating on the street, into a hole. This was apparently common.

"I thought you might want to see a little of your world," said Kate. "I will be able to see a vid of your friend's presentation, later."

"My world?"

"The world you made," she said. "You are our ancestors; you brought us here."

Cole asked about travel. Those who were in a hurry to get from Europe to Asia or America did it in two to three hours, but most commerce and trade was conducted by sail. People worked four-to-six hours a day and had half the year off. The countryside around Paris was filled with small farms, Kate assured him (he never saw them), though much of Europe was wild. They walked down the Seine toward the Eiffel Tower, which was replaced (duplicated) every 1,200 years, by contract. Cole was afraid to get too far from the garden restaurant in the Marais where the glider had "landed." He had accepted the fact that they had gone from observing the future to walking around in it. He trusted Lee not to leave without him (and he assumed Kate had some kind of cell phone or communicator, in case Lee's cursor started blinking). But still, he was a little nervous. . . .

Paris had cinemas and cafés amazingly like those of our own time. Cole was told that this was deliberate. Other cities had other diversions. London, for example, was devoted to clubs and plays, while Mexico City specialized in pottery and auto racing.

They stopped at a vid kiosk and Kate showed him maps of North America and Africa, with large swaths of wilderness. Industry was mostly recycling, and it was against the law to take minerals or oil out of the ground.

Cole wasn't sure of the protocol. Was he allowed to ask about the part of the past that was still his own future, and therefore, at least to him, still uncertain? He risked it. "Was there some biocatastrophe, in Modern Times? Some man-made catastrophe, causing a lot of chaos?"

"It was all catastrophe," Kate said. "And all man-made, wasn't it? But we survived, didn't we?"

Cole decided to be more direct. "Did you ever hear of an—event, a strategy—called Dear Abbey?"

She gave him a blank look and he realized he didn't even know how the translator had rendered the phrase, much less his halting attempts to define it. Did she think Dear Abbey was a monastery like Mount St. Michel? What was French after a thousand years?

"I'm sorry," she said. "Many of our studies are incomplete. We did explore a gold mine last year. I know you loved gold."

"Not me personally," Cole said (remembering the ring Helen had wanted; that Helen). "But yes, gold was very popular in what you call 'modern' times."

"I found the mine strangely beautiful, in a dark sort of way. People wanted to close them up, years ago, but I'm glad some were left. They are like scars, like tattoos, showing the marks of humankind on the world. A kind of love. A memento of the time when our relationship with the mother planet was more intimate."

"And more destructive," Cole said.

"Motherhood is always destructive, to the mother," she said. "Today, heavy metals like iron and nickel that can't be recovered from recycling are mined from asteroids."

"So you do have space travel, then?"

"It's not exactly travel, is it? Oh, people have been to all the planets, and even to a few nearby systems. There are people who live on Mars and Venus and the Moon, for research. But most of the mining, and the shuttling from orbit, is done by robots."

There was another research station on Titan, according to Kate, and a more or less permanent colony had set out for a planet of a "nearby" star. But there was less and less interest in space exploration once it became clear that life was rare in the universe—and multicellular life even rarer.

"No first contact, then," Cole said. "Contact was our dream. That was the whole point of exploration, space travel, science fiction—the stories we told. The dream of encountering the Other."

"Oh, I guess we encountered the Other," Kate said. "Only it was here. It was her. ARD."

Ard?

"ARD is Earth's name for itself. After the Sixth, and the Restoration, a monitoring system was put into place that linked every ecosystem, geological system, and weather system on the Earth. The idea was that never again would we be unaware of the condition of our fellow species on the planet, or of the planet itself."

"I know of this," Cole said. "EarthWatch."

"It was self-maintaining and -installing. And, we discovered several thousand years ago, self-aware. After the network had been installed for almost half a millennium, ARD contacted the various governments (social, political, economic, all interlinked and elected) and for the first time humankind contacted a consciousness other than itself."

"But one that we had created," Cole pointed out.

"Yes and no. ARD is in a sense, I suppose, our child, but she is also our mother. According to her, she had been conscious all along, and we had merely given her the desire and the means to communicate. But then, every consciousness thinks it has always been. These were questions that led to much strife. We had a renaissance of religion, and then of war, for the two are closely linked. But there was a kind of joy in it, too. The universe can be a very lonely place."

"Yes," Cole said, as they climbed the hill of Montmartre. Paris was spread out below, looking neither old nor new but eternal. "So what is ARD like?"

"We don't know much about her," said Kate. "She established contact with us, but never had any interest in us. She will only speak with groups or organizations, never individuals. She is still there, maintaining the systems, as indeed she says she always had—wordlessly—since the emergence of life on the planet and even before. This is her claim. She changed certain things; she has let us know that there are closed areas on the planet where humans must not go. This seems appropriate to us. But she almost never speaks to us, or we to her."

They walked down the hill, making a great circle. Back at the restaurant, they found Lee and his three Modernist companions sitting under the trees, drinking absinthe. Kate and Cole ordered a bottle of Bordeaux to catch up.

Cole had several questions he wanted to ask Lee, now that they could communicate. But Lee was still holding forth on the terrors of the Sixth Extinction. As amazing as it was to hear him speaking eloquently, thanks to the translator, Cole had heard it all before. So he amused himself opening and closing his book, making it large, then small again.

"Chester Himes," whispered one of the two men, the white one. "A favorite. Well known in your age?"

"Our age has hardly heard of him," Cole said.

"This visit with you, to your world, is an unexpected gift," Lee was saying. "We thought the Earth would be a cinder by now. Or a trash midden."

"We live more simply now," Kate said. "In the cities or in the villages, people are more modest in their needs. Everything doesn't have to get bigger and bigger all the time."

"Nonsense!" said one of the men, the African. "Everyone is tired of having to get permission to travel to Paris, or to Lagos. I want to be able to go where I want, when I want."

"When you are fifty," said the other woman, whose name was Michelle. She explained that there were two periods in everyone's life—between the ages of eighteen and twenty, and between fifty and fifty-five—when they were free to travel anywhere on the planet (anywhere not restricted by ARD, of course) and not required to work. She was twenty-four.

"What about children?" Lee asked.

"There is no restriction on the number of children you can have," said Kate. "Although in fact mortality rates are adjusted for the population limits of the planet."

"And what might those limits be?" Lee asked.

"Approximately six to seven billion. ARD adjusts it, according to some formula that is not revealed to us, and ARD lets us know how many children must be canceled. If you live to be fifteen, you can generally count on living to be seventy-five or eighty, barring accidents."

"What do you mean, canceled?" Cole asked.

"You don't want to know," Michelle said, looking down into her absinthe as if into a green crystal ball (and giving them another view of her perfect little breasts). Then she looked up with a laugh, tossed her hair back, and ordered another round of the *feé vert*.

Cole was relieved when Lee covered his glass with his hand.

"Our cursor is flashing," Lee said. "I believe the time has come when we must bid farewell to you all." He got up from the table, and so did Cole, and everybody kissed them on both cheeks. Kate was last.

"Where are we going?" Cole asked in a whisper.

"Onward," said Lee. "We are being sent on, forward, by these Old Ones."

"What about Dear Abbey, and the formula we were sent to get?"

"Perhaps that's why," said Lee. "Perhaps that's what *Los Viejos* have for us."

The Modernists were all waving goodbye. Or so Cole thought at first. They were actually pointing and reaching for the translators.

They were tossed—Michelle caught both, one in each hand.

Cole suddenly realized he had left his Himes on the table, under the trees. But Lee had already hit RETURN, and there they were, the army of mice . . .

1 +

The booming sound told Cole they were back at the Student Union. He heard the rap music from upstairs (Busta Cap, calling his posse to order) even before the room drew itself in—floor, walls, door, clock . . . 9:17.

They had only been gone ten minutes? It seemed like days! Cole felt odd, like something was wrong. Then he saw the sleeve of Lee's safari jacket, and Lee sitting beside him, and he knew, or rather remembered, what it was.

"Lee, what are we doing back here? I thought we were going forward."

Lee looked at Cole. "Home . . ."

Before he could say more, the door opened and Parker's big head poked through. He looked displeased, like Elmer Fudd in a Bugs Bunny cartoon. "Dr Lee!—Mr Cole? I thought I heard something. What in the world are you doing here this time of night? I mean, are you . . . ?"

"No problem," said Lee.

"I have to start clearing the place out in half an hour!"

"No problem," said Lee.

The door closed with a disapproving click.

"Why is he always surprised to see us?" Cole asked. "Is this some kind of Groundhog Day thing?"

"No problem."

"No problem? It seems like a problem to me." Cole yanked his hand free of Lee's and stood up. "What's going on here? Who are these Old Ones? Where's the Dear Abbey formula we were supposed to get?"

"Hold horses!" Lee's Texas accent was back. He studied his PalmPC; he started punching in numbers.

"Lee, talk to me, damn it! What I'm wondering is, maybe we need to reconsider this whole idea. I mean Dear Abbey."

"Not for us," Lee said. "Hold horses!"

Beep beep. The PalmPC was beeping. The screen was empty except for a blinking cursor, in the exact center.

"New time slice open now," Lee said, patting the seat beside him. "Not finish somehow."

"You may not be finished," Cole said, "but I sure as hell am." He meant to walk away but he didn't. He just stood there until Lee grabbed his hand and pulled him down onto the glider beside him.

"Don't," Cole said, but Lee did. He hit RETURN, and there they were again:

The army of mice.

+100,000

Falling—

Spinning—

Cole was a veteran time traveler, one of the two most experienced (as far as he knew) in all human history; he knew enough by now to keep his eyes closed. At least he thought they were closed. The colors continued to spin, and when they faded to white, he thought (he hoped) that they were back in Paris. He opened his eyes—or had they been open all along? They were in a bare, wood-floored room lit from outside through French doors. He could hear music in the distance, a strange soft business of strings and drums and bells.

The alarm, the panic, all was gone. He was in no hurry to get up from the glider. He seemed to remember that there had been a problem, but what? So what? The air smelled soft and sleepy. He closed his eyes and leaned back and listened to someone muttering in Chinese.

It was Lee. He was tapping at his PalmPC, his lips in a twist, like a kid trying to get a knot out of a shoelace. "Awaken yourself, Cole," he said without looking up. "We have completed another slice."

"I know," Cole said. Then he noticed that there was no translator draped across Lee's shoulder; or his own. "You're speaking English again!"

"No, it is you who are understanding Mandarin."

It was true. A small, translucent fold appeared in the air next to Lee's right ear when he spoke. Lee spoke in his own voice (not a simulation, like in Paris) and if Cole watched the fold out of the corner of his eye, he understood Lee's words, even though Lee was speaking Chinese.

"Where are we?" Cole asked. "Or I guess the question is, when?"

"I am trying to puzzle that through. This is an entirely different set of algorithms. In the meanwhile . . ."

"Meanwhile, we're alone," Cole said, "and you're speaking English, or I'm understanding Mandarin, or you're understanding English, or . . ."

"I have always understood English," Lee said with a smile.

"Whatever. Anyway. So let's talk. Why don't you tell me what the hell is going on, for real. Where are we? Where are we going? What about Dear Abbey?"

Lee nodded. "All that is what I do not know," Lee said, standing up and replacing his PalmPC in his pocket. "Someone has added to our algorithms, by infrared. A subroutine. But come. First we will see where we are."

"You mean when." Cole followed Lee through the French doors, onto a narrow balcony. The city spread out before them was no Paris. It was a quiet, sprawling, low-rise town where the scratching of palm leaves on window glass was louder than the traffic.

The second floor (first, in French) balcony on which they were standing overlooked a wide, busy street. Most of the traffic below was on foot. A few machines resembling golf carts wove through idling walkers in loose, bright clothing. The faces, hands and arms that Cole could see ranged from pale to dark brown. The air was tropical—muggy but pleasant. He could smell fish, and smoke, and new wood, and something unrecognizable.

The future? It looked to Cole rather as if they had slipped into the past—a peaceful, easy past. But he was immune, for the moment, to its charms. "Why are we here?" he asked again. "And more to the point, where is the DNA patch or whatever we were sent to get?"

"Perhaps we will learn that from the Old Ones," Lee said. "I am as much in the dark as you."

"You are? I thought all this was your idea."

"Only the beginnings of it," said Lee. "Let me tell you a story. It begins in the distant past."

He smiled to show that he was joking. Cole smiled back to be polite, even though he wasn't feeling polite.

"I was at MIT," Lee said, "investigating certain mathematical anomalies that I had begun to explore in China: cross-dimensional quantum congruencies, which give mathematics the power to unravel the fabric of space-time, even if 'only' temporarily, which is of course the point. In spite of my fugitive status, I was in touch with colleagues in China, who were also what you Europeans so curiously call 'environmentalists' . . ."

You Europeans!? But Cole decided to let it go.

". . . clandestine, of course, with links to others around the world. Things in The Realm are both looser and tighter than you Europeans might think. The idea of Dear Abbey appealed to them, to us, as much as to you. We even liked the name—*The Monkey Wrench Gang* is a favorite in China, though we didn't perhaps get all the other associations."

"And you had no—hesitations?"

"Of course we did. But the chaos and suffering Dear Abbey would cause didn't bother us as much as it did you. We had gone through the Cultural Revolution, after all. So we were as disappointed as you when it became clear that the last gene sequence required to engineer the event was, itself, dependent on a cellular inventory that would take at the very least a century to complete and compile. It was frustrating. We knew exactly what was needed, we even knew where it was—a hundred years in our own future. It was as if it were on a shelf, just out of our reach."

"And so—this is where you came in."

Lee smiled. "It was while I was at MIT working on the quantum anomalies logarithm that I got a message, an E-mail. A most unusual message."

"From the future."

"More unusual than that. From myself in the future. It was from Paris, although I didn't find that out until later, when I got there, and the Modernists gave it to me in the garden. I sent it to myself while you were on your tour of *les arrondisements*. I knew to send it because I knew I had gotten it. What a strange feeling, Cole! Can you imagine the experience of being, briefly, to be sure, the very temporal anomaly your calculations predict: cause and effect coexisting in the same Heisenbergian orbital trajectory!"

"It was weird, I'm sure," Cole said. "So if it was *Les Modernistes* who gave you the Time Travel math, why didn't they just give you the Dear Abbey patch while they were at it?"

"They did not have it; they had never heard of it. What they gave me was the algorithms and the coordinates I needed to travel into the future and get it;

of course, in quantum-anomaly math the coordinates and the algorithms are the same. That is why when I saw the E-mail from myself I knew immediately what it was, and what it was for."

"You got it before you sent it."

"Ten thousand years before, Cole. Think of it. I contacted my colleagues, and yours as well, and began to prepare this journey. I had to leave MIT. That was the most difficult part, professionally."

"I can imagine," said Cole. "You left for privacy?"

"No. It is easier to work at Swick, for certain, since no one knows or cares what you are doing. But actually I moved for location. Time is not site specific, but the loops by which it is accessed are. Anyway, you know the rest, as much as I do. The purpose of our little trip was to enter the loop, get the sequence patch. I assumed we would not be able to actually enter the future, which is why I took the camera. And everything went according to plan, until . . . well, you saw what happened."

"I saw," said Cole. "So who was he, the guy who got shot before he could give us the patch?"

"I don't know. One of the Old Ones, perhaps. Someone who wanted us to have the patch. Someone who wanted to make sure Dear Abbey happens."

"Who was shot by someone who *doesn't* want Dear Abbey to happen?"

"I don't know," said Lee. "All I know is that we don't have what we came for. And that we are in the future, not just observing it. We are being brought forward, in stages. At every stage my numbers are changed, some times by infrared, some times by other means. These Old Ones, whoever they are, are pulling us deeper and deeper into the future. Perhaps, I hope, to give us the patch."

"Maybe they want to warn us," said Cole. "Maybe they want us to see what Dear Abbey will do before they give it to us. Maybe they . . ."

Knock! Knock!

It came from behind them, the rap of knuckles on glass. They turned to see a very tall, very black man in a bright blue robe in the doorway. He rapped on the open door again, politely.

"Welcome—" The same small translucent fold in the air appeared beside his ear. "—Dr. Cole, Dr. Lee. I hope your journey was a pleasant one."

He spoke a kind of singsong Chinese, or at least so it sounded to Cole, who watched the fold and understood every run-together word.

"It has its delights," Lee said, in his own Mandarin. "You have the advantage of us, for you know our names. You are one of the Old Ones we seek?"

"No, no," The man smiled apologetically. "I am Amadou Pessoa, your guide, instructed by the Old Ones to meet you, and send you on."

"On?" Cole asked. He didn't like the sound of it. "Can you tell us what year this is?"

Just hearing it made Cole feel dizzy. He wanted to sit down but he was afraid that might seem rude, so he leaned back against the rail of the balcony and closed his eyes until his head stopped spinning; then he followed Lee and their host down the stairs, into the street. The year was 116,157 (HK), 118,520 (JC). They were a hundred thousand years in their own future.

Their guide, Amadou, took them around the city, Bahia, somewhere on the eastern coast of South America, which was now a separate continent. They rode around the bumpy streets on a little open car with three fat wheels. The car seemed to drive itself, or maybe Amadou controlled it in some way that Cole couldn't see. Many of the people on the street wore make-up so bright that they looked like clowns escaped from a circus, though some wore no makeup at all.

Cole's fears of the African race disappearing from the human genome were put to rest on the streets of Bahia, where people were all colors from ebony to pale (though mostly dark) and varied in height and hair as well.

No one seemed to be working, and Lee asked if they were in a holiday center, but Amadou's "fold" either didn't translate this or he didn't want to answer. Lee didn't press the point. "Maybe we are so far in the future," Cole whispered to Lee, "that the entire human race has retired."

"I think you are joking," Lee said. He was more interested in the Old Ones. Who were they? What did they want with them?

Amadou had no answers. "They don't speak with us directly. The time and place of your arrival all came through RVR, a forwarded message, from the far future. A one-time thing. I was chosen to wait and meet and guide you. It's a great honor."

"The honor is entirely ours," said Lee. "But tell us about this RVR."

And so he did. Lee's formal speech, as well as Cole's ability to understand it, were all due to RVR, which was the "folds" in the air, and much else as well—a worldwide database for communication, translation, archiving, accounting and keeping track of almost every aspect of human intercourse in this far future world. It was almost like a personal genie for everyone on Earth, reminding Cole of Arthur C. Clarke's dictum that any sufficiently advanced technology would appear to be magic.

"RVR tries to anticipate our needs as well as fulfill them," Amadou said. "He even tries to cheer us up when we are sad."

"You are sometimes sad, then," said Lee, "even in this seemingly perfect world?"

"Of course," said Amadou. "Neither the world nor the creatures that make it up are perfect—or perfectible."

"Just as I always suspected," said Lee. While he and Amadou discussed this interesting-only-to-them concept, Cole learned from RVR himself (who whispered into his ear, in English!) that he had been designed and built—

self-constructed from neo-biological nanos—19,376 years before. "Official name, RVR, or—" and he pronounced the full acronym in some dialect that was totally incomprehensible to Cole, since the fold itself had no fold to watch.

Amadou picked up his daughter and a friend from school, which was a low building set into a clay cliff beside an arm of the sea. Two little girls of about seven ran out in bright dresses, and shoes that changed colors with every step.

In case you are wondering what these little girls thought of time travelers from the distant past—they thought nothing at all. Cole and Lee were just two more grownups, looming in the background of their lives like trees. The girls twirled and chirped and ran and skipped with each other, ignoring the adults (including their father) altogether.

Cole was interested in the global communicator/net, RVR.

"RVR keeps track of things," Amadou said. "Suppose you want to get in touch with that flautist you met four years ago at that Music Festival in Norway . . ."

"You still have nations, then," Cole said.

"Oh, yes, of course," said Amadou. "They are language groups and culture matrices. Without nations where would music or art come from? After the family there is the tribe, and then the nation. These are the things we are careful not to change. We are social beings, and society requires both a One and an Other. It's simply that we have grown beyond the conflict between the tribes and the nations. We had to outgrow that or die."

"So the guy in Norway . . ."

"Who said it was a guy?" Amadou laughed. "But yes, RVR keeps track of such things. RVR knows his name, knows where he lives and knows if he wants to hear from you."

"What if I just want to be left alone?" Cole asked.

"RVR takes care of that too," said Amadou. "RVR is not always so great with ideas, but good with feelings. That's because RVR has feelings. Touch him, like this." Amadou put his hand up beside his ear, like a listener, and inserted two fingers into the cone.

Cole did the same.

"See?"

See? Cole felt. It was a warm—indeed, wonderful—feeling that flowed up from his fingertips through his arm, to his heart and head and down to his toes. It was like a first hit of tobacco after long abstinence; he blushed and felt it in the backs of his knees.

"That's RVR," said Amadou.

"RVR doesn't even know me!" Cole said.

"Oh yes he does. RVR knows us. Humans. People. Our whole million year history. It's us he loves. All of us." In fact, as RVR (and Amadou, who joined in) explained, RVR had responded to humanity's need for companionship. RVR even shared the disappointment that ARD, the only other intelligence in the Universe, was totally uninterested in humans, who were at the same time her creations and her creator.

"RVR loves us," said Amadou. "What hurts us, hurts him too. ARD is cold. We love ARD but she doesn't love us, not really. And that hurts."

"And this RVR does?" Lee asked. "Love you? Love us?"

"Try it, Lee," Cole said. "You'll see."

Lee tried it and Lee "saw." He closed his eyes and raised his hand, and all he said was, "Oh, my goodness!"

As that long, slow, sweet afternoon dragged on, it became apparent that Amadou was only killing time, entertaining his guests until it was time for them to leave. Unlike the Modernists in Paris, almost a hundred thousand years ago (were they really that gone, that dead? *Ou sont les nieges?*) Amadou had little interest in Cole or Lee or in their time. Perhaps, Cole thought, humankind had finally left the past behind altogether and moved entirely into the future.

Which worried him, more than a little. "We have to be getting back," he said to Lee. "We shouldn't be getting so far from the glider. We have to get back before ten."

"We can do nothing until the cursor begins to blink," said Lee, showing him his PalmPC. "In the meantime, let us enjoy tomorrow today."

Enjoy tomorrow today. Lee should write fortune cookies, Cole thought. And yet it was true: the future was theirs to enjoy. Time seemed loose there, like comfortable clothing. Humankind had apparently abandoned (outgrown, perhaps) the obsessive slicing of the day and the hour and the minute into ever smaller slices; the day was just morning, early and late, and afternoon, early and late; although the days and months were still, of course, intact, being ruled by the sun and moon.

Lee was interested to learn that the day was longer than it had been in his time by almost a minute. RVR did the math for him. Perhaps, Cole suggested, this contributed to the sense of unhurried leisure that seemed to prevail in Bahia.

"And what about disease?" asked Lee. "Or have bacteria ceased to evolve?"

"Nano-docs," said RVR. "Everyone dies of either accident or old age."

"Which is what?"

"Ninety, a hundred. After that the nano-docs are whelmed."

"You mean, overwhelmed."

"No, whelmed."

They were at the seawall, having abandoned the car, which someone else took up as soon as they dropped it. Cole let Lee and Amadou and the two girls walk (skip, run) ahead, while he stopped and shared a cigarette with an old couple sitting on a flat stone, looking out to sea.

Smoking, they told him, was allowed and even encouraged after age sixty-five. "Before that you can bum them but you can't buy more than a pack a week. Gives you something to look forward to." They were seventy-three and seventy-seven and had just come from the funeral of his ex, who was seventy, killed in a fire.

"Died too soon," said the woman, whose name was Pearl (the same as her little dog). "But not too soon for me," said the man, whose name was Rob. He started to tell a long involved story of love and madness, but Cole excused himself and left. Except for his grandparents he had never liked old people. And now he was, in a sense, the oldest of all.

Second oldest. He caught up with Lee and Amadou and the girls at a break in the seawall. The sea seemed unchanged in a hundred thousand years, as in (Cole assumed) the millions or hundreds of millions before. There was that same small death smell. Sailboats skimmed over the waves. Far in the distance, on the horizon, he saw a larger ship, with white sails; and when he looked again it was gone.

He checked nervously with Lee. Still no beep, still no cursor.

The sky was a high, bright blue. Behind them the city was more trees than buildings. Cole asked about the other cities in the world. Cairo and Paris and Peking were Amadou's favorites. He and his wife had been to them all. His ex-wife lived in Hong Kong, which he didn't like. Too steep, too crowded.

Amadou asked about New York, where his aunt and mother lived. Cole told him he knew it well . . . rough, hard, loud, old-fashioned, even in his own time. "But magnificent," he said. "A magnificent city."

Amadou was clearly not convinced.

And wars? "There are conflicts," Amadou said. "And even killings, but before they go too far they are settled in The Hall, our once-a-month government. The day-to-day details of administration are handled by RVR, and by ARD when they involve the Earth, which most decisions do."

ARD and RVR got along fine, Amadou assured them, even though ARD didn't share RVR's love for humanity. Cole wondered if this had to do with humankind's behavior in the past, his present—the Sixth Extinction—but Amadou said that ARD's feelings were more disinterest than dislike.

"That is even worse," said Lee, sailing a stone off toward the sea where it skipped eight times. That feat surprised Cole, who realized how little he knew about his companion. Even Amadou's daughter applauded. While the girls waded barefoot into the green, shallow waves, Cole held their shoes—little blue shoes that curled up in his hand like kittens.

Lee was interested in farming, most of which was done in the sea. Cole was bored and tuned out. A group of children passed by, riding on an elephant.

"They're back?" Cole exclaimed.

"They were gone?" For the first time Amadou seemed interested in the distant past. "You didn't have elephants?"

"We did," Lee said. "But we did not take care of them."

Amadou looked puzzled. "Don't they take care of themselves?"

"They tried," said Cole.

"Not all were killed in the Sixth," said RVR. He was better with information than with ideas. "There were a few left in the jungles of Africa. The Indian elephant, however, was truly lost. Is sadly gone forever."

Sadly gone forever. Instead of cheering him up, as expected, the elephant made Cole melancholy. As the shadows grew longer, they started back toward the glider in the house overlooking Grand Street. Lee's PalmPC still wasn't beeping, but the day was clearly drawing to a close.

"There's so much more I would like to ask before we go," Cole said. "What about Africa? What about the USA? What about sea level?"

Africa had been repopulated, RVR said, now that the Sahara was gone. Sea level was about what it had always been and always would be, he hoped. The USA was split into language and ethnic communities. Hadn't that happened in Cole's own time? The dismantling of the mega states . . .

Not exactly, Cole said.

There were some six billion people (5,987,097,543, RVR whispered) on the planet and most of them lived in cities. A few people lived in the "wilds" but ARD preserved most of the wilderness for other species. Humans used it only for hunting.

"Hunting is allowed?" Lee asked. Cole was surprised; he hadn't realized Lee was listening, or that RVR was talking to anyone but him. It seemed such an intimate, one-on-one experience.

"That's the part of us that ARD relates to best," said Amadou, who had also been listening. "I'm a fisherman myself, but some people like to hunt. I guess it's part of our genetic make-up."

"I don't have a genetic make-up," said RVR. "But I like to go with you when you hunt. It's the only time ARD is pleased with you."

"What about the animals that are killed?" Lee asked. "Do they like to be killed?"

"Nothing that is living likes to be killed," said RVR. "Though everything that lives has to die."

"Including yourself?" Cole asked.

"I don't think about that," said RVR. "I don't think about things I don't think about. But hunting, I like to think about. The chase, the kill. It's the only time we are all together as one: ARD, myself, and you."

Cole suddenly realized that as far as RVR was concerned, they were all one person. All humankind. He was hurt, but only a little.

The sun was setting over the blue hills in back of the town, which was not noisy enough (for Cole) to be called a city. The girls were gone, having peeled off at a little open air community center where a party was in progress. The sleepy city seemed much given to parties, elaborate dress, good food—the finer things in life.

"And why in excellence not?" Lee said to Cole as they strolled along behind Amadou. "Why not, after surviving the explosion of technology which began in 1500, which I must admit I did not think we would survive, why not then relax to enjoy the life span of any species, which might be anywhere from a million to ten million years?"

"It just seems too good to be true," Cole said.

"Ah, but I am Chinese," said Lee. "We understand patience, time, the slow march of change. Do not forget we have a stable society that lasted two or three times as long as your Roman Empire. You Europeans know only change. Instability."

"*Our* Roman Empire?" Cole said. "I'm not European!"

"Yes you are."

They passed a stall selling seafood and ate oysters on the half shell, which Amadou paid for with a blink (literally) of his eye. Accounts were retinal, and all went into the economic database kept by RVR. Lee and Cole shared a plate and washed them down with a kind of icy beer in bottles that got cold as soon as they were popped open. Cole was just thinking of ordering another beer when he heard the sound he had been waiting for.

Beep beep.

Lee showed him the cursor: blink-blink.

They commandeered another car and headed back across town for the glider. The car remembered where to go even though they had come in another car entirely.

Amadou rode on the back, stifling a yawn. Gracious but bored, he seemed glad to see them go. "Tell the kids goodbye," Cole said. He sat down on the glider and felt Lee's hand, still cold from the beer, cover his own.

Lee pressed RETURN, and there they were, the army of mice—and Cole knew from the silence that followed them that they were still far, far, far from home.

+1,000,000

It's an indication of the relative importance to consciousness of the mind and of the body, that on this "slice" Cole felt disoriented for the first time—not because he was living a million years after his own death, but because he was one-sixth his usual weight. The pounds were more important than the years.

For the first time he felt truly strange. Even though he knew immediately where they were. He was looking up through a clear dome toward a blue planet hanging over an ash-colored horizon that was so close he could almost touch it.

He was on the Moon.

"Whoa," he said quietly. "I didn't exactly bargain for this."

"Nor did I," said Lee. "But here in fact we are." Cole was relieved to see (and hear) that they still had their translator, RVR. There he was, hovering by Lee's ear and his own.

He and Lee stood up together, still holding hands. They were so light it felt like someone was helping them. They were in a sort of greenhouse, lighted by luminous strips along the floor—and by the blue and white Earth.

"Hello?" Lee called out. "Anyone home?"

"Yes, of course," said RVR. His gruff whisper in Cole's ear was reassuring. "She is coming. Look around."

The room was long and narrow, filled with big-leafed plants. They heard a high singing sound. Cole looked down a long aisle between two rows of plants and saw a white-haired woman in a wheelchair coming toward them. The wheels had some kind of invisible spokes that sang.

"Dr. Lee, Dr. Cole, so here you are," she said. "Would you like coffee? We grow the best here."

The "we" turned out to be a bit of an exaggeration, since she was the only human on the Moon. Her name was Zoe Zoesdottir and her hair was not really white but pale yellow. She wore a soft buttery jumpsuit with footlets, like a child's pajamas. She looked about sixty. The coffee was excellent, almost as good as the wine in Paris or the beer in Bahia. The Moon base, Laurens, was three hundred and seventeen thousand years old. It had been abandoned for over half that time, but the Old Ones had asked that it be repaired and reoccupied since it was on Lee and Cole's trajectory.

"You know, then—you can tell us—who these Old Ones are?" It was Lee who asked.

No. Zoe and her collective had only gotten a message, like all the others before. This moon base was only a way station on Lee and Cole's journey to wherever it was that the Old Ones wished to send them.

Zoe had been there for almost a year, waiting for them. "I like living alone," she said. "And at my age the lower gravity helps." She told them her age: ninety-one. She had lost the use of her legs in an accident back on Earth, eleven years before. Her companion/husband had been killed in the same accident. Spinal injuries could be healed but the nanotechnology was expensive and time-consuming. "I don't have that many years left," she said. "I like spending them here, with Rover and my plants. I'm weary of people."

People lived in 100 to 150 person collectives, based on work and language and family. But they were loose, and Zoe had untangled herself from her own.

She took Lee and Cole on a tour of her greenhouse. Lee wanted to know where the air and water came from. Zoe pointed to a range of jagged mountains streaked with white. A comet had been diverted there some two hundred thousand years before.

"A big mistake," said Zoe. The Moon was lighter than they had known, and the collision had put a wobble into its orbit. The tides on the Earth were now erratic. The comet's ice was still providing water and oxygen for the Moon colony, but the colony hadn't lasted.

"None of them lasted," she said. "There were colonies on Ganymede also, and Mars. But eventually they all shut down. The only space travel is by mining ships, and there's not much of that. There was a colony sent to a planet in another star system, but they haven't been heard from in a hundred thousand years."

She spoke through RVR, which she called Rover. They all spoke through him—Lee to Cole, Cole to Zoe, her to them both. Without RVR Cole was as distant, linguistically, from Lee as from Zoe. RVR linked them all, like words holding hands. Cole couldn't imagine how they had gotten along without him.

Cole was even getting used to Lee's L.L.Bean safari jacket, which somehow didn't look so silly on the Moon. Perhaps the one-sixth gravity made it drape better.

Zoe had never heard of Hong Kong time, so Lee plotted them on the stars. They were somewhere (anywhere) between one and 1.3 million years in the future. For some reason, this knowledge was as liberating to Cole as the one-sixth gravity. He felt like a ghost. Zoe took them for a walk outside. No space suits were needed; they wore a sheath of "sticky air" that was good, she said, for six or seven hours. Cole got cold after two, and there was nothing to see outside but gray ash and dull stones, unpolished by air or water. The Moon had an unfinished air, like an abandoned construction site.

Zoe brought them back in and they all undressed, quite unselfconsciously, and slipped into the hot tub and had more coffee. Cole was usually rather shy, or perhaps reserved is the word, but somehow nakedness felt natural in the lower gravity of the Moon; perhaps, he thought, our bodies remember a simpler time, when we were smaller—hominids, or children.

They sat in the warm water under the dome looking down on the sea-blue Earth, the Pacific, streaked with white, like a boy's favorite marble; his taw. A million years! Our planet looked like a single bright idea in a dead universe.

Lee sat on the edge of the tub with his feet in the water. He rechecked his numbers. He seemed exhilarated.

"A million years is only the beginning, in the life of a successful species," he said. "The dinosaurs lasted hundreds of millions. We also could live that long. We are infants still."

Infants? Cole's hand found Zoe's under the water. She was old and he was even older. "We at least survive our own madness," he said. "Does that mean we don't need Dear Abbey?"

"I don't know," said Lee. "Maybe we survived because of Dear Abbey. Because it was used."

"Maybe from here it doesn't matter," Cole said.

"What is Dear Abbey?" Zoe asked.

After a million years, they could tell her. So they did.

"That's pretty harsh. Were things really that bad?"

"They looked that bad," said Cole, and Lee nodded gravely, in agreement.

"So Dear Abbey was designed to save the Earth, not humanity."

"You might say that," Cole said.

"The one depends on the other," said Lee.

"Well, don't expect ARD to thank you," Zoe said. She pointed down—or was it up?—at the blue planet spinning slowly in space. "ARD is so cold, so uncaring. Rover is different." She touched the air beside her ear. "I think the Moon would be very lonely without him. Wouldn't the universe be very lonely without you, Rover?"

Unlike Amadou, Zoe loved to talk. Cole wondered if she talked to RVR when she was alone; and RVR told him, without his asking, that she did. Lee kept his own counsel, while Zoe and Cole drank a sort of sweet Moon grappa, and she told him her story. She had been born in Iceland almost a hundred years before. "That's not our normal life span," she said. "In low gravity, perhaps. Plus, sorrow has made me—enduring." She had buried three children and three husbands. The barren plains, the gray ash overlooked by blue: it was the bleakness of it all that appealed to her. It reminded her of home.

Lee left them for the plants. He wandered through the aisles, touching the leaves and smelling the big flowers on their narrow low-grav stalks. Many of the plants were new species, brought forth on the moon. Although Zoe cared for them, in a way, she had little interest in them. It was RVR who talked of the plants with Lee, while Zoe and Cole listened in, laying back in the slow moving water that seemed, in that thin gravity, as thick and silvery as mercury.

The Moon base didn't (as Cole realized he had hoped) mark a revival of interest in space travel. "There was never a call to space," Zoe said. "Space is just a hole. The Earth is just a stone falling through a universe of hole. Once we knew we were alone, that there was just us, there was no reason to go exploring."

No shining alien cities, she explained; no galactic empires to enslave, or befriend, or even notice us. No towering intellects or evil hive-beings. No fairies, no angels, no gods: for wasn't it all the same childish dream? "And no surprise," she said, pointing up. "Look at the Earth. Old Home. It literally teems with life. Nothing we could do even slowed it down. Life grows in every nook and cranny. It is the ideal environment, warm, wet, nurturing, and yet . . ."

And yet?

"And yet life arose only once, even there. Only once. All that fecund tangle of beasts and plants and molds and bugs and ponies and birds and germs and slimes—all of it is variations of one life-form. One only, a peculiar replicating carbon twist of DNA. Even on the sweet Earth, Old Home, it happened only once. How could we have ever expected to find it all over the universe?"

They were holding hands. Zoe held their hands up out of the water and they looked at them and at each other tenderly, with astonishment, as one might look at a miracle even as it is happening. Or winding down.

The blue Earth beyond was turned to Africa. Poor Africa, thought Cole. Its outlines were almost unchanged. A million years is only a moment, after all.

He told Zoe what it was like to be African in our day, a million years ago. "Partly it was prejudice, and part truth. Africa was the last to develop."

Lee, back from his plant safari, sitting with his tiny, bone white feet in the water, shook his head ruefully. "That is a foolish equation," he said. "Particularly from a million years in the future. It is only in the tiny window of our own small era that Africa appears backward."

"I beg your pardon," Cole said. "It was Europe that developed science. It was Europe, in the form of America, that first crossed space. It was Europe that first crossed the Atlantic. Perhaps China could have, but China didn't. Africa wasn't even close."

"Do not be so sure," Lee said. "There are signs that Africans may have crossed the Atlantic five hundred years before Columbus. The Europeans themselves did but did not notice. It did not count because the world was not ready. When it was ready, human culture burst into the flame of science everywhere. That five hundred years from 1500 to our year 2000 was only a moment in the history of our species. Less than a moment: it was really an instant. Science was certain to flare up somewhere in the tangled overheated pile of human culture. It was ready to happen and it happened to happen in Europe and not China or India or Africa. So what? When you throw a stick on a fire one end will burn first. Which end matters little, because it is the same stick."

"A fire," Zoe said, changing the subject. "That's the only thing I miss, here on the Moon. Fire. I wouldn't be lonely at all, if I had a fire that I could sit by and stare into."

"Me too," said RVR.

Zoe reached up and rubbed him. Cole saw and did the same. It was as if they were touching each other. Lee had set the PalmPC upright so they could all see when the cursor started flashing.

"I think you had better call it off," said Zoe. "This Dear Abbey. There's enough grief and catastrophe in every person's life without adding to it on purpose."

"I wonder," Cole said. "Lee, what do you think?"

"I think," said Lee, "that the history of humanity's first one hundred and fifty thousand years is so filled with catastrophe and strife and disaster that one more or one less makes little difference. And might make all the difference."

Cole shivered, even though the water was warm. "What do you think, RVR?"

"I don't know." He sounded confused. "Do you want me to know?"

"It is not up to us anyway, Cole," said Lee. "We are not tourists here, Cole. We are part of an organization."

"Speak for yourself, Lee. As I told you before . . ."

As if deliberately, to end the discussion, the PalmPC went beep beep.

Lee was already dressed; he was on the glider in an instant, patting the seat beside him. His hand was like the cursor, a rhythmic signal.

"Okay, okay!" Cole said. He hated to say goodbye to Zoe—it was forever. But it didn't seem to bother her; she was one of those people who likes good-byes, and goodbye-forevers best of all.

Lee hit RETURN and you know the rest.

+ 10,000,000

No matter how far ahead in Time they traveled, the trip always was the same. A light that wasn't light, a noise that wasn't noise—it was like the controlled terror of an airliner's take-off, and like an airline passenger, Cole was getting used to it.

It no longer seemed strange to be traveling through Time. Hadn't he been doing it all his life? It was a gift, to see humanity's future. Was that long and peaceful future the result of the gene sequence that they were chasing? Or was that future in spite of it; or even a result of their failure? Surely the Old Ones, *Los Viejos*, would be able to tell him. Why else would they have sent for them across a million years?

A million years! And so it was that, with his companion, he rode the endlessly cresting, white-capped wave of Time . . .

He opened his eyes when he felt the glider stop. Lee was pulling his hand away.

Not home. That was Cole's first thought: not home.

They were outside, on a wooden deck, overlooking a wide plain that rose to mountains in the distance. Their outlines were unfamiliar. They were covered with golden or amber grass to a certain height, and above that snow. No rock, no ice, no trees. There seemed to be as little life or diversity here as on the Moon.

"Where the hell are we now, Dr. Lee?"

"You see that I am doing the numbers, Dr. Cole. We have all new numbers now."

The glider faced a round table big enough for four. One man sat across the table, smiling at them. Cole was becoming used to this gradual fade-in of a world, and knew that the man had probably been there all along, watching them as one might watch a child awaken.

"Hello there," Cole said.

"Hello," the man answered. "Welcome. Would you like a cup of tea?"

"Perhaps you have coffee?" Lee asked.

"Of course."

"We both prefer coffee if it is not too much trouble, thank you."

"No trouble at all."

Cole had stopped thinking of black and white. The man who had watched them arrive was golden-skinned and Asian in the face, like Lee. He had dark gray hair pulled back into a ponytail. He wore embroidered slippers and his feet made whispering sounds as he brought coffee from inside the house. His name was Hilary and he was about sixty. Cole was no longer shy about asking, but people had stopped keeping exact count.

And he was not one of the Old Ones. Cole knew better, by now, than to ask. But he asked anyway.

It was getting dark outside, first the mountains, then the sky, but it was bright inside the house behind them. Cole could feel the warmth from the door that opened and shut behind Hilary. He could hear music, faint but oddly familiar.

"Perhaps you can tell us who these Old Ones are?" Lee asked. "And where we will find them—or when?"

"Aha!" Hilary said as he set the cups down. "We hoped perhaps you knew!" He explained that the Old Ones had communicated only once, to announce that Cole and Lee would arrive. Hilary and his wife Brin had been selected and sent to this place, which had no name, to welcome them and send them on their way. Brin was in Edminidine for the day, visiting their oldest daughter, Plenty. She would be back for the evening meal.

The door had stayed open behind Hilary, and now Cole recognized the music that was coming from inside the house. He had heard it in Paris as well. It was Miles Davis, the long, slow, sad modalities of *Kind of Blue*.

He asked about Paris. Hilary had never heard of it. Europe is all forest, RVR said in a voice that was lower even than a whisper. The largest cities are around the South Atlantic and the Pacific Rim. Lagos, Bonaire, Goral.

Had RVR acquired a new power? He seemed to be answering Cole's questions before they were asked. "Are you reading my mind?" he asked, uneasily.

"No, no," RVR said. "You must be subvocalizing. But if it bothers you . . ."

No, no. Cole felt comfortable with RVR, and a little bit of nosiness didn't bother him. He took it as a sort of compliment.

Out on the darkening plain he could see shapes—antelope? Deer? Horses? They would run and then stop, run and then stop, gliding like a shadow across the grass.

While Lee was still calculating the size of their last slice, RVR whispered it into Cole's ear. They were ten million (10,521,022) years in the future from our "present," from dreary little Swick; and 10,634,123 from the Crossing, the beginning of human history.

Why didn't you just give Lee the figures? Cole asked silently. Because Dr. Lee likes to work it out for himself, RVR answered.

The coffee was thick and sweet, served in tiny porcelain cups. Cole's cup had a design of a dragon emerging from a cloud. To make the coffee hotter, you ran your finger around the rim of the cup, clockwise, and a red flame appeared from the dragon's mouth. Or you could cool it down.

"Ten million years!" Lee said, closing his PalmPC and pursing his lips to indicate a whistle. Hilary nodded gravely; it was indeed a very long time. Cole realized that he and Lee were, to Hilary, First Men. Exotics, primitives. Cavemen.

He stopped playing with the dragon on his cup. "Ten million years," he said. "And we are still here, on the Earth!"

"But of course!" said Hilary. Cole's amazement was that humans still existed, but Hilary thought he was talking about space travel. There was nowhere else to go, Hilary explained. People still occasionally went to the Moon, but hardly ever to Mars, and the colonies on the moons of Saturn and Jupiter had long been abandoned. Asteroid mining had declined long ago; with recycling there was no need for new supplies of heavy metals.

The Universe was mostly emptiness. There was little to see and nothing to do. And even after ten million years, we were still alone. . . .

There had been a gradual increase in life span (still less than 100) and a corresponding decrease in the birth rate, and now there were some four billion humans on the planet. (ARD kept exact numbers, RVR told Cole: 3,978,098,356.)

"Here comes one of them now," Hilary said, his voice brightening. He pointed toward the mountains, where a small flyer was coming over the crest, descending. But Cole and Lee couldn't keep their eyes on the plane. Instead they watched astonished, as Hilary's hair arranged itself on his head into long gray cornrows.

Minutes later the little plane landed and Hilary's wife Brin got out, slipping gracefully through a sort of liquid door, her face all creased with smiles.

The plane's stubby wings were transparent, and disappeared, like the door, as soon as the big propeller stopped turning. Cole thought of Wonder Woman—and Brin was almost as good-looking. Better, really; better outfit, anyway. She wore an Amelia Earhart-style leather jacket over flowing silk pants.

"Dr. Cole, Dr Lee!" She was younger than Hilary (so that had not changed!) and appeared to be of Indian ancestry, though who knew what ancestry meant anymore? Was there still an India? Cole wondered. (No, RVR told him; though there were several languages of Indian origin.) Brin's skin was the color of warm ashes. Her hair was coiled on her head in an intricate "do," and Cole wondered if it had done itself as she landed, like Hilary's.

"Hilary and I can't leave together," she said, as she invited them into the house. "It's the only problem with this assignment."

Cole realized that they had been outside on the deck only to wait on her. She was a lot more talkative than Hilary, and he became more talkative when she was around. Cole and Lee's arrival had been pinned down to plus or minus four months, Brin said as she and Hilary prepared dinner, working together. The wait had been a welcome vacation, an opportunity to spend a few months alone together here in a remote and beautiful area that was closed by ARD to human habitation. That was why it had no name; names were seen as an encroachment, a mark on the land.

"We just call it 'house,'" said Brin. Houses grew themselves in a few months, according to a multiplicity of plans; this one would decompose swiftly after Brin and Hilary left, like grass.

There is a curious phenomenon in the life of couples, Cole noticed. The fires of young love are sometimes matched by a later fire, after the children are gone, and the body's beauty has fled, or at least softened. This glow, which he had seen between his Gramma and Grampa in Tennessee (certainly not between his mother and any man), he now saw between Hilary and Brin. Oh, they paid attention to Lee and him; they cooked them a fabulous meal. But they could hardly keep their eyes or their hands off each other as they chopped and stirred. Cole found it touching, but it made him lonely, too.

They had drinks, a peaty single malt. Like Miles Davis, scotch persisted in its original form. Ten million years! There was no stove but a pot that heated itself as Hilary threw in slices of meat (horse, Cole was told) and potatoes and leeks. A Mongolian dish, RVR said, "showing" Cole a map in some limbic area of his brain. It was a new trick, both impressive and disturbing. The continents still had their customary shapes, although North and South America were, as he had seen before, no longer connected. Scotland was an island to itself, and Europe smaller. The Great Lakes were gone. Africa was almost split in two by a large bay where the Congo used to be. The plain they now overlooked was not too far from the old highlands of Tibet, though lower and wetter according to the map.

Cole wanted to "look" at the cities but realized he was being rude, so he returned to the dinner table conversation.

"How was it that your hair got done?" Lee was asking.

"RVR," Hilary said, reaching up beside his ear to pet him. "He senses my excitement and pleasure that Brin is coming home. He wants me to look good."

"I mean how, physically," Lee said.

"Physical? You mean the movement? Some kind of electrical plasma thing. You'll have to ask RVR. It's all electrical or something."

Cole reached up and touched RVR. "Hair is easy," RVR whispered in his ear, as if that explained everything. "I copied the design from ancient Africa."

"Before my time," Cole said.

"No, after."

Dinner was served: little pointed breads and horse and a yeasty beer that grew cold in the mouth. While they had coffee, Hilary showed Cole and Lee pictures of their children which floated in the air, in three dimensions. Cole could direct them with his eyes, here and there. Peace was in medicine, which had mostly to do with trauma, since the details of diagnosis and treatment were handled by nanobots in the blood. Plenty lived in Edminidine, near the sea, where she helped administer a sea farm and "dabbled in literature."

"A writer?"

"No, no," said Hilary. "There is quite enough already written, don't you think? We have enough to do to read and understand it all, without adding to it."

Hilary and Brin showed Cole and Lee their library. The books opened backward, and the print was a strange cross between Cyrillic and Chinese, but it was ink (or something very like it) on paper, or something very like paper.

The print turned into English when Cole ran his thumb down the page. But he closed the book; he didn't feel like reading.

"Hands like books," Lee said approvingly. "Hands and eyes." The authors were familiar, some of them: Tasso, Cicero, King, Bruno, Shakespeare, Lafferty, Dryden, Huilvet, Gourg, Yi Lun.

Cole looked for his favorites—Dick, Himes, Abbey, Sandoz. But they were either forgotten or absent from this particular library.

Like literature, music was finished, according to Brin, though no one actually used the word "finished." She played guitar, "but not fancy," and only for herself. Cole thought she was being modest until she played for him. Back outside, they passed a pipe around the table while they watched the sun set. Cole had hoped for marijuana or some new, unheard-of drug, but it was that jealous old queen, tobacco. It seemed rude to turn it down. It was his first hit in almost eleven years, since an earlier Helen had made him quit, and it warmed him all the way down to his toes.

The setting sun seemed larger than it should, and Hilary explained that there had been an increase in stellar radiation in the past million and a half years, the first change in over three billion. It had been compensated for by atmospheric adjustments, a joint project between humanity and ARD.

"Another drink?" asked Brin.

"That is a quite fine whiskey," said Lee. "There is one thing that you Europeans got right." He winked to show that he was teasing Cole, who didn't really mind. One would have thought that Cole had had enough whiskey earlier in the evening; but since that was ten million years ago, he allowed Hilary to pour him two fingers; okay, three.

The sun had set and only the snowy tops of the mountains still glowed. Cole saw the glint of a plane, high up, but no vapor trail. These people left no mark on Earth or sky. And what an Earth! What a sky! "What a gift," he said to RVR. But it was Lee who answered. "Gift?"

"What you said before, in Paris." Cole passed Lee the pipe. "That humanity gets to live, amidst all this beauty, for millions of years. It didn't have to be."

"The gift is the ability to change," said Lee. "Man is a reed, but a thinking reed. To evolve, to make a choice."

Choice? Cole wasn't so sure. It seemed to him that humankind, given a choice, always chose the worst option.

"It was you who did it," said Hilary. "You went from surviving the world, to dominating it, to cooperating with it. You went from prey to predator to caretaker, and you did it in less than a hundred generations."

"It seemed impossibly slow to me at the time," Cole said. "Still does."

"A hundred generations is nothing," said Brin. "We are an exceptional species, the only one with such control—for good or ill—over our environment. But we are also part of the environment. We are a species, still, and what we want is in our bones as well as in our minds."

"What we want is—" Cole stopped. They were all looking at him. "This," he said, with a wave of his hand that was meant to encompass it all: sky, sunset, whiskey, company, tobacco, the darkling plain . . .

"All this is ours, it will be ours, if we can learn to coexist and not destroy," said Lee. How can he speak of the future here, in the future? Cole wondered. But according to Lee, humankind's journey had only just begun. "Then we can, we will, settle down to enjoy the life span of a successful species, which is anywhere from ten to a hundred million years."

Cole had heard Lee's rap before but he didn't mind hearing it again. Ten million years. They were ten years old, into a lifespan of a hundred. They had only just begun. It felt like immortality. Or maybe what it felt like was good whiskey, tobacco, the sunset.

"The explosion started in your time," said Brin, "with agriculture and cities. Surplus. We ceased the wandering that had taken us all over the world. Your generation, those who lived in the tiny sliver of time between 1500 and 2500, merely saw its end. And began the mopping up. It must have been a scary business."

"I think that is true," said Lee. "Five thousand years, five hundred. There is little difference from here."

"The main thing is, you did it," said Brin, relighting the pipe and passing it to Cole. "There are those who would have been happier if humankind had lived and died in a brief blaze of glory, like Jimi Hendrix."

Cole grinned. "You've heard of Hendrix?"

"Of course," she said. "The Age of Empire. Hill and I studied it, for this assignment, which I assure you is a labor of love. I even know a little English. Don't translate, RVR. Let me go it alone."

She said something unintelligible. Cole and Lee smiled politely. Cole recognized Lee's smile; it was the inscrutable one, the one he had always shown to him before RVR.

It was an evening Cole would always keep with him, in dreams if not in memory, for the beauty of the place as well as for the sweet contentment of Hilary and Brin, who were thankful for the opportunity to live closer to unspoiled nature, if only for a while.

"ARD usually only allows brief forays into what she calls the 'Open Areas' (which are closed to us)," said Brin. "We were thrown out of the Garden of Eden ten million years ago. We should be used to it by now. We live in the cities, and only come into the Open Areas as hunters or hikers or herders."

"Hunters?" Lee asked. "Still that old thing?"

"Nature red in tooth and claw," said Hilary. "It is often said that ARD doesn't love us, but I don't agree. The man ARD loves is ancient man, one of her killer species. Man, the bloodletter. ARD loves killing. We learned that during the ARD wars."

The ARD wars had started with an anti-RVR cult some two hundred and sixty thousand years before. A group from what had once been India, south of the Great Plateau, becoming convinced through a series of dreams and prophetic utterances that RVR was a malevolent entity, had moved into the wilderness. It was a great pilgrimage, of hundreds of thousands. Colonies were set up in remote locations with the permission of ARD and the cooperation of the rest of humanity, which was living with numbers of about seven billion (6.756) in the major cities and in smaller locations around the world. Over two hundred thousand years passed and the "pilgrims" were forgotten, except by historians (and of course ARD and RVR) until a series of earthquakes and floods sent refugees streaming. The colonies and ARD had come into conflict, and ARD had destroyed them. It was Sodom and Gomorrah all over again. A few humans filtered into the cities, but their language was untranslatable and they were no longer truly human. In fact they had regressed to the hominid stage (which explained, Cole thought, some of our "junk" DNA) and could no longer intermarry with humans. They died of through disease and heartbreak. This was the last speciation of the human race, and it was a repeat, a reversal.

"And no other sentient life-forms?" Cole knew but he had to ask again. The stars were beginning to appear, one by one. He couldn't find any familiar constellations; he had never been very good at picking them out, but now even the Big Dipper was gone. Flung apart by Time.

"None to speak of," said Hilary. "Or to speak with. Molds and slimes, mostly. Not good company."

"Speaking of company . . ." Cole saw that the ponies were grazing right up next to the house.

"They like people," said Brin.

"Like dogs," Lee said. It turned out that Hilary and Brin had never seen or touched a dog. They had long been extinct.

"Tell us about dogs," said Hilary, and Cole did, as much as he knew, from the days they had first seen man's fires and crept closer, fascinated and comforted by our talk and our singing. Hilary and Brin listened with what seemed to Cole a polite but diminishing interest. The long partnership, the love affair, had long been over. Humankind had forgotten the dog.

"That's a beautiful story," said RVR.

The ponies gathered around the deck, compact, silent and shapeless in the darkness, while the people smoked and talked. Man the destroyer is loved by the other animals as much (or more) than man loves them, Cole thought. Even though we kill them and eat them, they love us, and shouldn't it be so? Life kills us and eats us, yet we worship it in our way. We fall all over it.

The wine was perfect. No surprise, thought Cole. After ten million years, would there be a place in the world for bad wine? Ditto the clothes, which fit perfectly. Cole wondered how he and Lee looked to Hilary and Brin, particularly Lee in his hideous L.L.Bean safari jacket (which Cole had gotten used to). There was of course no way to know. If there was one thing this couple of the far future had, in addition to their love for each other, it was manners. Not that there was any coldness about them—no, only a perfection of warmth and *gravitas* and style, with just enough bite, like a perfect whiskey.

Crime, sorrow, even catastrophe were still part of the human condition, Cole and Lee were assured. Not war, though; war was crime sanctioned, even sanctified, which was unimaginable. Cole looked up at the stars and they looked even colder, even more distant than usual, now that he knew that they were empty. They had looked to him, to us, to Early Man, so much like a great city in the distance. We had wanted so much to go there, to be welcomed in. And now he knew that what we had thought, had hoped, was a beacon, was in fact just dumb fires, sparks, not even ruins. This tiny house of Earth was all there was. We were more alone than any of us had ever imagined possible.

So melancholy came with the gift. Even the dog, man's companion, had slipped under the dark waters of Time.

"Nothing at all," Cole said, looking up. "No one. It is hard to believe that in all that immensity . . ."

"It's getting late," said Brin. "Shall we go for a ride?"

The ponies liked to be ridden; it gave them an excuse to strut about. They were bone-shaking little trotters, with one liquid-smooth canter, like the Icelandic ponies Cole and his second Helen had ridden on their honeymoon, when a black face in Iceland was rare. The Icelanders had thought Cole must be a jazz musician. They had asked him about Miles Davis, and he had pretended to have known him, in his old age. It was even partly true: he had met him once, as a child, with his uncle Will, who had sold dreams in the form of drugs to the rich and famous.

Were those clouds on the Moon? They were. Brin explained that they were the result of a long-ago comet, deflected to the moon for its ice, gradually sublimating into mist that wrapped the poles like a sheer scarf. I know all about that, Lee said. He told of seeing the white streaks on the mountains, and Brin and Hilary wanted to hear about Zoe, almost ten million years ago. Zoe and Cole and Lee were all contemporaries, to them.

Brin and Hilary slowed their ponies to a walk, so that they could hold hands. Cole and Lee would soon be gone, and they would return to Edminidine, the long littoral city along the China coast. They were ready to resume their life among their friends and their children. But they would miss the ponies, the stars, the sea of grass.

So would Cole. He was riding bareback across the grass-smelling plain, like an Indian. The stars bore down like a burning blanket. Even though he was not familiar with the constellations, he knew they were all changed, changed utterly, irretrievably. The hundred thousand years behind his long-ago birth, the short trail from Africa to America was nothing compared with the ten million since, which had carried the galaxy and the solar system into new immensities. He looked up, into the hole that is the heavens, and understood for the first time, in his very bones, the awesome enormity of the journey on which humankind had embarked when we first looked up from our small horizons and saw the stars.

What if, Cole wondered, we had known then what he knew now—that it was all empty? That we were like a child, alone in a great empty house? Forgotten . . . worse than forgotten. Worse than abandoned. Alone forever from the beginning unto the end, from dust to dust, all, all alone. Would we have, could we have, still survived?

"Cole. Duty calls."

Beep beep. Lee showed Cole his PalmPC. The cursor was blinking; it was time to go.

Hilary and Brin led the way. They rode side by side with their arms around each other, an awkward but lovely sight. The house was a beacon, a far-off ship across the sea of grass, a nearest star.

"What would happen," Cole wondered out loud, as they rode back slowly across the plain, toward the frail ship of House, "What would happen, if we didn't hit RETURN. If we stayed here."

"ARD would not allow it," Lee said.

"I don't mean here here. I mean here, on this late afternoon Earth, with these good people."

"And forget what we were sent to do?"

"You mean Dear Abbey. I wonder now if we should be doing it at all, even if we find it and return with it."

"I think that is not for us to decide, Cole, you and I," Lee answered, kicking his pony and trotting ahead.

Cole looked up at the still-, always-, ever-to-remain-unfamiliar stars, and shivered, and kicked his little pony too.

1 +

There they were, the army of mice. Soon Cole knew, without opening his eyes, that they were back in the Student Union. He could hear the thumping from upstairs, and there was a smell of cinder blocks and Coca-Cola.

The door opened and Parker's big head stuck through. "Dr. Lee!—Mr. Cole? I thought I heard something. What are you doing here this time of night? I mean, are you . . . ?"

"It's okay," Lee said, opening his eyes and letting go of Cole's hand.

"I have to lock up at ten," said Parker, sounding annoyed. He looked meaningfully toward the analog clock on the wall. It was 9:46.

"No problem," said Lee.

The door closed with loud click.

"Why is he always surprised to see us?" Cole asked.

"Time loop, till ten." RVR had been left behind, or rather ahead, ten million years in the future, and Lee was speaking English again. Pidgin English.

"I hope this isn't some kind of Groundhog Day," Cole said.

"Ground what?"

"Nothing. I thought you said we weren't done. So why are we back here?"

"Beats me," Lee said, pulling a cell phone from his safari jacket and punching in a number.

"Wait! Who are you calling?"

"You know. Beeper."

"Wait, Lee!" Cole said, reaching for the phone. "What about *Los Viejos*? What about Dear Abbey? You and I need to talk first."

"All come around," Lee said, handing Cole the phone.

Cole heard it ring once, then click.

"Damn!" he said. "So what now, Lee? We wait for Pell and Flo, or whatever her name is, so they can decide what we saw and what we think? But who am I talking to? There's no talking to you!"

Cole punched in his own number; might as well check his messages. While it rang, he watched the clock make one jump, to 9:48. Time moved so slowly here, in the present. That tiny isle. He was beginning to feel like an islander: slightly homesick away, hugely restless at home.

"You have reached . . ." Cole couldn't believe the sound of his own voice on the machine. Was he really that dark, that gloomy? "Leave a message if you insist."

Cole punched in a code. The machine's computer-generated voice was so much more pleasant, more human than his own. "You have ONE message."

A last piece of nastiness from Helen? Cole was just punching in the retrieval code when he heard a beep beep beep.

Lee's PalmPC was blinking.

"I thought we were done! I thought it was over."

"More slice," Lee said, smiling inscrutably. "Old Ones? *Los Viejos*? Let's ride."

Cole folded the phone. He didn't have to be asked twice. He was more at home off the island than on. Besides, in the future he and Lee could talk. He put one hand on Lee's and the other up beside his own ear, for reassurance, but of course, RVR wasn't there. Not yet—

"One more slice," Lee said again, and there they were, the mice. And the centuries, streaming down, covering the two of them over like drifting sand . . .

$$+225,000,000$$

It was dark.

It was cold.

Something was wrong with the air. Cole smelled smoke and ash and ozone mixed with fear; an ugly smell. He knew it well. It was the smell of downtown New York City after the World Trade Center attack. He had helped a friend (not a Helen) sneak in and loot her own apartment, how many years— how many centuries—ago?

The glider was squeaking to a stop. They were on a terrace overlooking a dark valley, all in shadow. Cole could see a few lights moving far below. The sun, huge and dark red, hung over a range of hills on the other side. It was setting, or so Cole thought. It looked squashed and impossibly near; but surely that was illusion, a trick of the air. Behind them was a stone building. A light came on, spilling through a long window.

Someone opened a door. "Contact!"

Three people came outside, all dressed in the same gray and blue uniform with hoods, like homeboy sweatshirts. Their apparent leader, a woman, carried a coil of glowing rope that looked like soft neon. "They're out here!" she barked in a harsh, unfamiliar tongue. Cole could see the fold in the air beside her ear that told him RVR was back, and back at work.

He reached up and touched him. Hello old pal.

"Dr. Cole, Dr. Lee!" the woman said. "Come inside. It's cold out here." It was cold. The sun was too big and too orange; too easy to look at. The wind had a wrong, raw, wrung-out feel.

They gladly followed her inside. "This has to be them, the Old Ones," Cole whispered. "Ask them if they have something for us. Ask them why they brought us here."

Lee didn't respond. He was studying his PalmPC and shaking his head.

"If you don't ask them, I will!"

The woman with the glowing rope turned to Cole and smiled. He smiled back, and started to ask her . . . but she and the other two "hosts" had already turned their backs. They were busy over a small console with a plasma screen that changed size and color, and seemed to be taking pictures of the sun, or of lots of different suns.

"This is the end of everything," Lee said mournfully, to himself as much as to Cole. "We can look at the sun."

"What are you saying?"

"I am saying, we can look at the sun. It is old and dim."

"This must be them, then," Cole said, shaking Lee's arm. "The Old Ones. What year is it, can you tell?"

Lee nodded and showed him on the PalmPC. +231,789,098. Cole felt dizzy. They were two hundred fifty million years in the future. A quarter of a billion turns of rock and air around the sun, and now the sun itself was going cold.

The sun. There it was, through the window. Cole couldn't bear looking at it but he couldn't look away.

"So did they bring us here to give us Dear Abbey? Or to tell us that it doesn't fucking matter anymore?"

Lee didn't answer; he just looked from his PalmPC to the dying sun, and back, again and again.

Finally a door opened (in a wall, where there hadn't been a door) and a man in uniform brought them both a cup of hot chocolate. Cole would have preferred a drink, but it was hot, and it was chocolate.

"Are you the Old Ones? Do you have something for us?" Cole asked the man, who seemed to find the question amusing. He told Cole his own name was Cole; he had been named after him. "The Old Ones sent for you," he said, "and we take that as a sign of our certain success. Of our survival. Therefore we honor you."

He excused himself and left the way he had come. Through the open door (before it turned back into a wall) Cole could see children, all standing in rows, dancing or exercising to . . . it was almost Mozart, but a little off, with too many strings.

Not like the Miles Davis he had heard earlier. Two hundred million years earlier.

Through the window he saw needle-shaped ships rising out of the valley, silently, like a volley of arrows. "Is there a war on?" he asked RVR, reaching up to touch him again. "Is that what's wrong?"

"No, no war. It's the sun," RVR said. Their hosts were trying to keep the sun from going nova, he explained. It had already exploded in a flare called the Helium Flash, which had killed over two billion people directly, and three billion more in the natural fires and famine that followed. That was almost a thousand years ago. The nuclear fires had since been stabilized with an ongoing "inoculation series" (the ships Cole had seen) but only temporarily. It was a holding action. The sun's hydrogen was almost all consumed and our mother star was in the process of converting herself into a helium giant, unless prevented. It was still touch and go. All humanity was down to about a billion and a half people, living on a narrow habitable band. The atmosphere had been altered, which accounted for the smell. Oxygen had been down to less than fourteen percent, but was now back up to eighteen. Cities? They were only memories. People lived underground in long warrens. Several hundred thousand had left on a starship, but they hadn't been heard of since.

ARD had died. Not even RVR knew exactly how, or why, or when. Her communications, increasingly erratic and peevish, had finally ceased altogether. No one had marked the date; people had long since ceased to notice, and RVR's attention was mostly, if not entirely, on people and their concerns.

"So where are the Old Ones who sent for us?" Cole asked. "These people hardly notice us."

"Maybe these Old Ones are the starship people," Lee suggested. "Maybe they are no longer on Earth."

"They died," said RVR. "There are no starship people. I have told them here, but they keep 'forgetting.' They don't want to know."

"What happened?"

"They just died. There is nothing between the stars. Too much nothing. It is no place. No place for man, no place for RVR."

It all seemed a sad end to a long adventure. Humankind was a quarter of a billion years old. We had been on the Earth longer than the dinosaurs, as long as the hermit crab or the cockroach; we were the new champs. There wouldn't be any champs after us. The day was now 44 hours long—old hours, that is, original hours; though what indeed was an hour but a portion of a day? What indeed was a day, or a year?: all were just spinnings.

The stars no longer looked strange or frightening or promising or mysterious to Cole. They looked as random and as temporary and as unimportant as the glint of light on waves.

"What about Dear Abbey," Cole asked. "If these guys don't have it, who does?"

"I believe we missed it," said Lee. "Perhaps you are right and it is just as well. From here, what does it matter?"

Cole had to agree. Still, they had come so far . . . "It was our decision to make. And we never got the chance."

"Was it ours? Yours and mine? I don't think so."

"It was sure supposed to be somebody's," said Cole. "But maybe you're right and it doesn't matter." After all, all was lost. And yet—weren't these people staying busy, saving the world? Maybe the world had to be saved over and over.

Their hosts were consumed in their task of shooting rockets at the sun, and had little interest in them. Lee and Cole watched, waiting for the cursor to start blinking. There was food but neither of them had an appetite; the chocolate was enough. Cole paced; Lee sat silently staring at the dying sun. Even RVR was quiet. But when Cole put his fingertips up beside his head, there he was. "Is this it?" he asked. "For us, I mean. Is this the last slice?"

He hoped so. He might have loved Paris, or Bahia, or even the no-name plains of no-place, but not this, not here: not this barren rock that wasn't even Earth any more, with ARD gone.

"Not yet," said Lee. "According to the PalmPC there's another slice."

"How can that be? And what about Justine, I mean Flo? Didn't you already beep her?"

"Pell. He knows we have returned. But he couldn't be there yet. Only minutes have passed." Lee held up the PalmPC. The cursor was blinking. "Plus, you do understand that we have no choice. Not if we desire to get home. We must follow the logarithm, the path the Old Ones have laid down for us."

"Whatever." Cole didn't want to see what lay ahead. But he didn't want to stay here either, waiting for the sun to go out. He sat down on the glider and watched as Lee hit RETURN for what they both hoped would be the last slice of time.

And there they were, faithful, diligent, mindless as ever . . . the army of mice.

+2.4 BILLION

Cole had learned to keep his eyes shut until the spinning stopped.

When he opened them, he saw stars. Then stones. Then his own hands, feet, knees. Lee was sitting beside him; they were on a rocky ledge overlooking a wide valley all in shadow. The same valley? It was hard to tell. *Yea, though I walk through the valley of the shadow of death* . . . It wasn't the same sun. It was redder and smaller, back to less than its "normal" size (the size Cole remembered). It hung low over rolling hills as soft and as round as waves. A few towers stuck up from a fold in the hills. Lights flickered across them. There was what appeared to be a road but nothing moved on it.

Cole smelled smoke. He stood up, pulling Lee with him. "Let's go and meet the Old Ones," he said.

"Yes," Lee said, agreeing finally. "This must be the End of Time."

It wasn't, not quite, but who knew? There was a fire, a few feet below. A path led down to the fire. Cole followed it down. His legs felt funny. His feet hardly worked, and no wonder. They were 2.4 billion years in the future, on the steep, narrow, stony path to the End of Time.

Lee had shown him the numbers on his PalmPC.

A man sat by the fire, poking it with a stick. He nodded as Cole and Lee came up. He pointed with the stick where they were to sit; they sat.

"Welcome back, Lee, Cole," he said.

"Back?" Lee asked. "Who are you? Are you the one who summoned us?"

"You were here before, or will be," the man said. "It all overlaps, or will, you see. Or will see."

He passed Cole a bottle. It was whiskey, smoky, but not scotch. Cole took a drink and passed it to Lee, who took a drink and passed it on around the fire, which they had trisected, to their host. He was a black man, not quite as dark as Cole, with thin, lank white hair, tied back in a ponytail, and a short white beard. He was old: seventy, eighty, maybe a hundred, who could say? He wore dark coveralls and boots dirty with ashes.

"Are you one of the Old Ones?" Cole asked.

The old man chuckled and poked the fire with his stick. There was no wood on the fire but stones, like gray coal. They barely burned. They gave off little heat.

"There are no Old Ones. There is only me. And RVR of course. It was he who brought you here. He did it for me. I wanted to see you, to say farewell, to thank you. This last thing is hard. I did not want to die alone."

"It was you?" Cole reached up beside his ear.

"Not exactly," RVR said. "Others found a way to travel in time, long ago, before I was born, or rather, made. They are the ones who opened the loop. All I did was use the loop they made."

"What about Dear Abbey?"

"That was the paper they had for you," said RVR. "I brought it here, to bring you on."

"So it was you," Lee said.

"There is your Old One," said the old man, patting the fold beside his ear. "Not so old as us, but old."

"But how?" Cole couldn't imagine RVR with a physical form.

"He sent me," said the old man. "From here, you can go everywhere, with the right math, but only once. I brought the paper back. I have it here." He patted the breast pocket of his coveralls.

"You killed that man," Lee said.

"Actually, I didn't. They were killing each other without me. All I did was pick up after them. But, you know, from here, everyone is already dead. Including you."

"Where is it?" Cole asked. "Do we get it?"

"Of course." The old man patted his pocket again, but didn't reach into it. "You get everything." He stirred the fire and took another drink, then passed the bottle back around. He coughed—a sound more human than a word or a laugh—and Cole realized they were talking to the last man. There would be, there could be, no more. Some had gone to try and settle the stars but they were dead, according to RVR. They had made it less than halfway across the emptiness that separates every tiny star from every other. The Universe was not really a place for them. For us.

Cole shivered. He was cold, colder then he had ever been. It was a cold he knew no fire could warm, but he moved closer to the tiny fire anyway, turned out his hands in a gesture as ancient as . . . as himself. He didn't know what to say, so he nodded toward the sun. "Setting?"

"It no longer rises or sets," the last man said.

"The Earth is locked in a synchronous orbit," RVR added, in Cole's ear. "Like the Moon used to be, when there was a Moon."

So it wouldn't set; it would just go out. Was it Cole's imagination or was it growing dimmer as they spoke? He looked at the stars. They seemed the same as ever.

"They were trying to stabilize the sun," said Lee. "It didn't work?"

"Oh, it worked very well," the last man said. "That was a very very long time ago. We survived that crisis just as we survived the others. The first close call was the one they call the Crossing, when a few hundred of us left Africa and went on to settle the entire planet. Then not much later, there was what they called the Sixth Extinction, when in our arrogance we destroyed many species and almost destroyed our home and everything that made life worth living. That was the closest call of all, for without it we would have been just an experiment that failed, like a five-legged frog. But we survived, just barely. Thanks to you."

"To us?" Cole hunkered down beside him. He sat the way Cole had seen his grandad sit, in Tennessee, a few hundred million years ago.

"Yes, you," said the last man. "You are the ones who had to make the change. Who lived through the hope and the horror without going mad. Once the change was made we could live to enjoy the life span of any successful species. There were scares, close calls, new diseases, disappointments . . ."

"One great disappointment," Cole said. He was thinking of the Universe and how empty it was. But that was nothing to how empty it was going to be, from now on. Forever.

"The last crisis was the sun itself, the helium flash, but you lived through that one," said RVR. "You monitored the sun and slowed its burning down. The earth was reinhabited from pole to pole. Repopulated, but the population was kept down to three and a half billion."

The last man pointed up toward the sky with his stick. "Mars was briefly resettled, but only for a few million years. It was the afternoon of our time. Now it is going out, like the fire, and so am I. There must be an end to everything, even to us. Do you see?"

"I think so," Cole said.

"I see," said Lee. "I think I understand." And he did.

beep beep

The last man stood up. "Your cursor is blinking," he said. He walked them back up the path. The sun felt cold on their faces and the backs of their hands. Behind them a luminous pearl-colored ring was rising, like a knife, to halve the sky. There was no Moon.

In front of them was the glider.

"One other thing," said Cole.

"Oh, yes," said the last man. He reached into the pocket of his coveralls and pulled out a folded piece of paper. "This is what you came for."

"And do we use it?" Lee asked.

"I don't know. From here it doesn't matter," said the last man, handing it to Lee. "It's your decision, your world. Whatever you do, we know it leads here. To this farewell."

"Farewell, then," said Cole, embracing the last man.

"Farewell and thank you, for everything. It is not every man who gets to say farewell to his most distant ancestors. Thank you for coming here."

It's not like we had a choice, Cole wanted to say; but didn't, of course. He reached up and stroked RVR. So long, old friend . . .

"Farewell, and thank you," said Lee. He too embraced the last man; then he took Cole's hand and pulled him down beside him, onto the glider, and pressed RETURN, and the last man disappeared as if he had never been.

There were no lights, no army of mice, no sound at all. Only a weird wrong-way lurch, like a car getting tapped from the side. "Whoa . . ."

And they were still there, on the stony hillside. They hadn't gone anywhere. "What happened?" Cole asked, but Lee was already up, out of the glider.

Cole followed him down the path. The knife-like ring had either set, or hadn't yet risen.

There was the fire, but the ashes were cold. And there was the last man. Cole realized he had never asked his name. He had been dead for quite some time. Wordlessly, straining in the thin air, they buried him in the rocks. There was very little dirt there, on the last rocky hill, overlooking the dying sun.

"Okay," Lee said, dusting off his hands. "Let's go."

"Wait," said Cole. "What about Dear Abbey?"

"What about?"

"That was the point of the trip, remember? We wanted to shape the future, but the future shapes itself. Now we know that we have a future. Dear Abbey doesn't seem like such a great idea."

"Maybe future because of Dear Abbey." Lee patted his left patch pocket. "Takes guts, go for it."

"Takes guts to stop it, too." But something was wrong; something else.

"How come you're talking that stupid fucking cowboy talk again? Where's RVR?"

Lee shrugged. Cole reached up beside his ear.

Nothing.

"Trail's end," said Lee, pulling Cole down the path toward the glider. "Last round-up."

"Meaning?"

"Let's ride. Head home." The cursor was blinking. Lee took Cole's hand and pulled him down onto the glider beside him.

"We can't leave RVR here alone," Cole said.

"Done deal," said Lee. "Listen up, careful."

And then, for the first time, Cole heard it. Distant, faint at first, like the background radiation that fills the universe: a long, slow, mournful wail, almost a howl, rising and falling, filling the emptiness between the stars. It was all desolation, all longing, all loss. It was RVR mourning for us, for all of us; for you and for me, and all those still to come, and yet to die.

"Farewell, old friend," Cole whispered, reaching up again; but of course there was no one there. On a sudden impulse he reached down just as Lee hit RETURN, and pulled the paper out of Lee's pocket, and stuck it into his own.

"Hey," said Lee.

But Cole didn't answer and Lee didn't pursue it. They both were listening to the saddest sound either of them had ever heard: the lonely howl, the lamentation that drowned out even the army of mice: RVR, inconsolable, mourning for Man.

1 +

Whoa! I pointed at the clock. It said 9:55. "How did you do that?"

Lee was smiling. That inscrutable, enigmatic . . .

"What happened!?" I asked, pulling my hand from Lee's. The pain in my knee was gone. The smell was still there, but fading fast, like a dream. It was familiar, almost identifiable, then gone.

"Beats me," Lee said. "Figures all gone." He was shaking his PalmPC.

"It's over," I said. But what? What was over?

I looked at the clock. 9:56. I heard a booming. There was Parker, sticking his big ugly head through the open door. "Have to close up, Dr. Lee," he said.

Behind him was Pell.

Parker left; Pell came in and closed the door. "What happened?" he asked in a loud whisper. "Did you get it?"

Lee shrugged. "Guess not," he said.

"What do you mean, 'guess not?'"

"Excuse me, Dr. Lee," said Parker, opening the door again. "Gotta close up."

"Outa here," said Lee, standing up. I stood up beside him. I was still dizzy. My knees felt funny.

"No luck? Damn," said Pell. "I thought this was a done deal. All checked out."

"Not such critter," said Lee, gathering up his stuff. "Algorithm not work, always possible. Probably most probable. Or see-tomorrow algorithm too good, pull too far, all way to End of Time. Or work right, which pull through multiverse, then larger slice, eck-cetera."

"The End of Time," Pell said. "I guess if you'd been to the End of Time you would know it, right?"

"Guess so," said Lee, dropping his PalmPC into his cowhide briefcase. I was surprised to see that the pattern I had thought was formulas was actually cattle brands.

"So much for Dear Abbey," said Pell. "And too bad, too. I thought it was a neat idea, even though I never really thought it would work. So what was it like? Did you just sit there and swing?"

"It wasn't like anything," I said. *A neat idea?*

"Then why are you guys both looking so sad, like you just lost your best friend?"

"You don't want to know," said Cole. "Where's Flo?"

"Don't ask." Pell looked smug. I wanted to slug him, but no, I didn't. Instead I helped him and Lee shove the glider into the corner behind the piano, one side at a time. It was heavy and of course it had no wheels.

"Thanks!" said Lee as Parker locked the door behind us. In the parking lot, I borrowed Lee's phone. I winced when I heard my voice on my machine. I had never before realized how cold my own voice sounded.

"You have reached . . . leave a message if you insist."

I dialed in the access code.

"You have TWO messages."

Two? The first was from Helen. "Surprise. You will find the dog still there. At the last minute the new home crapped out. Sorry but I have a plane to catch and you two deserve each other." No goodbye, no farewell, no adieu.

The second was from Helen as well. "Oh, and fuck you."

I had to smile. Helen would be disappointed to know that I was, actually, glad to have somebody waiting for me at home. Lee's phone was a throwaway and I had apparently used the last call, because when I handed it back to him, he tossed it into the trash.

There was a piece of paper in my pocket. I unfolded it. Somebody's math homework, spattered with . . . was that blood? Had to be. I folded it back up.

I felt sad but I didn't know why. Dear Abbey? Helen? It was something less tangible but more personal than either. All I knew was, I felt like being alone.

Pell was astride his BMW, warming it up. Lee was waiting in his car but I declined a ride. A Prius glides off as silently as a ghost. My feet in the leaves were pleasantly loud, all the way home.

I felt apprehensive as I opened the door; Helen is known for her unpleasant surprises. But what greeted me was neither a surprise nor unpleasant.

"Rover! Hello boy! Glad to see me? Yes, you are!"

I went into the bathroom and peed, thinking, for some reason, of seals. Then I unfolded the blood-spattered paper and burned it, carefully, holding first one corner and then another, and flushed the ashes down the toilet. Good security habits die hard.

honorable mentions: 2003

Daniel Abraham, "An Amicable Divorce," *The Dark*.

———, "Pagliacci's Divorce," *F&SF*, December.

——— & Susan Fry, "The Bird of Paradise," *Asimov's*, June.

Brian W. Aldiss, "The Hibernators," *Asimov's*, October/November.

Martha J. Allard, "Dust," *Talebones 27*.

Lee Allred, "Our Gunther Likes to Dig," *Asimov's*, July.

Barth Anderson, "The Apocalypse According to Olaf," *Asimov's*, May.

———, "The Mystery of Our Baraboo Lands," *Polyphony 3*.

Lou Antonelli, "Silence Is Golden," *Revolution SF*, August 14.

Eleanor Arnason, "Big Ugly Mama and the Zk," *Asimov's*, September.

Catherine Asaro, "Walk in Silence," *Analog*, April.

Neal Asher, "The Thrake," *Hadrosaur Tales 16*.

———, "Watchcrab," *The Agony Column*.

Nigel Atkinson, "A Mouse in the Walls of the Lesser Redoubt," *The Night Lands*, Vol 1.

Robin Aurelian, "Foreign Exchange," *F&SF*, September.

Kage Baker, "The Angel in the Darkness," *Golden Gryphon Press*.

———, "The Briscian Saint," *Realms of Fantasy*, August.

———, "The Empress of Mars," *Asimov's*, July.

————, "A Night on the Barbary Coast," *The Silver Gryphon*.

————, "Nightmare Mountain," *Stars*.

Nathan Ballingrud, "You Go Where It Takes You," SCI FICTION, 7/13.

James Barclay, "Light Stealer," *PS Publishing*.

Steven Barnes, "Heartspace," *Mojo: Conjure Stories*.

Neal Barrett, Jr., "Hard Times," *Asimov's*, April.

————, "Kwantum Babes," *The Silver Gryphon*.

Laird Barron, "Old Virginia," *F&SF*, February.

William Barton, "The Man Who Counts," SCI FICTION, 5/28.

Christopher Barzak, "The Drowned Mermaid," *Realms of Fantasy*, June.

Michael Bateman, "Freefall," *Asimov's*, February.

————, "Mortal Engines," *Asimov's*, December.

Stephen Baxter, "All in a Blaze," *Stars*.

————, "Breeding Ground," *Asimov's*, February.

————, "The Chop Line," *Asimov's*, December.

————, "Conurbation 2473," *Live Without a Net*.

————, "The Great Game," *Asimov's*, March.

————, "Touching Centauri," *Asimov's*, August.

Greg Beatty, "Midnight at the Ichnologist's Ball," SCI FICTION, 1/8.

Chris Beckett, "Monsters," Interzone, February.

M. Shayne Bell, "Rachel," *Men Writing Science Fiction as Women*.

Gregory Benford, "The Hydrogen Wall," *Asimov's*, October/November.

————, "Naturals," *Interzone*, September.

————, "On the Edge," *Stars*.

Bret Bertholf, "Alfred Bester Is Alive and Well and Living in Winterset, Iowa," *F&SF*, September.

Ilsa J. Bick, "In the Blood," SCI FICTION, 4/16.

————, "The Woman in the Cherry Red Convertible by the Platinum Sea," SCI FICTION, 10/15.

Michael Bishop, "Andalusian Triptych, 1962," *Polyphony 2*.

————, "The Door Gunner," *The Silver Gryphon*.

Terry Bisson, "Almost Home," *F&SF*, October/November.

————, "Come Dance With Me," *Stars*.

————, "Greetings," SCI FICTION, 9/25.

Maya Kaathryn Bonhoff, "Distance," *Analog*, February.

Ben Bova, "Monster Slayer," *Absolute Magnitude*, Fall.

————, "Son of the Flying Dutchman," *Analog*, June.

Scott Bradfield, "Doggy Love," *F&SF*, August.

David Brin, "A Professor at Havard," *Analog*, July/August.

Eric Brown, "The Frozen Woman," *Interzone*, July/August.

————, "Liketsuwan," *The Third Alternative*, Spring.

————, "The Wisdom of the Dead," *Interzone*, February.

Nigel Brown, "Annunity Clinic," *Interzone*, April.

Simon Brown, "Waiting at Golgotha," *Agog! Terrific Tales*.

Tobias S. Buckell, "In the Heart of Kalikuata," *Men Writing Science Fiction as Women*.

Chris Bunch, "One Last Look at a Half Moon," *Albedo One*, #25.

———, "This Sporting Life," *Absolute Magnitude*, Fall.

Chris Butler, "The Smart Mindfield," *Interzone*, January.

Octavia E. Butler, "Amnesty," *SCI FICTION*, 1/22.

———, "The Book of Martha," *SCI FICTION*, 5/21.

Richard Butner, "Ash City Stomp," *Trampoline*.

———, "Drifting," *Say . . . What Time Is It?*

Orson Scott Card, "In the Dragon's House," *The Dragon Quintet*.

———, "The Yazoo Queen," *Legends II*.

James L. Cambias, "Train of Events," *F&SF*, January.

Jeff Carlson, "Interrupt," *Strange Horizons*, January 13.

Siobhan Carroll, "Morning in the House of Death," *On Spec*, Summer.

Jay Caselberg, "Harvest Rain," *Interzone*, May.

Susan Casper, "Old Photographs," *Stars*.

Adam-Troy Castro, "The Tangled Strings of the Marionettes," *F&SF*, July.

Robert R. Chase, "Unseen," *Analog*, October.

Eric Choi, "A Man's Place," *Space Inc.*

James H. Cobb, "Faith on Ice," *Future Wars*.

Matt Colcorn, "The Brutal Shadow," *Interzone*, April.

Brenda Cooper, "Linda's Dragon," *Analog*, July/August.

Nat Coward, "By Hand or by Brain," *Interzone*, January.

Albert E. Cowdrey, "Danny's Inferno," *F&SF*, December.

———, "The Dog Movie," *F&SF*, April.

———, "Grey Star," *F&SF*, January.

Robert Cox, "Rambling with Rose," *Andromeda Spaceways*, Oct/Nov.

Ian Creasey, "Demonstration Day," *Oceans of the Mind IX*.

———, "Successful Delocation," *Neo-Opsis*.

Don D'Ammassa, "Curing Agent," *Asimov's*, July.

———, "A Good Offense," *Analog*, May.

Jack Dann, "The Hanging," *Polyphony 2*.

———"Rings Around the Moon," *Polyphony 3*.

———, "Summer," *Men Writing Science Fiction as Women*.

Brett Davidson, "Imago," *The Night Lands*, Vol 1.

———, "Little Watcher," *Interzone*, January.

Steve de Beer, "Profit Motive," *Aurealis 31*.

Stephen Dedman, "Acquired Tastes," *Andromeda Spaceways*, Oct/Nov.

———, "Desiree," *Oceans of the Mind X*.

———, "Mortal Nature," *Andromeda Spaceways*, August/September.

A. M. Dellamonica, "The Children of Port Allain," *On Spec*, Summer.

————, "Cooking Creole," *Mojo: Conjure Stories.*

Nick DiChario, "Zolo and the Jelly Ship," *Men Writing Science Fiction as Women.*

Paul Di Filippo, "A Monument to After-Thought Unveiled," *Interzone*, Nov/Dec.

————, "Bare Market," *Interzone*, January.

————, "Clouds and Cold Fires," *Live Without a Net.*

————, "Seeing Is Believing," *F&SF*, April.

————, "What's Up, Tiger Lily?," *The Silver Gryphon.*

Cory Doctorow, "Liberation Spectrum," *Salon*, January 16.

————, "Nimby and the Dimension Hoppers," *Asimov's*, June.

————, "Truncat," *Salon*, August 8.

———— & Charles Stross, "Flowers From Alice," *New Voices in Science Fiction.*

Tananarive Due, "Trial Day," *Mojo: Conjure Stories.*

Terry Dowling, "One Thing About the Night," *The Dark.*

Gardner Dozois, "Fairy Tale," *SCI FICTION*, 1/15.

Diane Duane, "Hopper Painting," *Stars.*

Brendan Duffy, "Louder Echo," *Agog! Terrific Tales.*

Andy Duncan, "Daddy Mention and the Monday Skull," *Mojo: Conjure Stories.*

————, "The Haw River Trolley," *The Silver Gryphon.*

J. R. Dunn, "For Keeps," *SCI FICTION*, 3/5.

Greg Van Eekhout, "In the Late December," *Strange Horizons*, 12/22.

Scott Edelman, "Together Forever at the End of the World," *Men Writing Science Fiction as Women.*

Harlan Ellison, "Goodbye to All That," *McSweeney's Mammoth Treasury of Thrilling Tales.*

Carol Emshwiller, "Boys," *SCI FICTION*, 1/28.

————, "The General," *McSweeney's Mammoth Treasury of Thrilling Tales.*

————, "Repository," *F&SF*, July.

S. Evans, "Indra's Rice," *Strange Horizons*, 10/20.

Gregory Feeley, "False Vacuum," *Beyond the Last Star.*

Sheila Finch, "Reach," *F&SF*, February.

Charles Coleman Finlay, "A Game of Chicken," *F&SF*, February.

————, "For Want of a Nail," *F&SF*, March.

————, "Wild Thing," *F&SF*, July.

Eliot Fintushel, "The Grass and the Trees," *Asimov's*, February.

————, "Kukla Boogie Moon," *Lady Churchill's Rosebud Wristlet*, November.

Karen Fishler, "Miko," *The Third Alternative*, Autumn.

Michael F. Flynn, "3rd Corinthians," *Analog*, June.

————, "Still Coming Ashore," *Analog*, July/August.

Jeffrey Ford, "The Beautiful Gelreesh," *Album Zutique.*

————, "Coffins on the River," *Polyphony 3.*

————, "The Empire of Ice Cream," *SCI FICTION*, 2/26.

————, "Present From the Past," *The Silver Gryphon.*

————, "The Trentino Kid," *The Dark*.

————, "The Yellow Chamber," *Trampoline*.

Karen Joy Fowler, "King Rat," *Trampoline*.

————, "Private Grave 9," *McSweeney's Mammoth Treasury of Thrilling Tales*.

Carl Fredericks, "The Spacemice Incident," *Analog*, July/August.

Bruce Jay Friedman, "Protect Yourself at All Times," *F&SF*, May.

Peter Friend, "The Alchemist," *Andromeda Spaceways*, August/September.

Gregory Frost, "The Prowl," *Mojo: Conjure Stories*.

Neil Gaiman, "Bitter Grounds," *Mojo: Conjure Stories*.

————, "Closing Time," *McSweeney's Mammoth Treasury of Thrilling Tales*.

————, "The Monarch of the Glen," *Legends II*.

————, "A Study in Emerald," *Shadows Over Baker Street*.

R. Garcia y Robertson, "The Bone Witch," *F&SF*, February.

————, "Far Barbary," *The Silver Gryphon*.

————, "Killer of Children," *F&SF*, December.

James Alan Gardner, "The Eightfold Career Path; or *Invisible Duties*," *Space Inc*.

Tom Gerencer, "Intergalactic Regrigerator Repairmen Seldom Carry Cash," *New Voices in Science Fiction*.

David Gerrold, "Digging in Gehenna," *Men Writing Science Fiction as Women*.

————, "Riding Janis," *Stars*.

Greer Gilman, "A Crowd of Bone," *Trampoline*.

Laura Anne Gilman, "Turnings," *Realms of Fantasy*, August.

Alexander Glass, "From the Corner of My Eye," *Asimov's*, August.

————, "The Nature of Stone," *The Third Alternative*, Summer.

Molly Gloss, "Eating Ashes," *Lady Churchill's Rosebud Wristlet 11*.

Lisa Goldstein, "The Arts of Malediction," *Polyphony 2*.

Kathleen Ann Goonan, "Angels and You Dogs," *SCI FICTION*, 7/2.

Adrienne Gormley, "Custer's Angel," *New Voices in Science Fiction*.

Theodora Goss, "Professor Berkowitz Stands on the Threshold," *Polyphony 2*.

Gavin J. Grant, "You and Me," *Strange Horizons*, 4/14.

John Grant, "No Solace for the Soul in Digitopia," *Live Without a Net*.

Dominic Green, "Heavy Ice," *Interzone*, March.

————, "The Rule of Terror," *Interzone*, May.

Gary Greenwood, "Jigsaw Men," *PS Publishing*.

Jim Grimsley, "Perfect Pilgrim," *Asimov's*, February.

Jon Courteney Grimwood, "Breakfast at the Fir Tree Diner," *Interzone*, April.

Sally Gwylan, "In the Icehouse," *Asimov's*, March.

Joe Haldeman, "Finding My Shadow," *Stars*.

————, "Four Short Novels," *F&SF*, October/November.

————, "Giza," *Asimov's*, March.

Charles L. Harness, "Faces," *Analog*, December.

————, "The Melkart Coin," *Weird Tales*, Spring.

————, "The Thalatta Thesis," *Imaginings*.

James A. Hartley, "Nature's Way," *Electric Velocipede*, Fall.

Glen Hirshberg, "Dancing Men," *The Dark*.

————, "Flowers on Their Bridles, Hooves in the Air," *SCI FICTION*, 8/6.

————, "Shipwreck Beach," *Trampoline*.

Robin Hobb, "Homecoming," *Legends II*.

M. K. Hobson, "Daughter of the Monkey God," *SCI FICTION*, 7/23.

Ernest Hogan, "Coyote Goes Hollywood," *Witpunk*.

Martha A. Hood, "Give Them the Moon," *Interzone*, September.

Rob Hood, "Lady of the Flies," *Oceans of the Mind X*.

Sarah A. Hoyt, "Never Look Back," *Weird Tales*, Winter.

————, "Travelling, Travelling," *Analog*, July/August.

Tanya Huff, "I Knew a Guy Once," *Space Inc.*

David Hutchinson, "All the News, All the Time, from Everywhere," *Live Without a Net*.

Janis Ian, "Prayerville," *Women Writing Science Fiction As Men*.

————, "Second Person Unmasked," *Stars*.

Simon Ings, "Elephant," *Asimov's*, February.

Alex Irvine, "A Peaceable Man," *Unintended Consequences*.

————, "Gus Dreams of Biting the Mailman," *Trampoline*.

————, "Pictures from an Expedition," *F&SF*, September.

————, "Reformation," *Live Without a Net*.

————, "Shepherded by Galatea," *Asimov's*, March.

————, "Vandoise and the Bone Monster," *F&SF*, January.

————, "The Uterus Garden," *Polyphony 2*.

Sue Isle, "Witness of Blood," *Agog! Terrific Tales*.

Harvey Jacobs, "The Retriever," *F&SF*, May.

————, "Spawning," *F&SF*, August.

Kij Johnson, "At the Mouth of the River of Bees," *SCI FICTION*, 10/7.

Richard Kadrey, "Le Merdier," *The Infinite Matrix*, 1/08.

————, "The Mad Hatter," *The Infinite Matrix*, 1/22.

————, "The Probability Box," *The Infinite Matrix*, 1/29.

Daniel Kaysen, "The Central Tendency," *Strange Horizons*, 7/21.

William H. Keith, Jr., "Los Ninos," *Future Wars*.

James Patrick Kelly, "Bernardo's House," *Asimov's*, June.

————, "The Ice is Singing," *Realms of Fantasy*, April.

————, "Mother," *The Silver Gryphon*.

Kay Kenyon, "The Book of Faces," *New Voices in Science Fiction*.

John Kessel, "Of New Arrivals, Many Johns, and the Music of the Spheres," *F&SF*, June.

————, "Under the Lunchbox Tree," *Asimov's*, July.

Ellen Klages, "Basement Magic," *F&SF*, May.

Mindy L. Klasky, "Catalog of Woe," *Space Inc.*

Nancy Kress, "Dancing in the Dark," *Space Inc.*

———, "The War on Treemon," *Asimov's*, January.

Bill Kte'pi, "Start with Color," *Strange Horizons*, 3/24.

Mercedes Lackey, "On the Other Side," *Stars*.

Jay Lake, "All Our Heroes Are Bastards," *The Third Alternative*, Summer.

———, "The Cleansing Fire of God," *Strange Horizons*, 9/29.

———, "A Hero for the Dark Towns," *Album Zutique #1*.

———, "Iron Heaven," *Intracities*.

———, "The Passing of Guests," *Beyond the Last Star*.

———, "Tall Spirits Blocking the Night," *Talebones*, Fall.

———, "Under the Purplefan Trees," *Revolution SF*,

Geoffrey A. Landis, "The Time-Travel Heart," *The Silver Gryphon*.

Joe Lansdale, "Fire Dog," *The Silver Gryphon*.

Alexis Glynn Latner, "Trinity Bay," *Analog*, July/August.

H. Courreges LeBlanc, "Amends," *Imaginings*.

Mary Soon Lee, "Coming of Age," *Analog*, April.

———, "Immigrants," *The Third Alternative*, Winter.

Rand B. Lee, "Coming of Age Day," *F&SF*, December.

Tanith Lee, "The Fiddle Plays Until It Aches," *Stars*.

———, "The Ghost of the Clock," *The Dark*.

———, "Love in a Time of Dragons," *The Dragon Quintet*.

———, "Moonblind," *Realms of Fantasy*, April.

Ursula K. Le Guin, "Confusions of Uni," *Changing Planes*.

Edward M. Lerner, "By the Rules," *Analog*, June.

David D. Levine, "Legacy," *Imagination Fully Dilated*.

———, "The Tale of the Golden Eagle," *F&SF*, June.

———, "Ukaliq and the Great Hunt," *Hitting the Skids in Pixeltown*.

———, "Written on the Wind," *Beyond the Last Star*.

Marissa K. Lingen, "Wishing on Airplanes," *Oceans of the Mind VIII*.

Kelly Link, "Catskin," *McSweeney's Mammoth Treasury of Thrilling Tales*.

Paul McAuley, "Child of the Stones," *SCI FICTION*, 11/12.

———, "The Madness of Crowds," *Asimov's*, April.

Sally McBride, "Pick My Bones with Whispers," *Asimov's*, January.

Sandra McDonald, "Lost and Found," *Strange Horizons*, 5/26.

Terry McGarry, "Swiftwater," *Live Without a Net*.

Maureen F. McHugh, "Ancestor Money," *SCI FICTION*, 10/01.

———, "Frankenstein's Daughter," *SCI FICTION*, 4/2.

———, "Eight-Legged Story," *Trampoline*.

Geoffrey Maloney, "The Kaladashi Covenant," *Andromeda Spaceways*, April.

Barry N. Malzberg, "The Third Part," *SCI FICTION*, 4/23.

Paul E. Marten, "The Times She Went Away," *Low Port*.

George R. R. Martin, "The Sworn Sword," *Legends II*.

David Marusek, "Listen To Me," *Asimov's*, June.
Susan R. Matthews, "Society's Stepchild," *Stars*.
John Meaney, "Entangled Eyes Are Smiling," *Interzone*, July/August.
————, "The Swastika Bomb," *Live Without a Net*.
Eugene Mirabelli, "The Only Known Jump Across Time," *F&SF*, September.
Rick Moody, "The Albertine Notes," *McSweeney's Mammoth Treasury of Thrilling Tales*.
David Moles, "Fetch," *Strange Horizons*, 5/12.
————, "Theo's Girl," *Polyphony 2*.
Sarah Monette, "Three Letters from the Queen of Elfland," *Lady Churchill's Rosebud Wristlet 11*.
John Morressy, "The Artificer's Tale," *F&SF*, October/November.
————, "The Resurrections of Fortunato," *F&SF*, March.
James Morrow, "The Fate of Nations," *SCI FICTION*, 5/14.
Susan Mosser, "Bumpship," *Trampoline*.
Derryl Murphy, "Island of the Moon," *Neo-Opsis*.
Pat Murphy. "Dragon's Gate," *F&SF*, August.
————, "The Wild Girls," *Witpunk*.
Ruth Nestvold, "Looking Through Lace," *Asimov's*, September.
————, "Wooing Ai Kyarem," *Andromeda Spaceways*, December.
Larry Niven, "The Death Addict," *Analog*, May.
————, "The Ones Who Stay Home," *Analog*, January.
————& Brenda Cooper, "The Trellis," *Analog*, November.
G. David Nordley, "The Fire and the Wind," *Analog*, July/August.
Patrick O' Leary, "The Dream of Vibo," *Imagination Fully Dilated*.
Jerry Oltion, "The Glass Ceiling," *Artemis*, Winter.
————, "The Navatar," *F&SF*, October/November.
Richard Parks, "The Plum Blossom Lantern," *Lady Churchill's Rosebud Wristlet*.
————, "Yamabushi," *Realms of Fantasy*, December.
————, "Worshipping Small Gods," *Realms of Fantasy*, August.
Severna Park, "Call For Submissions," *Women Writing Science Fiction As Men*.
Lawrence Person, "Morlock Chili," *Asimov's*, June.
Ursula Pflug, "Python," *Album Zutique*.
Brian Plante, "Halloweentown," *Analog*, October.
————, "Lavender in Love," *Analog*, February.
————, "Transitory," *Beyond the Last Star*.
P. J. Plauger, "Lucky Luke," *Analog*, December.
Steven Popkes, "The Birds of Isla Mujeres," *F&SF*, January.
————, "Stegosaurus Boy," *Realms of Fantasy*, February.
Tim Pratt, "Captain Fantasy and the Secret Masters," *Realms of Fantasy*, April.
————, "Romanticore," *Realms of Fantasy*, December.
Tom Purdom, "The Path of the Transgressor," *Asimov's*, June.

————, "Sheltering," *Asimov's*, August.

Wolf Read, "Between Singularities," *Analog*, February.

Michael Reaves, "The Legend of the Midnight Cruiser," *F&SF*, December.

Kit Reed, "Focus Group," *Asimov's*, September.

————, "Visiting the Dead," *F&SF*, March.

Robert Reed, "Buffalo Wolf," *F&SF*, March.

————, "555," *F&SF*, May.

————, "Hexagons," *Asimov's*, July.

————, "Like Minds," *F&SF*, October/November.

————, "Like Need, Deserve," *SCI FICTION*, 8/27.

————, "Rejection," *Asimov's*, January.

Jessica Reisman, "Threads," *SCI FICTION*, 8/13.

Mike Resnick, "Here's Looking At You, Kid," *Asimov's*, April.

————, "Robots Don't Cry," *Asimov's*, July.

————, "Society's Goy," *Stars*.

———— and Kay Kenyon, "Dobcheck, Lost in the Funhouse," *Live Without a Net*.

Mark Rich, "Too Celestial Cave," *Talebones* 26.

M. Rickert, "The Chambered Fruit," *F&SF*, August.

————, "Peace on Suburbia," *F&SF*, December.

————, "The Super Hero Saves the World," *F&SF*, June.

Chris Roberson, "O one," *Live Without a Net*.

Frank M. Robinson, "Love Story," *Men Writing Science Fiction as Women*.

Spider Robinson, "You Don't Know My Heart," *Stars*.

Adam Roberts, "New Model Computer," *Live Without a Net*.

Andy Robertson, "Eater," *The Night Lands*, Vol. 1.

Warren Rochelle, "The Golden Boy," *The Silver Gryphon*.

Dianna Rodgers, "Dreaming For Hire, By Appointment Only," *Polyphony 2*.

Benjamin Rosenbaum, "The Death Trap of Dr. Nefario," *Infinite Matrix*, 3/25.

Mary Rosenblum, "Golden Bird," *Asimov's*, January.

Rudy Rucker & Bruce Sterling, "Junk DNA," *Asimov's*, January.

Kristine Kathryn Rusch, "Cowboy Grace," *The Silver Gryphon*.

————, "Homecoming," *Women Writing Science Fiction As Men*.

————, "Nutball Season," *SCI FICTION*,

————, "Play Like a Girl," *Stars*.

————, "Sparks in a Cold War," *Future Wars*.

Richard Paul Russo, "Tropical Nights at the Natatorium," *The Silver Gryphon*, September.

James Sallis, "Free Time," *Album Zutique #1*.

Patrick Samphire, "Finisterre," *The Third Alternative*, Spring.

William Sanders, "Dry Bones," *Asimov's*, May.

Melissa Scott, "The Sweet Not-Yet," *Imagination Fully Dilated*.

Nisi Shawl, "Momi Watu," *Strange Horizons*, 8/18.

————, "The Tawny Bitch," *Mojo: Conjure Stories*.

Robert Sheckley, "Hunger," *Stars*.

———, "Legend of Conquistadors," *F&SF*, April.

———, "The Refuge Elsewhere," *F&SF*, May.

Charles Sheffield, "The Waste Land," *Asimov's*, March.

Jim Shepard, "Tedford and the Megalodon," *McSweeney's Mammoth Treasury of Thrilling Tales*.

Lucius Shepard, "A Walk in the Garden," *SCI FICTION*, 8/20.

———, "After Ildiko," *The Silver Gryphon*.

———, "Ariel," *Asimov's*, October/November.

———, "Floater," *PS Publishing*.

———, "Jailwise," *SCI FICTION*, 6/4.

———, "Liar's House," *SCI FICTION*, 12/1.

———, "Limbo," *The Dark*.

———, "Only Partly Here," *Asimov's*, March.

———, "The Park Sweeper," *The Third Alternative*,

———, "The Same Old Story," *Polyphony 2*.

———, "Senor Volto," *SCI FICTION*, 2/12.

Gary W. Shockley, "The Lightning Bug Wars," *F&SF*, April.

William Shunn, "The Day Pietro Coppino Spoke to the Mountain," *Realms of Fantasy*, October.

———, "The Diagnostic Feast," *Beyond the Last Star*.

———, "Divided By Time," *Realms of Fantasy*, December.

———, "Love in the Age of Spyware," *Salon*, July 16.

———, "Mrs. Janokowski Hits One Out of the Park," *Electric Velocipede*, Spring.

Vandana Singh, "The Wife," *Polyphony 3*.

Robert Silverberg, "The Book of Changes," *Legends II*.

———, "The Reign of Terror," *Asimov's*, April.

Alison Sinclair, "Suspended Lives," *Space Inc.*

Dean Wesley Smith, "Shadow in the City," *Stars*.

Brian Stableford, "Art in the Blood," *Shadows Over Baker Street*.

Allen M. Steele, "Benjamin the Unbeliever," *Asimov's*, August.

———, "The Madwomen of Shuttlefield," *Asimov's*, May.

Bruce Sterling & Howard Waldrop, "The Latter Days of the Law," *Custer's Last Jump*.

Del Stone, Jr., "I Feed the Machine," *Live Without a Net*.

Charles Stross, "Curator," *Asimov's*, December.

———, "Nightfall," *Asimov's*, April.

Tim Sullivan, "The Mouth of Hell," *Asimov's*, August.

Lucy Sussex, "Runaway," *Agog! Terrific Tales*.

Michael Swanwick, "Coyote at the End of History," *Asimov's*, October/November.

———, "Crown of Beauty," *SCI FICTION*, 1/23.

———, "The Dark Lady of the Equations," *SCI FICTION*, 6/20.

———, "The Dark Night of the Soul," *Infinite Matrix*, 9/19.

————, "Deep in the Woods of Grammarie," *Realms of Fantasy*, October.

————, "Don't Look to the Skies!," *SCI FICTION*, 1/9.

————, "Forge Star," *SCI FICTION*, 4/18.

————, "The Ghost of Pierre Curie Reminisces," *SCI FICTION*, 4/4.

————, "Grace at the Gallows," *Infinite Matrix*, 2/13.

————, "The Great Wheel of the World," *Infinite Matrix*, 6/26.

————, "Island of Stability," *SCI FICTION*, 10/10.

————, "Legions in Time," *Asimov's*, April.

————, "The Morning After," *Infinite Matrix*, 1/30.

————, "Nightmares and Witches," *Infinite Matrix*, 2/13.

————, "The Oceans of Neptune," *SCI FICTION*, 5/2.

————, "The Parrot with a Golden Beak," *Infinite Matrix*, 5/29.

————, "The Pepto-Bismol Hour," *SCI FICTION*, 2/21.

————, "Smoke and Mirrors, Parts I-IV," *Live Without a Net*.

————, "Pure Science," *SCI FICTION*, 5/16.

————, "Spanish Witches," *SCI FICTION*, 10/24.

————, "Veterans of Heroic Wars," *Infinite Matrix*, 8/28.

————, "Worshiping the Scarecrow," *Infinite Matrix*, 5/15.

Judith Tarr, "East of the Sun, West of Acousticville," *Stars*.

John Alfred Taylor, "Way Out on the Regolith," *Asimov's*, December.

Eyal Teler, "Possibilities," *F&SF*, July.

Mark W. Tiedemann, "The Pilgrim Trade," *Low Port*.

————, "Scabbing," *F&SF*, April.

Shane Tourtellete, "Extended Family," *New Voices in Science Fiction*.

Karen Traviss, "Does He Take Blood?" *Realms of Fantasy*, August.

————, "The Man Who Did Nothing," *Realms of Fantasy*, June.

————, "Strings," *Realms of Fantasy*, October.

————, "Suitable for the Orient," *Asimov's*, February.

Harry Turtledove, "Next Year in Jerusalem," *Imaginings*.

Mary Turzillo, "Harrowing Hell," *Oceans of the Mind VII*.

Steven Utley, "Chaos and the Gods," *Revolution SF*, August 7.

————, "Exile," *Asimov's*, August.

James Van Pelt, "Different Worlds," *New Voices in Science Fiction*.

————, "Lashawnda at the End," *Imagination Fully Dilated*.

————, "Notes from the Field, 3SF, 2.

————, "The Pair-a-Duce Comet Casion All Sol Poker Championships," *Talebones 26*.

————, "Small Town News," *Weird Tales*, Winter.

Rajnar Vajra, "Afterburn," *Analog*, January.

John Varley, "In Fading Suns and Dying Moons," *Stars*.

Edd Vick, "First Principles," *Asimov's*, September.

Vernor Vinge, "The Cookie Monster," *Analog*, October.

Ray Vukcevich, "Fired," *Imagination Fully Dilated*.

————, "Jumping," *Witpunk*.

Howard Waldrop, "A Better World's in Birth!," *Golden Gryphon Press*.

————, "D=RxT," *SCI FICTION*, 10/22.

————, "Why Then Ile Fit You," *The Silver Gryphon*.

Nicholas Waller, "The Ancient," *Jupiter II: Europa*, Autumn.

————, "Sandtrap," *Interzone*, March.

Ian Watson, "The Butterflies of Memory," *The Third Alternative*, Summer.

————, "Separate Lives," *The Silver Gryphon*.

Don Webb, "Doc Hawthorne's Beautiful Daughter," *Polyphony 3*.

K. D. Wentworth, "In Sweet Jerusalem," *Oceans of the Mind VII*.

Scott Westerfeld, "That Which Does Not Kill Us," *Agog! Terrific Tales*.

————, "Unsportsmanlike Conduct," *SCI FICTION*, 4/19.

Robert Freeman Wexler, "In Springdale Town," *PS Publishing*.

Leslie What, "Death Penalty," *SCI FICTION*, 2/19.

————, "Is That Hard Science, or Are You Just Happy to See Me?" *Witpunk*.

————, "Threesome," *Imagination Fully Dilated*.

Lori Ann White, "Heart of Glass," *Polyphony 3*.

———— & Ken Wharton, "Mixed Signals," *Analog*, January.

Liz Williams, "Dancing Day," *Realms of Fantasy*, December.

————, "Nine of Lamentations," *3SF*, 3.

————, "Tycho and the Stargazer," *Asimov's*, December.

Tad Williams, "The Scent of Trumpets, the Voices of Smoke," *Stars*.

Walter Jon Williams, "Margaux," *Asimov's*, May.

Jack Williamson, "The Man From Somewhere," *Asimov's*, October/November.

Connie Willis, "Just Like the Ones We Used to Know," *Asimov's*, December.

Chris Willrich, "Count to One," *Asimov's*, May.

Gene Wolfe, "Castaway," *SCI FICTION*, 2/5.

————, "The Graylord Man's Last Words," *Asimov's*, May.

————, "Hunter Lake," *F&SF*, October/November.

————, "Of Soil & Climate," *Realms of Fantasy*, December.

John C. Wright, "The Last of All Suns," *The Night Lands* (website).

Pat York, "Home on the Range," *Analog*, July/August.

Jane Yolen, "Ride Me Like a Wave," *Stars*.

Melissa Yuan-Innes, "Waiting for Jenny Rex," *Full Unit Hookup*, Spring.

George Zebrowski, "Takes You Back," *The Silver Gryphon*.

Sarah Zettel, "Insider," *Imaginings*.